SCENE FROM
RED RALPH
OR
THE DAUGHTER OF NIGHT.

TORTURING A WITCH.

See No. 3, page 23.

RED RALPH

OR

THE DAUGHTER OF NIGHT

A ROMANCE OF THE ROAD
IN THE DAYS OF DICK TURPIN.

BY

PERCIVAL WOLFE

LONDON

Published for the London Romance Company by the

NEWS-AGENTS' PUBLISHING COMPANY LIMITED

147, FLEET STREET

LIST OF ILLUSTRATIONS.

RED RALPH;

OR,

THE DAUGHTER OF NIGHT.

[RALPH DRIVEN TO THE WATER'S EDGE.]

CHAPTER I.

THE THIEF AND HIS PURSUERS—A STRUGGLE FOR LIFE—THE LONELY HOUSE UPON THE RIVER'S BANK—THE STRANGE DISCOVERY—ALONE WITH THE DEAD.

ONE stormy December night towards the close of the last century, a strange and horrible scene was enacting in a lonely house upon the banks of the Thames, near to Old Westminster Bridge.

Scarce had the Abbey clock tolled the hour of twelve when in the hitherto silent streets arose a loud clamour of voices and the sound of hasty footsteps—of a thief flying with Justice at his heels. A wild tumultuous rush of hot and excited men, all out of breath, with running and shouting, and savage and eager, and jostling each other like ravenous hounds over a

No. 1.

SPECIMEN OF "RED RALPH."

Published for the LONDON ROMANCE COMPANY in Penny Weekly Numbers.

coveted bone, they scrambled down a narrow dirty lane, ill-lighted and badly paved, to the river-side, where, upon the top of a flight of steep steps, they came to a sudden halt, and broke out into an angry consultation.

"That's the way he went," cried one.

"He ran to the left," cried another.

"I'll swear 'twas to the right," a third exclaimed.

"I'll take my oath it wasn't this turning at all," vociferated a fourth.

"Which ever way he's gone," they all agreed, " he can't escape us, and we'll stretch his rogue's neck for him this time as sure as his name's Red Ralph."

Pale and panting, ragged, muddy, and blood-stained, the hunted man was at this moment crouching beneath the shadow of a wall at the bottom of the steps, and scarcely half a dozen yards distant from the foremost of his pursuers.

Driven from here he crawled along, still under the shadow of the wall, until he reached another flight of steps, and here flattened himself against the rotting woodwork, whilst the howling mob above crowded down to the water's edge.

The lanterns, which two old Charleys swung to and fro in their trembling hands, threw a flickering light upon the black waters beneath, as they rolled in upon the slimy stonework, green and slippery to the fugitive's feet.

The same light revealed in all their grim ferocity the savage faces of those behind, the sweepings of the back slums and blind alleys, who had joined eagerly in the sport—the sport of hunting a man to death.

But the runaway was hidden in the shadow, and though the lights danced round and about him, they had not yet fallen upon his pallid face and shrinking form as he stood trembling there in dread expectation, with fast beating heart and throbbing pulse, every moment expecting that some sharp eyes would find him out.

Expecting, too, that he would be dragged forth from his hiding-place like a rat from its hole, and carried off to jail, there to lie rotting beneath a load of iron, until it suited His Majesty's convenience to strangle him on Tyburn Tree.

Not long, however, could he hope thus to remain concealed.

A movement in the crowd indicated the arrival of a new-comer, who was elbowing his way to the front.

It was a man with a torch, which cast a lurid glare upon the unsightly group, and upon their bludgeons, firearms, and gleaming naked swords.

Upon the river, too, beyond, and on the green and moss-grown wall close to the spot where the fugitive was hiding, flattening his slim form as much as possible, and striving to creep more and more within the shade.

But he could not hope to escape notice many moments more, for the man with the torch was even now descending the steps, one at a time, cautiously and mistrustfully.

He had descended to within six feet of the skulking, trembling figure, when the fearful danger of his position urged the fugitive to take some immediate steps for self-preservation.

Casting a wild scared glance around he took in rapidly the chances for and against him, and decided upon a plunge into the river.

A wild and desperate chance was this, however, for he could scarce hope to swim beyond pursuit when boats were within hail, and indeed, as the sound of the oars informed him, were rapidly approaching.

He was now upon the lowest step, but, creeping away before his pursuers, he let himself down into the water, which he expected would engulph him to the throat.

To his amazement and delight, however, he found that he had unthinkingly chosen a shallow place—that he had indeed stepped down upon a narrow ledge running round the wall.

There was hope in this !

If he could possibly contrive to cling to the slippery surface of the wall and creep away out of sight he might yet be saved.

But his pursuers came crowding down upon him.

The hounds were upon his trail.

The myrmidons of the law athirst for his blood !

Another torch had now arrived, and another and another.

The faces of his pursuers were close at hand—wild and savage, clustering together upon the steps.

One man stealing towards him spread forth his long, thin, claw-like hands, and groped for him in the darkness.

Shrinking, shuddering, the fugitive clung to the woodwork, and clambered onward stealthily.

Above, the sky was pitchy dark ; no sign visible of moon or stars.

The noise of the robber's footsteps was lost in the shriek of the hurtling wind which furiously lashed the surface of the water, dashing the spray into the faces of the foremost of the watchmen.

But yet his pursuers pressed upon him.

One stretched out his arm and waved aloft a flaring torch.

Its light penetrated the darkness, and the thief crept away further and further from the treacherous glare.

But at the moment when further escape seemed to be impossible, the fugitive crawling along and clinging with desperate tenacity to the slippery woodwork upon which his cramped and aching fingers refused to fasten, he felt that what he was holding for support was yielding beneath his touch.

Yet there could be no doubt of it ! the woodwork was giving way—was leaning forwards towards him !

In another moment he would be swept from his foothold and dashed into the water beneath, which the furious wind lashed into froth around his feet.

At that instant a vivid flash of lightning revealed a boat rowing up to the steps ; the men in which, catching sight of him, raised a hoarse shout.

Clutching frantically at the woodwork the robber scrambled onward, for the lightning flash also revealed to him the fact that he was swinging to a door.

As it swung over, however, it swung him violently against the wall, and shook loose his hold so that he fell into the water.

An awful moment of wild confusion followed in which he struggled and fought for dear life.

The storm at this juncture was at its wildest. The gale raged furiously. The thunder rolled and crashed in deafening reverberations, and the broad expanse of heaven was one great flare of livid light.

Battling madly with the waters which seemed threatening to drag him back, he crawled up to the woodwork ; clinging despairingly, was dashed back ; scrambled up again, and dragging himself through the doorway drew it to after him.

Then seizing it with both hands upon the inside prepared to do battle with his pursuers.

But the sound of their voices without daunted him, and he turned to fly.

He was in an old-fashioned garden, grass-grown and neglected, and surrounded by a high wall.

There were no visible means of egress therefrom, but it was not safe to remain another moment where he was, and plunging through a tangled mass of shrubs and straggling weeds he made his way towards an old house, the quaint red brick angle of which the lightning had revealed to him.

Meanwhile loud shouts of " A boat ! a boat !" rang in his ears, and responsive cries from the water.

Then with a crash the door flew open and some of his pursuers scrambled through, whilst others, at the same moment, were scaling the garden wall.

By this time he had reached the house.

To find an outlet in the court beyond was now his chief aim.

But this was impossible, for the great gates were securely locked and barred.

The sound of footsteps in the garden drove him from his attempt to escape in this direction.

He turned towards the house, and in the despairing glance he cast around he fancied that he saw that one of the lower windows stood a few inches open.

It was only four feet from the ground and he had easily reached it.

In another moment he had effected an entrance and closed the window behind him.

His pursuers, who had forced their way into the garden, ran backwards and forwards past the house, and searched in vain for the fugitive.

With a scared white face and bated breath he waited and watched.

The sound of the footsteps died away. His pursuers had gone.

A deathlike silence reigned around.

A silence, unbroken, oppressive—the silence of the tomb.

Close to the window, with his hand resting upon the window sill, he stood motionless until the last faint sound had died away in the distance.

Then he heaved a deep sigh of intense relief.

And then he turned to cast an inquiring look into the room in which he had thus found providential shelter.

A heavy curtain of soft and thick material came in contact with his outstretched hand, and drawing this aside he felt his way cautiously into the intense darkness beyond.

Scarcely a yard further on his hand fell upon the richly carved back of an old-fashioned chair, and upon its soft velvet lining.

He was evidently in some handsomely furnished apartment.

A few steps further on and the drapery beneath his touch proved it to be a bedroom.

Having paused for a moment to listen he began feeling cautiously along the bed, satisfied that no one was asleep in the room, and intending thus to make a tour of the apartment.

But suddenly his hand came in contact with an object which filled him with unspeakable astonishment and horror.

It was the cold and clammy face of a corpse!

CHAPTER II.

THE CHAMBER OF DEATH — THE HOUSE OF MYSTERY — THE ROBBERY — THE HORRIBLE DISCOVERY—THE MUTILATION—TERROR!

THE horror of this discovery held the robber for a moment transfixed and unable to move hand or foot.

His blood curdled, and his heart for an instant seemed to stand still.

He had not strength enough to withdraw his hand from the fearful object which it rested upon.

This thraldom, however, did not long endure.

With a violent effort he recovered himself, and as he regained his lost presence of mind began to consider what course of action he should pursue.

It did not take him very long to arrive at a conclusion, for his was a wild adventurous life, and he had learnt by bitter experience that every thing depended upon promptitude and bravery at the proper moment.

Without farther hesitation, then, he began to feel in his pocket for a certain article which he was in the habit of carrying with him.

" I hope I haven't dropped it, though," he muttered to himself, finding that it was not in the pocket he expected. " Thank goodness, no; it is here."

And as he spoke he drew forth a small pocket lantern, and then feeling again produced a flint and steel.

Practice had made him expert in a rather difficult operation, and in a few moments he had struck a light.

Then he eagerly cast his eyes around the apartment.

A strange scene presented itself to his view—a scene which filled him awe.

The room was spacious, and the light of the lamp the robber carried did not penetrate to the furthest corners, so that for some time he could not discern the distant objects.

Presently, though, he made out that the walls were hung round with black velvet, and that the bed curtains and the canopy and coverlet were of the same material, and all richly embroidered with gold.

It was not the furniture of the room, however, which interested him.

Instinctively his eyes travelled in the direction of the occupant of the bed.

There, lying in state, was the body of a woman, young and beautiful.

White as marble was her face, upon each side of which, though confined by the white bandage intended to support the drooping jaws, struggled forth silken tresses of raven black hair.

The bandage alluded to was not, though, similar to that used upon such occasions, for it was very narrow, and fastened in such a way as to be as little visible as possible.

It was evident that great pains had been taken to dress the body of the beautiful woman in this her last toilet.

Round her white polished throat and arms glittered a mass of splendid jewellery, in which the diamonds sparkled like a thousand stars.

Twisted among her raven tresses were the most costly pearls, and rubies, and emeralds.

Upon every finger of both her hands were placed the most beautiful rings, some of diamonds and set in a modern fashion; others evidently relics of the wealth of those long dead and gone.

A perfectly bewildering accumulation of riches the whole presented, at the sight of which the robber stood aghast.

Stood like one in a dream—utterly unable to believe the evidence of his senses.

Here, before him, was wealth sufficient, could he but possess himself of it and escape—to enable him to live the remainder of his life in idleness and luxury.

Need we say that the temptation was a great one to this highwayman, who every day risked his life to obtain possession of as many shillings as any one of the hundreds of costly stones glittering before him was worth pounds!

Greedily, then, he approached the bed.

His eyes sparkled with cupidity.

His fingers hooked themselves into a clutching shape.

His heart throbbed with wild exultation and excitement.

But as he drew towards the treasure he suddenly paused.

A slight sound had startled him.

A sound he fancied he heard in the house below.

Raising his lantern high in the air he searched for the door.

He approached it cautiously; noiselessly turned the handle and peeped out.

Pitchy darkness enshrouded the staircase beyond the point to which the ray of the lantern penetrated.

The most profound and deathlike silence reigned over all.

"It's very extraordinary," the robber muttered beneath his breath, "it seems as though everyone in the house were dead."

Awfully oppressive was the silence.

Intensely black the darkness.

A cold breath of air, too, seemed to creep past him and chill his blood.

He fancied that he was surrounded by the inmates of the grave.

That he heard a faint murmur around, and that the faces of the dead pressed on him, their icy breath fanning his fevered cheek.

With these horrible thoughts upon him he was powerless, and his knees trembled beneath him.

But again he recovered his fleeting courage, which never long deserted him, and determined upon making a voyage of discovery.

He could not believe it possible that the dead woman in the room he had left could be the only occupant of the house.

But in which direction should he first of all make a search.

He decided in favour of the lower regions, and, having taken off his boots, stole down stairs.

All the doors he found standing open, and one by one he visited them.

They were all furnished in an old-fashioned style, but with furniture of a costly nature.

They and the kitchens and offices were alike silent and deserted.

Retracing his steps he made a cautious ascent to the upper rooms, which one by one he explored with a like result.

The beds in the bedrooms were made, but no one was to be found in any apartment.

All was cold, dark, and silent.

A blight—a curse seemed to hang over all.

Deeply impressed, disturbed, and astonished by the mysterious character of affairs, the robber returned again to the apartment containing the corpse.

Silently he stood gazing upon the face of the beautiful dead.

Who was she so wealthy — so lovely—so young thus to be deserted ?

Was it possible that she had thus adorned herself -before she died ?

No, that could not be the case, as under those circumstances she would not have put the bandage round her face.

She would not have placed the gold coins upon her eyelids.

No, she had died, and some loving hand must thus have decorated the corpse.

How was it then that she lay thus alone ?

But he had not time to waste in idle conjecture.

However much he racked his brain, it would not be very probable that he would be able to arrive at any solution of the mystery enshrouding this extraordinary affair.

And if he was to have the jewels, it was not safe any longer to delay.

Placing the lantern on a chain by the bedside, he approached the corpse.

Very gently and carefully he undid the clasps of the necklaces which surrounded the white and polished throat, and drew them off.

Then he raised one of the cold snow-white hands and busied himself removing the glittering baubles.

But while thus occupied a rustling sound in the room brought him to a sudden pause.

So deep was the obscurity caused by the sombre hangings of the apartment, and so completely had the jewels occupied his attention, that hitherto the robber had not any very distinct notion what the room contained.

Rigid and motionless there he stood leaning over the bedside, with the dead woman's hand in his, and listened.

The curtains at the bottom of the bed rustled again.

His widely dilated eyes pierced the darkness.

He held his breath and listened.

His gaze concentrated in intensity.

Then with a half-uttered cry he started forward, snatched up the lamp, and rushed to the bottom of the bed.

It was a lock of silvery hair lying upon the black velvet coverlet that had first attracted his eyes.

He found it now to belong to the head of an old man, who knelt upon the floor, leaning his face against the bed.

Involuntarily the robber's hand went to his heart in search of a pistol he carried there.

But the figure before him remained perfectly motionless.

"Was he asleep ?"

The light of the lantern but dimly revealed the outline of his form. Something in it, however, caused the robber to stoop and raise the head.

The old man was dead, and his silvery locks were dabbled in gore.

His throat was horribly gashed and his clothes saturated with blood which long ago had dried and congealed.

A razor was clutched in the dead man's bloodstained fingers tightly closed upon it.

His limbs were stiff and rigid, and there was that in the dreadful appearance of the corpse which showed that he had been dead for several days.

Strange and more mysterious did this horrible affair become upon each first discovery.

The corpse of the beautiful woman lying in cold magnificence upon the bed, looked as though life had but departed a few hours at most.

Yet were there some flowers which lay strewn upon the coverlet dry and withered.

With an oppressive weight upon his heart, the robber returned to his unholy work of despoiling the body.

Carefully but rapidly he removed the jewels from her hair and the bracelets from her arms, thrusting them away into his pockets as he took them.

Then he drew off and pocketed the rings, using as little force as possible, although it was a very distasteful task which now occupied him, for, robber as he was, he could not help looking upon himself as a pitiful miscreant to be thus employed.

More than once he hesitated, half inclined to fling down his ill-gotten spoil and beat a retreat.

Many a time had he committed a theft—many bold and lawless deeds had he done, but not deeds of this nature.

Out on the king's highway, beneath heaven's broad canopy, bestriding his brave black mare, had he robbed high and low.

Often enough had he single-handed stopped the king's mail.

Large amounts had been offered for his apprehension.

A large price had been set upon his head, and yet his head was safe upon his shoulders.

That very night he had slipped through the hands of the Bow Street Runners and made his escape.

He had done so a dozen—a score of times before. He had led a life of successful lawlessness, and, though scarcely twenty, the name of Red Ralph was the terror of the London Road.

Now, though at the horrid work he was engaged upon, his heart failed him, and his hand trembled.

But avarice! the demon avarice! urged him on.

He had reached the last ring.

This was by far the most costly of all.

In it blazed one large diamond, evidently of immense value.

But it was so fast on the dead woman's finger that it defied all his efforts to loosen it.

Obtain it he must, for it seemed to him worth all the rest put together.

In vain he struggled with it.

He could not move the costly jewel.

It was evident that the dead woman had worn it for some years. The joint of the finger seemed to have grown since the ring was put on.

Only one way was there—one horrible method.

He shuddered at the thought.

But again the demon avarice urged him on.

From his breast pocket he drew forth a dagger-knife.

The click of the blade sounded awfully distinct in the intense silence.

The light from the lantern fell directly upon the blanched hand of the corpse, but the face lay back in the midnight gloom.

The robber's form was dusky and indistinct, but the light played around his long thievish fingers, and upon the bloodthirsty steel.

But the silence seemed to grow more and more and more intense—overwhelming!—soul-crushing!

The faintest rustle of the clothes upon the bed of death was horribly distinct.

There was a pause of perfect stillness while the robber prepared for the horrible work.

Then the sharp blade grated against and crushed the bone with a sickening sound; and then—

Then a cold clammy hand clutched the robber's wrist, and a death-like embrace encircled him! wrenching himself from which he overthrew the lantern, and all was pitchy darkness.

A tomb-like blank, without the faintest glimmer of form!—

A horrible uncertainty, through which he groped and scrambled in fearful terror, madly striving to find an outlet.

Wildly, but fruitlessly! with the awful something at his back, creeping—creeping on him, hanging round him—groping for him, perhaps, in the dark!

Half lifeless, half idiotic with sickly terror, the robber at last wrenched open the window and sprang out.

Missing his footstep, though, as he sprang, he fell a dead weight to the ground, and lay stunned and senseless on the green sward beneath.

CHAPTER III.

FIRE! FIRE!—THE AWFUL FATE!—THE ESCAPE
—THE ROOKERY IN ST. GILES'S—THE SUBTER-
RANEAN BOOZING KEN—DICK TURPIN, JACK
SHEPPARD, AND BLUESKIN—THE OLD HAG'S
WARNING—THE BRANDED HAND.

But when again Ralph opened his eyes, a glare of light was on his face, and the air was stifling hot, and loud shouts rang in his ears.

Staggering to his feet, he reeled as though he was drunk, and clutched his aching head in his cold hands.

He thought at first that the police were again upon his track.

He fancied that he was again struggling frantically to distance his pursuers.

Struggling desperately and hopelessly.

But a moment's reflection convinced him that such was not the case, and brought back to his recollection all that had occurred.

Instinctively his hand sought the pocket where he had deposited his treasure.

It was safe.

What had happened, then?

What was the cause of the glare of light?

Whence came the voices?

Before him the house from which he had escaped was in flames!

The voices were those of a crowd of people attracted to the spot, and endeavouring to force an entrance at the outer gates.

Loudly they shout. Heavy blows batter the stout panels.

The gates rock and creak, and give way with a loud crash, and the mob pour into the garden.

The sky above is blood-red, and the flames are pouring from the window of the room from which Ralph made his escape.

The old house seems to be on fire from cellar to attic.

High rise the red-hot columns of sparks, and the black smoke is belched forth, reddened by the furnace.

The hoarse roar of the angry flames is echoed by the hoarse roar of the mob.

Down through them, clearing their way like battle chariots, come the engines with their strong swift horses.

But too late—too late!

From all the windows now red flame bursts forth.

Long tongues of fire lick the house side, and encircle the chimneys.

From top to bottom the house is one great blaze.

But suddenly in the midst there comes an awful crash!

Then comes a roaring burst, which makes the sky lurid.

Then comes an upward-driven explosion of sparks and red-hot fragments, as from a crater.

The mob fall back, shuddering in affright.

The roof has fallen in.

But ere this the robber has left the scene of terror.

Under the shadow of the house side he has crept away—has scaled the garden wall upon the west side of the house, let himself down into a dark narrow lane, and made off at the top of his speed.

Nor did he pause until he had placed a good mile between the burning house and himself.

Then, however, he came to a halt, and leaning against the wall of a garden, he set about collecting himself.

"Ralph," he said, casting a woeful glance upon his ragged and muddy attire, "I don't at all recognise you this evening; you have not been yourself; you are not worthy of yourself; you're disgracing yourself in fact. Ralph, I'm ashamed of you."

He was not laughing when he thus soliloquised. He *was* ashamed of himself.

He did not by any means approve of several little incidents which had occurred during the course of the evening. More than once he had been trembling—he who usually knew not what fear meant.

Then again that affair of the finger—that brutal mutilation which had been done for no good, for the ring had been lost.

He had dropped it in his flight.

Captain Ralph, somehow, did not at all relish this reminiscence, and he was ashamed of himself.

"Curse it!" he muttered, "I won't think of it any more."

It was a very fine resolve, only it was very difficult to banish the horrible recollection from his mind.

What was that death-clutch which had fastened on his wrist?

Was it the woman who had returned to life?

Had she been lying in a trance?

If so, what had been her fate? Had she returned to life miserably to perish in the flames?

Ralph resolved, though, that he would dismiss the subject from his mind, if possible, for a short time, and he walked forward at a rapid pace, bending his step towards Saint Giles's, in which unsavoury locality was situate a certain house of call for highwaymen and footpads he was in the habit of frequenting.

In those days the police were not then as they are now—all powerful.

Robbers consorted together, formed bands, got into their own strongholds, and set the law at defiance.

Once within the Rookery, a man was safe, whatever his crime, unless his fellows chose to give him up to justice.

Here the gentlemen of the road revelled in luxury.

Their days were passed in feasting and drinking.

They had the choicest viands, the rarest wines, the most beautiful mistresses.

Their lives were one round of wild sensual enjoyment.

No wonder, then, that they risked much—all to obtain a footing in this paradise—to get the means to live this life of luxurious delight.

Deeds of heroic daring were of every-day occurrence, and all the town rang with the names of the great robbers and prison-breakers of the day, the foremost among whom were the well-known Jack Sheppard, Dick Turpin, Red Ralph, and Tom King.

Hurrying along at a rapid pace in a northerly direction, Captain Ralph was not long before he reached the goal to which he was bound.

A low beetle-browed tavern. It was very closely shut and strongly bolted and barred.

Having knocked sharply on the panel, steps were heard approaching, and an extremely drunken potman, with elaborate caution and an outrageous hiccup, questioned the new comer through the keyhole.

"What's—hic—what's—hic—whatshure name, ole feller?" said the potman, hanging on to his side of the door to steady himself, and frowning ferociously at a candle which he held in his hand, and out of the flame of which for the life of him he could not keep his precious nose.

"It's all right," replied the robber from the outside, "open the door."

"I—hic—I—hic—bother the—hic—hiccups."

"Look sharp, will you?"

"Ain't I—hic—looking—hic—whatever ails the hic—candle; it keeps on—hic—hicking into my face."

"It's all right, I say."

"I—hic—hope it is."

"Look sharp, you old fool!"

"I ought to know that—hic—voice."

"You'll know my fist, my fine fellow, if you don't know it already, if you don't look sharp. Open the door."

The last order was given in so authoritative a tone, that the inebriated potman stayed no longer to parley, but began to undo the bolts, burning his nose awfully as he did so, singing his ears, and setting fire to a large portion of his ragged head of hair.

He certainly looked an extraordinary object, with his bloated face, dull sleepy eyes, carroty curls, and pickled-cabbage-tinted nasal organ.

The robber could not refrain from smiling at his appearance, and observed sarcastically, as he passed him by—

"You're a nice fellow, certainly, to pretend to take care of a door. You'll let in Jonathan Wild's men before the night's out, if you don't mind what you're about."

"I shouldn't—hic—let you in, my fine fellow, if I had my own—hic—way. You're far too high and mighty, Mr. Red Ralph. I'm bl—hic—blessed if you ain't—"

It was very evident that the robber was no stranger in the house into which he had just obtained an entrance.

Without hesitating he proceeded down a long narrow passage, up a flight of stone steps, across a yard, and down some steps leading to a cellar.

Thus far all was dark and silent.

He knocked in a peculiar way at what seemed to be a brick wall, but was in reality a door.

Responsive to his summons a small trap flew open close to his head, and a very villanous face with a very wicked eye—the other had been knocked out some time or other—presented itself.

"Hallo!" said the head belonging to the eye. "Who's that?"

"Can't you see?" asked the other, rather impatiently.

The man stared very hard in Ralph's face, and presently said—

"To be sure! Why, it's the Captain!"

"Of course it is; open the door."

With an ominous grating, the door, or as it seemed six feet by four of the wall, revolved on its hinges, and Ralph passing through found himself in a small cavernous apartment, with a small fire-place in one corner, before which crouched a blear-eyed old hag nursing her knees.

She raised her head when Ralph entered, and stared at him for a moment, in surprise, while the one-eyed man, who was formidably armed with two pistols and a naked cutlass, also turned round to stare at him.

"You've been in the wars, captain," said the man.

"Deary, deary, my pretty Ralph!" echoed the old crone. "His beautiful scarlet coat all rags and tatters, and his lovely gold lace torn off his cuffs, and those boots and ruffles that I take such pride in—and he's lost his sword."

"That 'll do," retorted the Captain, rather abruptly, nipping the old hag's endearments, as it were, in the bud. "Who's here?"

"They're all here, to-night, my pretty captain," said the old woman. "They muster most uncommon strong. There's Captain Dick, and Captain Jack, and gallant Tom King, in fine array, the lot of them, and that big blackguard Blueskin, the good-for-nothing ugly varmint; and there's all the gals, of course, Miss Edgeworth Bess and Mrs. Maggot, and Polly Peachems here, and Lucy Lockit—all flounces and laces and patches, and painted faces—you'd say it was his Majesty's Court at Saint James's instead of Cutthroat Court, Saint Giles's."

"There—there, I can see for myself," interrupted Ralph, moving away.

"But, my pretty captain, I don't like the notion of your going into this fine company all over mud, the way you are."

"I shall do," replied the other, angrily, and pushed past her.

He knew the way, and, touching a spring in the wall, opened a heavy door on to another passage.

At the end of this there was another door still, approaching which he heard loud sounds of merriment within.

Again he knocked, and in another moment stood in the presence of the strange company here assembled.

A very strange company it was, too, in a spacious cavernous apartment, brilliantly lighted by wax candles, flaring away apparently in the most reckless disregard of expense.

A large table stood in the centre of the room, round which sat a number of handsomely attired men of various ages, and a number of women, all most splendidly dressed, and the greater part very pretty.

They were engaged in what seemed to be a drinking bout of a formidable character, for the table was crowded with punch bowls, bottles, decanters and glasses, whilst the "dead men" strewed the floor in every direction.

A great burly red-faced man was on his legs, when Ralph entered, singing a song, in which the company joined vociferously.

At sight of Ralph, however, he suddenly stopped, and in a dead silence every one in the room turned to look at him.

"Why, mercy me!" cried one of the ladies, a handsome brunette with great eyes, and beautiful white shoulders she was not at all niggardly in displaying. "Why, mercy me, it's the Pretty Captain!"

"He's not a pretty captain now, though," cried Blueskin, who was the man on his legs. "Why, my pippin, what in the name of the scarecrows have you been a doing to yourself?"

He certainly was in a ragged condition, smeared with mud and blood, and his garments saturated with water.

But yet it was impossible, even under these disadvantageous circumstances, to disguise the exquisite symmetry of his form, and the remarkable beauty of his face, round which, contrary to the fashion of the day, he wore his own golden hair in clustering curls.

It was a very youthful face with delicate features, clear blue eyes, red pouting lips and dazzling white teeth.

One could not help thinking that it was pretty enough for a woman's.

His slender figure, too, though well knit and muscular, appeared far to slight for the deeds of daring bravery which it was certain Red Ralph was the hero of.

No wonder that he was called the Pretty Captain, and no wonder that all the ladies were in love with him, and that his reputation for gallantry, although so young, was the town's talk.

Not a fault, physically, did he seem to possess, allowing that the beauty of his face was none the worse for being the beauty of a girl instead of a man —not a fault, save one—one dreadful blemish in his hand.

His right hand, back and palm, fingers, nails, and wrist, was blood red.

A terrible hand it was, when uncovered—which somehow made you shudder to look at it.

A strange mystery, too, overhanging it which no persuasion had ever induced its owner to reveal the particulars of.

This circumstance caused our hero to be called RED RALPH.

"What on earth have you been doing, my pretty captain?" asked Blueskin. "You, who are always so hasty."

"I've been making a fool of myself," replied Ralph, rather surlily.

"How so?"

"I laid a bet and lost it."

"Well, that occurs to many people."

"Not to me, though. For I bet fifty pounds I'd rob a man, and I failed."

"How was it, captain?" asked a score of voices.

"You all know Roaring Dick, the bully."

"Yes—yes."

"It was he who twitted me the other night at one of the kens I go to, and said that I had a great reputation for robberies, and in reality I did nothing."

"Don't you; what does he do?"

"I told him I could dare do anything that he proposed, and he laid me a wager that neither I nor any man in town could rob a certain old Doctor of Divinity he had been for some time past trying to get the better of."

"A bungling idiot."

"I said as much, and I laid him fifty pounds I'd steal the very bed the doctor lay on."

"Ha, ha! That's coming to close quarters."

"I lost no time, of course, but got to work. The doctor lived with his wife, his son, and one servant. I made love to the servant, and got her out of the way, and got the street-door key from her, all in half-a-dozen hours."

"Bravo, captain!"

"Then I dressed myself as porter; waited till dusk, saw the old lady out, and got into the house. I soon packed the bed up and shouldered it, but in coming down stairs, as ill-luck would have it, I slipped my foot and fell with an awful crash. Then out of the parlour comes running the doctor and his son."

"That was awkward, captain."

"Very, but I explained, a gentleman of the name of Llewelwyn, says I, puffing and blowing as though I were out of breath, had sent me with this feather bed, which would the doctor kindly take care of with some more things I should bring, till the gentleman came to fetch them? 'Llewelyn?' says the doctor, 'I don't know him; who is he?' 'I've no idea,' said I, 'but he knows you and ordered me to leave the goods here.' 'I don't care,' says the doctor, 'I won't have them, for I don't know him, so take them back.' 'Pray, let me leave them, I am very weary already carrying them hither.' 'Take them away, or I shall throw them into the street.' 'I shall get into trouble if you send them back!' says I. 'I'll throw them into the street' says he. 'Well, if you won't have them,' says I; 'will you gentlemen kindly help me to lift the bed on to my back again?' 'With all my heart,' says the doctor; and they put the bed on my back, and I toddled off with it as happy as you please."

"Well, captain," said Blueskin, when the loud laughter which this story had elicited had subsided a little; "you won your bet."

"No, I didn't."

"You didn't?"

"No! I'll tell you what a mistake I made: you see Master Dick would not take my simple word that I had done what I wagered I would do. Together then we waited about in the neighbourhood until the servant girl came out again, and we learnt from her what had happened."

"Well, well!"

"It was a dreadful error."

"What was?"

"Simply this, I had taken the wrong bed."

"The wrong bed?"

"Yes, the son's bed. I had of course lost the bet, but I wasn't going to be beaten so easily; I bet him double or quits that I would take that bed back and bring away the other."

"Ha! ha! ha!"

"Bravo, captain!"

"How did you manage?"

"I managed worse than ever, for I had had a good deal to drink and wasn't quite myself, and when I had got into the house in the dark, and groped my way to the bedroom, I never noticed till I began tugging at the bed that the old doctor was asleep on it. He woke up and roared loud enough to awaken the dead, all the pack gave chase, and the lord knows how I have escaped as I have done; but I have been half drowned and half roasted, and almost scared to death."

"And you have lost a suit of clothes and a hundred pounds."

"I have."

"A pretty night's work that."

"I am perfectly aware of it."

"You won't be so ready to bet again, I suppose."

"I will not rest until I have retrieved my character, but in the meantime I must change my clothes, and then I'll be happy to drink all your good healths."

He left the room, and, retiring to the adjoining apartment, where the robbers kept their disguises, soon effected a change, and returned again.

The company saluted him with a loud cheer.

When it had subsided Ralph took a seat at the table, and filling a tumbler of brandy tossed it off without winking.

"Here's all our good healths," cried he with a laugh, "and if our lives be short, may they be merry ones."

"By the powers !" said Tom King, who had been sitting silent for some time, "while we are talking here, we have let something slip through our fingers."

"What is it ?"

"The Lord Chief Justice is coming to town this very night to open the Old Bailey sessions."

"Well ?"

"He'll have a handsome sum with him in his carriage, of which we might relieve him."

"A good job if we could put a bullet through his head."

"It would prevent his putting on the black cap on our behalf."

"I tell you what, Captain Ralph, if he were to be robbed you are the man who should do it."

"Why ?"

"Because he has sworn to see you swing, and to attend your funeral."

"I know he has, but I hope he will be disappointed. However, if there is yet time I am ready for the adventure."

"He is expected at Knightsbridge about four; there is hardly time, for it is three now."

"My mare is close at hand: I'll go."

"No, no, captain; stop and have some punch. You've done enough for to-night."

"Enough ? Nonsense, I have disgraced myself by my failure; I will go."

He rose from his seat as he spoke, but the ladies tried to stop him, and the old hag stood in the doorway when he reached it.

"Red Ralph," she cried, in loud harsh tones; "beware !"

"What is it, woman ?" he asked in amaze.

"Beware, beware !" she cried; "go not forth to-night for an awful fait awaits you."

"Pooh, let me pass."

"Nay, listen to me; a curse hangs over you, as well you know. The hand of God is raised, and this night shall you meet the woman who will drag you to the scaffold. Oh, beware, beware—beware of the fiend with the beautiful face who waits for you at this moment. Beware, beware !"

She waved her arms above her head and shrieked aloud with unearthly laughter.

Then suddenly becoming silent crept away to her old seat by the fire-side.

The company at the tables looked on in intense surprise, and laughed and said the woman was drunk.

The Captain said nothing, but as he passed through the door some said his face was strangely agitated.

Was there a curse hanging over him ?

Was a beautiful fiend waiting for him ?

We shall see.

Certain it is that a strange adventure was set in store for him this eventful night.

CHAPTER IV.

HURRAH FOR THE ROAD — SIXTEEN STRING JACK — THE HIGHWAY ROBBERY — HELPING HIS LORDSHIP OFF WITH HIS BOOTS — THE ALARM—LIFE OR DEATH.

DARKNESS still reigned around as Captain Ralph of the Branded Hand took his way up Piccadilly towards Knightsbridge—a very different sort of place in those days to what it is now.

When he came to a small public-house which stood where Apsley House stands now, and where it was the custom for travellers to wait for one another and form into bands before proceeding on their dangerous way to Kensington or Hammersmith, a horseman rode up and saluted him.

"Captain Ralph."

"Captain Rann."

"The ladies' highwayman."

"The hero of sixteen strings."

It was none other than Sixteen String Jack, the notorious robber, who thus claimed acquaintance.

"What brings you this way to-night ?" asked Rann. "I am afraid you will find nothing worth the fetching."

"Have you been long on the road ?"

"An hour or so. I have ridden down from Chiswick."

"Did you happen to pass a chocolate-coloured travelling carriage, may I ask ?"

"No; nor anything else worth emptying. But whose is it ? not Lord Jeffries, I suppose, because—"

"Because what ?"

"If it is, there's something in it worth carrying away."

"What's that ?"

"Five hundred pounds only. His share of blood-money at the assizes that he's bringing home with him."

"If that's the case I'll relieve him of its weight."

"I should like a finger in the pie, captain, if you've no objection."

"None, my dear Jack. Let's liquor first though. What ho ! hostess, bless your pretty black eyes. Come give us one of your brightest smiles and biggest tankards."

Either a very early riser or a very late goer to bed this black-eyed hostess must have been, for she readily opened the inner door when Ralph knocked against the panel with his riding-whip, and brought him out what he required.

"Is that to your liking, my pretty captain ?" she asked.

"Almost as sweet as your two red pouting lips."

"Give us a toast then," said she.

"Your own sweet self."

"No, no."

"What then ?"

"I'll give it you, captain—Hurrah for the road !"

The robbers drank it and proceeded onwards at a brisk pace, for they wished to meet his lordship's carriage at a certain lonely part of the road highly favourable to the adventure.

Both the highwaymen bestrode magnificent horses—black and glossy—with long flowing manes and tails; with flashing eyes, quivering nostrils, and high action, bespeaking blood and breed.

As they rode silently onwards the pricking of the ears of Captain Ralph's black mare betokened that some one was approaching.

Without waiting to be guided the sagacious animal immediately quitted the high road for the grass upon the roadside, where the sounds of its hoofs could not be heard.

The other horse followed.

[THE LEAP OVER THE GRAVEL-PIT.]

Then, at a spot where some trees cast a deep shadow upon the ground, they came to a halt.

"There's something on the road," said Ralph after he had listened a moment or two attentively. "I hear the sound of wheels."

"It must be his lordship's carriage, as this is the time you say he is expected. Let us prepare for him."

"Have you the rope?"

"Yes."

As he spoke Rann alighted from his horse, and producing a thin but very strong cord fastened one end to a tree near which they had halted, and carrying it across the road attached the other end to a tree on the opposite side.

Having done this one robber crossed the road, and took up his position there in the shade, leaving his comrade where he was, that is to say about eight feet from the rope on the opposite side to London.

Thus, in perfect silence, they waited for the traveller, their faces concealed by black crape masks.

The sounds of wheels were now distinctly audible.

A dark chocolate-coloured travelling coach came in view, drawn by four horses, the postboys on the leaders loudly cracking their whips.

But the rope stretched across the road brought them to a sudden stop.

One of the leaders blundered over it, the other stumbled and fell.

The two postboys simultaneously ploughed the mud with their noses.

The wheelers began to plunge and kick furiously.

The servant in the rumble thumped his head violently upon the top of the coach, and its inmates cried out in alarm and let down the windows.

A very red and puffy face appeared upon the left-hand side, into which, within an inch of his nose end, was intruded the barrel of a pistol, and carrying his eye along the glistening blue steel, and along the scarlet sleeves of the person who held it, Judge Jeffries detected a countenance with which he was well acquainted.

"Oh, you atrocious villain!" he gasped; "it's you, is it, Red Ralph? Spinning another inch of rope to hang yourself with, eh? However, you've hit on the wrong man this time."

"How so, my lord?" replied the highwaymen. "Have you really nothing to reward me for all my trouble; I've been waiting a long while?"

"I haven't a farthing about me," said the old lawyer; "I'm not such a fool as to carry money on the highway."

"Dear, dear!" cried the robber, in a vexed tone; "I must put up with a few trifling trinkets, then—that diamond brooch and those rings (I'm really ashamed to ask for such trifles), and your watch."

"You—you villain! you wouldn't dare!"

"I must trouble you for them—as quietly as possible, if you please, or I shall be obliged to blow your lordship's brains out."

Very small and delicate did that kid-gloved hand appear which pointed the pistol at his head, yet was there surely a wondrous latent strength in the well-turned wrist above it.

Soft and musical was that voice; inexpressibly sweet the smile which parted those red lips, and glittered on that glorious set of pearly teeth.

Yet in those fierce orbs there glared a lurid light of vengeful hate, and the well-formed mouth was compressed like a vice with fell determination.

A very plump and pretty young lady, who had been trembling upon the back seat, hiding as much as possible behind his puffy-faced lordship, here shrieked aloud, and in agonized accents implored the highwayman not to fire.

"Be not alarmed, fair mistress," said Captain Ralph, gallantly raising his plumed hat as he spoke; "his lordship, I am sure, will spare us anything so unpleasant."

"You murdering vagabond! I shall hang you yet, that's one consolation."

"It must be. In the meanwhile, though, I must trouble you for those trifling trinkets I mentioned."

"Wh—a—at?"

"If you please, my lord."

The pistol was still pointed at his lordship's head; and now was heard an ominous click, against which there was no appealing.

The old man with a groan handed his valuables through the window.

"Is this all?" asked the robber with one of his sweetest smiles.

"All? isn't it enough?"

"Scarcely. I must beg of you to add your purse."

"There's nothing in it."

"Oblige me with a view of it—thank you," he said, jingling and pocketing the proffered article, which contained about ten pounds.

"And now the contents of your lordship's other pockets."

"I—I haven't another farthing."

"Indeed; will you kindly step out, then, and allow me to look in the carriage?"

Opening the carriage door as he spoke, Ralph laid a gentle but firm hand upon the old man's collar, and pulled him, before he was aware of his intention, out into the road.

Ralph, alighting, helped the young lady out, whilst Rann kept guard with ready-cocked pistols, all watchful of surprise.

Then Ralph searched the interior of the carriage without effect, pulling out the cushions and ripping open the padding, but finding nothing there to reward him for his trouble.

"You are sure he has it?" he asked presently of his companion.

"Quite sure."

"He must have it on him then. May I trouble your lordship for your coat?"

"My coat?" groaned the old gentleman, yielding it up very reluctantly.

Ralph searched it, but found nothing.

"Now your waistcoat."

"I shall catch my death of cold, you villain!"

Ralph searched the waistcoat, and then cast a scrutinizing glance upon the remainder of his attire.

"You—you surely don't want anything else, in the presence of ladies, too?"

"I shall trouble your lordship for your boots."

"My boots?—impossible!"

"Why so?"

"I cannot get them off without a bootjack."

"We must help you, then."

They compelled the unhappy old gentleman to take a seat upon the road, and then Ralph wrenched off his boots with dislocating violence, finding in one of them, sure enough, a pocket-book crammed with Bank of England notes and other papers.

"I'll pay you for this, you miscreant!" screamed his lordship, hoarse with passion. "I'll pay you as sure as your name's Red Ralph."

"Yes, yes," replied the other smiling, "you repeat yourself, my lord; you said so before; but here I see there are other things besides notes in your collection. You seem to do a little in the money-lending way. Here are a lot of bills of exchange that are no good to me. What shall I do with them?"

"Stuff them down the old wretch's throat," suggested Rann.

"They can't hurt him," said Ralph, laughing.

And in spite of the victim's struggles and entreaties the documents were forced between his teeth, and he was compelled, with a pistol pointed at his head, to munch up and swallow a couple of hundred pounds worth of paper.

Having completed his meal, he was put back into the carriage, into which Ralph afterwards assisted the pretty young lady, stealing a kiss of her as he did so, and expressing his regret that he should have been compelled so long to delay her upon her journey home.

Then raising his plumed hat he bowed low, and wished her good night.

But just at this moment an exclamation from his companion Jack Rann caused him to raise his head in alarm.

"Quick, quick!" cried the other, "I hear horses; the Runners are upon us."

"Which way?"

"From London."

"Save youself, Jack; we will go in opposite directions."

"We meet then at the boozing ken in an hour's time if all be well."

"Yes, in an hour's time."

The other robber put spurs to his horse, and galloped up the road.

The sound of the horses' hoofs of the approaching party was more and more audible.

In another instant some twenty mounted policeman had swept round the corner and at sight of them, the old gentleman, gaining courage by their presence, shouted lustily for help.

To his cries also were added those of the postboys and the servant, hitherto as still as mice.

The young lady too screamed shrilly and began to think about fainting.

No time was to be lost.

An instant's delay might prove fatal, and Ralph turned to look for his faithful steed.

She was cropping the grass by the roadside, and responsive to a low whistle from her master, trotted to his side.

Placing his hand upon her back, he vaulted lightly into the saddle.

But the police were now close upon him, hemming him round.

"Seize him, seize him! it is Red Ralph the highwayman!" shouted the old law lord.

Ralph caught up the reins in his left hand, and threw an eager sweeping glance around to take in the difficulties and dangers of the situation.

The police spread themselves out to block up his passage.

At the same time the sound of horses' hoofs approaching in the opposite direction cut off his retreat.

"A bold stroke for life," muttered the robber betwixt his clenched teeth; "twenty to one are long odds, but they'll take my dead body if they take me at all."

CHAPTER V.

THE SURPRISE — THE ESCAPE — A GALOP FOR LIFE—THE YAWNING CHASM—THE FATAL SHOT —THE BATTLE WITH THE BLOOD-HOUND—THE MYSTERIOUS SCENE IN THE WOOD.

RED RALPH had in that brief moment of hurry and confusion calculated all his chances and resolved upon a course of action.

Bending down his head to a level with the horse's ears, he pricked its flank with his spur and dashed like a rocket through the straggling rank of police.

One of the men endeavoured to catch at the horse's bridle, but, instead of succeeding, he rolled ignominiously in the mud.

The remainder in some confusion, owing to the rapidity of the robber's movements, wheeled round as fast as they could, and discharged their pistols.

The bullets, however, whistled harmlessly round his head and about his horse's ears.

Twisting back then in his saddle, he discharged his pistol into their midst, raised a loud jeering shout of defiance, and galloped furiously onwards to London.

He had not gone far, however, when he saw the toll-bar gleaming white across the road.

There was no time to wait for it to be opened, and it was so high that the risk of injuring his horse would have been too great had he thought of jumping.

Wheeling round, therefore, he cleared a low hedge dividing the road from a market garden, and galloped across the cabbages, making for the open country with all the speed of which his high-bred steed was capable.

Ever and anon the moon was obscured by dense masses of floating clouds, and oftentimes the robber urged on his wild career in pitchy darkness.

Vaulting over a hedge and ditch which bounded the market garden, he found himself now in the fields beyond, the ground of which was horribly uneven, and compelled him to slacken his speed.

His pursuers' voices were distinctly audible.

They had followed him across the garden. They had reached the hedge, and some had sprung over into the field.

Struggling still upon the uneven ground, and in profound darkness, for the moon was again obscured, the robber was within but a few yards of them.

Every moment he expected that one of the police would be at his side.

He dreaded to feel a hand laid upon his shoulder.

He dare not pause, though, but stumbled onwards.

He was almost inclined to get off his mare's back and lead her along.

But if he did this, and the moon came forth from the screen of clouds, he would not perhaps be able to mount again immediately, and would thus lose most valuable time.

Would the light never return again, that he might make a dash forward?

He heard the policemen shouting to one another—

"He's close to us somewhere."

"Dead or alive, he shan't escape us to-night."

Oh! what agony was this delay!

What waking nightmare! To feel danger close t his heels, and yet to be powerless to help himself.

But, ah! the moon burst suddenly forth from behind the dark clouds obscuring her glorious face.

A broad expanse of country spread forth before him.

A broad green field, smooth as a lawn, lay just beyond the rugged ridges of ground over which he had been floundering.

Without waiting for a moment to look after his foes, he set spurs to his horse's sides and dashed onward.

With a yell they followed in pursuit—with a clump, clump, which seemed to shake the earth like the reverberations of an earthquake.

Loud echoed their voices in the clear night air, as they urged their horses onward in the exciting chase.

Fleet as the wind then fled the highwayman.

His faithful black mare strained every muscle and sinew to distance her pursuers.

On! on!—'Twas a race for life.

But what was that which at some fifty yards' distance spread a black streak across the green sward he was traversing?

Straining his eyes he endeavoured to make out the nature of this object which puzzled him.

"It must be water," he said to himself. "If so, we can swim through it. But is it water?—ah!—"

At this moment was the moon again obscured by clouds, and all before him plunged into darkness.

In dread uncertainty of what might be in store for him he galloped forward.

He dare not have paused.

His pursuers were still following in full cry.

They were rapidly gaining on him.

Then loud voices rang in his ears.

Within half a dozen yards of the dark object, the moon again came forth from behind the clouds.

Then it shone brightly down upon a black chasm.

Great heavens! it was a yawning gravel-pit upon which he was headlong rushing!

But it was now to late to save himself.

There was not time to draw in his steed.

A wild and desperate chance suggested itself to him.

He could scarcely calculate the breadth of the chasm, yet he fancied it was in the limits of possibility for his horse to clear it.

It required not the aid of his spurs to urge on the faithful creature he bestrode.

She seemed to know that all depended on her.

On she rushed like the wind.

Then gathered her strength for the fearful leap.

Again was the moon obscured.

Again did the pitchy darkness cover the earth.

She sprang out into the dense obscurity.

The robber felt her body quiver spasmodically.

An awful moment followed.

In which his heart seemed to cease to beat.

Involuntarily his knees tightened upon the saddle—his fingers clasped the reins like a vice.

His eyes dilated; his teeth clenched; he held his breath as he rushed through the air.

A moment afterwards with a shock the mare's feet rested on the edge of the chasm on the opposite side.

The earth crumbled, and the sandy soil gave way and scattered down below.

The horse fought frantically for a footing—lost it—regained it, and dashed wildly on again ere the robber could scarcely comprehend that the danger was past.

Some of his pursuers had not had time to rein in their horses, and chance directing their course to a wider part of the chasm to that which Ralph had safely passed over, they went thundering down into the pit-hole, and lay a confused heap of struggling men and horses, the living trampling down the dead.

But those who were fortunate enough to save themselves in time, roared loudly to those behind to hold hard.

Then, seeing that the highwayman was in a fair way of escaping scot-free, they sent a shower of bullets after him.

The murderous lead, however, rattled harmlessly around as Ralph galloped onwards, every stride of his brave steed lengthening the distance between them.

He had crossed the field now, and taking the stone wall beyond in a flying leap, found himself in a country lane with hedges on either side.

The shouts of the police still rang in his ears, and as he knew not whither the lane might lead him, instead of turning either to the right or left, he leaped one of the hedges, and galloped on again in a northerly direction, taking the route as well as he could judge to Hampstead.

The clouds continually obscuring the moon's face, rendered it almost impossible to keep up the rapid pace at which he had been going, and, as more than once the mare had stumbled during the last half-mile, he judged it advisable to come to a halt.

"Poor Nelly," said he, stroking its silky neck, "we are safe now, and I am sure you must require rest.

"Strange, though," he added, after a pause, "that she should be so soon beaten; she has had a longer bout of it than this before now, and yet scarce turned a hair. I hope she did not hurt herself with that nasty jump."

Even while he spoke the brave creature's gait appeared to grow more and more unsteady.

They were at that moment upon the confines of a small but thick wood.

Obedient, therefore, to his guiding hand the mare forced her way in between the brushwood and overhanging branches.

But she proceeded only a few yards further before she staggered and reeled.

Ralph had not time to disengage his feet from the stirrups ere she fell with a deep groan heavily to the ground.

He shook himself free, sprang to his feet, and next moment was kneeling at her head.

"Poor Nelly," he said, in deep sympathy and fast-gathering alarm. "What is the matter? What have I done? Besotted idiot that I am, I have ridden her to death!"

He placed his hand upon the horse's heart.

He held his breath as he listened, and felt eagerly for the pulsation.

But the heart was still in death.

Stupified by what had happened, he rose staggering to his feet, and stood gazing in a bewildered way upon the body lying before him.

"Dead!" he muttered; "dead! my own true faithful friend."

One of the bullets from the pistols of the police had struck her side.

A horrible wound gaped hideously, from which her heart's blood had ebbed away.

Thus, then, she miserably perished in her endeavour to save her master from his enemies.

The sound of a gun-shot, however, aroused Ralph from his painful reverie.

It was a shot fired somewhere close at hand.

He looked round in wonder—not unmixed with alarm, fancying that his pursuers had overtaken and were closing upon him.

A rushing sound at the same moment approached him—the sound of some large body forcing its way through the brushwood.

Hastily springing behind a tree, he waited for the coming danger.

Scarcely, however, had he concealed himself, when a magnificent stag rushed past and bounded into the open.

"Poachers," muttered Ralph to himself. "I'm glad it's no worse."

The words had only just passed his lips when two more shots, fired in rapid succession, smote upon his ear.

Then there came the sound of hasty footsteps, and the crackling of branches, and two men, with wild and disordered dress torn to rags by the violent wrenching of the briars through which they had forced their way, came panting past.

In front of the tree behind which Ralph was concealed, one of the men flung down his gun, exclaiming, "I must either lose my life or that," and rushed on again at redoubled speed.

"It's an ill wind that blows nobody any good," thought Ralph, as he picked it up.

But hardly had he done so when the bushes behind him gave way to admit of the passage of a large fierce dog, which flew with a low but savage growl at his throat.

To frantically battle with and beat off the furious beast was now sufficient for his attention.

He did not then hear the shouts of the gamekeepers rapidly approaching the scene.

Vainly was he striving to defend himself from the bloodhound.

Its blood-shot eyes seemed bursting from their sockets.

Its white teeth gleamed horribly in the ghastly moonlight.

It had sprang so suddenly upon him that he had not time to strike it down with his gun.

To grasp it, then, with both hands by the throat was his only chance.

To strangle the raging, howling, blood-thirsty monster.

Fearful were the exertions which the struggle called forth.

The perspiration burst out in beads upon Ralph's forehead.

The great veins swelled up to bursting.

Together they rolled upon the green sward trampled to mud in the fearful conflict.

At last his hands slipped from their hold.

His fingers relaxed.

His strength seemed deserting him.

With a fearful snarl the blood-hound flew open-pawed at his throat.

At this moment, however, when death seemed certain, help came at last.

The delay of another instant, and the fangs of the destroyer would tear out his windpipe, would bury themselves in his mangled flesh, and tear and worry out his life.

But at this fearful juncture Heaven sent help in the shape of two keepers, who, rushing forward, beat off the savage hound with the butt-ends of their guns.

Ralph, weak and breathless, now struggled to his feet, fancying that the danger was past.

He had, however, only escaped from one to fall into another.

Whilst upon his knees, one of the men raised his gun in the air, and struck the highwayman down senseless at his feet.

" We've caught one of them, at any rate," said the keeper, who had thus acted, " and he may think himself lucky that she did not settle his business for him before we came up."

" That's matter of taste, I reckon," said the other, with a grim smile. " Some might prefer choking that way to the regular scragging match with professional assistance."

" I say, Joe," said the first speaker, who had been stooping over Ralph's prostrate form. " Look here !"

" What is it ?"

" Here's a go !"

" What's happened ?"

" We've made a pretty mess of it."

" Have you killed him ?"

" No—no, not that only, look here ! This is no poacher. He looks like a gentleman."

" He's a stranger in these parts, it seems to me," said the other man, stooping down, and earnestly scanning the robber's features. " I don't know him."

" I hope we hav'nt cooked his goose. No, I feel his heart beating."

" Undo his waistcoat. Let me. Hallo !"

" What's that ?"

" Why, his breast pocket here is crammed with—with jewels, by all that's extraordinary. See, man—see. Here's diamonds by the thousand, and emeralds and pearls, and look you here, a purse full of gold and notes. Why he's richer than a mine in Peru."

" Look here at the pistols in his belt. What is he, do you think. By the lord, I have it."

" What ?"

" He's a highwayman, and this is the swag he had just made at some great robbery."

" What's brought him to this wood, do you think ?"

" Perhaps he came here to bury his treasure."

" Do you think so ? No; that can't be, for look here—here's a dead horse. He's galloped away from the Bow Street Runners, most likely."

" What do you propose ?" asked one of the men, after a silence, " what shall we do with him ?"

" We might as well stick to what we've found."

" And leave him here ?"

" He'd know us again."

" Not if—"

The sentence was not completed, but a significant glance of ominous purport was exchanged by the two villains.

A hellish glare illumed their evil eyes, and they looked about them stealthily and listened.

" No one is here to see," one said, at last, in a hoarse whisper ; " buried over there among the underwood, no one will ever find the body, and we can place the sea between us and the law."

So saying, he drew from his breast pocket a long bladed knife, and stooping by Ralph's senseless body his murderous hand crept stealthily towards the victim's heart.

But the growling of the blood-hound apprised the two keepers that footsteps were approaching.

The would-be murderer rose from the body of the senseless man, and thrusting the knife into his breast pocket looked hurriedly around.

Cautiously, noiselessly, but rapidly, they crept away dragging with them the savage blood-hound, one clutching its jaws to prevent it from barking.

Scarcely had they stowed themselves away in a hiding-place, when the branches parting with a loud rustling noise, two figures appeared, one of a man, short and muscular, humpbacked and illshapen, the other of a woman, tall and graceful, with an air full of majesty and calm repose.

The new comers had followed a narrow pathway, which led through the copse.

The woman came first, and, as one of the branches had somehow become entangled with a short cloak which the man wore, she turned to see what had occurred to detain him.

" Need we go any further ?" she asked ; " it seems to me that we shall not find him however far we go."

" I'm almost afraid that he is not coming."

" The wretch has played us false."

" I am afraid he has."

" In that case, what is to become of us ? The ceremony must take place before morning."

" Yes, it must take place before morning."

" Unless it does, all is lost."

" Yes ; all is lost."

" Don't jabber over my words, fool," said the woman, fiercely turning upon him.

There was a silence of some moments, during which the lady seemed to ponder over some course of action very difficult to determine upon.

Whilst so engaged the humpback watched her from beneath his red, shaggy, bristling eyebrows, a horrible leer disturbing his hideous features.

" There is no way left that I can comprehend—no way by which we can secure the money unless this fellow comes, and I cannot hope for that now after this long delay."

" I almost think he must have got wind of our intention, my lady."

" What do you mean ?"

" If he suspected that the honour of marrying your daughter would cost him his life—"

" How could he know that ?"

" I can't tell, I'm sure."

" He understood that he was to leave England immediately after the ceremony, and that he would be provided for in a foreign country, and be able to live at ease for the rest of his life."

" That was what I told him."

" Is it not a sufficiently tempting offer think you to such a vagabond outcast as he is ?"

" It ought to be."

" Did you properly explain the affair ?"

" Up to a certain point I told him the truth. I said that according to my lord's will your daughter-in-law must be married on or before to-day."

" The 10th of December."

" Yes, and that if he would act the part of bridegroom, and immediately after the ceremony leave the country, keeping henceforth his identity a dead secret, he would be supplied with a handsome income until he died."

" And he, you say, was utterly friendless."

" He had not a friend in the world."

" And sick of England."

" Sick enough. He could not keep body and soul together in it any longer."

" How do you account for his non-appearance, then ?"

" Why, he has been asking for the ship we said his passage was taken in, and found that it was not, and then he has thought the affair over, and come to the conclusion that we meant to play him false."

" Thank God, he knows so little of our secret, except a vague outline without any names, that he can do us no mischief."

" No, I took care of that. While he had the opportunity of blabbing I let him know nothing."

" Afterwards death would seal his lips, and our secret would go with him to his grave."

There was an awful silence after these words, during which the two keepers looked at each other blankly.

After a while the lady said,

"He will not come to-night; it is no good waiting any longer."

"No," said the hunchback, "but what is to be done? Who is to supply his place?"

"Hark!" cried the lady, suddenly seizing his arm, and pointing with a trembling finger to some object at a few feet from the spot where she stood; "see, see! what is that?"

"What?" asked the hunchback hoarsely.

"There on the grass. Great heavens! It is—it is my dead husband's face—it is he come back from the grave. Oh, hide me from him! hide me from him! Mercy, mercy!"

With a half-stifled shriek the shivering woman fell upon her knees on the green sward, and clutched her face convulsively in her icy hands.

CHAPTER VI.

THE WHITE FACE IN THE MOONLIGHT — THE ROBBER'S DOOM — THE OLD HOUSE IN THE WOOD — THE RETURN TO LIFE — MORE MYSTERY — THE BRIDE OF DEATH.

THE hideous humpback, though himself almost scared out of his wits for a moment or two, presently recovered sufficiently to crawl forward with the crablike motion which was habitual to him, to look upon the object that had terrified his mistress.

It was, of course, Red Ralph's face, who yet lay senseless, stunned, and blood-besmeared on the grass, the moonlight falling full upon his pale features.

The humpback slowly approached him.

When he saw that it was a man and not a spirit he had to deal with, his alarm subsided.

He knelt by the side of the prostrate form, and laid his hand upon Ralph's breast.

"He's not dead yet, though!" he muttered. "Who is he, I wonder? A gentleman, I should think, or—ah, he's a highwayman for a hundred!"

Having got thus far in his reflections, the humpback turned and motioned to the lady to approach.

She did so, though still trembling violently.

"What is it?" she asked, in a strange whisper.

"Only a wounded man," the hunchback replied. "He seems to have been knocked down and robbed, for his pockets have been rifled."

"What is he doing here?"

"I don't know, but— Hallo! Look, here is his horse, and dead. My lady, I have an idea. Suppose we availed ourselves of what chance has thus thrown in our way. This fellow is, no doubt, a reckless vagabond, and might be easily induced to take the place of the other fellow who has disappointed us."

"What reason have you for supposing that he is a vagabond?"

"The general cut of the fellow."

While speaking, the hunchback had been feeling in Ralph's pockets.

From one of them he drew forth a paper.

A poster which had been torn down from a wall.

Glancing over the words that it contained, which, being in large type, were easily discernible by moonlight, the hunchback uttered a loud exclamation. "By heavens!" he cried, "it is none other than Red Ralph, the famous highwayman. It must be he, for see—here is his description."

The lady read through the words, and handed back the paper to the hunchback.

"Would he consent, think you?" she asked.

"He is insensible, and cannot help himself."

"But should he refuse?"

"In that case," said the hunchback, with a horrible smile. "He only would die an hour or two earlier than he otherwise would do."

The hunchback, who was possessed of gigantic strength, raised the highwayman in his arms and carried him through the bushes out into a park.

For some moments after they had gone, the two keepers remained silently watching and listening.

Then they slowly emerged from their hidingplace, and peeped after the retreating forms of the lady and her ill-shapen companion.

The hunchback was carrying the highwayman's insensible form in his arms, and the moonlight revealed in startling distinctness Ralph's white upturned face.

Every now and then the lady paused, and turned to scan the horizon, as though fearing that some spy might be watching their movements.

The hunchback, however, with all the speed which the weight of the burden he carried would allow of, hurried onwards, nor did he pause until the shadow of an avenue of majestic chestnuts hid him from the watchers' view.

Not until then did either of the speakers give utterance to their astonishment.

"Well?" said one at last.

"Well?" repeated the other.

"What do you make of all that?"

"An extraordinary affair, is it not?"

"We hav'nt seen the most extraordinary part, though. Some horrible doings there must be up there at the Hall."

"I'd give my life to know what is the meaning of the mystery. Suppose we follow and watch."

In the track of the hunchback and his beautiful guide, the two gamekeepers stealthily followed.

Silently and cautiously they approached the Old Hall, within the walls of which, e'er dawn of day, a fearful tragedy was about to be enacted.

A deed of black and damnable treachery.

A cruel wrong, an outrage perpetrated upon one so young, beautiful, and innocent—friendless and defenceless in the hands of her cold-blooded mother-in-law and her monstrous accomplice.

Helpless to his doom was carried Red Ralph.

The prophecy of the Old Hag at the boozing-ken had so far come true.

Already had he been brought face to face with a beautiful fiend—already had he fallen into her snares.

It yet remained to be seen whether or not in the fulness of time she would drag him to the scaffold.

Certain was it, however, that from the earliest time a dark and terrible curse had hung over his race.

Through more than four generations had his forefathers, once amongst the greatest and most noble in the land, rendered the name monstrous among men by their foul deeds of blood and horror.

Upon him, Ralph, the last of a doomed house, the curse lay heavier than upon any other.

Also the memory of a father's violent and disgraceful death—broken upon the wheel in France, for sacrilege and murder—of a mother's shame and infamy and awful end, strangled and burnt at the stake in Smithfield.

Yes, sure enough, a curse hung over him, and Fate was pointing now to the road by which he must travel to the end.

The hunchback bore him onwards by the chestnut avenue and through a small plantation, to where, in a high red-brick moss-grown wall, they came to a small door, scarcely discernible for the tangled mass of blackberries and briars growing across it.

To a casual observer it would have appeared that the door-way had been for many years in disuse, for it was green with damp, and the bushes in front almost choked it up.

But the lady carefully drew the creeping plants on one side, and, applying to the lock a small key which she carried, without any difficulty effected an entrance.

The hunchback having carried the highwayman through into a garden beyond, she then carefully replaced the bushes, so that it would have been very difficult to have told that they had ever been moved, and, following her companion, locked the door again behind her.

They then made their way through another plantation, crossed another large old-fashioned garden, in the midst of which stood a great sombre mansion, and let themselves in at a side door.

Noiselessly, then, they crept on tiptoe up a narrow stone staircase, and entered a room above, in which a large lamp with a shade of crimson glass cast a subdued light around upon costly decorations and luxurious furniture.

The thick velvet pile of the carpet rendered their footsteps inaudible; and while the hunchback busied himself in loosening the insensible man's cravat, his beautiful companion glided to and fro as noiseless as a phantom.

The effects of the blow that had stunned him were already passing away.

A few drops of cold water sprinkled upon his brow caused him with a deep sigh to open his eyes and look languidly around.

" Where am I ?" he murmured softly.

The lady, raising her head, motioned her companion to withdraw, and, approaching the highwayman with a sweet smile, placed a crystal goblet to his hot parched lips.

Greedily he drank the cool and deliciously refreshing liquid which it contained.

Scarcely, however, had the last drops passed his lips when with a faint murmur, as though of exquisite bliss, he closed his eyes again, and lay back upon the soft couch on which the hunchback had placed him.

Whilst he there lay motionless, a smile of surpassing sweetness flitted across his handsome features, and his lips murmured gently, as though some ecstatic vision filled his imagination.

During the time that he was unconscious, those who brought him thither were not idle. The lady laid aside a dark hood and cloak which she had worn, and the hunchback lighted a number of lamps about the room, and while yet Ralph's eyes were closed crept away out of sight.

Ralph did not, however, remain very long insensible, and when again he opened his eyes a vision of seraphic beauty was before him.

He lay upon a soft couch in a magnificent apartment, rich in gilt mouldings, with countless lamps reflected again and again in great mirrors reaching from the floor to the ceiling.

Before him, in all her queen-like and superb beauty, was the mysterious woman.

She was not at most more than twenty-five or six years old, and her splendid hair, black and shiny and soft as silk, hung down upon her bare and snow-white shoulders.

She was attired in a magnificent robe of black velvet, and her naked arms and neck were ornamented with glittering diamonds, rubies, emeralds, and pearls in lavish profusion.

Never in his life had he looked upon one so lovely, he thought, as he gazed rapturously upon the woman before him with her angel's face, melting eyes, red pouting lips, and splendid form, faultlessly modelled and voluptuously developed.

Yet was there hidden beneath this superb beauty something dark and treacherous, false, snake-like—satanic.

It was the beauty of the rattlesnake, which lures to destruction.

Her soft languishing eyes seemed to eat their way into his very soul.

He shuddered and cowered beneath their gaze.

Vainly he strove to cast off the meshes which encompassed him.

Vainly, for he was her slave—her slave for evermore.

He almost fancied he could feel the corpse-chill of her lithe and slender fingers, covered with glittering rings as they hovered round his throat.

They seemed to his excited imagination to tighten and tighten like the folds of a snake slowly creeping round the doomed one's body, crushing the bones and flesh to pulp.

He felt those glowing burning eyeballs eating their way to his heart.

He felt a tress of her soft hair sweeping his face.

He felt her scented breath upon his cheeks.

" Who are you ?" she asked in soft winning tones.

" They call me Red Ralph," he answered, as it were involuntarily, for he appeared to be under a kind of spell.

" You are a highwayman," she said, " I have often heard of your bold and reckless deeds—of your gallant exploits—your hairbreadth escapes—your acts of gallantry, which are the town's talk."

Who was this mysterious beauty who thus addressed him ? he wondered,

Had she fallen in love with him and lured him thither to this strange house in the wood ?

In the same soft winning voice she continued :—

" Alas! bold Ralph, you are now in the power of those who will ruthlessly work your destruction, unless you consent to what I shall propose to you."

He looked up earnestly into her glowing eyes. The serpent's breath was still upon his cheek. The silk hair seemed creeping round his neck.

" I—I will what you choose," he murmured.

" A shameful and dreadful death awaits you," she said, " unless you agree to do what is proposed to you. I can save you, if you consent, and the means by which you earn this reward are not very disagreeable."

He listened eagerly, drinking in every word she uttered, but spoke not himself.

" You can save yourself, by marriage."

" Marriage, with whom ?"

He stretched his arms out, as though he would have encircled her beautiful form, but she glided from his embrace.

" No—no," she said, in a low voice. " It is not to me you are to wed, but to one younger and far more beautiful.

" More beautiful ?" he murmured, in amazement.

" Yes, will you consent ?"

What more she said, he could scarcely comprehend. He somehow felt that there were danger and treachery in store for him.

He knew that there was satanic influence at work.

He knew that he ought to have resisted—to have struggled for freedom.

But he was powerless!

The blow he had received, and the fatal draught which had been administered to him, combined to bewilder and confuse him.

He was like one walking in his sleep. Like one under the influence of opium.

He had been drugged!

His beautiful companion talked passionately, and, giving him her hand, helped him to his feet and led him, he walking with weak and tottering steps towards one end of the room where hung a thick curtain of crimson velvet.

Then, drawing this aside, he gazed wonderingly into a room beyond.

It was much smaller than that in which he stood, but was exquisitely furnished, and was fragrant with the perfume of the most delicious flowers, whilst the air was filled with soft and touching melody, coming he knew not from what source.

In the roseate light he saw, reclining upon a couch, a creature so beautiful that he could not believe the evidence of his eyes.

She was about eighteen years of age, of a delicate pink and white complexion, with golden hair which fell in rich silken tresses upon a neck and bosom white, polished, and beautifully moulded as the bust of the Medicean statue.

A flowing robe of gauzy, almost transparent material enveloped her beauteous form. She wore no ornaments, but a wreath of orange blossoms was entwined in her hair.

"This is your wife," the lady whispered in his ear, as he stood gazing unsteadily upon the lovely vision before him.

The beautiful girl appeared to be either asleep or dead, so still and statue-like was her attitude. Obedient to the call of the other lady, however, she slowly opened two orbs of heavenly blue, and faintly smiled as the lady, leading Ralph, advanced towards her.

Then she rose to her feet, and laid her hand in that which she held out towards her, and gazed into his face with a dreamy expression, as though she saw him not.

The hand she placed in his was very cold, and her manner had in it something indescribably strange and unnatural, like that of a somnambulist.

He stooped down towards her, intending to say something, though hardly knowing what, for he was confused and giddy himself, but, glancing round, he saw that the outer rooms were filled with strange faces, and the lady led him and the young girl towards them.

Next moment, with his senses all reeling, he found himself and his future bride standing together in a semi-circle ranged before a grey-headed priest, who, book in hand, began in low tones to read the solemn exhortation which opens the marriage ritual.

More and more, however, did the confusion of Ralph's mind increase.

When the time came for him to respond, he hardly recognised the hoarse sound of his own voice.

He heard not that of his bride, nor did he notice how it was that when the ceremony was concluded every one glided away again as mysteriously as they had come, and he found himself sitting by his wife's side, upon the couch, where she had reclined, when first he saw her.

As cold and silent as ever was she, with the same icy hand and dreamy sightless eyes.

An awful stillness in her manner, a kind of death in life, which chilled and terrified him.

Greater grew his terror, though, as he gazed upon her face, and through, the strange confusion of his mind broke the recollection of the dead woman lying in her jewels upon the bed in the Old House at Westminster.

Now for the first time did he trace the extraordinary likeness between the two women—a likeness he must have noticed before had it not been for the difference in the colour of the hair.

Yes, there were the same regular features, the same classic beauty.

Were they related? was it chance?

What awful mystery connected the two?

What mysterious destiny had brought him into the presence of both in one night?

Was he dreaming? was he mad?

CHAPTER VII.

THE TEMPTER AGAIN—THE SUBTERRANEAN PAS-
SAGES — THE TREACHERY—THE SNARE — TH
HORRIBLE DOOM.

WHILST Ralph was confusedly endeavouring t
collect his scattered thoughts, the lady he had just see
returned and spoke to his companion.

Presently, though how he knew not, they were bot
gone, and he was sitting alone in the room, the light
of which seemed to have almost entirely died out.

Too confused and bewildered, however, to feel an
alarm upon this account, he sat there for a long whil
in a dreamy state until he was aroused by a soft han
resting on his, and, looking up, found the lady in th
velvet dress bending over him.

"Come with me," she said.

Ralph tried to recollect what had happened durin
the last half-hour, and looked around for his bride.

She was nowhere to be seen.

"Where is she?" he asked.

"I will take you to her."

He rose obedient to her summons and followed he
and she led him from the room.

She led the way down a broad thickly carpeted stair
case, and along a seemingly interminable passage.

Then down a steep flight of stone steps.

"Where are we going?" he asked, pausing to loo
wonderingly around.

She only answered with one of her fascinating smile
and fixed her glittering eyes upon his.

She held out her soft hand to take his, and h
allowed himself to be led away again without
murmur.

Along a low narrow passage they now proceeded
the walls of which were green and wet.

At last they paused before a low door, which grate
on its hinges as the lady opened it.

He looked wonderingly forward into the dens
gloom beyond, and would have asked some ques
tions, but again the glittering serpent's eyes did thei
work of fascination.

She held the light in such a way that Ralph coul
not see what there was beyond.

Hitherto she had preceded him, and it was th
fact of her holding back for him to pass in front, whic
awoke, in his breast, a momentary suspicion of foul pla

He passed the fatal threshold, and the door close
behind him.

It closed with a loud clang, which vibrated throug
his heart.

He was alone in pitchy darkness.

For a moment, he was at a loss to understand wha
had happened to him. He thought that the doo
must have closed by accident.

Several moments elapsed, and yet the darkness an
silence remained unbroken.

He turned and flung himself against the door, an
battered wildly with his clenched fists, and shoute
with all the strength of his lungs.

Then the horrible truth began to dawn upon him—
he had been betrayed.

He had fallen into a trap.

The fair-faced fiend had lured him to his destruction

He listened intently, and he fancied that he hear
a low mocking laugh, full of bitter irony. A satani
mirth—the rejoicing of a demon at his misery.

But the horror of his situation had not yet reache
its climax.

He felt the floor was giving way beneath his feet.

He clutched wildly at the walls.

Their slimy surface slipped from his fingers.

A hideous vapour arose from underneath, hal
stifling him.

Great heavens! what fearful death awaited him?

[TORTURING A WITCH.]

Rapidly the floor sank beneath his feet, and the slimy walls glided from his grasp.

Then there was a grating sound beneath him, and the floor on which he stood gave way suddenly.

In another moment he was dashed violently down into a black abyss full of water and mud.

A loud cry escaped his lips, and even in that moment of confusion and terror he fancied that he could hear another shriek which was not the echo of his own.

Another shriek, long, shrill, heart-rending, full of bitter agony.

Hurled headlong downwards, he was almost stunned by the violence of the fall.

He somehow or other, though, saved his head by stretching out his hands, and thus warded off the shock.

But the filthy mess into which he had been plunged choked and stifled him.

A noxious odour arose from the black mud which half poisoned him.

He felt sick and giddy.

He stretched out his hand to save himself from falling, and his hands came in contact with the slimy wall.

Into what horrible place had he fallen?

Had the giving way of the floor been accidental?

His mind, however, was very soon settled upon that point, for presently he heard the trap close over his head with a crash.

No. 3.

Then he felt certain that this horror had been premeditated.

And what was his fate? Was he doomed here to wallow in this revolting place until his strength failed him, and he sank down choked and stupified?

No, the thought was too fearful.

He felt that his mind was giving way under the accumulation of terrors.

Then he made the roof ring again with his piercing shrieks.

And then, exhausted and panting for breath, he began to grope his way along by the wall.

Perhaps there might be a way out of the place into which he had fallen.

He might be able to escape.

Oh, how his heart bounded at the thought!

He groped his way onwards very slowly and carefully, for he was fearful of falling into some hole, and sinking over his head in the filth.

As it was, where he was now walking the water only reached up to his waist, and with intense delight he discovered as he progressed that it grew more shallow.

He walked so very slowly that the wall he was following seemed of enormous length, and he began to think that he was in some sewer, at the mouth of which he should in good time arrive.

Finding no obstacles in his way he grew bolder, and increased his pace.

But suddenly his progress was cut short.

He struck his head violently against a wall in front of him.

Very much crestfallen, he turned and began to follow the second wall.

All before him was dark and dismal, yet not quite hopeless, for surely there must be an outlet and it was only a work of time and patience.

But after he had crept along by the wall side for about twenty feet, his progress was again cut short.

There was another wall before him.

A deep sigh escaped his heaving breast when he made this discovery.

A horrible thought broke upon him. He was in a large square hole or cesspool, or cellar from which there was no outlet.

Wearily and despondently he turned the corner, and began slowly creeping along by the third wall.

He was now travelling in the direction from which he had originally come.

Only one of the four sides had yet to be explored. In this lay his last hope.

With a fast-beating heart, then, he crept onwards.

He scarcely dared to hope: the reaction would be too horrible: it would, he felt be more than he could bear.

The cold perspiration broke out upon his face.

His hair bristled upon his head.

His knees smote together.

Onward, onward, the journey seemed to be interminable.

Would he never reach the end?

As he proceeded, however, he made a terrible discovery. As he advanced, the water rose.

It continued to grow deeper and deeper, and had soon reached his breast and was rising towards his chin.

If he were obliged to travel much further, he must either travel under water or swim.

But when he was reflecting upon these dismal alternatives, and when the filthy water had reached his chin, he found himself, to his great delight, at the fourth wall.

He groped his way along now with a throbbing heart, for his only hope lay here.

A few moments more, and all would be decided.

Eagerly his hands followed the wall, but his heart grew heavier every step he took.

At last, when he was giving himself up to despair, the longed-for opening was found.

A narrow outlet through which he had no small difficulty in squeezing his body. He hesitated not a moment, however, but groped his way onward in the new direction thus afforded him.

He struggled onwards up to his neck in the black mud and slush, half stifled by the noxious vapours arising from it.

Every now and then he heard a squealing and scampering which he knew to be made by rats, although it was too dark to discern them.

Would these horrors never cease? he asked himself, as he felt his strength deserting him.

But at length his heart beat wildly with joy. A faint glimmer was descernible, though far ahead.

He worked his way laboriously towards it, and found that it came from above — from a trap-door partly open.

The door was about three feet above his head, and he could but manage to reach it by springing upwards and clutching at the edge.

It would have been an easier plan to cry aloud for help, but how could he tell to whom his cries would be audible?

Such a plan might only lead to his certain death at the hand of those from whom, by a miracle, he seemed hitherto to have escaped.

There was a bright light burning in the chamber above, but although he listened intently he could hear no sound.

Perhaps the room was empty. In any case it would be madness any longer to remain where he was without making an attempt, however desperate, to free himself.

Concentrating what strength yet remained to him, he sprang upwards and clung to the edge of the trap.

His head spun round as he did so, and every limb trembled violently from weakness, but he yet continued to maintain his hold.

Then he dragged himself laboriously through the aperture, raising the trap-door with his shoulders as he did so.

He found himself in a strange sort of cellar or cavern which appeared to have been hollowed out of a rock.

A dying fire smouldered in a roughly contrived fire-place, before which—stretched out upon the bare ground in a shaggy coat that made him look like some huge dog—a man lay asleep.

His face, upon which the fire-light shone, was almost hidden by a tangled mass of coarse black hair. His figure was sturdy and muscular.

In his belt he carried a cutlas and a pistol, and another pistol lay upon the floor close to his hand, in which he grasped an empty bottle.

He had evidently drunk himself to sleep.

Ralph—with all the care he was capable of—wriggled his way through the opening and crawled into the room.

He congratulated himself immensely upon the fact of this man's being asleep, for he had no doubt that he would, unnoticed, be able to find a means of egress from the cave if he were only cautious how he proceeded.

But such was not to be the case.

The same evil fortune which had pursued him relentlessly throughout the night overtook him here.

On working his body free of the trap he flung the trap-door upwards, and it fell over with a deafening crash against the wall.

Next moment, before Ralph could gain an upright position, the sleeping man had awakened and sprung to his feet.

His eyes alighting upon the crouching form of the

highwayman, with a savage curse he loosened his cutlass from his girdle and made a furious blow at him.

But his aim was unsteady, and the gleaming blade hissed through the air within an inch of the robber's head.

The violence of the blow made the man stagger against the wall.

Ere he could recover himself Ralph had seized the pistol lying upon the ground and hastily cocked it.

His antagonist in another instant had again raised on high his murderous blade and made a furious rush upon him.

But as he came Ralph levelled the pistol at him and fired.

The ball struck his foe between the eyes and instantly covered his face with blood.

His body for a moment retained an upright posture, quivering convulsively.

Then tottered, swayed to and fro, and fell backwards through the open trap.

A loud splash followed—a gurgling—and dead silence.

Motionless as a statue, Ralph remained in the attitude which he had taken when he fired the fatal shot —his arm still stretched out—the pistol still grasped betwixt his fingers.

He waited thus half fancying that the dead man's face might re-appear at the trap-door.

But all was still.

Slowly he rose to his feet and gazed down into the black abyss.

He took a blazing stick from the fire and holding it above his head peered into the blackness beneath.

The surface of the noisome ditch lay black and smooth as heretofore.

Heaving a deep sigh of relief, he turned away and began to make a more lengthened survey of the strange place in which he found himself.

By the aid of the blazing stick serving him as a torch he soon discovered in a distant corner of the gloomy cave a roughly hewn door-way into which was fitted an oaken door seemingly of immense strength, though unbarred.

Opening this he passed through into a long low passage beyond, then up a flight of rough stairs all hewn out of solid stone, and with some difficulty raised a heavy trap-door. Ralph then forced his way through a very narrow opening into what seemed to be a room in a miserable cottage, with bare walls and a thatched roof.

The door of the hovel, though very strong, was standing unfastened as the door was below.

There was no sign of human presence about this curious place, and, seeing that it was broad day without, Ralph had little fear of any act of violence.

The idea therefore occurred to him that it would be as well to institute a search for some dry clothes before he made his exit.

He had left the trap-door open leading to the staircase.

It formed the hearth of the cottage room in which he stood, and was evidently only to be opened from the outside by touching some spring which, though he searched for it for some time, he did not succeed in discovering.

Leaving the investigation, however, to some future period, he descended to the cellar and began to search for some wearing apparel.

He found two large chests—the lid of one of which, standing open, had before afforded him a passing glance of a confusion of clothes.

He dragged its contents out upon the ground and searched among them for what he wanted.

There was a great variety of dress both male and female, and of every quality.

Ralph in astonishment tumbled out rich silks and costly velvets, coats elaborately embroidered with gold lace, petticoats of every colour of the rainbow, ruffles, perukes, high-heel shoes, jack boots, cocked hats, chemisettes, silk stockings, and hoops of all sorts and sizes.

He might, had he so chosen, have attired himself as an officer in His Majesty's Guards, or a Bow Street Runner, or a beau or a belle of the first water.

"They can't be disguises and left all tumbled up in this way," Ralph thought. "But what are they?"

The mystery seemed difficult to solve, yet the solution was close at hand.

He had chosen from among the clothes a scarlet cloth coat, and was turning it round and round to examine it.

His eye fell upon a cut in the back.

He looked at the lining.

Upon it there was a black stain.

The stain of blood.

The mystery was cleared now. These were dead men's clothes stolen from the bodies of murdered victims.

It would appear that the man Ralph had shot was one of a band of robbers, and that these were some of the spoils.

It could not be possible that there was only one inhabitant of this mysterious cave?

Yet, again, it was not very likely that the band (if a band existed) would be abroad during the daytime: that was the period which robbers usually selected to take their rest.

He knew a good deal, too, about the gentlemen of the road and the celebrated cracksmen of the period, yet he had never heard of such a retreat as this.

Never—ah! he stopped suddenly in his reflections, for something in the darkness had caught his eye and rivetted him to the spot.

It was a white face watching him.

He sprang towards a sword hanging against the wall, unhooked it and stood ready for the expected attack. As no attack came he slowly advanced towards the face which still was stationary where he first had seen it.

But as he drew near a smile spread over his handsome features, for he now perceived that what he had been looking at was a yellow satin mask hanging on a rail.

But when he took it down and looked at it the smile gave place to a look of astonishment as a thought flashed through his mind.

"The Yellow Masks," he pondered, "the Yellow Masks. It surely is not possible that I have found out the hiding-place of that mythical band. It is true, then, that they exist. They are not really—as I have always supposed—horrible phantoms conjured up by the old nurses to frighten naughty children. No, this must be their stronghold or what was their stronghold, for who knows I may have killed the last survivor? And these were the clothes stolen from their victims. The blood upon them seems to bear witness to the truth of the horrible atrocities the Yellow Masks are said to have committed."

Horrible indeed were the atrocities attributed to the lawless band to whom Ralph supposed the cave to belong.

It was rather a dangerous experiment, though, to remain here long, for should they unexpectedly return he could hardly hope for a better fate than to have his throat cut and be flung back again down the trap.

In his place the generality of persons would have lost as little time as possible in effecting their escape. With Red Ralph, however, it was different.

As the reader who follows his fortunes will find, he did not turn his back upon any ordinary danger.

He was miserably wretched, too, in his soaking mud-clogged dress, and, although he felt some repugnance at putting on murdered men's secondhand clothes, still they must be more comfortable than those he wore, and he resolved to effect a change.

He had very soon selected the necessary articles of clothing, and had not much trouble about finding a good fit.

Then he dragged off his wet clothes and began to dress.

When he had finished he was about to fling the old ones down the trap, but with a start he stopped short.

"Good heavens!" he exclaimed, "what was I going to do?"

And he began to feel in the pockets. Very deliberately—at first. Then with a faster-beating heart—then in desperate haste. At last in despair he desisted.

"I must have dropped them down in the ditch," he muttered, "when that beautiful demon flung me down they must have fallen from my pocket."

It was the diamonds and jewels he had stolen from the dead body in Westminster about which he was speaking.

"By jove! and the five hundred pounds, too, I took from old Bigwig."

Ralph groaned at the recollection of what he had lost.

"Why, I've got rid of half-a-dozen fortunes in one night. Half-a-dozen times as much as ever I had in my possession. However, if they are down in the ditch, I won't rest until I find them again."

He made up his mind to bear with his loss as philosophically as possible.

It was time now to take his departure while he was yet safe and sound.

He lighted another stick at the fire, and made his way along the passage and up the flight of steps to the trap-door.

But to his intense consternation he found that it was closed.

Vainly he endeavoured to raise it.

There must have been a secret spring somewhere, but to discover its whereabouts defied all his efforts.

What was to be done?

How had the accident occurred?

He felt quite positive that he had not closed the door when he came through it.

Was it possible that he had fallen into another trap?

"Oh, what a fool I was not to go when I got the chance!" he thought.

But what was to be done?

He did not like to abandon the search, although he felt that it was almost useless.

Over every inch of the wall within his reach did he again and again pass his hands in the hope of finding a spring.

But in vain.

He stamped and kicked and thumped, but still the door remained tightly shut as before.

What was to be done, he asked himself again and again, without being able to find any satisfactory answer.

Nothing could be done, indeed, but to wait and see what fate should bring about.

He returned to the cave below and sat down by the fire listening intently for the slightest noise.

Every moment he expected that some one might steal in upon him from behind and stab him in the back.

And so impressed was he with this horrible idea that he was at last obliged to shift his place so that he might sit with his back against the wall.

Not very long had he been thus when he felt that sleep was taking possession of him.

He yawned and stretched himself and altered his position again and again.

But it was no good. Do what he would his eyelids grew heavier and heavier.

What was he to do now?

To sleep was to invite almost certain death.

Whilst he was slumbering the band would probably return. He would only be aroused by the thrust of a poignard or the blow of a bludgeon.

His only chance of escape lay in his watchfulness and vigilance.

Yet he felt that it was impossible to ward off the drowsiness oppressing him.

The only way to do, then, was to find some place where he could sleep a while, and where he would not be observed should any one return suddenly to the cave.

With the aid of a flaming stick he again made a tour of the mysterious chamber, and his eyes alighted on a sort of cupboard which he thought might serve his purpose.

A quantity of lumber was piled up in front of it, which he pulled on one side to allow for the passage of his body.

Then, dropping in a quantity of the clothes from the box, made himself as comfortable as possible.

Hardly had he been there five minutes before he was fast sleep.

Slumbering as placidly as a new-born babe—dreaming he had escaped from all danger and was again following a cross country upon his bonnie black mare.

Very far from free of danger, however, was he, for see the door of the cave opens with an ominous creak, and two dusky forms steal into the fire-lit chamber.

Two dusky forms with gleaming daggers in their hands.

CHAPTER VIII.

THE DRUGGED BRIDE—RECALLED TO LIFE—THE VICTIM—THE NIGHT JOURNEY—THE OLD HAG—THE ATTEMPTED ESCAPE—A WITCH! A WITCH!

WHOSE was that piercing shriek which had rung in Ralph's ears as he fell through the trap?

What had become of the beautiful girl to whom he had been so mysteriously wedded, and from whom he had been so suddenly separated.

These are questions to which our story obliges us to find an immediate answer, although to do so we are reluctantly compelled to desert our hero in a highly critical situation.

In a quaintly-fashioned chamber in the western wing of the Old Hall the fair creature who had played the part of bride in the strange ceremony lay in an unconscious state upon her virgin couch.

Cold, powerless, passive, she lay there, supremely beautiful, yet with the pallor of death upon her soft peach-like cheeks.

Helpless in the hands of those who pitilessly worked her ruin, the beautiful girl could not, though the internal struggle was absolutely terrific in its smothered violence, shake off the torpor weighing her down, numbing her senses, crippling her vital energies.

But as the hours crept slowly on the imprisoned soul struggled more furiously for freedom.

Violently ere now had it battled with his manacles.

When the hideous humpback was, at her mother-in-law's directions, carrying her away to her bed-chamber, the young bride had given vent to the piercing shriek which had reached the ears of Ralph when falling through the trap.

Instantly, however, were the cries stifled, and she was borne away.

But not before some of the inmates of the house had been alarmed, and in low whispers the mysterious lady and the hunchback consulted together upon the future course of action.

"The effects of the potion seem to be wearing off," the lady said.

"It is the long delay."

"There are only two courses open to us: we must get away at once or—"

"Or renew the draught."

"No, no; that must not be done. I fear it might cost her her life."

"It would certainly be a dangerous experiment."

"Too dangerous. I—I would not have my hands stained with her blood, much as I should gain by her death."

"The carriage we agreed should be here at six."

"That is very late."

"They will keep their time, though, my lady; I am certain that we can depend upon them."

"Let us hope so. If she recovers her senses before then, we are lost."

They carried the poor girl into her bedchamber and laid her upon the couch where her motionless limbs were extended, her face turned upwards, and as white as the pillow upon which it lay.

The mother-in-law sat silently watching in a small dark antechamber, where, upon a deep old-fashioned window-seat, she could command a view of the insensible form of the young girl, and could see what was taking place in the park without, in the plantation, and the gloomy garden close under the house side.

Very still and death-like lay the white figure, and not the faintest sound of breathing reached the listener's attentive ears.

Yet, nevertheless, the young bride's sleeping soul began, in spite of the potion's benumbing power, to shake off its shackles.

Something stirred within the depths of the entranced woman's existence, and she began to awaken slowly and painfully.

She felt, at first, something like inward shudderings which went palpitating from her heart to her brain.

Then the power of the will gathered strength, and at length, after a strong internal convulsion, the muscles of her eye-lids quivered, and her eyes opened.

Then her whole frame quivered with intense emotion, and then with a low husky cry she sprang up in bed, clutching the bedclothes between her thin white fingers.

With her wildly-dilated eyes, her streaming hair, and her white garments gleaming ghastly in the moonlight, she formed a terrible picture, which for a moment, as she turned and gazed upon it, chilled the watcher's blood.

Ere she could rush forward the young bride's frozen tongue seemed suddenly to loosen itself, and her tortured soul gave utterance to a piercing shriek of agony, succeeded by another, and still another, each louder and shriller than the last.

But, shaking off the momentary fear which had at first restrained her, the lady ran forward, and, flinging herself upon the other, struggled with her violently and held her down upon the bed.

It was doubtful, however, whether her strength would have been sufficient thus to keep her there had not the hunchback come to her help.

He, holding the young girl in his brawny arms, forced her head back upon the pillow, and with brutal violence wrenched open her mouth.

Quick as lightning then the woman dashed betwixt the victim's teeth some colourless liquid from a small bottle which she produced from a medicine chest standing on the table.

Only for a brief moment afterwards did the young girl struggle for freedom.

A grey shade crept over her face.

Her limbs grew stiff and rigid.

The pupils of her eyes grew large and darkened, and fixed in a sightless stare horrible to look upon.

The two accomplices laid her back upon the bed, and stood for several instants silently regarding her.

At last the lady spoke; and the low tones of her voice trembled with agitation.

"Do you think we—we have given her too much?"

The hideous hunchback bent over the unhappy victim of their cruelty.

His bony crooked fingers undid the fastening at the neck of her dress, and he laid his hand upon her bosom, white and polished as the finest marble.

"Does her heart beat?" the lady asked.

"Yes; faintly."

"Thank God for that. We could take her away now if the carriage were only ready."

"It is below."

"Will you carry her, then? But stay; let me listen first upon the stairs."

With noiseless footsteps the lady stole away into the darkness of the corridor, cautiously opened a small door, and passing through was lost in the dense obscurity beyond.

Silent as the tomb, however, was all within this strange house.

Presently she returned and whispered to her accomplice.

"Is all well?"

"Yes."

"Shall I bring her?"

"Yes."

In deep silence and pitchy darkness the hunchback bore his fair burden down a secret staircase leading from the ante-room to the garden without.

It was the staircase by which Ralph had been brought into the house.

By the same road that Ralph's insensible form had been brought thither, the young and lovely creature to whom he had been under such extraordinary circumstances wedded was carried away.

In the wood without there was a travelling carriage waiting with four horses, fresh and strong, and pawing the air with impatience to commence their journey before them.

Muffled in a thick cloak, the motionless, unbreathing, yet still living form of the beautiful bride was placed within, upon the back seat.

The hunchback also entered the carriage, and, as he slammed the door to, the figure of the mysterious lady who had taken so prominent a part in this strange drama disappeared from the shadow of the trees where it had been lurking, and flitted through the old garden towards the secret staircase.

The carriage containing the abducted girl then drove on at a rapid pace, and was soon beyond the limits of the park.

Daylight was breaking with a dull leaden hue, and the broad expanse of bleak open country through which they were travelling looked wretchedly cold and miserable.

They were tearing along at a rapid pace, now that they had reached the high road.

The hedges on either side of the road seemed to fly past them.

Yet the hunchback was not satisfied by the pace, but again and again called out in anger to the postillions.

"Faster, faster, faster! a thousand curses on you, faster!"

Vigorously the postboys plied their whips.

The panting horses strained every muscle and sinew.

The sparks flew in showers from their clattering hoofs.

"Faster, faster, faster!"

It was more like the shriek of a demon than the sound of a human voice.

His hideous face, distorted by passion, glared at them through the carriage window.

He shook his fleshless fist, and howled and jabbered and cursed.

They might have thought they had the devil for a passenger.

"Faster, faster! you cursed dogs! you slouching hounds! you bungling idiots! I'd like to wrench your ears off, I'd like to job out your eyes, I'd like to twist out your tongues. Why don't you drive faster? why don't you whip? why don't you spur? why don't you bring blood?"

Thus did the horrible hunchback scream discordantly through the carriage window as they tore along the road.

He was in a fever lest they should not be able to reach their destination before the world was up and stirring in the work of the newborn day.

As it was, their clattering steaming progress through a village on their way brought many white frightened faces to the windows, and some very early risers to the doors.

A man at the toll-bar gate through which they passed asked with a wondering face whether it was an elopement, and added to his good lady, when he had got into his house again, that if it were, and he were the bride, he for his part would as soon have run away with Old Nick.

On they rushed again, the postilions furiously lashing the panting horses, the hunchback shrieking more and more hoarsely, like a bird of ill omen in their rear.

They reached at last their destination, which was an old house standing by itself, at the bottom of a lane, which the branches from the high trees growing by the roadside cast into deep shadow.

Leaving the young girl in the carriage, the hunchback made his way across a neglected garden to the house, and hammered long and persistently at the door.

A blear-eyed old crone at last replied to him.

"Well?" she said, in a week weedy voice.

"Well?" he repeated, imitating her tone, "will nothing short of an earthquake waken you?"

"What do you want now you have awakened me?"

"I've brought you the young lady I spoke to you about."

"Where is she?"

"Outside. I'll bring her in. You must take care of her. I have got to go back, but will be with you again to-morrow; and now watch her closely, and remember your life depends on her safe keeping."

The still insensible girl was brought into the house and carried up stairs.

They placed her on a bed in a close-smelling room, with a low ceiling, black panels, and a four-post bedstead, heavy and cumbersome, and surrounded by feathers similar to those upon a hearse.

Here she lay still as death—as white as a corpse—when the carriage had driven away, and the old hag sat watching by her side.

She was a frightful old hag, toothless and slobbering, with tufts of iron-grey hair growing here and there upon her head, which, otherwise, was bald and red, and hideous to look upon.

With long claw-like fingers she hovered round the form of the sleeping girl, and stealthily searched in the pockets of her dress with thievish intent.

"Not a brass farden," she muttered, discontented, and with a dismal expression of countenance, "not a stiver, not a rap, not a bodle, not nothink; and, oh! how thirsty I am; my poor throat's like a lime-kiln."

The breath coming from her poor throat was odorous of alcohol, and there was that in her bloated face, her trembling fingers, and unsteady gait, which told her story very plainly—she was a gin-drinker.

Before the hunchback had left, however, he had most particularly cautioned her against quitting the house during his absence.

The house stood by itself far away from any other habitation.

It was wretched, poverty-stricken, and in ruins.

It had also the reputation of being haunted, so that it was no wonder the old hag had no visitors.

The day passed without any one coming.

The old woman watched at the window, fondly hoping that some one would heave in sight to whom she could beckon and send on a journey for gin to the nearest village.

But no one appeared; at least, no one who would have undertaken the errand.

Thus did her devouring thirst remain unappeased.

Excruciating her torments at length became, and she could endure them no longer.

White and motionless the beautiful girl still lay upon the bed.

Could not she be safely left for half an hour? the old hag asked herself.

There was no lock to the door, but it was not in the slightest degree probable that the drugged girl would arouse herself from her lethargy.

The old hag crept up to her and listened to her breathing, raised and let fall her hand, and shook her again and again.

But the girl lay still and motionless.

"She's all right," the old hag muttered, "and I won't be gone a minute."

With this she hurried off as fast as her tottering limbs would carry her.

But she was absent much longer than the minute she talked about.

Half an hour after the old hag had left the room the young girl arose from the bed; weak, faint, and giddy.

In vain she strove to stand; the room swam round her, and she sank with a deep sigh into a chair near to the open casement.

It was night again, and the moon had risen.

Without were tall dark trees with outstretched branches that assumed demon forms to her excited fancy.

The young bride remained for nearly a quarter of an hour motionless at the window, the cool air fanning her fevered brow.

Then she started to her feet and looked wildly around.

Where was she?

Into whose power had she fallen?

What motive had prompted her abduction?

How long had she thus been helpless and senseless?

As she asked herself these questions the wildest terror took possession of her.

What horrors might not be in store for her at the hands of the unscrupulous wretches whose victim she had fallen?

One course only was there open to her.

She must fly!

Yes, flight—instant flight—was her only resource.

She paced the room eagerly, but with cautious footsteps.

She gazed anxiously from the window.

A black gulf yawned beneath, and she turned from it with a shudder.

Then she crept to the door, opened it, and listened.

A dark corridor was without, ending in a steep flight of stairs, upon which the moonlight shone through a small passage window.

The fugitive, groping her way in the darkness, crept onwards.

With suppressed breath and a heart that beat until

she sickened with the violence of her emotion, she crept onwards.

Partially supporting herself by the railing she descended step by step.

The staircase was old, and creaked fearfully beneath her light tread.

Again and again she paused to listen, and lingered and wasted valuable time, little dreaming that the danger was without, and not within, the house from which she was bent upon escaping.

Little dreaming that the old hag was hurrying homewards as fast as she could walk—that she was even now in sight of home.

Every moment lessened the space between them.

Yet did the fugitive slowly creep onwards.

She reached the outer door at last, when the old hag was within a couple of yards of the garden gate.

She opened the door, passed through, and closed it as the old hag opened the gate.

But catching sight of her jailor's face—more horrible than ever in the moonlight—she crept shivering into the shadow of the wall, and allowed her to pass into the house.

Then, summoning all her strength, fled like the wind.

Not for a very great distance, however.

She was too weak for that.

She managed to reach the bottom of the lane. She contrived to stagger some hundred yards further on, and then fell fainting upon the threshold of a cottage door.

Presently the door was opened, and a woman, coming out, started back with a shrill cry at the sight of her.

"What is it?" asked a man's voice from within.

"Come here! it's a dead woman. Quick! quick!"

The man came with a light, and his wife stooped over her prostrate form.

But ere she could touch it the man had pulled her back, with a low cry, and a look of unutterable horror on his face.

"It is the witch!" he cried, "it is the witch! Take care, or the touch of her will wither your flesh."

Then, with a piercing shriek, his wife ran from the prostrate body, and the cottager, spurning it with his foot in a perfect paroxysm of terror, howled with all the strength of his lungs—

"Help! help! help!"

CHAPTER IX.

THE WITCH IN THE HANDS OF THE MOB—FIENDS IN HUMAN FORM—TO THE STAKE! TO THE STAKE!—THE RAGING FLAMES—THE MARTYR—THE MYSTERIOUS HORSEMEN—THE STRANGE MEETING.

THE cries of the frightened rustic reached the ears of the dwellers in a cottage at some fifty yards distance down the road, and they came hurrying to the spot.

Soon, like wildfire, the news spread far and wide, and the villagers crowded round the scene of action.

The hoarse and angry voices of the men contended with the shrill vindictive tones of the women as they wrangled over the prostrate form of the insensible girl.

But all were agreed upon one point: that was, that she was a witch who had visited their village a month before, and left behind her a withering curse and blight upon their homes and children—their land and crops.

"Where has she came from?"

"They told us she was dead."

"Such as she is never die. The grave is no prison to them."

"The stamped-down soil can't keep them under."

"It is because she was not put to death when we had her in our power."

"We should have drowned her."

"No, no! we should have burnt her."

"Yes, yes! let us burn her to ashes now."

"She shall not again escape us."

"To the stake! to the stake!"

A dozen hands were eagerly stretched forth.

The unhappy girl was roughly seized and dragged along the ground.

Her garments were torn into rags and wrenched off her body.

Her lovely form was revealed through the huge rents in her apparel.

Cruelly bruised and scratched, and stained with dust and dirt, the still senseless and half-naked girl was borne away to the place of execution.

Savagely the wretches howled around their victim.

The air was rent by their hoarse cries for vengeance.

They capered, and clapped their hands, and burst into loud and fiendish laughter.

"To the stake! to the stake!"

Soon the mob had reached a prodigious size; not a soul was left in the squalid huts and hovels of which the village was composed.

The old and infirm—the crippled, palsied, and blind—came to swell the throng.

Some shrieking fiends of women had brought with them their babies at the breast.

This is no exaggerated picture, reader. Years have brought about great changes even in highly-civilized England, where now-a-days there are no ignorant wretches who believe in witchcraft, or anything so absurd. ("Oh, no!" as the artful dodger says, "Not at all, by no means.")

These howling brutes of men and screeching hags of women dragged their victim onwards to the centre of what, for want of a better name for their litter of pig-styes, must be called the High Street.

In the centre of this was a stout oaken post driven deep into the hard ground, and fast as a rock.

It served at other times as a whipping-post, whereat wretched tramps, turnip-stealers, and such like miscreants were flagellated vigorously by the village constable by the order of the lord of the manor.

To this, with cords which were produced with lightning rapidity almost as soon as asked for, they bound the poor girl.

She had recovered her senses by this time, thanks to the brutal treatment she had received at the hands of her persecutors.

In wild terror she gazed upon the savage faces glaring at her.

In plaintive entreaty she stretched out her naked arms towards them.

"What have I done?" she asked. "What are you going to do to me?"

But in reply they only howled at her.

"A witch! a witch!"

"Silence her!"

"Gag her!"

"Strangle her!"

Some of the women, mad with fury at the sight of one who they supposed had wrought so much misery upon them and theirs, would have flown upon her.

They would have torn her limb from limb had not the strong arms of the men restrained them forcibly.

A fearful howl of vengeance, however, expressed their hatred and determination to be revenged.

Only one among the struggling crowd put in an appeal to save the condemned, but to her no one would give heed.

This was an old woman more long-headed than the rest, and with a better eyesight than the rest, though her age was wellnigh threescore.

"You are committing murder," she cried. "For shame of you! for shame of you!"

"What do you mean, Mistress Swift?"

"That it is not the witch."

"Not the witch?"

"No."

"How do you make that appear? Why, here is one who can swear to her. Can't you, Mistress Giles?"

"Ay, that I can if I were on the rack."

"And I."

"And I."

A score of voices joined in chorus.

"You are wrong, I tell ye," the old woman persisted; "the witch that cursed our village was a dark-haired witch, and see this woman has hair of the colour of gold."

For half a moment—not more—public opinion was on Mistress Swift's side, and a murmur ran through the crowd.

Had the witch black hair or golden?

Could there be any mistake?

But there arose a loud clamour of tongues; everybody talking together; each screaming her loudest to scream the other down.

"I will take my oath it's she, fair hair or dark."

"Look at her face; can there be any mistake?"

"It's just her mouth, and nose, and cheeks, and all her doll's face that my John, the lazy ne'er-do-well, took such a fancy to, od rot him."

"Isn't she the same height too? and see her hand; she has got a wedding ring on her finger."

"Ah! who is she wed to, I wonder?"

"She's Satan's bride, I will be sworn."

"Let her go to him then as quickly as she pleases. Heap up the faggots. Bring a light there; bring a light."

The poor girl could not doubt the fate that was in store for her.

Greedily her ears drank in the awful words she heard around.

What availed her innocence? for she was as innocent as she was ignorant of the evil imputed to her.

The villagers were bent on her destruction.

A horrible doom awaited her, from which there appeared to be no earthly hope of escape.

A fatal resemblance she certainly bore to a certain woman whom her would-be murderers supposed her to be.

The same likeness, it will be remembered, Red Ralph had noticed with amazement and alarm.

To what awful end would it lead?

We shall see.

The raging howling mob crowded round and jibed at and menaced her.

"Fire the pile! fire the pile!" some shrieked, thinking there was an unnecessary delay.

The poor girl, pale as death and half fainting with fear, stretched forth her arms in pitiful entreaty.

"Mercy! mercy!" she shrieked.

"Hear her," yelled one of the hags; "she asks mercy of us."

And then a yell of devilish laughter followed from the rest.

"She who has withered our limbs, and blinded our eyes, and blasted the land on which she looked, she asks for pity."

"Burn her! burn her! the death is far too easy for such as she."

"Mercy! mercy!"

"See she is pointing to us now. She will curse us yet; I feel her curse upon me now."

"And I; and I."

"Pile up the faggots! Light the fire! Burn her quickly!"

"Look at her eyes fixed on us. Blind her with the flames that she may not see us."

"Cut out her tongue that she may not ask the devil's aid to injure us."

"Mercy! mercy! I am innocent."

But it was in vain for her to appeal to her executioners.

Their hearts were hard as steel.

They were deaf to her prayers.

They thirsted for her blood with a devouring thirst, which her blood alone could appease.

"Mercy! mercy!"

Her voice was drowned by the yells of the mob.

A flaming torch, passed from hand to hand, now set light to the faggots and straw which surrounded her.

The straw blazed fiercely up, but the wood was green, and as yet only hissed and spluttered.

A shout was made for more straw and for dry wood, and soon plenty of both was brought to the scene of torture.

A light was applied to the fresh material, and the flame caught it and blazed fiercely.

A dense black smoke arose and hid the victim from those who were eager to gloat their eyes upon her excruciating sufferings.

Long and painful they seemed destined to be, for the wind was blowing the smoke away from her, and the flames were steadily creeping upwards.

She would not be choked; she would be roasted alive.

Like fiends from hell the rabble danced and screamed around her, stirred up the fire, and fanned the flames.

Their savage cries drowned her agonizing shrieks of terror.

They also drowned the sound of the tramp of approaching horses.

Before any one had heard the noise of the horses' hoofs, the horses and their riders were in their midst.

Bright naked swords gleamed fitfully in the firelight.

The male brutes fled roaring, or rolled stunned and bleeding in the dust.

The female fiends flew to all points of the compass, shrieking a thousand murders and other calamities.

But who were the horsemen who had come only in the nick of time to save our lovely heroine?

They were all magnificently mounted, and dressed in scarlet coats richly laced. There was one peculiarity about them, though, which struck the beholder at the first glance.

They all had orange-coloured faces; they wore masks.

They were the famous Yellow Band.

At their head was a young man whose figure displayed the same matchless symmetry as did the form of the superb black charger which he bestrode.

This gallant stranger, springing from his horse, dashed bodily through the flames, scattering the blazing faggots right and left.

With a slash of his sharp sword he severed the cords which held the poor girl prisoner.

She had fainted from the intensity of her terror and the suffocating heat.

He caught her half-naked palpitating form in his arms, and sprang back through the roaring furnace.

Then, depositing her in a place of safety, he knelt by her side and removed his mask to gaze into her face.

But as he did so he uttered a loud cry of astonishment.

It was the face of his wife!

Yes, thus did Red Ralph again meet his mysterious bride.

But, before proceeding further with his adventures upon this occasion, it is necessary to return to the point where we left our hero in a considerable fix.

Some startling adventures had occurred to him in the interval, and some more startling still are to follow all in good time.

["YOUR MONEY OR YOUR LIFE!"]

CHAPTER X.

THE TWO MYSTERIOUS FIGURES—THE TRAITOR CAPTAIN — BLOOD-MONEY—THE SURPRISE— RALPH'S BRIDE — THE EXTRAORDINARY DIS-APPEARANCE.

WE left Red Ralph in his hidingplace in the cupboard in the cave, peeping out at two dusky forms stealing towards him, with daggers in their hands.

He thought at first that they were stealing in upon him to take his life.

He drew himself up, clenched his fists, and set his teeth.

No. 4.

He was ready for the struggle.

But it came not, and the figures passing by approached the fire.

There they appeared to be looking about and listening.

They spoke in a low tone of voice—a smothered tone, as though they were fearful of arousing some one.

" Where is he ?" one asked.

" I left him sleeping."

" Where ?"

" Here before the fire."

" He must have gone out, then."

" No, that is impossible ; he was **dead drunk**, he hasn't had time to sleep off the effects yet."

"What on earth can have become of him?—Ah!"

The exclamation came from one of the men, who had staggered upon the edge of the open trap, and saved himself, by little short of a miracle, from falling head first down into the black abyss beneath.

Dropping down upon one of the chests, he trembled violently, whilst his face assumed an ashy paleness.

"Good God!" he muttered, "he must have gone down there. How did it come open?"

"I unbolted it myself, some hours ago, thinking we might want it if he gave us any trouble."

"To pitch him down?"

"Ay. He has gone down of his own accord, it seems, though I don't know how he came to open the trap; I only left it a few inches open, and propped it open with a stick."

"He must have gone down, I suppose."

"Yes, there's no hidingplace here."

"Let's fasten the door, then, and talk this matter over."

They dragged two stools up to the fire, and began to converse in a low tone of voice.

Ralph listened intently.

"What I'm to have for this job is five hundred pounds," said one; "that's clearly understood."

"Yes, captain, that's the price, and a handsome one it is."

"Handsome you call it: what! for betraying into the hands of justice twenty as gallant young fellows as ever straddled pigskin; and my comrades too?"

"Deuced lot you care about that, I should think."

"No matter whether I care or not, the sum is a very small one. However, I have agreed to it, and I will carry it through. You see thus far all has been easy enough for you, as I said it would be. Indeed easier: I drugged the man left on guard, and I got rid of the rest of the band on an excursion up the country. They will return at noon, and having done their work will carouse and go to sleep. They usually sleep all day after one of our expeditions. Then you and the rest, concealed down here, can take a sudden rush up the steps into the other cave, and capture all."

"You are to remove their arms, you know."

"Yes, you may rely on me for that."

"Would it be possible to have a peep at this other cave? I should like to take the geography of the place."

"Yes, but we must do it at once; we have very little time to spare."

"It is ten now, I see," said the officer, consulting his watch.

"Yes, delays are dangerous."

With these words the two left the cave by another door, which Ralph had not yet discovered.

No sooner had they gone than he sprang out of his hidingplace and followed them.

The act was almost one of madness, so great was the risk he ran; but, had the danger been a hundred times greater than it was, he would have braved it.

Passing through the door he crept along the passage after the two men.

They opened a door which was almost hidden in the rough face of the rock, and entered another cave larger than the one they had left.

The two men walked forward, and the robber, carrying a torch he had lighted, raised it above his head and flashed it to and fro, to show his companion the nature of the place they were exploring.

But while thus engaged a shrill whistle struck upon their ears.

"Ah!" exclaimed the robber, "that is the signal."

"Your comrades are here?"

"Yes; shall we admit them?"

They turned suddenly, and Ralph had not time to retreat.

Quick as lightning, though, he glided behind a curtain covering a narrow recess.

They passed him by without noticing the trembling of the drapery, and leaving the cave closed the door behind them.

Once more was he a prisoner.

"I hardly know whether I am awake or asleep," he said to himself; "so much has happened to me lately, I think I must be either mad or dreaming."

He pinched himself, and found that he was not asleep, whether mad or sane.

"Was that awful scene of the river real?" he asked himself. "And was the likeness between the dead and the living a truth, or only my fancy? And am I married or am I not? And shall I ever live with my wife? Shall I ever see her again? Shall I, for that matter, ever learn her name?"

The darkness which enveloped him was highly favourable for reflection, and he went on wondering.

"Shall I ever get out of this place alive? Shall I ever see my my old friends again, and the beauties of the Rookery—Nancy, and Bess, and Moll, and Polly, and Lucy? Bless their bright eyes and moist red lips! I'd like a kiss from one of them now to keep my courage up. And Maude—ah, Maude, I don't like thinking of her now, I'm a respectable married man with a prospective chance (a very vague chance, though) of being the parent of a family."

While he was thus reflecting he fancied he heard the sound of footsteps overhead.

"It is the police officers," said he to himself; "they are coming in to be stowed away. Won't there be an awful scrimmage presently!"

The door opened at this moment. Ralph screwed himself as close as he could to the wall.

The persons he expected, however, did not enter the cave, but in their place a number of men, booted and spurred, and travel-stained

These were the robbers, he could see at a glance, and they had returned from their expedition, whatever that might have been.

Directly they entered the cave one of them lit a fire, and almost immediately cooking operations commenced.

The food they were preparing was very soon ready, and they took their places round a large wooden table, which already was ornamented by a number of bottles and glasses.

Loudly they laughed, deeply they swore and drank, and ravenously they devoured their food.

They were a fierce rough lot, and Ralph could not help thinking that the constables would find their capture rather a tough job.

In the middle of the meal the man entered whose treacherous plot Ralph had overheard.

"The captain! the captain!" resounded on all sides, and the men rose to their feet.

"What cheer, comrades?" said he, taking his place at the head of the table, close to where Ralph was concealed.

"Not much luck," replied one of the men in a surly tone; "they must have deceived you, captain."

"How so?"

"It was a wild goose chase, that's all."

"What! was there no treasure in the house?"

"Nothing worth carrying away."

"You've had very bad luck of late, it seems to me."

"We've not had very good. It's not my fault for one, anyhow."

"Whose fault do you suppose it is?" asked the captain angrily. "Is it mine?"

There was a pause.

"Well, captain," said the man who had before spoken, and who appeared to be a sort of lieutenant, "you've not led us lately as you used to do."

"Do you want a fresh leader?" the captain asked, in an agitated voice. "Is there anything you have to complain of? Ain't I true to you?"

There was a dead silence. It was evident that there was something wrong in the camp.

"Which is he who dare say I am not true to you?" asked the captain in a loud voice, and he drew, as he spoke, a pistol from his belt.

"I dare," cried an unknown voice, and next moment Red Ralph stood in their midst.

For an instant there was a deathlike silence—a panic, in which everybody stood motionless as though turned to stone; the most astonished of all being the captain himself.

Ere he could sufficiently recover himself, however, Ralph had sprung upon him, wrenched the pistol from his hand, felled him to the earth, and placed his foot upon his neck.

Then the Yellow Band rose with an angry roar, and the air bristled with their naked swords.

"Cut him down!" was the cry of all.

But Ralph waved them back imperiously.

"Listen to me first," he said, authoritatively; "kill me if I speak not the truth. This man is a traitor."

"A traitor?"

"Yes; at this moment and with his consent there are some constables concealed in the lower cave."

"Constables in the cave?"

"You can easily overcome them if you act with promptitude. But in the meanwhile secure this man."

The captain was very quickly bound hand and foot, and then the robbers, concentrating their strength, made a rush down into the other cellar.

Almost immediately afterwards there followed the sound of firearms and the clashing of steel.

The battle raged furiously for a few moments.

Then there followed several dull splashes, and then dead silence!

The robbers came pouring back, and in another moment the traitor was pierced a score of times and lay a corpse upon the ground, his late followers forming a circle round him.

"And who are you?" asked the one who acted as lieutenant of the band, addressing our hero.

"My name is Ralph," he answered boldly—"Red Ralph, whom they call Ralph of the Bloody Hand."

"Three cheers for Red Ralph!" roared the robbers, to whom his name was as familiar as their own.

"And who is to be our chief now?" one inquired.

"Will you try me?" asked our hero.

There was a pause of uncertainty, and then a loud hurrah rent the air.

"Long live our new captain—Red Ralph for ever!"

Thus summarily was Ralph made captain of the Yellow Band, and that night led them on an expedition by which they secured a heavy plunder.

On their way to the scene of the robbery they passed through the village where the scene already described was taking place.

It would indeed require a skilful pen to describe the astonishment of Red Ralph when he recognised his mysterious bride, but to do so would be a much longer task than to describe his blank countenance at an event which now occurred.

He had wrapped the fainting girl in a thick cloak with which one of his men had supplied him, and had laid her in the shade under some trees whilst he went a few yards off to give some orders.

When he returned she was gone.

Yes; she had disappeared, though how nobody could tell.

In vain he questioned all around.

No one could tell him.

Was she indeed the witch that they had called her? The cloak lay there, but the fainting girl had vanished.

They searched the village and country around in vain.

"I must give it up," said Ralph; "I believe I must have married a Will-o'-the-wisp."

From that time forward he resolved to think no more about her, and devoted himself entirely to the interests of the Yellow Band.

Their deeds became famous throughout England, and they were the terror of all classes.

It is with their wild and terrible career that we have to do.

Yet the strange mystery of the Bride of Death will be revealed in a future chapter at no great distance.

CHAPTER XI.

NIGHT — THE PROJECT — THE YELLOW BAND — STAND AND DELIVER!—A TOUGH CUSTOMER—TOM KING, THE HIGHWAYMAN, ASTONISHES JONATHAN WILD, THE THIEF-TAKER.

THE moon had risen.

A bright clear night of silver clouds, strong lights and shadows, and not a breath of air.

Not a leaf stirred.

Presently there was a slight noise in the thick brushwood, a crackling of twigs, and the bushes were parted by two gloved hands, and a man enveloped in a long riding cloak stepped forth.

He glanced about him in all directions before quitting the shadow of the trees, and then gave a low whistle.

This signal was unanswered.

"Not here!" muttered the man. "Strange! It is already past the hour—I feared that I was behind the time."

The man repeated the signal rather louder than before, but there was no response.

"Something is wrong," he continued, "or he would not have failed. Perhaps some of the men have seen him."

He drew from beneath his cloak a small hunting-horn, and raising it to his mouth gave a shrill loud call, and then listened attentively for an answer.

The echoes of the call had scarcely died away when the answering note of a bugle was heard, apparently at no great distance from the spot.

He then repeated his summons, and in a few seconds he was joined by ten or twelve men, who pushed through the brushwood in every direction.

"What is it?" demanded the first comer.

"Are you all prepared?"

"Yes," returned the men, with one voice.

"Are we all here?"

"No," returned the man who had first spoken. "Jarvis has gone with the captain."

"And he has not yet returned?"

"No."

"Have none of you seen Jarvis or the captain since they quitted, this morning?"

"No."

"Then I fear that there's something amiss."

"Why?"

"The captain was to have been here nearly half-an-hour ago."

"He may have been detained."

"Of course he has—but how? He's punctuality itself, ordinarily, you know."

"True, lieutenant—but you know that he didn't speak positively about returning. In fact, he must have thought it probable that he wouldn't be back in time, as he said that you were to lead us up if he didn't arrive."

"He did—but I scarcely like leaving the spot, just yet."

"And yet you may do more wrong by remaining, lieutenant."

"How so ?"

"He may be in danger."

"Do you think so ?"

"Nothing more likely. You know how venturesome he is."

"True, and, as he counted upon us, he may not have observed his usual caution."

"Then we had better lose no——Hah !"

There was a shrill shriek of some night bird at a little distance from the spot.

"Dart !" cried several of the men.

"Is he the scout ?" demanded the lieutenant.

"Yes."

"What does he mean by that cry, then ?"

"Some one approaching, I take it—but we shall soon discover that."

The result proved that the man's surmise was correct, for the next minute the distant tramp of a horse was heard, and undoubtedly coming in that direction.

"You're right," said the lieutenant. "Stand clear, all. We must see who approaches."

Saying which, he withdrew into the brushwood whence he had emerged, and the men disappeared on the instant, as if by magic.

The tramp of the horse drew nearer, and a cavalier shortly appeared upon the scene, mounted upon a dark chestnut mare.

He was about to draw up by the thicket where the lieutenant was concealed, when the latter stepped forth from his hidingplace and seized the bridle with his left hand, while with his right he presented a pistol at the horseman.

"STAND AND DELIVER !"

But, had the traveller intended compliance with this command, it would have been impossible.

Simultaneously with the lieutenant's words the horseman was seized from behind in a powerful but invisible grasp and borne to the ground.

"Gently, gently," remonstrated the traveller as soon as he could speak.

"Resistance is useless,"

"I don't mean to resist."

"Your purse."

"Pshaw," returned the horseman, impatiently ; "how could I give you anything while my arms are pinioned ?"

"Search him, then."

"Wait : I bear a message to you, I believe."

"From whom ?"

"I must first be assured that I make no mistake. *Ralph !*"

"*A true man*," returned the lieutenant at once. "The countersign ?"

"*A good man and true.*"

"That's enough," said the lieutenant ; "you can't have managed to get at that from any one but the captain. We can trust you."

"Of course you can."

"Where is the captain ?"

"Captain ?" repeated the traveller.

"Ay ; he that entrusted you with the message for us."

"I can't say that. I met a horseman about twenty minutes since two good miles from here, and he politely requested me to deliver the letter to an individual I should meet at this spot."

"A letter ?" exclaimed the lieutenant impatiently ; "pray give it to me without further parley."

"Gently, gently," said the stranger ; "I am not so sure now that I shall give it up."

"And wherefore ?"

"I must have some further information in return for my services."

"On what point ?"

"Who is that captain, as you call him ?"

"He would probably have told you that if he had desired you to know."

"Well, then, unless I do know——"

"What ?"

"I shall not give up the letter he gave me."

"You will not ?" said the lieutenant ; "it would be a sorry return for the service you are to render us to offer you further show of violence."

The messenger started back a few paces and threw himself into a posture of defence.

"Violence, say you ?"

"Yes," returned the lieutenant ; "therefore appreciate duly my forbearance and give me the letter."

"Be this my answer !" retorted the traveller.

He whipped his sword from its sheath and made a rush at the lieutenant.

Another instant and it had been but short work for him. Thanks, however, to his wonderful agility, he bounded aside, and the sword of the traveller slit the lace ruffle which adorned his right wrist.

"Say you so ?" exclaimed the lieutenant ; "have at you, then. I have given you a fair chance, I think."

He drew his sword, and the next instant they were engaged in a deadly conflict.

For some minutes the combat was carried on with great vigour upon either side.

They were well matched. Both young, both lithe as eels and active as greyhounds.

Meanwhile the band remained quiet spectators of the duel. These lawless men appeared to have the proper esteem for the bravery of the stranger which prompted him single-handed to attack a whole horde.

At first, however, they had made a movement as if about to interfere, when a sign from the lieutenant restrained their half-formed purpose.

Blow after blow was given and returned upon either side with such good earnest that the wood rang again with the clashing of their swords.

And yet no blood was shed. At length, however, a trifle decided the fight in favour of the stranger.

The lieutenant, having chanced to step upon the traveller's hat, which had fallen during the conflict, stumbled slightly, giving the other a slight opening of which he was not slow to avail himself.

Before the lieutenant could recover his equilibrium the sword of his adversary entered his left arm just above the wrist, causing him to utter an exclamation of pain.

"Curse your chance !" he exclaimed.

"You are hurt badly ?" demanded the stranger.

"Not too badly," retorted the lieutenant, " to cry quits with you before we part. On guard, sir !"

"You are a man after my own heart," exclaimed the traveller, enthusiastically.

"I've no time for further parley," said the lieutenant, smarting with his hurt ; "come on, sir."

The men now began to murmur.

"No, no, lieutenant," said one ; "that's quite enough ; win or lose, we must have the captain's letter."

"Ay, ay," said several.

"Come and take it, then," cried the stranger.

"That will I," said the first speaker stepping forth.

"Stand back, Wolff," said the lieutenant ; "this is my job."

"Not more than mine."

"Come on, all of ye," exclaimed the traveller excitedly.

Two or three replied to this by drawing their swords and advancing in spite of the lieutenant's command to fall back.

"The first man that raises an arm against this gentleman makes me his foe."

This was spoken by the lieutenant in such serious

earnest that once more they paused, and once again the lieutenant and the stranger crossed swords.

How the conflict would have ended it is impossible to say, had not an unexpected termination been put to it by one of the men crying—

"See, see; what is that paper on the ground?"

"The letter!"

"He has dropped the captain's letter."

And at the same instant the stranger was seized from behind and held firmly in spite of his most frantic struggles, while one of the men possessed himself of the paper.

As they had surmised, it proved to be the disputed missive, which had escaped from the traveller's doublet during the struggle.

"Plague take your numbers!" cried the traveller. "I thought that I could scarce hope for fair play here."

"Release him," said the lieutenant.

"No, no."

"Sir," said the lieutenant, stung with the other's words, "we shall resume this upon a future occasion,"

"And in the meantime you secure by numbers what you failed to accomplish single-handed," sneered the traveller.

"This letter contains matters which affect us all."

"Doubtless."

"And, as I have scarcely the right to trust the issue of so important a matter to my arm—"

"You discover this," growled the pinioned stranger, with a curl of the lip, "when you get pricked—more valour to you!"

"Sir," exclaimed the lieutenant, goaded to madness.

"Ay, threaten, bluster now," continued the other; "strike away now; you can have no further fear."

"Beware!"

"Ay, bully."

"It appears to me, sir stranger," said the lieutenant, with forced calmness, "that, although you have a due sense of the cowardice of striking an unarmed and defenceless foe, you quite overlook the fact that it is equally unjust to insult a man of honour when your very helplessness precludes all possibility of administering the chastisement which your insolence would otherwise provoke."

"A man of honour, forsooth. A rogue, a knave, a cutpurse!"

"And yet a man of honour."

"Pah!"

"Why else should I have endeavoured to reserve the quarrel to myself when a word from me would have settled it in this fashion before a blow could have been struck."

The traveller made no reply to this.

"But now for the captain's letter," resumed the lieutenant. "What says he?"

One of the men handed him the letter, which he opened and read as follows:—

"The Lady Maude has been removed, whither I am not yet assured, but I have a strong suspicion that I could guess the direction. Instead of meeting me at the appointed spot, be within an hour by the Palmer's Cell. I shall signal you from there, and we shall go to work upon other tactics.—RALPH."

"Humph!" murmured the lieutenant, as he finished the perusal of the missive; "I could give a shrewd guess myself, I suspect, as to his meaning."

"What says the captain?" demanded the man who had handed the note to the lieutenant.

"Read for yourself," said the other, glancing at their prisoner, and handing him the note.

The letter was read and passed round to the men.

"An hour, you see," said the lieutenant; "we are

nearly upon the time now. It was twenty minutes before our messenger delivered it that it was written."

"But how shall we dispose of him?" asked he who had been called Wolff.

"Bind him, and leave him here until we return."

"Accept my thanks," said the stranger in bitter sarcasm; "a great decision for a man of honour."

"My object in doing this is to have you ready for the conclusion of our quarrel when I return," said the lieutenant.

"Doubtless,"

"Lieutenant," said Wolff, "we are wasting time."

"True; bind him; use as little violence as possible to make him sure, and come."

These commands were readily obeyed, and the whole troop left the spot, pursued by the malediction of the luckless traveller.

Five minutes had perhaps elapsed when the sound of horsemen caught the prisoner's ear.

"They are returning already," he murmured; "perhaps they have decided that I should be safer removed altogether. Dead men tell no tales."

But here he was mistaken. The sound came from a direction opposite to that which the men had taken.

"Ah!" he exclaimed, as soon as he ascertained this fact, "it may be that assistance is at hand. Oh! oh! hallo! oh!"

"Oh! oh! hallo! oh!" responded a distant voice.

"Help! help! this way!" shouted the prisoner.

Now he could hear by the increasing sound that the horsemen were galloping in that direction.

In a short space of time three or four horsemen galloped up the glade, and one of them hastily pulled up and sprang from his saddle.

"The cries came in this direction," he said, panting.

"Here! here!" cried the prisoner. "For God's sake come and release me; these cursed thongs cut into my flesh."

"Ah, there you are!" said the new comer, slipping towards him

"Ay, come and cut these cords," groaned the other.

"But, man, don't be impatient; there you are."

He drew his sword and severed the ropes.

"Hah!" said the late prisoner, shaking himself together, "that's better; those cords there have half cut my arms through."

"How came you there?" demanded his rescuer.

"Some knaves fell upon me and bound me there."

"Then you must have fallen into the clutches of some of Ralph's yellow boys."

"The Yellow Band?"

"Ay."

"Never!—and yet—"

"Oh! it's more than likely. This is their beat."

"Then you must be right, and the captain thus alluded to——"

"Ah, they spoke of him?"

"Yes—'twas him doubtless I met—Red Ralph!"

"Yes; you say you met him?"

"When I was riding along nearly an hour since, I was accosted by a horseman, who asked me to deliver a note to some one I should meet upon the spot by signalling. The romance of the incident took my fancy and I consented. Then here I was set upon by a whole mob; the wood seemed alive with men; and I began to suspect, from certain words which they let fall, that I had unintentionally abetted some lawless purpose, and I refused to give up the letter until I had been informed who and what they were. Then they fell upon me, seized the letter, and bound me to yonder tree. That's the whole history of my mishap."

"And what did this letter contain?"

"I know not."

"You didn't even look at it?"

"What! would you think me capable of such a meanness?"

"Pshaw!" muttered the other contemptuously.

As he uttered this exclamation his attention was attracted by one of his companions, who had dismounted for the purpose of picking up a paper which lay almost hidden from sight under a hedge.

"What have you got there, Nicholls?"

"I don't know—a letter apparently—but it's written so vilely that I can't make head or tail of it."

"Here it is, Mr. Wild."

"Wild?" exclaimed the newly-released prisoner.

"Yes. What then?" said the person alluded to.

"Jonathan Wild."

"Yes, sir," said Wild (for it was he), "Jonathan Wild is my name, and I'm not ashamed of it."

"Indeed?" said the other, drily.

Jonathan Wild took no further notice of the man he had just served by setting him at liberty, but hastily opened the letter.

"Confound it!" he ejaculated, "it is written in cipher."

"What is it?" demanded the late prisoner.

"The very note you brought here."

"Then they must have let it fall in the hurry. But can you make nothing of it?"

"No."

"Then hand it to me. I may be able to do something with it."

Wild took the letter from the man's hand and passed it on to the speaker.

"What do they say?"

"I scarce can say yet; that looks like 'Cell'— 'Palmer's Cell;' can that aid you at all?"

Jonathan Wild started.

"Aid us?" he exclaimed. "Indeed it can. That's a rendezvous, doubtless, with the Yellow Boys to whom you brought this letter."

"Ay," said the other, a sudden light breaking in upon him; "now I understand what their half-words meant. They are to meet at a place called the Palmer's Cell, in an hour."

"An hour?" said Wild.

"Ay—that is, it *was* an hour; but we must be near upon the time now."

"Then, let's get on. Stay, did they muster strong?"

"I counted a good dozen," was the reply.

"Humph!" muttered Wild, glancing uneasily round at his four associates, "were they armed?"

"To the teeth."

"Mounted?"

"No."

Jonathan Wild was silent for a few moments, and from his gestures the stranger judged that he was mentally calculating the chances of an encounter with such odds as the Yellow Band would present at the appointed trysting-place.

"Four—five," he muttered; then, looking up at the stranger, he demanded, abruptly, "Will you make one of us?"

"I?—what! do a little thief-taking?"

"Yes; there's plenty of money to be gained."

"Hang your money."

"And as much excitement as you can wish for— but perhaps you rather fear a cracked sconce?"

"Not I; I'd give a good round sum to have this Red Ralph for five minutes to myself."

"It strikes me you'd give something to be away from him, if you did come across him," sneered the thief-taker.

The stranger clutched his sword-hilt threateningly, but choked his resentment for the moment, and bade Wild lead the way to the Palmer's Cell.

"One word before we start," said Jonathan Wild, glancing doubtfully at the stranger. "How comes it that you should be able to decipher the hieroglyphics in which Red Ralph and his Yellow Band correspond?"

"That's my business," said the stranger.

"Nay, but I'll make it mine."

"Tut, tut," retorted the other, "if you accept my services, let us move forward. We must be full late now. If you mean quarrelling, I shall be nothing loth after we have squared accounts with Captain Ralph."

"Stay," said Wild. "One last word. What may your name be?"

"King."

"Tom King;" repeated Wild, in the greatest amazement.

"That is my name," answered Tom King; "and now, hey for Captain Red Ralph and the Yellow Band!"

CHAPTER XII.

THE PALMER'S CELL—TREACHERY—THE STRUGGLE—THE CAPTURE—THE WOMAN IN WHITE— JONATHAN FOILED.

THE lieutenant of the Yellow Band moved onward with his little troop at a rapid pace until they were safely out of hearing of the luckless messenger who had brought them the letter from Red Ralph.

"Wolff," said the lieutenant, "call a halt."

This command obeyed, the lieutenant desired the men to form a circle around him for the purpose of holding a council of war.

"Now, my men," said the lieutenant, "we have, as near as I can calculate, about ten minutes to reach the Palmer's Cell; of course it would frustrate all our schemes to be seen together: secrecy and despatch must be the order of the day. Wolff and I will take the road; Joyce, William, and Burdett will go across the Lime-tree path; and the rest of you branch off as you please, but let silence and speed be your watchword. Now, then, for the Palmer's Cell!"

With a low murmur of assent the band set off in accordance with these instructions.

Now, although the roadway was by no means as near a route to the trysting-place, the other paths were so obstructed with the great growth of briars and thorns and all kinds of wild vegetation that the lieutenant was the first upon the spot with his right-hand man Wolff.

The Palmer's Cell was one of the antiquarian relics of the locality, and deserves a word of description.

A rude rocky cavern, which had evidently been made habitable in some remote age by the hermit who had given the name to the spot, by some rough masonry, brickwork, and certian equally rough efforts at ecclesiastical sculpture,

Upon the right of this cavern was a dark recess, which upon entering from the light appeared only to contain a range of natural shelves formed in the rock. A nearer glance, however, when the eye grew more accustomed to the shadows, proved it to be the entrance to a second cave of a like nature.

From this branched a second and a third apartment of artificial formation, and from one of these inner caverns was a second communication with the wood.

Immediately facing the the entrance to the Palmer's Cell was a wooden gate, upon which was written "Saint Geoffrey's Retreat," which was one of the few Roman Catholic religious establishments in existence at the period of our history in this country.

The lieutenant and his man entered the cavern.

"Not arrived yet, Wolff," said the former.

"No; I thought we should be the first here—hullo! what's this?"

He picked up from the ground a piece of white muslin apparently torn from a feminine garment.

"Why, there's blood upon it. There's been some ugly piece of work carried on here; see, too, there are very evident traces of a struggle."

It was indeed as the lieutenant had said. Upon examining the earth more closely by the aid of a lantern which Wolff carried they could discern several moist patches, and experience taught them that it was the moisture of human gore.

"I hope that no harm has come to the captain," muttered the lieutenant, uneasily.

"The captain?" iterated Wolff; "you surely don't think it possible."

"And wherefore?"

"The victim in this job is doubtless a woman."

"Pshaw; because we find a scrap of a woman's dress bedabbled with blood you conclude that it is a woman who has come to grief. But we shall see."

The noise of some one approaching caught his ear.

"The men are coming up," said Wolff.

"They make noise enough for a regiment of cavalry," muttered the lieutenant, angrily; "one would think they wished to be discovered."

"Stay," interrupted Wolff; "we are in error; it is not they who come."

"Ah! how know you?"

"I hear the tramp of horses," replied Wolff uneasily.

"Some late travellers, I presume. We must not let the present job blind us for anything else that may turn up in the way of business."

"Stand close, lieutenant," said Wolff, "whilst I go and reconnoitre."

The sounds of horses now drew near, and the two men judged that they could not be a minute's ride from the spot.

Wolff walked warily to the mouth of the cavern, and, clambering into the strong thick creeping plant which grew about the entrance, there waited till the cavaliers should draw sufficiently near for him to take observations.

On came the horsemen. Six in number.

One of them rode a little in advance of the rest, and the first glance that Wolff caught of his face in the bright moonlight served to fill him with the most lively apprehensions.

Quick as thought he slid from his hidingplace and stepped back into the cavern.

"Well?"

"Danger!" breathed Wolff, with his finger upon his lip.

"Ah! say you so?"

"I see that there are six horsemen heavily armed making for this spot."

"Six?"

"And I recognise in their leader the traveller with whom you fought."

"Never!"

"I'm certain of it. I never forget a face that I've once seen."

"But we left him bound hand and foot scarce a quarter of an hour since," said the lieutenant.

"True—but hush!"

They approached!

The six horsemen had reined in their steeds immediately in front of the entrance of the cavern.

The next instant the two Yellow Boys could hear the dismounting.

"It is high time for action," thought the lieutenant.

He grasped Wolff by the wrist and stepped noiselessly through the entrance to the first inner chamber.

Here, however, the sound of the voice of one of the horsemen arrested their attention.

"Marks," said a gruff voice, "withdraw a few paces to the left—keep a sharp look out."

"Yes, sir,"

Shoot down any fugitive!"

They recognised the tones. That voice once heard was never to be forgotten.

"Wild!" breathed Wolff into the lieutenant's ear."

"Then there has been treachery at work," returned the lieutenant.

"Ah!—the traveller."

The lieutenant gave the other's arm a silent squeeze to show that his suspicions were understood."

They believed that they had been taken in an ambush. That the letter which Tom King had brought them was a forgery.

Their attention was so thoroughly absorbed in their present danger that they did not think of the improbability of another one—of the uninitiated being able to write their cipher!

"Come on," whispered the lieutenant.

Wolff silently followed, and in an instant they had gained the other exit.

Wild and his men were already searching in the adjoining cavern.

"They have been here," the fugitives heard Jonathan Wild say, "and lately too: I can detect a recent presence in the atmosphere."

"Then it's true what they say of him," muttered the lieutenant: "he has all the instinct of a bloodhound in his devilish trade."

They passed on through the aperture, pushing aside the briars which covered it, and—

"Yield!" exclaimed a voice close to them.

They glanced upwards and found that they were covered by a pair of horse pistols held by one of Jonathan Wild's Janissaries.

It was Marks. When Wild had ordered him off to the left the two fugitives had been so astounded and alarmed at recognising the voice of an old and implacable enemy that they had not noticed the instruction which his speech conveyed.

"Yield!"

"Never!"

"Then I'll shoot you down."

"Try it."

As if by a previous understanding they both feinted to fly in opposite directions, and then suddenly threw themselves forward upon their faces.

There were two reports, followed by a cry of pain.

"Ah!" cried the lieutenant, "I am struck."

"Say you so, lieutenant?" ejaculated Wolff with an oath; "then, by heaven, it's short work with our friend here."

Marks uttered a shout of alarm, and the next instant Wolff was upon him.

The former was a big powerful man, and for that reason always chosen by his chief, Jonathan Wild, for any post of danger—an enviable mark of distinction for the fellow!

Wolff was considerably his inferior in size and strength, no doubt, but the suddenness of the attack completely took the other by surprise.

In far less time than the incident has taken to record Marks lay stretched upon the turf, pinned to the ground by the robber's knee.

"Lieutenant!" cried Wolff.

But there was no reply. The cavern only returned the call with a dismal echo which filled him with thoughts of blood and revenge.

"Dead!" he exclaimed, horror-stricken. "Lieutenant, answer me."

No reply.

"You've shed the best blood of us," cried Wolff, "and now prepare for the worst."

He drew a short knife shaped something like the modern American bowie from his belt, and flourished it before the eyes of the hapless Marks.

"Mercy! mercy!" cried the officer.

But Wolff's only reply to this was to make a third call to his lieutenant, which but met with the former results.

"Now, heaven have mercy upon your soul."

"One minute," supplicated the terror-stricken wretch.

"Quick, then; it's a short shrift you'll get at my hands. Lieutenant!"

"Help! help! murder! mercy! hah!"

Wolff raised his hand to strike the fatal blow.

Marks closed his eyes and ceased to struggle. There was a sharp bustling noise close at hand, and the upraised arm of the robber was caught in a grasp of iron ere it could descend.

Then Wolff was toppled over and fell beside his late prostrate antagonist to find himself in a like predicament.

It was Jonathan Wild himself who, at this critical juncture for his functionary, thus reversed chances.

"Silas Wolff," exclaimed Wild, joyfully; "so, so, my old friend, we meet again!"

The robber struggled frantically to free himself from the thieftaker's clutches, but in vain. A man of Wild's well-known prodigious strength was not to be shaken off.

"Struggle away, Silas," said the thieftaker; "I could cry quits with you now if I chose, but I've sworn to have the pleasure of hanging you, and you know me for a man of my word."

"Liar!" gasped Wolff.

"Fool," retorted Wild, ferociously; "to-night you accompany your friend the lieutenant and Red Ralph to Newgate."

"Never!"

He renewed his efforts to escape, but Wild pressed upon him so cruelly that he was nearly suffocated.

"What, ho!" shouted Wild; "bring some cords. Here, you Marks, jump up—idiot! the danger's over now."

But Marks did not stir. He had swooned from fear.

A second cry from the thieftaker brought assistance, and the robber was securely bound.

"Bear him into the cave," said Wild.

This command was readily obeyed, and Wolff had the satisfaction of seeing that the lieutenant still breathed, although in a similar sad plight.

Thus his silence was explained:—

Wild and his men had fallen so suddenly upon the lieutenant and his men that he was bound and gagged before he could warn his companions.

"So far," said Wild to Tom King, "all has proceeded satisfactorily."

"No casualties?" demanded the other.

"None. That idiot Marks, who has about the stamina of a girl, has fainted—that's all."

"We had better see about restoring him," said Tom King.

"I suppose so," growled the thieftaker; "though the proper reward for him would be to let him shift for himself; but we shall shortly need his assistance, I think."

"You think so?"

"Yes."

"But if the rest of this precious gang are within shot they will have been put upon their guard by the report of the pistols."

"What of that?"

"They'll never venture to attack us here."

"Pshaw! you little know the men you speak of."

"But they would never venture to attack us without knowing our number."

"Wrong again. You don't know what these fellows would venture. Besides, they know our number as well as we do."

"How is that possible?"

"They have scouts in every direction."

In the meantime one of the officers had procured a bucket of water from the well in the cave and had succeeded in restoring the swooning Marks to consciousness.

As he opened his eyes he glanced about him, affrightedly, and was reassured after Wild had abused him roundly for his cowardice.

"I had a narrow squeak, Mr. Wild," mumbled the crestfallen Marks

"You'll be nearer the end one of these days," said Wild.

"I say—stop—I think I can hear something."

His hearing was sharpened by having his head close to the ground.

"What do you hear?"

"I fancy I can hear footsteps in the distance."

"Go and look out, then."

Anxious to recover his chief's good opinion, the man sprang to his feet and obeyed with alacrity.

"Yes," said Marks, from the mouth of the cave, "I was right; I can hear some one, I'm sure."

"Let us go," said Wild to Tom King, "and see if the idiot has spoken the truth for once."

"I suppose that they are all right?" said King, glancing at the two captives, who lay side by side bound hand and foot.

"They're safe enough," returned Wild; "come on."

They went to the entrance and looked about them.

"I can hear nothing," said King.

"Nor I," said Wild, "but still I believe the fellow; he has wonderfully long ears—an hereditary feature!"

"Then, all that remains to be done," said King, "is to post the men advantageously, and we can take them in ambush; we can hold our own against a host."

Whilst the thieftaker and his temporary colleague Tom King were occupied in their meditated surprise for the Yellow Band, a little scene of some importance was being enacted within the cave.

As soon as their captors had withdrawn, Wolff shifted his head towards the lieutenant.

"Are you hurt?" he demanded in the lowest of whispers.

The lieutenant could only reply with a glance.

"Put your head nearer mine," said Wolff.

The other obeyed as well as he was able, and the faces of the two robbers touched.

However, instead of embracing as the ordinary spectator might have supposed they were about to do, Wolff merely seized between his teeth the gag which choked the lieutenant's utterance, and tugged at it violently.

It was a hard pull, and tested severely the strength of Wolff's masticatory organs.

But perseverance gained the day, and the gag was shifted.

A few minutes had elapsed.

"Now I can hear something," said King.

"Hah!" said Wild; "you see now that we were right to make preparation, eh?"

"I do."

One of the men came running up to the spot where Wild and Tom King were conversing.

"What is it now, looby?" demanded the thieftaker.

"There's a woman running along the road pursued by a whole mob of the Yellow Band."

"What do you mean by a whole mob?"

"Three or four?"

"Ass!" exclaimed the irritable Wild; "let the woman come; are you afraid of a woman?"

Before the man could reply a female voice was heard calling for assistance, and the next minute a woman dressed in white, with her hair streaming down her back, rushed to the Palmer's Cell.

"Here you are," cried Tom King, "come here! we're friends; you're quite safe here."

[THE ESCAPE FROM THE NUNNERY.]

"Thanks, thanks," said the woman, panting for breath, "this is a miraculous preservation."

"What's the matter?"

"I have been pursued."

"By whom?"

"Two robbers."

"Only two."

"Yes, that's all, but I am half dead with fright."

"Come in here and rest; this is Mr. Wild, he's here to capture these ruffians."

"Fool!" cried Wild, "what's the use of blabbing about my affairs to every woman you meet."

"A little more civility, Wild," said Tom King, as he conducted the frightened lady into the cavern.

No. 5.

"Hullo! what's this?" exclaimed Tom King.

"What's the matter?" demanded the thieftaker.

"Come here."

"I can't; these knaves are coming up."

"But—"

"Peace!—Ha! they have smelt danger, I suppose, and are retreating. Never mind, we shall bide our time."

"But, Mr. Wild, the prisoners."

"What of them?"

"Where are they?"

"Where are they? Why, where should they be?" He entered the Palmer's Cell as he spoke.

"Ten thousand furies!" he roared, "they have escaped."

CHAPTER XIII.

JONATHAN'S RAGE—A LADY WHO COULD WHISTLE
—THE HAND-TO-HAND COMBAT—A SURPRISE
FOR WILD—RED RALPH FOR EVER!

JONATHAN WILD was furious. He stamped and swore, and cursed every individual about him—but there was no mending the matter.

The prisoners had escaped!

How they had contrived to effect this was a matter of the profoundest mystery to all.

Every nook, every passage and cavern was searched, and the bushes beaten in every direction, but still they could find no traces of the fugitives.

Jonathan Wild could barely comprehend the possibility of their loosening the thongs which, but a few minutes before, held them so securely.

But, not to invest their escape with too much wonder, he got over this point by mentally admitting its possibility. But then how could they contrive to get clear off when his men guarded every point about the Palmer's Cell?

There was only one solution of the mystery, and this the thieftaker did not hesitate to announce to his colleagues.

"We have a traitor amongst us," he said, glancing about him suspiciously; "who is he?"

The men looked inquiringly at each other, but one expression alone filled every countenance—wonder.

"A traitor!" iterated Tom King.

"Ay," said Wild; "a traitor; and I'd give a year's perquisites to be able to drop my hand upon him."

"Impossible."

"I say we have, and he shall swing for his treachery, I swear."

One of the scouts ran in to announce that the Yellow Band were approaching in force.

"How many do they muster?"

"I counted a dozen, Mr. Wild," replied the man.

"And we are six," said Wild; "two to one, humph."

"But then the attacked will always have an immense advantage," suggested Tom King.

"Possibly. We must endeavour to get a volley at them before they are upon their guard."

"Oh!" cried the lady, "I am lost—undone."

"Have no fears, madam," said Tom King, "we will protect you."

"But you will be outnumbered," she said.

"We have justice on our side."

"True, sir, but—"

"Cease your prate, woman;" said Wild, brutally, "we have no time to bluster to a woman's fears."

"Sir," said the lady, "you would not dare insult me in my father's presence."

These words were barely uttered before Tom King, disgusted with the thieftaker's brutality to a lady, struck him a smart blow in the face.

"Tom King," cried Wild, livid with passion, "I swear you shall repent that blow."

"And I swear I never shall," said King, "since it was but a just reward for your insolence to a lady."

"Nay, do not quarrel on my account, I pray you. If you would but give me an escort to—"

"We can give no escort now," snarled Wild.

"Where to?" demanded Tom King, without heeding Wild.

"To the Manor House."

"The Manor House?" said King.

"The Manor House?" repeated Wild. "Might I ask your name, madam?"

"Certainly; my christian name is Blanche—my surname the same as my father's."

"Doubtless: and that is—"

"Mordaunt."

"Sir John Mordaunt?"

"The same, sir."

The thieftaker was thunderstruck. Sir John Mordaunt was the richest commoner of England, and one of the most influential men of the day.

"Plague upon my tongue," he muttered; "I've spoilt myself there, that's very certain."

"Madam," said Tom King, raising his hat respectfully, "it were worse than madness to attempt to leave this place at present. We should be pursued and taken by these ruffians, and you would be subjected to great indignities. Rely upon us to check them—have no fears. They are superior in strength, but we are all armed and have the advantage in every way. Be reassured, I pray you."

"I will, I will," said the lady; "I am a soldier's daughter, and not altogether deficient in courage."

"You don't fear the firing."

"Not I, sir; I shoot myself a little."

"Then you can render us a very material service."

"Indeed; then you have but to command me. I can load for you while you fire."

"Precisely what I was about to say. I am now more than ever assured of success."

"Hand the pistols, then, while there is time. I can hear footsteps," said Lady Blanche.

"Good," said Jonathan Wild; "this is indeed a service, madam."

His tone was wonderfully subdued since he had been informed of the lady's rank, and he stood respectfully uncovered before her.

One of the scouts ran in to say that in the space of a few seconds the Yellow Band would be upon them.

They had halted to reconnoitre a few paces distant.

"Load and give them a volley," suggested Lady Blanche.

"Excuse me," said Tom King; "I think that the great point is patiently to await their attack here. What do you think?"

This was addressed to Jonathan Wild. The thieftaker, albeit an adept in the art of dissimulation, could not so far disguise his resentment to Tom King for the blow he had received as to reply with anything like civility, and therefore, being conscious of his weakness in this particular, he would not trust himself to answer.

"As you please," said Lady Blanche Mordaunt. "Of course you are the best judge."

"But whatever we do, it must be done at once. They come!"

"Give me the pistols and powder-flasks, then," said the lady.

Jonathan Wild hastened to obey, and the weapons of his men were collected in an instant, and the lady accomplished the unladylike operation of loading them with a dexterity which confirmed her assertion of her knowledge of their use.

"Mr. Wild," said Marks, entering the cavern.

"What now?"

"We have no shelter where we are placed; shall we retreat to the cave and await their attack?"

"No."

"But—"

"Silence, you jackanapes! You poltroon! You white-livered rascal! Do as you are bid and say nothing."

The man retired grumbling.

The arms were redistributed, and Lady Blanche Mordaunt retired into the cave.

As soon as her ladyship was within the cavern, her bearing underwent a sudden and most remarkable change.

Her ladyship whistled!

A very low note, but still a whistle.

"Hallo!" whispered a voice from above.

"Hush! keep dark until I give the word. It's working beautifully."

"Are they coming?"

"Who—the men?"

"Ay."

"Yes. They are pausing there for something. I suppose that they are waiting there for the signal to advance."

"You cannot manage to give it?"

"No," replied her ladyship. "Stay. I might manage it from the other exit. It must be done, at all hazards!"

She gathered up her skirts in a most graceful manner, and tripped lightly through the cavern to the door at which the lieutenant and Wolff had been confronted by Marks, and then, raising a small silver whistle to her lips, she blew a loud shrill note.

"Hullo!" exclaimed Wild, "there's something very wrong here."

An answering signal was heard from the Yellow Band, and then they once more advanced.

"Now, then, or never!" ejaculated Tom King.

"Now, my men," said Jonathan Wild, "take a steady aim! Pick out Red Ralph, and the game's our own."

"Fire!"

There was a loud report, but, as far as the officers could see, no damage had been done.

The pistols were again passed on, and were reloaded by the Lady Mordaunt with surprising rapidity.

"Give the knave another volley!" cried Tom King.

"Pick out Red Ralph!" roared Jonathan Wild.

A second report followed, but the Yellow Band still came on! Not one out of their number was wounded!

A third time were the pistols passed into the cave, but this time they were not charged with the same rapidity.

"Where are they?" exclaimed Wild. "The pistols, madam. Give them at once, or we are as good as gone, every man of us!"

But there was not any reply this time. Her ladyship had disappeared!

Nothing could be heard now but a voice which Jonathan Wild recognised as belonging to Red Ralph, the captain of the Yellow Band, inciting his men to action.

And strangely enough it sounded quite close at hand!

"Come on! Charge them, my men! Smite the villains, hip and thigh, and the day's our own. Take Jonathan Wild alive; he shall die to-night, or I'm no true man."

"Rascal!" roared the thief-catcher, "if I were near you now!"

"Don't fear, now," continued Red Ralph; "they have no fire-arms!"

"Confound him!" cried Wild, "he even knows that. He must be in league with the foul fiend himself."

This was an imprudent speech, for his men had already began to waiver, and were but too glad to accept this assertion as truth.

Red Ralph was reported by the vulgar to have a charmed life, and the present state of things seemed to corroborate this idea.

The six men had fired twice into the advancing body, and without any perceptible result!

As Red Ralph spoke, the men gave a lusty cheer and charged the constables, sword in hand, at full galop.

Tom King and Wild placed themselves to the front and received the attack of the twelve men with commendable coolness.

Their example served to steady their men, who immediately took part in the struggle, and stood their ground, in spite of the unequal odds.

"Cut them up!" called a voice which sounded remarkably like the lieutenant's.

"Ha! You are there, are you?" shouted Tom King.

"Yes, King," returned the lieutenant, "here I am, sword in hand, awaiting my opportunity of finishing our little matter."

"And here am I," cried King, withdrawing a pace, and flourishing his weapon.

"Now for one fire," said the lieutenant. "You have blazed away at us, and I should say that's now our turn."

Wild's men began to grow uneasy, and to give ground at this terrible threat.

"Now's our time!" cried a voice immediately in the rear.

Jonathan Wild turned round, and there stood the Lady Blanche Mordaunt, sword in hand, preparing to attack them in the rear.

"Hullo there!" ejaculated Jonathan Wild.

"Come on, Wolff," said her ladyship.

"All right, captain," said the same voice which had before responded to her ladyship from above. "I'm with you."

A scrambling noise was heard, and in a trice Lady Mordaunt was joined by Wolff, who had all the time been concealed in a hollow in the rocks at the top of the cave.

"Treachery!" shouted Wild.

"A man!" cried Marks.

"A trap—an ambuscade!" said a second and a third.

"Down with your arms, then," cried Lady Blanche Mordaunt; "yield, or I'll make mincemeat of every man of you."

All, save Wild and Tom King, dropped their weapons affrightedly and cried for quarter.

"Yield then, Jonathan Wild!" said the Lady Blanche Mordaunt, in the rear.

The thieftaker's only reply to this was to dash savagely at the speaker; but Tom King, who appeared to have entirely lost himself in the confusion of the front and rear attack, turned from his foes, and beat up Jonathan Wild's sword.

At the same instant the enemy closed with them, and Jonathan Wild and his men were worsted.

Tom King, at the same time, was beaten to the ground and menaced by the upraised swords of the Yellow Band.

"Victory!" shouted the Lady Blanche Mordaunt, waving her bonnet triumphantly.

"Hurrah! Hurrah!" shouted the Yellow Band.

"Tie them up," said her ladyship. "Bind them securely—hand and foot! Not after the style that they tied up Woff and the lieutenant."

"Ay, ay, captain!" responded the band.

"Captain?" iterated Tom King.

"Captain?" repeated Jonathan Wild, in amazement.

"Then you," said Tom King, staring aghast at her masculine ladyship—"then you are—"

"Red Ralph," answered the pseudo Lady Mordaunt, with a laugh. "Red Ralph. At your service, Tom King."

CHAPTER XIII.

WILD VOWS VENGEANCE—THE HIGHWAY ROBBERY — THE BEAUTIFUL GIRL — THE PASSIONATE ENTREATY — KIDNAPPING — TO THE NUNNERY! TO THE NUNNERY!—THE BLOOMING DAMSEL AND THE RIGHT REVEREND BISHOP OF BONDESTRET.

WHO shall give a due description of Jonathan Wild's rage and mortification upon discovering that the beauteous Lady Blanche Mordaunt was no other than Red Ralph, the Captain of the Yellow Band?

There—there in his grasp, and yet to lose him!

Nay, not simply to lose him, but become his prisoner! The gibe, the scoff of the whole world; for he well knew that he was as much detested as he was feared by his Janissaries, and that the knaves would not fail to publish his defeat and ridicule him to the scandal-loving public.

Not so, Tom King, however.

He was so thoroughly struck with the audacity of the highwayman's exploit—so possessed with admiration for the dash with which it had been executed, that his position lost all it's ignominy in his view.

He had fallen a victim to a bit of daring, which undoubtedly merited success.

"What shall we do with them, captain?" demanded Wolff.

"Bear them as they are to the glade. There they will be free from chance observation. Stay, fasten them upon their horses, backwards.

Jonathan Wild cursed both loud and deep, but he might have saved his breath.

Tom King merely laughed at the malediction of the thieftaker.

"Plague take you, you jibbering fool!" cried Wild, savagely.

"Ha! ha! ha!" laughed Tom King. "You look scarcely so majestic, sitting backwards upon a horse, Mr. Wild."

"Curse you," roared the thieftaker, "I believe that you are pleased with the failure—failure for the nonce, I may say."

"Pleased—delighted."

"Indeed?"

"Verily."

"And I believe, Tom King, that you are in league with the Yellow Band."

"Right again."

"Hah!" exclaimed the thieftaker. "You are, are you? Hark you [this was addressed to his men]— Hark you that! He says that he is in league with the Yellow Band, and I swear that the day will come when those words will be brought forward as evidence against you."

Tom King endeavoured to scoff at this threat, but he well knew that the speaker was a man whose resentment was to be avoided.

"Tom King," said the pseudo Lady Blanche Mordaunt.

"Captain?"

"You see now that if we let this rascal free he will sacrifice you as mercilessly as he would me or any of my band, if we were in his power."

"I never questioned that for a moment," replied King."

"Then do you not think that we are justified in sacrificing him?"

"Villain!" cried Jonathan Wiid, "would ye murder me?"

"No; only put you out of the way in self-defence."

"I think that nothing could justify such a proceeding, Captain Ralph," returned Tom King, gravely.

"Perhaps not; but off with them, my men; we will decide after. And hark you, Wolff."

"Captain?"

"If he murmurs—shows the faintest signs of wishing to escape, toss him into the pond."

"Yes, captain."

The thieftaker took this for a tacit understanding that he was to be slain, and his cheek blanched with fear.

The four men, strapped as the Captain of the Yellow Band had ordered, upon their horses backwards, were carried from the spot, followed by their humiliated leader.

The last to depart was Tom King, who, although in this undignified position, made the best of it, and nodded his adieux to Red Ralph.

"There goes a game fellow!" said Ralph, as he returned his vanquished foe's salute.

As soon as they had departed Ralph turned to the lieutenant.

"Walters," said he, "what is that about the blood in the cave which you mentioned to me?"

"Wolff and I found this here, and beside it was a pool of blood—and apparently fresh," replied the lieutenant.

"Indeed."

Ralph took the piece of white muslin and examined it with interest.

"Strange," he muttered, half-aloud; "she was dressed so too. My life upon it, the Lady Maude is in some way connected with this.—Walters!"

"Captain."

"You got a note, of course?"

"Else we had not been here."

"Certainly. Then you are aware that the Lady Maude has been carried off to the nunnery?"

"You mentioned it in the note, captain."

"I did. And are you willing to join me in a venture to-night—a venture from which we can hope to obtain no personal advantage?"

"I know what you mean, captain," replied the lieutenant. "You would rescue the Lady Maude from what is, doubtless, her prison—is it not so?"

"Right," said Red Ralph; "and what is your answer?"

"Is my answer necessary?" demanded the lieutenant. You know that I am yours for anything and everything."

"I do, Walters; then here are my tactics—as we have been so successful with our arch enemy, Jonathan Wild, I mean to adopt something of the same style of proceeding in the present instance."

"Proceed, captain."

"You must know, Walters," continued Captain Ralph, "that I have gained the information, from the same quarter as I learnt that the Lady Maude had been carried to the nunnery, that the Lady Abbess is awaiting the arrival of a novice—possibly another victim, of the name Arnold. Now, this Miss Arnold is to arrive to-night.—What's that?"

The sound of carriage-wheels was heard approaching.

"A carriage."

"We must look after it."

"Stay here awhile, captain," said Walters; "I'll go and see about it."

"Quick, then."

The lieutenant sprang upon the nearest horse and galloped off.

As he turned the angle of the road he found himself out in the bright moonlight open to observation, and he almost feared that he had been perceived.

However, he reined his horse quickly up to the side of the hedge, where he was completely hidden by the shadows of some giant elms.

On came the carriage, a lumbering old vehicle drawn by four horses and richly decorated, showing it to be the property of a family of importance.

As it drew near the spot where the lieutenant was concealed, a head was put through the carriage window, and a voice shouted out—

"Drive on, James! faster, you rascal! I'm sure I saw a horseman on ahead, and I know that this road is reported to be dangerous. Drive on faster!"

The coachman lashed up the horses, and they came dashing up to the lieutenant.

As soon as they reached him he darted from his hiding-place, and rushed to the horses' heads.

"Stand!"

"Hah?"

"Halt!" cried the lieutenant, "or I'll blow you to atoms."

But the coachman, maddened with fear, did the best thing to be done under the circumstances, which was to endeavour to drive on.

It is just possible, too, that he would have accomplished his purpose, had not the lieutenant seized the bridle of the nearest of the leaders and forced him almost back upon his haunches.

"Drive on!" cried the voice from within the carriage.

"Do so at your peril!" said the lieutenant.

The coachman in terror had let fall the reins.

Seeing this, the highwayman drew up to the carriage window.

"Now, if you please, sir."

"Ruffian!"

"Come, come," said the lieutenant, "hand over."

"What?"

"Your loose cash."

"Never!"

"You're wasting time."

The old gentleman raised his hand quickly, and the lieutenant perceived that it held a pistol.

There was a report, but when the smoke cleared off the highwayman was still in the same position.

He had seen his danger just in time to duck and avoid it, and then resumed his place as coolly as if nothing had occurred.

"Now it's my turn," said the lieutenant, with admirable *sang froid.*

"Ruffian! would you slay me?" cried the old man.

"Well, I don't know, unless you hand over your watch and purse."

"Give it up, father," entreated a female voice.

"Never!"

"You are running a useless risk—wasting our time and unnecessarily alarming the lady."

The highwayman presented his pistol as he spoke, and the old gentleman turned aside in terror.

"It is on full cock, sir," said the lieutenant, "so don't keep it presented at you too long. It might go off by accident, even."

The old man stooped down as if about to comply with the robber's demand, but the light of the carriage lamp flashed upon the polished barrel of a pistol.

"Hah! treachery?" exclaimed the lieutenant. "Move from that position, and I swear by heaven that I will blow your brains out."

At the same time, growing impatient at the long delay, he raised a small silver whistle to his lips and blew a long shrill note.

"What ho! captain?"

The next minute he was joined by Red Ralph.

"What's this?"

"Just empty this obstinate old man's pockets, whilst I clean out the carriage."

"I think, Walters, we had better clear the carriage out altogether."

"Altogether?"

"Ay—we can make use of it. Will you step out?"

This was addressed to the young lady, who had well-nigh fainted from terror.

"Oh! spare me, spare me," she cried.

"Fear nothing, Miss Arnold."

"You know me?" exclaimed the young lady, in amazement.

"Let my words prove it to you," returned Red Ralph.

"Then, whoever you may be," entreated the girl, "I pray you have mercy upon my father's gray hairs."

"But he has had no mercy upon you, Miss Arnold."

"What mean you?"

"Simply, if I am not mistaken," answered the Captain of the Yellow Band, "that you do not go to the nunnery voluntarily."

"Ha! you know that too?"

"Then I am correct?"

"You are, you are," returned the young lady, in tears.

"And your unnatural parent here was carrying you there by force?"

"Alas! yes."

"Then let him look upon your deliverance from his cruel persecution as providential—upon the present business as a just punishment for his crimes."

"Villain!" ejaculated the old gentleman.

"Silence, old man!" said Ralph, sternly, "provoke me not to a course of action which I would fain avoid."

"Who are you?"

"It matters little; suffice it for you that I know you and your nefarious scheme, and, that your daughter may suffer no further violence at your hands, you may consider yourself my prisoner!"

"Prisoner?" repeated Miss Arnold, in the greatest alarm.

"Fear nothing, Miss Arnold," said Ralph, "your father is safe for your sake; but he must go with me—"

Then he turned and said in a low voice to the lieutenant—

"Walters, summon assistance. Give the signal for some of men."

The lieutenant blew a call upon the bugle he carried, and in the space of three minutes some seven or eight men came running to the spot.

"This way," said Red Ralph; "secure this old man; clear out the carriage, and place him and the lady in a secure part of the haunt; let them be treated with every respect and attention."

"Yes, captain."

Ralph's attention was at this moment attracted by seeing the old man attempting to conceal a letter.

"What is that?"

"What?"

"That paper he is hiding there—give it to me."

The old gentleman struggled to retain possession of it, but his efforts availed him but little.

"What is this?" said Ralph, as he hurriedly perused the note. "The Bishop of Bondestret! so, so, Mr. Arnold, he is in league with you in this pretty piece of business. A bishop of the established church engaged in a conspiracy to imprison a young lady—and that young lady your daughter—in a nunnery! Then will I defeat your whole scheme. This will sufficiently prove to the world that no fanatical zeal for what you would conveniently choose for your faith has led you to adopt this step, and Miss Arnold will, doubtless, be removed from your paternal tenderness."

Mr. Arnold groaned.

"And you have succeeded in creating a reputation in society for piety," resumed the leader of the Yellow Band. "Fie upon you, old man. You had better, far better, far better have adopted my calling. At any rate, I only prey upon the wealthy and the powerful.

"Slave!" cried Mr. Arnold, "you shall hang for this."

"Silence! Away with them! Fear nothing, Miss Arnold; you shall be free to depart almost immediately."

The captain's commands were obeyed, and once more he was alone with the coachman, who sat upon his box half frozen with terror.

"Now, coachman," said he, "I wish you and me to be friends."

"O lor! Mr. Highwayman," gasped the man.

"Peace! Will you do as I bid you?"

"Any mortal thing."

"Obey me, then," said Ralph, "and not only shall I allow you to go scot-free, but I will reward you handsomely."

"Reward?"

"Ay."

"What do you wish, sir—that is, honoured sir?"

"I wish you to remain here for ten minutes; take no notice of anything you may see or hear."

"Yes, sir."

"Then drive me to the nunnery; do you hear me?"

"Yes, sir."

"And will obey?"

"Faithfully."

"And you shall have five guineas."

"Five guineas?"

"Ay, and if you perform my bidding faithfully—"

"I promise."

"Enough; I say that if you perform my bidding faithfully, it shall be doubled."

"Oh! honoured sir," exclaimed the man, "I'm yours for life."

"That's more than enough. Half-an-hour will suffice."

The man reiterated his assurances of fidelity, and Red Ralph returned to the Palmer's Cell.

In the course of three or four minutes the coachman saw a white figure moving along the road, in the direction in which the highwayman had departed, and he began to entertain some superstitious qualms.

As the figure drew nearer, however, he perceived that it was a woman dressed in white, and who was making for the spot in very unfeminine strides.

The woman did not pause as she passed the carriage, but merely uttered a word which caused the coachman to start, and almost to tumble from his seat—

"Remember!"

"O lor' yes," answered the coachman, "I will indeed, sir."

He recognised the voice of the Captain of the Yellow Band.

Red Ralph had for his present scheme returned to the Palmer's Cell, which served him upon this occasion as a dressing-room, and hastily re-arrayed himself in the feminine apparel.

Contenting himself with this passing admonition to the coachman, Captain Ralph hurried down the road in the direction of London.

"I left her here," he said, pausing before the stump of a tree which had been destroyed by lightning; "she must have got loose and strayed away; perhaps she's nibbling at the sweet herbs in the next field—st—st—Hey! Nancy, lass!"

His summons was responded to by the neigh of a horse, evidently close at hand.

"Hey, Nancy, lass!" repeated the captain. "This way, lass."

The next minute a horse was heard galloping across an adjacent field, and then, taking the hedge at a fling leap—no small matter—the "Nancy" that Captain Ralph had summoned stood by his side.

"Brave lass," said Red Ralph, patting her neck. "Brave Nancy."

The horse, or rather mare, returned his caress with a neigh of pleasure.

"Now then, Nancy," said Ralph, springing upon the saddle sideways. "Hey for the road! Off and away!"

And Nancy flew off with her strangely attired master, like the wind.

When they had proceeded about a mile along the London Road the captain drew rein and began to look about him.

At the same instant the distant sound of a church clock striking came faintly upon his ear.

"There goes St. Paul's," murmured the captain; "the wind's in this quarter, and we shall have a stormy night of it. It must be nearly upon the hour. Ha! here comes my lord bishop. I may as well

ride up to him. His grace bears a reputation for gallantry, and will never fear a petticoat."

A light touch of the rein once more set Nancy in motion, and they mounted a rather steep hill, at the foot of which he had drawn up.

Not a hundred yards in front of him came on a single horseman at a gallop. He wore a long riding cloak which half covered horse as well as rider, but a broad-brimmed hat ecclesiastically fashioned and fastened with black cords and tassels announced that it was the traveller whom the Captain of the Yellow Band had expected.

"Good night, sir," said Ralph, as the traveller approached.

"Good night to you, madam," returned the traveller, with a very gallant bow.

"A fine night."

"It is: you are abroad rather late, methinks, madam," said the traveller, halting awhile.

"Indeed, I am, sir," returned Ralph, in a low voice. "And I am very fearful."

"Fearful—of what?"

"Robbers."

"There is no fear here, madam," said the traveller.

"Indeed? But there is," said Ralph: "it is reported that this road is infested by the Yellow Band."

"Nay; it *was*, perhaps. But Mr. Jonathan Wild has swept them all off to-day."

"Indeed?"

"Ay, madam, and their rascally leader, Captain Red Ralph, as he designates himself, is by this time safely lodged in Newgate."

"This is glorious news. But are you sure?"

"Certain, madam. He gained such information to-day as must have ensured the success of his undertaking."

"Whose?"

"Jonathan Wild's: who but he could do it? He is the greatest—"

"Rogue living!"

"Eh?"

"Nothing."

"Oh! I thought you said something," said the traveller.

"No, sir, I was listening to you."

"I was about to say that Jonathan Wild is the public benefactor of the age."

"Doubtless, if he has effected the capture of this robber. I have a mission of importance to fill which calls me out so late at night, but was just returning with my object unaccomplished."

"Why so?"

"I feared to pass a portion of the road up higher. It is so dark, and I was returning."

"Will you accept my escort? Will you come with me?"

Ralph turned his horse round and stood side by side with the traveller.

"With all my heart, my lord bishop."

"Madam."

"But stay, your grace;" and here Ralph produced a pistol and presented it at the bishop. "Suppose instead you go with me?"

CHAPTER XIV.

THE BISHOP FALLS INTO THE HANDS OF THIEVES —THE CONVENT—A NUN BY FORCE—RALPH'S LOVE—LADY MAUDE—THE PLAN OF ESCAPE— THE PURSUIT—RED RALPH AGAIN VICTORIOUS.

"TREACHERY!" cried the bishop. "What ho! Murder! Robbery!"

"Silence."

"Help! Mur—"

"You'll get into trouble, my Lord Bishop of Bondestret."

"Jezebel!" cried the astounded ecclesiastic.

"Softly."

"Put down that pistol."

"Sit quiet, or I warn you 'twill explode," said Ralph.

"Whither would you lead me, fiend?" demanded the bishop, reining in his horse.

"To my residence."

"I'll not go."

"Indeed?"

"At least, not with a pistol at my head."

"Then you would not object if I offered more gentle inducements?" said Ralph, lowering the pistol for an instant.

The old bishop endeavoured to look unutterably killing, but the comical expression of his countenance, as he tortured his fat cheeks into a smile, so tickled Ralph that he burst into a roar of laughter.

"Hallo! young woman."

His grace was astonished at the masculine laugh.

"You're a sad rogue, your grace!" exclaimed Red Ralph.

"Gad, if it were not for the cloth," laughed the bishop—

"Fie upon you, my Lord Bishop of Bondestret."

"How came you to know me?"

"Let us proceed a little further, and you shall learn that."

"Nay."

"But I say yes."

Ralph raised the pistol to the bishop's head, and they rode on.

"I suppose I must," said his grace, whose countenance wore an oddly mixed expression of curiosity and fear. "But I never was wooed in this fashion before."

"I can well believe that," said Red Ralph, laughingly.

They had now reached the spot where the lieutenant had stopped the travelling carriage, and three of the men were still engaged in their work of plunder.

Every vestige of property had disappeared, and nothing remained but the carriage and horses.

It had been a rich booty, for the proprietor of the carriage had come with a well-lined purse, prepared to satisfy any scruples of conscience which the lady superior of the convent might choose to entertain with regard to the business in hand.

"Hawks," said Captain Ralph.

"Is that you, captain?" said one of the men, looking up.

"Yes; I want your assistance here."

"Ay, ay, captain."

"Captain!" iterated the bewildered Bishop of Bondestret.

"Ay, captain," said Red Ralph, with a light laugh.

"Then you are—"

"Red Ralph, the Captain of the Yellow Band; at your service."

"Merciful goodness!"

"The knave that Mr. Jonathan Wild, the greatest public benefactor of the age, has secured and safely lodged in Newgate this night."

The bishop could not utter a word for several minutes.

He was utterly dumbfounded.

"Audacious scoundrel!" at length he cried.

"My gallant churchman!"

"Unblushing ruffian!"

"Most virtuous prelate!"

"You laughing thief! You jibbering rogue! Jailbird!"

"Proceed, your grace," said Red Ralph, laughing boisterously.

"Gallows Jack!"

"Don't exert yourself too much, my lord bishop," said Red Ralph. "It's dangerous; you are just the style of man who pops off with apoplexy!"

His grace was silenced in an instant.

"Now comes my turn," said Ralph, "as your grace is quiet for a moment. Perjured guardian!"

"Liar!"

"Traitor! Betrayer of the innocent! False priest and—"

"Sir!" reiterated the churchman, changing colour.

"Hah! my lord bishop," exclaimed Ralph; "my words touch you nearly."

"Ruffian!" faltered the bishop.

"None of your abusive epithets touch Red Ralph, the Captain of the Yellow Band; outlaw—robber—though he be, with a price upon his head?"

"What do you mean by these idle words?" demanded the bishop, but with reduced importance.

"Mean, my lord bishop?" said Red Ralph. "Why, that I know you—that I am acquainted with all your rascally proceedings—with the object of your presence here to-night."

"It is an idle boast," said the bishop, eyeing him curiously.

"Nay, it is none; one word will suffice to prove the fact."

"Indeed?"

"Ay!"

"And that word is—"

"Arnold."

"Hah!"

"You see, my lord, it was no idle boast."

"Man, demon, fiend—whoever you may be—"

"I am Red Ralph, Captain of the Yellow Band."

"And leagued with the foul fiend, I'll be sworn."

"Believe it not, your grace," returned Red Ralph, sarcastically. "And therefore the presence of so much piety can harm me little."

"Answer me one question."

"Willingly, if in my power, my Lord Bishop of Bondestret."

"Hush."

His grace glanced about him affrightedly.

"Wherefore?"

"Fool!" said the bishop. "Would you betray me to your men?"

"I have no secrets from my associates," said Red Ralph.

"And your men—"

"Know all. I deem it prudent. I might be caught in ambush. It is known to me that the Bishop of Bondestret's cunning is greater even than his piety, and so I provide against it thus. Should any harm occur to me, every man of the Yellow Band is prepared to publish to the world your grace's peccadilloes —to disgrace you before all—to ruin your reputation, and, possibly, to lose you your liberty."

With a half-suppressed curse the bishop withdrew his hand from a pocket in the lining of his riding-cloak, in which it had been fumbling for the last few minutes, and dashed it vexatiously upon his knee.

Red Ralph observed the action, and did not fail to take advantage of the inference which he drew from it.

"And what may be the object of all this?" demanded the bishop.

"The immediate object is to secure your person, and only to release it upon the receipt of a heavy ransom."

"And do you think that such a proceeding is practicable in free England in the eighteenth century?"

"Where a bishop of the established church would imprison a helpless girl in a nunnery!"

"It is monstrous! and I'll never consent."

" You will."

" Never ! "

" You will —you are half consenting already to accede to any demand I may make, my lord bishop."

" Do you profess to read the hearts of men as well as cut purses, Sir Captain of footpads ? "

" That do I, your grace," returned Captain Ralph ; " and I can read in yours vice, treachery, and cowardice."

" Indeed ? and what price may you set upon me ? "

" Five thousand pounds."

" Pshaw ! "

" And I shall not budge one half-a-groat, your grace."

" 'Tis plain," said the bishop ironically, " that your thiefship does not read men's pockets as well as their hearts."

" I could read yours."

" Indeed ? "

" Ay ! I can say that the pocket of your cloak contains a weapon."

The bishop started.

" I strike home again," said Ralph. " But the game begins, as I anticipated. Hey, Hawks, accompany this gentleman to the haunt; keep him snug and away from other guests. Good night, your grace. Five thousand is the price. I shall leave you a month to think it over."

The Bishop of Bondestret was dismounted, and marched off between two of the men.

" Send Walters to me, Hawks," shouted Red Ralph.

" Ay, ay, captain," answered the man, as he disappeared in the wood.

It was perhaps a quarter of an hour after the incident just related that a carriage was drawn by four horses up to the principal entrance of the nunnery, a garden door of which faced the Palmer's Cell, as we have already described.

There was a harsh clanking of chains and shooting of ponderous bolts as one of the servants gave a loud summons at the gate, and the heavy lumbering gates creaked upon their rusty hinges as they were thrown open.

" Who is it that claims admission at this hour ? " demanded a harsh and unpleasant female voice.

" One who would speak with the lady superior," returned an occupant of the carriage.

" It is after hours, and the lady superior is at her devotions."

" But my arrival is expected by the lady superior."

" Then, if you will wait awhile I will take your name to her, and say if you can be seen to-night."

" Arnold."

The woman departed, and in the course of a few minutes returned, saying that the lady superior was ready to see the visitor.

A gentleman stepped from the carriage and handed out a young lady, thickly veiled, and they both passed into the nunnery.

They were shown into the presence of the lady superior, a tall bony woman of a stern forbidding aspect, at the sight of whom the veiled lady appeared to tremble and shrink away in fear.

" Reverend mother, I salute you," said the gentleman.

" Benedicite, my son," replied the lady superior.

" This is my daughter Alice, of whom I spoke to you, reverend mother."

" She wishes to take the vows ? "

" Yes."

" Willingly resigns the vanities of the flesh ? "

" Yes, reverend mother," again said the gentleman.

" Nay, Mr. Arnold," said the lady superior, " let your daughter speak for herself; answer me, daughter of man — child of sin."

The girl shook visibly.

" Are you prepared to devote the remainder of your life to holiness ? Speak, girl."

" Nay, n—"

" Hah ! " exclaimed Mr. Arnold, seizing the trembling girl by the arm. " Answer the lady superior —answer her truly, I command you."

" Yes, yes," faltered the girl.

" 'Tis well, daughter," said the lady superior. " But the night grows late; have you nothing further to say ? "

" But one word," said Mr. Arnold, " and I will not longer detain you, reverend mother. In gratitude for the motherly protection you extend to my wayward worldly child, I shall endow—"

Here his voice sank, and the remainder of the sentence was heard alone by the lady superior.

The eyes of the abbess glistened with cupidity.

" Good, my son," she said. " And now good night. I am already overstepping the rules of the convent in admitting you at this hour."

" I would speak one word with my child ere I depart."

" Let it be brief, then."

" It shall."

The abbess stepped to the door to give instructions to one of the nuns about the disposal of their new sister for the night.

" Farewell, my daughter," said Mr. Arnold, tenderly embracing her.

The daughter's reply was curious to hear, and would have considerably startled the lady superior had it not been given in a very low whisper.

" Hand me your barkers, Walters."

" Here."

And " Mr. Arnold " hastily passed a pair of pistols into his daughter's hands, who immediately concealed them in the folds of her dress.

" Shall I remain, captain ? " asked Mr. Arnold, in a whisper.

" If possible," replied his daughter.

" Are you prepared to depart, my son ? " demanded the abbess.

" My daughter fears to leave me just yet."

" What ! would you take her away ? "

" No; but she would like me to remain for to-night."

" Impossible ! "

" You hear, my child," said Mr. Arnold, mournfully ; " but never mind ; I shall be close at hand."

He squeezed her hand, and the pressure was silently returned, implying a mutual understanding.

" If it must be so," said Alice Arnold, in a voice broken by emotion, " farewell, my father —farewell."

And then in a breath she said, ere the echoes of her words had died away—

" Be at the gate by the Palmer's Cell. Have Wolff and Hawks with you."

" Yes."

And father and daughter were parted.

" Sister Ursula," called the lady superior.

" Yes, holy mother," answered a nun, appearing upon the threshold.

" Conduct Sister Alice to a chamber for the night; we will arrange future proceedings in the morning."

The nun bowed, and beckoned " Miss Arnold " to follow her from the room.

The nun preceded Miss Arnold through several long passages, each of which was only dimly lighted by a small flickering oil lamp in the middle.

" Let me hold you by the hand, if you please," said Miss Arnold.

" Wherefore ? "

" I don't like the look of these long passages.

" You are fearful—timid ? " said Sister Ursula.

" Dreadfully

[THE MIDNIGHT DUEL.]

"Then walk with me," said the nun, good-naturedly placing her arm around the new sister's waist.

After they had proceeded a few paces like this the nun paused with an exclamation of affright.

"The saints protect us!" she said. "Are you not well, sister Alice?"

"Yes, thank you. Why do you ask me that?"

"Your heart beats so strongly."

"It always does when I have an arm round my waist."

"Sister Alice!" exclaimed the nun reproachfully.

"I mean a woman's arm," added Miss Arnold hastily.

"Of course."

Miss Arnold reciprocated the Sister Ursula's ten-derness by encircling her waist (a remarkably small one, by-the-bye, and well-shaped) with her right arm, and they continued traversing the passage until they arrived beneath the oil lamp.

Here Miss Arnold held her companion by gentle force for a few minutes.

"You are remarkably pretty, Sister Ursula."

"Fie, sister," said the nun, blushing with pleasure; "your words and thoughts are far too worldly."

But she was gratified nevertheless.

Not a lifetime of monastic severity could entirely eradicate all traces of the woman.

"How came you to be a nun?" demanded Miss Arnold.

No. 6.

"I entered this retreat at my father's request."

"Request?"

"Yes; not command. I had a liking—scarcely a liking—but—"

"You have shut yourself up for life here in mistaken religious fervour."

"Nay, I believe that I have a vocation for a monastic life."

"Never believe it, pretty Sister Ursula," said Miss Arnold; "woman was born for the wife of man and the mother of children—not to shut herself up in a gloomy prison-house."

Sister Ursula sighed, and her eyes filled with tears.

"I beg you will not speak thus to me, Sister Alice," said the nun; "I have chosen my life and—"

"Would willingly change it if it were possible."

"It is not possible."

"What is your name?"

"My worldly name is Mary Powell; I am the only daughter of Stanley Powell—"

"Stanley Powell!" iterated Miss Arnold.

"Yes; do you know him?"

"By name only."

"He is well known for his earnest pious life; it was that he feared he could not take due care of me that he wished me to take the vows and enter the retreat."

"And you?"

"Obeyed my father."

"Would you change your life if it were possible?"

"I—oh! I—sister Alice, you break my heart!" cried the poor nun, bursting into a torrent of tears.

The new sister did all in her power to console the nun. She kissed away her tears with astonishing fervour, and protested a dozen times that she would not for worlds hurt her feelings, accused herself of being brutal and unkind, and administered a thousand self-reproaches which Sister Ursula gently repudiated through her tears.

"Pray, Sister Ursula," said Miss Arnold, "before you leave me for the night, will you tell me if the Lady Maude who was brought here yesterday is still an inmate of the retreat?"

"Yes, Sister Alice," was the reply; "and not simply an inmate, but she sleeps in the adjoining cell."

Miss Arnold started as if she had received a strong galvanic shock.

"Did you know her, then?" continued Sister Ursula.

"Slightly."

"Poor girl; I sadly fear that she—" here the nun sank her voice into a whisper and glanced about her apprehensively—"that she is not a voluntary inmate."

"I know it."

"I feared it. 'Tis thus that the well meaning of these establishments is so perverted."

"I am glad, though, that I am so near to her. I should have felt dull the first night."

"The lady superior has had some consideration upon your behalf," said Sister Ursula.

"Indeed? In what way?"

"Your cell—"

"Say bedroom, please," said Miss Arnold, with a shudder.

"Bedroom, then, overlooks the garden."

"Ah!"

"Why that start?"

"Nothing; but what portion of the garden? It surrounds the retreat."

"The glade entrance."

"The Palmer's Cell?"

"Yes."

"By heavens!" muttered Miss Arnold, "there's a special providence in all this."

"I do not understand you, Sister Alice."

"No, no. Good night, dear Sister Ursula—pretty Mary Powell."

"Hush."

"And hope."

The door was closed and Sister Ursula was gone.

The new sister listened intently at the door until the echoes of the nun's footsteps died away in those gloomy long passages.

Then she gently opened the door.

"There is no time to be lost now," she murmured; "let me see the next cell—this must be it."

She tapped gently three times but there was no response.

Again she knocked, and this time there was a rustle of a feminine garment.

"Maude! Maude! Lady Maude!"

"Who's there?"

"'Tis I."

"Who?"

"'Tis I—here to aid you, Maude!"

"Ah! Ralph!"

"Yes; Ralph," answered the highwayman, for it was he; "open the door and fly with me."

"Alas, I cannot; it is barred without."

"So it is," exclaimed Ralph; "fool that I was not to have seen it!"

But he made up for the few seconds lost time by the haste with which he took down the fastenings.

A moment more and the Lady Maude was enfolded in the arms of the Yellow Band's adventurous captain.

"Ralph."

"Maude."

These two monosyllables were all that they could utter for several moments.

But these were more full of expression, more replete with ardent affection, than volumes could have spoken.

Red Ralph was first to recover his presence of mind.

"Maude," said he "we must see about escaping."

"I fear there is no hope, Ralph."

"Pshaw! my love, was there hope of my being here at all?"

"True, there was not."

"Then believe me, Maude darling, the rest shall be accomplished; let me see this window."

"It opens."

"Good."

"But those bars—"

"Are nothing; the fastenings are rotten with age; see, I can almost shake this one out. Ha! that's it, you see, Maude."

Lady Maude stood gazing in admiration at her lover's efforts upon her behalf.

One by one his strong arm demolished the iron fastenings which stood between them and liberty.

"There!" said Ralph, "now what do you say, Maude? Now place your foot in my hand—so—jump down; it's quite safe; I come. Hah! what's that?"

Footsteps were heard approaching Lady Maude's cell.

"Lost, lost!"

"No, no; are there no fastenings? Ha! these bars."

Red Ralph hastily caught up two of the bars which he had just removed from the window, and shortly succeeded in fastening the door of Lady Maude's cell on the inside.

Another second and it had been too late.

There was a knocking on the outside, as soon as the fastenings had been removed and it had been discovered that it was secured within.

"Come, Ralph! come," said Lady Maude affrightedly.

The Captain of the Yellow Band sprang through the window, and stood beside the trembling girl.

"Come, Maude, darling," said Ralph, placing his arm around her; "you have no cause for fear now; this way."

"If we should be overtaken?"

"I am armed."

"Oh! Ralph."

"Where can that door be?" he muttered impatiently.

They had walked some little distance along the ground by the boundary wall, and still he had not observed it.

An idea occurred to him, and he signalled the lieutenant.

The signal was returned a few paces behind him, which showed him that in spite of his vigilance he had overlooked the exit.

But now a fresh difficulty presented itself; the gate was secured by a strong lock, and he had no means of forcing it.

It far too massive a portal to be kicked in.

At this critical juncture the loud tolling of the convent bell was heard, and a rushing to and fro in the building, accompanied by the flashing of lights and the cries of the nuns, ensued.

"Oh! Ralph, Ralph," cried the highwayman's fair companion, "what shall we do? we shall be taken and forced back."

"Never!" said Red Ralph. "Hey there, Walters!"

"Yes, captain," replied the lieutenant from the other side of the nunnery wall.

"You can't manage to force the door?"

The lieutenant replied to Ralph's appeal by delivering the portal a mighty blow which shook the wall.

But still it resisted stoutly.

"Confound it, captain," said Walters, "it must be built in with the masonry."

"No, it is but locked."

"Ralph, Ralph! they are upon us," cried Lady Maude.

Lights were now flashing in different parts of the grounds, and Ralph understood that the search and pursuit had begun in real earnest.

"We must scale the wall," cried Ralph; "there is not a moment to lose."

Quick as lightening Ralph, encumbered though he was by his female attire, cleared the difficulty before him, then helped up his fair charge, and in a moment the two fugitives were safe on the other side.

The shrieking of the sisters was something terrible to hear.

They could be heard scampering wildly across the grounds, and then the banging of doors told the Yellow Band and their leader that they had given up the pursuit for that night.

"Now, Maude, darling," said Red Ralph, "whither shall I lead you?—to my home?"

"Oh, no!" said Lady Maude; "to London, Ralph."

"To-night?"

"Yes, I should not compromise myself by remaining in the wood to-night."

"And I should not compromise you, Maude," said the highwayman tenderly—"not for worlds."

"But I can go alone," said Lady Maude.

"Never."

"But you would be no protection for me dressed as you are."

"A greater protection than in my natural garb."

"How so?"

"Dear Maude," said Ralph, I am too well known in connection with the gallant Yellow Band."

"Alas!"

"Where do you purpose staying in London, Maude?"

"At old Mr. Mountjoy's, in Maddox Fields; he was an old lover of mama's, and has a great affection for me, although I believe he detests such of my father's qualities and manners as he detects in me."

"Good," said Ralph; "I think he is the man to be relied upon."

"He is indeed."

"Horses, Wolff."

Horses were brought, and the captain lifted the Lady Maude into the saddle, and then mounted himself.

"Now for London!" said the captain of the Yellow Band.

The nunnery was yet in sight when they heard the sound of horses' hoofs behind them.

"Hah!" cried Lady Maude; "we are pursued."

"Never fear, Maude."

The sounds drew nearer, and Red Ralph turned in his saddle to ascertain who were the two riders.

"Sir Launcelot! by all that's awful," he exclaimed.

The Lady Maude gave a faint shriek.

"Hey! up then, lass," cried Red Ralph, "I give 'em leave to put us back into that den we have escaped from provided they can overtake us, Maude."

Red Ralph was mounted on his mare Nancy, and so might have defied a locomotive, had such a thing been known at the period of our history; but the companion of his flight was indifferently horsed, and it was more than likely that they would be ultimately overtaken if Ralph could not devise some scheme.

He saw the danger, but unhappily could think of nothing, when the pursuers gave him an idea which placed the winning cards in the hands of the fugitives.

"Halt there!" cried one of the horsemen as soon as they were within hail.

But the fugitives only urged on their steeds with redoubled vigour.

"Halt! I say," repeated the horseman, "or I shall fire upon you."

This threat was repeated several times, but no notice of it, when suddenly there was a report, and a bullet whistled past Ralph's ear.

"Ho, ho!" he cried; "that's it, eh? Tit for tat is my motto."

Saying which he reined in his mare, and turning short upon his pursuers he levelled deliberately, and fired at the foremost.

Horse and rider came down. The horse was killed upon the spot, and the rider considerably shaken and bruised.

The other cavalier reined in upon seeing his companion's mishap, and hastened to render assistance while the fugitives passed on unmolested.

That night the Captain of the Yellow Band and his fair charge reached the metropolis in safety.

CHAPTER XV.

THE HUNCHBACK AGAIN—THE TERROR OF THE OLD HAG—BRUTAL CRUELTY—THE SWOON—THE BEAUTIFUL CAPTIVE—THE CUPBOARD—THE JACK-IN-THE-BOX—THE SKELETON'S EMBRACE.

ALTHOUGH a deep mystery enveloped the disappearance of Ralph's bride, and the efforts to find her which his trusty band of Yellow Boys had made in his behalf were entirely fruitless, yet a few words will suffice to let the reader know what had become of her.

Scarcely had Ralph left her side when a dark figure crawled towards her through the brushwood.

It wriggled itself onward with a snake-like motion.

It writhed and twisted like a crushed worm.

The beautiful girl had not yet recovered her senses, or the sight of the monstrous object would have scared her out of her wits.

It was scarcely possible to believe the livid face, blood-shot eyes, and black and crooked fangs to belong to a human being.

It was, however, the head of the hunchback which appeared between the bushes as Ralph retreated, and the hunchback's misshapen carcase was it also which wriggled and writhed its tortuous course towards the insensible girl.

Noiselessly but rapidly he approached, and, glancing around to see that he was unobserved, seized the girl in his arms and sprang back among the brushwood.

Then, with almost inconceivable quickness for one encumbered with a human burden, he bounded onwards down the hill-side, burst his way through a high hedge, and traversing several meadows was out of hearing of the robbers long before they had discovered the girl's absence.

He paused when he reached a willow copse by the edge of a small stream, and strained his ears to the utmost to listen.

Afar off he could hear a confused murmur of voices mingled with shouts and shrill cries.

"They've found it out," said the hunchback, with a fiendish chuckle; "they'll have to look sharp, though, before they catch me."

As he spoke a red glare burst out in the sky over the village.

The hunchback shook his clenched fist in the air and laughed loud and long.

The glare grew more intense.

The sky was blood-red.

Shrieks of terror mingled with savage threats reached his ears.

"They're sacking the village," the hunchback yelled in fiendish delight; "they're laying waste all before them. I wish I were there to see. How I love sights like that—blazing homes, and screaming women, and slaughtered brats! but I must away or they will catch me and take away my prize—my beautiful prize—my loved Leonore—my beautiful and scornful lady whom I love so much and who scorns me so intensely. Ha! ha! I can bide my time. It will be her turn next to pray and weep, and mine to laugh. Ha! ha! ha! ha!"

Horribly ugly did this misshapen wretch appear as he stood rubbing together his long bony hands in goblin merriment, gloating his eyes as he did so upon the lovely face and form of the helpless captive.

But a sound resembling the galloping of a horse suddenly struck upon his ear, and aroused him from a reverie into which he seemed to have fallen.

The noise warned him that he was yet within easy reach of the Yellow Band, and that he had no time to lose.

He, therefore, again took up the beautiful girl in his arms and hurried onwards.

In about ten minutes more he had reached the old house where Leonore (for such appeared to be the name of Ralph's mysterious bride) had been taken by the hunchback upon the previous day.

The blear-eyed hag was in readiness to open the door for him, and as soon as he had entered the bolts and bars were shot into their sockets.

The old hag was evidently in a great state of terror, and her hands trembled so violently that it was only with the greatest difficulty that she could prevent a candlestick that she held from falling out of her hands.

With watchful eyes, full of shrinking dread, she followed every movement of the hunchback, keeping always at a respectful distance from his fist.

She certainly expected that she was going to catch it.

There was also another certainty—her expectation would be fulfilled.

The hunchback carried his beautiful burden up stairs, and gently laid her upon the bed in the room where she had before been placed.

She was still insensible.

The hunchback looked at her with an evil smile lighting up his cat-like eyes.

"She'll be safer this time, I'll warrant, for I shall be her jailor myself."

He gave a glance at the fastening of the window, and then, very carefully locking the door, put the key into his pocket and walked downstairs.

The old woman, who had been holding the light for him whilst he was so engaged, scampered down before him as fast as her old legs would carry her.

She was in a mortal fright, and was in as great terror of being within reach of his feet as of his fists.

When the hunchback turned away from the door she turned back to allow him to go first, but he roared out at her—

"Go on, or I'll help you."

"Don't'ee hit me, then," she whined.

"Get downstairs."

"Don't'ee, don't'ee."

"I'll break your wretched old neck if you don't look pretty sharp."

"Oh, oh, don't'ee."

His fist and his foot were raised as she darted past him with the look of a hunted hare.

He made as though he would have kicked her furiously as she bounded down stairs, slipping and stumbling, and bumping her poor old bones, and flinging her limbs about in awkward terror, with very much the same sort of action as you might expect in a crippled daddy-long-legs.

Upon the last flight he made a dart at her, and she sprang forward and fell down half-a-dozen steps, and rolled on the floor of the passage, extinguishing the candle, which, in falling, afforded only a fleeting glimpse of two thin, bony, black stocking-encased legs, kicking frantically as their owner strove vainly to adjust her drapery and regain her feet.

Cursing her fiercely, the hunchback made several ferocious lunges in the dark with his heavy boots and roared to her to get up.

Groaning pitifully, the old woman collected her scattered limbs as well as she could and followed him.

"Oh, deary! deary! Oh my poor bones!" sobbed the old woman.

"I'll poor bones you directly!" cried the hunchback savagely. "I'll black you and blue you, my charmer. I'll wrench off your wretched old ear and poke out your wretched old eye. I'll jerk out all your rheumatic old joints, and bang you in your lumbagoey old back with a big stone."

The unhappy old woman shivered with terror at these dreadful threats, which the hunchback accompanied by the most awful curses and blasphemies.

She was a very long while indeed in following him, but she did come at last, and, having picked up the fallen candle, relighted it.

The room into which she had followed the hunchback was one upon the ground story, with a stone floor, dark panelled walls, and one small diamond-paned window securely guarded by heavy iron bars.

In it there were but two chairs, one of which was an old arm-chair with a high back; there were also a rickety table, a few shelves containing some cracked crockery, and a fire-place holding a handful of mouldering ashes.

By the side of the hearth stood a thick stick, reared up in the chimney corner.

The hunchback took up this stick, examined it with a smile, and proceeded to lock the room door.

"Oh, deary! deary! deary!" cried the old woman in great terror.

Her eyes seemed to be starting out of her head.

She shivered miserably with abject fright, and her teeth chattered like castanets in her loose jaws.

"Now, beldame," cried the hunchback, turning up his coat-sleeve as he spoke. "Have a care."

"Oh, deary! deary! deary!" sobbed the old woman,

wringing her hands in dire consternation at the fate in store for her.

"You miserable, drivelling, old, addle-headed hag!" cried the hunchback.

"Oh, deary! deary! deary!"

"You drunken, stupid, blind, deaf object of misery, look out!"

Heaping such abuse as this upon the unhappy old creature, he brandished in the air the stick he had taken up for the purpose, and brought it down with tingling thwacks upon her back and legs and arms, though she vainly endeavoured to defend herself.

Wildly she fled before him. She tried to dodge him round the table and chairs.

But her efforts were fruitless. Wherever she got to, the stick he held was quite long enough to reach her.

The more she struggled the faster she ran, and the louder she screamed for mercy the more delighted was the misshapen monster illusing her.

Laughing and screaming himself, he danced like a goblin before her. He fenced with her with the stick, and chose his time for hitting her, when he saw a good opportunity of doing so, upon her bony elbows, or on her shins, or across her back, and more than once upon her head.

But upon one of these occasions, hitting her harder than he intended, he struck her senseless to the ground, where she lay with the blood pouring from her nose and mouth, a dreadful object to look at, with her eyes fixed and glazed and her scanty white locks bedabbled with gore.

"I wonder whether she's dead," said the hunchback to himself, as he contemplated the form of his fallen victim.

To discover whether or not he had really killed her, the ruffian gave the poor old woman a kick.

She replied with a hollow groan.

"Ah, I thought she was too tough to go off quite so quickly," said the hunchback. "I shall give her a reviver, and then leave her to come to."

With this he fetched a bucket of cold water and dashed it into the face of the wretched old woman, after which he locked the door and left her to come to as best she might.

"I'll lock up all the doors and take the keys with me," he said; "they must be safe then. The girl will be too weak to help herself until I return, if she regains her consciousness; and as for the old woman, it will be all she can do to save herself from croaking."

He stole on tiptoe upstairs, unlocked the bedroom door, and peeped in at the unconscious girl.

She lay there motionless, pale, and death-like.

A horrible smile crossed the misshapen wretch's face.

He chuckled softly to himself, and stole away again like a thief, having once more carefully locked the door.

"She's in my power, now," he muttered: "she is mine, and nought can save her."

*　　*　　*　　*　　*　　*

The beautiful girl lay for a long while in an insensible state; at last, towards the end of the night, she slowly and painfully returned to consciousness.

She opened her eyes and gazed around her in terror.

She started up in bed, stretched forth her arms, and cried out wildly—

"Mercy! mercy!"

She thought that she was yet at the stake in the hands of the bloodthirsty fanatics from whom Ralph had delivered her.

She clutched the bedclothes in her small white hands, and uttered a half-suppressed shriek of terror.

But soon the truth began to dawn upon her.

The pale moonlight pouring into the room revealed to her certain articles of furniture which she recollected.

"It is the same place that I was at before," she murmured; "why have they brought me back here?"

The more she reflected upon the subject, the more the horror of her helpless situation crushed and stupified her.

But she would not lie there to await her doom without making an effort to escape from her unknown jailors.

She very slowly and painfully got off the bed.

The floor seemed to spin round with her, for she was faint and giddy.

A death-like silence reigned around, and so intense was it that she could hardly believe the house had any other occupant.

It was a strange close-smelling room, and the gloomy house had the appearance of a building over which hangs some awful curse.

Perhaps it was cursed.

It was a house where you heard dim rumbling noises in the dead of the night, and echoing taps against the mould wainscoting.

Spectral footsteps, too, creaked in dark nailed-up rooms, and the nibbling and scampering of rats in cellars and choked-up drains, and the beating of death-watches in damp crumbling walls.

As she listened some such noises as these filled the beauteous Leonore's heart with dread and apprehension.

She was, however, almost entirely without apparel, and it would be necessary to find some garments.

With this idea she began to search the room, and, approaching the door of what seemed a cupboard, with some difficulty contrived to open it.

The door suddenly swung open with an ominous creak, and at the same moment Leonore started away with a faint scream, putting up her hands as she did so to ward off some approaching horror.

A white and grizzly death's head was suddenly protruded from the doorway.

Two long fleshless arms were stretched out and encircled her waist.

She shrieked and struggled, but struggled in vain.

No efforts of hers could free her from the horrible embrace.

She battled frantically, but the monster held her still in its iron grasp.

She was in the arms of a hideous skeleton; its fleshless jaws pressed against her pale cheek, while its eyeless sockets and something that appeared to be a head of straggling white hair, looking indescribably horrible in the ghastly moonlight.

CHAPTER XVI.

RED RALPH AND THE DRUNKEN FOP—STANLEY POWEL GROWS TOO LOVING—A YOUNG LADY WHO COULD FENCE—THE FIGHT—THE INTERRUPTION.

HAVING seen the fair Lady Maude safely housed with her old friend Mr. Mountjoy in Maddox Fields, Red Ralph was retracing his steps in the direction of Piccadilly, in which quarter he was in the habit of putting up with a friend when in town, when he met with a little adventure, which as it is in some way connected with a previous chapter of this narrative, we shall here relate.

He was passing a house which was brilliantly illuminated, and from which the sound of boisterous revelry was issuing, when an unsteady gallant, descending the stone steps, got his sword between his legs, and came down head first, almost capsizing Red Ralph.

"Hulloa!" cried Ralph, who was still in disguise.

"A thou—thousand pardons, a mere slip of the tongue; no, d— it, I don't mean that ; but you understand, madam, no offence."

"Not in the least " said Ralph.

"That's right, then, let's be friends—gish a kish."

Red Ralph pushed the maudlin wine-bibber from him in disgust.

"Don't be coy, my gipsy."

"Can you tell me whose house is that, pray, sir ?" asked Ralph.

"That I can."

"Thank you, sir."

"And shall I ?"

"If you please."

"And what if I don't please ?"

And here the drunkard smiled superciliousy with the look of tipsy importance which men at a certain stage of alchoholic aberration frequently wear.

"I don't mind telling you, though," he resumed, "that, hic ! that house belongs to the hardest drinker in the country ; I'll match him against any man at his own liquors."

"Who ?"

"Stanley Powell."

"Hah !"

"Goograshus, you frighten me."

"Is Mr. Stanley Powell in the house at present ?"

"Coursh," anwered the reveller with a disdainful curl of the lip at Ralph's ignorance. "Hulloa there ! by Bacchus ! she's going into the house. Hi ! you madam, Powell won't see any woman to-night, there's a bachelor party on."

But Ralph, heedless of the drunkard's words, had knocked at the door and gained admittance.

"Excuse me, madam," said the servant, "but Mr. Powell is—"

"Enough," said Ralph, "I must see Mr. Powell to-night."

A guinea dropped into the man's willing palm, and this little difficulty was smoothed over.

"Now go to Mr. Powell and say that a lady would speak with him for an instant."

"I dare not ; I—"

"Go."

And a second guinea sent the servant bounding up the stairs to the apartment whence the sounds of revelry proceeded.

The next instant proved, however, that the fears of the domestic had not been without some foundation, for a door above was thrown open with great violence, and a man's voice was heard showering abusive epithets upon the servant's head.

At the same time a scuffling was heard, and a dull thud announced that the hapless servant's head was not alone suffering for its owner's temerity."

"Knave ! varlet ! " cried the irate Mr. Stanley Powell, pursuing the footman downstairs and administering pedal applications to his nether extremities at each word.

"You lying filching jackanapes ! how dare you interrupt me against my express order ? D'ye think I keep you in idleness and vagabondism for the pleasure of gazing upon that hideous face? Answer me, you scoundrel; not a word, you villain ! Eh ? go hang yourself, and rob Jack Ketch of his fee."

Mr. Stanley Powell had reached the foot of the stairs by this time, and perceived Ralph, who stood with his head turned aside as if in great alarm.

Now Ralph, as the reader must have surmised, by his frequent adoption of the disguise, looked remarkbaly well as a woman.

His figure was slight but graceful, and possessed all the muscular power of a strong man with the feminine proportions.

Ralph, too, from his long experience was remarkably well versed in all the little coquetrics which are the attractions in the gentler sex.

He always were a thick veil, through which shone a pair of lustrous black eyes with killing effect, and the mode and quality of his apparel impressed one with the idea of a lady of superior rank.

"Your pardon, madam," said Mr. Powell, bowing to the ground.

Ralph returned his salute with frigid courtesy.

"A thousand pardons, very dear madam, I beg," said Mr. Powell obsequiously. "I was not aware who it was that desired to see me."

"The man is not to blame, Mr. Powell," said Ralph in a low tone, as if not yet recovered from the effects of Mr. Powell's harshness to his servant. "I told him that I had business of an important nature. I should have said that Lady—"

Here Ralph paused abruptly, and glanced at the servant as if about to commit an indiscretion.

"Fore gad !" muttered Mr. Powell to himself, "here's an intrigue."

Then he added aloud to the discomfited servant— •

"Is the walnut room prepared as I desired ?"

"Yes, sir."

"Very well ; now remember, Thomas, that I shall be particularly engaged, and under no pretext under the sun let me be disturbed. D'yo' hear me ?"

"Yes."

"Mark you ; obey.

"But, sir—"

"What now ?"

"If Mistress Flagon should call ? "

"I am out."

"Yes, sir."

"Unexpected business has called me suddenly out of town—to—oh ! say to 'The Retreat.' Mistress Flagon will understand."

And so did Captain Ralph.

"This way, madam," said the old gallant, handing Ralph into a superbly appointed chamber to the left of the passage.

The Captain of the Yellow Band chuckled inwardly as he perceived the old roué double-lock the door behind them, but did not make any remark upon the action.

"Now, madam," said Mr. Stanley Powell ; "now we are alone."

His fair visitor appeared to be in great alarm.

"We are alone, I say, madam," continued the old debauchee. "I pray you to remove your veil."

"Nay, sir," said Ralph in low tremulous tones, "I pray you—"

"Fie on it, madam," said the old gallant, with a light laugh ; "there is no occasion to use further caution here."

"Not caution, but—"

"But what ?"

"Oh, sir—"

"Tut ! tut ! we can dispense with anything in the way of coquetry, madam ; we are alone, remember."

But Ralph's only reply was to seat himself at the table, which was spread with every delicacy that could tease the most fastidious appetite, and to begin a furious onslaught upon the viands.

The Captain of the Yellow Band was almost famished.

While with the beloved Lady Maude the cravings of nature had been silenced, but as soon as she was disposed of Ralph became aware that he had taken nothing to eat since noon.

Mr. Stanley Powell was so taken by surprise at the freedom of his visitor's movements that he could not speak a word for several minutes, but stood gazing stupidly upon Ralph, who was devouring everything that came to hand.

At length the old libertine found his voice.

"S'death, madam!" he exclaimed, "but your appetite is greater than your conversational powers."

Red Ralph, with his mouth full, merely looked up and nodded his assent.

"Now, madam," said Mr. Stanley Powell, after a few minutes' pause, "I swear I'll have that veil down and satisfy myself that—"

"What?" asked Ralph, looking up.

"That I am not being hoaxed."

"How hoaxed?"

"Tut! tut! down with the veil, I say," cried the old beau pettishly.

But Ralph quietly resumed his repast.

This was too much for Mr. Stanley Powell's patience, and with a final appeal to the lady, which was disregarded as before, he advanced towards her with the intention of using violence to accomplish his purpose.

However, Mr. Powell's hand no sooner touched his visitor's face, than a vigorous push sent him staggering back.

But the old beau was not thus lightly put off.

He advanced once more, and Ralph, unwilling to use violence, sprang to his feet and placed the dining table between them.

"Come, come, my hungry coy one—come here," said Mr. Powell.

But the hungry coy one declined, and Mr. Stanley Powell at once began an animated but undignified chase round the table.

In his second run round, the old man tripped over a fallen chair, and staggering against the dining-table sent it, with its weighty and savoury burden, smashing to the ground.

This blocked up one side of the room, and further flight was an impossibility for Red Ralph.

However, when matters were growing critical, he chanced to perceive a small dress sword and belt lying upon a couch, which had been hitherto unnoticed.

To possess himself of this, and place himself on guard, was the work of an instant.

Mr. Stanley Powell drew and endeavoured to disarm his fair antagonist, but without avail.

Ralph was a master of the fence.

The host soon discoved this, for Ralph pressed him so hard that he began to cry lustily for assistance.

The next minute the door was burst in, and Mr. Powell's valet de chambre came running to the rescue.

CHAPTER XVII.

THE FOP AND HIS FRENCH VALET — RALPH PLEADS MARY'S CAUSE—THE HARD-HEARTED FATHER—WITCHCRAFT—RED RALPH IN THE TOILS — THE RECOGNITION—HO FOR NEWGATE!

RALPH was now unquestionably in an unpleasant predicament.

As yet his true sex had not been discovered, but he doubted not that a few minutes more would disclose it.

Mr. Stanley Powell had been in his youth an expert swordsman and a noted duellist.

But age and a life of hard living and debauchery had weakened the wrist of steel of former days, and he had been at the mercy of the Captain of the Yellow Band any time during the past five minutes if Ralph had chosen to exert himself.

But the only object of Red Ralph was to free himself from the obnoxious flirtation of the old roué, and not to do him any personal violence.

The French valet came running to his master's assistance as we have stated.

Now, it would not have answered Red Ralph's purpose to be seized by Mr. Stanley Powell's menials, for at such close quarters his masculine development would most surely have betrayed itself and he would get into hot water.

There was therefore but one chance left, and of this Red Ralph was not slow to avail himself.

With him to think was to act.

As the French valet was struggling to remove the dining-table, which impeded his progress, Ralph made a sudden and violent feint which drove his aged antagonist back several paces.

It was a fortunate thought. A chair was in the way, and Mr. Stanley Powell stumbled and fell over it, and his sword was sent spinning to the further extremity of the apartment.

In an instant Ralph was upon him.

"Send that man away," said Ralph in an undertone.

"Jezebel! I—"

Ralph shortened his sword and offered to strike. There must have been something which spoke of danger in his glance, for the old man was cowed in an instant.

"Tell him to go," said the Captain of the Yellow Band; "or—"

"Go away, François," said Mr. Stanley Powell faintly.

"M'sieur?"

"Go away."

But the man, not understanding that he should be ordered off when his master was in such a startling fix, only renewed his struggles with the dining-table.

"He doesn't hear," said Ralph. "Your master says you are to go away. Don't you hear? He doesn't care for his frolics to be interrupted in this way."

"But he call, madame," said François.

"Tell him to go."

"Leave the room, François."

"And Mr. Powell doesn't wish to be interrupted again," said Red Ralph.

Monsieur François shrugged his shoulders and left the room.

"Now, madam," said Mr. Stanley Powell, "allow me to rise."

"Certainly, Mr. Powell," said Red Ralph, delighted.

He extended his hands, and Mr. Powell was once more upon terra firma.

"Now, pray tell me what may be your object in paying me this untimely visit?" said Mr. Stanley Powell.

"I am glad to come to the point," said Ralph. "You have a daughter, Mr. Powell?"

"Sir!"

"I say you have a daughter."

The old man coloured to the temples, and stared into the face of the Yellow Band's Captain, through the thick veil which he still wore, as if he would read the inmost thoughts of his soul.

"Do you know where that daughter is?"

"Undoubtedly."

"In a nunnery."

"S'death, madam!" cried Mr. Stanley Powell, "I say I know it."

"In a nunnery," pursued Ralph—"a prison-house —wasting her youth, withering her young heart in obedience to the mandate of her cruel, heartless parent."

"Madam!" said Mr. Stanley Powell, "to commence, I may say that your reflection on my actions is unjust— that your interference in my personal matters is d—d impertinent; and I may further add, madam, that my daughter's mode of life is her own free and unbiassed selection."

"You lie!"

Mr. Stanley Powell grew scarlet. He hastily clapped his hand to his side, but his sword was not there.

"Pooh!" said Ralph, coolly, "you see how little your anger affects me. You see that even with your own manly weapon I am more than your match; so smother your anger, I implore you. I repeat, sir, you lie. Your daughter, the unhappy Mary Powell, has been lured into that den under false pretences."

Mr. Powell had passed into another stage of indignation, and was now quietly boiling with suppressed rage.

"Listen, madam," said Mr. Stanley Powell, "I know not who you may be, nor by what right you force your presence upon me here for this purpose. But for the nonce I will waive the question of your right to take up the cudgels in my daughter's behalf, and simply content myself with assuring you that all hope of removing her from her self-elected mode of life is useless; she has taken voluntary and irrevocable vows, which no earthly power can set aside."

"I shall not go," said the Captain of the Yellow Band deliberately, "until I have effected my purpose."

As he said this he set himself down upon the couch. Fatal chance!

As he reached the soft, springy cushions, he heard a sharp grating sound like the smothered noise of a watchman's rattle.

Before he could ask a question—ere he could even give the occurrence a second thought—he felt himself seized and held as if in a vice.

Red Ralph was utterly bewildered—lost.

He could see no one about him—no one was present but Mr. Stanley Powell and himself—of that he was assured; and yet he had been grasped by an invisible power and held down.

He was soon convinced that no human grasp held him, for, if not able to release himself from a powerful clutch, he well knew that he was never literally immoveable in such a predicament—a circumstance which had too frequently occurred to him to give him any undue alarm.

That he could always shift himself to the right or left a little, and that when making a violent exertion the grasp upon his person tightened, and grew firmer in proportion to the strength of his effort.

Now it was different. He was held by witchcraft, he imagined, or by some supernatural agency, for the bondage was not bodily painful, and yet he could not move an inch to the right or left—backwards and forwards.

"Ha! ha! madam," cried Mr. Stanley Powell, in wild joyful triumph, "I have you now; you have placed yourself in the lion's den, and you shall suffer for your temerity. You have had your turn, and now comes mine."

The aged libertine's face flushed with excitement.

He advanced to the couch upon which lay the Captain of the Yellow Band, bound by an invisible power, and helpless.

"The first thing," grinned the toothless old libertine, "is to look at those killing black eyes, which have been doing such execution during the last twenty minutes upon the humblest of your adorers."

Ralph gnashed his teeth in silent rage.

Mr. Stanley Powell, eager to glance at the fair incognita's face, tore away the veil.

Here he met with a slight rebuff.

"Hallo!" he ejaculated in the greatest astonishment; "gad's life, I've seen those features before."

Ralph's position was becoming critical, and he would willingly have sacrificed the whole of that week's large but unlawful gains to be free and outside Mr. Stanley Powell's mansion.

Mr. Powell was evidently much puzzled, and yet his former interview with the Captain of the Yellow Band had been of so striking a nature that it had left a lasting impression upon his mind, and he could not, in spite of himself, have done the problem and given his attention to the realization of his triumphs with his helpless prisoner.

"Where can it be?" he muttered. Then he added, addressing Red Ralph, "We have met before, madam."

"No," said Ralph.

"But I say we have; your features and some tones of your voice are indelibly impressed upon my mind."

"Impossible."

"Not so," said Mr. Powell; "and now I understand why I am not quite clear upon the point."

"Upon what point?" demanded Red Ralph, endeavouring to appear at his ease.

"You are disguising your voice, and—" here he began, to Ralph's disgust, to fondle his cheeks and chin—"by gad! madam, you have forgotten to shave this morning. Ha! ha! ha! ha!—this then explains the freedom in the use of my dress sword—a bully in petticoats."

Ralph bit his lips and was silent.

"A cutpurse, a rogue, I'll be sworn," continued Mr. Stanley Powell. "Hi! ho! John, James, Thomas, François!"

"Go for assistance," said Mr. Powell, as a whole tribe of domestics came running to the room in obedience to his summons. "Let some one fetch the officers. Here, Thomas, mount and ride off to Newgate; say that I have entrapped—"

Red Ralph's heart beat like the ticking of a clock.

"Never mind," resumed Mr. Stanley Powell; "I won't mention names."

The servant quitted the room, and the Captain of the Yellow Band was left a prey to the mingled sensations of rage, disgust at his imprudence, and fear for the result of the mishap when the officers should arrive from Newgate.

CHAPTER XVIII.

MORE ABOUT THE SKELETON — THE GLOOMY HOUSE AND ITS MYSTERIES—THE ROOM OF DEATH—THE UNDERGROUND ROOMS—A FEARFUL SIGHT—THE STRUGGLE WITH THE MANIAC WIFE.

In vain did the beautiful Leonore struggle in the arms of the horrible skeleton.

The greater her efforts to release herself from its hateful embrace, the tighter did its clutch seem to become.

For a few moments she was wellnigh out of her wits with fright.

The attack had been so sudden and unexpected. Her assailant of such an extraordinary nature.

Many women, under like circumstances, would have fainted from terror, or continued to scream and struggle unavailingly.

This brave girl, however, was not so silly; she summoned all her courage and reason to her aid, and looked the difficulty in the face.

The skeleton was not alive, although it jumped so nimbly out of its hiding-place, and clutched her so tightly. It was, after all, but a sort of horrible jack-in-the-box—a mechanical contrivance of fiendish ingenuity.

How to free herself from its clutches was now the matter which required her consideration. When she stood still it was still also. When she pulled away it tightened its hold on her.

Then she recollected that it had sprung out at her

[THE HUNCHBACK THREATENING LEONORE.]

with open arms. She pulled the door towards her, and worked herself round towards the cupboard.

As she did so the skeleton released his hold.

Suddenly he left go altogether, and, in a way at once grotesquely ludicrous and horrible, scampered back into the cupboard.

Then she slapped the door to in a moment, and leaned against it, and drew a long breath of relief.

Decidedly that was a cupboard to be avoided. There was another cupboard also of which she had no very favourable opinion, although she had not tried it.

After a little reflection upon the difficulties of the situation, she concluded very naturally that only two ways of escape was open to her—the door or the window.

As regarded her clothes, there was no time to think about them now. She determined to wrap herself up as well as she could in a blanket, and throw herself upon the mercy of some passer by.

She must not go near the village, or who could say what horrible tortures would be inflicted upon her?

She first of all turned her attention to the window, but here her hopes were soon blighted when she came to examine the fastenings.

It was not only, as the moonlight enabled her to see, very high from the ground, but it was securely guarded by iron bars of enormous strength.

No. 7.

The door, then, was her only hope, but this was locked upon the outside.

The wood, however, was old and rotten, and the doorpost had, to a small extent, given way, so that there was a possibility of forcing back the bolt from the inside.

What implement was she to use, though, to effect this purpose?

She looked about the room and, to her great delight, discovered a knife lying behind some litter on the mantelpiece.

With this in her hand she approached the door, and was about to operate upon the lock when a creaking noise on the stairs arrested her hand, and sent her scared and trembling back to the bedside.

She remained for some time silent as death and listening intently.

But then she came to the conclusion that she must have been mistaken, and, with the knife in her hand, once more approached the door.

All was still now.

She forced the blade of the knife under the lock, and, without any great exertion of strength, forced it back.

Then she opened the door very cautiously, and peeped out.

All was very quiet and dark. If the house contained any other inmate but herself, he or she, as the case might be, must be asleep.

As yet, as the reader will remember, Leonore had not set eyes upon either of her jailors.

She had recovered from her fainting fit, opened the door, gone downstairs, escaped from the house, and wandered towards the village, only to faint upon another doorstep, and, on recovering her consciousness, find herself in the hands of the bloodthirsty fanatics from whom Ralph had set her free.

Having fainted again, she had returned to her senses once more to find herself in the same gloomy unknown house from which she had run away.

It almost seeemed like magic that she should thus travel to and fro, knowing not whither she went or wherefore she was a captive.

But it would not do to sit down and wait patiently for the issue. She must at once take a decisive step.

She descended the stairs very slowly, and cautiously pausing more than once to listen.

But she heard nothing, and she soon came to the conclusion that she was alone in the house.

Reaching the bottom of the stairs, she groped along in the darkness until her hand encountered the handle of a door. She turned it, but found that the door was locked.

Groping her way along she came presently to another door, which she tried with the same result.

At last, having tried two more, she found that she could force the knife-blade under the lock of the last, and thus manage to open it.

The first faint streak of dawn was struggling through the iron bars of the window, but the room was yet almost entirely plunged in obscurity.

As Leonore advanced, however, she was able to make out indistinctly the objects which the room contained.

One thing at once attracted her attention—a long dark something upon the floor.

Straining her eyes to the utmost, she approached, and was within a yard of it before she perceived what it was.

Then she started back, and her blood curdled with horror.

It appeared to be the corpse of an old woman, the skull smashed in and the face covered with blood.

The girl shrank back in terror from the fearful sight.

Into what den of horror had she been brought?

What would be her own fate if she remained any longer?

She crept out of the room again, shuddering as she went, and closed the door after her.

Then she stood, uncertain what to do next—whither to bend her steps.

She found her way to the outer door by which she had before escaped, but this time it was double-locked, and fastened in such a way that to open it was impossible. To open any of the other doors of this landing was also beyond her power, and she now turned her attention to the floor beneath.

She found a staircase which led down below, and, feeling certain that she was alone in the house, fearlessly descended.

At the bottom of a flight of steep stone steps she came to a heavy door, very strongly bolted and barred. With some trouble she undid these fastenings and entered a sort of vaulted chamber, beyond which was pitch dark.

She knew not what to do now. She was afraid to return to the room where the old woman lay, though she fancied that she had noticed a small piece of candle and some lucifer matches lying on the table.

After a momentary hesitation she groped her way onwards in the dark.

Opposite to the door by which she had entered she found another door also securely bolted. This she opened, and entered a place which appeared to be either a cell or cellar, lighted by a small grating high up against the ceiling.

There was a dreadful stench in this place, and it was very cold and damp.

Leonore glanced round despairingly, and saw that it contained nothing but an old broken earthenware pitcher, and what at the first sight appeared to be a heap of dirty rags and straw in one corner.

As she was turning round again towards the door the clanking of a chain startled her.

She started violently, for at first she thought that the cellar might contain some savage dog, which would rush out upon her.

But there was no further movement, and she was fast coming to the conclusion that the noise must have been made by rats, when a deep and hollow groan struck upon her ear.

She stood motionless, her eyes fixed upon the spot from which the sound had proceeded.

After a moment's interval the groan was repeated.

Wellnigh frightened out of her life, the young girl's first idea was to fly, but then a thought flashed through her brain, and as rapidly altered her determination.

Suppose there was another captive in the house!

Single both were weak, but together they might successfully struggle against their jailors.

Conquering her fear, then, she drew near the dark corner.

As she did so a sight met her eyes which filled her with amazement and horror.

All at once a horrible object became discernible in the obscurity, and she stood transfixed before it.

The object which terrified her was the figure of a woman, miserably dirty and neglected, sitting crouched up like an ape nursing her toes, and half-hidden by straw.

It would be impossible to give the reader any just idea of the fearful condition to which cruelty and neglect had reduced this unhappy creature.

Her lean emaciated body had for its only covering a few filthy rags.

She was, to look at, nothing but a bag of bones. Her arms and legs were fleshless.

Her face was shrunken, and her deep-set eyes and hollow jaws gave her the appearance of a death's head.

A ragged mass of hair hung over her eyes and down her back.

She had long nails like the talons of a bird. Her joints seemed to be bursting through her tightly-drawn skin.

She was also covered with dreadful sores and bruises, the effects of brutal violence.

Poor unhappy creature, what misery she must have suffered ere she arrived at this state!

Such was the thought which passed through Leonore's mind as she gazed upon the miserable captive, and the first involuntary feeling of loathing and disgust gave place in the young girl's gentle heart to one of deep commiseration.

The object of misery looked up at her from among the straw, half covering its face with its hands in doing so, as though afraid.

" My poor woman," said Leonore in a gentle tone, " what are you doing here ? "

The captive made no answer, but stared at her in stupid terror.

Leonore repeated the question after a pause.

" I am dying," replied the other in a low faint voice, scarcely audible.

" What is the matter with you ? "

" I am dying of cold and hunger."

" How long have you been here ? "

" Years."

" Years ? "

" Ever since I can remember ; I can recollect nothing before the awful night he brought me here."

" Who brought you ? "

" Hush, hush ! He will hear you if you speak so loud. He will come back and beat me again with his cruel whip, which cuts so deep into my flesh."

" There is no one to hear you, my poor creature. Of whom are you speaking ? "

" Of him—upstairs."

" Of whom ? "

" Of my husband."

" Your husband ? But who is he ? "

" Jabez. Don't you know him ?—Jabez the hunchback."

" Ah ! " cried Leonore in sudden terror, glancing around—" the hunchback."

" Yes, yes," continued the other. " Do you know him. If you do you know a devil."

" I know him well enough," said Leonore in trembling tones. " Is it possible that this house belongs to him ! "

" Yes, this is his house, and the old hag upstairs is his housekeeper. They two together are killing me by inches. They starve me and beat me, and leave me half mad with thirst for days together. Sometimes I pray of them to kill me at once with one blow, and put me out of my bitter misery."

" But why does your husband keep you thus a prisoner ? "

" I know not, except that he was disappointed in the fortune he thought I should bring him ; and because he is as vindictive and unforgiving as a fiend."

" I wonder, though, that he does not kill you at once, instead of keeping you thus buried alive."

" He keeps me alive to watch my sufferings. He often comes down here and gloats his eyes upon my misery. He dances and laughs and claps his hands with joy when I shriek out in agony."

" The monster ! "

" Yes, he is indeed a monster. He has no heart to which I can appeal. He is a stone. He is dead to all human feeling."

" You must not remain here to be killed, and I must lose no time either, if I am to make good my escape."

" Escape ? Have you come here, then, to help me ? God bless you ! God bless you ! "

" I will try all I can to do so, but I do not know the house, and am unacquainted with its economy."

" Are you, too, a prisoner, beautiful lady ? " asked the other captive.

" Yes, I have been brought here in some mysterious way, and for some unknown reason."

" For no good purpose, I am certain, lady. For no purpose but your ruin, dishonour, and death. But let us lose no time. Let us fly."

" Yes ; let us fly," murmured Leonore thoughtfully. " But how ? "

She was moving towards the door, when the other woman suddenly sprang from the corner and caught her by the wrist.

" Stay," she cried in an excited tone ; " you must not leave me."

" No ; I do not intend to do so ; I will come back directly."

" No—no, you must not quit my sight."

" I must do so for a short time."

" No—no—no."

" Rest assured I will very shortly return. I want to find some means of egress from our prison-house."

" Stay ! stay ! I dare not trust you away from me. You will not come back. I feel certain you will not come back."

" My poor creature, I promise you faithfully that I will not be gone many minutes."

But it was in vain to reason. The half-witted wretch clung wildly to her, screaming and sobbing.

Then, as Leonore struggled to free herself, the other's tears gave place to an ungovernable fury.

" I will murder you," she shrieked. " I will have your life if you try to get away."

" Loose your hold ! " cried Leonore in terror.

But the idiot's hold seemed to tighten.

At that moment, too, a sound in the house above reached their ears.

There was a heavy footfall in the passage over head.

" Release me, release me ! " cried Leonore, struggling madly with her assailant. " Release me, or we are lost ! "

CHAPTER XIX.

JONATHAN GAGGED — A FRIEND IN NEED — THE THIEF-TAKER AND HIS MYRMIDONS — DANGER —ESCAPE—THE BLASTED TREE—THE UNDERGROUND MYSTERIES — BLIND MAN'S BUFF— TOM KING IN TROUBLE.

RETURN we for a while to the glade in the forest, where Jonathan Wild, Tom King, and the myrmidons of the former worthy lay bound at the mercy of Captain Red Ralph and his redoubtable Yellow Band.

So securely had they been bound by the men that escape was deemed an utter impossibility.

They were, therefore, placed upon the ground, tied hand and foot, and left there in a circle grimly helpless and silent.

The lieutenant had taken the precaution to order that they should all be gagged. Had he but taken his other precautions as wisely all might have been well—his chief might have been saved from a fearful peril.

But we must not anticipate.

The last of the Yellow Band had scarcely quitted the glade when the branch of a tree, immediately above the spot upon which lay the thieftaker bound and helpless, was shaken violently, and a man appeared scrambling through the thick foliage.

Then he endeavoured to clutch the branch, with the ostensible purpose of taking an easy drop to the ground, but unfortunately missing his hold he came to the ground with fearful velocity and a loud thud.

We have said "to the ground;" but here we are in error. He chanced to alight exactly in the softer portion of Jonathan Wild's stomach.

The latter was, of course, almost annihilated, but the new comer was thereby saved an unpleasant mishap.

"Pheugh!" he cried, as he regained his equilibrium and shook himself together. "That was likely to do me some harm if it hadn't ha' been for— Why, hallo!" and here he began to look uncomfortable, for he recognised the thieftaker in the victim of his misadventure. "Hullo! Why it's Mr. Wild!"

Jonathan Wild glared upon him in a terrifying manner.

"I'm very sorry, Mr. Wild; I am, indeed."

Mr. Wild intimated, as well as he could by a glance, that he wished to be set free.

"Yes, Mr. Wild," said the other obsequiously, interpreting the thieftaker's meaning; "in a minute—where is my knife?—I really—"

Here he began an animated search all over his person for the missing weapon, and, failing in his object, he had resource to the aid of Jonathan Wild's readier invention.

"Take mine," said the thieftaker, as plainly as eyes could speak.

But it had to be repeated several times ere the other could guess his meaning.

"Oh! I see, Mr. Wild; here it is. There you are, Mr. Wild."

A stroke of the knife had severed the cords which held the gag so tightly within the latter's mouth.

Jonathan Wild's first speech upon the recovery of his freedom was wonderfully characteristic of the man.

"You thickheaded booby!" he cried. "You numskull! Idiot! Ass!"

"Mr. Wild," said the man, all humility, "'pon my life, I—"

"You lying jackanapes, you did!" cried the thieftaker, anticipating the man's speech. "You did, you rascal—you knew that I was there, and jumped upon me intentionally—knocked all the breath out of my body."

"I assure you—"

"Silence!"

"But—"

"Cut these infernal cords, unless you like to see me a prisoner."

"Certainly, Mr. Wild."

And the man hastened to obey his leader's mandate with such precision that he cut rather more than the cords in setting free his wrists.

"Hah! O-oh!" cried Jonathan Wild. "You ruffian!"

"I'm very sorry."

"You lie, you jackanapes!" cried the thieftaker. "You tried to cut me, and you have only succeeded in your purpose—you have cut me to the bone. But hang me if I don't have the law of you for it; I'll cry quits, or my name isn't Jonathan Wild."

In vain did the luckless man protest his innocence. His despotic leader would hear no excuses, but insisted that it was all done with intent, and that he had only failed to accomplish his murder for fear of the witnesses who lay upon the ground about them.

"Silence!" cried Wild. "Speak under your breath, unless you want to bring Red Ralph and his Yellow Band about our ears; and I almost believe that you wouldn't care about that."

Another of the men was set free, and then the two set to work upon the thongs which held their comrades.

In the space of five minutes from the appearance of their emancipator in the tree, the whole party, including the doughty Tom King, were set at liberty.

"Now," said Jonathan Wild to the new comer, "now, Turnbull, give an account of yourself, where have you been?"

"Scouting as you ordered, Mr. Wild," returned the man.

"And why were you not at hand when we needed your services?"

"Because I saw that I could be of no service to you in a fight against such odds, and—"

"And you actually saw us engaged?" said Mr. Wild in amazement.

"Yes, sir."

"You hear that, all?" said the thieftaker, appealing to his myrmidons and Tom King. "He owns having seen us, and yet didn't come forward when he was wanted."

"Yes, Mr. Wild," said the man, "but I reserved myself for this."

"Liar!" cried Wild, "I wish you had reserved yourself as you call it altogether before you had jumped your filthy carcase upon me."

The speaker still looked pale from the results of his mishap.

"However," continued Jonathan Wild, "you hear what he says; just note it down, Jeffries; I shall want you as a witness when we get back to town; just note down the particulars."

The man knew from experience this was likely to prove no idle threat, and he already quaked in anticipation of the promised punishment.

"Hadn't we better leave all our little rows for the present, Mr. Wild?" suggested Tom King.

"As you please," said Wild, assuming a bland complaisance, which his men well knew boded no good for the last speaker.

"Then, if so," said Tom King, "I do please. Just give up this dispute till a more fitting occasion, and think how we can repay this Captain Ralph for his kind attention. We shall have some of his men looking us up if we are not sharp."

The thieftaker merely nodded his head in token of assent, and was immediately lost in a brown study of the matter in hand—vengeance on his late conquerors—a sensation which occupied a large share of his sympathies.

"Hark you, Mr. Wild," said Tom King, "I have a proposition to make."

"Then let's have it," returned the thieftaker."

"What do you think of hunting out the Yellow Band in their haunts, Mr. Wild?"

"It cannot be carried out."

"There you are mistaken, Mr. Wild," said Tom King in a determined tone; "it can and shall be."

"And by whom, pray?"

"By me."

"Singlehanded?"

"Yes."

The thieftaker looked upon Tom King with a contemptuous curl of the lip for a few seconds, and then burst out in a derisive mocking laugh.

"Laugh on," said Tom King, "but let those laugh who win."

"Mr. Wild," said one of the officers, "I think I hear some one approaching."

"Hah! then we must be brief. Hark you, Mr. Tom King; you are determined to follow up this wild goose chase?"

"I am."

"And I am half inclined to set my face against it."

"Gad! but that would be a sad pity," said Tom King, laughing. "And for what reason would you object? No nice consideration on my behalf, I'll warrant."

"'Tis, though," said Wild; "I wouldn't have you come to harm at the hands of Red Ralph or his Yellow Boys, because—"

"Finish it, Mr. Wild," said Tom King. "Because of what, pray?"

"Because I've sworn to hang you, Tom King," said Wild viciously.

"Have a care, Jonathan," said King seriously—"have a care."

"Pooh. pooh!"

"I warn you that I might be tempted to cut your throat."

The thieftaker drew back a few paces, and stood between two of his myrmidons.

"You hear that, men—you hear that—he threatens to cut my throat. I call you all to witness that."

The sounds of footsteps, of which one of the men had advised the thieftaker a minute or so before, were now audible to all.

No time was now to be lost.

With a few hurried words of threat to Tom King, and defiance on the part of the latter, Jonathan Wild disappeared in the winding of the road followed by his five associates.

Tom King clambered into the tree from which the man Turnbull had fallen upon Jonathan Wild, and there awaited the arrival of the new comer.

When the individual who had thus alarmed Jonathan Wild and his party appeared in the glade, Tom King perceived at a glance that he had met him before.

He was, in effect, Tom King's old enemy Walters, the gallant Lieutenant of the Yellow Band.

He bore no traces of his late tough struggle with Tom King. The wound which he had received was so slight that it had merely sufficed to extract as much blood from a vein in his wrist as any barber surgeon of the period would have let for any mortal ailment with which the lieutenant might have been afflicted.

"I wonder what he'll think to find us all cleared off," thought Tom King.

Whatever the lieutenant might have thought, he did not allow a word to escape him.

He glanced about him at first as if rather surprised, but settled the difficulty with a toss of the head, implying, as plainly as a toss of the head could, "Oh, it's all right."

With this he pushed aside the bushes and disappeared in the thicket.

After this there was a low whistled signal, which was presently answered.

"That's the way in," murmured Tom King in his hiding-place.

But he had a very ticklish task to perform in this self-allotted business, and he was determined not to fail from incautiousness.

He resolved, therefore, to lie snug for a while.

The result proved that his caution was not ill timed. In less than five minutes the lieutenant reappeared, followed by two of the Yellow Band.

"Lieutenant—" began one of the men.

"Hush!"

The only shaded spot in the glade chanced to be the identical tree in which Tom King was hidden, and beneath its overhanging boughs the cautious lieutenant beckoned his two men to converse.

The consequence was that the only man that they had to fear overheard the whole of what ensued.

"Lieutenant," whispered one of the men; "they must have taken the road to the Miller's Point."

"Ay, I see their tracks plainly, lieutenant," said the other.

"Of course," said the lieutenant; "but the question is, how did they contrive to get free? I saw them bound up myself."

"And I helped to do it."

"And I too; and I know very well that the devil himself couldn't have untied the knots."

"And yet— But stop," said the lieutenant; "there's been something down by this tree. Do you see how the leaves are knocked off?"

"Yes," said one of the men; "and here is a branch torn off."

Tom King began to experience an uncomfortable sensation.

"What does it mean, leiutenant?" demanded the latter speaker.

"It means," replied Walters thoughtfully, "that whoever rendered them this assistance was concealed in this tree."

"That's strange."

"It is."

"Not so very strange, either," remarked the lieutenant.

"Not so?"

"No; didn't you tell me that a fifth man had been seen lurking about the forest?"

"Yes."

"And that he was recognised for one of Jonathan Wild's men?"

"Yes."

"Then there's the whole explanation of it," said the lieutenant. "This fellow has been lurking about, and the instant you left the spot he did all the mischief."

"Curse him!"

"Hang him!"

"If I had but known it!" said the former. "I stood under here all the time, too, and he was probably only a few feet above my head."

"I dare say," mentally muttered Tom King.

"If I had only fired into the tree, or if my pistol had only gone off by accident, or—"

"Or if they hadn't escaped," said the lieutenant. "But they have; so all the 'ifs' in the world are useless."

"But it might have gone off, lieutenant, you know."

"Let's hope it won't now," thought Tom King, slightly alarmed.

"Regrets are alike useless and absurd now," said the lieutenant. "The fact is, we have let them slip through our fingers nicely this time, and there only remains one slight chance of remedy."

"And that is—"

"Pursuit."

"I'm with you, lieutenant."

"I too."

"Good," said the lieutenant. "Then back with you to the haunt. Put on your cutlasses, and look to the primage of your barkers."

"All right, lieutenant."

"Be sure and speedy; and I can promise you some tough work if you mean fighting."

The two men responded with a faint cheer, and darted back into the bushes, followed by Walters.

"That's decidedly their haunt, as they call it," mused Tom King; "and I will be there in a few minutes more. Wait until the coast is clear."

He had not long to wait.

The lieutenant and his two men, booted and spurred, and armed to the teeth, speedily reappeared through the bushes.

"Where are the horses?" demanded the lieutenant.

"Waiting for us at the Palmer's Cell. Dan Parker has them."

"Call him hither."

One of the men signalled, and an answering call came faintly along upon the night wind from the direction of the Palmer's Cell.

A galloping of horses was heard, and three fine-looking hacks were trotted into the glade by one of the Yellow Band.

"Here, Parker," said the lieutenant, beckoning the man.

He placed his hands lightly upon the neck of one of the horses, and vaulted into the saddle with all the grace and ease of an accomplished equestrian.

"Now then, my men," said he, "be quick. To horse and away!"

"Ay, ay, lieutenant."

"They cannot have made much progress a-foot. Forward!"

And the three horsemen cantered out of the glade.

"So much for them," said Tom King, once more at his ease. "And now for the haunt of the Yellow Band."

He scrambled out of the tree, and made his way at once to the part of the thicket from which the lieutenant and his two men had emerged.

Here, however, he began with a great difficulty. The shrubs had been twined in such a way that the entrance was almost inaccessible to one of the uninitiated.

But Tom King was not the man to be baffled by a trifling obstacle when he had set his mind upon accomplishing a difficulty.

He tore such of the bushes away, therefore, as impeded his progress, and, in doing so, sadly lacerated his hands, and left a bleeding track behind him.

But his purpose was accomplished, and he had passed the first barrier.

"That's over," he muttered, as he paused awhile to breathe, for his exertion had been by no means of the lightest. "I'm sorry that I knocked it about so—it would leave a track to a sharp-sighted fellow. If that lieutenant, as they call him, or Red Ralph himself were to return, I might consider myself as good as departed this existence."

Pity he had not thought us seriously as he spoke.

If so, he might have yet retraced his steps, and escaped the lions' den with a whole skin.

Before him was a zig-zag straggling path, apparently leading into the thick of the forest.

To the right was also a path, but scarcely so defined as the other.

To the left was apparently a way to somewhere, but no path had ever been formed. The grass was trodden underfoot, the bushes and trees had been cut away in some places, and the general appearance clearly indicated that some person or persons had made their way through there recently.

Tom King was fairly puzzled between the choice of three paths.

"It's confusing," he muttered; "and yet—let me see—it is not that—and—I have it, it must be this to the left. As I must make up my mind to try all three, I think I stand a better chance of success at once by beginning this."

He therefore proceeded to carry out this intention forthwith.

Progress here he found scarcely less difficult than the previous portion of his journey had been.

For half an hour did Tom King do battle bravely with briar, thorn, and thicket, and at the expiration of that time paused to rest at the foot of a tree-stump, not three minutes' walk from his starting-point.

"This is a strange adventure," thought King; "and a still stranger place I've got to. Now, this is rather a natural curiosity to begin with."

His attention was attracted by the tree-stump against which he leaned.

Although shut in on every side by trees, bushes, and shrubs, this tree had apparently been struck down by lightning, whilst all the vegetation about had escaped unscathed.

"Singular," muttered Tom King, "that the electric fluid should have singled out this old fellow; and I'll warrant he was no sapling."

In the examination of the tree he was handling it rather roughly, and he fancied that he felt it move!

"Impossible! and yet—hah!"

He pushed heavily against it, and this time there was no doubt as to its having shifted several inches.

Renewing his exertions he had the satisfaction of pushing the tree-stump back, discovering an aperture sufficiently large to admit the passage of an ordinary-sized man with ease.

The blasted tree formed a kind of cap covering to the hole, one side of it being fastened to the ground by hinges.

"Chance has no doubt discovered for me what I might have sought for eternity and failed to find," mused Tom King. "This is—must be the entrance to the haunt of the Yellow Band. But it looks plaguey dark."

And it did indeed look dark. It was no small proof of Tom King's courage that he pursued his scheme beyond this point.

Smothering his qualms as they arose he sat down, passed his legs through the dark aperture, and let himself gradually down.

He commenced resting upon his elbows, but, stretch as he would, his feet could find no landing-place.

"And yet there must be," he muttered. "I must risk it."

He let himself down to the full extent of his reach, and his foot kicked some post or pillar!

"What can this be?" he thought, as he rested his foot upon the moveable support; "surely not a stepping-stone? No man would trust himself to such a place in this pitchy darkness."

As he kicked about he felt that the place was hollow from two or three feet below the surface of the soil.

Presently, growing bolder, he released the hold of the left hand and lowered it into the aperture, feeling for some further hold, whilst with his right hand, and the slight rest from this invisible projection at the bottom of the pit, he contrived to support himself.

As he had conjectured, he was not long in placing his foot upon a huge wooden staple.

"I'm getting at it by degrees," he murmured, hopefully; "it is certain that I am upon the right tract now. This secret entrance has not been formed without some reason, and good reason too."

Grasping the wooden staple with his left hand he released his hold of the pit's mouth, and trusted himself to the black void beneath him.

A second shift downwards and he was upon *terra firma.*

Carefully groping his way along, he proceeded in a stooping position down a low vaulted passage cut out of the solid earth.

After a while he came to an iron gate, and then he experienced another bar to his progress.

But his undauntable perseverance overcame this, and a gate which opposed him was forced open.

True, it had created rather more noise than he would have chosen to make; but the gate was passed, and he pushed his way on through the darkness.

A few steps further brought him to a door, through a chink of which he fancied that he perceived a faint glimmer of light.

It was now growing exciting, and it was no wonder that the heart of the adventurous Tom King went somewhat faster as he paused to consider his next step.

He stooped and applied his ear to the small aperture through which the faint thin streak of light proceeded.

All was silent.

Then he tried the door.

It yielded to his touch, and he pushed it open and stepped on.

He found himself in a boarded vault of an unhealthily low pitch, and smelling damp and mouldy.

"A night here," thought Tom King, "would be rheumatics for life."

But was there no outlet? This was the next consideration.

He soon perceived that there was. A dull oil-lamp, flickering miserably as if about to give up the ghost, was suspended by a chain from the centre of the cavern, and seemed only to throw the gloomiest of shadows over this subterranean cell; so that the visitor had not at first discovered that three pillars of earth, fashioned evidently to imitate the dungeon of some old castle, each concealed a passage.

There was that by which he had entered, and one upon either side of it.

For what purpose these clay columns had been built up before the entrances to the passages Tom King was at a loss to divine.

However, he was not then in exactly the mood to study architectural curiosities.

He, therefore, proceeded at once to examine both the outlets.

Both were equally dark, gloomy, and silent, and he chose one of them at hap-hazard.

Some eight or ten yards of this were traversed, and then he found himself in a second vault of larger dimensions than that which he had just quitted.

But here a startler was in reserve for our adventurous spirit.

Two men lay sleeping upon the ground!

Smothering an ejaculation of surprise as it arose to his lips, he turned to retreat.

One of the men moved.

Tom King at once perceived the danger and hastened his movements, but alas! he met with a sad mishap which wellnigh proved fatal to him.

His foot kicked a cutlass which lay in his way, and sent it clattering along the ground two or three paces.

The two men opened their eyes.

"Who's there?"

"What's that?"

But, fortunately, Tom King was already out of sight.

He scampered along the passage as fast as his legs would carry him, and made for the starting-point.

A few strides brought him once more to the first cavern.

But here was a terrible dilemma! he could not make out which of the passages he had come from.

Both of them were exactly alike. Both columns precisely similar.

Then, turning about him in despair at this hapless mischance, he lost himself altogether.

He felt as if engaged in a game of blind man's buff.

He had turned about until he could not even say which of the three passages he had just last traversed.

And now, to heighten his perplexity, he fancied he heard a click like the cocking of a pistol.

This was almost immediately followed by a sharp ringing report, and he felt a sharp pain in his shoulder.

CHAPTER XX.

THE HUNCHBACK AND HIS CAPTIVES—THE LIE—THE WARNING—THE BRUTAL OUTRAGE—THE BEAUTIFUL GIRL IN HER DUNGEON—THE TERRIBLE DISCLOSURE—THE SHRIEK—A DARK MYSTERY.

THE unhappy half-witted creature who called herself the hunchback's wife still maintained a tight hold upon Leonore in spite of her struggles.

The steps she had heard in the passage above approached nearer.

Leonore, in speechless terror listening, heard the door at the foot of the stairs grating upon its hinges.

In a moment afterwards the door of the cellar was thrust open and the hideous face of the hunchback appeared before her.

Leonore stood motionless, her eyes fixed upon the hateful countenance of the intruder; but the other captive, with a cry of fear, shrank away from her, crouched in the corner like a dog, and endeavoured to hide herself among the straw.

The face of the hunchback, when first it passed the threshold of the door, wore a savage and vindictive scowl, but presently it gave place to an ugly smile almost as terrible to look upon.

"What!" he said; "so I have caught you, have I, my pretty dicky-bird? Where were you flying to, I wonder?"

As the girl made no answer, he came sidling towards her with a sort of crab-like motion horrible to look at.

"Was my pretty dicky-bird flying away?" he asked, mouthing and grimacing with an evident effort to be agreeable. "Why should she wish to run away from her poor Jabez?"

With a violent effort Leonore restrained her rising wrath sufficiently to speak to her questioner with some degree of calmness.

"Why have I been brought to this place?" she asked.

The hunchback smiled.

"Will you answer me?"

"Your ladyship has been brought here in accordance with the orders I have received."

"Orders? From whom?"

"From your lady mother."

"From Lady Glyde? Impossible!"

"Nevertheless the fact, though."

"And for what reason?"

The hunchback shrugged his shoulders.

"In any case I will remain here no longer; you will therefore please to allow me to pass."

"But your ladyship would not think of going away now."

"I insist upon going."

"But until your ladyship's apparel is sent it is impossible."

"When will it be sent?"

"This afternoon."

"And I shall then be allowed to go?"

"Certainly, if your ladyship wishes to do so."

Leonore, or, to use the captive's entire name, Lady Leonore Darcy, was, for a moment, almost inclined to believe the statement he made to her; but then the thought flashed through her mind, if she was so easily to be allowed to depart, why had she been brought there at all?

She hesitated, and looked distrustfully at the evil face of the hunchback, whose eyes were fixed intently upon her beneath his shaggy red eyebrows.

"If your ladyship will allow me," he said, after a brief silence, "I will conduct you to a room where you will find breakfast prepared for you."

He bowed low as he spoke, and his tone was as respectful as his manner was cringing.

After a momentary hesitation she stepped forward.

But as she did so the idiot woman, rising suddenly from her crouching attitude amongst the straw, caught her by the hand.

"No—no!" she cried in a pleading tone. "Do not go!"

"Is your ladyship ready?" asked the hunchback, pretending not to notice the interruption.

Lady Leonore moved towards the door a step, the other woman still clinging to her.

"For heaven's sake no!" cried the idiot in a voice

of passionate entreaty. "Do not listen to him. Do not follow him. If you go, you will go to death."

Lady Leonore stood still, gazing wonderingly at the mad woman.

"Do not heed what that poor benighted creature says to you," exclaimed the hunchback, with a savage frown. "She is raving."

"She cautions me against you," said Lady Leonore, "and I fear that there is reason for her alarm."

"Reason for it?" cried the hunchback. "She is as mad as a March hare! She is a babbling idiot—a jabbering fool!"

"I am mad only because it is your cruelty which has scared away my wits," replied the poor creature. "But I am not mad now when I warn this lady not to believe you. Would to God that I had not done so myself!"

"Silence, fool," roared the hunchback. "Come, my lady."

Still Lady Leonore hesitated. Then the idea occurred to her, would it not be better anywhere than in these cellars? No; she must not be separated from the other woman.

"Come," repeated the hunchback more impatiently.

The lady shrank back from him, but made no answer.

Then his eyes blazed up with wrath, and he advanced towards her with outstretched arms.

Again she shrank from him—shrank nearer to the wall.

"Come," he said once more. "Come you shall, whether you choose or not."

As he spoke he encircled her beautiful form with his long ape-like arms.

In vain she endeavoured to repulse him.

His strength was enormous, and she was weak as a baby against his will.

But the idiot woman came to her rescue and clang to her.

She used her long claws as weapons to aid her fellow captive, and dug them into the wretch's cheeks.

As the blood trickled down his face he uttered a savage howl, like a wild beast wounded, and dropped his victim.

Then, clenching his teeth, he rushed at the idiot, who fled screaming before him.

Flinging herself upon the ground, she crouched and writhed, and shrieked for mercy.

But she might as well have implored pity from a fiend.

With his eyes flashing fire, and uttering the most fearful blasphemies from between his set teeth, he glared at her for a moment. Then flung a glance around in search of some instrument of torture.

But, seeing nothing which would serve his purpose, he raised his foot and kicked the miserable woman furiously in the face.

She fell back with a hollow groan, her face instantly suffused with crimson blood; a sight so horrible that Leonore, sickening with terror and disgust, would have fainted had she not clung to the wall for support.

Next moment, however, the hunchback turned towards her, and she endeavoured to escape from his clutches.

But her efforts were in vain. She was caught in an instant.

She struggled frantically from his grasp, and sprang away.

In doing so, however, she dashed her head with fearful violence against the cellar door.

Then she reeled for a moment and fell senseless to the ground.

*   *   *   *   *   *   *

When she opened her eyes again she knew not how much time had elapsed since she swooned away.

It was twilight, and she was in a dark, damp, noisome cellar.

She awoke with a shriek, for, as she opened her eyes, they fell upon the figure of the hunchback, threatening her with an upraised knife.

"Silence!" he roared fiercely. "Silence, or you die this moment."

She shrank from him, and gazed in terror at her hideous jailor.

"Would you kill me?" she said.

"I will, if you make any more noise. What makes you scream in that way?"

"I screamed because I saw that knife."

"You screamed before. Why was that?"

"I must have done so in my sleep," replied Leonore, bewildered, "if I screamed at all."

"Perhaps so," mumbled the hunchback. "Don't do it again, anyhow. See, here is some food I have brought for you—some warm milk and some bread and butter; you must be dying for want of some refreshment. Be reasonable, and your lot won't be so very terrible."

As he spoke he moved towards the door.

Leonore called to him as he reached the threshhold.

"Why am I confined in this dreadful place?" she asked.

"Because you cannot be trusted, except under lock and key."

"But it is so cold: I shall die."

"As soon as you are reasonable I will give you a better lodging."

"How long am I to be kept a prisoner?"

"As long as I choose."

"Heaven help me! What have I done to deserve such treatment?"

"What have you done?" cried the hunchback, with a loud mocking laugh. "You have brought all your sufferings on yourself. Had you listened to my love—"

"Wretch!" cried Leonore, with a shudder, "do not desecrate that word by uttering it from your vile lips."

"Ha! ha! You are still proud, then," cried the hunchback; "you still despise me, do you, my proud beauty?"

The lady answered him only with a look of deep scorn.

"You will not listen to me now?"

"Neither now nor any other time."

"And yet, remember, you are at my mercy."

"You may kill me—you may torture me, monster, but I will never—never—consent to be your wife. You know that I am betrothed, and that I would rather perish—"

The hunchback interrupted her with a loud laugh—savage and ironical.

"If you knew all—" he cried.

"Knew all?" she repeated, trembling.

"Yes; if you knew all you would know that you never can be the wife of the man you love."

"Why so?" she asked, in a low and agitated tone. "Has anything happened to him?"

"Oh, no; he is well enough."

"Thank God for that!"

"But when you are the wife of another—"

"That I will never be."

"You think so."

"I swear it before heaven."

"Stay; pause a moment before you take an oath to it, my pretty lady; look at your hand."

The girl's eyes turned inquiringly in the direction he suggested.

She gazed upon her hands in silent wonder, then started violently.

[TOM KING IN DANGER.]

At this moment, for the first time, did she become conscious of the presence of a wedding ring upon the third finger of her left hand.

"What does it mean?" she murmured in bewilderment. "What is this mystery?"

"The solution is simple enough," cried the hunchback, with a fiendish laugh: "it means that you are already wed."

"Wed?—When? when? I do not believe you."

"Your not believing it signifies very little. It is the truth."

"But—but—when?"

"While you were under the influence of a drug administered to you by Lady Glyde's directions—a subtle drug which rendered you unconscious and yet capable of action, though for the time deprived of reason—then you were married by her directions to a husband of her choice."

The terrified girl covered her face with her hands and uttered a piercing scream.

"Merciful heaven!" she murmured; "it was not to this demon I have been united. Oh, surely, it was not to him!"

"Not to me," said the hunchback, catching the words; "though you won't be proud of him, I dare say."

"To whom was it, then? Speak, and torture me no longer."

" It was to a common felon, then, if you must know —an outlaw—a highwayman—a man on whose head the government has set a heavy reward; and whom you will, if you live long enough, have some day the pleasure of seeing hanged at Tyburn."

The poor girl groaned bitterly, and her head sank upon her breast.

" What was his name ?" she asked.

" His name?" said the hunchback, with a laugh; "his name is a celebrated one; he is called Red Ralph!"

With a bound the girl sprang to her feet.

Her frame quivered convulsively.

Her eyes seemed to be starting from their sockets.

" Red Ralph!" she cried in a hoarse shriek, and covered her eyes in shuddering horror. " Not Red Ralph! No—no. It cannot be he—he of all other men in the world—oh! no, no—this is too horrible!"

The hunchback looked on in dumb amazement.

" There is some mystery here," he thought; " what is it?"

And he was right. There was a mystery—dark and terrible—a mystery which it will be our duty to unveil in the future chapters of this strange narrative.

CHAPTER XXI.

THE PURSUIT—A HOT CHASE—THE THIEF-TAKER IN TROUBLE—SAVED AGAIN—A CHARMED LIFE —THE YELLOW BOYS DEFEATED.

THE Lieutenant of the Yellow Band and his men galloped off in pursuit of Jonathan Wild and his myrmidons, as we have related in a previous chapter.

Although the pursuing party was well mounted, and the pursued were on foot, the latter made considerable progress before the Yellow Boys came up with them.

A ten minutes' gallop, however, sufficed to bring them within sight of their late prisoners.

" Come on!" shouted the lieutenant; who was a few yards in advance of his men; " I see them; Jonathan Wild must be made sure."

The men answered with a cheer, and set spurs to their horses.

On they went at a breakneck pace, in the greatest excitement, in anticipation of the fray.

" Mark, my men," continued the lieutenant, making himself heard with difficulty, on account of the rapidity of their pursuit; " mark, I say, that the thief-taking vagabond must not escape us; if we cannot take him alive, shoot him with as little compunction as you would a dog!"

" Ay, ay, lieutenant."

And, with a hasty cheer, the detachment of the Yellow Band dashed after their avowed enemy.

The sounds of their horses had attracted the attention of the fugitives, and they had taken to flight.

Jonathan Wild, who, to do him justice, possessed a certain amount of bulldog courage or ferocity, was heard calling frantically upon his men to stop and face their pursuers.

" Halt, you knaves!" he shouted hoarsely. " Stop, you poltroons! Stand and fight it out!"

But this did not jump with their tastes.

Onwards they tore, as if his Satanic majesty were at their heels.

" You rascally cowards!" cried the thieftaker. " I'll report every man of you when I get back to Newgate!"

" When you do."

The latter speech came from the Lieutenant of the Yellow Band, who was still some few yards in advance of his followers, and within hearing of Jonathan Wild's words.

The thief-taker, who had been forced by the cowardice of his men to retreat (for he was unable, single-handed, to cope with such odds as his pursuers presented), here redoubled his exertions, and, by his superior activity, succeeded in placing some of his men between himself and his pursuers.

" Halt!" cried the lieutenant, close upon them.

But on they flew.

The Yellow Boys galloped up, and one flew on ahead of the fugitive party.

The thief-taker and his myrmidons were now forced to halt and make a fight of it, or again yield themselves prisoners to the Yellow Band.

There is little doubt that the men would have yielded, superior as they were in numbers, had not Jonathan Wild perceived them wavering, and settled it before they could determine for themselves.

" We are six to three," said the thief-taker exultingly.

Hearing this the men drew their hangers, and awaited the attack of the Yellow Boys.

" Yield!" shouted the lieutenant.

" Never!" shouted the thieftaker, flourishing his weapon.

" Never!" echoed two of his myrmidons, with a faint cheer.

Without another word the speaker drew his right holster pistol, coolly examined the priming, and levelled with deliberation at the thieftaker.

" Murderer!" cried Wild, darting behind one of his men.

The man, however, did not seem to perceive the object of this movement, and, having a decided dislike for being a deputy-target for his leader, he at once reversed their positions.

This was carried on with great spirit by both Jonathan Wild and his man in a ludicrous manner, and the Yellow Boys could but laugh at his terror.

" One word ere we proceed to extremities," said the Lieutenant of the Yellow Boys: " I would not willingly take life—"

" Of course not," said Wild, hopefully.

" Unless yours."

" Hah!" cried the thieftaker, again darting into the group of men.

" But," resumed Walters, " unless you yield, or at least accede to the request which I am about to make to you, we will certainly shoot you down."

The men groaned.

" What do you want?" demanded one of the officers.

" You must give up Jonathan Wild to us."

" Never!" cried Wild, affrightedly.

" Or else we fire. Give him up, and you will all of you be at liberty to depart unmolested from the forest."

Jonathan Wild was in no trifling consternation at this proposition.

He saw that his men were more than half inclined to agree.

" Do you consent?"

" We do."

" Certainly."

" You treacherous cowards!" exclaimed Wild, " you shall suffer for this."

" You will, Jonathan Wild," said the Lieutenant of the Yellow Boys.

" Never!" shouted Wild. " If these villians desert me now—if they dare to play the traitor, let them look to it."

" They need have no fear," said one of the Yellow Boys.

" I'll hang every man of them."

" You won't have the chance."

" No," said the lieutenant; " they need have no fear upon that head."

"Then let's give him up."

"Rascals !"

"Every man for himself, you know, Mr. Wild."

Jonathan Wild was naturally enough greatly alarmed.

Glad to get off thus lightly, the men stepped it and left their leader to the mercy of his enemies.

"Yield ! Give your arms up, Jonathan Wild," cried the lieutenant.

"Never !"

"Your hour has come."

"Come, then, and take me," said the thieftaker.

With this he turned suddenly and darted to the right.

"Fire !" said the lieutenant.

Jonathan Wild, by an effort almost superhuman, bounded into the air and cleared the hedge.

There was a loud report.

The three Yellow Boys fired simultaneously at the thieftaker.

There was a loud howl of pain, which told him that he was hit.

In effect two of the bullets had struck him in the shoulder as he was in the air.

"He's hit !"

"His blood be upon his own head," said the lieutenant.

"They've done for him," cried one of the officers. "Off we go."

And the unhappy thieftaker's men turned to fly from the spot, and leave their leader to his fate.

"After them !" cried one of the Yellow Band, setting spurs to his horse.

And off the three Yellow Boys galloped in pursuit of the faithless janissaries of the thief-taker.

This was an unfortunate step, as future events will show.

The officers, now perceiving that they were pursued, began to separate, and darted out of the road through the hedges in every direction, a course of action which had been open to them from the first, and which it is surprising that they had not thought to adopt before.

Thus the pursuers were foiled.

"Dismount and after them, lieutenant," suggested Wolff.

"It is useless."

"But—"

"No, no, Wolff," said the lieutenant; "we have made a mistake; let us return and seek for Jonathan Wild."

He wheeled round and galloped back to the spot where the thief-taker had been shot.

"He must have fallen into the bushes," said one of the men.

"True," said the lieutenant. "Now then, dismount."

The three men sprang from their saddles and commenced an active search for the wounded thief-taker.

But he was nowhere to be seen.

Long and vigilantly was the search pursued, but without avail.

They discovered, after some time, traces of his fall and marks of blood.

The latter proved that his wounds had not been of the simplest character.

"He must have contrived to crawl off," said the Lieutenant of the Yellow Band. "But how ? Where to ?"

This remained unanswered.

"He can't have got far, lieutenant," said Wolff.

"Too far for us, I fear."

"Nay; see this pool of blood; he must be seriously wounded."

"The villain bears a charmed life, Wolff."

"It would almost appear so; but see—this is the direction."

Wolff here called the attention of his comrades to some of the long blades of grass, which were glistening with the thieftaker's blood.

"If we only had Snarl it would be an easy matter."

Snarl was a pet dog—a bloodhound which the Yellow Band kept.

"Ay," said one of the men; "but while we were fetching Snarl he would be able to get clear off."

"True."

"Then there is but one thing to be done."

"And that is—"

"Spread out from here and search."

"Good."

Accordingly they resumed the search as the lieutenant had directed, but without any success.

They were all three some little distance from the spot where they had left their horses when a footstep in that direction caught their ears.

"What was that ?" cried the lieutenant to the nearest man.

"A footstep."

"And— Hah !"

This exclamation was caused by hearing a sound, from the same direction, of the horses being violently lashed.

Then the animals were heard galloping wildly away. What could it mean !

The lieutenant was the first to run back to the spot.

A single rider was galloping furiously to the left, and the two other horses were running away riderless in the opposite direction.

"Ho, ho !" cried the lieutenant. "Ho, Wolff ! Edwards, ho !"

"Ho, ho ! lieutenant," answered the two men simultaneously.

"Quick, quick ! He escapes ! "

"Who ? "

The two men came running up to the lieutenant.

"See, see, Wolff," cried the lieutenant, pointing to the rider to the left, who was fast disappearing from view ; "Jonathan Wild escapes, for a million."

"Confusion ! "

The alarm was sounded, and in the space of two minutes the Yellow Boys came running to the spot from every direction.

But, had the whole band assembled, their numbers could have availed them little in the present intance.

The fugitive was mounted, and had a start which warranted his safety.

There was now little doubt in the minds of the Yellow Band that Jonathan Wild had escaped.

To afford them additional proof of this blood-tracks were found upon the spot where they had left the horses.

The pursuit, notwithstanding, was carried on with great spirit, but without success.

One of the thieftaker's men was discovered lurking behind a hedge, and brought back in triumph.

In the meantime Jonathan Wild galloped on towards the metropolis at a breakneck pace.

He never drew rein until he had placed many miles between himself and his pursuers.

"Safe, safe !" he cried exultingly. "The man is not yet born who is to put an end to Jonathan Wild !"

CHAPTER XXII.

TOM KING IN THE ROBBERS' CAVE—THE DWARF —A QUEER CONVERSATION—CAUGHT AGAIN— THE THREAT OF VIOLENCE—THE STRUGGLE— TOM KING A PRISONER.

To return to Tom King.

Unexpectedly attacked by an unseen enemy, the gallant Tom King was struck down in his hasty retreat from the haunt of the Yellow Band, whither he had most incautiously ventured with the determination, as he had expressed to Jonathan Wild, of rooting out the nest of robbers who infested the forest and took toll upon the king's highway.

It would be nearer the truth, however, if he had said that he was about to satisfy an almost feminine curiosity upon the subject of the Yellow Band, and to gratify an insatiable thirst for adventure and peril.

Of the latter he had already had sufficient; indeed, he thought it far too much for the amount of the former experience up to the present.

As Tom King lay upon the ground he felt the blood slowly trickling down his arm.

A few minutes elapsed after the firing of the shot before any one appeared.

"It must be a single individual," thought Tom; "had there been more than one person they would never have hesitated to advance. It is evidently a wary customer. I must lie still and see what is going to happen. Jack may prove as good as his master yet, in spite of the shot. 'Sdeath! it smarts."

As yet the pain of his hurt was comparatively trifling, but Tom King, in pursuance of a mental scheme quickly hatched in his ready brain, pretended to be suffering mortal agony.

He groaned and gnashed his teeth, and panted as about to give up the ghost.

Then grew quieter by easy stages, and finally lay back tranquil, with his eyes fixed upon an object in the ceiling.

A few seconds now proved the correctness of Tom King's conjecture, for shortly a footstep was heard, and an undersized large-headed fellow of outrageous proportions made his appearance.

Tom King was so thoroughly astonished at the quaint figure which presented itself, that he began to have some doubts as to whether he had been assailed by human or supernatural agency.

The man, or boy, whichever it was (for at a first glance it was impossible to determine), was certainly not more than four feet in height, and preposterously broad across the shoulders.

There was no deformity in the back, beyond the strange proportions. A huge head was adorned or disfigured by a ragged red shock, which did not bear the slightest traces of a comb having been applied to it within the remotest period of time.

The legs of this singular personage were naked and strangely malformed. We can only give something of an idea of them when we say that they were literally as thick as they were long.

The arms, on the contrary, were long and muscular, and appeared to belong to a person of gigantic proportions.

Altogether this quaint figure impressed one with an idea of prodigious muscular power.

Warily, stealthily he advanced to the spot where the wounded Tom King lay prostrate upon the ground.

"Hah, hah! my bird," he muttered as he drew near, "you have got into the trap somehow, and now you've paid for your fun dearly."

"Not yet," mentally muttered our adventurous friend.

The dwarf surveyed him cautiously awhile at a few paces distance, and then drew a little nearer.

"Dead."

"Not quite," thought Tom King.

The dwarf advanced close to the wounded man, and stooped over him.

Tom King felt his heart beat quickly, for a decisive moment was at hand.

The dwarf placed a hand upon Tom King's breast. Now was the time!

Tom King suddenly clutched at the manikin, and dragged himself up to a sitting posture.

Then, by a sharp push forward, he contrived to upset him before he could even utter a cry.

The next instant they had reversed their positions.

The dwarf lay struggling upon the ground, with Tom King's knee upon his breast.

A loaded pistol was stuck in a girdle which the dwarf wore, and Tom King pounced upon it in a twinkling and presented it at the struggling dwarf's head.

"Let me go," cried the dwarf.

"Silence."

"Let me go—let me get up—what are you holding me for?" demanded the dwarf in a shrill treble voice.

"If you speak again above your breath," said Tom King in his ear, "I'll blow your brains out."

"What have I done to you?" whined the dwarf piteously.

"Silence."

"Hah—h!"

The blood trickled from Tom King's wounded shoulder into the eye of the dwarf, and caused him to give utterance to the last exclamation.

"Now you may get up."

He shifted his knee from the breast of the dwarf to allow him to rise.

The dwarf, with a cry of joy, was about to spring up when Tom King steadied him with the pistol which he still held at his head.

"You won't shoot me?"

"Silence."

"But—"

"Once more I bid you silence," said Tom King. "Obey me, and you shall not come to harm by me."

The dwarf signified his implicit obedience at once.

"Take off your girdle."

"What for?"

"Obey me."

The dwarf slowly undid his girdle and stood awaiting his conqueror's further commands.

"Now," said Tom King, "bind up my shoulder; carefully, I say."

"Trust me, sir," said the dwarf, all humility.

He proceeded very slowly to convert the girdle into a bandage as directed.

"Quicker," exclaimed Tom King. "You are wasting time idly, and, if you dare to play me false, by heaven you shall repent it!"

"Sir, I swear—"

"Enough; do your best to remedy the evil you have caused, and you are safe from all harm; but let me see anything like treachery, and that moment is your last!"

The dwarf trembled violently at these words.

They were uttered so seriously—with such significant earnest—that there was no mistaking Tom King's resolution.

He therefore set about bandaging Tom King's wounded shoulder in the best manner open to him with such scanty preparations at hand.

"You have some knowledge of surgery, I should say."

The skilful way in which the bandage was applied drew this remark from the wounded adventurer.

"Slight," replied the dwarf.

"Where did you pick it up?"

"In Flanders."

"With the army?"

"Ay."

"You have served, then?"

"I have," said the dwarf, "and have done some good service, too; at least, I have frequently been credited by my superiors for such."

"In what regiment?"

The dwarf frowned.

"You mock me, stranger."

"Not I, in truth; why should I?"

"You know that I—a poor half-grown, deformed, unfinished object—am not exactly a military figure," said the dwarf with much bitterness.

"Of course," said Tom King, "I perceive that you are not up to any military standard; but you say you have served?"

"I have."

"Then again I ask in what regiment?"

"In none in particular. I was simply a hanger-on to the army. I was allowed to fight without the advantages—and many of the disadvantages, too, it is true, of a regular soldier."

"And you engaged in battle as a labour of love?"

"Yes."

"Singular taste!"

"Not so," said the dwarf. "From my earliest infancy I have been an object of ridicule to my fellow men."

"Ridicule?"

"Ay, ridicule," continued the dwarf bitterly; "sneered at and ill-treated; and I might have suffered much violence even, had not the same Providence that cursed me with this shapeless body blessed me with these two good protectors, which have generally won me something akin to respect as soon as their power has become known."

As the dwarf said this he swung round his two ponderous muscular arms.

Tom King looked at the dwarf pityingly.

"Jeered at by some," continued this singular personage, "and by the rest of humanity pitied—ay, pitied for my hideous person."

"Nay—"

"Oh, I know it," interrupted the dwarf. "In this state of things it is little to be wondered at that my nature became somewhat soured. I've reason to believe that I am by nature kindly disposed—gentle and forgiving. Even now—believe me as you will—I feel much greater satisfaction at healing your wound than I did in giving it."

"You are a strange man," said Tom King.

"I know it," said the dwarf; "and strange has been the change effected in me by the contempt heaped upon me by man on account of my deformity of person. From being kindly-natured I turned to hate, despise, detest my fellow men. For this reason I followed the army to the war."

"For what purpose?"

"To take a share in the authorised murder then going on: to revenge upon a foreign foe the indignities I had received from my own countrymen."

"You are indeed a singular being," said Tom King.

"Am I not?"

The bandaging of the wound was now completed.

"Now, what would you of me?" demanded the dwarf.

"You must conduct me hence."

"I?"

"Yes, you."

"What! lead you to liberty, that you may bring down destruction upon the Yellow Band?"

"Be that as it may, you must conduct me hence."

"Upon one condition."

"I make none."

"Then I refuse."

"Beware."

"Fire if you will. The second shot will bring down the whole band upon you, and my death will be speedily avenged."

"True," said Tom King; "name your conditions, then."

"I will lead you to the forest upon condition that you swear to me solemnly never to molest us further —never again to venture hither yourself—never to betray what you have learnt—never to speak of it—of us—to living soul."

"I cannot swear that."

"Then hear my determination, and believe in my sincerity when I speak it. Sooner than commit an action which might endanger the safety of Red Ralph or one of his Yellow Band I would lose a thousand lives; slay me if you will—shoot me dead upon the spot, and, in so doing, sacrifice yourself."

"I care not," said Tom King. "The Yellow Band shall learn to their cost that Tom King did not sell his life cheaply."

"Tom King!" repeated the dwarf, as if greatly surprised.

"Yes; you know me?"

"It struck me that I knew you when I first caught sight of your face, as you lay there upon your back."

"You have seen me before, then?" demanded Tom King in surprise.

"But once," returned the dwarf. "But I've often heard of 'Fighting Tom.'"

Tom King's face flushed with pleasure at the words of the dwarf.

"And would you, Tom King, have me play the traitor to Red Ralph and his gallant Yellow Boys—men whom I grasp by the hand and call brothers. Tom King, you mistake your man. I never was other than faithful to friends: treacherous as you like to foes!"

Tom King held out his hand.

"Take my hand, my friend," said he with warmth; "take my hand, and with it my esteem. I agree to what you propose. No harm shall ever come to the Yellow Band or its leader through me."

"No?"

"None; you cannot think me capable of such. You have ever known me by report, I feel assured, as loyal and true, and I would not be guilty of a meanness."

"I know it."

The dwarf took the proffered hand, and wrung it warmly.

"I will swear to it, if you please," said Tom King.

"Nay," said the dwarf; "Tom King's word against a host of oaths."

"Thanks, my friend."

"Follow me."

They were about to quit the vault when they were alarmed by the sound of footsteps close at hand.

The dwarf turned pale.

"Who is it?" demanded Tom King in the lowest of whispers.

"I know not—hush! follow me quickly, and with as little noise as possible, and all may yet be well."

But they were already too late.

"Who goes there?"

"It is I," answered the dwarf readily.

"Reuben?"

"Yes."

"Come on," whispered the dwarf, clutching Tom King by the coat-sleeve, and dragging him gently forward.

"Stay, Reuben," said another voice: "who have you with you?"

The dwarf made no reply.

"Reuben!" again called the former speaker.

"Yes."

"Who have you with you?—I can hear another footstep."

The dwarf paused awhile, and Tom King could feel that the hand by which he grasped his coat-sleeve was trembling violently.

"Hush, Mathews," whispered the dwarf in a tone intended as confidential. "It is all right."

"Oh, one of our new prisoners, I suppose?"

"Yes; precisely."

"I see; but where's the necessity for such a deal of mystery?"

"All right."

And with this the dwarf endeavoured to pass on.

But the curiosity of his comrades was aroused.

"Reuben's got a woman there, I'll wager, and we all know the captain's scruples in these matters. Let us look him up."

The dwarf and his companion had overheard the latter speech, and, seeing the danger, endeavoured to seek safety in flight.

Tom King, however, being unacquainted with the subterranean passages through which they were passing, stumbled in his eagerness over a projecting stone and fell violently to the ground.

An exclamation of pain escaped him, for he had fallen upon his wounded shoulder, which was now beginning to trouble him.

The dwarf stopped, and dragged the fugitive to his feet by a sudden jerk and pushed him forward.

The Yellow Boys were close behind, following in their track.

"On, on," whispered the dwarf in an imprudently loud tone; "you know the way now?"

"Yes."

"Fly, then; do not pause—don't draw breath until you are safe out of the forest."

"Good; farewell."

"Away! I will detain them here until you are safe. On! on!"

Tom King sped onwards in the pitchy darkness, but soon was brought to a halt by overhearing what was being carried on behind him.

The Yellow Boys had come up with the dwarf, and were offering him violence.

"Treachery!" cried one.

"Seize Reuben!" said another.

Then followed a scuffle, and the dwarf was heard in loud and angry expostulation with his comrades.

"Where is she?"

"Who?" demanded the dwarf.

"The woman you had with you."

"You are mistaken."

"We are not."

"It is false," said the dwarf; "who is the man that can call Reuben Wharton traitor?"

"I."

"And I."

"You lie, then," exclaimed Tom King's preserver. "You lie, all of you, to a man—foully lie!"

A scuffle ensued.

"The dwarf is coming to grief on my account," thought the fugitive. "This must not be. Sooner would I return and sacrifice myself to their vengeance than that he should suffer."

He could now hear that the dwarf was being dragged off struggling.

"It is just possible that he would be hardly dealt with," thought King, "should they really become aware of my presence."

And that they undoubtedly would.

As this thought occurred to him he suddenly missed his hat.

In the struggle with the dwarf it had fallen from his head, and, in his haste to escape upon the sounds of approaching footsteps, he had quite forgotten to recover it.

"That is just sufficient to prove the poor wretch's death-warrant with these lawless men."

It was indeed.

Tom King then, without a second thought of his own security, began hastily to retrace his footsteps.

He paused upon the entrance to the cavern to witness what was taking place.

Two of the Yellow Boys held the dwarf in their clutches whilst two more of them were searching about the cavern for proofs of his supposed treachery.

"Confess, Reuben, said one of the men. "Confess, now; you have been playing the traitor to your comrades."

"I deny it."

"You were not alone when we came up?"

The dwarf preserved a sullen silence.

Then he suddenly slipped to the ground, and toppled over his two guardians.

Then sprang to his feet, and, placing himself in a posture of defence, awaited the attack of the others.

"Yield, Reuben," said the Yellow Boys; "you cannot cope with us, and we would not willingly harm you."

"Never!"

"Then down with him! Cut him down!"

One of the men drew his sword, and his example was immediately followed by the other three.

"Come on!" said the dwarf, calmly folding his arms. "Come on, and cut away! I'm ready for your swords! You shall see how a true man should die—how I can fall a victim to the stupidity of false comrades and bullies!"

"Reuben," said one of the Yellow Boys, stepping towards the dwarf, "be reasonable. You have been caught in an act which, at any rate, looks like treachery."

The men advanced slowly, evidently still loth to strike.

As soon as they got within a few feet of him the dwarf broke ground, dodged their weapons, and made for one of the three exits from the vault.

This, however, was foreseen, and instantaneously blocked up by one of the Yellow Boys, sword in hand.

With lightning rapidity the dwarf had bounded for another of the exits, but again met with opposition from another of the Yellow Boys.

This could not last much longer.

Maddened by his resistance, and their scruples got under by his presumed treachery, the Yellow Boys would not be trifled with, and Tom King plainly saw that his preserver must inevitably fall a victim to their vengeance."

Single-handed and wholly unarmed, the manikin stood at bay opposed to four desperate men.

"See, see," suddenly cried one of the Yellow Boys; "here are stains of blood—fresh too."

"What does it mean?"

"It means that Reuben has been playing the traitor with one of the captain's prisoners."

"I deny it."

"You have had one of the prisoners here: answer that?"

"I admit it."

"And have offered her violence."

"I admit that I have offered the prisoner violence, too," said the dwarf.

"And slain her?"

"I have not seen one of the female prisoners."

"Then who is it?"

The dwarf made no reply.

"He will not answer," said one of the Yellow Boys.

"Then we are justified in taking his life."

"Ay, ay!"

They were advancing upon him from four points with uplifted weapons.

This time there could be no escape for him. He couldn't even hope for a second respite.

It was something grand to witness the calm defiance with which the dwarf now awaited his impending fate.

"It shall never be said that I allowed a man of that pluck to be slain for the want of my arm to protect him," said Tom King to himself.

Another minute and he would have been too late.

Whipping forth his sword, he dashed forward into the vault, and ran full tilt into the amazed Yellow Boys.

With two sweeps of his sword he beat down their four weapons, and grabbed at the dwarf, saving him from immediate danger.

"An enemy!"

"A foe! a spy!" cried the men, recovering themselves upon the instant.

"Death to the spy!"

"Down with the traitor!"

"He is no traitor," said Tom King.

"He is: he has conived with you at our destruction, and doubtless at Red Ralph's fall."

"It is false, he fought against me for you; here are the proofs!"

Tom King pointed to the bandage upon his wounded shoulder, through which the blood was still oozing, the hurt having been roughly handled in the bustling encounter and the stumble which he had had.

"And then he would have aided you to escape."

"He had no choice," said Tom King: "I should have shot him had he not obeyed my commands, and I ordered him to set me free."

"How came you here?"

"That I decline to answer."

"Lower your point, then, and give up your sword."

"Only with life."

"This is trifling," said one of the men: "you cannot hope that we should set you at liberty."

"I shall set myself at liberty, or die in the attempt."

"You will most undoubtedly die, then."

"Of that I must take my chance."

"There is no chance in the matter: you have intruded upon us, ventured here in enmity to us, and, having bearded the lion in his den, you must take the consequences."

"It is not reduced to such a certainty as you might suppose," said Tom King. "You may slay me; probably you will; but I warn you I shall sell my life dearly. This will settle accounts with one of you."

Here Tom King held out the pistol he had taken from the dwarf.

"And here is the life of at least one more in this trusty blade, which has done its owner good service in its time."

The Yellow Boys began to advance.

"Stand aside!" said Tom King, "stand aside, but let me go free, and I will swear never to divulge to living souls anything I have witnessed here, as I promised your comrade here. before he could be induced to accept my proposition, and then only the choice between that and certain destruction awaited him from this same bullet which shall find a home in one of your breasts, if you refuse to grant my request. Do you consent?"

"Never!" cried the four Yellow Boys with one voice.

With uplifted swords they dashed at him.

Tom King levelled the pistol at the advancing robbers and fired, but at the very moment his finger pressed the trigger the pistol was knocked upward, and the bullet was lodged harmlessly in the roof of the vault.

At the same moment he was seized round the middle in a pair of powerful arms, and fairly lifted off his feet.

Then he was thrown to the ground, and Reuben Wharton stood over his prostrate body.

"Traitor!" cried Tom King bitterly.

"Not so," said the dwarf; "say rather 'friend;' you were about to shed blood uselessly; you could not hope to resist numbers."

Then turning towards his comrades he continued, with a wave of his arms—

"Stand off; do him no harm; he cannot oppose you further; secure your prisoner, and give him a fair hearing before Red Ralph and the whole band."

"It's all very strange," said one of the Yellow Boys.

"It can all be explained," said the dwarf. Bear him gently away; his shoulder is badly hurt."

Without more ado the four Yellow Boys raised their prisoner in their arms, and bore him with as much care as possible from the vault.

"Reuben Wharton," said Tom King, "I'm sorry you have ever served the King and country."

"Wherefore?"

"You have done this night an act of treachery which no man should be guilty of who has ever carried arms in a lawful fight."

"Not so, Tom King," said the dwarf: "you mistake my motives still: wait patiently, and all may yet be well."

CHAPTER XXIII.

THE MECHANICAL SOFA—RALPH'S OLD ENEMY—JONATHAN WILD'S AGONY—RED RALPH SHOWS FIGHT—A HUNDRED TO ONE—THE TERRIFIC LEAP.

To return to Captain Red Ralph.

We left him, as the reader will doubtless remember, held firmly in the grasp of an ingenious mechanical sofa in the house of Mr. Stanley Powell.

The captain's object in forcing his way into the old profligate's presence was to obtain, either by entreaties or by force, some change in the cruel destiny of his daughter, Mary Powell, the pretty novice of the Retreat.

The result of the adventurous Ralph's scheme we have told.

In an unfortunate moment he had seated himself upon the sofa, which proved to be a mechanical contrivance, made, doubtless, with sinister purposes, and which held its occupant immoveable.

Mr. Stanley Powell had sent to Newgate for officers upon piercing the feminine disguise of the Captain of the Yellow Band and discovering his true sex.

In a very short space of time the officers arrived.

"Where is Mr. Powell?" demanded a voice in the hall.

"That voice," murmured Red Ralph—"surely I know that voice."

The owner of it crossed the threshold of the apartment, and advanced towards the master of the mansion.

"A thousand furies!" said Red Ralph, mentally.

The new comer was an old enemy.

In a word, it was no other than Jonathan Wild.

"Ha! Mr. Wild, I'm glad to see you," said Mr. Powell.

"The pleasure is mutual, sir," replied the thief-taker.

"I've a customer for you."

"So I heard," said Jonathan Wild; "and I hastened here at once, although I'm not exactly in a fit condition to attend to business at present."

He carried his arm in a sling.

"Are you badly hurt?"

"Not dangerously, I'm told. I have had a couple of balls in my shoulder, but they are safely out, and I shall mend if I can only lay up a little; but where is the person for whom you want my assistance?"

"Here."

"This lady?"

"Yes, this *lady*."

"Indeed; of what has she been guilty?"

"Disguising her sex."

The thieftaker looked towards Mr. Powell for an explanation.

"It is not a woman at all," said Mr. Stanley Powell, chuckling.

"Oho! a cracksman?"

"A housebreaker?"

"How came he here?"

"He forced his way in with some cock-and-bull story about my daughter. You know my daughter, Wild?"

"I have the honour of Miss Powell's acquaintance."

"But why he came dressed up like this I'm at a loss to imagine."

"Probably thinking that a petticoat would be more likely to gain favour with Mr. Stanley Powell."

The old profligate grinned with pleasure at the thieftaker's jocularity.

"And then," said Mr. Powell, growing suddenly serious, "then my man-woman attacks me with my own sword."

"But you were too much for her ladyship there?"

"Faith! I wasn't."

"Indeed?"

"No; I'm not as young as I was, Mr. Wild, and my wrist has lost some of the power for which it was once celebrated."

"Celebrated truly!"

"And I doubt not that some further violence would have been offered me had he not placed himself in my power by a fortunate accident."

"The sofa?"

"Yes."

"A great and wonderful contrivance that, Mr. Powell."

"It is, Mr. Wild, and I am indebted to you for it.'

The thieftaker bowed his acknowledgments.

"True that I paid rather stiffly for it, but—"

"You have found it fully worth the sum paid for it Mr. Powell?"

"I have."

Red Ralph was in the greatest agony all the time that this conversation proceeded.

However, he continued to preserve a calm exterior until the thieftaker drew nearer to his prison-couch.

"Now, then, for the prisoner, Mr. Powell," said Jonathan Wild.

Jonathan Wild drew nearer and stared upon the prisoner curiously.

"I know that face."

"You do?"

"Yes, Mr. Powell; I shall think in a moment of his name."

The feminine toilet had even preserved Red Ralph's incognito for the moment from the eyes of hate.

"I'm sure I've met you before," said Jonathan Wild.

The Captain of the Yellow Band was silent. His voice he knew would betray him.

"He has a wig on."

"Off with it, then," said Mr. Stanley Powell.

The thieftaker obeyed, and shorn of his ringlets there was not a doubt of Red Ralph being speedily recognised.

"It is not possible!" said Jonathan Wild, half aloud.

"What is not possible, Mr. Wild?" demanded Mr Stanley Powell.

"Mr. Stanley Powell," said Wild, "you have no other than Red Ralph, the Captain of the Yellow Band, for a prisoner."

"Red Ralph," iterated Mr. Stanley Powell, in amazement.

The fame of the valorous Yellow Band, and the audacious exploits of its leader, had reached London,

and were ordinary subjects of discussion in every drawing-room.

"Yes, Mr. Powell," said Jonathan Wild, "this is my old friend Red Ralph, and before another hour has elapsed he will be safe in limbo—eh, captain?"

Red Ralph made no reply.

In his confusion he feared that he might betray himself, and there was yet a chance of deceiving them.

A sad misapprehension. The lynx eye of the thieftaker could never be deceived.

"You don't seem to enjoy it, captain," sneered the thieftaker.

"Ha, ha, ha!" laughed Mr. Powell; "you are a droll dog, Mr. Wild."

"Yes, I like my joke."

And the two chuckled and laughed till their sides ached.

"Off with him."

"Yes, sir," replied the thieftaker. "Where are the daubies? Oh-h-h!"

An exclamation of pain escaped him as he attempted to move his wounded shoulder, in a moment of mental abstraction.

"Are you badly hurt?" demanded Mr. Stanley Powell.

Wild glanced towards Red Ralph, and seeing a smile upon his lips he replied,

"A scratch, Mr. Powell," as carelessly as possible.

In the present case, however, nature was stronger than human will, and he could not disguise his sufferings.

A deathly pallor overspread his countenance, and the blood forsook his lips.

He felt himself growing faint, and he bit his nether lip nervously.

"Mr. Wild, you are ill," exclaimed Mr. Stanley Powell, alarmed.

"No, no," said Wild, looking towards Ralph with a last effort.

"Here, Grant! Barker, come up; I—"

His voice quivered and grew much fainter.

He trembled violently, and clutched the edge of the dining-table.

Then tottered to the door, making almost superhuman efforts to steady himself until out of Red Ralph's presence.

He had reached the doorway.

There was a sound of a body falling.

He had fainted in the passage.

The two men he had summoned, however, came running upstairs.

"Hulloa," cried one of them, in no great concern, "jiggered if the governor ain't gone and fainted."

"I think it's all up," said the other, giving Wild a shake.

The swooning man groaned.

"Here, men, here's your prisoner," said Mr. Stanley Powell—"here is your prisoner."

The two men entered the room; one of them Ralph recognised immediately, but as they had only met on one occasion he hoped that his disguise would be able to pass muster.

"Secure him," said Mr. Stanley Powell.

The men hastened to obey, and as a preliminary movement they had to release him from his present bondage.

Before Mr. Powell could offer a word, they had dragged back the sofa and released Captain Red Ralph.

"Beware!" cried Mr. Powell, "secure his hands first."

But it was too late.

With a loud cry of joy the Captain of the Yellow Band sprang from the sofa, shooting out his fists on either side.

[STANLEY POWELL AND HIS VICTIM.]

The two officers who were to secure Red Ralph were both floored simultaneously.

To repossess himself of the sword of Mr. Stanley Powell was the work of a moment.

"Down with him!" cried Mr. Powell to the officers.

The two men drew their hangers, and at once commenced a furious onslaught upon the gallant Captain Ralph.

Nothing now but the greatest activity could possibly give him a respite, and that only of the briefest duration.

The two officers were armed with short stout weapons, in the use of which they were by no means unskilled, whilst he had but a delicate court rapier to oppose them.

A chance blow of any strength must undoubtedly shiver his frail weapon to atoms.

Here and there flew Red Ralph, now springing over a chair, now leaping the table, and then placing the mechanical couch between him and his three opponents.

This last was a favourite position of Red Ralph's during the short encounter which ensued.

"Run into him, you cowards!" exclaimed Mr. Stanley Powell.

"It's all very well," said one of the men, pausing for breath; "*you* have a try what *you* can do."

"Come on, Mr. Powell," laughed Red Ralph, derisively; "have another turn and try your luck."

"Rascal!"

"Ah, you can talk."

"I can act, too," cried the old man, rushing at the highwayman.

Red Ralph met him half-way, and with a well-directed blow, sent his sword spinning from his grasp.

Then, before the officers could interpose, he grasped the old man round the waist and, with a violent effort, threw him on to the sofa.

One of his antagonists was disposed of.

"So much for Mr. Stanley Powell!" cried Red Ralph. "Now then, you fellows, come on; I'm awaiting your pleasure."

"Let's finish this," said one of them; "this is all nonsense."

"I quite agree with you," said Red Ralph. "Finish it."

The former speaker answered the captain's challenge by darting forward with his sword uplifted.

Ralph darted aside as the man dealt him a terrible cut, and the blow fell harmlessly upon a chair.

The force of the blow, however, did Ralph good service, for his adversary was quite overbalanced with the swing, and left his agile opponent an opening of which he did not fail to take immediate advantage.

A smart thrust through the sword arm rewarded the officer for his failure.

"Hah!" cried the fellow, in the greatest fright, "I'm slain! I'm killed!"

The whole had taken place in so short a space of time that the man's comrade had no opportunity of interposing.

As soon, however, as the officer fell, his companion advanced to the attack.

But Ralph was more the man's equal than ever, and, judging from the previous efforts of the Captain of the Yellow Band against his three adversaries, there was but little doubt as to the issue of the conflict, which was reduced to an ordinary duel.

Red Ralph, too, hastened to snatch the fallen man's sword from his grasp, and confronted the other officer as he rushed upon him.

"Give in, give in," cried the officer. "Resistance is useless!"

"This doesn't look like being useless," said Red Ralph, laughingly.

"It is impossible that you should escape!" said the man.

"Pshaw!"

And the Captain of the Yellow Band pressed furiously upon his antagonist.

Blow after blow was exchanged, and the officer was bleeding from an ugly gash in the forehead.

The whole house was now aroused with the sounds of the conflict, and the clashing of their swords rang out loud above every other sound.

Servants and visitors could now be heard rushing for the scene of the strife in every direction.

In another minute help would be there for his enemy, and the Captain of the Yellow Band would be again a prisoner.

All the while Mr. Stanley Powell lay struggling in the arms of the mechanical sofa—fairly caught in his own man-trap, and shouting frantically to Red Ralph's opponent to "cut the villain down."

"Down with him!"

"It's all very well, Mr. Powell— Ha!"

Red Ralph had taken advantage of an opening, and dealt the man a cut upon the left shoulder, which spouted with gore upon the instant.

"Fiend!" shrieked the man, "you should die now if I had a thousand lives to lose in the fight!"

"Bravo!" cried Mr. Stanley Powell, with a futile attempt to rise.

The sounds of assistance were by this time close at hand.

"Keep off!" cried the officer to the servants, as they appeared in a body upon the threshold—"Keep off! I can manage him now; he belongs to me."

Bleeding from every part the officer kept to it with wonderful pertinacity.

But stab, thrust, or cut were alike put aside by the Yellow Band's Captain, who never once lost his coolness and presence of mind.

"Bravo!" again ejaculated Mr. Stanley Powell. "Cut him down, and I'll add a hundred pounds to the reward already offered for his apprehension."

"Here goes for it, then," said the man.

He feinted and aimed a terrific blow at Red Ralph, which, however, was quickly put aside and replied to by a more certain stroke, which again drew blood from the unfortunate officer.

"Death and damnation!" roared the officer. "You shall die."

"Not by your hand," retorted the Captain of the Yellow Band.

"Yes, by mine, I swear!"

They renewed the combat, which had for the moment ceased, and the servants began to advance to the rescue in spite of the wounded officer's admonitions.

"Come on, you rascals," shouted Mr. Stanley Powell.

Some of the visitors, Mr. Powell's select circle of bachelor friends, began to push through the servants towards the combatants.

Another cry from the officer announced a fresh wound.

"To the rescue!" cried Mr. Powell, fearful that Red Ralph would obtain the mastery.

"No, no, Powell," said one of the gentlemen; "never spoil sport; it's a fair fight."

"Ay, ay," said another, pushing back the domestics. "Stand back, you knaves, and let us see the end of this little job."

"Fools!" cried Mr. Powell, struggling in the toils of the sofa, you know not what you do; secure him, I say."

"And we say no," cried one of the gentlemen.

"To be sure not."

"No, no."

"Let us see it out," continued the first speaker, "and see fair play."

"But I tell you—"

"Nonsense, Powell; we're ashamed of you, positively."

"Bravo!" cried one of them, "that was a doughty blow, in truth."

Red Ralph, until this moment unscathed, here received a flesh wound of no importance in the arm.

Ralph, albeit perfectly cool, still was rather nettled at being hit by a wearied and wounded antagonist, who when the conditions of the combat had been equal was unable to touch him.

He therefore retaliated upon the officer with great fury.

The officer was almost beaten to the ground.

Still he persevered in what was visibly a hopeless cause with a gameness which elicited the admiration and applause of the excited spectators.

"If you let that man escape," said Mr. Stanley Powell, "you will regret it all your lives—I warn you."

"But why?"

"Don't you know who it is?"

"No."

"Who is it?"

"Red Ralph!"

"The Captain of the Yellow Band?"

"Yes."

Red Ralph's antagonist let fall the point of his weapon, and was at the mercy of his enemy.

It created the reverse effect upon his auditors to that which Mr. Stanley Powell had intended.

Red Ralph, as we have previously had occasion to remark, bore the reputation amongst the civil authorities and the lowly generally of being invincible—having a charmed existence—being shot and sword proof, and various other absurdities.

It must be remembered that we write of a period at which superstition was ripe. A hundred years ago the world still had faith, to a certain extent, in witchcraft, phantom robbers, flying Dutchmen, and other marvels.

The Captain of the Yellow Band, however, when he perceived that his antagonist was helpless and at his mercy, most generously forbore to exercise his prowess further.

He now turned his attention to the visitors who had been surveying the combat.

"Red Ralph!" said one.

"The famous Yellow Boy!" said another.

"The prince of highwaymen."

"Here's a treat—quite a show," observed a jocular fellow.

"Stand aside, gentlemen, and let me pass," said Red Ralph.

"Secure him!"

The voice was Jonathan Wild's. He had barely recovered his senses, but his first thought was to secure the person of his old enemy, whom he had now in his grasp—

As he believed, we might have added. Events will show if Ralph was indeed destined to succumb to this reverse of fortune.

"I warn any one who attempts to bar my progress," said Ralph. "I am a desparate man, and will not be baulked by trifles. I would not willingly take life, or do harm to any living creature, but blood will be spilt if I am molested."

Determination was in his every tone and gesture, and the gentlemen hesitated as the Yellow Band's Captain made for the door.

But there was something so outrageously absurd in a single individual bidding defiance to a whole mob that the pause was but momentary.

Several of the gentlemen drew their swords and presented an alarming array to Red Ralph's well-used weapon.

"I have warned you," said Red Ralph, "and now the consequence be upon your heads."

"The rascal begins to bully," said one. "I thought his trade must shortly come out."

"Pity, too, and such a game fellow," remarked another.

"Death to the first man who strikes a blow!" cried Ralph.

"That's me, then," said one of the gentlemen, stepping forward.

Ret Ralph advanced to meet him.

Their swords crossed, clashed once, striking fire by the violence of the blow.

Then, the gentleman's weapon was shivered, and the hilt alone remained in his hand.

"Hah! death!" he ejaculated.

The highwayman's sword passed through his body. The blow and the thrust followed so quickly upon each other that Red Ralph could not stay his arm.

This settled the matter. Seeing their friend fall mortally wounded, as they imagined, the rest of the company with a shout rushed forward.

Then Ralph, as a last resource, dragged forward the fallen table.

It was a sudden and a mighty effort, and did him good service.

The gentlemen, servants and all, came sprawling over it, and all was confusion for a second.

This moment was sufficient for the ever ready Captain of the Yellow Band.

He glanced about, taking in the whole apartment with a sweep of his eagle eye.

Made a rush towards the window.

A spring into the air, a wild leap forward, and he had dashed through the casement, carrying with him glass and window-frame.

CHAPTER XXIV.

LEONORE IN HER DUNGEON—SILENCE AND DARKNESS—THE TERRORS OF THE NIGHT—THE DEAD HAND—THE IDIOT AGAIN—THE SECRET PASSAGE—HORROR—THE HUNCHBACK AND THE CORPSE.

THE life to which the unhappy Lady Leonore supposed herself to be doomed at the hands of the hunchback was one of such cruelty and hardship that she had little doubt that death would soon come to rescue her from the hands of her brutal jailor.

He brought her some coarse food, and left her there, in the cold damp cell, for several hours. He had also brought an armful of straw and some old ragged blankets, with which she endeavoured, though with but indifferent success, to keep herself warm.

She felt, however, very little uneasiness respecting her food and lodging, and the food stood untouched by her side whilst she sat throughout the livelong day a prey to the most poignant mental anguish.

Cold and silent, motionless, and white as death, her beautiful head resting against the wall of her dungeon, her hand pressed to her faintly-beating heart, she remained many hours with scarcely an alteration in her attitude, which was full of despair.

Sometimes, bowing low her head, she would burst into a violent fit of sobbing.

"Heaven grant that I may die!" she murmured. "I am not fit to live now that I have broken my oath."

Then she would fling herself prostrate upon the cold wet floor of the noisome dungeon, and the faint motion of her bosom was the only sign of the flickering life yet remaining in the body of the unhappy girl.

Once, though, she sprang to her feet and rent the air with her piercing shrieks.

"Oh, Everest, Everest, save me! Save me!"

There was a wild, heart-broken, hopeless misery in this wailing cry; but alas! 'twas only heard by the four stone walls encompassing her, or wafted away on the night air to startle the drowsy cattle far away in the fields.

It could not, however, reach the ears of any one capable of rendering her any assistance. The loutish villagers, slumbering heavily in their hovels, heard nothing of it, and he to whom she appealed, alas! was far, far away. Perhaps now, too, he knew all, and loathed and despised her for her falsehood.

As yet the reasons which had prompted her stepmother to act so treacherously towards her she could not comprehend, and the object of her imprisonment in this horrible dungeon was a dark mystery.

So intense were her misery and despair during the earlier part of her captivity after the hunchback left her, that she had only hoped that death would come to her relief; and so sick, weak, and ill did she feel, that she could easily believe that she was dying.

But she was very young, and life was strong in her and asserted itself.

As the weary hours wore away and the hunchback did not return, hope again began to spring up in her heart, and she asked herself why she should not make one more attempt to escape.

She found upon investigation that the hunchback had left some wine and water, of which she drank a little, and also ate a small quantity of bread.

Greatly refreshed and strengthened, even by this frugal repast, she raised herself to her feet and made a tour of inspection of her dungeon.

The door was very strong and was locked upon the outside; she shook it violently, but it resisted all her puny efforts to force it open. The window was high up from the ground, and secured by iron bars.

She wandered round and round the cell in which she was a captive, and vainly looked for some weak place where there might be a hope of escape. In one corner there was a quantity of lumber—rusty iron and wood-work—and, reckless of the bruises which she inflicted upon her soft, white, delicate hands, she dragged this on one side, with a faint hope that she might find some small doorway hidden behind them.

But the search was fruitless, and she returned in despair to her miserable straw bed.

Whilst she was sitting here in a despairing mood she presently heard heavy footsteps approaching, then a key grated in the lock, and the door of the dungeon opened.

The light of a lantern which he carried revealed the hideous features of the hunchback.

"Aha!" he said, with a Satanic grin, "how does my little dicky-bird like its cage? See, I have brought you some clothes; you must be very cold."

"I am very wretched," she answered.

"And yet you were not happy when you were better off."

"Why have I been brought here at all?" she inquired. "How long am I to remain a prisoner?"

The hunchback smirked and shrugged his shoulders, but made no answer.

"Is it my mother at whose will I am a prisoner!"

"I will tell you to-morrow, perhaps," answered the hunchback; "I cannot tell you now; therefore be patient, my little bird; be patient."

He had brought her some more food as well as the clothes, and he left it by her side.

When he had gone she raised to her lips a small jug which he had left, and, much to her astonishment, found it to contain some hot wine and water. The food consisted of some pieces of cold chicken and some bread.

Very strangely did this delicate diet contrast with the dungeon in which she was confined, and she could not help thinking that it had alone been her own folly which had prompted the hunchback to resort to so much severity.

She could now only hope to be able to effect her escape if he took her back to the upstairs room which she had so unwisely quitted.

Having attired herself in the clothes that her jailor had provided her with, she again wrapped herself up in the blankets, and, lying down upon the straw, prepared to pass away the hours until morning as best she could.

The night was dark and starless.

A dense obscurity prevailed in the dungeon, and it was with the greatest difficulty that Leonore could discern the dim outline of the small window.

She still felt very weak and ill, and yet she was extremely wakeful.

She several times closed her eyes, and endeavoured to doze away some of the long weary hours which must be passed before daylight came again.

But her efforts were fruitless.

The darkness was still as dense as heretofore, and a grave-like silence prevailed in which she could almost have fancied that she heard the violent throbbing of her own heart.

She would have given the world, she thought, for some light, some companionship, some sign of life.

But the night seemed to grow blacker than ever, and her strained eyes, filled with tears, were unable any longer to distinguish the difference between the black wall and the black sky.

Soon the oppressive silence and darkness seemed to crush her.

She choked for air as though she had been in a coffin—as though she had been buried alive.

An awful shuddering dread took possession of her. She sat motionless as a statue.

Her head was burning hot, but her limbs were icy cold. She was too frightened to move a finger.

She dreaded even to breathe.

But at this crisis—when with throbbing temples and fast-beating heart she felt that she must shriek aloud or fall down dead—a strange noise broke the deathlike silence.

It was a scratching scampering noise, close to where she lay, and she started into a sitting posture with a sickening terror, for she thought that the noisome place was swarming with rats.

She was thinking of screaming, and hammering against the wall to frighten the filthy wretches away, and had raised her hand to do so when the scratching suddenly sounded so close to her side that she could not doubt that it was inside the cell with her.

Then she drew back shuddering, with a half-suppressed scream.

She would in another moment have sprung to her feet, but ere she had time to rise something cold and clammy passed over her hand.

In another instant it encircled her wrist.

She gave a shrill cry of terror, and struggled to free herself.

But her unknown assailant held her tightly, and in speechless terror she became conscious that it was a hand which was upon her.

A cold clammy hand clutched her wrist.

A dead hand—it seemed bony and bloodless. Fear deprived her of all power of movement.

She could not, to save her life, have freed herself from the unknown terror which had thus crept upon her.

Her tongue clave to the roof of her mouth and choked her utterance.

But while thus dumb and paralysed, a voice in a harsh whisper hissed into her ear—

"Silence, or you die!"

There was, however, no occasion to threaten her, for Leonore was too terrified to speak.

Trembling like a leaf, she waited until the voice again addressed her.

"Who are you?" it asked.

"A prisoner," replied Leonore.

"A prisoner?" repeated the voice. "Are you the woman I saw yesterday?"

Leonore listened intently: she fancied that she recognised the tones of the speaker's voice.

"You are Jabez's wife, are you not?" she said.

"Yes, I am."

"Then I am Lady Leonore."

"And you are a prisoner here?"

"Yes, I am confined in a terrible dungeon, from which I cannot escape."

"Do not be too sure of that. If you will have faith in me, I will help you."

"God bless you, if you will do so—but how? It is so dark I cannot see you. Is there a door in the wall through which you have passed your arm."

"A door? No, it is a hole that I have made."

"When? I only heard you scratching a moment before I felt your hand."

"Ha! ha! I have scratched for many days— many weeks—many weary months for that matter; I was only removing the loose bricks when you heard me. Remain quiet for a moment, and I will strike a light."

The cold hand was removed from her wrist, and for a moment or two all was silent.

Then a faint scratching noise struck upon the listener's ear; the other woman was using a flint and steel.

Then there was a faint glimmer, and presently Jabez's wife had ignited a small end of candle she had got with her, the light of which revealed her thin haggard face, horribly bruised and swollen, from the effects of the ruffian's violence.

When the candle was lighted, the half-witted creature handed it through the opening in the wall, and busied herself with removing the bricks and widening the aperture.

When she had done so sufficiently to allow for the passage of her body, she crawled through and sat down by the other's side.

"Yes," she said, " I have come to save you."

Leonore, slightly trembling, made no answer.

"I should have escaped myself, last night, only I did not know who was here. I thought it might be Jabez, when I heard some one moving."

"And you were afraid to touch the wall?"

"Yes. I waited as long as I could, though; and at last my patience was exhausted, and I determined to make an attempt."

"But how do you propose to escape now?"

"That will be easy enough, for I have done all the hard work."

"Done it all?"

"Yes. I have made my way through the wall by wearisome toil. I had completed my task by daybreak yesterday, just before you came into my cell, but I had been afraid to go on, because I thought Jabez might surprise me, and it is only safe to work at night."

"But now you have broken through the wall you are in another dungeon."

"Yes, yes; I know that well enough."

"But you can only escape by the door, and that is securely locked and barred."

"Ah! you do not know what I know, but I will show you another way."

Leonore looked at her companion with wide-opened eyes.

She must be raving, she thought.

"I will show you a secret passage."

"A secret passage?" echoed Leonore.

"Yes, see here! Under the straw."

"I see nothing."

"Not yet; but now—don't you see that iron ring?'

"Ah!"

"It belongs to a trap-door, and I will raise it."

As the woman spoke, she laid hold of a small iron ring upon the floor, which, being covered over by straw, had hitherto escaped the notice of the beautiful captive.

Without much effect, she raised a trap-door by the aid of this ring, and disclosed a flight of stone steps leading down into pitchy darkness.

"How is it that you knew of this?" asked Leonore, with some faint misgivings of treachery.

"I know all over this strange house," she said, " and have often explored its mysteries before I became a prisoner here."

"But why have you not escaped before, if you knew you could escape by this passage?"

"I had only just completed my work at the wall, as I told you, when daylight surprised me."

"But why not have escaped then?"

"Because I should have been afraid of going out in the daylight. I should have expected to be overtaken and brought back."

Leonore felt satisfied with this explanation, and asked no more.

Jabez's wife, carrying the candle, led the way. Leonore, not without some fear and trepidation, followed.

"Pull the door to after you," said the other.

"Pull it to? Will that be safe?"

"What do you mean?"

"If we should want to go back?"

"We shan't go back that way."

"You are certain that there is another outlet."

"Yes, quite certain, and if not?—"

"If not?"

"I would die, rather than go back."

Not without some secret dread of coming evil, Lady Leonore pulled to the trap above her.

It closed with a dull sound, which smote heavily upon her heart.

Then they slowly descended the steps.

At the bottom they found a narrow passage, very cold and damp.

They cautiously proceeded for about a dozen yards, and then found themselves in a sort of vaulted chamber profoundly dark, but apparently of great size.

"What a dreadful place!" said Leonore, with a shudder.

"We shall soon get out of it, though," whispered the other. "Trust to me. I know the way."

In silence they proceeded together for some time, but suddenly the woman stopped still and seized her companion by the wrist.

"What is the matter?"

"Hush!" said the other : "listen."

"I hear nothing."

"Listen again. Do not you hear a footstep?"

Leonore, still as death, and clinging to the cold slimy wall for support, heard the sound of approaching steps.

"Great God!" murmured her companion. "We are lost."

"Let us run back," whispered Leonore.

"No, no; I will put out the light. Creep close to the wall."

As she spoke, she extinguished the candle, and at the same moment a faint light glimmered in the distance.

Slowly it approached, and the two women, almost dead with fright, recognsied the hideous face of the hunchback.

Creeping as far away into a dark corner as they could get, they waited in deadly fear.

The hunchback slowly approached.

He was carrying something over his shoulder.

As he drew nearer, they saw with horror that it was a dead body.

The dead body of a woman.

The body of some other of his victims.

CHAPTER XXV.

RED RALPH'S ESCAPE—HIS ADVENTURES WITH THE WATCH—PAUL JONES IN PETTICOATS—A STAND-UP FIGHT—THE CAPTAIN AGAIN VICTORIOUS.

RED RALPH, the bold leader of the Yellow Band, fell with a violent crash outside the window of Mr. Stanley Powell's mansion.

Rapid as had been his exit from the dining parlour he had taken sufficient time to gather a host of cuts, scratches, and small bruises.

Windows were not then formed with the frail delicate frames of the present day; and, although the force of his leap had carried the whole of them away, the consequences were disastrous to the beauty of his countenance for some considerable period to come.

Besides this the skirts of his dress caught in the window frame and tore them to shreds.

Stunned, bleeding, and half naked, Red Ralph lay upon the ground for several minutes, motionless, breathless.

And yet no one arrived to secure him.

A great commotion was taking place in the house, but no one had as yet ventured to the street door.

At length the sound of approaching footsteps aroused the swooning highwayman.

He sighed, opened his eyes, and looked about.

"Hullo!" exclaimed a voice close beside him.

He looked up, and perceived a watchman, with his lantern, standing over him.

"Where am I?"

Several seconds elapsed before he could recall to himself his late stirring adventure.

"What's the matter, mum?" asked the watchman.

"I—I scarcely know," said Red Ralph wearily; "I—oh! heavens!"

He passed his hand over his face, and withdrew it covered in blood.

"How did you do this, mum?" demanded the watchman.

"This—I—I—" stammered Ralph, all abroad, "I have been molested by some ruffians who—"

The attention of the watchman was here directed to the broken window, and the fragments of glass about the ground.

"Was it in there?"

"Yes."

"In Mr. Stanley Powell's?"

"Yes."

"The old blackguard!"

"And not he alone: he has a number of friends of his there, and they would have offered me violence."

"Do you know Mr. Powell?"

"No."

"Then how came you there?"

"I went there upon a business matter, not knowing the character of the man I had to deal with."

"And then, to escape them, you jumped out of the window?"

"Yes."

"Poor woman!"

The window being all broken, they could distinctly hear the buzz of voices in the parlour, and at this moment the words of the various speakers reached them.

"Look him up!" shouted Mr. Stanley Powell: "he'll escape us yet!"

"He hopes so," thought the Captain of the Yellow Band.

"Get out—into the street!" again cried Mr. Stanley Powell.

Then followed a confusion of sounds—the upsetting of furniture and the scrambling of a mob of servants and guests from the parlour.

All was eagerness to adopt Mr. Stanley Powell's suggestion.

"Save me! Oh! save me!" said Red Ralph, imploringly, to the watchman.

"Yes, mum," said the watchman; "you may depend upon me."

"Thanks! thanks!"

"If they should dare to touch you whilst I'm here I will soon let them see what's what."

"But let us be off; if they should come."

"Never fear."

But Red Ralph did fear. He well knew that nothing could save him if they once arrived upon the spot. Half a word of explanation and the watchman himself would count amongst his foes, already a too numerous list, since Jonathan Wild's alarming disclosure of the highwayman's identity.

"Aid me to rise," said Red Ralph, struggling to get up.

"Give me your hand."

"That's it. Heavens! I'm terribly giddy."

Red Ralph staggered and reeled like a drunken man.

"You've been awfully treated," said the watchman.

"I have, indeed."

"Don't fear, mum," said the watchman; "they wouldn't attempt to touch you whilst I am here."

"What could you do against a number?"

"Nothing."

"Then—"

"It ain't that, mum," said the watchman; "I know that I shouldn't be much use if they attempted to use violence, but they'd be afeard to try it on with an officer of the law. There's something in a watchman that frightens them all."

Red Ralph smiled, but could not help admitting the reason of the watchman's words.

"Let me lean upon you. That's it. Thanks; let us hasten away."

The door of Mr Powell's house opened.

"Here they come."

"Help me away, then, for God's sake."

The watchman at length moved off, and they had reached a turn in the street before a pursuit had fairly commenced.

"There he goes!" cried a voice at the street door. "After him! After him!"

"Run him down!"

But there would not be much need of this, for Red Ralph was so thoroughly enfeebled by his late exertions, and the shaking received in his leap through the parlour window, that flight was perfectly out of all question.

His only hope of escape depended upon stratagem, and on his ready wit alone he relied for success.

The pursuing visitors and servants from Mr. Powell's house came running along the street.

"They're upon us," said the Captain of the Yellow Band to his companion, apprehensively.

"All right, mum," returned the watchman; "you rely upon me. I'll see you all right through this."

One of the gentlemen here overhauled them.

"Stop!"

Red Ralph clung to the watchman's arm with well-feigned feminine alarm and consternation.

"Come along," he said tremblingly. "Save me! Oh, save me!"

"All right, mum," said the old Charley; "I'm right enough. You needn't hold me so tight; I'll do it."

"Here, watchman," said the gentleman; "stop; d'ye hear!"

"Be off."

"I tell you to stop!"

"I shan't!"

"But I say you are aiding a robber to escape!"

"It is false!" said Ralph.

"Get home with you," said the watchman; "get home, I say, or you'll get into trouble."

"But—but—"

"Off with you!"

The rest of the party came running up, and amongst them Red Ralph, to his no trifling consternation, perceived the two officers who had been with Jonathan Wild.

If they should step forward he was undoubtedly lost.

The watchman would most probably know the men, and then nothing upon earth could possible save him from capture.

"Here, you old fool, stand aside," cried another of the gentlemen.

"What for?"

"And give up that fellow."

"Which?"

"No quibbling; that one."

"I don't see no fellow but your lot," said the watchman.

"Then you refuse?"

"And not only refuse," said the watchman, "but I'll have all of you to the lock-up if you ain't off."

"The man's mad," suggested one of the gentlemen.

"Raving!"

"Rabid!"

"Let's take them both back."

"Ay, ay."

"Glorious fun," said one of the company, a fair lisping young man of twenty; "immense joke! let's lock up the Charley; eh, lads?"

"Ay, ay."

And a roar of cheers and laughter greeted this jocular proposition.

The watchman thought matters were beginning to look serious, and he stepped back a few yards as they advanced to secure his person, and produced a ponderous rattle.

"Now, I tell you what it is, gents," said Charley: "if you come any larks with me I'll spring my rattle, and have you all carted off to the lock-up."

"Nonsense, my man."

"Stuff!"

"You'll find that it's no nonsense," returned the watchman.

"But he's under a misapprehension," said one.

"He must be."

"Do you know who you are guarding there, Charley!" demanded another.

"No; I know that it's a woman, and I know that she is being ill-treated; and I'll look after her; so off!"

"Thanks, thanks!" said Red Ralph, encouragingly.

"You are an old fool, Charley," said one of the gentlemen.

"Thank'ee; I'm too wido for you, my fine gentleman."

"Ha, ha, ha!"

And they all roared again at the gross deception under which the honest and gallant guardian of the night was labouring.

"Why, that's no woman!"

Ralph trembled.

But the watchman only saw in this an attempt to throw him off his guard, and he replied accordingly—

"And you're no man."

The gentlemen all laughed again, and one of the officers who had come with Jonathan Wild to effect Red Ralph's capture pushed his way through the crowd up to the watchman.

"Here, you come with me," said he, laying his hand upon Red Ralph's shoulder roughly.

The Captain of the Yellow Band shook off his grasp, and, putting forth what feeble strength remained to him, dealt the officer a blow in the face which floored him in scientific style.

"Bray-vo!" said the watchman; "now, who's the next."

"This is absurd," said one of the gentlemen. "Do you know, watchman, that you are protecting a robber and a highwayman?"

"Oh, indeed," said the watchman, sarcastically. "I certainly didn't know it, gents; but so much the better; it's something out of my line—quite a novelty for me."

"The old idiot!"

"Fool! ass!" said another, "don't you really know who that man—woman—is?"

"No."

"Then learn that it the notorious highwayman, Red Ralph, the Captain of the Yellow Band!"

"Ha! ha! ha!" laughed the watchman. "A Paul Jones in petticoats; Dick Turpin in skirts; Sixteen-String Jack and Captain Kidd!"

Red Ralph was immensely delighted at the watchman's obstinacy, and he made the most of it at once.

"You see how they would seek to deceive you?" he said.

"All right, mum."

The gentlemen and the officers now began to consult together upon the best means to be adopted to capture Red Ralph.

"You see," said one, "that this old fool's obtinacy will force us to use violence."

"Yes."

"Then there's nothing to be done but to secure him."

"Very good."

"The idea of one man escaping from all of us would be too absurd, and get such a laugh against us if ever it became known."

"Which it certainly would."

"True."

These words were not unheard by Red Ralph, who still entertained the most lively apprehension for his safety.

"They will use violence," he whispered to the watchman.

"Never fear."

"Come, come, Charley," said one of the servants, stepping forward. "You're making a fool of yourself."

They all came on in a little mob now, and Red Ralph felt his heart beat violently.

"Let me fly," he whispered. "I can run now, I think."

"No, no; stay where you are. You shan't be hurt."

But they were unpleasantly nearing, and despite his protector's assurance of safety Red Ralph felt anything but comfortable.

One of the more venturesome of the party stepped up to Ralph and laid hands upon him, but was speedily rewarded for his temerity with a violent blow upon the sconce from the watchman's rattle.

This brought matters to an alarming climax for Red Ralph.

The pursuers passed round in a body.

Right and left did the watchman strike out, and Red Ralph himself, as it is scarcely necessary here to remark, did his own cause as much service as his slightly returning strength would allow.

But numbers must overcome the bravest hearts.

Cries, oaths, and blows were exchanged, and Red Ralph, in the excitement, quite forgot his sex for a few minutes.

Happily for him, the watchman, his sturdy protector, did not notice it. He was too much engaged with a couple of active young men who were squaring up to him upon scientific fistic principles.

But the watchman made short work of both of them, however.

The rattle he carried was a most formidable weapon, and brought a man to the earth at each doughty blow.

But while he was thus engaged Red Ralph had been overpowered and borne to the ground.

When the watchman, having disposed of his two youthful adversaries, next looked up, he found that the object of all his execution was being dragged from the spot.

"I have done all I could alone," cried the watchman, "and now I must have assistance."

Whiz! whiz! whiz! went the rattle, with a tremendous noise.

Whiz! whiz! whiz! came the answering rattle from every direction.

The watchman continued to spring his noisy instrument, and in the space of a few seconds his brothers came running to his assistance in every direction.

Red Ralph was by this time, in spite of his greatest exertions, dragged half-way back to Mr. Stanley Powell's house.

"Hi! hi!" cried the watchman in his colleagues; "after these fellows—these brawling gallants are dragging off that poor lady. After them!"

"After them!" cried the watchmen with one voice.

"Help! help!" exclaimed Red Ralph, never ceasing his struggles.

The watchmen, never doubting for a moment that they were aiding justice and humanity, dashed after the party.

And now once more the disturbance began.

A conflict with the watch was by no means an uncommon occurrence in those days, and both parties entered into it with spirit.

The young bloods of the period appeared to imagine themselves the personal enemies of the respectable old guardians of the streets; and the watchmen themselves fully reciprocated their sensations.

The consequence was that the object of the conflict was almost entirely lost sight of, and black eyes, bloody noses, and bruises of every description were administered as a labour of love.

At one part of the battle the whole of the combatants engaged rolled in one huge mass upon the ground, striking out indiscriminately at friends or foes, upon the glorious Hibernian principle of "Wheriver ye see a head, hit it."

The flunkies began to have enough of such rough usage, and two of them skulked off.

However, the remainder of the combatants were so greatly interested in the proceedings that their departure was quite unnoticed.

This may explain the singular and mysterious termination of this comedy of errors which we are about to relate.

At length the fiercest spirits must succumb to violent exertions, and the watchmen and their foes paused for breath, as if by a mutual understanding.

"Pheugh!" said one of the gentlemen, "this is a nice little job."

"It is," said another; "to be fighting against a regiment of Charlies to secure a highwayman."

"Where is the rascal?"

"Who?"

"Red Ralph."

"I don't see him!"

"Nor I."

"No—nor I. Where is he?"

The watchman took up the question, and began looking about them, but they could see no traces of the lady (!) upon whose behalf they had been so bravely doing battle!

Red Ralph was gone!

Yes, the Captain of the Yellow Band had most mysteriously disappeared during the conflict, and no one had seen him depart.

"Gone?"

"Gone?" echoed the watchmen in astonishment.

"Yes," said one of the gentlemen, endeavouring to stay a troublesome bleeding at the nose, "gone. You've done your work well. He's escaped."

"He?" repeated several of the watchmen.

"Yes, he."

"But it was a lady."

"Nonsense—"

"Don't believe them," said Red Ralph's original protector; "they would deceive you."

"Obstinate old fool!" said one of the gentlemen, "I tell you that it is yourself that is deceived."

"It could not have been a gal, Dogberry," said another of the watch. "Look how she—I mean he —fought—like a lion!"

"Of course not," said the former speaker. "No woman that ever lived could hit out like that—straight from the arm-pit!"

And the gentleman tenderly wiped his ensanguined proboscis, which testified sadly to the absent Ralph's prowess.

"Then who, in the devil's name, is he?" asked the watchman.

"Who? Who should he be? I told that obstinate idiot. Who should it be but *Red Ralph, the Captain of the Yellow Band?*"

CHAPTER XXVI.

FOILED AGAIN—RALPH ONCE MORE IN WILD'S POWER—THE SECRET ENEMY—MYSTERY—THE TABLES TURNED—"MERCY! MERCY!"—A MIRACULOUS ESCAPE—ANOTHER ADVENTURE, AND ANOTHER DISGUISE—THE OFFICERS UPON THE ROBBER'S TRACK.

MYSTERIOUS, inexplicable as the escape of the Yellow Band's leader appeared, it was in reality the simplest thing imaginable.

Even as the flunkies had escaped from the conflict, as related in another chapter, so had Captain Red Ralph released himself from their most embarrassing attentions.

Patience is the greatest of virtues, and had been brought into great requisition in Red Ralph's late adventure.

A well-chosen moment and a little of his wonted activity had saved him from the skirmish which had sent all his friends and adversaries scrambling upon the ground in a confused and stirring mêlée.

Darting aside from the bustling mob, he had only waited to see them engaged in the exciting battle which he had originated, and then he sped from the spot, amazed, astounded at his providential escape.

"Red Ralph was never born to succumb to such a set of rabble as that!" he exclaimed triumphantly.

"Then yield to me!" said a familiar voice at his elbow.

"Hah!"

He turned to find himself face to face with his arch-enemy, Jonathan Wild the thieftaker.

"At length, Red Ralph, you are my own!"

"Not yet."

"You are—if you would save your life for the present."

"I would save it altogether."

"You cannot."

"Then I'll die in the attempt to preserve my freedom."

"That you're welcome to," said Jonathan Wild; "but you certainly shall not leave me with life until you are safely lodged in Newgate."

The thieftaker toyed with a huge horse-pistol which he held presented at the highwayman.

"Pistols miss fire."

"Not mine, Ralph."

"Not generally, I admit, Jonathan," returned the highwayman in the same bantering strain; "but even yours, you know, can be hocussed."

"Hocussed!"

"Ay, that's the word," said the Captain of the Yellow Band.

"S'death! Confusion! you don't surely mean to say—"

[LEONORE ENTERS THE SECRET PASSAGE.]

The thieftaker, taken aback by the cool assurance of Red Ralph, pulled back the lock to examine the priming of the pistol.

For once in his life Jonathan Wild, the great—the prince of thieftakers—was overmatched in cunning.

As the tiger springs upon his prey, so did Red Ralph, the Captain of the Yellow Band, spring upon the thieftaker.

A sudden and a well-directed blow sent the pistol spinning in the air.

And, as the weapon quitted his grasp, Red Ralph seized the thieftaker by the throat and hurled him to the ground with terrific violence.

"Lie there, mighty Jonathan," said Red Ralph.

He turned to fly from the spot, but a sudden idea caused him to halt awhile.

"I might as well clear out his pockets," murmured Ralph.

Jonathan Wild did not offer to stir for several seconds, although perfectly conscious.

Better, indeed, had he been insensible, for, seeing the highwayman return, he began to tremble for his life.

The agony he suffered in those few brief seconds is undescribable.

Ralph stooped over him.

"Monster!" ejaculated the thieftaker; "would ye murder me?"

No. 10.

"I don't know."

The coolness of the highwayman's reply struck terror to his heart.

"Would you stain your soul with blood, Red Ralph?"

"Not human blood."

"Then—"

"But I would take your life, Jonathan Wild, with as little compunction as I would a dog's."

"Wherefore?"

"Because I don't look upon you as human."

"That's a poor excuse for my murder, Red Ralph."

"Oh, oh!" laughed Red Ralph, ironically; "and so you think to reason me out of my just retaliation."

"You have retaliated."

"But not sufficiently to satisfy my vengeance."

"Have mercy."

"Why should I?"

"As you hope for mercy."

"When—where?"

"Here, and hereafter."

"Silence! you blasphemous dog!" exclaimed Red Ralph. "Would you dare to allude to the dread hereafter with a catalogue of crimes like yours about to be accounted for at the judgment-seat?"

"No, no; oh, no."

"I tell you yes. Prepare to die."

"Murder! help! Mercy, mercy!"

"What mercy would you have shown me? None."

"I would—I would."

"Swear, it then, and load your soul with the guilt of perjury before you die."

"I will not," said the thieftaker, turning deadly pale.

"This is a great vengeance," thought the Captain of the Yellow Band, as he perceived his prostrate foe change colour.

"But, Ralph, Ralph, you will not slay me?" whispered Jonathan Wild.

"Why not?"

"Because in hunting you down you know I but do my duty."

"And something more."

"No."

"You lie, dog!" said Ralph. "You know that you are paid by my unnatural relative to hunt me to the death."

"Hah!"

"You see I know all."

"Spare my life, and I will confess all—all; I swear it, Ralph."

"No; I should reduce myself to your own degraded level by making a bargain with you."

"Then spare my life."

"No; I cannot reconcile it to my conscience, Jonathan Wild."

"How?"

"A butcher is no assassin; he slays an ox or a sheep, and sleeps none the worse for it—"

"But you, Ralph—"

"A vulture, a hawk, a kite, a wolf, are man's natural enemies—are detested by humanity as preying upon the inferior brute creation: you are still more odious, more vile! You prey upon your own species, and therefore well deserve the death I am about to give you."

Ralph raised his hand above the thieftaker's head.

This time Jonathan Wild looked forward to a speedy death as a certainty.

He did not even cry for mercy, as he had previously done.

He closed his eyes, and, with clenched teeth and a knitted brow, prepared for death.

In his terror he had not observed that Red Ralph possessed no instrument wherewith to deal the fatal blow—that he was, indeed, quite unarmed.

"He has gone through more than a dozen deaths," thought Red Ralph. "I think I may leave him now."

The highwayman's hand descended, not, as his helpless enemy had supposed, upon his shrinking brow—but into his coat pockets!

"This may be of some use to me," said Red Ralph, securing a pocket-book, very bulky, and tied round with a tape.

This action seemed to arouse Jonathan Wild more than the thoughts of a speedy dissolution had done.

He struggled to shake off the highwayman's hold.

But Red Ralph had no light grasp of him, and was not to be got rid of in this easy fashion.

"Silence!" said Ralph, administering Jonathan Wild a playful dig in the chest, which deprived him of utterance for several seconds. Silence! I am going to clear out your pockets, to begin with."

"And then—"

"I shall—"

Red Ralph drew his fore-finger significantly across the thieftaker's throat.

He felt Jonathan Wild's huge frame quiver beneath his clutch as he touched his flesh, and he felt that he was having a glorious and ample vengeance upon him."

He therefore recommenced the rifling of the thieftaker's pockets, and secured such papers as he was possessed of, together with his watch, purse, and some few valuables.

"There, that's done," said the Captain of the Yellow Band. "And now, Jonathan Wild, I wish you a good-night, and a good journey—downwards."

"Have mer—"

Red Ralph rose to his feet, and cut short the abject wretch's supplication by spurning him with his foot.

The thieftaker rolled a few paces and remained motionless, half persuaded that Red Ralph's vengeance was really accomplished.

In other words, he believed that he ceased to exist.

After a few seconds, however, a smarting in the side, the result of the last blow he had received from Red Ralph's heavy riding-boot, caused him to open his eyes, and he looked round to see whether or not the coast was clear.

It was, and after some slight consideration, he scrambled to his feet, shook himself, felt over his carcase, counted his bones, as it were, and crawled off.

Catching sight, however, of Ralph's form upon the point of disappearing in the far distance, Wild shook his clenched fist at it, and muttered between his set teeth, with an expression of demoniacal fury illuminating his fiend-like face.

"Wait a while—wait a while, Master Ralph. Ere long we will settle the long-standing account betwixt us. I can bide my time, for I know that your doom is as certain as God's vengeance. Try as you will, you cannot escape it. The owners of the bloody hand have all fallen one after the other—have all died a sudden—a fearful death, and you shall not escape. No—no, before open Heaven, I swear it."

Heedless of these awful words, the hero of this strange story pursued his way, never looking back at his fallen foe.

"I am very weary," he muttered, as he walked along, "and did it cost me my life I must have an hour's sleep before I do any more. But where?—Ah! Michael's place is close by. Good old Michael's, I am certain of shelter there."

He stood still to think and looked doubtfully around him.

He was at the top of the street in which Stanley Powell's house was situated, and he did not like venturing too near, although in that direction certainly lay his nearest way.

When he came to look, too, he saw that the old rake's residence was a blaze of light, and that the door and several of the windows were open.

Most people in Ralph's place would have taken to their heels, but Ralph did not very rarely adopt that course.

Making the best, therefore, of a most unpleasant job, he walked boldly past Mr. Stanley Powell's mansion.

As he did so one of the domestics engaged in the temporary repair of the window raised a light which he held in his hand for the convenience of the acting workman, and its unwelcome rays fell full upon the form of the fugitive highwayman.

But no one spoke.

"They haven't noticed me," thought Ralph; "I'm glad of that; I've had enough adventure for this night, at any rate, and I heartily wish myself safe back at the haunt, surrounded by my true and faithful Yellow Boys."

He paused before the house which was his chosen destination for that night.

Every window was dark, and all was silent.

Red Ralph picked some gravel and some pebbles from the road, and threw them up at a window upon the first floor.

Twice or thrice did he repeat this without any result.

At length he began to grow impatient, and he knocked rather loudly at the street door.

Presently the window at which he had thrown the pebbles and gravel was raised, and a head stretched forth.

"Who's there?"

"Michael?"

"Yes. Who is it?"

"Hush! it is I, Michael; come down."

"What! Gerald?"

"Yes, Michael; come down and let me in—quick! quick!"

"Wait a moment, Gerald."

"As short a one as convenient; I am in danger."

"I'm with you in a crack, Gerald," said Michael.

And the head was withdrawn and the window reclosed.

The next minute (which seemed the next hour to Red Ralph) the door was opened, and the owner of the head from the window appeared in night costume to welcome the wearied fugitive.

"Who are you?"

"Gerald."

"But in that dress?"

"Yes; a disguise."

"Good. But, Gerald, in truth, I can only recognise the voice as belonging to you. How changed you are!"

"Only in sex."

"I know—but come in—nothing ever can change Gerald."

"Hush!" said Red Ralph, "You must no longer call me by that name."

"Wherefore?"

"No matter; you must call me Ralph, or anything you will, but not Gerald. I have learnt to-day that another possesses my secret—our secret."

"And he is—"

"Jonathan Wild!"

"Never! How came he by it?"

"No matter. I imagine that I have a clue; but of that we must speak further. I want to be put to bed at once. I have been knocked about and roughly handled, and am in great need of rest."

"This way, then."

Michael led the way upstairs to a little bedroom upon the first floor.

"Here you are, Geral—I mean Ralph. Here's your old bedroom, always ready for you."

"Thanks, Michael, thanks; one trusty heart is always here, ready to succour a friend at a push.,,

"Your thanks insult me, Gerald," said his friend.

As they carried on the conversation Red Ralph was divesting himself of his female attire, preparatory to retiring for the night.

Wearied and exhausted with his prodigious exertions, Red Ralph was getting into bed in delicious anticipation of sweet repose when there was a loud summons below.

"What's that?"

Alarm was depicted upon both countenances.

The knocking was repeated.

"What can it mean?" said Michael, uneasily.

"Some drunken fellow's practical joke," said Ralph.

But the expression of his countenance plainly indicated that he had no belief in the words he uttered.

In vain did he endeavour to convince himself that his uttered surmise was the probable truth.

Again was the knocking repeated, and this time several voices angrily demanded admission.

"Go and see what it means, Michael," said Red Ralph.

"Very good."

The speaker ran, half naked as he was, to the next room, and, throwing open the window, demande dwho it was that claimed admittance at that unseemly hour.

"Open! open!" cried half-a-dozen voices at once.

"Who to?"

"To us—the king's officers!"

"What do you want here?"

"Red Ralph."

"Ralph?" repeated Michael in dismay.

"Yes; Red Ralph, the Captain of the Yellow Band; we know that he is concealed here."

"You are mistaken."

"No! no!"

"I say you are. I have no one at all concealed here."

"Then open your door, and let us search for ourselves."

"And if I refuse?"

"Open, in the name of the law."

"You must prove your authority."

"We have a warrant."

This was an alarming thing to oppose.

Michael stepped back to the passage, and spoke in a hurried whisper to Red Ralph at the bedroom door.

"Ralph."

"Yes."

"They claim admission."

"I know; I have heard all," said the Captain of the Yellow Band.

"What is to be done?"

"Admit them."

"But you know that they have a warrant for—"

"My apprehension? Yes, I do; admit them."

"But what will you do?"

"No matter. Is my trunk still here?"

"Yes; just where you left it."

"Good; then I am safe."

Michael ran lightly down the stairs, and began to unfasten the bolts and bars.

Impatient at the long delay, the officers without kept up a great noise and clamour for admission.

"Wait a little," said Michael, "all in good time, you know. Gently, my friends; you're coming in; that's it."

The last chain was removed with a great apparent show of labour on the part of Michael, and the officers, four in number, were admitted.

"Now, what is it?"

"We've come to arrest Red Ralph, the Yellow Boy."

"What of him ?"

"He is concealed here."

"It is false : no one is concealed here, I tell you."

"We must assure ourselves of that."

"Where is your warrant ?"

"Here."

The officers produced the required document, which Michael was a long time perusing.

So long, indeed, that they made disagreeable remarks upon it, and threatened him with a criminal prosecution for conniving at the escape of a traitor and a felon.

"You are ridiculous," said Michael, calmly ; "I merely wish to ascertain the truth of your authority. I see here that you are provided with a search warrant, but here is an irregularity in it which fully warrants my opposing you to the full extent of my power."

"What mean you ?"

"Simply that the warrant is not made out in my name."

"It is ; there is your name plainly enough."

"It is not. My name is—"

"Michael," interrupted one of the officers, pointing out the name upon the search warrant.

"It is ; but warrants are not usually made out in an individual's Christian name."

"And Michael ?"

"Is my Christian name."

The officers were greatly annoyed at this.

"No matter," said one of them, "Christian name or surname, we know enough to warrant our search without any legal authority."

"I shall oppose you."

"Then we shall use force."

"Force, will you ?"

"Yes ; and we would advise you not to oppose us. If Red Ralph is found here, and you were known to have opposed the carrying out of the sentence of the law, you would get into trouble."

"Then, as I cannot—dare not—oppose such odds successfully, the wisest thing is to let matters take their course ?"

"Precisely."

"But I warn you that I shall make a complaint in the proper quarter, if anything is wrong : I'm not the man, I assure you, to allow you to annoy me illegally and with impunity."

"We will stand our chance of that."

After looking about them carefully they proceeded to mount the stairs.

The first room they came to was that in which Red Ralph was to sleep for the night.

Here they endeavoured to force an entrance, but a stout lock opposed them.

Opposition only tended to increase their ardour, and they now felt assured that their expected prey was within.

"Open the door !"

"Open in the king's name !"

"Open ! we charge you."

"Lost ! lost !" mentally ejaculated the faithful Michael in despair.

CHAPTER XXVII.

ANOTHER FIX—THE OFFICERS BREAK INTO THE BEDROOM—A STRANGE OLD MAN—MORE OF RALPH'S TRICKS—HURRAH FOR THE ROAD !

"CONFOUND them !" muttered Red Ralph ; "they are determined that I shall have no sleep this night. I would fain rest awhile now, for I am weary and sore at heart."

And in truth the highwayman's countenance bore testimony to his sad words.

Want of sleep and his great exertions had done their work, and his courage had almost departed.

The knocking was repeated.

Open this door in the king's name !"

"Open, open, in the name of the law !" said another voice.

"And at once, too," continued the first speaker, "unless you would have us break it in."

Impatient at receiving no reply, the four officers dealt the door several determined blows.

It began to creak ominously.

"I must open the door," said Red Ralph ; "they will break it down else. Courage ! and I shall yet defeat them."

"Open ! open !"

"Patience, patience, I implore you," said the trembling querulous tones of an old man within the room.

The four officers looked into each other's faces, and then at Michael.

As the latter had caught the words of the occupant of the room, a smile of triumph had lit up his countenance, which had still lingered upon his lips as the officers glanced at him.

"Who's there with him ?" demanded one of the men of Michael.

"No one."

"Then who's that old man ?"

"My father."

"Then Red Ralph is with him ?"

"No—I tell you he is all alone."

"That remains to be seen."

Again did they renew their knocking and clamour, and noisily demanded to be admitted.

"Patience, patience, Michael ; I'm coming," said the voice within the chamber, which Michael said belonged to his father.

"You'd better," said one of the officers hastily.

"Ay, and quickly too."

"Gently, if you please, gentlemen," remonstrated Michael ; "my father is far advanced in years, and at fourscore and ten you may yourselves find it difficult to skip about with the activity of your youth."

"We don't want to hurry the old man," said one.

"No, no, only we don't want no humbug. Let him open the door immediately, or I'm jiggered if we don't have it down, and make our way in."

"I shall take care to resent this violence," said Michael.

"Pooh, pooh."

"Your warrant, as I have pointed out, is not in accordance with the law, and I am persuaded that an action for trespass will lie."

"You do, if the action don't," said one of the officers, with a coarse laugh, which was quickly taken up by his three comrades.

"No more parley now," said another ; "down with it."

They put the proprietor of the house aside in the most unceremonious manner imaginable, and prepared to rush at the door.

At this moment the lock was turned and a bolt withdrawn, and the door gently opened.

The four men immediately rushed precipitately into the room, nearly upsetting the person who had admitted them, an aged patriarchal-looking man, nearly bent double with long life.

He was a most venerable-looking old man, with a few thin gray hairs upon a polished head. He wore his beard long and snow white, and a large green shade protected his eyes from the light.

"What want ye at this time of the night ?" demanded the old man indignantly.

"Nothing of you, father," said one of the officers, impressed with the patriarch's venerable appearance ; "we only seek an outlaw, and a fugitive from justice."

"Justice?" iterated the old man.

"Ay, father."

"Then wherefore seek ye here?"

"Because he in this house."

"It is false!—think ye I would harbour an outlaw?" exclaimed the old man, indignantly. "Have I reached fourscore and ten years to be suspected as a traitor to my king and country, and to keep a house as a refuge for outlaws and robbers?"

"But we tell you, father, that the man we are in search of has been seen to enter this house, and we have the king's warrant to seek for him."

"Seek, then, seek and welcome," said the old man; "but do your duty quickly, and let me return to rest; my aged limbs can ill brook such a break upon their accustomed repose."

The four men entered, and commenced active search for the object of their pursuit.

Everything in the apartment was ransacked without affording the slightest clue to Red Ralph.

The bed from which the aged occupant of the chamber had just risen, apparently, was pulled open, and vicious thrusts given underneath, and the bed and mattresses stabbed through and through.

But without success.

The old man, leaning upon his son Michael's arm, stood calmly surveying the devastation which these ruthless officers of the law were creating within his little snuggery.

Once only did he betray the faintest emotion. This was when one of the men dragged off some of the bed-clothes in his zeal to prosecute the search.

"Nay, nay, my friend," said he, hobbling up and interposing; "you can do no good by this mischief; I pray you leave my humble shelter in such order as your duty will allow you."

"Nonsense, father," said the man, angrily; "offer us no further opposition. We don't want to do you any harm, but if you oppose us any more we shall take good care to represent it in the proper quarter, and you would find yourself in the wrong box."

"Yes, yes," said several of the men, speaking at once.

"Our suspicions are already aroused by the long time you have kept us waiting at the door."

The old man held up his hand to his ear, as if unable to catch their words.

"Don't you see that my father is deaf?" said Michael.

"Deaf, is he?"

"Yes, and has been these twenty years," said Michael.

"Poor old man!"

"Well, we must finish our search, and then we'll go."

"But are you not already satisfied that we have no one here?" asked Michael.

"No."

"What makes you suspect our house, then?"

"A man answering the description given of Red Ralph was seen to enter here not an hour ago."

"You are mistaken."

"No, I am not. The man who saw him enter is without, aiding the rest of our men to guard your place."

"Then my house is surrounded?"

"It is."

The old man glanced up at this, and one would almost have imagined that he had caught the last words of the officer.

The men then left the room, and continued the search all over the house, but with the same result.

No traces of the highwayman could be discovered.

"Now are you satisfied?" said Michael, as they descended the stairs to quit the house.

"No."

"Suspicion is part of your nature."

"Perhaps."

"Indeed it is; I verily believe that a thief-taker would suspect his own father, or the mother that bore him."

"Say on, sir," said one of the officers, "we shall not be put off by your coolness, believe me. We shall keep a sharp look-out upon this house in future. Beware! We would willingly spare that old man's gray hairs from shame and disgrace, and we believe him to be true enough, but we have strong suspicions about his son. Once more we warn you: if you are discovered giving refuge to Red Ralph, or to any hunted felon, it will go hard with you, I can promise you."

"Enough," said Michael: "I can dispense with your threats. I can answer for my own actions in the proper quarter."

The officers departed with many warnings and threats, and once more the fugitive highwayman and his faithful friend were left in peace.

Michael ran up the stairs, and pushed open the bedroom door.

The old man sat upon the side of the bed, evidently in great expectation.

His bent feeble appearance had departed, and he was as upright as a dart.

"Michael," said he, in a voice very different from that in which he had addressed the officers—"Michael, we may score another victory."

"Ay, Gerald."

"Not that name."

"Nor yet Ralph under existing circumstances."

"Yes — Ralph! — hang the fear. The cowards haven't the discernment of an infant."

"Nay, don't say that, father," laughed Michael; "they fancy themselves wonders in artifice."

"Doubtless."

"But at all events the Ralph must be sunk for the present."

"No, no; I am, and always will be, Red Ralph, the Captain of the bold Yellow Band!"

The tramp of horses could now be plainly heard without.

"They are patrolling the street," said Red Ralph; "one of those servants at Stanley Powell's did perceive me after all. We must proceed warily, Michael."

"But, Ralph—"

"Nay, nay, I'll be gone at once. They have plainly told you that you may only count upon their forbearance through the respect which they pay to your father's gray hairs—ha! ha! ha!"

"Ha! ha! ha!"

"But I must be gone. Have you a horse I could have?"

"The old mare is in the stable," said Michael; "leave by the stable door. We must muffle her hoofs, and then you will cross the field down Grove Lane, and you are safe."

"Good," said Ralph. "And now once more for the road!"

CHAPTER XXVIII.

DOWN THE VAULTS—THE HUNCHBACK AND HIS VICTIM—THE HUNTED SHADOW—GHOSTS AND RATS—THE GRAVEDIGGER—THE EMBRACE OF DEATH.

IT would be difficult to describe the intense anxiety and terror which agitated the hearts of the beautiful Leonore and her companion, the idiot woman, while they stood crouching in a dark corner of the cellar, awaiting the arrival of the hunchback carrying the corpse of his murdered victim

As, however, the hateful monster drew nearer, a

sickening dread that she would be discovered caused Lady Leonore to creep further and further away into the darkness, leaving her companion crouching in a dark corner, where she had hidden herself at the first alarm.

Nothing so unwise as the course that the beautiful girl had adopted could she have hit upon, for she soon became aware that the hunchback was making towards her.

Presently he had passed the corner where the idiot was hidden without noticing her hiding-place.

He was walking slowly, but was advancing straight towards Leonore, who fled like a guilty shadow before him.

With her eyes fixed upon him she glided onwards, guiding herself by one hand, with which she felt the cold slimy surface of the wall.

But how could she escape?

Rapidly he neared her, and she expected nought else than that presently she would find herself in some corner unable to go any further, and that then she and her hated jailor would be face to face.

But all at once she unexpectedly felt space instead of slimy brickwork beneath her outstretched hand.

She had reached some sort of opening, and she might creep in there out of the way.

She peered wistfully into the obscurity.

There seemed to be something like a passage before her, and, without a moment's hesitation, she plunged into it, and groped her way a few paces onward.

Then paused for breath.

The heavy footsteps approached; the light glimmered at the entrance of the passage.

Great heavens! he was coming that way.

He had entered, and was close upon her.

With a wildly palpitating heart she turned again and fled.

She never turned to look after her now.

She never paused to think what danger might lie in the dark path before her.

She flitted onwards with wondrous rapidity. She reached the top of a steep flight of steps, and descended them without accident.

Still groping her way on she came to a door standing ajar. She pushed it open, and entered a damp dismal place, which had a choky smell in it of some noxious exhalations.

And here she paused again to listen.

The heavy splay feet of the hunchback sounded with dull thuds upon the passage floor above.

In a moment or two afterwards he came shuffling down the steps, followed by a horrible trailing sound, which she knew to be the limbs of the dead body dragging down the steps.

But her terror wellnigh approached a maddening pitch when the hunchback stopped in front of the vault in which Leonore was hiding.

Creeping behind the door she flattened herself against the wall, and waited motionless for her doom.

The hunchback thrust the door open upon her, thus hiding her from his sight as he entered.

The poor girl, trembling like a leaf, expected every moment that she would be discovered, and, holding her breath, stood motionless, holding the wall to save herself from falling.

But the hunchback did not close the door behind him, and she was as yet in safety.

He placed the light he carried upon the floor, and then laid his awful burden by its side.

Leonore presently heard a heavy fall, which made her heart beat violently.

Then there was a peculiar grating noise.

She peeped through a crevice of the door, and saw with terror that the hunchback had jumped down into a half-dug grave, and was busy digging and throwing out the soil.

He worked in silence and with great energy for some little time, every movement he made being followed by the girl's scared eyes.

The yellow light fell upon the sallow, bruised, and blood-stained face of the corpse, and now and again upon the visage of the murderer. It was difficult to say which of the two presented the more horrible sight.

After he had laboured for about a quarter of an hour —a time which to the trembling beauty seemed an age of agony—he flung down his shovel and scrambled out of the grave.

"That's deep enough for her," he muttered. "When she's been well stamped down and the bricks replaced over the top, it'll puzzle her ghost to find a loophole, I'll wager— Hah?"

He stopped suddenly, and listened with an expression of astonishment.

Leonore listened also, but could hear no sound in the deathlike silence of the vaults.

"I'll take my oath there was something moving about," said the hunchback in a low but distinctly audible tone. "What the devil was it, I wonder?"

He listened and wondered for a moment or two, and then chuckled to himself.

"It's rats, I guess," he said with a laugh; "there's only rats and ghosts in these parts, that's one comfort, and I don't care a curse for neither on 'em."

With another chuckle the wretch stooped to take up the body of his victim, but, while in the act, he paused again, and looked round him in fear.

This time his face was blanched, and his hand trembled as he took up the light and crept to the door.

The half-fainting girl fancied, in her terror, that it must have been the violent throbbing of her heart, so audible to herself, which, in the deep silence, had reached the ears of the murderer.

The suspense which she suffered required an almost superhuman effort on her part to refrain from shrieking aloud.

When the hunchback had listened for a short time, however, he seemed to make up his mind that he was mistaken, and returned to his work.

Again he placed the light upon the ground, and once more stooped to pick up the dead body.

In her death agony the old woman had clasped her hands over her head, and the joints had stiffened in this shape.

As he raised the body, by some accident the arms fell, and his neck was encircled in their icy embrace.

With an awful curse he strove to free himself, but was unable to do so.

The weight of the body swayed him over into the pit-hole.

Reeling and staggering, wrenching and striving, he lost his footing and fell with the corpse into the grave.

In falling he kicked over the lantern, and the vault was enveloped in pitchy darkness.

Half dead with fright the wretched Leonore then, with a gasping cry, sank in a swoon upon the ground.

CHAPTER XXIX.

THE HUNCHBACK, THE PURSUER, AND THE CORPSE—THE FASTENED DOOR—THE SOUND OF TERROR — BURIED ALIVE — THE MURDERER'S FRENZIED FRIGHT.

WHEN Lady Leonore again opened her eyes, the cellar was still enveloped in darkness.

She listened. All was silent as death.

She waited for a long time, dreading to move a muscle for fear that the noise she made might betray her presence.

At length, as the silence still continued, she spread out her hand.

It encountered an object which at the first touch she knew was the lantern overturned by the hunchback's fall.

Stretching forth her hand a little further, she drew it back again with a shudder, for it had rested upon the edge of the grave!

What had happened during this period of unconsciousness which she had passed?

Had the hunchback scrambled out of the grave and beaten a hasty retreat?

Was he still lying down there with the corpse of his victim?

A horrible uncertainty overhung all, and the poor girl still lay upon the ground too much terrified to make any movement for the purpose of discovering the truth.

As, however, the silence still continued, she very slowly and noiselessly rose to her feet.

An idea of escape had again entered her head.

She would grope her way by the stairs to the passage above, leading into the upper vaults.

There, probably, she would find the idiot woman, and they might escape together.

This plan was very well in theory, but there was a terrible obstacle in the way.

That obstacle was the door, which was fastened upon her.

She groped her way to it and found it fast.

She pulled at it, but it yielded not to her efforts.

She pushed at it with an equal want of success.

How had this occurred?

There could be only one solution to the mystery, and that was that the hunchback had closed it after him when he left the vault.

As she moved away from the door, however, her feet came in contact with a mound of earth.

He had, then, left the corpse unburied at the bottom of the pit!

It was a fearful situation.

To be thus entombed alive in the presence of a corpse.

Could any position more horrible be imagined?

Alas! events proved that the horrors had only just begun.

Whilst the unhappy girl stood motionless, endeavouring to collect her fast-fleeting senses, and to calm the violent throbbing of her heart, the sound of a sigh suddenly fell upon her ear.

She started back with a half-suppressed shriek.

Her blood curdled, and the hair bristled upon her head.

All was again silent. Had she been mistaken?

But no; again was the awful sound repeated.

It came from the grave.

Then followed a rustling noise which was more fearful still to listen to—to listen to powerless and incapable of flight.

Her knees smote together.

A clammy dampness burst out upon her forehead.

Was it the dead coming to life?

A laboured breathing now issued from the pit, and then some muttered curses, low and deep, apprised the listener that it was the hunchback recovering his senses.

He had struck his head violently, as he fell, and had hitherto lain unconscious at the bottom of the pit, the terrible weight of the dead body pressing him down.

After some vain struggles he now released himself from this dreadful burden and scrambled out of the grave.

Leonore crept closer than ever to the wall, and held her breath.

"Curse her!" she heard him growling to himself,

"she very nearly managed to do for me at last. Where are the matches?"

The matches!

If he struck a light all was lost!

He fumbled for some time in his pockets, swearing savagely as he did so.

"I could take my oath I had them," he muttered; "but they're gone now. What have I done with them? Dropped them down the hole, perhaps. If that's the case, I must leave 'em there."

Still he continued his search, but without success.

"It'll be an infernally awkward job, groping my way to daylight through those vaults. They're worse than Rosamond's bower a precious sight, but I suppose I must; and to begin with, where's the door?"

As he spoke the hunchback spread out his long thin hands, and began to grope his way in the pitch darkness.

Sick at heart, Leonore crept away from him.

The ends of his fingers scraped against her dress.

His breath almost fanned her cheek as he crawled by

Then she heard him feeling over the slimy walls.

Presently he stopped. A horrible curse escaped his lips.

"Where is it? What the devil has become of it?" she heard him say.

Then he groped his way on again.

Then she heard him kicking and shaking violently at the closed portal.

A perfect volley of blasphemous imprecations now escaped the wretch's lips.

"Its closed," he said. "But how? It's stuck fast. I haven't got the key. I'm buried alive!"

He flung himself again with all his strength against the door.

He dragged at it with the fury of a wild beast.

But in vain.

It was as firm as a rock, and resisted all his efforts, terrific though they were.

A fearful howl, more like a savage beast's than a human being's, then escaped him, and he flung himself upon his knees upon the floor, searching in vain for the fallen matches.

Crawling upon his hands and knees, he approached the shrinking girl, who crept away from him upon tip-toe.

But it was impossible to avoid making some noise in thus moving about in the dark, and presently her foot struck against the fallen lantern.

The hunchback uttered an exclamation of alarm.

He was perfectly silent for an instant, and then the girl fancied that he must be creeping towards her, noiselessly.

Full of terror lest next moment she might fall into his clutches, she crept away again.

The faint rustling of her garments, however, met the ears of the murderer.

He uttered a loud yell.

"Keep off! keep off!" he screamed. "I can hear you coming. Keep off!"

The miscreant thought that it was the spirit of his murdered victim creeping upon him.

His shrieks and howls were of so awful a nature that the girl was almost tempted to call out to him that he was mistaken.

While this thought was uppermost in her mind, however, the ruffian had seized hold of the shovel lying at his feet, to use as a weapon of defence.

Then, shrieking and howling in terror, he whirled it round his head.

The poor girl, crouching upon the ground, spread out her hands to save herself, expecting every moment to receive her death-blow.

But in his mad fright the monster stumbled, and for the second time went head-first down into the grave.

CHAPTER XXX.

A NIGHT OF EXCITEMENT—RED RALPH ON THE
ROAD AGAIN—THE SECRETS OF HIS PAST LIFE
—A CURIOUS SCENE UPON THE HIGHWAY—
THE MAN WHO WAS SICK OF HIS LIFE—THE
GLOVED HAND—ANOTHER MYSTERY.

It was a night of stirring and terrible excitement
for the bold Captain Ralph.

And now when he had fondly hoped that his dangers
for the night were over, he found himself forced to
quit the hospitable roof of his staunch friend Michael,
and seek elsewhere that repose of which he stood in
such great need, and which the vigilance of the Bow
Street Runners would not allow him to take beneath
that shelter.

With a parting grasp of the hand and a hasty farewell, Red Ralph descended to the back of the house
and made his way to the stable.

Here, as Michael had informed him, he found a
trusty steed awaiting him.

In a trice Red Ralph had saddled and bridled the
horse, and then by way of extra precaution, at such
a critical moment, he carefully muffled the hoofs.

Gently, warily was the stable door opened, and Captain Red Ralph led out the mare, vaulted lightly
into the saddle, and walked her gently across the field
of which Michael had spoken.

Then, when a hundred yards from the house, he
urged her into a trot, canter, and finally a gallop.

"Hurrah for the road!" cried Captain Ralph, with
a merry laugh.

He had put half a mile between himself and the
house he had just quitted, and he felt his spirits rise.

The indomitable courage and energy of the bold
highwayman had always befriended him at the proper
moment in his wild and adventurous career, and now
returned to him when any ordinary man would have
been cast down and prostrate.

"They may watch now," said Ralph to himself,
with a chuckle; "they may stop around Michael's
house until doomsday if they like—I only wish they
would, provided that rare old Michael was not bothered
with their attention. The prison is not yet made—the
man not born who can secure Red Ralph—until—"

Here the robber's manner underwent a sudden and
remarkable transformation.

"Until my fate is fulfilled. When and how—when
and how will that be? Pshaw!" he added, with an
effort to shake off the temporary gloom which oppressed him. "Pshaw! I really believe that the
old hag's predictions and croakings of evil at the
boozing-ken have had some influence upon me."

And that is little to be wondered at, seeing the singular and startling fulfilment of the first part of her
prophecy in his marriage with the beauteous unknown.

This threw him into a long train of thought.

"Those jewels, too," he muttered—"that princely
prize which I had within my grasp and lost—a fortune
—a mine of wealth. I must have lost them in the
sewer—I must have lost them there, and there I must
seek them. It is a great chance—a very rare chance,
in truth, if I find them! But the search must and
shall be made nevertheless. A prize of such magnitude must not be lost for the want of a little perseverance upon my part. Yes, to-night, I must seek
our haunt—repose with my trusty Yellow Band, and
to-morrow, if possible, the search shall be made. Our
sure companions will be all there, and I shall need—
it shall be done."

In order to avoid the town and his enemies Red
Ralph had been obliged to take a very circuitous
route, and he now began to experience an annoyance
from it.

The part of the country in which he found himself
was quite unknown to him.

"I must make for the nearest house and ask the
way," he said.

Upon looking about him he perceived a faint light
in some distant dwelling, and towards this he directed
his steed.

However, he had not ridden far when the necessity
for this was obviated.

The sound of horse's feet reached him, and he soon
distinguished that they were coming towards him from
a cross road at which he paused.

Soon a single rider appeared in sight, and Red
Ralph halted under the shadow of an oak until he
came up with him.

Then Ralph touched his horse lightly with the spur
and sprang forward.

"Halt, sir traveller."

"Hah!"

"Excuse me," said Ralph, politely; "your pardon
for startling you."

"Who said that I was startled?" demanded the
stranger, gruffly.

"I merely inferred it," said Red Ralph.

"Then you are mistaken; I am prepared for all
emergencies."

"No preparations are necessary in the present
case."

"Humph!"

"I assure you, I merely wish to ask you the direction to—"

"Pray keep your distance."

Red Ralph saw that the suspicious traveller held a
pistol in his hand.

"Put your pistol by," said Red Ralph, "and tell
me the name of this road."

"You have an unceremonious way of making your
demands."

"I am accustomed to be obeyed, sir traveller," said
Ralph.

"Indeed?"

"Ay, sir; and I would beg you to answer me at
once—I have no time to waste in idle parley."

"Gad's life! but you are amusing."

"You will find me so before we part company,"
said Ralph.

"I have," retorted the stranger; "and now let
our interview end. Go your way and annoy me no
further with your impertinent demands."

The stranger held his pistol pointed threateningly
at Ralph as he made a step away.

The man's obstinacy so annoyed Red Ralph that he
was determined to make him give the information
which he so haughtily refused.

"Very good, sir," said Ralph: "since you so un-
courteously refuse to give me the information, I must
wait for a more civil traveller."

"Enough."

"Good night."

The highwayman raised his hat and made the
stranger a low bow.

The traveller returned his salutation as haughtily
as he had met his advances, and was about to depart
when an unexpected incident completely changed the
aspect of affairs.

By a sudden movement Red Ralph knocked the
pistol from the stranger's hand with his hat.

Then whipping forth one of his own holster-pistols
he presented it full at the sullen traveller, and the
positions were completely reversed.

"Villain!" ejaculated the stranger, in consternation.

"Softly, softly," said Red Ralph; "you must be
careful in the selection of your epithets now; your
discourteous reply to my very civil demand has not
put me in the best of humours, and unless you imme-

[RED RALPH ROBBING JONATHAN WILD.]

diately do as I wish you I shall certainly blow your brains out."

"Would you murder me?"

"Possibly."

"Ruffian!"

"Beware! You seem to slight my admonition."

"What would you with me?"

"Your purse."

"Hah! as I suspected. Would you rob me?"

"That is such a harsh term; I would beg a loan."

"Then you may beg for what I care. You'll get no loan from me."

"You are mistaken; I shall get all I desire from you."

"Pshaw! an idle boast."

"You will find I am no boaster."

"Stand aside and let me pass."

"My worthy friend—"

"Beware," said the stranger; "I am not a man to be molested with impunity, I warn you."

"Indeed?" said Red Ralph, ironically; "it seems to me that you are given to idle boasting more than I. What chance have you to stand against me now? I am more than your match, you see."

"I do not."

"No?"

"No; that remains to be seen."

"Come, come, sir," said Ralph, growing impatient;

"time is precious, and I am waiting for your purse, watch, valuables. and information of this outlandish locality."

"Then you shall have neither from me, I can assure you."

"You are mistaken."

"Not while I have life to protect them."

"Then I shall commence by depriving you of that protection."

"Wretch!"

"Gently. You have brought it all upon yourself; a little civility on your part, and—"

"I should have fallen by other means into the snare which your hellish cunning had set for me."

"No; I swear it—"

"Pshaw!" said the traveller, ironically; "think you that that the oath of a cutpurse is worth that?" (contemptuously snapping his fingers.) "Spare your oaths, young man; you make your way downwards more certain, and uselessly waste your breath; for, let me tell you, did you swear by every saint in the calendar—nay, did you commit your soul to hell upon the truth of your asseverations, you would fail to convince me of your truth: a thief is ever a liar."

"Say on, say on," said Ralph; "if I take your valuables the least I can do is to allow your tongue a little freedom. Have you finished?"

The stranger would deign no reply.

"Now hear me," said Red Ralph; "you can believe me or not as you wish; I care not—"

"That's fortunate."

"When I crossed you to-night it was with the purpose, the sole purpose, of seeking information of the locality."

"Truly!"

"Ay, truly, sir traveller, in spite of your sneer. But, since you so rudely repelled my advances, in pure revenge I seek the only retaliation open to me. Sir, your money or your life!"

"My life be it, then."

The stranger uttered these words with a bold defiance which completely won the admiration of Red Ralph.

"You are a brave man, and I honour you," said Ralph.

"Spare your sarcasm," said the stranger, angrily.

"I swear I speak in all sincerity."

"You lie."

"Hah!" cried Red Ralph: "say you so? No man ever yet gave me the lie with impunity."

"Then take it now. I hurl it in your teeth. Liar, dog, cutpurse, footpad, ruffian."

"Thank you," said Red Ralph, with a comical suavity of manner; "I am obliged for your flattering epithets, and am now determined to take what you offer with so little embarrassment."

"My life?"

"Ay."

"Take it and welcome; it has long since been burdensome to this weary body."

"Weary of existence?" said Red Ralph. "Well, I never took life, and would not now commence with that of a brave man. Your pistol lies there; pick it up."

"For what purpose?"

"We shall be equal."

"Then you would propose a duel?" said the stranger.

"Precisely."

"I refuse to pick up my pistol."

"Upon what grounds?"

"I should only seek to gain the mastery by some act of treachery."

"You belie yourself; treachery and candour cannot thus be linked together," said Red Ralph.

"A youthful error."

"Then you refuse to meet me in fair and lawful combat?"

"I do."

"Upon what grounds?"

"Why, in truth," replied the stranger, haughtily, "it scarcely suits my humour to be questioned by a man of your stamp; but since my reply is not of the most agreeable, I don't so much mind giving it."

"I await it, most disagreeable of travellers," said Ralph.

"You know the laws of the duello?"

"I believe so."

"Then you must know that a man of the humblest position in society must inevitably lose caste in an encounter with one who is the lowest, the vilest scum of the earth."

Red Ralph coloured to the temples, and his lips quivered with rage at the traveller's words.

His hands trembled violently, and his fingers nervously clasped the butt of the pistol which he held presented at the stranger.

"No, no," he said, half aloud, letting fall his hand; "I cannot shoot a man thus. Ride on, sir traveller, and take your chance of escape."

"I refuse."

"This, too? Wherefore, I pray?"

"I cannot brook the accent of command from you."

"Then go, I beseech you, in your own good time; I cannot shoot an unarmed man, and to-night you will surely die by this hand."

"Then shoot."

"I cannot; ride off and I shall fire when you are twenty or thirty paces distance."

"Then I most emphatically decline."

"Again—"

"Ay, if I must die let me receive my death-wound in front; I would not that the charitable world should discover my cowardice in a wound received in flying from danger."

"You are a singular man," said the Captain of the Yellow Band.

"I am what Fate has made me," said the traveller, gloomily; "but come, we waste time in further parley; why do you pause in your work?"

"It seems to me that you are eager for death?"

"I am."

"I thought so."

"And knowing it, you would pause before perpetrating the murder upon which you erst were so intent."

"Sir," said Ralph, his fancy completely won by the singularity of the encounter—"Sir, I never yet shed human blood save in loyal and open combat, and I would not now begin. Go thy ways in safety and in peace. I can honour bravery and respect a courageous man."

The stranger burst into a low mocking laugh.

"Or is it that you have a wholesome dread of the gallows?"

"Nay, you wrong me there," said Ralph; "I risk my life almost every day I live. Besides, my life would be forfeit in robbing you as much as if I took your life."

"True."

"And now farewell."

"Farewell."

"I have taken a strange and sudden fancy for you," said Ralph, "and it is more than likely that we shall never meet again upon earth."

"I hope not," said the traveller, most ungraciously.

"I would ask one favour of you," said Ralph, without noticing the other's testy rejoinder.

"The loan of a shilling?"

"Nay," said Ralph, smiling at the cynic's remark: "I would grasp your hand in friendship."

The stranger withdrew his hand out of reach.

"You refuse?"

The stranger was silent.

"You feel you would be contaminated by contact with a robber?" said Red Ralph, bitterly.

"No, no; it is not that," said the traveller, hastily.

"Then why refuse? I tell you frankly that my hand is not stained with blood."

The stranger shuddered.

Ralph silently extended his gloved hand, and presently the stranger, after looking into the robber's handsome countenance with a more kindly expression, advanced his hand too—*also gloved!*

They exchanged a warm hearty pressure, when Ralph's glove accidentally slipped off and revealed his blood-red hand.

The stranger looked upon it for a minute with a fascinated glance full of wonder and alarm.

Then, with a cry which appeared to break the spell which momentarily held him, he set spurs to his horse, and galloped wildly from the spot.

Red Ralph, wonder-stricken at the stranger's manner, sat gazing after him until his receding figure was lost in the shadows of the night.

The cry which the traveller had given was repeated, and its echoes struck upon the highwayman's ear dismally in the solitude of the road.

"Wonderful!" murmured Red Ralph. "Others, (not many, it is true) have seen this cursed mark of my hereditary shame, and have been greatly struck by it, but I never yet knew it to have so singular an effect. There is another mystery to add to that which has spoilt my career — soured a young life; a mystery which I would give much to solve. And yet we may possibly never meet again in life. No, no, something convinces me that I have not seen the last of that man. Time will show."

And the Captain of the Yellow Band rode slowly from the spot.

CHAPTER XXXI.

RALPH AT HOME AGAIN—THE SPY BROUGHT OUT FOR JUDGMENT—THE FALSE ACCUSATION—THE DWARF PROVES HIS STRENGTH — TOM KING WOUNDED FATALLY—THE NIGHT ENTERPRISE—THE HIGHWAYMAN'S COMMAND.

DAY had dawned as Red Ralph, the Captain of the Yellow Band, passed the Palmer's Cell.

"My brave Yellow Boys all sleep," murmured Ralph. "A few moments more, and I shall share their repose."

He had reached the glade as he uttered these words.

Barely had they passed his lips when a dark figure sprang from the bushes and caught at the head of his horse.

"Stand and deliver!"

"Music!" ejaculated Red Ralph, in ecstacy at once more hearing those familiar words.

"The captain!"

"Ay, Walters," said Ralph, "returned once more —dead beaten."

"You have been over-exerting yourself, captain," said the lieutenant, for it was he.

"Almost, Walters," said Red Ralph, wearily; "call one of the boys to look after my horse; I can go no further; aid me to dismount."

The lieutenant half lifted his chief from the saddle, and bore him by the secret entrance to the haunt.

"Anything occurred during my absence?" he demanded.

"Yes, captain," said Walters; "but I shall not speak of these matters until you have slept."

"But anything of moment?" asked Red Ralph anxiously.

"Well, yes; but it will keep until the day has fairly set in."

And, in spite of Red Ralph's anxiety, this was all the information which he could gather from his faithful friend.

Forced to content himself with this, the Captain of the Yellow Band was led, not unwillingly, to his sleeping chamber, a rude but fantastically decorated cavern in which the little sovereign of this lawless tribe reposed alone—a mark of his supremacy there.

It was late in the afternoon of that day before he awoke—still stiff and in some pain from his exertions overnight, but withal greatly refreshed with his slumbers.

As soon as he had fairly recovered his consciousness his active mind was upon the work.

He called for the lieutenant, who was waiting close at hand.

"You have rested well, captain," said the lieutenant.

"I have; now tell me what happened here in my absence?"

"We have caught a spy."

"Hah! Where?"

"In the vault by the glade entrance."

"Never!"

"'Tis true."

"But how came he there?"

"He discovered the entrance by accident, he says.'

"An ugly chance for us."

"It is; but he assures us that it is known only to himself—as far as his knowledge goes."

"You have interrogated him, then?"

"I have."

"We must see him again together, and see what is to be gathered from him, Walters."

"One word more," said the lieutenant, "before you see him."

"What now?"

"You know the man, I believe, captain."

"The spy?"

"Yes."

"Who is it?"

"He is called—that is, he calls himself Tom King."

"Tom King?" iterated the Captain of the Yellow Band.

"Yes, he said that he was known to you."

"He spoke the truth," said Red Ralph; "let us see him at once; have him brought out."

Red Ralph hastily completed his toilet, and repaired to a larger cavern in which the Yellow Band were assembled.

His entrance was greeted by the men with three cheers which verily appeared to shake their subterranean dwelling.

The captain thanked his men for their affection, and addressed a few words of kindness to each individually which made them more his own than ever.

"Now for your spy prisoner," he said.

Tom King, pale and weak from loss of blood, and bound securely—though, from his sad condition, it was apparent that this was scarcely necessary—was led into the cavern.

"Red Ralph!"

"Tom King!"

This was the only greeting which the friends of former days gave each other.

"Tom King," said Red Ralph, after a while, "I cannot say how I feel to see you here — my prisoner."

"Ralph," said Tom King in low tones, in which might be traced some well-suppressed emotion—

"Ralph, you can ask yourself the cause of my presence here."

"I am at a loss to comprehend your meaning," said Ralph.

"Your comprehension is intentionally dull, I think."

"'Pon my life I cannot understand you," said Ralph, "unless you would seek to throw me off the scent by a subterfuge—a line of conduct well in keeping with your present treachery."

"Ralph," said Tom King, "I shall attempt no subterfuge. To attempt to deny that I entered your haunt with no friendly intentions to you would be useless; but you well know that you might ever have counted upon Tom King's friendship had not your faithlessness to your pals turned their hearts from you."

"You speak in riddles," said the Captain of the Yellow Band.

"My meaning is not apparent?"

"No, i'faith."

"Then, to be clearer, for I suppose you would have me denounce your treachery to your followers here—"

"Say on."

"You set the officers of the law upon the men you called your friends — sold them for a few paltry guineas."

"Are you really speaking sincerely?"

"You may understand that I am sincere," said Tom King. "Why else should I have so turned against you?"

"True," exclaimed Ralph; "there must have been some gross misunderstanding here. I always knew Tom King for a true and faithful friend, and, although rash, I am sure that he would never have turned traitor without good reason—real or presumed."

"Beware of him," whispered Wolff in his ear; "he would deceive you by an assumption of pretended wrongs."

"Fear not, Wolff," said Red Ralph in reply. "Now, Tom King, answer me. Why have you sought to betray me—your sworn friend—I, whom you swore to be true to, with our friends Dick and—"

"Hush! name him not," said Tom King.

"What do you mean?"

"Let not your hypocrisy be carried any farther. Poor Dick Turpin has fallen a victim to your treachery, and I, in seeking to avenge him, have paid part of the penalty for my imprudence; the rest of the penalty, whatever it may be—the cruellest death you can prepare for me—I am ready to receive. Your faithlessness, Red Ralph, has grieved me more than could any reverse, however severe, which I might have suffered at the hands of a foe."

As Tom King concluded this indignant defiance his lip quivered, and his cheek grew, if possible, even paler than before.

He set his teeth, and made a violent effort to control his emotion.

Red Ralph sprang forward and caught him as he staggered forward and was about to fall.

"Get a stool."

A stool was brought, and Tom King, half fainting, was placed upon it and supported by two of the robbers on either side.

"Tom," said the Captain of the Yellow Band, "hear me, old friend; as I suspected, you have been and are still labouring under a misapprehension upon something which concerns me."

"Would that I could believe it!"

"Tell me the nature of your doubts; I am sure that they will admit of explanation."

Tom King turned his pallid countenance towards the Captain of the Yellow Band imploringly.

"Ralph," said he earnestly, "don't speak me falsely."

"No, no."

"If ever you did care for us—for me, and I think you did—"

"Can you doubt it?"

"No, no; I believe you did. Well then, by the memory of your old esteem for your old companions, deal fairly with us for once."

"I swear it."

"Enough. I feel singularly ill," said Tom King, now speaking with great effort, "and it is just possible that I am dying at this moment."

"Dying?" ejaculated Red Ralph.

"Ay, dying; and therefore your words could never do you any harm. Moreover, I will swear, should I recover, never to breathe to mortal soul what you may wish."

"I have no secrets to give you," said Red Ralph; "I will answer you everything I can candidly; but in truth I am quite at a loss to understand your meaning as yet."

"One question will alone suffice," said Tom King sadly.

"And that is—"

"Where is Dick?"

"Who?"

"Dick Turpin?"

"I really cannot say—possibly on the road—no, not yet; it is too early for him to have begun work for the night. I should say that he is most probably at the boozing-ken."

Tom King regarded the Captain of the Yellow Band earnestly for several minutes before he spoke.

"Ralph," he said at length, "I am determined to give you a clear statement of this affair. It may be that you know all—more than I do of the matter; but as there is still a bare chance of us having been in error all this time, I shall risk a little ridicule in addition to my present humiliation."

"Say on, Tom."

"You remember the last occasion we met at the boozing-ken?"

"Alas! too well."

"I thought so."

"Nay; not for any reason which you could have been acquainted with," said Red Ralph hastily.

"You know that the old woman spoke a lot of rubbish to you—bored you with some of her fanciful predictions in which she is so fond of indulging.

"I do."

"You may remember that you left the place shortly before Dick?"

"I think I did."

"I am sure you did."

"Well, well, agreed; what of that?" asked Red Ralph.

"Patience, patience," said Tom King; "I am rather weak from loss of blood, and cannot get along as fast as I could wish. Well, you had left perhaps ten minutes when a man came running into the place in a great state of consternation, and asked for a man named Richard, saying that he had been sent by Captain Ralph for him. Not suspecting anything like treachery, Dick followed the man, and we haven't clapped eyes upon him since. They hadn't left the ken long before we heard the report of a pistol, and we all of us rushed out, but the galloping of horses dying away in the distance was all that we could hear to tell us that he had been taken in ambush."

"And you suspected me of being party to this treachery?"

"We did, and not unnaturally," said Tom King.

"It was most unnatural," said Red Ralph indignantly.

"You had just before left the house, and one of our party remembered that you and Dick had had a few words recently—besides which the man asking for you—"

"All a conspiracy," exclaimed the Captain of the Yellow Band.

"You swear it?"

"I do."

"Then I believe you," said Tom King. "But rare Dick Turpin languishes now in the jug."

"Newgate?"

"Ay."

"How know you that?"

"I have seen it in print."

"Strange!"

"Yes; and moreover, our old enemy Jonathan Wild claims credit for his capture."

"Jonathan Wild! is it possible?"

"I read it myself."

"And you were in league with him against me?"

"No; this is how it has all come about. As soon as I heard that you were 'doing' this part of the country I set off in quest of you. I am not much given to calmness or reasoning, and I jumped with my wonted rashness at what now appears to me to be an absurd conclusion. I came off with the avowed purpose of seeking revenge upon you for your treachery to poor Dick."

"The sentiment does you honour, Tom," said Red Ralph; "or it would have done had the object of your resentment been other than Red Ralph."

"I know it," said Tom King, sadly. "However, I have paid for my headstrong rashness dearly. You see I bear a pistol-ball in my shoulder. But listen. I prowled about this part of the wood until yesterday, when a horseman accosted me, and, without any introduction whatever, begged me to deliver a letter to an individual on the glade above. I need not enter into further details respecting that."

Red Ralph regarded him for several moments, unable to catch his meaning.

"You mean—"

"That you were the horseman, and that I was the messenger you chose."

"Never."

"Ask any one here."

"There is no need for that if I have your word for it. But you astonish me. I thought that I had a little discernment."

"And I too, Ralph; but I knew you not. I accepted your mission, because I thought it likely to further the object of my visit to the forest. Then it was by accident that my curiosity was aroused before the delivery of your mission, and I refused to give it up. A scuffle ensued, and I had a little bout with your lieutenant here."

"In which I got worsted," said the lieutenant, smiling frankly.

"By accident," added Tom King, generously. "Then, having secured the letter and tied me up in the glade, they left me. But they had been only gone about five minutes when Jonathan Wild and his bulldogs came up upon the same errand as myself, and they soon set me free. What occurred subsequently you have no doubt learnt from some one here."

"But how came you released from your bonds the second time?" demanded Wolff.

"When you bound Jonathan Wild and his men as well?"

"Yes."

"Oh! one of his men lay hiding in a tree looking upon the glade. As soon as you were fairly off he came forward and released us. How Jonathan Wild and his man fared you know. I avowed my intention of remaining behind, and seeking out your haunt, but the thieftaker had too much prudence for the task."

"Then no one knows our secrets but yourself?" asked Ralph.

"As far as I can say," was Tom King's reply.

The speaker had been growing paler and paler during the foregoing conversation, and the deathly hue which his handsome countenance now wore was such as to cause Red Ralph the greatest alarm.

"You feel faint, Tom?"

"Yes, I do."

"Let him be seen to," said Ralph. "Where is Reuben?"

"He's under arrest," answered one of the Yellow Boys.

"Reuben under arrest?" repeated Red Ralph.

"Ay, captain," said Walters; "he was caught conniving at Tom King's escape, and so we have tied him up until your return."

"Set him free, then. My life upon it, he is honest and true."

"He is—he is," said the wounded man faintly. "It is true that he would have aided me to escape, but had he not done so I should have shot him. Afterwards, in the course of conversation, we found that we had been fellow-soldiers in Flanders, and so, out of sympathy for an old comrade, he bandaged my wounded arm, and was leading me to liberty when the men came up."

"You see, captain," said Wolff, "although it turns out that this is a pal of yours, Reuben wasn't to know that, and yet he would have set him free—that would have probably been our ruin had not these explanations taken place."

"Of course."

"One word more," said Tom King. "One word, and I have done. Before he would budge an inch, although menaced by my pistol, Reuben exacted an oath from me that what information I had gathered respecting your secret haunt should die with me."

"Did he so?"

"I swear it."

"I believe you," said Red Ralph; "I have ever had the greatest confidence in Reuben's attachment to us all."

"And I."

"And all of us."

"Let some one bring Reuben in; he can tend your hurt."

"You never told us when you got that hurt?"

"From Reuben's hand."

"He fired the shot?"

"He, and none other."

"And yet they would not believe his truth," said Red Ralph; then, turning to the lieutenant, he added, "That alone should have convinced you, Walters."

"This is the first I have heard of it, Ralph."

At this moment, Reuben, the dwarf, was led into the cavern.

His arms were securely fastened behind him, and he strode into the midst of the Yellow Band, scowling sullenly upon those nearest him.

Immediately that he caught sight of Tom King he walked eagerly up to his side, and questioned him anxiously as to his wound.

"How are you, now?"

"Sadly," replied King.

"If these fellows would but loosen my arms, I could attend to you; but generous as they are with a friend, with a foe they are remorselessly cruel.—Rascals!" he exclaimed, turning upon the Yellow Boys, indignantly, "will you let a man die before your eyes like this, by slow torture? If I cannot attend to him, brain him upon the spot, and be merciful; mortification must ensue if the wound is not properly dressed, and you kill the unhappy wretch by torture! Be men, be men!"

"You shall do as you please, Reuben," said Red Ralph.

"Red Ralph!" exclaimed the dwarf.

He had not seen the Captain of the Yellow Band upon entering the cavern, his whole attention having been so engrossed with the wounded man.

"Yes, Reuben; wait an instant patiently.—Let him be untied."

But, before they could release him, the dwarf's impatience had effected a marvel of strength.

By a violent exertion he had snapped the cords which bound him! When we say that the cords were ordinary hempen ropes, it will give some idea of the prodigious strength of the dwarf!

The Yellow Boys, knowing as they did his great muscular power, could not repress their astonishment. The dwarf stretched out his ponderous arms, which were cramped with long bondage, and then waved them triumphantly above his head.

"Your hand, Reuben," said Red Ralph.

The dwarf hastily gripped the proffered hand of Red Ralph, and then turned to Tom King.

"He must have my first attention," said Reuben.

"Right," said the Captain of the Yellow Band. "Do your best for him; he's as game a fellow as ever cried 'Stand!' to a true man."

"I know it," returned the dwarf.

He had already commenced unfastening the bandages upon the wounded shoulder.

"Let me have a basin of water and a sponge."

These were speedily brought.

The Yellow Boys gathered round Reuben and his patient, and anxiously awaited the former's opinion as to the danger of the wound.

In the first instance it had been comparatively slight, but, aggravated by inattention and the rough usage which it received, it had assumed a very ugly appearance.

"Is there any danger?" demanded the Captain of the Yellow Band.

The dwarf made no reply.

"He fears to answer you in my hearing," said Tom King, with a faint attempt to smile.

"No," said Reuben—"not that. I know well that you are too much of a soldier to fear to learn the worst."

"Then there is danger?" demanded Red Ralph, anxiously.

"No."

"Let us learn the worst at once," said Tom King. "I have faced death too often, to fear to look the grim tyrant in the face when and wheresoever it may arrive."

"Then," said the dwarf, after a lengthened survey of the wound, "the worst we may anticipate is a few weeks' repose."

"Is that all."

"All."

"Then that may easily be got over. We shall see that your imprisonment is rendered as agreeable as possible, Tom."

"Do you think that there is any necessity for calling a surgeon, Reuben?" demanded the lieutenant.

"None."

"I know you would not rely upon your own skill alone, unless—"

"Unless perfectly satisfied with the results," interrupted the dwarf. "Right, I would not. Rest and attention is all that will be required."

"And that he shall have," said Red Ralph. "You must have my cabin prepared for him. Make as soft a couch for him as our means will allow. Send at once for anything you may require. Drugs or bandages."

"I have everything at hand," said the dwarf. "Lift him into the captain's cabin."

Two of the Yellow Boys were about to execute this command when Tom King requested them to pause awhile.

"And Dick?" he asked, looking anxiously towards Red Ralph.

"Make your mind easy upon his account," said Ralph. "I shall do all that is possible on his behalf."

"Thanks, thanks!"

And Tom King was borne into the cabin of the Captain of the Yellow Band.

That night Red Ralph, accompanied by Walters and Wolff, sallied out into the forest in quest of adventure.

Not even the dangers which the former had undergone upon the previous day could satiate the thirst for excitement which urged Red Ralph on in his wild and lawless career.

"We shall have no moon to-night, Walter," said he, as they gained the forest glade.

"So much the better," returned the lieutenant.

"Not so, say I," said Wolff: "my motto is, 'a moonlight trip for plunder.'"

"It's more amusing, perhaps, but less safe."

"And I care nothing for the amusement without a little danger," said Red Ralph.

"I know it, captain," said Wolff. "You are rather too fond of that sort of thing to suit us."

They rode along chatting upon their lawless calling, some ten minutes, without meeting with a living soul. The road and country all around appeared to be quite deserted.

"We shall have no sport to-night," said the lieutenant.

"You are mistaken," said Red Ralph, listening intently. "I can hear some one coming this way—at a gallop, too."

"Indeed?"

"Ay, you will know directly."

"What an ear you have, captain!"

In a few minutes both Wolff and the lieutenant understood the truth of Red Ralph's statement.

A single horseman could be seen galloping along the road.

"Stand aside," said Ralph. "This must be my job."

The three highwaymen walked their horses down a bye lane, and then, motionless and silent as statues, they awaited the traveller's coming.

"A government messenger!" muttered Red Ralph, as the messenger appeared in sight.

"Then take care."

"Wherefore, Wolff?"

"He is armed."

"That for his arms!" said Red Ralph, snapping his fingers contemptuously.

"Look out. He's here."

"Stand close!"

"Now for it."

Unsuspecting of danger, the rider came along at a smart canter, evidently taking great enjoyment in his exercise.

A minute more, and Ralph touched his horse lightly with the spur and sprang in the traveller's path.

"Stand and deliver!"

CHAPTER XXXII.

NEWGATE A HUNDRED YEARS AGO—THE MYSTERIOUS LADY VISITOR—THE LOVELY FACE UNVEILED—THE RECOGNITION—AN EXTRAORDINARY SCENE BETWEEN THE ROBBER AND THE LADY—HELP! HELP!—A VISION OF DEATH AND TERROR—THE FINGERLESS HAND.

ABOUT a couple of hours after the events just recorded, a man in the uniform of a government messenger pulled up a hard-ridden horse before the door of the dwelling of the Governor of Newgate adjoining the prison.

The horseman sprang from the saddle and tugged at a huge bell-pull upon the doorpost.

The whole street, dull, dark, and deserted, re-echoed with the violent appeal.

The importance of the messenger's mission was shown in the clamour of his summons and duly appreciated within, for the door was opened while yet the bell was ringing.

"Show me to the governor."

"The governor has retired for the night," was the reply.

"No matter," said the messenger; "I must see him at once."

"You cannot."

"Don't you see by my dress that I am upon an errand of death."

"You have a death-warrant!"

"Yes."

"You can leave it."

"Impossible!"

"Why?"

"I have particular instructions to see the governor himself."

"But the governor has retired to rest an hour ago, and left particular orders that he was on no account whatever to be disturbed."

"Enough; who is the deputy?"

"Mr. Warren, the secretary."

"Show me to him."

The porter admitted the government messenger without further opposition, and ushered him into a reception room, there to await the arrival of the acting governor.

In the space of a few minutes Mr. Warren arrived. He was a small pompous personage, evidently impressed with the importance of his office.

"You wished to see me?" he asked upon entering.

"Well, no," said the government messenger quietly; "I wished to see the governor himself."

The deputy coughed.

"I am the governor for the present, sir," said he.

"You mean you replace him until he wakes up in the morning."

"That I presume can have little to do with your errand?"

"You are mistaken; it has much to do with it, sir."

"How, pray?"

"Because my instructions say particularly the governor."

"My good man," said Mr. Warren pompously, "don't trouble—"

"Stay," interrupted the messenger; "I am a government official, and not your good man."

"Very good," said Mr. Warren, turning very red in the face; "no offence was meant."

"And none taken."

"I'm glad of it."

"When I do take offence I also take steps to show it."

Mr. Warren looked uncomfortable, and failed ignominiously in an attempt to smile.

"But to my business," resumed the messenger: "I shall not need to disturb your master—"

The secretary winced.

"Your master," repeated the messenger maliciously—"providing you can do what I want."

"I have no doubt I can."

"Here," said the government messenger, producing a formidable-looking parchment: "I bear a warrant for the execution of a prisoner."

"Who?"

"Richard Turpin."

"So soon?"

"Yes; he is to be executed on Monday next."

"But the trial is only just over."

"I am aware of it. But they mean to make short work of them now; hanging doesn't seem to stop highway robbery."

"And the object is to strike a decided blow by stringing them up upon a very short notice?"

"Yes."

"And a very good idea too."

"You think so?"

"Certainly; do you not too?"

"I—oh, yes; but this—this—what's his name?"

"Richard Turpin—more familiarly known to our criminal reports as Dick Turpin—he has only been in custody a day or so?"

"Not long it's true—tried and found guilty on Wednesday, and on Monday morning at eight o'clock the gallows and a short trip into the next world."

The messenger shuddered.

"You are not much used to this sort of thing, but it comes quite natural to us."

"The hangman?"

"Yes."

"So I should imagine," said the government messenger drily.

The secretary glanced up in the other's face, but the messenger's countenance was stolidity itself.

"As regards the warrant for the execution of this Dick Turpin," he said, "I can take the charge of that."

"But that is not all."

"You have something else to deliver to the governor?"

"Yes, simply a message."

"To what effect!"

"Something which I believe—which it is beyond your power to take authority in."

"Sir," said the deputy with great dignity, "I am invested with full authority by the governor."

"Then I have to see the prisoner."

"The condemned prisoner?"

"Yes."

"Humph!"

"You cannot give me an order to that effect?"

"Well, I—"

"No matter; will you please to send your master to me—"

"Stop, stop!" exclaimed Mr. Warren, "I can give you any order which I may deem correct."

"The same as the governor's?"

"Yes."

"Then give me the order at once, for it grows late, and I have travelled far to-night; moreover, I am not in the habit of conversing with highwaymen and condemned prisoners, and I wish the disagreeable job over as soon as possible."

"But at least tell me the nature of your business with the prisoner," said the deputy governor.

"My instructions specify nothing upon that head whatever."

"Then you decline?"

"Positively."

"Cannot this business be transacted by some one here?"

"My dear sir," said the Government messenger petulantly, "do you imagine that I should have been entrusted with this important mission if you or any of the warders were capable of doing the business?"

"I don't know, I'm sure," quoth the indignant deputy.

"Then show your discretion by meddling no further in the business."

"Meddling; well, I—"

"Enough, sir. Please to prepare me the order to see the prisoner. I have already foregone some of my instructions in stating my business with you instead of your master, and, unless I am attended to at once, I promise you I shall make a representation of the whole affair in a quarter which both yourself and the governor might find unpleasant."

The deputy, without another word, seated himself at a table, and rapidly penned the order to see the prisoner, Dick Turpin, in the condemned cell.

When he had finished he rang a bell, and one of the warders entered the room.

"Ha! Mathews," he said, "you're just the man I wanted."

"If you please, sir," said the warder with a bow and a scrape, "you're wanted."

"Who by?"

"A lady, sir."

The secretary coloured up to the temples.

"Don't you see that I'm engaged, booby!"

"It's a lady visitor, please, sir," said the warder hastily.

"Visitor? Oh; well, will you show the lady in here?"

The secretary was anxious to show a little of that authority before the messenger of which the latter personage appeared inclined to make so light.

A lady, thickly veiled, was ushered into the room.

"I wished to see the governor," she said in an undertone.

"Yes, madam," replied the secretary.

He handed her a seat with considerable flourish, and then he sat down, crossed his hands, and calmly awaited for her to commence.

"I said the governor," she said after a few seconds.

"Yes, madam," said the secretary, "I am the governor."

"You?"

"For the present: the governor is at present invisible."

"I'm sure that he would see me if you would take my name to him."

"Madam, I am deputed by the governor to transact all business for him until to-morrow."

"But my business is of a strictly private nature: I must see the governor alone."

"Then you cannot see him to-night," said the secretary, greatly annoyed that he had not been able to appear to greater advantage before the government messenger.

"Will you take my card to him?"

"Impossible!"

"Or send it?"

"Equally impossible."

"The governor will be greatly annoyed when he learns that I have been and that you refused to allow me to see him."

The secretary looked from the messenger to the lady, and then from the lady to the messenger.

"Well, madam," said he at length, "I will have your card delivered to him; although I assure you in so doing I am not fulfilling my instructions."

He took the card which the lady tendered him, and left the room.

As soon as he had gone the lady breathed a heavy sigh of relief.

Then she murmured a few words half-aloud, which appeared greatly to astonish the Government messenger.

She was speaking her thoughts, evidently ignorant of his presence.

The fact was that the messenger was seated at the further extremity of the room—a spacious chamber, and but imperfectly lighted by an indifferent oil lamp.

The lady was seated under the rays of the lamp, and all her movements were observed by her invisible companion.

"Thank Heaven!" she murmured, "I have succeeded so far. If I can but see the governor, I know

that his mercenary spirit must accede to such a powerful argument as I shall be prepared to offer him. In these matters, as well as every concern in life, half the battle is to know the people you have to deal with.—Ah! how stifling this veil is—I feel as if I were about to faint! I must undo it awhile and breathe—there—ah!"

She unfastened the veil as she spoke, revealing a countenance of surpassing loveliness.

Pale as a stature of marble, but adorned with a pair of rich lustrous violet eyes, shaded by long dark eyelashes.

A regular set of features of wondrous beauty.

A face that a dreaming poet pictures, but that mortal never sees!

The grandeur of her beauty appeared to have an immediate and remarkable effect upon the Government messenger.

As she removed her veil he gave a start of surprise.

A gesture which would rather denote the recognition of an acquaintance, however, than aught else.

He never once now removed his eyes from her; a puzzled expression was upon his face, giving one the notion that he had met the lady before, but failed to trace the occasion in his memory.

Suddenly it came to him.

With an ejaculation of surprise—joy and misgiving combined—he started to his feet.

"Who's that?" exclaimed the lady, hastily replacing her veil.

The messenger strode across the apartment, and advanced close to the lady.

"Who are you?" she asked.

"One who knows you well," replied the messenger.

"And you were placed there while your master was away, to play the spy upon my movements?"

"No, no, by Heaven!" exclaimed the messenger. "I was here upon business before you come in. I was talking with the secretary when you called his attention from me. I sat there by accident, unobserved by you, until you raised your veil. Then I recognised—"

"Whom?"

The alarm with which the lady put this question astonished the Government messenger.

"I recognised a face that I had seen before—for a few short minutes—a few blissful happy minutes which will ever stand out in my memory as the brightest of an erring career."

"You are mistaken, sir," said the lady, in a low tremulous tone. "We have never met before. Never!"

"We have."

"Where?"

"Look upon me—can you not remember?"

She glanced upwards into the messenger's face.

"No, no," she said, "and yet there is something about your person which I cannot help connecting with a startling hideous vision that I was once troubled with.

"A vision!"

"Yes—a dream, nothing more—but a dream of terror—of death!"

"Then it is just possible that you were under the influence of some hellish spell when—"

"When—what? Say on."

"When we met before."

"You were about to word your phrase otherwise."

"I admit it—I admit it," said the messenger, hurriedly. "Think well, madam, I beseech you. Do you not remember a hasty wedding with a strange bridegroom, and a sudden parting when the ceremony was concluded?"

The lady regarded him with a blank look of astonishment.

[TERROR OF THE HUNCHBACK.]

"Do you not remember?" demanded the messenger.

"No."

"Oh, false one!"

"Sir," said the lady, "I tell you that you are mistaken."

"I am?"

"You admit it."

"Thus far—that I took you for an angel from your angelic presence—that I find you a fiend in cunning and cruel deception."

"Sir!"

The lady rose indignantly from her seat, and moved towards the door.

In an instant the Government messenger was by her side.

"Stay, madam," he exclaimed, clutching her by the wrist—"Stay awhile; let me wring that hardened heart with fear—the only emotion it can feel."

"Unhand me!" exclaimed the lady.

"Silence!"

"Help!"

"Quiet, perjured woman! false wife! traitress!"

"Oh! he is mad!" exclaimed the lady. "and I alone and helpless, at his mercy. Oh! for the love of mercy, don't harm me. Spare me, spare me!"

"Vile woman!" said the messenger, "is it possible that one so fair can also be so false?"

"How false?"

"Dissembling syren," cried the messenger, "you enrage me with your cool deception."

"Help! oh, help!"

"Silence! or I shall forget myself and slay you."

"Hah! mur—"

The cry died upon her lips.

She turned ashy pale.

He felt her wrist quiver beneath his clutch.

She sank a dead weight into his arms.

"She has fainted," he muttered: "I must call assistance. Yet no; it would be dangerous, and I must not forget even now the great object of my visit to Newgate."

He tore off her veil and once more revealed her lovely face.

A deathly pallor had now overspread her countenance, and the absence of all expression really made her appear the chiselled divinity of some great sculptor.

"It is she," muttered the messenger. And yet— that pale face: it seems to me that I connect it with something more fearful than that even—as she said, a fearful vision—a vision of death and terror!"

He took her hand, which was lying helplessly at her side as he spoke.

And gently raised it to his lips.

Suddenly his eye rested terror-stricken upon the tiny glove.

One of the fingers was wanting upon the hand!

With a wild cry he let the fainting beauty slip from his arms to the floor.

A rush—a bound, and he fled maddened from the room!

CHAPTER XXXIII.

THE GIRL'S TERROR—A WHISPER—LOST IN THE VAULTS — THE BRICKED-UP DOORWAY — THE ATTACK OF THE RATS—THE WELL-HOLE—THE IRON TRAP—THE TORRENT.

WE left the hunchback when he had fallen for the second time into the grave of his victim.

Poor Leonore, still crouching on her knees by the edge of the pit, awaited the renewal of hostilities.

However, she waited in vain.

The monster in falling had again knocked himself senseless, and lay at the bottom of the grave incapable of further atrocities for some time to come.

But the unhappy girl was too much terrified to move, and remained upon her knees trembling and helpless.

All at once a faint sound caught her ear.

She listened intently.

Could she be mistaken?

No; it was a whisper.

At first she was almost benumbed with fright, for the sound seemed to come from the grave.

But presently, still listening, she fancied that she heard her name—

"Leonore!"

Yes; she was certain of it now.

The voice addressing her came from the direction of the door.

Rising to her feet she crept round the cellar, guiding herself by the wall.

As she reached the portal the sound was again repeated.

"Leonore!"

"Yes."

"Are you alone?"

"No," she answered, with an involuntary shudder.

Then, after a few moments' pause, she added in an eager whisper—

"Hush, hush! open the door."

"I will try."

There was a grating noise, very faint indeed, but still loud enough to fill Leonore's heart with an agony of fear lest the hunchback should hear it.

The opening of the door was a long and tedious process, but at length it was accomplished, and Leonore passed through into the passage beyond. The idiot was there awaiting her.

"I've been watching and listening a long while," she said. "What has become of him?"

"He has fallen into the grave, and lies there stunned."

"Now is our time, then; we must not waste another moment."

"But it is all so dark; what can we do?"

"The darkness matters little; I can find my way easily if you will trust to me."

"That I will, willingly."

"Let me lay hold of your hand, then."

Leonore stretched forth her delicate little taper fingers, not without some slight repugnance, however, and they were grasped in the claw-like hand of her companion.

Together, then, they ascended the steep flight of stone steps leading into the vault above.

Here all was black as night, and to Leonore it seemed incredible that any one should be able thus to find his way blindfold through the intricacies of this dismal place.

"Are you sure that you are going right?" she asked.

"Yes, quite sure."

"Are you, then, so familiar with the place?"

"Yes."

"But I understood you to say that you had been a prisoner in the cell above for a very long while."

"It was before he locked me up there that I was accustomed to wander all over the house."

"What a strange place it is, and of what an enormous extent!"

"Nobody would think so, to judge from the outside, though."

"What is it? some sort of a castle?"

"The house above is a small mean place enough— a kind of farm-house, much more modern than these vaults."

"What are they?" asked Leonore, who felt, in spite of the danger of her position, a vivid curiosity about the wonders surrounding her.

"They originally belonged to a nunnery. I could tell you all the horrible tales connected with the tortures that have been perpetrated here."

"Indeed?"

"They would make your blood curdle in your veins."

"The horrors of the present are sufficient to do that," responded the trembling girl. "But what a long way it is!"

"We have not much farther to go now; there is a small flight of steps somewhere by which we can escape."

"Thank God for that!"

"A little farther only, and we shall have done."

They moved on again more slowly than before, and her companion seemed to be groping for some landmark in the darkness.

At last she uttered an exclamation of pleasure.

"Have you found them?"

"Yes."

They were now at the bottom of a flight of steps which they rapidly ascended.

"There is a door here through which we can get into the rooms above."

"But suppose it is locked?"

The idiot chuckled.

"I can manage the lock; never fear; I know the trick of old."

Whilst she spoke they had reached the top of the steps.

She then quitted her hold of her companion to pass her hands over the wall.

Presently she uttered a cry.

"What is the matter?"

"We're lost, we're lost!" answered the other with a groan."

"But what has happened?"

"Everything has happened; the door is gone!"

"Gone?"

"Yes; it has been bricked up: the communication with the floor above has been cut off. We are prisoners without hope."

"Not without hope," responded Leonore. "Why cannot we get out by the way our jailor came in?"

"That is our only chance; but we must find out the way first."

"I do not understand you. You said just now that you knew the vaults so well."

"I thought I did, but they have been altered since I was here. I thought when we saw Jabez that he had entered by this door which has been bricked up."

"Ah! I see now. But cannot we find the real outlet?"

"If we had a light we could do so very easily, I dare say, but in the dark it is more difficult."

"Let us try, anyhow."

They descended the stairs again, and began their search in earnest.

The task which they had undertaken was, however, fraught with even more difficulty and danger than Leonore had imagined.

"We must go very carefully," said Jabez's wife, "for there are dreadful holes— Ah!"

At that very moment she clutched her companion's arm and dragged her back.

"What is the matter?"

"A well! In another moment you would have been down."

A cold shudder ran through the girl's frame. The truth of her companion's statement was only too evident, for on her stretching forth one foot it encountered space instead of the brick floor upon which the other rested.

Creeping on more cautiously than before, and proceeding always with outstretched hands, they worked their way slowly onwards.

At last they came to a door.

"Perhaps this is it?" said Leonore, and pulled at a rusty key sticking in the lock.

The door flew open with an ominous creak.

Then there was an extraordinary sound—a scrambling and squealing and squeaking.

Then past them rushed a troup of rats, and Leonore, with a shriek, covered her throat only just in time to save herself from the attack of one of the hideous monsters.

When they were gone at last the two women passed through the doorway.

They were in a small passage, and proceeding up this came to another door, which, when they had opened and passed it, slammed to behind them.

They were now in darkness, which seemed, if possible, more intense than that which had preceded it.

Leonore, groping her way onwards, found at last beneath her hand something which seemed like an iron grating.

She raised a bolt with a violent effort, and the trap flew suddenly open.

In another moment she was dashed to the ground by a torrent of water pouring in upon her.

"Good heavens!" she heard the idiot exclaim, "it is the moat. We are lost!"

CHAPTER XXXIV.

DICK TURPIN IN THE CONDEMNED CELL — THE MEETING OF TWO FAMOUS HIGHWAYMEN — FILING OFF THE MANACLES — THE COIL OF ROPE — THE INTERRUPTION — RALPH AND THE JAILOR — BRIBES AND THREATS — THE STRUGGLE — FLIGHT.

RETURN we now to Newgate. As soon as the Government messenger gained the passage he stumbled against Mr. Warren, the secretary and deputy to the governor of Newgate.

"Hullo!"

"Beg your pardon," said the governor's deputy, picking himself up in a great fluster, "I didn't know."

The Government messenger interrupted him, in confusion, saying—

"No matter—the fault was mine."

"No, no," quoth the secretary, mollified at finding the hitherto disagreeable visitor so gracious. "I'm sure I—"

"No matter," again interrupted the messenger, testily. "Yours or mine—where is the warder to conduct me to the condemned cell?"

"The man."

"Yes, yes—don't I speak plainly?"

"Sir, I—"

"Tut, tut; call the man, or I must seek the prisoner alone."

The secretary now could not fail to notice the other's strange and excitable demeanour.

"You seem to be in confusion, sir?" he remarked.

"Confusion? No; I—"

"Indeed you do."

"Not I—I waited long, and—"

"You grow more and more excited every minute. Has anything happened during my absence?"

Mr. Warren regarded him doubtfully.

The Government messenger passed his hand across his brow with a gesture of pain.

"Stay," said he, suddenly looking up: "something has occurred."

"I thought so."

"The lady you left in the room with me has fainted away."

"Fainted?"

"Yes."

"But how? Why? Alarmed at anything?"

"No—not that I know of—how should I? What could alarm her? Why do you put such a question to me?"

The secretary regarded him again, not comprehending his singular agitation.

"I cannot understand what you mean," he began.

At this moment the warder appeared in the passage.

"Is this Matthews?"

"Yes."

"Here," cried the Government messenger—"lead me to the condemned cell. Here is the governor's order."

And before the secretary could say another word he had caught the warder by the arm and hurried him from the spot."

"Here you are, sir," said the warder, pausing before a massive, strongly barred, unbolted door, in which there was a small grating.

He opened the door and entered the cell with the messenger.

"You may go," said the latter to the warder.

"You have to see the prisoner alone, sir?"

"Of course."

"The order doesn't say anything about that, sir."

"No matter: I must see the prisoner alone. Be gone!"

"I would sooner have express orders to that effect."

"You have them."

"No, sir."

"You have—my express orders. See you obey them at once."

He placed a gold piece in the warder's hand as he spoke.

This was a most conclusive proof of the correctness of his authority, and the warder departed at once.

The Government messenger advanced into the cell, closing the door after him.

The prisoner, Richard Turpin, whose death-warrant the Government messenger had brought to Newgate, was seated upon the edge of a low wooden bedstead, humming some popular melody, in a low tone, as they entered the cell.

Then he simply raised his eyes and glanced at the two new comers, without discontinuing the ditty.

The notorious highwayman was, in person, above the middle height, a strongly knit figure but slight, and had a light jaunty air, which not even his present reverse of fortune could entirely eradicate.

Undoubtedly he was aware of the doom in store for him, and yet his bearing was light and buoyant as ever!

"What's your pleasure?" he asked, as the visitor drew nearer.

"Dick!"

"The prisoner looked up.

He appeared to recognise the Government messenger's voice.

"Who are you?" demanded Dick Turpin.

"A friend."

"Indeed?"

"Ay, a true friend, Dick."

"Then you're welcome," said the highwayman—"very welcome. I haven't many friends in the world."

"You have."

"Pshaw!" said the highwayman, his light-hearted manner giving way to a bitterness of expression; "the only friend I believed myself in possession of has deserted me in this strait."

"You think so?"

"I know it—here is the proof of what I say. Had the friend I allude to been as true-hearted as I deemed him he would have been here."

"Impossible."

"Nothing is impossible to true friendship. The word doesn't exist for it, sir. Had I been in—in—"

"Tom King's place," suggested the Government messenger.

"You know to whom I alluded?" said the prisoner in surprise.

"Of course."

"Who are you?"

"You do not recognise me?"

"We have never met before."

"We have."

Dick Turpin glanced into his face with a puzzled expression.

"There seems something familiar, too, in your voice," he said; "and yet I cannot call to my memory where I have heard it."

"Think again."

"It is useless; I cannot remember you."

"Now do you recollect me?" asked the Government messenger, removing a false wig and whiskers.

Dick Turpin sprang to his feet, with a cry—

"Red Ralph!"

"Hush!"

It was no other than the bold Captain of the Yellow Band, who in the disguise of the Government messenger had obtained an entry into Newgate, and by a bold stroke succeeded in reaching the condemned cell.

The reader must understand that this was then, as at present, an almost impossible thing.

Imminent and great was the peril which the Captain of the Yellow Band ran, but he would have willingly ventured a dozen lives, had he possessed them, in Dick Turpin's behalf.

However, his disinterestedness was ill met by the prisoner.

As he uttered the name of the Captain of the Yellow Band, he gathered up his fetters in his two hands and made a violent and sudden dash at him.

Red Ralph, however, found no difficulty in evading this vigorous attack.

Dick Turpin's activity was marred by his fettered condition.

"Dick," said the Captain of the Yellow Band, stepping aside, "you are mistaken. I come here to aid you."

"Traitor!"

"Hush!"

"I shall not. I must relieve my feelings and denounce you, little as an exposure here may affect you."

"You are deceived."

"I am! I am!" exclaimed Dick, bitterly.

"But not in the way you supposed," said the Captain of the Yellow Band. "I have heard from Tom King the history of your capture by Jonathan Wild. He is convinced that you have been the victim of a conspiracy, and that some one has proved false to you."

"And I too."

"And he is also convinced," said the Captain of the Yellow Band, "that I am guiltless of your misfortun."

"Pshaw!"

"I swear it, Dick!"

The prisoner shook his head sadly, and turned away.

"Dick, Dick," said Red Ralph, "pray have a little consideration. How hard is it to have your word doubted by the man you would serve!—by the man whom you are running imminent peril to save!"

"Ralph!" said Dick Turpin, sadly "I have lost confidence in humanity."

"Because you believe me false."

"Ay!"

"Then be reassured."

"Because," interrupted Dick—"because I know you are false."

"You wrong me, Dick," exclaimed the Captain of the Yellow Band, "I will swear it by any oath you propose."

The earnestness with which he uttered these words did not fail to make an impression upon the sceptical prisoner.

"Would I could believe you, Ralph!" he said, doubtfully.

"You can believe me."

Dick Turpin looked into the frank open countenance of his comrade for an instant, and then thrust forth his sturdy but heavily-ironed hand, which Red Ralph grasped cordially.

"Now, Dick," said the latter, "we have no time for any explanations, so they must be put off until our present job is over."

"What job?"

"That which I am here to manage for you, Dick."

"You cannot mean—"

"Everything. Indulge your wildest dreams, Dick."

"Ralph," said the prisoner, his face flushing with the excitement of hope—"Ralph, your words fill me with hopes and fears—hopes that—"

"Hush!"

Red Ralph had heard a faint sound at the door, and glancing upwards he perceived an eye glistening at the grating.

"The jailor!"

The countenance of the Captain of the Yellow Band underwent an instantaneous change.

He regarded the prisoner with a stern forbidding look, and addressed a few harsh words to him in a rough voice.

Then he stepped backwards a few paces, and with a sudden spring dragged open the door of the cell before the eavesdropper could make good his retreat.

"Hah!" said Red Ralph, "you're there, are you?"

"No, sir—I."

"Tut, tut, man. Never listen at a door; you run the useless risk of getting kicked."

"I assure you, sir," stammered the jailor.

"Your assurances are as false as you are sneaking and mean."

"'Pon my word, sir."

"Enough! be off!"

The man slunk away.

"He's gone."

"Yes," said Red Ralph, "but we won't trust to him again. We'll make sure of him, thus."

Saying which, he took off his riding-cloak and hung it over the door, by fixing one of the buttons to the grating.

"Now, I think that we shall be free from interruption," said the leader of the Yellow Band.

He did not, however, rely too much upon the warder's forbearance, but placed himself near the door, as he hastened to produce a short iron instrument which was screwed into a round handle.

Then he listened intently at the door for a second.

"All right."

He ran lightly across the cell, and in an instant was digging desperately at the manacles which held fast the prisoner's wrists.

"Thanks, thanks!" murmured Dick Turpin, fervently.

One of the handcuffs was removed.

"Patience! patience!" said Red Ralph, working hard at the other, "this is a tough job. Now, Dick, you must tell me what you have ascertained about the position of your cell since you have been here—not much, I suppose?"

"Not a great deal," said the prisoner, "but still I haven't been quite idle. Hope never entirely deserts me, though I must say that I never was nearer despair than I have been this last squeak."

"But what course can you take when you are freed from these irons?" asked Ralph.

"That I can soon see to. Set me free to begin with."

"Gad! but it is a difficult matter, Dick. Ha! victory!"

With a clatter the irons fell from his wrists and he was free!

His hands, at least, were released, and this gave the prisoner such great satisfaction that he waved them triumphantly over his head, and breathed a murmur of joy.

"Hush!" said Ralph, "your fetters have yet to be removed."

"Oh! it's a delightful thing, liberty!" said Dick Turpin.

"And you shall taste its delights shortly, Dick!"

"Ha!"

The fetters were fastened from his ankles to his waist, from whence they were supported by a stout girdle of iron.

This it was no trifling matter to loosen.

The ankles were speedily set at liberty, but the belt around the waist presented a terrible obstacle!

"We shall never manage this," said Red Ralph.

"Haven't you a file?"

"Yes."

"Leave it with me."

"I intend to use it on these bars, but I had hoped to leave you little work to do with the irons."

The Captain of the Yellow Band threw off his coat, and disclosed a huge length of rope coiled around his body.

"Untwist this; aid me," said Red Ralph.

"One moment."

"No, no; minutes are precious now; leave the iron girdle until I have gone."

The uncoiling of the rope was the work of some few seconds, which appeared as ages to them.

It was a desperate venture of two desperate men!

Both fully comprehended the extent of the danger, and it is no disparagement of their courage to say that they felt remarkably nervous upon the chances of discovery.

If an attempt at escape were discovered it would render all chance of such a thing impossible.

Impossible for both! Red Ralph had ventured rashly into the lion's den, and it was highly probable that, if discovered, he would have to pay for his temerity with his life.

Nothing could protect him should his incognito be pierced by one of the many officers with whom he was unhappily acquainted.

At length the rope was removed from his body.

Dick Turpin gathered it up in his arms and secreted it beneath the mattrass of his bed.

"Now for the irons," said the latter: "how can I contrive to keep my freedom from the jailor should he come back?"

"I have provided against that, too," said Red Ralph.

He drew a ball of twine from his pocket, and with this he proceeded to tie the irons to the prisoner's wrists and ankles as nearly as possible as they had been before.

"Now, Dick, you must take this pistol; but be sure only to use it at the very last extremity."

"Trust me."

"I do."

"It would not be safe to use it here; I should have the whole staff of warders upon me in a second."

"And the chance would be irrecoverably lost."

"It would."

At this moment the warder's footsteps were heard without, approaching the door.

"Quick, quick!" said Red Ralph; "sit upon the bed. There, now."

He immediately donned his riding cloak and placed himself by the door.

Then, as the jailor drew within hearing, he addressed a few words to the prisoner calculated to throw the former off his guard.

"Unhappy man," quoth Red Ralph in a drawling puritanical voice; "would you but confess."

"Never," said the prisoner, catching at the other's meaning.

"Then prepare for a violent and ignominious death."

"That I am prepared for, unless I can—"

He paused.

"What?" asked the Captain of the Yellow Band.

"Unless I can escape."

"Hullo—hullo!" said the jailor, entering the cell; "who talks of escaping?"

"I."

"Then you may make your mind easy upon that score."

"I do."

"You can never hope to escape from here."

"Indeed?"

"You will never leave here again, Dick Turpin, until—"

The jailor glanced towards Red Ralph meaningly.

"I understand you," said the prisoner; "but I assure you, my friend, that before—"

Red Ralph frowned warningly.

"Before ten days are over I shall be outside the old jug."

"Oh, yes!" laughed the jailor; "you can manage *that* before a week is over."

There was an ugly significance in the jailor's words which caused Dick Turpin to shudder.

"Yes," continued the jailor brutally, "before a week is over you will be taking an airing in front of the jug, upon a nice little wooden stage erected in your honour."

"Silence!" said Red Ralph sternly; "don't sport with the guilty man's death moments."

The warder slunk away thoroughly abashed by the reproof.

As he moved from the door Ralph placed his finger warningly upon his lip and frowned at the prisoner.

"Hush, Dick; take this."

He hastily passed him a knife, and the instrument with which he had released him from his fetters.

Dick Turpin concealed them hurriedly beneath his waistcoat.

"This looks into the prison yard," whispered the prisoner.

"The Old Bailey?"

"Yes."

"I shall be there at hand with aid until—"

The jailor returned.

"Come, sir," said he; "I should think that it's nigh time you had finished with the prisoner."

"Your opinion is not wanted," said the visitor sternly.

"May be," said the jailor; "but it is always against orders to admit visitors to prisoners under sentence."

"Is not the order I brought you in due form?"

"Yes; but—"

"Then speak no further upon the subject, I beg you."

The warder bowed his head in deep humility.

"Farewell, unhappy man," continued Red Ralph, addressing the prisoner; "and may you repent your evil ways."

"Thank you, sir," said the prisoner in a broken voice.

"May better fortune be in store for you; farewell!"

"I hope so with all my heart," said Dick Turpin with a smile of intelligence; "farewell, sir."

Red Ralph nodded meaningly to the prisoner, and quitted the cell.

"You must lead me back, Matthews," said Red Ralph.

"Yes, sir."

The jailor carefully locked and bolted the cell, and then led the way back.

"Do you wish to see Mr. Warren again, sir?" he asked.

"No," replied the Captain of the Yellow Band; "I have no further need of his services."

"Very good, sir."

"Why do you ask?"

"Because you can go out by another door."

"So much the better."

"We shall get out sooner, sir, by this passage."

"Through the prison?"

"Yes."

"But will there be no difficulty for me to pass?"

"Not with me, sir."

"Oh, I see," said the visitor: "a warder can always pass?"

"Of course, sir."

"Good."

They had now gained a door which opened on to the prison yard, which they had to traverse.

"Stay one moment," said Red Ralph; "I want you to take the prisoner back something for me."

"Beg pardon, sir," returned the man; "prisoners ain't allowed to receive anything at all."

"Sure?"

"Positive, sir."

"But a condemned prisoner is surely allowed some little extra indulgences."

"In some ways, sir," answered the warder; "but they are most particular not to let them have any present of any kind."

"Wherefore?"

"They are afraid of them receiving any means of escape."

"O-ho!"

"Or poison."

"But there can be no danger of that from me—a Government messenger, you know."

"Of course not."

"Certainly; then you will take a scrap of paper for me?"

"Couldn't, sir."

"Nonsense!"

"No, sir; it's against the rules; we mustn't infringe them for any one at all, sir."

Red Ralph, without greatly heeding the warder's words, produced a pocket book and pencil, and hurriedly wrote a few words upon a leaf, which he tore out and gave to him.

"There, give him that."

"Really, sir—"

"Tut, tut!" said Red Ralph, slipping a sovereign into the man's hand; "you may read it, and then deliver it if you see fit."

"Very well, sir."

The warder took the paper, and, after stowing away the golden bribe, read the note aloud, which ran as follows:—

"Guilty man; turn your thoughts to better things. Repent! Confess, and the King may have pity upon your sad condition."

"The King!" iterated the warder as he concluded.

"Ay, the King!"

"Is it possible, then, sir, that his Majesty himself is interested in the prisoner?"

"I should betray a great indiscretion did I *say* anything," observed Red Ralph, with a glance which insinuated volumes; "I can only tell you to judge of the importance of my mission here by the urgency of my request to see the governor in the first place, and afterwards the prisoner himself."

The warder was immensely impressed by these words.

"Very well, sir," said he, with fast-increasing respect; "you may be sure that the paper shall reach the prisoner."

"To-night?"

"At once."

"Thank you; you may count upon my gratitude."

The jailor bowed his acknowledgments.

"And possibly," continued the visitor, with yet deeper significance—"possibly not upon mine alone. Good day, and remember."

"Certainly, sir."

Ralph had just stepped into the prison yard when the jailor called after him—

"One word, sir."

"What now?"

"I see that there is something else written upon this paper, sir."

"Indeed?"

"Yes, sir," said the jailor; "upon the back of it."

"Let me see," said Red Ralph, with well-assumed surprise. "Oh, it's nothing—some scribbling—a problem in Euclid—I had worked it out—it is of no use."

"Thank you, sir."

Ralph walked once more towards the exit from the prison yard.

However, before he could gain the door he was again stopped by one of the warders.

"Beg your pardon, sir," said the man; "Mr. Warren has sent me after you."

"What for?"

"He wants to speak with you before you go."

"Impossible!"

"He says he will not detain you a minute, sir."

"My friend," said Red Ralph, "I know that he will not detain me half a minute, because I shall not go to him."

"Beg pardon, sir, but I would much rather that you came."

"Oh! *you* would," laughed Red Ralph; "'pon my word, my man, you are deuced amusing!"

He moved on towards the door, but the warder stepped before him.

"You cannot leave, sir, until you have seen Mr. Warren."

"Stand aside!"

"I cannot."

"I shall report this insolence, remember."

"I'm very sorry, sir, but I am only obeying orders."

"I don't care what you may be obeying; I shall not obey."

"They are the governor's orders."

"That I am to be insulted?"

"No, sir," said the man respectfully but firmly; "I was to request you to return to him."

"And I refuse."

"In that case you are to be taken back."

"By force?"

"At the last extremity."

"Then, now hear me, my man," said Red Ralph; "unless I pass out immediately, and unmolested, I shall take such steps that all concerned in this outrage shall be punished for it. I must see that his Majesty's officers are not disgraced in this way. S'death, sir! it would be nothing short of petty treason."

The warder was not a little startled at these words.

Red Ralph moved on to the door.

"Open here and let me pass out."

"Have you got an order?" demanded the door-keeper.

"This is my order."

He threw open his riding cloak and displayed the Government livery.

The man at once obeyed the order and Ralph passed through.

The warder who had brought the order from the governor had recovered from the temporary alarm into which the supposed Government messenger's words had thrown him, and he called to the door-keeper to stop him.

"Don't let him pass!"

But it was too late. Red Ralph was already out of Newgate!

The warder now, perceiving his folly in not carrying out his instructions to the letter, darted out after the visitor and laid his hand upon his shoulder.

"Stop, sir," said he: "at any risks you must go back with me."

"Begone!" said Red Ralph angrily.

"I cannot; you must come back."

"Must, forsooth!"

"Ay, sir; you must."

"We shall see to that."

He endeavoured to shake off the warder's hold and to move on, but the man only clutched him with greater firmness.

He was a big powerful fellow, and Red Ralph began to be fearful that he might be detained longer than he would find perfectly convenient.

"I have warned you."

"No matter—come back, sir."

Red Ralph turned savagely upon the warder and grappled with him.

The man was heavily built, weighing possibly some four or five stone heavier than the light supple highwayman.

But Red Ralph was as active as a kitten—a quality which goes far in a wrestle!

He clutched his opponent round the middle, gave him a sudden lift from the ground, and by a great exertion pitched him fairly over his hip!

The warder fell with a deep heavy thud!

"Help! help!"

But the highwayman sped from the spot like a hare!

CHAPTER XXXV.

DICK TURPIN'S ANXIETY—THE STRANGE SCRAP OF PAPER—SOMETHING ON THE OTHER SIDE —VERY MYSTERIOUS—THE JAILOR COMES TO GRIEF—A CHANGE OF CLOTHES—A RUN FOR DEAR LIFE — SCALING THE WALL — THE MISHAP—THE FEARFUL DESCENT.

WE leave our hero and his fortunes a while to follow up the more interesting movements of the sturdy Dick Turpin.

Half an hour had perhaps elapsed after the departure of his comrade, the Captain of the Yellow Band, when he heard the tramp of the warder in the stone passage anterior to the condemned cell.

Naturally full of alarm upon the eve of a daring project and a desperate venture, he hastily glanced about him to see that there was nothing about which could create the least suspicion in the jailor's mind.

His anxiety had already caused him to see to this very carefully.

The next minute the jailor entered the cell.

As each bolt had been withdrawn the prisoner's sensation had grown more and more painful.

He well knew the jailor's footsteps, for in close confinement the ear grows speedily accustomed to distinguish such few little things as break the monotony of the prisoner's existence.

And yet he had been endeavouring to pursuade himself to hope against hope that it was the Captain of the Yellow Band returned.

What could the warder want with him at that hour?

It was not the time he usually made his round.

Something must have gone wrong!

Red Ralph had possibly committed some imprudence and had aroused the suspicions of the authorities!

Perhaps he had been arrested; perhaps all was discovered!

The prisoner felt a cold sweat break out all over him at this terrible thought.

But he was not long left in this fearful uncertainty.

The jailor entered the cell as we have already observed.

"Dick," said the man, advancing towards the prisoner.

"What now?" the highwayman replied, without looking up.

He felt that he dared not trust himself in his present agitation.

"The gentleman who was here just now—"

"Well!" interrupted the prisoner hastily, "What of him?"

"How you snap one up."

"What do you want?"

"I was going to tell you," replied the jailor, "the gentleman who was here just now—"

"Yes, yes!"

"Patience; the Government messenger has sent you this."

Dick Turpin looked up in amazement!

The jailor held out a paper to him—the note with which he had been entrusted by Red Ralph.

"For me?"

"Yes."

Dick Turpin yet hesitated to take it. He could not understand the jailor, the individual entrusted with his safe keeping, should have undertaken to act as a go-between to himself and the leader of the Yellow Band.

"Take it, man," said the jailor; "it won't bite you."

Dick took the paper and read the short admonition to reform his sinful life, which Red Ralph had written as a blind for the jailor.

"What can this mean?" thought the prisoner, "surely he cannot—"

As he thus mused he had turned the paper over and his eye caught something which he seemed to study with much interest.

The warder observed the action.

"Oh! that's nothing much."

"What is nothing?"

"Oh, that side."

"No, no; I see."

He looked up inquiringly at the warder as he spoke.

"No," contined the warder, "it's only a mathematical problem."

"I see."

"And can't be of much interest to you Dick, eh?"

"I don't know that."

"Do you mean to say that you understand mathematics?"

"Yes."

"Then you are more learned than I should have thought."

"Oh, I have had some little education, my friend."

"Indeed?"

"Yes; so you may as well leave this with me."

"I can't."

"Why not?"

"Against orders."

"But this can't do any mischief, you know."

"Perhaps not; but I can't leave it, nevertheless."

"It's a cruel thing, this prison discipline," said Dick.

"It's a very necessary thing. Give me the paper come."

The prisoner, with an impatient gesture, threw the paper from him.

It fell upon the ground *close to the bedside!*

"Well, you might be a little more civil, master Dick," said the warder, angrily.

"Why should I?"

"It don't encourage one to do you a good turn again."

"You've been paid for it."

"How do you know that?" demanded the warder, hastily.

"Because you are too hard-hearted to do any poor wretch a good turn unless you are paid."

The jailor only replied to this by a coarse brutal laugh, and stooped down to recover the paper.

This was an unfortunate action for the jailor.

He heard the fetters of the prisoner clank violently, and he endeavoured to spring up.

But Dick Turpin was too quick for him.

In the space of a second he had sprung upon him and toppled him over upon the bed.

Here he held him pinned down in a grasp of iron.

"Help! hel—"

"Hush!" breather the prisoner, hoarsely in his ear.

"Release me, or —"

"Silence! a word, a movement, the least sound, and by heaven it is your last."

The jailor turned deadly pale.

"You would not slay me?"

"If necessary."

The warder resumed his struggles, but in vain.

"If you are wise," said the highwayman, "you will not move."

"What do you mean?"

"To escape."

"Impossible!"

"You will see."

The fetters of the prisoner had slipped from the string which bound them to his limbs and fell to the ground.

The jailor heard the fall, and began now to anticipate the worst.

Released from these the highwayman could do with the warder as he pleased.

History tells us that the physical strength of Dick Turpin was something prodigious, and as the prison authorities well knew this they had secured him with fetters of a crushing weight.

It is therefore little to be wondered at that the jailor began to entertain some serious misgivings.

He ceased to struggle.

Fear deprived him of all power to oppose the athletic highwayman, and he was helpless as a babe in his grip.

"Now I think that we have come to something like an understanding," said the highwayman; "now sit up."

The jailor obeyed him without the least opposition.

"Now, off with your coat."

The jailor showed some signs of opposition to this command.

The prisoner, however, made a step towards him, and he hastened to obey him at once.

"That's it, my friend," said Dick; "now your waistcoat—look alive!"

A threatening gesture accompanying this demand at once induced the warder to remove the garment.

"Now your breeches."

The jailor sullenly removed his knee-breeches, and stood shivering in his shirt awaiting the prisoner's further pleasure.

Dick Turpin now began to undress himself, but without once removing his eyes from the warder.

When he had finished he tossed his clothes to the jailor.

"Now, my friend," said he, "you can dress yourself in those."

The man had no choice but to obey.

At the same time the highwayman hastily donned the warder's clothes, still keeping a sharp watch upon his movements.

"Confound these things!" exclaimed the prisoner; "they won't meet; whatever shall I do?"

He tugged as hard as possible at the knee-breeches, but it was with the greatest difficulty that he contrived to make them meet at the waist.

At this instant the warder, who had been casting sheep's-eyes at the door of the cell, sprang to his feet and darted towards it.

"Ha ha!" cried Dick Turpin, bounding after him like a deer.

But the man had already gained the passage.

With a wild bound he fled along, hotly pursued by the alarmed prisoner.

Terror lent wings to the warder, and he seemed to fly.

[RALPH'S FRACAS IN NEWGATE.]

But the same desperation possessed his pursuer.

The highwayman's legs, too, were a trifle longer than his late jailor's, and he speedily shortened the distance between them.

Now he was within half-a-dozen feet of the warder!

The latter heard his pursuer's footsteps close behind him, and with a cry he bounded into the air, and desperately redoubled his exertions.

"Curse the fellow's throat!" muttered Dick Turpin.

Three desperate leaps forward, and the highwayman was beside the warder.

An instant more, and he had dragged him to the ground.

"You have given me a nice trot, my friend," said the highwayman.

He stooped down and raised the jailor in his arms.

Struggle, kick, plunge as he would, the jailor could not offer an effectual resistance to Dick Turpin.

In less time than we can write the words, the warder was borne back to the condemned cell.

"Now," said the highwayman, "I shan't trust you again. Kindness is thrown away upon some people."

Saying which, he proceeded to bind the unfortunate jailor upon the bed with as much speed as possible.

When this was effected he tore off a portion of the coverlid, and hastily fashioned it into a gag.

No. 13.

"You'll stifle me," cried the jailor.

"No matter."

"You'll murder me—I shall choke—have mercy!"

"Nonsense!" said the highwayman; "make your mind easy upon that score, my worthy jailor. I don't want to take your life. I only seek to secure my own. There, you breathe like that. Now, pray remember that I have treated you with all the consideration which your obstinacy permitted. If we had changed places, and you had been making a dash at escape, I think that it is probable Dick Turpin would have been rather more roughly treated by you."

The binding and gagging of the warder being completed, Dick Turpin turned his attention to the window.

During the brief period which had elapsed between the departure of Red Ralph and the jailor, and the return of the latter with the note which the Captain of the Yellow Band had written him, Dick Turpin had commenced experiments upon the bars which guarded the window.

One of them was nearly cut through!

It was a fortunate thing that he had lost no time.

All depended upon a few minutes now, as the reader will presently understand.

He worked away at his file with a will, and a second bar was cut through.

"It's a tough job," he muttered, as he dragged at the bars, endeavouring to loosen them in the sockets.

But they were deeply imbedded in solid masonry.

Perseverance and a powerful arm, however, finally gained the day.

Two of the bars were dragged away, leaving an opening sufficiently large to allow the body of a man to pass through, with a little squeeze.

"Now for the rope."

The highwayman hoisted up his jailor upon the mattrass, and dragged out the coil of rope which the Captain of the Yellow Band had brought with him wound around his body.

This he fastened to the stumps of two of the iron bars, and tugged at it with his whole strength to test its security.

"That's right," said Dick; "it would support a young elephant at a push."

He clambered up to the window, and peered down into the prison yard below.

It was a fearful height, and made the prisoner quite giddy to look at it.

But there was no hesitation in his manner now!

"Good-bye," said the highwayman, gaily; "I hope that we shan't meet again in a hurry, old friend!"

And, nodding jovially to the captive jailor, he pushed through the window.

The next minute he had trusted his body to the mercy of the strong, but certainly not stout-looking rope!

He seemed to have been descending for an hour!

"What was that?"

Something overhead!

Some commotion, certainly.

And in the condemned cell!

The cell from which he had just escaped!

"It grows exciting now," he muttered between his teeth.

The noise above did, indeed, grow alarming.

They must have discovered his absence already.

He let the cord glide faster yet through his hands, until his flesh felt as if on fire.

But his haste was ill-timed!

A jerk had unhooked the rope above, and down it came.

Down, down fell the hapless highwayman with a violent shock.

CHAPTER XXXVI.

QUEER GOINGS-ON IN NEWGATE — THE RUSTY-BROWN GENTLEMAN — JONATHAN WILD AGAIN — THE ALARM-BELL — SOMEBODY AGAIN IN A FIX.

MR. WARREN, the pompous little secretary and deputy of the Governor of Newgate, was in a great flurry of excitement.

The first night of his deputyship had brought some of the most unpleasant and difficult jobs with which a poor deputy-governor could be afflicted.

In the first instance, the Government messenger's singular demeanour and still more singular demand to see the prisoner whose death-warrant he had brought was a great startler.

Then, upon returning to the reception room, he had found the veiled lady fainting upon the floor.

He had raised her, and succeeded in restoring her to consciousness, when he learnt that it was the strange behaviour of the Government messenger which had so alarmed her and caused her to faint away.

Then he sent one of the warders in pursuit of the Government messenger, with instructions to persuade him to return to the deputy-governor.

Care was to be taken not to give offence to the haughty Government messenger, but at all hazards he was to be brought back.

In the course of a few minutes the warder entrusted with the mission returned to acquaint his superior with the result of it, which we have already related.

Then the deputy-governor was thrown into no trifling consternation.

He felt that any way this time he had committed some fearful blunder, and that mischief must result from it.

If the Government messenger was free from blame in the matter of the veiled lady he would undoubtedly resent the insult which had been offered in attempting to detain him by force.

Supposing, upon the other hand, that the veiled lady's statement were true, and that the Government messenger had been guilty of some outrage, would not his failure to secure the ruffian's person be resented by the injured lady?

He was fuming and fretting at the equivocal duties which had been forced upon him when a warder entered and announced a visitor.

"Who is it?"

"Mr. Wild, sir."

"I can't see him to-night."

"He says it is particular business, if you please, sir."

"No matter."

"Concerning the highwayman Dick Turpin."

"No matter, I say: if it concerns twenty highwaymen—forty Dick Turpins,—I can't see Mr. Wild to-night!"

The man departed to carry the message to the thieftaker.

He had barely quitted the room when the door bell of the governor's private entrance was violently rung.

Mr. Warren called back the warder.

"Yes, sir,"

"Go and see who it is, and bring me word immediately."

The man departed, and ran back in a few minutes.

"Who is it?"

"A Government messenger."

"A WHAT?"

"A Government messenger, sir—so he says; he's not in uniform, sir, as far as I could see."

"Then I can't see him to-night. I've had enough of Government messengers for the present."

Before the man could carry this message to the porter at the door a second warder came running along the passage.

"What now?" demanded the deputy-governor, very angry.

"A gentleman wants to see you, sir, if you please."

"Who is he?"

"A government messenger," answered the jailor.

"Hang the Government messengers!" ejaculated the deputy-governor; "I can see no one to-night."

"He says he has something to tell you of the greatest moment."

"But—"

"He insists on seeing you, sir," continued the warder.

"Insists?"

"Ay, sir."

"You're mad, my man."

"No, sir," said the warder; "them's his very words, sir."

"This is strange," said the deputy-governor. "Well, I suppose I must see him; show him in quickly, too, for I am sick of Government messengers, veiled ladies, and of everything else."

The warden ran off, and presently returned, accompanied by the gentleman who called himself a Government messenger.

He was an ordinary-looking individual, very ordinarily dressed in a suit of rusty brown.

"What may be your business with me, sir?" asked the secretary.

"Allow me to preface that by asking a question," said the gentleman in the suit of rusty brown.

"Be quick, then."

"Sir?"

"I say be as quick as convenient because my time is precious, and I wish to retire to rest."

"Very well, sir: then have you received a Government messenger here to-night?"

The secretary looked black as thunder.

"I have."

"You have?" exclaimed the rusty-brown gentleman, starting up; "then I was right in my conjecture. Hang the fellow's impudence!"

"What do you mean?"

"I mean this, sir," replied the visitor; "pray sit down, and allow me to take a seat; my story will take some few minutes to relate."

"Will it?" quoth the deputy-governor drily.

"A few minutes—yes."

"Then we will reserve it until a more convenient opportunity."

"I cannot put it off," said the rusty-brown gentleman in an authoritative tone.

"You cannot?"

"No, sir; I cannot."

"Sir, your presumption is tremendously amusing."

"Enough, sir," said the visitor; "I cannot waste precious moments in idle wrangling; oblige me by remaining silent, and listen to what I have to say."

The secretary looked as if he could have exploded with wrath and indignation.

"You must know," began the rusty-brown visitor, "that a few hours since I was riding hither with a warrant to execute the highwayman Dick Turpin—"

"Who?"

"Dick Turpin."

"Another warrant?" exclaimed the deputy-governor.

"I know not what you mean by another warrant. I say—"

"But, sir," said the perplexed deputy-governor, "I tell you that I have received the warrant you speak of half an hour ago."

"Received it?"

"Yes, yes."

"Then he actually delivered it?"

"He did, of course; but who the deuce is he?"

"The robber—the highwayman who stopped me in the forest glade, robbed me of the warrant, forced me to change clothes, and galloped off and left me in charge of two ruffians in the forest."

"Is it possible?"

"It is indeed, since I tell it you, sir governor."

"Dear, dear!" said the secretary, in trouble again, "I merely put an ordinary question; I meant no offence."

"Sir, I don't take offence so easily; I'm not quite so thin-skinned."

"Certainly, sir."

"When I do," continued the gentleman, whose temper was as rusty as the brown of his apparel, "I take immediate steps to resent it."

"That's just what the other fellow said."

"Who?"

"The man who brought the death-warrant."

"The highwayman?"

"Dear me, yes."

"S'death! but no matter if he has delivered it."

"But that's not all, he has seen the prisoner."

"He has? Then, by Jove, sir, you must look out for squalls. The fellow has the impudence of the Prince of Darkness himself."

The deputy-governor was all upon the alarm for danger, and he now began to anticipate the most desperate things.

His courage, as we have seen, was not great, and he had a wholesome dread of any of the desperate inmates of Newgate being at large in the prison.

He hastily rang a bell, and a warder entered the room.

"Has Mr. Wild left?"

"No, sir; he's waiting until the governor awakes."

"Send him to me."

The next minute Jonathan Wild entered the room.

"So, so, sir," said the thieftaker maliciously, "you are obliged to have resource to my services after all, I find."

"No offence, Mr. Wild," said the deputy-governor, all humility; "but listen to what this gentleman has to say."

"With all my heart," quoth the thieftaker, bowing to the rusty-brown gentleman, who forthwith related his adventure with the highwayman in the forest.

"And was this near the Palmer's Cell?" demanded Wild.

"By the forest glade, I tell you."

"Then, by heaven!" cried the thieftaker, jumping up, "you've had a distinguished visitor, Mr. Warren."

"Who?"

"Red Ralph, the Captain of the Yellow Band!"

"Never! But he has not yet left the place."

"Haha! say you so? Ring the alarm-bell, and shut all the entrances!"

The next instant Newgate was all noise, bustle, and confusion.

CHAPTER XXXVII.

THE RISING WATERS—A FEARFUL STRUGGLE FOR LIFE—THE TRAP—THE IDIOT'S FATE—THE MYSTERIOUS CHAMBER OF DEATH—THE BLOOD-STAINED GARMENTS—THE ONE CHANCE OF ESCAPE—LOST! LOST!—THE FALL.

HIGHER and higher rose the threatening waters upon the hapless Leonore and the imbecile wife of the hunchback

It poured into the room like a miniature cataract, threatening the two shrinking fugitives with instant annihilation.

Now the Lady Leonore, who had taken the initiative all through, both on her own and her companion's account, was forced to relinquish all hopes of escape for the unhappy idiot.

Escape for either seemed a terrible doubt.

For both, by the single exertions of either, escape seemed an utter impossibility.

The Lady Leonore perceived a trap-door in the ceiling, which she immediately began a scramble to reach.

But how to attain her object?

There was not a single object in the place by which she could climb to the ceiling.

True, it was not a lofty room, but some sixteen or eighteen inches divided it from her grasp when stretched to her extreme height.

Had the floor been clean it would have been a matter of no very great difficulty to spring up to it; but the rapidly-rising waters thoroughly impeded her movements.

And now it began to grow alarming!

"Come, come, unhappy creature," exclaimed the Lady Leonore to the companion of her sufferings.

But the woman crouched down in the rising flood, and muttered some low indistinct sounds, apparently comprehending that a great danger existed without understanding the nature of it.

This was the only effort which the Lady Leonore attempted to make upon the poor creature's behalf.

But, although the wife of the hunchback could not offer to aid herself in her great peril, she chanced to afford the Lady Leonore great assistance.

The latter was making frantic efforts to spring up to the ceiling and catch at the handle of the trap when a sudden ray of intelligence appeared to cross the idiot woman, and she sprang forward clutching at the Lady Leonore and jabbering unintelligibly, as if imploring her not to leave her alone to her fate.

"My poor woman," said the Lady Leonore, compassionately, "I cannot aid you; I am as powerless as yourself in this terrible place."

But even as she spoke she perceived a chance of reaching the trap above them.

The dwarf's wife standing by her side gave her an idea that the desired object could be readily accomplished by one raising the other in her arms.

Vainly did Lady Leonore endeavour to impress this upon the poor idiot, who only regarded her with alternate looks of blank astonishment and a meaningless smile.

Time was slipping rapidly on, and the water was rising.

Suddenly Lady Leonore placed one hand upon the idiot's shoulder and sprang upwards.

The aid thus derived accomplished her purpose. The trap-door was reached, and yielded to her touch.

Now she began to entertain hopes of escape once more.

She could reach the bottom of the trap as it swung down, and did not doubt that she should thus be enabled to drag herself through.

Again did the idiot endeavour to drag her back, but Lady Leonore, as quick as lightning, placed her foot upon the idiot's shoulder, dragged herself forward, and—she had clambered through!

As she gained her feet she heard the poor brainless thing fall back with the shock from her foot in springing up.

There was a splash—a choking gurgling sound—and all was still!

The Lady Leonore turned from the trap with a shudder and looked about her.

She now found herself in a small apartment similar in size and shape to that which she had just so fortunately quitted.

Without pausing to examine the contents of this chamber, she cast a searching glance around her for an exit from the room, and her eye alighted upon an iron-barred door upon her left.

In an instant she was trying to undo the fastenings.

With great difficulty she succeeded in shooting back the bolts and unfastening the heavy massive bars which secured the door, but a terrible obstacle to further progress presented itself in the form of a huge lock.

She shook and tugged at the door, but it resisted her utmost efforts.

She glanced about her for some weapon wherewith to prise open the door.

Close at hand, a huge crowbar lay upon the ground, as if placed there by Lady Leonore's good genius for her special service at the present critical juncture.

The difficulty of using this weighty and formidable instrument was conquered by her perseverance and terror.

The point of the crowbar inserted in the small aperture by the lock, and the weight of the instrument did the rest, with trifling exertion upon her part.

The door yielded with a crash that sent the blood to the fugitive's face!

Before entering the room, she paused an instant upon the threshold, to see if the noise she had created in her progress had alarmed any inhabitants of the house.

But all was silent.

She stepped on to find herself in a bed-chamber, the first glance of which sent a thrill of terror through her body.

Everything in the room was in great disorder, and many appearances told a tale of blood and violence!

The bed was tumbled and the clothes bloodstained.

Clinging to the coverlid was an ivory-handled stiletto, the blade of which was snapped off halfshort, and rusty with human gore!

Hanging over chairs were many articles of female apparel of the richest materials, several of which denoted that their unfortunate possessor had been the victim of the assassin's steel.

A richly brocaded dress of white satin was spotted with blood, and a murderous cut in the body told how the wearer of the dress had met her fate.

Lady Leonore gazed upon those objects half-wild with fright.

Everything about her inspired her with awe, and there was a fearful stillness in the place, which spoke of death.

The very atmosphere seemed thick and foul with murder!

For a while her spirit seemed held down—her energies cramped with terror. The awe of the presence of death was upon her, and she felt momentarily spell-bound in that scene of murder.

Presently rousing herself to the sense of her present danger, she managed to shake off these terrifying thoughts, and to look about her for the means of flight from the chamber of death.

In her movements she came upon a treasure which had hitherto escaped her notice.

Upon the table, prominent enough in the objects about, lay a number of rich and costly jewels, probably, she thought, the property of the owner of the blood-stained garments.

With the sight of these precious trinkets came the desire to possess them.

Not, indeed, any desire to enjoy the possession of an assassin's plunder; but might they not purchase freedom and safety for her ?

She hastily secured them about her person, and made for the door of the room.

This, like every mode of entrance or egress which she had met with, was secured by bolt and lock.

But the crowbar which had gained her an entrance into the bed-chamber secured her a safe exit from it.

The door forced open, a flight of stairs presented itself, down which she ran rapidly towards the street-door.

As yet she had met no one in her progress—not even heard the sound of human voice, and yet she felt assured that the house was inhabited.

The door was locked, bolted, and barred by a dozen fastenings of immense force *upon the inside!*

These were rapidly removed, but still the door was secure—immoveable!

What could it mean?

Was it possible that it was locked both inside and out?

Somebody must yet remain in the house.

The thought of coming across any one did not at all tend to reassure her, and she redoubled her exertions to force open the door.

No wall was ever more firm, however, than the massive portal before; she might as well have used her efforts against solid masonry.

With a sigh she relinquished her labourious task, and began to retrace her footsteps towards the chamber she had quitted.

Every natural egress seemed closed to her, and but one means remained—the window!

It was a desperate venture, but the only chance that remained to her of freedom—possibly of life!

She threw up the window and looked out into the darkness.

Beyond a few feet from the window nothing was visible, and it was with no very agreeable sensations that Lady Leonore contemplated trusting herself to the mercy of a cord, or whatever she should chance to find, by which she meditated effecting her flight from the window.

But there remained to her no time to indulge in nervous fancies.

She tore the coverlid from the bed with averted eyes and proceeded to fasten it to the window frame.

This done, she ventured through the window, grasping the sheet with the tenacity of a drowning man.

As she slipped downwards her flesh came in contact with some portions of the sheet which were stiff with blood, and a shudder thrilled through her entire body.

No girlish qualms, however, could stand in her way at this extremity, and onward she went to liberty.

Presently she reached the end of the coverlid, and her feet hung downwards without a resting-place!

"Great heavens!" murmured the poor girl in terror, "the sheet is not long enough! I am lost!"

To add to the great terror of this critical moment, the sound of a footstep within the house reached her.

What could it mean?

Had a pursuit commenced?

Had the abstraction of the jewels been discovered, and were the assassins of their original possessor upon her track!

As these thoughts flashed through her excited brain her cheek grew pale and she turned faint.

The footsteps grew more audible.

She must drop.

Better, far better, to take the only remaining chance of escape that presented itself than await an almost certain death by the murderer's knife!

With a half-murmured prayer for preservation, she resigned herself to the mercy of Providence.

The sheet slid through her hands and she fell downwards!

CHAPTER XXXVIII.

LEONORE STUNNED AND BRUISED — HOUSELESS AND FRIENDLESS — THE LONELY INN — THE BRUTAL LANDLORD—MYSTERIOUS WHISPERS—THE DRUGGED WINE—A NIGHT OF TERROR—THE ATTEMPTED MURDER—THE YOUNG GIRL'S VENGEANCE.

THE distance which Lady Leonore fell from the window did not certainly exceed three feet, and yet she slipped and stumbled, half stunned, to the ground.

Rising as soon as she was able to her feet, she drew her scanty garment around her and crawled onwards.

Bruised and shaken by her fall; faint, weary, and almost naked; she knew not where to turn for assistance.

She did not dare to beg a cup of water in the village to quench her parched lips.

The most intense sufferings seldom make the unhappy wretch who suffers altogether reckless of life, and it is scarcely to be wondered at that the fair fragile Lady Leonore turned in her agony from the dwellings of the fiends who had sought her destruction at the faggot.

No! On, on, on she must push to some more humane quarter.

Her forlorn condition must certainly inspire the most flinty-hearted with compassion and pity.

To add to her bodily torments, she endured the most exquisite mental agony, for, to a pure spirit like hers, the very fact of being in the broad open world alone, unprotected, and her shivering limbs but half covered, was the most profound and humiliating suffering.

One thought now alone occupied her mind.

Could she but contrive to convert into money the jewels which she had found in the deserted house, she might purchase garments.

Then, oh, how trifling would be her difficulties! Indeed, she looked forward to this as the termination of her sufferings.

But how? Where to accomplish this? If she attempted to sell those jewels, would she not probably be suspected of having come by them unlawfully? And what troubles might then not accrue to her?

Should she be prosecuted for being in possession of the property of the slain, how should she defend herself?

Who would give credence to her wild and improbable tale?

But she did not pause to meditate upon her danger and difficulties. On, on she pressed, not knowing—scarcely caring—whither she went, so that she put miles between herself and the village in which she had been so cruelly maltreated.

The weary distance she wandered ere she came in sight of human habitation—the fatigue, cold, and suffering she endured—are beyond description.

Presently she fancied she perceived in the distance a faint flickering light, and, buoyed up with the hope of obtaining relief and rest, she sped onwards, with renewed courage and vigour.

Yes! there was hope for her once more; she had found an asylum for the night.

The spot from which the light glimmered was a roadside public-house which was yet open, notwithstanding the untimely hour.

She knocked faintly upon the door twice or thrice before any notice was taken of her summons, and then a gruff voice rudely demanded her wishes.

"Shelter," said the shivering Leonore in reply.

"No shelter here unless you can pay for it."

"I can and will pay anything you require," urged Leonore.

"Then, that's a very different matter," said the voice.

The door was immediately unbarred, and the weary fugitive was admitted into a sorry cheerless-looking habitation, the aspect of which did not at all tend to raise her drooping spirits.

By the side of a dying fire, in a wretchedly tumble-down chimney, was a broken bench.

A deal table, not over clean, stood in the centre of the room, and upon either side of it were two rush-bottomed chairs, apparently not long vacated.

This was the whole furniture of the place, upon which was fixed the unmistakable seal of squalid misery.

The landlord of this apology for a tavern was a huge ruffianly-looking fellow, who scowled desperately from a ferocious pair of ferrety eyes, nearly hidden beneath his lowering beetle brows.

"Hullo !" he exclaimed, gazing in surprise upon the half-naked shrinking object before him, "what on earth are you about at this time of the night ?"

"I want shelter and food," stammered Lady Leonore.

"Shelter and food—"

"Yes, I can pay for all I have of you ; indeed I can."

"Of course you can," said the man, with a coarse brutal laugh, "or else you will get deuced little out of me, I can tell you."

Lady Leonore shrunk back affrightedly.

"You ain't too well covered up neither, my gal," said the landlord, coarsely.

Leonore shrunk still further off, and coloured to the temples as she drew her thin garment around her shivering limbs.

The fellow noticed the action and the poor girl's embarrassment, but was not disposed to allow her to avoid the disagreeables of her position.

He commented freely upon her appearance, until the poor girl rose up, and indignantly silenced him.

"You are insolent !" she exclaimed, her eye flashing fire : "I come here as a customer, and not to listen to your insulting words. If you are inclined to entertain me, attend to my wants at once : if not, I will be gone at once."

"Certainly—oh ! of course, yes," said the man, all humility at once. "No offence, I'm sure."

"Enough !" said Lady Leonore ; "get me some refreshment."

"Yes, ma'am."

And the man bustled out of the room.

When he was gone Lady Leonore began to look about her to ascertain the nature of the house into which chance had directed her steps.

The effrontery of the man, now that she meditated upon it, alarmed her more than it had insulted her.

She feared the worst from his bold demeanour. There was something in it more than was apparent.

The dangers undergone of late by Lady Leonore had so sharpened her wits that now to suspect danger was to be upon her guard against it.

In glancing around the room her eye rested upon a small object which lay upon the floor, beneath the broken bench.

She stooped to possess herself of it, and found, as she had suspected, that it was a knife—a short-bladed weapon, with a large black-horn handle—apparently a dinner knife, of which the back had grown as sharp as the edge, by long service.

The dagger-shape which it had assumed gave Lady Leonore a shock, and she hastily concealed it in her sleeve.

"Here is your supper, ma'am," said a low voice.

A woman bearing a small tray had noiselessly entered the room.

"You—you have brought it ?" stammered Leonore.

"Yes, this is it. What have you dropped ?"

"Dropped ? Oh ! nothing—nothing—my handkerchief. I have it, thank you."

The woman merely nodded her head gravely and turned to leave.

"Have you a bedroom for me ?" demanded Lady Leonore, anxious to detain the woman in conversation awhile.

"Yes."

And she walked on towards the door.

"Stay a moment," said Leonore ; "will you return to conduct me to it ?

"Yes."

"I would prefer your attendance to—to *his*."

"My husband's ?"

"Yes ; he is your husband, then ? "

"Yes, ma'am."

Lady Leonore felt considerably relieved at these words. She now could fear no molestation at the landlord's hands whilst his wife was present.

The woman, evidently thinking that there was no further need for her services, was again about to leave the room when Leonore looked for something further to detain her.

"You—stay—you have brought me nothing to drink."

"No ; what do you wish for ?"

"Can I have some wine ?"

The woman looked at her surprised, but made no reply.

"Did you hear me ? "

"Yes," answered the woman ; "but (you mustn't mind the question) can you pay for wine ? "

"Of course," said Leonore, the blood rushing to her face, "or else I should not ask for it."

The woman again nodded her head in that grave manner which so puzzled Leonore, but never offered to stir.

"You see that I can repay you for everything," said Leonore rather angrily, "your trouble included."

She produced the jewels which she had concealed upon her person.

"Certainly, ma'am, certainly," said the man, appearing at the door ; "you can have anything you please. Why didn't you get the lady wine, wife ? "

The woman again nodded her head in assent, and quitted the room without a word.

As Lady Leonore glanced up her eyes met those of the landlord, which were fixed upon her, twinkling with cupidity.

He turned away confusedly, and hastily followed his wife from the room.

"You shall have the wine directly, ma'am," he muttered.

Lady Leonore began to entertain some serious misgivings.

She felt that she had committed an unpardonable imprudence in showing the rich prize of which she was possessed.

"Fool, fool !" she murmured half aloud ; "I fear my indiscretion has led me into trouble here ; that glance as he left meant mischief. I must be upon my guard."

Faint and weary as she had previously felt, she pushed the food from her almost untasted. The new alarm had quite destroyed her appetite.

A footstep—a faint shuffling sound—struck upon her ear, and she leaned over the table appearing to eat.

It was the landlord returned with the wine.

As he drew near the table she could hear that the bottle was being violently shaken behind her.

A horrid wild suspicion flitted across her mind, and she made a mental resolve not to drink of the wine.

"You can put it down," said Leonore ; "I will call when I want your wife."

"Very well," growled the landlord.

There was something in Lady Leonore's manner which smacked of the habit of command and at the same time compelled obedience. He left the room at once.

"What do I dread here?" Leonore asked herself; "alas! I know not. My fears are of the vaguest description. I cannot say to myself even what form they assume. This wine, let me be right or wrong, I am determined not to touch. The manner of these people inspires me with dread—an indefinite sort of terror. I am sadly alone and helpless. To the all-seeing care of Providence I must resign myself, trusting for a merciful release from the peril which awaits me."

As she murmured these fears half aloud her eyes wandered restlessly about the room, and she thought seriously more than once of making a rush from the house.

To accomplish this it was necessary to remove the door fastenings, which was not to be done without creating much noise and clatter.

This would speedily bring the people of the house upon her, and probably give the brutal landlord an excuse for open violence.

No, she must remain and see what the night would bring forth.

In order not to arouse in the landlord's mind any notion that she suspected treachery, she poured some of the wine into the glass, and, after watching that there was no one near to observe her, sprinkled it under the table and over the ashes in the fire-place.

A whitish sediment which remained in the tumbler more than confirmed her half-formed suspicions.

The wine was drugged!

This discovery that her fears were so well founded only increased her agitation, and at every faint sound she started and trembled, whilst a deathly pallor overspread her countenance.

Anything to put an end to this killing suspense and anticipation!

She called the woman, to be shown to her bedroom.

The words had barely quitted her lips when the woman glided into the room with that same quiet stealthy step which had so startled her before.

Where had she sprung from? Was it possible that they could have been watching her movements from some unseen corner?

"Will you show me to my bedchamber?" said Lady Leonore.

The woman nodded in her characteristic fashion.

"Have you finished supper?"

"Yes."

"Then I can take it away; you will have the wine saved for you?"

Lady Leonore felt that this was thrown out as a feeler, and she merely nodded her head in the woman's manner, not trusting herself to reply.

The landlady then looked gravely round, and motioned Leonore to follow, by grimly bending her head.

As they passed to the stairs Leonore heard a faint scuffling sound, and upon glancing around her perceived a dark object moving about in a still darker recess to her right.

"Stand off!" said the woman. "It is the lady—she is going to her room."

The shadowy form retreated, and was lost in the darkness of the recess.

"What is that?" demanded Lady Leonore.

"My husband—he thought that it was me alone."

Leonore was by no means satisfied, although silenced by this reply. She could not help thinking that some immediate outrage had been in contemplation.

The recess alluded to was close beside the door of the room in which Lady Leonore had been taking her supper, and she began to fear that they had been watching her movements from there.

At any rate it explained their sudden appearance as she called for them.

The woman led her upstairs to a meagrely furnished bedroom, of a dull forbidding aspect, the window of which was cross-barred with stout iron bars!

"Here is a light!" said the woman.

"One moment," said Leonore: "can you furnish me with any clothing? I can pay for it, you know."

"I have nothing; here is an old dress of mine, which you are welcome to. I can let you have some more clothing in the morning."

"I would have preferred it to-night," said Leonore.

"Impossible!" said the woman, drily; "you shall have them before you see me in the morning."

And with this promise she was forced to content herself.

She could not help fancying that there was a hidden significance in the words the woman uttered as she left the room.

Was it possible that she should be destined never to see that morrow to which the woman alluded?

Then, the first thing to which she gave her attention was the door. This was furnished with a lock and two small bolts, so that she was enabled, she thought, to secure herself from intrusion.

Still, she could not make up her mind to sleep in such a state of uncertainty, although her eyes were heavy, and she would have given much to slumber in security.

She made a close investigation of the apartment, but the only mode of entrance which presented itself was the door which she had secured.

And yet a certain something seemed to whisper her a caution against venturing to sleep.

She accepted it as ominous, and resolved to struggle against fatigue until the night had passed. With this idea, she drew to the bedside the only chair which the room boasted, and seated herself in it.

For upwards of twenty minutes she sat thus, making a desperate effort to shake off the drowsiness which oppressed her.

Not a sound was heard; all was silent as before; and yet she did not feel satisfied.

"If they thought of molesting me," she thought, "they would put off an attempt whilst I had a light burning."

The first step was, therefore, to extinguish the candle. This done, she reseated herself in the chair, and breathed very heavily, that any listener might be impressed with an idea that she slept.

She had resolved to try this experiment as a last resource, and then, if no attempt were made, to retire and rest her wearied spirit.

For she would then have settled it within her own mind that she had been mistaken altogether—that the mysterious movements of the host and hostess were simply the imaginations of her over-heated fancy.

But in the space of a few minutes a sharp click in the wall caused her heart to stand still.

She held her breath, and listened in terror for the sound to be repeated!

All was silent from the spot whence the sound had come, but a low, dull, grating sound succeeded it, coming apparently from *beneath the floor!*

"Was it possible," she asked herself, "that they were about to effect an entrance through the floor?"

Another instant, and a phenomenon more startling than anything which she had yet seen in her journey of terrors made itself apparent.

The bed against which she leaned, and in which she was doubtless supposed to be sleeping—was moving!

She could scarcely believe the evidence of her senses at first.

But a minute—nay, less —served to convince her of the startling reality of he. surmise, for, from an almost upright posture in wh ich she had been sitting, she found herself nearly lying upon the bed !

She stretched out her hand and pushed herself off as the bed gave a jerk and fairly revolved.

Had she been in it she must have been precipitated into a frightful-looking chasm beneath, of which she caught a faint glimpse as the bedstead was displaced.

This, then, was the fearful mystery of the house, of which a kind of instinct had happily warned Lady Leonore ! The unfortunate traveller was lured into this place, and in the dead of the night was slaughtered in cold blood. His tomb that frightful well beneath the bedroom floor !

Lady Leonore breathed a silent acknowledgment for her merciful preservation from this new peril, and quietly awaited the next movement of her murderous host and hostess.

She had not now long to wait, for at the expiration of five minutes she heard the landlord's shuffling footsteps on the landing outside her door, and the handle was tried.

Had he discovered that his intended victim had escaped the trap set for her ?

Had he come for the purpose of accomplishing the work which his hellish machinery had failed to fulfil ?

In the meantime the bedstead had righted itself, and was in the same position it had held when she had been shown into the room.

The instant after the handle of the door was tried the lock was turned.

They, then, possessed a duplicate key !

Still more strange—the two bolts which Lady Leonore had shot were drawn back from without !

The critical moment was arriving. Courage ! courage ! Lady Leonore !

She felt now that she must be prepared for any emergency.

She still possessed the knife which she had found beneath the bench in the room below, and this she grasped, determined to sell her life dearly.

Grasping it firmly, she stepped up to the bedside and drew one of the curtains around her, as the door was opened, and the ferocious landlord entered the room.

With his catlike stealthy tread he advanced towards the bed, brushing the terrified girl's skirts as he passed.

He flashed the light of a bull's-eye lantern around him, and she could perceive by his actions that he was searching for something which he was greatly chagrined and disappointed at not finding.

"Confound the wench !" he muttered between his clenched teeth ; "she never took them into the bed with her ? If she has I shall have a nice job to get them out of the lime ! "

Out of the lime ?

The well into which Lady Leonore would have fallen had she remained upon the bed was, then, filled with quicklime to destroy the body of the slaughtered victim.

To what a den of infamy had she not strayed !

The object of his visit Lady Leonore now well knew must be the jewels which she had so imprudently shown to his wife.

He proceeded to search the room minutely, but, fortunately, up to the present had not touched upon the spot where Lady Leonore stood, breathless and motionless, concealed by the bed curtain.

Presently he again muttered a few words respecting the missing treasure which caused Leonore the most lively apprehensions.

"Curse the girl !" muttered the ruffian, "she must have taken them to bed with her after all. I must see after them there. If they are not there, nothing remains but the lime, and ugh ! hang me ! if I like the thoughts of it."

With this he advanced to the bedside and leaned over close by Lady Leonore, dragging the clothes aside to search for the jewels.

Now, Leonore, is your chance for liberty and life ! No feminine qualms must stay your hand now.

Strike deep, and rid the world of a ruffian and a pest to society !

As the assassin leaned over the bed in his search for the missing treasure he presented a huge back to the trembling girl's avenging knife.

Nor did she pause.

Raising it high above her head, she brought it down with such force as to bury it up to the hilt between his giant shoulders !

The most subdued groan !

A slight tremor of the bedstead, and all was over !

The murderer-landlord would never prey upon his fellow-creatures more !

CHAPTER XXXIX.

SCENES IN NEWGATE—THE CONDEMNED CELL—JONATHAN WILD AND THE JAILORS — ONE'S AFRAID AND THE OTHER DAREN'T—CONFUSION —THE ESCAPE—GROANS—THE DISCOVERY.

WITH his wonted astute perception, Jonathan Wild at once pierced the incognito of the Captain of the Yellow Band.

And that, too, without having seen him, but simply judging from descriptions received.

The thieftaker had no sooner proclaimed his opinion that the first Government messenger was no other than Red Ralph, the leader of the bold Yellow Band, than the alarm-bells of the prison were set ringing, and messengers were hurried off in every direction.

Men were sent to every outlet.

Orders were issued that no one should pass out of the building.

Jonathan Wild hastened from the room, and summoned three of his men who were in attendance.

"Now," said he, "where's Matthews ?"

"Not here," answered one of the warders present.

"Who will conduct us, then, to the condemned cell ?"

"I can do that," said the jailor who had answered before.

"Lead on, then."

The first thing to confirm the thieftaker's suspicions upon arriving at the condemned cell was to find the door unbarred and unlocked !

"Here's something wrong !" he said, hesitating to open the door.

He scarcely liked the idea of being the first to venture into the cell.

More than one instance was known to him of a prisoner dashing out his jailor's brains with his iron manacles.

What if the prisoner should be upon the other side of the door, ready to spring upon them ?

Ugh ! the thought was decidedly unpleasant.

Dick Turpin, too, being possessed of more than ordinary strength, and probably at the present time with more than ordinary ferocity, it was just such an exploit as he would be likely to perform.

"Open the door," said Wild to one of his men.

The man hesitated.

"What are you waiting for, idiot ?" said Jonathan Wild, savagely.

"I'm waiting to follow you in, Mr. Wild," replied the man.

"Ass ! I tell you to go first."

The man grinned uncomfortably to his comrades.

[DICK TURPIN'S ESCAPE FROM NEWGATE.]

"You rascal!" exclaimed the thieftaker, "I'll teach you to mock me. Open the door, I say."

"I shall not."

"So so! mutiny!" said the thieftaker.

The man would not reply, but simply showed his positive refusal by walking back a few paces from the door and making a sullen halt.

"Coward!" said the thieftaker, now thoroughly enraged.

"You don't seem over plucky yourself, Mr. Wild."

This quite nettled his superior, who, although perfectly unscrupulous, was not deficient in courage, and was wonderfully tenacious of a reputation for bravery, which he had contrived to establish.

No. 14.

Without another word, therefore, he pushed open the door and walked boldly into the condemned cell.

All this discussion, however, had given the highwayman time.

"Asleep, are you?" said the thieftaker, perceiving, as he imagined, the prisoner in bed.

Dick Turpin had taken the precaution, before taking to the window, to fasten his jailor securely upon the bed, and then he had covered him with the counterpane, so that the cords which held him were not visible.

The coverlid was drawn up to the man's nose, and the gag was perfectly hidden.

At a first glance, therefore, the thieftaker and his men were naturally enough deceived.

A few steps nearer the bed, and Jonathan Wild perceived that the face was not that of the sturdy highwayman Dick Turpin.

"Hullo!"

But the jailor, for very good reasons, did not reply.

"Hullo!" repeated the thieftaker; "who are you, then?"

"He's gagged."

"Gagged!" iterated the astounded Jonathan Wild.

"That's it—precisely."

To drag off the counterpane and disclose the thongs and ropes which held the jailor prisoner, was but the work of an instant.

"*Matthews !*"

The luckless jailer could only reply by a lamentable roll of the eye.

"Cut the ropes," said Wild. "Release him—double quick."

The men cut the ropes which bound the jailor, and in the space of a few seconds set him free.

"By the window," gasped the jailor, as soon as the gag was removed.

"How did he do it?"

"He had a coil of rope hidden under the bed."

"How could he have got that in here?" asked one of the men.

"Red Ralph," suggested Jonathan Wild.

"Who?" asked Matthews, the jailor, not a little astonished.

"Red Ralph—the man who came here to visit the prisoner."

"But he has had no visitors—that is only one."

"The Government messenger, you mean?" said Jonathan Wild.

"Yes."

"That was he."

"What! Red Ralph?"

"Yes; the Captain of the Yellow Band. But where is he?"

"Gone!"

"Left the building?"

"Yes."

"Are you sure?"

"Certain: I let him out."

"And how came you in such a miserable plight as this?"

"Dick Turpin had managed to slip his fetters."

"By Red Ralph's aid, of course," said the thieftaker.

"Possibly. Well, just before he got to the West gate, he wrote a few words on a slip of paper."

"For what purpose?"

"To give to the prisoner.

"But how could he get them to him?"

"By me!"

"What!" thundered Jonathan Wild; "do you mean to say that you were fool enough to carry a note to a prisoner?"

"I read it first."

"What of that? They could mean a thousand things in a few cant words, which you wouldn't be able to see through."

"Oh!" said the jailor, "there was nothing upon the note to excite any doubt at all."

"Of course not. It wasn't calculated to excite suspicion—more likely to allay it."

"Here's the very note," said Matthews, as his eye lighted upon a paper lying on the ground.

Jonathan Wild pounced upon it and eagerly ran through its contents.

"There's not much here," he said, after vainly endeavouring to twist into something mysterious the admonitory epistle which Red Ralph had sent to Dick Turpin as a blind.

"I told you so."

"Stay. What's this?"

He turned it over, and endeavoured to trace some strange unintelligible scribbling upon the back of the back of the paper.

"Can you make anything of it?"

"Not I; but I know that Dick Turpin could. It's written in cypher. He knows a dozen different secret alphabets and handwritings. I'd give something to be able to make out this one."

"Will you let me see it, Mr. Wild," said one of the men.

"Here it is, Harris," said the thieftaker; "do you think that you can make it out?"

The man took the paper and studied it attentively for a few seconds before he spoke.

"Do you make anything of it?" demanded Wild.

"I see that he speaks of the jailor in it."

"Hah !"

"Yes; I can scarcely understand, but I rather fancy that he says ' change with the jailor !' "

"Change with the jailor?" repeated Jonathan Wild.

"Yes; I'm sure those are the words, but I can't understand it."

"I do, though!" exclaimed Matthews, the jailor, suddenly; "it means, change clothes. I see it all now."

"See what?"

"The note, the note—the meaning of it all—fool! fool !"

"I'm glad of that, at least," said Jonathan Wild.

"But he will be able to pass in my dress. Let's see after him quick, quick !"

"One moment more," said Jonathan Wild. "How did he get out of window?"

"By a rope, I told you."

"You are wrong."

"How so?"

"There is no rope here now, and it would still be hanging here if he had really escaped that way."

This seemed inexplicable.

The explanation of it, however, was simple enough, as we have already shown.

Half-way down upon his perilous descent, the fugitive highwayman, alarmed by the voice above him, had suddenly increased his speed; the jerk had slipped the rope off the iron bar, and it had fallen with him to the ground.

"He can't have got out here," said Jonathan Wild; "there's no means of escape, and it's a fearful height."

Aided by one of his men, he clambered up to the window and looked down into the prison yard.

Dick Turpin and rope had both disappeared.

Whether he had contrived to effect his escape we have yet to learn.

"You must be mistaken," said Jonathan Wild: "he cannot possibly have got that way."

But the jailor persisted in the statement he had made about the rope.

However, such was Jonathan Wild's influence in the prison that even his surmise had more weight than the jailor's evidence.

"Then, how *can* he have got away, Mr. Wild?" asked the jailor.

"I should say that he has managed to avoid us in one of the passages."

"That's no great conclusion," sneered the warder, angrily, at having his assertion controverted : "if he ain't got out of window, and he's got somewhere else, he must be in one of the passages. Why, there's not another place to go to."

"No matter," said the thieftaker; "we have already wasted too much time in idle discussion. Let us begin the hunt in right real earnest."

Saying which, he led the way into the passage, and made immediate and active steps in the proposed search.

"We must divide," said Jonathan Wild, "and go on different tacks, all of us."

The thieftaker hastily pointed out one of the labyrinth of passages which he had mentally devoted as his own field of operations.

Then he gave his men the necessary instructions, and they separated in all directions.

Of course they met with a disastrous failure.

Disastrous because, had they lost no time here, but departed at once to the prison yard, in all probability Dick Turpin would by this time have been safely reinstated in the condemned cell—more heavily ironed than ever.

They had been some time engaged in this search, when the folly of not giving attention to the prison yard at the same time occurred to Jonathan Wild, and he called one of his confidential men to him.

"You must continue the search here," said the thieftaker, "whilst I see to the yard."

Then, accompanied by several of the warders, the thieftaker made his way to the prison yard.

Presently, arriving at one of the prison doors, which had received from the prisoners its ill-sounding appellation, they called the warder who was on duty there.

"Has any one gone out here?" demanded Wild.

"No, Mr. Wild."

"I mean within the last hour."

"No one."

"That's all right, then," said Wild. "Has any one attempted to pass out here?"

"Yes."

"Who?"

"One of the men."

"A warder?"

"Yes, Mr. Wild."

"Hah! how long since?"

"About twenty minutes."

"Did he seem much hurried?"

"Not particularly."

"Did he press you much about going out?"

"Oh! yes; he insisted upon passing out."

"And you refused?"

"Yes, Mr. Wild; the alarm-bell had rung, and I know my duty."

"And what did he do when he found you wouldn't let him pass?"

"Do, sir?"

"Yes, yes—what did he say? Answer, my man, for moments are precious now; a prisoner has managed to escape to some part of the yard in a jailor's uniform. We are endeavouring to find him. This man, I am convinced, was he."

"It's very likely, Mr. Wild," answered the jailor, "for I remember that his face was strange to me; and although I can't of course know every one personally, I remember most of their faces."

"What plea did he urge for wanting to go out?"

"Private business for the governor."

"Then, what made you refuse to let him through?"

"I knew more about the governor than he appeared to. He didn't seem aware that the governor was ill."

"Dear, dear!" exclaimed Jonathan Wild, anxious to find some cause for complaint: "why didn't you secure him?"

"I had no right to."

"Since you suspected him—"

"But I have no authority to arrest every man I suspect."

"Then, you should make the authority, you fool!"

"If I arrested every man I suspected, Mr. Wild, retorted the warder, "you wouldn't be long here."

"Oh, indeed!" said the thieftaker, scowling viciously upon the man; "say you so? Then I must look after you."

The jailor only smiled the threat.

"Laugh on," said Wild; "but when you talk about arresting true servants of the king when in pursuit of a traitor your own honesty must be suspected; nay, it *is* suspected—"

"By whom?"

"By me."

"Ha! ha!"

"It is my opinion that you have connived at this Dick Turpin's escape."

"Dick Turpin?"

"Yes."

"No, no," said several of the warders, who were standing around the disputants, "you're wrong, Mr. Wild."

"If I'm wrong," said the thieftaker, "how has the prisoner managed to effect his escape? Answer that."

The opinion of Jonathan Wild had always great weight with the authorities.

The jailor and his own men began to glance at each other, and then at the door-keeper.

"Wait a bit, Mr. Wild," said the warder. "How can you say that I've aided his escape?"

"Because you admit he was here."

"And that he couldn't pass."

"So you say."

"But if you believe part of my statement you must believe the whole of it."

He turned appealingly to the men, who murmured their assent.

"Besides," continued the jailor, following up his advantage, "how do you know that he has escaped yet, Mr. Wild?"

"Know it? Of course I know," said Wild, savagely.

"Then as you are so positive about his movements it seems that there are greater grounds for suspecting you than me."

Several of the jailors began to smile, which thoroughly enraged the thieftaker.

Jonathan saw that the man was too quick-witted for him to gain anything in an argument, and with a final curse he quitted the spot.

Several of his men followed him immediately, but his flight was so sudden and so rapid that they failed to keep him in sight.

"Which way did he go?" said one of the men.

"Straight ahead!"

The prison yard was so badly lighted and the night was so dark and misty that they could see nothing a dozen yards in front of them.

They ran on, but, failing to come up with the thieftaker, they paused, and held a hurried consultation.

"He must have returned to the prison," suggested one.

"What shall we do, then?" demanded another.

"Search on alone."

At this moment a dull sound reached them, as if from some heavy falling body!

The men started simultaneously.

"What was that?"

"Something wrong."

"Where?"

"In which direction?"

The sound had been so slight that they could not catch the direction from which it came.

The next moment, however, these doubts were satisfied.

A faint cry reached them.

A low wail of pain!

A note of suffering; slight, almost inaudible, but withal eloquent of anguish!

Greatly startled at the sound, the men, without a word, ran off in the direction from whence it came.

One of the men in advance stumbled and fell over a projecting substance upon the ground

His comrades stooped to raise him up, and found that he had tripped over the prostrate form of a man.

The men picked the body from the ground, and bore it to an adjacent oil-lamp.

"My!" ejaculated one of these men; "it's Mr. Wild!"

"Lor! so it is Mr. Wild! And ain't he bleeding, just!"

CHAPTER XL.

DICK TURPIN'S EXTRAORDINARY ESCAPE FROM NEWGATE — HIS STRUGGLE WITH JONATHAN WILD — THE ALARM—THE CHASE — THE ENCOUNTER WITH THE WATCH — THE HACKNEY COACH — THE HIGHWAYMAN KIDNAPPED — DRIVE FOR YOUR LIFE!

BUT where has the prisoner himself got to by this time?

As we have already shown, the search of Jonathan Wild and his myrmidons has proved fruitless.

A lamentable failure!

Lamentable, indeed, to the thieftaker himself, as we have seen.

But to explain how this has come about.

When we left Dick Turpin, he had fallen with the rope by which he was effecting his descent from the condemned cell—fallen heavily to the ground.

And this from a considerable height; so considerable, in fact, that it is little short of a miracle that he was not dashed to pieces.

But Dick Turpin would appear to possess the feline plurality of lives.

He was a big man, and, although slimly made for his height, was very weighty, and yet he managed a fall of fifteen or twenty feet without any very serious damage.

Half-way down he bumped against a projection in the wall.

This gathered him a few slight bruises, and shook him a great deal, but at the same time it served to break his fall.

And he reached the ground upon his feet.

"Pheugh!" he muttered, as he shook himself together; "that was a narrow squeak!"

Then his first thought was to see that he had no broken bones, for his limbs were so numbed with his fall for several minutes that he was by no means assured of this until he had examined his legs and arms.

"Fortune favours the bold!" he muttered, exultingly; "and, by all that's fortunate! here's the rope come down with me. This will very likely prove of great service to me."

Indeed it did, as we shall show!

He gathered up the rope in his arms, and began to look about him.

"This dark night will rather hinder my success now, I fear," said Dick Turpin to himself. "So far it has rather aided me, it is true. If I could only see the gate, now. Wherever can it be? I did know it. But my fall has quite upset me. Let me see. It must be this way."

He groped his way along in the dark for some distance, without any signs of the gate he sought.

At length, however, his perseverance was rewarded by seeing at some little distance ahead the faint glimmer of a lamp.

"Victory!" exclaimed the prisoner hopefully. "Now I may consider myself free indeed."

But he scarcely believed the words he uttered. It was too much to hope that escape could be so easy a matter.

One of the warders was standing at the door, as Dick Turpin came to a standstill in front of it.

"Good night!"

"Going out so late?" said the warder.

"Yes; private job for the governor," replied the prisoner.

And with this Dick Turpin endeavoured to pass on.

But the warder was loquaciously inclined, and not disposed to part so shortly with one who was making a welcome break in the terrible monotony of his night post.

"Stop a bit," said the warder: "how is it that the governor is sending you out at this hour?"

"I can't say; and what's more," said Dick, petulantly—"it is not my business. He sends me on an errand, and I'm only to go."

"Well, you needn't lose your temper over it," said the warder: "I only made a simple remark."

The man prepared to unfasten the door.

The fugitive felt his heart beat quicker and quicker.

The turning of a key was all that remainded between himself and liberty!

The key was in the lock. The warder applying both hands to turn it.

"The old lock is as rusty as it can be," grumbled the warder. "Confound it! it won't turn."

As he was about to renew his efforts to turn it the alarm-bell in the building was rang.

Ding, dong, its warning notes rang out a death-knell to poor Dick Turpin's hopes.

The warder listened a second, and then withdrew the key from the lock and carefully replaced the many fastenings to the door.

"What are you about there?" demanded Dick Turpin, quite alarmed at what he saw.

"That's settled the matter."

"What?"

"The alarm-bell."

"You'll surely let me pass."

"Not to-night."

"I tell you, you must."

"Nonsense!" said the warder, with aggravating deliberation; "don't you know what that alarm-bell means?"

"Not I."

"Then I'll tell you. Something's wrong inside, and no one must leave the grounds."

"What is wrong?"

"I can't say. Probably a prisoner has got out of his cell."

Dick Turpin eyed the warder steadfastly, but the man had, evidently, no suspicion that he was the cause of the alarm in the prison.

Dick would not trust himself to reply to this, as he was fearful of raising the warder's suspicions.

"Since you won't listen to reason," he said, "I'll go and get an order from the governor himself."

"Do that, and you can pass out and welcome."

Without another word Dick Turpin hurried from the spot, greatly chagrined at his failure to pass out by the hangman's gate, as the door was called.

"There only remains one thing," muttered the fugitive, as he went, "and that is the wall. It's a terrible chance, I know, but it is my only one."

He hastened to untwist the cord which he had taken the precaution to conceal upon his person.

This he cast up at the iron spikes which crowned the wall, using the rope as the Indian hunter uses the lasso.

Two or three times he cast it up unsuccessfully.

Perseverance, however, mastered this difficulty. It had caught one of the spikes above and was firmly fixed.

Just then he fancied that he caught the sound of voices at a little distance from the spot.

"Hah!" he thought, "they're after me, I suppose; I must be brief."

Better had he not lost even the time to listen to the warning sounds.

He commenced the ascent of the rope.

He applied himself vigorously to the task, and the progress he made was such as must have astonished the smartest jack tar that ever scorned to go the lubber's hole on the rigging of a man-of-war.

Ten good strides were accomplished and the distance to perform lessened by half as many yards when the fugitive highwayman heard a footstep below !

Here it was that Dick Turpin made a great mistake.

" If I move I must be heard," he mused, " and if I stop still it's just possible that they may not notice the rope's end on the ground."

And, therefore, he paused until the person below should have gone past.

A violent tugging and jerking at the rope, however, speedily convinced the prisoner that he had made a great mistake to pause there.

Had he continued his ascent without noticing the arrival below, by this time he would have been nearly at the top of the wall.

" Come down !" cried a voice below.

" Jonathan Wild !" exclaimed Dick Turpin, in an instant.

" Come down, then," cried the thieftaker, dragging desperately at the rope. " Down with you !"

" Hang him," muttered Dick, " his cries will bring assistance, and it will be all over with me in a trice. I must settle this at once."

The jerking of the rope below was carried on more vigorously than ever.

The thieftaker was endeavouring to shake off the highwayman's hold by dragging him away from the wall and then suddenly letting go.

Dick Turpin got some cruel knocks, but still he clung with desperation to the rope.

" I have it," said Dick, at one of the pauses in his punishment : " prisoner or at liberty I'll cry quits with Jonathan."

He listened intently for a second, and then suddenly loosened his hold of the rope and fell.

His right foot, which was encased in a heavy riding-boot, happened to land fairly upon Jonathan Wild's three-cornered hat.

The hat, however, averted the more serious consequences of the blow, which, upon the head, must inevitably have proved fatal.

And Jonathan Wild was simply toppled over.

With him fell the highwayman, who was unable to recover his balance.

As they reached the ground both instinctively lunged out and clutched at the other.

" Good !"

This came from Dick Turpin, who was delighted to find that he had taken possession of the thieftaker's neckerchief.

Jonathan Wild managed to take good hold of his adversary at the same instant, and they closed in mortal strife.

Both held their breath with excitement.

The strength of both was great : Dick Turpin had perhaps the advantage, but in a scramble like the present the chances were almost equal.

Over and over they rolled upon the ground, locked in each other's arms.

In the course of the scramble Jonathan Wild contrived to get his claw-like fingers entwined in the long glossy hair of the highwayman, and he tugged at it cruelly.

Thoroughly exasperated at this unmanly attack, Dick Turpin butted at the thieftaker with his head, and caught him an ugly knock in the mouth which caused him to swallow several teeth.

This released him from Wild's clutches, to whom he delivered a blow upon the chest and sprang to his feet.

But the thieftaker was not to be disposed of with so little ceremony.

Dick Turpin had barely risen when Wild was upon him.

With a cry he flew at his throat, but Dick stepped aside and managed to avoid him.

" Now, Jonathan Wild," said he, warningly, " beware of interfering with me ; I'm desperate, and blood must come of it."

Again the thieftaker sprang upon the sturdy Dick Turpin.

But the latter was now thoroughly aroused, and he plainly saw that his only chance of escape lay in administering a decisive punishment to the persevering thieftaker.

He met Wild half-way with a blow in the face, which staggered him momentarily.

With a cry of execration, the infuriated thieftaker dashed the blood from his face, and returned to the combat.

" Headstrong fool !" said the highwayman, " you slight my warnings ; so now take the reward of your obstinacy !"

As the thieftaker rushed in, Dick Turpin suddenly stooped forward and caught him in his arms around the middle.

Jonathan Wild had made such a mad rush that he could not stop himself, and he fell a victim to the highwayman's manoeuvre.

Dick Turpin, quick as lightning, took his enemy in his arms as if he had been a child.

Raised him above his head and dashed him to the ground !

Jonathan Wild fell, with a low, dull, hollow groan.

A huge motionless body lay there, seemingly without life, until the thieftaker's myrmidons, and the warders arrived upon the spot, as we have described.

" So much for Jonathan Wild !" said Dick Turpin.

Not pausing to look upon his defeated foe, the stalwart highwayman returned immediately to the rope.

The strongest of men, of course, could not have undergone the tremendous exertion which the highwayman had just passed through without experiencing some effects from it, and Dick Turpin felt considerably blown.

But he did not dare to pause.

On, on he went. The rope was then before him to mount. The task had to be performed, and he went boldly at it.

When some length of this apparently endless rope had been climbed, he heard the warders and Jonathan Wild's men approaching the spot, and, taking a wholesome warning from his late-gathered experience, he redoubled his exertions.

Fortune once more played into his hands, and he had made good his footing upon the top of the wall beside the threatening iron spikes before his pursuers arrived upon the spot.

Nay, more : he had succeeded in drawing up after him the rope to which he owed his preservation.

This was most important.

Had the cord been perceived by the new-comers, it would have given a clue to his flight, and they would have immediately been put upon the right track again.

Jonathan Wild's disaster had occurred so immediately beneath the spot at which Dick had climbed up, that the highwayman could actually overhear the men's remarks as they picked up their leader's insensible form.

" How has this come about ?" said one of the warders.

" He's had a fall."

" Something more than that," said another. " See here : he's been very roughly handled."

Dick did not wait to hear another word, but began his preparations to descend upon the other side.

He let the rope gradually drop, that its fall might not be overheard by the pursuers.

Still, a great amount of caution was necessary to avoid the iron spiking.

Slipping across, with all the caution he could possibly observe, he chanced to catch his coat-tail in one of the revolving irons, and it spun round in its rusty sockets with an alarming sound.

"Hullo!"

"What's that?"

These and similar exclamations from the men who had carried the body of the leader to the lamp to ascertain the extent of his injuries, caused the fugitive most lively apprehension.

The remainder of his descent was accomplished in about half the time that this portion had taken.

The adventures of the night, however, had not yet reached their termination.

His foot had barely touched the ground before he felt himself seized by the shoulder.

"Hullo there!"

He looked up to find himself himself in the clutch of a watchman, who had chanced to pass at that moment.

"Unband me?"

"What are you about?"

"Let me go!" said the highwayman, "or by heaven—"

"Help! help!" shouted the old Charley.

And as he cried he sprang his rattle vigorously.

The fugitive closed with the watchman, who was but a plaything in his powerful grasp.

A trifling exertion and the watchman was flung off.

"Help! help!" shouted the man.

The answering rattles came from every direction, as Dick Turpin bounded off.

The men, too, on the other side of the prison wall, recognising the sound, shouted lustily to the watchman to detain him.

Meanwhile some ran round to the nearest exit.

"Now for it," said Dick Turpin: "neck or nothing!"

As he gained the corner of the street he perceived a hackney coach standing in the way, and he darted aside to avoid it.

As he gained the spot, however, two men sprang from the ground, toppled him over, and in a trice had bundled him into the coach.

The door was closed before he could offer the least resistance, and one of his captors, who held him in the coach, called out directions to the driver, as they rattled along.

"Drive on!"

"All right!"

"Saffron Hill—"

"Yes, yes."

"If it grows too hot for us, make for the Oxford Road."

"Ay, ay."

"Now, on for our lives!"

CHAPTER XLI.

MORE DANGERS YET — THE SUPPOSED GHOST— A WOMAN'S BATTLE — THE FRIENDLESS GIRL AGAIN AT LARGE — HAMPSTEAD HEATH — THE AMOROUS WAGGONER — HELP! HELP! — THE KNIGHT OF THE ROAD.

LET the reader, for an instant, picture to himself the dreadful position of the fair Leonore.

A houseless deserted wanderer, a fugitive from the fiends her false friends who sought her destruction, she had claimed asylum for the night in an assassin's den, and had nearly been sacrificed to the infernal practices of the host and hostess.

But the former had paid dearly for his villany.

The situation in which she found herself placed had converted the trembling shrinking girl into a desperate woman, determined to do battle for her life to the utmost of her strength.

The brutal landlord was thus sent to his long account, with a huge catalogue of crimes upon his head. His death-blow received from the hand of a girl of tender years and gentle blood, whose life, he deemed, had been already taken by the machinery of the fatal bed-chamber to the lime-filled well!

Happily for Lady Leonore, the confusion of that awful moment did not allow her fully to realize the horrors of her position, or certain it is that she would not have been able to carry out that drama of blood unto the end.

She drew forth the reeking knife from the still quivering carcase of the would-be assassin, recoiling in terror from the destruction which her fair hand had wrought, and turned towards the door.

First, to see whether the treasures which had tempted the landlord to seek her life were safe.

Yes. Fortunately, they were as she had placed them, undisturbed by the adventures of the night.

Then there was the dress which the woman had pointed out to her in the room, which had yet to be put on. She felt that she could not again venture forth, unless her shivering limbs were better hidden from the curious gaze of the world, no matter at what peril she remained.

She hastily put on the dress, and once more made for the bedroom door, shuddering, as her eyes caught sight of the fatal bed and its bleeding burden.

She grasped the knife firmly and descended the stairs.

What was to be the next step in this fearful drama?

Would she now be able to quit the house and fly for refuge towards the metropolis?

Her foot was upon the stair when the voice of the dead man's wife from the parlour arrested her progress.

"Have you got them?"

Leonore felt that she was trembling violently, and she clutched at the handrail of the balusters for support.

"Is it all over?" again spoke the woman. "Do you hear me?—Shark!"

But no reply came, and the woman's next words were given in a voice which betokened alarm at her husband's silence.

"Why don't you answer, Shark?" she exclaimed, in the way that we speak in the presence of death. "Are you afraid of anything?"

Lady Leonore bit her lips, and made a violent effort to suppress her emotion.

And then stepped on with as little noise as her trembling state would allow of.

Arrived at the bottom of the stairs, she paused, motionless, with her right hand grasping the blood-stained knife, and held at arm's length, that the landlord's life-blood might not fall upon her garments.

Thus she stood when the woman, not receiving any reply to her repeated demands, advanced into the passage bearing a small candle lamp.

As the light flashed upon Leonore, motionless as a statue, the effect was ghastly in the extreme. Her pale face contrasting fearfully with the ensanguined weapon which her right hand convulsively clutched!

The woman gazed for an instant upon the startling object before her — transfixed with supernatural terror!

Fascinated—rivetted to the spot.

At length she spoke in a low hoarse voice, her distended eyes fixed immoveably upon her less frightened guest, and evidently with the notion that she was addressing the immortal part of their supposed victim.

"Back! back!" she whispered, whilst the perspiration stood out in thick beads upon her brow. "Back to your grave! You are not here in the flesh, I know well! Escaped the fall, even, the lime does its work too surely to allow of any such chance! Back, back, I say."

Leonore made a step forward, and the effect upon the guilty woman was terrible!

She gave a wild piercing snriek, which seemed to shake the crazy old den of slaughter.

The lamp fell from her hand, and she turned and fled.

Leonore now saw that this was the moment for her to effect her escape.

By the light of the fire, faint as it was, she made her way into the room, and speedily found the door.

She had taken particular notice of its fastenings as she sat at her supper, for the thought that such an emergency might arise had crossed her, and she made but short work in removing them.

Her struggles, however, were not got over.

Another scene in this drama of horrors had yet to be played.

As soon as Leonore's movements were accompanied by earthly sounds the hostess recovered her wits.

The supernatural terrors disappeared upon the instant.

"Ha-ha!" she ejaculated; "you are there, are you? Back with you!—Here, Shark, Shark!"

And, without awaiting the reply from her husband, which he could never give, she sprang upon Leonore and dragged her violently from the door.

Leonore struggled boldly with the woman, but was no match for the muscular power opposed to her.

Still she persevered, unwilling until a last extremity to use the fatal weapon in her defence.

"Shark! Shark!" the woman still continued to call, as she dragged the unfortunate Leonore towards the stairs.

The continued silence at length appeared to strike fatally upon the widow's ear.

"Wretch!" she exclaimed, clawing violently at poor Leonore, "you shall be torn piecemeal. Where is my husband?"

"Unhand me!" said Leonore.

"Where is my husband?"

"Your husband has fallen a victim to his own treachery!"

"Liar!" shrieked the woman, "you have slain him!"

"In self-defence."

"Then, by ——, you shall die!"

Leonore saw that she must yield to the prodigious power of this fiendlike woman.

Her frail strength could scarcely offer a faint resistance.

Leonore clutched the handrail of the stairs for support, and offered a temporary check to the woman's impetuous attack.

Then the woman, with a yell which appeared to proceed from some wild beast rather than from human lungs, clutched her savagely by the throat, and Leonore struck at her with the knife.

"Hah!" she shrieked, "murderess! I am slain! Hel—"

Her grasp of Leonore relaxed, and she fell to the floor.

Leonore did not wait an instant to see the result of the blow, but returned at once to the door, tore it open, half mad with the dreadful scenes she had enacted, and rushed wildly from the house.

She had no knowledge whatever of the country, nor did she pause to consider what route she should take.

No matter whither she flew so that she escaped the sight of that scene of horrors which she had just quitted.

Nor did she pause until, thoroughly overcome with fatigue and exhaustion, she sank panting against the roadside.

"When, when," she murmured aloud—"when will these horrors have an end? What have I done? What wrong have I done to my fellow-creatures that I should suffer thus?"

Then, with a sad sigh, she continued—

"Ingrate that I am! Rather let me return thanks for my merciful preservation. I, a helpless and feeble girl, to be so strengthened in that moment that I escape such a peril and am free!"

She now began to look about her for shelter. There was a house a little way before her, a lordly-looking mansion, at the end of a long avenue of poplars, shut in by large iron gates.

But she dreaded applying for shelter here.

What reasonable explanation could she give of her being abroad at that untimely hour?

Who would believe her wild and improbable history?

No; onwards she must trudge—continue her sad weary pilgrimage until she came to a house of public entertainment. At a private house that terrible explanation which *must* be given created in her new position an embarrassment which she felt that she dared not face.

At length there was a faint break in the clouds in the east which made her hope that the long grim night was dying and another day was being ushered into existence.

This thought inspired her with fresh courage, and she pushed onwards, still ignorant of the direction in which she was journeying, until she came up with a man whom she had observed to cross a stile into the road a little way in advance of her.

"Can you tell me the name of this road?" she demanded.

The man stared at her as he replied, "Yes; this is the London Road."

This was not very decided information; every road leads to London.

"Can you tell me the name of this part, then?" she continued.

His only reply was a repetition of the rude stare at her question, which alarmed whilst it annoyed her.

"Can you not reply to my question?" she demanded impatiently.

"Yes, I can, my lass; but whatever's been the matter wi' ye?"

"What do you mean?"

"I mean, have you cut your hand?"

Lady Leonore perceived that the hand he pointed at still bore signs of the blood which she had shed.

Being quite off her guard, she imprudently endeavoured to conceal the tell-tale stains, which naturally aroused a suspicion in the man's mind that all was not right.

"It strikes me, young woman," he said, severely, "that you've been up to something that—"

Ere he could finish the sentence Lady Leonore fled from the spot, leaving the man gazing after her in astonishment.

Presently she came to a pond and ran eagerly to it and washed herself free from the stains of the dead assassin's blood.

She had now reached a large tract of open country, hilly and covered in patches with furze and a low stumpy brushwood.

The morning had now set in, but was grey and

misty, and she could not see more than twenty feet around her.

She was now at a loss as to what direction she should take.

She might wander about upon this dreary common far away from any human habitation, and her great hope was now to seek refreshment and shelter at the earliest-opening house.

She therefore seated herself upon a wooden form placed for the accommodation of weary travellers, until she heard the sound of horses approaching.

A waggon-load of vegetables for market was coming along the road, and to the waggoner walking at the front horse's head she addressed herself—

"What is the name of this place, if you please?"

"This?" answered the waggoner, somewhat scared —"this, mum, is Hampstead Heath."

Leonore could not conceal her satisfaction at finding herself so near to the metropolis.

"We are not many miles from London?"

"About four miles."

"Thank you. Are you going to London, pray?"

"Yes, mum; I be going to market."

"And would you object to—to—" she paused, and scarcely liked to proceed.

"What is it?" demanded the waggoner.

"Would you let me ride in your waggon a little way?"

"Will I? To be sure I will. Hi! woa! woa! there!"

The waggon stopped, and the man took her in his arms and lifted her into the vehicle as though she were a child.

"I think I'll get in too," he said, climbing up the wheel, "for the morning's plaguey sharp."

There was something in the fellow's manner which disagreeably impressed Lady Leonore.

He stared rudely at her pale face and her comely person painfully developed by the scant clothing she possessed.

"Thee bain't a bad-looking gal at all," said the waggoner, "by no manner or means. What might be thy game out here?"

Lady Leonore made no reply, but turned her head away.

"Dang'd if she ain't coy, too," soliloquised the waggoner, with a laugh. "Come and sit by me, my lass."

"I beg you will not annoy me," said Lady Leonore.

"By no manner or means, mum—gee up!—if tha' won't come and sit by me I'll bring myself over there."

Lady Leonore sprang indignantly to her feet, and endeavoured to jump out, but the waggoner restrained her.

"Gently, my lass," he said, enfolding her in his loathsome embrace. "Give us a kiss. Don't 'ee be shy."

Leonore struggled in vain in the arms of the stalwart waggoner.

"Help! help!" she cried.

"Don't be silly," said the man; "I don't mean thee no harm."

"Let me go, then."

"Not if I know it, my lass."

"Help! help!"

"Call away, my lass; there's no one about to hear thee."

In vain did she wrestle with the huge ruffian.

In vain did she struggle; in his arms she was weak and powerless as an infant.

She felt, with alarm, that her little remaining strength was wellnigh spent; she was becoming exhausted.

She feared that she was about to faint.

Vainly did she struggle with the dreadful sensation which was gaining upon her.

She exerted herself to the utmost, and with what power she yet possessed uttered one long sustained cry for assistance.

What sound was that?

A horseman came galloping up the road towards the waggon, and assistance was at hand!

"What are you going to do with that lady?" demanded the cavalier, stopping beside the waggon.

"Save me! oh! save me!" implored Lady Leonore.

"Be off!" cried the waggoner, "or darned if I don't lay my—"

The horseman stopped him short by giving him a smart cut across the face with his riding whip.

The waggoner looked up roaring with pain.

"Hullo!" he cried, springing out of the van, "the Yellow Boys!" Saying which, he ran off as if pursued by the evil one.

The horseman who thus arrived so opportunely for Lady Leonore wore a Yellow Mask!

CHAPTER XLII.

RED RALPH AND DICK TURPIN IN THE COACH— THE OFFICERS IN PURSUIT—GIVE AND TAKE —A TOUGH JOB—HELP ARRIVES—A GENERAL ROW.

As soon as Dick Turpin could recover his presence of mind he began to struggle with his captors.

But they held him firmly down at the bottom of the coach.

"Quiet!" said one.

"Don't jump about so," said a voice, the tones of which did not strike unfamiliarly upon his ear; "you'll upset the trap."

The highwayman glanced up in astonishment into the speaker's face, to recognise the welcome features of a friend.

It was Red Ralph, the Captain of the Yellow Band, again!

"Red Ralph!"

"Yes, Dick," answered Ralph; "but keep quiet now; our only chance depends upon it."

Dick Turpin was all amazement.

They were evidently going at a rattling pace, and yet the carriage wheels appeared to make not the slightest noise.

The horses' hoofs could not be heard either.

"Where are we?"

"In the hackney-coach."

"But I don't understand."

"What?"

"Are we moving along?"

"The explanation of the mystery is simple enough," answered the Captain of the Yellow Band; "we have muffled the wheels and the horses' hoofs."

"Then we are safe."

"Not yet."

"We are; for here's Saffron Hill: once in the old familiar haunts, and we can defy all the authorities together."

But a few minutes proved that the fugitive had rather underrated the vigilance and perseverance of the minor civic magnates.

Horses were heard in pursuit.

Red Ralph leaned out of the coach, and then perceived some three or four horsemen riding desperately towards them.

"We shall have to make a fight of it, I suppose," said Ralph.

"Stay," said Wolff, who was the third passenger in the vehicle; "suppose he gets out, captain, whilst the

[FLIGHT OF LEONORE FROM THE HUNCHBACK'S.]

coach goes on—makes a turn off, and then they'll be sure to follow on; he'll get clean off."

But Dick Turpin positively refused to listen to this.

"No," said he, resolutely; "I'll stay with you and fight also; I'll take my chance with you."

"Well, well," said the Captain of the Yellow Band; "if it must be so, then look out, for here they are down upon us!"

It was as Red Ralph said.

One of the horsemen a few lengths in advance of the others galloped up to the horse's head and caught it by the bit.

"Stop!"

But the driver only replied to this by aiming a terrific cut at the horseman, which, however, he nimbly avoided. The blow fell upon his horse, making the animal rear and snort with the pain, and nearly unseating his rider.

And the hackney-coach tore up Saffron Hill faster than ever.

But the pursuers were not thus easily to be baffled.

The coach could not proceed at anything approaching the speed of the officers in pursuit, who in a trice were up with it again.

The coachman lashed up his horse and struck out right and left with his whip, but he was dragged from his box immediately.

One of the officers presented himself and a pistol at the coach window.

"Yield!"

But, far from yielding, the late prisoner made a grab at the pistol, and secured it.

"Off with you," said Dick Turpin; "fly, or I fire!"

The officer needed no second warning.

Dick then leaned out of the window and presented the pistol at the officer's comrades.

A flash and a report were succeeded by a snort of terror and pain, which announced that one of the horses was struck.

"Stand aside, Dick."

Dick Turpin withdrew from the window, and his place was immediately occupied by Red Ralph.

"Now," cried Ralph to the officers: "molest us no further, or your blood be upon your own obstinate heads."

"Red Ralph!" shouted one of the officers.

"Red Ralph!" echoed the rest.

"Yes; 'tis he, for a million!"

"Then, this *is* a prize."

"Not yet," exclaimed the individual in question, and as he spoke he levelled and fired at the nearest horse.

The poor animal tottered and fell, dragging his rider beneath him.

"Who's the next?"

"I am, Red Ralph," cried another in reply to the challenge of the Yellow Band's leader.

The officer gallantly charged up to the door of the hackney-coach, and grabbed at the intrepid Ralph.

But the officer's bravery met with a terrible reception.

A blow from the butt-end of Ralph's recently-discharged pistol sent him reeling in his saddle.

"There he goes," said Wolff.

The officer fell a dead weight from his horse, which at once galloped off.

Meanwhile three of the officers had dragged open the opposite door of the coach, and seized Dick Turpin by the collar.

"Hah! Master Dick," he said, "you'll spend the rest of the night in Newgate yet."

"Never!"

"Or else I'll blow you to atoms."

He pressed a pistol to the late prisoner's brow.

It was a critical moment.

Red Ralph turned from his successful encounter with one of the officers to find that they were attacked in a totally unexpected quarter.

"Ha! ha! Red Ralph," said the officer triumphantly; "so we get the best of it after all, it appears."

"Only at present."

"Ho! ho! and what may be your next trick, my noble captain?"

The reply came from behind the officer.

"*This!*"

And a knife was buried to the hilt in the gallant officer's shoulder.

"Hah! traitors!" cried the unfortunate man.

The pistol fell from his grasp, and his hand hung helpless by his side.

He groaned deeply and sank fainting to the bottom of the coach.

The perpetrator of the deed paid for his rashness on the instant, for one of the unfortunate officer's comrades, who was coming to him as the blow was struck, hit him heavily upon the head with the butt-end of a loaded riding-whip.

There now remained only two of the officers who were capable of molesting the fugitives any further.

To these Red Ralph addressed a few words of caution.

"You two, pray, depart in peace," he said; "we wish you no harm, and would fain avoid shedding any more blood."

But the two officers stood still, without offering to touch Dick Turpin, and yet determined not to move away without him.

As Red Ralph spoke, additional officers came within sight.

"Now we shall see," exclaimed one of the officers exultingly.

"We shall," said Red Ralph: "I can hear the noise, and am prepared for emergencies."

He raised a silver call to his lips and blew a long shrill note.

Several windows were thrown up, and more than one voice was heard demanding the cause of the untimely outcry.

"Help! help!" said Dick Turpin.

"Who for?"

"Me—Dick and Red Ralph. The Philistines are upon us, and unless you come, we shall all be carted off to jail for the night."

A dozen voices responded to this appeal.

In the space of a few seconds the officers arrived upon the spot, and were very speedily followed by the men who had answered Red Ralph's summons.

"Down with them!" cried the Captain of the Yellow Band; "down with them!"

The officers, now mustering in great force, were prepared for any emergency, and a terrible fight ensued!

Oaths, blows, and shots were exchanged freely.

All was now noise, confusion, and universal *mélée.*

CHAPTER XLIII.

A SKIRMISH WITH THE POLICE — ANOTHER ESCAPE — THE BENIGHTED TRAVELLERS — THE DRUNKEN LANDLORD — THE SHOWER-BATH — THE RICH GUEST — A PLOT — THE ROBBERS — THE SLEEPING BEAUTY — "ONE TASTE OF THOSE POUTING LIPS" — DANGER — THE BURGLARY — TERROR — ALARM — FLIGHT.

A TERRIBLE skirmish was that which was now taking place between the mob of lawless ruffians and the mounted officers of justice upon Saffron Hill.

Oaths, cries, and the clashing of swords mingled with the springing of the watchmen's rattles and an occasional report of a pistol, rendering the *mélée* of most alarming aspect.

Although the officers were in a great minority, the justice of their cause, and the immense superiority of their weapons of offence and defence (which had, probably, most to do with it), gave them a decided advantage over the rabble.

The fight had been waged warmly for some ten minutes when two men might have been seen to make a sudden attack upon the officers in the rear.

Two of the officers were thrown from their horses, which were immediately secured by the men.

Then the horses were artfully drawn away from the crowd of combatants, and, at a few yards from the noisy fray, mounted quietly by the two men, and walked as quietly down a bye-street.

"Now for it, Dick," said one of these men, with a low chuckle.

The other replied by an assenting laugh, and they rode rapidly from the spot.

Avoiding the main thoroughfares they cantered on westward, and did not speak again until they arrived in the Oxford Road.

Here they drew rein before a low thatched hostelry, where one dismounted and knocked sharply upon the door with his fist.

"House, house !" he cried.

But no reply came.

It was the dead of night, and the inhabitants had long since retired to rest.

But he renewed the knocking vigorously, and still called lustily to be admitted.

Full five minutes they must have been there, shouting and knocking, when the individual who had not dismounted began to show signs of weariness.

"Come, come, Dick," he said; "we had better be moving again."

"Another minute, Ralph," said the other.

"Nay, nay, Dick; we may knock and call till we are hoarse. He'll never hear us."

"But the pretty Margaret may."

"Gad!" exclaimed the other, laughing heartily; "you'll never change your ways, Dick."

"Never!"

"You escape the gallows by the luckiest chance that ever befell a poor condemned wretch, and a few minutes have scarcely elapsed when you are longing for a sight of Mistress Margaret's bright eyes."

"Ah!" said Dick, with a mock-heroic sigh, which appeared to come from the depths of his riding-boots. "Faith, Ralph, they *are* bright.

The thought of the damsel's good looks caused the reckless Dick Turpin to apply to the hostelry door with renewed vigour.

At length a window was opened above, and a red woollen night-cap appeared, followed by the round rubicund visage of mine host of the Wheatsheaf.

"Who's there ?"

"Me!"

"Come down, good Jock; we are benighted, and seek rest and entertainment; come down."

"What do you want?" demanded mine host, in a voice smacking suspiciously of having been aroused from a drunken slumber. "What do you want disturbing the peace of a res—respectable house and a respectable family at this time at night. Be off, or hang me but I'll douse ye!

Saying which he withdrew his woollen night-cap and closed the window.

As may be supposed, the two highwaymen were greatly disgusted at this, and not in the least inclined to submit to so unceremonious a dismissal.

"Besotted old rascal!" exclaimed Red Ralph.

"Drunken old villain!" added Dick Turpin.

"We'll beat down his door if he won't open. Open! open!"

And he recommenced a noisy hammering upon the oak.

He had not continued this clatter more than a few seconds, when the window was reopened, and down came the threatened bucket of water, drenching the clamorous Dick Turpin.

Red Ralph laughed heartily; as for Dick Turpin, he could not refrain from laughing also, but we are by no means sure that he enjoyed the joke.

"Be off, you rapscallion," shouted the irascible Jock.

"You perverse old idiot," shouted the Captain of the Yellow Band, "don't you recognise our voices ?"

"Lor, captain!"

"Ah! you hear me now."

"Is it really you, captain ?"

"Yes; and Dick too."

"What's left of him after your cursed showerbath."

"Really!—upon my life!—my noble captain, wait a bit."

And, jumbling up a score of apologies to the two highwaymen, the host of the "Wheatsheaf" quitted the window, and hurried down stairs without waiting to refasten it.

Then sundry ponderous bolts and chains were withdrawn, and the doors were opened by the shivering landlord.

"Bless me!" he exclaimed, as he grasped them both eagerly by the hand in turn; "this is a pleasure."

"It ought to be," laughed Dick Turpin; "at least, it ought to be to you, for it has been some pain to me."

"Come, come in, my noble captain; we'll soon remedy that."

They entered the house, and whilst the landlord busied himself in refastening the door they strolled into a parlour upon the left of the entrance.

A few sparks of a dying fire were lingering in the grate.

"Why, Jock," said the Captain of the Yellow Band to the landlord, "your fire is not out yet."

"No, captain; I've had a latish customer here."

"Late, indeed, for you."

"Yes; but, as he stayed for the night and paid for his share of bottles with a right liberal hand, I couldn't well refuse him the use of the parlour."

"No, no."

"He stays for the night ?" repeated Dick Turpin.

"Yes."

The two highwaymen exchanged significant glances.

"What's he like ?"

"I scarce can tell."

"But what does he here ?"

"He's a traveller, captains, like yourselves, and benighted."

"Rich, think ye ?"

"I should say yes."

"Good."

Dick Turpin laughed gleefully and rubbed his hands.

The Captain of the Yellow Band grew moody and silent.

This marked difference between these two lawless men is not unworthy of note.

The sturdy Dick Turpin was in the greatest spirits when contemplating an enterprise of the character of that which now began to float about in his reckless mind.

We must do him the justice to say that the greater the danger involved in the transaction the greater relish did he betray for it.

Red Ralph, on the contrary, always appeared to have a struggle within himself when upon the eve of a robbery, if there was time for deliberation.

A difficulty to keep himself in the criminal track he followed out.

When, however, the job was there before him on the open road—man to man upon the king's highway—he entered into the business with that wonderful spirit and dash which had made him so notorious.

The landlord was so "foggy" with his broken slumbers and the many spirituous liquors which he had imbibed that he did not observe the significant glances which his visitors exchanged.

"What'll ye drink, my noble captains?" asked he presently.

"Brandy for me," said Turpin.

"And you, captain ?"

"I'll think over it, Jock," said Red Ralph; "bring brandy first."

Boniface departed, and the two highwaymen could now carry on their conversation unrestrained.

Dick Turpin gave a long but subdued whistle.

"We're in luck, Ralph."

"Perhaps," returned the Captain of the Yellow Band; "but who knows? it is just likely to be some poor devil."

"Not likely, Ralph, from what old Jock says of him."

"We must learn more surely before doing anything."

"Of course."

"And then he must say where he sleeps."

"True."

"It wouldn't do to go prowling about the house at the dead of night."

"No, no."

"I'm with you, then, Dick," said Red Ralph, "although I must confess that it scarcely likes me."

"Pshaw, man," exclaimed Dick Turpin, "you're not growing scrupulous in your old age!"

"Scarcely."

"I believe in, and always shall, a fair, an equal division of property."

"Bravo!" said the Captain of the Yellow Band with a light laugh; "bravo, Dick! it is a glorious principle—what's yours is mine."

"And what's mine's my own," added Dick Turpin.

And they grew merry with laughing, until the the landlord returned with the brandy.

"Brandy grog," said Dick; "give us some of the real brew, Jock."

"Some of the right down real original, my noble captain," responded Boniface.

And he forthwith commenced formidable preparations with hot water, sugar, and lemon.

As the process of manufacture continued, Dick Turpin put some questions to the landlord—about the lodger—not very artfully framed, but still not likely to arouse any suspicions in Boniface's mind, in his present foggy condition.

"What's your traveller like, Jock?"

"What d'ye mean by that, my noble captain?"

"Is he short or tall? Old or young? Handsome or ugly?"

"Old, ugly, tall."

"Very well answered, Jock," said Dick Turpin. "And he's rich as Crœsus, I'll warrant."

"I can't say."

"Oh! but he must be, to lay out his money as you say he has."

"Perhaps."

"And is he armed?"

Red Ralph frowned warningly upon his comrade.

Sleepy as the landlord was, the question of the highwayman was so plumply put, that it was more than probable that his suspicions would be aroused if some little caution were not observed.

"Leave that to me," intimated Red Ralph, in eloquent pantomime. "I'll manage it."

Dick Turpin bowed his acquiescence and was silent.

"Hullo! my noble captain!" exclaimed the landlord, glancing up at this moment, and catching sight of the signs they were exchanging. "What's all this?"

"Nothing, Jock."

"Nothing? Gad! but it looked very like something."

"No, no," said Red Ralph, "we were only expressing our satisfaction at the grog."

"Oh, oh!"

And he took a sip—a very large one—himself, and smacked his lips, in ecstacy.

"It is nectar!" said Dick Turpin, enthusiastically.

"You are judges of a tipple, my noble captain!"

"I think so," said Dick Turpin, modestly.

"Ay; but it is good, is it not?"

And he sipped again.

"Indeed! it is, Jock," said the Captain of the Yellow Band.

"So our traveller up-stairs thought."

"UP-STAIRS!"

"Yes."

As he gave the answer, it appeared to strike the landlord that his questioner was showing an undue curiosity upon the traveller's behalf, and he looked rather sharply up at him.

Dick Turpin was, however, earnestly engaged in peering to the bottom of his tumbler of grog.

An hour or more they sat smoking and drinking, growing more and more silent as the night advanced.

At length the landlord, stupefied by his second carouse, dosed upon his chair.

His pipe fell to the ground, but the sound failed to disturb him.

However, Red Ralph warily forbore to move yet in his half-formed project.

Soon though a thick irregular breathing announced that Boniface was safe for the night.

Red Ralph rose to his feet.

Stepped lightly across the floor, and made for the door.

He listened for an instant, to assure himself that all was silent in the house, and then he beckoned to Dick Turpin to follow him.

As the latter rose to his feet, the candle upon the table sank in its socket, flickered, and expired.

Here was a misfortune!

"Hist!" said Dick Turpin, "what shall we do now?"

"I can't say."

"We must have a light."

"There's a lamp upon the chimney-piece there."

"Get it, then."

The fire remaining in the grate gave such a feeble light that Dick Turpin could see nothing in the room but the objects immediately facing it.

The consequence was, that in feeling his way across the room he stumbled over a chair.

Both the chair and the highwayman fell scrambling to the floor.

"Who's there? Hullo—" cried Jock, the landlord.

"Hist—hush!"

The two highwaymen remained immoveable—breathless!

"What's tha-at—who—who—o?"

With a few sleepy exclamations of this nature, the landlord slumbered and snored again.

"Now then, Dick," said the Captain of the Yellow Band. "Gently, my lad. Get the lantern."

Dick Turpin stooped and fondled his damaged shins, and then reached the lantern as desired.

"Now for a light."

"But how?"

"Here are the matches."

"No—hush!" said Red Ralph, in a whisper; "we can't venture upon striking a match now."

"What then?"

"Ha!—the fire."

"One moment—here's a piece of paper."

He stooped and picked up a small scrap from the floor.

He thrust it into the fire, but the dying embers had not sufficient fire left in them to ignite it.

He stooped down and blew one of the brighter coals until it caught, but even then it refused to rise into a flame.

"What is it?" asked Ralph.

"A piece of card."

"Glazed?"

"Yes; that is why it will not blaze up."

"Give it to me."

Dick passed the card to him, and he stooped to the fire and examined it attentively, to see if there was any writing upon it.

"There is something on it," said Red Ralph, "but what I cannot make out."

At this moment, as if for his especial service, one of the coals burst forth into a tiny flickering flame.

Red Ralph eagerly availed himself of the opportunity and read aloud—

"Mr. Stanley Powell!"

"Who?"

"Mr. Stanley Powell," answered Red Ralph, all amazement. "Is it possible that he is here?"

"Stanley Powell—the old profligate of Maddox Fields?"

"The same."

"Then he *is* a prize."

"Doubly a prize for me, Dick. But come along."

On tip-toe they crept from the parlour, and began mounting the stairs which were immediately without.

Oh! how they creaked!

It seemed to the two adventurous highwaymen that a regiment of soldiers could not have made more noise!

They must surely alarm the traveller!

"Careful, Ralph," whispered Dick."

"All right."

"He has his barkers with him, without doubt."

"Probably. This is the door."

As he spoke he tried the handle.

It turned—but the door was fast!

"Locked?"

"Yes."

"Wait a minute."

Dick Turpin had yet in his pocket the instrument with which Red Ralph had loosened his fetters.

He rather prided himself upon his proficiency in the "fancy branches" of his profession, and the picking of the lock, which to less skilful hands would have been a labour of time, was accomplished in a second.

He pushed the door open gently and entered the room.

"He sleeps with his window open," thought Red Ralph.

"We might have got in that way," said Dick Turpin, pointing to the open window.

"True."

To the left of the window was a four-post bedstead, with the curtains closely drawn.

"He sleeps soundly," said the Captain of the Yellow Band.

"Yes: the wine that he took with Jock makes him safe for us."

"Fortunately."

Red Ralph drew nearer to the bed and listened.

Not a sound—not the faintest breath could he detect to confirm his suspicions.

Before proceeding any further, it was absolutely necessary that he should know if it really was Mr. Stanley Powell, as he imagined.

He felt that having him there in his power, as it were, might lead to a change in the sad fate of his unhappy daughter.

The reader has, probably, not forgotten the fair Miss Mary Powell, the daughter of the profligate Stanley Powell, whom Red Ralph found immured in the dreary convent by the hermit's cave.

Ever since he had had the poor girl constantly before him, and he would have given much to rescue her from her sad doom.

With a light touch he drew back the bed curtains.

Yes—there he was in bed. That is, they could see the outline of some individual snugly esconced in the sheets.

The face was turned from them.

Red Ralph, to catch a fair sight of the face, leaned over the bed, balanced upon one foot, whilst Dick Turpin grasped his hand to prevent him slipping.

Imagine, then, his astonishment upon discovering that the occupant of the bed was a woman!

He drew back with a suppressed exclamation.

"What is it, Ralph?"

"See for yourself," answered the Captain of the Yellow Band.

Dick Turpin stooped forward, and drew back immediately, as Red Ralph had done.

His astonishment was not less than Red Ralph's, but his countenance was full of admiration for the beauty of the unconscious sleeper.

"The fair Mistress Margaret, by all that's wonderful!"

"Hush!"

The damsel shifted in the bed, and murmured a few words, which they failed to catch.

"She speaks—"

"Of me," said Dick.

"As vain as you are wild, Dick!" whispered Red Ralph.

Dick Turpin smiled, but never offered to move from the spot.

"Come, come, Dick."

"Don't hurry, Ralph," said Dick Turpin. "Doesn't she look lovely there? Beauty divine!"

"Yes, yes. But come."

"I swear, Ralph," said Dick Turpin, with his eyes still fixed upon the coverlid, as it rose and sank with the fair sleeper's heaving bosom, "I swear that the sight overcomes me."

"Hush, man, hush!"

"A lovely wench!"

"You said so before."

"And did her but scant justice."

"Granted; but come away."

"One taste of those pouting murmuring lips, and I'm with you."

Red Ralph drew the love-sick highwayman back affrightedly.

"Dick, Dick!" he whispered, "your rashness will undo us quite."

"The angel!"

"Come, come."

But he had to drag him from the bedside forcibly.

Dick Turpin heaved a deep sigh, and turned to his companion with a most comical expression of sadness.

"We must have mistaken Jock," said Red Ralph.

"No; I'm sure he said 'up here.'"

"No; I have it; of course ther's another room there, you know."

"Beside this?"

"Yes."

"Come, then."

They gently closed the door, and made for the adjoining room.

"Confound this!" muttered Red Ralph; "we have all the same work to go over again.

"And no such reward in view," sighed Dick Turpin.

"Pshaw!"

But they were mistaken.

Only one door in the house (that is, one bed-room door) could boast of a lock.

This, as we have seen, was meant to secure the apartment of the fair Mistress Margaret.

When they raised the latch of the adjoining door it gave way a little—perhaps a few inches—but then was immoveable, and no effort of theirs could effect an entrance.

Of course, we do not mean to say that the two highwaymen could not have achieved their object had they been in a position to use all the means at their disposal.

But it must be remembered that all their movements had to be made without alarming the occupant of the apartment.

They were in a fix!

"This is a puzzler."

"It is."

"But we must not be baulked thus," said Dick.

"I'm determined not to be," said Ralph, resolutely.

"Then, how to proceed. Stay, Ralph: I have it!"

"Speak!"

"The window!"

"Useless—how can we get at it?"

"Easily."

"No, no: to get at it we must go down and open the door; all those bolts and fastenings being shifted cannot fail to arouse Jock."

"You do not take me here," said Dick Turpin: "I mean to get in by the other window."

"In this room?"

"Ay; you know that the window in Mistress Margaret's chamber is open."

"Yes."

"We have but to get out creep along the parapet, and open the next one."

"Good! Go on—I follow. But no noise—as carefully as we can."

Treading so lightly that neither could hear the footsteps of the other, they ventured again into the bed-chamber of the landlord's fair daughter.

Dick Turpin was the first to step out on the parapet.

"Have you got there?" demanded Red Ralph.

"Yes—hush!"

"You can see him?"

"Yes—silence—he's moving in his sleep. I can see now why we failed to get in by the door."

"Why?"

"There's all the furniture of the room against it."

"Wary old fox!"

Dick Turpin now tried the window, but it was fastened by a crazy old catch which held it secure.

There was no means of opening it but by turning the latch.

Forcing it open was out of the question.

"Ralph!" whispered Dick.

"Yes."

"Come here; I want you to give me a hand with the window."

Red Ralph joined him, and they contrived to cut a piece out of one of the panes of glass with the diamond in a finger-ring he wore.

The latch was turned, the window opened, and they entered the room.

The first thing which the Captain of the Yellow Band then perceived was Mr. Stanley Powell's walking sword lying across a chair.

As he had been tilted at so very recently with this identical weapon he could not fail to recognise it, and it at once confirmed his suspicions.

The room was precisely of the same dimensions and shape as the apartment adjoining, and a four-post bedstead with white hangings—a fac-simile of that occupied by Mistress Margaret—was in precisely the same position.

Red Ralph, however, to assure himself more fully of the correctness of his surmises, drew back the curtains of the bed and gazed upon the sleeper.

What a sad contrast he presented to the tenant of the neighbouring bed-chamber!

The old *roué* lay flat upon his back, with his mouth wide open, and snoring most discordantly.

"You old villain!" muttered Red Ralph; "I should dearly like to cry quits with you for the fright you gave me, but I think I almost got the best of the bargain—even then."

Whilst Red Ralph thus mused Dick Turpin was busying himself in making free with Mr. Stanley Powell's garments.

He had ransacked the pockets of the knee-breeches, coat, and waistcoat, and was now applying his industrious fingers to the riding-cloak.

He felt some papers in the lining of it, but, deeming these of little service, he gave over the search.

"What have you there, Dick?" demanded Red Ralph.

"Only papers."

"Let me see."

Red Ralph was of opinion that he might find the papers particularly useful, and he hastened to secure them.

"Bear a hand here, Dick," he said: "hold me a light whilst I see what this is. Hah! '*To the Lady Superior of the Retreat.*' The very thing. But let me read on."

"What is it?"

"I'll tell you anon; but this is a real prize."

He finished reading the paper, and carefully replaced it as he had found it.

"What are you about?" demanded Dick Turpin.

"Hush! we must put all back."

"What?"

"We must replace everything as we found it, Dick."

"Nonsense!"

"Dick, I have my reasons; do as I tell you, and you shall have a rich prize, I promise you: I have read there something that may render us independent for years. Do as I ask you, and trust to me."

"But, Ralph—"

"Not a word; you know that I never deceived you yet."

"True."

"Then trust to me now."

"I will—but it's deuced hard, Ralph," sighed Dick Turpin, grunting, as if to say that this was but a sorry compensation for resigning the prize.

However, the things were all replaced in their original position, as Red Ralph desired.

"We must go back the way we came," said Red Ralph.

"Cannot we go by the door now?"

"No; the noise would awaken the old man, and all our cares and caution prove fruitless. Back this way. Come along."

Dick stepped out on to the parapet first, and Ralph was about to follow, when Mr. Stanley Powell called out in alarm.

"Who's that?"

Red Ralph stood there, motionless as a statue.

"Any one there?" again demanded Mr. Stanley Powell.

Ralph motioned Dick away.

All was silent for a minute or two, and he began to hope that the old man had fallen asleep again.

He made another step towards the window, and paused.

The bed-curtains at this instant were pulled aside by a trembling hand, and the shrivelled-up countenance of the debauchee Powell appeared.

His expression was of the greatest alarm, and his eye wandered in fearful anticipation around the still moonlit chamber.

The first object it rested upon was the form of the Captain of the Yellow Band, half hidden by one of the window-curtains.

His eye remained immoveable upon him—fixed and fascinated with fright!

Red Ralph had caught the sound, and turned his head slowly round to ascertain the cause of it.

Thus he unintentionally gave his old adversary a greater start than ever, for the moonlight, resting strong upon his pale beardless face, gave him a wild weird aspect, which was greatly aided by the window-curtains hanging around him in fantastic folds.

He appeared to the old man freshly aroused from a heavy sleep, like a ghostly statue heavily draped.

Mr. Stanley Powell gave one loud unearthly shriek and sank back upon his pillow.

(When assistance came he was in a deep fainting fit.)

Ralph advanced to the bed, took one glance at the swooning man, and then hastily returned to the window.

"Dick," said he, "we must begone, We shall have to make a run of it again, I expect."

"Why?"

"He knows me."

"What of that?"

"It will spoil us with Jock. Now, as he believes profoundly in us, we must not give him any suspicion of our real—real *profession*."

"But, if we fly in the middle of the night, what will he think?"

"What he pleases; we can explain anything away."

"I don't exactly see it, but I rely upon you again."

"Good: you know where the horses are put?"

"Of course."

"Drop into the road and get them out quick. I can hear somebody stirring below stairs."

The words were barely uttered ere Dick Turpin had dropped from the window.

Their haste was well timed, for Red Ralph very shortly heard a footstep in the passage outside the door.

It was the landlord who was awakened by his daughter Margaret. The scream of their guest had aroused her, and she had hastened to awaken him.

He knocked at the door repeatedly, but Mr. Stanley Powell was quite unconscious of their presence.

Then, growing alarmed at the continued silence within the chamber, Jock endeavoured to force open the door, but the old profligate's precautions had shut out assistance from him.

The door was immoveable.

"Something is wrong," Ralph could hear him say.

"You must get in by the window through my room," said another voice, which he recognised as belonging to the pretty Mistress Margaret.

This was enough for Ralph.

He only waited to close the window and replace the fastening.

Then dropped into the saddle which Turpin had placed immediately beneath the window.

CHAPTER XLIV.

THE YELLOW BAND PREPARE FOR ACTION—THE ARTFUL TRICK — FILLING THE FIRE-ARMS WITH BEER—THE CAPTAIN'S STRANGE DESERTION — WHAT DID IT MEAN? — MR. POWELL'S BOND—A CAROUSE—THE PARTY IN THE SMOCK-FROCK—THE AMBUSCADE.

Two days after Dick Turpin's escape from Newgate and his flying visit to "The Wheatsheaf" hostelry in the Oxford Road with the leader of the Yellow Band, a great commotion was taking place in the forest, near the haunt of the mysterious gang which was the terror of that part of the country.

Some twenty men, all well mounted and armed with cutlasses and holster pistols, were drawn up for inspection in the forest glade.

They all wore the same uniform, and, from the regularity of their movements and the military precision with which their various evolutions were performed, they might have been taken for a regularly organized body of the state.

One peculiarity, however, in their appearance would have at once dispelled any such idea.

They all wore the yellow masks from which they gained their title.

Up and down the two lines into which they formed themselves rode their leader Red Ralph.

His dress was of the same colour as the others, and corresponding in every particular, with the exception that it was of a richer material.

His wrists, too, were adorned with costly lace ruffles, whereas his men only wore white linen cuffs.

He was mounted upon his favourite bay mare, which pranced and curvetted as if proud of the honour of bearing the chief of this formidable band.

Red Ralph addressed a few words to each of his men in turn, respecting the priming of their pistols and the necessity for taking every precaution to ensure the success of the enterprise upon which they were about entering.

"Lieutenant Walters," said Red Ralph.

"Here, captain," answered the lieutenant, riding out from the head of the nearest column.

"Have you seen anything of Dick Turpin?"

"I saw him but five minutes since."

"And has he decided upon joining our expedition?"

"Yes, captain."

"Then, why does he linger?"

"He wished to stay until the last moment by Tom King's side."

"Good. And how fares the patient to-day?"

"He improves rapidly."

"Does he know of our project?"

"No: Reuben says that it would be dangerous for him to move."

"Then I sincerely hope that Turpin has not mentioned it. Nothing could keep him back if he happened to hear of it, you know."

"True!"

A shrill cry of some forest bird was heard.

"The scout!" said Red Ralph. "What does it mean?"

"Probably that some one is coming by this way."

"Sound a challenge."

The Lieutenant of the Yellow Band complied, and it was answered almost immediately by a similar call.

"It is Wolff."

Wolff shortly rode up, dressed as a farmer in leather leggings and a drab coat and breeches.

"Well, Wolff," said Red Ralph, advancing eagerly to meet him, "what news?"

"The best."

"They come?"

"Within an hour they will be passing the Palmer's Cell."

"Good!"

"But the escort will be more formidable, captain."

"Than what?"

"Than we anticipated."

"But will it be more formidable than ours?"

"Yes."

"Hah!"

"The military alone will outnumber us, I hear."

"What is their number?"

"Thirty of the household troops."

"Pheugh!"

"Then Old Powell has provided additional protection."

"Indeed?"

"Yes—he has hired about a dozen determined fellows, who will all be well armed and regularly sworn in for this service."

The Captain of the Yellow Band began to look serious.

"That seems like danger, Wolff."

"It does: at least, danger from the military."

"The other counts for something, surely."

"Not much."

"A dozen, say you?"

"Yes."

"And armed?"

"To the teeth."

"Then they count for a very good dozen, I should say."

"But one of them is a particular friend of mine."

Red Ralph's expression changed in an instant.

He burst into a light laugh and held out his hand to Wolff.

"Bravo! bravo! Wolff," he cried; "a traitor in the enemy's camp!"

"Ay."

"Then a fig for their dozen!"

"Yes; they halted at the half-way house for refreshment, and I managed to exchange a word with Morris."

"It it Morris, then?"

"Yes, captain."

"And what did he say?"

"That he had taken one or two wholesome precautions to render their fire-arms useless."

"That is brave!"

"Yes; he has poured a little malt liquor down the barrel of each, and they might as well endeavour to fire off a walking cane!"

"Good! good! But the soldiers?"

"He could do nothing with them for fear of arousing their suspicions."

"I see."

At this juncture the scout signalled again and Dick Turpin rode up to the glade.

"Well, captain," said he, saluting Red Ralph in military fashion, "how goes the enterprise?"

"Bravely, Dick."

"I'm glad of it."

"We are to have a regular pitched battle, it appears."

"With the military?"

"Yes; they muster thirty. But you are with us, I suppose?"

"If you'll have me."

Wolff, who had taken advantage of Dick Turpin's arrival to exchange a few words with his comrades, here rejoined Red Ralph.

"I would beg to offer a suggestion, captain," he said.

"What is it, Wolff?"

"We must have recourse to some kind of stratagem to make sure of success, captain."

Red Ralph regarded him earnestly for several seconds.

"You must not think, captain," said Wolff, hastily interpreting the look, "that I am showing the white feather upon my own account."

"I know that," answered the Captain of the Yellow Band, "and I have already been thinking of what you suggest. But I am rather puzzled, I must confess, as to what I must be after."

"If we could lead them into an ambuscade, captain."

"Ay; but how—how?"

He walked his horse a few paces away from the group, and for some few minutes was lost in meditation.

Red Ralph's inventive genius was never long called upon in vain, and he had speedily resolved upon a line of conduct.

With what success his project was attended we shall show as we proceed.

He presently rode up to Dick Turpin, Walters, the lieutenant of the band, and Wolff, who were conversing in a group.

"Well, captain?" said the latter.

"I have it, Wolff," returned Red, "somebody else must take the lead."

"How!" exclaimed Dick Turpin.

"I must leave you."

"Wherefore?"

"You will soon learn that—will you take the command in my absence, Dick?"

"Nay, answered the highwayman, courteously, "the command must devolve upon the lieutenant."

Walters modestly enough demurred, but Dick Turpin was firm, and it was settled that the lead should rest with the lieutenant.

Red Ralph too, in truth, was better pleased with this arrangement, although he had paid Dick Turpin the compliment of asking him.

He knew that the men would rather be led by their own lieutenant, who understood them, and knew every inch of the ground which they were about to contest.

"Well then, Walters," said the Captain of the Yellow Band, drawing him aside, "a few words in your ear before we separate. You will proceed at once to place the men in the brushwood about the hermit's cave. From there they can fire upon the horses of the household troops; the horses, bear in mind."

"Ay, captain."

"I wish that distinctly borne in mind, for I must have no life taken unless at the last extremity. Disable their horses, if you like, and the day is our own. I do not doubt that we should gain the best of a skirmish if we could only manage to close with the soldiers. It is only their fire-arms that we have to fear. At the broadsword I could venture to put our men against any in the world."

"Ay, that you could!" said the lieutenant, enthusiastically.

"I give you these instructions, Walters," continued the Captain of the Yellow Band, "for preparations to meet our worst emergencies. I am in great hopes that we shall not have need of violent measures."

"I hope not."

"You must not make an assault in a body, unless you hear me signal thrice."

"Good."

"If I am in danger, I shall take some precaution to forewarn you of it. You understand me?"

"But surely," exclaimed the lieutenant, taking alarm at once, "you are not about to run into danger, captain?"

"Not heedlessly."

The lieutenant shook his head doubtfully.

"And now we understand each other, Walters?"

"Perfectly."

"You need not tell the men at once that I shall not be with you; it might discourage them."

And with this; they returned to the band.

Red Ralph then consigned his horse to the care of Wolff, and hastily returned to the haunt.

* * * * * *

Whilst the Yellow Band was making the preparations for the reception of Mr. Stanley Powell and the military detachment, as we have seen, the expected enemies were carousing at the half-way house of which Wolff had spoken.

He had given a correct estimate of their numbers.

Thirty chosen men of the household troops were there with the avowed intention of rooting out the Yellow Band!

These were aided by a dozen men whom Mr. Stanley Powell had hired as body-guards to protect him in his passage through the forest.

Mr. Stanley Powell had given them a *carte blanche* at the hostelry, for he thought that he could not better prepare men for an enterprise which he anticipated must be attended with considerable danger than by allowing them to imbibe freely of intoxicating liquors.

His own courage, too, had somewhat decreased with the increase of years, and he endeavoured to brace up his nerves with strong waters.

The consequence was, that before they contemplated putting an end to their carous none were too steady upon their legs.

But happily, thought Mr. Powell, all of them were the more prepared for a desperate emergency.

They were assembled in a large parlour, all talking

[DICK TURPIN'S ENCOUNTER WITH JONATHAN WILD.]

at once and making a dreadful noise and clamour, and keeping the landlord fully employed in running backwards and forwards to supply their frequent commands.

Two or three habitual topers were in the room, and apparently greatly interested in the proposed expedition against the Yellow Band.

At length, however, Mr. Stanley rose from his seat, and suggested a move.

The officer in command of the soldiers experienced some little difficulty in getting his men under weigh; but the prospect of a brush with the reported invincible banditti at length achieved the desired object, and they prepared to depart.

"Before we leave," said Mr. Stanley Powell, rather thickly, "does any one know the country well?"

No one answered. The soldiers to a man were perfectly ignorant of the locality.

"Landlord!" called Mr. Powell.

"Sir?"

"Can you give us a man who knows the forest well—one who could act the part of guide for us?"

Before the landlord could reply, an individual in a smock-frock, with red head and sandy whiskers, stepped into the parlour, and made his way up to Mr. Stanley Powell.

"I'm the man," he said, with a strong country dialect.

"Where have you sprung from?" demanded Mr. Powell.

"The bar, sir."

"And you can undertake to conduct us through the forest?"

"Yes, sir? for a trifling consideration; you understand."

"Of course you shall be paid for your trouble."

"Thankee, sir."

"You are well acquainted with the forest then?"

"Every inch of it."

"You know the nunnery?"

"The Retreat, sir?"

"Yes."

"Ay, sir, well; do you want to go there, sir?"

"Yes; and if you can take us a near way you shall have a guinea for your trouble."

"A guinea! Gad, sir! I can do that for you."

"Good: then you are just the man I want."

The soldiers and Mr. Stanley Powell's body-guard were called together and formed into marching order outside the house.

"March!" said the officer of the troops.

And off they started, headed by Mr. Powell, his body-guard, and the newly-acquired guide.

They had not proceeded far, however, when Mr. Powell found reason to object to the path which the guide had chosen.

It was a narrow footpath down which he proposed leading them, so overgrown by the thick foliage that they had to stoop in their saddles as they proceeded.

"Why are you bringing us this way?" he demanded.

"The nearest way, sir."

"Is there no road then?"

"There is, sir, but we save half a mile by taking this path."

"But the road must necessarily be the safest."

"Not at all, sir," responded the rustic; "no one would ever dream of your attempting this narrow footpath upon horseback."

"True," returned Mr. Stanley Powell, "there's something in that."

"A goodish bit, sir," rejoined the guide: "if we took the road, it is more than likely that we should be caught in an ambuscade."

Mr. Powell looked considerably startled at the word.

"You see, sir," pursued the rustic, "the Yellow Band by this time most probably know of your intentions against them, and they are a desperate lot of fellows, if report says true."

"They are."

"And they would think no more of firing upon you from the cover of a tree than they would in shooting down a mad dog."

"Upon me?"

"Ay, sir, upon you: they would choose you for their first shot, for most likely your dress would mark you out as the chief man among us.

"Go on this way, my man, by all means—any path you like—but I hope sincerely that it is not much longer, for it is truly a cutthroat-looking spot, and I shall not feel easy until we are well out of it."

"Here we are, then, sir; this is the end of it."

They emerged one by one into a broad open space.

One circumstance here caused the officer of the household troops some annoyance and a great deal of mistrust.

No less than three of his men were missing!

CHAPTER XLV.

THE MISSING MEN—THE INVISIBLE ASSASSIN—THE WORK OF DEATH—THE HAUNTED CELL—THE HORRIBLE APPARITION—TRIUMPH—DANGERS TO COME.

GREAT was the chagrin of the officer and Mr. Stanley Powell to find, on emerging from the path through which their volunteer guide conducted them, that several of their number were missing.

No one could offer the least explanation of the mystery.

No one had heard any cry or the faintest indication of a scuffle, and some sound would undoubtedly have been noticed had the missing men been struck down by the knife of an invisible assassin.

"There is a traitor amongst us!" exclaimed the officer, looking about him.

The men glanced suspiciously from one to the other. Of the troops there could be no doubt. The only suspicions, therefore, could point to the men hired by Mr. Stanley Powell.

"The traitor must be there, Mr. Powell," said the officer pointing to his men.

"Unless," returned Mr. Powell — "unless the guide—"

"Of course," exclaimed the officer; "why, he was the first man to be thought of here!"

He beckoned, and the countryman came up with a scrape, and pull at a ragged lock of sandy hair which hung over his forehead.

"My man," said the officer sternly, "I believe that there is a traitor amongst us."

"A what?"

"A traitor."

"Lawk, sir!"

"And I believe that you are either a great knave or a decided fool, and I rather incline to the former belief."

"I don't quite follow'ee, sir," returned the man, "I be on'y a poor humble man, quite on'arned, and your fine words on'y bother me. Speak me plain in straightfor'ard English, and I'll give ye an answer."

"In plain English, then," said the officer, "I believe you are a traitor—a rascal. *Now* do you understand?"

"I hear what you say, but 'pon my life, sir, I can't understand what you mean."

"Ah! you can doubtless assume a deal of innocence," said the officer, "but let me tell you, my fine fellow, that if I was assured of your treachery six feet of stout rope should settle your accounts with this life."

"Lawk, sir! you frighten me."

"I only speak the straightforward truth. If I but fancied you guilty I'd hang you like Haman!"

"But, sir, I don't see why you should talk like this to me: you hired me to guide you to the glade, and I'm doing it. I call upon any one to say if I ain't brought you a short cut through the wood. Ask any one of the men who knows the part."

One of Mr. Powell's men was appealed to, and certified to the truth of what the guide advanced.

He did not know the country sufficiently well to undertake the post of guide, but yet he recognised the place into which they had emerged from the crosspath, and he gave it as his opinion that they had saved at least half a mile by taking the path.

"Enough," said the officer. "Now you may lead us on to this precious Yellow Band's haunt; but beware! I shall have my eye upon you all the time; you are covered with this pistol, and the faintest suspicious movement will be the signal for me to fire. Now lead on."

The guide looked greatly alarmed as well as astonished at this threat, and led on again, followed immediately by the officer, who held the pistol at his head.

A few paces on the guide stopped short to warn the officer of a hole almost concealed by twigs and fallen leaves into which he nearly stepped.

This told capitally in favour of the guide, and they resumed the march.

A short distance further, however, they were not so fortunate. The ground was full of holes, similar to that which of he had but just warned the officer, and into one of them the horse of the latter stumbled, and could not extricate his fore leg.

The guide immediately profferred his aid, and very dexterously drew up the horse's leg, without causing the rider to dismount.

"See if he has hurt his leg," said the officer.

The guide took up the horse's leg and examined it critically before giving his decision.

"I fear, captain," he said, shaking his head, "that the pastern is damaged."

"Seriously?"

"No—only a trifle."

"Never mind—st—st!"

And the troop moved on again. But, sure enough, as the guide had said, the horse appeared hurt in the fore leg, for it limped most painfully.

However, there was no help for this now. The critical moment of their enterprise was fast approaching, and he could not afford to waste the time in getting another horse.

"What place is this?" demanded the officer, pointing to a rocky projection in the embankment, half hidden by the thick foliage.

"This is the Palmer's Cell."

"Indeed?" said the officer. "Then we must be close upon their haunt. Is this place remarkable for anything?"

"The Palmer's Cell, sir?"

"Ay."

"Nothing beyond the remarkable echo in the cavern."

"An Irish echo?" demanded the officer, laughing.

"Yes, sir," said the rustic gravely.

"O-ho!" laughed the officer; "it will answer any question put to it?"

"Anything, sir."

"Then, s'death!" he shouted, "where's the Yellow Band got to?"

The words had barely passed his lips when the answer came from a volley of small arms.

The shots flew about them in every direction, but they could not see whence they came, so well hidden were the attacking party.

Eight of the soldiers were unseated, their horses having been struck down by the bullets of the invisible enemy.

Amongst the first to fall were the officer and Mr. Stanley Powell; the latter considerably shaken and greatly frightened, but no bones broken.

The former quite heedless of his bruises, but instantly upon the alert.

His first impression was that the guide had led them into an ambuscade, and, clutching the pistol, which had never quitted his hand, he eagerly sought him.

A glance at the poor fellow, however, very quickly dissipated any notions of treachery from this quarter.

The guide, to all appearance badly wounded, had staggered against the bank, and was supporting himself upon one arm, whilst his other hand was pressed upon his brow as if in great agony.

Singularly enough not one of the soldiers was wounded. Eight of the horses had been shot down, but beyond this no harm had befallen the attacking party.

It struck the officer at once that the object of the enemy was to disable them simply; but, if so, why deal so severely with the unfortunate rustic who acted as their guide?

Probably they regarded him in the light of a spy.

"See to that poor fellow—" began the officer.

But, ere he could conclude his humane order, a second volley was fired with still more disastrous effect.

Whizz—whizz! came the balls in every direction from the bushes, and some of the troops even declared that they could perceive the muzzles of the muskets gleaming through the foliage.

Still not one of the soldiers had been injured, although only five men remained mounted!

"We shall all be hopelessly slaughtered here!" cried the officer as soon as he could make himself heard. "Charge into the bushes! Drive your carbines into the foliage and blaze away!"

The men responded with a cheer, and a rattle of musketry succeeded.

But a dead silence followed their fire. Not a sound was heard to announce the success of their volley.

Not a cry to tell that any of the intrepid Yellow Band had been struck!

"Load again!" cried the officer in a loud clear voice. "Make ready! Into the bushes with you; fire!"

Another report succeeded, and with no better result.

"They must be about this cavern!" said the officer, quite puzzled as to what they should next be after. "Follow me! we'll root 'em out if they're here!"

"Stop, stop!" said the guide faintly.

"Who calls?"

"It is me, colonel."

The officer could but pause to listen when saluted as colonel!

"What do you want?"

"Don't ye venture into that cavern; they say that the Palmer's Cell is haunted by the Yellow Boys."

"Haunted? Pshaw! how can any place be haunted by living flesh and blood?"

"But you don't think that them Yellow Boys are real nateral flesh and blood surely?"

The officer burst into a loud fit of laughter, but his men were rather impressed by the wounded guide's words, for they wavered and seemed half disinclined to follow their officer into the Palmer's Cell.

"What!" cried the officer indignantly; "are you women that you heed the croakings of a poor bleeding peasant! Pah! Let those who feel craven-hearted hang back; that's all!

Waving his sword the gallant young soldier dashed into the Palmer's Cell, followed by the whole troop.

The five men whose horses remained to them even dismounted and followed the rest into intricacies out of the range of hermits' caverns.

As soon as they had fairly disappeared, the wounded guide, who alone had been left behind, whistled a low call!

The signal was answered instantaneously, and a man sprang forth from the bushes.

"Wolff!" said the guide.

"Captain!"

"Yes."

And the guide sprang lightly up from his reclining posture, all traces of his hurt disappearing as if by magic.

"See to the horses, Wolff."

Two men came out of the bushes as Wolff had done in answer to the latter's summons, and immediately secured the five horses which alone of the whole troop were unhurt.

"Mount and ride off full gallop!" said the pseudo-guide.

Then, turning to Wolff, he added hastily—

"The men are distributed in the Palmer's Cell as I directed?"

"Yes, captain."

"Good; and what have you done with the three troopers?"

"I have them near at hand bound securely."

"I'm glad of that, we can make use of them."

The two Yellow Boys were by this time mounted and ready to start, and they signified the same to Red Ralph.

"Off and away, then," said Red Ralph. "Shout out, as you go, as loud as you like. Gallop!"

The men obeyed, and right lustily did they shout, as if attempting to drown the clattering of the five horses' feet as they rode off full gallop.

With oaths and wild shouts the soldiers and Mr. Stanley Powell's men rushed out of the cavern.

"Hah!" cried the officer, mad with chagrin, "the only horses which were let to us—there they go—galloping like fiends. Fire upon them. Two pounds to the man who hits a horse!"

But the soldiers had to reload their carbines, and by the time that this was accomplished the two Yellow Boys were safely out of range.

It was now that several of the men who had flung away their carbines and drawn their swords upon entering the Palmer's Cell made the discovery that the five horses were not all of which their wily enemy had robbed them.

All the carbines which had been left behind had disappeared with the horses!

The officer grew more and more perplexed every instant, and in vain did he cudgel his brains for a project!

He endeavoured to get some assistance from Mr. Stanley Powell, but the old *roué* was in no condition to give advice. He was too much occupied with his fears for his own personal safety, and, indeed, he began to wish himself heartily at home.

"Something must be done," said the officer, in trouble: "call the men together."

Now a fresh alarm awaited them. When the soldiers were called over, ten were missing! whilst only one of Mr. Stanley Powell's men returned from the Palmer's Cell.

Had they been struck down in open combat—had even a cry or a groan betrayed that they had fallen in ambush, the soldiers would have thought nothing of it.

But there was something startling at the least in this inexplicable disappearance of thirteen of the troops without the least warning!

"It's all that devil of a captain of theirs!" said Mr. Stanley Powell: "he's the fiend himself at stratagem."

"I would I had him here," exclaimed the officer.

"*He's not far off!*" said a voice from the Palmer's Cell.

The officer and several of the men might have been seen to change colour.

The next instant there was a loud cry of terror, and out of the cavern rushed one of the soldiers, throwing his arms wildly above his head.

"What is it? what's the matter?" demanded a dozen voices at once.

"Oh! help! help!" shouted the soldier.

"Speak, man," said the officer: "what's the matter?"

The man could not reply for some few seconds.

"Have you seen the foul fiend?"

"Himself!" cried the soldier, his eyes starting from their sockets, and trembling from head to foot; "himself! the fiend himself! I was there in his grasp—spell-bound by his damnable arts!"

His hearers shivered with horror!

"Nonsense, man!" remonstrated the officer; "you are mad."

"Mad or not mad," said the soldier, "I would not return to that cavern to be made commander-in-chief."

The troops who had crowded round their comrade began to grow fidgetty and exchange glances, whilst those nearest to the Palmer's Cell sidled round to the further side of the group.

"This is sheer folly, Mr. Powell," said the officer.

"Ye—es—"

"We must form again and make a regular search in this cavern. Depend on it there is some ingenious juggle going on that a little care with a little boldness cannot fail to discover."

"You return there, then," said Mr. Powell: "I will keep watch here with some of the men."

A smile of contempt curled the officer's lip.

"Where is the guide?" he asked: "he may be able to enlighten us."

The guide, however, had disappeared, and vainly did the soldiers seek him.

This was fresh cause for uneasiness. The guide had appeared wounded unto death, and yet he had contrived to move off!

With great difficulty, however, the officer formed his men into a body for a fresh investigation of the Palmer's Cell, and they advanced to the mouth of the cavern.

Here a startling vision met their view, which had such an effect upon the men, that the expedition against Red Ralph and the Yellow Band was utterly routed and broken up.

Just as they reached the cave, the wildest, most unearthly shrieks arrested their footsteps. Pandemonium appeared to be let loose, and the legions of fiends yelling in horrible discordance their approval of their liberty!

Then followed a loud explosion which seemed to shake the earth, and the cavern was filled on a sudden with one huge flame.

In the centre of the flames appeared a tall gaunt figure clothed in yellow from head to foot, resembling, save in the uniform hue of his person, the mystical Herne the Hunter.

Motionless, and with a fixed sardonic grin upon his yellow face, this strange apparition surveyed the awe-stricken soldiers.

The effect was wondrous—appalling!

For a minute all seemed transfixed by the unearthly vision!

Then the soldier who had rushed from the cavern and informed his sceptical leader of the terrors he had witnessed, broke the silence, and ran off crying wildly for mercy!

His example was followed by the whole body, even including Mr. Stanley Powell and the officer. In justice to the latter, however, it must be said that he exerted himself to the utmost to avert the panic, and was the last to quit the spot.

In the flight, however, the soldier who had led the way, and who was the only one who averred to have seen the diabolical practices of the Yellow Band of fiends, bounced into an adjacent hedge, from which he emerged as soon as the spot was clear of his comrades and Mr. Stanley Powell's reduced retinue.

Then a whole mob of the Yellow Band ran out of the Palmer's Cell, headed by Wolff, who was clothed all in yellow.

Wolff had personated the unearthly individual in yellow, who had put the climax to the chapter of horrors which had served to rid the Yellow Band of the unpleasant attentions of the military.

"Wolff," said the soldier, who as the intelligent reader has, doubtless, divined was no other than Red Ralph—"Wolff, you looked your devilish character to the life!"

"Thankee, captain," said Wolff, laughing grimly,

"but I'm deuced glad that you broke ground as you did. Those flames nearly choked me, not to mention my disgust at seeing so much good brandy burnt to waste."

"Scarcely to waste, Wolff," said the Captain of the Yellow Band, "since it has contrived to rid us of a very disagreeable enemy, and that too without bloodshed—without striking a blow."

"It was a wonderful scheme!" said Dick Turpin.

"Indeed it was," said the lieutenant. "Three cheers for the captain, my lads."

And three lusty cheers rang through the Palmer's Cell, but without producing the marvellous echo of which the quondam guide had spoken!

"And three cheers for Wolff," cried Red Ralph, "for he put the finishing stroke to the job."

"Nay, captain," said Wolff, modestly, "I was but an actor in your pantomime. All would have been nothing but for your idea of the flames. You raised their fears, and so laid the foundation of the whole affair, by bringing them through the bridle-path where our men who hired themselves to old Powell managed to secure three of the soldiers so quietly. And then, in making one of the prisoners change clothes with you, you settled the job, for I don't believe that they would have run even then had you not led the way."

"As you please," said Red Ralph: "I see you are determined to load me with honours."

"Well deserved!" shouted Dick Turpin, lustily.

"So let us return to the haunt," resumed Red Ralph, "give our poor maimed comrade Tom King a history of the attack, and have a carouse. To-night, lads, I leave you again for a while. I have a job on Hampstead Heath."

Better had he not quitted the haunt that night!

A dreadful shock was in store for him when next he returned to the scene of his triumphs.

But we must not anticipate the startling adventures that Red Ralph has to encounter.

CHAPTER XLVI.

LEONORE AND RED RALPH—THE HORRIBLE REVELATIONS—THE CHASE—"ON, ON, BRAVE NANCY!"—THE FALL—THE FOREST—PURSUIT—THE SWOON—THE GIPSY ENCAMPMENT—JONATHAN WILD—THE PLOT—THE BROKEN BRANCH.

LADY LEONORE had well-nigh fainted when the horseman in the yellow mask upon Hampstead Heath rushed and rescued her from the odious familiarities of the waggoner.

It needed no more than the cavalier's presence to render Lady Leonore the service of which she stood in such need, for, as we have already related, the waggoner no sooner caught sight of the yellow mask than, with a cry of fear, he rushed from the spot.

The masked horseman leaned over the Lady Leonore for the purpose of raising her up, when the sight of her face appeared to affect him no less than the yellow visor had alarmed the waggoner.

"Never—never!" he cried.

Leonore perceived that her features were familiar to her preserver, and her old fears returned immediately.

The unhappy resemblance she bore to somebody who had incurred the displeasure or suspicions of the villagers from whom she had so narrowly escaped, was about to get her once more into trouble!

"Sir, hear me, oh! hear me," she ejaculated: "you fancy that you recognise me, but, oh! for the love of mercy, believe me when I tell you that you are mistaken."

"Never!" returned the horseman. "Would you deceive me?"

"No, no—I swear it. But I (so it appears to me) have the misfortune to bear a close resemblance to some one who has created herself some terrible foes."

"Madam," said the horseman sternly, "in attempting to deceive me you but mislead yourself. I have great and dreadful reasons for knowing you."

"How?"

"You are one who should be nearer and dearer to me than all the world."

Lady Leonore shrank back alarmed at these strange words.

"Sir, I implore you—"

"Nay," said the horseman, "fear me not; I love you too tenderly to wish you harm. Love you with a depth and devotion which can only cease with life."

At first the Lady Leonore had fancied that the horseman was deranged, but the earnestness of his manner and the clearness of his enunciation soon convinced her that he was sane.

There then remained but one conclusion to her: he was labouring under the same delusion as the maddened villagers who had attempted to burn her at the stake.

The fatal resemblance would ultimately undo her—of that she felt assured.

However, she was spared further embarrassment upon this head by the appearance of a new danger. A sound of horsemen came along the road across the heath.

"What is that?" exclaimed Lady Leonore and her preserver simultaneously.

"Can I be pursued?" said the former, in alarm.

"Nay," said the horseman; "fear nothing. I will protect you with my life."

Lady Leonore glanced into the masked face to express her gratitude. Vainly did she strive to pierce the mask, as the tones of the horseman's voice struck somewhat familiarly upon her ear.

The sounds of the horses now grew nearer and nearer, and Lady Leonore's fears grew momentarily greater.

"Let us fly!" she exclaimed.

"Fear nothing," said the horseman; "you are under my care, and no power upon earth shall tear you from me."

"Thanks, oh! thanks!" said Leonore; "I felt a great security in your protection, but they may be too powerful for you."

"They were not too powerful before—when this good blade and this right arm smote them right and left in your cause."

"What mean you?"

"I mean, lady," said the horseman, "that but for me and the timely intervention of my gallant followers you would have been by this time a charred and hideous corse!"

"Great heavens!" ejaculated Leonore, with a shudder at those fearful words, "'twas you, then, who saved me from that dreadful fate?"

"'Twas I."

"And you are—"

"Your husband!"

And with these startling words the horseman removed his yellow mask, revealing the handsome face of Red Ralph, the Captain of the Yellow Band.

Once more had his wondrous fortune put him in the way of his beauteous virgin wife, at a most terrible moment for her.

For an instant they forgot the danger from the presumed pursuit, until a warning shout bade them be upon their guard.

"Come on!" called a voice in the distance, "it was just at this part of the road I left him."

"Come," said Red Ralph; "we must leave the road until this fresh danger is past; give me your hand—so—"

He lifted her on to the horse and then sprang up behind her, clasping her slender waist with the hand that grasped the rein.

"Ho! Nancy lass! off and away!" and the mare bounded off with a snort of intelligence.

The double burden did not allow the mare to put forth her best speed, but she gallopped off at a very respectable pace.

But, unfortunately, the noise of his retreat set the pursuers upon the scent, and he could presently hear them urging their steeds on the right track!

Leonore could now only wring her hands in silent terror. The pursuit she felt assured was for her. Her cruel enemies who had so persecuted her were now hunting her down.

Red Ralph urged on the gallant mare to further exertions, but the hard labour she suffered soon became painfully apparent.

At each pat of her beloved master's hand she renewed her struggles, but failed to increase her lead.

Unless some happy chance befriended them Red Ralph could easily foretell the end.

He must succumb to his hard fate. Once more yield himself the prisoner of that justice which he had outraged. Leave his wife after another interview of such sad brevity alone and unprotected.

No, never! This last thought made him resolve to battle for his liberty with his life.

"On—on, my brave Nancy!" he cried; "off and away, lass! Ho for the haunt of the bold Yellow Boys!"

And again did the noble animal respond to her master's summons with wondrous courage.

But cruel fate was against them.

After breasting boldly a small hillock, a ditch of considerable width had to be leaped.

Ralph, in the confusion, had not perceived it, and was therefore not prepared in time to clear it. The mare, however, gallantly took the jump, but her hind legs slipped back, and she stumbled and fell.

Ralph in an instant had succeeded in disentangling both himself and Leonore from the fallen mare, and was prepared to renew the journey on foot.

In the fall he had, however, encountered a serious misfortune. One of his legs had been beneath the mare, and a painful sprain of the ankle was the consequence.

With the prospect of a long journey on foot, this became, to say the least, unpleasant.

But Red Ralph was not the man to be daunted by trifles, and he stepped boldly onwards, bearing his newly-recovered wife, half fainting, in his arms.

In the course of a few minutes, the falling of the mare proved to be a piece of good fortune rather than otherwise, for he had at once avoided the road and made his way by a narrow bridle path into a thick wood.

Here pursuit appeared doubtful—capture almost an impossibility.

He pushed on boldly, until he could no longer hear the sound of his pursuers. The hurt of his ankle began to make itself apparent, but, setting his teeth and making a determination not to heed it, he continued his way.

Presently he felt the arms of his lovely burden (which encircled, almost lovingly, his neck) slip from around him, and Leonore hung a dead weight in his arms!

An alarming suspicion crossed him.

He glanced down into her face. It was pale and death-like!

She had fainted. The dangers and privations to which the poor girl had of late been subjected were now beginning to tell upon her at a most unfortunate moment.

"Poor girl!" said Red Ralph, "this has been too much for her. I must get some water, though. But how? Where?"

He placed the insensible Leonore gently upon the ground, and began to look about him.

He had walked into the thick of the wood, and he would, no doubt, have great difficulty in extricating himself from its labyrinth.

He looked upon the beauteous Leonore in the death-like stupor, until he felt frantic. There was she perhaps dying—and he powerless to aid her!

Hither and thither he rushed, but could not see the faintest sign of human habitation.

Then he would run to her side, clasp her cold hand, white as alabaster, and call upon her to look up. But in vain. The poor girl was still in the same deep swoon, unconscious to all that was passing around her.

"Selfish fool that I am!" exclaimed Red Ralph, springing to his feet once more, "I have been no distance from her yet. I must get water, wherever I go for it."

Then, with a hasty glance at his pallid bride, he rushed wildly away.

On, on he went, never heeding the briars and bushes which tore his clothes and his flesh most cruelly.

Suddenly, as he paused to look about him, a low faint sound caught his eager ear, like the dripping of water, and shouting joyfully he bounded off in the direction.

But he must have been mistaken. His ear had surely deceived him!

For a few steps the sound appeared to grow louder and more distinct, and then it suddenly ceased altogether.

Hither and thither he ran in his anguish, but unhappily failed to discover any traces of the brook, which he felt convinced was somewhere close at hand.

When his chagrin and grief had wellnigh reached a climax, and he was upon the point of despairing, his hopes were restored by perceiving, a little distance ahead, a wreath of smoke curling gracefully above the trees.

"A house! a house!" he exclaimed joyfully, "at last. Thank heaven for this!"

There was no path leading to the spot whence the smoke proceeded, so Red Ralph dashed boldly into the bushes and briars once more, and battled his way through them.

Presently the shrubs grew less thickly, and he progressed more easily. Anon he could plainly perceive the direction from which the smoke had issued.

Half-a-dozen yards on was a gipsy encampment, and the whole of the vagrant tribe were gathered about a huge cauldron swung upon a tripod over a flaming wood fire.

In the midst of them stood a big burly man, whose different apparel denoted him to be a house-dweller, and who was engaged in an earnest conversation with one of the gipsies, apparently making a compact of some kind.

Red Ralph paused, scarcely liking, in spite of his urgent need, to venture abruptly into the camp of this band of wild rangers.

It was well he did so!

The stranger in conversation with the gipsy king turned round towards the fire, and the bright glare reflecting upon his face revealed to Red Ralph the well-remembered features of his arch-enemy, Jonathan Wild the thieftaker!"

"Wild!" ejaculated Ralph.

The word had burst from him ere he could think to restrain himself.

"Hullo!" exclaimed the gipsy king, whose ready ear had immediately caught the sound.

"What is it?" demanded Wild.

"Somebody mentioned your name."

Red Ralph now saw and regretted his imprudence, but fortunately no immediate harm came of it.

The gipsies looked carelessly about, and Jonathan Wild resumed his conversation with their chief.

Red Ralph, in his hiding-place, could see by their gestures that something of great importance was being discussed, but he was too far off to overhear what was the nature of the discussion.

Close by the fire was a large oak, whose branches overhung the encampment, and by making a short *détour* Red Ralph was enabled to reach this unobserved.

Then he proceeded as noiselessly as possible to climb it, and to his infinite gratification overheard the following conversation.

"You grow chicken-hearted, Master Jonah," said the thieftaker; "but consider the reward."

"A paltry half a century!" said the gipsy scornfully.

"The Government offers that," rejoined the thieftaker, "but there are no less than a dozen rewards offered by different parties. Mr. Stanley Powell offers two hundred, dead or alive; and a bishop, who shall be nameless, offers a like sum—"

"And even that does not pay for the risk," said the gipsy king, scornfully. "*You* know what *that* is."

"Pshaw!" said Jonathan Wild, snapping his fingers; "I don't value Red Ralph *that!*"

The Captain of the Yellow Band grew infinitely more interested than before.

Jonathan Wild was here, then, plotting his capture with the gipsies, all his previous schemes having but heaped defeat and shame upon his head.

This was a cunning move, for of all people Red Ralph would have been less inclined to suspect the gipsies than any one.

"I shall spoil this little job nicely, Master Jonathan," muttered Red Ralph, between his set teeth.

And he pressed eagerly forward to catch the remainder of the remarkable project for his destruction.

Fatal chance!

The branch upon which he crept was rotten with age, and the sapless wood snapped like a piece of glass, precipitating Red Ralph into the midst of the wonderstricken gipsy band!

CHAPTER XLVII.

RALPH IN THE HANDS OF THE GIPSIES — AGAIN AT THE MERCY OF THE THIEFTAKER — THE ROBBER'S AGONY — NIGHT IN THE CAMP — THE STRANGE VISITOR — A CHANCE OF ESCAPE — THE KISS — THE MUTILATED HAND AGAIN — ONCE MORE A PRISONER.

As soon as the gipsies perceived that the falling body was a human form, they were upon it like a pack of famished wolves, and poor Ralph got rather roughly handled.

"A spy! a spy!"

"What is it?" said the gipsy king, pushing his way through the crowd up to the crest-fallen Ralph.

"A spy."

"Where did he come from?"

"He was holding on that tree, and the branch gave way with him."

"Why—surely I know that face," said the gipsy king.

"Let me see him," said Jonathan Wild, pushing his way up.

Red Ralph now trembled for his life.

"The very man!" ejaculated Jonathan Wild.

"Who?"

"Red Ralph."

"Never!"

"It is. I could swear to that face in a million."

The gipsies looked from one to the other, and the gipsy chief and Jonathan Wild exchanged glances of astonishment.

It appeared to them little short of miraculous that he should have fallen into their power at the precise moment that they were plotting his destruction, and that of his adventurous followers.

Jonathan Wild's first idea was that this was some new trick, and that the Yellow Boys were lurking at hand ready to fall upon them.

He immediately communicated the nature of his fears to the gipsy king, who sent out scouts in every direction forthwith.

Red Ralph's agony at this is indescribable. Should they chance to discover his fainting bride, the beauteous Leonore, to what indignities might not her helpless condition subject her?"

"What do you propose doing with him?" asked Wild.

"I mean to get the reward."

"But you haven't taken him," said the thieftaker.

"Nor you either yet," said the gipsy, significantly; "and what's more to the purpose, Master Wild, you don't lay a hand upon him until I touch the canaries."

"You never have any confidence, Master Jonah," said the thieftaker: "I believe you would suspect your own father."

"I would," retorted the gipsy king, "if his name happened to be Jonathan Wild."

"Tut! tut!" said the thieftaker, "we needn't quarrel over such a trifle—it isn't worth while. Give him up to me, and I'll see you have your reward."

"Ha! ha! Master Wild," laughed the gipsy, ironically, "you're wondrous cunning; but since when, pray, have I appeared such an arrant fool to ye that you should try a poor dodge like that on me? Pshaw!"

The thieftaker bit his lip, and was silent for a moment.

"No matter, Jonah," he said, presently, "let the prisoner be bound and carried into the tent. It isn't absolutely necessary that they should hear all we have to say in this matter; you understand."

The gipsy gave the instructions, and Red Ralph was bound securely and borne into the tent.

Now his bodily sufferings were quite eclipsed by the mental anguish he endured.

Not a thought, however, had he for himself, though his position was not the most enviable. All his ideas were engrossed by that one topic, his newly-recovered Leonore.

Surely there was some wondrous fatality in all this!

Upon each occasion that he had seen the lovely but unhappy girl whom he had sworn before heaven to cherish through life, he had been torn almost immediately from her by a strange combination of circumstances.

Was it the punishment of Providence for his crimes? he more than once asked himself.

Was it decreed that the rash words which he had uttered, when fascinated by the surpassing loveliness of Lady Leonore, should bring their own punishment?

"If so," muttered the Captain of the Yellow Band, in anguish, as he writhed with the cords which cut into his flesh," if so, I can only accept my lot. But, oh! it is hard, cruelly hard, that the poor girl should so suffer for my crimes! Could I but be sure that she was secure from harm, I could meet the worst which may befall me."

Here, his meditations were interrupted by the entrance of Jonathan Wild into the tent.

"Well, Ralph," said the thieftaker, maliciously, "so we have you at last."

Ralph was silent.

"Lost your tongue?" pursued Wild: "so much the better. But I've come to tell you that Jonah, the gipsy and I have come to an arrangement about you."

The thieftaker paused again, evidently hoping to draw Red Ralph into conversation with him.

"The result is," resumed Jonathan Wild, with killing deliberation, "that you are to be hung at midnight!"

With a ferocious expression in his snake-like eyes, the thieftaker regarded his captive.

But the bold Captain of the Yellow Band preserved the calmest exterior, notwithstanding the startling nature of Jonathan Wild's information.

Wild, upon his part, was greatly disappointed. He had come in delighted by the gipsy king's decision, with the idea of gloating over the doomed victim's agony, and listening to appeals for mercy.

Not caring, therefore, to show his disappointment to the captive, Jonathan Wild left the tent without another word.

Had he been able to read what was passing in the unhappy Red Ralph's mind, in spite of the calm bearing he preserved, Wild would have been immensely gratified.

"Leonore!" exclaimed Red Ralph, half aloud, and in the bitterest anguish of spirit—"wife—lost, lost for ever! Would to heaven that we had never met! Then this blow would have fallen less lightly. Now I feel that my time approaches: for the first time, in my wild career, I feel that I am upon the eve of something terrible—which can but mean the end of life. Never! never! By heaven, I cannot die thus. It cannot surely be so doomed. Leonore, oh! Leonore ——"

And with her name upon his lips he sank into a dreamy kind of stupor.

How long he remained thus he could form no idea, when suddenly he became conscious of another presence in the tent.

He had heard nothing—seen nothing, and yet he felt that he was not alone!

Languidly he opened his eyes, for, although fearfully anticipating a hasty summons to a violent and awful fate, he had suffered and still endured so much that he could not rouse himself, even at the thought of the dread moment's near approach.

Beside him stood a female figure with her gaze temporarily averted from him.

She was glancing towards the entrance of the tent.

The next instant she turned her head round, and there he beheld, to his unbounded amazement and joy, the face of his beloved!

It was Leonore!

Yes, there could be no doubt of it—it was Leonore again. And yet there was something about her which Red Ralph scarcely comprehended.

She was no longer the fainting pallid creature whom he had quitted in such trouble but a little time before.

Her dress, too, was quite changed. She was now habited in a dress of gay varied colour, denoting her to be one of the Zingari, and, from the superiority of its texture and make, she must have been some one of note in the band.

All this he noted with one glance of his quick eye.

"Leonore!" he breathed, rather than said—"Leonore."

The woman regarded him compassionately for a while without speaking.

"You suffer," at length she said.

"No, no," said Red Ralph, endeavouring to smile: "not now that you are here, Leonore."

"You wander in your mind," said the woman; "you do not know me, I am assured."

"Not know you!" iterated the captive, faintly.

"No; you are light-headed with suffering."

"No, no, my own love. I know you. Had suffering even destroyed my mind, your face would at once restore my reason."

The gipsy was evidently puzzled by these strange words.

"Speak," said Red Ralph, as a strange suspicion crossed him; "are you not my Leonore?"

"I am called Mina," said the gipsy.

"Mina!"

"Yes; I am the queen of this tribe; you mistake me for another."

"Never!" exclaimed the captive; "no, no, it is not possible; the same—even the same voice."

"Some strong likeness I bear to another misleads you."

"It cannot, cannot be!" said Red Ralph; "and yet this change from weariness—nay, almost death—to health and life—what can it mean? Is it possible that what you say of me is true—that suffering has destroyed my reason—that my diseased fancy has likened you to *her*."

"I scarce can answer that," said the gipsy, smiling; "your words now seem rational enough. Is there anything you wish for now?"

"A little water, for the love of mercy," said Red Ralph.

A brown jug close at hand speedily supplied this want, and Red Ralph, after gulping eagerly at it, was profuse in his acknowledgments.

"My head is burning," he said; "the skin upon my brow feels like parchment, and my temples throb most painfully."

"Shall I bathe them?"

The sufferer gave his assent, in a look of the profoundest, most unutterable gratitude.

"You are an angel of mercy, in the midst of demons," said Red Ralph, fervently. "Grant me but one request, I beseech you."

"If reasonable."

"Place your hand to my face, that I may touch it with my lips."

The gipsy smiled and blushed visibly with pleasure, but did not offer to grant the prisoner's demand.

"Thank heaven!" murmured Ralph, earnestly, "that I am permitted to see one fellow-creature more to love—that my last moments may be thoughts of love."

"Of what do you speak?"

"Of you; nay, do not smile, for I swear I speak in all sincerity. You think that my love will be short-lived: alas! that's true; but Red Ralph never yet feared to die, nor will he shrink now."

"What mean you?"

"You must surely know that at midnight I am to be hanged."

"By whom?"

"By the tribe."

"For what?"

"Because Jonathan Wild the thieftaker, and my foe, has willed it, and because there is a price upon my head."

"Hah!" exclaimed the gipsy queen; "a price—say you so? Then no words of mine could save you. There are yet other means, but—"

Here she glanced about, as if fearful of being watched. Then from her waist-belt she drew a short stiletto, with which she immediately set about severing the cords.

One stroke, and his hand was at liberty!

[THE HIGHWAYMEN AND THE SLEEPING BEAUTY.]

In an instant he had taken advantage of this to seize her unemployed hand and cover it with kisses.

He could feel that she trembled violently, as she endeavoured to disengage it, and the stiletto fell to the ground.

In stooping to regain it, her eye chanced to fall upon his right hand, upon which it rested fixed—fascinated for several seconds!

The glove which he always wore upon it had been torn in the recent struggles, and its blood-red hue was revealed!

Then she suddenly averted her gaze, as if from some loathsome object. A shudder, momentarily, convulsed her entire frame!

Then, with a loud piercing shriek, she fell to the ground insensible!

Ere the terror-stricken Red Ralph could offer a word or even a thought, the gipsy tribe flocked into the tent and fell upon him!

"What is it?" demanded a score of voices at once.

But before a word was spoken they had drawn their own conclusions from what they observed.

Their queen lay fainting upon the ground, and her drawn stiletto lay there within her grasp!

"See, see," said the chief of the Zingari, "he has insulted your queen."

"He has—he has!"

"Then what shall be his doom?"

No. 17.

" Death !"

" Ay, ay—death to the man who has insulted our queen !"

" Rend him piecemeal !   Death to Red Ralph !"

CHAPTER XLVIII.

STRANGE SCENES IN THE GIPSIES' CAMP—PRE-
PARATION FOR TORTURE—THE RESCUE—THE
ESCAPE—THE RETURN TO THE CAMP—TERROR
—THE BREAK-UP OF THE BAND—THE DWARF'S
DEATH.

" HOLD !"

As a loud commanding voice uttered this word the gipsies instinctively turned round, and there beheld Jonathan Wild at the entrance of the tent.

" Gently, gently, my friends," said the thieftaker. " What would you do with your prisoner now ?"

" Slay him !" responded some twenty voices at once.

" He has insulted our queen, and we have sworn that he dies ! "

" Down with him ! "

" Stay, stay !" said Jonathan Wild; " I, too, have sworn that he dies; but rather let it be by the hang-man's cord."

" No, no ! "

" Down with him now ! "

" As you please," said Wild; " I have given my opinion ; agreements are made with you but to be broken.

" What do you mean by that, Master Wild ?" asked the gipsy king.

" Simply that our last understanding was that the prisoner should hang at midnight. Now you seem to forget all about that. However, I warn you that no reward will be forthcoming without my assistance, and that you certainly shall not have unless my will is fol-lowed in this matter."

The gipsy king grew grave at these words, and he held a hurried consultation with the band in Romany, which the thieftaker was unable to comprehend.

Not so Red Ralph.

He understood all that was uttered, and it did not at all tend to reassure him.

The band were to assemble at midnight to put him through a series of tortures worthy the invention of Red Indians, previous to hanging him, in revenge for the presumed insult offered their queen.

One of the tortures they spoke of as the whip; and, in order to make his sufferings the more acute, the instrument of torture was to be manufactured before the prisoner's eyes.

It consisted of a kind of cat or knout made of leather thongs, in the tips of which were inserted pieces of jagged iron.

Red Ralph was not at all deficient in courage, and yet he felt the flesh creep upon his back at the thought of being mutilated with this hideous instrument be-fore the assembled gang.

The only thing of which he could now think was the chance he should stand in a struggle for liberty when they should unbind him for the torture.

This was his only remaining hope, he thought.

But he was happily mistaken.

The time fixed for the perpetration of the crime grew terribly near, when, as Ralph lay back in his helpless condition, nervously twitching a cord which lay in reach of his hand, tantalising him in his in-ability to grasp it, he fancied he heard a sound of some one in the tent.

Then something cold touched his hand, and a

bearded mouth bit at the thongs which bound his wrists.

It was apparently a tough struggle, but at length successfully accomplished.

His arms were free !

He held out his right hand in gratitude to his in-visible liberator, and it came in contact with the shaggy coat of a large hound !

" What, Snarl !" said Red Ralph as he recognised the rough skin of an old pet dog.

The hound gave a whine of pleasure, more eloquent far than speech could possibly have been.

With his arms at liberty the work of freedom was very shortly performed, and once more did Red Ralph stand upright and fearless.

But the odds were fearful yet against his escape from such a host of enemies, and he could only hope for success in stratagem, and by observing the utmost caution in his proceedings.

The necessity for this was apparent the next instant.

There was a footstep without, and Red Ralph had barely time to throw himself down into his old position ere Jonathan Wild once more stepped across the thres-hold of the tent.

" I'm glad you're awake, Ralph," said the thief-taker in a bantering strain, " for I want a few minutes' conversation with you before this little affair comes off."

Here he made an upward jerk from the throat, to intimate the midnight execution of Ralph.

" You'll never live to see that, Jonathan Wild," said Red Ralph.

" O-ho ! Indeed ! "

" Never ! I swear it ! "

" And what, pray, my very good friend, is to prevent it ? " said Wild with great deliberation.

" This ! "

With this exclamation Red Ralph sprang up from his recumbent position, and before the astonished thieftaker could dream of offering resistance had seized him in a powerful grip by the throat.

The act was so sudden that Jonathan Wild could not even utter a sound.   When he had recovered from the momentary amazement into which the unexpected attack had thrown him, the grip upon his throat was so firm as to preclude all possibility of appealing for help.

Wild's arms hung helplessly by his side.

His eyes rolled fearfully, and he grew purple in the face.

The veins upon his forehead swelled nigh to burst-ing.

The tongue protruded, the face grew blacker, and the eyes appeared starting from their sockets.

Still the vengeance of the Captain of the Yellow Band was not satisfied.

His enemy was there in his grasp. The rascal's fate lay within his hands, and Red Ralph was full of thoughts of murder.

Suddenly the huge form of the thieftaker sank with-in his foe's clutch, and appeared to collapse.

" *Dead !*" said Ralph to himself. " There's the end of that ; justice is done to him, then."

Saying which he cast the lifeless body from him as if it had been the carcase of a beast of prey which he had brought down.

Then he stepped lightly to the entrance of the tent and looked out.

At a short distance from the spot some of the band were engaged in erecting a post—for the purpose of tying up their unfortunate prisoner, no doubt—but now, happily, their prisoner no longer.

The night was beautifully moonlight, and the sky clear and cloudless, but Ralph was in no mood to admire the beauty of the night.

He would rather have preferred it dark and cloudy.

As it was, every object in the open space in which the gipsies had encamped was as visible and distinct as at noontide.

Still he was not to be daunted. No hanging back now. He had never been known wanting in courage when the occasion demanded it, and it was not likely that he was now going to show the white feather.

He stepped boldly forth, but the gipsies were too much occupied with their task to heed his footstep.

They had heard it, and probably taken it for the return of the thieftaker, their worthy ally.

Congratulating himself upon exciting so little attention, he walked round the tent and stepped along a narrow path.

Still he scarcely liked quitting them without a parting effort at retaliation for the cruelties which they had been guilty of towards him, and still more for the viler atrocities which they had in store for him.

"I would give much," he muttered half aloud as he went, "to have half a dozen of the bold Yellow Boys with me. The time will arrive though; of that I am assured. In the meantime I must cherish the memory of the gipsy king, Master Jonah. Oh! let me not forget that name—Jonah! Jonah!"

"Who speaks my name?"

It was the voice of the gipsy king himself, who the next instant stepped forth from the hedge and confronted Red Ralph!

For a second they surveyed each other in silence.

The astonishment at this unexpected encounter was mutual.

Red Ralph had immediately recognised the voice and person of the man he had learned to hate so deeply upon so early an acquaintance. But the gipsy king evidently was scarcely so quick to remember the form of the man whose life he had contracted for with Jonathan Wild.

A minute, however, or less sufficed to acquaint the latter with the real state of affairs, for Red Ralph broke ground and flew upon his foe.

Hatred for the gipsy and desire of escape nerved his arm in the moment of trial.

The gipsy was a far more stalwart man than the Captain of the Yellow Band—hardened by the rough life of the tents and open air exercise.

But the apparently delicate frame of Red Ralph was possessed of marvellous strength and flexibility.

His muscles appeared to be of steel, highly tempered and delicately fashioned, and possessing all its elasticity.

As Red Ralph came on, Jonah the gipsy clawed at him, but his grasp was easily shaken off by the former, who seized him in his arms and raised him high above his head, as if he had been an infant!

Then he cast off the huge vagrant with a violent jerk, and he fell with a desperate thump to the ground stunned and bleeding.

"So much for Jonah the gipsy!" said Red Ralph triumphantly as he strode past the motionless body. "But I haven't seen the last of that gentleman yet, I hope. However, I think that both he and my old friend Jonathan Wild will keep clear of Red Ralph for awhile."

* * * * * * *

Vainly did Red Ralph search the part of the wood in which he had left his fainting wife.

Vainly did he call upon her by name, until the wood resounded with a mournful echo of the word "Leonore!"

She was gone, and not the slightest trace of her remained.

He now felt, in his anguish upon her account, that he would give much to know that she was only safe, if even the knowledge separated them for ever.

Hopeless and sad he wandered away, now heedless of what direction he took or what became of him.

For a second he was foolish and wicked enough to regret his escape from the gipsies, and the fate which awaited him at their hands.

Suddenly the neighing of a horse close at hand aroused him from the despondent reverie into which he had fallen.

With a smile of delight, he started and gazed around him.

"Ho! Nancy, lass!" he called, "ho! ho! Nancy, lass!"

In a moment his favourite mare ran up to his side, neighing and snorting with pleasure scarcely less intelligible than that of her master.

She had scarcely moved from the spot where Red Ralph had been compelled to quit her when escaping from the officers with Leonore after the chase over Hampstead Heath, and was now rested and prepared for work again.

This was a wonderful stroke of good fortune, of which Red Ralph did not fail to avail himself.

He fastened the girth and sprang into the saddle, and cantered across the smooth turf.

But now the ride failed to restore his spirits. He felt oppressed, and not only upon Leonore's account.

Something was going wrong he was sure. He was a great believer in presentiment, and he felt sure that he was about to experience a dire calamity.

He was not unfrequently low-spirited, for the violent excitement consequent upon his irregular mode of life brought terrible reactions; but in his worst fits of despondency a canter upon the soft turf would restore his humour.

With a sigh, he stroked the mare's sleek coat, and started off in the direction of his haunt.

Upon the road he passed several travellers who would have excited his cupidity upon ordinary occasions, but now they were allowed to pass on their way unmolested.

So engrossed was he with his own meditation that even the courteous "good-night" of the travellers he passed went unheeded.

He did not draw rein until he arrived at the glade in the forest, when he sprang from the saddle and, leaving the mare to shift for herself, made his way with all haste through the intricacies of the forest to the haunt.

"Hullo!" he muttered, as he stepped across the threshold of the dark passage. "No challenge?—what can it mean? Surely they are not neglectful of my orders whilst I'm away—their carelessness will ruin us."

He walked on, but met no one!

Every passage of the haunt was traversed, and not a living soul had he seen.

Red Ralph felt a vague dread stealing over him. Was he now about to meet with the great calamity which he had been so sadly anticipating that night?

No, no—they must be in the large hall—the cave in which they took their meals together.

Yet he dreaded to turn his steps thither. A sickening feeling was about his heart, and he dreaded to know what had befallen him—what had happened to the Yellow Band in his absence.

Suddenly a low moan struck upon his ear—a note of agony of some suffering fellow-creature, and it came from the direction of the larger cave—the only spot unsearched.

To run thither was the work of an instant,—there to meet a sight which sent a chill to his very heart's blood!

Stretched upon the ground lay the dwarf, Reuben, writhing with the agony caused by two horrid gashes upon the cheek and brow!

From the two hideous wounds the blood was trickling sluggishly, in thick drops, down his cheek, the deathly palour of which was rendered yet more ghastly by the fearful contrast which the bright purple hue of his life's-blood presented to it.

The unhappy man panted violently.

It was a terrible struggle for breath, which told its own sad tale at a single glance.

"Reuben, Reuben!" cried Ralph.

The poor dwarf glanced up at the speaker, and the light of love shone for an instant in his fast glazing eyes.

"The captain?" he said, with an effort.

"Yes, Reuben, yes—'tis I. What does this mean—what has happened?"

"You know nothing?"

"Nothing."

"Oh! 'tis a sad tale—a sad, sad tale, captain."

"What is it—speak, oh, speak, Reuben, I beseech you."

The dwarf struggled bravely with the grim enemy which was fast gathering him in its folds.

Getting his breath, he spoke once more, but with great difficulty.

"Tie up this hole in my forehead, captain. It seems to let the air in and cut short my breath."

Red Ralph tore off his lace scarf and bandaged it round the wounded man's brow, which seemed to have the effect of affording a temporary relief to the sufferer.

"It's an ugly cut, that one, captain," said the dwarf, with a sickly smile, "and has done me for this existence. The soldier gave me that."

"Which one?"

"The very man we took prisoner in the path you led the military and old Powell through."

"The man with whom I changed clothes afterwards?"

"The same."

"But how?"

"By some means he contrived to escape from here—found entrance—brought back soldiers—old Powell—the lot—I was too forward—cut down—left for dead—Newgate—the other—all—every man—res—rescue, God bless you, captain."

The unhappy man's voice trembled ominously.

"Ah! great Heaven! captain—"

Reuben, the dwarf, was no more.

CHAPTER XLIX.

THE ENTERTAINMENT AT LADY GLYDE'S — THE EXTRAORDINARY ROBBERY—THE ACT OF VIOLENCE — THE ALARM — THE THIEFTAKER — SECRET INFORMATION — THE DISGUISE — THE REVELATION.

ALL was noise and bustle at the Glyde mansion.

The Prime Minister was there, and a grand crush of fashionables, including most of the ambassadors from foreign courts.

Amongst these notables the greatest excitement was created by the representative of one of the Eastern courts, on account of the splendour of his apparel, which dazzled all beholders.

From head to foot he was one mass of brilliants and precious stones, and one of the chief occupations of the guests was to give rough estimates of the value of his gorgeous attire.

But, alas! he paid the penalty for his vanity by having to suffer the presentation of every lady in he ball-room.

One lady who appeared to be alone in the assembly was especially attracted by the eastern ambassador.

Once having fixed him, she never quitted his side for an instant.

Indeed, her attentions became so marked that many of the company—the female portion more especially—commented rather freely thereon.

This lady, who was veiled (almost the only lady in the company, although the practice of wearing veils was not at all remarkable at the period of our tale), was heard to complain of the heat of the rooms, and to invite the ambassador on to the verandah.

This unfeminine advance elicited much scandal from every one in the room. Many of the gentlemen did not fail to pronounce it scarcely respectable.

Presently, as they had not returned to the ball-room. two young sprigs of nobility, who rather enjoyed the joke, strolled on to the verandah, "sorry," as they expressed it, "to spoil sport," but unable to repress their curiosity as to the movements of the eastern ambassador and his fair inamorata.

They were no sooner out than one of them gave a cry of alarm, which speedily brought the whole room running to the spot.

Here a surprise was awaiting them—a sensation which was the next nine days' fashionable scandal.

The lady had disappeared—flown no one knew whither—no one could see how!

The ambassador was lying insensible upon the ground.

A huge red lump upon his forehead told that he had been stunned by a blow of some heavy instrument.

But what was the meaning of it all?

This they had yet to learn, when the unfortunate foreigner could be brought to his senses.

Restoratives were administered, and then he indignantly explained.

Whilst conversing with the lady, in what he described as a tender manner, he had suddenly perceived that she was fondling, with suspicious tenderness, a necklace of precious stones which he wore.

This had aroused his suspicions, and presently he perceived that a brilliant of rare value had been abstracted from his person.

Now, convinced that his suspicions were well founded, he charged her with robbing him, upon which she produced a short stick or bludgeon—evidently a life preserver—and struck him down.

It had all taken place so suddenly that he had no opportunity of giving an alarm.

His hearers looked doubtful at first, but presently the veracity of his statement made itself apparent.

He had been, in vulgar phraseology, literally cleaned out!

But how had the audacious marauder made off?

And not a whit less wonderful was it how she had contrived to gain her entrée to that assemblage of fashion and rank.

Lady Glyde was in despair.

Her mortification at the unhappy occurrence was indescribable.

All eyes were turned upon her for information, but in vain. She could not say who was the mysterious woman who had introduced herself into the ball-room.

No one knew her in the company. All had remarked her strange isolated appearance in the ball-room, and still more her peculiar behaviour with the ambassador, who had come to such signal grief, but no one there could say who she was.

Lady Glyde questioned the door porter, who admitted the guests, but strangely enough the man knew nothing about the lady, and he had seen no veiled lady enter the house.

All inquiries that were made resulted in nothing, and nothing tangible could be ascertained about the mysterious fair one.

It remained a profound mystery.

Terribly startling! For there was no egress from the verandah but by the ball-room.

Alarming, for the princely value of the gems of which the unfortunate ambassador had been robbed!

An hour later in the night a fresh visitor arrived, but his announcement passed unheeded by the guests, who were still occupied with the gigantic robbery.

Sir Digby Roscoe, as he had been called by the servant, was an elderly gentleman, of about the middle height, rather grey, and stooping slightly.

Upon entering he made his way at once to the side of Lady Glyde, and with a gravely elaborate salutation requested the favour of a few minutes' private conversation with her ladyship.

Lady Glyde at once assented, and led the way into an ante-room, when a servant provided them with seats.

"Sir Digby Roscoe, madam," began the gentleman, "is merely a name which I have assumed, for the purpose of gaining an immediate audience of your ladyship."

"How sir?" said Lady Glyde. "Who may you be, that you are obliged to visit me *incognito*?"

"Nay, my lady," said the visitor, "I beg you will speak lower; I do not wish my presence here to be remarked."

"Sir," exclaimed Lady Glyde impatiently, "as little as you please of this nonsense. I am in trouble, and—"

"I know it."

"What; has the unhappy affair then so soon reached the outer world?"

"Everything reaches me. I knew the particulars of this unfortunate robbery before yourself."

"Impossible!"

"A fact, I assure you."

"Pray, sir," said Lady Glyde, "make no further mystery of this; who and what are you?"

"My name is Wild, my lady."

"Wild, Wild," said Lady Glyde; "the name is unknown to me."

"Jonathan Wild."

Lady Glyde started up from her seat.

"The thieftaker!" she ejaculated in astonishment.

"That is my occupation, my lady."

"What is your business here?" demanded Lady Glyde.

"The capture of the robber of the ambassador's jewels."

"Then you have arrived most opportunely, Mr. Wild; you needed no assumed name to gain this interview."

"True; but I do not wish my presence here to be known to any one but yourself."

"As you wish it, it shall be so; but may I inquire the object of this mystery, Mr. Wild?"

"Decidedly, my lady," responded Mr. Wild. "The fact is that this is an audaciously clever robbery."

"Truly."

"And the thief could not have worked it unless she had confederates in the house."

"Good heavens!"

"Nay, do not alarm yourself unnecessarily, my lady. I've no doubt that I shall secure them before the night is over."

"Do your suspicions point to any one in particular?"

"They do."

"To whom?"

"That it would be scarcely prudent to disclose at present; I only wish to secure your ladyship's co-operation."

"In what way?"

"You have been robbed lately?"

Lady Glyde expressed her utter ignorance of the fact.

"Nevertheless, you have. You had a diamond bracelet similar to that which you now wear?"

"I had and have."

"Pardon me, your ladyship, you have been robbed of it."

"Nay, Mr. Wild, there I am sure that you are in error."

"You think so because you saw it in your jewel case when dressing?"

"The correctness of your information both astounds and startles me."

"I am generally pretty sure before I advance a statement, Lady Glyde; this bracelet, allow me to tell you, has been abstracted from your jewel case within the last hour."

Lady Glyde was all amazement.

"But, Mr. Wild, since you knew of this, it was assuredly in your power to prevent the robbery, or to arrest the thief."

"Both were, my lady," said the thieftaker coolly; "but I permitted the robbery, to serve the ends of justice."

"Justice?" repeated Lady Glyde; "you speak in enigmas!"

"But, nevertheless, the truth, as you shall see. Would your ladyship trust that bracelet which you now wear to my care for a moment?"

This strange request startled Lady Glyde, and she rose to her feet, about to quit the room.

"Nay, madam," said the thieftaker; "do not be alarmed, I beseech you; I can prove that I am sincere in what I advance. See here."

He coolly produced from his coat pocket as he spoke the fellow bracelet to the one which was upon Lady Glyde's arm.

"What!" she ejaculated; "you have it?"

"As you see; I want the other merely to justify the accusation, which I am about to bring against a lady of rank and position, in the eyes of the authorities."

Lady Glyde unclasped the bracelet from her arm and handed it to the thieftaker.

"There, Mr. Wild," she said, "take it; I cannot understand your object in wanting it, but—"

"Oh, I can easily explain that, if what I have already said is not sufficient for your ladyship. I am well informed—"

"You are, truly," interrupted Lady Glyde; "the extent of your information is startling."

"So you would say if you knew the real extent of it."

"Is it indeed so wonderful?"

"It is."

"Then I pray you to tell me more, and pardon my feminine curiosity, Mr. Wild."

"Nay, you have been sufficiently startled for to-day."

Lady Glyde changed colour, and looked up in the thieftaker's impassive face.

"What do you mean?"

"I allude simply to the phantom you saw."

"Great heavens! is it possible you know of that, too?"

"It is; nay, more—that same phantom is not far from you at this moment."

"Your words terrify me," exclaimed Lady Glyde.

"I intend that they should. Know, Lady Glyde, that this phantom will never leave you; more, will be eternally by your side, breathing destruction in your murderous ear! Behold him!"

The speaker tore off a wig and false beard, and stood revealed RED RALPH, THE CAPTAIN OF THE YELLOW BAND!

The unhappy Lady Glyde uttered a suppressed

groan, and sank cowering upon the floor, burying her face in her hands.

All was silent.

Presently she looked up and she was alone!

CHAPTER L.

THE PHANTOM — RALPH'S WONDERFUL DOINGS AT THE BALL — THE SCENE AT THE JEW'S — BARGAINING FOR THE JEWELS—TO NEWGATE.

LADY GLYDE sprang to her feet and hastened to the ball-room.

The visitor she had received was no phantom, of that she was assured. There was a startling flesh and blood reality about his terrible denunciation; an unmistakeable proof of an earthly presence in the abstraction of her jewels.

At every risk she determined to secure her enemy.

His tongue should be silenced—terribly silenced—if by her own hand.

She could not prevent his giving utterance to something unpleasant, but it was even preferable to risk this than to endure the continual terror with which this man of mystery threatened her.

But in vain did she seek for him in the ball-room. He had disappeared.

No one had seen him leave the room, and the servants were positive that no one had left the house.

Then he must still be there. The only conclusion which Lady Glyde could arrive at was that he had contrived to change his disguise—how she did not attempt to explain to herself.

However, she was a thorough woman of the world, and was by no means affected with vulgar superstition.

If phantoms existed, and she would barely admit the possibility, she had never heard of their thieving propensities.

She immediately issued orders that no one was to leave the house under any circumstances, unless with her special orders, provided that the doorkeeper did not know the individual by sight.

Then she looked about for a messenger. Near the ball-room door stood a servant in private dress, and she beckoned him to her side.

"Take a hackney coach at once," she said, "and drive with all haste to the house of which I will give you the address, and ask for Jabez, the hunchback; they will know who you mean."

"Yes, my lady."

"You will give him this card from me, and say that I desire his presence here immediately."

Whilst Lady Glyde wrote in pencil on the back of a card the servant, as if in imitation of her ladyship, was similarly occupied.

When she had finished she handed him the card and walked to the hall door with him, and nodded to the porter to allow him to pass.

Then, with a final admonition to her messenger to lose no time, her ladyship returned to the ball-room.

However, she had barely crossed the threshold when the door porter came running after her with a slip of paper screwed up in to a note.

"I beg pardon, my lady," said the man, "he's left this for you."

"Who?" she asked, taking the note.

"The man you just told me to pass out."

"You mean the servant?"

"Yes, my lady."

"Then why say 'the man?' Don't you know his name?"

"No, my lady; he's one of the visitor's men, my lady."

"One of the visitor's servants? Gracious! I thought that he was one of the household."

"No, my lady."

"No matter; you may go. How provoking! Still, perhaps it is as well as it is. This man will go my errand and think no more about it. The servants about one are apt to tattle of every movement of their superiors. But what can he have to write about here?"

She opened the note and read—

"It is gratifying that you should have furnished my passport with your own hand! At the same time you give me the whereabouts of the vile hunchback, worthy partner of your black deeds; his destruction is now as certain as your own. Tremble, and dread the vengeance of THE PHANTOM!"

Red Ralph hastened from the Glyde mansion, congratulating himself upon the marvellous success of his daring schemes.

Chance had played into his hands at every turn, and he had never once failed to take advantage of an opening that offered.

Startling and improbable as his adventures may appear, a little explanation of the means by which he worked his seeming wonders at Lady Glyde's renders them simple enough.

When Lady Glyde quitted her boudoir he had taken the liberty of appropriating one of the ball dresses which he found in her wardrobe.

Then by the aid of a rich head-dress and veil, he had completed a capital disguise, and thus made his entrance into the ball-room.

Here his cupidity was at once excited by the dazzling richness of the Eastern ambassador's jewels.

His coquetries charmed the Asiatic, and they repaired to the verandah as described.

The rest is known.

Red Ralph having secured a rich booty, also secured his excellency's silence with a well-directed tap on the head from a life-preserver which he had concealed upon his person, clambered over the balcony verandah, and made off quite unobserved in the bustle and confusion of the ball.

When away from the house, he was suddenly surprised to find himself in a locality which was perfectly familiar to him—the scene of many of his most audacious exploits.

This was an excellent chance for him. He lost no time in seeking the aid of a Jew with whom he had dealings, close at hand.

This Jew soon furnished him with a complete court suit—not the best fit, but sufficiently good for the emergency.

The coat was decidedly "baggy," but out of this very misfit grew a rare chance, which led to his final success in his succeeding adventures.

The Jew suggested that his customer should put another coat on beneath it, and Ralph agreed to it, observing, almost prophetically, that it might turn out a service to him.

A powdered bag-wig and hat put the finishing stroke to his metamorphosis, and Red Ralph sallied forth, emboldened by success, to return to the Glyde mansion.

The carriage of one of the guests stood alone by the corner of the street, but a few doors from Lady Glyde's, and the coachman sat dozing in his seat.

Ralph opened the door and sprang in, calling out, "to Lady Glyde's."

The startled coachman, alarmed at being caught napping, answered sleepily, "yes, my Lord," and drove up to the door.

Red Ralph gave the name of "Sir Digby Roscoe,"

and thus effected his second entrance into the Glyde mansion.

Then came the interview with Lady Glyde, as narrated. The highwayman threw off his bag-wig and false beard, and, taking advantage of her ladyship's temporary alarm at his denunciation, removed his upper coat, leaving only the close fitting black garment beneath it.

Thus transformed once more, he had made his way unnoticed through the ball-room to the hall, where the servants of the visitors were collected in groups.

Not deeming it prudent to appear hurried in his departure, he strolled about, until he was alarmed to find it too late!

No one could leave without her ladyship's special orders.

Remonstrances with the door porter were in vain, and Red Ralph began heartily to wish that his temerity had not led him into this fresh dilemma.

Presently his fears were by no means diminished by the appearance of Lady Glyde at the entrance to the ball-room.

"Pheugh!" muttered the highwayman to himself, "she's beckoning me. I must brazen it out. She has recognised me, and wants to make conditions."

But no. Red Ralph's lucky star was still in the ascendant, and her ladyship, seeing him standing alone, away from the other domestics, hit upon him for her messenger to Jabez, the hunchback!

* * * * * *

A rich booty had the bold highwayman secured!

But still a difficult portion of his task remained to be accomplished—how was he to dispose of them?

The question was readily answered. He well knew where to dispose of them, within the hour, too, provided he was inclined to sell them for about a tithe of their value.

But he was working now with an object, and it was necessary that the most should be realised upon the fruits of his daring robberies.

"I must make up my mind for a desperate risk," muttered the highwayman. "I must take them to a jeweller, a west-end court jeweller, or—no, a good thought!—they shall go to that house next to Hazard's."

"Hazard's" was a notorious gaming-house of the period, which was frequently honoured, according to rumour, by the presence of royalty itself.

Adjoining it was a jeweller's shop, that drove a thriving trade by the desperation of the gamesters who visited its neighbour.

It was by no means uncommon for a young "blood" to step out of Hazard's, next door, to dispose of his valuables, for the purpose of enriching the more fortunate gamblers, or the sharper blacklegs, by his own ruin.

Thither Red Ralph repaired, and, as he had surmised, found the jeweller stirring, notwithstanding the late hour.

"I want to dispose of some jewels," said Ralph.

"Certainly, sir—my lord," quoth the jeweller, obsequiously, "step in—allow me—"

Red Ralph first produced the case of brilliants which had decorated the person of Lady Glyde.

"Lady's trinkets!" said the jeweller, elevating his eyebrows in surprise.

"Yes; are you particular as to the sex of the wearer of your purchases?"

"No, no—no offence sir, my lord—no offence—by no means. Do you wish to dispose of these?"

"Yes," said Ralph, "I am here for that purpose."

"Yes—decidedly—no offence, my lord. I merely put the question, because I have before now—although quite out of my custom,—advanced money upon security for gentlemen."

"No—I wish to sell these outright," answered Ralph, "and for their utmost value."

"Humph!" muttered the jeweller, eyeing them critically, "good, no doubt, but—excuse the term—antiquated. Fashion is all with jewellery, as with everything else, and the intrinsic value of them is comparatively trifling."

"Trifling!" exclaimed Ralph.

"Comparatively speaking," hastily added the jeweller.

"We shall not haggle about the price—I have urgent need of the money, or I should not be here. Name your price."

"Well, say—ahem—say three hundred—"

"Eh?"

"And fifty pounds, I couldn't say more. They, doubtless, cost—"

"Twice that sum," said Ralph.

"So I should say," mentally added the jeweller, "and I should like to know who you bought them of at the price."

However, Red Ralph was astonished at the rare value of his prize, and buyer and seller were mutually satisfied.

"I will give you a draft," began the jeweller.

"Draft! I must have notes—gold if you have it. They won't take drafts next door."

"Certainly, my lord."

"I have some more jewels here—very rich, I believe. Could you advance me cash upon them? It will be repaid to-morrow with interest."

Ralph here produced the unfortunate ambassador's jewels.

A collection of rubies, emeralds, and brilliants of the first water, which completely dazzled the jeweller.

"'Sdeath!" muttered the jeweller, "they must be playing high at neighbour Hazard's to-night. Distinguished visitors, too, I'll be sworn. I wonder who my customer may be, that sells his family jewels for a sixth of their value—silly fool! He'll blow out his sheep's brains on his hearth-rug before the morning."

"Well," said the highwayman, coolly, "are you disposed to do this business?"

"Decidedly, my lord, if in my power. How much would cover your immediate wants?"

"That I am scarcely prepared to say. I have received them as security for a debt—they will be redeemed to-morrow. I wish you to give me a note of the amount you can furnish me with. The individual who owns them will call in person to-morrow for them, and you will receive five per cent. for the loan. Will those conditions suit you?"

"Well, my lord, I think that five per cent. is scarcely—"

"Enough? Then we cannot do the business. However, I rely upon your discretion not to mention that the royal jewels—ahem,—tut! tut! that is, that these jewels have been presented to you. His highness—ahem, no—I mean the gentleman to whom they belong would not be pleased. You take me?"

"Certainly, my lord," answered the jeweller, breathless.

Then he added, to himself, "royal jewels! His highness! pheugh! These are the Regent's then, for a thousand! I must secure his highness in a delicate transaction of this nature, and I secure him as a customer for ever!"

Red Ralph pretended to grow impatient, and moved towards the door, which at once brought the jeweller up to the mark, as he had anticipated.

"Stay, sir. Name a sum, and, if in my power, it is yours of course."

"That I cannot do, I tell you. The more you advance me, the higher will be the interest you will have to take. The gentleman will probably call in a private carriage to-morrow to redeem them—that is, if we do business together, and it will be his particular wish to see you alone. You may attribute your own motive to this if you please. I can say nothing on that head. You understand?"

"Decidedly, my lord," answered the jeweller, with a kind of semi-confidential significance.

An amount of money was proposed which staggered the highwayman, who had no notion of the value of his booty, and accepted; and he departed with a huge roll of bank notes.

As soon as Red Ralph left the jeweller's house he made his way to the nearest coach stand, where he hired a vehicle.

"To Newgate. The governor's entrance," said the highwayman, springing in and closing the door. "Double fare for you if you do it in less than a quarter of an hour."

"All right, your honour," responded the Jarvey, and away he rattled.

With what startling results Red Ralph's second visit to Newgate was attended we shall relate presently.

For the moment, our neglected heroine, Lady Leonore, demands our attention.

But of her in another chapter.

CHAPTER LI.

LEONORE'S ADVENTURES IN THE WOOD — THE STRANGE MEETING — THE WONDERFUL LIKENESS — THE HUT — DANGER.

WE quitted Leonore in the wood, whither she had been borne by Red Ralph after their escape from Hampstead Heath.

If the reader will retrace his steps he will remember that upon Leonore falling faint and exhausted in the wood Red Ralph quitted her to search for assistance, and that he had been unable to return.

His surprise and capture by the gipsy band, and the subsequent narrow escape he ran, have kept us from the movements of the robber's virgin wife, whom he seemed destined to meet but by chance, to render her some signal service at each fresh interview—as if in some way to repair the cruel wrong he had done her in their strange marriage, at his first introduction to her—and then to be parted from her almost upon the instant.

Now, whilst Red Ralph was passing through the strange scenes which we have related, Leonore was again in jeopardy.

For long after Ralph's departure from her side she lay swooning.

So long did she continue insensible that it was more like a deathly trance than aught else.

At length she sighed and opened her eyes.

She looked about her fearfully, striving vainly to recall her scattered senses.

It was long before she could realise her present position, and when it did come to her in all its fearful reality she turned sick and cold with alarm.

Unhappy girl! alone in the wood, no company but the shrubs and trees, which cast their long fantastic shadows around her, giving a weird and wild aspect to the dismal place in which she found herself.

And where was he? Had he really deserted her, left perchance to perish of cold and hunger in that dismal wood?

No, no, she could not believe that. Had he not twice rescued her in deadly peril, and at imminent risk and danger to himself?

As she essayed to rise she found that the night dews of the turf upon which she had lain so long had chilled and cramped her limbs, and it was with the utmost difficulty that she could regain her feet.

"Alas!" she exclaimed aloud, "unhappy girl that I am! Why do I not die? Why do I not die? For what but misery and suffering am I reserved? How gladly would I now welcome my last hour could I but behold him once more!"

In spite of her despairing words, the instinct of self-preservation was yet strong within her, and she struggled boldly with her weakness.

As she grew warmer she contrived to move onward. She knew not, thought not of her destination. Her only thought was to get out of the wood, whose grim silence and darkness terrified her.

Onward she walked, her fears overcoming her bodily weakness. Pushing her way through bushes and briers, she presently perceived that the wood grew less abundant, that the brushwood was more scanty, and the trees fewer as she proceeded.

She was then, doubtless, nearing the limit of the wood.

This gave her renewed hope and courage, and she pushed forward boldly, until she found herself in an open tract of country, with a narrow road branching off upon either side.

By this time she began to perceive, by a break in the clouds, that the night was nearly gone, and that another day was about to set in.

This was comparative happiness for her. It was the night which she so much dreaded in those gloomy labyrinths of tree and bush.

She paused here to look down each road, with a view to discover, if possible, the nearest habitation.

But no. It was too much happiness to hope for at once. She felt that she could not possibly be so near the termination of her immediate sufferings as to hope for assistance.

And, truth to tell, she almost dreaded to come upon another hostelry or house of public entertainment. The recollections of her fatal adventure in the chamber of death at the low road-side house were yet strong upon her.

Her hands were yet stained with the blood of the ruffian landlord and his inhuman wife who had sought to slay her, but upon whom she had so fearfully retaliated.

As these fearful remembrances came upon her Leonore started off again, taking the right hand path, without any object but to fly from the thoughts which rendered her unnerved and despairing.

She had not pursued this road long when she thought she perceived a cottage some distance ahead.

At length, then, the trials of the night were over!

As she neared the spot she discovered that it was simply a wood hut, of the rudest construction she had ever seen.

No matter. It was a human habitation, and the occupant must have some pity for her sad forlorn condition. She did not now pause an instant to consider if it were prudent to trust herself in that isolated wood hut, but hastened to knock upon the door-post for admission.

Better for Leonore had she shunned this place. Better, far better, had she still battled with fatigue, and pushed onwards until she reached some town or village.

But fate had willed it otherwise.

At first no heed was taken of her summons. It was yet early morning, and the inhabitants of the hut were apparently still sleeping.

Again did she repeat her demand for admission, and now she was rewarded by hearing some sounds within.

A few minutes elapsed, and a fastening was removed on the inside of the door, which was drawn cautiously back, and a woman fantastically arrayed in bright-coloured garments appeared.

In her hands she carried a gun, which she hastily

[FLIGHT OF RED RALPH AND LEONORE.]

cocked, as the door swung back, and presented it threateningly at Leonore, who started back affrightedly.

But, startling as was the woman's sudden appearance, as well as the finding herself so suddenly menaced by a deadly weapon (or, rather, startling as it would have been under ordinary circumstances), Leonore's whole attention was drawn to another remarkable fact.

This was the marvellous resemblance which the woman bore to herself! In every respect—height, build, and feature, she appeared her very double—her second self!

This also seemed to strike the other in a no less degree the next instant, and she remained in the same attitude, gazing upon Leonore in astonishment, for more than a minute.

Leonore was the first to break the silence.

"Grant me some assistance, I beseech you," she said.

"What do you want?" demanded the other.

Both paused more astonished than before.

The singular resemblance which they bore to each other did not cease with their persons. Their voices and every gesture were alike!

"This is very strange," said Leonore.

"It is more than strange—it is wondrous. Enter and tell me who you are. You are friendly to me?"

No. 18.

Leonore thought this a rather singular question, but she replied in the affirmative.

"How could I be otherwise? Do we not meet for the first time?"

"True, my sister; come then. It seems that in addressing you I speak with my shadow. What can this marvellous resemblance mean? Tell me who you are?"

"My name," began the weary fugitive, "is Leonore. I have fled from cruel foes who would take my life. I am faint and sick unto death. I beseech you to give me a crust of bread and a sup of water, or I shall sink."

"You shall have both. I see that you are truthful, that you mean me well, and are not the spy of my enemies?"

As this was put in the form of an interrogation, Leonore hastened to reiterate her assurances of truth and sincerity.

Still the hostess appeared to cherish some lurking doubts, until the fast increasing pallor of Leonore's cheek told its own sad tale.

Then she took her by the hand and gently seated her upon a low rude bench, which was the only seat the cabin boasted. From a shelf she reached a small jug containing cider, and filled a drinking-horn with it, which Leonore drained with avidity.

A piece of dry and uninviting coarse bread was placed before her and devoured on the instant.

"Poor girl!" said the owner of the wood hut, compassionately, "you are famished. You have then wandered far in the night?"

"I have, indeed," answered Leonore, "I cannot say how far. I have passed a whole day in the wood insensible."

"Poor creature!"

"How I contrived to crawl on I know not; fear of the darkness and solitude lent me strength, or I should have been starved. My thanks—my heartfelt gratitude for your charity."

"Never mind that," said her hostess kindly, "but tell me who you are. I perceive that you have remarked with myself the extraordinary resemblance which exists between us. What can it mean?"

"I am as ignorant as yourself," replied Leonore; "it has astonished me as much as you. Pray tell me your name."

"My name is Mina," answered the woman; "I am a gipsy, and therefore there can be no tie of blood; and yet, were it not for the difference in the colour of our hair, the resemblance between us would be perfect."

"True."

At this moment the sound of footsteps in the wood without reached them.

"Mina the gipsy changed colour, and started to her feet in very evident alarm.

Then she snatched up her gun from the ground and once more turned it upon Leonore.

"Traitress!" she exclaimed, her eyes flashing fire, "you have betrayed me!"

"I don't understand you," said Leonore.

"Not understand me?" iterated Mina. "You have sold me to my enemies—taken advantage of my pity to betray me: your famished looks and the fatigue were all assumed—an idle tale. But bitterly shall you repent it. Ha! they're here; I shall conceal myself here. Beware! for I shall cover you with my gun."

As she uttered this hasty menace the gipsy dragged back a huge bundle of straw, tore it open with a jerk, and completely covered herself in it in such a way that she could perceive Leonore's movements and hold the gun presented at her all the while.

Leonore was so thoroughly amazed at all this that she could not utter a word.

Barely had the gipsy concealed herself when the tramp of feet without paused at the door of the hut, which was thrust rudely open.

Five men, headed by Jonathan Wild the thieftaker, entered the hut.

CHAPTER LII.

LADY LEONORE AT THE MERCY OF JONATHAN WILD—THE ACCUSATION—THE MAIDEN'S DOOM—NEWGATE—THE EXPLANATION—THE VICTIM OF FATE—THE DAY OF DEATH IS FIXED.

LEONORE was so thoroughly alarmed at the threatening words of Mina the gipsy, so suddenly followed by the appearance of Jonathan Wild and the other men at the door of the wood hut, that she could not utter a word of explanation or remonstrance.

"Ha-ha!" cried the thieftaker, with an oath, as he gained the threshold; "at length we have her."

Leonore shrank back affrightedly.

"What would you?" she demanded.

"You don't know, of course," exclaimed Wild, with a coarse brutal laugh; "pretty innocent!"

The men, in obedience to their leader's orders, advanced to seize the shrinking Leonore.

"Stand off!" cried the girl indignantly; "by what right do you presume to persecute me?"

"Oh!" exclaimed the thieftaker, "you are trying a new tack, are you? I'll precious soon show you my right to act in the way I do. Off with her!"

The men again drew near to seize her, but ere they could put their hands upon her she sprang to her feet and bounded off to the further end of the hut.

Here she threw herself back against the straw in which Mina the gipsy was concealed, thus silently appealing to her for aid.

Nor was her appeal unheeded!

"Beware!" cried Leonore, warning them off with her uplifted arm; "you shall suffer for this indignity!"

The men started back in such great alarm that Leonore herself was astounded.

Did five burly ruffians, who would dare to offer her an outrage, so fear the menaces of a helpless girl?

"Curse her witchery!" ejaculated Jonathan Wild, seeing his men pause irresolutely.

"We had better give it up, Mr. Wild," said one of the men.

The thieftaker responded to this by dashing his gloved fist savagely into the speaker's face, drawing blood from his mouth and nostrils.

"Who will next presume to suggest that?" demanded Wild, glaring furiously round upon his men.

They shrank back from the avenging arm of their irascible leader, but still did not offer to molest Leonore further.

"Now, hear me, my men," said Wild: "unless you take this woman I will report you to a man. You shall be dismissed the service."

"It's no matter, Mr. Wild," grumbled one of the men; "we cannot work against witchcraft."

Witchcraft! This was the second time that this astounding accusation had been brought against her.

"Idiots!" ejaculated the thieftaker, with a lunge at the speaker, who adroitly avoided it. "What do you mean by this humbug? Seize that woman, unless you would have me do my own dirty work."

The men only retreated a few paces nearer the cabin door.

With a cry of execration, Jonathan Wild rushed upon the unhappy Leonore and seized her by the arm.

Ere he could proceed to further violence, however, there was a flash of fire in the straw.

A loud report, and a howl of pain from one of the men near the door.

The thieftaker himself was staggered for the moment, and fancied that he was struck, for the flash was so close to him that it well-nigh singed his face, and he relinquished his hold of Leonore.

The latter, finding herself at liberty, sprang up and dashed towards the door.

The men were now thoroughly terror-struck, and made a scramble towards the door, blocking up the egress in their anxiety to get out.

It was a fearful squeeze for them, but their fears prompted them to far greater exertions than their leader's orders could have done, and they burst through, carrying some of the woodwork with them.

One of the men fell to the ground, and was left there half breathless by his comrades, who flew through the wood like a herd of frightened deer.

Leonore followed on the instant, treading over the man, and sprang away in the opposite direction.

In the meantime Jonathan Wild had not taken long to recover himself, and in an instant he was bounding along the road in pursuit of the fugitive.

Presently Leonore could hear him behind her, and she redoubled her speed, flying for her very life—yes, her life, although at that instant she did not know that it was sought.

Much less did she imagine for what object—with what terrible intent—they were there to make her their prisoner.

It now became an exciting chase—a race for life and death—a race which must inevitably terminate in the capture of the unhappy girl.

Poor Leonore, temporarily strengthened by her fears—aroused to great exertions by the presence of immediate danger—had used all her strength with a burst, and would shortly fall into the clutches of the thieftaker, who pursued her hotly.

It was soon decided.

At every step the distance between them was lessened.

A few more yards, and Jonathan Wild was up with her.

He seized her in his hateful clutches.

"So-ho!" he exclaimed, panting freely; "at last, my lady, I have you; and now the devil himself shan't release you from my possession until you are safely housed."

Leonore could only reply by prayers and entreaties, which of course fell unheeded upon the callous ear of the brutal thieftaker.

"Now then," cried Wild when he had recovered his breath, "off we go again. Move forward!"

"Whither would you lead me?"

"To Newgate," was the brief reply.

Leonore could not comprehend the meaning of this alarming word, and she pressed for an explanation.

Her demand was met with a scornful laugh, and Jonathan Wild only reiterated his command for her to proceed, adding threats of blows unless obeyed upon the instant.

"Go on," he said, "or else you'll repent it, by ——!" You shall have plenty of explanation in the witness-box—more than you want of it there, I'll warrant."

"Witness-box?" repeated Leonore. "Surely no charge of crime can be brought against me?"

"Crime? Oh, no!" said Jonathan Wild, laughing brutally, "not crime. We don't hang people for crime now-a-days; only for amusement, sport, just a little delight for the mob. And to see a woman swing will be quite a novelty—a regular tit-bit."

Leonore shuddered at these brutal words, and shrank away from him.

"No, no, you don't, my lady—not quite so fast. Now that I've taken the trouble to secure you I don't mean to let you go in a hurry. No power upon earth shall snatch you from me!"

"Of what am I accused?" demanded Leonore.

"Bosh!" said Jonathan Wild contemptuously.

"I insist upon an answer," said Leonore firmly.

"O-ho! you do? You insist! Very good: since you insist, you must be accommodated. I didn't think you would care to hear it repeated here. However, since you find it agreeable, and I'm agreeably inclined towards you, I don't mind telling you—"

"What?"

"Goodness! you do it well—bewitchingly! No, no, no; not that," he added hastily—"not that; for I promise you you'll find it a devilish hard matter to do anything bewitchingly with me. You are by no means ill-favoured, though, and, were it not—not—not, in fact, what you are said to be, I might be tempted—"

Leonore turned from him in terror.

"The coy fiend!" exclaimed Wild. "Curse me! but she is enough to seduce the Lord Chancellor himself with her fair face; but it shan't be said that Jonathan Wild could be put off the scent with a pair of bright eyes."

The thieftaker was evidently undergoing a struggle with himself, but we need not speculate on the result of his deliberations, as they were cut short by a loud voice close at hand, exclaiming—

"Stand off!"

Both Jonathan Wild and his prisoner glanced up at the sound.

There stood Mina, levelling her gun at the thieftaker.

"Hell and fiends!" he shouted, "the woman's double, by all that's horrible!"

"Fly!" said Mina.

Leonore struggled to her feet, and would have flown; but the possibility of her escaping brought Jonathan Wild to his senses, and again he seized her.

"Release that girl," said the gipsy, "or I fire."

She repeated her warning; but Wild was not to be put from his purpose now. His only reply to her admonitions was to draw suddenly from his belt a pistol, which he levelled and fired as he turned round.

Almost at the same instant the gipsy fired; but apparently neither shot had taken effect.

When the smoke cleared off Mina had disappeared, and left the thieftaker master of the field, still the captor of poor Leonore.

However, during the journey to Newgate Leonore suffered nothing further from his odious familiarities.

That night Leonore rested—scarcely slept—in Newgate.

At every step she grew more and more amazed. She was received and recognised by the authorities at the prison as a condemned prisoner who had escaped.

But condemned for what? This she could not learn. No one paid the slightest attention to her reiterated demands for an explanation of the crime with which she was charged.

All alike treated her entreaties and protestations of innocence with scorn and derision.

It was a terrible mystery. In vain did she think over any action of her life which could have called down upon her the wrath of Providence. How had she rendered herself amenable to the laws of the land?

Surely the just retaliation upon the landlord of that den of infamy, the road-side inn, could not be looked upon in the light of murder?

Impossible. Moreover, there were no witnesses to the deed of blood, and therefore she could not thus readily have been recognised as the perpetrator of the crime, if crime it were.

One fearful day, followed by a still more fearful night, did she pass in the condemned cell, with no companion but her own sad thoughts.

Then, upon the second day, early, she was waited upon by the governor of the prison and several of the authorities, all of whom wore an expression of solemnity which filled her with a new and inexplicable alarm.

But speedily the agony of suspense gave place to a more tangible fear.

They were there to read to her a warrant for her execution in two days, upon the charge of murder.

The governor had scarcely begun reading the document, when the unhappy girl sprang to her feet, with a piercing shriek, which echoed fearfully through the prison passages.

"No! no!" she cried, in anguish, "you cannot call it by that awful name. The act was justifiable in the sight of Heaven and man."

"Justifiable?" iterated the astonished governor.

"I swear it. Pray hear my explanation, gentlemen, I beseech you."

"Allow me to conclude—"

"One moment, if you please," said the prison chaplain, stepping forward: "the unhappy woman is about to confess her crime."

"If crime it can be truly called," said Leonore.

"Say, did your hand direct the blow?" asked the governor.

"Yes."

"Then let me finish the reading of the warrant."

"Nay," urged the chaplain, "it appears to me, both for the ends of justice and for the satisfaction of the jury who have convicted her—"

Leonore interrupted him with a startled cry.

"That the confession should take precedence of any legal forms," pursued the chaplain. "Say, unhappy woman, are you guilty of the crime imputed to you?"

"I am," said Leonore; "but before Heaven I can swear that I am guiltless of murder. It was my hand that dealt the fatal blow, but had I not struck I should not now be alive to tell of it."

"Explain yourself."

"He entered the bed-chamber where he thought I slept, and this was the only means of escape which I possessed."

The gentlemen glanced from one to the other, evidently quite at a loss to comprehend her meaning.

"She wanders," said one.

"The fear of death has turned her brain," said another.

"What do you mean to imply by that?" asked the chaplain.

"Imply?" said Leonore. "Is it possible that the character of the house is not known? The bedstead and the lime-filled well would surely bear the best witness to the truth of what I state."

The gentlemen shook their heads."

"It seems to me," said the chaplin, "that her reason is clear enough. These are not the words nor is this the manner of a mad woman."

"True," said the governor.

"Then but one inference remains," said another of the gentlemen, "and that is, that she has exerted her invention, of whose activity we have already abundant proof, to defeat the ends of justice with a plausible tale. But we may undeceive her at once with the whole truth. Tell her."

"I swear I speak the truth," said the girl, earnestly.

"Know, unhappy girl," said the chaplain, apparently much shocked, "that before he expired the poor youth who fell by your hand made a clear statement of the whole circumstances of his death."

"Youth?" exclaimed Leonore, more and more confounded. "But he that died by my hand was advanced in years."

"Pshaw!"

"I speak the truth, as far as my judgment will carry me. His hair and beard were grey."

They could not but be impressed with Leonore's earnestness as she spoke these words, but unhappily she failed to convince them.

"Woman, woman," said the chaplain, in a tone of sad reproof, "the testimony of the dying youth is too clear to admit of doubt now. He described your person—your gipsy garb; nay, more, he even identified your portrait taken in the prison before your mysterious escape!"

For an instant Leonore was confounded by these strange words.

Suddenly a new light broke in upon her, and she started to her feet, with a cry of joy and relief.

"I have it now, gentlemen," she said; "all is explained—all clear to me."

"How?"

"I have been mistaken for a woman to whom I bear a strange resemblance."

The chaplain shook his head incredulously.

"Nay, hear me out ere you condemn me."

"Be brief then."

"I will," said Leonore. "I am a lady of rank in society; my name is Lady Leonore Glyde—or it was," she added, hastily, as the thought of Red Ralph crossed her.

"What audacity!"

"I swear I speak the truth! I can get witnesses to vouch for the truth of what I assert. Torn from my home and friends, by a cruel combination of misfortune and persecution, I found myself in the wood where I was captured by him who brought me hither."

"But how?"

"That involves a long explanation, which I can give presently. Let it suffice then, for the moment, that at the wood hut, exhausted by fatigue and hunger, I sought food and shelter, and was met there by a gipsy woman, calling herself Mina, who bears a wonderful resemblance to myself in form and face. We are alike in voice and manner, too—so much so that I do not wonder at the mistake's occurring. We both were strangely impressed with it."

The gentlemen looked incredulous.

"What jury in the universe would believe this tale?" said one of the gentlemen.

"None."

"No," said the governor; "such things have been known, but there has always existed some mark, some peculiarity, by which the two might be distinguished."

"And there does here," said Leonore eagerly.

"Name it."

"The colour of our hair—mine is fair, as you see, whilst hers is either black or of a deep hue."

Her hearers were startled at this.

"Stay," said the clergyman; "the statement of the murdered man mentions this, I believe. He describes the person of his assassin."

"He does," said the governor, "and speaks of her raven tresses."

"You hear, gentlemen?" exclaimed Leonore eagerly.

"We hear," said one, sternly, "but it only appears to me another link in the chain of guilt. To disguise your person more effectually to your destined victim, you wore a wig."

"No, no! oh, no!"

"I fear that the evidence is too conclusive," said one.

"Alas! yes," added the clergyman mournfully.

"You see, sir," said the governor, "that the near approach of death cannot change the guilty woman's nature. False she has lived—false she will die."

With this he was about to conclude the reading of the death warrant, when Leonore again interrupted them.

"Gentlemen, gentlemen," she cried, in heart-rending accents," this is too awful. Surely I am not to be condemned unheard. I have evidence the most conclusive of the truth of what I state.

"Name it."

"Where is he who captured me and brought me here?"

"Jonathan Wild?"

"Yes."

"Let him be called."

The thieftaker, who chanced to be in attendance at the prison, was shortly brought to the cell and confronted with the prisoner.

Leonore then related the history of the shot fired at Wild by Mina the gipsy from the straw in which she lay concealed.

Wild admitted the truth of this assertion, which cleared up a mystery in his mind.

Then Leonore proceeded to speak of the violence offered to her by the ruffianly thieftaker, which he stoutly denied.

The sudden appearance too of Mina the gipsy at this critical moment for Leonore also cleared up some most unpleasant doubts in his mind, but, as it was the sequel to a tale which must have damaged him in the estimation of his superiors, he boldly denied the whole occurrence.

Unhappy Leonore!

Poor doomed girl! wedded to misfortune, and now condemned to death for a crime of which she was guiltless.

Fated to meet but falsehood and treachery at every step she took.

"No, no," reasoned the wily thieftaker, "if I admit that I must go the whole hog, and then it would look unpleasant with me. Besides, if I swear that all she says is false, she is as good as gone, and I am safe again. Besides which, I cry quits with my coy beauty for her cruel repulses. I never go half-measures with women who please my fancy for a moment; love or hate; and if the latter, it pretty generally goes hard with them. Ta ta, my coy charmer."

And the vile ruffian left the cell, and went calmly to breakfast, as if he had just done the state some signal service and eased his conscience.

All the protestations of poor Leonore now availed her little.

The stern sentence of the law must be carried out.

One short day, in addition to that which had already set in, was to be allowed her to prepare for a future state, and on the following day she would close her account with life.

Heaven have mercy upon her at this extremity!

CHAPTER LIII.

AGAIN IN NEWGATE — THE RESULT OF RALPH'S NEGOCIATIONS—BRIBERY AND CORRUPTION— MORE DANGERS—ANOTHER SQUEAK FOR LIFE.

RED RALPH speedily gained admission to the presence of the governor of Newgate, who, by an extraordinary chance, was at the building.

With some little difficulty he also succeeded in obtaining a private audience, and then followed a few words which are worth narrating.

"Will you take a seat?" began Red Ralph, handing the governor a chair, with admirable *sang froid*.

The governor was greatly astonished at the visitor's manner, but yet he could not help availing himself of his singular act of politeness.

"Now, sir," he began, "may I inquire your business?"

"To be sure," answered Red Ralph. "I have come to speak of the men you hold here in your charge, who are, I believe, condemned to death."

"To whom do you allude?"

"The batch of Yellow Boys."

"What of them?"

"They are condemned?"

"They are."

"And when are they to suffer?"

"That is kept a secret."

"For what purpose?"

"Well, sir," said the governor, eying his visitor curiously, "I can scarcely yet recognise your right to put the question. However, I don't mind telling you that the authorities have deemed it prudent to decide upon that course, because they fear that they may meet with some opposition from a mob."

"Are they to be hanged privately?"

"No, not privately; but the time is not yet made public."

"And the place?"

"Tyburn, of course." Then he checked himself, and hastily added, "Unless the authorities should see fit to alter their decision."

"Very good."

"And now for your business, if you please," said the governor.

"I have already said that it relates to the prisoners."

"You have."

"Then I may tell you," continued Red Ralph, "that I have been exerting myself for days past to procure a reprieve for these unhappy men, and that I have—"

"Signally failed."

"Right. I have. All my endeavours have proved in vain. It seems that highway robbery is a fast spreading evil, and that no punishment has yet been severe enough to check it."

"True," said the governor," and therefore it has been decided to strike a terrible blow to stop the evil. This blow is the execution of the gang who have latterly infested the country for thirty miles around the metropolis."

"I know it," said Ralph; "but that execution must never take place."

"Indeed!"

"Truly."

"And who is to prevent it?"

"I."

"You? Why you said but now that you had failed in every way to obtain their pardon."

"I have another resource."

"And that is—"

"Yourself."

"Pray explain yourself, sir; I detest all mysteries."

"By all means," said Red Ralph. "Now, although those persons high in office to whom I have applied could not grant my request, it has been hinted to me that it might be accomplished through you."

"How so?"

"Not exactly according to rule, or legally, but—"

"Pardon me," interrupted the governor, "if not legally we may as well put an end to all further discussion. It is an idle waste of time, and can be productive of no result—that is, of no good result—to yourself."

"One word more—"

"It is useless."

"Nay," said Ralph; "I must insist upon laying my propositions before you. I anticipated much opposition upon your part before coming here, but I am convinced that I shall succeed before I take my departure."

"Your confidence is amusing and commendable," said the governor; "your perseverance upon this subject is rather—excuse the word—a bore."

"I am sorry to annoy you, but my motive is purely philanthropical."

"Sir," said the governor, "your philanthropy is decidedly misplaced here, and very annoying."

"Sir," replied Red Ralph, determined not to be put off by a rebuff, "I am grieved that I prove an annoyance to so courteous a gentleman as yourself, but my object is pressing, and I must not hesitate."

"Come to the object at once then, I beg," said the governor testily.

"Then I have been led to believe that you would do all in your power to save these guilty men from the ignominious fate which threatens them—"

"Then both yourself and your informant have been labouring under a misapprehension, believe me."

"I trust not."

"I know well the duties of my office, and be assured that no earthly consideration would induce me to forget them."

"There is one consideration, I believe," said Ralph.

"Not one; let that content you, I beg."

"You will excuse my doubting that," said Red Ralph. "Nay, more; you must allow me to contradict you. It is a favourite axiom of mine that every man has his price."

"Sir!"

"No offence."

"Gad! sir," said the governor, "you are amusing. You come here throwing out hints of bribery, and then beg me not to be offended. Let me tell you, then, that your words are too absurd to offend. Once more—it is useless to discuss the matter further. I wish you a very good night."

This very broad hint was quite thrown away upon the imperturbable Ralph.

"I wish, sir," he said, calmly, "that you would name a sum of money, or any dignity or gift, which you could wish for as a return for this service, and I think I could promise you almost anything."

The governor looked serious, but remained silent.

Ralph saw that he had secured his attention, and hastened to take advantage of it.

"Since your modesty will not allow you to mention any gift which my influence in a certain nameless quarter could procure, I can only make an offer myself. Would five thousand pounds offer any inducement?"

The governor started. The magnitude of the sum naturally surprised him.

"Money down!" said Ralph.

The eyes of the governor glistened, and his fingers twitched convulsively, as if he had already clutched the money in anticipation.

Ralph watched him narrowly. He could see that cupidity and a sense of duty were struggling together for the mastery in his bosom.

Now was the time, then, to strike. Red Ralph took from his pocket a portfolio, from which he drew a huge bundle of bright, crisp, new bank-notes, which he spread out upon the table.

Then from his coat pocket he produced a weighty sack of gold pieces, which chinked most musically as he laid it upon the table.

The governor wavered. The man of such an iron determination the moment before was upon the verge of destruction.

Mammon sent virtue to the right-about, and the governor of Newgate was a lost man.

Unfortunately, however, for Red Ralph's plans, a slight chance spoilt him. At this instant—the instant which would have decided the case in his favour—there was a knock at the door without.

The governor started to his feet, and turned pale and red by turns in an instant, as if detected in the act of committing some crime.

"Who's there?"

"Me, sir," answered a male voice, which was familiar to Red Ralph. "Harris."

"Don't let him in," said Red Ralph, rather uneasily.

The governor nodded. He only understood a desire upon Ralph's part not to have the nature of their interview suspected.

"Gather up that," he said, pointing to the money.

In an instant it was placed in the pockets of the visitor, and the governor went to speak with the man at the door.

"What is it, Harris?"

"You are wanted immediately below, sir."

"By whom?"

"Mr. Wild, sir."

Ralph started.

"I hope my old friend won't come here," he thought; "it would be unpleasant to come across him just now."

"You can say that I am engaged, Harris," said the governor.

"He said that it was very urgent, sir, and that you would rather see him at once, he knew."

"Very good. Then I must go, I suppose."

Then he turned to Red Ralph, saying, "I shall return in a few minutes, sir."

"Very good," said Ralph.

But the governor had no sooner left than Ralph grew uneasy.

Out of the presence of his temptations, he feared that the sense of duty would gain the day. If so, it might lead him to take some unpleasant measures.

As this thought recurred to him he rose and followed the governor out of the room. As he neared the entrance he overheard the voice of Jonathan Wild in conversation with the governor himself, and the first words he caught served to convince him that he had taken a wise precaution in leaving the room above.

At the foot of the stairs was a small ante-room, in which visitors waited their turn to see the governor upon the various affairs of the prison. Unobserved by the governor and Jonathan Wild, he stepped in here, and listened to their conversation at the entrance.

"So the execution is fixed for Thursday," said Wild.

"Yes. We are to have a small body of the household troops to accompany us. We shall leave here at sunrise. I count upon your assistance here, you understand."

"Yes, sir."

"One word now before you leave, Mr. Wild. I have a visitor upstairs who has come upon a most singular errand."

Then their voices sank into a whisper, and Ralph could distinguish nothing further.

Presently he caught a few words which alarmed him.

"Will you come up with me?" said the governor, "and if we see fit he can be apprehended."

Wild assented, and they proceeded up the stairs, passing within six feet of the spot where Red Ralph was concealed.

No sooner were they gone than Ralph stepped forth

and sauntered to the gate with as easy and unconcerned an air as he could assume.

"What is it, sir?" asked the doorkeeper.

"I want to go out," answered Red Ralph, as if astonished at the question.

"Certainly, sir. You have seen the governor?"

"To be sure, I have. Good night."

"Good night, sir," answered the man, unfastening the ponderous door and dwarf iron gate, with a coolness and deliberation which was agony to the highwayman.

But the door was opened! Red Ralph was stepping out when he heard some one running down the stairs above, and the voices of Jonathan Wild and the governor shouting out.

"Wilkins!" called the governor.

"Sir?" replied the doorkeeper.

"Keep your gate closed."

Ralph jumped down the steps, and bounded off full gallop.

"That's a narrow escape!" muttered the highwayman. "Another moment and it would have been too late! I have failed so far, true, and it was just on the cards that I should succeed. No matter; I have gained some information from my visit, and Red Ralph shall turn up at the moment that they least expect him."

CHAPTER LIV.

IMPORTANT NEWS—RALPH'S STRUGGLES, VEXATIONS, AND DANGERS—THE SECRET PLOTS—TREACHERY—DESERTION—A FIGHT—FEARFUL ODDS—"DOWN WITH HIM!"

ONE important piece of information had been gathered by Red Ralph by his visit to Newgate.

The time and place appointed for the execution of the members of the once renowned Yellow Band.

Only one doubt occurred to him upon the subject. As he had escaped by flight from Newgate, might not the authorities, fearing an outbreak upon his part, deem it expedient to alter the previous arrangements?

No. He reasoned that it was not known to them how he had left the building.

His retreat had been effected in a very quiet manner, and the doorkeeper himself who had allowed him to pass had not been able to detect anything hurried or suspicious in his manner.

Moreover, his identity—was that discovered?

The audacity of the visit would avoid all possibility of such a conclusion being arrived at.

However, to ensure success in his meditated project for the final effort upon his unfortunate comrades' behalf, Red Ralph placed a trusty scout near the prison, always upon the look-out.

The result proved that his precaution was not misplaced.

In the meantime Red Ralph was always upon the move. Hither and thither he fled, gathering together a horde of ruffians of the lowest and most desperate class of humanity.

He procured the fidelity of these by purchase, and the fruits of the robbery at Glyde House secured him a small army, who were all well clothed and provided with pistols carefully secreted upon their persons.

Then a store of arms of every description was conveyed in barrels to a house in the vicinity of the fatal Tyburn Tree, which Red Ralph purchased for a large sum of its occupant.

In this house, too, they met to arrange their final preparations, and to concoct the plot for the release of the Yellow Boys—the feat of unparalleled daring which was shortly to startle the whole of England.

Of one thing Red Ralph was assured. That was the time of the day at which the secret execution would take place. It was invariably early morning, and he doubted not, whatever day might be fixed upon for the carrying out of the extreme penalty of the law, that this arrangement would be adhered to.

To guard against surprise, therefore, Red Ralph kept his men at repose by day and carousing by night.

By this arrangement he guarded against all possibility of losing the scent by any premature stratagem which the officers of justice might devise.

The execution, according to the information which Red Ralph had so boldly gathered at Newgate, was fixed for Thursday.

Now they had already arrived at Wednesday morning, and there was no sign of preparation for the fatal moment.

It was, then, to remain as originally settled, for Thursday.

Red Ralph therefore made up his mind for a tough struggle upon the following morning. He would have preferred to intercept an expedition which was intended to be conducted in secret.

Then it was possible that they would have been almost unattended. But, from the little that he had caught of the conversation between the governor of Newgate and Jonathan Wild, he well knew that a tough job was in store for them.

It would now assume the aspect of a pitched battle upon a small scale, and Red Ralph, alive to the necessity of being acquainted with the spot upon which it was to take place, went to take observations in person, accompanied by two of his most trusty followers.

It was early in the afternoon when Red Ralph and his two companions arrived beneath the fatal tree.

It was just beginning to drizzle with a cold thin rain, which no garments could keep out, and Red Ralph was very soon induced to terminate his observations.

Just at the moment that they were about quitting the spot one of the men announced that some soldiers were appearing in the distance.

"Soldiers!" said Red Ralph, in consternation; "this looks as if they meant to bring an army to ensure the administration of justice, as they call it."

"Ay," said one of the men, "and a rare muster of them there is by all appearance."

"See, sir," said the other, pointing in the direction, "it appears to me that they are only the escort for some procession."

"Procession!" echoed Red Ralph, jumping round, "what can that mean?"

"I don't know," answered the other, "but I can see a white figure (and it's a clergyman's gown, I'll be sworn) in an open carriage."

"It cannot be possible," said Red Ralph, in alarm, "that they have so broken through all rule in this matter. By Heavens! it is, though. Back! back to the house! I'll give ten golden guineas to the man that beats me in the chase!"

And he was sincere in this. Gladly would he have rewarded either of them who proved more swift of foot than himself.

But his eagerness outran their avidity for the golden bribe, and he distanced them both by many yards.

Arrived at their meeting-house, another blow to his hopes awaited him.

Of the whole body of men he had hired, but six were within. The remainder were returned to town, according to a previous understanding with their leader, but which Red Ralph in the pressing emergency had entirely forgotten.

Bitterly did he reproach himself for not having guarded against this mischance.

He should have been prepared at any moment for the great event for which he had risked so much to assemble the body of gentlemen of easy conscience at such an extravagant cost.

However, what would have been the death-blow to the hopes of any less audacious adventurer simply raised in Red Ralph a still stronger interest in the business in hand.

Here was real danger in plenty for him. His only annoyance was, that in order to gratify his passion for risk and excitement he endangered the lives of his doomed followers.

The bold Yellow Boys!

With the aid of his motley band, he had counted upon their rescue from the clutches of the law at the eleventh hour as a certainty.

Now it was reduced to a chance.

How much more would have been his anxiety had he known the full extent of the risk he was running!

But on this it is useless to speculate.

Nothing remained but to make the effort with such resources as were left to them.

He hastily called his men together, and found that they mustered only eight besides himself.

A mere handful to pit against a body of picked men of the household troops!

However, this was no moment for considerations of this nature. Minutes seemed ages, and the fatal preparations at Tyburn were doubtless by this time fast progressing.

Red Ralph then addressed his men, briefly sketching out the nature of the enterprise. He did not venture to acquaint them with the real strength of the force to which he was about to oppose them, lest they should refuse the risk.

But, in spite of his caution, he met with some opposition.

One of the men suggested that this was the enterprise for which he had assembled so many, and that it must naturally be impracticable to so few.

Murmurs of doubt and mistrust greeted this suggestion.

"What, you rascals!" exclaimed Red Ralph, "would ye dare to hang fire now? What have I clothed ye and fed ye and filled your pockets for?"

"That's all very well, captain," said the man who had raised the first objection; "but we understood that we were engaged in a scrimmage, not for eight or nine of us to have to go in against all the lot."

"No, no."

"We should be chopped to mincemeat."

"Ay, ay."

"Every man of us," said another.

"Why, you white-livered scoundrels!" ejaculated Red Ralph, "you never questioned my business before you accepted my bounty."

"Because it all seemed fair and square enough, captain."

"Tut, tut," said Red Ralph, "let us have no more idle parley on the subject: while we are wasting precious moments here all the mischief is being done. Come on!"

Not a man offered to stir.

"What, all alike? Fools! don't you see that as we have to do the job alone, so much greater will be each man's share of the reward I promised you."

"But what use would the reward be to any of us, captain?"

"Ay, ay, what use?"

"It will make every man here independent for life."

"And give him a house to rest in," said the self-elected spokesman of the party—"six feet of clay."

"No, no; not for us," said several in a breath.

"Then must I go alone?" demanded Ralph, indignantly, as he buckled on his sword.

"You had better give it up, captain, as a bad job."

The words had barely passed the man's lips when Red Ralph, in a phrenzy of passion, dashed at him, and with one blow of the fist felled him to the ground.

"Slaves!" he shouted, now maddened with rage and indignation, as he turned, glaring furiously upon them. "Who is the next one who will dare propose such a thing to me?"

The men murmured at his violence, and stooped to raise their fallen comrade from the floor.

"But I do but waste my breath upon you," said Red Ralph, his choler giving way to scorn and contempt. "You are not worth a brave man's anger. What you refuse to attempt (eight brave hearts!) I go single-handed to accomplish. To accomplish, mark me; ay, and single-handed, too. Else do I swear never to return alive. Give me my pistols, rascals!"

No one offered to obey him. However, he managed to perform these little offices for himself.

His toilette in this respect complete, he stood there ready to depart, armed cap-à-pie, literally glistening with pistols and offensive weapons.

But now an obstacle presented itself to the accomplishment of his purpose.

He began to perceive that he would find it difficult even to venture forth single-handed!

Whilst he had been engaged in buckling on his sword-belt and otherwise arming himself, the faithless men he had hired held a whispered consultation amongst themselves, which he had not noticed.

One had suggested that it would not be proper to allow such a bold fellow as their leader to rush upon certain destruction.

But how to detain him! This was a difficult matter, for they had seen how violently he had resented the suggestion of their fallen comrade.

Argument or persuasion would be worse than useless, they well knew.

There remained, then, but one means—Force!

Without any demonstration, they veered round towards the door and placed themselves before it, whilst one of them silently secured it, and removed the key.

And now the unsuspecting Red Ralph turned to depart.

They had moved away from the door, and one man, well secured from his leader's vengeance by the comrades who stood around him, began to remonstrate with Red Ralph.

"Captain," said he, "let us beg you to reconsider this step."

"Silence!" said Ralph.

"You cannot possibly do any good, captain, and may—"

"Silence!" again thundered forth Red Ralph, purple with passion. "Ah! the door fastened!"

"Yes, captain."

"You have presumed—!"

"To detain you by force. Yes, Captain, since persuasion won't do."

"Idiots!" shouted Red Ralph, "dare you dictate to me what line of conduct I shall pursue?"

"Let our actions speak for themselves," was the answer.

Red Ralph drew a pair of pistols from his belt.

"See here," said he, pointing them at the nearest of the men, "I command two of your lives, and, by everything, I swear to take them unless I am allowed to pass out upon the instant."

Still they did not offer to stir.

"Let us chance his fire," suggested the former spokesman.

["DEATH TO THE MAN WHO HAS INSULTED OUR QUEEN!"]

"Yes," said another, "and then fall upon him altogether."

"Brave lads!" said Red Ralph, with a scornful curl of the lip, "see here. You are not worth powder."

And he replaced his pistols.

Seeing this, the men would have fallen upon him, but his quick eye divined their intention, and, springing back, he whipped out his sword.

"Now I would have you beware!" said Red Ralph.

"Now, captain, do hear reason," said one of the men.

"Ay, sir. What can your single arm avail against eight of us?"

"Any more than against a whole expedition at Tyburn, captain?"

"Headstrong fools!" said Red Ralph. "The time has been when, with less reason for the job than that which prompts me now, I have cut my way single-handed through three times your strength."

Two of the men drew their swords, and advanced towards their redoubtable leader, with the intention of disarming him.

In an instant, before an eye could wink, Red Ralph was upon them.

Their swords met, two noisy clashes followed, and the weapon of one was beaten from the holder's grasp and sent spinning to the other side of the room.

The second man was beaten to the ground, with an ugly gash upon the cheek as a reward for his temerity.

"Who is the next?" cried Red Ralph, like a lion at bay.

The men, amazed at the sudden and marvellous discomfiture of their two comrades, hung back.

"Pooh! pooh!" said Red Ralph, snapping his fingers at them, and laughing derisively, "a fig for a hundred such white-livered ruffians; a curse upon you all. You shall rue this day's work if one of my trusty Yellow Boys has come to harm!"

"Yellow Boys!" repeated the men, with one voice.

This was startling news for them.

Red Ralph had carried out all his arrangements *incognito*, and so effectually had he preserved his disguise that not one of the men he had engaged even dreamed who he really was until this moment.

Now it came upon them a startling piece of intelligence.

But whilst it raised their respect for his world-famed prowess in his lawless career, it also excited thoughts of treachery in their minds.

A rich reward was offered for his capture!

Seeing their amazement at his imprudent disclosure, Red Ralph hastened to take advantage of the temporary cessation of hostilities.

In vain, however, did he endeavour to force the lock of the door.

A well-directed kick from his heavy riding boot sufficed to shiver the bottom panels.

But still the door—an old-fashioned and heavily constructed oak portal—stood firmly.

A second kick; a third, and Red Ralph felt himself seized from behind.

Borne to the ground by numbers!

His treacherous myrmidons had taken advantage of his helplessness to fall upon him.

"Traitors!" shouted Ralph.

Like a lion in their toils did he struggle and fight against hope, with a wondrous courage and perseverance.

Up and down they wrestled all over the room, and prodigious was the strength displayed by the slightly built and apparently delicately constituted highwayman!

Overpowering were their numbers, and yet all seemed panting alike with the struggle.

And all the while Red Ralph's ideas were fixed upon the terrible tragedy which he judged must by this time be enacting at the fatal gallows tree!

Agony—anguish of the most acute nature—did he endure, and thought not of the many hard knocks, the bruises which he was gathering in this unequal struggle.

But what could bravery avail against such fearful odds?

Treachery appeared to be gaining the day, when Ralph, by a prodigious exertion, contrived to throw his assailants off for a moment.

Never pausing to consider danger, he gathered up his little remaining strength for one grand final effort.

Drawing back for a spring, he bounded into the air, and dashed through the fastened window, carrying glass, sashes, and the thick window-frames with him!

By a miracle he was almost unhurt.

He, however, fell heavily to the ground, though in an instant he was again upon his feet—but for what?

To find himself confronted by some eight or ten of his hired band, who had at that minute returned.

"Down with him!" shouted one of the men inside the house.

"Have at you!" cried Ralph.

CHAPTER LV.

A PRISONER IN NEWGATE—THE YOUNG WIFE'S REVERIES—LEONORE AND THE JAILOR—UNAVAILING PRAYERS—THE PREPARATIONS FOR THE EXECUTION—THE FATAL HOUR HAS COME—THE MOB—THE HANGMAN'S TOUCH—THE LAST MOMENT.

WHILST the bold captain of the once famed Yellow Band is employing such desperate measures, with, alas! but slight appearance of ultimate success, for his doomed followers already at the fatal Tyburn Tree, what has become of the hapless Lady Leonore?

All unknown to Red Ralph, his virgin wife lies in Newgate, sentenced, like his well-loved Yellow Boys, to an ignominious death.

Death by the hands of the common hangman, and for a crime which her soul abhors!—a crime of which she is innocent as the unborn babe!

The fatal day is fixed. Broken down with the mingled sense of indignation at the charge brought against her, and terror at the near approach of death, Leonore awaits her doom!

Of late, it is true, she had little to make life of any charm to her.

But although, in her despair, she frequently wished herself beyond the trials and sorrows of this life, now that the awful moment approached a fearful all-crushing dread was upon her soul!

Unhappy girl!

Devoted to so horrible a doom at her tender years —she who had been reared in the lap of luxury—who her life through had known no care nor anxiety, no trial nor hardship, until within these last few dreadful days—at an age which should have seen her the admired of all beholders—the envied of her own sex!

And what fault, what crime had brought about this awful punishment?

The crime of loving too well. Had she not formed that fatal attachment she would never have called down upon her the wrath of her interested relatives.

But of late her lover's name had never passed her lips.

Since the fearful words of Jabez, the hunchback—an assertion which had been borne out by the presence of the wedding ring she wore—her maidenly virtue had shrunk from all thought of her former lover.

Truth to tell, her heart was not now, as it had been, Everest's. The services which Red Ralph had rendered her had not been without their influence upon her.

His bold handsome form and his dashing bravery were ever foremost in her mind.

At times she would repeat to herself the words he had spoken during their few brief interviews, and in her calmer moments she would even think that she could die peaceably could she look upon him once more.

But no, no; this was too much to hope for.

They were destined to be separated; else why had they parted as soon as they had met upon each occasion?

It was the morning before the day appointed for the fatal ceremony which was to close her account with life.

Leonore was slumbering restlessly upon her rude prison couch, and in her sleep rehearsing the fearful tragedy which was shortly to take place at Tyburn.

In the stone-paved corridor without the prison cell there was a heavy tramp, which ceased as it arrived at the door.

Then the heavy bolts and chains were unfastened, and the key grated harshly in the lock.

Leonore turned upon her side and murmured some

inarticulate words as the door opened and the jailor entered the cell

He bore in his hand a tray containing the prisoner's morning meal.

"Here you are," said the man. "Oh, she's asleep, poor devil! I wonder that she can do much of that."

Leonore moved about restlessly, and at this moment held up her hands imploringly.

"Mercy, mercy!" she murmured. "I am guiltless of crime. I am so young to die!"

"That she is," said the jailor, "poor wench. Confound it! she's crying now. I never did like to see a woman cry, even in her sleep. Wake up!"

Leonore started up, with an exclamation of fear.

"What is it so soon?" she exclaimed, with a shudder.

"Is what so soon?"

"The—the—oh! I cannot speak it," and she burst into a torrent of tears.

"Don't take on so, my girl," said the jailor, with rough good nature. "We must all die once, you know."

"But not thus."

"True; but then we shouldn't provoke justice."

Leonore shook her head mournfully.

"There it is," she said, "that I find my fate so hard: to die so young, and upon a cruel and unjust accusation."

The man nodded his head in a way which said, as surely as words could have spoken it, that her protestations of innocence were utterly lost upon him.

"You, too, believe me guilty?" demanded Lady Leonore.

The jailor made no reply.

"I'm very sorry for that," continued the prisoner sadly, "for you have shown me much kindness—"

"In my own rough fashion, ma'am—that is, my good woman."

He corrected himself thus because he feared to show a condemned prisoner that respect which her bearing evidently provoked.

"Before I die," said Leonore, with a heavy sigh, "I would fain have you believe in my innocence."

"What for?"

"It would be some consolation to have one being upon earth who would feel some respect for my memory, if not regret for my loss."

"Well, ma—my girl," said the man, "it's a rum notion, but if it will be any consolation to you I'll believe anything you like."

Leonore turned from the man full of disappointment.

"Look here," said the jailor: "you must eat your breakfast this morning."

"I cannot."

"But you must."

"I cannot; I have no appetite: the sight of food is loathsome to me. Do not press me, I beg."

"Lor bless me, ma'am," said the jailor coaxingly, "I've seen many a bold fellow tuck in the best meal he had ever seen only an hour before he was turned off, and—"

The jailor perceived that he had caused his charge much pain, and he hastened to change the subject.

"Look here, my girl," he said, "the governor asked for my report, and I heard him say that you mean to starve yourself—"

"Would that I could!"

"Ah!" exclaimed the jailor; "I thought that he wasn't far out. Now, I tell you what, unless you take the food that is given to you, you will be forced to eat: you'll have the doctor about you."

"Surely they would not use violence at this moment?"

"Wouldn't they, though?"

"Then they must be cruel by nature," said Leonore,

"and take a delight in a poor wretch's torments under the name of justice."

"You must not be so hard upon 'em," said the jailor, "we don't allow prisoners knives to cut their throats with, nor ropes to hang themselves with; nor we don't allow 'em to starve themselves. Why should one manner of committing suicide be allowed any more than another?"

"Suicide!" repeated Leonore, startled at the name of the fearful sin which she had contemplated in thought; "oh! give me the food—I wouldn't for worlds die with that sin to my account."

"Come, come," said the jailor, "you ain't unreasonable after all. There you are, and may you enjoy it."

The prisoner thanked her rough guardian with a sad smile.

"Is there anything you would fancy?" asked the jailor.

"Nothing."

"Prisoners are allowed anything they like before—ahem!—that is at certain times."

Leonore thanked the man, but assured him that there was nothing she could desire.

"I would that it was in my power to reward your kindness," she said; "but, alas! I have nothing."

"I don't want rewarding," said the man. "I tell you what: if you like to cut me off a bit of your hair, you might. I should like to give it to my missis. I'm a married man, you know, and my wife's rather a rum un. That sort o' thing would please her, I know."

Leonore readily consented to this, and the jailor left the cell with a bright golden tress of his prisoner's hair—not for his wife, as he said, for that was an innocent little fiction of his, which had spared him the appearance of any unjailor-like tenderness before his charge.

An hour later the prison chaplain visited Leonore, according to custom.

His visage was sterner than usual, and he wore an expression of solemnity which Leonore failed to construe.

After the usual exhortations to relieve her guilty soul by a clear confession of the crime for which she was to suffer, he begged her to be composed and to listen to what he had to say.

"Willingly," said Leonore. "I am sorry that you should think me hard and obdurate, but I cannot confess myself guilty of a crime of which, by Heaven, I swear I am innocent!"

The chaplain looked shocked.

"All is excusable, unhappy woman, to mortal ears," said the clergyman. "The terrors of your position and the hope of mercy at the last moment have sealed your lips; but though I would not willingly cause you to despair, if it gave one moment's anguish, yet let me beg you, for a more urgent cause, to banish all hope of earthly salvation. No power upon earth can spare you now."

"Believe me, I implore you," said Leonore earnestly, "that no such thought possesses me. I have no such hope."

"Then confess to me."

"I have nothing to confess."

"You will ease your soul of a load of guilt. Your confession will be heard by my ears alone, and cannot affect your fate, should there happily be a change in your doom."

"I quite understand that," said Leonore.

"Then confess the truth."

"I have," said Leonore. "To make any other statement would be to stain my soul with the guilt of falsehood at this awful moment."

The chaplain regarded her earnestly. There was

such evidence of sincerity in her manner that his former conviction was shaken.

"And now," said he, "are you prepared for a piece of information of a sad nature?"

Leonore trembled violently.

"You mean—the—the—to-morrow?"

"No; it is not to-morrow."

"When then? If not to-morrow, a brief respite but prolongs my agony and suffering."

"I am glad that you contemplate it thus," said the chaplain eagerly; "for instead of a respite, as you say, it is rather the reverse. It is to be hastened, rather than retarded."

"What mean you?"

"Can you hear it?"

"Yes."

"It is fixed for to-day."

The prisoner spoke not—stirred not.

After a while she pressed her hand wearily over her eyes, and looked sadly around the cell.

So singularly quiet and tranquil was her manner that the good clergyman began to fear that her reason had flown.

He moved towards her and held out his hands, about to beg her to join him in prayer.

As he approached she threw up her arms, and fell sobbing upon his breast, as if her heart would burst with burning, but tearless, grief.

*　　*　　*　　*　　*　　*

A few hours later in the same day a procession formed outside Newgate, and proceeded westwards.

Six men were to be hanged that afternoon; but, from the unusual hour appointed for their execution, none suspected the real nature of the expedition, and it had, therefore, but very few followers to Tyburn.

To destroy all suspicion more effectually, the malefactors were borne in close carriages.

The first three contained the six men who were to be hanged for highway robbery.

These were members of the once formidable Yellow Band. Their crime had not been most clearly brought home to them, but it sufficed for the ends of justice that their connection with Red Ralph had been clearly established.

In those good old hanging days much clearer proof was not necessary.

Behind these three carriages came a fourth.

It was occupied by a gentleman in plain garments, which looked like a somewhat premature mourning for the wretched culprits who were about to suffer, and beside him sat a young girl, beautiful and pale as a piece of statuary.

The gentleman spoke unceasingly to her, but apparently his words fell unheeded upon her ear.

Had not her eyes been open it might have seemed that she slept, so utterly insensible did she appear to all passing around her.

The procession had left the metropolis behind, and presently it halted by a pleasant piece of country, but one of terrible associations—in a word, Tyburn!

At the suggestion of Jonathan Wild the procession at starting preserved some of its customary forms, which was the cause of a fresh indignity being offered the guiltless Leonore.

From the diabolical nature of the crime with which she was charged she was the only one of the prisoners to be conveyed to the place of execution in an open cart or tumbril.

The vicious thieftaker then took means to circulate amongst the crowd collected about the prison that she was the witch whose crimes had startled all the world so recently.

In this fiendish piece of vengeance, however, he overreached himself.

A regular riot ensued, and poor Leonore would have been torn to pieces by the infuriated mob but for the interference of the soldiers.

They had to put back to the prison and start afresh.

As the carriage stopped the girl started up and looked around as if just awakened from a trance.

"Have we arrived?" she asked the gentleman.

"Yes."

"Mr. Meredith," she said, "I have had a kind of waking vision."

"A vision, Leonore?"

"Yes."

"Of what nature?"

"I shall not die to-day."

Her words were uttered in such a tone of conviction that the clergyman was startled.

"It is as I thought," said he; "as the drowning man clings to a straw, so you cling to hope until the last."

"I feel a conviction of what I say."

"Enough, Leonore."

"I hope I don't offend you, Mr. Meredith," said Leonore; "I don't slight your kind consolation, believe me, but I speak the truth."

"I believe you," said the chaplain. "But see, they come. Are you prepared?"

"Yes."

They descended from the carriage."

As they moved towards the huge machine of death upon which was fixed the cord which was to strangle this fair creature, in the name of justice, she could not repress a shudder.

"Don't leave me, Mr. Meredith," she whispered.

"I will not; I am by your side until—"

"Until the last moment," concluded Leonore. "Thank you."

"Then you now think that all is over!"

"No."

The preparations were made with all possible haste, in pursuance of the good chaplain's entreaties, in order to spare the poor girl as much pain as possible.

The six men still remained at some few paces off.

Leonore was to be first dealt with, that she might not witness their execution.

It was the final moment, and their fetters were removed.

The hangman went from one to the other, with a hasty hand preparing their last toilette upon earth.

It was curious to see the different effects which the solemnity of their position had upon the men.

Some were the picture of terror, whilst others were utterly indifferent to the fate awaiting them, and coolly surveyed the preparations for death.

One man was even indulging in some low coarse ditty of the period, to show his utter contempt of the gallows—a piece of levity which was duly reproved by the chaplain.

"Now!"

Fatal signal!

Holding Mr. Meredith's hand, Leonore, in obedience to the hangman's word, took her place beneath the wooden structure.

The cord was placed round her neck.

But, beyond a slight tremor which passed through her frame as the executioner's coarse fingers came in contact with her flesh, she appeared unmoved.

"Leonore!" said the chaplain imploringly.

"Mr. Meredith," said the fair girl, "you believe me to be upon the point of death?"

The chaplain bowed gravely.

"Grant me one last request."

"Name it."

"Have faith in my innocence."

"At this time, Leonore, I must; and would to Heaven it were in my power to save you!"

Leonore silently pressed the good clergyman's hand.

And now the signal was given for the hangman to proceed.

"See, see!" cried Jonathan Wild; "a troop of horsemen approaching."

"Ah!" exclaimed the officer of the troops; "an interruption! Men, look to your arms!"

But so suddenly had the troop galloped to the spot that all was confusion.

One in advance of the rest dashed into the throng and threw himself from his horse.

His sword leapt from its scabbard, and he sprang to the gallows.

"Fire!"

Too late!

A cut from his sword severed the rope, and Leonore sank swooning upon his breast as the rest of the troop dashed up.

CHAPTER LVI.

RALPH BETRAYED—HIS ESCAPE—PREPARATIONS FOR A STRUGGLE—THE FIGHT AT THE SCAFFOLD—JONATHAN'S RAGE—THE SOLDIERS AND THE MOB—"DOWN WITH THEM!"—WOLFF'S BRAVERY—HIS WOUNDS — HAND-TO-HAND FIGHT—VICTORY OR DEATH.

IN vain did the soldiers endeavour to rally against the sudden and impetuous attack of Red Ralph and his followers.

But we remember that we left our hero in such a plight that his opportune arrival at Tyburn requires some explanation.

Betrayed by the ruffians he had hired, clothed, and fed, it was only by his undaunted courage and almost superhuman efforts that he had broken from the room from which they had barred his exit.

And now, at the moment when, having achieved thus much, he rose to his feet, cut and bleeding from the broken glass, and half stunned by the violence of his fall, he found himself opposed by the remaining portion of his troop, who had just returned.

It was a piece of cruel fortune; but, nothing daunted, Red Ralph was instantly prepared to resist further hindrance or molestation.

"Hullo, captain!" exclaimed one of the foremost.

"Stand off!" cried Red Ralph, threateningly. "I am desperate now, and there is danger in me!"

"What mean you, captain?"

"Those ruffians I have paid so well have turned traitors," said Red Ralph, "and would invite you to share their treachery."

"Never! never!" shouted the former speaker, and his cry was immediately taken up by his comrades.

At this moment one of the men called from the house.

"Stop him! don't let him pass!"

"You hear?" said Ralph.

"Stop him! Cut him down! He has maimed two of us."

The men looked from one to the other, as it were for the cue.

Red Ralph was not slow to perceive this hesitation, and he hastened to turn it to his own account.

"What!" he exclaimed, in affected astonishment, "is it possible that you pause? S'death! gentlemen, honour among thieves is never forgotten."

"No, no, captain," said one, "I am with you."

"Good!" cried Red Ralph, grasping him eagerly by the hand; "it is something to find one true man amongst you."

This example was the chalk egg in the hen's nest.

The remainder of the men vowed fidelity to Red Ralph in a breath.

So much time had been lost, however, by all this that Red Ralph feared he could not arrive upon the field of action in time to prevent the execution.

There was, therefore, no time to arm themselves in a fit manner to oppose such a force as the representatives of justices presented.

But Red Ralph preferred now to risk all, in an effort for the release of his brave comrades, to the possibility of letting the delay end fatally to any one of them.

He formed the band hastily, and with a cheer he led the way, mounted upon his favourite mare, at a breakneck pace, arriving upon the spot, as we have seen, in the very nick of time.

The scene that ensued it is impossible adequately to describe.

The soldiers were borne down before they could make use of their fire-arms, else it had fared badly with Red Ralph and his troop.

"Close round the prisoners," shouted Jonathan Wild, at the outset.

But prudent as this piece of forethought appeared, it ultimately turned out most disastrous to the cause of the thieftaker.

The soldiers obeyed with true military precision.

Immediately, however, the attacking party turned to this part of the fray and brought all their strength upon it.

Manfully did the troops oppose the lawless band; but they were manifestly at a disadvantage, for no sooner did the trembling criminals see how matters stood than they attacked the soldiers fiercely in the rear.

Occupied with the foes in front, the soldiers could offer no resistance to the new enemy.

Three of them were disarmed in a trice, and a fierce and bloody struggle ensued.

The clashing of swords and the cries of the poor wounded wretches rent the air, and, aided by an occasional pistol shot, created all the appearance, on a small scale, of a regular battle-field.

Boldly did the soldiers struggle, but, in spite of their utmost efforts, the doomed Yellow Boys contrived to force their way through their ranks and join in the combat for their own emancipation.

The rage of Jonathan Wild was beyond description.

With the self-same blow he saw the men he had vowed to hang slipping through his fingers, and also the failure of his fiend-like vengeance upon the guiltless Leonore.

His chagrin too was greatly increased by the fact of its being the hand of his avowed enemy Red Ralph which dealt the blow.

As Ralph, bearing Leonore upon his arm, was turning to fly from the spot, to put his fainting burden in a place of security before joining in the fray, Wild, whose eyes were never removed from him, levelled a pistol at Leonore and fired.

Red Ralph, however, quick as lightning divined his hellish purpose, and with a jerk dragged her behind him.

The shot whistled harmlessly past.

Ralph, however, was more successful in his retaliation. A sharp turn—a hastily-aimed shot— and Jonathan Wild was bleeding in the face from a flesh wound.

Without staying to watch the effect of his shot Red Ralph made a dash for his mare and was very speedily in the saddle with Leonore (who was still speechless with amazement at the singular fulfilment of her vision) seated before him.

"Ho, Nancy, lass," cried Red Ralph; "off, and away."

The mare answered with a snort of delight, and bounded off for Ralph's house.

Meanwhile the fight raged furiously at Tyburn Tree.

The men hired by Red Ralph for this especial service now that they were in it fought desparately, and were valiantly opposed by the soldiers.

The released Yellow Boys battled too as men only do battle when life and liberty are the stakes fought for.

Those who had contrived to provide themselves with weapons in the conflict did good execution with them, whilst those who were unarmed flung themselves furiously upon the soldiers and the civic authorities and fought with their fists alone.

And still the issue of this strange contest appeared doubtful.

The opposing parties were nearly of a strength. The soldiers, it is true, were picked men, stalwart fellows and well trained.

But what could their training avail them in a skirmish like the present?

The flight of Red Ralph was unnoticed in the fray by all save the watchful Jonathan Wild.

As soon as he perceived the most formidable of his enemies flying he rushed from the field calling upon several of his men to follow him in pursuit.

This gave the Yellow Boys and those fighting in their cause some advantage.

"See! see!" cried Wolff, who was in the thickest of the skirmish and covered with blood; "see, they are already turning tail! Give it to them lads! Down with them!"

A deafening shout greeted these words, and they attacked the soldiers with renewed vigour.

"Retreat and form!" cried the officer to the troops.

But he might as well have ordered the instant arrest of the whole party.

The thing was utterly impossible.

The Yellow Boys saw how much depended upon preventing the execution of this command, and it was not probable that they would quietly submit to be charged in body by the military.

Wolff, hearing the officer's command, shouted to his comrades to oppose it with all their power.

At the same time he made prodigious exertions to burst through the crowd and get at the officer, who was dismounted and fighting bravely with his men.

"Come on," shouted Wolff, waving his reeking sword above his head.

One of the soldiers, perceiving Wolff's intention, made a sudden lunge at him, which would have proved fatal had not one of his comrades perceived the blow in time to turn it aside.

"Ha! ha," shouted Wolff, turning furiously upon the soldier; "you will take precedence of your superior, eh? Let that last you until I return."

Their swords crossed, but the soldier's weapon was beaten from his grasp by the impetuosity of the other's attack.

A second blow split the unfortunate man's skull, and he fell back a corpse as Wolff pushed madly onwards.

At this stage of the combat scarcely a man was unhurt.

Wolff himself might have counted his wounds by dozens; but, heedless of pain or hurt, he battled on wildly, performing prodigies of valour, which did much to incite his party to further exertions.

"At last," he cried, with ferocious joy, dashing at the officer of the troops, "at last we shall have a little bout to ourselves, my noble captain."

"Surrender!" shouted the officer.

"I might offer you that chance of salvation," retorted Wolff, "but it is too late now; too much blood has been spilt."

"Misguided man," said the officer, "how can all this end?"

"Thus!" replied Wolff.

A furious cut at the officer was parried with great coolness and swiftly returned.

But here neither party had a very manifest advantage. The soldier was, of course, well trained in the use of arms, but it will be remembered that the Yellow Band specially prided themselves upon their proficiency in the use of the broadsword.

The officer possessed a decided superiority by his youth; but Wolff, although much older, was remarkably tough and wiry.

His greater experience, too, gave him greater coolness, and thus the differences were pretty fairly balanced.

Many and mighty were the blows exchanged, and, beyond a few slight flesh wounds, which only excited them to more vigorous attacks, they were both unhurt.

Presently they paused for breath, almost, as it seemed, by a mutual tacit understanding.

"You're rather smart for a youngster," said Wolff, grimly.

"And you're not slow for an old one," said the officer.

"My boy, said Wolff, in a paternal tone, "I can admire your pluck, but you're as good as a dead 'un, unless you cry enough."

"Brag is unworthy of such a swordsman," retorted the young soldier. "As for a dead 'un, you show far more signs of approaching defeat than I."

And in truth he did.

From head to foot Wolff was bleeding from wounds of no vital importance, but which rendered his appearance at once ghastly and ferocious.

"Come on, then, boy, to the finish!" shouted Wolff.

The officer responded boldly to the challenge, and once more they cut and slashed at each other for their very lives.

As their weapons met the young officer feigned to be unprepared, and as Wolff hastened to take advantage of the opening, he parried a well-directed blow, and lunged in return with lightning rapidity.

This was with better effect, however. His weapon passed through the less fortunate Wolff's left arm.

"Hah!" yelled Wolff, as his arm hung helpless at his side, "a curse upon your chance."

"Nay," said the officer, "it was well and fairly played for."

"True," replied Wolff, with great magnanimity, considering that he was writhing with pain, "it was. The words escaped me in spite of myself. I would not undervalue your courage or your skill."

"Generously spoken," said the young officer; "surrender, and I'll see you through this job safely."

"Never!" shouted Wolff, all fire at the word, "never, whilst I have this good arm free."

"You had better surrender," again said the officer.

"Pink me here, youngster," said Wolff, holding out his sword arm, "and then—no. d—— it! then you may chop me to sausage-meat. Silas Wolff never surrenders!"

"I like your pluck," said the officer, "but you'll rue it."

"Come on; no further parley, please," cried Wolff.

The young officer replied to this by a vigorous onslaught.

But although the blows rained upon him thick as hail, Wolff managed to ward all off with wonderful coolness.

Presently the soldier pressed him hard, and Wolff had to retreat several paces.

Then, gathering his whole strength, he replied to the attack with such a formidable blow that caused the officer to spring back, with much sacrifice to personal dignity

But Wolff's blow, although it must have determined the contest had the officer simply attempted to parry it, was a disastrous one for the striker, from the unexpected defence.

Wolff was staggered with the violence of his effort, and before he could recover himself his adversary's sword passed through his body.

He felt that he had received his mortal thrust, but would not die unavenged.

As the soldier pressed forward at the lunge, Wolff suddenly seized him by the wrist, holding the fatal weapon still quivering in the wound.

Then, ere the young warrior could disengage himself, Wolff drew back his right arm, shortened his own weapon, and thrust it up to the hilt in the other's breast.

It had passed through the officer's lungs.

The blood founted from his mouth in a torrent.

There was an instant's pause; then both staggered, and fell side by side, the soldier expiring before he reached the ground.

"VIC-TORY!" shouted Wolff with his last breath.

CHAPTER LVII.

THE CHASE—HUNTED DOWN—BESIEGED—FIRE! —ONE MORE CHANCE—THE ROOF—WILD'S MYRMIDONS—THE TRAP DOOR—LOST! LOST!

WHILE the fight around the gallows at Tyburn raged thus fiercely Red Ralph, with his beloved Leonore, was dashing at full gallop to the house which he had engaged for the furtherance of to-day's audacious exploits.

It was not very long before Red Ralph saw that they were pursued.

"No matter," he exclaimed aloud, "once within doors, with such arms as I have there, I can hold my own against a legion, at least until the decision of the fight."

As yet they were a safe distance from their pursuers.

In spite of the weighty burden which the gallant mare carried, Jonathan Wild could not gain upon them.

Arrived at the house, Red Ralph gently lifted Leonore from the saddle, and then sprang off.

"Come in, Leonore," said Ralph; "come and fear nothing."

"But they must soon recapture us here," said Leonore.

"Never; never with life!"

They entered as they spoke, and hastily barred the door.

Then they set about barricading every entrance, and were thus engaged when they heard the pursuing party gallop up.

A violent blow upon the door announced that Jonathan Wild had lost no time in commencing operations.

"Ha, ha!" said Red Ralph, with a laugh of triumph, "you may try that as long as you please."

"It cannot hold out long," said Leonore in alarm.

"Long enough for our purpose," answered her husband.

"Would it not be possible to escape by the back?"

"No."

"Why?"

"The wary Jonathan Wild (and I am sure that I recognise his voice) would never leave unguarded so simple a means of flight."

But as he spoke he hastily ran off to take observations in the direction indicated.

A glance showed Red Ralph that it was as he supposed.

Two of the thieftaker's myrmidons, with drawn swords, guarded this outlet.

"As I suspected," said Ralph; "there is nothing left us but to hold out to the last, and await assistance from my victorious Yellow Boys."

The thieftaker's voice could now be plainly heard issuing orders to his men.

Then after a while a pistol was fired through the keyhole.

The lock was shivered to atoms.

But happily for Red Ralph and his charge, they had taken the precaution to fasten every bolt and bar before the erection of the barricade, which alone was sufficient to guard the door for some time.

"All seems pretty secure here," said Ralph; "let us go upstairs and see what is to be done."

This was a fortunate thought.

As he entered the apartment immediately overhead he perceived a pair of hands upon the window-sill.

One of the men had contrived to climb up while his comrades were engaged below.

Red Ralph flew to the window and hastily flung it open.

"That's for your pains!" he cried, dealing the unfortunate man a blow upon the head which sent him back, performing a series of summersaults before he touched the ground.

Ralph at the same instant saw an officer below level a pistol at him, and ducked just in time to avoid a well-directed shot.

The bullet whistled unpleasantly close to his cheek, and lodged harmlessly in the ceiling.

"Leonore?" said Ralph.

"Yes."

"Nay, nay, do not come nearer to the window. Can you fetch me a pair of pistols from below?"

"Yes."

"You do not fear?"

"No, no."

"Then you can materially aid me. You will find them in the room we have just quitted. Go; I will keep watch here. Be speedy."

Leonore hastily descended and shortly returned with the pistols.

"Now," said Ralph, "can you take your station beside this window? Thus. Hold this hat so that they may just see the corner of it from below; but do not upon any account advance, I charge you."

"I understand," said Leonore.

This arranged, Red Ralph collected his pistols, which he had reloaded while speaking, and withdrew to the next window.

The success of his stratagem was soon apparent.

The bullets came whistling up thick as hail at the visible corner of the hat.

Almost at the same instant two shots were fired from the other window by Red Ralph, with excellent effect.

Two of the attacking party were put at once *hors de combat*.

"My curses light upon the hands that fired those shots!" shouted Jonathan Wild. "Fire upon the other window."

This was also a signal for the besieged.

In an instant Red Ralph was beside Leonore, and a repetition of his attack was attended with the same success as before.

Two more of the thieftaker's men were struck down.

"Death and furies!" shouted Jonathan Wild. "We shall all be potted here like partridges! Batter down the door!"

This was more alarming for Red Ralph than aught else, for he had already heard his temporary barricading below creak most ominously at their repeated assaults.

A blow was delivered at the entrance which shook the building from the foundation to the roof.

But still it held out stoutly.

Then Red Ralph heard the thieftaker issue a command whose import he failed to catch, and nearly all the party ran off.

"They fly!" exclaimed Red Ralph triumphantly. "Leonore, they run, and we are safe."

"Is it possible?" said Leonore doubtfully. "It is too much to hope."

"Unless," said Red Ralph, with a sudden change of expression, "it is merely some ruse to lure us forth."

"It is, it is," exclaimed Leonore; "see, one remains behind."

This they thought conclusive, but they soon found they had been mistaken.

Back came the whole troop of constables, with two huge branches of a tree and a quantity of dry twigs and leaves.

"Ah!" ejaculated Ralph, "a battering-ram! we are lost!"

Leonore uttered a faint shriek.

'Nay, fear nothing," said Ralph. "All hope is not yet gone Give me my pistols again."

Leonore placed them in his hands, imploring him not to run wildly into danger.

Red Ralph leaned forward from the window, and suddenly fired upon the men as they were bringing up their battering-ram.

Success once more attended his exploit.

Two of the men were wounded, and their scheme was for the moment frustrated.

"Could I but renew the barricade below, or strengthen it," murmured Ralph half aloud.

Leonore ran to the foot of the stairs to see if it were yet safe below, and immediately returned full of fresh alarm and apprehension.

"What is it?" asked Ralph.

"I smell fire!"

"Fire!" exclaimed Ralph. "Ah! by Heaven! They mean to burn us out, the fiends!"

The twigs which they had brought were evidently for that purpose, and they blazed and crackled by the door in a manner which filled the two inmates of the house with terror.

The smell of fire and the smoke were soon painfully apparent above.

The door had caught and was burning slowly but surely.

But the thieftaker's impatience would not allow of the completion of this fiend-like piece of vengeance.

The battering-ram was again dashed at the door, which, now half burnt through, yielded with a terrific crash.

In burst the officers, trampling out the fire as they came, and flying up the stairs.

Red Ralph in an instant dashed to the room door and turned the key.

This gave them a moment's respite.

"Come, Leonore," he cried, "exert yourself; we shall not yield until the last extremity."

He dashed out of the room by another door, closing it after them.

Immediately outside this was a ladder which communicated with the roof.

He carried Leonore up this, then drew it after them, and closed the trap.

In the loft Red Ralph took a coil of rope which he had providentially placed there for future service, and darted on to the house top, closely followed by Leonore.

"Outwitted!" he ejaculated. "Leonore, we shall foil them yet!"

Saying which he hastily fixed one end of the rope around a stack of chimneys.

The other end he swiftly fashioned into a noose, which he placed round Leonore's waist.

"Now, Leonore," he said; "take this pistol; defend yourself fearlessly: it is life and death!"

"And you?"

"Fear nothing; I shall follow immediately. Farewell."

He pressed her tenderly to his breast.

"Now, Leonore," he added; you must not look below; fear nothing; I shall let you down safely. Hold the rope thus—so. It will not cut you so much. I am with you."

Leonore reached the ground in safety. The whole party of thieftakers were within the house, engaged in the search for Ralph.

They were evidently nonplussed.

As soon as Leonore had disengaged the rope from around her Red Ralph drew it up and began to follow her.

Barely had he quitted the parapet when a violent dash at the trap announced that the enemy was upon the track at last.

Red Ralph, hearing this, let the cord glide through his hands until it burnt like a red hot wire.

"See! see!" cried Jonathan Wild, dashing on to the roof; "he will escape us yet! Back! back! some of you. Fire upon him! Death and furies!"

Several reports followed this command, and matters looked desperate for the bold Red Ralph.

CHAPTER LVIII.

THE HOUSE ON FIRE — RETREAT CUT OFF — WILD'S AGONY — THE EXPLOSION — MORE TROUBLE FOR RALPH — WOLFF'S CORPSE — CAUGHT AT LAST.

WHEN the smoke of the pistols had cleared off Red Ralph had disappeared.

The rope by which he had descended dangled from the stack of chimneys.

"Back! back!" again shouted the thieftaker to some of his men below. He dashed up to the parapet and leant over, nearly overbalancing himself in his eagerness.

But no signs of Red Ralph or the girl he had rescued from the hangman's clutches!

"He certainly did go down by the rope," muttered Jonathan, half doubtfully. "Yes, yes; of course I saw him. S'death! I shall soon begin to doubt the evidence of my own eyesight with this devil of a man!"

This settled beyond the possibility of a doubt, he came to a very speedy conclusion that it was useless to waste further time upon the house-top.

As he turned towards the trap in the roof the faint clatter of a horse's hoofs upon the hard road caught his quick ear, and upon glancing about him he perceived a horseman (as he imagined) mount a rise in the road at some distance from the house, and gallop away.

But the horseman was out of range.

"Confound his luck!" exclaimed Jonathan Wild, in a frenzy of passion, "he's fairly off at last!"

Nothing then remained but to descend and recommence the pursuit.

With this purpose he was passing through the trap-door, when his attention was attracted by the cries of one of his myrmidons from below.

It was a cry of the most terrible significance!

"Fire! fire! The house is all blazing! Save yourself!"

The thieftaker scrambled down the ladder and darted to the door of the room, draging it open with a jerk, and flew to the stairs.

[RALPH AMONG THE GIPSIES.]

There he perceived true cause for alarm.

The whole of the lower part of the house was one huge sheet of flame!

"Furies!" ejaculated Jonathan Wild, "we shall be smoked to death as helplessly as a lot of rats!"

The passage below was absolutely unapproachable.

Nothing remained therefore but to return with all speed to the roof, and adopt the means of flight used by Red Ralph and Leonore.

Quick as lightning the thieftaker carried this purpose into effect.

But now arrived upon the roof, a fresh disaster awaited him, and one which filled him with well-grounded alarm and dismay.

The rope was gone from the chimney-stack!

He had quite forgotten this, and, to add to his terror and chagrin, it was his own hand which had severed the cord and thrown it over the parapet, lest Leonore, whose flight he could not account for, should still be hiding upon the roof, and contrive to effect her escape by its aid.

His position was now desperate in the extreme.

"Help! help!" he shouted, in hopes that some of his men below would hear his cries.

But no one replied.

The agony which the inhuman wretch suffered in those few brief moments fully compensated for the brutal persecution of the guiltless Leonore.

No. 20.

His own brutality had recoiled with terrible effect upon himself.

What was to be done?

He looked earnestly over the parapet into the road, and for an instant contemplated risking his neck in a leap.

But the venture was too great, and the idea was banished as soon as entertained.

He returned once more to the trap-door, and gazed wistfully down.

But here the horrors were fast accumulating. The flames were mounting with awful rapidity.

The house was an old structure, and built almost entirely of wood—well-dried timber, which blazed as if it had been steeped in tar.

It was an awful moment.

The ruffianly thieftaker quaked with fear, and the perspiration stood out in thick and distinct beads upon his forehead.

The agony of a lifetime was compressed into those few brief minutes.

"Great Heavens!" exclaimed the thieftaker, clasping his hands wildly, "what must I do to save myself?"

It was curious to witness the abject terror of this ruffian. He who, to do him justice, never feared to meet any man in mortal strife, who would have opposed himself unflinchingly to any fatal weapon, was now utterly helpless with fear of the flames which were rapidly encompassing the house on which he stood.

"Help! help!" he shouted again and again, "mercy, mercy! Help, oh, help!"

But there was no help for him now.

He had ordered off his men in pursuit of the bold highwayman who had that day dared to thwart the execution of justice at Tyburn.

Now, too, he imagined that the very slates upon the roof grew hot beneath his feet.

But this was purely the effect of terror upon his overcharged imagination. The fire had not yet reached the floor below.

Presently he heard the sound of voices in the road, and upon looking over the parapet he perceived that it came from some of the nearest neighbours, who had been attracted by the flames, and had run there post-haste, to render what assistance lay in their power in subduing the fire.

Hope revived within him, and he called wildly upon them for aid.

Happily for him, his shouts were heard, and immediate help promised.

"Hold hard, there!" shouted a man in the crowd. "Don't move yet a while; we'll have a ladder in a brace of shakes."

Jonathan Wild responded, for the first time in his life perhaps, with truly heartfelt gratitude.

Off galloped one of the spectators, and in a trice reappeared, staggering under the weight of a long ladder.

The crowd greeted his arrival with a deafening cheer, in which the thieftaker himself heartily joined.

A dozen eager hands placed the ladder against the wall, and Jonathan Wild sprang forward.

Just then a singular rumbling noise seemed to pervade the house from top to bottom, which shook volently, as if in the grasp of some huge monster.

Then followed a terrific explosion, like the simultaneous discharge of a dozen large pieces of ordnance, and the house was blown to atoms.

*   *   *   *   *   *

Red Ralph had glanced upwards as he descended by the rope, at the very moment when the thieftaker fired at him.

The bold highwayman felt nothing at the moment, but doubted not that he had been hit, and that he was thus sent scrambling to the ground.

At the same time the idea came to him, like a lightning-flash, that if he were struck it would but add to the satisfaction of his destroyer to gloat over his expiring agonies.

Quick, then, as thought, he crawled into the house, not even taking time to regain his feet.

In the terror and confusion of the moment, in re-adjusting his rope, he made his descent upon another side of the house to that on which Leonore had gone down.

This was a dreadful mistake, leading, as the reader will find by the sequel, to much suffering and misery.

Fortunately, however, as far as his immediate safety was concerned, he had fallen by the door-step; indeed, one of his hands rested upon it as he touched the ground, which accounts for his sudden disappearance from Jonathan Wild's view.

As he crawled over the smouldering embers of the door he discovered that he still grasped a piece of the rope by which he had escaped from the house-top.

The pistol shot of the thieftaker had simply severed the cord a few inches above Red Ralph's grasp!

"Humph!" muttered the fugitive, "the fire is scarcely out yet. I should like very well to rekindle it. It would certainly be a glorious vengeance. Leonore must be safely off by this time. I'll do it!"

He hastily collected some of the wood which the besieging party had brought, and he piled it in such a manner that it would ignite rapidly.

At the same time fire would most effectually block the entrance to the house.

This done he turned his attention to the door communicating with the stairs.

His temporary barricade lay scattered by the constables all over the place.

To collect this was the work of an instant, and he began piling it before the door.

Barely had he commenced, however, when a slight interruption occurred.

One of the officers came downstairs at full speed, burst open the door, and dashed into the room.

"Hullo!" he cried.

But before he could utter another word the highwayman dashed a weighty oak chair at him, which most effectually silenced him for a while.

"Who's there?" cried a second officer, drawing up short upon the stairs.

Red Ralph made no reply, but silently awaited beside the door the man's coming.

The doomed constable advanced warily, and glanced cautiously about before stepping forth, but Red Ralph being close up to the wall, the officer could not see him without protruding his head.

This was sufficient for the highwayman's avenging arm.

The unfortunate man's sconce was no sooner visible than down came the chair with a terrific thwack, which floored him without a groan.

And then the bonfire was proceeded with.

The barricade of the stairs was completed in such a way that it would be most difficult to break through, and the outer door was effectually blocked by the fire itself.

Red Ralph now raised a trap in the floor and descended to the basement, where he had stored two small kegs of gunpowder.

In each of these he bored a small hole with the point of his sword, and sprinkled some of the powder over the vaults.

Then he hastily ascended, leaving the trap open and plenty of combustible matter near it, so that a falling spark even would complete the work of vengeance.

"Now for liberty!" he cried triumphantly, dashing towards the back outlet.

But he paused a while.

The two unfortunate officers lay upon the floor, insensible to all that was passing around, and awaiting a speedy and inevitable doom.

"Poor devils!" muttered the highwayman, "I cannot leave them to so horrible a fate. No; my retaliation upon Jonathan Wild shall be worthy the knave's persecution of me, but never shall it be said that Red Ralph was guilty of such a monstrosity as leaving two poor helpless wretches to perish when his hand could avert their doom!"

With all possible haste he dragged the two inanimate bodies to the door at the back.

Every minute seemed an age.

The fire was communicating rapidly from one object to another, and now a piece of woodwork was crackling over the very mouth of the vaults!

"Death!" cried Red Ralph, alarmed; "but my time's nearly up!"

There now remained no time to be gentle, and the only way to get the senseless constables out of the burning house in time was by taking them by the feet and dragging the two forth at once.

They got rather damaged by this undignified style of locomotion, but their lives were spared.

"Free once again!" cried Red Ralph, throwing up his arms joyously. "And now for Tyburn!"

Several horses were grazing peaceably enough upon the lawn at the back of the house, and Red Ralph was mounted in an instant.

Fortunately, too, the holster pistols were still in the saddle ready loaded and primed, so that he was in good condition to oppose any molestation.

"Now for Leonore!" said Red Ralph. "Ah! What's that? By heavens, 'tis she! Heaven be praised that she is safe! So, so; she takes the Oxford Road! God speed you, Leonore!"

It was at this time that Jonathan Wild, from the housetop, saw her mounted upon the gallant mare Nancy, and ride out of the hollow in the road, as described in the opening of this chapter, and mistook her for the highwayman himself.

A few moments brought Red Ralph to the scene of the bloody conflict which had taken place between the soldiers and his men.

The ground was strewn with dead and dying, and the groans of the wounded were terrible to hear.

The turf around the gallows was sodden with the blood which had been so freely shed upon either side.

Of the host engaged in the late combat six only remained able to keep their feet.

These were four of the rescued Yellow Boys and two soldiers, who had now ceased all enmity, and were passing from one to the other of their wounded comrades, administering such help and comfort as lay in their power.

The first object which met the highwayman's startled gaze was the corpse of Silas Wolff.

Stiff and stark it lay there in its hideous ghastliness, covered with bloody wounds.

A fixed sardonic grin was upon the countenance, now rigid in death, and his distended right hand pointed to the gallant young officer whom he had fought to death.

"Wolff!" exclaimed Ralph, horror stricken, "Wolff, this battle has been bravely fought, and victory, if victory it is, most dearly won! Rare Wolff, we shall not find your mate readily!"

"Hullo!" exclaimed one of the Yellow Boys, pausing in his office of mercy to a badly-wounded comrade; "the captain, by all that's wonderful! Are you unhurt, captain?"

"Ay, Walters; and you?"

"A few scratches; nothing more: but we had some warm work, I warrant you."

"I know it."

"But you were not engaged yourself, captain?"

"Not here, Walters," replied Red Ralph. "But think not that I deserted you. I have had some sharp work myself up at the house yonder."

"You were engaged, then, captain?" said the lieutenant, for it was he who was one of the few almost unhurt. "I heard the firing, and thought for a while that it was you making some diversion in our behalf."

"Right, Walters," answered Red Ralph; "but should we part suddenly now (and it is just probable we shall be forced to), a word in your ear. In two days from this, at sunset, I shall expect what men we can muster at the Boozing Ken."

"Right, captain."

"Spread it about amongst those of our poor fellows who are in anything like condition."

"I will."

"And assure them that I left nothing undone to serve you all. But this last business (I mean the interruption to the execution) was the only course left open to me at last."

"Captain," said Walters, wringing the highwayman's hand, "they understand that perfectly."

"And Silas Wolff is gone?"

"Alas! yes."

"We shall find it hard to replace him, Walters, I fear."

"Truly, captain; but he fell gallantly! He fought like a demon, and struck out until he could strike out no longer. His left arm was nearly lopped off some time before he fell, but still he fought on, doubtless in a very purgatory of torment!"

"Poor fellow!" said Ralph in a broken voice; "game until the very last! Well, well, he died as he has lived, undaunted, and laughing at death itself."

At this time several persons began to straggle up to the spot.

They did not arrive very quickly, for they were not sure which party claimed the day, and in case the victory lay with the attacking party, the lawless victors might turn upon any one at hand.

One of the soldiers, who up to the present had appeared to ignore Red Ralph's presence, turned suddenly upon the spectators and pointed out the notorious highwayman.

"See there," said the soldier; "he is Red Ralph, the Yellow Boy! Secure him, good people, and claim the reward for his apprehension."

"You play the traitor, my friend," said Red Ralph, riding over to the soldier; "you pretend to cease hostilities while you are only two to four, but when assistance arrives you turn traitor!"

"I only do my duty," retorted the soldier.

At the same time he clutched the bridle of Ralph's horse, but Ralph soon dealt him a blow with the butt end of a pistol which sent him reeling back.

"He speaks the truth," said the highwayman, defiantly; "I am Red Ralph! And now who claims the reward for my apprehension?"

CHAPTER LIX.

THE CHALLENGE — "WHO FOLLOWS?" — THE CHASE — A LEAP FOR LIFE — THE HACKNEY COACHMAN — SAVING THE WOUNDED.

THE challenge which Red Ralph thus boldly offered to the crowd which had now assembled round the survivors of the conflict at Tyburn very soon met with a response.

A sturdy fellow, mounted upon a fleet little cob, rode out of the crowd.

"Claim the reward for your apprehension?" said he. "That will I, you jackanapes!"

"Come on, then."

Red Ralph waited coolly until the man was nearly up with him, and then he pulled his horse sharply round and ran full at him.

Over they went, horse and rider, only, unfortunately for the latter, the cob got the best of the fall.

"So much for number one!" cried Red Ralph, laughing boisterously. "Now, who's the next?"

"I."

Everybody looked round.

The voice proceeded from one of the officers, who had at that moment ridden up, quite unperceived in the confusion which prevailed.

"O-ho! old friend!" said Red Ralph. "So you will have another tussle?"

"Indeed I will, Master Red Ralph," was the man's reply.

"Come on, then."

The fellow advanced, but the bystanders shouted to him to beware.

"He has more tricks than Old Harry himself," said one.

"Ay, and they're first cousins, I'll swear," said another.

The officer would evidently have preferred being out of the job, but, having volunteered, he could not well avoid it now, as the eyes of the whole assembly were upon him.

"Who will lend me a hand?" he demanded, looking round.

"O-ho!" shouted Red Ralph derisively. "So you can't venture to tackle me alone!"

"Why, if it was merely a matter of cutting you to mincemeat Master Red Ralph," responded the officer tartly, "I would ask no aid from mortal man."

"Truly?"

"Ay, truly. But you are reserved for another fate."

"You lie."

"Nay, the lie is yours."

"Not so, I swear. I give it back to you in your teeth."

The bold highwayman snapped his fingers contemptuously in the other's face, and the bystanders all laughed until the officer bit his lips, bringing the blood.

"Nay, don't grieve, man," continued Red Ralph in a mock soothing tone. "You have talked big enough for a very Goliath. Now come out and show what fight you have in you."

"Go on, man," shouted a voice from the crowd. "I'm with you."

"And I."

"And I'm another."

"Bravo!" cried Red Ralph. "You'll have an army presently."

But, as some half-dozen fellows stepped forth for the purpose of aiding the constable to apprehend Red Ralph, the latter deemed it high time to make a move.

"So, so!" he exclaimed, surveying them calmly, at the same time, however, keeping his eyes fully open for any surprise which might be contemplated. "Well, as you are a pretty fair number, I shall give you a run for it. Off and away!"

He pressed his horse's girth with his heel, and bounded away like the wind, shouting out to Walters as he went—

"Remember, Walters, two days hence I shall expect you. I shall be with you again when you are not looking for me."

The party set spurs to their horses and galloped off in pursuit, quite elated at the prospect of a chase.

They were all, with the single exception of the constable, amateurs at man-hunting.

None of them had hitherto run down anything more formidable than a rabbit or a fox, and therefore the present was a decided treat for them.

At the start they mustered six, but, from the rapid pace Red Ralph had taken up at the start, two were discouraged before proceeding many yards.

The remaining four, however, kept boldly to the work.

From time to time Red Ralph would turn round in his saddle, and laughingly bid them defiance.

The constable was in a great rage, and pressed the poor beast he rode most cruelly, but without much result.

Red Ralph had made a long start for himself, and every minute visibly improved his position.

And now three of his four pursuers fell off, their horses distressed with overwork, and the constable alone continued the chase.

In the excitement he had not observed that he was alone.

The highwayman, upon turning round and seeing how matters stood, gradually slackened his pace, for he disdained to fly from a single foe.

"He falls off!" cried the officer aloud, in great excitement. "Huzzah! Huzzah! He's mine!"

He pressed his horse on to further exertions, and in a few minutes the distance between them was considerably lessened.

And now they were within call of each other.

"So-ho! my gallant cutpurse!" cried the officer derisively.

"So-ho! my prince of jail crows!" responded Red Ralph.

"I shall run you to earth yet."

"You think so?"

"I'm sure of it."

"Truly?"

"As sure as we are—"

"Alone!" added the highwayman, with such ominous emphasis as the smart pace would allow him to give.

The officer for the first time glanced about him.

"Alone?"

"Ay," said the highwayman, "and I did think of stopping to give you a tussle, and death to the worst man!"

The officer drew rein a little, but Ralph perceived the action, and twitted him smartly with it.

"Nay, nay, man," he cried, with a mocking laugh, "never fall off. Come on, come on! You'll run me down yet?"

"Ay, that I shall," answered the officer, with a faint attempt at boldness, which, however, proved abortive.

"Nay, then, I'll tease you no longer," cried Red Ralph. "I see you don't relish the prospect of a tussle."

"You lie!"

"Ah! Say you so?"

The speaker rained in so suddenly that he brought his horse up on its haunches.

At the same time he turned sharply round, presenting a full front to the lukewarm courage of the officer —an act of imprudence for which he nearly suffered the next instant.

"Take that, then!" shouted the officer, hastily levelling a pistol and firing.

But the sharpness of the act prevented the aim being very correct, and Red Ralph was still unscathed.

"Tit for tat!" said the highwayman, drawing forth one of his holster pistols.

The officer ducked with so undignified a gesture that Red Ralph burst into a fit of laughter.

"Don't be alarmed, my friend," he cried. "You're

welcome to your shot; only don't try it again. A second time I shall not be so generous, and remember, pray, that I very seldom miss the mark."

The officer could scarcely believe in the highwayman's wonderful magnaminity.

"Come on, my courageous jail-kite!" said Red Ralph, turning his horse round and riding off again. "You don't like the prospect of getting at any closer quarters, although you must be a much heavier man than I."

"Braggart!" said the officer, feeling compelled to repudiate the charge.

"Eh? You are whispering defiances?" pursued Red Ralph laughingly. "Now, I'll not be hard upon you. I promise you that if you can run me down as you boasted you shall secure me without further trouble."

"You swear it?" exclaimed the officer with eagerness.

"I do."

"Agreed."

"Follow, then. Off and away!"

"After him! Hist, hist!"

At the outset Red Ralph tantalised his pursuer by allowing him to get pretty nearly up with him; then he would shoot away at a pace which defied all pursuit.

Presently, growing tired of this amusement, he set spurs to his horse, and fairly galloped away.

The highwayman was a splendid horseman, and the consciousness of his own superiority to his pursuer in this respect made him desire to put him to an equestrian trial which would close the chase in ignominy for him.

Two hedges were cleared by Red Ralph in magnificent style.

But on came the officer.

The first was cleared, if not with grace, at least with fair success. But in the second either his horse was jaded with over exertion or he did not know the precise moment to make so trying a demand upon it, for he just scraped the top of the shrubs and scrambled upon his knees on the further side.

However, the rider was not unseated, and the chase continued.

"You think that you have got over the difficulties," thought Red Ralph, chuckling, as he flew along; "but a day's steeple-chasing would be mere child's play to the dance I'll lead you, if you'll follow me fairly. Ah! a brook! Now, now, my friend, I'll try your courage once more."

Not a great many yards in front was a bright clear stream, which presented a very wide leap for a horse.

The highwayman was surprised at its width when he came near it, but there was now no time to pause.

The officer was coming on fast, and Red Ralph had sworn not to offer him any further oppositon should he overtake him.

He pulled up his horse, turned round, and rode back.

"He means to yield," thought the officer.

And he pressed eagerly forward to secure the prize he had worked so hard for.

But another of the cruellest deceptions awaited him.

The highwayman had only ridden back to get room for a run, preparatory to taking the leap.

Now he dashed forward, loosing the horse's head, and, as if able to inspire his steed with fresh vigour at a word, away he bounded, like lightning!

It was a terrific leap!

"Now!"

The gallant horse bounded forward and sprang into the air.

The next instant he was upon the other side of the stream. His hind feet slipped upon the bank, and he could not mount it, but Red Ralph in a trice was out of the saddle and tugging at the bridle.

And then he paused a while, to see if the officer would venture to take the leap.

But he was perfectly safe here, for as soon as the officer perceived the startling width of the stream, he reined in his horse so suddenly that he was nearly pitched over its head.

"Ha! ha! my friend," said the highwayman, "I thought that this would punish you. Come on."

"You have a better mount than I," growled the man.

"Granted. And a better man to mount him you'll admit?"

"Well, you havn't so much to brag about. My beast refused the leap, or else I—"

"Enough, my gallant friend," said the highwayman, with aggravating raillery; "it is an old saw and a wise one, that a bad workman always complains of his tools."

The highwayman then untied his lace neckcloth, and, dipping it in the river, used it as a sponge to bathe his hard-worked horse.

This odd grooming was most gratefully received by the horse, who neighed with evident pleasure, as if ready for a second course over a country as rough as that already traversed.

When this was completed Red Ralph mounted again and prepared to ride off, his actions all the time being closely watched by the officer upon the opposite bank, who was gnashing his teeth with shame and humiliation at his failure after such a hot chase.

"Good day to you, my friend," said the highwayman, saluting the crest-fallen officer with mock courtesy, "and may your next job be conducted with more spirit and meet with better success."

"Devil!" shouted the officer, boiling over with rage, "you shall not escape me thus!"

He drew forth his loaded holster pistol, and, poising it upon his left hand, took a slow and deliberate aim.

There was a report, and Red Ralph felt a sharp ping in his leg.

At the same time his horse gave a wild cry of pain and terror, and fell, well nigh crushing his rider.

By a quick movement, however, Red Ralph contrived to disengage himself from the fallen horse, and to regain his feet.

"Traitor!" cried Ralph to the constable, who was anxiously surveying the result of his shot from the other side of the stream; "you shall pay for that. I warned you once, but you slighted my admonition."

The officer would have fled, but ere he could start his horse he was covered with the highwayman's pistol.

Red Ralph aimed low, for he could percieve that the officer was about to "duck" in the saddle, and fired.

"Murderer!" shrieked the officer, springing half out of the saddle. "I'm slain! Help! help!"

He slid off the horse, and rolled upon the ground in torture.

"You are well and rightly served," called the highwayman across the stream. "You called for it and have got it."

"Villain!" said the officer, writhing with pain; "You've killed me."

"I've no remorse upon the point," said the highwayman coolly.

And with this he turned and walked rapidly from the spot.

Now, although he had got over a great deal of ground since the commencement of the chase from Tyburn, he had the wise precaution to go no great distance from the spot.

He had only a short walk before coming to the Oxford Road.

Arrived here, he called a hackney coach, which

happened to be passing at the time, and told the Jarvey that he required him to perform a piece of work for him which demanded secrecy and caution, and that in payment he should receive ten guineas.

The sum caused the coachman's eyes to twinkle with delight, and he swore the most faithful execution of his trust.

"First, then," said Red Ralph, "you see I've fallen into the river, yonder, and I want you to lend me an old coat."

"I've only one here, your honour," answered the Jarvey.

"You have an old cape, havn't you?"

"Yes, sir."

"That's the very thing—anything, so that I don't catch cold."

"It's as your honour pleases."

"Thank you, friend."

"Now I want a hat."

"I've only one, your honour."

"I'll buy it of you."

"But I shall have none to wear."

"You can go and get another."

"Will your honour wait?"

"Yes. Stay though; can you get another coach?"

"When?"

"Now, this minute?"

"In a twinkling, your honour—my stables are in this road."

"Off with you, then, and bring another coach with you, double quick."

"Yes, your honour."

"Now, I'm going to drive on to Tyburn. There's been a squabble there—some fight or something."

"So I've heard, your honour."

"Oh! you've heard of it?"

"Yes."

"What was it all about?"

"I was told, your honour, that Red Ralph, that devil of a highwayman, had interfered at some execution which was going to be conducted in secret, and an awful battle has taken place between the thieves and the troops."

"I've heard something of that, and I want your carriages to get away some of the wounded."

"Very good, sir."

"So follow on, as quickly as you like, and take your cue from me. Come along. Mind and don't mention the contract to any one."

"All right, your honour."

Red Ralph, in his new character of Jarvey, proceeded with all speed to the scene of the sanguinary conflict.

Notwithstanding the deal of ground which the highwayman had got over since quitting the spot, very little time had been lost, and scarcely any preparations had been made to bear off the wounded from the field.

Walters, the lieutenant of the once great Yellow Band, was still at liberty, and busily employed in tending his wounded comrades.

Red Ralph drove up to him at once.

"Want a coach, your honour?" he asked, with the peculiar salute of the Jarvey of the period.

"Yes, yes, my man," answered the lieutenant eagerly.

A dozen voices, at the same instant, would have engaged the coachman, but he found no difficulty in keeping to the lieutenant.

"Will you give me a hand?" asked the lieutenant.

"Certainly."

Red Ralph went up to one of the wounded Yellow Boys, and assisted him to rise.

"One moment," said the lieutenant, looking up from a fast-dying man with whom he was engaged in his merciful work, "this poor fellow first."

"I think not, your honour."

The lieutenant looked up, indignant at the coachman presuming to offer a suggestion.

"No offence, your honour," said Red Ralph, perceiving that they were still within hearing.

"Then give me a hand here."

"I beg your pardon, your honour," said Red Ralph again, "I think this will be best done first."

"Why?"

"Because that poor chap won't need a coach or anything else in five or ten minutes."

"Do you think he's so far gone as that?"

"Death is in his face."

"But we may get him some relief, if it is not possible to preserve his life," said Walters.

"Hadn't we better secure a good man?" said Red Ralph.

The lieutenant looked up at the supposed coachman, evidently at a loss to comprehend the meaning of this strange observation.

"Secure a good man," he repeated, "what do you mean?"

"I mean that" (here the supposed coachman drew closer to Walters and lowered his voice to a whisper) "that poor fellow would be dead before we could reach the Boozing Ken."

"Ah!" ejaculated Walters, "you know then?"

"Of course, lieutenant."

"Hush!"

"All right. Don't be alarmed, Walters. I did not think that you would so soon have forgotten me."

"Good Heavens! the captain."

"Hush," cried the highwayman, "don't look so astonished. See, see, we are attracting notice. Help me to put some of the men into the coach. I have another coming along. Ah! here it comes. Now then!"

"But I shall never be able to get off," said Walters.

"Pretend to be badly hurt," said Red Ralph. "But I see they're bringing one of the red coats to put in our coach. There's no help for it. He must go with us too. Plague upon it! it will embarrass us nicely."

CHAPTER LX.

LEONORE—THE "WHEATSHEAF"—BOUND TO THE HORSE—WILD RESUSCITATED—ON THE TRACK — RALPH OFF THE SCENT — LADY GLYDE — WILD'S NEW VILLANY.

LET us follow up the movements of Lady Leonore a while, from the time that she escaped from the house by Red Ralph's assistance.

She had barely loosened the cord from around her waist when she found herself confronted by two of Jonathan Wild's men.

"Hullo! here's one of 'em. The other can't be far off," exclaimed one.

Leonore earnestly begged them not to molest her, but her entreaties might as well have been addressed to Jonathan Wild himself.

They cut off a piece of the rope with which Leonore had effected her descent from the housetop, and hastily tied her hands together.

Then they put her upon Red Ralph's mare, which was quietly grazing upon the lawn, and fastened her in the saddle.

"Untie my hands, I beseech you," implored Leonore, "I shall fall off."

"So much the better for you," was the reply. "You may, by a lucky chance, come to grief, and save yourself from a more unpleasant wind-up."

"But my feet will get entangled in the straps."

"Then you'll drag along a bit, and that won't

harm the likes of you. You must bring your witch-craft to the rescue."

"Inhuman wretches!" exclaimed the unhappy Leonore.

"Now she's going to abuse us."

At this moment Jonathan Wild's voice was heard from within, calling loudly upon his men to follow him upstairs.

"Come on," said one, making for the house.

"But the prisoner?"

"Oh! she's safe enough for the present. Come on."

They rushed into the house, obedient to their leader's summons, leaving Leonore alone, but bound and helpless upon the horse's back.

As soon as she was alone she tugged at the cords, but they cut into her flesh, and made no difference in her awkward position.

After a little perseverance, however, she contrived to support herself in her seat, by resting the cord between her two wrists upon the point of the saddle.

Then she started the horse off at a gentle trot.

Happily, she was an expert horsewoman, or she would never have managed to save herself from falling.

She experienced considerable difficulty in guiding the horse, but the graceful accomplishment acquired in happier days enabled her to conquer this, and in a few seconds she was out of danger.

Still her situation was by no means a pleasant one.

The cords which bound her cut into her flesh in a cruel manner, and each moment the pain grew worse.

What was to be done?

It was unendurable now, and, at any risk soever, she must stop and ask assistance.

As she cantered down the Oxford Road she en-countered many horsemen and pedestrians making with all speed for the scene of the strife at Tyburn.

The news then had reached the town already.

Would not her own escape be known with the rest?

Of course. Then, in the face of this, how could she ask assistance of any passing traveller?

Her strange position would undoubtedly arouse suspicion. She would probably be retaken, after all the perils she had run in that day of terror.

Never!

Rather should the cords cut off her delicate hands, rather would she die of the agony than endure again the humiliation of a public disgrace!

Onward she rode, enduring indescribable torments, until she approached a road-side hostelry.

The "Wheatsheaf," kept by our old acquaintance Jock!

Red Ralph's gallant mare had been so thoroughly trained to pause at this house when passing that it was quite natural for her to stop.

By all that was fortunate, too, the worthy Jock was standing at the door, and he ran up at once to proffer his assistance.

"Good lud 'a mercy!" he ejaculated. "Why, how comes this?"

Leonore, thinking he alluded to the thongs which bound her, replied accordingly.

"Some ruffians, taking advantage of the confusion prevailing further up the road, have robbed me and bound me thus."

"Ah? The scoundrels!" quoth honest Jock in-dignantly; "but how came you mounted on the captain's own Nancy?"

"I do not understand you."

"Why this is the captain's—"

Jock drew up short.

Perhaps he was saying too much. Should Red Ralph be really concerned in this outrage, and he had frequently suspected his dashing customer to be a knight of the road, he might run the risk of betraying him.

This he was too politic to do.

Red Ralph was an excellent customer, profusely lavish with his lightly-gotten gains.

Moreover, he was not the man whose displeasure he could venture to incur with impunity.

"I see," said Leonore, getting over her momentary embarrasment, "you recognise this horse?"

"Yes — no — that is, I have seen him before, madam."

"And now, please, loosen these cords."

"Your pardon, madam."

Jock released Leonore in a trice and aided her to dismount, and set about grooming the mare.

"I think that I will continue my journey now," said Leonore.

"You had better rest a while," said the landlord. "The road is full of all manner of knaves, who would not hesitate to offer you violence in open daylight. They are going up to Tyburn in shoals to see the scene of the battle which has taken place there."

"Indeed?"

"But as you have come in that direction you must have seen something of it."

"No, no," answered Leonore, with a blush and a stammer.

"Truly?" quoth Jock, preparing to open the flood-gates of his eloquence upon her. "Then, madam, you don't know of the horrible fight which has oc-curred?"

"No."

"Well, they had a regular pitched battle, and a regiment of soldiers is cut to pieces, and a dozen of the Yellow Boys who were going to be strung up. And the witch—"

Leonore started.

"Oh, yes, madam," continued Jock, "they were going to hang up a witch as well, but she got away nicely. The ground opened, and she sank through, and they do say that the smell of sulphur was some-thing awful choking!"

Poor Leonore was so immediately concerned in this that she could not even smile at the loquacious boni-face's monstrosities.

She merely made some commonplace expression of surprise, with as much calmness as she could.

Then she reiterated her desire to continue her journey.

"Pardon, madam," said Jock, "but I warn you that you will continue at your peril at present. Besides, if you remain here you will have an oppor-tunity of learning all the news of the fight. Some of the wounded soldiers or constables are sure to pull up here."

"Ah? Then I must certainly go on," exclaimed Leonore affrightedly. "Will you please get my horse ready again?"

"Oh!" said Jock, "you don't like the idea of seeing the wounded men? Well, if you please to re-main, you can have a chamber above; my daughter Margaret shall attend you, and no one need ever know you're here."

"Then I think I'll stay."

"Very good, madam. Will you walk this way?"

Jock led the way into the house, and handed her over to the care of his daughter, the fair Margaret.

This lady, the reader will remember, has already been introduced into these pages (but only asleep in bed), upon the occasion of Red Ralph's last visit, in company with the sturdy Dick Turpin, after the dashing rescue from Newgate.

Presently Jock returned to the door to witness the long procession which still hurried westwards.

He had not been long here when two hackney coaches with drawn blinds, each bearing a man upon the box beside the coachman, pulled up before his house.

"What is it, my masters?" demanded Jock. "Have ye seen anything of the battle at Tyburn?".

"We are just from there," answered the driver of the first coach.

"Come in, then."

The old gossip was all eagerness for the news, and he almost dragged the man off the box.

"Gently, gently, Master Jock."

"Hullo! you know me?"

"Aye, for a knave."

"Knave yourself, you villain!" retorted the boniface.

"Nay, nay, good Master Jock," said the Jarvey, soothingly; "I do but jest. We have a poor wounded soldier in the carriage who is badly hurt, and we fear that the jolting of the coach will be more than he can bear much further. Aid us to carry him into the house."

Jock readily assented to this.

It was some solace to his thirst for the latest intelligence to have one of the very men housed in his dwelling.

When they came to lift the soldier out of the coach, what was Jock's surprise to see that it contained four wounded men besides the soldier.

"Do all of them get down here?" he demanded.

"No, Master Jock," replied the Jarvey; "the remainder are well enough to proceed to the hospital."

Before resuming the journey, however, the coachman went to the stables to procure some water for his horses, and then the first object which caught his view was Red Ralph's mare Nancy.

"What, Nancy lass!" he said, patting her sleek coat.

The beast, with a neigh of delight, returned the coachman's caress.

"Why the mare seems to know you!" remarked Jock.

"Yes. How came she here?"

"Do you know her owner?"

"I do," returned the coachman. "But you reply to my question with another. How came the mare here?"

"A lady brought her—no, no, I mean—and yet, why not?—a lady came with her."

The coachman started, and gave utterance to an exclamation of very evident satisfaction.

"Look you, Master Jock," he said, "if you value the consideration and goodwill of the captain who owns this mare—"

"Which I do."

"Treat the lady with all respect and attention. I will guarantee you the reimbursement of any expenses you may incur."

You? And who are you? What assurance have I—"

"Tut, tut!" interrupted the coachman, with an austere wave of the hand which ill suited his humble calling. "You must content yourself with the assurance of the captain."

"The captain?"

"Ay, through me. Havn't you got his mare there? He will return here—that is, come here—for he hasn't been here before to-day—"

"No."

"In the course of an hour. On no account allow the lady to quit before he arrives. You hear me?"

"Ye-es," said the terrified Jock, terrified because he thought that he saw in this injunction the confirmation of his suspicions of Ralph's unlawful calling.

It was, then, he who had committed the outrage upon the poor girl who was now in the house.

Now Jock was to a certain extent a rogue, but at the same time a most decided coward.

He did not mind entertaining a robber, and being the best of friends with him, but he decidedly objected to sharing his exploits.

The coachman having refreshed the horses, left the wounded soldier to the landlord's care, and departed.

Poor Jock was now in a great state of perplexity.

What was to be done?

If he pressed the lady to stay he would probably become party to a transaction which would render him amenable to the law.

The least it could do was to risk the reputation of his house.

If, on the other hand, he got rid of his guest, would he not incur the gallant captain's displeasure?

And of this he had a most wholesome dread.

No matter, he was resolved.

At any risk Leonore must be sent on.

He had an excuse.

He did not know the driver of the hackney coach.

Might he not be an enemy of Red Ralph's?

Might it not be some plot to his prejudice?

Or, at the worst, he might aver that the lady had persisted in her intention to proceed in spite of all he could do, and that he had not the power to detain her against her will.

No sooner had he resolved upon this than he put his project into execution.

Leonore had departed perhaps half an hour, when who should arrive at the "Wheatsheaf" but Red Ralph himself.

"Well, Jock," he said on entering, "you have a guest!"

The landlord changed colour, and stammered out his excuses, which he had been studying with much care ever since Leonore had left.

"Idiot!" exclaimed Red Ralph in great disgust. "You don't know what mischief you have caused. But beware: if any harm comes to that lady you shall answer the consequences to me!"

"I—I—I'm very sorry. I didn't know she was a friend of yours, captain."

"You lie, Jock. I told you myself not an hour ago."

"You?"

"Ay, I told you. Only you were fool enough not to recognise me because I had on a coachman's hat and coat!"

"Lor, captain!"

"Silence, fool! Which direction did she take?"

"The main road to town."

"And you know nothing further?"

"Nothing."

"That is no information at all, then."

Red Ralph sprang into the saddle, and dashed off without another word. But he had not proceeded a dozen yards before he returned.

"Jock."

"Yes, captain."

"Should any one come and ask information about this lady, you know positively nothing."

"Yes, captain."

"You understand me?—nothing whatever."

"Yes, captain."

"Look you, make no mistake, or dread the consequences."

And Red Ralph rode off full gallop towards town.

A few minutes after his departure two mounted constables galloped up to the "Wheatsheaf" and called for the landlord.

"You have received a lady here?" said one of them.

Jock was so lost by the startling fulfilment of Red Ralph's information that he stammered out something which was taken as an assent.

"She is here now?" pursued the former speaker.

"No, no," said Jock hastily. "She hasn't been here. She's gone. I havn't seen her."

"The man's mad. Is she here or is she not?"

"No, no. She hasn't been here."

"Then why all this stammering and confusion?"

[RALPH'S ADVENTURE ON THE ROOF.]

Jock began to collect himself a little.

"This is the third time I've been asked the same question within an hour."

"Ah! by whom?"

"By—by—a stranger."

"Mounted?"

"Yes."

"And he rode off at once?"

"Yes."

"In this direction?"

"Precisely."

Without a word the two officers set spurs to their horses, and gallopped off in Red Ralph's track.

Poor Jock was now in a greater dilemma than before

Without intending it, he feared that he had done the captain an ill turn.

The officers were yet in sight when a lady, thickly veiled, and in an equipage which denoted her to be of superior rank, stopped before Jock's hostelry.

"Are you the landlord?" she demanded of Jock.

"Yes, madam—that is, my lady," answered Jock obsequiously.

"Has a lady arrived here, tied upon horseback, within the last hour?"

Jock was positively dumbfounded.

He opened his ponderous jaws and stared idiotically at his questioner, but could not offer a word of reply.

No. 21.

"Do you hear me?" demanded the lady in a tone of irritation.

"Yes, my lady, but—"

"But what?"

"I know nothing."

"She has not been here?"

"N—n—no."

"Then why not answer me at once?"

"You're number three," stammered the landlord.

"The man has been drinking!" said the lady indignantly. "Drive on!"

The carriage rattled off, leaving Jock more confused than ever.

"Well!" he muttered, "if this continues I shall certainly be what they said I was—mad, and an idiot. I'm quite in the clouds!"

He had just retreated to the back of his counter when in rushed a man all over plasters and bandages.

His head was strapped in every direction, and a white neckcloth envelopped his jaws, through which the blood was oozing from a gash upon his cheek.

"Landlord! landlord!" called this ghastly object.

"Sir!" said the startled Jock.

"Who was that that left just now in the carriage?"

"Don't know, sir."

"A lady?"

"Yes."

"Then, curse you! why not say so?"

"I—I—"

"Silence!" bawled the wounded man. "My name is Wild. I daresay you know it."

"Lor yes, sir. You are wounded in the battle at Tyburn?"

"What the mischief is that to do with you? Where did that lady come from?"

"She came from town—I don't know where."

"Good. Have you seen a girl pass the house, bound to a horse?"

The landlord collapsed.

"Answer me, you fool," said Wild, with an oath.

"Number four!"

"What?"

"Nothing."

"Answer my question. Is the man mad or drunk? What do you mean by number four?"

"You are the fourth person who has asked me about a lady tied upon horseback."

"Ah!" exclaimed the thieftaker. "Who were the others?"

"I don't know."

"What did that lady in the carriage want here?"

"The same business."

"How? She asked you for a woman tied upon horseback?"

"Precisely. She was number three."

"Number three! What's that?"

"The third person, you understand, Mr. Wild, who asked."

"Curse your number three!" interrupted the thieftaker savagely. "Do you know what crest the panel of the carriage bore?"

"No, sir."

"Humph!" muttered Jonathan Wild aside. "If it should indeed be the Lady Glyde, as I suspected, then the girl's statement was correct, and I really see no reason to doubt it. I must be after her ladyship at once and introduce myself. Thus I invariably turn a mishap to good fortune. Out of this devilish business of to-day may grow wonders untold. I have had fair vengeance on the girl already, and so can spare her, if Lady Glyde will. But Red Ralph's doomed. Fate must have rescued me from almost certain destruction in the burning house, by a miracle, for this especial end! Look to it Red Ralph!"

CHAPTER LXI.

PLOT AND COUNTERPLOT — JONATHAN WILD'S LAST MOVE — LEONORE IN HIS POWER AGAIN —THE THIEFTAKER'S PASSION AND LEONORE'S PERIL — A PROPOSAL — DEATH BEFORE DISHONOUR!

AND now plots afresh are hatching to work the ruin of Lady Leonore and the destruction of the bold Ralph.

They are surrounded by a new peril sprung out of the very danger which Red Ralph's last and boldest stroke has happily averted.

After leaving the hostelry of Jock upon the Oxford Road, Lady Glyde (for, as Jonathan Wild had surmised, it was her ladyship who had called upon the same errand as himself) proceeded to the scene of the conflict.

The reason of her ladyship's sudden and unexpected appearance upon the exciting scene was this.

At the eleventh hour Lady Glyde heard the astounding news that the unhappy girl who lay in Newgate, condemned to an ignominious death upon the scaffold for murder, had given her name as Lady Leonore Glyde.

Upon ascertaining this Lady Glyde summoned her carriage, and drove post-haste to Newgate.

Here she obtained an interview with the governor, and made known her business, only to find, alas! that she was too late.

The anticipated execution had already taken place.

So, at least, the authorities in town imagined. How signally it had been frustrated the reader already knows.

The agony which the guilty Lady Glyde suffered upon learning these fearful tidings fully compensated for much of the agony which she had caused the unhappy Leonore.

Her daughter had perished upon the scaffold!

Horrible thought! True, she did not bear the poor girl any overwhelming affection. But were not her name and her family disgraced by this fearful act?

She well knew, too, that it was impossible Leonore could be guilty of the terrible crime laid to her charge.

She had never been from her sight since her birth until the late events had separated them, and she had watched the growth of the child to girlhood and finally to womanhood.

Every action of her life had shown her gentle, good-natured, loving, and the essence of truth and virtue, and she could not believe that her nature had so strangely changed.

No, no; such a metamorphosis was utterly impossible.

Lady Glyde poured out a torrent of invectives upon the governor of Newgate which utterly overwhelmed that pompous official, threatening him with the vengeance of the supreme authorities for neglecting to forward her intelligence of the assertion which Leonore had made as to her identity.

Then she left the prison, regardless of the terrified governor's prayers and entreaties to hear reason, and directed her carriage to the west.

Before she had proceeded very far the carriage was overtaken by a mounted messenger, who had been immediately despatched upon this business.

He brought the intelligence from Tyburn, whence he had ridden at a desperate rate, that Lady Leonore had escaped, and the manner in which this escape had been effected.

Then followed Lady Glyde's inquiries upon the road, ending as we have seen, and her ladyship returned with all speed to town to set fresh means at work to find the missing Leonore.

Lady Glyde was but an hour returned home when

A servant announced that a gentleman of the name of Wild desired to see her.

"Some tradesman, I suppose," said Lady Glyde. "Say I am particularly engaged, and cannot be seen to-day."

The servant departed, but returned in a few minutes.

"Mr. Wild says, my lady," said the man, "that he cannot leave without seeing your ladyship."

"Cannot?"

"He says so, my lady."

"Nonsense. Dismiss him!"

"But—"

"Do you hear me?" interrupted Lady Glyde imperiously. "Am I mistress here or not, pray?"

"He says, if you please, my lady, that he is sure you will see him, for he comes upon a matter which occupies your whole attention at present."

Lady Glyde started to her feet, and was interested at once.

"Send Mr. Wild to me, then, since he persists," said her ladyship.

Accordingly Mr. Jonathan Wild—obsequious to a degree in the presence of aristocracy—was ushered into the apartment.

Lady Glyde returned his salute with a freezing inclination of the head, but did not attempt to rise.

"My name, my lady," began the thieftaker, "as your servant has doubtless informed your ladyship, is Jonathan Wild."

Lady Glyde half rose to her feet, and changed colour visibly.

"The phantom!"

"I beg your pardon, my lady," quoth the astonished thieftaker.

"Nothing, nothing," said Lady Glyde, hastily collecting herself.

The reader will readily account for her ladyship's agitation when he calls to mind Red Ralph's last introduction to Lady Glyde, upon the occasion of the ball, and the audacious robbery of the Eastern ambassador.

The highwayman had used Jonathan Wild's name as one of his several aliases upon this occasion.

But to resume.

"Your ladyship," began the thieftaker, "has been to-day to Newgate, where you have had an audience with the governor."

"I have."

"The subject of this interview was Lady Leonore Glyde."

Her ladyship bowed.

"From the prison your ladyship proceeded to Tyburn, to ascertain if the condemned prisoner was really whom she asserted, Lady Leonore Glyde, your missing daughter."

"And what is your object in telling me all this, Mr. Wild?"

"I'm coming to that, my lady."

"Then come quickly, if you please," said Lady Glyde. "It seems to me that you appear desirous of creating an effect by showing how well versed you are in my affairs. This is an old trick of quacks and conjurors, and I wonder that you play it upon me."

"Pardon me, my lady," said the thieftaker, "I am merely arriving as fast as possible at the object of my present intrusion."

"The expression is well chosen," said Lady Glyde quickly.

Wild winced.

"You are under an impression," he continued with forced calmness, while he secretly writhed at Lady Glyde's cutting contempt, "that this condemned murdress is your missing daughter?"

It was now Lady Glyde's turn to look uncomfortable.

The terrible truth put to her by the remorseless thieftaker in all its hideous disgrace was a severe rebuke to her misplaced *hauteur*.

She was unable to reply; so she simply bowed assent.

"Now, my lady," pursued the thieftaker, who perceived the effect of his smartly-worded address, and was inwardly chuckling at it, "I merely come here to offer my services in seeking the lady and bringing her to you."

"And you think you can do this?"

"I can."

"How soon?"

"I cannot say; but I shall proceed at once in the business if your ladyship engages me."

"You may consider it an engagement, if my terms—"

"Oh!" interrupted the crafty thieftaker, "your terms are my own, my lady."

"Good."

"Your most obedient servant, my lady," said Wild humbly.

And with an elaborate bow he retired from the austere Lady Glyde's presence.

"So much for her cruel ladyship," muttered Jonathan Wild as he left the Glyde mansion. "I think I got the best of that little skirmish. My Lady Glyde is a sharp practitioner; but I rather think that Jonathan Wild is too 'cute for her. My terms are hers, are they? Good! Now, then, for that little snuggery where I have so nicely secured Miss Leonore. S'death and the devil! My Lady Glyde little dreamt that I had already secured the prize!"

* * * * * * *

The thieftaker upon arriving in town had been met with the inspiring intelligence of the recapture of the persecuted girl.

Two of his officers had, by a lucky stroke of fortune, chanced to overhear two men speaking of the singular circumstance of a girl of apparent high breeding riding a magnificent mare and halting at a tavern in the vicinity.

This was the fugitive's precise description of course, and they lost not a moment in recovering her.

She was borne away to Jonathan Wild's residence in triumph.

Here in silent terror she awaited the accomplishment of that awful fate from which Red Ralph had so opportunely rescued her.

The doom, she imagined now, was only retarded for a few brief hours, not averted.

Judge, then, the alarm of the maiden when, after an hour's captivity in the thieftaker's house, Jonathan Wild himself was ushered into her presence.

The ruffian had now a fresh line of conduct cut out for him.

A scheme it was which would undoubtedly make him for life.

But this fresh piece of rascality must be developed in the thieftaker's own words.

"We meet again," he said as he entered, hatching his plot the while.

Leonore could not repress a shudder at the sight of her fiendlike persecutor.

This was duly noticed and appreciated by Jonathan Wild.

"Accept my congratulations upon your escape," continued the thieftaker. "I am heartily glad of it."

Leonore was silent.

"Your manner would seem to imply," pursued Wild, who found it difficult to open the campaign, "that you doubted my sincerity; but of that in the present instance you shall have ample proof."

The wording of this phrase raised apprehensions of violence in poor Leonore's mind, which showed themselves so palpably in her face that the thieftaker remarked upon it.

"Nay, fear nothing from me," said he; "the devotion I bear to you is born of respect."

This astonished Leonore more than anything he had said.

"Respect!" she repeated.

"Ay, Leonore."

"Then you are falser than I ever deemed," said Leonore indignantly. "You say that you respect me, and speak of devotion, and yet you would have sworn away my life. Nay, you did, for should I not now be a corpse had not another's hand—"

"Nay, nay, I swear it!" exclaimed Wild with such apparent fervour that Leonore was for the moment staggered. "I had busied myself with the highest authorities in the land to procure your pardon, and at the very moment when you were cut from the cord my messenger arrived upon the field with the document."

"And you swear this?"

"I do."

Leonore looked upon the hideous seared countenance of the thieftaker, which wore an expression of the the most profound truth and sincerity.

Vile as she knew him to be—perjured as she had seen him in the witness-box at her own trial—she could scarcely believe him base enough to swear away his soul with such deliberation.

A faint hope sprang up from this for the captive girl.

"Then you mean to say that I am free?"

"Precisely."

"Why, then, am I brought here?"

"For your own good."

"How so?"

"I would save you from the perils which encompass the lone maiden in this city of vice."

"If you speak truth—"

"I swear it."

"Then I can but be grateful for your good intentions, but I should have preferred choosing my own counsellors."

Wild looked upon her with a glance which was intended to convey a gentle reproach for her ingratitude, but the scars, cuts, and blood-stained patches which covered his face considerably damaged the effect of what was an excellent effort in dramatic art.

"You are too cold," said the thieftaker tenderly. "I would show you kindness, but you repulse every advance I make."

"Enough of this," said Leonore shortly. "To the point at once."

"Eh?"

"I say to the point at once. What is the object of all this?"

"I don't understand—"

"Nor I," continued Leonore, following up the attack so spiritedly commenced with a degree of smartness which completely staggered the thieftaker. "I only see that all this is simply the prelude to something of which I am ignorant as yet. Cease your hypocrisy and deceit. What do you want?"

Jonathan Wild took a minute to collect himself after this, and then returned to the charge.

"Leonore, I love you," he exclaimed with a sudden burst, as if torn by a dozen conflicting emotions.

"You lie."

"Madam?"

"I say that it is false. You say this with a purpose."

"Humph! You think so?"

"I know it."

"Well, perhaps you're right. But in good sooth I admire you."

"What do you wish?"

"I want to make you mine."

As he advanced his prisoner sprang back a pace with a gesture of loathing and detestation.

"Monster!" she cried; "sooner would I dash my brains out against the wall than accept such infamy!"

"Nay, you misunderstand me."

"No; now I understand you perfectly," exclaimed Leonore. "You would have me purchase my life with my honour."

"Nay."

"Silence! Hear my answer. Did your gallows tree await me here—were the cord around my neck, as—as it was—and you the hangman awaiting my answer for the signal, it should still be the same. And now sell me again to the justice which is to murder me!"

Wild had never seen her to such advantage as when making the present indignant reply, and the dignity of her bearing for the moment completely overawed him.

"Now, madam," he began, "allow me to assure you that you have entirely misconstrued my meaning. I would make you my wife, love or no love, since you put it in such admirable and business-like form."

Poor Leonore was fairly perplexed at this.

She could not now comprehend his meaning. She well knew that there was some hidden purpose in all his actions; but this was a puzzle.

It could not be that he really bore her any affection. No; of this she was assured.

Jonathan Wild saw that she was now at a loss, and he watched her expression anxiously, to see whether she could assign any reason for his strange conduct.

Meanwhile Leonore got at an inkling of the truth, and was determined to meet craft by duplicity.

Adversity had sharpened her wit, and she was now a fair antagonist for the nonce for even the thieftaker himself.

"You are sincere in this?" she asked, half doubtfully.

"I swear it by any oath you may propose," exclaimed the thieftaker with unassumed eagerness.

"You would marry me, a vagrant girl—a gipsy—a murdress perhaps?"

"Nay, I know you are neither one nor the other," said Wild.

"I thought that you suspected as much," said Leonore, anxiously watching the effect of her words.

"Suspected?"

"Ay, that my words at the trial had not been without their effect upon you."

"You don't surely mean that you are really Mina?"

"And not Leonore Glyde. But really I did not even hope that so perfect a master in the art of dissimulation could be deceived by my poor playing."

"Fool, you have overreached yourself," shouted Wild, with a burst and a torrent of invectives. "You have spoken too soon. Had you held your peace a while I should have settled the matter; but as it is—no—"

Here he broke suddenly off, and fell into a long train of thought.

"No," he mused, "thanks to the wonderful resemblance, I can sell her to my Lady Glyde before the trick is discovered. Once I've made my money—possession—but first—" and here he muttered his thoughts half aloud, "but first I can now take possession of my prisoner upon my own terms. She's a devilish handsome girl!"

Leonore caught these last words, and having now achieved the object for which she attempted to deceive the thieftaker, she hastened to reassure him as to her identity.

"I now understand the motive of your little love scene," she said, in a tone of triumph.

"No matter."

"I may as well inform you," said Leonore. "that in endeavouring to marry into my family you play for too high a stake."

The thieftaker looked perplexed.

"You mean then that you are—"

"Leonore Glyde."

"Plague!"

"Nay," said Leonore, "spare yourself all chagrin upon the point. On no account could you have succeeded to gain my hand in marriage. The boldness of your project deserves some recognition, but it is a failure."

"Not yet."

"An utter failure."

"Madam, you are yet in my power," said Wild significantly.

"Ruffian and coward!" she exclaimed, "but death by my own hand should preserve me from dishonour."

"Nay, if you provoke me," exclaimed the thieftaker advancing.

"Stand off!" ejaculated Leonore, catching at the nearest object to use in her defence.

This chanced to be a small metal statuette, and was not to be despised at a shift.

The thieftaker, however, was too quick for the helpless girl when proceedings arrived at open violence.

In an instant he had wrested the object from her grasp.

"Help! help!" she shrieked.

"Nay, my coy beauty!" said the thieftaker, "we are far from all hearing here."

This was a falsehood, for he was trembling with apprehension lest her cries should be overheard and draw attention to the house.

"Ruffian!" ejaculated Leonore "I swear you shall repent this."

"Never," said Wild.

"By Heaven you shall."

She appeared as nothing in his iron grasp.

Every struggle she made grew weaker than the effort which had preceded it.

She felt that her strength was rapidly leaving her, and she burst into tears—the reaction from the bold and open defiance with which she had met all the thieftaker's advances.

"Tears certainly do become you, my dear," said the thieftaker. "Now, some men object to see a woman weep, but I rather like it. It sets off some styles of beauty to good advantage."

His grasp of her relaxed somewhat as she ceased to struggle.

Taking advantage of this, Leonore sprang from him, and with one bound was by the room door.

Wild, however, was beside her before she could touch the latch.

"Stand off!" she cried frantically, "or I will dash myself into the street below."

"Pshaw!" exclaimed the thieftaker contemptuously, "you would'nt have the courage to do it if you could, but you cannot."

Leonore glanced towards the windows, and saw that they were strongly barred.

The poor girl struggled, but she was weak and powerless.

Helpless as an infant in a giant's grasp.

"Help! help! mercy!" she shrieked in piercing tones, "murder! help!"

CHAPTER LXII.

AN INTERRUPTION—THE CAPTIVE'S DEFENCE—THE THIEFTAKER'S FURY — WILD UPON ANOTHER TACK—REDUCING THE GARRISON BY FAMINE—LEONORE'S LETTER—THE LAST RESOURCE—A GLEAM OF HOPE!

THERE was a knock at the door.

"Curse them!" muttered the thieftaker. "Who's there?"

"You are wanted below, if you please, Mr. Wild."

"Who is it?"

"I don't know."

"I'm out."

"What, sir!"

"Out—engaged—not within—not to be seen. Rot you, be off!"

But the man was not to be disposed of thus easily.

"The man says, sir, that he will not go away until he has seen you. It is most important business."

The thieftaker was forced to leave Leonore, who was in the greatest joy at this unlooked for reprieve.

"Curse his officious tongue!" muttered Jonathan Wild half aloud.

Then, turning to Leonore, he added, with a malicious grin, "Do not think to get off thus, my charmer. I can promise you—"

"Mr. Wild."

"I'm coming."

"Sir?"

"I'm coming. Be off. I'll break your cursed neck, you villain!"

Jonathan Wild left the room, carefully locking the door outside with as much noise as possible, that Leonore might understand how utterly useless it was for her to contemplate escape for an instant.

As soon as his footsteps died away upon the stairs Leonore sprang to her feet and proceeded to secure the door.

Taking one of the stout oak chairs which constituted the chief furniture of the apartment, she pressed the top of the back beneath the projecting lock—forming a foundation for her barricade which would defy any ordinary strength.

This was prized up by other articles, and every object which the room contained was made to aid in this service.

Leonore was busily employed in her work when the thieftaker returned.

The lock was turned in an instant; but the door was fixed!

"Thank Heaven!" murmured the prisoner with heartfelt gratitude.

The thieftaker was in a violent passion at this discovery.

He stormed and swore, but all his oaths and invectives could not burst open the door.

In vain was blow after blow showered upon it.

It groaned and creaked, but only gave note of its great strength and solidity.

"Let me in!" cried Jonathan Wild in a voice of thunder.

"Never!"

"I warn you that you shall suffer for it if you offer me further resistance."

"I should suffer for it if I offered none," said Leonore.

"Nay," said Wild craftily. "I swear that you should not."

"Pshaw!"

"Never! by all that—"

"You need not perjure yourself," said the captive. "All your eloquence could not now induce me to admit you."

"But something stronger than eloquence might, madam!"

"Possibly."

"And it shall be tried."

Leonore was silent.

"I say, madam," repeated the thieftaker, "that it shall be tried!"

The prisoner said nothing, and Jonathan Wild grew furious at her silence.

He spared no exertions to reduce the fortress which his prisoner had established in her own defence, but all without avail.

At length he ceased, and Leonore was left alone.

But now that she was relieved from his immediate persecutions she felt not a whit less alarmed than before.

She well judged that he had but retired for a while, to return with fresh schemes to force an entrance.

All she could do was to pray for strength in the fearful emergency.

Again and again did she gaze out of the iron-barred windows, but escape in this direction was an utter impossibility for many reasons.

First, the bars were immoveable.

But supposing this difficulty got over, the height from the street was so great that it would be certain destruction to attempt to reach it without better means at her disposal than those she possessed.

The next day the prisoner heard a knocking at the room door, and then Jonathan Wild spoke.

"How are you by this time, my coy Lucretia?" he chuckled. "Eh? Oh, she's lost her tongue, has she? *But has she found her appetite?*"

This, then, was the explanation of the thieftaker's forbearance tactics!

He meant to starve the hapless girl into submission!

"Can't find a word for her own pet?" continued the thieftaker after pausing vainly for Leonore's reply. "Well, well, you've made a very effective barricade, and I confess myself beaten so far. How you have managed it is, I must own, a mystery. Now don't sit so still. I know that you are there. You haven't escaped; I'm sure of that. Many a more substantial fortification than yours, my pearl of virtue, has been reduced by famine! We shall see how long you will hold out."

Then he paused and listened intently for several minutes.

But the prisoner did not move or utter a word.

This was the most aggravating conduct which she could observe, for, in spite of Jonathan Wild's words, he could not help doubting from time to time if it were really possible that she could be still within the room, and yet not speak.

His long experience in prison matters taught him that the most fearful thing connected with solitary confinement was that awful silence which the prisoners were forced to preserve.

"Ah! well," he said, as he prepared to make a move, "you can hold your tongue as long as you please. I know very well you haven't got out, and, what's more, you can't get out. Plague her! why the mischief don't she answer?"

And then he ran off and hastened to the street to see if the window-bars had been tampered with, for her silence was a constant torment to him.

From time to time he half feared that she had committed suicide, as she had threatened.

This was by no means a pleasant prospect. Not that the thieftaker was troubled by any qualms of conscience upon the matter.

The only disagreeable thing was that he would have found the affair so difficult of explanation to the authorities.

The next day Leonore began to consider what could be done to avoid the fearful doom to which she must succumb if her captivity lasted much longer.

She must attract attention from without if possible.

And yet if she called to a passer-by for assistance she would probably be taken for a mad woman, and her cries meet with no other result than the jeers of her captor.

If she had writing materials she might be enabled to call upon the humanity of a casual passenger in the street.

This idea was no sooner entertained than Leonore commenced a vigilant search in all the corners of the room.

Every box and drawer was ransacked, and at length she discovered a packet of paper and a blacklead pencil.

She then wrote a note as follows:—

"*I, Lady Leonore Glyde, being held prisoner in this, the house of Jonathan Wild, the thieftaker, most earnestly beg and entreat the humane consideration of the reader of the present in my behalf, that he or she will give such information to the authorities as shall lead to my release from this place, where I am subject to the grossest indignities, and am now sinking with exhaustion from want of the common necessaries of life.*"

To this she affixed the date, and, folding it into the form of a note, she cast it from the window.

The next moment she saw a man stoop and pick it up.

"Heaven be praised!" she exclaimed, "and grant that it may produce the desired effect."

Within five minutes she heard a footstep upon the stairs without, and her heart beat quick with joyful anticipation.

But a cruel disappointment was awaiting poor Leonore here.

"Ha, ha, my coy charmer!" exclaimed the hated voice of the thieftaker, "so you have pleased to let me know after all that you live. You have set my mind at rest, if that is any comfort to you, and I know it is. Ha, ha!"

Leonore turned sick.

"Here it is," continued Jonathan Wild with a chuckle, "and a tender appeal it is too. You ought to get a helping hand at once, I'm sure, poor creature. But it's foolish to ask the assistance of justice. You'd only be removed from here to be strung up. That was a foolish move!"

"You forget the pardon your messenger brought to Tyburn," said the prisoner, who could keep silent no longer.

But the next instant she could have bitten her tongue off with vexation and annoyance.

"Ha, ha!" shouted the thieftaker in ecstacy, "so you have found your speech at last, have you? Now you set my mind doubly at rest, and I know that that is a double satisfaction for you. But, to undeceive you upon that other little matter of the pardon, you did'nt surely believe that tale, did you? Oh, no. I merely told you that to keep you amused. The fact is that you are still under sentence. I have it in my power to save you; but it is a matter of consideration whether it will be more to my interest at last to take the reward offered for your apprehension or make you my wife. Let that comfort you until our next interview. I'm off upon a little matter of business concerning our nuptials. Ta, ta, dearee!"

Then followed a smacking, to intimate that he was kissing his hand to his prisoner in adieu.

Leonore then took her station at the window, and there watched until Jonathan Wild went out.

Then as soon as he was out of the way she made several copies of her letter of appeal for aid, and waited patiently for the passing of the next foot passenger.

One of her letters was thrown with but a very sorry result.

The man who picked it up read it attentively through, and then looked up at the window where poor Leonore stood awaiting in painful anxiety the result.

He pantomimed to her in gestures of assenting condolence with her woes, gave a soothing wave of the right hand, and walked on, tapping his forehead significantly, and shrugging his shoulders.

"Great Heavens!" exclaimed the unhappy Leonore, "it is as I half feared: he evidently deems me insane. And yet my letter is carefully worded. I must change the style."

More letters were written and thrown out with various results.

Several persons tossed them away unread.

Some scanned them over and crumpled them up in their pockets, but no one took any notice of the affair.

At length a young man read it attentively through and then came to the house.

A few words of explanation seemed to satisfy him, and he walked away, shrugging his shoulders and shaking his head with sad compassion.

"They have told him that I am mad," said Leonore, bursting into tears. "This is sorry work! Ah, me! But it will never do to despair. Courage and patience, Leonore. Here's for another venture, and may better fortune attend it! Ah! he reads it. Come, that's a point gained, at any rate. He looks this way! Surely! Yes! He holds out hopes. He catches my meaning, and he will return with assistance. Heaven be praised, and prosper his good intent! Grant that this last hope may not be raised up to be dashed from me as the others. I surely have met that person before somewhere. Let me think. Yes, it must be. And does he recognise me at this distance? He bows. Yes, yes, he means that as a token of recognition. There is yet hope, then!"

CHAPTER LXIII.

RALPH IN WHITEFRIARS—THE LETTER—DEATH TO WILD—ON TO THE RESCUE—WILD AND LADY GLYDE—BOLD STROKE FOR A WIFE—DISAPPOINTMENT — WILD'S ALARM — HOME—THE PRISONER HAS ESCAPED.

Red Ralph gallopped from the Wheatsheaf Tavern, to London, and did not discontinue his search for Leonore until the night was very far advanced.

Then, footsore and wearied, he sought an asylum for the night with his trusty friend in Maddox Fields.

Here the same cordial greeting as of old awaited him.

On the morrow he started out again. London was traversed from east to west—from north to south.

But still no result.

Red Ralph had to meet Walters by appointment, in Whitefriars, at noon upon the second day.

Walter was there to the minute, but Red Ralph only arrived at the rendezvous very late, and looking worn and jaded with disappointment and fatigue.

"Ah, captain!"

"Well, Walters, what news?"

"Plenty. Ay, and of the sort to interest you, captain."

Red Ralph smiled sadly.

"I think not, Walters," he said.

"Nay, but I'm sure of it. And you seem to want something to cheer you up. You are pining for the green fields, the open road, and a moonlight trip for plunder!"

"Not that alone at the moment, Walters," said Red Ralph wearily.

"You're not so deep in love?"

"Ay, I am, Walters—with my wife."

"Your wife? Never! Surely you are not married?"

"I am. But do not question me further on the matter now. It slipped from me in an unguarded moment."

"Count upon my discretion, captain," said Walters.

Red Ralph silently pressed his proffered hand.

"Now, come, Walters," said Ralph, with a forced attempt at lightness, "what shall be our loving cup?"

"I care not."

"Then, here, landlord, tapster, a bottle of good Burgundy."

"Yes, my master."

"Now for this startling intelligence, Walters," said Red Ralph.

"This is the first thing I have to show you. Read it through, and let me know what you make of it."

So saying, the lieutenant spread open a letter, written in pencil, and laid it before Red Ralph.

He read it through to the end; but his cheeks flushed, and he was all excitement after the first line.

As he proceeded he ground his teeth fiercely and clenched his fist, dashing it violently upon the table, and upsetting the wine, as he came to the concluding words.

The missive which so agitated Red Ralph ran as follows:—

"*I, Lady Leonore Glyde, being held prisoner in this the house of Jonathan Wild, the thieftaker, most earnestly beg and entreat the humane consideration of the reader of the present in my behalf, that he or she will give such information to the authorities as shall lead to my release from this place, where I am subject to the grossest indignities, and am now sinking with exhaustion from want of the common necessaries of life. I also would beg the reader to judge of my sanity by the clearness of my thoughts here expressed under trying circumstances, and not to be deceived by any statement that my persecutor shall advance as to my being of unsound mind.*"

Red Ralph sprang to his feet as he concluded the letter.

"Where did you get this, Walters?"

"The writer threw it to me herself from the window of the room in which she is confined."

"Come there at once, Walters. Minutes are ages now. No time must be lost. We cannot tell what awful consequences may result from a minute's delay."

"You are strangely interested in this business, captain."

"And why not?" ejaculated Red Ralph fiercely. "And why not? If you object to go with me, I can go alone."

"Tut, tut, captain," remonstrated Walters. "I meant not that. I am with you always. I but remarked—"

"True, true," interrupted Red Ralph, grasping him by the hand. "This indignity offered my wife—"

"Your wife?"

"Ay."

"Pheugh!"

"That's it, Walters," said Red Ralph. "You can understand that it has maddened me."

"I can and do."

"She speaks here of gross indignities having been offered her by that villain Wild. If he has dared to—I'll cut his throat. I swear it. Let me but live to meet him!"

"And I will be your deputy, should you not be able to avenge yourself, captain," said Walters.

"Good," cried Red Ralph. "I accept your offer. Swear it!"

"Willingly!"

"Now then for action. Let me see. I have it. Jonathan Wild evidently keeps her there at his own residence to suit some hellish plot of his counting. That must be in direct opposition to the law."

"Undoubtedly."

"Good. Then I have a plan."

"To work at once, then, captain, for to-night at sunset—"

"I know. The rendezvous at the Boozing Ken you mean, Walters?"

"Yes."

"Fear not. I shall be there."

*   *   *   *   *   *

Jonathan Wild, when he left Leonore after his last interview, told her that he was going upon a little matter of business concerning their nuptials.

For once in his life he spoke the truth.

He started for Glyde House, and upon sending in his name was ushered immediately into the presence of her autocratic ladyship.

"Well, Mr. Wild," began Lady Glyde, with ill-concealed anxiety in her tone, "have you succeeded?"

"Yes and no, my lady."

"Mr. Wild, have the goodness to quit your figurative address and speak to me in the plainest English which you have at your command. Have you found Lady Leonore Glyde?"

"In plain English, then, yes," responded the thieftaker.

"Where is she?"

"Oh! In safe company at present, my lady," said Wild.

"Has she been removed to Newgate again? Answer me."

"N-no-no. Not exactly to Newgate," said Jonathan Wild.

"What do you mean by 'not exactly to Newgate?' Is there never any frankness in your words? Answer me straightforwardly, please. No circumlocution, I beg, and no attempt to attach a secret importance to the information you have."

"My lady—"

"To the point at once. Do you seek to raise the price of your services in the matter? I shall submit to anything. I have told you that cannot be called extortion."

"Well, since you put it so plumply, my lady, I will reply in your own way," said Jonathan Wild.

"Do so."

"In a few words, then, I don't wish to sell your daughter. I wish to—to—in short, to—"

"Come, sir. What?"

"To marry her!"

Lady Glyde stared at the thieftaker as if she thought that he was deranged.

"What?"

"I think I speak plain English now, my lady."

"If the man is not mad," said Lady Glyde with cutting contempt, "he is decidedly impudent."

"Now, my lady, it is you who speak in riddles," said Wild.

"My meaning is," said Lady Glyde sternly, "that if a low-bred carle, like yourself, talked such nonsense upon an ordinary occasion I should order him to be whipped and thrust into the kennel."

Wild winced.

"Your ladyship appears to consider my proposal extravagant," said the thieftaker calmly.

"It is beyond the pale of consideration. Therefore say no more nonsense, but to the work upon which I employed you. Have you recovered the Lady Leonore Glyde? If so, why is she not here?"

"For two reasons—"

"Oh! Then there is the matter of your payment for this work. Tell me what you consider adequate payment, and my steward will attend to you."

Jonathan Wild was so thoroughly crushed by the haughty Lady Glyde's sarcasms that it was some time before he could recover himself sufficiently to speak.

"One word, Lady Glyde," said Jonathan. "You treat with scorn an alliance which I propose out of the pure affection which I bear to the lady, and which I believe is reciprocated by her. Ahem. In fact, I think I may say that I have fair proofs of her affection for me."

"What are these proofs?"

"The best is that she has sought refuge in my house."

"In your house?"

"Yes."

"I'll not believe it."

"That is scarcely courteous," said Jonathan Wild. "However, I don't expect much courtesy here. Nevertheless, it is the fact. I rather fancied, too, that the sacrifice was rather upon my side than hers; for it is not every man who would wed a girl who has had the hangman's rope about her neck."

Lady Glyde bit her nether lip nervously.

"Unblushing rascal!" she exclaimed violently. "No more of this, or I shall have you thrust from the house. Name your price, and take your leave—"

"My price," said the thieftaker doggedly, "is the hand of the Lady Leonore Glyde. Nothing else."

"You are mad as well as insolent!" said Lady Glyde. "Would you condescend to marry a bigamist, as well as a woman who has had the hangman's rope about her neck?"

Wild started!

A bigamist?"

"Ay."

"What mean you?"

"Simply that Lady Leonore Glyde is already married!"

He changed his tone as if by magic, and all his humility returned in a trice.

"Lady Leonore will be here within an hour, my lady."

"Good," said Lady Glyde. "And as for your madness, I look over that. I shall direct my steward to pay you fifty pounds for your trouble."

The thieftaker expressed his acknowledgment and departed.

It was a terrible come down, though, for him. He had played for a high stake, a princely fortune, and it had subsided into fifty pounds.

No matter, this was better than nothing.

One thing troubled him, however, and this was the conduct he had observed towards Leonore.

However, he should do the magnanimous to her now and secure her pardon.

All things considered, too, it was a rare stroke of fortune that his vile designs upon the poor helpless girl had gone no further.

He would have found it difficult to get over much worse than that which had already occurred.

Thus musing, he arrived at his residence.

As he entered, his servant told him that "The men had brought his order all right." But Wild paid no heed to his servant, being so thoroughly engrossed with the thoughts of the difficulties to get over with regard to Leonore.

He tapped at the door as usual.

And as usual he received no answer.

[THE WITCH ON HER WAY TO TYBURN.]

"Lady Leonore," he said, "my Lady Glyde has sent for you. All difficulty is removed, and—why don't you answer?"

The thieftaker continued talking at the door for nearly twenty minutes, until his patience was exhausted.

"Why, it seems to me," he muttered, as he peered through the keyhole, "it seems to me that she has taken down her barricade. Lady Leonore, my Lady Glyde, your august mother, has sent me to you. You are to return. All is over, and—death! my lady, I wish you would answer me. I'll swear I speak the truth now by every saint in the calendar. No, no, if I talk of swearing she is sure to doubt me."

He turned the handle as he spoke, and, to his unbounded astonishment, the door yielded to his pressure!

He stepped forward a pace or two, nervously enough, anxious that Lady Leonore should not deem him rude in forcing himself into her presence.

This extraordinary conduct will be duly appreciated when we reflect upon the ruffian's former treatment of the helpless girl.

Then, getting no answer. he stepped in and looked around.

The bird was flown!

"Gone!" he cried in amazement. "Gone! Death and furies! How?—when?—where?"

CHAPTER LXIV.

WILD'S PLANS FRUSTRATED—HIS RAGE—VEN-GEANCE UPON HIS SERVANT—HOW LEONORE ESCAPED—THE TWO OFFICERS—RED RALPH REUNITED TO HIS YELLOW BAND—"DEATH TO JONATHAN WILD!"—PROSPECT OF ADVENTURE —A DASH FOR A RICH PRIZE.

The thieftaker's plans were now frustrated in every direction.

Upon returning to his house from the Glyde mansion he found that Leonore had escaped from his clutches.

How, when, or where it was utterly beyond him to decide.

All was a perfect mystery to him.

He paced up and down the chamber which had been the hapless Lady Leonore's prison in a torrent of rage, vainly endeavouring to solve the problem.

In the course of a few minutes the servant came to him.

Before he could utter a word the thieftaker sprang upon him, and pinned him to the ground, demanding, with the bitterest oaths, where was the prisoner he had left in his charge.

As soon as the man could speak he explained the matter.

It appeared that shortly after the thieftaker had quitted the house two men arrived, to all appearance government officials.

These two men demanded, in Jonathan Wild's name, the prisoner then in the house.

The man asked their authority to take her, upon which one of them produced a paper, said to be written by the thieftaker himself.

At this point in the man's narration Jonathan Wild could no longer contain his rage.

"Idiot, if not liar!" he cried, "how could you accept that as an authority for what you have done?"

"But they said it came from you, Mr Wild," remonstrated the man in piteous accents.

"They said, fool? Do you believe all that is told you?"

"But they showed it to me, Mr. Wild, showed me the paper."

"But you can't read!"

"No, sir, but—"

"Fool! Go on, though," exclaimed the thieftaker, "or I shall strike you to my feet before you have time to make your idiotic explanation."

The man withdrew from reach of his irate employer's arm and tremblingly continued his narrative.

"Then, sir, we all went upstairs. They wanted to make me stay behind, but I suspected—"

"Cunning fool!" said Jonathan Wild with a cutting sneer.

"Yes, sir."

"And if you suspected, if you had the smallest doubt, why did you allow them to take off the prisoner?"

"Why, sir, you see—"

"Ass! Go on!"

"Well, sir," continued the man, still trembling with fear, "when we got to the door it was a long time before the lady would answer."

"Of course."

"But I assured her that it was not your worshipful self."

"Oh! you did?"

"Yes, sir," said the man, all eagerness.

The poor wretch imagined he perceived a tone of forgiveness in the thieftaker's words.

Unhappy wight! he was most cruelly deceived in this.

Jonathan looked around him with silent viciousness. Then suddenly pounced upon the nearest object at hand.

This chanced to be a metal inkstand.

The man saw mischief in his master's eye, and ducked to avoid punishment.

But the thieftaker allowed for this, for the man's fearful anticipations betrayed him.

"Take that, you officious fool!" ejaculated Wild.

It flew from his hand, and the next instant the unfortunate man lay stretched upon the ground.

A cruel gash upon his forehead, covered with blood mixed with the ink from the inkstand, very speedily made him a sorry spectacle.

"Get up!" shouted Jonathan Wild. "Get up, you villain, and go on."

But the man only groaned, without offering to stir.

In truth he did not feel great pain from his hurt, ugly as was its appearance, only he feared a repetition of the chastisement.

"Oh! you won't get up, won't you?" said his torturer.

However, as soon as the thieftaker made a move in that direction he sprang to his feet.

"Oh! I thought you would soon recover yourself. Now go on."

The man wiped the blood and ink from his face with the sleeve of his coat and proceeded fearfully.

"Well, sir, she would'nt open the door even then."

"But you persuaded her?"

"No, no, no, sir."

"Oh! I thought you did?"

"No, no, sir," said the man with comical eagerness. "Not I; on the contrary."

"No lies!"

"N—n—no, sir. She said that she would never unbar the door, and that she should stand by the window, and as soon as she heard that we were likely to break in her barricade she would throw herself into the street."

"And did you break in?" demanded Wild eagerly.

"No, sir."

"Why not?"

"One of the men appeared to be very much frightened at this, and begged her not to fear violence, that they were come to deliver her up to justice, and that her ultimate escape was a certainty."

"Oh! he said that, did he?"

"Yes, sir."

"And you, you muddy-pated rascal, could not divine that it was all a farce—a sham?"

"No, sir."

"Go on."

"Then he said something else, sir, and she opened the door and came out meek as a lamb."

"And then?"

"They got into a coach and drove off, and—and, sir—"

"What then?"

"Then—that's all."

"Fool!"

He glanced about him restlessly, but the man, smelling mischief, made for the door in most undignified haste.

"Come back!" roared Jonathan Wild, with an oath.

The man rattled the door handle with a trembling grasp.

"Leave that," said the thieftaker. "Tie up your ugly face and run off to Morris's. Fly! and try to repair the mischief you have done."

"Yes, sir."

And, as an earnest of his obedience, he flew down the stairs four at a time.

"Come back."

"Yes, sir."

"Where are you going to?"

"Mr. Morris's."

"What for?"

"For—for——"

"Idiot!" growled the thieftaker. "Tell him to come to me this instant. Now be off. 'Sdeath! d'you hear me?"

"Yes, sir."

And off dashed the man full gallop.

"We shall see," muttered Jonathan Wild. "Fortunately, she doesn't know anything of my little arrangement. If she has not left London, I think I can yet pounce upon her. She will be sure to attract notice by her desire to avoid publicity, and thus I hope she may not be difficult to discover. We shall see. But how has this devilish business been contrived? Things are going badly with me of late. I would give much to know to whom I owe this little grudge. No matter; by to-morrow I hope to hold my lady again in my power, and then her ladyship's clever and austere mother shall have her—at a price—at a price—for the fifty pounds scarcely pays for all the trouble I've had in the matter."

* * * * * *

Delighted at her release from the captivity of the odious thieftaker, Leonore had willingly embraced another imprisonment which was offered, although it was destined to result, she deemed, in that death at Tyburn which Red Ralph's exploits had but for the moment averted.

She entered the coach with her new captors, a singular sensation of joy overcoming the alarm she had felt while in the clutches of the thieftaker.

But why joy? she asked herself.

Were her sufferings, then, so great that she could now contemplate with gladness a release from them at so fearful a price?

No. Something, she felt assured, was about to occur which was to ameliorate her condition.

But what?

This she learnt before the hackney coach had proceeded many yards.

"Leonore," said one of her new guardians, in a well-remembered tone, "is it possible you don't know me?"

"Ah!" she cried. "You, my husband again! Is it indeed real?"

"It is I, Leonore," said Red Ralph, for it was he as the reader has doubtless divined.

This, then, was the plan which he had in contemplation before leaving Whitefriars with the lieutenant, who was his companion and the third occupant of the vehicle.

But, not to dwell upon the rapture of this brief but blissful reunion of Red Ralph and Leonore, we must content ourselves with simply relating that the latter was conducted to a place of safety in Whitefriars, near the tavern in which Ralph and Walters had met.

Here she was left for a while by Ralph, with the strictest injunctions not to venture forth until he should return.

Then he mounted his horse, and, accompanied by Walters, rode off post-haste to the Boozing Ken, to keep the rendezvous which he had made with the wounded survivors of the fray at Tyburn.

Here his entry was greeted by the deafening shouts of his wounded band.

His delight at seeing them there together, sadly reduced in numbers and condition though they were, was inexpressible.

As soon as the cheers had somewhat subsided Red Ralph addressed them in a short harangue, which he concluded by promising them very speedily a little stirring work.

"How many have we fit for active service?" he demanded.

"All of us."

"Ay, ay, all—to a man."

"Nay," said Red Ralph, "I can see one or two who are unfit—at least to-night. But let them get all right at the earliest, for we shall no doubt be troubled by our friend Mr. Jonathan Wild very shortly."

A growl of execration went round the room as Red Ralph mentioned the thieftaker's name.

"I know that you bear him no love," said Red Ralph.

"Death to Wild! Death to Jonathan Wild!" shouted one of the wounded.

And in an instant the cry was borne from mouth to mouth with an energy which would have alarmed that autocratic functionary had he chanced to be within hearing.

But, unfortunately for the future peace of the two most prominent characters of this history, the thieftaker was actively engaged elsewhere plotting mischief.

But of this we shall presently have occasion to speak.

"Now, my men," said Red Ralph, "I have sworn to cut Jonathan Wild's throat with this hand—"

A deafening shout of approval cut short their captain's words.

"Or, failing that—that is, should I chance to perish before the accomplishment of my design—the lieutenant here will do the little job for me."

"Bravo! Bravo! A cheer for the lieutenant!" cried one.

And a lusty cheer was accordingly given.

"Now, then, to business," said Red Ralph. "I have a little job cut out for a few of us to-night."

"Huzzah!"

"It will only serve to keep our hands in. The mail from the North will pass the cross-road below in a few minutes if I mistake not."

"Be careful, captain, then," said one of the Yellow Boys.

"Ay," said another, "they're devils with their powder and slugs."

"Never fear me, boys."

The distant sound of a horn was heard, and Red Ralph, the lieutenant, and three or four others dashed from the room.

CHAPTER LXV.

THE NORTH MAIL—"STAND AND DELIVER!"—AN ECCENTRIC OLD MAID—RED RALPH'S WEAKNESS—THE SNEAKING TRAVELLER—A SURPRISE—"RALPH OF THE RED HAND, BEWARE!"—ALARM AND FLIGHT—HO! FOR LONDON.

THE moon was up and shining brightly when Red Ralph, the lieutenant, and such of the Yellow Boys as were fit for active service stepped forth from the Boozing Ken.

"Your horse, captain," cried one of the men as Ralph ran off.

"No matter," he replied. "None of you are mounted, so we'll do this little job afoot."

"Never," said Walters. "The captain mustn't stop a coach on foot."

"No, no," answered the men with one voice.

"Very well," said Red Ralph. "Since you wish it, I will ride, but I would give much if I had my own Nancy."

"What has become of the mare?" demanded the lieutenant.

"Oh! she has got into the clutches of that devil Wild!"

"No matter, captain," said Walters, "we'll have her again before the week is over."

"I hear the wheels of the coach nearer," said Red Ralph.

"Quick then! Gallop!"

And off they raced after their leader, helter skelter down the hill.

Lining the little valley was a row of lofty elms upon either side of the road, and behind these the adventurous Yellow Boys ensconced themselves.

Up came the unsuspecting mail coach, the guard still blowing his horn in the most cheerful manner.

As they rode into the shade of the elms he ceased his music for an instant to address the driver.

"This is a nice bit of road for an ambuscade, Wells."

"Eh—oh—h!"

"STAND AND DELIVER!"

Red Ralph rode out so suddenly that the leaders reared suddenly back upon their haunches.

The coachman was half jerked from his box.

The guard got an ugly rap upon the head with the violence of the concussion.

And the occupants of the coach were precipitated into each other's laps.

One old gentleman came to sad and sudden grief. A luxuriant wig, which looked wonderfully natural when cocked on with a rakish hand, was dashed into the gaping mouth of an old maiden lady opposite to him, who was dozing at the moment of the disaster.

And the same blow caused her to swallow several of a set of very expensive false teeth she wore.

"Come, your valuables!" said Red Ralph.

The driver, recovering himself, lashed his horses furiously, but their heads were securely held.

"Strike again," said Red Ralph, "and I blow you to atoms!"

"You villain!"

"Silence!"

The guard, who supposed himself unobserved all the time, slyly produced a huge blunderbus from the top of the coach.

This he suddenly levelled point blank at Red Ralph.

Bang! There was a deal of fire and smoke, but when it cleared away the highwayman was still there untouched!

"Curse on my aim!" cried the guard in the utmost vexation.

"Nay," said the highwayman with a light laugh, "your aim is very good. I should advise you only to see always that your slugs have not been removed when you make a halt."

"You mean then that—"

"They were taken out at the Pretender's Head."

"It never quitted my possession," said the guard doubtfully.

"I leave you to judge for yourself if what I say sounds like truth or not," said Red Ralph.

"Curse your handiwork!"

"Now, my men," called Red Ralph to his followers, "are you done there?"

"There's one old woman who refuses to give her money."

"Old woman yourself, you knave!" said the maiden lady.

"Madam," said Ralph, riding up, "you must deliver up your property."

"Never!"

"If you would preserve yourself from indignity."

"Indignity!" shrieked the old maid. "Take all I have, take everything, but—"

"Enough. Fear no violence from us."

"Well, sir—here is my purse, and it is cruelly hard to have to give up that, the savings of a year, and for such a purpose too."

"I'm sorry, madam."

"Wretch!" cried the old lady. "But the ruin of a family be upon you for this."

"What mean you?"

"Mean? Why, that this money was to pay my nephew's creditors, to release him from the debtor's prison, and to restore him to his wife and children. But now they may starve. You'll rue the day that ever you touched a halfpenny of it."

"True, I should," said the highwayman. "Put back your purse."

"What?"

"Keep your money."

They were about to turn from the coach door when the lieutenant pointed out to Red Ralph a passenger crouching down as if hoping to escape observation.

"Come, come," said the highwayman. "Don't attempt to skulk off in that paltry manner. Pay your black mail and let us depart."

The shrinking traveller never attempted to rise.

"You haven't the courage of the old woman," said Walters.

He leant forward and gave the traveller a tap upon the back with the butt of his pistol.

Up sprang the man in an instant, glaring with rage and indignation.

"Ruffians!" he cried, "fly for your lives—fly, and this instant, or I blow your brains out."

As he presented a brace of pistols Red Ralph turned to fly.

But, growing suddenly ashamed, he veered round again.

"No," he said, "I'm not to be frightened out of my wits like that."

"Go, go, young man," said the traveller, lowering his pistols. "Depart in peace, for I swear that I shall not give you one sou. I would not stain my hands with *your* blood, but warn your companion there ; I may not have the same consideration for him."

"Who are you?"

"No matter, I know you."

"Very probably," returned the highwayman. "Many travellers do upon this road."

"Sad boast!"

"What is it, then, that you know of me?" asked Ralph doggedly. "What is all this mystery for?"

"Ralph of the Red Hand!" said the traveller with stately emphasis, "I know you—none better. If you would avert your fate, if you would change the doom you were born to, like all your race, avoid me!"

"You know that too?" said Red Ralph, strangely impressed.

"I do. And now depart in peace," said the traveller mournfully. "Mend your way of life if you can, and you shall hear of me when you least expect it. Away, I can hear the sound of horses upon the road."

Red Ralph turned and rode slowly away.

There was a tone of command in the old man's voice which, ill as Red Ralph would have taken it from another, appeared to come quite naturally from him.

There was something familiar too in his voice.

When and where had they met before?

This he was determined to know, and he rode back to the coach door.

"Still here," began the traveller.

"One word," said the highwayman. "We have met before?"

"Many years since."

"Probably. I mean, though, quite recently. You remember when?"

"I do. It was upon the Hounslow Road. We parted suddenly."

"I remember now."

"Well you may, Ralph of the Red Hand, for then you were nearly accomplishing the doom of the house of—"

He stopped short.

"Go on," said Red Ralph. "You will not speak !"

"No."

"Say, is it possible that you are—"

"No matter who. Away! In an instant it will be too late."

Red Ralph with a sigh turned again from the coach door, and rode off.

"Marvellous!" he muttered. "For what am I reserved at last? If it can indeed be he! 'Beware of the third meeting,' says the legend of our house. Then must I live but to dread that which I would fain believe a joy. Pshaw!"

His reveries were suddenly interrupted by the lieutenant warning him of approaching danger.

"Captain!"

"What now?"

"Fly for your life!"

"Wherefore?"

"The Philistines are upon us!"

And the Yellow Boys spread themselves about in every direction, whilst Red Ralph turned his horse's head once more towards London.

CHAPTER LXVI.

A MYSTERY — THE AGE OF BLOOD — NEWGATE UPON THE NIGHT PRECEDING AN EXECUTION —THE OLD JEW — PRAYERS AND ENTREATIES — CAPTAIN RANN — EDGEWORTH BESS — THE LOVELY CAPTIVE — THE SUDDEN ATTACK — VENGEANCE—THE FURIOUS MOB—THE HANGMAN'S TERROR.

A DARK mystery!

A terrible and unfathomable mystery overshadowed the early life and career of Red Ralph.

An awful destiny his seemed to be.

Struggle as he would, the course of events slowly but surely drove him onward towards the awful doom in store for him.

A doom which the sequel of this strange and eventful history will reveal.

Reluctantly leaving him for a while, surrounded by perils and dangers, we are compelled by the necessities of our narrative to introduce the reader to a fresh scene, where other extraordinary occurrences are taking place, which, as time will show, had a great influence over the life of the lawless captain of the famous Yellow Band.

It is a scene to which the reader has already been introduced under other circumstances.

Yes, it is Newgate, that black and frowning edifice which rears its head amidst the haunts of busy commerce—that dreary prison-house from which, on the fatal Monday morning, even now, in these days of enlightenment and ultra civilisation, the shivering wretch is dragged forth to be strangled like a dog before the assembled scum and refuse of society, congregated at the scaffold's foot, only too greedy to partake of the feast of blood, which the law gratuitously provides them.

In the days of which we write hanging was a weekly, nay, an almost daily occurrence, and yet, strange as it may seem, the spectacle lost none of its charm.

As great a mob appeared to gather together for every execution.

Yes, there were always spectators for the sight, and as certain as there were spectators, so there was always some one who seemed to be only too eager to perform the principal part in the hideous drama.

If Jack Sheppard was strung up on Monday, Blueskin was ready for Tuesday, then Dick Turpin would make his bow on Wednesday, and Claude Duval follow suit on Thursday, while for Friday and Saturday, and the following week, there were any number of Sixteen String Jacks, Colonel Jacks, Tom Kings, Jenny Divers, and suchlike, all only too eager to "ride up Holborn Hill in a cart," and go to glory underneath the fatal tree, amidst the applause of the assembled thousands.

In those days, when hanging was so much the fashion, and when public executions were such very trifling checks upon crime, you may be sure that all his Majesty's prisons were filled to overflowing.

Prisons were not then what they are now.

There highwaymen drank and ate of the best that money could purchase.

There was card-playing and dicing and dancing and flirting in any quantity.

The pretty lady pickpockets had plenty of time and opportunity to fall in love with the gentlemen highwaymen before the cart called for them, and they did too, and there were even marriages solemnised in those days within grim Newgate's walls.

In those days there was not only one condemned cell, as there is now, but a whole passage full of them—a dozen at least.

Sometimes each cell had its occupant.

Very often the doomed men passed the night before the day of their execution roaring and singing, mad drunk.

Very few except the women would listen to the chaplain—sometimes not the women either.

Now and then there were too many waiting for Jack Ketch's nimble fingers (his name was Dennis at the period of our story, and he was hanged himself at last).

There were so many sometimes that many of the condemned cells contained two occupants.

Such was the case on the night following the incidents described in the last chapter.

In one of the cells were two persons condemned to death.

One a young and beautiful woman, the other an old man with long straggling locks of grey hair, bushy eyebrows, and wolflike teeth.

A strange contrast did the demeanour of these two prisoners present.

The girl was deadly pale, with a cold statuesque beauty, but not a muscle of her lovely face quivered.

Her hand was as steady as that of a practised duellist.

The rise and fall of her bosom was slow and steady, as she reclined in an easy attitude upon the coarse pallet.

She did not sleep, although at times her eyes were closed.

No, it was easy to see that she was deep in thought, that her fertile brain was busy—busy at what?

Was she hatching some deep and elaborate scheme of escape?

Was she planning some fearful vengeance against those who had betrayed her?

It is impossible to say. To no breast but her own was the dark secret of her thoughts communicated.

As, however, the weary hours slowly passed away, and the ghastly daylight crept like a thief through the gratings of the cell, she still was silent and thoughtful, heedless of all earthly objects around.

Heedless of the monotonous tramp of the jailor in the paved passage without.

Heedless of the brutal merriment of the drunken wretches in the adjoining cell.

Still more heedless of the fitful groans and miserable complaints of her companion, the grey-headed old man.

The most pitiful and abject of God's creatures was this.

A wailing, groaning, crawling, self-debasing wretch.

He sat upon the edge of his hard couch biting his

clawlike nails, nursing his knees, rocking himself to and fro, in indescribable agony of mind.

He was an old gipsy—a black-hearted old scoundrel, who had committed as many crimes as he had lived days.

A miscreant whose hands were stained with blood and whose soul was blackened with perjury.

Not the first by any means of his family who had gone Tyburnwards.

He, indeed, had had relations executed for every offence that we have a name for.

Some had passed bad money, and some had stolen horses and sheep. A good many had robbed upon the king's highway, and a good many more had committed murder.

There was one who had had a wife or two too many, and one (but he was a gentleman and a scholar) had signed somebody else's name—a beautiful imitation, hardly to be told from the original.

Yet, with all these precedents before him, this old man did not like to take his turn at the halter.

He was suffering tortures—not tortures of remorse, though. For that matter, he would have liked to live twice as long and to commit twice the number of crimes, and then perhaps he would have been ready.

Why not? He was not much more than sixty. Let us say sixty. Well, twice that—a hundred and twenty.

Suppose he began his crimes at the age of ten. That leaves a hundred and ten years of villany. That surely ought to be enough for anybody.

Even this miserable old wretch was of that opinion, but you see he had only lived half the time.

It was an awful thing to have to die!

So young too! To be cut off in the flower of his youth, or, if you like it better, in the prime of his life. He rocked himself to and fro and groaned and moaned.

He snivelled and whimpered and whimpered and snivelled.

He tried to go to sleep and could not.

He would have got drunk as the other prisoners did, only he had no money to buy spirits.

He asked the turnkey keeping watch outside the door to go and beg a half-pint of brandy from one of his rollicking neighbours.

But when the turnkey went upon this errand they inquired—

"Who's it for?"

"For Ikey Moses," replied the turnkey.

"What?" roared Captain Rann, of whom he had begged the favour. "Who did you say?"

"Ikey Moses, captain. You know him, don't you?"

"Know him!" replied Rann in a fury. "Who does not? By Heavens, I have just cause for knowing him."

"It aint through him, though, captain, that you're in trouble."

"Is'nt it?"

"He did'nt peach on you, sir, did he?"

"I was'nt lagged this time through him, it's true."

"No, I thought not."

"But I should never have been lagged at all, I should never have been a thief, if it had not been through that old scoundrel's handiwork."

"That's true enough I believe, but then the wretched old crittur is laid up by the heels himself now, captain."

"Serve him right. Hanging's far too good for him."

"We oughtn't to bear malice, though, captain, at such a time as this, on the very brink of Tyburn."

"I daresay not, Johnson, but I'm not an angel, and I can't forget."

"You won't give him a drink then?"

"No."

"Nor send the poor devil half a crown?"

"Not half a farthing."

"What am I to tell him?"

"Tell him to go and hang himself, and save Dennis the trouble."

"Ah, he's not likely to do that, he's too much afraid of the pain."

The turnkey turned away upon his heel when the conversation had gone thus far, seeing that it was quite hopeless to try and soften Jack Rann's heart towards his fellow-prisoner.

There were the other condemned men, however, to whom he could appeal. Perhaps they would not all be so obdurate.

Ikey Moses's name, though, was not very sweet, it would seem, among the gallant knights of the road.

Tom Callogan, the cut-purse, was the next to whom he appealed.

"What's he want for?" asked Tom.

"He's so thirsty, sir, he says."

"He'll be thirstier next journey," answered Tom.

Jerry Aberville was the next appealed to. This famous highwayman waxed very wroth at the mention of Mr. Ikey.

"An atrocious old miscreant. He's sent many a brave boy to the last reckoning, he has, and now he's afraid to go himself."

"He says he's so dry, your honour."

"He want's to get drunk I suppose."

"I suppose that is about it."

"He has'nt pluck enough to face the hangman sober."

"I suppose he do feel just a little nervous, your honour."

"Devil a drop he'd a stood for any of his poor victims. No, tell him to send to Mrs. Maggot or Edgeworth Bess. Perhaps they'll oblige him. I know they doat on him."

The two ladies alluded to occupied a cell at the further end of the corridor, where they had been throughout the night alternating between shrill choruses of popular thieves' songs and piercing shrieks, when the turnkey recommended silence.

At the first overture respecting Ikey's brandy they burst out into the most violent invective against the ancient Israelite.

"Oh, if they had got him there!" they said.

"Oh, wouldn't they like to tear his eyes out!"

"Oh, wouldn't they mark him!"

No one should know him for the same when he stood up in the cart next morning under the fatal tree.

In spite of their violence, however, these young ladies were tender-hearted, and when the jailor had described old Ikey's miserable condition they softened towards him.

"Poor wretch!" said Bess.

"He is, miss," chimed in the jailor.

"I think I'll send him a crown."

"Do, miss. You do an act of charity. He's in a very bad way."

Kind-hearted Bessie handed over the required five shillings, and the turnkey departed.

"A drop of something warm wouldn't hurt me very much," he thought, as he retraced his steps. "Half a crown's worth would be enough for the old man."

But a moment after this thought had passed through his brain he felt ashamed of himself.

"I've never been a prig all my life," he muttered. "I'm dashed if I begin upon a dying man to start with."

He therefore took the money to the Jew, and asked what he should get him.

"How much is it?" asked the old man greedily.

"A crown."

"Is that all? Ugh!"

"Well, I'm blessed if you ain't a nice deserving object, after all the trouble I've had."

"What do you mean by trouble? I shall pay you, shan't I?"

"Oh, if you will, that's another matter, only I thought you hadn't got any tin."

"I've got five bob. haven't I?"

"Ah, to be sure."

"Well then, if I give you a groat —"

"A what?"

"The price of a pot of porter."

"Ah, you'll ruin yourself. Don't do that, I beg of you."

"Well, of course, if you wont. Only I don't like the idea of your not having anything. Here, I say, suppose you take twopence. Come you must. If you don't accept it I shall think you are proud."

"I am a little, that's the truth. Good night to you."

As the jailor spoke, he shut the cell door with a bang.

Scarcely had it closed, however, when the old Jew began to sing out at the top of his voice.

"Hullo! I say, stop! stop!"

"What now?" asked the jailor, looking in again with a surprised expression.

"Why, I say, you haven't got it for me."

"Got what?"

"The drink."

"I've got you the money; that's enough."

"What's the use of the money? I can't spend it."

"Don't say that. Money is all-powerful even in Newgate. You've only got to bribe one of the other turnkeys to go for the liquor."

"tuI say. Stop a minute."

"Well, what is it?"

"What a hurry you're in."

"Yes, I am rather."

"Couldn't you manage to get it me?"

"I'm afraid not."

"But why?"

"Well, it is very dear at the shop where I deal. You wouldn't have very much for your money."

The old Jew pulled a very long face at this intelligence.

"How much?" he presently inquired.

"Well, I'm afraid not much more than you would get at any respectable shop for a shilling."

"Oh dear! oh dear!" groaned the old Jew. "Here's a heartless robbery. There's an awful swindle upon a poor unhappy creature unable to defend himself."

"What do you say?" asked the jailor.

"Oh, nothing, sir. I beg your pardon. I shall be very much obliged to you if you will only get me a thimblefull."

So saying, Ikey Moses disgorged the crown piece, parting with it as unwillingly as though it had been a back tooth.

The jailor then departed, chuckling, and presently returned with about a quartern of brandy, which he handed to the prisoner.

A longer face than ever he pulled when he received it. But he could not help himself, for there were no other turnkeys whom he could employ.

No, he was done; and, what was more, he had only his own meanness to thank for it.

He was certainly a foolish old man, this Jew felon, for even now, when he had got the much-coveted liquor, he did not husband it out, but took it all at one gulp.

There he sat, huddled up, rocking himself to and fro as before, and groaning and whimpering for more.

When an hour had passed he appealed to the jailor.

He begged of him in a playful tone at first.

Then he entreated piteously.

But he sued in vain.

"Hold your noise, you old wretch!" retorted the man fiercely. "There's no peace for you."

There had been no peace for hours.

The poor wretch was scared out of his wits by the horrid fate before him. and could not be quiet.

When he had rocked himself to and fro until he was weary he rose to his feet and began to pace the cell like a wild beast.

Then he went and hammered at the door, and called upon the turnkey and the other prisoners for more liquor.

The other prisoners at the sound of his voice roared out angrily, and threatened him with their vengeance did they ever again obtain their liberty.

For a long while he bore their jibes and insults patiently, only replying by whining prayers for drink.

But when he found that they would give him nothing he changed his tactics and loaded them with abuse.

"You pack of cutthroats," he cried, "I shall yet live to see the lot of you strangled. Yes, I shall. I shall have a reprieve and you will be hanged, and I'll be there to see in the best place that can be bought for money."

Many times during that dreadful night the old Jew appealed to the turnkey for information respecting this same reprieve.

"I know it's come," he said. "I feel quite certain it's come. Why don't they send it in to me? It's an awfully cruel thing to keep it back. They must know what I am suffering—that is, if I wasn't sure the reprieve was all right."

"But, as you are so sure, what does it matter?"

"It would be more satisfactory if they let me know at once. Besides, I don't like being herded up here with all this scum."

"You're very particular, all at once, Mr. Moses. But, then, if you're to be reprieved, it won't be for long you've got to stop here."

"I'm sure his Majesty would not have allowed me to stop half as long. There'll be an awful row about this, I can tell you, when his Majesty knows of it. I've been of great service to his Majesty, and I'm certain he won't desert me."

"Well, if you're so certain you'd better shut up, because we've had quite enough of your row."

Left to himself, the unhappy old Jew fell back again upon his rocking and his prowling, groaning, and whimpering, as before.

In his prowls, however, he was very careful not to go near his fellow-prisoner.

Stretched upon her hard pallet she still lay perfectly motionless.

Her eyes were open, as they had been all along, and fixed upon vacancy.

She was superbly beautiful.

Her hair was black as the raven's wing.

Her large dark eyes seemed filled with a devouring fire.

Her dress was mud-stained and ragged, and her silky hair hung about her head in tangled masses, yet in it were twisted strings of large coloured beads.

The strangest thing about her, however, was that, though her feet were bare, she wore gloves.

Stay, there was something stranger still.

One of her hands had only three fingers.

The old Jew, it was very easy to see, stood in great dread of this beautiful captive.

The slightest movement that she made caused his eyes to wander in her direction; but he never ventured within her reach.

Finding, however, that she did not interfere with him—indeed, that she seemed to be unconscious of his presence—he gained courage, and no longer put any restraint upon himself, but shook and battered furiously at the door, screaming the while with all the power of his lungs.

Suddenly, whilst thus engaged, a hand was laid upon his shoulder.

It was that of the beautiful captive, who had risen silently.

She clutched him with a grip which it was vain to try to shake off.

She thrust her fingers down his neckerchief, twisted it round, and half strangled him.

Then, with one tremendous effort, tore him away, wheeled him half across the cell, and sent him full length upon the floor.

"Lie down," she hissed between her white and gleaming teeth. "Lie down, dog! Lie where you are!"

To make the order more intelligible, perhaps, she strode to the spot where the prostrate Jew was grovelling abjectly, and placed her foot upon his head.

He might have been dead, so motionless was he.

If it had not been for the rolling of his eyes, there was no sign of life about his livid face and motionless form.

She stood for some moments grinding her heel into his cheek, grinding his head upon the flags, and then, with a contemptuous laugh, strode away.

"Get up," she said fiercely. "Go to your corner and sit still."

"I—I—didn't mean to disturb you."

"Go to your corner and sit still."

"I—I—"

"Silence!"

He said no more, but crept away like a bruised reptile.

"What a fiend it is!" he muttered to himself. "What a fiend! I hope they won't reprieve her, at any rate."

From this time forward, he made no disturbance.

The fearful night of terror and suspense slowly wore away.

Day broke, and the jailors came to open the door.

At sight of them though, the Jew gave a piercing shriek, and, running to the other end of the cell, crouched in a corner, glaring at them with bloodshot eyes, like some wild beast at bay.

"Ikey Moses," said the governor, who accompanied the turnkeys, "Ikey Moses and Esther Brandon, I have come to tell you to prepare yourselves, for the law must take its course."

The woman did not move a muscle of her face.

Still was it, as white and motionless as death.

She rose slowly and calmly, and in a low, but distinct and perfectly firm, tone of voice said—

"I am ready."

The state into which the announcement threw the old Jew was, on the contrary, terrible to witness.

He clasped his hands and sobbed like a child.

He stamped and tore his hair.

He crawled about on his hands and knees, and groaned—

"For God's sake, gentlemen, don't murder me." It will be murder and nothing else, if you hang me before you have heard from his Majesty."

"There is no hope of pardon," said the governor.

"Yes, yes, I am sure there is."

"I am sure there is not. Let me entreat you to prepare yourself."

"I can't. I won't. How can I?"

"There is no hope."

"Oh, don't say so. Please don't say so."

The governor turned away without making any reply.

The old Jew, however, clung to him tenaciously.

"Oh, sir, please put it off till to-morrow."

"It is impossible."

"No—no! You can if you like."

"I tell you it is impossible."

"Well, this afternoon then!"

"No."

"For a few hours!"

"No."

"For two or three hours—only two or three!"

"I tell you it is impossible."

"For an hour then, only one short hour!"

"I have no power to delay the execution. The procession will leave the prison at eight o'clock."

"Shall we go together?" asked the old Jew presently. "May'nt I go last?"

"You will go in separate carts. That with Esther Brandon will leave the prison last, but her execution takes place before yours."

Even this delay seemed to afford the cowardly wretch some gratification.

The motive for this arrangement had not been to spare his feelings, though, as may be supposed.

On the contrary, it had been prompted by a desire to save the woman the horror of seeing the male prisoners executed first.

The same plan had been adopted, as the reader may remember, upon the occasion when Leonore was taken to Tyburn, in a mistake for the very woman who was now about to suffer the extreme penalty of the law.

The interval between the time and the hour fixed for the departure passed wearily enough. The old Jew, as heretofore, groaning and sobbing, the woman, as she had ever been, still silent and calm.

At length the fatal moment arrived.

The jail doors opened and the Jew was led forth.

An enormous concourse of people had assembled.

A sea of savage faces surged tumultuously before his eyes.

The old man turned deadly sick at the sight of them, and his knees gave way beneath him.

Like a limp rag he was carried by the jailors and lifted into the cart.

Then the journey commenced, amidst the hooting and groaning of the mob.

But it was not for the Jew that this dense concourse had assembled.

It was not upon him that they had come there intending to wreak a bloody vengeance.

It was upon the witch.

That such was their intention there was little doubt.

To guard against an interruption of the usual course of the law, the military had been called forth in far more than the ordinary number.

The street was alive with red coats.

The sun shone brightly on the glistening steel of a hundred drawn swords.

And it would seem, if one might judge by the appearance of the mob, that these preparations were quite necessary.

Dark and lowering faces were to be seen on every side.

Scores of hideous ruffians menacingly grasped their bludgeons.

Haggard, half naked, fiendish-looking women shrieked forth discordantly the name of the condemned murdress, Esther Brandon.

When the Jew had passed along in his cart there was a pause, a deathlike silence.

Then, the prison gates closing, a hoarse murmur arose, which, waxing louder and louder, grew at last into a savage howl scarcely human.

The bloodthirsty mob fancied itself about to be cheated of its victim.

But such was not the case.

The gates again opened.

[THE STORM ON THE THAMES.]

A cart came forth.

It contained three occupants.

The hangman, who drove, sitting on a coffin, the clergyman, and Esther Brandon.

Still deadly pale.

Still calm as ever.

At sight of her the mob raged fearfully.

Like black billows they swayed to and fro.

The air was rent by piercing shrieks and harsh and savage cries for the life of the hated witch.

The priest, with an ashy face, prepared to read his book.

The hangman, as white as a ghost, looked nervously round at the fearful mob.

The soldiers charged upon the crowd and drove them back with howls and curses.

Thus the procession started for Tyburn.

CHAPTER LXVII.

ON THE WAY TO TYBURN—THE FURIOUS MOB—THE FAIR CAPTIVE—THE UNHAPPY CHAPLAIN—THE HANGMAN HANGED—" DOWN WITH THE WITCH "—TO THE STAKE—THE MURDRESS AND HER VICTIM.

THE tidings had spread like wildfire through the town.

The witch had been captured.

In vain had the authorities endeavoured to keep the fact a secret.

The occurrences which have been already related respecting the wrongful capture of Leonore had added fuel to the fire of popular indignation against the famous criminal.

The whole populace rose and howled aloud for her blood.

The outpourings of back slums, filthy courts, and tortuous blind alleys had come to see her die.

The veriest refuse and scum were they of the lowest dregs of vice.

Yet even they felt themselves pure in comparison to this monster.

No, she should not escape.

An innocent girl had very nearly suffered a shameful death on her account.

But now her time had come, and she should not slip through their fingers.

What awful crimes, then, blackened the soul of this fair fiend, on whose death they were so determined ?

Of what fearful atrocity had she been guilty, thus to stir up the fury of these wretches, themselves the vilest of the vile ?

She was a witch !

A thousand crimes had been attributed to her, though none had been proved.

But proofs were not required.

This was an age of darkness.

An age of cruelty.

She had been branded witch, and her death had been determined on.

At daybreak, then, did the mob assemble.

Forth from all the hotbeds of crime they poured in one continuous stream.

They gathered thousands strong around the precincts of the jail.

They lined the road down Snow Hill, along Holborn, along the Oxford Road, and all the way to Tyburn.

The hoarse roar which saluted the appearance of Esther Brandon apprised those far away that she was coming, and was echoed again and again all along the line of route.

Thus travelling with inconceivable celerity, the news that the witch was coming reached Tyburn in a very few moments after she had left Newgate.

Not that the calvacade was ever destined to accomplish half that distance.

A raging mob surrounded the cart from the very moment that it quitted the gloomy prison gates.

So enormous was the assemblage that before it had arrived at the bottom of Snow Hill, in spite of the sharp swords of the soldiers wielded mercilessly on every side, the vehicle was blocked up in the centre of one dense mob of human beings.

In vain did the soldiers fight and struggle with the crowd which hemmed them in on every side.

So confined was the space that they could not use their weapons with any effect.

The mob pressed upon them, and endeavoured to force their way to the prisoner.

Some of the bolder of the mob used their bludgeons, and soon both parties were waging a hand-to-hand battle with a savage fury which showed that the conflict could but terminate on either side by victory or death.

Dennis, the hangman, knowing well enough that he was anything but a favourite with the roughs, was quaking with fear for his precious skin, should he fall into their hands, and, drawing forth a pistol from his belt, threatened with it the foremost of his assailants.

The most deafening yells and howls and the most fearful execrations were heard on every side.

Horrible missiles filled the air.

Dead dogs and cats, filth from the gutters, and, worse than these, sharp stones were hurled with fiendish intent at the beautiful woman who was the cause of this terrible scene.

Pale as a statue, and almost as unmoved, she sat there in the hangman's cart, whilst the savage wretches around scrambled and fought their way towards her.

Placid and calm, inexpressibly lovely, was she, and an almost angelic smile, such as a martyr at the stake might have worn, passed from time to time across her beautiful features.

At such times as these the roaring of the angry mob was terrible to listen to.

The poor parson, well nigh scared out of his wits by the horrors of the scene in which he found himself most unwillingly performing a principal part, was too much occupied with the contemplation of his own approximate *finale* to comfort anybody else whose latter end might be speedily approaching.

He certainly stuck to his book with a perseverance worthy of the cause.

But there were too many dead cats flying about for him always to be very sure where he was to a line or two.

Whether or not the woman to whom his discourse was addressed listened to the spiritual consolation he thus offered to her it is difficult to say.

Her face wore an expression of gentle resignation, and she murmured gently between her blanched lips some faint words, which might either have been prayers or curses.

Once, when the howling of the mob had reached its loudest, she suddenly raised her clasped hands on high, as though imploring Heaven's intervention.

At sight of this an extraordinary change came over the appearance of the crowd.

A moment before they had been striving one against the other, like hungry cats fighting for a bone.

All were eager to strike the fatal blow which was to deprive her of life.

A sudden panic seemed now to seize them.

There was a momentary lull in the storm.

They watched her with white scared faces.

The foremost of the struggling wretches shrank back trembling, seeming to fear that her eyes might fall on them.

They thought that it was some fearful malediction which she was about to pronounce.

They thought that they were going to be crippled or palsied, struck lame or blind.

That they were going to be bewitched.

But the terror which fell upon them thus was but of momentary duration.

One in the crowd, more strong-minded than the rest, rallied them on their cowardice.

A stalwart ruffian—a blacksmith, seemingly, by trade—with a hot perspiring face, all smoke besmeared, and with bare arms, on which the muscles stood out like knotted cordage, roared, with cast-iron lungs—

"Down with her ! Down with the witch !"

Rallying under this man's generalship, the mob made a terrific rush upon the cart and its occupants.

A headlong rush which carried all before it, like waters bursting open the gates of a lock.

The soldiers—fighting furiously, but overcome by the large odds against them—were driven back in a confused struggling mass.

A blow on the side of the head hurled the hangman from his seat, and, a score of hands clutching at him at once, he was dragged away, howling for mercy, to be hanged with his own rope from a neighbouring public-house signpost.

The unhappy chaplain, torn out of the cart by the heels, was in a trice stripped of his surplice and wig, which, ripped into a thousand tatters, were spread over the heads of the people, and fought and scrambled for with savage playfulness.

Upon the fair captive, however, were those immediately concerned in the last attack intent upon wreaking a bloody vengeance.

Seized by the wrists, she was dragged roughly from the cart, and next moment the air bristled with the knives of her would-be assassins.

" Beat her brains out !" howled the wretches in the rear.

" Trample her to death !"

" Tear her limb from limb !"

" No, no !" others screamed vociferously. " Pass her this way. Let us all have a share in her death."

So greedy were the wretches for her death, so loth to lose the gratification of torturing their victim, that all struggled round her, each thrusting back the other that he alone might be the one to strike the blow from which their very rapacity had hitherto saved her.

She could not die more than one death was the notion uppermost in the minds of her self-elected executioners.

What, then, should that death be ?

" Burn her !" screamed a frightful hag, with straggling locks of grizzled hair, and long thin arms and naked breast.

The proximity of Smithfield seemed to favour the monster's suggestion.

" To the stake with her !" howled others.

But even about this there seemed a difference of opinion.

There were some who thought that this death was not cruel enough.

Some there were who panted for the perpetration of some hideous atrocity, for the very nature of which they racked their inventive faculties mercilessly.

Torn, bruised, and panting from the effects of their brutal violence, the witch lay on the moist greasy stones, looking in her deathlike pallor already a corpse.

Yes, a corpse, had it not been that from her eyes there yet flashed an angry glare.

A glare of deadly venomous hate.

Heeding not her sufferings, untouched by her peerless beauty, her ferocious assailants dragged her onward, those in advance cleaving a way through the mob with their knives and bludgeons.

Excruciating were her sufferings from their ill-usage.

Scarcely a limb but seemed to be dislocated, scarcely a joint but was half dragged out of its socket.

Her bare feet were cruelly trampled on, and cut and bleeding.

A stone had struck her on the cheek and cut it deeply.

Something else had bruised her soft white shoulder, from which the blood trickled slowly down upon her bosom.

She was evidently in great pain, but scarcely a sign of her agony was visible upon her face.

There was no fear in her glittering eyes.

Nothing but hate, burning hate for her enemies, not unmingled with bitter contempt and disdain.

They dragged her along through the crowd towards Smithfield.

The soldiers, thoroughly routed, had now turned tail, and were making the best of their way back to the prison.

No one was there to stretch out a helping hand for the unhappy woman.

No one to save her from the horrible fate threatening her.

As they neared Smithfield, however, another crowd seemed to be approaching the one which surrounded the fair captive.

A hoarse roar of voices imperatively ordered the captors to halt.

The second crowd then parting, there was disclosed to view a livid corpse, stretched upon a hurdle.

At sight of this ghastly object the captive, hitherto firm and courageous, shrank back in evident terror.

With a suppressed shriek she strove, though vainly, to cover her eyes, and hide the dreadful object from her view.

What was the meaning of this sudden fear ?

Was this the body of one of her victims ?

Yes—this was the corpse of the man she was accused of slaying.

The murdress was face to face with her victim.

CHAPTER LXVIII.

RALPH AND THE BOW STREET RUNNER — THE STRUGGLE IN THE PASSAGE — INVOLUNTARY MURDER — LOST LEONORE — THE FRUITLESS SEARCH—THE MOONLIGHT—A RUN FOR LIFE—THE WHITE FIGURE IN THE BOAT—"SAFE ! " SAFE !"—NOT YET.

RETURN we now for a while to our gallant hero, Red Ralph, whom we left, as the reader will remember, making his way to London after his attack on the mail coach.

Upon reaching London, he at once directed his steps to the house in White Friars at which he had placed his loved bride, the Lady Leonore, for temporary safety.

He paused for a moment in front of the quaint old carved porch and listened.

The street was quite still.

He cast his eyes anxiously around.

He was unobserved. He might venture to knock.

He gave a sharp rap with his knuckles against the panel, and then paused to listen again.

He was surprised after a time, however, to find no response.

But, losing patience, after a short delay, he hammered again, this time louder than before.

Again he waited.

All was still as death within the house.

Not a sign of light or life visible.

Ralph's heart beat fast with fear and apprehension—not fearing for himself. His brave heart was a stranger to such emotion, but he was deeply concerned for the safety of his lady-love.

He walked back into the road and looked up at the front of the house.

All was dark and silent.

Again he returned to the porch, and once more was going to knock, when suddenly the door opened, and he found himself confronting a man who at the first glance he could see was a Bow Street runner.

The man standing in the shadow of the door, Ralph was unable to see his features, but the moonlight streamed directly upon our captain's handsome face.

" Red Ralph," cried the officer, at the same moment seizing the highwayman by the collar, " in the king's name, I arrest you."

Ralph was so astounded by this unexpected capture that for an instant his presence of mind deserted him.

The man, taking advantage of this circumstance, made good his hold, and now had him as tightly as though his fingers were a vice.

" Leave go," cried Ralph, shaking him to and fro in his efforts to free himself.

But the man only laughed.

" Nay, nay, my pretty Yellow Boy," said he, " not quite so easily as that I trow."

" Leave go, I say."

"Not if I know it."

"It will be the worse for you if you don't."

"It will be much the worse for you, captain, if I manage to take you, and I mean to try my best. I've been looking for you a very long time."

"Look here, fool!" said Ralph, between his set teeth. "You will not take me alive and single-handed. There is very small chance of you're taking me at all. Leave go."

"Never."

The man clung to him with the tenacity of a bull-dog.

But Ralph by this time was losing all patience.

The officer would not loose his hold, and Ralph was at all times strongly averse to violence.

But this sort of thing could not go on much longer. Our hero clenched his fist and struck the officer a tremendous blow in the face.

The man dropped like an ox beneath the butcher's axe, and Ralph turned to fly.

But the Bow Street runner recovered as though by magic. He was up again almost as quickly as he had gone down.

In another instant he had again seized the captain, and at the same time producing a pistol from his breast pocket, presented it at Ralph's head.

Ralph delayed not a moment, but, clutching the pistol so as to direct the barrel against its owner, began to struggle desperately to free himself.

Tightly locked in a bearlike hug, the two men wrestled silently for several moments, and passing the doorway, slammed the door to, and continued to struggle in the dark.

Suddenly, however, the pistol went off with a sharp report.

The instantaneous flash revealed to Ralph the man's agonised face.

With a deep groan he fell backwards.

He fell a dead weight to the ground, and then there followed an awful silence, unbroken by she faintest sound.

"Good God," muttered Ralph, "he is dead! Heaven knows I did not intend to do this deed, if it was through my instrumentality that he thus died."

He remained in the pitchy darkness for some moments, hesitating what he should do.

He was afraid to open the door, lest the sound of the pistol-shot might have alarmed some of the neighbours.

It would not be safe to remain here, though.

It was clear that nobody was in the house; but how long it would be before some comrade of the dead man might return it was impossible to say.

Better far it would be now to beat a retreat.

But he did not quite relish that notion either.

He was far too anxious about his young bride.

Somehow or other he must find her. At least he would try.

"If I only can manage to get clear of this hateful city," he said, "and can carry off my pretty bird with me, I'll warrant they don't find me again in these parts for many a long day. But, alas! how can I hope for such good fortune? I have lost her once more, and it is more than likely that we shall never meet again. Surely no one since the world was made ever spent such an extraordinary honeymoon."

As he made these reflections he produced from his pocket a tiny dark lantern. Then striking a light by the aid of a flint and steel, in the handling of which he was extremely dexterous, he proceeded upon a voyage of discovery.

He lost no time about it, for he knew how valuable every minute might prove to him, but hurriedly passed through the rooms one by one.

There was not a soul in the house.

He tried the first, second, and third floors, and the attics, the kitchen, and the cellars, with the same result.

There was no good end to be gained by stopping here any longer; and, descending again to the passage, he strode towards the street door.

He could not refrain from a shudder as he gazed down into the face of the corpse, horribly mangled and blood-besmeared.

"Poor fellow," he muttered to himself. "It was an unlucky day for you that threw you across my path."

And thus speaking he passed out at the door.

Scarcely, however, had he closed it behind him and crossed the threshold, when the sound of a well-known voice struck upon his ear.

The voice belonged to his arch enemy—Jonathan Wild.

"Curse the loitering idiot," exclaimed the thief-taker. "What does he mean by giving me all this trouble?"

"I beg your pardon, Mr. Wild," said another voice, "but don't you think, sir —"

"Think what, you booby?"

"Think we oughtn't to have left the boat?"

"Left it! We're going back directly, I suppose."

"Yes, sir. Only if one of us had stopped—"

"I should have stopped if I had not known you were such an infernal idiot. You could not be trusted alone."

"But, sir, I —"

"The girl is safe enough, too, as I've fastened her. But I know your motive."

"Mr. Wild, I assure you —"

"You want to get out of the row, if there is one, but you need not be afraid. There's not likely to be any trouble. That scoundrel Ralph's far enough from here, unless my plans have failed."

The two men had reached the house by this time, and paused before the door.

Ralph meanwhile had darted out of the porch, and, hiding in its deep shadow, screwing himself close to the wall, waited until they had passed by.

He could hear every word they said as they approached, and from the conversation he, as may be supposed, formed a very shrewd guess respecting Leonore's whereabouts.

Jonathan Wild was now hammering at the door.

Ralph thought to himself, "If I can only keep within the shadow of the houses, and creep cautiously along, I shall be able to get down to the river. Then no doubt I can find the boat."

It was a very difficult matter, though, to keep in the shade, for the moonlight was very strong, and the gable ends of the houses did not overhang the pathway, so that the moon shone full upon him.

The worst part of the matter was that Wild's man was standing at the door looking in the direction in which Ralph was going.

Several times Ralph looked back, and always saw his face in the same direction.

"Can he see me, I wonder," he muttered.

He hesitated about coming out into the light, but he knew that he was wasting valuable time, and he could not possibly hesitate much longer.

Wild all this time was banging loudly on the panels.

"He'll get tired of that directly, and then perhaps they'll retrace their steps. Shall I try? Yes, I will."

He made a sudden dart into the light, and hurried onwards.

But he had not gone more than a dozen yards when a loud shout was raised behind him.

"Hullo! hullo! you there!"

Ralph, however, quickened his pace instead of replying.

"Hullo! hullo!"

He heard footsteps now.

Some one was running after him.

What was to be done? He had better take to his heels.

How far was the river off he wondered.

Decidedly they were chasing him.

He glanced round. Yes, Jonathan and his man were coming down the lane at a strapping pace.

Ralph did not wait to see any more, but set off at a run.

Seeing him do so, the others ran after him.

At the bottom of the lane there was the river, and some boats were moored up close to the bank.

Ralph looked hurriedly around, at the same time drawing forth a clasp-knife from his breast pocket.

"Leonore! Leonore!" he said aloud.

There was no answer.

"Leonore!" he repeated in tones of passionate entreaty.

The footsteps of his pursuers were rapidly approaching.

Another moment and they would be upon him.

"Leonore! Leonore!" he cried.

Ah! What was that he saw in one of the boats?

Yes, something was moving—something white.

He sprang towards it.

It was a woman's figure, enveloped in white, lying at the bottom of the boat.

He jumped lightly into the boat.

The moon at the moment revealed to him the face of his beloved.

Once more they were together.

But Wild and his man had by this time reached the river's bank.

Ralph clutched the handle of his knife, and swept it across the ropes of the boat moored close to the one into which he had sprung.

Then, seizing the sculls, he pulled vigorously out into the stream.

Two shots were fired at him, but the bullets whizzed past his ears.

"Safe! safe!" he cried, triumphantly, as he rowed along.

But he spoke too hastily.

His danger had only just begun.

CHAPTER LXIX.

JONATHAN AND HIS MINION—IN A FIX—JONATHAN'S CRUELTY—TAKING A HEADER—ALMOST DROWNED—THE DEATH STRUGGLE IN THE WATER—THE FIGHT ON THE BANK.

WHEN Jonathan Wild found that the ropes had been cut he howled with rage.

Just at that particular landing-place the water was very deep, and although the thieftaker was very anxious again to place his hand on Captain Ralph's coat collar, he did not at all relish the notion of a dipping.

What was to be done?

"Curse your lumber-head!" he roared out at his companion. "Why don't you suggest something?"

"Well, sir, I would, sir— "

"Well?"

"Only I can't, sir."

"Why don't you hold your tongue, then? What do you mean by wasting precious time by your infernal tomfooleries?"

"I beg your pardon, sir."

"Hold your tongue, will you, when I tell you?"

Mr. Wild's minion was silent, and his master looked about in a disconsolate way, wondering what on earth he could do.

Presently he turned so savagely upon his companion that the unhappy man jumped six inches off the ground in terror, thinking that he was going to be struck.

"What now?" roared Jonathan. "What are you jumping about for, you wretched idiot? You'd better scramble down into the water, and try and get hold of a boat."

"Do what, sir?"

"Wade through the water."

"But, sir—"

"Well?"

"It's so deep."

"Not at all."

"I shall be drowned, to a certainty."

"No such luck."

"I shall catch my death with cold."

"I'll tell you what you'll catch if you don't very soon do my bidding, without any more dilly-dallying, and that's a good thrashing."

The man, who was evidently scared out of his wits by Jonathan's threats, began with many pitiful groans and moans to let himself down into the water.

The method he adopted was very similar to that of those small boys who bathe in the canals on very cold days, and whom you may see sitting nursing their knees.

He tried the water, a toe at a time.

So enraged, however, was the thieftaker, by the waste of time which these tardy operations occasioned that he presently lost all patience.

Then raising his foot he gave his man a tremendous kick, and sent him flying like a spark from a blacksmith's hammer.

Head over heels and heels over head the unfortunate myrmidon of the law went into the water.

As he had not the remotest notion how to swim, the agony of mind which he suffered whilst he spluttered and struggled, gulping down pint after pint of mud and water, can be more easily imagined than described.

Somehow, though, luckily for him, for he had no idea what to do to save himself, fortune threw in his way one of the boats, clutching at which with frantic tenacity he scrambled into it more dead than alive, and lay on his back groaning.

"Now then," roared Jonathan Wild in a fury. "Bring it alongside, will you?"

But the poor minion was not in a condition to bring anything alongside.

On the contrary, he lay where he had fallen, feeling as though he were going to give up the ghost.

Then Jonathan began to think that he had not acted quite as wisely as was his wont.

Here was he in this man's power, and yet he could not do without insulting him.

"If the vagabond doesn't bring the boat here in a moment," he thought with agony, "we shall lose all chance of ever catching them."

There seemed but small chance, however, of the man bringing the boat to the shore, and indeed it is very probable he never would have brought it there had not the tide saved him the trouble.

No sooner did it come within reach, though, than Jonathan made a spring at it.

He was in an awful hurry, or he would probably have waited another moment before he ventured upon such an energetic measure.

Unhappily, he rather miscalculated the distance, and springing upon the gunwale of the boat upset it.

Next moment, therefore, master and man were struggling in the water.

Poor Jonathan!

His fury was only equalled by his terror, and, to make matters worse, his minion clung to him to save himself from sinking.

Jonathan Wild swore frightfully, whenever he could get his head above water, and kicked and plunged, in the hope of shaking off the incumbrance that had fastened upon him.

"Get off! Leave go! Will you leave go?"

But he would not.

He seemed only to have one idea left in his head, and that was that if he was to be drowned it should be in company.

Unless he escaped he would take good care that Jonathan did not do so either.

Up and down they bobbed in the water like a fisherman's float when a fish is nibbling at the hook.

Happily, at each fresh immersion the tide washed them towards the bank.

Jonathan, being foremost, grasped the woodwork at the waterside.

The man hanging on to his back, though, was such an enormous weight, owing to his soaked clothes, and Wild was so weak and exhausted, that he could not pull himself up.

Frantically then he lunged out with his spurs.

But his efforts were in vain.

Kick as he would, he could not manage to reach him.

And as he still continued to kick out the minion avenged himself by garrotting him.

All the while they were kicking and struggling the woodwork was creaking ominously.

It was very rotten, the nails were old and rusty, and a very little more straining would certainly tear it away.

Wild, perspiring in spite of the cold water, panted and struggled.

The minion clung to him like a leech.

The woodwork gave way suddenly with a great crash, and souse they both went back again.

As they did so Wild gave a despairing howl for help.

It was heard by some watermen at the moment approaching the scene of action.

One of them plunged into the water.

At first it seemed likely that all three would have been drowned together, as the two men in the water immediately fastened upon the newcomer.

But others came to the rescue, and after a desperate struggle the lives of Wild and his minion were saved.

What did they do then?

Give thanks to Heaven for their preservation?

On the contrary, as soon as he got his breath a little, the thieftaker fell upon his subordinate with the fury of a demon, and they fought like Kilkenny cats.

But all this while the reader may suppose that Ralph was making good headway against his pursuers.

Unhappily, he had but gained a very small advantage by the good start that he had made, as will be seen.

CHAPTER LXX.

A NIGHT OF TERROR — THE STORM ON THE THAMES—THE SCULLS UNSHIPPED—DANGER AHEAD—A COLLISION.

WHILST Jonathan Wild and his companion were fighting a storm was brewing overhead, unheeded by the combatants.

Ere they had finished their dispute the storm broke out.

Now it was at its wildest.

A sudden gale had arisen, and raged furiously.

The thunder rolled and crashed in deafening reverberations.

The broad expanse of heaven was one great flare of lurid light.

The hurtling wind lashed the water into froth-tipped ridges.

"Rather an ugly night," thought Ralph as he rowed along. "I must get on shore as soon as possible, for I fancy it will presently begin to rain in torrents."

Not many minutes elapsed before he felt pretty sure that they were not pursued, and he now eagerly turned his attention to his lovely young bride, who still lay silent and motionless.

He found that the reason she did not speak was because the cruel ruffians had tied a handkerchief tightly across her mouth.

They had also bound her securely hand and foot.

Ralph, however, very soon freed her from her bondage.

Poor girl, she was weak and faint.

She was almost frozen stiff with cold, for she had been in the boat nearly an hour.

"Dearest Leonore," said Ralph in a low musical voice, as he bent over the lovely head of his virgin wife, "when will our troubles come to an end?"

"It seems as though Heaven sent you to my rescue," murmured she. "I don't know how ever I can repay you for what you have suffered on my account."

"Shall I tell you, Leonore?" asked Ralph in a low tone. "By your love."

Whilst, however, they were thus conversing the fury of the storm momentarily increased.

A violent rocking of the boat caused her to look hurriedly around.

It is very rare that the wind has much effect upon the generally placid waters of old Father Thames, but sometimes, as on this particular occasion, there rages upon it a miniature tempest.

Quite sufficient was its violence, however, to make a voyage in a small boat extremely hazardous.

Ralph knew this, and also that he was wasting valuable time.

He, therefore, resumed his seat, and prepared to take up the sculls again.

But, oh! horror! What did he see?

The lurch of the boat had unshipped the sculls, and they had drifted far away.

What was now to be done?

He was entirely at the mercy of wind and tide.

Should the thieftaker and his men now come in pursuit of him he was entirely at their mercy.

He sat down despondingly. He racked his brains vainly for some means of conquering the difficulty.

Shading his eyes, he more than once peered anxiously through the gloom in the direction of the landing-place where he had left the thieftaker.

As yet he saw no one, and he wondered very much at the circumstance.

But he could not hope that they were thus easily going to let him depart without an effort.

"If the tide should only drive us towards the shore we might very well effect a landing," Ralph thought. "Or even there would be a chance for us if we came across one of the many lighters moored up and down in the river. We might hide on board."

Neither event, however, seemed likely to occur.

The swollen tide was driving them along at a furious pace down the middle of the stream.

They were not at all likely to reach either bank for a mile or two yet.

As for the lighters, Ralph soon found that he had made a miscalculation.

Approaching the first at a tearing rate he in vain clutched at the slimy side, but it slipped past, and he could not keep his hold for a single instant.

As the tide drove them onward he called loudly, in the hope that some one on board might hear him.

But he received no reply, and in another moment had left the lighter far behind.

On, on they went, the boat rocking fearfully to and fro, so that every moment Ralph expected that they were going to be capsized.

On! on!

The moon was now totally obscured by dense clouds. The sky was black as ink, save when vivid flashes of lightning from time to time illuminated the scene with ghastly distinctness, only, however, to make the succeeding darkness appear more intense.

Presently, glancing ahead during one of these livid glares of light, Ralph saw that they were drifting straight upon another barge.

The idea of clinging to the side he had long ago abandoned. Now he was fearful lest the concussion might overthrow the boat.

At such a rate were they being driven along that he felt that did they come in contact with the bulky monster before them it was scarcely possible that they could escape being upset.

He scarcely dared to move in his seat, so nicely was the boat balanced, but he must do so, or there was no chance for him.

Very cautiously he crawled over the seats and reached the head of the boat.

There he prepared to the best of his power to ward off the coming collision.

With his heart in his mouth he waited silently.

They approached rapidly.

They were going full tilt against the barge. Nothing could save them, unless—

Ah! a sudden gust of wind springing up, the head of the boat was swayed round, and they glided past the danger, grating the boat's side against the barge as they went.

"Thank God for that," murmured Ralph.

As he spoke he scrambled back to his place.

Lady Leonore sat where he had left her, pale and silent.

"Are you afraid?" he asked.

"Not while I am with you," she replied.

He stooped and pressed her hand to his lips.

"Bless you for those words," he said. "I could die happy now if needs be."

If this were an empty boast, it seemed that his courage was soon to put it to the test.

The tide was now driving them onwards at a more furious pace than ever.

At a loss to account for the white-tipped ripples which dashed past him in countless myriads, he turned round again to look ahead.

Something of enormous size, blacker than the surrounding darkness, loomed close upon them.

In another moment a flash of lightning revealed the dreadful truth.

But too late.

Almost at the same instant that Ralph saw that it was a bridge upon which they were driving they were whirled furiously against the stonework.

With a terrific crash the boat's side was stove in.

The water poured through the aperture.

In wild terror Leonore clutched the wooden seat, whilst Ralph made frantic but futile efforts to keep the boat off the thick masonry.

It was a brief but fearful struggle, and then the boat was spun round and hurled violently against the stonework on the opposite side of the arch.

"Leonore!" cried Ralph in a tone of passionate energy.

His strong arm encircled her waist.

The dark and turbulent waters engulphed them.

The lightning lit up the sky with a blue blinding glare.

The thunder rolled and crashed with fearful reverberations.

Then all again was pitchy dark, and the hurtling wind shrieked shrilly through the arches of the bridge,

drowning the wailing cry of the unhappy Leonore as the waters closed for the second time above her.

CHAPTER LXXI.

SHIPWRECKED—A BATTLE WITH THE WATERS— THE MANIAC—"OUR QUEEN!"—RESCUED—THE SUBTERRANEAN CHAMBER—CASTING LOTS FOR LIFE—THE OATH.

It was a moment fraught with such pain and terror as would haunt a man's mind until his dying day.

Death stared him in the face.

There seemed no possible hope that he could escape with his life and save the beautiful girl who was solely dependent on him for succour; and, as the reader can imagine, never for an instant did he dream of making any effort at self-preservation, unless he could also rescue his young and lovely bride.

Cruelly, though, was he encumbered by the young girl, who, knowing not how to swim, nor how she imperilled her young husband's life by the course she was pursuing, clung in terror round his neck, and frustrated all the efforts that he made to save her and himself.

To swim, then, was impossible. To float equally so.

When he first reached the surface after the upset of the boat he had clutched at the stonework of the bridge, being close to his hand, and by its aid had kept their heads for a moment above water.

But it was only a moment, the fury of the tide washing him from his hold.

Thus they passed through the arch.

Were they drifted out by the strong current into the middle of the stream they must be lost. But how to prevent it?

Half blinded by the spray, and half stunned by a violent concussion against the stonework, Ralph struggled madly to drag himself round the bulwark of the bridge.

Desperately he clawed at the slimy stonework.

It glided eellike from his grasp.

Again he clutched. Again his hands slipped over the greasy surface.

He felt that his strength was fast leaving him.

The wind howled around like the sound of demoniacal exultation.

The darkness was intense, and added, if possible, to the horror of the moment.

To die thus—to perish miserably *in the dark!*

Therein lay the terror beneath which the brave heart of the highwayman quailed, spite of his lion-like courage.

Again and again did he make a struggle towards the stonework.

Again and again did he madly, desperately cling to its slippery surface—only, alas! to fall back more and more exhausted into the black waters.

Yet, however, did he still persevere, and at length his labours were rewarded.

Struggling up for the last time, half stunned, half blinded, a sudden glare of lightning revealed to him an iron ring within his reach.

Summoning all his remaining strength, he sprang upwards and clutched at it.

He passed his right arm through, and thus was able to keep his own head and that of his fair charge above the water.

"Thank God!" he murmured, "We are safe. Another moment, and I could have done no more."

The position in which he now was placed, however, was extremely critical.

The strain upon his arm was very great, and his strength was almost exhausted.

Unless he were not soon seen and rescued, he could not hope very long to be able to keep his hold.

The lightning came now at longer intervals.

The thunder was fainter and more distant.

A pitchy darkness enveloped all the objects at the foot of the bridge, and it would have been impossible for any person from the parapet above to see what was passing in the dense obscurity below.

Ralph raised his voice, and called loudly for help.

The rushing of the waters between the arches drowned his voice.

"Help, help!"

The wild shrieking wind carried away the sound.

"Help, help!"

The darkness engulphed him. Afar off the lights glimmered faintly in the windows of the houses. There was no sign of life.

"Help, help!"

It was a cry wrung from him in the intense bitterness of the mental and physical agony he endured.

To die thus miserably, when a bright and glorious career was before him, it was hard indeed.

The girl whose insensible form he was supporting seemed to grow heavier. She lay a dead weight on his arm.

She was awfully still, white, and cold.

Was he but supporting a corpse?

The pain in the other arm, which he had passed through the iron ring, was now becoming so intense that he could scarcely bear it any longer.

He was also growing stiff with cold, and felt as though his hold of Leonore was slowly, but surely, relaxing in its tightness, and that soon she must slip from his grasp into the grave.

It seemed as though death were dragging her down by the feet.

For the last time he raised his voice, and yelled with all the remaining strength of his lungs for assistance.

There was at that moment a lull in the storm, and his cry rang shrilly through the night air.

Scarcely had its echo died away, than the window of a house close at hand was suddenly flung open.

A red light in the room to which it belonged revealed to Red Ralph a dark figure, which rushed forth into a wooden balcony before it, and wildly waved on high its long thin arms.

Ralph shouted again, and was again silent.

At the sound of his voice the figure violently waved its arms once more, and shrieked discordantly in answer to the cry.

Then danced and laughed in a frenzy of fiendish mirth, and clanked a chain which it held in its hand.

Ralph shouted once more, but was answered only by a loud discordant laugh, and an unintelligible jabber, and then other figures rushing out from the red glare beyond seized the first, and carried it back struggling and screaming into the house.

Then all again was dark and silent.

As the light died out, so also died out our hero's last hope, and his strength failing him, he slipped down, with a hollow groan, into the water.

The struggle was at an end; he could do no more.

*   *   *   *   *   *

Happily, though, other ears than those of the strange object in the balcony—maniac, demon, or whatever it was—had heard Ralph's cries.

A boat's crew rowing up the river had been attracted by them, and arrived at the bridge just before Ralph loosed his hold of the ring and fell into the water.

By the light of a torch which a man in the bow waved above his head a glimpse of the highwayman's figure was dimly discernible.

"What is it?" inquired one of the men, a tall dark-complexioned fellow, evidently possessed of gigantic strength, who appeared to be the leader of the band. "Can you make out, Zekiel?"

"Two persons in the water, I fancy," said the other. "One looks like a city gallant: probably been fighting in some house on the bank and jumped into the water. Shall we row on?"

"No, we might as well have a look at them. Some of these young bucks at times carry a goodly store of shiners in their pouches. Row towards them."

The men, in obedience to this command, altered their course and rowed rapidly towards the arch to which the iron ring was fixed that Ralph was clinging to.

"He seems as though he could not cling much longer," said the man with the torch.

"Ah, he's gone!"

"We shall reach him in time yet. If not it can't be helped. The cold water, at any rate, won't damage the shiners very much."

They rowed on vigorously, and with less than a dozen more strokes of their oars reached the spot.

"He seems nearly dead," said one of the men, when, having grasped Ralph by the collar, he began to pull him up the boat's side. "The woman also."

"It would take more time to revive them than we have got to spare, at any rate. Shew a light here will you, while I try his pockets?"

Some one handed over the torch and held it down close, while the leader was engaged in the work.

"Whoever he was, he seems to be a brave fellow. He sacrificed his life on this woman's account."

"How so?"

"Don't you see how tightly his arm is twined round her, and that his fingers clutch her dress?"

"Her hair so covers her face that there is no seeing whether or not she's pretty. I should like to see, too."

As the man spoke he supported the body of Lady Leonore with one hand, and not ungently removed her golden tresses from her face.

Then bent down to look at her more closely.

But scarcely had he done so when he uttered a loud cry of astonishment and terror and started to his feet.

At the same moment, the leader leaving go of Ralph, the two bodies sank.

"What is the matter?" said the chief in an angry tone. "We have lost them now."

"But we must not lose them. Row for your lives. Row for your lives. You know not who it is."

"Who is it, then? Speak!"

"Our queen!"

"You lie, man," roared the chief, seizing him by the throat. "How can that be?"

"I swear it. For Heaven's sake lose no time."

"If this be the truth, and through your bungling she has perished, look to yourself."

No more passed. There was not a moment to spare if they were to rescue the woman from a watery grave, even were it not already too late.

Pulling with all their strength, they rowed the boat backwards and forwards, to the right and to the left, flashing on high the torches to scan the surface of the water.

Their search was at length crowned with success. Entangled among some floating spars and planks which the storm had cast adrift, Ralph and his fair charge were above the water, although for several minutes they were hidden from the sight of those searching for them.

In another moment they were drawn up into the boat, which rapidly pursued its course.

In about a quarter of an hour it had reached Westminster.

There, at the foot of some moss-grown and slippery steps, they alighted and made fast the boat.

Carrying Ralph and his bride, they crossed a large

[THE HANGMAN HANGED.]

neglected garden, and entered what seemed to be a spacious mansion, which had been allowed to fall into decay.

As they approached nearer, however, it proved to be no more than a pile of ruins, ravaged by fire.

Entering at what had been a hall door, they cautiously proceeded for some time until they came to a wall, over which hung a mass of ivy.

Pulling this on one side, an opening was observable, then a precipitous flight of stone steps.

Carefully and noiselessly they descended into a passage below, out of which, by a secret door, they presently reached a series of spacious subterranean chambers.

An old gipsy woman took charge of Leonore, and carried her to a couch before a blazing fire, while the men busied themselves in restoring animation to Ralph's almost helpless form.

When at length he slowly and painfully opened his eyes he found himself the centre of a group of strangely-attired men, whose wild and severe figures and faces filled him with amazement.

Before, however, he had time to raise himself or speak, a score of knives were pointed at his breast.

"You are in the power of those," said the leader of the band, addressing him, "who will treat you well if you will not betray them."

Ralph was silent.

"Do you swear not to divulge the secrets of this assembly?"

"Yes," said Ralph faintly, "I swear."

"'Tis well. Now administer the oath."

At these words the room suddenly became dark, and Ralph felt as though the floor were giving way beneath his feet.

He made an effort to rise, but a hand on each arm pressed him down to the chair on which he sat.

Meanwhile the floor trembled underneath him, and from the motion of the air he was sure that he was on some sort of mechanical apparatus which was sinking down—down to unknown depths below.

"They can't mean to murder me, however," Ralph reflected, "or they would surely never have taken the trouble to revive me."

He felt weak and confused as yet, and could but very dimly call to mind the particulars of the fearful scene through which he had so lately passed.

His clothes were quite dry now, he felt, and when he had an opportunity of looking at his coat sleeve for a moment he noticed that it was not the coat he wore when he fell into the water.

It was now pitch dark, but yet he could feel that the journey was not quite ended.

Suddenly, however, there was a slight shock, and he was still.

Then there was a deathlike silence, and he could almost have fancied that he had been let down into some dark pit and left there alone, only that he felt at that moment the hands of his captors grasping his arm.

Presently there was a rustling and a faint whispering.

Then he felt that the chair and platform on which he sat were being moved forward.

The apparatus stopped again. There was a dead silence for a moment, and then a blinding glare of blue light revealed a scene of a most extraordinary character.

Round a table, at the head of which he found himself seated, there were ranged a dozen mysterious figures, wearing dark cloaks, which covered them, with the exception of their faces.

These were deadly white, hollow-cheeked, fleshless, indescribably ghastly.

In the hand of each of these figures was grasped a pistol, the barrel of which was pointed at his head.

Turning his eyes slowly to the right and to the left, he saw that the figures standing by his side were similarly attired to those before him, and that they also had pistols pointed on either side of his head.

At the other end of the table sat an old man with a snow-white beard. Before him was a book covered with strange characters, to which he added others as he spoke.

"Stranger," he said, in low solemn tones, " who are you?"

"My name is Ralph," replied our hero.

"What else?" asked the old man.

"Some call me Red Ralph. Some call me Ralph of the Bloody Hand."

"But your surname?"

"That," replied their prisoner, " is my secret, and one which I do not feel at liberty to divulge."

There was a hoarse murmur of discontent among the cloaked figures, but the old man silenced them with an imperious wave of his hand.

"There is no harm in his keeping his secret," he said. "What does it matter to us what he is called? Now tell us what you are."

"I am a captain."

"A captain of what?"

"Of cavalry."

"Are you a soldier, then?"

"A soldier of fortune."

"What do you mean?"

"A knight of the road, some would say. Others would call me a dashing highwayman. Others a thief. I'm not particular myself what name you give to my profession."

"You then are the robber for whose capture such large rewards are offered?"

"The same."

"Whose description is posted on all the dead walls of the metropolis?"

"They do so honour me."

"Did we then give you over to the authorities we should receive upwards of a thousand pounds."

"Well, if you like risking your own necks by going so near to the hangman, I suppose you would."

"At any rate you would be hanged."

"I do not think so. It is difficult to say, of course. I think, however, that I possess sufficient influence in a certain quarter to escape."

"In what quarter?"

"That is another of my secrets."

"Hark ye, Red Ralph, this is not a time for joking, as you will find. We have already rescued you from death. We have consulted upon the subject, and had almost decided upon admitting you as one of our society. Upon reflection, however, I should advise that such shall not be the case."

"What, then?"

"That you be put to death."

"But since you rescued me?"

"It was not my wish that it should be done. Having done so, be yours the misfortune of suffering the agony of two deaths."

"But will you not give me a choice before you kill me? I have not refused to belong to your society. I have not the remotest notion what it is."

A low murmur passed among the cloaked figures, and then the old man spoke again.

"Lots will be drawn. Your fate will be decided by the cast of a die. Pray that you may be fortunate, and wait."

At the last word the light again died out, and all was once more dark and silent.

Full twenty minutes passed thus—minutes which seemed like ages to the prisoner anxiously awaiting the decision.

Suddenly the same blue glare revealed the same cloaked figures, and the old man sitting as before at the opposite end of the table.

"Red Ralph," he said, "your lucky star is in the ascendant. You are one of us. Swear to keep our secret, and it shall now be revealed to you. Swear by all that you hold sacred here and hereafter. Swear, and now drink."

A goblet was handed to him at this moment.

A crystal goblet, containing a purely transparent liquid, which looked and tasted like water.

Ralph put it to his lips.

"Drink," said the old man.

He took a mouthful.

"Drink," repeated the others in chorus.

Ralph drained the goblet, but as he reached the last drop it fell from his hand.

A film came over his eyes.

His head spun round.

He fell back in his chair in a deathlike swoon.

CHAPTER LXXII.

THE MURDRESS AND THE MURDERED —"DEATH TO THE SORCERESS!"—THE ORDEAL— BLOOD—DEATH BY THE STAKE—SMITHFIELD — JONAS THE GIPSY — UNEXPECTED CHANGE OF FORTUNE—THE GIPSIES STAND BY THEIR QUEEN.

FACE to face with her victim!

Yes.

Such was the terrible position in which Mina, the gipsy queen, now found herself placed.

In the clutches of an infuriated mob, roaring with fearful cries for her instant destruction !

Death—death of the most awful nature—now appeared imminent.

And Mina the gipsy queen shivered with terrible anticipations.

Yet still something of her wonted pride and demeanour remained to her, and she gazed around upon her captors with a glance of contempt and disdain, even while she trembled with fear of their vengeance.

"You condemn me for a crime of which I am innocent," she began, in a loud clear tone, which was heard above the cries of the mob.

"Guilty, guilty !" cried a dozen voices at once.

"And who is my accuser here ?" demanded the gipsy.

"I," cried a voice.

"And I, and I," shouted a host of voices together.

"And what are your proofs ?"

The nearest persons in the crowd, who were her more eager denouncers for the moment, were rather staggered by this.

In fact they had no proofs whatever.

They were utterly unreasonable, as King Mob ever is.

No proofs had even been asked by the majority of the persons assisting in this disgraceful proceeding.

It sufficed for all that some two or three individuals, who were now not even distinguishable, had declared Mina the gipsy queen to be a sorceress and a murdress.

Their words inflamed the superstitious people, and one and all fell upon the woman, whom they did not know to be guilty.

One man, however, amongst the crowd who was a little calmer than the rest here interfered to prevent them going to extremities.

"Stay !" he cried, holding up his hands, "let us not do murder."

Several of the crowd shrank back, appalled by the terrible sound of the words he uttered.

"We demand justice," he continued, "and justice only."

"Justice, justice !" shouted the mob in a chorus.

"Ay, and justice we will have," resumed the former spokesman.

"I ask for no more," said Mina the gipsy, eagerly availing herself of this temporary respite.

And in an instant the volatile mob, who would the moment before have condemned her to a violent death without mercy and unheard, were loud in their cries for justice.

"Bring hither the body."

Half a hundred eager hands were stretched forward to aid in this ghastly office.

The hideous corpse was now placed before the avowed assassin.

Once and once only did the gipsy quail before this ghastly object.

It was when a white cloth was removed from the face of the corpse, revealing a countenance distorted with the agonies of its final moments.

Although no great length of time had elapsed, the body was no longer in a fit condition to be handled in the way it was now being used.

But the maddened people only saw one object in their frenzied thirst for vengeance upon the assassin.

"See, see," cried one, who was by the unhappy Mina's elbow, and narrowly scanned her features all the while, "she trembles. She fears to look upon it !"

"You lie !" exclaimed the gipsy, commanding herself with a great effort. "I fear to look upon nothing on earth."

"Truly," said a bystander viciously. "Then your present coolness cannot be taken as a proof of your innocence."

"Any more than emotion could indicate guilt," said Mina.

"Then for another trial," said the former spokesman.

"Name it," said the gipsy queen defiantly, "and you shall see how I will shrink from any ordeal !"

"Ordeal !" cried the man. "Aptly named. Let us try her by the ordeal of touch !"

"Good, good !" shouted a dozen voices at once.

"I accept," said the gipsy, eagerly jumping at this ridiculous proposal. "Put me to the proof."

They made way for her in the crowd again, and she approached the corpse once more.

Here she paused for a few seconds.

"She fears !"

"She dare not brave the ordeal !" cried several voices.

"Silence, silence," said the man who had proposed the ordeal by touch. "She wishes to speak. Let us give her a fair hearing."

"Ay, ay."

"One word, and I have done," said the gipsy, holding up her hand.

"Say on."

"I accept the trial you propose upon one condition only."

"Name it."

"That after this—"

"No, no," cried a voice. "No conditions with a murdress."

The cry was caught up by the mob in an instant.

"Nay, nay," cried the former speaker. "Let us hear what she has to say before we decide anything."

"Say on, then."

"My only condition is," said Mina the gipsy, "that if I come out of this ordeal free I may be allowed to depart in peace, and on the instant."

This was demurred to at first, but after a while assented to.

And then the proceedings commenced in earnest.

It consisted in this.

The accused was required to place her hand upon the body of the victim, and swear solemnly her innocence of the crime imputed to her.

The face of the gipsy grew livid, and her dark eyes glistened fiercely as she stretched forth her hand—showing how painful was the effort to subdue her emotions.

A momentary spasm shook her from head to foot as her hand came in contact with the cold clay of the murdered man.

But now she was upon her trial, and these signs, which would at another moment have been accepted as evidences of her guilt, were allowed to pass unheeded.

"I swear," began the man, proposing the form of oath to the accused.

And fearlessly she followed his words.

By the most fearful oaths she swore to her innocence.

Unfalteringly did the gipsy, if guilty in truth, consign herself to eternal perdition.

Thus swore Mina the gipsy, solemnly, with her hand upon the lifeless corpse of him of whose destruction she was accused—so solemnly, and with such an appearance of truth and earnestness in her manner, that even her most violent denouncers were silenced.

A low murmur went through the crowd, and many even did not hesitate openly to sympathise with her wrongs, so capricious and so sudden are the changes of opinion of such a gathering.

The ordeal is well-nigh complete.

The accused has but to remove her hand from the corpse and depart.

With an intense sigh of relief, Mina the gipsy queen withdraws.

But, great Heavens! what is that?

Upon the breast of the corpse is seen a blood-stain which was not there before the ordeal.

And this blood-stain bears the exact form of the supposed murdress's hand, which has just quitted the breast of the corpse.

A cry of horror went round the circle who were within sight of the proceedings.

From mouth to mouth the appalling intelligence was conveyed.

And with this was tacitly understood the doom of the gipsy queen.

Meanwhile Mina had not understood the meaning of the cries.

Death she could see plainly enough upon every face, but why she could not understand.

At length she turned her eyes once more upon the body, and there perceived, to her terror and dismay, the dreadful signification of the hisses of execration which were hurled upon her by the infuriated rabble.

And now, for the first time, did hope entirely desert her.

And well it might, for the ordeal had failed.

Not to dwell too long upon this painful scene, with the proof of her guilt established beyond a doubt to the mob of accusers, the doom of Mina the gipsy was sealed.

Nothing now remained but to decide upon the manner of death.

Many were the suggestions offered and rejected as not worthy of the crime thus established.

"Smithfield!"

Awful word!

In an instant it was caught up by the mob, with loud cries of assent, and the unhappy woman was hustled by her persecutors in a way that would probably have spared her all further vengeance at their hands had it continued many minutes.

But never a word of supplication escaped her now.

They soon gained the spot where they intended to witness the last hours of the unhappy gipsy.

And now were hasty preparations made for the execution of their vengeance.

"Justice" they fanatically called it.

A huge pile of faggots, steeped in tar and inflammable matter, was collected together, and Mina the gipsy was held upon the wood whilst several tied her to the stake.

As these preparations proceeded a tall swarthy-looking fellow of muscular proportions, and wearing a large Spanish sombrero, hastily pushed through the crowd, and strode up to the destined victim.

"Who is this woman's accuser?" he sternly demanded.

"Jonas!" exclaimed Mina, in a voice of joy. "Jonas!"

"Ay, Mina," said the man, "it is I. What does this all mean?"

"That this woman dies," said one of the bystanders.

"Fool!" exclaimed Jonas.

"Stand back! Stand back!" cried the mob.

"Ay. Stand off, and don't interfere in the execution of justice."

"Justice be hanged!" said the newcomer, defiantly. "Set this woman free."

"Never, never! Death to the murdress!"

"Death to the sorceress!"

"Cease this mummery. Release this woman at once."

"You will but bring yourself into trouble," said one.

"See here," said the gipsy king (for it was he, as the reader will doubtless remember). "This is how I fear your trouble, as you call it."

With these words he drew a large dagger-shaped knife, and before any one could divine his intention he severed the bonds which bound her to the stake with one single stroke of its keen blade.

"You will get trounced for interfering, I warn you," said one.

Barely had the words been uttered when the sturdy gipsy dealt the speaker a blow in the face which stretched him senseless upon the ground.

"Now," he exclaimed proudly, "who shall dare to oppose me?"

And then, taking advantage of the temporary panic created by his boldness, he began to push through the crowd and move away with Mina.

But this could not be accomplished so easily.

Another instant, and the mob had recovered from their momentary stupefaction, and cried aloud for vengeance upon the gipsy sorceress and her champion.

Jonas raised a small silver whistle to his lips and blew a loud shrill note.

A dozen of his followers seemed to spring from the stones with the summons.

"Make us a way here," he said. "Preserve your queen from these ruffians and maniacs."

The dozen gipsies no sooner showed demonstrations of hostility than the hundreds to whom they would have opposed themselves shrank back.

They were not at all prepared to oppose men in combat.

Their vengeance was against one helpless and defenceless woman.

Jonas and Mina were not slow to take advantage of this turn of chance in their favour, and speedily they made good their retreat.

A few of the mob would have followed, but, seeing that pursuit was not the general order of the day, they refrained from incurring the displeasure of so formidable a champion as Jonas.

"Now then, men," cried the gipsy king, "you can rejoin me at your pleasure at the retreat in Westminster."

CHAPTER LXXIII.

THE RUINED HOUSE AT WESTMINSTER—A STRANGE ENCOUNTER——TWO GIPSY GULLIES——RED RALPH—WHY A PRISONER?—JONAS THE GIPSY—THE ROMANY'S VENGEANCE——DEFIANCE—RALPH IN DANGER.

WHILE this diversion in favour of the gipsy queen was taking place at Smithfield, Red Ralph had been conveyed to the ruined house in Westminster, as we have narrated.

Here, overcome by the strong narcotic which the gipsies had administered to him, he sank into a profound slumber of several hours' duration.

When he recovered his senses he had quite forgotten the events which had preceded his introduction to the ruined rendezvous of the gipsy band.

By degrees, however, it came to him, and he began to think of taking his departure, for the aspect of the place was by no means cheering.

He staggered to his feet, yawned wearily, for he had scarcely yet recovered from the effects of the drug which he had taken, and moved towards the door.

He pushed at it lazily, but, strangely enough, it failed to yield to his pressure.

"The door sticks fast," he muttered, half aloud.

And again he pressed it, but with no other result.

"This is rather odd," he murmured. "It must be fastened."

But no fastening could he discover.

"I am still asleep," he continued, with an endeavour to shake off the drowsiness which seemed to benumb his faculties. "Confound it! What ails me still?"

He yawned sleepily, and then began to shake himself together, preparatory to a second attempt to push open the heavy door which opposed him.

Again and again did he strive, exerting himself to the utmost, but with no more result than before.

Now he began to grow just the least bit uncomfortable.

Only one reason could he assign for this impediment. The door must be fastened—and heavily fastened, too—upon the outside!

For what purpose, then?

The gipsies had made him their prisoner, but he was quite at a loss to divine the object of this singular proceeding.

However, he did not long pause to consider this.

No matter the object, the fact of being held prisoner by any one ill suited his free roving spirit.

Immediately he resumed his assault upon the door, but it never budged an inch.

It appeared as if constructed of solid masonry.

"This is beyond a joke," thought Red Ralph uneasily. "What can they mean by it?"

Only one thing it could mean, and this was that he was a prisoner!

But for what purpose? Did the gipsies intend to play him false after all the expressions of friendship which they had lavished upon him?

There was certainly something in it which had yet to be explained.

And Red Ralph very much feared now that such an explanation would prove anything but satisfactory to him.

When he had striven to burst open the door until he was thoroughly exhausted, but without making the slightest impression upon it, he resolved to wait patiently until his captors, for so he deemed them now, should return.

Then he must take advantage of the first opportunity which should present itself to escape.

It was "Hobson's choice," and therefore a wise resolve.

He had recovered from the effects of the narcotic about two hours, when he was not a little pleased to hear footsteps without, and the door was unfastened, with a very apparent desire to make as little noise as possible, in order not to arouse Red Ralph's suspicions of his forcible detention.

At least so thought the leader of the once formidable Yellow Band.

"Plague take them!" muttered Red Ralph. "They are as cunning as their fellow-thief the fox. I must be wary."

Two gipsies entered.

The prisoner was seated where he had been sleeping, and he looked up with an affectation of that drowsiness which he had really experienced a few minutes before.

"How goes the day?" demanded Red Ralph carelessly.

"It is late," answered one of the gipsies. "You have slept."

"A little."

The newcomers exchanged significant glances.

"Good," muttered Red Ralph, chuckling mentally. "It takes!"

"Have you any need of refreshment?" asked the gipsy.

"No," replied Red Ralph. "I am not hungry now, I thank you."

"Will you drink?"

"I am not thirsty either. I drank something just now."

"Just now?"

"Yes, before I slept."

"Oh!"

"The only thing I stand in need of is a little fresh air. I stifle here."

The gipsy adroitly changed the conversation, but Red Ralph was fully a match for him now.

Without appearing to notice the intention, or being greatly pressed upon the subject he turned the subject again to this.

"It is oppressively close here," he murmured, with a yawn.

"Because you are unwell."

"No. I think that I have quite recovered my late accident."

"No, no; you are mistaken."

"Indeed? Verily, my friend, you appear to know the state of my body better than I do myself."

The gipsy was slightly staggered by this unexpected retort.

"I merely speak from what the doctor reported of you," the gipsy managed to mutter after a while.

"The doctor?" said Ralph.

"Yes."

"Have I then been so bad as to need his services?"

"Ay, truly you have."

"And therefore you think that I must necessarily be in a bad state at the present moment?"

The gipsies evidently did not relish the tone which the conversation was assuming.

"We are told to ask you if you want anything?" said one.

"Yes."

"You do? What is it?"

"A little fresh air."

"That you cannot have."

"Granted—unless you assist me. I am powerless to rise."

"You had better rest. In a little time Jonas will be here with the rest of our tribe, and he will consult with you on what is best to be done."

"But until then?"

"You had best remain here."

"But I had rather not."

"You must."

"Must?"

"Ay. Such are the doctor's orders."

"But I don't care for the doctor's orders, and I would prefer—"

The gipsy cut him short with a wave of the hand, and they both quitted the place.

So suddenly had they taken their departure that Red Ralph had no time to follow them.

He sprang up and darted to the door, but too late!

"It wanted but this to confirm my suspicions," he said, rather alarmed. "I am their prisoner. Of that there can be no doubt. It only remains to determine what is the object of this apparently friendly captivity."

This, however, was no easy matter to decide.

The return of the remainder of the gipsy tribe, too, was an event to which he looked forward with no pleasurable emotions.

As yet he had not been recognised by them.

But he remembered his last interview with the band, and upon that occasion, too, he had been their prisoner.

Then they had bartered his existence with his bitterest enemy, Jonathan Wild the thieftaker.

Upon that occasion, too, he had effected his escape by the downfall of one of their band.

This was the stalwart gipsy whom he had encountered and overcome in a brief but deadly struggle.

What, then, if this individual should return with the rest of them?

He would inevitably be recognised, and his doom would be reduced to a certainty.

The Romany never forgives—never forgets an injury!

These and other meditations equally unpleasant were all he had to comfort him for the next few hours.

But all the time his greatest discomfort was his ignorance as to the fate of Leonore.

How had she fared in the hands of this wild and unscrupulous people?

They had loaded her with honours, it is true, but this was whilst mistaking her for their queen.

When the mystery of the wondrous resemblance which they bore to each other should be cleared up by some of the keener-sighted of the tribe, what would be the result?

A hundred different pictures, each more terrible than its predecessor, were conjured up, and their separate horrors mentally discussed, before his solitude and his musings were again broken in upon.

In the meantime a singular scene was enacting without.

Shortly after the visit of the two gipsies to Red Ralph Jonas the Romany king arrived with Mina, rescued from the stake at Smithfield.

It is impossible to describe the astonishment of all at seeing Leonore and Mina together.

At first they could not at all comprehend which was really their queen.

However, a certain boldness in the manner of Mina soon informed them that they had been mistaken with Leonore.

"Leonore," said the gipsy queen, advancing towards her with outstretched hands, "do you not remember me, my sister?"

"Yes," replied Leonore, sadly. "Indeed I have good reason to remember you. For you I have suffered much. For you I had well nigh seen my last day's life?"

"What mean you?"

"Mina," said Leonore, in a voice of gentle reproof, "it is useless to dissemble now."

The gipsy queen frowned sternly and appeared to be about making an angry retort, but, checking herself hastily, she motioned to Leonore to follow her a few paces away from the tribe, in order to be out of their hearing.

"Now, Leonore," said Mina, taking the fair girl's hand affectionately, "you must explain to me. What is the meaning of these things with which you reproach me?"

Poor Leonore shuddered to be thus in contact with one whom she had heard denounced as a murdress.

So little, too, were her sensations disguised that Mina at once remarked them.

"You shudder, Leonore," she said. "And wherefore? You have heard—"

"That your hands are stained with blood? Yes," added Leonore.

"And you believe it?"

"How can I think otherwise? Have I not been condemned to death—death by the hands of the hangman, and all through the fatal resemblance which exists between us?"

"You!" exclaimed Mina, in amazement. "Is it possible that you were taken for me?"

"It is. Nay, you must have known that. It was from your wood hut that I was taken prisoner by that odious Jonathan Wild."

"True."

"And you knew why I was taken. You well knew that it was yourself they sought."

"I did," said Mina. "I grant you all this, but make some small allowances. Startling as the like-ness between us is, I knew that there was sufficient difference for them to discover their error before proceeding to extremities, as indeed you see they have done."

"They have not."

"What do you mean?"

"That I could not establish my identity."

Mina's face brightened with satisfaction as Leonore spoke.

"Then, since you are here," she said, "I must judge that there was a second trial, resulting in an acquittal."

"No."

"How, then, are you here?"

"There is such a terrible confusion in my ideas upon this matter, and everything connected with those fatal moments, that I can scarcely remember now. But the verdict of the former trial—your trial—stood good. The sentence was not to be altered simply because you contrived—by witchcraft, they pretend—to escape from the prison after condemnation."

"But how come you here now?" demanded the gipsy queen, with nervous impatience.

"I was rescued from the scaffold."

"The scaffold!" exclaimed Mina, with a shudder.

"Ay. The very rope which was to strangle me was around my neck, tightening in the last fatal embrace, when his ever ready hand severed it and bore me from the spot."

"Whose? To whom do you allude?" asked the gipsy queen.

"My husband."

"You are married?"

"Yes."

"To whom? Where is your husband now? Why do you leave him?"

"He is here."

"Here?" repeated Mina, looking about her in the greatest amazement.

"Ay. Your people will explain how we came here, for verily I cannot understand why that man should so pursue us with such inveterate hatred."

"Who?"

"Jonathan Wild."

"The thieftaker?"

"Yes."

"Strange! That man is the bane of a hundred lives. His sole pleasure in life would appear to be to prey upon humanity generally. Give me your hand, Leonore."

But Lady Leonore shrank back in unmistakeable horror.

"Do you fear me, Leonore?" asked the gipsy queen.

"No, no."

"Then do you despise me?" she continued, with a frown which gave her beauteous face an expression which was almost demoniacal.

"No, no; believe me," said Leonore.

She felt in her present critical position she could not afford to incur the enmity of so powerful an authority as the queen of that wild vagrant tribe.

Mina looked upon Lady Leonore curiously for several minutes, studying her meditations, which were plainly depicted upon her face.

A furtive glance of doubt and fear which Lady Leonore stole at her at length acquainted the gipsy queen with the state of the case.

Leonore believed her to be guilty of the terrible crime with which she (Leonore) had been charged, and for which she had nearly suffered, and her pure spirit shrank from contamination with a murdress.

"Good. I am glad that it is no worse," murmured the gipsy queen. "I half feared that your aristocratic pride despised the proffered friendship of the Romany."

"No, no," said Leonore hastily. "Believe me, it is not that."

"I know it. You cannot love one whom you believe guilty of the crime of murder."

Leonore silently hung her head.

"Leonore," said the gipsy queen tenderly, "I can but respect you the more for your purity. But, believe me, you judge me wrongly."

Leonore turned away.

"Nay, more," continued Mina the gipsy. "Leonore, I could give you good explanation of all this, but I wish that you should rely upon my word first. Still you disbelieve, you who have suffered so much from false condemnation?"

This appeal won over Leonore upon the instant.

She threw her arms around Mina's neck, and embraced her tenderly.

"Now, Leonore," said Mina, "take me to your husband. I will give you an explanation to chase away all your doubts at the earliest."

* * * * *

While this interview was taking place between Leonore and the gipsy queen Red Ralph had received an unwelcome visitor.

This was no other than Jonas, the chief of the tribe.

Jonas, it will be borne in mind, had excellent reason for remembering his prisoner.

"So-ho!" he ejaculated. "At last you are in my power again, and I can cry quits for that little matter."

"Jonas!" cried Ralph.

"You have hit it, Red Ralph," said the gipsy, "and now you may tremble as much as you like."

"Red Ralph doesn't know what that word means," said the highwayman proudly.

"Don't you? Then you will shortly experience a novel sensation, for I mean to give you good cause for the greatest fears, my friend. You are here surrounded by my people, and I have but to say the word to them, and a dozen are ready to—"

Here he drew his finger across his throat with dreadful significance.

"If I find it suits my pleasure better, Red Ralph," he continued, "I may sell you to government. Yes, perhaps that would be the better plan; for, with such handsome rewards as are offered for your apprehension, it would be but an expensive luxury to cut your wizen here. Yes, Ralph, still your fears—you shall die without bloodshed. The Romany never forgives!"

"Liar!" exclaimed a voice at the entrance.

They looked up and perceived Mina and Leonore standing upon the threshold together.

CHAPTER LXXIV.

MINA THE GIPSY—A ROMANY'S VENGEANCE—RED RALPH IN A CRITICAL POSITION—JONAS FRUSTRATED—RALPH'S SUCCESS—JONAS MEDITATES MISCHIEF—THE VOW—"LEONORE! LEONORE!"

MINA, holding Leonore by the hand, advanced into the room.

"Mina!" exclaimed Jonas in a tone of angry surprise.

"Yes," answered Mina, "It is I, Jonas, and it is I who forbid you to raise a finger against that man."

"And by what right do you presume to dictate to me?"

"The right! Would you have me name it before all?"

"Yes; speak out."

Mina's eyes flashed fire for an instant, and she was about to say something hastily when she checked herself, and, looking upon the gipsy with a glance which he could not encounter, said in a low and impressive tone—

"No, Jonas, I will not say by what right. You are heated, and you forget yourself at present."

"You—that is—it is false. Say now why you thus dare presume to dictate to me."

"Dare! Presume!" uttered Mina. "You are insolent."

Jonas bit his lip and was silent.

"You well comprehend my meaning," continued Mina significantly;" but I will not touch on that subject. I simply assert my authority by the right which your spirit will best comprehend."

"And that is?"

"The right of might."

"Indeed," said Jonas quickly, as if he had not expected this answer. "That is a right which I can't acknowledge."

"It needs not your acknowledgment. All here know it, and none will *presume*—the word is yours—to cross my wishes."

"If your wishes mean the escape of that man, you are mistaken."

"Not so."

"I swear it. This night he will be delivered over to justice."

Leonore uttered a faint cry of alarm.

"Nay, fear nothing, Leonore," said Mina. "This fellow forgets himself."

"But I shan't forget him, I promise you," said Red Ralph.

"You hear him," said Jonas; "he threatens me."

"And you—do you not threaten him?"

"Mina," said the gipsy doggedly," you know that the Romany never forgives an injury."

"And I fear no Romany's threats or boasts," said Ralph.

"Hush," said Mina to Red Ralph in a low voice. "Do not taunt them any further, or you will set the tribe against you, and then my utmost efforts to save you must inevitably fail."

But the quick eye of Jonas caught the glance exchanged between Mina and their prisoner.

"See you that?" he cried triumphantly, addressing the few members of the tribe who had now arrived upon the spot. "Mina our queen is in league with the house-dwellers against her own people."

"'Tis false."

"Yes," said Red Ralph quickly. "There is no league, and as for my being a house-dweller, I'm no more deserving that title than yourselves. I dwell in the woods. I rest upon the green turf, and the most part of my time with no better coverlid than the bright heavens above me."

This was a happy thought.

It gained the sympathy of many of the tribe at once.

He was a wanderer—a homeless vagrant like themselves—and therefore one of them.

Red Ralph at once perceived the advantage he had gained by this chance shot, and was not slow to follow it up.

"And now," he said, addressing two or three of the tribe who were conversing together in undertones, "do you know why I have earned this man's enmity?"

"Because you have proved yourself the foe of my people," said Jonas quickly.

"You lie!"

Jonas advanced threateningly, but Red Ralph turned sharply upon him and he stopped short.

That slim supple figure looked exceedingly dangerous when at all animated.

"No," said Red Ralph. "He lies, and he knows it. When have I proved the Romany's foe? I have ever loved the gipsy as a brother. He has suffered the same wrongs as myself—the same persecutions at the hands of the house-dwellers, and the similarity of our woes has created sympathy—sympathy, love."

There was a rough eloquence about him as he spoke these words which at once secured the favour of his rude auditors.

"He speaks false," said Jonas. "He would sell our whole tribe if it but suited his purpose."

"Of that I leave you to judge," rejoined Red Ralph immediately. "This man would surely sell me to our common enemy—the law!"

"That's true," said the gipsy, with ill-concealed malice. "I would, for vengeance!"

"You lie in your teeth!" said Red Ralph. "Vengeance has no point in it. It is for the cursed gold of the thrice-cursed house-dwellers."

A cheer burst from the lips of the gipsies.

It was spontaneous, and plainly showed how their sympathies were; for they had evidently been suppressing them before, out of consideration for their leader Jonas.

But they could not but admire one who spoke with such virulence against their common enemy the house-dwellers.

Jonas bit his lip until the blood came, and was silent.

He saw that it was useless for him to struggle now. All that he could now urge would be of little avail, and so he was silent.

"What do you desire?" asked one of the gipsies of Ralph.

"Simply to go free," said Red Ralph. "Not that I would quit a people whom I would fain love as brethren, but I have been wounded here."

"Wounded?"

"Ay, in my affections."

"How so?"

"I was brought hither in friendship, and when I wished to depart I found myself a prisoner."

"You are at liberty to leave us when you will," said Mina, with a glance of tenderness, which Red Ralph well knew how to interpret.

The love which the highwayman bore his wife he felt was almost shared with the gipsy queen.

Perhaps it was simply a feeling of warm gratitude for the signal service rendered.

Perhaps the strange likeness which she bore to Leonore had something to do with it.

Now he did not wish to depart.

But Mina, perceiving with a glance the sudden change in his determination, gave him a look so full of meaning that it could not be misunderstood.

This woman spoke as eloquently with her rich dark eyes as most men with words.

He read in that glance that there was danger in remaining there—that the volatile nature of the Zingari might destroy him to-morrow, as it had preserved him to-day.

"Come, then, Leonore," he said. "Let us be going."

"Nay, my sister," said the gipsy queen to Leonore, "I think that you will be safer here with me."

Leonore would have preferred to accompany Red Ralph, but he in an instant comprehended the benefit of the arrangement Mina proposed.

Together they formed a people, and were some protection for the helpless houseless girl.

He was but a hunted felon, and could not tell what minute would drag him from her arms.

He knew, too, that he could always trace the pilgrimages of the gipsies, while he should lose all traces of Leonore alone.

"Yes, Leonore," he said, clasping her tenderly in his arms, "what Mina says is for the best. Alone I could offer you but a sorry protection. Here you are

safe from molestation, at all events. And now, my love, I go to busy myself in your behalf. I shall ere long be at Glyde House once more. I shall assert your rights. I shall denounce the author of your wrongs—"

"My mother!" said Leonore.

"Your mother!" exclaimed Red Ralph. "Is it possible that a mother can thus treat her child?"

"No matter, Ralph," said Leonore. "We can do nothing."

"Nothing, say you?"

"No. Remember, I beseech you, that, no matter what wrongs we may suffer, she is still my mother—our mother!"

"Angel of mercy and gentleness!" exclaimed the highwayman, embracing her rapturously, "pleading for your destroyer. But fear nothing. Let time and her crimes bring their own punishment; and they will. Never fear me. Farewell!"

A last long lingering embrace, a parting glance with the gipsy queen, and Red Ralph, the captain of the Yellow Band, was gone.

Once more he was separated from his wife!

And now, when would they meet again?

Leonore fell sobbing on Mina's bosom, and was led from the spot.

Presently Jonas the gipsy looked up as if awakened from a dream.

"Gone!" he murmured aloud. "Is it possible? And he was here—here surrounded by our people; and yet he gets away! Death! he must bear a charmed life. Some spell encircles him, which only one versed in the hidden mysteries could fathom. It is useless to attempt to harm him. Strange—and how I hate him! Oh! how bitterly! And I could have crushed him here before me. And why did I not do it? Why? Because he cowed me with a glance of his eye. It must be some cursed jugglery by which he charmed me—else I am a coward! No, no, not that. It is well known that Jonas the gipsy never feared to meet any man living in mortal strife. Could I but reach him, though! Let me think. He loves this girl—this pale-faced child of the house-dwellers. I must reach him through her, then. Good! Thus I shall revenge myself with one blow, for Mina loves her too—ay, and loves her well, or I am deceived. So be it. Leonore, your life's in danger! Look to it!"

CHAPTER LXXV.

"HEY FOR THE ROAD!"— A NOVEL ROBBERY — THE DEVIL ON HORSEBACK — AN OLD FRIEND APPEARS — THE ROBBER IN JEOPARDY — THE BITERS BIT — LYNCH LAW — JUDGED — CONDEMNED—EXECUTED.

RED RALPH was no sooner clear of the ruined house in Westminster than he procured a sturdy and fleet horse and dashed off for Epping Forest.

Here he encountered Walters and six chosen men, all mounted, and prepared for anything that was desperate and adventurous.

They greeted the arrival of their beloved leader with a cheer.

"Well, Walters," said Ralph, "and what information got you from Leytonstone respecting the matter of which I spoke to you?"

"About old Skinner, the steward, you mean, captain?"

"Ay."

"Everything. The most complete information we could wish."

"That's glorious!"

"Ay. He has sent on a despatch to Master Taverner, the maltster, to be prepared with his rent for to-day. He says that he will arrive towards even-

[THE DEATH-STRUGGLE IN THE LONE HUT.]

ing. It seems that he has to collect for miles around the country to-day."

"Good. Our golden goose will be all the better stuffed."

"So say I. But, captain, Master Taverner did two of our men a good turn lately—Jasper and Wilton, you know, who were so badly hurt at Tyburn in the skirmish. He took them in and had them nursed for nearly a week."

"Then he must be rewarded somehow."

"I knew you would say so."

"Think it over, Walters, and suggest some means of doing it."

"I will. By-the-bye, captain, another word re-

specting old Skinner before he arrives, which will not be long hence. He travels armed."

"Armed? A riding whip and a blunderbuss, I suppose."

"A splendid pair of holster pistols, of the latest make, I am told he carries."

"Indeed?"

"Ay. And beautiful weapons they are, too, from report. Something quite new. Go off with the lightest touch, and never miss fire."

"You rouse my curiosity, Walters. I must have these pistols."

"But you must be very careful in getting them, captain."

"Never fear, Walt"—

He stopped abruptly, and looked up.

"What is it?"

"Some one coming along the road. Don't you hear? There."

"No, captain. It can't be Skinner. It is an hour before his time."

"No matter, we must see. We cannot be sure to an hour with a man like Skinner."

Red Ralph gave the word, and in a trice his six followers had disappeared.

Walters rode up to a turn in the road to scout, and came back full gallop.

"You're right, captain," he cried as he advanced. "It is somebody, and it is our man, too."

"Skinner?"

"Yes."

"Good. Take my horse."

Saying which, he sprang from the saddle and gave the reins to Walters.

"You are going to do this alone, captain?"

"Alone."

"And afoot?"

"As you see. Begone. He's turned the angle of the road."

"He hasn't observed us."

Red Ralph darted nimbly behind a huge oak—a forest patriarch of gigantic size—and waited until his destined prey arrived.

Unsuspicious of evil, Mr. Ephraim Skinner, steward and collector of the Weirton estate, rode along at a gentle trot.

Then, as if fate was playing into the hands of the lawless men who meditated his ruin, Mr. Ephraim Skinner drew rein as he passed the spot where Red Ralph was hiding, and proceeded at a walk.

No sooner had he passed than Red Ralph sprang lightly from behind the tree, and darted after the rider.

With three enormous strides he had reached the horse's flank.

Then he made a desperate bound, and landed upon the horse's back behind Mr. Skinner.

"Murder!" cried Skinner.

"Silence, you old fool!" said Red Ralph, grasping him round the middle.

"It must be old—ahem—himself," said the old man in an agony of despair. "Please, sir—"

"Silence!" said Red Ralph, quietly transferring the renowned pistols from the holsters to his own belt. "Give me your money-bags!"

"Money-bags?" gasped Mr. Skinner, with a faint shriek.

"Ay. You need not echo my words. Give me every halfpenny you have about you, and without loss of time, or you shall suffer for it, I promise you."

Old Skinner endeavoured to turn and look at the face of the man who made this fearful attack.

But Red Ralph squeezed him so tightly as to nearly deprive him of breath, and butted him in the face with his head, inflicting such injuries upon him that he roared aloud for mercy.

But while Red Ralph was thus busily engaged with Mr. Ephraim Skinner, the arrival of three individuals upon the scene of action who had not before appeared led to an exciting little incident, which we shall relate.

Red Ralph heard some one approaching, but he deemed that it was Walters or some of his followers, and he simply proceeded calmly enough in his interesting labour of clearing out Mr. Skinner.

With a stroke of his knife, previously flourished before the terror-stricken steward's eyes, he severed the strap which secured a weighty bag of coin to his belt.

This he threw to the ground, and it was immediately picked up and secured by one of the three new-comers.

At the same instant another of them seized Red Ralph by the right leg, and, with a sudden push, succeeded in tumbling him off the horse on the other side.

So tightly, however, did the highwayman hold Mr. Skinner that both went over together, and, unfortunately for the steward, Red Ralph was uppermost.

Then, like a pack of hungry wolves upon their prey, the three men, without a word, fell upon the highwayman, pinning him to the ground.

One of them especially appeared to exercise a deal of unnecessary violence in his efforts to secure Red Ralph.

Indeed, so marked was this that of the three the highwayman turned his attention to him alone.

By a powerful effort he succeeded in disengaging one of his arms, and delivered his enemy a blow in the face that cooled his ardour for a moment.

"Ah!" cried the man, with an oath. "You shall repent that blow, Red Ralph. It shall be wiped out in blood."

"Yours be it, then," cried the highwayman, struggling like a second Hercules.

"No. Yours, I swear."

"Ha, ha!" cried Red Ralph, getting a glimpse of his brutal adversary for the first time. "I know you now, JONATHAN WILD!"

True it was.

Jonathan Wild the thieftaker had once more turned up at this critical juncture.

"Ah! You know me, do you? Well, then, look upon me, for you won't have many more chances. I am going to kill you now."

"You have grown tired of hanging, then, Jonathan?" said Ralph.

"No," said the thieftaker. "I shall hang you afterwards, before the breath is out of your body, just by way of keeping my word."

Ralph struggled violently.

But what could he accomplish at such a terrible disadvantage and opposed to three stalwart men?

The thieftaker took a pistol from his belt, clicked the lock, and examined the priming with cruel deliberation.

Red Ralph saw all this, and he saw also the motive with which it was done, but he would not give the thieftaker the satisfaction of witnessing the fears which he could not but feel at the critical nature of his position.

Of a sudden, then, his struggles ceased, and he lay quietly upon his back, closing his eyes.

"Brought him down at last," said Jonathan Wild, triumphantly. "At length, then, you really fear me, Red Ralph? You feel, I know, that your last hour—your last minute—of life has come."

But Red Ralph did not reply.

The thieftaker then, kneeling upon Red Ralph's chest, to cause him as much pain as possible, deliberately poised a pistol over his face, covering his right eye.

"No, no," he said. "That would do the job too quickly. I want a little amusement with it."

He changed his aim and pointed at the prostrate highwayman's cheek.

"Good bye, Ralph."

There was a double report.

One of the men who held Red Ralph rolled over upon the ground, bleeding in the face.

Simultaneously with this, the pistol which the thieftaker held was struck from his grasp, and the hand which had grasped it was wounded slightly.

Then there was a rush and a scramble in the bushes, and in much less time than we have taken to record the fact the lieutenant of the Yellow Band and his six followers were down upon the thieftakers.

And now the positions were completely reversed.

With the wounded man they did not choose to busy themselves, but Jonathan Wild and the other were kicked and buffeted in a way which would have soon put an end to the existence of both had it continued much longer.

"Nay, nay," said Red Ralph, interposing. "Spare them."

"Spare them?" cried Walters. "You intercede for the man who was within an ace of taking your life but half a minute since?"

"Nay, but we should be brutes of their own level if we took advantage of their helplessness."

"A high-flown reason, with which I certainly cannot agree, captain."

"Nor we, either," cried the Yellow Boys.

And, as if to prove how thoroughly they were opposed to Red Ralph's idea, they thumped and kicked Jonathan Wild until his knees refused to support him.

Upon searching the thieftaker's man they found a coil of rope in his pocket.

"Hullo!" said one of the Yellow Boys. "What was this for?"

"To string him up with," said the man, pointing maliciously to the captain of the Yellow Band.

"Say you so?" cried Walters. "Then you have spoken your own doom. I swear it."

His meaning was caught at once by the Yellow Boys, who assented to this suggestion with loud acclamations.

One end of the rope was thrown over the branch of a tree and made into a running noose.

This was placed around the neck of the shivering wretch, and the other end was held by one of the Yellow Boys, ready to do summary justice upon him when the word should be given.

"Your turn is next," said Walters to the thieftaker.

"Let us bind him to this tree here, that he may see his mate go off first," said one of the Yellow Boys.

This suggestion perfectly suited their present humour, and it was therefore greeted with a loud cry of assent.

Jonathan Wild was instantly dragged to a tree, and, in spite of his most frantic struggles, pinioned and bound securely to it.

"Now, then," said Walters.

"Stay!" said Red Ralph. "This is nothing less than murder, and I oppose it with all my power."

"In all else, captain, you shall have every consideration," said Walters, "but in this we are determined. Are we not, men?"

"Ay, ay," cried the robbers, with one voice.

"Nay. But hear me, I entreat of you," said Red Ralph, who was now thoroughly alarmed for the miserable wretch.

"Captain," said Walters, "you must not oppose the men further. They do but justice upon them. An eye for an eye, a tooth for a tooth. He would have hung you with but little remorse, I can assure you."

"I believe it."

"Enough, captain. That is his death-warrant, then."

The Yellow Boys arranged themselves solemnly in a line and each took a hold of the cord, that the terrible deed of retribution now in contemplation might not be the work of an individual.

"Now," said the lieutenant, "say, men, has this fellow earned the death which we are about to give him?"

"He has."

"And you think sincerely that you do but justice in killing him?"

"We do. Justice, and justice alone."

"Then Heaven have mercy upon the wretched man's soul!"

A deep and solemn "Amen!" came from the lips of all.

In vain now did the captain of the Yellow Band attempt to assert his authority.

Upon ordinary occasions Red Ralph was more absolute than the most despotic of monarchs, but now his remonstrances were unheeded by all.

The enmity of the men to the officers of the law had been deepened by the unnecessary harshness with which they had been treated previous to the fracas at Tyburn.

Foremost, too, amongst their tormentors had been that human vulture, Jonathan Wild.

And now they had him in their power.

"My men," said Red Ralph. "Believe me that you will repent this deed until the last day of your lives."

"No matter, captain."

"No," said Walters. "We do but slay these men in self-defence. There is no other way of securing them, and we are not safe while they live. You are not safe."

"Nay," exclaimed Red Ralph, shudderingly. "I wash my hands of the matter. Do not mix me up in it, I beseech you."

The six men stood in a row, impatient to execute Lynch-law justice upon their victim.

Jonathan Wild looked on, frozen with terror, the most abject picture of suffering anticipation which one can conceive.

"Now," said Walters.

"Stay!" cried Red Ralph, imploringly. "Hold, I command you. Ah! How terrible is this!"

The six men dragged together at the rope, and the unhappy wretch dangled in the air!

The fate he had intended for Red Ralph had recoiled upon his own head, and the would-be hangman was himself hanged!

CHAPTER LXXVI.

MR. SKINNER—HIS ESCAPE—A PLEASANT COMPANION IN PECULIAR LODGINGS—THE STORM— A GHASTLY SPECTACLE.

WHILE the tragic episode which we have just related was taking place Mr. Ephraim Skinner, the steward and collector of the Weirton estate, had quietly sneaked off unobserved.

But not alone had he contrived to make good his retreat. His sack of money, which had fallen to the ground during the struggle between Red Ralph and the thieftakers, he had also managed to secure and bear with him.

Unfortunately, he could not contrive to procure a horse, or rather he did not care to risk waiting longer, and so he proceeded on foot upon his way.

He knew the country very well upon ordinary occasions, but the fright that he had suffered had so unsettled him for the present that he wandered on at hazard.

Presently, when he stopped short to reconnoitre, he found himself in a part of the forest which was quite unknown to him.

This was an unpleasant discovery, to say the least. Darkness would be shortly coming on, and then he would possibly have to pass the night in the forest, a prospect which was anything but inspiring.

However, he had got his money, and that was some consolation.

He hugged his beloved bags to him, and started off to reconnoitre in every direction, in the hope that he should find some leading path.

Vain hope!

Mr. Epraham Skinner ran about until his legs ached most painfully, but not the faintest trace of such a path could be discovered.

Presently the heavens grew a little foggy, and gave Mr. Skinner a foretaste of the darkness which would now shortly ensue.

How could he hope to survive the terrors of a night in Epping Forest, and alone?

Every expedient which could be imagined was thought of by Mr. Skinner, but of course unavailingly.

In vain did he rack his fevered brain. There was but one remedy for his woes.

Night had set in with all its disagreeables, and, as if to enhance them, a low drizzling rain began to fall, which very soon wetted Mr. Ephraim Skinner to the skin.

The atmosphere was sultry and oppressive to a degree, and Mr. Skinner's coat streamed like a laundress's wash-tub.

Presently there was a low rumbling noise in the heavens of distant thunder, and down came the rain immediately after in a deluge.

"This is pleasant!" muttered Mr Ephraim Skinner, with grim satire "Devilish pleasant, 'pon my soul!"

Then, by way of amusement, he began cursing the authors of his woes.

And volumes of anathemas were rained down upon the devoted heads of the bold Yellow Boys—harder than the waters of the heavens rained down upon the curser himself.

Mr. Skinner had contracted a bad habit at the desk of stooping.

A kind of chronic lumbago had prevented him bending his back; but his neck was bent so much forward as to make it almost at right angles with his body.

This left a nice opening between his shirt collar and his flesh, down which poured the rain in the most afflicting manner.

"Oh! oh-h-h! my eye!" cried Mr. Skinner. "Ain't I full of water—oh-h-h! It's a regular bath, and shan't I catch cold after this! And oh! the lumbago. Gah-h!—it's trickling down my stockings into my boots now."

He suddenly assumed a perpendicular position, and out poured the water from his neck like a water-spout.

"This is really too awful!" said Mr. Skinner. "I must find some shelter, or I shall die of cold and damp."

In front of him was the very thing. Apparently an immense tree. Apparently we say, for it was so terribly dark that he could see nothing immediately in front of him with anything like distinctness.

"If I could only sit down for a little!" murmured Mr. Skinner, for his poor old bones began to ache most dreadfully. "The ground here is woefully damp, and that would be death. If I could only climb up this tree. Now I know I haven't climbed a tree for forty years. I wonder if I really could manage it."

Just then something moved on the other side of the tree, and sent Mr. Skinner's heart leaping to his mouth with fright.

"Good gracious!" he whispered hoarsely, "what's that?"

He wiped away the perspiration from his forehead and looked about, but nothing could he see.

Then he settled that it must only be his imagination.

But now he was more than ever determined to climb the tree and rest upon its broad and powerful branches until daylight.

Some large bunion-looking notches in the bark, and a few young sprigs favoured the old man's ascent, and with a deal of panting and blowing he succeeded in reaching the first floor—that is, the lowest branch.

"Pheugh!" he cried, holding on with his left hand, whilst with his right he pressed his aching sides. "Oh! what a terrible job this is! And what will the servants at the hall say? They'll think that I'm lost, or dead, or something. And won't they rejoice? curse them! And curse those roving vagabonds, and those others—the villains who prey upon their fellow-wolves. What would I not give to be face to face with them in the witness-box in the Old Bailey! However, I am amply revenged upon them in having rescured my money. They have got my horse, and my holster pistols, it is true, but they both belong to my Lord Weirton, and he must find me more. But the money; well, they are our mutual properties, since I deduct my little percentage before accounting for it. *What was that?* Oh! how dreadful this darkness is! If it were only a little light."

As if in compliance with his desire, the heavens were at that moment brilliantly illuminated with a flash of lightning.

Mr. Ephraim Skinner bobbed down his head affrightedly, as his eyes encountered the sudden glare, and he perceived something which at once aroused his curiosity.

Some dark object was there, beneath a branch of the same tree, but upon the further side.

"Strange," thought Mr. Skinner. "I didn't see anything before."

But there was nothing so very remarkable in this after all, for until the lightning had come he had not been able to see anything whatever.

Whatever it was that stood beneath that branch, it appeared to possessed a strange fascination for the benighted steward and collector of the Weirton estate, for from the moment that his eye had been caught he never once removed his gaze from the spot.

He was anxiously awaiting a second flash of lightning for further information.

Thanks to the boisterous nature of the night, he had not long to wait.

A lightning flash—more terribly grand than any which had preceded it—revealed the object of Mr. Skinner's curiosity a little more distinctly.

But even now he could resolve nothing clearly.

A strange sensation, however, took possession of the curious Mr. Skinner.

A kind of creeping sensation, similar to that of having an insect crawling up one's arm.

He felt that his heart began to beat rather more quickly than before.

He began to grow rather warmer, and presently he felt that he was perspiring violently.

And why?

Simply because this time the lightning had revealed that the object which the steward had perceived did not stand beneath the tree, as he had at first supposed, but that it *dangled from the branch!*

Mr. Skinner, without having anything definite in the way of fears or anticipations, trembled violently.

"I think I will—I will—get down," he muttered, with an endeavour to convince himself that he was not afraid of anything, and that he simply desired to pursue his journey in the storm.

But although he wished himself from the spot—and of this there could be no possible doubt—he felt drawn towards the further branch of the tree by a kind of mesmeric fascination.

And there, stretched out along the broad branch of the oak, he lay with his dilated eyes fixed upon the now invisible object of his curiosity.

Fully ten minutes he lay there, never speaking, for he was past that point now.

Never scarcely breathing, until the forest gloom was again dispelled for an instant by the electric fluid.

Presently it came.

There was a terrific crash, as if some mighty planet had fallen from its sphere, and cracked our globe from pole to pole.

And Mr. Skinner watched with more anxiety—a greater and more feverish interest than ever.

The object, he could now plainly see, was suspended from the tree by a cord fastened round the branch.

"Oh!" cried Mr. Skinner in an agony of fear. "Oh! horror, horror! Oh! horror!"

Nature could no longer sustain this fearful shock.

A fearful and prolonged cry burst from his lips, and his senses forsook him.

He still lay there clutching at the branch of the fatal oak, but even the loudest peals of thunder failed to arouse him from his deathlike swoon.

CHAPTER LXXVII.

RED RALPH AND THE BAND—RETRIBUTION—THE BLASTED OAK—A SOLEMN OFFICE—THE GRAVE —THE RESTORATION TO LIFE.

THE fury of the storm was spent.

With one tremendous peal of thunder and a lurid glare of lightning the deluging rains were over.

In that part of the country some of the inhabitants declared that a thunder-bolt had fallen in the forest.

The precise spot no one could venture to fix, but several declared that it had fallen.

A deliciously cool temperature succeeded the sultry heat, and the stars came out in brilliant array.

Red Ralph pushed aside the thick foliage which had grown apace during the long time it had been undisturbed by the Yellow Band, and stepped into the glade, followed closely by Walters and the six men who had been with them earlier in the evening.

"It is a glorious night after the storm," said the former.

"It is, captain," said Walters. "The elements have had a rare time of it all to themselves while it lasted."

Red Ralph walked on moodily for a little way.

Something disturbed him, and his followers refrained from breaking in upon his meditations, with that singular consideration which always characterised this rough and lawless band in the treatment of their leader.

"Walters," said Ralph.

"Well, captain."

"Come here," said Red Ralph. "Walk beside me."

The lieutenant was by his leader's side in an instant, and silently awaited his further speech.

For some distance they continued in silence, as if Red Ralph had grown suddenly absent, and had forgotten his previous words.

"I am here, captain."

"Ah! yes, Walters," said Red Ralph, "I am out of spirits, Walters. I feel ill at ease."

"I perceive it."

"And would you know the cause of that, Walters?" asked Red Ralph.

"Ay, tell me, captain."

"That awful deed has shocked my nervous system."

"What?"

"The mur—the execution of that unhappy man this evening."

"Never, captain!"

"Ay, but it has, Walters," said Red Ralph, with a shudder, which he struggled vainly to repress. "To-night I have received a shock which I feel will last me for the remainder of my life."

"Surely not, captain," said Walters, with brotherly tenderness, mingled with respect. "Believe me, it should never have happened had I thought that it would have caused you one moment's pain. The lives of Wild's whole carrion crew were not worth a twinge of remorse—not the faintest, believe me."

"Walters," said Red Ralph in a tone of solemnity, "in all our unlawful and sinful doings there has been a kind of excuse—something to palliate the nature of the wrong inflicted. Not an excuse perhaps of any solidity, but at any rate something that was sufficiently tangible to offer an excuse to ourselves."

"Granted."

"Hence the absence of remorse which has ever characterised us and our Yellow Band."

"True. And has not this some excuse? Do not even your qualms of conscience disappear when you reflect that the deed perpetrated by our men and myself—and in which you have had no hand whatever—is simply reduced to a matter of necessity?"

"Necessity?"

"Ay."

"Where is the necessity, pray?"

"It was but a matter of self-defence. Had we not arrived at the moment we did you would have occupied the place which the knave himself has far more worthily filled."

"Vain and false reasoning!"

"Not so."

"It is, Walters," said Red Ralph solemnly. "And you feel it to be so, Walters, in spite of these words which you utter, merely to disposess me of my sadness."

"No, no."

"I appreciate the effort, and am grateful for it, believe me," said Red Ralph, pressing the lieutenant's hand. "But let us not attempt to deceive each other or ourselves. Hunger may excuse robbery, but no excuse whatever can be allowed for murder!"

The word had an ugly sound, and the speaker shuddered in a way which communicated a shiver to the lieutenant himself.

For some distance further they proceeded in silence.

Presently Red Ralph branched out of the main path to a narrower footway upon their left.

"Captain," said Walters, stopping short. "Let us keep to the open way. Some fresh game may be stirring, and—and—"

"No," said Red Ralph. "You know that that is not very likely so soon after the storm. Come on, or, if you would rather, I will go on my way alone, but I intend to take this path."

"As you will. I go with you wherever you lead—into the jaws of death itself."

They did not exchange another word. The path was so narrow that they had to proceed in single file along it, Red Ralph leading the way.

He was the first to emerge from it.

He drew back suddenly, with a cry of wonder.

"Gracious powers!" he exclaimed. "What is this?"

The fatal tree which had served as the gallows for the doomed follower of Jonathan Wild was razed to the ground.

The lightning had struck and charred it up as if it had been a piece of tinder.

Close by the tree lay a looking object, burnt and grim.

Red Ralph silently pointed it out to the lieutenant.

"See there," he said. "We have defiled that noble tree by bringing it to such a use, and the God of storms has destroyed those fatal traces of our crimes. It is a fearful lesson this, Walters!"

The lieutenant was not a whit less impressed than his leader by the awful occurrence, but he said nothing.

Red Ralph passed his hand nervously over his eyes, and with his other pointed to the charred corpse of the constable who had met his fate at their hands.

The men understood without a word what was meant by this gesture, and they silently proceeded to carry out the instructions conveyed.

Two drew their swords and lopped off some branches of an adjacent tree, and proceeded hastily to fasten them into a litter.

One of the men who was tearing some twigs from a bush suddenly called to his comrades to come to his assistance.

"What is it?" asked Walters.

"See here, lieutenant," they cried. "What is this?"

Ralph and Walters went up, and there they saw a second body lying half buried in the foliage.

It was Mr. Ephraim Skinner, steward and collector of the Weirton estate.

"Take him up," said Red Ralph, after an oppressive silence, which had lasted full five minutes. "Gently. Let us at least pay what remains of the poor miserly old man some respect."

The bag of money was still tightly clenched in the old man's hand, and one the robbers endeavoured to draw it away.

"Let it be," said the captain of the Yellow Band. "Nay, I command you. Let us bury in one grave all traces of this night's dreadful work."

The men yielded the point with a faint murmur, and what remained of Ephraim Skinner was placed upon the litter beside the body of the constable.

Then they formed a solemn procession and retreated in the direction they had come, Red Ralph and the lieutenant holding back the bushes for them as they advanced with their fatal burthen.

"Set it down here," said Red Ralph, pointing to a mound of earth. "And now you know what to do. In Heaven's name, let us complete it at once and begone. I stifle."

As they again raised the litter the corpse of the constable rolled accidentally from the litter into its last resting place, the ditch.

"Now for the other," said Red Ralph, "and may their immortal parts meet with more mercy!"

The litter was raised again, but this time the men dropped it with a cry of alarm.

The second dead man had moved.

"Mercy! mercy!" cried Mr. Ephraim Skinner. "Have pity upon a poor miserable old sinner, I pray you."

"What!" exclaimed Red Ralph. "Is it possible, Mr. Skinner?"

"Yes, sir," groaned the steward. "Have mercy, I beseech you. I am an old man, noble gentlemen —old enough to be your father, your grandfather. Take my gold, every farthing I possess, but oh! do not doom me to so fearful a death!"

The Yellow Boys were all dumbfounded at this sudden restoration to life, and, to do them justice, rejoiced most heartily at it.

"Fear nothing, old man," said Red Ralph. "You shall not be harmed."

"Thanks, thanks—a thousand thanks!"

And, in an excess of gratitude, he held out his darling money-bag to Red Ralph.

"No, no, old man," said Red Ralph. "Keep your money. I have but one thing to ask of you."

"Name it, oh! name it."

"That you will keep your own counsel upon this night's doings."

"I swear it," said Skinner, fervently.

CHAPTER LXXVIII.

JONAS PLAYS TRAITOR—THE MEETING OF TWO WORTHIES — THE MINIATURE — THE RUINED HOUSE IN WESTMINSTER—THE HUNCHBACK'S RETALIATION—THE MEETING WITH LEONORE —"MERCY! SAVE ME FROM THAT MAN!"

WE now quit Red Ralph and his Yellow Band for a while to take a glance at the doings of another personage in our narrative, who, although he has not hitherto played a very prominent part in it, has become so mixed up in the adventures of two of our leading characters as to necessitate some portion of our present labours being devoted more especially to his movements.

In a word, this individual is none other than Jonas the gipsy.

The fiery blood of the Zingari boiled for revenge upon Red Ralph, who had so contrived to overreach him.

To accomplish this he now could think of but one plan—a plan diabolical and unscrupulous, born of the devilish cunning of the revengeful gipsy.

Leonore was to be the victim of his fiendlike contrivances.

Thus he could strike with one blow his hated enemy, the captain of the Yellow Band, and Mina.

Against the latter he now cherished the most violent animosity.

She had thwarted him on the eve of a brilliant stroke of business, and humiliated him before the tribe and Red Ralph.

And therefore she should drain the cup of humiliation to the dregs, if it lay in his power to bring it about.

In the meantime Lady Glyde was by no means idle.

The search for Leonore was still prosecuted by her ladyship with the utmost vigilance.

All London had been ransacked, and yet no traces of her could be discovered.

Jonas the gipsy now could no longer contain himself.

The sight of Leonore maddened him, and for many days he absented himself from the tribe.

While in the metropolis, or in any of the adjacent outskirts, the gipsy not unfrequently put up at a low inn in Whitefriars, the resort of the vilest of the vile—thieves, rogues, and sharpers.

Jonas had a business connection here.

His size and his bullying propensities procured him the respect of the ruffians he met here, and also got him employment for his own particular abilities.

For instance, young men of doubtful courage, who had some little affair of honour upon their hands (and these matters were of very frequent occurrence in those days), would apply to Jonas with a well-lined purse to get them out of trouble by disabling their destined antagonists upon the eve of the appointed meeting.

Here, too, Jonas, it was whispered, had undertaken a business which, while it stamped him amongst his ruffianly associates as a thoroughly unscrupulous and desperate fellow to oppose in any way, and therefore enhanced their consideration, rendered his life not worth an hour's purchase should justice once secure him.

Jonas had passed two days at this tavern when the landlord introduced a customer to him.

This was Jabez the hunchback and the agent of Lady Glyde in the search for her lost daughter.

Jabez was at his wit's end for means to prosecute the search, and had come to the landlord of the inn for assistance.

"Your servant, sir," said Jonas to the hunchback, smelling a job.

Jabez nodded his acknowledgments of the salutation.

"You have some business with me?"

"I have. This is it. A young lady of good family has left her home—it is feared with some low-born churl—disgrace and ruin hang over the family unless the girl is very speedily recovered."

"I understand you," said Jonas. "And you wish me, then, to—"

"To aid in the search."

"Good."

"That she is in London I am very sure. It only remains for you to tell me her whereabouts, and fifty pounds is yours."

"Do you limit me to time?" demanded the gipsy eagerly.

"No."

"Then you may count upon the job as good as done."

"Very well, but no trickery, mind. I must see her before—"

"Before paying?"

"Yes."

"You shall be fully satisfied of that, believe me."

"I must."

"Good. And now let me have what information you can upon the matter. What is she like?"

"I have her portrait here," said Jabez, tapping his breast pocket. "You shall have it presently. As for information, I cannot give any—that is, any beyond the fact that she is yet in London. With this and her portrait you will have to start on your search."

"Very well."

"Before you accept my business," said the hunchback, "let me tell you that it is no trifling task which you undertake. I have already spent much time and money in it, and have utterly failed to obtain the slightest clue."

"Possibly," said Jonas. "But then I have means of obtaining information which you cannot have."

"You have? Then exert it to the utmost, and receive the reward which I am all eagerness to pay."

"And I am none the less eager to receive, believe me."

"I can believe that. Any information you may gain you can bring at once to that address. I shall then be ready to aid you. But in any case, your reward will be assured of if it is by your means that I am put upon her track."

Jonas took the address and silently read it over.

"You may rely upon me, sir," he said. "Do you mean to pay me anything on account for this job?"

"No."

"Not a fiver?"

"Not the ghost of a stiver," exclaimed the hunchback. "If that's your meaning, you may as well undeceive yourself at once. I am not to be gammoned into anything of that sort, I can promise you."

"Oh! you're not?"

"Not I."

"Now that may be all very well, but you may as well be civil, my friend, or perhaps—"

"Oh! that's it, is it? Now let me tell you, my friend, as you call me—curse your impudence!—that I am not to be bullied by any man."

Jonas the gipsy scowled ferociously and rose to his feet with an ominous gesture.

The hunchback never appeared to notice the movement, but sat still, as if perfectly unconcerned.

Jonas laid a hand upon the hunchback's collar, but the next minute he repented it.

Jabez turned upon the gipsy with a snarl, showing a pair of doglike fangs as his lips parted before his clenched teeth.

With a sudden grip he seized the gipsy's wrist in his huge paw, and shook off the hold upon his collar.

Then he pressed with such violence upon the gipsy that, in order that his arm might not be broken, he was forced to bend to the ground.

"You'll break my arm."

"Down! down!" said the hunchback, livid with passion. "Down! you worm. Down on the ground, or I'll snap the bone like a twig. Down, and grovel in the dust! Beg for mercy!"

The pain was excruciating.

But Jonas had his pride. Sooner than ask for quarter he would have been torn piecemeal.

His body was bent to the ground by the muscular power of the misshapen little Hercules, but his spirit was erect as ever. It could only be humbled to suit his purpose.

"Now get up," said the hunchback, when he had tired of this cruel pastime. "Get up, and grow wiser."

As soon as he was free from that iron grasp Jonas turned savagely upon his antagonist, and would have at once resumed the contest.

Jabez, however, did not choose to continue this—not that he was by any means deficient in courage or confidence in his own powers, but it was a digression from the business in hand.

As the gipsy advanced, therefore, he brought him up short by drawing a pistol from his pocket and presenting it.

"Another step," said the hunchback, "half a step more, and I'll blow you to pieces."

"Put down that pistol," said the gipsy.

Jabez declined, of course, and the gipsy laid his hand on the bell pull.

"Oh!" cried Jabez. "That's it, is it? I warn you, before you make a fool of yourself, that I am prepared for any trick that you may be up to. See here."

Saying which, the hunchback produced a second pistol and a huge bludgeon from his capacious pocket.

"Now sit down," said the hunchback, "and listen to reason."

It was the best argument he could possibly have used with the gipsy, who obeyed without further discussion.

"Now it just strikes me," said the hunchback, "that I am thoroughly deceived in you, or rather that I might have been, but for your precious rascality. You needn't bite your lips and look savage. You see that it hasn't much effect, and has shown me that your boasted power of obtaining information is a villainous fiction, merely invented in the hope of defrauding me by receiving payment in advance."

Controlling himself by an effort, the gipsy replied to this as calmly as his irritation would permit.

"You see, sir," said he "that you press me rather hard. No man likes to be called a rogue and a thief until he has earned the title."

"And you—"

"Haven't yet earned it."

"Oh!"

"Not from you."

"Perhaps not," said Jabez. "At all events, you tried it on."

"No. I only asked for something in advance," said Jonas. "You must know, if you've tried it, that this business is not to be done without some expense."

"True."

"And I only wanted something to go on with."

"And I don't give a penny. Now, do you still accept my job?"

"Yes. Let me see the likeness."

The hunchback took a little ivory miniature from his pocket and laid it before the other.

Jonas half jumped from his seat as his dark eyes glanced upon the picture, and he stifled an half-uttered exclamation as it rose to his lips.

"What's the matter?"

The hunchback had not seen the other's remarkable agitation, or he must have divined the cause of it at once.

Had he not been looking in another direction he might have saved himself at least half of the promised reward for the truant young lady's recovery.

"The matter?" said Jonas, controlling his amazement. "I thought there was some one outside—nothing more."

"And is there?"

"No, I was mistaken, I find. But this girl?"

"This is her portrait. And now before I go and leave it in your hands tell me one thing."

"Willingly."

"You are not deceiving me?"

"In what way?"

"You are not undertaking my mission without any prospect of ultimate success?"

"No," answered Jonas. "I can swear to that if you wish it."

"No," said Jabez. "Your word is as good as your oath for me—both are equally reliable."

The gipsy appeared not to notice the sneer which the tone of the speaker conveyed, and hastened to continue the subject of the miniature.

"In proof of what I say," said Jonas, "I am willing to stake the promised reward against the like amount of yours that not only do I succeed in this business, but that I take you to see her within an hour."

"An hour?"

"Ay."

"Impossible."

"No matter. Do you agree to my terms? If I lose I do this job for nothing."

"I agree, of course," said the hunchback. "But I believe it to be all a farce. But beware how you again deceive me."

"You need not threaten me," said the gipsy. "Come with me now, if you like, and satisfy yourself."

"I will."

But the gipsy appeared in no way disconcerted by this ready compliance with his proposition, and Jabez was quite at a loss to understand his meaning.

His only means of accounting for the gipsy's unconcern was that it was merely a mask to hide some meditated mischief.

He therefore determined to be fully on his guard that no surprise should lay him at the mercy of the crafty gipsy.

A smart walk of half an hour brought them to the ruined house in Westminster.

Here Jonas bade the hunchback enter, and Jabez grasped his pistols tighter than ever, now making sure that some stroke of treachery was intended.

Still the signal failure of his efforts hitherto to discover the retreat of Leonore determined him not to allow trifling obstacles or unworthy fears to stand for a moment in his way.

Still he clutched his pistols tightly in his pockets, and bade the gipsy to lead the way.

By all that was unfortunate Leonore and Mina were in the place at that time, and all the mischief was worked.

As they threaded the gloomy labyrinths of the subterranean passages two female voices were heard in earnest conversation close at hand.

As the voices struck upon his ear Jabez the hunchback started with astonishment.

In one of them he recognised the original of the ivory miniature—Leonore!

"Go on," he said to the gipsy, pressing eagerly forward. "Where is that girl—the owner of that voice?"

"Gently," said the gipsy, holding him back. "You will alarm her by your impatience. Wait."

Arrived at the end of the passage which they were traversing, the gipsy opened a door, and led the hunchback into a kind of cellar in which were seated several members of the tribe.

"Ah!" muttered the hunchback. "Treachery, as I thought."

"Hold your peace," said Jonas surlily, "if you would find your way out of this place alive."

"Who have you got there, Jonas?" asked one of the tribe.

"A pal."

"Square?"

The gipsy nodded.

"But where is she?" demanded the hunchback impatiently. "Will she come here?"

"No."

Just at this instant, however, as if to belie the gipsy's assertion, the door opened, and the object of their conversation and Mina entered.

Jonas at once placed himself before Leonore, so as to shield the hunchback from her view, and demanded how she liked her new friends, and other trifles which astonished his companion, who could not comprehend the sudden amiable turn in his leader's humour.

The hunchback, however, was so eager and impatient to get a better view of Leonore that he pressed forward, and, in spite of Jonas's efforts, revealed his unsightly form to her startled view.

The poor girl turned pale as death as she caught sight of the hunchback, and the hand with which she clutched Mina's arm quivered as if suddenly palsied.

"What is it?" asked Mina, looking at her. "Good Heavens! what is the matter? Are you ill, Leonore?"

"Take him away," said Leonore, pointing to the hunchback. "Oh! that fearful man! Mercy! Save me from him, I pray you."

And the poor girl fell in Mina's arms, nearly fainting from fear.

CHAPTER LXXIX.

JONAS IN TROUBLE—THE HUNCHBACK'S DANGER—DEFENCE—AN EXCITING INCIDENT—OVERPOWERED—LEONORE'S PRAYERS—THE LETTER—THE MYSTERIOUS STRANGER—THE ABBEY CLOISTERS—NIGHT.

IT would be impossible to render an adequate description of the disgust manifested by Jonas the gipsy at the eagerness of the hunchback.

He felt that he had spoilt an excellent chance of wreaking his vengeance on Leonore and the gipsy queen, and by the very same stroke of policy securing a rich prize.

But now not only were his prospects for the moment baffled, but he deemed it not at all improbable that he should get into hot water with Mina.

Jonas quailed beneath the piercing gaze of her rich full eye as she looked round sternly upon the gipsies.

"Who has done this?" she asked.

No one could reply. Jonas was summoning up such remnants of his courage as he could muster.

"Who has brought this man here?" demanded Mina, pointing to Jabez.

"It was I," said Jonas, with an attempt at his wonted bullying tone. "I, and I have done quite right."

"Yes," chimed in the hunchback, "of course. We've been on the search for Lady Leonore since—"

"And he comes to claim his daughter," said Jonas.

"Not my daughter," began Jabez.

[THE SPY.]

"Silence," growled Jonas between his teeth.

And planting his heavy boot on the toe of the hunchback he well nigh crushed it.

"You hear this?" said Mina, addressing the gipsies. "Jonas, you see, is hatching up some conspiracy."

"It's false," said Jonas.

"'Tis true," said the gipsy queen. "And you should have had the wit to arrange your lies before coming here. As it is, it may be hard with you. That misshapen object there will rue the day he crossed my path, too, if I find that Leonore has ever received an injury at his hands. Let him look to it!"

The hunchback felt that he had made a bit of a mistake, but it was now too late to retrieve his error, and he therefore resolved to put a bold face upon the matter.

"It is useless," said Jabez, with a sneer of contempt, "to try on your mummery with me. I value your threats about that!"

He snapped his fingers scornfully in the gipsy queen's face, but the next instant repented of it.

The tribe began to murmur in a manner that made the hunchback's flesh creep upon his bones, and he felt that he would have been much more at his ease outside those gloomy ruins.

His right hand was in his coat pocket, nervously clutching one of his pistols.

"What claim have you upon the girl?" said Jonas to the hunchback. "Why don't you speak out? You were fast enough with that long rigmarole to me a while ago."

"The only claim I have is as the agent of her family," said the hunchback. "And they have commanded me to seek her out, bring her home, and restore her to her friends and relations. That's all the harm I wish her."

"What do you say to this, Leonore?" asked Mina.

"Oh! no, no, no!" cried the shrinking girl, "What he says is false. If it were even true I would not, dare not, return with him."

"You hear?"

"Leonore," said the hunchback, "think of my lady, who has waited so long—the anguish and grief she feels at being thus separated from you—the anxiety and doubt as to your fate. Lady Leonore, if you have any humanity left in you you will at once return to her ladyship, who is dying to be restored to you."

However, this touching appeal had only the effect of drawing tears from Leonore.

She remained as firm as before in her resolve not to go with the hunchback.

"What makes you fear that man so?" demanded Mina.

"Because," answered the girl, in a frightened whisper, "because he has already attempted my husband's life—because he would have slain me, too, had I not escaped his clutches by the merest chance."

"Is it indeed so?"

"Alas! yes."

"Then he shall not have a second chance of harming you, Leonore," said Mina, and then, turning to the tribe, she raised her hand, and, pointing to the hunchback, cried suddenly, "Secure that man!"

Half a dozen of the men had pounced upon the hunchback ere the words were barely spoken.

But they had not reckoned on meeting in that little stunted figure so much muscular power.

With a savage growl, Jabez shook them off in every direction, and jumped back some eight or ten feet with a bound that completely took the gipsies by surprise.

Then he whipped out a pistol from each pocket and presented them full at Mina.

"Now," he cried, "advance another step, attempt to detain me one moment against my will, and I will blow you to pieces!"

Had the hunchback looked before leaping he would possibly have chosen another spot.

As it was, he had just got to the entrance, and here the little manikin stood at bay.

His defiance, however, lasted but an instant.

Some one from behind struck him two violent blows upon each arm, which knocked the pistols from his grasp, and quite staggered him.

Then, before he could even contemplate further resistance, the whole tribe fell upon him, and pinned him to the ground.

Jabez struggled like a lion in their toils, but what could all his efforts avail him against such numbers?

"My curses upon ye all, ye thieving sons of fiends!" hissed the panting hunchback between his set teeth. "Ye despoiling vagabonds!"

At every fresh epithet which the hunchback bestowed upon them—and they were not a few—the gipsies gave him a fresh proof of their enmity in the shape of a kick or a squeeze, which stopped his breath for a while.

"And now what would you do with him?" asked Jonas.

"That is yet to be decided," answered the gipsy queen, turning sharply upon the speaker. "If his offence merits a severe punishment, *then let him look to it!*"

There was a terrible significance in Mina's tone which caused Leonore to spring up from her recumbent position with a cry of alarm.

"Oh! no, no, no!" she cried. "Do nothing violent, I beseech you. Not for worlds would I have upon my conscience the thought that I had caused harm to that wretched man."

"Fear nothing, Leonore," said Mina. "Whatever may be the result of this night's business, you can in no way be answerable for it."

This speech, however, instead of quieting Leonore, only conveyed to her the confirmation of her apprehensions, and added to her fears.

"Come, come, Leonore," said the gipsy queen, endeavouring to lead her away. "Pray be calm. Remain in the adjoining place, and fear nothing."

But Leonore refused to stir.

She read in the determined tone of Mina that some fearful retaliation for the many sufferings she had undergone was meditated upon the hunchback.

She implored Mina and the tribe to have mercy upon him—begged them in tears.

But for a long time her prayers and entreaties were disregarded.

And now the poor girl's agony was great.

In every tone, in every gesture, she read the hunchback's condemnation for the indignities which she had suffered at his hands, and the sufferings which had resulted from them.

But now sufferings and indignities were all forgotten, if not quite forgiven.

She only thought that there were there a set of desperate men who would pause at nothing to accomplish the commands of their queen.

And her entreaties grew more loud and fervent in the unhappy hunchback's behalf.

Upon her knees she implored Mina to allow him to depart—the tribe to spare him, and let his punishment fall to other hands than theirs.

Had the prisoner of the gipsies been any other than Jabez the hunchback, he could not fail to be impressed with the earnestness of the poor girl's prayers in his behalf—in the behalf of one who had not only attempted her life, but who had caused her so much subsequent suffering.

How much the deformed manikin's generous feelings were touched by this we purpose to show hereafter.

After much time and an endless supplication Leonore's prayer was granted.

It was resolved that Jabez the hunchback should be allowed to depart, upon condition that he would no longer seek to harm Leonore or persist in his project to restore her to her friends (?), as he designated his vile employers.

Jabez was the quintessence of craft and knavery, and he easily persuaded his captors that he had given up all thoughts of carrying out his previously avowed projects.

Then he was allowed to depart.

As a precaution, his eyes were bandaged, and the cloth was not removed from them until he was some distance from the ruined house.

One little piece of by-play, however, escaped the gipsies—fortunately for the hunchback—and this was an agreement between Jonas and the worthy Jabez for an early meeting.

Jabez then took his departure, with signs of the greatest humility and contrition for the wrongs which Leonore averred had been offered her.

"Farewell, Lady Leonore," said the crafty hunchback. "Farewell. But remember and ponder over what I have told you. Lady Glyde pines in secret for you, and her ladyship's physicians are of opinion that the consequences will be disastrous unless you are almost immediately restored to her."

Leonore put several questions to the hunchback touching Lady Glyde's malady, but received no further answer.

Only one thing could restore Lady Glyde to health, and that was the immediate return of Leonore.

Having, craftily enough, laid the seeds of much unhappiness and self-reproach for poor Leonore, the wily hunchback was allowed to depart.

Jonas was now rather worse off than ever.

Not only did Mina continually heap reproaches upon him, but the whole tribe did the same.

And once more he quitted them in disgust, to return to his haunt in Whitefriars.

A day or two passed, and Leonore was in the greatest uneasiness.

The words of the hunchback had not been without effect.

This effect, as we purpose showing, led to a fresh chain of disasters to our unhappy heroine, which came about as follows.

Every day at dusk Leonore and Mina left the ruined house in Westminster to take a short walk as a constitutional.

Their general route was the Abbey cloisters.

Here they could breathe the fresh air, and were not likely to attract observation.

Mina well knew that danger was still to be apprehended from Jonas, whose animosity was now greater than ever, on account of the failure of his schemes.

To guard, therefore, against any act of violence on his part, two of the tribe were always following in attendance upon them at a short distance.

One evening they were examining the time-worn stones upon one of the old Abbey tombs, when a person in a long Spanish cloak brushed hurriedly past them.

Quite unobserved by the gipsy queen, he contrived to thrust a piece of paper into Leonore's hand, and immediately vanished.

So sudden had been the action that Leonore had not even time to call Mina's attention to the singular occurrence.

So she simply concealed the paper and held her peace.

Whatever prompted her to this strange line of conduct it would be impossible to say.

It would almost seem that fate was working her destiny without allowing her the smallest chance in it herself.

Be this as it may, Leonore, as soon as she could find an opportunity, perused the note in secret, and sad were the results of her want of confidence in Mina, who had proved herself so far such a staunch friend.

Thus ran the missive :—

"*If you would see Lady Glyde before she expires you will not lose an instant in hastening to her side. The doctors have stated most positively that she cannot survive for two days longer unless some remarkable change were to suddenly set in. This it is in the power of one individual alone upon earth to bring about. The writer need scarcely remark that this individual is yourself. Fly then, and preserve the mother who bore you, or live for ever with the terrific crime of matricide upon your head. Think over this well, and your heart will most surely prompt you to the right course of action, in spite of the persuasion of one who would work your ruin in endeavouring to overrule you in such a project. Keep this to your own bosom, and no harm can possibly result from it. Remember! silence and despatch!*"

There was surely in the repetitions contained in the foregoing singular effusion enough to have shown the most ordinary observer that the writer was strangely eager in pressing the point.

But still Leonore could not listen to the warning which was thus so very palpably conveyed.

It was a short struggle between heart and head, in which the latter stood a very poor chance.

What though her mother had caused her so much unhappiness? Was she the less her child?

And where, then, was a daughter's place when a parent was breathing her last?

Fatal reasoning !

So Leonore kept her own counsel and bided her time.

The opportunity, alas! soon presented itself for the execution of her imprudent project.

Next day at dusk the two girls were starting upon their wonted excursion when one of the gipsies came running after them to say that Mina's presence was desired for an instant by the tribe.

" Wait for me here, Leonore," she said. " I shall return immediately."

As soon as Mina was fairly out of sight Leonore started off in her wild flight.

The Abbey cloisters were passed, when from behind one of the large stone columns started the mysterious individual in the Spanish cloak who had given Leonore the letter.

In an instant he had detached his cloak from his shoulders and thrown it over his arm.

Then with a few rapid strides he overtook Leonore, waved his large cloak in the air above her, and dexterously enwrapped her completely in its folds.

Simultaneously he gave a low but shrill whistle, and a coach drove up to the spot.

Leonore in vain endeavoured to cry out.

The cloak effectually stopped every attempt to be heard.

Then the stranger took her lightly in his huge arms and lifted her into the coach as easily as one would a child.

" Home !" said the stranger, in a voice that sounded like the grinding of two millstones.

And away they started at a gallop.

Now, Leonore, alas for your imprudence !

CHAPTER LXXX.

THE SPY.

THE tragical termination of the last exploit we related of Red Ralph and his bold companions threw such a gloom upon them for a time that not even the sudden and unexpected restoration to life of Mr. Ephram Skinner, the steward and collector of the Weirton estate, could bring back their wonted buoyant appearance.

The steward, we may observe, in conclusion of this little incident in our hero's chequered career, was restored to his property and his friends by the Yellow Boys.

Strange to say, instead of cherishing a spite against the lawless fraternity for being the authors of his woes upon that eventful night, he only remembered with gratitude the conclusion of the startling little drama.

How he proved his gratitude to the Yellow Boys we shall take occasion to show a little later.

It was a day or two after the events above alluded to that Red Ralph and Walters were wandering together about the border of the forest, when they paused to refresh themselves at a rustic tavern, where they encountered a person, the meeting with whom led to a variety of singular adventures which we now purpose to relate.

Red Ralph and the lieutenant were seated in the parlour, drinking, when a person entered, and peered curiously about him in such a way as to attract the immediate attention of the leader of the Yellow Band.

He glanced up, and his eyes encountered those of the newcomer.

Apparently the man interpreted this look as an exchange of significant understanding.

After a variety of pantomimic gestures of the most extravagant nature he came up and addressed Red Ralph, who was not a little perplexed to account for his singular behaviour.

"You are waiting for somebody?" he demanded, pursing up his eyebrows and peering into Red Ralph's face significantly.

"Oh! am I?"

"I—I put the question," quoth the stranger, very tartly.

"And I answer," replied Red Ralph, "that I may or may not be; but whether I am or am not, it is my business alone, and cannot in any way concern you."

"So you think," said the stranger, with an inward chuckle, which he appeared extremely desirous of suppressing before our hero. "Now, I don't mind telling you that I'm—" Here he looked about in the utmost melodramatic style, before he concluded, in an impressive whisper, "I'm Barker!"

"Oh! indeed," said Red Ralph laughingly. "And who's Barker?"

"Pah!" said the stranger, with an expression of the most profound contempt. "Cease this nonsense. I tell you that I also am aware of the meditated attempt upon the old baronet and his treasures."

"What?"

"The old baronet and his treasures."

Red Ralph looked first at the lieutenant and then at the singular personage, quite in the clouds.

"My good man," said our hero, "if you would only give yourself the trouble to make this mystery a little clearer I should not be able to express my gratitude in proper language. What do you mean?"

"Simply," replied the man, "that I am aware that when the baronet passes the glade at sunset, laden with all his plate, you will be there. I shall be there too. Dick has sent me to explain."

"O-ho! I begin to perceive," exclaimed the lieutenant. "Turpin has got hold of a good thing, and wants you to share it with him. This fellow—Barker—is his messenger, only he does not make himself very clear, through a slight misapprehension under which he apparently labours. He appears to me to imagine that it is merely a preconcerted plan between you and Dick Turpin."

"That's it," said Barker. "Why, didn't you know?"

"No. This is the first word I have heard of it. Pray explain, therefore, what is the nature of this new enterprise."

"You must know, then, captain," said Barker, "that Sir Thomas will pass the glade at sunset, laden with all his family plate."

"How have you become possessed of this knowledge?" demanded Red Ralph suspiciously.

"That is rather Dick's secret than mine," replied the man. "I am only a messenger of his. But I hope to be an acting party shortly in one of the boldest little stratagems which have lately come to my knowledge."

"And Dick? At what time does he intend to join us?"

"Only at the latest moment," answered the man, "for he is busily employed elsewhere at the present time."

Red Ralph glanced up sharply into the other's face.

He fancied that he had detected a tone of significance in his words which gave his speech a hidden meaning.

However, the man's expression in no way confirmed any doubts which might momentarily have crossed his mind.

"Now, then," said Red Ralph, "if we are to work together in to-night's venture, just give me an idea of your plan of action."

"Willingly."

"At sunset you say the abbot will pass the glade?"

"Yes."

"Then he will probably pass this point of the road a little earlier?"

"Precisely."

"Then I vote that our venture be carried out here."

"S'death! no, no!" cried the man, jumping up in a great state of excitement. "Hang it all, that will never do!"

"Why not?"

Mr. Barker cooled down instanter, as if he had committed an unpleasant mistake in displaying so much vehemence upon the subject.

"I mean, of course, that that would be much too near the inn. That's all my fear, I assure you."

"I see."

"I have to return to Dick Turpin," said the man. "He will be waiting close at hand for me."

"Where?"

"The Boozing Ken."

"Very good. You may tell him that we shall await him here."

"I will. Good day, captain, for the present."

"Good day."

And the man vanished.

No sooner was he gone than Red Ralph rose to his feet, and carefully closed the door.

Then he drew his pistols from his belt, and examined the priming.

All this much to the astonishment of the lieutenant, who could not at all comprehend the reason for the observance of such an amount of unnecessary caution, as it appeared to him.

"Walters," said Ralph.

"Captain."

"That fellow means to play us false."

"Never!"

"I could swear it."

"How do you judge that?"

"From several causes. First, that he seems to know nothing himself about this project of which he speaks."

"Nothing?" said the lieutenant. "Why he knew the time appointed for the job, and the precise spot at which it was to take place."

"Pshaw! That was merely an after-thought. Did you not observe his singular conduct when he entered?"

"Certainly."

"And did you not see that he was merely playing a part, and, moreover, not playing it naturally, as he might have done?"

"I certainly did notice that his manner was singular, captain, but it seemed to me that it was only to be attributed to his doubts as to whether you were really the person of whom he was in search."

"A very little time will show, Walters," said Red Ralph, "and, I mistake not, you will find what I say to be correct."

"That this fellow is a traitor?"

"Yes."

"But for what purpose?"

"That remains to be seen."

"But I only know of one enemy that we have to fear."

"And that is—"

"The law."

"True."

"Then you think, captain, that the man is an emissary of justice."

"Yes. Probably of Wild's."

"Wild's? Ah! captain, why would you allow that fiend incarnate to escape us a second time?"

"You well know why," replied the captain of the Yellow Band. "Was not too much blood already shed in the unnecessary execution of that unhappy wretch?"

"Execution — not unnecessary, captain," said Walters.

"Murder is never necessary," said Red Ralph severely.

The lieutenant felt the justice of the rebuke, for he hung his head in silence.

Just then a crackling noise above caught their ears, and a fragment of the plaster of the ceiling fell upon the table between them.

Both looked up simultaneously.

There was a small round hole cut in the plaster, about the size of a shilling.

Through this hole the point of a knife protruded about an inch.

Red Ralph rose to his feet without a word, and moved upon tiptoe towards the door.

Here he beckoned to Walters to follow him, placing his finger upon his lips to invite caution.

Walters silently obeyed, he knew not why, but he had implicit confidence in the penetration and talents of his leader.

Red Ralph walked to the stairs, followed by the lieutenant, and was mounting when the landlord came forward.

"Hullo! my friends," he said, "where are you going to?"

"Only to my friend upstairs," answered Red Ralph.

"Your friend?"

"Ay. He told me to come up to him."

"Oh! Well, that's rum. He told me that no one was to go to him upon any pretext whatsoever."

"Oh! I know. But he did not mean to exclude us."

"Very good," said Boniface. "I suppose it's all right."

"Of course it is."

And without further opposition Red Ralph and the lieutenant ascended the stairs.

Arrived upon the first landing, Red Ralph applied his eye to the keyhole of the nearest door, peered into the room for several seconds, and withdrew.

Then he motioned to his companion to place a hand upon the door, which he did.

"Now then," whispered Red Ralph, "when I give the word. Both together, mind. He must have no time. One, two, THREE!"

Both dashed at the door simultaneously, and it gave way with a loud crash!

What they saw there we reserve for another chapter.

CHAPTER LXXXI.

A FEARFUL AWAKING—THE HUNCHBACK—TAUNTS
—THREATS AND FEARS—THE CLOCK—THE HAND
UPON THE HOUR—"MERCY! MERCY!"—"LEONORE, FAREWELL!"

WHEN Leonore recovered consciousness she found herself in a wretched-looking hut, whose solitary aspect filled her with renewed terror.

She was lying upon a rude couch, the hardness of which made itself apparent as soon as she remembered the preceding events of her strange career.

She essayed to rise, but the effort was painful in the extreme, and she was forced to relinquish it at once.

Her whole body was stiff and in pain, as if she had been sleeping on a dew-damp lawn.

She was forced to rest, and await in physical, if not mental, quiet the next phase in the new drama of violence which she now felt that she was called upon to perform.

"Alas! alas!" she murmured, while the tears trickled down her fair face. "What is to be the next step—the new terror for which I am reserved?"

The words were yet upon her lips when the sound of an opening door close beside her caused her to look round in dismay.

She could see nothing.

Nothing whatever, and yet she was conscious that she was no longer alone in the room.

She became aware of this by a kind of secret intuition—by the same reason that one is conscious of being the object of another's fixed regard without actually seeing the person.

Leonore, with an effort which was scarcely less painful than the previous one had been, contrived to raise herself on her elbow and look about her.

Still she could perceive no one, and she sank down with a faint groan, closing her eyes.

A slight sound beside her couch caused her now to look up with a start, and then she beheld something which but strengthened her fears.

By her side stood the terror of the unhappy girl's existence.

In a word, the hunchback.

Jabez stood glaring with a fiend-like chuckle upon his helpless victim for several minutes without a word, evidently awaiting her speech.

But Leonore was frozen with terror, and could not utter a syllable.

After waiting thus for a while Jabez spoke.

"So, so," said he, with a sneer, "we have your ladyship at last, have we?"

Leonore looked up into his face, as if to implore his mercy.

"Indeed, my lady," continued Jabez, "I thought that we had really parted company for good."

"Would that it were so!" muttered Leonore to herself.

"But it seems that we are destined to come together again, and all by accident, too. He! he! ain't it droll? Such a strange accident, ain't it?"

Leonore now comprehended the whole of the simple and shallow stratagem by which she had fallen into the clutches of Jabez the hunchback.

How bitterly did she now reproach herself, but alas! to what use at this period?

Had she but listened to the voice of prudence before, had she but taken counsel with Mina, who had proved herself so staunch a friend in the hour of trial, all might now have been well.

But, alas! it was not to be.

"But really, my dear Lady Leonore," said the hunchback, with a cynical sneer, "I don't see why you should weep so much at the prospect of being restored to the arms of a loving mother."

Leonore looked up.

"Sir!" she exclaimed, with some remnants of that spirit which had formerly characterised her, but which had been a stranger to her demeanour of latter days, "remember our respective positions."

"Sir! What a spirit!" exclaimed the hunchback mockingly.

"Or you may have cause to repent your insolence."

"So, so!" exclaimed the hunchback. "You threaten me?"

"No; I warn you."

"Warn do you?"

"Yes," said Leonore, with growing spirit. "And

not that alone. I also warn you that only one line of conduct can now by any possibility save you from well-merited punishment for your former baseness and deceit."

"And that is—"

"That I am treated with every respect at your hands."

"Of course."

"And—"

"Oh! that's not all?"

Leonore did not choose to observe the palpable sneer with which these words were uttered, but proceeded quietly.

"And the other condition is that he is no further molested."

"He?" exclaimed the hunchback, with well-feigned ignorance of her meaning.

"Yes. You know well to whom I allude," said Leonore.

"No, really."

"I allude to my husband," said Leonore, with pride.

"Your husband?"

"Yes, he."

"Oh!" exclaimed the hunchback, with a look of the profoundest wonder. "You mean Red Ralph, the robber, the footpad, and blackleg!"

Leonore turned purple with indignation.

But the remorseless hunchback continued, with a grin—

"Red Ralph, the gallows cheat! Eh, Lady Leonore?"

"Silence, ruffian!" exclaimed Leonore indignantly. "Were he here you would not dare to speak thus!"

"Oh, no? forsooth!"

"No; and well you know it."

"Gad, my lady! Do I?"

"Ay. See, you change colour at the mention of his name!"

Jabez turned in an instant.

His expression was one of the most diabolical hatred, the most virulent passion which it is possible for the human countenance to assume.

"Look you here, my Lady Leonore," he said, as deliberately as his passion would allow him to speak, "you have no prudence, or it would teach you to remember one thing."

"What mean you?"

"That you are not yet handed over to your lady mother."

"Insolent!"

"Pah! You know that I am not to be frightened with any words, however big. Remember that."

"You will repent this."

"Well, even that is possible, but I doubt it much. I am not given to repentance."

"A sad boast."

"Not so," continued the hunchback. "And I would have you moderate your words a little, Lady Leonore, for you are not yet out of my power, and you know what that means."

"Would you dare?"

"Dare?"

"Ay, dare," retorted Leonore. "You know how much I have already dared."

Leonore shuddered.

"And I may, perchance, even dare still more if I find that it suits my interest."

There was a tone of significance in this which caused Leonore the most lively apprehensions.

"I see you appreciate the importance of my words."

"I?"

"Yes. You change colour now," said the hunchback. "And believe me, my lady, that your fears are not without foundation."

Leonore began to feel excessively uncomfortable.

"When am I to see Lady Glyde?" she asked, in rather a subdued tone.

The alteration was so marked as to cause the hunchback to grin with satisfaction.

"So-ho!" he exclaimed, with a brutal laugh. "We are getting a little subdued, eh?"

"What do you mean?"

"I'll tell you what I mean," said Jabez. "And in the plainest English I can command. Leonore, you are too wise."

"I do not understand you," faltered our heroine in dismay.

"Must I speak plainer, then? Well, in a few words, Leonore Glyde will never see another sun rise."

Leonore started to her feet with a cry of apprehension.

"You surely would not again offer me violence?"

"Violence? Oh, no, not I. I shall simply prevent all possibility of your damaging my character, and I have a character to lose, believe me, my Lady Leonore."

"You need not fear me," said Leonore. "I bear no malice."

"Doubtless; but you shan't have the chance."

"Sir, I implore you by all—"

"Tut! tut! You may spare yourself the trouble, for I shall not believe a word you utter."

His desire was evidently to terrify Leonore.

But, poor girl, she had already experienced the enmity of this villainous little wretch, and it is not to be wondered at that she trembled for her safety at the words he uttered.

After pausing for some moments in silence to watch the effect of his words, he resumed.

"Lady Leonore," he said, "if you have anything further to say, I beg of you to be speedy."

"Wherefore?" faltered the unhappy girl, in terror.

"That you divine."

"Nay, I—"

"Ha! ha! You would have me put my intention into words. Well, well, if it will afford you any pleasure, I don't mind. Leonore, *I am about to slay you!*"

Leonore gave a wild shriek, and darted to the door.

Jabez did not attempt to intercept her movements.

The reason of this was simple.

The door was fast!

She had not observed that, upon entering, the hunchback had locked the door and withdrawn the key.

Had she done so, her fears might have been aroused earlier.

"Do you see that?" said the hunchback, pointing to a clock.

"Yes."

"Note the hour well, for when the long hand is upon the twelve Leonore Glyde will be no more."

"Mercy! mercy!"

"Mercy? Oh! plenty of that. I shall do it as quickly as possible, for my own sake."

"Oh, man, man!" cried Leonore, "this is a cruel jest."

"You'll find it none."

"I know it is. You seek only to fill me with alarm."

"'Tis false."

"Nay, I know it, for I know that you would not dare—"

"Dare again?"

"You would not, at least, risk—"

"Risk!" echoed the hunchback. "Oh! the risk is nothing. *I have made my arrangements.*"

Another devilish pause to watch the effect of his words.

"No, no," he resumed. "We are all to ourselves here. I shall slay you."

This with the cruellest deliberation.

"And then your body will be dropped down the well, and all trace will disappear."

Leonore was frozen with terror and apprehension.

The clock now tolled the hour.

The death knell sounded of the unhappy Lady Leonore.

"The time has expired," said the hunchback, with sonorous emphasis.

"Mercy! mercy!"

"At last," said the hunchback, grinning sardonically. "This is certainly some satisfaction. A little earlier it might have prolonged your life; it could not have preserved it. Take what consolation you can from that."

Again and again did Leonore cry for mercy.

But as well might she have addressed her supplications to a savage beast of the forest.

"Leonore, farewell!"

With a growl of savage hatred he rushed upon the trembling girl and seized her fair throat in his claw-like hands!

CHAPTER LXXXII.

THE SPY—THE DOOM—STARTLING REVELATIONS—A THIEFTAKER'S OATH—A DASH AT ESCAPE—LEAP FOR LIFE—"AFTER HIM!"—A NARROW SQUEEZE—RED RALPH'S GOOD GENIUS.

LET us return for a glance at the further doings of the captain of the Yellow Band.

Red Ralph and the lieutenant, the reader will doubtless remember were at an inn at the outskirts of Epping Forest.

Here they had—or Rather Red Ralph had—discovered that a man was playing the spy upon their actions from one of the rooms above that in which they were seated.

In order to overhear their conversation the man had cut through the flooring and bored a hole with a dagger-knife in the plaster of the ceiling.

This had betrayed him.

Red Ralph had with his eagle glance perceived it in an instant.

Then he made his way upstairs, as already narrated, in spite of the landlord's opposition.

One little matter, however, we omitted to mention.

Previous to quitting the parlour Red Ralph threw open the window, and leaning out blew a long shrill note upon a small silver whistle.

The call was answered close at hand, and in the space of a few minutes four of the Yellow Boys made an appearance.

They, too, followed their captain and Walters upstairs, and were beside him as the door was burst open by the combined efforts of the two former.

In they all rushed in a body.

There they beheld a man upon his knees with his head laid flat upon the floor, covering a small aperture in the planks.

This was the result of the fellow's patient handiwork.

The unhappy wretch had not even the time to look up before they were upon him.

Immediately an exclamation of alarm burst from his lips.

But any cry which he might utter could not now bring succour.

They had him in their power.

"What do you want here?" he began, with an effort at boldness.

"You."

He looked up at the speaker, and apparently recognised Red Ralph upon the instant.

He started and changed colour.

"So, so," said the captain of the Yellow Band "You begin to see that it is all over with you now."

"What mean you?"

"Simply that you are about to quit the world."

"Quit? I?" stammered the man.

"Yes, yes," answered Red Ralph, "and you expect it."

"Nay, I swear—"

"Hush!" said Red Ralph, with solemn emphasis. "Do not perjure yourself at this awful moment."

The man turned ashy pale.

"But, captain, I implore—"

"Captain!" cried Red Ralph, catching him up sharply. "So then you avow that you know me?"

"Nay, I—"

"Oh! 'tis too late now, my friend. You have incautiously let slip the whole truth," said Red Ralph.

"But I merely said captain as a title of honour one habitually gives—"

"Knights of the road?"

"Precisely."

"'Sdeath! man," cried the lieutenant, with a laugh of triumph, "you are sinking deeper and deeper into the mire at every step."

"You wilfully misunderstand my meaning," growled the man.

"Indeed."

"You will find our meaning much more easy of comprehension," said Red Ralph.

A most significant gesture with which the speaker accompanied his words caused the unhappy wretch the most lively apprehensions.

Red Ralph drew his hand ominously across his throat.

"Look here, captain," said he, "I know very well that you but seek to frighten a fellow."

"Not I."

"You do. And well I know, too, that, whatever you may be, you are not bloodthirsty nor cruel."

"Are you attempting to get over my determination with long-winded compliments?"

"Determination?" faltered the poor wretch trembling violently.

"Ay, my fixed determination."

The man looked up into the handsome countenance of the captain of the Yellow Band earnestly.

"Well," he muttered, more as if speaking to himself than addressing his words to the others, "if that is a murderer's face, then I may never look upon another sun. But, by Heavens! I am immensely deceived."

"You are truly."

There could now be no deception he imagined.

Yes, he was doomed to death at the hands of the Yellow Boys and their leader, upon whom he was there to play the spy.

As they had quitted their hold upon him during the foregoing controversy, he rose to his knees and earnestly supplicated for mercy.

But his punishment was not yet complete.

"Here, take your stand about him," said Red Ralph to his four men.

The Yellow Boys, with that military discipline which always characterised them, ranged themselves about the unhappy spy.

"Draw!" said Red Ralph solemnly.

The spy gave a sort of spasmodic jerk at every word that Red Ralph spoke.

The four Yellow Boys each drew a pistol from his belt and awaited further commands.

"Examine the priming and present," said Ralph.

One loud click of the four pistol locks followed, and then were presented at the spy simultaneously, with mechanical precision.

"Await the word," said Red Ralph.

"Captain, captain," cried the spy, who was now a most pitiable object to behold, "what you contemplate is the cruellest murder."

"I can't admit that."

"How else can you designate it?" demanded the fellow. "It is none the less your deed that your hand directs not the fatal blow."

Ralph shuddered.

The words of the spy brought to mind a scene of terror in the forest which he had seen enacted by his men.

He thought upon the fatal oak—upon the steward Skinner—upon the blasted tree!

"Humph!" he muttered. "You are not quite a fool. The wonder is that a man with your wit could have been persuaded into accepting such an office."

"I had no choice."

"No choice?" echoed the captain of the Yellow Band. "That's a strange tale, my friend. It strikes me that a man need not accept any means of earning a livelihood that are repugnant to him. The army, the navy, are open to every man."

"I admit it," said the man, with a sigh, "and perhaps I should have resisted him."

"Who?"

The spy paused before replying to this question.

"Do you mean to say that you have been forced to accept your present degrading position?"

"Ay, truly."

"By whom?"

"By that fiend, Jonathan Wild the thieftaker."

"Indeed?"

"Ay. Do you know the man?"

"Well."

"Then you know the blackest fiend that ever polluted earth with his presence."

"You speak truth now," said Red Ralph. "But what is the particular wrong you have suffered at his hands?"

"They are not to be numbered," answered the spy. "By an act of imprudence I have placed myself in his power, and now you see with what effect he exercises it."

"How?"

"By forcing me into these devilish works."

"And he forced you to play the spy upon me?"

"Ay."

"For what purpose?"

"That we might learn your projects and fall upon you in an unguarded moment."

"Oh!"

"Ay. And you may know that no less than four separate parties are at work from different points upon your ruin."

"How so?"

"They are all equipped and mounted by Jonathan Wild, and despatched with strict injunctions to shoot you only at a last extremity."

"That's kind."

"Moreover, if you should chance to be shot by one of them—no matter how severely—you are to be hurried off to town upon the instant."

"And to what purpose, may I ask?" said Red Ralph.

"That he may fulfil his oath and hang you."

"He's a friend to be remembered," said Red Ralph.

"Ay," said Walters. "This is the man who swore so solemnly to cease all acts of animosity to you or any member of the Yellow Band."

"Ay."

"And upon the strength of this you set him at liberty—scot free, whilst his less guilty follower—"

"Hush!"

This was an unfortunate speech, and Walters was sorry for it before it was half completed.

But he could not resist the pleasure of satirising upon what he deemed effeminate scruples upon the part of Red Ralph in having allowed the thieftaker to go free when they last had him in their power.

Whist thus engaged, however, with their conversation they gave rather less attention to the spy.

The poor wretch had never once ceased to think of escape.

His eyes wandered restlessly around the room.

Twice it alighted upon the window and rested there.

Longingly he looked towards it—his heart beating violently the while, as he thought of the dangers of a leap through it.

He must decide quickly.

The chances were decidedly in favour of the window, if he could manage to reach it.

It was life or death.

In remaining he believed it to be certain death.

A final glance at Red Ralph and the lieutenant.

Their eyes were momentarily averted in the interest of their conversation.

Suddenly—with one bound—scarcely seeming to rise to his feet before leaping—he was up.

He dashed at the window, and went through, carrying half the frame with him.

"After him!" cried Red Ralph.

"After him!" cried Walters.

"Follow!" shouted the men.

And downstairs they dashed, headed by the lieutenant.

Red Ralph, however, was too impatient for this mode of descent.

The spy had just leapt the window, and it was, therefore, practical.

Why not use it?

He dragged down the broken sash, and took the leap.

Fortunate it was, too, that he came that way, for had he descended the stairs with the others an assassin's knife would have drunk his life-blood ere he could have gained the road.

Of this, more a little further.

CHAPTER LXXXIII.

HOUNSLOW HEATH — THE LONELY TRAVELLER— THE GALLOWS TREE—A FIGHT WITH A BLOOD-HOUND—THE RUN—MYSTERY—WHAT NEXT?

THE progress of our story brings us now to a strange episode in the life of Red Ralph.

We come now to his meeting with a woman destined to exercise a great and terrible influence over his future career.

Slowly, but surely, had he been journeying onwards towards the awful—the inevitable doom.

Little recked he now of that terrible warning of the old hag.

Little dreamt he how near was the end.

*   *   *   *   *

One wild and stormy night, when the heavens were black as a pall, and not the faintest glimmer of a star visible upon the broad surface of the sombre firmament, a lonely woman's figure might have been observed slowly and painfully wending its way across Hounslow Heath, in the direction of London.

Weary and footsore was she.

Her clothes were old, worn, and ragged, and saturated with rain.

[THE EXPLOSION.]

She crept along at a snail's pace, but every now and then was obliged to come to a standstill altogether.

The wind swept across the bleak desolate heath in sharp cold blasts, and she shivered miserably and drew her rags about her.

She was very young—twenty at the utmost.

Her hair was of a rich golden colour, her eyes a heavenly blue, deep and earnest in their gaze.

She would have been surpassingly beautiful had not her face worn an expression of pain and fatigue.

Who was she to be thus wandering alone and at the dead of night, in a wild and dangerous country?

At first sight a careless observer might be led to suppose that she was some poor medicant—some houseless wanderer tramping from parish to parish, sleeping sometimes in barns, sometimes under haystacks and hedges, and so tramping on until she reached the goal to die, at last, perhaps in a ditch within sight of the home which had so cruelly closed its doors against her.

Thus might a person have thought upon glancing at the sad figure wearily pursuing its painful course amidst the wind and rain.

But a more careful study of the face and form would have led to a different conclusion.

The girl's skin was not freckled nor sunburnt by exposure.

She was pale and delicate.

Her features were exquisitely chiselled and Grecian in their beauty.

Her hands were small and pretty.

Her fingers slender, her nails carefully pared and filbert-shaped.

Ragged and worn as was her dress, it was easy enough to see by the way in which she wore it, that in any other attire, in elegant and costly garments, perhaps, she would be at her ease.

It was impossible that one so beautiful and delicate could be accustomed to a life of hardship — that this journey which she was now performing could have lasted for any length of time.

That there was a deep mystery overhanging her past life, and was the cause of her thus travelling alone, was very certain.

What that mystery was the course of our story will reveal.

Wearily she progressed until she reached the centre of the heath, and here, pausing, she endeavoured, with hands shading her eyes, to make out the distant objects, only distinguishable as a blacker blackness amidst the surrounding gloom.

There was something not very far ahead which stood up black, and she fancied that perhaps it was a signpost.

"If I could possibly make out the words upon it," she muttered to herself; but the darkness was too great for that.

The darkness was, indeed, so intense that although now but two or three yards distant from the black object, she could not yet discern more of its outline than that there was an upright post, high and thick, rising from the ground.

"Perhaps it is after all a tree," she thought.

And the next moment she laid her hand upon it.

In another, she would have gazed upwards, but almost in the very act of doing so, a faintness stealing over her, she clung with one hand to the post, to save herself from falling, while she pressed the other to her head.

This weakness presently began to pass away again, but as yet she dared not trust herself without support.

As she stood waiting for her strength to return a clanking noise overhead caused her to raise her eyes.

Then, with a shudder and a half-uttered shriek, she shrank from the post and cowered upon the damp earth.

Slowly to and fro, 'twixt her and heaven, revolved some dark mass, bearing an indistinct likeness to a human form.

It was a dead body.

The corpse of a gibbeted malefactor hung in chains over her head, its bones rattling dismally in the wind.

Shivering violently, she strove to rise again to her feet, but her weakness overcame her.

"O Heaven," she murmured faintly, "lend me strength to escape from this horrible place."

She laid her hand upon the ground and strove to rise, but fell back again heavily, and lay motionless and prostrate.

At that moment she heard the sound of breathing close by her side.

She raised her head and gazed in terror around.

Something was moving slowly along a few feet from where she lay.

It was creeping towards her.

In frenzied terror she struggled to rise.

But she was as helpless as though she had been paralysed—as though she were asleep and suffering from some hideous nightmare.

Her efforts were in vain, and she lay in shuddering dread, waiting the approach of the unseen horror.

Breathing heavily, it approached.

Nearer and nearer.

Her blood curdled, and her flesh crawled.

It shuffled along the ground beneath the gibbet, and presently she heard a crunching sound.

It was crunching one of the dead man's bones!

What was this monster—this unclean thing—crawling round the corpse of the murderer?

It crept up to her, and its bloodshot eyes glared into hers.

Its sickening breath fanned her ashy cheek.

Its bristling teeth gleamed savagely, as it drew back an inch or two and regarded her menacingly, with a low and angry snarl.

It was a great monster of the bloodhound breed, as well as she could judge in the uncertain light, and the darkness seemed to lend gigantic proportions to its long body and strong limbs.

To struggle with such a beast as this, did she even possess all her accustomed strength, would have been a hopeless contest.

She lay perfectly still, hoping that it would not attack her.

But the hideous brute had tasted human blood.

It was greedy for more.

She saw it drawing itself together and preparing for a spring.

She knew, then, that if she would save her life she had not a moment to spare.

Instantly one of her hands covered her throat, while the other drew from her breast a tiny dagger, bright and glittering, and sharp as a razor.

The hound sprang towards her, and made, open mouthed, at her throat.

But as he came she raised the dagger, and turned its point towards him.

It entered the roof of his mouth, and with a fearful howl he sprang back.

At the same moment her intense terror seemed to lend her strength, and she scrambled to her knees.

Again the raging beast rushed upon her, but again she received it upon the dagger's point.

With a deep groan, it fell again, and lay perfectly still.

Now she rose to her feet and turned to flee.

She ran along at the top of her speed.

More than once she slipped and fell, but scrambling again to her feet, madly pursued her wild career.

On, on she flew, with a rapidity which seemed almost incredible after the state of weakness and prostration in which she had been but a few moments previously.

But not for long could she hope to keep up this pace.

She began to fail again.

She tottered and stumbled—her limbs ached painfully—her brain reeled, and she grew giddy and sick.

"O Heaven, grant that I may escape from this fearful place," she murmured.

In front of her was a large dark object, which she fancied must be a house.

As she approached she found that this was the case, and, moreover, that the building was an inn.

"I will seek shelter here," she said to herself, "though I am doubtful whether I shall be able to obtain it."

It indeed seemed very questionable, for the house was dark and silent.

Not the faintest glimmer was to be seen betwixt the chinks of the closed shutters in the lower rooms, or through the diamond panes of the lattices above.

Certainly it was not to be expected that the house should be open at this hour, for it was now considerably past midnight.

She was, however, so faint and weary that she resolved upon making the attempt.

That one so ragged and woe-begone should expect

to obtain admission to a house of public entertainment may seem to the reader somewhat extraordinary.

Perhaps, however, she knew her own business best. Let us see.

Approaching the door, she raised her hand to knock, but as she did so the sound of voices struck upon her ear.

She paused to listen.

There was a confused whispering, in which she seemed to recognise the sound of a man's gruff voice.

There was nothing very alarming in this so far, and yet she dreaded to go any further into the mysteries of this lonely hostelry.

Hounslow Heath just about this time was a famous resort of the gallant knights of the road.

Bold fellows, most of them scorning petty knavery, unnecessary cruelty, or brutality, and yet among the less scrupulous there were some very ugly customers.

Some dark stories were afloat respecting the treatment of belated travellers in the lonely inns in this part of the country.

A poor unprotected beautiful girl might fare badly did she fall into the hands of these lawless desperadoes.

Most probably this house was the resort of highwaymen and footpads.

It would be wiser and better to journey onwards.

But she could not do so.

She way dying with fatigue.

Therefore, raising her hand again, she knocked at the door.

In an instant the voices ceased.

The girl's heart beat quickly, as she waited and listened intently.

Suddenly the door opened in front of her.

The traveller started back almost as though she expected to receive a blow.

But in front of her, instead of a burly ruffian, as she anticipated, there was a young girl of about fifteen.

A fair young girl, with an open innocent face, who held a candle in her hand, and, shading her eyes, gazed upwards at the beautiful stranger.

"Can I have a bed here for the night?" asked the latter.

The girl looked at her in silence for a moment or two, and then said—

"Step inside."

Silently the other obeyed.

The girl then closed the door, and put up a short chain inside.

Then she led the way through a wide hall, past a bar, into a kitchen beyond.

Upon the way the stranger gazed apprehensively around, but could see nothing of any man.

By the side of the fire an old woman sat in an armchair, nodding and mumbling to herself.

The young girl approached and said—

"Grandmother!"

"Ye—es, my child."

"There is a young woman who wishes to stay here for the night."

"Who is she?"

"Here she is, grandmother. Look."

The old woman, screening her eyes with her hand, peered wistfully across the room to the spot where the stranger stood.

She was a very old woman indeed, with snow-white hair and a long pointed nose and chin, closely approaching each other, nut-cracker fashion.

She had small restless colourless eyes, and long white lashes, which gave her a strange appearance.

But there was nothing very terrible about them. Nothing, indeed, to make the young traveller so suspicious.

Certain, though, was it that as she approached she cast distrustful glances around.

She was wondering what had become of the man whose voice she had heard.

She wondered more presently, when the old woman spoke.

"How late for one!" she said.

"Yes, I have lost my way."

"Have you travelled a long distance?"

"Yes, a very long distance."

"You have money?"

"Enough to pay for what I require."

"Let me see it."

"What?"

"We give no trust, you know."

The stranger hesitated.

"I thought so," said the old woman. "You hardly look like a person who can afford to pay for accommodation at an inn."

"Indeed?" said the fair traveller, and as she spoke she produced from her bosom a small leather packet.

"Look here," she said.

The old woman uttered an exclamation of astonishment.

CHAPTER LXXXIV.

INSIDE THE INN—A STRANGE OLD WOMAN—SUSPECTED TREACHERY—THE LONG ROOM—THE FACE AT THE WINDOW — THE MANIAC — THE MURDER — THE FALL — IN THE RUFFIAN'S CLUTCHES—THE HORSEMAN ON THE HEATH.

A MOMENT'S silence succeeded the speech which the fair stranger had made.

An avaricious gleam lit up the eyes of the old woman as she gazed greedily upon the object revealed to her from the leather covering.

A gorgeous necklace glittered there in the unknown woman's hands—a necklace so costly that its value must have been enormous.

"What is that?" asked the old woman in a low scarcely audible tone.

"They are diamonds."

"Yes, yes—I see—and real?"

"Yes, they are real?"

"Where did you get them?" she asked quickly.

But seeing that the other was somewhat confused by this question, she hastily added—

"Never mind, my dear—never mind."

"I do not think that I am called upon to make any explanation."

"No, no—of course not. They're yours now."

"Yes, they are mine."

"To be sure they are yours now, and that's enough —quite enough."

"I hope so," said the other uneasily.

"Quite, quite," repeated the old woman more eagerly still.

Then, after a moment's pause, she added—

"You want a bed you say?"

"I want shelter till the morning."

"To be sure. It is a dreadful night to be abroad in."

"Yes, it is a dreadful night."

"And for one so young, too—so young and so fair."

The old woman rubbed her hands and stared with greedy eyes at the owner of the jewels, an attention which by no means set the other at ease.

She, however, made no rejoinder.

"A bad country, too," continued the old woman, "to carry about so much valuable property. Were you not afraid, my dear?"

"No."

"No?"

"I can defend myself, if needs be."

"Ah!"

Again there was a pause. Sincerely, but vainly, did the young traveller wish herself beyond the walls of this house where she had sought shelter.

It would not do, though, now to seem afraid.

She had come there, and if she must escape, decidedly this was not the moment.

What on earth could have induced her to exhibit the jewels? That was a piece of rashness which might have very serious effects.

But now the evil was done, and she must be wiser in future.

Perhaps, though, it would not be so very difficult to explain the reason which had prompted her to show the old woman the gems.

When she first entered the inn she was well-nigh dead with fatigue. She felt that she could not possibly crawl any further upon the way—that if she did not obtain shelter she would inevitably sink down and die of fatigue upon the road.

The idea, then, of being turned out of doors again frightened her out of her prudence.

Although a houseless wanderer, it was not very difficult to see that she was unaccustomed to the way of the world.

She was unable to bear much hardship or privation. This mysterious pilgrimage of hers might have been a long one, but it was very certain that it was her first.

Now, however, that she began to suspect there was danger here the fatigue was banished before her fears, and she was fully determined upon making her escape, or at least making the attempt, directly an opportunity should offer itself.

Perhaps the old woman read something of these suspicions passing in her mind.

She changed her manner, and was now quite kind and cordial.

"You must want something to eat and drink," she said. "You must be nearly famished."

"No, thank you. I only require rest."

"It will be no trouble you know. My grandchild can get everything you would like in a few moments."

"I want nothing, thank you."

"I've got a teapot standing here upon the hob. I am sure that a nice cup of tea would be very refreshing."

The girl was afraid of taking anything, and yet afraid to refuse.

After all she thought there could be nothing very terrible in a cup of tea.

She would watch the old woman and her grandchild closely and see that they did not practise any tricks.

She watched them, but they did not appear to have any notion of any underhand business.

The granddaughter fetched a cup and saucer from a cupboard and placed them before her, by the fireside, on a small round table.

She then from a sideboard brought a sugar basin and a milk jug.

After this she brought the teapot from the hob where it had been standing, and left the stranger to pour out for herself.

There could be no treachery here.

She did not for a moment suppose it possible that the contents of the teapot could have been kept there ready drugged for the first unfortunate traveller who made an appearance.

The girl, therefore, filled up her cup and drank the tea without fear.

Meanwhile the old woman got to be quite chatty.

"If you'd been a minute later you would have been too late, my dear," she said.

The traveller sincerely wished that she had been.

"We are generally very early folks," said the old woman. She had very much the appearance of having sat up ever since she was born, without ever washing herself.

"Indeed?" said the person addressed.

"Yes. Only you see I've been rather poorly and restless of nights, and we've had company."

"Have you any people staying here to-night?"

"Oh, yes, there are one or two travellers."

The visitor was much relieved by this information. Supposing it were true, they might be appealed to in case of danger.

Presently the old woman said—

"You look very pale and tired, my dear. I suppose you'd like to see your room."

"I should indeed."

"Show the way, then, Jane," said the old woman. "The blue room."

"Yes, grandmother."

She took up a candle as she spoke and led the way.

It seemed a large rambling house, and on their way to the bedroom they passed several doors.

Outside these the young traveller looked, hoping to see the boots belonging to some of the persons supposed to be in the house, but there were none visible.

However many lodgers there were, too, they slumbered in a very peaceful fashion, and without snoring.

Another thing struck her as very peculiar, and not very satisfactory.

The passage at the end of which the blue room was situated smelt very cold and damp.

There was moisture glistening on the walls, and the wind sighed mournfully through the chinks and crevices.

She noticed these matters, but made no remark, and presently they reached the door of the room where she was to sleep.

The girl soon unlocked it, apparently with some little difficulty, and she passed in, holding the light, and waiting for the other to follow.

"This is the room," she said.

Having thus spoken, she placed the candle upon the top of a chest of drawers and immediately withdrew.

The traveller heard her pass along the passage, and down the stairs, and then all was silent.

For her own part, she stood perfectly motionless where the other had left her.

The way she had been treated, when she came to think of it, was very extraordinary.

At first the old woman had seemed to doubt whether she was able to pay for her accommodation.

To convince her that she was she had shown her the jewels.

Then immediately, without any further questions, she had agreed to find her a bed.

How did she expect to be paid?

Did she think that the jewels, or some portion of them, were to be hers?

But the smallest of the stones would be worth far more than a month's board at such a place as this.

What idea had she, then? Nothing but robbery—nothing else could she intend.

While the fair traveller was turning this over in her mind she glanced anxiously around, to see what sort of a room she had been put into.

There was, however, nothing remarkable about the apartment.

It was large and well-furnished. In the centre stood a four-post bedstead, with dark and heavy hangings, surmounted by plumes of feathers, black and dusty, which waved gently to and fro, nodding in the wind that crept into the room through the badly-closed window.

She examined the fastening of the door. It was of a very fragile nature, and she dragged a heavy chair across the floor and placed against it, hoping thus to make a surprise impossible, should such be attempted.

How to escape, though, was the idea uppermost in her mind.

Her thoughts turned naturally towards the window.

She approached it, pulled on one side the heavy red curtain, and looked out.

All was dark, and she could discern nothing.

The light inside the room, too, dazzled her.

She pulled the curtain round her, so that the rays from the candle might not confuse her vision.

Thus arranging matters, she found that she could make out the dim outline of a tree right in front of her.

The branches on the side nearest to her brushed the wall of the house, close to the window.

It seemed to be a great distance to the ground, but perhaps it would be possible to descend by the aid of the tree.

To ascertain whether such a proceeding were practicable it would be necessary that she should open the window.

As she raised her hand to undo the catch she fancied she heard a sound behind her.

She turned hastily.

The room was pitchy dark.

She stood silent and motionless, in awful dread of what might happen next.

There was not, however, the faintest movement audible within the room.

She listened silently.

Not a sound.

What had happened? Could it be possible that the candle had gone out of its own accord?

It was only a small end of candle, about three inches long, but it could not have burnt out in the few moments she had been in the room.

She listened.

Still there was no sound.

But she dared not move hand or foot. She dared not advance into the room.

While she stood undecided a faint sound outside the window caused her to glance in terror in the direction from which it came.

The tree was shaking violently.

From out the branches a dark form emerged.

It seemed to swing forward towards the window.

As the shrinking trembling woman stood transfixed, gazing in shuddering horror upon the mysterious object, it reached the window frame.

Next moment a face was pressed against the glass.

Clutching the woodwork by the side of the window to steady herself, she stood motionless, crouching against the wall.

The face on the outside of the window seemed to be peering into the room, but she could not see its features.

In a moment the sash rattled, and the catch was raised from the outside.

Some one was coming into the room.

Without waiting to see more, the girl sprang back.

Stealthily and noiselessly she withdrew into the room.

She groped her way along in the darkness.

Presently her hand rested upon the drapery of the bed.

At the same moment she heard a sound behind her.

A heavy footfall on the floor.

It was the man getting in at the window.

What could she do? she asked herself. Suppose she escaped by the door, would she find succour in the house?

Was not this man employed to come and murder her?

But even in this moment of terror the thought occurred to her that they would not so soon have made an attempt upon her life. They would surely have waited until she had gone to sleep.

While thinking thus she was searching for the door.

But in her haste and terror she had taken the wrong side of the room.

She heard the footsteps approaching. They were close upon her.

She expected every moment that the man's hand would seize her by the shoulder.

At that moment the curtain of the bed came again under her fingers, and the thought occurred to her that she had better conceal herself under the bed.

Stooping then, she noiselessly crept beneath it.

Scarcely had she done so when she heard the click of a flint and steel, and then the room was suddenly lighted up.

Still as death she lay there listening.

A fearful dread of the vallance being raised, and of a horrible face glaring in at her, held her spell-bound.

But the person who had entered the room seemed to have no such intention.

He was moving about, making a clanking sort of noise as he went, which she could not account for.

He seemed to be pacing the floor.

The light still continued, so that he must either have relit the small end of candle, or have brought one of his own.

Presently, her fears for the discovery of her hiding-place somewhat subsiding, she ventured very gently to raise the drapery before her, and to peep into the room.

So horrible a sight, however, met her eyes, that for a moment she remained perfectly paralysed with fright.

It would be difficult to imagine a more unsightly object than was this man who had entered thus clandestinely by the window.

Some dreadful accident had at some past time occurred to his face, horribly distorting all the features, and depriving him of the sight of one of his eyes.

The miserable rags he wore scarcely covered him, and through their tatters his gaunt limbs might be seen, covered with dirt and sores.

Around his waist was a circle of iron, in some places bound with rags, as though to prevent its cutting into his flesh.

From this hung the end of a broken chain, which, as he walked about, swung and clanked in the way she had heard.

While she looked at him he closed the window and drew the curtains, shivering as he did so.

Then he approached the fireplace, and, stooping down, endeavoured to set fire to some wood lying there ready to ignite.

To aid him in this design he dragged off some of the paper which hung loosely from the wall near to the window.

Then he went down on his hands and knees, and, thrusting his face close to the smouldering wood, blew it into a blaze.

Before this fire he sat, crouching and shivering, and, from the way in which his miserable rags steamed, she could see that he must have been soaking wet.

Lost in wonder, the frightened girl watched his movements.

Who or what could he be?

It was hardly possible to suppose that he was one of the ordinary inmates of the inn.

This could surely not be his usual style of entering his bedroom.

No, he could not live here.

What was he?

The only probable solution of the mystery was that he was a felon who had escaped from jail.

That was the only way she could account for his conduct and appearance, unless—

Ah! there was one other explanation which might apply to him.

One fraught with such horror that she shuddered as the thought passed through her mind.

Was he a maniac escaped from a madhouse?

She lay there watching him for more than an hour.

His back was still turned towards her.

He sat nodding over the fire, every moment threatening to fall headfirst into it.

His steaming clothes emitted a close stifling smell, which filled the room, and made her feel very sick and ill.

Every now and then, when his loud breathing told her that he was asleep, she had a vague idea of crawling from under the bed, and making an attempt to escape.

Every time, though, that she was about to make a movement the man woke up.

To make up her mind to wait patiently until he fell fast asleep was, then, the only course open to her.

She waited with what patience she could muster.

She was herself miserably cold and wretched.

Her own clothes were soaked by the rain, and her limbs ached.

She got so dreadfully cramped by lying so long in one attitude that the pain was intolerable.

When, however, she made the slightest movement it seemed as though it always startled the sleeping man, and he woke with a start and a muttered exclamation to gaze around.

Overcome with fatigue at length, after vainly struggling against the drowsiness stealing over her, she closed her eyes and slept.

All at once she awoke in great terror.

Strange and horrible cries echoed in her ears.

Tremblingly she raised the drapery and gazed into the room.

Upon the floor before the fire the maniac was rolling and fighting as though in convulsions, shrieking, grinding his teeth, and clanking his chains in a manner horrible to behold.

As she continued to gaze upon him, however, he grew calmer, and presently, awaking from the fearful dream which was agitating him, he rose to his feet, wiped the perspiration from his brow, and crawled towards the bed.

In unspeakable terror, she watched and listened, as he drew the curtains on one side.

It was not safe yet, she thought, to come from her hiding-place.

His sleep seemed scarcely to last more than two or three minutes at a time.

Whenever she ventured to move he was awake again, starting up in bed, listening, crying out, " Who is there?" or venting his rage upon his unknown disturber in savage threats and curses.

Presently she again fell asleep, but for how long she had no means of judging.

When, however, she again awoke, it was to hear the sound of voices in the room and a struggle upon the bed.

"Quick, quick!" she heard one voice say. "Give me the knife. She wakes."

"Here!"

Then followed a blow. Then a deep sigh, a half groan, and a death-like silence.

"Do you want a light?"

"No. Let's come away now."

"But the jewels. Had you not better look for them?"

"Why should we?"

"It will be over then, and we need not return."

"Never mind. I would rather return presently than stay now. I feel sick. Let's come away. The jewels are safe enough."

The footsteps moved away, the door closed, and the sound of the voices died out.

The listener, however, remained silent where she was.

"Great Heaven!" she murmured to herself, "what has happened? The old woman and her granddaughter have committed a horrible murder. They thought I was in the bed."

While she was thinking thus a fearful sound met her ear.

It was the sound as of water trickling slowly. It was the dead man's blood, dripping from the saturated bedclothes to the boards below.

Some of it fell upon her hand, and she drew it back with a shudder.

She waited no longer then, but began to crawl from under the bed.

Upon her hands and knees by the side of the bed she placed her hand upon the bedclothes to help herself up.

As she did so she placed it upon the hand of the supposed corpse.

She drew back in affright, and in another moment would have started to her feet, but the hand closed like a vice round her wrist.

She uttered a half-stifled shriek, and strove to free herself from its hideous clutch.

Was the man not dead after all?

The fingers encircling her wrist were icy cold.. They held her with the stoney grip of death.

Frantically she struggled to free herself, but in vain.

Striving to wrench herself free, she dragged the body towards her, until it lay on the edge of the bed.

Another violent jerk, and she dragged it over, so that it fell with its other arm round her neck, and its frightful head, gashed and blood-stained, resting on her bosom.

With a mad, despairing effort she tore herself free, and fled to the window.

She dragged it open and gazed down wistfully.

Day was breaking now, and she could see the flags of a court-yard about ten feet below.

But how was she to descend?

The man must have reached the window by the aid of the tree, but he had done it only by moving himself forward on one of the branches, which, relieved of his weight, had resumed its place again.

Somehow or other she must descend.

She climbed upon the window-sill and looked down.

As she did so she heard footsteps in the passage, and the handle of the door being turned.

Not a moment was to be lost.

She hesitated no longer, but sprang upon the window sill, and leaped down.

She fell with stunning violence upon the flags, and lay for some seconds unable to move, until the old woman's voice at the window above aroused her.

"See, see!" she cried, "she has escaped."

"Quick, quick! Follow her, or she will get clear away."

The fugitive vainly struggled to regain her feet.

In falling she had struck her head against something, and was half senseless from the force of the concussion.

But she must make an effort.

She crawled on her hands and knees towards the wall.

By its aid she regained an upright posture and steadied herself.

Then made an effort to run.

But before she had got two yards from the house she was seized by the arm and dragged back.

A scowling ruffian held her prisoner. He took her in his arms, and, in spite of her efforts to free herself, carried her back into the house.

As the door closed she uttered a piercing shriek—a heart-rending wail of terror, which echoed shrilly across the lonesome heath.

Heaven ordained that it should reach the ears of some one willing and able to assist her at this moment of dire distress.

A solitary horseman passing slowly and thoughtfully along the high road reined in his steed as the cry was wafted towards him on the morning air, and listened intently.

No other cry followed it, and he was for a moment doubtful from what direction the sound had come.

He, however, did not allow any time to elapse before he took some steps to find out the cause.

Springing lightly from his steed, he knelt upon the road and placed his ear to the ground.

For an instant only he remained thus; then, jumping up again, he bounded into the saddle, and set off at a gallop for the inn.

"I fancied it was so," he said to himself. "They are again at their old work of murder and robbery; but perhaps this time I may be able to see fair play."

He had no need to do more than shake the bridle, and the handsome creature which he bestrode carried him at lightning speed across the heath.

In a few moments he had reached the inn.

He sprang from the saddle, and hammered with his riding whip at the door.

As, however, he received no answer, he wasted no more time in that direction, but, glancing at the priming of his pistols, ran round the house.

He presently came to a window about four feet from the ground.

Into this he scrambled, smashing away the sash with almost superhuman strength.

Scarcely had he alighted on the floor when the piercing shriek again rang in his ears.

He rushed forward through the room, broke open the door, and bounded into the passage.

Following the sounds, he soon came to another apartment, where the unhappy girl was struggling with the ruffian and the old woman.

They were tying her hands with a rope.

In the corner of the room was a horrible well-hole, down which it appeared the wretches were about to hurl their victim.

But without pausing to make an inquiry, the newcomer raised a pistol, and discharged it at the ruffian's breast.

With a fearful cry, he sprang into the air, and fell dead.

The old woman dropped on her knees, shrieking piteously for mercy.

Heeding her not, however, the gallant stranger took the half-fainting girl in his arms and bore her from the room.

"Who are you?" she asked, when the fresh air fanning her face recalled her to consciousness. "Who are you that have thus saved me from a fearful death?"

"They call me Red Ralph," replied the man. "I am an awful scoundrel, according to accounts, but still between whiles I occasionally do a good action that nobody hears of."

"Heaven bless you," said the beautiful girl covering his hand with burning kisses.

CHAPTER LXXXV.

CHASE OF A SPY—RED RALPH ALONE—FORTUNATE ESCAPE—WHERE ARE THE YELLOW BOYS?—THE SPY'S COMPACT—BACK TO THE INN—A SCRAMBLE—OPPOSED TO AN ARMY—A SPIRITED ATTACK—RED RALPH'S PROWESS—FLIGHT OF THE YELLOW BOYS.

RED RALPH, when he jumped from the window of the inn at Epping Forest in pursuit of the spy, with his wonted good fortune, alighted safely upon his feet.

The spy, less lucky, had sprained his ankle, and, although he was putting himself into untold tortures to fly from the Yellow Boys, he made but little progress.

Off darted Red Ralph, and in an instant came up with the unfortunate wretch.

"Stop!" cried Red Ralph.

But the man only endeavoured to hobble the faster, howling with the pain of his ankle as he went.

With one bound Red Ralph overtook him and brought him to bay.

The spy had grown desperate.

It was life or death, and he attacked the captain of the Yellow Band with a courage of which the latter had not deemed him capable.

But Red Ralph could afford to despise him.

The man was unarmed and helplessly lamed.

"My friend," quoth Red Ralph, "you had certainly better keep quiet. You'll not improve your condition by resistance."

"Cold-blooded villain!" said the spy breathlessly. "Would you have a man quietly submit to be murdered?"

"Pshaw!" said Red Ralph. "I think that you have now been sufficiently startled."

The man's face brightened up in an instant, as if by magic.

"And—"

"And we shall let you off cheaply—too cheaply, doubtless."

"By Heaven you shall not," cried the spy. "I confess I have merited your vengeance, though perhaps not death. Do but look over this matter, and count upon my eternal gratitude."

"Gratitude?"

"Ay."

"And what is your gratitude worth to me, pray?" asked Ralph.

"Much."

"Explain."

"Shall I not continue to be near your avowed enemy, Jonathan Wild?"

"Possibly."

"Enough. He hates you and your band as never mortal hated mortal yet. Many are his foes, but he would willingly forego all thoughts of vengeance upon any but you—dear as it is to his bloody-minded nature—provided he could be assured of that."

"I well believe that," said the captain of the Yellow Band.

"You may, indeed," resumed the spy eagerly. "I have heard him say as much upon several occasions."

"But even then I do not see how you could aid me."

"Not see it?"

"Not I i'faith."

"'Tis clear enough," said the spy. "The thief-taker's life is spent in devising schemes for your capture. He has suffered more reverses and more defeats at your hands than at those of the best moonlight cavalier that ever cried 'Stand!' to a true man."

"I think that he never gains much by his interviews with me," said Red Ralph laughingly.

"In truth he hasn't—and yet he is never tired of following upon your track."

"I marvel much, however," said Red Ralph, "that his men are not, for they all along have had to share the reverses of their leader."

"They are," answered the spy, "and therefore you see me here. He can get none but new men to engage in the service. An idea has got abroad that you are something supernatural."

"A kind of vampire," laughed Red Ralph, "or a Flying Dutchman, eh?"

"Ridiculous as it is," pursued the spy, "they presume that you bear a charmed life, and will not attempt your capture again."

"Indeed I'm sorry for it," said Red Ralph, "for

their polite attentions have always afforded me some amusement—a little distraction. Some violent excitement is the food of my fevered blood."

"That accounts, then, for it," murmured the other thoughtfully.

"For what?"

"Seeing you follow this strange career, captain."

"Partly. I have other motives."

"Indeed!"

"Yes, family matters, which—"

The spy leant forward eagerly to catch his words, but Red Ralph turned abruptly off.

"Which do not concern any one."

The other dropped back somewhat abashed.

It suddenly occurred to Red Ralph that he alone of the six they mustered in the inn had followed in the chase of the spy.

What had become, then, of Walters and the four Yellow Boys?

"Where could they have stayed?" muttered Red Ralph half aloud.

"I know," exclaimed the spy.

"Ah?"

"Yes—I never thought of it before—a small detachment of constables were to arrive at the inn about the time that you burst into the room. They probably arrived later."

"I see."

"And found that you had gone upstairs."

"From the landlord," exclaimed Red Ralph, "and waited to see who your six visitors were."

"No doubt," said the spy. "But if that is the case, how is it that you alone have eluded them?"

"By my usual luck," said Ralph. "I jumped through the window after you."

"And they?"

"Went out of the house in a rational manner."

The spy looked up into Red Ralph's face in wonder.

"In truth," he said, "it would almost appear that there is a special providence hanging over you."

"I must return to the inn. If you have any truth in you, you will not venture to join our enemies against us now."

"I swear it by Heaven!" exclaimed the other fervently.

"Enough."

"Nay—'tis not enough. I will do you a service. You shall know by some sign when our mutual foe Jonathan Wild is hatching new treachery."

"Your hand upon it," cried Red Ralph.

The spy took the proffered hand and pressed it cordially.

"Remember!" said Ralph.

"I will, never fear."

"Farewell."

"God speed and preserve you."

And the spy—the enemy whom Red Ralph had so suddenly transformed into a friend—stood watching the receding form of the bold Yellow Band's captain until it disappeared in the distance.

As Red Ralph neared the inn once more the sounds of a noisy struggle struck upon his ear.

A violent clashing of swords, mingled with oaths and blows, could be heard for some considerable distance.

In an instant Red Ralph had whipped forth his own bright blade, and hurried to the scene of the conflict, grasping a pistol in his left hand.

As he entered the inn a most exciting spectacle met his view.

Walters, the lieutenant of the Yellow Band, was struggling upon the ground in the arms of two stalwart constables, and wrestling like a lion.

One of the four Yellow Boys had been also beaten to the ground, and a constable was standing over him threatening him with an uplifted sword.

"Tell me," cried the constable as Ralph entered, "what has become of him. Where is he?"

"I don't know."

"You lie."

"The lie is yours," cried the prostrate Yellow Boy. "Out upon you for a man-hunting vagabond!"

"Tell me where is Red Ralph, or I'll brain you as you lie there."

"I know not," returned the Yellow Boy, "and, moreover, I would not utter a word if I knew."

"One more chance I give you," said the constable, with fast growing choler, "and then you are a dead man. Where is Red Ralph?"

"HERE!"

All eyes were turned to the door when the highwayman just paused momentarily upon the threshhold.

"Be this Red Ralph's answer to you," cried the captain of the Yellow Band.

And bounding to his side, he delivered the man a blow upon his sword arm which left it dangling helplessly by his side.

Up sprang the Yellow Boy with a wild cry of delight.

Delight more at the return of their beloved leader than for the rescue at such a perilous juncture for him.

Red Ralph now turned his attention to the lieutenant.

Two blows of his stout sword, delivered with lightling rapidity, sent the lieutenant's two captors to grass.

Up sprang Walters, snatched a sword from one of the fallen constables, and threw himself upon some fresh foes.

"Another debt of gratitude I owe you, captain," he cried.

"Then pay it at once, Walters," cried the captain of the Yellow Band, "by settling accounts with as many of those rascals as possible."

"Good," cried the lieutenant.

And in a trice he was cutting and hewing away at the constables with a will.

Up to the present three of the Yellow Boys had been making a desperate stand against a whole host of constables.

At least a dozen of them remained in fighting condition.

The three Yellow Boys were back to back, forming a small triangle, and cutting away desperately.

But the odds were so prodigious that their utmost efforts could only keep the others at bay.

To assume an offensive position was utterly out of the question.

Red Ralph speedily joined his mighty weapon to those of the men and Walters, and in the space of three seconds as many of the constables had bitten the dust.

But a mighty force yet remained to be disposed of.

It was almost an impossibility to cope successfully with all.

This Red Ralph saw at a glance, and he determined to make some sort of a diversion by which they could beat a strategic retreat.

Presently an opportunity offered itself.

One of the foremost constables lost his balance, and Red Ralph made a grand charge at the very moment.

Back they fell in a disordered mass, leaving the doorway clear.

"Now for it!" cried the captain of the Yellow Band.

All charged the poor constables in a body, and their confusion became hopeless.

A few final blows, and Red Ralph with his sword pointed to the door.

The men comprehended his meaning in an instant.

Then, before the constables could recover them-

[A LAST CHANCE FOR LIFE.]

selves, or dream of offering any resistance, the whole troop of highwaymen had fled.

"After them!" shouted the leader of the constables.

Every man echoed the cry, and the whole body flew to the door.

And now it became an exciting chase.

Red Ralph and his followers set off at a breakneck pace, hotly pursued by the constables.

Unfortunately for the latter, the Yellow Boys had got such a start that they were not very likely to be overtaken, for some little time at least.

Moreover, they were so thoroughly acquainted with every part of the country that they had an immense advantage over the constables.

No. 28.

CHAPTER LXXXVI.

AN EXCITING CHASE —"FIRE!"—A BAD SHOT— A HUNTER'S LEAP—OUT OF THE RACE—RALPH ON THE ROAD—A BOLD EXPLOIT—THE THREE TRAVELLERS — THE STRANGER WHO WISHED TO BE ROBBED—THE PURSE AND THE GUINEA —THE ESCORT — THE KING—"BY HEAVEN! I KNEW IT."

THE Yellow Boys kept together for some time, until Red Ralph gave the signal to separate.

Then they spread themselves about in every direction.

This bothered the constables terribly.

But of all of them they only desired to secure their far-famed leader, Red Ralph.

Then, without a word, as if upon a tacit understanding, they started off in a hot pursuit of him alone.

Red Ralph, however, of the whole party was the most fleet of foot.

He bounded along like a deer, increasing the distance between them at each stride.

This he continued for some considerable time.

It afforded him some amusement to hear them panting behind him, when he would double his speed, and dart away from them laughingly, with the adroitness of an experienced professional pedestrian.

But presently he heard them making preparations which caused him to abandon this agreeable pastime and take to the briars and thickets.

"Load and fire!" cried one of the constables breathlessly.

The words seemed to take away what breath remained to him.

He had to fall out, and relinquish the chase exhausted.

"Come on!" cried Red Ralph.

The constables replied to this taunt with a shout.

Red Ralph, however, had a startler in reserve for them.

His wind was prodigiously long, probably because he had been so thoroughly seasoned to this kind of thing.

He increased his speed slightly, and bounded into the air, clearing a tall hedge in a style which would have done credit to a hunter.

One of the constables ran wildly forward in advance of his comrades, and drew up short.

Then presented a pistol, and fired at Red Ralph hastily.

Alas! too hastily.

The bullet went so very wide of the mark that they could hear the highwayman's jeers, although they could no longer keep him in sight.

Red Ralph might now be said to have eluded them.

Further pursuit they saw would be madness — folly.

"Curse the fellow!" said one of them, panting as if he could never recover. "He's not to be caught."

"So say I."

"And I too," said another.

"Then why were you so hot after it all along, eh?"

This seemed likely for a while to provoke the constables to a little dispute among themselves.

However, they wisely smothered their little private chagrins, and held a council of war upon the next steps in the pursuit of the captain of the Yellow Band.

The only thing which remained to them was to follow up such traces of Red Ralph as they could find.

Thus they were as likely to take him by surprise as they would have been to effect his overthrow in making a dash.

The latter course was now impossible.

With commendable caution they carried this wise resolve into execution, and started off in a very short space of time upon the business.

What effect attended this expedition we shall show.

*   *   *   *   *   *

Red Ralph, when free from the attentions of the constables, once more grew impatient, and longed for action.

Something to keep him from thought—thought which was maddening.

He made his way to a beautiful little dell in the forest, where he found his horse tied to a stake beneath a thick rain-proof foliage, a spot admirably selected by the highwayman as his forest stable.

Then, with a light hand upon the neck of the horse and the back, he vaulted into the saddle.

"Hey for the road!" he cried, starting off at a brisk canter.

For more than an hour he rode about his wonted promenades, but not a single traveller appeared in sight.

"The rough weather has kept the roads clear for to-night," said the highwayman, walking his horse gently up a hill. "And yet I scarcely feel inclined to give up my trip without a little excitement, and, egad! my purse wants replenishing sadly, too."

The incline he had mounted was wonderfully steep, and being at all times a most considerate master for his horse he paused to give it a long rest after its exertions.

The hill-top was one of the highest points in that part, and commanded an extensive view of a very beautiful country for miles around.

Our highwayman, who was, as the reader will say, a bit of an anomaly throughout his whole way of life, was not insensible to the beauties of nature, and could not fail to be impressed with the glorious panorama which lay stretched at his feet.

The sky in the west was of a blood-red hue, and had a beautiful and rich effect upon all the country round.

Its crimson shadows were reflected with most pleasing effect upon the foliage in every direction.

"This is truly a most glorious sight!" murmured Red Ralph enthusiastically. "Brilliants and—and—" here he sank at once from the sublimity of his nature-worship to his lawless calling with an alarming slip—"and should tempt some travellers forth for my game."

As he spoke these words he gently stroked his horse's mane and patted his neck.

The crimson sunlight reflected upon the pec blood-stained colour of his hand rendered it of a yet deeper hue.

For a moment it almost appeared as if it were moist with blood.

The highwayman shuddered, and hastily concealed it beneath his doublet.

Red Ralph, the bold and unscrupulous robber—the man who feared nothing upon earth—who would take the purse of another with as little compunction as possible—apparently held his own blood-stained hand in the greatest horror.

The secret of this we shall have occasion to explain later.

For the moment it must suffice that the whole of Red Ralph's past and present wild career of sin was connected with it.

It was the dread secret of his family, and one which he was very anxious to preserve.

But out of this very shunning of notice had grown the reverse effect.

Thus had he received the title of Red Ralph from one of his lawless companions, and the name had clung to him throughout his wild career of crime.

Lost in painful meditation, our robber-hero sat motionless on his horse until a faint sound in the distance caused him to look up.

At first he could see nothing, but presently he perceived the dark outline of a figure moving along beneath the shadow of a row of wide-spreading trees.

"I'll ride and see," said Red Ralph, rousing himself by an effort. "May be a chance will present itself."

He set off in a gentle canter down the hill.

Presently he drew near enough to distinguish the moving objects.

He was not a little surprised to discover that no less than three horsemen were riding towards him.

One rode on ahead, and a glance showed him to be a man of superior rank.

The two riders behind were not at all to be mistaken for grooms.

The foremost rider was a man of middle age, and rather above the ordinary height, well proportioned, and rather prepossessing in appearance.

As they drew near Red Ralph halted in the centre of the path and met them with a low salute, bending over his horse's neck.

The three horsemen returned the bow with much politeness.

But the highwayman could not help observing that, whilst the two rear horsemen uncovered to salute him, the foremost only bowed with a stiff grace.

"Good evening to you, gentlemen," said Red Ralph.

"A good night to you, sir," returned the foremost horseman.

"I beg your pardon, sir traveller," said one of the other two to Red Ralph, "could you guide us to the Wharton Manor?"

"Yes," returned the robber, "willingly—it is no distance."

"Many thanks."

"Spare your acknowledgments," said Red Ralph.

"Nay—not so."

"But I beg you will. I have a small favour to demand."

"Demand?"

The tone of the speaker indicated clearly enough that he did not approve of Red Ralph's form of speech.

"I mean," returned Red Ralph, "that I have a particular favour to ask of you in return."

"Oh! ask it by all means," said the horseman. "We do not care to remain under an obligation to a stranger."

Red Ralph waved his hand, to intimate that he did not consider the favour so great.

"Your pardon," said he, "I merely have to beg of you a trifling service—nothing more."

Then have it, in Heaven's name!" said the foremost rider.

"It is a trifling loan."

"A loan?"

"Ay," said Red Ralph. "The loan of your purse."

"Sir!"

"And those of your two friends here, together with such valuables as you possess about you."

The three travellers looked from one to the other, and appeared to be quite alarmed at the magnitude of his demand.

"What may you please to mean by that, sir?" demanded one of the two travellers.

"Robbery!" thundered the other.

"Robbery?" echoed the foremost traveller with a slight start. "Surely the knave could never attempt to despoil our persons upon the open highway!"

"I beg your pardon," said the robber, turning to the speaker, "but such is precisely my intention, by whatever title you choose to designate it."

"Villain!"

"As little bother as possible, if you please," said Red Ralph.

"Rascal!"

"Ruffian!"

"Treason!"

The cry of the last speaker considerably astonished the highwayman.

Treason! What could he have wished to imply by that?

Surely they could not turn highway robbery into injury by thought or deed to the state.

"Scarcely treason," said the robber, hoping to draw them out.

"Treason most damnable!" persisted one of the travellers.

The words were barely spoken when he would have recalled them.

The foremost rider turned upon him with a frown, which appeared to give him a desire to shrink into the saddle.

This was not lost upon the captain of the Yellow Band.

A sudden thought flashed through his mind.

At first he had imagined that this was no common person he was stopping, but now he was impressed with a singular notion that he was addressing one of the highest possible rank in the realm.

Red Ralph turned from him to the two horsemen who formed his escort.

"Now, gentlemen, oblige me," said Red Ralph, "with this little loan we are about to negociate."

"Never!"

"Never!" echoed the other.

And they endeavoured to push by the highwayman and continue their journey.

However, Red Ralph was never to be disposed of with so little ceremony.

Very coolly he brought them to a stand, by presenting a pistol at them.

"Now, gentlemen," he said, "oblige me by not forcing me to proceed to extremities. I have the greatest desire to treat you with every consideration."

"Hang your impudence!"

"D—n his politeness!"

"Most extraordinary!" said the horseman in advance.

"Never heard of such a thing in my whole life."

"Possibly," said the highwayman, "but will you oblige me with your valuables?"

The cocking of the pistol seemed to gain upon the nerves of the two travellers, and they produced their purses with a simultaneous jerk.

A glance convinced Red Ralph that they were well lined.

Ralph bowed his acknowledgements, and, bending low in the saddle, saluted them with a parting "Good night."

The other traveller, however, presented a purse to him.

The robber waved back the proffered purse with a gentle and respectful gesture.

Then, hat in hand, he made a profound obeisance.

"Sir," said he, "I do not wish for your purse. The liberality of these gentlemen has replenished my exchequer for the present."

"Exchequer?" repeated the stranger, with a chuckle. "Egad! but the knave would share royalty with the king, eh, gentlemen?"

The two gentlemen laughed at this sally, as well they could be expected to do under the circumstances.

"But I must insist," said the former speaker, "if these gentlemen have had to pay you black mail, then so will I. Take it, sir."

But Red Ralph still refused.

"'Sdeath! sir," cried the traveller, "my purse is as well lined as theirs, and its contents are as good and sound coin."

"Nay," said Red Ralph, "I doubt it not, sir; but I am particular to confine my misdoings to taking toll upon the king's highway."

"And not the king's person," said the stranger in a whisper to one of the escort.

"Precisely."

"Eh?"

"I said precisely," said Red Ralph, whose quick ear had at once detected the words.

"What do you mean, sir?"

"That I must still refuse your gift," said Red Ralph. "I am what you will, but still a loyal subject. My name has often figured foremost in defence of the king and state, and I shall not be the first of my race to turn traitor."

"A strange fellow!"

"Truly."

"But what may your name be, then?" asked the stranger.

"Red Ralph."

"Red Ralph? I do not remember any such name."

"That is my present appellation, said the highwayman."

"Oh, oh!" cried the stranger. "And you have a string of aliases as long as my arm I'll warrant."

"Red Ralph!" exclaimed one of the rear horsemen. "Is it possible that you are the fellow we have heard so much about?"

"You do me honour—"

"Unenviable."

"This is the highwayman, sir," said the former speaker, in explanation, to the gentleman who sought to be robbed, but failed, "of whom your—I mean you have heard so much of late."

"Truly."

And immediately our hero became the object of the fixed regard of the three horsemen, and was subjected to a scrutiny which he found embarrassing in the highest degree.

"'Sdeath!" cried the stranger. "This is that formidable rascal of whom I have heard so much. I thought him a very devil—a Flying Dutchman, I swear!"

"And I, sir," said one of the others, "I am all amazement. I pictured him a ferocious giant!"

"Well, well—come along, gentlemen—and here, Sir Red Ralph."

"*Sir* Red Ralph?"

"Well."

"I might claim the honour of knighthood for those words at some future day."

The travellers exchanged glances of great significance.

"Tut!" said the gentleman," but the knave is as ready with his wit in repartee as he is with his fingers in our fobs. But take the purse, sir."

"Nay, I cannot."

"Cannot?"

"Dare not."

"Dare not? Sir, you speak in riddles," said the stranger. "As for daring, when you have dared thus far—"

"Oh! pardon me, sir," said Red Ralph hastily. "When I say dare not, I mean that it would sit heavily upon my conscience. I fear no man else."

"You rogue, if you knew all you would only be too glad to take the purse. See what a boast it would give you when you were squandering its contents in getting mad with liquor with your thieving companions."

"May I ever be spared so sad a boast," said Red Ralph. "But since you press your gifts upon me so, I accept a portion of it only."

Taking the purse, he opened it and took out a guinea.

Then he returned the purse.

"I take this as a souvenir of this honour," said the highwayman.

"How, sir?"

"As a gift from the most illustrious—"

"Sir!"

"I accept it only as a *portrait*," said the highwayman. And then bowing humbly he turned once more to the two horsemen, who were listening to the foregoing conversation in silent astonishment.

"Gentlemen," he continued, "I salute you. Accept my humblest apologies for this night's work. I would at once repair the wrong and return your valuables did I not think that my conduct might be possibly attributed to fear."

Thus speaking, the highwayman rode off, hat in hand, leaving the three horsemen staring after him in the utmost amazement.

He had not ridden far when he encountered two more horsemen.

They stopped Red Ralph as they drew near.

"Pardon me, sir traveller," said one of them. "Have you seen any one go past this road?"

"I have."

"Attended?"

"Yes."

"By two horsemen?"

"Yes."

"The road was clear?"

"Quite."

"Accept my thanks. I almost feared that they would be molested by those rascals who infest these roads."

"No fear of that," said Red Ralph.

"But there is great fear—the more especially if they chanced to recognise his Majesty."

"His Majesty?"

"Ay, sir."

"By Heavens! I knew it."

"How, sir, have you seen him?"

"Yes, yes—that is, I told you but now I have seen him escorted by two horsemen."

"To be sure. Good night, sir, and my best acknowledgments."

"Good night to you, sir."

And Red Ralph and the two horsemen rode off in opposite directions.

CHAPTER LXXXVII.

AN ADVENTURE—THE HAUGHTY STRANGER—THE NARROW PATH—THE ENCOUNTER—VICTORY—THE COUSINS—THE HAND OF BLOOD—THE GLADE —THE CONDUCT TO THE HAUNT—ON THE TRAIL —VENGEANCE—"HOLD YOUR HAND!"—TOO LATE —THE DOOMED CONSTABLES—THE EXPLOSION.

SLOWLY and thoughtfully Red Ralph returned to the present haunt of his bold Yellow Boys.

The adventures of the night had almost satisfied for the present his thirst for excitement.

Still one more adventure was in reserve for him before he rejoined his followers.

As he rode along in a contemplative mood—a mood which he studiously shunned, but which grew upon him in unguarded moments—he came suddenly across a solitary traveller.

They were both advancing along a narrow bridle path, and it was only possible for one to pass at a time.

Red Ralph was so thoroughly absorbed in his thoughts that he did not observe the traveller advancing until he got quite close.

Then both looked up.

However, neither of them appeared to be inclined to move from the path.

The traveller was not less pre-occupied than our hero.

"Your pardon, sir," said the stranger, with an unpleasant kind of hauteur in his tone which ill suited his words. "One of us must dismount."

"Indeed?"

"Ay, sir."

Red Ralph looked up just the least bit disgusted.

"And then, sir?"

"I certainly shall not."

"Nor I."

Then came an ominous and most unpleasant pause.

"I must pass," at length quoth the stranger testily.

"By all means."

"Then pray stand aside."

"Impossible."

"Sir?"

"I say it is impossible," said the captain of the Yellow Band. "The path is too narrow."

"Then I must dismount?"

"Certainly."

"I shall not, sir."

"As you please," said Red Ralph. "I have no wish to force your inclinations in any way."

"Force my inclinations!" echoed the stranger. "You use strange expressions it appears to me."

"Indeed?"

"Ay, sir, indeed."

"And it seems to me, sir traveller," said Red Ralph. "That you would force a quarrel upon me."

"Not I."

"Then why is your manner so strangely disagreeable?"

"Sir?"

"Ay, more than that, sir, it is devilish unpleasant."

"Enough, sir," said the stranger angrily. "I am a peaceable man, but as you appear to desire that I should quarrel with you—"

"Not I."

"I say, sir, that since you appear to desire that I should quarrel, I have no objection."

"Oh!"

"I never refuse a quarrel with any man."

"Nor I."

"Nor at any moment."

"Nor I."

"Then I think that any difference could be well and fairly adjusted upon the spot."

"With all my heart. I ask for nothing better."

As coolly as if about to discuss some ordinary topic of the day, the two men jumped from their horses, and fastened them to a tree.

Then both drew.

"Now, sir," said Red Ralph. "Do you mean seriously to press this singular quarrel?"

"Oh!" cried the stranger with a jeering laugh. "So, so, sir braggadocio, you hang fire?"

"You think so?"

"It looks like it."

"Indeed? Then, sir, let me tell you that if I hesitated to enter into this quarrel it was more out of consideration for you than myself."

"Then let me tell you that your consideration is sadly misplaced," said the other.

"Not so, for I am experienced in the use of arms."

"Truly?"

Not wishing to notice the sneer that accompanied the word, Red Ralph continued—

"Yes, sir, such were my motives; but since you have let fall certain expressions which might be construed into an imputation of cowardice upon my part, I shall at once proceed."

He held forth his sword and stood on the defensive.

The stranger advanced to meet him, and their weapons crossed with a clash.

At the onset Red Ralph would have treated his adversary very cavalierly, but he speedily found that he was now opposed to no mean skill.

He was a perfect master of the sword, and handled his weapon with a grace and dexterity which would have reflected credit upon a *maitre d'armes*.

"One," cried the stranger.

"Nay."

"A hit—just a touch."

"Nay, sir," said Red Ralph. "I assure you—your point just grazed my coat."

The stranger seemed vexed.

It had been very near indeed, and the captain of the Yellow Band had grown wary and cooler upon the instant.

Now both began to see the metal that was in the other, and to bring the utmost pressure to bear upon their play of life and death.

The most skilful passes were exchanged.

Still the two duellists were unhurt.

At length, by mutual consent, they paused to rest.

Both were greatly heated by their exertions, and upon the front of the traveller more especially the perspiration stood out as if a shower of dew from some overhanging tree had fallen upon him.

"You fence well, sir," said the stranger, wiping his brow.

"Thank you, sir."

"May I ask the name of your master?" pursued the stranger.

"I haven't had one since I was twelve years of age."

"Indeed? An early age that to learn the use of arms."

"I had foils made expressly for me when I was but eight years old," said Red Ralph.

"Eight?"

"Ay, sir."

"Then you must have been shot out of the cradle to the riding school I should say."

"Almost."

"Destined for a military life?"

"Yes."

"Father a soldier?"

"No."

Then Red Ralph abruptly terminated the conversation.

"I am wasting your time, sir," he said, rising from the trunk of a tree upon which he was seated.

The other noticed the action, and sprang to meet his enemy.

Red Ralph could not help noticing that the stranger blushed like a girl as he advanced.

The reason was doubtless that he had thought to understand in Red Ralph's hasty turn off in the conversation an imputation upon his courage.

By those questions he might wish to prolong the delay which had occurred whilst they rested.

"Your pardon, sir," said the highwayman. "You will excuse my abruptness."

"Sir?"

"I would not for worlds affront so noble a foe."

The stranger bowed.

"You merely touched me nearly just now in conversation."

"Hit upon some little family matter?"

"Which I should prefer avoided—buried in oblivion, if that were possible."

The stranger regarded Red Ralph curiously before replying.

"Sir," he said, after a pause, "the apology is due from me, then—nay, but it is—I thoughtlessly hurt your feelings."

"Scarcely that."

"Accept my apology, then."

"I do in all gratitude."

After this warm interchange of courtesy both prepared to renew hostilities once more.

"On guard, sir?"

"On guard."

And the second bout was a display of such address and skill as would have delighted a school of students.

"The first blood?" asked Red Ralph.

"Sir?"

"The first blood parts us?"

"As you please. We fight à l'outrance, if you desire it."

"Not I, by Heaven!"

"Nor I."

"Then the first scratch shall decide the battle."

"Good."

And both applied themselves to it so earnestly that it would almost have appeared to the casual observer that they were engaged in the bloodiest conflict.

Presently Red Ralph had his weapon nearly beaten from his grasp by an adroit cut of his adversary.

In an instant, however, he had recovered it, and returned the attack with such sudden vigour that the other was taken completely by surprise.

He retreated rapidly to make a firm stand, but Red Ralph pressed him too hotly.

The duel drew near its close.

When his adversary was nearly stumbling from being backed into a tree, Red Ralph made a feint, sprang nimbly forward, and succeeded in reaching home.

It was a mere scratch which he inflicted with his sword's point upon the other's brow.

"A truce!" cried Red Ralph, throwing down his sword.

"Right well and nobly played for," said the stranger.

"An accident."

"Not so, I swear," said the stranger, graciously. "You fence with a precision and judgment I have rarely seen equalled—never surpassed."

"Sir, you do me honour—you flatter."

"Not I, I swear. I would not so far insult you nor forget myself as to offer flattery to a man who has carte and tierce at his fingers' ends."

Red Ralph bowed his acknowledgments.

"One word more, sir," said the stranger. "Before we part would you oblige me?"

"In what way?"

"By telling me your name."

Red Ralph started and looked confused.

"Not if it troubles you at all," added the stranger, hastily.

"Not at all."

"Pardon me," said the stranger." I fancied that I perceived a kind of hesitation in your manner."

"You did for a moment," said the captain of the Yellow Band; "but I most willingly give you my name."

"Thank you.

"Upon one condition."

"Oh! impose any you please," said the stranger.

"Then it is that you do not mention me to any living soul."

"Granted."

"Nor couple my name with that of any one of whom you may hear strange things told."

"Well, I consent to that," said the stranger, looking up into the highwayman's face in astonishment.

"Then I am called Rowland Wharton," said Red Ralph.

"Wharton?"

Ralph bowed.

"Surely not of the Wharton family?"

"I believe so," said Red Ralph. "And now if you will pardon an abrupt leave-taking."

"By all means."

"Good night."

"Good night, sir."

"And remember your promise."

"My word's my honour," said the stranger. "My honour is my life."

They were parting when Red Ralph suddenly bethought him to ask his adversary's name.

"By all means," said the stranger. "It is an exchange of courtesy which is your due."

"But do not mention due if you would prefer keeping silence upon the point."

"Not I!" said the stranger." "You can take it and publish it to the world. I have no wish nor reason for suppressing my name."

Red Ralph winced.

The stranger perceived this, and was sorry the next instant for his thoughtless speech.

"A thousand apologies, I'm sure," said the stranger. "I did not think of what I said, or believe me I would not—"

"Not a word, I beg," said the captain of the Yellow Band, interrupting him graciously. "Your name is,—"

"Cecil Wharton Vane."

"Indeed."

"You know the name?"

"Well."

"Then you are related to the Wharton family."

"Yes."

"And consequently to mine."

"Then, my cousin, your hand."

Red Ralph extended his palm to the stranger.

"Why, whoever would imagine that this delicate woman's hand had such an iron wrist at the end of it that it could so handle a sword? Cousin, may we know more of each other."

After these remarks upon the delicacy of the palm he grasped he was about to examine it, but Red Ralph tore his hand away with a jerk.

Mr. Cecil Wharton Vane looked rather astonished, but was silent.

"Once more, good night."

"Good night."

And thus they separated.

Red Ralph was not long in reaching his haunt.

It was a cave adjoining the old spot—the scene of so many of their former exploits.

Above the cave were still the ruins of the old house of which we have already spoken.

As Red Ralph gained the glade one of the Yellow Boys darted out of the thicket, and with a most significant gesture enjoined him to silence.

Then to follow him.

Red Ralph obeyed.

The man led him by a most circuitous route to the cave.

The reason for this, however, he was not long at a loss to divine.

The sound of strange voices in earnest conversation at no distance reached them.

A little nearer yet the Yellow Boy drew Red Ralph, and now he could hear the conversation which ensued.

The officers of justice were upon the track. The Yellow Boys were hunted down like a pack of destroying wolves.

It was the party of constables, who had proceeded warily, as determined in the consultation held after the flight of Red Ralph, and had come unexpectedly upon the robbers' haunt.

Unfortunately, their proceedings here had not been conducted as warily as their advance.

The constables had been overheard by the Yellow Boys, and a terrible end was awaiting them.

The hunted banditti were about to resist the attack of the police by a measure which would be a terror to the country.

Upon arriving near the mouth of the cave Red Ralph saw two of the Yellows Boys busily employed in arranging gunpowder in small kegs, with other combustible matter, for an explosion.

"What is this?" demanded Red Ralph in consternation.

"Hush!"

But it was too late.

The constables above had overheard, and could be heard upon the top of the cave scrambling along.

"Now then," cried one of the Yellow Boys. "They are all there!"

"Good!"

A train of powder was laid to the kegs in the space of two seconds.

"Stop!" cried Red Ralph.

Too late.

The match was blown and applied.

Then a flash of fire twisted its hasty and tortuous course along the ground with a hiss.

Then a terrific explosion!

CHAPTER LXXXVIII.

THE FATAL DEED — RALPH LEAVES THE BAND — TO LONDON — THE ABBEY CLOISTERS AGAIN — THE WITNESS TO AN ABDUCTION — RALPH TO THE RESCUE — TOO LATE — THE STRANGE ENCOUNTER — THE ASSASSIN'S KNIFE — "I'M SLAIN!"

A FEARFUL deed was done—a deed of violence to be repented of at no distant date by the band of desperate men who had committed it.

The cave was blown up.

The constables, who had collected in a body in the ruins of the house above, had been hurried into a terrible fate without a moment's warning.

Their bodies, many of them dismembered by the violence of the explosion, were blown to fragments in every direction.

Limbs were flying about in a way that was truly awful.

So sudden and so complete had been the vengeance of the Yellow Boys that not one of them remained to tell the sad tale.

To a man they were killed upon the spot.

Desperate had been the persecution of Red Ralph and his followers, and desperately had the latter avenged themselves.

Hunted to the death, the Yellow Boys had turned like a herd of stags at bay.

And now their retaliation began to be awful and severe.

This tragic event, too, could not be known in the metropolis for some time.

The batch of constables who had come to such an untimely end would be missed, and various causes assigned for it, no doubt.

But for the present the authorities could only proceed by guess work.

The dangerous and desperate nature of the errand upon which the constables had started would render their absence at once the signal for the most astounding stories amongst the newspaper quacks.

And yet they would be, doubtless, far short of the truth.

Red Ralph now grew moody and silent.

The fearful events — the two awful tragedies which the Yellow Boys had recently enacted—filled him with alarm and grief.

His path was smeared with blood.

Against fate itself had he striven to avoid the taking of life.

He had passed through a wild career.

A career of danger, skirmish, and pursuit.

He had been brought to bay a hundred times, and had always contrived to keep that main principle in view.

And yet now, after all he had undergone to preserve himself from these crimes, other hands than his

had wrought two of the bloodiest massacres, with which his name must now be for ever associated.

To remain longer there for the present was impossible.

In spite of the utmost entreaties of the Yellow Boys and the warm-hearted lieutenant, Red Ralph started off early that night.

His first care was Leonore.

How had she fared all this time?

At first he silently reproached himself for having forgotten her.

Yet no—she was not forgotten.

Even in his wildest, most exciting moments of danger, and often of deadly peril, he had given his beloved wife a thought.

Arrived in London, he turned his horse towards Westminster.

With all possible speed he was by the ruined house.

Here he met with an adventure which not a little startled him, and caused him much annoying afterthought.

As he passed by the abbey cloisters a coach drove up.

Out sprang two men—ferocious-looking ruffians.

One of them carried a cloak, which appeared of a most unreasonable size and weight.

"I wonder much," said Red Ralph to himself, "what these fellows are after. I'll keep watch."

Red Ralph dismounted, left his horse in the care of a porter at some short distance, and then made his way back to the cloisters.

Here he secreted himself behind one of the columns, in such a position that he could overhear nearly all that was said in an ordinary conversation pitch.

But without risking observation he could not well see all that passed in this business.

Barely had Red Ralph taken his place when he heard a female shriek.

A wild piercing cry, which rang out an alarming echo through the abbey cloisters.

This was too much.

At all risks Red Ralph sprung from his hiding-place.

There he saw a tall black looking fellow struggling with a female, who was completely enveloped in the folds of the cloak he had noticed before.

One of the two men he had at first noticed—the possessor of the cloak which they had put to such treacherous service—opened the door of the hackney coach.

In spite of her struggles, the woman was thrust in with her ruffian antagonist.

The door was closed, and off dashed the coach at a rattling pace.

All had been effected so momentarily that the coach was far ahead before Red Ralph could advance a dozen strides.

However, he determined to regain his horse, and follow in pursuit.

He had not now exercised the necessary caution.

His object was too palpably demonstrated.

So, before he had quitted the cloister, he suddenly found himself confronted by the man who had opened the coach door.

The owner of the cloak.

The man had so suddenly sprang before him, appearing to dart out of a timeworn old column, that Red Ralph was completely taken by surprise.

"Where are you going?" demanded the fellow.

"Ha-ha!" cried Red Ralph. "I'm going to look after this devilish ill-looking business.

"Truly?"

"Ay. And you shall accompany me."

"O-ho!"

"Come on, you rascal. We've no time to lose."

And then, as Red Ralph attempted to pass, the fellow put up his arm.

"Stand back!"

Red Ralph's blood was up to his front in an instant tathis insult.

,'Knave!" he cried. "You dare presume to raise your arm to me!"

"Dare!" echoed the fellow. "Look you here, I've half a mind to trounce you well."

He caught at our hero as he spoke.

But he made a sad mistake here.

The slight figure and delicate appearance of the captain of the Yellow Band did not seem to conceal muscles like the finest-tempered steel.

The hands were barely upon his shoulders when Red Ralph caught at him and seized him by the wrists.

Then, by a sudden turn, he twisted them so painfully that he was toppled over.

Then, as he rolled in the gutter, Red Ralph, to show his utter contempt of him, spurned him with his foot.

"Roley!" cried the prostrate ruffian. "Help, help!"

Red Ralph turned round, anticipating a second encounter.

He was not disappointed in this.

But, alas! he turned too quickly round.

At the very instant he turned his head a second fellow, who might have been the worsted villain's twin brother, from their extraordinary resemblance, sprang forward.

A long knife glittered in his clutches.

One blow at the highwayman staggered him, and he fell.

"Miscreant!" cried Red Ralph. "Assassin! I'm slain!"

───

CHAPTER LXXXIX.

RALPH WOUNDED — TO THE RUINED HOUSE — —THE DISAPPOINTMENT—THE MISSING GIRL— "AH! 'TWAS SHE!" — RALPH IN PURSUIT— THE HUNCHBACK'S HOUSE—THE GARDEN—THE CRIES—TO THE RESCUE.

THE wound which Red Ralph had received was rather a severe blow for the moment than aught else.

This he soon discovered.

After a second he rose from the ground bleeding rather profusely from a stab in the arm.

A little inspection of the hurt, however, showed it to be but slight.

It had not touched either of the arteries.

The weapon of the assassin had glanced through the sleeve of Red Ralph's coat, catching a slight hold of the flesh, and just punctured the skin upon his breast.

This it was that had deceived him, making him for the moment imagine himself past surgical aid.

However, the roughest of surgery sufficed for the present.

Taking off his neckcloth, he bound it tightly round the wounded arm.

The two ruffians who had made this murderous attack upon him had long since disappeared.

They had vanished upon the instant.

Pursuit without any possible clue meant no pursuit at all.

Ralph, therefore, very wisely dismissed the subject from his mind as well as he could, and made his way once more towards the ruined house.

But still that piercing shriek rang in his ears.

Still, by a strange and unaccountable impulse, he felt urged to exert himself in the woman's behalf.

It was surely something far greater than an ordinary sympathy with a helpless victim to villainy.

Brooding upon this, and vowing to take a great vengeance upon the first of the precious trio that he should meet, Red Ralph arrived at the ruined house.

He paused.

A footstep caught his ear.

Then he drew back, for he knew that the gipsies kept their residence in the ruined house a profound secret, and that they could only enter or leave their abode when quite free from observation.

Without this wise precaution they would have been driven off, and hunted from the metropolis.

In the days of which we write these vagrant tribes were regarded as a pest, and really suffered much unnecessary persecution at the hands of justice.

Hence the violent hatred which the Zingari bore the house-dwellers.

To resume.

Hearing some one approach, the captain of the Yellow Band drew back until the person should pass.

It was useless, however, to observe this precaution.

A woman stepped from the door of the ruined house.

"Leonore!" cried Red Ralph.

And, bounding forward, he clasped her in his arms.

The woman coloured slightly at the warmth of his embrace.

"Not so, Red Ralph," she said, gently repulsing him. "'Tis Mina."

The highwayman changed upon the instant, as if by magic.

"True," he said, "and right glad I am to see you, Mina."

The gipsy queen could not fail to notice the sudden change from fire to ice, and she turned heartsick.

Wildly, devotedly, she loved Red Ralph.

Loved, and in secret.

"And Leonore?" said Ralph.

"Is well."

"Thanks, thanks," said Red Ralph, "a thousand thanks, dear Mina."

"For what?"

"For your love."

"Love?"

"To Leonore. How can we ever hope to repay all we owe you?"

"Ralph," said the gipsy queen, in a low, but earnest voice, "I am already repaid—amply repaid."

"How?"

"By your words."

"Dear, dear Mina," exclaimed Red Ralph, warmly.

And seizing her once more in his arms—not an unwilling prisoner! — he imprinted a kiss upon her brow.

Suddenly he looked into her face, encountering the glance of her upturned eyes.

So full of passionate love—of tender affection.

"But Leonore?"

As the words were spoken Mina gently but firmly disengaged herself.

A stifled sigh broke from the gipsy queen.

Then she was herself again.

"Leonore?" said Mina, looking around her. "I was about to question you."

"Me?"

"Ay."

"But wherefore?"

"She was here but now."

"Here!"

"Yes. She came out with me."

"But how comes it you are alone, then?" demanded Ralph.

"We came forth together, but I returned for an instant. 'Twas but an instant. When I got back I missed her, and—"

Ralph turned sick.

[RALPH, TURPIN, AND KING STOP THE MAIL COACH.]

The expression of pain upon his countenance was so marked that Mina grew alarmed at once.

"What ails you?" she asked. "Are you unwell?"

"No—a slight twinge. But tell me, where were you to go with Leonore?"

"Merely for a ramble to breathe the fresh air. We have latterly been about the Abbey cloisters."

Ralph gasped.

"The cloisters?"

"Yes. We go there as soon as it grows dark. Before then we have thought it unsafe to venture forth."

"Great Heavens!" ejaculated Red Ralph, with a burst of agony.

"What is it?"

"The Abbey cloisters!" replied Red Ralph. "Oh! monstrous!"

"What is?"

"Sister, I passed the Abbey cloisters but now on my way hither. Suddenly I was startled by a loud shriek, and upon going to ascertain the cause of it I found a woman enveloped in a large black cloak struggling in the hands of a huge ruffian."

Mina shrieked.

Already she apprehended the worst.

"But did you not interfere to save her?" she demanded.

"I did, vainly," replied the captain of the Yellow

Band. "Before I could gain the spot the woman was thrust into a hackney coach waiting at hand and driven from the spot."

Mina clasped her hands in bitter anguish.

"But why did you not follow the coach?" she demanded.

"I essayed to," returned Red Ralph. "But ere I could quit the cloisters I was set upon by two ruffians. One I disabled, but a second attacked me in the rear, and I was felled to the ground by a stab from a Spanish stiletto. See here."

As he said this he held up his arm for her inspection.

"Great Heavens!" exclaimed the gipsy queen. "You are wounded."

"Slightly."

"Let us see a surgeon."

"Nay, there is no danger for me, I have bandaged it up. It is but a little blood-letting."

"And this woman who has been abducted you think is—"

"Leonore. I do."

"Merciful Heavens!" said Mina. "What shall we do now?"

"I know not," said Red Ralph. "Let me think over it a while."

The peril in which he now believed Leonore to be drove all possibility of reasoning from his mind.

He clasped his hands wildly across his brow, as if to force thought.

"Mina," he said, "can you give no idea to whom we owe this villany?"

"None."

"Think, I beseech you."

"The thieftaker?"

"Ay, 'tis he."

"But if he had been acquainted with our hiding-place I should have been the first to fall to his enmity."

"Ay."

"Stay. I've yet another notion."

"Tell me quickly."

"Shortly after you left us in the ruins a person of whom Leonore had the greatest fear found his way into the place by the aid of Jonas."

"Jonas?"

"Ay, he—the traitor."

"And this person?"

"Is one Jabez the hunchback."

"Jabez!" cried Red Ralph wildly. "Then I have it now."

"What. You think—'

"That 'tis he who has carried off Leonore."

"In person?"

"No. These are hired ruffians. That was plainly to be seen by their expertness at their damnable trade."

"But how to find this hunchback?"

"I know his house."

"This is indeed a marvellous chance!" said the gipsy queen.

"Ay. There must have been a special providence in this. By a fortunate accident I was put in possession of a letter addressed to him. Then it preserved me from great danger—possibly saved my life."

"Heaven grant, then, that it may prove as propitious now."

"Amen."

We must here be pardoned a slight digression.

To connect the incidents of our narrative the more effectually, we would recall to the mind of the reader that the letter addressed to Jabez the hunchback had been given to Red Ralph by the writer, Lady Glyde, upon the night of the memorable exploits of our hero at her ladyship's mansion, upon the occasion of the grand ball.

The letter was given to Red Ralph when disguised as a domestic, and had been his passport from the house when the doors were barred against all, to prevent any possibility of his issuing from the place.

"I must fly," said Red Ralph.

"Ay, lose no time."

"Farewell, Mina."

"Stay. Have you all you desire?"

"All."

"Means? arms?"

"Yes, yes. A thousand thanks. Fear not. Your sister shall be restored to you, or I shall never more see you."

"Farewell."

"Farewell."

"Courage and success."

Red Ralph waved his hand to Mina and rushed off.

Poor Mina stood watching his receding figure until it disappeared.

Then, heaving a heavy sigh, she returned to the tribe.

Red Ralph found his horse awaiting him in the charge of the porter.

He sprang into the saddle, took a coin from his pocket, and tossed it to the man.

It was the first that came, and, being a guinea, made the porter a far happier man than the donor felt at that particular moment.

Off dashed Red Ralph post haste.

As he rode along he took a packet from beneath his waistcoat, opened it, and took out the very letter to which we have just alluded.

Having read the address, he galloped to the hunchback's house.

Now Red Ralph well judged that if he endeavoured to obtain admission into the house in the ordinary way—the door—that the hunchback would be put upon his guard.

This would be fatal.

At the back of the house was a garden, only protected from the road by a back wall.

An ordinary brick wall would not have presented much difficulty to the captain, but this chanced to be covered with broken bottles and the sharpest flint so effectually that not a square inch was left to give an intruder the smallest advantage.

This was a puzzle.

How could it be got over?

Red Ralph was not the man, however, to be brought to a standstill by such an obstacle.

He lopped off a branch of a handy tree and, placing it upon the top of the wall, rested it securely between some of the stoutest bottles.

Then, placing his left hand upon the branch, he sprang up and vaulted cleanly over.

He looked about.

So far his progress had been unobserved.

At the nearest end of the garden was the cottage.

There were two entrances. One upon the level of the garden.

A second by some stone steps leading to the basement.

He tried the nearest.

"By all the infernal chances!" ejaculated Red Ralph. "How shall I get over this?"

This was soon answered.

His hand yet lingered upon the door latch, when he heard a loud female shriek.

A piercing cry.

A wail of woe which must have proceeded from a poor wretch bodily and mentally afflicted.

For an instant the captain of the Yellow Band stood motionless.

Then his eyes flashed fire, his breast heaved, and he bit his nether lip until it bled.

There was a second cry.

As loud as before, no doubt, but scarcely so distinct.

It seemed as if another door now partly killed the sound.

"The villain!" cried Red Ralph, with a burst.

Then he threw himself on the door with his whole strength—by no means a force to be despised in his present humour.

Beware who shall cross Red Ralph now!

In went the door—shivered—splintered to a thousand fragments.

The highwayman strode across the broken wood into the passage.

Then listened.

A cry was heard again from above.

Less distinct this time.

A smothered shriek.

So distinct was it, however, that Red Ralph at once divined the cause of the sound.

"Heaven and earth!" he exclaimed, "she's stifling!"

So low was the sound that he had not been enabled to distinguish in which direction it proceeded.

He listened again.

No further cry, however, was heard.

Not the faintest sound to guide him.

He must try every direction.

Oh! agony! The mischief might be completed in the time which he should lose.

With a rush he darted into the nearest room.

Then a second. But they were empty.

As he turned to fly from the latter, he perceived that there was a second door at the further end of the room.

He rushed towards it.

His attention was now arrested by a faint sound.

So faint, so slight, that it was a wonder that he caught it.

It proceeded from the room which he was on the point of entering.

He could hear that several men were engaged within in earnest conversation.

It could not be there, then.

Back he came.

Darted into the passage.

Then upstairs.

A scuffling noise now caught his attention.

He listened.

It was in a chamber upon the right.

With the thought his hand was upon the door.

"Mercy! mercy!"

The voice proceeded from within the chamber.

The tones were Leonore's.

The door was burst open in a trice, and in dashed Red Ralph.

CHAPTER XC.

A CRITICAL MOMENT—THE KNIFE—RALPH IN TIME — A BOLD ENCOUNTER — JABEZ OVERTHROWN—AID FOR THE HUNCHBACK—FEARFUL ODDS—A DESPERATE COMBAT—"FLY, LEONORE!"—RALPH VICTORIOUS—THE WINDOW—THE SHOT—THE WOUND—"AM I HIT?"

HE was within the room.

And now what a fearful spectacle met his view!

What a sight of horror!

The robber's wife — his beloved Leonore—was struggling upon the ground with Jabez the hunchback.

The hideous wretch was clutching her fair throat.

With his disengaged hand he grasped a knife—a large and murderous looking weapon.

The knife was in the air ready to descend upon the alabaster throat of Lady Leonore.

But her struggles were frantic.

She wrestled as only mortal can wrestle when in a strife between this and eternity.

Else had she been lost some minutes since.

"Dog!" cried Ralph.

His sword leapt from the sheath, and he bounded forward.

Such an impetus did his fury give that he fell upon the hunchback with the sword.

Then cut wild at him.

The blow was given with prodigious power, but with the flat sword.

Otherwise the hunchback had lived no more to prey upon suffering humanity.

As it was, however, the force of the cut did service.

He staggered, and quitted his hold.

And Leonore, released, sprang forward towards Red Red Ralph, and sank sobbing upon his breast.

"Never weep, my Leonore," said the captain of the Yellow Band.

"Oh! Ralph, Ralph!"

"You're safe now."

"Never!" cried the hunchback.

And, springing up, he darted towards Red Ralph.

The highwayman met him, however, with such a steady point that he drew up.

It was rushing upon certain death to advance further.

The hunchback leapt into the air, displaying an agility of which no one would have deemed him capable, and grabbed at a sword which hung suspended over the chimney, together with a variety of small arms.

"Devil!" cried the hunchback in a fury, "you shall die the death. I swear it."

And with this he commenced a furious onslaught.

But Red Ralph met him with a smile upon his lips.

Coolly he turned off every cut or thrust.

While Jabez was white and speechless with rage Red Ralph met him with the coolness of a *maitre d'armes* in the fancy school.

As yet the captain of the Yellow Boys had only acted upon the defensive in the combat.

"Now, Jabez," quoth he, as he warded off a desperate stab, "now on your guard!"

"Hellhound!"

"On your guard, I say."

"Bastard dog!"

"On guard!"

A third abusive epithet rose to the hunchback's lips.

But no time had he to utter it.

Ere it could be given he found the threatened blow come upon him with a shock.

One cut from the highwayman's sword beat the other's weapon to the ground.

A second cut did but little damage, but was quickly followed by an effective thrust.

A delicately aimed thrust.

So neatly done, in fact, that the robber's sword passed through the hunchback's cheeks—damaging his beauty and impairing his future speech.

"There!" said Red Ralph.

Then he withdrew his sword, wiped it, and awaited the further attack.

"You shall repent that," roared the hunchback.

"You will," said Ralph.

"Never shall you leave you this place alive," ejaculated Jabez.

"And who will prevent me?"

"I."

"Fool!"

The little wretch stamped upon the floor violently at this fresh taunt.

"Dog! devil! cut-purse! rogue!" screamed the hunchback, stamping violently between each word.

His gestures suddenly raised some suspicions.

Red Ralph began to mistrust.

Did so much stamping mean only the ebullition of the deformed ruffian's rage?

No, surely.

Something more was to be apprehended from it he deemed.

Was it a signal?

Another instant proved the truth of his conjecture.

Suddenly a smile of triumph lit up the hideous physiognomy of the hunchback.

A demonical laugh, which might have been the rejoicing of the Prince of Darkness at the overthrow of a once virtuous mind.

"Ah!" cried Ralph.

"Now, my friend," said Jabez, spitting out the blood from his mouth between each word, "now I think that we shall be equal."

"Never!"

"I shall cry quits with you for this scratch."

As if to prove the unworthiness of the title which he gave to a wound which was really severe, the blood founted from his mouth in a very cataract at this moment.

His person was deluged with the ensanguined stream.

And now he looked more hideous and ghastly than ever.

Just then a noise was heard without.

Some one was ascending the stairs.

Assistance for Jabez!

"Traitor!" cried Red Ralph. "But your life is forfeited now."

"Or yours."

The hunchback, with a boldness worthy of a better cause, presented a ready weapon to the highwayman's eager attack.

Their swords crossed.

"Defend yourself," cried Red Ralph.

"To the last gasp!"

"Fool! You leave yourself uncovered every instant," said Ralph.

"Then find your opening," retorted the hunchback.

"I cannot."

"Ha! ha!"

"To slay you thus would be nothing short of murder."

"No!"

It was true. A dozen times could Red Ralph have given his deformed adversary the *coup de grace*.

But he forbore, even now that his temper was up.

His main principle was yet strong before him.

He was strengthened in his mind by the recent run of tragic events.

Time grew precious.

The footsteps were outside upon the landing.

"Enter!" cried the hunchback. "Ho! ho! To the rescue!"

"Open, open!" said a voice without.

A voice, too, which struck familiarly upon the ear of the highwayman.

"Leonore," said Ralph, "can you hold the door a while?"

"Yes, yes."

The poor girl was now becoming almost accustomed to these exciting and dreadful scenes of danger and hair-breadth escapes.

She preserved her presence of mind in a way to be highly commended.

What strength the delicate girl possessed was at once exerted in keeping fast the door.

And effective it proved.

As the door opened outwardly they could not gain much purchase from the exterior.

Leonore held the handle firmly.

The lock was turned.

Thus a brief respite was gained.

But yet it could not long endure. In a few brief moments assistance for the hunchback would arrive.

What then would be the result of all Red Ralph's struggles?

Failure, defeat, and ignominy.

Leonore's death, or worse.

The latter thought caused our hero such a twinge of agony that in an instant all his scruples vanished.

Jabez should die.

One foe removed, he could hope to resist the others.

"Jabez, you're doomed," said the highwayman, determinedly.

"Braggart!"

"Nay."

"Braggart!" cried the hunchback. "Braggart and fool!"

"You'll find I but speak sincerely," said Red Ralph.

The dwarf's only reply to this was to feint, and make a sudden lunge, which changed their positions.

He was veering round!

Nearing the door!

The highwayman was only upon guard for himself at this moment, and Leonore had well nigh come to harm.

Suddenly the dwarf raised up his sword aloft.

Red Ralph, thinking that a mighty attack was meditated, met it with an ordinary guard.

But, no!

With the cunning of a fiend, the hideous hunchback had awaited his moment to strike home.

He sprang from the ground.

Made a wild rush at the door.

Aimed a blow at Leonore.

All this in the space of a second.

An instant later, had Red Ralph paused for a moment to consider the chances, his wife had been slain.

He bounded forward, with an agility rivalling that of the hunchback.

Struck up his weapon as it was within an inch of Leonore's bosom—thirsting for her heart's blood.

Then in rapid succession delivered him a blow upon the forehead which laid bare his head, and passed his sword through the deformed body.

"Ugh!"

A sob burst from his lips.

He rolled over against the door, and there lay in mortal agony.

The life-blood gushing from his mouth in a torrent.

It was a fearful spectacle!

The hatred expressed still upon the manikin's face was fearful to behold.

His passion struggled with his agony for the mastery, and it was difficult to say which gained the day.

"Ho, ho!" cried Jabez. "To the rescue, you knaves! Ho! ho! ho."

"Ho, ho!" answered a voice from without. "Open! open!"

"Force it."

Leonore was no longer there to guard the entrance.

Still, as if by a kind of justice, a retaliating justice, the hunchback's own helpless body impeded the opening of the door.

And he was powerless to move.

A blow was delivered upon the door from without.

It yielded.

But in pushing it open it mangled the body of the hunchback in a pitiable manner.

Still he never murmured at the treatment.

His anguish he could not suppress, in spite of himself.

A hollow groan burst from him, and with it a cry of rejoicing and encouragement to the newcomer.

Ralph smelt danger.

Since the hunchback was so sanguine it could be no mean power he was to oppose.

Springing forward, he raised his sword above the hunchback.

"Another word, and I brain you," he said, in a determined tone.

Jabez was silent.

Even now he could hope for life.

With his whole soul in the emergency, the highwayman awaited the entrance of the newcomer.

Grasping his trusty sword, still reeking with the proofs of his vengeance, he awaited.

The violence of the shock broke the upper hinges of the door, and it fell with a crash over the prostrate body of the hunchback.

Three men appeared at the doorway!

The nearest, grasping a long sword with a basket hilt, strode over the fallen door.

He had not advanced into the room when Red Ralph met him.

Met him with a rush.

So impetuous and so unexpected upon the part of the man that he was completely taken by surprise.

A cut and lunge from Red Ralph, and he bit the dust.

Two remained yet to be disposed of.

Both sprang simultaneously over the fallen door and the two bodies, and rushed upon Ralph.

Like a rock, our hero withstood their united attack.

But still he could not now hope to run successfully through such a series of dangers.

His strength, too, was not inexhaustible, and the two foes were now quite fresh.

We have seen, upon the other hand, what Red Ralph had undergone in that eventful day.

Still he did not feel inclined to shirk an encounter.

His prowess already served him well.

The two bleeding bodies of his already worsted foes created for him an amount of respect which was highly serviceable.

The two men lacked confidence.

Still, with even this advantage, what could he hope to achieve?

"Cut him down, you rogues!" shouted the hunchback, faintly.

His breath was nearly spent, and yet, to show his hatred to the last, he used so much of it in words.

"Down with him!"

"Come on!" cried Red Ralph. "You play with me, you rascals!"

"He mocks you!" said the hunchback, hoping to provoke them to anger by his words.

He succeeded in part.

One of the three grew enraged, and made a slight mistake.

His safety lay in his coolness.

Once deprived of this, he gave Red Ralph an opening which in his present critical position the highwayman was not likely to miss.

A severe wound upon the left arm cooled his ardour.

At the same time it staggered both his adversaries.

Here was Red Ralph with his single arm opposing a host!

Two were severely hurt, a third had an ugly cut in the arm, and the fourth was terribly blown, and apprehensive of his punishment coming next.

And Red Ralph was unscathed!

Untouched!

"If I could but secure a retreat for Leonore," thought the highwayman.

From the defensive he made a vigorous onslaught, beating his two adversaries from the doorway.

Now the exit was free.

"Leonore," said Ralph, his eye still fixed upon the opposing ruffians.

"Yes."

"Fly! Escape at once."

"And you?"

"Fear nothing for me. I shall wait until I have finished these two villains, and then I will follow you."

"Where?"

"To Westminster again."

"Stop her," said the hunchback, whose voice had now sunk to a hoarse whisper.

"At your peril!" cried Red Ralph. "Move but an inch towards the door, and, by my soul, I swear never to leave the spot until I see you both dead at my feet!"

Both paused.

The words of the highwayman sounded rather alarming.

"Fools!" exclaimed Jabez, who was now scarcely audible. "Are you to be cowed with words?"

"Nay."

"Ah! my friend," cried the robber with bitter sarcasm. "And you? Have you been cowed by words?"

"No! no! no!"

"Truly, you haven't. But you have something to remember me by. I warned you. Away, Leonore! Fly! You embarrass me. I will rejoin you, fear not."

"Heaven protect you!" said Leonore.

She was deathly pale.

Still though her heart stood—still at the thoughts of the deadly peril her beloved husband was encountering for her sake—she had such confidence in his prowess that she scarcely thought it possible for him to encounter defeat.

As she stepped over the fallen door Jabez raised his hand to intercept her.

Red Ralph, albeit so greatly occupied, found time to glance there and aid her.

He sprang back, and jumped upon the hunchback, silencing him for the present.

But it was useless.

Jabez had not now even the power to offer the smallest opposition to her progress.

Leonore passed out.

Fled down the stairs.

Free!

Escaped once more from a deadly peril.

Freed from a fatal clutch, and at the eleventh hour.

"Free! free!" cried Red Ralph in a tone of triumph. "Liberty!"

Then he applied himself vigorously to his adversaries.

"Look to it now," he said.

As he spoke he sprang upon one side, and applied the whole force of his attack to one of the men alone, before the other could aid him.

A slight wound was the result of this successful feint.

"Confound him!" ejaculated the man. "He'll escape us yet."

"Has he pinked you?"

"Ay."

"Curse him! Let us fall on him both together. Don't let us heed his toasting fork, or we shall wait patiently here whilst he chops us up."

This was precisely what Red Ralph feared.

They had now worked him into a corner.

The position was dangerous—full of peril.

Still he would not shrink from the fight after his great success.

"Look out!"

"All right."

"When you're ready."

"If you mean me," said the highwayman, with a light laugh, with was scarcely in accordance with his present sensations. "I am ready and willing always you know. Come on."

"Here, then."

" Now."

And with fury they did come on.

Their two blows were aimed at his head, and he took both upon his sword in good style.

Still the shock was too much for his weapon to sustain.

The force of the shock shivered it up to the hilt !

Red Ralph was unarmed.

Defenceless !

And two armed adversaries had yet to be dealt with.

Red Ralph beware !

Another minute and you must cry " Hold, enough !" for now, at length, the chances are against you.

But all hope was not yet over for the highwayman.

Quick as lightning the danger flashed through his brain.

The chances and the results had been cogitated in the space of a few seconds.

Before either could recover from the violence of their blows—ere their weapons could be upraised for a fresh attack—Red Ralph was at work.

He struck at one, giving him a violent blow in the face with the hilt of the sword.

This sent the fellow reeling against his comrade in villainy.

Then with lightning rapidity he turned to the other.

Rushed upon him, and seized him by the throat.

His grasp was yet as firm as ever.

The muscles were not yet relaxed, in spite of the terrible fatigues he had undergone.

The throat of the ruffian suffered much damage, although the grasp was but momentary.

Then, with a prodigious effort, Red Ralph hurled him to the ground.

He fell with a mighty crash against the other, who was rising at the instant.

" Come on !" cried Red Ralph, now thoroughly worked up. " Come on to the end !"

But ere they could rise Red Ralph bounded over the door, which was still resting on the now insensible form of the hunchback and the first of his hired assassins.

" Victory !" shouted the robber, taking the whole flight of stairs at a jump.

" I conquer !"

He hurried to the door.

With cries of triumph, he tore it open and issued forth.

Free was he, too, from what had appeared such a fatal chance.

" I have settled accounts with all," cried the highwayman joyfully. " I knew my vengeance upon my black-muzzled assailants of the Abbey cloisters would come, but did not deem it would be so speedy."

He had now gained the main road, and was passing the front of the house in which he had just spent such an exciting hour.

Suddenly a window was thrown open.

He looked up, and perceived his last two assailants.

Both grasped pistols, and were taking aim at Ralph.

Quick as thought our hero threw himself flat on his face.

Just in time it seemed, for the report came at this precise moment.

As he rose he felt a sharp pain in his arm.

" Ah !" he cried. " I am hit. I hope it is not dangerous."

The blood was pouring through his sleeve.

The next moment, however, he remembered whence he had taken this wound.

It was the old hurt from the Abbey cloisters.

The bandage had got loose in the scuffle, and the slight pain he experienced was simply the result of the blood having dried the wound and stuck to the coat sleeve.

A second shot now followed.

But Ralph was out of reach.

" Now for Westminster once more," he cried.

He soon found his horse quietly grazing where he had left it, and was speedily galloping back to town.

CHAPTER XCI.

RETURN TO WESTMINSTER—THE CLOISTERS ONCE MORE—THE STRANGER—THE WARNING—AN OLD ENEMY—A BOLD SALLY—IMPRUDENCE—OVERCOME — THE PRISONER — THE PROCESSION — CHARING CROSS—THE BARONET'S INVITATION—THE HANDCUFF—THE ROMANY CULLS—THE RIDE FOR LIFE—THE BRIDGE—SURRENDER—LIBERTY OR DEATH—A DESPERATE LEAP.

THE events which we have just recorded of the captain of the Yellow Band led him to retrace his steps with all possible haste towards Westminster.

His destination was the ruined house, the abode, for the time, of Mina and her tribe.

As Red Ralph was issuing from the Abbey cloisters he encountered a person whose face and form were familiar to him.

The man, too, evidently recognised him, yet, singular to relate, passed him by without any sign of recognition.

Red Ralph turned and gazed after him.

Arriving at some little distance off, the man beckoned to him and Red Ralph followed.

Then as Red Ralph drew near him he pressed his finger upon his lips and motioned him to silence.

" Pass on," he whispered.

Ralph walked on slowly.

As he lingered by the man the latter whispered —

" *Beware !*"

" Of what ?"

" Wild."

" One word," said Red Ralph in the same tone.

" Hush !" said the other, looking round affrightedly. " I am watched, and I would not give an hour's purchase for my life did it come to his ears that I was seen speaking to you.

" But what is the danger which I have to apprehend ?"

The man looked about him with a deal of mysterious precaution before replying to this.

Then he leant his face across to Red Ralph's and whispered—

" Go not to Westminster."

" What do you mean ? Here I am at Westminster."

" Ay, but not where you propose going."

" Ah !" said the captain of the Yellow Band, " how know you that I had any particular destination at Westminster ?"

" From Wild."

" But he ?"

" I know not."

" Strange," muttered Red Ralph. " But it is out of all question that he could be aware of it."

" Not at all."

" But how ?"

" I know not how," returned the man. " But that he does know it is very certain."

" How certain ?"

" An ambuscade is prepared for you by Jonathan Wild."

" Ah ! For when ?"

" Now."

" Ah ! my friend," said Red Ralph, looking upon his informant with something of suspicion in his glance. " I am grateful if you would really do me a service, but—"

"You neglect my caution," exclaimed the man annoyed.

"I do."

"But wherefore?"

"Because I doubt the correctness of your information."

"You will be ruined."

"No. It is impossible that Jonathan Wild should know of my visit to Westminster."

"Why impossible?"

"Because an hour since I knew it not myself. Because an hour ago I was miles from this spot, and so placed that the bare possibility of ever reaching here was doubtful."

The man looked puzzled.

Nevertheless, he stood boldly to what he had advanced.

"What it means," he said, "I cannot explain, but this I know, Jonathan Wild has been informed of your meditated visit there."

"But my visit was never meditated an instant."

"No matter—he knows of it."

"Impossible."

"How else do you find me here to warn you?"

"I know not."

"How should he be able to fix the precise moment?"

"Well," said Red Ralph, "it certainly does look singular, but I am bound to say that I cannot upon such doubtful grounds forego my visit."

"Ah!"

As the man gave utterance to this exclamation Red Ralph looked up not a little surprised.

"You appear to me to be strangely interested in my welfare," he said, suspiciously.

"Interested?"

"Ay. That was the word."

"I admit it, but not strangely," returned the man.

"Indeed, but it is."

"Is it possible then that you have so soon forgotten?"

"What?"

"The debt of gratitude I owe you."

"Really," said Red Ralph, with a laugh, "it is gratifying that you haven't forgotten it. But 'pon my soul I don't know what you mean."

"Already forgotten?"

"What?"

"The poor wretch—the spy—whom you would have hanged in the forest," said the man.

Red Ralph uttered an exclamation of wonder.

"In truth," he said, "I had forgotten you. But how is this? You appear another man."

"Merely a disguise," said the fiend's spy. "I have changed the colour of my hair and beard."

"And very effective it is."

At this moment the tramp of a pair of heavy riding boots was heard close at hand.

Ralph looked up.

The spy vanished.

It was all very strange.

So quickly transacted had been the warning that it appeared as if it had been a dream from which he had just awakened.

Then as Red Ralph looked round him another thing struck him as being rather remarkable.

It was the precise spot in the cloisters where he had witnessed the abduction of Leonore by the hunchback's myrmidons.

The very place where he had been struck down by their knife.

Singular coincidence.

It could not fail to produce a strong impression upon the highwayman.

As he glanced along the cloisters he perceived two men advancing in that direction.

One of them he could not fail to recognise.

It was Wild.

"The thieftaker!" mentally ejaculated Red Ralph.

Then there was some truth in what the spy had advanced.

Fortunately the highwayman was well concealed by a projecting column and its dark shadow.

He withdrew a little further, and silently awaited the thieftaker's arrival.

On they came.

They proceeded slowly as they drew near the spot.

Then stopped to converse exactly facing Ralph's hiding-place.

Now a second surprise awaited the captain of the Yellow Band.

Jonathan Wild's companion was one of the highwayman's late antagonists!

Less than an hour since he had left him scrambling upon the floor in the hunchback's house.

And yet he had found time to put the thieftaker upon his track.

"Are you sure of what you state?" Red Ralph could hear the thieftaker ask.

"Positive."

"But this is all a most improbable story."

"It seems so, possibly," said the man. "But this fellow fights like the devil himself!"

"I know it."

"And as for his coming here, I haven't the remotest doubt of that."

"How so?"

"Because when the girl skipped off—curse her!"—

Red Ralph's hand rose instinctively at these words.

"I heard him say distinctly, 'Back to Westminster!'"

"Oh!" murmured Red Ralph in his hiding-place. "This is where he learnt it."

"Then we must lose no time," resumed Jonathan Wild. "I will place the men about the den of these cursed gipsies. He shall not escape me this time."

This was a most alarming piece of intelligence for Red Ralph to acquire.

He did not so much fear for himself.

But Leonore and Mina. To what persecution might they not be subjected?

This flashed through his mind at once, and he had speedily resolved upon a means of putting them off the scent.

A bold stroke and good fortune must stand his friend once more.

"'Sdeath!" exclaimed Jonathan Wild. "I would give all I possess to have Red Ralph secure in Newgate once again—all, all—life itself."

"*Then I claim it!*" said Red Ralph in a voice of thunder.

And stepping forth, he confronted the thieftaker.

"Red Ralph!"

"Ay."

"By Heavens! 'tis he!"

The effect upon Jonathan Wild and his companion was such that neither could make the least movement for a while.

They stood still, surveying the audacious robber.

Petrified with wonder.

Dumbfounded.

The boldness and audacity of this movement upon the part of the highwayman will be duly appreciated when we remember that Red Ralph was totally unarmed.

His sole remaining weapon, his trusty sword, had been shivered to the hilt in his encounter with the very man who stood before him now with his hated foe—Jonathan Wild.

Wild soon recovered his presence of mind.

Red Ralph, however, started with one advantage.

He had never lost his.

Then before they could either of them act upon the

offensive they had to defend themselves from a sudden and spirited attack upon the part of the bold highwayman.

Dashing forward, he delivered Wild a blow in the face which sent him staggering back.

Almost at the same instant he struck at the other with good effect.

The man fell to the ground as if his sconce had encountered a modern steam hammer.

This accomplished, with creditable prudence, he started off at a run.

A smart pace it was, too, and there is but little doubt that he would have soon rendered pursuit a mere farce had not Jonathan Wild, with characteristic presence of mind, summoned assistance, even as the blow from Red Ralph's hand was delivered.

A note upon a shrill whistle which he carried brought a dozen men to his aid.

They seemed to spring from the ground.

Two sprang upon Red Ralph from behind a column as he ran.

But only to meet with a reception which was even a trifle warmer than that which the thieftaker-in-chief had received.

Both were hurled to the ground with such violence that they did not move for some time.

On he ran.

But not far.

Fresh assistance for the thieftaker arrived at every turn, and Ralph began to look serious.

In his impetuous rush he managed to dash past several of the nearest.

But it was impossible that this could long continue.

The odds were fearful.

One man more venturesome than his mates threw himself upon the redoubtable highwayman.

Heedless of all risk, too, for some punishment he was certain to receive from Red Ralph.

However, before Red Ralph could well disengage himself he was dragged by a dozen hands.

One threw himself upon the ground and clutched his legs.

Another seized him by the arms from behind.

Another fell upon him in front, and he was toppled over upon the ground in a trice.

Then ensued a regular scramble, until Jonathan Wild came up with the man to whom Red Ralph owed the present dilemma.

For a dilemma it was most unquestionably.

Although resistance was useless — madness, in fact — the highwayman struggled like a lion in the toils.

At length even Red Ralph must yield.

So he suffered himself to be dragged along.

But it must be said with a very bad grace.

They endeavoured to force the bold captain into a hackney coach, but they soon found this to be an utter impossibility.

He struggled so successfully against all their efforts that they were soon forced to abandon the matter in despair.

So Red Ralph was dragged by the triumphant constables through the London streets towards the prison.

The crowds who followed, as soon as it became known that the prisoner was one of the notorious Yellow Boys, were prodigious.

"Confound the chance!" muttered the highwayman between his clenched teeth, as he went along. "Why did I not take the fellow's warning?"

At length they reached Charing Cross, in spite of mobs, and of all the prisoner's struggles.

Here they made a pause.

A gentleman who was mounted upon a superb chestnut horse stopped the procession to make inquiries of one of the highwayman's captors.

"Mr. Wild," said he, beckoning the thieftaker to him.

Wild ran up to his side and touched his hat obsequiously.

"Yes, Sir Harry?"

"You've got a prisoner there."

"Ay, Sir Harry, and one of some consequence, too."

"So I presume by the unusual strong gathering following in your wake. What is the rascal's name?"

"It is Red Ralph, the captain of the Yellow Band."

"Never!"

"Pardon me, Sir Harry."

"'Sdeath! but I had forgotten the knave."

"Indeed, Sir Harry, have you ever known him, then?"

"Unfortunately."

"So say most of the knave's acquaintance."

"Ay, but I have good reasons myself. The last interview I had with the gallant captain cost me over one hundred guineas."

"You were robbed?"

"Ay. He stopped me close home—on Hounslow Heath."

"What audacity!"

"So you would say if you knew all the circumstances, Mr. Wild. His coolness was astounding."

"Ay, Sir Harry, he's a cool hand."

"I knew it to my cost," said the baronet. "He drew out my purse in the most gentlemanly way you could imagine."

"And would you like to appear against him?"

"Not I."

Red Ralph was here brought near enough to take part in the conversation.

He raised his hat to the baronet.

"How do you do?" said he. "I am happy to renew our acquaintance, Sir Harry."

"Thank you, you dare-devil villain!"

"Hope to have the pleasure of meeting you again shortly, Sir Harry."

"I hope not," said the worthy baronet dryly. "I shall scarcely hope to have the honour of your rogueship's company to supper to-night."

"Why not?"

The baronet laughed heartily at the robber's coolness.

"Am I to consider that as an invitation?"

"What?"

"I ask you, Sir Harry, if I am to consider it as an invitation to supper at your house to-night?" demanded Red Ralph.

"Yes—oh! yes."

"Thank you."

"Gad's life!" said the baronet, laughing so heartily that he almost appeared in danger of falling from the saddle. "But you are the most consummately impudent rascal I ever clapped eyes upon."

"I'll be there, Sir Harry."

"And at what hour?" demanded the baronet with mock gravity.

"When you will."

"Then at ten o'clock I shall expect you—eh?"

"At ten."

"Good."

"Will you do me the honour?" said Red Ralph, holding forth his manacled hand.

"What? Oh! to shake hands. With all my heart."

And the good-humoured baronet leant forward and took the indomitable Red Ralph by the hand and shook it heartily.

"Good bye, you prince of rogues. Good luck to you, and an easy jump from the box."

"Not yet, Sir Harry," said Red Ralph, still grasping the baronet's hand, "though these pretty toys

[THE ATTACK.]

seem to hold me pretty secure. Just take this in your hand."

The baronet good-humouredly took hold of the right handcuff and examined it.

Suddenly, and to the surprise of all, the highwayman's right hand was at liberty.

He had only got the baronet to hold the handcuff whilst he slipped his hand out.

The fact was that it was loose for him, but still tight enough to hold him unless he could get the handcuff held square for him.

It was a dexterously performed trick of Red Ralph's, by which he had frequently escaped from apparently fatal bondage.

A trick too which in more modern times has excited the wonder of all the world, and the execution of which has been ascribed to some supernatural agency.

Red Ralph had no sooner one hand at liberty than he hastened to take advantage of the chance.

He struck out vigorously right and left, staggering his guardians upon either side.

Seized the baronet's horse by the bridle and backed it into the mob of constables.

Then a dig in the animal's side, well delivered, caused it to throw up its hind legs in a terrifying manner.

But this diversion in his own behalf could scarcely

have given him the least hopes of escape had he not assistance in view.

Amongst the crowds following the *cortège* he had observed many acquaintances.

Low rascals who were perfectly prepared to lend a hand to any one to defeat the ends of justice.

"Ho! ho! my chums," he cried out, "a hand for a pal in trouble. Rescue, my Romany culls!"

A shout from all parts of the mob greeted this appeal.

Red Ralph at the same time, before the thieftakers had barely the time to know what it all meant, made a bound upon the horse's back behind Sir Harry.

Then, stretching out his hand, he grasped the reins.

"Now then!" shouted Red Ralph. "Off and away! Ho! ho! hi! Way there, or I run you down!"

The horse, goaded by the active heels of the desperate highwayman, sprang forward amongst the constables.

Down they fell upon each side.

And now ensued a regular (or rather irregular) scramble.

Screaming, the women and children sprang aside.

There was a tremendous rush everywhere, and every one was in every one's way.

"Make way there!" cried Jonathan Wild, in a fury.

But the constables had now got so thoroughly mixed up with the mob that it seemed almost impossible to extricate them.

A singular accident, too, for no one seemed to act openly against the officers.

And yet not less than half a dozen of them were scrambling upon the ground at the same moment.

They had been tripped up at the heels by some busy invisible hands.

"Make way!" roared Jonathan Wild, in a voice of thunder. "Make way!"

And he delivered such serious thumps right and left as he spoke that the surrounding mob was only too glad to obey.

And now he had a pretty clear path to proceed in the highwayman's pursuit.

Red Ralph and the startled baronet, on the still more startled horse, rode wildly down Whitehall.

Then as they neared the bridge (old Westminster) some officious fellows sprang forward to tender their assistance for what they deemed a runaway horse.

"Away!" cried Red Ralph. "Stand aside!"

But they could not at once comprehend his meaning.

A little delay was thus occasioned, and Red Ralph quickly changed their route.

"For God's sake don't turn over the bridge!" said the now terrified baronet.

"There's no danger."

"Nay, but there is. The horse will fly over the parapet in his present wild state."

"Never."

"Then I'll throw myself off. Nay, but I will."

"Confound it, Sir Harry."

"Loosen the rein."

"There."

With this the highwayman sprang from the saddle and ran over the bridge.

"My best thanks, Sir Harry, for your ride."

"You audacious rascal!"

"Good bye for the present, Sir Harry. I'll keep my appointment yet, in spite of you."

"By my soul I hope you may," shouted the baronet enthusiastically. "You deserve to get off for this."

"Farewell. Ha, ha! Here they come hot after you."

Then the baronet could not help murmuring half aloud—

"May he get off scot free. He's game to the back-

bone. But, hang the fellow! he rides like a New-market jockey, and he's knocked every bit of breath out of my body!"

Up came Jonathan Wild, snorting and puffing like a walrus.

"Which way, Sir Harry?"

But Sir Harry did not appear to hear the question.

"There he goes!" cried one.

"Where?"

"Over the bridge."

"After him!"

"Stop him," cried Wild to the passengers who were crossing the bridge from the further side.

"Stop thief!"

"A highwayman!"

"A robber! a robber!"

At this many people ran forward and stretched themselves across the road.

This was fatal.

Then they advanced.

Red Ralph now drew up and paused to consider.

Certain capture lay behind him and a great probability of it in front.

The moment's pause did not favour his cause.

On came the officers with a rush.

"Death and the devil!" exclaimed the excitable baronet, standing up in his stirrups to witness the pursuit. "But they'll have him now as safe as— Hullo!—no, by Jove he has, though! Well, well, the bravest fellow that ever breathed has died the gamest death I ever read of."

The highwayman stood at bay.

Springing upon the parapet of the bridge, he felt for his pistols.

Alas! he did not remember the scuffle at the dwarf's house.

"Surrender!" cried Wild.

"Never!"

"Then take him down."

The officers advanced.

"Liberty or death!" cried the highwayman.

And he sprang over the bridge.

CHAPTER XCII.

DROWNED--THE BOAT--THE ANIMATED SAIL-CLOTH —A FAMILIAR FACE—THE WATERSIDE TAVERN —THE DISCUSSION—THE DAMAGED BOAT—AN ACCUSATION — DANGER AGAIN — SAVED.

"He's gone!"

"Drowned for a hundred!"

"Dead for a ducat!"

"Then curse him!" cried Jonathan Wild. "The old proverb is all infernal bosh."

Red Ralph's desperate leap over Westminster Bridge seemed to settle the pursuit.

No one could imagine that he would survive it.

No, not even the marvellous run of luck which had hitherto attended the bold and audacious career of the captain of the Yellow Band could bring him in safety through such a desperate dash at liberty.

"Down to the shore!"

"Off—away!" cried Wild.

"It is useless," exclaimed the worthy baronet. "He's gone, poor fellow. Game to the backbone!"

Jonathan Wild turned savagely upon the speaker.

Had it been any other than a man of the baronet's rank and position he would have retorted.

As it was, he smothered his resentment as best he could.

The thieftaker bitterly hated Red Ralph for the many defeats and disasters which he had encountered in his pursuit, and he felt no more amicably inclined towards any one who could entertain the slightest sympathy for him.

Useless as it appeared to fly to the drowning man's rescue, it was attempted.

We had better have chosen the word "capture" than "rescue."

Down the officers dashed in a body to the waterside.

But no sign of Red Ralph could be discovered.

He was lost.

Father Thames had at last closed the career of the bold Red Ralph.

* * * * *

While the hue and cry after the drowned highwayman is kept up along the banks of the Thames—whilst the bloodhounds of the law are busily and eagerly engaged in dragging the waters where Red Ralph has disappeared—we would draw attention to a little crazy boat fastened to one of the long wooden piles in the water.

At the bottom of the little leaky vessel lie some pieces of sail-cloth and tarpaulin.

To these especially we would for the present direct our notice.

If they were observed attentively for a few minutes they would be seen to move a little.

From time to time they rise and fall slowly, with a gentle movement, as if some panting animal slept beneath.

The cries of the thieftaker and his men resounded upon the bridge and along the shore.

Boats were hastily manned and pushed into the river.

Cries for boathooks and drags were heard in every direction.

And now one of the boats laden with Wild's men passes close by the little crazy wherry.

So close, in fact, that their bows touch as it passes.

The empty boat is nearly capsized, but soon rights itself.

And the other boat passes on in safety, the weight it carries preventing all ill effects from the shock it has incurred.

Had not the occupants of this boat been so throughly pre-occupied by their eager search in the water for the drowned highwayman they must have remarked one singular fact in connection with the little wherry they were so nearly upsetting.

As it rolled upon its side the sail-cloth and the tarpaulin slipped aside.

Beneath peeped out a man's face.

Pale and breathless.

Panting—struggling for breath.

Half dead.

His mouth opened to its full extent, as if to drink in at a gulp as much as possible of the welcome air.

Then his head rolled restlessly, wearily, on one side.

Then after a while the poor panting wretch begins to look about him.

Gradually his face assumes a calmer and more natural expression.

Then he grows familiar, and we recognise the welcome features of an old friend.

The drowning man.

Yes, the miserable wretch who has battled so hardly for breath is none other than Red Ralph.

The captain of the Yellow Band is not yet sacrificed.

The highwayman yet lives, as we shall see.

But how?

How can he possibly have contrived to avert the terrible and apparently certain doom?

How has his good fortune befriended him at this juncture?

That we shall see.

Presently Red Ralph had so far recovered as to be enabled to breathe out a few words.

But what are those words?

Curses, both loud and deep, upon Jonathan Wild the thieftaker and his men.

Bitterly did he hate that man.

So frequently had he spared his life—for many times had he had it within his grasp,

And yet he would not slay him.

Jonathan Wild of course had no consideration for this.

He was never much troubled with scruples of conscience.

No weak effeminate sensations of gratitude troubled the thieftaker's tranquillity.

Not one.

"Plague upon them!" muttered Red Ralph, "they have well nigh finished me this time."

True it was, too.

For seldom had the bold Red Ralph had so very narrow an escape.

Thirty seconds longer under water would have been fatal to him.

Jonathan Wild's voice at this juncture was again heard in loud and angry command.

"After him, you blockheads! After him! That way!

"Surely they can't have seen me," said Red Ralph.

It was distressing.

What could he now do if such should really be the case?

It would be impossible for him to again elude them.

Still he would not be recaptured.

Of this he was resolved.

No, the worst might arrive, and then—then the waters should indeed receive him.

However, Red Ralph was never much given to despair.

He was ever upon the look-out for a chance.

And, by all that was fortunate! the chance arrived.

Red Ralph arose from the bottom of the boat where he reclined—dripping wet.

At all hazards he resolved to endure these tortures no longer.

Every limb was fast growing cramped and stiff.

Fortunately the boat was fastened close to one of the abutments of the bridge, so that he could not very well be observed from above.

He took off his coat.

Then proceeded to bale out some of the water which was slowly rising.

"By Heavens!" exclaimed the highwayman, "it was a narrow escape! Had I not chanced to dive so near to the boat I was a lost man beyond all doubt."

This, then, was the secret of the bold highwayman's escape.

His dive for life had taken him deep into the water beside the boat.

A lengthy immersion had of course been the result of so desperate a leap.

Then he had risen to the surface close beside the boat.

His hand had grasped it.

A wild hope of freedom had even then possessed him, and he dragged himself up.

A struggle it was—a terrible struggle for the boat.

A struggle for life.

The stake was desperate, and none the less so were his exertions to attain the victory.

Half drowned—nay, rather more than half—he had dragged himself into the boat.

Then, while scarcely sensible, he dragged the tarpaulin and sail-cloths over him.

Slowly and painfully he recovered.

Then, as we have seen, he arose, threw off his coat, and endeavoured to destroy the traces of his recent immersion.

His hair was now so flat and straight over his face, that it was almost a disguise in itself.

However, disguise or no disguise, a venture must be made.

He put out the oars.

Then prepared for the start, with a vigorous pull.

His shirt sleeves clung to his arms, and would have told any ordinary observer everything.

They were yet dripping with water.

Leaving the oars for an instant, he hastily rolled them up and then started afresh.

Even now his escape was extremely doubtful.

All depended upon his not being observed.

If noticed from the bridge, or by any of the numerous rowers about the river, he might look upon recapture as a certainty.

That is, recapture or the only other alternative—death!

For his strength was spent.

Boldly he kept to his work.

About him upon every side rowed the constables and watermen recruited for this service.

And through the midst of them went the very man of whom they were in search.

At length the shore was gained.

Many and exciting were the chances Red Ralph ran.

Still his good fortune stood him in good stead now—one of the most exciting moments of his life.

He sprang ashore.

Then, throwing his coat carelessly over his arm, walked up with a swaggering easy air.

Entered a tavern by the waterside, full of people.

In the parlour a large fire blazed away in a most cheerful manner, and Red Ralph hastened to take advantage of its genial glow.

His coat was first to be dried.

"Hullo! mate," said one of the watermen to Red Ralph, "what's up? Had a ducking?"

"Yes."

"After that chap?"

"Who?"

"That fellow as fell over the bridge?"

"Yes. I've been looking for him."

"A fool's errand, mate."

Ralph was paying so little attention that he did not notice this rather rough speech.

Moreover, he would not have deemed it prudent to pick a quarrel under the circumstance.

"D'ye know anything of the matter?" asked the waterman.

"No," said Ralph.

"Then how came you to be out in the river after him?"

"Business."

"What? You mean that you thought to pick him up?"

"Of course."

"They ain't found him?"

"No."

"Then between you and me, mate," said the waterman, "I can say I'm very glad of it."

Ralph looked astonished.

"How glad?"

"Why, he was a regular good 'un."

"Who?"

"Who? He, the man as jumped over the bridge."

"Then you know all about it?"

"Yes. On'y wanted to see first if you was one of the runners. I couldn't tell what you was. You ain't in our trade rig?"

This was put in the form of an interrogation.

However, as inquiries would have proved unpleasant to the captain of Yellow Band, he simply pretended not to comprehend what was meant.

"Ah, yes," continued the waterman, "that fellow as jumped over the bridge was the gamest chap as ever went to the bottom."

"Indeed?"

"Ay, that he was."

"And who was he?"

"Red Ralph, the captain of the bold Yellow Boys."

"Never!"

And to see the profound expression of amazement upon the face of the speaker, no one could have possibly imagined that he was speaking of himself.

"By-the-bye," resumed Red Ralph, "I'm not quite clear on one point."

"Which?"

"Who is Red Ralph?"

The waterman looked most profoundly disgusted.

"Who!" he iterated.

"Ay. What is he? Some robber I have heard, wasn't he?"

"Don't I tell you that he was the captain of the Yellow Band."

"Precisely."

"That is, or rather was, a band of the boldest fellows that ever trod the greensward."

"You appear to be enthusiastic upon the matter."

"What's that?"

"Seem rather to like the idea of highwaymen and robbers."

"Not I. I like pluck," said the waterman. "But none of your fine words for me, my friend."

"Fine words?" said Ralph.

"Ay. I can see well enough that you are no waterman now."

"No waterman?"

"No. You keep on repeating what I say, and why—because you don't know how to get out of it."

This was precisely what the highwayman wished to avoid.

Anything that could attract attention was likely to prove fatal to him at this juncture.

He was silent.

Seeing this, the waterman fancied he detected in it a confirmation of his hastily-formed suspicions.

"It strikes me," he continued, "that you are some dirty informer."

"Not I."

"I'm not so sure of that."

"I swear it."

Just at this moment, to add to his embarrassment, another difficulty arose.

A man entered the parlour of the tavern in great wrath.

It was a waterman who had found his boat alongside.

Now this boat, he positively averred, had been towed to a wooden pile near the centre arch of the bridge.

"It won't do, you know," he said, as he entered, and abusing the company generally. "I don't choose to have my wherry knocked about at everybody's pleasure."

"What's the matter, Bill Stevens?" demanded one.

"Oh! you know well enough," he answered surlily. "Whether you've done it in a lark, or not, I can't say, but you've lost one of the oars and damaged one of the rullocks."

"Me? Why, I ain't seen your boat."

"Well, if it ain't you, it's somebody else in the room."

"How do you know?"

"Somebody told me so."

"But didn't they say who?"

"No—only saw a chap shove in shore in my boat and run up here into the parlour."

Ralph grew uneasy.

However, he did not allow his unpleasant sensations to appear upon his face.

He found about this time that his coat was nearly dry.

Then, with as much deliberation as he could now use, he proceeded to put it on.

Then strolled to the door.

He had not reached it, however, before he became aware that he was the object of much attention upon the part of the company.

He saw one man—his late questioner, by-the-bye—point and nod significantly at him.

The irate waterman, Bill Stevens, confronted him.

"I say, you sir," said he in a bullying voice, "what do you mean by knocking my boat about?"

Ralph endeavoured to pass.

The waterman, however, was not to be disposed of thus easily.

"My good fellow, I haven't seen your boat," said Ralph.

"That's a lie!"

"What?"

"A lie."

Ralph grew angry.

"Have a care, my friend."

"What of? Who of?"

"Of me."

"I tell you what, unless you pay me something for the damage you have done my boat, why off you go as sure as my name's Bill Stevens!"

"Where to?"

"To the lock-up."

This was not to be thought of.

Any way in which Red Ralph could be confronted with the representatives of justice must inevitably prove fatal to him.

"Once for all," said Red Ralph, "pray understand that I know nothing of your boat—nothing of you. And I wish to have as little to say or do with you as you can make convenient."

"Oh, no doubt."

Ralph moved aside, and again essayed to pass out.

Again did the waterman place himself in the way.

"No, you don't."

"Stand back, you idiot!" said Red Ralph, growing rather red in the face.

"The devil a bit!"

And with this the waterman placed his hand upon the highwayman's shoulder.

"Hands off!"

"You shall go to the lock-up."

"Hands off!"

"Not I."

A crowd now began to collect.

Of all the things in the world this was what he wished most to avoid.

The chances were that he would be recognised by some one.

Then he could expect the worst.

Ralph pushed the waterman outside the tavern.

Still the man preserved his hold upon the adventurous highwayman.

And now two or three fellows came running up to the scene of the fracas from the waterside.

Amongst them were two of the constables, whom Red Ralph recognised upon the instant.

No time was now to be lost.

If he would get clear off he must make a rush at liberty now or never.

"Loose your hold," said Red Ralph, warmly.

"I shan't."

"Unhand me, I say. I don't want to use violence; but I warn you that I am dangerous now."

"Ha! ha! ha!"

"Obstinate fool!" cried the highwayman. "Take that!"

"Ugh!"

A smart blow between the venturesome waterman's eyes, a playful tap upon his chest, and Red Ralph was disengaged from the painful attentions of the owner of the boat to which he owed his life.

Mr. Bill Stevens fell to the ground with a groan.

Red Ralph coolly adjusted his coat and sleeves and walked off.

"I say," cried one of the bystanders, "look how he's been a-playing at skittles with Bill Stevens!"

"Let's go after him."

This suggestion, however, met with no very gracious reception.

"You go," said one.

"What alone?"

"Ay."

"And get a little more of what he gave Bill Stevens? No thank'ee."

CHAPTER XCIII.

MADDOX FIELDS—RE-EQUIPPED—RALPH HIMSELF AGAIN—THE "WHEATSHEAF"—OLD FRIENDS THE ROAD—THE CHESNUT GROVE—A BOLD VENTURE—THE TWO MASKS—"STAND AND DELIVER!"—DOG BITE DOG—A DANGEROUS EXPERIMENT—THE NIGHT MAIL—THE ROBBERY—THE BARONET—A STRANGE ENCOUNTER.

As soon as Red Ralph got clear off from the scene of the great danger which he had just escaped he made his way to the house of a faithful friend.

We have already seen this place in an earlier portion of our history.

It was in Maddox Fields.

Here he provided himself with a change of garments and borrowed a strong and fresh horse.

Then he bade his trusty friend an affectionate adieu.

"Now for Hounslow!" said Red Ralph.

One would almost have imagined that the captain of the Yellow Band had had sufficient adventure for a while to satisfy the most morbid craving for strong excitements which ever cursed a poor hot-spirited wretch.

Yet no.

A wild idea possessed him.

An idea which he felt that he must carry out. Else he could not rest.

Off he dashed, murmuring to himself as he rode through the Oxford Road.

He saluted old Jock and his daughter, the pretty Mistress Margaret, as he passed by the Wheatsheaf Inn, and was earnestly begged to make a pause there for a while.

"What is the time, Jock?" demanded Red Ralph, before acceding to their request.

"It is gone nine, or thereaway," answered Jock.

"Then I must refuse. Good night."

And blowing a kiss to the landlord's pretty daughter, off he rode at a brisk trot.

It was already past nine.

Before ten he had many little adventures to go through.

Of these, however, we shall but touch on two.

As the time drew on, Red Ralph increased his speed.

He had a rendezvous to keep, and his word was pledged.

Throughout his wild and rough career Red Ralph had always continued to preserve his reputation for strict adherence to a promise given.

And he rode onwards with renewed fervour.

Presently, arrived in a woody country in the vicinity of the heath, he had to pass through a grove of chesnut trees.

A dark road it was, shaded upon either side by a splendid row of lofty chesnuts.

Majestic trees they were, and called down the high-wayman's admiration at once.

"Beautiful," muttered Red Ralph. "This is the very spot of all others for a little excitement."

We well know what the robber meant by this now.

He would have liked to forward his trade a little.

The spot was indeed favourable.

Far removed from any habitation.

Silent as death.

The words which Red Ralph had just spoken were barely uttered when something attracted his attention.

A sound of horses !

He pricked up his ears, and began to look about him.

Two horsemen had just entered the grove from the further end.

Ralph coloured with pleasurable excitement at once.

"'Sdeath !" he muttered, "it is tempting. I've no barkers, though."

The horsemen slowly advanced.

"They come," said Red Ralph. "No matter—barkers or no barkers, I must have a turn to keep my hand in."

The two horsemen were close by at this period.

Red Ralph hastily donned a black mask, with which he had provided himself.

Then drew up in the centre of the pathway.

"Stand and deliver !"

"Hullo !"

"Money or your life !"

"The devil !"

"No pleasantries, gentlemen, if you please," said Red Ralph, with affected sternness.

This seemed to cause the two horsemen some mirth.

They laughed outright.

One thing Red Ralph remarked as singular—and still more singular that he had not observed it before.

The two horsemen were also masked.

Red Ralph was thoroughly exasperated at their laughter.

It could only be that they were laughing at him for his boldness.

No matter, he would carry it through as he had commenced it, and then they would see which way the laugh should go.

"Now then !" said Red Ralph once more. "Your purses !"

"Confound it !" ejaculated one of the horsemen, doubling up the violent exuberance of his mirth, "he's the devil himself !"

The other seemed scarcely less amazed.

Red Ralph grew furious.

Nothing perhaps did the highwayman so much dread as ridicule.

He lost all patience now and grew determined.

Achieve his object or fail—fail ignominiously—he was determined to make a dash at it.

A gentle pressure of the spur upon his horse's flank threw him close up between the two horsemen.

He lunged out upon each side, and caught each of the travellers by the shoulder.

The sudden violence with which they were assailed nearly unseated both the horsemen at once.

"Hullo ! hullo !" cried one.

"Hullo, what's all this ?"

"You wouldn't surely eat us both, my bonny Red Ralph ?"

The captain of the Yellow Boys started.

"Who are you ?" he demanded. "You know my name ?"

"And who are you that so soon forget an old pal ?"

"What my rollicking Romany cull !" said the other.

Red Ralph was amazed.

Both voices sounded familiar to him.

"Who are you ?"

"Well," said one of the travellers, a stalwart fellow, "try if your memory will serve you now."

He removed his mask.

A well-known face was revealed.

"What !" ejaculated Red Ralph. "Is it possible ? Dick Turpin !"

"Ay."

"And he ?"

This was said pointing to the horseman accompanying the notable Turpin.

"A friend."

"In truth ?"

"Ay, and true friend."

And the second horseman removed his mask also.

Wonder upon wonders !

The second horseman stood revealed a none the less familiar acquaintance of Red Ralph.

"Tom King !"

"Ay, Ralph," said the bold knight of the road, "Tom King once more, or what's left of him."

"Well, egad ! but I meant to practise upon you both."

And the merry trio grew uproarious with laughter.

"You knew me at once ?" asked the captain of the Yellow Band.

"Ay," said King.

"At once," said Dick Turpin. "For we well knew that no one but your dare-devil self would have tried on such a job as this."

"Hang it, Red Ralph !" said Tom King. "You grow ambitious !"

"How so ?"

"To aim at such game."

"There lies the fun of it."

"And the danger."

"Which means the fun."

"You're right there," said Dick Turpin. "There would'nt be much fun in it else. It's a miserable game."

"At times."

"But how come you upon these roads ?" asked Red Ralph.

"Accident."

"Yes," added Turpin. "We learnt by chance that there was to be a heavy prize upon the road before morning."

"Indeed ?"

"Ay, the night mail."

"Then I'll join you, if you will."

"With all my heart."

"And mine too," said Tom King. "I ask nothing better."

"Hark, then. Now's our turn I should say," said Dick Turpin.

The sounding of the guard's horn reached them faintly.

The sound was in the opposite direction, too, they noted.

Then it must be close at hand, or it would not have been heard in that part of the heath.

"Come on !"

"Now for it !"

"I'm with you, my pals !" cried Red Ralph. "But who's to lend me a pair of barkers ?"

"That will I," said Turpin. "I have two pairs with me."

"Thanks."

Thus prepared for an emergency, Red Ralph started off with his two companions.

As soon as they had gained the coach road the mail was seen in sight.

Out came the lumbering old coach from the hollow.

Breasted the hill, and dashed boldly up at a gallop.

"Now for it !"

"Close together."

"Advance !"

And with this the three highwaymen sprang forward.

Two dashed to the horses' heads.

"Thieves!" cried the coachman.

"Robbers!" shouted the guard.

"Hullo! Oh—h—h!"

A prolonged burst of agony came from the interior. A wild shriek.

A prayer for mercy in wild and shrill feminine tones.

The sudden dash at the leader's head had startled the team.

They reared and pranced aside, dragging the lumbering old conveyance over a rise in the ground, and—

Upset it.

As it tumbled over a wonderful scramble was heard within.

The female voice was heard in angry expostulation.

As Red Ralph ran up to the coach door a head peeped through.

Another startler for the captain of the Yellow Band.

It was the face of the baronet upon whose horse he had ridden in escaping from Wild.

And yet he had only left him in Westminster a few hours since.

"What's all this?"

"Your purse!" said Red Ralph in an assumed voice.

"A robber!"

"Call it what you will," said Red Ralph. "But give it, and quickly too."

"Never."

"Ah! you will not?"

"Never. Blaze away as you please, you scoundrel. Never will I part with a sou unless by force."

"Indeed?"

"I swear it. I never was robbed by any but one man, and never shall another hand than his take a penny from me."

"You mistake," said Red Ralph, highly enjoying the joke. "I have met you before upon the road."

"Possibly."

"Ay, and I have borrowed a trifle of you, too."

"Never."

"I swear I have."

"You lie, you black-hearted villain. Never was I stopped successfully but once, and he who did it—an infernal scoundrel—but he's gone, and I'd give five hundred pounds to have him stop me again."

"Then give me your purse on account."

"No. Be off, or I fire!"

Ralph saw that the worthy baronet's hand grasped something in his breast.

It might be his purse.

He raised his hand, clutching his pistol by the barrel, and brought it down with a swing, suddenly arresting it when within a few inches of the baronet's head.

But he succeeded in the object of this shallow trick.

The baronet drew his hand from his breast, clutching a pocket-book and held up his arm to ward off the approaching blow.

With a dart forward, and a sudden grab at the upraised hand, the pocket-book had changed owners.

"Now," cried the masked highwayman triumphantly. "Now how about your boast, eh, sir?"

"Be this my answer," retorted the enraged baronet.

A pistol report.

But the highwayman, half anticipating this, had ducked in the saddle, and the shot whistled harmlessly past.

In the meantime Tom King and his companion in mischief, the redoubtable Dick Turpin, had pretty well cleared out the luggage of the unfortunate travellers.

It was a rich prize.

Not even their most eager anticipations had estimated it at a quarter of its real value.

Much plate, jewellery, and valuables fell into their possession.

Strange things were revealed, too, in this exploit.

The guard of the night-mail was a renowned fire-eater.

Now, singularly enough, as soon as the robbers had made their appearance he had quietly slunk off his seat after a few feeble cries.

The coachman, too, had even been heard to declare that no robbers would ever dare to attack his coach.

Indeed, it was some such boast which had caused Tom King and Dick Turpin to venture there when Red Ralph had met them in the chesnut grove.

"Ready?" cried Red Ralph.

"Ay, I am."

"And I too," said Turpin. "Are you?"

"Quite."

"Off with us, then."

"Good night, sir," said Red Ralph to the worthy baronet, who was foaming with rage.

"Villain!"

And the old gentleman made the most desperate exertions to squeeze himself out of the coach door, but it was impossible.

Utterly impossible.

Ralph saw his struggles, and could not refrain from laughing at the genial old baronet.

"Good night for the present, sir. I shall see you again before the night's over."

"I hope so," roared the old gentleman.

"Thank you."

"Ruffian! Villain! Knave! Var—"

But he might have saved himself so many hard words.

The bold highwayman was by this time far removed from hearing.

Red Ralph had not yet done with the worthy baronet for the night.

He intended to have another interview with him, in fulfilment of his old agreement.

But this deserves a chapter to itself.

CHAPTER XCIV.

THE BARONET'S RETURN — HIS VENGEANCE — WILD'S MESSENGER—A FRESH ARRIVAL—THE STRANGE GUEST — A VOICE FROM THE GRAVE — THE APPOINTED HOUR — SUPPER FOR TWO — A WARM WELCOME — ACCOUNT OF THE FLIGHT—THE CAPTAIN OF THE YELLOW BAND.

THE old baronet, after the robbery of the northern mail by the captain of the Yellow Band and his two companions, Tom King and Dick Turpin, pushed his way home.

He arrived without further molestation at his mansion.

Here he vented his ill-humour upon every one.

His pocket-book, containing the most valuable papers, private memoranda, and various documents, had been robbed from him in his encounter with Red Ralph, whom, by-the-bye, the baronet believed to be at the bottom of the Thames.

And so all the servants—the cook more especially —suffered for Red Ralph's peccadiloes.

The baronet grumbled at everything that was brought to table.

He swore at his valet and footman to such an extent that they were obliged to leave the room.

In the midst of his fury a servant came in to announce a visitor.

"Who is it?" demanded the baronet.

"A messenger from Mr. Jonathan Wild."

"What does he want?"

"I don't know, sir."

"Then, confound you! show him in."

The servant ducked in time to avoid a glass which the irate baronet threw at him.

Then left, and ushered in Jonathan Wild's messenger.

It was one of his janisaries, who had just arrived from Newgate.

"Well, fellow, what is it?" demanded the baronet.

"Oh! If you please, sir, Mr. Wild has sent me to beg you to give some evidence respecting the last escape of Captain Red Ralph."

"Captain?"

"Ay, sir; so he is called."

"What can I say of that?"

"It was by your aid that he managed to effect his escape."

"What?"

The vehemence of the baronet quite startled the man.

"Leastways, sir," he added hastily, "he managed it by the aid of your horse."

"What's that to me, you infernal scoundrel, eh? Answer!"

"N—n—nothing."

"Then what the devil do you mean by your confounded insinuations and innuendoes?"

"I—I meant nothing, sir."

"Then say as little, you thief."

The man was so alarmed at this that he was afraid to speak until again addressed.

"Now then," said the baronet, "what is it you want with me?"

"Only to beg your honour to give a statement in writing of the manner of his escape."

"What's the use of that?"

"Every use, your worship."

"For what? For whom?"

"For the authorities."

"Pish! There were a hundred witnesses to the matter besides myself. You know that well."

"Yes, sir."

"Well, then."

"But Mr. Wild is a-feared of getting called over the coals upon the job, unless some one of influence, like your honour's worship, should be speaking for him."

"Oh! that's it?"

"Yes, sir."

"Then, by Jove, I won't."

"Oh, sir."

"Hold your tongue, you villain. What? I speak a word that would would save that villainous rascal from a trouncing? Never! I swear it!"

"But, sir, consider."

"Hold your tongue."

"And Mr. Wild—"

"Will trounce you for not succeeding in your errand."

"Yes, sir," said the man, with a shiver. "That he will."

"So much the better."

And the old gentleman turned good-humoured at the thought and laughed heartily at this.

The man was in despair.

When the baronet's mirth was at the highest the footman re-entered the room.

"What now?"

"Another gentleman, sir."

"Another *what*?"

"Another gentleman."

"Get out, you fool!" exclaimed the baronet, picking up something to throw at the footman. "Where's your first gentleman?"

The footman glanced towards the thieftaker's messenger, but did not venture to speak.

"You idiot!" cried the old gentleman. "Can't you distinguish a thief from a true man?"

The servant and the messenger of Jonathan Wild both quaked, but were silent.

"Who is this?" demanded the baronet after a while.

"I don't know, sir."

"Then go and ask his name."

"Yes, sir."

The footman left, but shortly returned to say that the gentleman would give no name.

"What does he want, then?"

"He says he comes by appointment."

The baronet cooled down for a moment.

Looked thoughtful, and put on his considering cap.

"I asked no one to see me here," he said, "but—no matter, he's far away now, poor devil."

"But he insists that he has an appointment, sir."

"Insists, does he?"

"Yes, sir. He begs you to remember an invitation."

"An invitation!" iterated the baronet changing colour.

He paused again to think for a second. Then shook his head doubtfully.

"Impossible," he muttered half aloud. "Impossible. But show him in, you villain."

"Yes, sir."

And the footman left.

"Now, you sir," said the baronet, turning to the messenger.

"Ye—es, sir."

"Make yourself scarce. It would damage my character to be seen here with a rogue of your stamp."

"Yes, sir."

"The villain even admits his own roguery," laughed the baronet. "Be off with you. Not that way, you'll meet the gentleman, and I don't mean that he should see you."

"No, no, sir."

"Get into that room," said the baronet pointing to a door behind him.

"Yes, sir."

"Wait there until I have got rid of my precious visitor. I want to speak to you about a robbery."

"Yes, sir."

"I've been stopped on the road."

"By whom, sir?"

"How the devil should I know, you infernal fool?"

"No, sir."

"Get off. Here comes the gentleman. Be off with you."

The baronet picked up something to throw at the thieftaker's messenger, but the man disappeared before he could quit his position.

In walked a gentleman—the visitor—enveloped in a riding cloak and wearing a slouched hat which almost concealed his features.

He bowed as he entered with the grace of a courtier.

"May I inquire whom I have the honour of addressing?" said the baronet with stiff politeness.

"So soon forgotten?" was the visitor's only reply.

The baronet glanced up surprised.

"Pardon me, sir, but I don't remember exactly."

"I thought not, but you see I am here to my time. You said ten, and I was here—or rather in your hall. So I have kept the appointment after all."

The old gentleman was fairly staggered by the visitor's words.

"Pardon me, sir."

"I see," interrupted the visitor. "You have forgotten?"

"I cannot well remember what has never occurred."

"Enough, sir," said the other, assuming a tone of offence which he by no means felt. "I go, sir. Farewell."

[THE QUARRY.]

"Excuse me."

The visitor moved to the door.

Then he let fall his cloak and raised his hat.

It was Red Ralph.

The baronet bounded from his seat with the activity of a youth of twenty.

Darted after the highwayman and caught him by the hand.

"Red Ralph?"

"Even he."

"'Sdeath! Why I saw you drowned," cried the old gentleman.

"Not quite."

"But how is this?"

"Oh! it's a long story," said the captain of the Yellow Band. "I was gone as near as possible."

The baronet looked lost.

He was so eager to express his satisfaction at the highwayman's restoration to life that he was puzzled where to commence.

"Sit down, sit down, and let me hear all about it."

"Well," said the captain of the Yellow Band. "I must say in all truth that I shouldn't have exerted myself so much to save my life if it hadn't been to keep your invitation."

The baronet literally roared with merriment at this.

"What a dog you are, Red Ralph!" he cried, while the tears streamed down his cheeks.

"At least the thief is a man of his word, eh?"

"He is, he is," cried the old gentleman.

And he wrung the highwayman's hand again and again.

"Now for it."

"For what?" asked Ralph.

"The story."

"My escape?"

"To be sure."

"But I came to supper, not to tell stories."

This set the old baronet off again, and he roared with laughter until a stitch in his side doubled him up.

"Ralph, you'll kill me."

"I hope not. But truly I came to be entertained, not to entertain my host."

"Thank you. But what you say is perfectly true. What will you take?"

"Anything."

"Drink?"

"Ay."

"What?"

"Anything. I'm dying with thirst, and starving at the same time."

"Indeed? Haven't you eaten?"

"Not since morning."

"Gad! then you shall go on until you explode, you rascal, you shall."

He called for attendants, and a sumptuous repast was placed before the famished hero of these memoirs.

Red Ralph fell to with a will, and the toothsome viands fell before his rapacity in an alarming fashion.

The baronet all the time looked on quite delighted.

He jumped about, handing up the different dishes to his guest, and seemed eager to anticipate his wishes before they could be put into words.

He laughed every now and then with pleasure to see the havoc which the dashing highwayman was creating in the comestibles.

At length, however, even Red Ralph's appetite must come to an end.

And then, with a few more potations—a few only, for Red Ralph did not count intemperance amongst his vices—the baronet pressed him for a relation of his miraculous escape from the Thames.

Red Ralph, as modestly as possible, related the different chances he had gone through.

At the conclusion the old baronet, who had listened throughout in breathless interest, seized the highwayman in his arms.

"Red Ralph!" he exclaimed with fervour, "I'd give a thousand pounds if you were other than—than—"

"A thief."

"Than what you are."

"Nay, nay, sir," said Red Ralph. "Speak the word, sir."

"I'll not."

"The truth should never offend."

"It should not."

"But you mean to say that in my case it would."

"It might."

"Nay, sir," said the highwayman, "nothing from you would offend me, since it would not be uttered with that intention."

"Right, lad, right."

And he again embraced Red Ralph with such warmth that our hero was much affected, and said—

"It is gratifying to find that one so lost—a scapegrace—"

"Ah, that you are."

"Nay, worse—a vagabond and a cutpurse—I have heard it often, sir—it is gratifying, I say, to one so lost as myself to find such friendship in you—a man, the soul of honour."

"Tut! tut!"

But although the old baronet spoke thus petulantly it was clear enough that he was not unmoved.

"I want to speak a little seriously now to you, Red Ralph," began the baronet, after a pause in the conversation.

"I guess the subject."

"Do you?"

"Ay. Reform.

"You are right. And I could not be the friend I would have you think me unless I had some thought for your future welfare."

"True."

"For a terrible remorse for all this business must come one of these days,"

"It has already."

"And yet you do not alter your dangerous mode of life."

"There you have it. It is the danger, sir, which keeps me bound so fast to it."

"I believe it."

"Else I had long since quitted a life whose very joys are but fevered excitements, and dishonourable ones too."

"Then why not take some other line of dangers more compatible with respectability?"

"Too late."

"It is never too late."

"It is too late when honour is lost."

"Never. The day might come when you would look back upon all the wild freaks of to-day as a dream—the dream of a madman."

"I would it could be so."

"It might—it can."

"How?"

"Leave England."

"Impossible."

"Join some foreign service. You will win distinction I am well assured, Red Ralph."

"I might have done so once, but now it is impossible."

"Why so?"

"I have others depending upon me."

"You mean the Band?"

"Ay, sir, and not they alone, though they would be sufficient to keep me chained to this fatal existence, for I could not now desert them."

"And why not?"

"Are they not hunted down by the law? Is there not danger in every step they take? I have to be eternally upon the alert to ward off threatening dangers."

"But you are ever in greater danger as their leader."

"True."

"And they could shift for themselves."

"No, no, sir," said the captain of the Yellow Band. "It is impossible, sir. 'Tis I who have brought them to this strait. It is I to whom they owe their wild and precarious mode of life, and I must and will see them through it."

"It is a false idea."

"No."

"I insist that it is."

"But you are not aware of the circumstances which led to our connection, and so, sir, believe me, you cannot judge."

"As you please, Ralph," said the baronet. "I but advise you for your own interest, you know."

"Of course."

And Red Ralph pressed the old man's hand affectionately.

"However, sir," he resumed, "there is another circumstance which would prevent my listening to your kindly-given counsel."

"What is it?"

"I have a wife."

"A wife?"

"Ay, sir."

"Some pot-house wench of a hundred loves, I'll swear."

Red Ralph coloured to the temples as he thought of his gentle and beloved Leonore.

He was about to reply hastily, but he checked himself.

The baronet was not to blame. The inference he had drawn was but natural.

"No, sir," said Red Ralph. "The lady I have married boasts of a noble name."

"Noble?" ejaculated the old baronet in amazement.

"Ay, sir, noble."

"Some romantic crazy girl, then, I suppose."

"Sir?"

"Nay, nay, Ralph, be not offended. I mean no harm, you know; but who could Red Ralph the highwayman have married boasting a noble name, unless, indeed, under false pretensions."

Here he eyed the captain of the Yellow Boys doubtfully.

Ralph met his glance fairly.

"No, sir," he said, shaking his head. "There are atrocities at which even such a villain as I stop short—"

"Ahem—I mean no—"

"Enough, sir. I cannot expect that you should believe Red Ralph the highwayman the soul of honour. But I am a strange contradiction. For the present I banish the highwayman and stand to the truth, believe it or not as you may."

The baronet eyed the handsome highwayman for a second in silence.

Then once more proffered his hand, which was eagerly grasped by the captain of the Yellow Band.

Red Ralph then, feeling that he owed the worthy gentleman some explanation, related the history of his secret marriage with Leonore.

Told him of her mother's treachery, and the attempt to slay him.

"And what is the name of your wife's family?" demanded the baronet.

"That you must pardon my not revealing."

"Wherefore?"

"My wife, poor girl, is the soul of truth and virtue, but in the eyes of the world is doubly disgraced."

The baronet shook his head with killing significance.

"A slight *faux pas?*"

The blood once more found its way into Red Ralph's face.

"You misunderstand me," he said. "I mean that she is disgraced in having a fiend for a parent, a—a robber for a husband."

"Red Ralph," said the baronet, "you are a wonderful contradiction, as you say; but henceforth I will maintain—against the world, too—believe me I am sincere—that you are a noble fellow!"

"And you will maintain this in spite of the injury I have done my wife in linking her lot to that of a villainous character like—like—"

"Like Red Ralph. Ay. But that of all is the only thing for which I can scarcely forgive you."

"Why not?"

"You would have me speak plainly?"

"Yes."

"Then you must know (I cite your own words) that Leonore is not honoured in wedding—"

"A thief again?"

"No. A man of your humble origin."

"There speaks the patrician," said the highwayman, smiling. "But I have yet to tell you that my family are not less noble than her own."

This was a startler for the old baronet.

For an instant he could scarcely believe what he heard, and his doubts of Red Ralph's veracity were clearly expressed upon his face.

However, before our hero's earnest look all doubts gave way.

This led to further explanations, and Ralph gave the baronet a sketch of his early life.

As this embraces incidents up to the moment of his introduction to the reader, and which are necessarily connected with our story, we propose giving it as nearly as possible in Red Ralph's own words.

But this deserves a chapter to itself.

CHAPTER XCV.

RED RALPH'S EARLY HISTORY — THE FAMILY DOOM — THE LEGEND OF THE BLOOD-RED HAND — RETROGRESSION — SAD RECOLLECTIONS — A FATHER'S HATE — THE FORGOTTEN MESSENGER — "SURRENDER, IN THE KING'S NAME!" — PROFFERED HOSPITALITY — RATHER TOO MUCH WINE — A SKIRMISH — THE CONSTABLE IN GRIEF — A SHAM FIGHT — A SAFE RETREAT.

"SINCE you desire it," began Red Ralph, "I will give you in as few words as possible a sketch of my early career.

"I came, as I said, of an ancient and honourable family, of Saxon origin, and consequently dating prior to the Conquest.

"In the sixteenth century an event happened to one of my ancestors which, strange and remotely connected with the present age as it may seem, has had a singular influence over the family up to the present generation.

"To this event, of which I am about to speak, I may attribute all the unhappiness I experience.

"All the woes which I have ever suffered may date from this period.

"The griefs and woes in questions arose in this wise.

"One of my ancestors, a fierce and warlike soldier, in an angry discussion with his son concerning a love match which he had contracted with the daughter of one of his tenants—a thriving farmer—drew upon the youth, and would have slain him had not the son defended himself with spirit.

"Then, in the skirmish which ensued, the father, in uncontrollable indignation that his own son should draw upon him, even though only with the object of defending himself, threw away his own weapon and precipitated himself on the weapon of his son.

"He fell mortally wounded, and denounced his unhappy son in loud and cruel terms with his expiring breath as his assassin, cursed his boy and the girl he had espoused, and pronounced the most horrible anathemas upon his progeny to all generations.

"Well, singular enough, ever since the unhappy occurrence a curse has clung to our family. The son of the self-murdered man gained the name of Hubert of the Red Hand, and had to quit the country on account of the scandal which was caused by the fatal event.

"In France he had a son born, and his boy's right hand was marked like mine."

Here Red Ralph withdrew his glove and showed the blood stain which gave him his name.

"This name," continued Red Ralph, "has been handed down in the family from father to son ever since, and I am the last of my race—with me it must die. Since then each generation has verified the strangely ominous curse—almost prediction—of the dying carl."

Here the old baronet interrupted the captain of the Yellow Band.

"Earl!" he exclaimed. "Then you are of truly noble family ?"

"Yes," said Red Ralph, "I am direct successor to the earldom."

The old gentleman was all amazement.

"Truly," he exclaimed, "you are a strange contradiction."

Red Ralph now noticed an alteration in his worthy host's tone.

There was a change in his familiar address, and he no longer called him by his name.

"The relation of my family troubles," said the captain of the Yellow Band, "are given at your request, sir—not to alter our relations—friendship, if I may use the expression."

"You may," said the old gentleman grasping him warmly by the hand. "You're a noble rascal."

"Thank you," said the captain of the Yellow Band. "But to continue my history. The son of my unhappy ancestor, who was born in France, the first of our race who bore the brand of shame which has since become hereditary, was brought up by his family in all tenderness and love. It seems that he inherited his father's passionate loving temperament, which was the cause of the sad calamity which influenced his whole future life. This boy as he grew into manhood—almost before—became engaged to a young girl, and, with all the ardour of youth, would have made her his wife. As the family were living in France in simple retirement and under an assumed name, the parents of the object of his passion objected to the match, and the lover in a hot-headed letter to his mistress besought her to fly with him.

"The letter was intercepted by her brother, a proud young upstart, with more temper than wit, and he took occasion to insult the youthful lover upon the first occasion they met.

"This chanced to be in public, and when the young man was in the company of his father. The father resented the insult. The brother of the girl retorted, and the two youths drew upon each other in great fury.

"The father, alarmed for his son's safety, endeavoured to part them, and, in a skirmish which ensued, the young lover's sword passed through his father's lungs.

"The unhappy exile had merely time to murmur, ' The doom of my race is verified,' and he expired.

"These fearful words provoked an explanation from the mother. The nobility of his birth became known, and his alliance with the lady of his love was contracted, to the satisfaction of all parties, and they returned to take possession of the long-neglected property in England.

"Like the two preceding generations, this earl had but one offspring of this alliance—a boy—who again bore the fatal mark of the race—the blood-red hand.

"The recent unhappy end of the father he had so well loved, coupled with the present calamity—for so he deemed it—drove the unhappy father from his senses.

"For years he was a hopeless maniac. Constant care and attention, however, restored him, but his constitution was greatly shaken, and his intellect impaired. Still he lived to an advanced age, and hope began to revive in the family that at length the fatal curse of the dying earl was at an end. The boy grew to manhood, and appeared to cherish only one weakness—a passion for the chase.

"The family seat upon which they resided was renowned for the beauty of the grounds, and the richness of the game preserves, and the young heir of the earldom was jealous of every hare or partridge that his father owned.

"He waged a terrific warfare against the poachers.

"Night after night he would sally out armed to the teeth, and accompanied by his servants and dogs, and some desperate skirmishes took place.

"It was upon one of these occasions that the son encountered his father in the grounds, taking a solitary moonlight ramble. Not knowing his parent at the moment, he presented his gun, and challenged the supposed poacher to stand.

"The earl, horrified to perceive this, imagined he saw in it the realisation of the hereditary curse hanging over our house. He had a wild notion that his own son sought his life from interested motives.

"He turned and fled. The son fired, and the father fell.

"The unhappy parricide fled the country, vowed to lead a life of celibacy, and thus avert the doom of the house. Well, he kept his resolution until he had reached the advanced age of fifty. Then he was forced to marry a young lady of family, for his honour was concerned in the matter. Time passed on, and the father found, with a mixture of sad misgivings and joy, that his lady was about to become a mother.

"Again the fatal sign of our race—the blood-red hand—was there.

"The babe was not yet a week old when his father, in a low despondent state of mind, put violent hands upon himself.

"In his will he stated that he had committed the deed in full possession of his faculties, and that now the doom of the house was averted. He earnestly besought the prayers of his descendants for the crime of suicide which he had been guilty of to save them from destruction.

"That child, an orphan before he had seen the world a week, was my father."

"Was?" said the baronet. "Does he not live, then ?"

"I believe so, but know not."

"How so ?"

"I will tell you. The age was now become more enlightened. The march of intellect forbad people to believe in hereditary curses, fatal signs, and other like mysteries.

"My father married, I was born, and—O Heavens that it should be so !—branded with the accursed mark of my race."

Here Red Ralph had again to pause in his narrative, overcome by the agonising recollections which his own words conjured up.

Then he resumed.

"I have nearly concluded, sir," he said. "From the moment of my birth my father eyed me with distrust. He affected at first to place no reliance on the family legend, but was most visibly affected by it. A daughter was also born to him, a gentle loving girl, who got the whole of his affections lavished upon her whilst I was treated as a ne'er-do-well.

"My mother loved me well, and did her utmost to protect me from my father's unjust anger. At length on one occasion I lost all patience, and a break between my father and myself consequently ensued.

"He cursed me with great bitterness, and Heaven knows without any fault, for I had never earned the slightest reproach from him, and I indignantly rejoined. Exasperated at my retort, he ventured to raise his hand to strike me.

"Now I have something in my accursed hot blood which would not allow me to receive a blow, even from a parent's hand, and I retaliated."

"One word," interrupted the baronet. "You say your father yet lives?"

"I believe he does. Fear nothing. Ere a blow could be delivered I felt a chill go through my veins. My father trembled and turned pale, as if at the last moment of his life. He threw up his hands imploringly and fell upon the ground before me.

"'Unhappy boy!' he exclaimed. 'Would you then murder me?'

"'Father,' I replied, in anguish, 'You have severed the last tie which bound us together. I leave you now and for ever.'

"'Go, accursed son of a thrice accursed race!' said my father. 'Never let me look upon you again.'

"'I go,' said I, 'and you shall yet hear of me in a way that shall cause you to regret the harshness of your treatment of me.'

"'Begone!' said my father.

"I left the house, and have never since crossed the threshold. My mother I would fain have seen. From time to time I have addressed her an anonymous letter, stating that her unhappy boy was well in body but wounded desperately in spirit. Well, sir, mine was an active daring spirit, and unless I had had some excitement to keep me going I should have come badly off. So in a fit of mad boyish love of adventure I formed together a number of young men and old disbanded soldiers into the band which I think has gained some notoriety since—unenviable you will say—as the Yellow Band."

"So, so," said the old gentleman. "This is the history of your famous gang of robbers?"

"Yes," said the captain. "In a wild search for adventure I formed this band. They were ready enough to follow me. The young man I chose as my lieutenant, one Walters, was my servant. He had served in the army, and he followed me, obeying all my orders as if I had been holding the king's commission, instead of fighting against his subjects."

"But I cannot understand," said the baronet "whatever led you to begin such a wild course of existence."

"It is not so very wonderful either, sir," said our hero.

"Why not?"

"I was only seventeen."

"Never—so young?"

"That was my age, sir, but I looked much older. I came of a martial race, and inherited all the fire and love of adventure of my ancestors. I did not pause to think that I was debasing myself. I looked upon myself as a hero. I became one, in fact, with a certain class."

"You have with all classes."

"A sad one."

"You have astonished the world with your daring escapes."

"And yet my only idea when I took to this extraordinary existence was to punish my father for the harshness with which he had ever repelled all my advances to his affection."

"And did you never return to the home of your ancestors?"

"Not until a twelvemonth had elapsed."

"And then?"

"And then I found the house to which I am the heir in other hands. The family seat had actually been let—let to a wealthy parvenu—as if it had been a lodging-house. The family had gone abroad. I fancied at first that it was to avoid the disgrace which I had brought upon the name, but I did not reflect in my hasty conclusion that there were but three men in the whole world who knew of my secret."

"But these men. Did you never fear that they would betray your secret to the scandal-loving world?"

"No."

"You believe them true?"

"I am assured of their truth."

"How so? You have much confidence in human nature, it seems to me."

"Not too much here. One of them is Walters, whom we call the lieutenant of the Yellow Band; a second is a member of the gang; and the third was the bravest fellow that ever drew breath—one Silas Wolff. He had served in the army, and was a bold soldier."

"He died?"

"Ay," returned Red Ralph, mournfully. "He fell in a hand-to-hand combat with the young officer commanding the troops who guarded the procession of my Yellow Boys to Tyburn."

"A brave fellow!"

"He was."

The old baronet paused thoughtfully, musing upon the remarkable history of his guest.

Presently he looked up, as the thought of the late attack upon the night mail occurred to him.

"Red Ralph," he said, "I have been robbed again recently."

"Indeed?"

"Ay. And by highwaymen."

Red Ralph never thought for the moment upon his late exploit and the stolen pocket-book.

As it occurred to him a smile stole over his countenance.

"Oh, sir! I thought that you never had been stopped upon the road by any man but I."

"I never was robbed by any but you until this night."

"To-night?"

"Ay. Three masked ruffians stopped the night mail, in which I was riding from town, and one rascal robbed me of a pocket-book containing valuable documents."

"Valuable? I'm sorry for that."

"Ay. I was thinking that you might perhaps be able to assist me in the recovery of it."

"I can, no doubt," said Red Ralph. "Describe the villains."

"He that robbed me was an ugly villain."

"Ugly?"

"Villainous."

"Thank you."

"Eh?"

"Never mind me. Continue."

"A rascal. He said that he should see me again before the night was over."

"Then he will."

"I only hope he may."

"He will, depend upon it. These fellows have strange notions of having pledged their words to anything."

The baronet caught the leer with which the highwayman accompanied these words, and he shook his head reprovingly.

"Nay. You must not put yourself upon the base level of a common footpad."

"And what would you give to have this rascal here to-night?"

"A hundred pounds, providing he had my pocket-book in his possession at the time."

"Then I claim the sum."

"You?"

"Yes. He's here."

"Where?"

"Here."

"In the house?"

Ralph bowed.

"You have brought him with you?"

"Yes," answered the captain of the Yellow Band. "I couldn't well have come without him."

"What do you mean?"

"Here's your pocket-book," said Red Ralph, throwing it upon the table, "and here's the robber."

"You?"

"Even I."

The old gentleman was lost in wonder and astonishment.

However, he was delighted to recover the pocket-book.

"So," he exclaimed, "you are the rascal also. 'Sdeath! Red Ralph—my lord, I mean—you're a marvel."

"Red Ralph, if you please. We must forget the lord."

"Not so, for you must give over this way of life, Ralph."

"Impossible."

"Wherefore?"

"Until I have made my peace with my father. That I dread to do. The curse of my race yet haunts me, and I fear myself."

"Pshaw! this is superstition."

"I know it. But I cannot shake it off. Until my father is no more—until he has sunk into his grave (God grant happily), and is at rest with all mankind—I shall never return to the home of my ancestors. I love my roving mode of life."

"But your wife?"

"Ah! spare me, I beseech you," said the captain of the Yellow Band. "It is for her sake that I fear to look back into the past, and yet had it not happened as it has I should never have known her."

"Well, then," said the baronet, "I yield a point. But grant me at least one slight favour. Give over such portion of your wild life as reflects dishonour upon your ancient name."

"Willingly, but how to live?"

"I will see to that."

Ralph shook his head.

"No," said he, "I prefer even my own courses to living upon the charity of any man."

"Then you are a contradiction," said his would-be benefactor. "But what I would propose to you is simply to allow me to advance you sums of money to keep you from dishonesty until you are master of your wealth."

"Ah! that must be thought of."

"You might join some foreign service, as I was but lately suggesting to you."

"True."

"Take your wife with you."

"Ay, but there's one difficulty yet remaining."

"What?"

"The bloodhounds of the law are yet upon my track."

"Never, they think you dead."

"But I am too well known to make it an easy matter to leave the country."

At this moment the door behind the baronet opened.

The messenger from Jonathan Wild had been quite forgotten.

"Who's this?" said Red Ralph.

"Hullo!"

"I grew tired of waiting, sir," said the man, "and I've been—"

"Listening," suggested Ralph.

The man looked up.

The sound of the Yellow Boy's voice quite frightened him.

"He knows you," said the baronet in dismay.

"I haven't the pleasure of knowing him," said Ralph.

"It's one of Jonathan Wild's men—a special messenger."

"Wild's? Pheugh!"

"Red Ralph!" exclaimed the thieftaker's man. "Is it possible?"

"And if it were, how can that affect you?"

"I can tell you how it would affect me," returned the man.

"How?"

"Thus," he answered, slyly taking a pistol from his belt. "I shall get a hundred pounds from the guvnor."

"For what?"

"Your capture."

"Indeed?"

"Yes. Yield!" he cried, presenting the pistol full at Red Ralph. "I arrest you in the king's name!"

"I do," said Red Ralph coolly.

"I thought so. You're a sensible fellow," said the man.

"But what are you going to do with me?"

"Take you back to Newgate."

"Direct?"

"Ay."

"Thank you."

The constable looked uneasy at the ironical tone in which the captain of the Yellow Band spoke.

"Will you not take a little refreshment first?" asked Red Ralph.

"No, no, I never drink anything when on business like this."

As the fellow said this he leered in a way which implied that he feared that the wine might be doctored.

"You infer a poor compliment on this gentleman's hospitality," said Red Ralph. "His wine is excellent."

But the man still refused.

He never moved his pistol from the first position he had taken up.

The highwayman was fatally covered by it in case of an attempt to escape.

"Then you refuse?" said Ralph.

"I wouldn't touch a drop."

"Then take the bottle!" cried Ralph.

Before the officer could divine his intention he took the decanter by the neck and hurled it full at his face.

It was well aimed. The pistol was dashed from his grasp, and the decanter cannoned from his arm to his head, and brought him to the ground.

Up sprang the captain of the Yellow Band and dashed at the officer.

In the space of a few seconds he had transferred the fallen man's pistols and sword to his own person.

Then he released him, and the officer was not a little pleased to get off thus easily.

Ralph moved to the door.

"I charge you, in the name of the law, sir," cried the officer, "to prevent that man's escape."

"Take that, you fool!" ejaculated the baronet, quite exasperated at the other's attempt to secure Ralph.

And he accompanied his angry words with a second missile.

It was another decanter, full of wine, and it would have done the officer some damage had it taken effect.

As it was, he bobbed and just contrived to avoid it.

Ralph, however, understood that the baronet might get into some trouble in conniving at his escape, and so he endeavoured in a few meaning glances to explain the position to him.

He flourished the officer's sword as he reached the door, although no opposition was now offered him.

"I'll run any man through who attempts to molest me!" he cried. "Beware, I say, I will escape or die!"

The baronet perceived the meaning of this, and he entered into the deception with great spirit.

Drawing his sword, he jumped up and ran after the captain of the Yellow Band.

Their weapons met at the door, but the old gentleman's was beaten from his grasp with marvellous rapidity.

With a great deal more noise and show than was necessary Red Ralph dashed open the door and darted into the road.

The officer sprang forward, and would have hurried off in pursuit, but the old gentleman had yet to be picked up.

He lay right across the doorway, holding up his hands to the officer, who could not refuse his assistance.

Then it took so much time to get the old gentleman upon his legs, for he slipped down no less than three times in the strangest manner, that by the time the officer arrived at the front door pursuit of Red Ralph was a hopeless matter.

"Now be off," said the baronet. "Your answer to your scoundrel of a master is that Red Ralph is not quite dead yet, and, moreover, that he will most probably live to see you both hanged."

"Sir," replied the man, "my errand is now more embarrassing than ever. Mr. Wild will resent these painful tidings upon me."

"He will?"

"Undoubtedly."

"Then off with you. That's some comfort, at any rate. Off you go, or, by the Lord Harry! my servants shall drag you through the horse pond!"

CHAPTER XCVI.

RALPH'S RETURN TO DICK TURPIN—THE WOOD HUT—A CAROUSE—TOASTS AND SENTIMENTS—RALPH'S RIDE—THE INN—"TO THE RESCUE!"—THE GIRL—SAVED FROM OUTRAGE—HER DOUBTS—THE HUT AGAIN—THE LADY'S HISTORY—A TALE OF BLOOD—A DARK DEED—THE ACCUSED—SAFE FROM PURSUIT—A FRESH ARRIVAL—"WHAT CAN IT MEAN?"

QUITTING the hospitable roof of the worthy old baronet, the captain of the Yellow Band hastened with all possible speed to rejoin his friends and comrades in the last deed of daring committed upon the king's highway—the stoppage of the night mail.

Dick Turpin and his staunch ally, Tom King, were awaiting Red Ralph at a hut in the wood adjoining the heath.

Here he recounted his adventures at the house of the baronet, and provoked the mirth of the doughty knights of the road at the expense of the police constable who had come to such signal and undignified grief.

It must not, however, be imagined for an instant that the captain of the Yellow Band imparted to his lawless and unscrupulous companions the secret of his birth and noble parentage, as confided to the old gentleman whose house he had just quitted.

"Ha! ha!" laughed Dick Turpin, "its a glorious adventure."

"True."

"But unfortunate," quoth King.

"How so, pray?" asked Red Ralph.

"They believed you dead."

"What then?"

"Now that Jonathan Wild finds out that you still live, he'll be after you again in no time."

"Pooh!" said Red Ralph, snapping his fingers carelessly, "I can afford to despise him."

"Gad! you can, Ralph," exclaimed Dick Turpin.

"Ay, that he can," said Tom King. "You have up to now."

"Ay, and shall."

"Moreover," said Dick Turpin, "it would have been useless attempting to keep such a secret."

"As what?"

"Your resuscitation, I think one may fairly call it."

"Indeed you may."

"But you'd never have kept it dark for long."

"No, no. Some dare-devil prank would have told all the world that the captain of the Yellow Band was still amongst them."

Whilst they were thus chatting merrily Tom King produced a bottle of good wine and a drinking horn from a shelf.

"Now, Tom," said Dick Turpin, "fill me a bumper."

"How, Dick—first?"

"Ay, first. The first toast to-night shall be mine."

"As you will."

The drinking horn was filled to the brim, and the three highwaymen rose to honour the toast which their bold comrade was about to propose.

However, it was rather awkward, as there was but one drinking cup, and they had to drink one after the other.

Dick Turpin, as the proposer of the toast, claimed priority in amiability only.

"Here's to future successes of Red Ralph—"

"Bravo!" cried King.

"And of his bold and dare-devil fellows, too—"

"The Yellow Boys for ever!" cried Tom King.

"May they confound their enemies—"

"Hurrah!"

"Set the body-snatchers and the big wigs at defiance—"

"Bravo!"

"And never dance upon nothing!"

"With a hip, hip, hurrah!" roared Tom King. "Confound it, I can't wait for the drinking horn, Dick."

And with this the daring highwayman seized the bottle, and honoured the toast without having resource to the aid of any intermediate vessel.

"Here's confusion to our enemies," said Ralph.

"Bravo!"

"And eternal perdition to Jonathan Wild the thief-taker."

"Amen to that."

They drank toast after toast, but the sentiment of all was pretty much the same.

The lauded each other to the skies and consigned the thief-taker to Hades, one and all.

When the carouse had lasted some considerable time Red Ralph as usual grew weary of it.

These debauches were very little to his taste.

It was deep in the night, and he was leaving the two highwaymen in the middle of a thick wood, with whose tangled labyrinths he was by no means well acquainted.

However, he mounted his horse and rode away, never heeding and little caring whither he roved.

The truth was that his late conversation with the old baronet, at whose hospitable board he had just been entertained, had not been without some effect upon him.

He no longer felt any enjoyment in the presence of the good-hearted but lawless men who made so much of him.

He hurried off to the right, judging that this direction would bring him again to the heath.

He had barely gained the open heath once more when his ears were saluted with a loud cry.

What it could mean he was utterly at a loss to comprehend.

Then there was a second cry, and this time much louder than before.

He noticed, too, that it appeared to be close at hand.

A few strides brought him through a narrow path into the open road.

Near the cross road was a low thatched tavern, dull and sombre in appearance.

Just as the captain of the Yellow Band gained the road opposite the tavern, lights were flashed in two windows simultaneously.

There were sounds of a scuffle, and Red Ralph, anticipating some foul play, rushed forward to the rescue.

We have already related—somewhat prematurely—

how he arrived in the very nick of time to save a young and beautiful girl from the murderous clutches of the owners of the lone house on the heath.

Bearing the girl in his arms, he regained the road rapidly, sprang into the saddle, and set spurs to his horse.

In an instant more it would have been too late.

He had barely started off when the door of the inn was dashed open with a bang, and a man rushed forth.

"Stop!" he cried as soon as he perceived the state of affairs.

But Ralph knew better.

Without replying, he buried his spurs deep in his horse's flanks and galloped off.

Very little of this rapid progress served to carry them far out of all danger.

The poor girl, however, was still trembling with fear.

A bold and determined courage had sufficed to save her life at a moment of extreme peril, and yet now that danger was lessened—nay, averted—her whole stock of courage seemed exhausted.

"Come, come," said the captain of the Yellow Band to his fair trembling charge. "You have nothing now to fear."

"I have, I have," cried the girl, burying her face in her hands.

"How so?"

"I recognise something terrible in this persecution."

"What?"

"Retribution!"

"Retribution?"

"Ay—Divine retribution."

"What do you mean?"

"Oh, for the love of mercy, do not press me for an explanation."

Red Ralph was utterly bewildered by her frantic words.

"You quite confuse me," he said, "for really I cannot possibly understand what you have to apprehend from any persecution now."

"You do not know all."

"Nor do I seek to know," said the captain of the Yellow Band, "if an explanation would be painful to you in the slightest degree."

"It would, it would."

"Enough."

But still the girl refused to be comforted.

Much to the annoyance of her preserver, she continued to lament and bewail her hard fortune.

"What do you intend to do?" asked Red Ralph presently.

"What do you mean?"

"Whither would you go?"

"I know not."

"But you have surely some destination, have you not?"

"None."

"Then whither shall I conduct you?"

"Where you will, so that I do not quit your side."

Red Ralph looked considerably startled at this. He was a smart showy fellow, but had never been made love to in this fashion before.

"My poor girl," he said, "it is impossible that you should stay with me."

"Why? Oh, say that you will not desert me!"

And she burst into a flood of tears.

Now all this was woefully embarrassing for the captain of the Yellow Band.

He never could endure to see one of the softer sex in tears, and the poor creature's grief was desolating.

He could not imagine what to do with her.

He could not leave her there without a home or shelter, and there was no house for miles but the den

of infamy from which he had so opportunely rescued her.

He could not venture to cast her off.

Humanity and gratitude for the tenderness with which she repaid his services alike forbad such a course.

It suddenly occurred to him that the only way to get rid of her decently was to take her to the wood hut where he had so lately quitted his jovial comrades, Dick Turpin and Tom King.

In spite of their rough ways of life, both of the redoubtable robbers entertained a certain amount of respect for the opposite sex.

Where a character was spotless—rather a rare occurrence at the period of our history, which was remarkable for a certain laxity of morals—they entertained a respect for the lady almost reminding one of the days of chivalry.

As they gained the hut she looked up into the face of her preserver, and he could see that a momentary doubt crossed her.

"Surely you do not fear me?" he said in surprise.

"No, no."

"Surely not after your singular expressions just now."

She looked alarmed.

"I have spoken wildly."

"Well you have, I must confess, rather wildly."

"And you have misinterpreted my meaning, doubtless?"

"I think not."

"Nay, but I can detect something in your voice and manner which assures me that you have misunderstood me."

"Nay, believe me."

"Nay, hear me," she continued wildly. "Forced by the cruellest combination of circumstantial evidence to quit my home upon a minute's notice, I fled I knew not whither. I came to Hounslow, rested at the inn, and you know the rest. Almost at the last moment of my existence, as I then thought, you rescued me."

"Happily."

"And Heaven reward you for your goodness to me."

"I am already sufficiently rewarded by you," said Red Ralph.

He looked upon her with such an ardent glance that the crimson blood flew to her head, dyeing it to the very roots of her hair.

"Nay, I beseech you not to misinterpret my warm expressions of gratitude," she ejaculated.

Red Ralph could now perceive that she was really in trouble.

"Lady," said he, taking her hand within his own and raising it tenderly to his lips, "you have nothing to apprehend from me."

"Oh, sir."

"I have not preserved you from those miscreants to take advantage of your solitary position."

"You have a noble nature, sir," said the girl, gratefully.

Her hand yet lingered in his.

He felt too that as he held it, pressed ever so lightly, it trembled in his grasp, and send a tremor through his whole frame.

Her eyes sank beneath his burning glance.

Yet something whispered in his ear to beware, a warning was uttered there in a single word.

Leonore!

He started as if he had heard her voice reproaching him, and turned from the girl.

"Come," said he, rousing himself from the dream of tenderness in which he had ventured for a moment to indulge. "Let us go into the cottage."

"Who is there?"

"Only two friends of mine."

"Men?"

[A LADY TO THE RESCUE.]

"Yes, but you have nothing to fear. Nothing to apprehend from them. They will treat you with every consideration, be sure."

She glanced up inquiringly into the face of her preserver.

Truth was there.

"I rely implicitly upon you," she said.

"And your confidence is not misplaced you will find."

"I know it."

"Come, let us go in."

He knocked at the door of the hut with his riding whip.

"Open, open!"

"Who is there?" demanded the voice of Dick Turpin.

"It is I."

"Who?"

"Why, Ralph," said the bold Tom King to Turpin. "Don't you recognise his voice?"

"Ralph?"

"Ay."

"'Gad! I didn't."

"Here you are—"

And the door was opened by the doughty Dick Turpin.

As he caught sight of the companion of the captain of the Yellow Band he jumped back.

An exclamation of the greatest astonishment burst from him.

"By all that's horrible, Red Ralph with a petticoat!"

"A what?" demanded Tom King, not a whit less surprised.

"A petticoat."

"Never."

He sprang towards the door, and the rescued girl shrank trembling behind her preserver.

"Gentlemen, gentlemen," said the captain of the Yellow Band, reprovingly, "gently please."

At this Messrs. Tom King and Dick Turpin exchanged glances of great significance, which were observed by the newcomers, as, indeed, the wags had intended they should be.

They both imagined that they perceived an intrigue.

"Enter, lady, and welcome," said Tom King gallantly.

"Thank you."

"What an ankle!" said King, in an audible whisper, to Turpin.

The girl looked frightened.

"One word," said the captain of the Yellow Band rather severely. "Before we proceed any further let me explain to you how I came to be honoured with this lady's society."

"It needs no explanation," said Dick Turpin laughingly.

"Nay, but—"

"None whatever."

"Not a bit," cried King.

And they laughed boisterously, while the poor girl's colour came and went from her cheeks in a most painful way.

"Stay, stay, comrades," exclaimed Red Ralph, now growing a little angry. "Don't you perceive that you are distressing the lady?"

"Eh? What?"

"Distressing?" cried Tom King. "A thousand pardons."

"You misunderstand."

"Oh! doubtless."

"Of course."

"Nay, but you shall hear me, you madcaps!" cried Red Ralph. "This lady I happened most fortunately to preserve from the clutches of a nest of the greatest villains who ever poisoned the face of the globe."

"How do you mean?"

"I rescued her from the inn yonder. You know the house."

"By the cross roads?"

"The same."

"We remarked it as we came, if you remember rightly."

"True."

"They would have robbed, and, doubtless, murdered her."

"The ruffians!"

"Then we should do well, perhaps, to make a journey thither, and repay them a little for their kind attentions."

"It is useless," said the captain of the Yellow Band, "for already they have reaped the reward of their treacherous malpractices."

"I'm glad of that."

"But how?" asked King.

The girl then gave them an explanation of the whole occurrence, as we have related.

They then grew curious as to her presence in that part of the country at so late an hour, and quite alone and unprotected.

She was, therefore, obliged to give an explanation.

But they had less consideration than the gallant highwayman who had rescued her, and she was obliged to enter into details.

"Well, gentlemen," she said, "I quite understand that an explanation is due to you."

"Nay," said Red Ralph.

"But it is. And none the less to myself," she added.

"How so?"

"To secure the continuance of your respect for me."

"That is scarcely wanted, madam," quoth Tom King gallantly.

She bowed.

"I see it is," she said, "and I shall give it, with your permission, in as few words as possible."

"Thank you."

"We are all attention."

"You will at once comprehend the nature of my domestic troubles," began the girl, "when I tell you that our home is governed by my step-mother—my father's second wife. A young family has sprung up, and are the household pets, whilst I and my sister—the only two children of my father's first wife—are unpleasantly looked upon by the whole of the household. In short, we are shamefully neglected. The servants even are not accustomed to treat us with proper respect. The governess of the new family has grown so bold and full of effrontery that it has been noticed by many visitors to our house. A person of some importance in our little family circle—I shall beg to be spared names—had formed an attachment to the governess, and I have every reason to believe that it was of such a nature as to reflect but little credit upon either party.

"A few nights ago I was awakened from my sleep with a start.

"I heard a cry of a child. I could plainly hear that it came from the governess's room, and thither I made my way with all speed.

"As soon as I arrived there a horrid spectacle, to which I was an accidental witness, greeted my view.

"A man was in the room, standing with the governess beside the child's cot.

"The woman held the pillow tightly grasped over its head.

"The man looked anxiously on—oh, heavens! when I record it!—looked anxiously on whilst the darling babe—the infant pet of the whole household—was being stifled.

"For murder was being done.

"I was so horrified with what I saw that I could neither move nor speak, but there I stood, stock still, to witness one of the most cruel acts which it has ever been my lot to see perpetrated.

"They held the pillow over the child's head until all was still.

"Then the fatal object was removed, and disclosed the pale features of the dead child.

"But was it dead? No. Notwithstanding the pale and settled expression of the face, the precious babe yet lived.

"It opened its eyes after a while—oh, Heaven! when I recall it how fearful is the remembrance of that dreadful night!—and prattled a few words in a painful choking voice, calling by name upon the governess and the guilty wretched man who stained his soul with crime.

"My—the man left the room, almost brushing my skirts as he passed me, and presently returned with something in his hand which I failed to distinguish at first, but shortly a phase of terror and blood in this drama of crime told me that the object in his hand was a razor.

"I will not dwell too long upon the fearful scene which ensued. The pretty babe, my sister, was cruelly sacrificed to their own safety. Their guilty secret was preserved, but my piece of mind, and that of the whole house, was for ever destroyed.

"The body of the poor little babe was discovered the next day cut so deeply about the throat that the head was well-nigh severed from the body."

"One word," said King. "I am glad to hear that the daughter escaped."

"Alas! that is no matter," said the girl. "One after another of the household has been arrested and tried for the murder, but the evidence has failed to convict any one—happily, happily. At length my turn has come."

"And you have fled."

"Yes."

"But why?"

"I have fled in fear."

"Of what?"

"The law."

"But you would run no risk in answering the accusation."

"Alas! I do."

The three highwaymen grew more and more interested.

"Tell us the nature of the danger which you think would threaten you," said the captain of the Yellow Band.

"There is a damning piece of evidence against me which has been brought to light by the aid of the governess."

"Infamous!"

"Villainous!"

"Well, to meet this I should have to enter into such explanations to clear myself as would implicate others."

"What matter?"

"The governess, I suppose?" said Ralph.

"And he. You forget the man I spoke off."

"But why should you so fear to implicate the murderer?"

"That you cannot understand of course until you know who that man is. But that shall never be known if it rests with me. Sooner would I be hunted through the world a condemned murdress than he should be accused."

"But you cannot hope to escape the vigilance of justice."

"Then I shall take my chance. If they can find sufficient proof of guilt, then I shall quietly submit. It was in the first moment of terror that I fled."

"That was unwise."

"Alas! I know it."

"You see it must naturally excite suspicion."

"Of course. But I saw at once that as soon as suspicion pointed its black finger at me it would go hardly with me."

"Why?"

"Because, being of the first family, the cold treatment of myself and my brother might be supposed to excite jealousy in us of the young family."

"True."

"But it is a sad pity," said the captain of the Yellow Band, "that you allowed your fears so far to mislead you."

"I scarcely know that."

"Nay, but it is, for with your power of reasoning such trumpery proofs as you say they possess could easily be explained away."

"But at what cost?"

"And do you so fear to bring the foul assassins to justice."

"Justice!" cried the girl wildly. "The scaffold you mean."

"And then—"

"Ah! forbear. Would you urge me to save my own miserable existence and commit parricide."

The robbers started.

The girl hastily endeavoured to recall the word, but it was too late.

However, they saw the pain it caused her, and they forebore to notice it.

"What is your name?" asked the doughty Dick Turpin.

She hesitated before venturing to reply to this.

"Oh, you must soon know that," she said after a second's consideration. "My name is Laura Delane."

"Delane!" repeated Red Ralph in astonishment. "Surely it is not the murder which has been so much talked of lately?"

"It is."

"Then for once public opinion has pointed to the true murderers."

"Oh, never, never."

"Indeed it has. The general opinion is that—"

"Hush! Forbear I implore you."

"As you please," said the captain of the Yellow Band. "But were it left to me, I confess that I should feel bound to bring the murderers to justice."

"Under any circumstances?"

"Ay, even should the miscreant prove my own father."

The girl clasped her hands over her throbbing brow.

"Man, man," she cried, "this is far easier said than done. You cannot say this much without realising the position. You cannot realise the position unless you had found yourself placed as I am placed."

"Possibly."

"Ah! yes," said Dick Turpin. "I can well understand the motives which restrained you, Miss Delane. But yet we must condemn your line of conduct."

"Alas! I know it."

"However," said Tom King. "You will be pretty free from all danger of pursuit here."

"You think so?"

"Oh, yes. And you are welcome to stay here as long as you please. If our presence here should embarrass you, we can make ourselves scarce very speedily."

"Oh, no, no, no," said Miss Delane. "Not for worlds. My earnest heartfelt thanks for your kindness. I have some money, and if you will permit it will pay."

But this they positively refused to listen to.

"No, no," said Turpin. "Pray allow us to offer you the poor hospitality we can without return."

"Yes," said King. "Stay as long as you will, and welcome. You are safe from observation here."

It was the second time the speaker had made the same remark, and, as if to contradict it, as it was spoken a knock came at the door of the hut!

The three highwaymen sprang to their feet.

The girl changed colour and was the very picture of consternation and alarm.

CHAPTER XCVII.

THE STRANGER—AN OLD FRIEND—THE SPY'S WARNING—THE HUNT FOR A MURDRESS—THE ROBBERS' OBSTINACY—RED RALPH AND HIS CHARGE—FLIGHT—TEMERITY—"BEWARE!"—DANGER AHEAD.

"WHO'S there?"

"Open, open!" cried a voice which did not strike unfamiliarly upon Red Ralph's ear.

"What would you?"

"No matter."

"Nay, but it matters much."

"I am alone."

"And I too," said King.

"But I'm unarmed."

"And so am I."

They could hear the man without playing an impatient tattoo upon the door.

"If you are so fearful," he said petulantly, "look from the window and speak."

"What for ?"

"I would speak with you."

"For what purpose ?"

"You shall learn."

"But what assurance am I to have that no harm is intended me ?"

"Your cowardice will undo you, you will find."

This was too much for King.

His patience was worn out before that of the new-comer, and he burst into an angry exclamation, which set both Red Ralph and Dick Turpin laughing.

"'Sdeath, you knave !" he cried. "I'll slit your villanous ears for you."

With this, before either of his companions could prevent the imprudent act, he slipped off the wooden bar which guarded the door and threw it open.

A man envelopped in a long riding cloak appeared at the entrance.

He appeared rather startled at seeing so many persons where, according to Tom King's little fiction, he had thought to meet but one individual.

Moreover, he was both surprised and disappointed upon beholding Tom King.

He had evidently thought to meet another person there.

"Hullo, friend," said the highwayman. "You appear all abroad."

"In truth I am," said the stranger confusedly.

"Come next door, perhaps ?"

"I don't understand."

"You must have wanted next door."

"I certainly am mistaken."

"Ah, well, next door is about two miles from here, my friend. Good night."

"Stay."

"Good night."

"One moment, Tom," said the captain of the Yellow Band, rising and coming forward. "It is I you want, I think."

The stranger uttered an exclamation of pleasure.

"Then it is true ?" he cried.

"What is ?"

"That you escaped that leap over the bridge."

"It would seem so, since I am here at present."

"Marvellous."

"Nothing wonderful—a series of fortunate chances."

"I thought it scarce possible."

"But now," said Red Ralph. "Pray tell me how you came here at this strange hour."

"I come to seek you."

"Me ?"

"Ay, yourself, captain."

"But how knew you ?"

"Oh ! it has already reached town that you have escaped again."

"So soon ?"

"Ay. And your old pal, Jonathan Wild, is going mad with excitement."

"Come, that's news."

"Yes. And he's already organised a large force to scour the country all around."

"So soon ?"

"Ay. Preparations, more extensive than any yet made, are now on foot."

"But I cannot understand how he has had time to discover our retreat even."

"He does not know precisely. He knows the locality and has had his eye on this hut for some time past."

"Oh ! has he ?" cried Dick Turpin.

"Then I'll have something more than an eye upon him if he chances to come across my path," quoth Tom King.

"Yes. His attention has been drawn hither as the lurking-place of two fellows he's most anxious to come across."

"And if he did," said Red Ralph, with a significant leer at his two comrades, "he'd give something to be out of their way as soon as possible. Eh, lads ?"

"It shouldn't be my fault if he didn't," said Dick Turpin.

"No, nor mine."

"None of you appear to cherish any good feeling towards him," said the stranger.

"We none of us love him to distraction," said King, laughing.

"And we shan't wear crape when he has his wizen slit."

"Nor I."

"And there is soon a probability of that happy event."

"Indeed ?" said Ralph.

"Yes. John Blake has sworn to do the job."

"Egad ! Then he'll keep his word," cried Turpin, "for he's the most determined young fellow that ever handled a jemmy."

"John Blake ?" repeated Red Ralph, musingly.

"Ay. Blueskin. You surely remember Blueskin, Ralph."

"Ay. He that was with that young dare-devil, Jack Sheppard ?"

"The same."

"He's in trouble, then ?"

"In the strong-room of Newgate, and loaded with irons."

"He *was* taken, but they can't keep him anywhere."

"Escaped again ?"

"Ay. And so would Blueskin, too, have escaped, but he wasn't aware that his young pal had succeeded. The love he bears the boy is something wonderful. Would you believe it, he wouldn't attempt to escape because he thought that Jack Sheppard was in the prison yet ?"

"Strange devotion that."

"It is. But I must not spend more time here in idle parlance. Every minute is an age now. It has happened most unfortunate for you again. A force of men have been engaged for a day or so in strict investigation of these parts for an escaped murderer."

"Murderer !"

The three highwaymen started and turned towards Miss Delane.

The poor girl, too, gave a faint cry and sank back.

"See, see ! She faints !"

"No. I—I shall be better immediately," she breathed.

The newcomer had not up to the present noticed that there was a female present.

At once, now, the circumstance appeared to strike him as being most remarkable.

"One word, captain," he said to Red Ralph. "Does that girl answer to the name of Laura Delane ?"

"I can't say."

"You have no need to speak," said the man, "for her face assures me that I have spoken aright."

"Mercy, mercy !" cried the girl, in earnest supplication.

"Fear nothing, Miss Delane," said Dick Turpin, stoutly.

"No, no. You are safe with us."

The stranger beckoned Red Ralph aside to whisper.

"What is it ?" asked Ralph.

"If you like to give up the girl quietly I can undertake to throw them effectually off the scent."

"What ?"

"And not only that," continued the man, not observing Red Ralph's indignant reception of the proposition, "but make a profit by it."

"You infernal scoundrel !" cried Red Ralph.

"Hullo !"

"What do you mean by making such a proposition to me?"

"She's a murdress."

"It's false."

"She's accused, at any rate."

"And do you think that I'd take blood-money?"

"Well, I'm not supposed to anticipate every little freak of fancy in which you indulge. However, I must begone now. Bear in mind the warning I gave you."

"I will."

"You would not heed my last, and you paid dearly for your temerity."

"I did."

"Farewell."

"One word. Promise me that you will not attempt to molest this unhappy girl."

He hesitated.

"Why, you see, captain," he said, "my arrangement only related to yourself."

"Ay. And I know that you have repaid all you owed me."

"Not yet. But this girl?"

"Is innocent of the crime with which she is charged. Of that I am assured. I only ask of you not to make use of the knowledge you have accidentally acquired to do her harm."

"Very well."

"You promise?"

"I do."

"Your hand upon it."

"There."

And with a hearty grasp this compact of mercy and forbearance was sealed.

"Farewell, and be speedy in your flight."

"Thanks."

And with this the stranger vanished.

"Come, we must bustle," said Red Ralph. "We must make a journey forward at once."

"But how are we to be assured of the fellow's truth?"

"I am," said Red Ralph. "He's one of Jonathan Wild's own confidental men, and once already I have neglected his caution. It nearly cost me my life. I had to leap over Westminster Bridge, and escaped by a miracle."

"Gad! I should say so."

"But come. We must begone."

But neither of the two highwaymen made the least sign of moving.

In vain did Red Ralph urge them to go.

They were obdurate, and would positively remain.

"To tell the truth, Red Ralph," said Dick Turpin, "I have but little faith in this strange fellow's story."

"As you will," said Red Ralph, tired with endeavouring to convince them against their inclinations. "I feel that I have a duty to perform towards this helpless girl, and I shall not quit her until I have placed her in some safe asylum."

"My eternal gratitude be yours!" exclaimed Miss Delane warmly. "Heaven will reward your goodness."

And they quitted the wood hut together.

A little later, and we shall see how foolish were the two highwaymen to pay so little heed to the warnings of the captain of the Yellow Band.

But the fortune which pursued our hero upon all occasions attended him upon this one likewise.

A deadly peril was averted by the merest accident, and this same peril was slighted by the dashing Dick Turpin and the sturdy Tom King.

But they had soon to repent their temerity.

CHAPTER XCVIII.

THE ATTACK ON THE WOOD HUT — A SPIRITED DEFENCE—TWO TO AN ARMY—HOPELESS RESISTANCE—TURPIN HIT—A FATAL DISCOVERY —THE BEGINNING OF THE END.

THE captain of the Yellow Band had barely quitted the wood hut with Miss Delane ten minutes, when Dick Turpin and Tom King found reason to repent of not heeding his warning.

The spy, out of gratitude to our hero, had kindly come at great personal risk to warn them.

And yet they had slighted his words.

Fortunately, Red Ralph had felt himself bound for the moment by the responsibility of watching over the safety of his new charge, Miss Delane.

Heedless of everything, the two mad-brained highwaymen continued their carouse, which the appearance of Red Ralph with Miss Delane, and the latter's singular and interesting history had interrupted.

"A fig for the red coats!" cried King.

"That for them!" said Turpin.

And he snapped his fingers contemptuously in the air.

"I should rather like to see them," cried Tom King, with a laugh.

"No such luck."

"I'm afraid not."

Dick Turpin poured out a huge goblet of liquor— that is, he filled the only jug they boasted from a barrel, and held it aloft.

"Here's perdition to the red coats, every mother's son!"

"I'll honour that," said King.

And the two mad revellers with a shout drained off the cup.

But a reverse was in store for them, which caused them to revise their previously expressed desire.

Their carouse proceeded for a few minutes, when there was a tramp of feet without.

Then a knock at the door.

The highwaymen now exchanged very curious glances.

Here was a singular and speedy fulfilment of the alarm which the spy had brought Ralph.

As neither of the highwaymen replied, the knocking at the door was more loudly repeated.

"What shall we do, Dick?" demanded Tom King of the other.

"I don't know."

"Shall we open?"

"As you like."

Before they could proceed further in their conference the door was assailed by a succession of violent blows which made the old hut creak again.

"Open, open!" cried a voice without.

"Open the door!"

"Open we charge you!"

The occupants of the hut could remain silent no longer.

"Who's there?"

"Officers of the law."

"Open, in the king's name."

"Open, or we break in."

And the attack upon the door was resumed more furiously than ever.

"It must give way, Dick," said King.

"It sounds like it."

"What can we be after, then?"

"'Pon my life I can't say. I almost begin to wish that we had—"

"Taken Ralph's advice?"

"Precisely."

"And I, too. Curse the door, how it shakes!"

"Hi!" cried Dick Turpin aloud to the attacking party without. "Cease your fun there."

"Then open."

"I decline."

"Then we break in."

"I shall fire upon you if you don't make off quickly."

"We can stand fire," answered a fresh voice.

"Ay, blaze away!"

"Then, confound you!" cried Dick Turpin. "You shall stand fire!"

"Are we all loaded up?" demanded Tom King eagerly.

"Yes."

"Where are the long 'uns?"

This was a fancy term of the bold highwaymen for fowling pieces.

"At the back. There, under that heap of straw to the right."

"Good."

Whilst Tom King was making these hasty preparations for retaliating upon the military the attack upon the stout little door of the wood hut was carried on with such zeal that it appeared every minute as if it must give way before the repeated blows.

Dick Turpin had to exert himself now to the utmost to make himself heard.

The din and clamour without had grown terrific.

"Hullo! ho, ho!" he shouted again and again. "Stop that noise there."

"Open, then."

"Curse me if I do."

"Then down goes the whole concern," shouted a soldier.

And the attack was renewed more furiously than ever.

The little hut shook now in a most ominous manner until the two besieged highwayman thought that every minute must send it rattling about their ears.

However, their blood was up now, and they took to their work in an earnest manner.

In the space of a few seconds Tom King shouted to his companion that the weapons were all ready loaded and everything prepared.

"Then blaze away at 'em," shouted Turpin.

"I will."

There was a window in the loft over the room in which the two highwaymen were carrying on their carouse.

To this they at once repaired, loaded with weapons of offence.

They had got a very fair stock of firearms, and, as they were all loaded, a very fair defence by the two highwaymen might be anticipated.

Dick Turpin was the first at the window, musket at shoulder.

The first sight he caught of the soldiers quite startled him.

There seemed to be a regiment of them, and all taking an active part in the attack upon the hut.

One fellow seemed particularly active in the business.

He darted hither and thither, delivering orders and snatching up pieces of wood to throw against the hut.

At first Dick Turpin could not comprehend the meaning of this, but he very speedily learnt the state of affairs.

And a very alarming piece of intelligence it proved to him.

The soldiers were going to burn them out.

This was not a very pleasant thing to discover.

"Quick, quick, Tom!" called Dick Turpin. "We must blaze away, or we are as good as gone. Come on?"

"I'm there," said King.

As he spoke he ran up the ladder into the loft and joined his companion.

He was loaded with firearms, all charged.

Indeed, it would have assumed the appearance of a skirmish between the military and the highwaymen had the inmates of the wood hut been more numerous.

As it was, their audacious resistance appeared hopeless.

As soon as Dick Turpin was at the window he put the musket he held to his shoulder.

Took a steady and deliberate aim.

Fired!

As soon as the smoke cleared off he could perceive that his shot had taken effect.

A serious gap had taken place in the ranks of the besiegers.

"Bravo!" cried Dick.

"Hit one?" asked King.

"Ay, and a leader."

"Good."

"Hullo! Down we go."

As Dick Turpin uttered these words he threw himself upon his face, and there was a quick succession of reports immediately.

The muskets balls rattled about the window of the wood hut in a most alarming fashion.

"Make some loopholes for firing, Tom," said Dick Turpin.

"Down here?"

"Ay."

"Good."

And, while his comrade was thus occupied, Dick Turpin contrived to employ himself aloft in a more dangerous manner.

He crawled up to the window, and, resting the muzzle of his musket upon the edge of it, waited for a minute impatiently for an opportunity to take aim.

The opportunity came before many minutes had elapsed.

The firing ceased for a second, and the doughty Dick Turpin raised himself upon his elbow and peeped over the window ledge.

It was but momentary, but he contrived to single out one who seemed by his activity to have been elected leader in place of the young soldier who had fallen.

Again he fired.

At the very moment he shot a report below announced that Tom King was already at work.

The new leader was brought to the ground as the former had been.

Tom King, too, did most signal service, for his exertions were entirely directed against the men who were collecting fuel with very apparent and alarming intentions.

Two men who had been chosen to execute this unpleasant business very soon bit the dust.

Others filled their places, but Tom King was there, and ready.

As he never fired two shots consecutively from the same spot, he contrived to do good execution without receiving any proofs of the beseigers' enmity in return.

The attack had scarcely commenced with anything approaching seriousness when no less than ten of the red coats had fallen.

Still the brave-hearted fellows kept to it manfully.

It cannot be said that they were not a little disconcerted by the disasters which they had reaped so early, without being able to retaliate, but they were not utterly discouraged as yet.

"Pheugh!" said Dick Turpin, panting and puffing freely with his exertions. "If we can only manage to do as much as we have already done, in the next five minutes—"

"We are safe."

"Almost."

"Then here goes."

The speaker applied his eye to a small aperture in

the wood caused by one of the bullets of the attacking party.

Then removed his eye, and filled up the hole with the muzzle of his musket.

A flash, a report, and a loud wail of woe told its own sad tale.

It was a lucky shot, and brought down two more of their enemies.

At the same time his companion in this exciting business had closed the account of one of them in another place.

The members of the military *hors de combat* were now swelled to a baker's dozen.

And all this mischief wrought by two pair of hands.

But, although the two highwaymen had fought like the bravest of the brave for themselves, they could not hope to struggle against the overwhelming numbers by whom they were assailed.

They continued to direct their principal atttentions to the leaders of the attack, and those who were charged with the firing of the hut.

The soldiers stood to it boldly, but still it appeared to them that they were being hopelessly slaughtered by the hidden foe.

Fortunately they could not form an estimate of their numbers, or else it is probable that they would long since have made an assault upon the sturdy little hut in a body, and carried it by storm.

But it could not last for ever, under any circumstances, however favourable to the besieged highwaymen.

The walls upon every side were now riddled in an alarming fashion with the bullets of the attacking party.

Dick Turpin, too, losing his caution once, presented too much of his stalwart person as a mark to the enemy, and speedily learnt that he was not shotproof.

A ball in the shoulder rewarded his temerity.

The wound was not either deep or dangerous, and more calculated to annoy him than aught else.

" Ah !" he cried.

" What now ?" asked King, startled.

" I'm hit !"

" Never !"

" I am, indeed !"

" Badly ?"

" Don't know."

" Stick to it, Dick. If you go I'll go too, I swear it !"

" You're a true pal," said Dick Turpin gratefully.

A noise was heard without during this momentary cessation of hostilities upon the part of the highwaymen which caused them to feel some little fresh alarm.

They were evidently shouting triumphantly.

In an instant the two highwaymen flew to their several posts of observation, and reconnoitred.

The first discovery they made was indeed terrible.

" We're done for !" cried Turpin. " It smells strong of smoke !"

" Smoke ?"

" Ay."

" Then they are going to burn us out."

" It's true."

" The devil ! The cursed flames have caught at last, then."

" Yes."

" Then we may count upon five minutes' grace at the utmost."

" Nay, not so much."

" Perhaps not. It burns like tinder."

" Back to our posts."

" Ay, let's take what retaliation now lies in our power."

And they continued their defence boldly, in the face of defeat, for several minutes.

But it was the beginning of the end.

CHAPTER XCIX.

THE HUNCHBACK ALIVE YET—HIS PLOTS AND COUNTERPLOTS—MANŒUVRES—THE WOOD HUT —A CONVERSATION OVERHEARD—RESOLVES— A BRAVE REVENGE—ON THE TRACK.

WHILST the attack upon the wood hut continues with such fury, and whilst it is defended by its only two occupants with equal spirit, the hero of these memoirs and Miss Laura Delane have contrived to effect a safe retreat.

That is, when we use the expression " safe," we would wish to imply safe from the menaces of the soldiers and their ostensible foes.

But a hidden enemy is at hand.

As the soldiers arrived upon the spot an old acquaintance of the leader accompanied them.

Jabez the hunchback.

He looked scarcely so healthy as when we last saw him, but yet active and tolerably strong upon his legs.

The fact is, he had lost so much blood upon the occasion of his encounter with the captain of the Yellow Band that he had never recovered from the effects of it.

The reader will remember the startling encounter we here allude to.

It was upon the occasion of Red Ralph's sally to preserve the life of Leonore.

And well had he contrived to achieve his object.

At the very last moment—at the instant previous to that which must have inevitably closed the unhappy girl's account with this existence had not assistance arrived.

So much for Leonore, of whom we shall give more anon.

To continue the movements of Red Ralph and the lady he had in his charge.

When Jabez the hunchback and the soldiers arrived near the wood hut, the former—who had been all through engaged in earnest conversation upon plans for the capture which they now meditated—drew off and went alone to reconnoitre.

In this pursuit a singular incident occurred to him.

It was this.

As soon as he perceived how matters stood he thought how much more easy and safe it would be to attempt a surprise.

Experience had taught him how a defence of such a little fortress might be conducted, even though so short of men as were the besieged.

To this, therefore, he devoted his whole attention.

The hut, we must here explain, was built upon the extreme edge of a shaw, or little wood, grown thickly with shrubs and brushwood.

So thickly, in fact, that it was almost impossible to penetrate its strange labyrinth.

However, the difficulty it presented was not sufficient to deter the little ruffian in his object.

The artifices of love are many—of hate there are a legion.

He made a wide but speedy *détour*, and at length he succeeded in working his way round to the shrubs and trees immediately backing the hut.

One giant tree completely sheltered the little building, an oak whose overhanging branches completely sheltered the spot from view.

This was possibly why it had been selected by the architect as his building site.

However, it sufficed to attract the attention of the diabolical little hunchback.

He threw off his coat at once and began to climb. His withered-up shrivelled little legs encircled the stately trunk before him, and his wiry little fingers clutched tenaciously wherever he could secure a hold.

It was a hard task, as the lower branches were young and not very strong.

Yet he kept to it boldly enough.

At length, after a tough struggle, his patience was rewarded by arriving at the desired point successfully.

From below he fancied that he had perceived a small crevice in the woodwork, but upon arriving at the spot he was exceedingly disappointed to discover that it was only a difference in the shade of the wood which had caused the illusion.

However, by instituting a diligent search he very soon discovered that in some points the woodwork was worm-eaten and could not present much resistance to a well-directed attack.

He had a knife in his belt.

A long ugly weapon, which had already been in such fatal proximity with Leonore's fair throat.

He plucked this forth with nervous haste, and made an eager search for some vulnerable point for assault.

The spot found, he commenced his attack.

A little judicious scraping—carefully performed, in order to avoid noise and alarm to the occupants of the hut—and the woodwork was in the space of three or four minutes cut through.

It was with feelings of joy, and anticipations of a rich treat of revenge, that the vicious little hunchback applied his eye to the small hole thus carefully made to discover—nothing!

Positively nothing.

The part of the hut which he looked into was pitch dark, and not even the outline of the place could be discovered.

"A curse light upon him!" muttered the hunchback.

As this amiable sentiment escaped him his ear caught the sound of voices.

A smile of triumph lit up his hideous countenance.

In an instant his ear was upon the little opening in the woodwork and he listened intently.

Now, by the expression of his face, it was clear that he could hear something of a satisfactory nature.

A shade of disappointment crossed his face at first it is true, but as he listened it was clear that this had given way to pleasure.

Pleasing and satisfactory beyond measure at the anticipation of some glorious piece of vengeance upon the bold captain of the Yellow Band.

"It was all very well for Red Ralph to go," said one of the inmates of the hut, whose voice and person were alike unknown to the listener.

"Perhaps," said another.

The former, we may observe, was Tom King, and the latter his only companion, Dick Turpin.

"But my opinion is that he takes more pains than necessary over that girl."

The hunchback pricked up his ears at these words.

"A girl?" he muttered.

"Yes," added Dick Turpin. "And I believe, too, that he's an artful rogue."

"In what way?"

"His morality."

"Ha, ha, ha!" laughed Tom King. "Yes, he looked demure enough for some old canting priest."

And the two highwaymen laughed until the wood hut rang with their mirth.

"Fools!" muttered the eavesdropper. "They little dream of the danger in store for them."

But, although he thus spoke, the hunchback well knew that the ostensible object of the forest excursion was to secure the captain of the Yellow Band.

He knew also that they had another object in view—the capture of Miss Laura Delane, the supposed murdress; but his mind was so full of his meditated revenge upon Red Ralph that all other ideas were confused in the intensity of his passion.

Had it been otherwise he might not have derived so much satisfaction, for he would have guessed that the girl the two highwaymen spoke of was none other than the said Miss Laura Delane.

As it was, he augured, not very strangely, that it was the highwayman's bride.

This it was that so gratified him.

The thought of taking a twofold vengeance upon Red Ralph and Lady Leonore was soothing to his wounded spirit on account of his many recent failures, and at the same time solace to his wounded body.

For his hurts were of so serious a nature that none but the strongest possible constitution could have recovered them—at least, not in the marvellously short space of time that had elapsed since the recent battle at his house.

But to return to the highwaymen, from whom we are beginning to wander.

Presently a word of information caught the hunchback's greedy ear, which was the most important part of the conversation.

"Do you know where he proposes to go to?" demanded King.

"No."

"He spoke of the village yonder."

"But he would never be stupid enough for that."

"Why so?"

"Why so, forsooth! Why, to move hence to go into that little nest of chatterboxes? If he means to leave the girl there alone perhaps he may escape all right."

"That's what he does mean."

"Not he."

"Why not?"

"The girl has caught Red Ralph's eye—it's clear enough."

"I don't believe it."

"I'd swear it."

"He seemed little inclined towards her here," said Turpin.

"That was a ruse upon the part of the wilful Yellow Boy."

"I think so, now that we are upon the subject, for, truth to speak, the girl herself seemed to have eyes for no one but Red Ralph."

"Yes."

"And I know what that means."

"Yes, it's palpable enough."

"Ay, indeed."

The hunchback only felt these words to be a confirmation of his previous suspicions.

"With all, I see that the knave keeps the secret of his marriage with her."

The highwaymen were speaking again, and the hunchback gave them all his attention at once.

This time the sentiments of the speakers jarred unpleasantly upon the nerves of the listener.

"At any rate," quoth the sturdy Dick Turpin, "I hope he may be safe wherever he goes."

"Do you?" muttered Jabez.

"And I too," cried Tom King. "For Red Ralph's a glorious fellow, with all his strange ways."

"Ay, that he is."

"Here's a health to gentleman Red Ralph."

"With all my heart."

A short silence ensued, which told the hunchback that the toast was being duly honoured.

"Curse them!" muttered Jabez. "May it choke them!"

This pleasant sentiment, however, was not to be fulfilled.

[THE DEATH OF BLUESKIN.]

"I'll very soon set my friends, the military, upon these fellows," said the hunchback, "and we'll see how far their sympathy with Red Ralph may carry them."

He was just about to descend from his perch, in pursuance of this pleasant idea, when it occurred to him that such a proceeding would not be exactly reasonable.

"No, no," he muttered, "that jackanapes of an officer was rather smart at my expense before his men. He called me mannikin. By Jove! I'll leave him here. He's likely to get peppered, and after all they are sure to take these fellows. They'll resist, no doubt, and he's sure to fancy that Red Ralph is still here. If he knew that he had gone they wouldn't stop. No, no, I'll leave them to fight it out. They'll do some damage to each other, and I shall have my revenge out of all of them at once. It's a glorious day's work. Everything seems to play into my hands at last. It only remains to discover which way my worthy friend Red Ralph and my young mistress of beloved memory have gone. Red Ralph, when next we meet, I swear your life will be in danger!"

There was a fearful intensity in the passion of the hunchback as he spoke these words.

A determination which must have startled a listener had any been near.

But he was alone.

The little hunchback preserved this as his one leading characteristic.

He was very careful never upon any occasion to allow his real sentiments to be expressed in his words or his face.

Down he slid from his perch.

Looked about him carefully, and, pushing his way through the thick shrubs and brushwood, started off upon his errand.

With what result it was attended we shall show as we proceed.

But now for a word with the captain of the Yellow Band and his fair charge, Miss Laura Delane.

CHAPTER C.

RED RALPH AND HIS CHARGE—THEIR RAMBLES—TENDER EMOTIONS—MOONLIGHT—RALPH RAMBLES SOLUS—THE WAITER'S SHOT—WHENCE COMES IT?—AN UNSEEN FOE—FLIGHT—THE FALL—A FATAL ACCIDENT.

AFTER leaving the wood hut Red Ralph and Miss Laura Delane journeyed apace for more than half an hour.

The poor girl was much fatigued, but she kept boldly to the task, never murmuring in the least.

The captain of the Yellow Band saw her sad plight, and deep as was his commiseration for her he did not venture to express it too freely, lest his sentiments should be mistaken for something more tender than ordinary sympathy.

He saw already that the fair creature was not at all indifferent to him.

Her eager glances and rising blushes told their own tale with great eloquence.

It must not be imagined that our hero felt any vain gratification at the thought.

His whole love was concentrated on one object.

This bore the form of his beloved wife, his virgin bride, the beauteous Leonore.

It was therefore with feelings of sympathetic regret that he perceived the tender emotions now so rapidly springing up in the bosom of the fair girl at his side.

Strict prudence would have bidden him to quit her there and then.

But no. No man can preserve his prudence under some temptations, and this was one of the most trying.

"How am I ever to repay your kindness?" murmured Miss Delane, looking down, as she walked by his side.

"I will tell you."

"Do, do, do, oh! do."

"By never alluding to it," said Red Ralph rather cuttingly.

The young girl turned away evidently disappointed.

"You must know," continued the captain of the Yellow Band, "that nothing so much embarrasses a man who has the smallest particle of modesty in his composition as to receive thanks for services, no matter of what nature and whether real or imaginary."

"Imaginary?" she said.

"Ay."

"But pardon me," said Miss Delane. "There can be no doubt as to the reality at least of the services I have received at your hands, and as for their importance—"

Red Ralph interrupted her with a gesture of impatience.

"My dear lady—"

"Well, well," she said interrupting him as he was about to say something scarcely pleasant, "since you say that thanks embarrass you, I will not pour out my gratitude, as I fain would. For it would be but a sorry return to do anything which could annoy you in the slightest degree."

The highwayman was netted.

He stopped short and pressed her hand warmly.

She did not attempt to withdraw her soft white palm, but walked on, with her rich violet eyes shaded by the long silky lashes turned upon the ground.

Her bosom heaved rapidly, and the tenderness in her young guileless heart was clearly apparent.

But Red Ralph had lost himself for a while.

He had for the moment no longer the presence of mind to abstain from temptation.

The way he had rebuffed the young girl's advances did not at all suit his own ideas of the respect due to the opposite sex.

And so from time to time he relapsed into a display of tenderness most singularly at variance with his forced demeanour towards the young girl.

As they walked on their pace gradually decreased.

By slow degrees his arm stole round her waist.

He could feel her heart fluttering beneath his hand, like a frightened bird in a cage.

He gently pressed her to his breast, and, gazing down upon her rich full eyes, imprinted a kiss upon her forehead.

The deep purple blood dyed her face to the roots of her hair.

She endeavoured gently to disengage herself from the highwayman's embrace.

But so gently that it but increased the ardour of the entranced Red Ralph.

And onwards they strolled, utterly oblivious of their perils.

Lost to all and everything but themselves.

Beware, Red Ralph! You are treading now upon dangerous ground.

If you are sincere, where is your love for your wife, Leonore, in whose behalf you were but now so stern towards the gentle maiden?

If you are not sincere—if it is but passion, and not love, you feel towards the fair girl whom chance has thus thrown in your way—then you must play an ugly part towards her.

The robber could do no one—much less a woman—a deliberate wrong, but his passion for the time conquered his more stern resolves.

As he now perceived her blushes rising again he was recalled to prudence.

Startled at the pitfall before him, his arm slipped from around the fair girl, and he stepped from her side.

Thus for the third time in their flight had he cruelly dispelled love's young dream.

"Have you any destination?" asked Red Ralph abruptly.

The girl looked up, evidently astonished at the question.

"Alas! I've none," she replied.

"This is really awkward," said the captain of the Yellow Band. "And I'm at a loss to know what to do."

"Oh! leave me, then," she said. "Pray do not let me trouble you. I'm grateful for your kindness, but I must not impose further upon you."

The words fell upon Red Ralph's heart reproachfully.

He hastened to re-assure her and to beg her not for a moment to consider him harsh or unkind.

He could not explain to her the reason of his singular behaviour, however, and he remained, as before, an enigma to her.

But the night was far advanced, and both the captain of the Yellow Band and his charge stood in great need of repose.

He did not dare to seek the village, as he had originally intended.

So they walked on until they came upon a snugly-sheltered spot in the wood, which he at once decided upon as Miss Delane's resting-place for the night.

For himself he would seek another spot near at hand.

He did not wish to shock the poor young lady's maidenly scruples by offering to remain near her as she slept.

Evidently she did not much like the notion of passing the night alone in the wood, but she could not in propriety make any observation upon the matter.

And so they parted.

Red Ralph cast lingering looks behind him, but walked away.

He was so thoroughly lost in thought that it never occurred to him that he was wandering very far away from the spot where Miss Delane was resting for the coming day until he suddenly found himself in a large open tract.

The forest boundaries were then passed.

As he rambled on in the bright moonlight—thinking of Leonore, of Laura Delane, and of the jovial baronet, Sir Harry—his ears were suddenly assailed by the report of firearms.

A pistol shot whistled close to his ear and caused him to jump back alarmed.

He looked around, but failed to see the perpetrator of the outrage.

Before he had again turned his head a second shot was fired.

This whistled so very close to his head that Red Ralph, setting his dignity at nought, took to his heels.

He ran on rather wildly, for he was really alarmed.

The shots were fired so quickly one upon the other that he could not but imagine that he was fallen into an ambuscade.

Still he could see no one—hear no one.

As he ran on, alarmed at the danger and startled by the singularity of the occurrence, he did not take any particular heed of whither he directed his steps.

The consequence was a most disastrous accident.

Suddenly his feet slipped beneath him and he fell forward.

Judge, then, his horror when he found himself precipitated forward down a terribly steep incline.

Down, down he fell with a fearful shock.

A hundred agonising thoughts passed through his mind in those brief seconds.

Terror indescribable.

His descent was brought to a sudden stop.

Sudden and violent.

His whole body felt dislocated.

Breathless and swooning lay Red Ralph upon his back.

CHAPTER CI.

THE FALL — THE QUARRY — THE HUNCHBACK'S WANDERINGS — A DISCOVERY — RALPH IN HIS POWER—TORTURES — THE FIEND'S MALICE— RALPH'S WRITHINGS—DEATH TO RED RALPH —THE ROBBER'S CHARGE—HER DREAM — THE RAMBLE—A FEARFUL SIGHT.

STUNNED and insensible lay the captain of the Yellow Band.

It was a dreadful fall—sudden and dangerous.

And a prolonged swoon was the result of this mishap.

Still and motionless as death itself lay the unconscious robber hero, Red Ralph.

While he thus passed through the night, in tranquillity at least, another personage claims our attention.

This is no other than our old acquaintance, Jabez. The little hunchback is not far from the spot.

With a tenacity of purpose worthy a better cause he had at length succeeded in getting upon the track of the captain of the Yellow Band.

He had passed through the whole night in arriving at this.

But nothing could deter the little ruffian in his self-allotted task at present.

He owed such a debt of vengeance to Red Ralph for the injuries—personal as well as others—that he had received at his hands that he felt a glow of pleasure as he contemplated the thought of again coming up with him.

Vengeance was the master passion of the little pigmy's life.

For vengeance he would have sacrificed everything —almost life itself.

In feverish haste the hunchback had rushed off to the village after hearing the conversation of the highwaymen at the wood hut.

Inquiries were made at once, notwithstanding the advanced hour of the night.

But nothing here could be learnt.

It was clear as day that Red Ralph and his Leonore (as the hunchback imagined his companion to be) had not paused to rest in that village.

Enraged and disappointed at his failure, Jabez started off in another direction.

Hours and hours he wandered about that wild country, upon a hopeless errand.

But still he kept on tenaciously at his search.

At length his exhausted condition could no longer support the fatigues he had undergone, and he was forced to rest.

He selected an open spot, in order that the first rays of sunlight might reach him and awake him to continue his search.

"Here," he muttered, "I must rest. The foul fiend sieze the villain who has reduced me to this plight. But the first rays of morning light will find me up and doing. I feel as if I had success close to my grasp, and yet could not take it."

Strange presentiment !

He slept on in a troubled sleep for an hour or so, until the morning had set in.

Then, as he had predicted, the first rays of light found him active and stirring.

As his opening eyes encountered the sunlit sky he sprang to his feet, and was fully awakened to the continuance of the self-allotted duties of the new day.

He began to look about him.

"This is a strange place that I've wandered into at last," he muttered aloud. "I wonder what this is."

He was surveying an opening in the ground—a large kind of pit it appeared to be—the mouth of which was surrounded by pieces of rough stone.

"This must be a quarry," thought the hunchback. " A strange out-of-the-way place for a quarry, too !"

He walked around some distance surveying it, when suddenly his attention was attracted to the bottom of the quarry by a singular appearance.

Some kind of body was there—a large human form.

A closer inspection—that is, as close an inspection as the distance would allow of—showed him that it was the body of a man.

He was lying upon his back, apparently asleep.

" I wonder who that is," said Jabez. " And I wonder still more how he contrived to get there. He seems to have chosen a strange resting-place—a strange resting-place."

As the hunchback repeated these last few words his voice died away into a whisper.

He gazed down at the motionless body beneath him in breathless astonishment.

Its outlines he discovered were familiar to him.

That form he could surely never mistake.

" It must be, or the eyes of hate deceive me," muttered the hunchback uneasily. " Surely it can be no idle fancy—no disordered vision of a heated brain !"

He ran round to another side of the quarry and peered eagerly down upon the upturned face.

And now his expression showed a confirmation of his thoughts.

" It is he !" muttered Jabez. " It is indeed Red Ralph !"

It was true.

By an accident which would appear to have something in it more significant than an ordinary chance Jabez the hunchback had wandered to rest in the very spot where Red Ralph had come to his disaster.

And what is almost as singular to relate, he had arrived upon the spot within a few minutes after the occurrence of the disaster.

Joy, the wildest and most overpowering, at the delicious prospects of revenge filled the hunchback's heart.

He felt that Red Ralph was now all his own.

What should he do with him ?

Should he slay him at once ?

" Decidedly," was his first mental reply to this strange question, but this involved another little difficulty.

How was this deed to be accomplished ?

He had no firearms. He possessed a sword, but at the distance which separated them it was utterly useless to him.

He looked about him for some instrument with which to close accounts with the helpless foe at his mercy.

His eye lighted upon one of the stones which were strewed about the quarry, and he pounced upon the nearest.

This, however, was at once given over for another—one larger and more certain to secure the vengeance he meditated.

With a refinement of cruelty, he selected one which was rough and jagged.

Should Red Ralph not be killed outright by the first blow, it would at least inflict such cuts and injuries upon him as would give his executioner some ferocious joy to witness.

" Yes, yes," muttered Jabez in fiendlike glee. " I must have a little sport !"

This determined him to endeavour to arouse the sleeping Ralph.

For sleeping he imagined him to be, from the tranquil appearance he wore as he lay there.

No. He decided that the captain of the Yellow Band must not be slain sleeping.

Else there would be no fun or amusement. He might even pass away from earth without a murmur or a struggle.

And he, Jabez, had already undergone more than a dozen deaths at his hands.

And should he be let off with less than a return ?

Never. Else it would be no vengeance at all.

As he thought over it in this light the hunchback hastily collected some large stones together, ranging them in a little pile by his side.

This done, he proceeded to awake the doomed Ralph.

" Hullo ! ho ! ho ! ho !" he cried. " Wake up, Red Ralph, my deary. Wake up and be smashed !"

But he failed to break the heavy sleep of the hapless captain of the Yellow Band.

" Ho ! ho !" shouted the hunchback. " Wake, I say."

He continued to shout and call upon our hero to wake, but all in vain.

He appeared to be sleeping the sleep of death.

This idea at last occurred to the hunchback, and his expression changed upon the instant to the bitterest disappointment.

But no, he could not be dead !

It would be too cruel thus to deprive him of his feast of vengeance.

At length, finding that his shouting did not appear to take much effect, he had recourse to another method of achieving the desired object.

He began to pelt the insensible man with some smaller stones.

At length the pelting and the shouting together awakened the highwayman from the deathlike stupor which had succeeded the fall that he had met with.

Red Ralph opened his eyes, and looked about with a pained and at the same time a puzzled expression.

" This way !" cried the hunchback. " Look up here !"

As he said this he lifted up one of the largest stones he was able to raise, and held it up ready to cast into the quary.

Unfortunately for the little fiend's vengeance, Red Ralph did not hear himself thus addressed.

He merely continued to groan and rub his eyes painfully.

" Well, there is one comfort," said the hunchback, maliciously grinning. " He's been knocked about a bit, although I haven't had the pleasure of doing it myself. Lor, how he's groaning !"

And the little wretch capered about, clapping his hands with delight.

At length Red Ralph, attracted by the noise as he was more fully recovering his senses, looked upwards and perceived the hunchback.

For a second his glance rested upon him—fixed.

He could scarcely believe that it was Jabez, for he had left him so thoroughly damaged that he could not understand how he had contrived to bring himself up to such a lively pitch in so short a space of time.

Jabez saw his look of wonder and astonishment, and hastened to assure him that it was himself *in propriâ personâ*.

" Here I am, my deary !" he exclaimed. " Look up, bless ye, deary !"

Red Ralph now could make no mistake.

There stood the hunchback, capering about in a fiendish manner, which caused Red Ralph some grave doubts as to the flesh-and-blood reality of the little imp.

This is scarcely much to be wondered at, however, for he appeared so promptly upon the occurrence of a severe accident that the highwayman began for the moment to look upon Jabez as his evil genius—ready to turn up at any moment of disaster or peril.

" Now, Red Ralph," cried the hunchback. " Prepare yourself for the worst. I'm going to finish you now."

And he held the stone once more poised aloft.

The captain of the Yellow Band shuddered and closed his eyes.

Death stared him in the face.

" Ha, ha !" cried the hunchback. " So we cry quits !"

" You would not slay me thus !" said the helpless Ralph.

" Wouldn't I ?"

" Inhuman monster !"

" That's right ! I like to hear that !" cried the hunchback.

Ralph bit his lip.

He knew that it had given the little wretch some gratification to see him thus humiliated, and he could have cut out his tongue for having uttered the words.

Still the bravest man that ever drew breath must feel some fear in the immediate presence of danger and of death.

Red Ralph, as we have seen frequently, was no coward.

Yet it was but natural that he should make some endeavour, even though he believed it to be hopeless, to preserve himself from such a hideous death.

The first words, however, having escaped him, he regained his pride and presence of mind.

Nothing now should allow him again to humiliate himself before the vile little rascal.

"You don't speak," cried the hunchback derisively. "What's the matter with you, Ralphy dear?"

The captain of the Yellow Band preserved a stately silence.

This only provoked the hunchback more than words could possibly have done, as Red Ralph knew.

"You ain't frightened, Ralph?"

No reply.

"Dear, dear," said Jabez, turning his eyes upwards in a mock affectation of astonishment. "If Red Ralph ain't been and got the funk fever, with all his boasting!"

"You lie!" roared Ralph.

"Ha, ha, ha!" laughed Jabez. "So you've found your tongue?"

"Enough to tell you to your teeth you lie."

"The lie is yours," said the hunchback enraged. "Yours, and your's only, you cutpurse dog!"

"Yours alone, in your black-hearted villany!" cried Ralph. "Yours, in your craven throat!"

"Fool!" cried the hunchback. "You but precipitate your doom with this!"

"I care not."

"A lie."

"I swear I do not."

"Then you curse yourself to all eternity, for the fear you now feel is as clear in your ugly face, in the deathly pallor of your cheek, in your quivering lip, and your quailing eye, as if it were writ in black and white."

"Hell hound!" cried the panting highwayman. "Know to your own confusion that the pallor of my cheek is the result of injuries already received."

"Pshaw!"

"And that I am more than half killed already."

"You will be quite killed almost immediately, Ralph."

"It will be an act of mercy!"

"Bosh!"

"You will rid me of a suffering by a speedy death."

Now, although the hunchback believed most implicitly that this was said but to tantalise him, if not to put him off the satisfaction of his vengeance, the thought that he might possibly be rendering Red Ralph even a doubtful service was so distressing to him that he half paused in his meditated vengeance on the knight of the king's highway.

"No, no, Red Ralph," he cried, with a sudden determination, "think not to put me off the execution of a cherished project by your lies and dissimulation."

"Knave!" cried Ralph.

"Lies and dissimulation!" repeated the hunchback, gladly perceiving that the highwayman was aroused at his words.

"Dog!" cried the captain of the Yellow Band. "You would not dare to speak thus did you not know that a fatal distance separated us."

"Pooh! pooh!"

"But I leave the execution of fitting vengeance upon your ugly head to others."

"Whom?"

"Those who know well where to seek you out."

"Your friends at the hut?"

"Ay, even they."

This was only a chance shot of the hunchback's. He had no previous notion that the inmates of the little doomed wood hut were friends of his gallant enemy.

"Well, well, Red Ralph, my gallant fob-tickler," he said jeeringly, "I may as well tell you, if it can afford you any gratification, that your friends and their wood hut have all been burnt up together!"

"Never!" cried Ralph.

The hunchback jumped about gleefully again.

At length he had succeeded in finding a topic which was hurtful to his disabled foe.

His own peril could not alarm him, but he was not invulnerable to the disasters of his friends.

It was a refinement of vengeance worthy the diabolical little brain that hatched it.

"Yes, yes, Ralphy dear," cried the hunchback. "If it will afford you any gratification to know it, the information is yours. I saw your friends and their house burnt up together. The house was rased to the ground, and your dear friends were grilled. They died in horrible tortures!"

Now Red Ralph was fairly affrighted.

The words of the hunchback filled him with terror.

Jabez was watching him with the eagerness of hate, and was not slow to perceive this.

Of course he enlarged upon it until he overreached himself and spoilt the whole illusion.

"Yes," he continued. "And not only that, but *they've taken her, too!*"

"Who?" cried Ralph.

"Leonore!"

"Ah! inhuman dog! ruffian doubly dyed!" he ejaculated in a breath. "You don't mean that Leonore is again—"

"In their power."

"Liar!"

"Or in mine, Ralph deary, if you like that better."

The prostrate highwayman twisted and rolled over in torture at this.

His own beloved Leonore in the power of her inhuman foes, after all he had gone through to preserve her.

It was too cruel.

"No, no," he said. "I'll not believe it. He says it but to alarm me—to raise my fears."

"No, no. Oh, no," said Jabez. "*We caught her just after we left the burning hut!*"

This was a mistake again.

"What?" cried Red Ralph. "You captured Leonore?"

"Yes, here."

Red Ralph was infinitely relieved at these words.

He saw in an instant that it was nothing more than a ruse to excite his fears.

At once he saw through the misapprehension under which Jabez laboured, and it had the very reverse effect to that intended.

However, he intended to satisfy his doubts at once.

"Then you found out Leonore's hiding-place?"

"Yes."

"That she escaped with me from the wood hut as you came up?"

"Yes, Ralphy dear, and we tracked you both through the wood."

"I'm glad of that."

"Are you, though?"

"Heartily."

"And for what reasons, may I ask?"

"That it proves beyond all doubt that you lie most foully."

"Eh?"

"Hah! hah!" laughed the prostrate highwayman. "Now it is my turn to laugh, friend Jabez."

"What mean you?" demanded the hunchback, as a sudden suspicion crossed him.

"Mean? Why simply that the woman who left the wood hut with me was not Leonore."

"Ah!"

"And that consequently both of them are safe."

"Nay, I swear."

"Pshaw!" cried Red Ralph, scornfully. "If they were not both safe, you would have been better informed upon this little matter."

There was no gainsaying this.

It was the inevitable conclusion, and the hunchback bitterly repented his hasty words.

He was clearly foiled, and at his own particular game.

"No matter," he cried, with a bitter ringing laugh. "I have still the original consolation remaining to me."

He looked around him for his stone once again.

Then, having selected it, he raised it with cruel deliberation.

Held it high aloft.

"Prepare!" he cried in sonorous tones.'

Red Ralph trembled in spite of himself.

Death was facing him in grim and violent terrors.

He closed his eyes and uttered a mental prayer.

But even now he could not refrain from mixing up his better part with earthly vanities.

His lips never moved, lest his self-elected destroyer should perceive and gloat over his fears.

He even opened his eyes again almost immediately, lest they should be construed by the hunchback into an exhibition of fear of the death which he was about to receive at his hands.

The moment arrived.

Ralph felt his heart stand still in dread expectancy.

He bit his nether lip until the blood started from it, to subdue his emotions, for he must die, no matter how or when, as became the last of his race—of one who bore the noble name of his family.

The hunchback's arms quivered for a second or two.

This was, of course, his devilish cruelty to prolong the agonies of the doomed Yellow Boy.

"Death to you, Red Ralph!" he cried, unable longer to play with his victim.

Ralph never spoke.

"Thus do I send you to death," cried Jabez again, with greater ferocity than ever, "and may this crush your soul to eternal perdition!"

*   *   *   *   *   *

Miss Laura Delane slept but ill in the spot selected for her by the captain of the Yellow Band.

She closed her eyes and earnestly courted repose.

But the coy goddess refused to be wooed in this rough rustic place.

Miss Delane had been more used to rest her fair form in a bed of down, and upon pyramids of the softest of pillows.

Therefore she was restless.

Perhaps Red Ralph had also some slight share in her perturbation.

She could not but contemplate in wonder and surprise his singular conduct upon their journey there.

His earnestness, tenderness, and effective wooing.

Then his sudden change to rigid silence and reserve.

"What could he mean by this?" she asked herself a dozen times, without obtaining any satisfactory reply.

Surely he could not mean cruelly to sport with her feelings.

No, no, she had seen him too large-hearted and noble to play such a paltry part.

There must be some cause more worthy than this.

Perhaps he already loved another.

A chill smote her to the heart as the thought occurred to her.

Yes, this could be the only solution of his strange demeanour, so fitful and changeable.

At length far into the night she slumbered lightly.

A troubled sleep it was, and disturbed by unpleasant visions.

She fancied, in her flight in dreamland, that she saw her guide and protector walking in some gloomy dark place, and come to the edge of a fearful precipice, where he tottered and swayed to and fro for several minutes.

Those minutes were hours of torture to the dreamer.

She endeavoured to spring forward to his salvation, but a demon—hideous and deformed—held her back.

She struggled in the monster's clutches, but failed to disengage herself.

She sprang boldly forward, but the prowess of the demon who held her was so superior to her most frantic efforts that she utterly failed to accomplish her purpose.

She saw Red Ralph turn towards her.

How fearful was his expression! How earnestly he besought that assistance which she was unable to render!

All was silence.

Yet he asked her for life in terms more eloquent than any words could make them.

He tottered.

Then with a fearful shriek fell down the fatal abyss.

That shriek rang out with such fearful terrible distinctness that she started up and looked around her frightened.

"It was but a dream," she muttered, with a sigh of relief.

And the tears of satisfaction coursed down her cheeks.

But still the shriek of her vision was in her ears.

The whole dream stood before her so distinctly, so vividly, that she could even now realise it again.

A shudder thrilled her entire frame, and she endeavoured to banish it from her mind.

But no. Some fatal power chained her senses to that, and that alone.

So strong was this influence upon her that she could not resume her rest.

This she would fain have done, as night had given place to early morning only, and she thought it probably that her protector would not rise from his arcadian pillow until the day was more advanced.

For the fatigues which they had both undergone upon the previous day were terrible.

She rose to her feet and strolled away.

She made a circuit of the spot upon which she had rested—a long wide circuit—but failed to discover any traces of her gallant companion.

Surely he had not deserted her!

No, he was too upright and noble to quit her thus, in the dead of the night in that lone wood, without a word of explanation.

Perhaps he too had already risen, and was walking about as she was, unwilling to disturb her slumbers.

She hoped it was so.

In this idea she rambled onwards, thinking it just possible that she should come up with her truant protector by a fortunate chance.

It was a beautiful spot into which she had emerged from the thicker wood.

An open country, well wooded still, but not so dense as was the part in which she had rested for the few hours of the past night.

She rambled on heedlessly now.

In spite of herself, her thoughts were momentarily drawn from her protector by the extreme beauty of the scene and the serene and glorious weather.

As she looked around her she could not help wondering how—with such peace, such placidity and tranquillity—any earthly creatures could make for themselves such artificial woes.

But upon these and similar meditations it was not given that she should long pause.

A circumstance was at hand to change the entire current of her thoughts with a rude start.

A shock too was in reserve for her which recalled to mind the very cause of her early rambles in the woods.

A voice suddenly struck upon her startled ears.

The words, too, uttered were such, of so terrible a nature, as never to be forgotten.

She looked up.

Just before her stood a hideous figure—a dwarfish hunchback of hideous proportions, with overgrown shoulders, and a huge rough head surmounting them.

His long muscular arms—bare to the arm pit and hairy as the coat of some denizen of the forest—were held over his head grasping a huge stone.

So large was the stone that Miss Delane could scarcely believe the figure she saw before her at the moment to be real.

She could not deem it possible for human arms to hold so ponderous an object so easily poised aloft.

But as he stood there motionless some fearful words were spoken which caused her a sickening sensation at the heart.

"Thus do I send you to death, and may this crush your soul to eternal perdition!"

CHAPTER CII.

THE QUARRY'S VICTIMS—THE FATAL STONE—TIMELY AID—THE HUNCHBACK'S REVENGE—A BRUTAL ATTACK—A BRAVE GIRL'S STRUGGLES—RED RALPH AT HAND—JABEZ TRIUMPHANT YET—POSITIONS REVERSED—THE HUNCHBACK'S FALL—ISRED RALPH CRUSHED?

A WILD unearthy shriek burst from the lips of Miss Delane.

She sprang forward.

A terrible suspicion was in her heart.

With a singular precision she jumped at once at a correct conclusion.

Probably because that he whose life was thus menaced alone filled her constant thoughts, and, therefore, there is no chance so remarkable after all.

Ere an eye could twinkle she was by the hunchback.

The cry which she had uttered had paralyzed his movements for a while.

Else had the vengeance been carried out upon the instant.

For a moment he paused thus, but speedily regaining his presence of mind, he was about to dash forward the stone before looking round, lest the vengeance for which he had striven so much should be again snatched from him at the eleventh hour.

How many times had he not been already foiled?

But the eyes of a lover are ever quicker than those of hate, and his purpose—his foul intent—was again to be frustrated.

And this, too, by a gentle girl.

The stone of death could not quit his grasp ere she had seized it by the top.

A sudden pull, and the stone was dragged from his clutch, capsizing him with it.

Red Ralph had seen the action from the pit, and was all animation upon the instant.

What would he not have given now to be upon the spot?

He struggled to his feet, but, alas! could do no more.

"Fall upon him now, Miss Delane," he shouted to the girl. "Brain him as he lays, or he will slay you remorselessly."

But the girl thought no more of such a course of action than of attacking a sleeping tiger.

The aspect of the fallen hunchback was so ferocious and terrible that she shrunk from him in horror!

At all times the appearance of our friend Jabez was calculated to inspire a woman with fear, but now, when his hideous physiognomy was so vilely animated with the bitterest hate, it was positively devilish to behold.

He glared upon her with such vengeance in his seared and hideous face—such a glisten of murderous intent in his blear eyes—that she shuddered and felt inclined to fly.

With a snarl like the growl of some ill-taught mongrel he bounded to his feet, and leapt upon the terrified girl like some savage beast.

She shrunk in terror away; but before she could move from him far he had her in his clutch.

"Ha, ha!" he cried. "You have dared to brave my anger, and you must beware my wrath!"

And with this he clutched her round the throat.

A stifled shriek—stifled by his clawlike fingers—burst from Miss Delane.

She struggled violently.

Then, by a powerful effort, dragged herself from his grasp.

Then dashed off around the pit.

The hunchback flew after her, with an oath.

Then ensued a spirited chase, which was kept up with much animation upon both sides.

The girl was of course all eagerness to escape, and flew rather than ran.

But the hunchback was not a whit less eager, and he bounded over the ground like a cat.

At length, with a wild yell, he fell upon her again.

Clutched her wildly.

"Now, I have you!" he cried, panting in fierce exultation.

"Mercy!" she cried.

But the hunchback only turned upon her with a withering mocking laugh.

"Fool!" he hissed in her ear. "You think to escape me. Never, never! I swear it."

The girl, now seeing that all hope of flight was vain, turned upon her persecutor.

At first she imagined that she might by prayer and entreaties turn his obdurate heart to mercy and forgiveness, but very little soon served to convince her that this was worse than foolish.

Every fresh attempt she made to soften him was met with contumely and abuse, and she was fain to desist.

And now her only hope remained in being able to resist the hunchback.

A very faint hope this.

The muscular arms of the little monster closed around her shrinking form.

She felt as if screwed into the clutch of some ingenious mechanical contrivance, which held her powerless.

"Oh! mercy, mercy!" she cried.

"Pshaw!" said Jabez, ironically. "You'll get fine mercy from me I can promise you."

"Oh, have pity."

"Baah!"

"Have you no heart?"

"That I have," said the hunchback, with a brutal laugh, "and thus I prove it."

"How?" she demanded, in eager expectation of release from his hideous embrace.

"I'm going to toss you down the quarry."

"Ah!"

And with this piercing shriek, which resounded through the wood for miles, she dragged herself from hunchback's clutches.

But ere she could rise from the ground he had pounced upon her again, and seized her once more in his ponderous muscular grip.

"Down you go!" said the hunchback. "You like his company I should say."

It was simply death, and the poor girl struggled with a strength of which few persons would have deemed her capable.

All else proving fruitless, she contrived to squeeze through his arms and slide to the ground, where she obstinately, or rather, resolutely, maintained her position.

It is no easy matter to one even of very superior strength to raise another from the ground against his will, and Jabez the hunchback found it no trifling task to perform with Laura Delane.

He dragged her ferociously by the hands, but met with a most successful opposition.

Being a girl of great spirit, she seized the nearest of his hands between her teeth, and bit it with such vengeance that they met.

"Ah!" he yelled, dragging away his bleeding hand. "You dare to bite, eh? Well, you shall suffer for that. By every tie that binds you to life I swear it."

As he spoke he dealt the brave girl a savage blow in the face.

The blood spurted from her mouth in an instant.

The captain of the Yellow Band was there below, helplessly surveying the unequal combat.

Helplessly? No.

Had he not his pistols? He had brought them from the wood hut with him, and, notwithstanding that he had been in such great need of their services a short time before, it had never occurred to him that they were yet in his possession.

With nervous eagerness he felt for them in his belt.

He drew one of them forth, and hastily examined the priming.

Then watched his opportunity to get a fair shot at the hunchback.

In the meantime it threatened to go hardly with the unfortunate Laura Delane.

The brutal hunchback, seizing her rudely by the shoulders, dragged her, in spite of her utmost resistance, towards the quarry.

The poor girl divined the object of this movement, and her shrieks were terrific.

But by degrees she neared the fatal spot.

Another yard, and all would be over with Laura Delane.

By Heavens! the distance was accomplished!

Her head hung over the precipice.

But here occurred a moment's pause, and Red Ralph gained the opportunity he sought.

There was a loud report, and the hunchback shivered from head to foot as if struck with a sudden ague, tottered, and released his hold of Laura Delane.

But her struggles never once ceased, for in her fears she had not heard the report of the pistol.

The consequence was that Jabez fell, dragged by the girl over her prostrate form.

With a sudden and violent push she threw him from her over the verge of the precipice.

The hunchback clutched frantically at the earth, and fell to the bottom of the quarry, carrying two large handfuls of the crumbling mould with him in his descent.

Miss Delane heard the fall, and it created for her in that brief moment a world of troubles.

Agony of mind unendurable.

His fall must inevitably bring destruction upon the man who had risked so much to preserve her life.

Yes. Red Ralph must have been crushed by the falling body of the hunchback.

She rose to her feet with her eyes averted from the fatal quarry, dreading to look down to learn the confirmation of her fearful suspicions.

CHAPTER CIII.

THE PROGRESS OF THE FIGHT AROUND THE WOOD HUT—HOW TOM KING AND DICK TURPIN ESCAPED—DICK TURPIN'S ENCOUNTER IN THE BRAKE—THE SOLDIER'S MISHAP—VIEW OF THE BATTLE FIELD — VENGEANCE DEFEATED—THE HIGHWAYMEN SPECULATE ON THE FATE OF LOST FRIENDS—A RECOGNITION—THE WOMAN BY THE PIT.

MEANWHILE the fight round the wood hut raged furiously.

Dick Turpin, the sturdy highwayman, alone was hurt.

Outside the hut the case was very different indeed.

The unfortunate soldiers were strewed about the ground in every direction.

The fatal aim of the two knights of the road had indeed told upon the attacking party with most startling effect.

The officer of the party, a young and enthusiastic soldier, lay weltering in his gore close by the door of the wood hut.

The fire, too, had caught by slow yet sure degrees upon the door of the hut, and threatened very speedily to destroy the whole building.

It was a desperate position for the robbers.

Still they resolved to fight it out to the last.

"Stick to it, Dick!" cried Tom King, excitedly.

"Ay, ay."

"Stand to it! Don't budge an inch."

"I'll stand to the last."

"And I too," cried King, "whilst there's a bit of timber left in the old hut."

"Huzza!"

With these and similar cries they excited each other on.

Braving death itself.

In the very teeth of danger the most terrible these two bold men kept uttering defiances to the strong party without.

Courage unparalleled.

It was little to be wondered at that the soldiers should have supposed the inmates of the hut who made such an effectual and determined resistance to their own large force to be more numerous.

The smoke grew suffocating.

Denser and denser at each instant.

Still there was one excellent effect with the quantity of smoke, unpleasant as it was.

Whilst it choked the two bold knights of the road, it also impeded the progress of the flames, which were now rapidly consuming their stronghold.

"Ugh! Ugh! Ugh!" coughed Turpin. "I shall choke."

"And I too," said King.

"Confusion!" cried the former. "What with this accursed shot, and the smoke together, I shall come to certain grief."

"Bear up," said King.

"Bear up?" echoed his comrade. "You tell me to bear up against this infernal smoke, and yet your own voice is scarcely audible whilst you utter your exhortation!"

"'Sdeath and the devil, it is thick!" cried Tom King.

"Curse the smoke," cried Turpin. "To the window again, Tom."

"Ay! ay!"

[THE WELL-HOLE.]

And the bold highwayman staggered once more under difficulties to the window.

In an instant he quitted it to look to Dick Turpin, who had suddenly fallen to the ground sharply wounded.

As he dodged past the window a shot was fired, whistling so close to his ear that he began to fear the worst from their vigilance.

If they gave him no further opening than this, he could scarcely hope to do as much execution from the window as Dick Turpin had done.

Suddenly his attention was attracted by the sound of voices shouting in triumph.

This was sure to be something unpleasant.

"What can that mean?" asked Tom King. "Such jollity in the enemy's camp can surely bode no good to us."

He listened again.

He could hear them shouting something, but the precise sense of what was spoken he was unable to catch.

Presently, however, a word set him upon the *qui vive*.

"It catches! It catches!"

What catches?

"Ay! ay!" shouted another voice, which could be heard above the din and clamour which accompanied the attack upon the resolutely-held fortress. "Ay! ay! *The wind has changed!*"

Ominous words.

Another minute, and the full force of this phrase struck Tom King.

The smoke, which had so troubled him and his bold comrade before, cleared off, and was succeeded by a still more alarming phase.

The flames began to make themselves apparent.

"By the Lord Harry!" cried Dick Turpin, "we're in for it now. Here's fire with a vengeance!"

"What shall we be up to?"

"'Sdeath!" cried Turpin, "that's difficult to decide."

"I have an idea."

"Out with it, then."

"The roof."

"Bah! There's no outlet."

"No matter; we can make one."

"I doubt it."

"Pshaw! it's easy enough."

"If we had time."

"But we are losing more valuable moments here in idle discussion than we shall find it easy to recover."

"True."

"To the roof!"

"On with you."

"Can you follow?"

"Ay! On you go!"

Tom King sprang up the ladder, closely followed by his comrade.

Once in the loft, Tom King produced a hatchet, with which he had previously armed himself, to be prepared in case that it should by chance come to a hand-to-hand fight, and made a vigorous onslaught upon the timber walling.

Such a mighty blow was the first that the hatchet shivered a plank the whole of its length.

"Bravo!" shouted Dick.

"That was well hit."

"Ay. At it again."

"One for freedom."

And he struck again, but not nearly so effectually.

"A failure," he said.

"Almost," cried Dick Turpin. "Now then, the whole weight of the body in the blow. Fancy that you strike at that arch devil, Jonathan Wild."

Tom King greeted this speech with a roar, to express his hatred of the great thieftaker.

"This one for Jonathan!" he shouted.

And gathering all his strength into one mighty effort, he made play again with the axe.

It was a formidable blow. The hatchet went through the wood with such force that it remained there fixed.

Immovable.

In vain he tugged at it with might and main.

He tried coaxing and force alternately.

The axe was fixed as firmly as if imbedded in the solidest cement ever fabricated.

"Confound it!" ejaculated Dick Turpin. "You've overdone it."

"Ay!"

"Let me give you a hand."

This was no easy matter.

It was almost impossible for both of them to get a hold of it.

However, perseverance conquered this difficulty.

Then the main object remained unachieved and unachievable.

"Now!"

"Together!"

And they both did pull together.

Away came—the handle!

This was mortifying in the extreme.

Not alone at the failure, but every instant added to the danger which they ran.

The flames began to encircle the wood hut.

The smoke was suffocating.

The heat intense.

"'Sdeath and the devil!" cried Dick Turpin. "We shall be smoked to death here, Tom."

"Never!"

He snatched up the handle of the hatchet from the floor, where he had thrown it in disgust, and dashed violently at the woodwork about the spot of his former attack.

The plank upon which he struck shivered.

A second blow, and it was stove in.

"Bravo!" echoed Turpin.

Incited by this success, Tom King struck at it again with such right good will that a second opening was made.

There was a plank beyond.

If they could now remove the middle plank an opening would be made sufficiently large to allow the body of a man to pass through.

Would there be time to accomplish this feat as well? It was a question.

However, the present emergency did not admit of any loss of time for consideration.

He dashed at it once more with tremendous force.

The board resisted, but the handle of the hatchet, a stout piece of ash, was split by the violence of the shock.

"Curses upon the miserable chance!" ejaculated King.

"Fate is against us!"

"Never believe it!" cried Tom King. "Fate helps those who help themselves!"

And with this courageous speech the undaunted highwayman dashed against the plank with the whole weight of his huge body.

There was a crash which made the whole of the stout little structure tremble.

Then the board gave way.

But the shock was so violent that Tom King could not put any stop upon his movements.

The plank was carried away, and he with it.

He fell through the aperture thus caused, and disappeared.

Dick Turpin sprang up to the opening in a minute.

"Hullo, Tom!" he cried.

But no answer came.

"Tom, are you hurt?"

"All right."

He was clearly not much hurt.

He spoke in a whisper, and of course Dick Turpin guessed that there was danger abroad.

"Hist!" he cried. "Is the coast clear, Tom?"

"Ware hawk!" answered the latter from below.

Dick Turpin felt the hut growing unpleasantly warm.

The flames were rising rapidly upon every side, and threatened in a few minutes to demolish the whole of the sturdy little structure, which had resisted so successfully up to the present.

The wood crackled in an ominous manner.

Several of the planks below could be heard giving way.

Just now the flames began to curl up the trap which led into the loft, and caught some straw which was strewed over it.

Dick Turpin thought it high time to make good his retreat if it was over to be achieved.

He squeezed through the aperture, caught hold of the splintered woodwork, and leant over.

The distance to the ground was not very great.

In spite of his wound, he would have ventured upon dropping, had not the way been impeded by the straggling branches of trees.

These would perhaps have caught him half-way, and held him there dangling.

Perhaps have tumbled him over upon his wounded part, which was not to be thought of.

Dick Turpin was not greatly hurt, but yet his wound was of such a nature as to cause him the most acute suffering.

He stretched out a little further, and looked around.

Immediately upon his left was a large oak—a great patriarch, whose stout branches might be guaranteed to bear any weight.

It was the identical tree and branch up which Jabez the hunchback had climbed.

Dick saw in an instant that it was the very tree to give him a helping hand in this hour of trial and need, and he made some exertion to reach it.

"Hey, Dick!" called Tom King, in a whisper from below.

"Hullo!"

"Toss out the muskets and the powder-flask."

"All right."

"Don't forget the barkers."

"Trust me."

These instructions complied with, under the greatest personal difficulty and risk, Dick Turpin once more gave his attention to his own salvation.

Supporting himself partially by a slight hold of a very frail twig of an overhanging branch, he crept along a narrow projecting ridge in the woodwork.

Two strides upon this very insecure foundation brought him to the branch of the oak, as he desired.

The remainder was comparatively easy.

He crept along the branch, and slid down the trunk to the next branches, from which he contrived to drop safely to the ground.

But even now he could not perceive Tom King.

He crept along, crushing out some of the falling sparks and pieces of burnt wood and twigs of the surrounding trees as he went.

Quickly securing the powder flask and both muskets, he made off with all speed.

To have stayed much longer there, although the bottom of the wood hut upon that side had not yet generally caught the flames, was to submit quietly to being roasted alive.

So Dick, with the two muskets, squeezed through the overgrown shrubs and foliage which formed a wall around the back of the wood hut of no mean solidity and strength.

"Pheugh!" muttered Dick. "This is a tough job."

"*That it is*," said a strange voice close to him.

He started and looked round.

Before he could budge another inch a heavy hand was placed upon his shoulder.

"You're my prisoner, mate," said the same voice as before. "So take it quietly."

The highwayman did take it quietly, with a vengeance.

In an instant he had turned upon the speaker.

It proved to be one of the soldiers, who, having been ordered round to the back of the hut to reconnoitre, had contrived to penetrate the thick foliage so far.

Dick Turpin, with the quickness of the lightning flash, dashed his huge fist into the soldier's face.

This staggered him for an instant, but did not suffice.

As soon as he perceived that it had not brought him to grass he closed with him, ere he had yet recovered from the effects of the blow.

The soldier was a bold brawny fellow, and could scarcely comprehend the unwelcome treatment he received at the hands of the highwayman.

He had not generally found people so glad to accept an offer of a tussle with him.

However, the prodigious strength of the highwayman showed very speedily why he had entered upon such a step.

Dick caught his powerful assailant in his arms so unexpectedly that he had hugged the breath nearly out of his body before the other could offer the least opposition to so unceremonious a mode of treatment.

The soldier struggled, but had literally no chance.

Dick, upon his part, although aroused to great exertion by the urgency of the danger which threatened him, could not perform so effectually upon the soldier as he would have done had it not been for the wound he had received in the wood hut.

However, he soon obtained the mastery of his assailant.

The sound of the scuffle brought Tom King to the spot at the very last moment of it.

The unfortunate soldier, knocked clean out of time, sank senseless upon the ground.

"Bravo, Dick!" cried Tom King. "Right well struck!"

"No, no, Tom," said Dick in a vexed tone. "All the power is out of my right arm by that devilish shot."

"Not all," said Tom, pointing to the prostrate soldier.

"Pick up his arms and ammunition," said the conqueror.

Tom King secured these, and then they pushed their way deep into the wood.

"Confound it!" exclaimed Dick, before they had made much progress in this direction. "I hardly relish the idea of retreating like this after a victory."

"An indisputable victory," added his comrade.

"Ay."

"What do you wish, then?"

"Let's work our way round to the front of the hut and reconnoitre a bit."

"Good."

"If they are yet too strong, we will rest contented. If only half a dozen men we will take up as good a position as we can find and pink 'em off at our ease."

"A magnificent notion!" ejaculated the other.

"Come, then."

They veered off to the left, and made their way to the scene of the action.

As soon as the two highwaymen could obtain a view of the field of battle they were greatly shocked.

The carnage which their two arms had wrought was terrible indeed to behold.

The unhappy soldiers lay about the ground on every side.

Some dying—many dead.

Some severely wounded and crying aloud for water.

The highwaymen exchanged glances.

"This is very awful," said Tom King in a hushed whisper.

"Ay, indeed."

"I think that we had better perhaps give up our project."

"With all my heart."

"Away, then."

"One moment. See what they are about first."

The soldiers, by command of a corporal—the only leader now alive—formed and marched up to the blazing hut.

They fired three rounds into the flames successively.

"See," cried Tom King. "They are determined to make sure of us if possible."

"We can afford them that little gratification," said Turpin.

"Truly we can."

"They may even pour three more rounds into our snug little castle if it pleases them."

"With all my heart," said Tom King, "although, truth to speak, I am heartily sorry for the old hut, for we have had many a jolly game in it."

"True, Tom."

"We'll do it the funeral honours at the nearest hostelry."

"Ay, shed a tear to its memory."

And they continued their progress in silence.

Every step they took lightened their journey and their hearts, for the danger was over.

"I wonder how Red Ralph got on," said Dick Turpin.

"Ay, and the girl—Miss Laura Delane, I think, was it not?"

"Ay."

A loud female shriek caught their ears at that moment.

They looked around them. Then dashed through the interwoven shrubs into an open space beyond.

"Why, hullo!" cried Dick Turpin. "There's a woman."

"There is, and she's looking down there. There's a hole there I suppose."

"Yes, and it appears to me that somebody has tumbled down it."

They increased their speed, and soon drew near enough to discover that the woman was no other than she whose name had last been upon their lips.

Miss Laura Delane.

There stood the poor girl, wringing her hands in piteous but helpless lamentation over the fatal quarry.

———

CHAPTER CIV.

THE QUARRY—CONCLUSION OF A FATAL STRUGGLE — RED RALPH'S DANGER — THE LAST MOMENT—A FRIENDLY HAND—THE HOUR OF NEED — THE HUNCHBACK'S REVERSE — HIS RIVAL'S TRIUMPH—DEAD AS A DOORNAIL.

TOM KING and Dick Turpin ran up to the quarry.

"Hullo!" cried the latter. "What's the matter, my girl?"

Miss Delane was too much in grief to notice the robber's unceremonious greeting.

"See, see them!" she cried.

Dick looked in the direction indicated, and there perceived that a scene was enacting in the quarry which possessed the highest interest for him.

Red Ralph, the captain of the bold Yellow Band, lay there.

With him, grasping him by the throat, lay Jabez the hunchback.

Yes, he yet lived.

The fall had failed to destroy the life which appeared to cling with such wonderful tenacity to that misshapen form.

And not only did he live, but he was doing battle with the bold Red Ralph.

He had been more fortunate than the Yellow Boy this time, and had got so little injured by his tumble that he was by far the more vigorous of the two.

The battle seemed going with the hunchback.

Red Ralph's prodigious strength seemed to have left him.

He was almost powerless in the arms of Jabez.

"At last! at last!" cried the hunchback exultingly.

"Ah!" said Red Ralph. "By my soul I'm undone!"

"A good oath," said Jabez.

"Monster!"

"Don't call names," said the hunchback. "Here goes."

He dashed his foot savagely at the highwayman.

And some execution would have been the consequence of the attack had not the highwayman drawn his head suddenly away.

The ancle of the hunchback, as it chanced, came in contact with nothing softer than a piece of jagged rock.

There was a species of retribution in this very action, as the hunchback himself had cast this identical piece of rock down the quarry at the highwayman.

Red Ralph had not dodged the blow intentionally, for he had grown slow in his perception by excessive exhaustion and fatigue, but his eye had chanced to catch the form of the girl above with the two highwaymen.

The hunchback roared with pain, and grabbed the unfortunate Yellow Boy's hair with his blood-bedabbled fist.

He tugged at it with such vengeance and spite that handfulls of the black glossy curls were left in his grasp.

"See! see!" cried Tom King. "It's going plaguey hard with Ralph."

"Curse the little fiend!" said the sturdy Dick Turpin.

He loaded his musket as he muttered the malediction.

Then, bringing it up to his shoulder, he took a deliberate aim at the hunchback.

"Move again, and I fire!" he shouted.

But Jabez did not hear the menace, and he continued to pound poor Red Ralph until a shot from Dick Turpin's musket attracted his attention.

"Hullo!"

He looked up, but without once quitting his hold of the fallen Red Ralph.

"What is it, mates?"

"Touch that man again, and I fire!" cried Dick Turpin.

"Dick! Dick!" cried the exhausted leader of the Yellow Boys.

"Ay, ay, Ralph."

"He told me you were burnt to death."

"He lies."

Ralph had barely uttered the words when the hunchback dashed his fist savagely in his face.

The blow did not do much execution, but the blood from the hunchback's wounded hand sprinkled over the robber's face and gave it a ghastly aspect.

Dick Turpin literally roared with indignation.

He loaded and fired so hastily that he missed again.

"A plague upon my shaky arm!" he cried.

"It grows warm," said the hunchback between his teeth. "I must be brief."

He still grasped the prostrate highwayman by the throat with one hand, whilst with the other, which was disengaged, he picked up a stone which lay close by.

He raised it above the highwayman's head, and was about to bring it down, when, for the second time in the execution of his vengeance, his hand was arrested.

He struggled with the impediment, not knowing and little thinking what it might be.

But all in vain.

A force not a whit inferior to his own was there to oppose the execution of his fiendlike malice.

He felt himself siezed by a powerful grip on the collar.

He was thrust off the helpless form of Red Ralph and hurled, stunned and bleeding, to the other end of the quarry.

"Thanks, thanks!" murmured Red Ralph. "You have saved my life, Tom King, and you shall—"

Ere he could complete the grateful sentence which was upon his tongue his eyes grew fixed in their gaze, and he sank back.

He had fainted.

It was indeed Tom King.

The doughty highwayman, whilst Dick Turpin had the villanous Jabez covered with his musket, had run round to the further side of the quarry and discovered the means of descending.

Thus he had arrived in the very nick of time.

"Come on, Dick!" he shouted.

"I'm there," answered Turpin.

And off he set, full trot, closely followed by the startled girl.

The side of the quarry was gained, and in a few seconds they had joined their friends at the base.

Turpin produced a small spirit flask from his breast pocket, and at once proceeded to bathe the temples and nostrils of the swooning Yellow Boy.

Miss Delane was invaluable, too, at this moment.

She had been drinking some water from a clear little stream adjacent, and she ran to fetch some in Tom King's hat—considerably damaging the gallant highwayman's property in this charitable work.

At length the captain of the Yellow Band opened his eyes.

He gazed around upon them all in turn, with looks of the profoundest gratitude for the services rendered.

But he spoke not.

This clearly indicated that his suffering must have been of no ordinary stamp, for he was not the man to be daunted by trifles.

Dick Turpin and Tom King both knew this well, and they exchanged glances of the deepest significance.

They began to think that it looked but so-so with him.

Miss Delane saw their glances, and with woman's wit divined the danger which menaced her gallant preserver.

"You do not think he is dangerously hurt?" she demanded, in eager and agonised accents.

"Eh? Oh, no. *When he can speak he'll tell you so!*"

This implied clearly enough that the speaker did not think Red Ralph capable of further utterance.

He was mistaken.

The words were barely spoken when Ralph murmured something.

So low was it, however, that it was only with the greatest attention that they could catch the words.

"*Th—the hunchback?*"

"Dead as a door nail!" said Tom King.

"And now, Ralph, do you think we can move you away?"

The bold highwayman's eye flashed fire yet.

"Ay," he replied, "if—if—you're sure—"

"Of what?"

"*That Jabez is dead!*"

CHAPTER CV.

THE BOLD RED RALPH SUBDUED—FRESH QUARTERS—HIS NURSE—CONVALESCENCE—THE WARNING—PERSISTENCE—THE FACE AT THE WINDOW—ALARM—THE HIDDEN PISTOL—A SECOND WARNING—ON THE TRAIL—RALPH'S TEMERITY PUNISHED—ARNOLD THE THIEF-TAKER—A LADY TO THE RESCUE.

WITH gentle care and kindly action the two highwaymen bore the captain of the Yellow Band from the quarry which had been the scene of such terrors.

They selected a quiet and secluded spot, where they deemed that he would be safe from molestation.

Then, their own inclinations calling them away from the spot, they left him well provided for, and in the tender care of Miss Laura Delane.

The grateful girl volunteered her services as nurse.

This had been jumped at immediately by the two highwaymen, as they almost feared at first that it would prove rather a tie to have to devote their time exclusively to the captain of the Yellow Band until he should have perfectly recovered the severe shock he had sustained both mentally and physically in the recent events.

Weeks, weary weeks, elapsed, and Red Ralph yet lingered upon the sick couch.

Still, with unremitting care and attention, Laura Delane waited by his side.

Unselfish and devoted girl!

She knew that there could be no hope for her of obtaining the love of the bold captain of the Yellow Band, for the secret of his love, if not of his singular marriage with Lady Leonore Glyde, had become known to her.

Red Ralph, as soon as he perceived that the fair girl really loved him, had been honourable enough to confide the utter hopelessness of her cherishing a passion for him—a passion which would certainly be unrequited.

No matter.

Still she stood there by the side of the man she loved, and by her attention no doubt added materially in preserving his existence.

It must be admitted that this occasionally struck her, and then she could not repress the notion that she had only succeeded in saving his life for another.

But, to do her justice be it spoken, she checked all these rebellious thoughts as they arose, and endeavoured, but vainly, to think that she was merely there to repay him in gratitude for having already saved her life in the memorable inn upon Hounslow Heath.

Such was the state of affairs when an incident occurred upon which we shall have occasion to touch as we pass on our way.

As soon as the captain of the Yellow Band had sufficiently recovered to rise from his couch—the couch of which he had grown, alas! so weary—his active spirit could not brook the restraint which they would fain have set upon him as dictated by prudence.

In spite of every opposition, he would go out and breathe the fresh air.

One trip passed off rightly enough, but in a second he was less fortunate.

He chanced to come across a fellow who recognised him instantly, and, knowing that such information would be well remembered by Jonathan Wild, he followed the invalid home.

The fellow then pushed with all possible speed to Newgate for the thieftaker.

But at the present Jonathan Wild was engaged in a piece of fiendlike malice which was almost as gratifying to him as the persecution of Red Ralph.

John Blake—or Blueskin—as he was known to robber-fame, lay in Newgate tightly bound in the well-hole and beyond all hope of rescue.

Jonathan Wild had already thrice captured Blueskin, but he was a resolute determined fellow, and had each time escaped, in spite of all the efforts of justice to detain him.

Blueskin had at one time been the follower of Jonathan Wild, but the latter's knavish practices in one or two matters had been of so outrageous a nature as to disgust even a housebreaker.

The more especial reason for quitting him was his persecution of a young carpenter's apprentice—one John Sheppard—whom he had, with devilish cunning, hurried into the downward path he was now treading, out of a paltry revenge he bore his widowed mother.

This boy, a nimble-fingered youth of nineteen or twenty, had already done such deeds as had startled the world.

The escapes he had made were the most marvellous ever heard of.

Thrice had he broken from Newgate, and now, for a fourth time, he was there, confined in the stone vault —a dungeon deep below the surface of the earth, and remote from all the rest of the prison.

But enough of this for the present.

We shall have occasion yet as we proceed to mention one or two circumstances in connection with the more extraordinary doings of this young robber and the redoubtable Blueskin.

As the spy who had seen the captain of the Yellow Band in his promenade could not by any possibility obtain an interview with Jonathan Wild himself, he was forced to content himself with a minor magnate.

He therefore confided what he knew to one Arnold, a thieftaker of some talent, and well known at the period.

However, all the talent and energy displayed by this useful body of men at that time were so thoroughly eclipsed by the great Jonathan Wild that none but him have survived to fame.

Arnold lost not a moment in going to the spot indicated by the spy.

For hours he watched without Red Ralph's presumed domicile.

Hour after hour did he watch, with that dogged perseverence which is one of the thieftaker's—modern or of that period—peculiar characteristics.

A day passed, but no signs of the captain of the Yellow Band.

Still Arnold was not daunted.

His solitary rambles around the present dwelling of the invalid highwayman were persevered in as steadily as if the interest of a nation were at issue in the success of his capture.

A second day passed.

It must be admitted that Arnold began to grow fidgetty.

The prize for the capture of the bold Red Ralph was a princely one, and, therefore, was not of course to be too lightly won.

Yet he confessed to himself that he would have preferred a glance, if nothing more, at the object of his solitary vigil.

But no such luck.

The fact is that Red Ralph had had a relapse.

He had, with his wonted impatience, stewed and fretted at the restraint of the sick room.

The consequence was that he found himself upon his back again for a day or two.

Even now he could not learn prudence, and was no sooner able to stir than he insisted upon going out of the house.

Previous to leaving the gallant Yellow Boy to Miss Delane's custody Dick Turpin and Tom King had begged her to use every caution with him.

She represented how highly dangerous it was for Red Ralph to be seen out of doors.

Capture, in his present sickly condition, would have been reduced to a positive certainly.

He could not resist the feeblest foe as yet.

Upon the fourth day of Arnold's watch—the fourth and final day, as the thieftaker mentally determined—Red Ralph's impatience burst through all restraint.

"It is useless, Laura," he said. "I must breathe the fresh air again. I must. I stifle here."

"Consider," urged his gentle nurse, "how venturesome you are."

"What danger is there?"

"Every danger."

"Pshaw, Laura. I'm strong again."

"You deceive yourself."

"Not I."

And he rose to his feet to show his boasted strength.

But it resulted in a lamentable exposure of his feebleness.

He tottered painfully and sank back upon a chair thoroughly exhausted.

"See, see," said Miss Delane, sadly, for it grieved her to see her bold champion so completely overthrown. "You can scarcely stand erect. Pray do not think of leaving the house, at present."

"I must."

"Then let me accompany you."

"No. I will go alone."

Miss Delane turned imploringly towards him, but he was inexorable.

"Laura," he said, "forgive my petulance, with your goodness and patience. The thought that I have grown enfeebled thus, that I am powerless as a helpless babe, is more galling to me than the bitterest sufferings. If I do not see the outside of the house this day I am sure that I shall grieve myself into a more miserable plight yet. A few degrees lower, and it might be a difficult matter to bring me round."

Having put it in this painful light, Laura Delane could not oppose him further.

They were in an out-of-the-way spot, as we have already stated, and therefore did not apprehend much danger from the vigilance of the officials.

Yet Red Ralph did not care to travel unarmed.

He took out a pair of pistols, carefully loaded and primed one himself, and placed it upon the table in readiness for his meditated ramble into the green fields.

Then he made a hasty toilet, donned his hat, and prepared to depart.

Miss Delane, seeing his preparations, stealthily secured the pistol, in the hope that prudence alone would have prevented his going out unarmed.

But she little knew the determined mind (another expression for obstinacy) she had to contend with here.

Having fixed his mind upon going out, no small matter could induce him to forego his project.

He looked about for the missing pistol, but failing to find it, it occurred to him how it had been removed.

Now, as he appreciated the object of his nurse's little deceit, he would not speak to her upon the matter, lest she might take it unkindly, and therefore he quietly started to take his ramble unarmed.

Whilst he was unfastening the door Miss Delane was suddenly startled by a shadow obscuring for a moment the light from the window.

She looked up at once.

There was the face of a man flattened against the glass and peering into the room.

It was but an instant that she caught sight of the face, but it was enough to fix the features deeply upon her memory.

A square face, closely shaven, and of the peculiar bull-dog type which marked a certain class of men of that epoch which now no longer exists.

"Who's there?" she exclaimed.

She darted to the window and looked out, but she could see no one.

Then she hastily threw open the window and looked up and down on every side.

The mysterious face at the window had most mysteriously disappeared.

While she was yet at the window Red Ralph walked out.

He had some difficulty in keeping himself erect, but his giant will preserved him in some measure from falling a victim to his present physical infirmities.

He tottered painfully once or twice, and Miss Delane felt that he was about to fall.

No. By a powerful effort he saved himself.

She watched him earnestly until he turned the corner of the road into a by-lane.

Then she closed the window and came away with a sigh.

"Poor fellow!" she said. "How he struggles to overpower this weakness! It is really heart-breaking to see such a noble spirit thus cast down. Ah! that man again!"

This latter exclamation was caused by seeing the same shadow that had startled her so before.

The same face at the window.

She ran forward again.

But again had it most unaccountably disappeared.

She picked up the pistol which she had so uselessly concealed from the highwayman and ran to the door.

As she gained the road she looked to the left, the direction which her fractious patient had taken.

Then, just as she turned her head, she caught a glimpse of a flying garment disappearing upon the right, the very lane into which the invalid highwayman had turned.

In an instant it flashed across the girl's mind that this boded Red Ralph no good, and she flew along the road, and turned sharply down the lane to the right.

As she gained the corner she heard a cry, and, by all that was terrible! the voice was his.

She ran on, and in the space of a second found how truthful had been her forebodings of evil.

The captain of the Yellow Band lay struggling upon the ground in the hands of a Bow Street runner.

The square close-shaven face—Arnold, the thief-taker, as the reader has doubtless divined—was that of the man who held Red Ralph down.

As she ran up she could see that the undaunted highwayman was making what feeble struggles he was capable of.

But he was as nothing in the herculean clutch of Arnold.

Laura waited not to consider the criminality of the deed, but, levelling the pistol which she had brought with her, she fired.

Arnold fell over his fallen victim instantly.

He appeared to fall as the pistol flashed.

CHAPTER CVI.

RED RALPH'S RECOVERY — STAUNCH FRIENDS — SIR HARRY JERROLD — A PRESENT — THE PROPOSED TRIP — AN OLD REMINISCENCE — NEWGATE — A STRANGE ADVENTURE — THE PRISONER ESCAPING — SIR HARRY AIDS JUSTICE — A GRAND BUSTLE — ASSISTANCE AT HAND — THE WRONG MAN — WHO HAS ESCAPED? — AN INTERVIEW WITH JACK SHEPPARD.

"LAURA, dear Laura," said the captain of the Yellow Band, "you have saved my life again."

And he fainted.

The thieftaker, Arnold, lay motionless and silent beside the prostrate highwayman.

A fatal tableau!

There was a stillness about the thieftaker which might be seen at a glance was no ordinary symptom of insensibility.

Engrossed as Laura Delane's attention was by Red Ralph's danger, she could not help remarking that there was an ominous pallor in the cheek of the Bow Street runner.

And she shuddered.

Had her foes seen her then, the most sceptical must have been convinced beyond a doubt that this was no murdress.

It was unmistakeably the shudder of one who was ignorant of crime, much less the perpetrator of such a deed as that of which she had been accused.

There was no blood about the fallen Arnold to denote that her shot had taken effect.

He lay pale and motionless, but there was no appearance of his having suffered violence.

Laura Delane knelt over the prostrate form of her robber patient and endeavoured by every means in her power to restore him to consciousness.

But he continued in the same deathlike trance for so long that she was in despair.

It appeared as if he would never awaken.

It was no enviable position for a young girl to be placed in.

Between two helpless men.

No, not two. One was certainly no more.

The other was so still that his existence even was doubtful.

"It is not possible!" she murmered, not daring to put her fears into plainer words even to herself. "He cannot be. No, no, I'll not believe it. It would be too awful, too cruel! After all the care and trouble—no, not trouble, for every step I have made in his behalf has been a pleasure, a delight. Yet, I cannot believe that he is dead."

While thus she poured out her fear and alarm, she quite forgot that she might every instant be interrupted.

Suddenly it occurred to her, and then she sprang up in great alarm.

But how to get Red Ralph back to the house?

This appeared no trifling object to accomplish, when the robber opened his eyes, with a deep-drawn sigh.

He looked up into his nurse's fair face—fair, but pale with grief.

The emotion which he saw there depicted he knew was upon his behalf, and he seized her willing hand and pressed it to his lips in grateful fervour.

A deep blush suffused the poor girl's cheek.

"Come, come," she said. "You must endeavour to move. It is a wonder that we have not already been interrupted. Come, pray rouse yourself."

Red Ralph pressed her hand and retained it, smiling as he said—

"I wonder much that you take any further interest in your fractious patient."

"Why so?"

"After my disobedience."

"Ah!" she replied, with a smile, "I can well understand how irksome is the confinement of the sick room to a man like you."

"You are a dear girl."

And as he said this he embraced her hand with fervour.

There was dangerous fascination in the highwayman, which his nurse was not slow to perceive.

Yet she had lost command so of herself in his presence that she felt no power to break off the conversation which had sprung up between them under such peculiar circumstances.

And now Red Ralph's obstinacy had brought about a relapse which would undoubtedly throw him back a week or so.

This would keep her by his side, of course, still longer.

For how could she desert him now, after having so long tended him in his sickness?

Indeed it was not to be contemplated.

Weeks elapsed, and Laura Delane yet lingered beside the overthrown highwayman.

But not in the same residence.

After the narrow escape which Red Ralph had had from the hands of Arnold the thieftaker Miss Delane at once procured him other lodgings.

She introduced herself everywhere, when introduction was necessary, as the robber chief's brother.

She also intimated that he was suffering from a pulmonary disease which required the utmost care and attention.

From time to time the faithful comrades of the bold robber visited him in his affliction.

As he again approached convalescence Red Ralph one day sent a message by Tom King to Sir Harry Jerrold, the kindly-disposed old baronet, who resided at Hounslow.

The next morning found the old gentleman by his side.

His greeting was kind and good-natured as before.

He eagerly pressed his services upon the bold Yellow Boy, and at the same time observed such respect in his bearing that it excited the attention of the two highwaymen, Dick Turpin and Tom King, who chanced to be present at the interview.

They could not help attaching some significance to this, for the position and high name of Sir Harry Jerrold were well known at the period of our history to every one.

"Ralph," said the baronet severely, "you have grievously offended me in this matter."

"How, sir?" demanded the captain of the Yellow Band in surprise.

"By not letting me know at once of your condition."

"You are very kind, Sir Harry."

"Pshaw!" interrupted the baronet testily. "I say that you should have let me know."

"Indeed I should, but—"

"But, but—but me no buts. I shall send Ransome to you."

Ransome was the name of the king's physician, and one of the most prominent men of the day.

"Nay, Sir Harry—"

"I say I shall."

"But it is too late now. Unfortunately, I am perfectly recovered."

"Unfortunately?" quoth the baronet, laughingly. "Hark at that now, for a dying man."

"Not quite dying, Sir Harry," said Red Ralph.

"Very nearly, you rascal."

"No. My best doctor now is plenty of good living."

"You shall have that."

"And exercise."

"And you shall have that too. I shall see to it. I haven't got the carriage with me now, as I did not know if you would like me to make a visit of ceremony of this."

"You are very thoughtful."

"Stuff! I shall send down the carriage for you at once, and you shall spend a month at Hounslow with me."

But Red Ralph most positively refused to listen to this.

"No, no, Sir Harry," he said. "I must decline this."

"Decline it?"

"Yes, Sir Harry."

"And why, forsooth?"

"For several reasons."

"Enough of several, you rascal. Give me one of them."

"Well, then, I have too much regard for such a friend as you as to cast the faintest shadow of disgrace upon your name."

The baronet, it was plain enough, was not untouched by the highwayman's words.

"Ralph," he said, in an undertone, that his words might not be overheard by Tom King or Dick Turpin, who yet lingered in the room with Laura Delane, "you are a noble fellow. But away with all nonsensical scruples at such a time as this. Come with me. Your nurse shall come with you, if you desire it. I see a little something in that nurse, you dog you. Gad, Ralph! you are a devil amongst the petticoats, I believe."

"No, no, Sir Harry," said the captain of the Yellow Band. "I am not ungrateful, believe me, but I cannot accept your kind offer."

The baronet growled something unpleasant at this.

"Hang it, sir," he exclaimed, "if you refuse my offer at least do me the favour to dispense with your infernal adjectives."

The sick robber smiled at his good patron's vehemence.

"You know, Sir Harry," he said, pressing the old gentleman's hand, "that my reasons are no selfish ones."

The baronet drew away his hand with another growl.

"I know," he said, surlily, "that you don't want to be humbugged with an old fool like me."

"Fie, Sir Harry."

"I know it, I say."

"No, no! You cannot know that. You cannot even think so, I am sure; for you must feel assured that I respect you more than I can express—that I feel towards you some of that love which should have been given to my father had fate willed it that we should be to each other as father and son."

The crusty old baronet was moved at these words.

His eyes looked moist, and when next he spoke his voice was a little thick. He wrung Red Ralph's hand warmly, and spoke to him now with his glance averted.

"Ah! Ralph!" he said, "you are a noble fellow! You shall be cured, however, in spite of yourself."

"Nay—"

"Tut, man. Don't interrupt me. I shall send you down some few things here to-morrow, that you may live a little freely—a dozen of the green seal—as thick as porridge, my lad—makes blood fast enough to choke off an apoplectic subject with one bottle at an hour's notice, or drive a gouty Indian mad in a single night."

Red Ralph would have also refused this courtesy.

However, Sir Harry was firm in this, and would take no denial.

"And the day after, if you are fit to go out, I shall take you for a drive. What says the nurse?"

Miss Delane blushed and answered tremblingly.

She was evidently very ill at ease in the presence of strangers.

"Yes, sir," she said. "I think that open-air exercise would be highly beneficial."

"Good. He shall have it."

*   *   *   *   *

The following day early a carriage bearing the well-known crest of Sir Harry Jerrold upon the panels drove up to the door.

A servant got down and carried in a heavy hamper.

This was found to contain the dozen of the promised green seal and luxuries innumerable.

The finest hot-house fruits were there.

Chickens, jellies, and pasties were there, also sufficient to feed a garrison for a week.

They were thankfully received and gratefully acknowledged by the highwaymen and his comrades.

They devoured all, and had a regular (or rather an irregular) carouse with the present.

And thus a day passed.

Red Ralph was rapidly improving in condition.

*   *   *   *   *

The next day, true to the appointed hour, Sir Harry Jerrold's equipage drove up to the door.

The baronet entered, full of the anticipated drive.

"Ralph," said he, "I've got a capital trip in contemplation to-day."

[THE FIGHT WITH THE BLOODHOUNDS.]

"What is it?"

"I propose a visit to Newgate."

Red Ralph opened his eyes in surprise.

He looked into the baronet's face for an explanation of the riddle, but none was forthcoming.

He could not understand it at all, for it was clear enough that he was not jesting.

"Ah! I thought I should startle you," said Sir Harry Jerrold. "Now you must know that there is a young jail-bird there now safe in limbo who has broken out of Newgate three times—one Sheppard."

"Oh! Jack Sheppard?"

"Ay. You've heard of him?"

"Frequently."

"Well, they've nabbed him again. Your friend Jonathan Wild has taken him and another notorious housebreaker with him, one John Blake."

"Blueskin?"

"Ay, he's called Blueskin I know. Well, all the fashion are visiting Newgate to see these famous rascals. Hogarth and Sir James Thornhill have already been. They say he's a desperate fellow."

"And are you going to see this Jack Sheppard?" said Red Ralph.

"I thought so. We can easily manage it if you think that it is safe for you."

"Undoubtedly," said the captain of the Yellow Band.

No. 35.

"Well, I don't think that you would be recognised."

"Not I. I can so disguise myself as to defy detection."

"Ah, Ralph, if you had but seen yourself in a mirror lately, you would well know that no disguise is necessary."

"Am I indeed so changed?"

"You are truly."

During the highwayman's long and tedious illness his beard had been permitted to grow, and his long hair hung in ringlets on his shoulders.

His cheeks, too, had grown pale and sunken.

Altogether he was as different from the Red Ralph of a few weeks before as he well could be.

The change, in fact, was so marked that Miss Delane, fearing to shock her patient, had studiously kept a looking-glass out of his way.

However, changed as he was, the highwayman was not ill-favoured now at all.

* * * *

They started upon their excursion to Newgate.

Just as they arrived at the door of the governor's house—the entrance which our hero so well remembered—they heard a sound of scuffling within.

"Something wrong there I should say," remarked the baronet.

"It sounds like it," said Ralph.

They little thought how wrong.

The door was immediately opened by a slightly-built youth of about twenty.

His features were sharp and intellectual, with a small twinkling eye and a firm-set expression about the mouth.

He wore his hair cropped close to the head, in a fashion which was most remarkable.

At the epoch of which we write long curled wigs with huge flaps upon the shoulders were in vogue.

Thus it was quite out of the way to wear the hair short.

The youth was all excitement, and by the disorder of his dress it was clear that he was one of the persons whom the two newcomers had heard scuffling from without.

"A bit of a rumpus here," observed the baronet.

"Yes, sir," said the youth. "A prisoner trying to escape."

And as he spoke a powerfully-built fellow sprang towards him.

He had just risen from the ground, where he had apparently been thrown by the youth.

"Is this he?" said Ralph.

"Yes, sir," answered the youth.

The man grappled with the other savagely.

"Let go!" said the lesser of the two combatants.

"It's no go," said the man. "You can't manage it this time."

"That's to be seen."

As he spoke he feinted to give ground, and then by a dexterous turn dragged his opponent to the ground.

He pounced upon his fallen adversary and held him firmly pinned down.

The fellow struggled violently, but it was of no avail.

"Lend me a hand, gentlemen," said the youth, "whilst I run for assistance."

"Certainly," said Sir Harry. "You're a plucky young fellow. You're the governor's servant, I suppose."

"Yes, sir."

The old gentleman, who was a thorough enthusiast when there was any display of courage, pounced upon the fallen man and held him down.

"What are you about?" he cried. "You're aiding a pri—"

The youth drowned the rest of the phrase with a slap upon the fallen man's mouth.

"Hold him there, sir, please. I'm off for assistance."

He jumped up, and, springing to the door, dashed out.

"Let me get up," cried the other, struggling frantically. "He's escaped—the prisoner."

"It won't do," said the old gentleman, with wonderful cunning in the shake of his head.

"I tell you—"

"Tell me what you like. You don't move from here until I give you up to the jailor's hands."

The fellow actually foamed at the mouth with rage.

But it was all of no avail.

The baronet yet possessed some of his youthful vigour, and he held the man down with a power of which few persons would have deemed him capable.

Red Ralph proffered his assistance, but the old gentleman would not accept it.

"It's very hard if I can't hold down a fellow who was knocked over by that stripling," he said.

The next minute there was a rush of jailors and officials from all parts.

Before a word was asked touching the singular position of Sir Harry Jerrold a great outcry was raised that a prisoner had escaped.

"All right," said the baronet. "I've got him here."

"Hullo!" said a voice, which Red Ralph recognised.

"Why, what's this?" said another.

"I've caught the prisoner," said Sir Harry Jerrold.

"Bosh!" said the first speaker, contemptuously. "That's Biglow, the door keeper."

The baronet was literally electrified at these words.

"What do you mean?" he said, releasing his hold.

Up sprang the fellow he had so energetically held pinned to the ground all this time.

"It means," he exclaimed, "that this old fool has held me down while the prisoner made off."

An immense excitement ensued upon all sides.

"Silence, Biglow," said Jonathan Wild, dashing his fist in the man's face. "This gentleman is his Honour Sir Harry Jerrold."

Biglow slunk off.

"He's quite right," said the baronet good-naturedly. "I am an old fool—although it isn't very pleasant to learn it from strange lips—a meddling old fool."

"Oh! Sir Harry."

"Silence, Mr. Wild, and you're an infernal toady."

"Oh, sir."

"Hold your cant. But is it a prisoner of consequence that has escaped?"

"One of the greatest consequence, unfortunately."

"Indeed? I'm sorry for that."

"Yes, a dare-devil young rogue. That's the fourth time he's got out of Newgate, Sir Harry."

"Indeed? A formidable young rascal. Who is he, Wild?"

"Who? Oh! that's JACK SHEPPARD!"

CHAPTER CVII.

THE GIPSIES AGAIN—MINA—LEONORE—LEAVING THE RUINED HOUSE—THE SPIES—A GIPSY'S STRATAGEM—MICHAEL THE HARE—LEMUEL—HIS DEPARTURE—AN OLD FRIEND—BROTHERLY LOVE—FRANKNESS AND TREACHERY—CANDOUR AND CUNNING—THE ROMANY'S HATE.

WHILST we have been giving the captain of the Yellow Band, and other personages in our history immediately connected with his adventures, our undivided attention, some important changes have been occurring in the eventful career of Lady Leonore.

We left her in Westminster.

The scene of her then abode our readers will readily recall to mind, as it was there that our hero himself had so narrowly escaped death at the gipsies' hands.

It was there, moreover, that Jabez the hunchback (whom we have now left lifeless in the stone quarry) had made such a bold stratagem for the recovery of the lost Lady Leonore.

Jonas the gipsy, his instrument in this nefarious transaction, has quitted the gang of gipsies, in which he was a kind of chief, under the sovereignty of their queen, Mina, and has not been heard of for some time past.

The gipsies, after the various troubles which had occurred to them in their old metropolitan haunt, longed for the green fields.

The free woods and forests to roam in.

The green sward their pillow, with no covering but the blue canopy of heaven.

The queen of this singular tribe called a meeting of her people, and it was resolved that they should at once commence their departure.

We use the expression "commence" with intent, as it was a matter of time to leave their present abode under existing circumstances.

They had to clear off by two at the time, in order not to excite the curiosity of any persons about.

Mina well judged too that their house was watched by the enemies of Leonore, if by no foe who would touch her nearer.

Had Mina kept to her original resolution of clearing out the band by twos, all would have been well.

Unfortunately (as we shall show in the course of our narrative) an incident occurred which caused her to alter this rule.

Mina decreed that the departure was to be in the following order:—

At sunrise on the morrow Lucas, and Zenga, his wife, should leave together.

By ten o'clock in the forenoon Black John and Michael the hare should depart.

And soon after they had left, Isaac and Lemuel. Here we pause.

Lemuel was the foster brother of the outcast Jonas, and it was well known bore the latter a strong brotherly affection.

Indeed, the absence of the traitorous gipsy chief from the camp of the Zingari was a great source of grief to the boy.

The first couple left and repaired to the spot appointed to await the tribe.

The second pair, Black John and Michael the hare, had not left an hour when the latter most unexpectedly put in an appearance, as the third couple, consisting of Isaac and the foster brother of Jonas, were taking their leave of the tribe.

The gipsy appeared much excited and blown from great exertion.

He was eagerly pressed for explanations of his return.

"One minute," said Michael the hare, panting freely. "Black Jack and I was watched."

"Watched?"

"Ay."

"By whom?" demanded Mina.

"Some cursed house-dweller has been playing the fox about our hole!"

"How know you this?"

"It is as clear as the bright day," returned Michael the hare.

"Explain."

"Well! we had only turned down by the Abbey cloisters, when Black Jack, with the eagle twinkle in his Romany ogle, spied a cull lurking behind a gravestone."

"Yes! Proceed."

"He whispers to me what he sees, and we walks on into the street, so that if we was really foxed on, the house-dwelling snake should show in the open."

"And he did?"

"Yes."

"Did you recognise him?"

"No."

"Do you know what he was like?"

"I did not remark particularly, for I did not wish that the lurking cull should know that we was up to his dodge."

"No matter. Go on."

"Well! there was no mistake about us being followed now, and so we determined to lead him off the scent, and a pretty dance we took him, I can tell you."

"I'm glad of that."

"You may be."

"You think that he is quite off now?"

"I'm sure."

"Where did you leave him?"

"Well! we led the way down Back Lane, through Duck Lane, and into Tothill Fields. There, as we passed down Mary-the-Martyr's Court, Black Jack says to me, ' I'm going to slope off down here. You walk on, and our foxy cully is off in a jiffy.' 'I twigs,' says I. Down Black Jack pops before our sneak could turn round the corner. I walked on smart, and on he comes after me. Well, then I led my chum a blessed dance. Up and down every court and alley in Westminster. He was rather a swell cove, and I knew that he'd get in grief with the rum un's down the slums."

"And so you lost him?" said Mina, beginning to tire of the gipsy's narrative.

"Not a bit of it."

"Ah?"

"No."

"Then he has discovered—"

"Nothing. I lost him."

"Well, of course," said Mina petulantly. "That is precisely what I understand."

"No, no," continued Michael the Hare. "He was a pluckt 'un for a swell cove, and although he got rather damaged once or twice down Tothill Fields, he kept to it like a downright Romany."

The tribe, who were listening, were interested, and he had to conclude his story, although the gipsy queen had early had enough of it.

"Well I wanted to get a good look at my swell, and so I waited for him in this way. Just as I'd turned the corner of the street I pulled up sharp. I'd been running, and so in a twinkling up he comes full trot, bounces round the corner, and upsets my applecart.

"' Hullo!' says I. ' Where are you driving to like that?'

"Well, he stammers out something in a bit of a tantrum, and tries to put his paws on my shoulders.

"' Hands off!' says I, and with this I planted my right between his two peepers, a regular stinger!"

A murmur of approval greeted his words.

"Bravo, Mike!"

"Thankee, Azael," said the Hare, with a friendly nod to the speaker.

"Go on, Mike," shouted one or two of the tribe.

"How did you get off?"

"Bolted!"

"Bravo!"

"Yes, and a precious run I've had for it, I can tell you. I'm not exactly slow on my pins, as you all know."

"No, no."

"No, I'm not. Well, I had to put on all the steam I had in me to distance him. His long legs cut through the streets like a racer: in fact, I question if

I should have got off so if it had been a fair race in the open; but I led him through such nice slums to throw him off the scent that he was regular done up, and here I am."

A shout of applause greeted the conclusion of Michael the Hare's adventure.

When the enthusiasm had subsided Mina addressed a few words to her people.

"I see that it is as I feared," she said. "We have enemies among the house-dwellers who are upon the track. We must meet stratagem by stratagem, cunning by cunning."

"Ay, ay."

"Our plan of departure we must arrange differently I find. Two leaving together are sure to excite attention. We must leave singly. Thus it shall be arranged:—Isaac must leave at once and alone; and mark, Isaac, if you should see any one lurking about—"

"I shall know how to treat him," said the gipsy.

And he drew out a long Spanish knife, with a murderous gesture which caused Leonore to turn shudderingly away.

Mina frowned him into silence as she observed this.

Then she resumed her instructions for the departure.

"Lemuel will follow you in twenty minutes; but, in order to make the way more pleasant, he shall meet you by the 'Boar's Head.' Mark well the spot, so that you can continue your journey. You know when you will meet with Lucas and Zinga?"

"Yes."

"Away, then."

And, with a hasty leave-taking, the gipsy Isaac left the tribe alone.

The twenty minutes passed, and, as he did not return, Lemuel was started.

As he came to bid the gipsy queen farewell she observed that his cheek was pale and sad, and his bright black eyes cast down with grief.

"Lemuel," said Mina.

The youth looked up.

"What is it that so weighs upon your heart?"

He hung his head again and did not offer to reply.

"I'll tell you, Lemuel," resumed the gipsy queen. "You are grieving after the renegade Jonas. Fie! He's an unworthy brother, a false friend, an outcast of of the tribe—"

"He's my brother," interrupted the youth meekly.

"Your foster-brother, true; but he's no Zingaro now."

"You are too severe upon him."

"I am not sufficiently severe, Lemuel, or he would not now be spying and hovering like a jackal about our camp in the treacherous night."

"Mina, Mina," said the gipsy imploringly.

"Beware of him."

The gipsy youth drew himself up proudly.

"I am no traitor, Mina," he said, with a flashing eye.

"I know it," said Mina. "You love us all; we well know that. But you bear the outcast of our tribe too much love, and we fear some evil consequences. In this case you see that a warning was due from us to you."

"Perhaps so," said the youth sadly. "But have no fear; I am true to my people."

"Yes, yes, Lemuel's true enough," said one of the tribe.

"And so farewell," said the youth. "In a few days we shall be re-united and out of this stifling city, away from the noisome presence of the house-dwellers, where everything breathes falsehood and deceit, into the fields, where all is liberty—in God's free air, the Romany's only home!"

A shout of applause greeted the rude eloquence of the young enthusiast.

"He's a brave boy," said Mina, as Lemuel took his departure.

"Ay, that he is."

"But I fear he is far too free-hearted and frank to hold those in mistrust who are unworthy of confidence."

Several of the older members of the tribe began to cry down Mina's fears as unworthy.

And so she spoke no further upon the matter.

And now for a moment our way is with Lemuel.

As the Zingaro issued from the ruined house a tall swarthy fellow, who had been lurking close by for some time, uttered a low cry of satisfaction and started in pursuit.

Then, as they gained one of the narrow streets in Westminster, the spy darted down a turning, ran at a tremendous pace, and turned into the main street again.

By this *détour* he had arrived in the same street about fifty yards in advance of Lemuel.

Then he threw himself hastily upon a doorstep, and, resting his elbows upon his knees, buried his swarthy face in his sunburnt hands.

Lemuel came on, unsuspecting that he had been the cause of so much artifice.

Just as he got up to the man he raised his head, and looked up with a sob.

The gipsy youth started back, with an ejaculation of astonishment.

The spy, upon his part, appeared not a whit less astonished at the meeting.

"Jonas!"

"Lemuel!"

Such were the mutual ejaculations of astonishment —real in the former case, and excellently well performed in the latter.

It was no other than the outcast of the tribe, whom Mina had just before warned Lemuel about.

But the gipsy had already forgotten her admonitions.

"Lemuel, my brother!" said Jonas.

"My brother!" said Lemuel.

And they embraced tenderly.

"Lemuel," said Jonas, with a well-affected sigh of woe, "I'm wretched."

"Alas! Jonas," said his foster-brother, "why have you left the tribe?"

"Why? But do not ask me, brother. My gipsy blood boils at the injustice I have suffered, and I could do such deeds as would freeze the blood with horror!"

"Jonas, Jonas," said the gipsy, "do not talk thus."

"Not talk thus, Lemuel?" said Jonas. "Why am I cast out of the hearts of the people that I love, and who loved me? Why am I an outcast from the tents of my fathers? Why am I—a pure Romany—a true Zingaro to the bone—sent to the right-about by this Mina, who we know is but a house-dweller's brat after all?"

"Mina?"

"Ay."

"A house-dweller's daughter? I never yet heard that."

"Eh? Well, perhaps not," said Jonas, colouring up to the temples. "But there is no need to speak further of that. It is sufficient that I—Jonas, the son of Ishmael the Leopard—am cast out of my own tribe for this woman. And for what? Another accursed girl—a house-dweller, too—whom Mina thinks proper to bring into the tribe without a word of consultation."

"Stay," said Lemuel. "If you allude to Mina's fair sister, Leonore, I cannot hear you."

"And why not?"

"Because Leonore is all gentleness and goodness."

"Falsehood and deceit."

The gipsy boy's face flushed, and his eyes flashed fire.

"You lie!" he said.

"How lie?"

"Foully lie."

Jonas's hands clutched nervously, and a menace rose to his lips.

But he suppressed it with a powerful effort.

It was not his policy now to anger his foster-brother.

With devilish cunning he divined the meaning of Lemuel's warmth upon the subject.

"I see," he said, smiling. "This fair girl has caught your eye, boy."

Lemuel eagerly denied it, but his deepening colour gave the lie to his protestations.

"No matter," said Jonas to himself. "I must work upon another tack, that's all."

"Lemuel," he said, "I am wretched, to be thus a castaway. I must rejoin the tribe or die."

"Die?" repeated Lemuel, pressing his hand tenderly. "That cannot be, Jonas."

"I fear it."

"But if you will return, I am sure that you will be received as one of us again."

Jonas shook his head sadly.

"Alas! I doubt it much, Lemuel," he said, with a sigh.

"We must see."

"Will you intercede with Mina for me?" he asked, in the deepest humility.

"That I will," said Lemuel, eagerly.

"Thanks, thanks, my brother. You give me renewed hope and life. There is nothing upon earth so strong as the Romany's love."

"Nothing."

"And although my anger at first blinded me, it is now past. I love the tribe. I love you, my brother. Without you my path is but a barren plain. I sigh for the canvas roof of the Zingari—the camp fire and the songs of the night-bird."

Such sentiments, so strictly in accordance with Lemuel's own sensations, could not fail to provoke his sympathy, and he was vowed to his service instantly.

"Brother, brother," he exclaimed, "you are every inch a Romany. I shall speak for you. But you must get over your enmity to the pale sister of our queen."

"Get over it?" exclaimed the outcast Zingaro. "Since I read in your flashing eye that the girl has caught your fancy, I have nothing for her but the deepest brotherly love. You can offer my excuses to the fair Leonore. Pray her to pardon me. Put my excuses in the best form you may. Tell Mina that I am repentant. I shall remain at the house in Whitefriars until I hear from her."

"You shall soon."

"Thanks, my brother."

"Of that be assured."

"Be you the messenger, my brother, to convey to me the glad tidings of my pardon."

"I will, I will."

"And when?"

"As soon as Mina arrives at the camp with Leonore."

"Will it be far hence."

"No, in the north. Finchley, you know."

"The old spot?"

"Ay."

Jonas's eyes twinkled with satisfaction at these words.

"I'm going there now," said Lemuel. "Before the week is out you may expect me back to Whitefriars."

"Farewell, then."

"Farewell, my brother."

And, embracing each other tenderly, they separated.

For an instant the thought occurred to Lemuel that he had done wrong to tell his foster-brother so much.

The warnings of the gipsy queen struck him forcibly, and he began to regret his confidence.

"I know that Jonas means us well, and that he is true and faithful," mused Lemuel, "and yet I wish that I had not neglected Mina's warning. She was so strict in her injunctions upon that head. But no matter."

He went on his way.

Still the regrets stuck by him.

He could not help wishing that he had not been so confidential with Jonas, sure as he felt of his foster-brother's truth and faithfulness now.

How different were the meditations of the two!

Jonas, the outcast, all perfidy and deceit, was meditating treachery at once.

"So, so," he muttered. "From what that upstart boy has babbled about, it is plain that Mina and that girl have not yet left. So, so. Well, I must see what kind of a job I can make of it. Unfortunately, my friend and patron the hunchback has not been seen for some days, so I must work the job alone. So much the better. I have found where the needful is to be got, and it is sure to be some more first hand than passing through a dozen thieves' paws. My proud Lady Glyde may yet hear of the prodigal, although her right-hand man is out of the race for the present. But I would sooner cut her throat than give her up. No matter. That's a luxury I can't afford at present. *It shall come after!*"

CHAPTER CVIII.

EXPLANATIONS—JACK SHEPPARD'S FEATS — THE PRISONER — THE PRESS-ROOM OF NEWGATE — WILD'S AGGRAVATION — SAVAGE ASSAULT — THE PRISONER'S FETTERS SNAPPED—A SCENE —A VOW FULFILLED—THE ATTACK ON JONATHAN WILD — HIS LIFE IN DANGER — THE KNIFE— BLUESKIN BORNE DOWN.

NOTHING could exceed the surprise manifested by Sir Harry Jerrold and the captain of the Yellow Band at hearing that the youth whom the former had so singularly aided to escape was none other than the desperate boy of whom the world, fashionable and vulgar, was then so full.

"But, but," stammered the baronet, "how on earth did he come to this part of the building?"

"Simply enough, Sir Harry," answered Jonathan Wild.

"Simply! What do you mean, Wild?"

"Simply for Jack Sheppard."

"Indeed?"

"Yes, he cut through twenty-four inches of solid wall."

"And you call that simple?"

"Simple for Jack Sheppard, as I said before."

"'Sdeath, man! you would make out this boy burglar to be a second Cæsar."

"Not quite that, your honour," returned the thief-taker. "But he's quite a wonder in the housebreaking way, I assure you, Sir Harry."

"So I've heard."

"The last time that he got out of the jug—prison I mean, Sir Harry—he had to pull a whole chimney to pieces, and then he only got into the stone-room.

Now to get out of this there was only one way, the door, and this was locked and bolted on the outside."

"Poor devil!"

"Not at all."

"What do you mean?"

"That he was not yet done."

"How? He never got out of there?"

"He did, Sir Harry."

"The boy is a wonder. Well, he deserves to get off."

"You think so, Sir Harry?"

"Yes."

"Ah, I know that your honour likes to see these rascals escape from justice."

"No such thing," said the baronet tartly. "I admire pluck in any man, sir."

"Yes, Sir Harry."

"But I know why you made such an impertinent observation, Mr. Wild."

"Sir Harry!"

"Yes, sir, it is because that Red Ralph managed to get clear of your clutches on my horse the night he was drowned."

The speaker's companion glanced eagerly at the thieftaker to watch the effect of these words.

But Wild was even now apparently not aware of the captain of the Yellow Band having been at the house of Sir Harry Jerrold on the very night of his desperate leap for life over Westminster Bridge.

"This man hasn't dared to say anything about it," thought the highwayman, "as I got away from him so readily. Chance plays my game well. But how about that fellow who found my hiding-place out?"

Ralph meant the thieftaker Arnold, from whose clutches he had so narrowly escaped.

Jonathan Wild stared fixedly at Sir Harry Jerrold for some few seconds before speaking.

"What's the man staring at?" said the baronet sharply.

"Nothing, Sir Harry," replied the thieftaker.

"That's a complimentary thing to say, Mr. Wild."

"Beg pardon, Sir Harry," said the thieftaker humbly, "but the fact is that I was not, am not, quite sure that Red Ralph really perished upon that night."

"Not sure?"

"No, Sir Harry."

"But how could any man possibly escape such a foolhardy jump as that?"

"I know not."

"Nor any other rational being."

"But Red Ralph is no rational being, Sir Harry."

"Is not? Was not."

"If it should be he was not, but I'm not positive of that."

"What makes you doubt?"

"Several things."

"Indeed?"

"Yes. One is the non-appearance of the body on the river."

"That's nothing out of the way."

"Beg pardon, Sir Harry. Dead bodies always turn up sometime or other somewhere."

"And so may this."

"Perhaps."

"It's likely enough now that his body is rotting under some coal barge or lighter, and will be picked up by one of the watermen or 'prentices who go rowing about there."

"I don't think so," said Wild dryly.

"Oh!"

"No, for another reason."

"And what is that?"

"He made an appointment while stopping to chat with you, Sir Harry, at Charing Cross."

The baronet looked profoundly ignorant of the fact.

"Appointment?"

"Yes, to sup with you."

And as Jonathan Wild spoke he stared into Sir Harry Jerrold's face as if he would penetrate the inmost depths of his soul.

But the baronet preserved an admirable composure.

He never moved a muscle or appeared to consider himself the object of such a close scrutiny.

"Well, well," he said, after a while, "I think that we'll go now. I only brought this gentleman, Mr. Wild, to see your remarkable prisoner, but since he's escaped."

"I can show you some who are equally curious, Sir Harry, if you would like to see them."

"I should."

"There's one who is a desperate fellow."

"By all means show him, then."

"If you'll come with me, Sir Harry, to the press-room, you shall see him."

The thieftaker led the way, and the baronet and Red Ralph followed him.

The press-room of Newgate is a square stone vault of moderate dimensions, and was formerly used as a torture chamber, as its title indicates.

It now preserves but little of its former appearance, happily, the wood presses being now long since done away with.

In the centre of the press-room, seated upon the edge of a wooden bench, was the ferocious prisoner of whom the thieftaker had spoken.

There was certainly nothing desperate in his appearance, any more than in that of Jack Sheppard.

He was a trifle more muscular and a bigger man.

There was a certain expression of determination about his mouth which told that it must be something more than a mere trifle to put him off a resolution once formed.

He looked up as the visitors entered, but his eye only rested upon the form of Jonathan Wild.

There was an intensity of hatred conveyed in that brief glance which showed that the life of the thieftaker would unmistakeably have been endangered had the prisoner been at liberty.

"This is the housebreaker, John Blake," said Wild.

"Blueskin?"

"Ay. You have heard of him, have you?"

"Ay, he's a remarkable pal of Jack Sheppard's."

"The same, your honour," said Blueskin, looking up at the speaker, with a smile.

"You're not so fortunate as your comrade," said Sir Harry.

Blueskin looked up eagerly.

"What, you don't mean that Captain Sheppard has slipped his darbies?"

"No, no, no," said Wild hurriedly, before the baronet could reply. "The gentleman means because he's in better quarters than you are."

"So much the better," quoth Blueskin. "He'll be out before the night is over, then."

"I swear that he won't."

"I swear he will. You may double your precautions, Wild. When Captain Sheppard says he's off you may pretty surely conclude he means it."

"And as for yourself?" said the baronet.

"Me? Oh! I'm nothing," said the housebreaker.

"But how is it you did not get out yourself, since it comes so easy to you?"

"'Tisn't easy."

"But it is to be done."

"The captain's done it five times, your honour," said Blueskin, "and I should have been off too, only I could not go without the captain."

"Fool!" said Wild brutally.

"Fool yourself, Jonathan Wild," iterated Blueskin.

"Silence!" said the thieftaker sternly.

Then. turning to the visitors, he added—

"What this fellow says is simply an idle boast, your honour."

"It's no boast, and he knows it," retorted the housebreaker.

"Silence!"

"I will speak. You can't stop my tongue, curse you!"

"No, but I may teach you obedience with the whip."

"Oh! you thrice accursed dog!" said the fettered prisoner bitterly. "If I had you here in my grasp, I swear you should not have another hour's life."

And he clenched his manacled hands with passion.

But the thieftaker only laughed at this ebullition of phrenzy of the prisoner.

"Another hour's life? Humph! *you* may not have so much."

There was an apparent significance in his tone, and the visitors glanced up curiously.

"I'll tell you what, Wild," said Blueskin, with an effort to suppress his passion. "I'll wager that I've enough life left me to cry quits with you before long."

"Ah?"

"Ay, it's true."

"Blueskin, you mistake, you'll never leave here."

"What!" exclaimed Sir Harry Jerrold, "Never leave?"

"Not until he takes his trip to Tyburn."

"The day that Captain Sheppard escapes I'm off," said the housebreaker with dogged determination.

"You speak too confidently upon the subject," said the thieftaker. "I'll look to your fetters."

Blueskin turned sharply round to face the thieftaker.

"Don't come too near me," he said, significantly.

Wild looked uneasy, and really appeared to consider the advice worth following.

Instead of attending to this matter personally, therefore, he contented himself with calling to some of the warders who were in attendance.

"Here, send Black Jim to me."

In the course of a few seconds a woolly-headed negro made his appearance, armed with a hammer, a chisel, and a knife.

"What is it, Mathter Wild?" demanded the negro.

"Just look to the prisoner's fetters."

"Yeth, mathter."

And, ducking down, he began to examine the anklets.

"Golly!" cried the negro.

"What is it?"

"Um cut slap through."

"Ah!"

The thieftaker drew near and examined them carefully.

"Is it true?" said Sir Harry.

"Yes, Sir Harry."

The baronet and his companion drew near also and examined the fetters.

As the negro had said, the anklets were sawn completely through.

The slightest exertion would have been sufficient to snap them asunder.

How he had contrived to accomplish this marvel they could not discover, for, although the place was most diligently searched afterwards, they failed utterly to discover any file or instrument of any kind with which it could have been effected.

"You see, gentlemen, that it was no idle boast."

"Indeed it was not," said Sir Harry. "You're a desperate character, Mr. Blueskin."

"You may pile them on as thick as you please, Wild," said Blueskin. "I shall never attempt to get out of this until Captain Sheppard is free."

"Humph!" muttered the baronet. "Captain Sheppard, as you call him, didn't appear to have quite so much consideration for you."

"What do you mean?"

"Nothing," interrupted Jonathan Wild uneasily.

"You lie," said Blueskin.

"Silence!"

"You lie I say," cried Blueskin. "In your throat you lie, you dog! I can see the lie trembling in your cursed throat now."

"Silence!"

"The ugly throat I'm going to cut."

At this the thieftaker's patience was quite exhausted.

He could contain his passion no longer.

Heedless of the presence of the two visitors, he dashed his fist savagely into the face of the helpless prisoner, drawing blood.

"Coward!" cried Sir Harry.

"Inhuman dog!" cried Red Ralph, unable to contain himself.

But the next instant Jonathan Wild suffered for his brutal conduct.

With a roar of indignation and passion the prisoner sprang up, overturning the negro armourer.

A loud and distinct crack was heard.

The fetters of the prisoner were snapped as if they had been but feeble cords.

He dashed forward, snatching the knife from the negro.

Then, with a bound like a ferocious beast of the forest, he was upon his tormentor.

Wild, though powerful and a bigger man than his assailant, was as nothing in his hands now.

His fury lent his arm a force which was irresistable.

Seizing the thieftaker round the middle, with a sudden jerk he threw him over his hip.

There he held him by the neckcloth, which he tugged at until Wild was almost choked.

"I shall strangle him," said the maddened prisoner, "and I've sworn to cut his throat. Never! Blueskin shall keep his word."

As the neckcloth was not to be removed, he stabbed at it viciously.

It offered but a weak protection to the neck of the ill-starred thieftaker.

It was quickly cut through, and with it the throat of Jonathan Wild laid bare from ear to ear!

* * * * * *

"Help! help!"

All had taken place so suddenly that neither the visitors nor the black armourer had the time to interfere.

As soon as they had recovered from the first shock they hastened to release the thieftaker from the grasp of the infuriated Blueskin.

"Help! help!" shouted the negro.

"Help!" said Wild faintly.

The warders came rushing into the press-room by dozens.

Blueskin was torn from his tyrant, with the blade reeking with the thieftaker's blood yet in his grasp.

Now he allowed himself to be taken quite tamely.

"No matter now," he said. "Do with me as you will. I have kept my oath!"

Wild was supported by two of the jailors, but refused to quit the cell.

"Bind him, bi—bind him," he murmured.

"All right, Mr. Wild."

"Shackle him."

"All right."

"I shall get—"

But his utterance failed him now.

He was forced to content himself with shaking his fist feebly at the prisoner.

"No you won't, Wild," said Blueskin, divining what the thieftaker failed to speak. "You won't get over it, and you won't live to see the last of me, I know."

Wild endeavoured to speak.

"Bear him out," said Sir Harry.

"A moment," said the thieftaker faintly.

"It's no use whatever, Wild," said Blueskin. "The knife went too deep."

"But not deep enough."

"You lie."

The wounded man struggled to rise at this taunt, and the blood gushed out from his throat in a terrifying manner.

"Bear him down, bind him down!" cried the thief-taker hoarsely.

His command was promptly obeyed.

Blueskin, manacled and bound hand and foot, was fastened securely to the bench.

"Now I shall triumph!" said Wild, with a gleam of passionate vengeance in his eye.

And he fainted.

"Bear him off at once, and fetch a surgeon," said Sir Harry. "And let us be gone, for the sight of that poor wretch, and his retaliation upon that villain, Wild, have turned me sick."

"It is too awful."

CHAPTER CIX.

WILD'S DANGER — HIS IMPATIENCE — ANOTHER VISIT TO THE PRISONER—THE HORRORS OF THE PRESS-ROOM — A FEARFUL VENGEANCE—THE PRESS — THE DEATH STRUGGLE — TAUNTS — —HORRORS—WILD'S CRUELTIES—THE ENGINE OF DEATH—BLUESKIN'S LAST BREATH.

BEFORE returning to follow up the further movements of the captain of the Yellow Band, or the remainder of our *dramatis personæ*, we propose finishing with this portion of our narrative, and closing the account of the housebreaker John Blake.

After the departure of the two visitors the unfortunate prisoner was treated with much unnecessary cruelty.

All the people about—jailors and thieftakers—were eager to do anything which could gain them the approving nod of Jonathan Wild.

The thieftaker-in-chief had gained himself such a prodigious reputation, and was so universally feared by great and small, that all about ran hither and thither madly at his will.

The consequence was, as we have stated, that poor Blueskin got cruelly maltreated as soon as the officers and the jailors were relieved from the presence of the two visitors.

Had this not caused some restraint upon their movements, Sir Harry Jerrold would have had some startling particulars to carry into the world touching the treatment of the prisoners in Newgate.

As it was, his indignation was more greatly excited against Jonathan Wild himself than his prisoner.

"He quite deserved all he got," said the baronet warmly to Red Ralph.

"You know I agree with you there," said the captain of the Yellow Band.

"Ay."

"Should it go hard with this fellow, you will speak for him."

"I will. You know that I bear Master Wild no great love."

"I do."

"Depend upon it that it will go hard with the fellow."

"Ah! that it will, under any circumstances."

"Yes, and if Wild recovers, he will punish him mercilessly."

"And if he dies?"

"Which looks the more probable, from what we have seen."

"Ay," said Red Ralph.

"Why, then they'll hang him for murder."

"They'll do that under any circumstances I should say."

"Perhaps."

In the meantime the subject of their sympathy did indeed fare badly in the press-room of Newgate.

Jonathan Wild was removed to a remote part of the prison, where he was carefully put to bed.

A surgeon was promptly in attendance.

The throat was examined. A fearful gash had been inflicted on it, which was speedily sewn up and bandaged.

The surgeon pronounced his patient at once out of danger.

The wound was much more horrible in appearance than actually dangerous.

The only thing necessary to a speedy recovery for Jonathan Wild was time and repose.

He possessed, as the surgeon averred, a most marvellous constitution—a constitution of iron.

As soon as he recovered his senses his first inquiry was for the prisoner.

Vengeance was ever uppermost in his mind—even now, when he believed himself to be on the brink of destruction.

"Let him be doubly ironed," he whispered to a jailor.

"Yes, Mr. Wild."

"Go and see to it."

"Yes."

Then to another, as soon as the first had quitted the room, he addressed some fresh order.

"Strap him down to the press."

"Yes, Mr. Wild."

"Why don't you go and see to it? Be off, curse you!"

"Yes, Mr. Wild."

And thus he kept on.

Meanwhile the orders which the thieftaker blurted out upon what he believed to be his death bed were most faithfully executed.

Nay, more, for so enthusiastic were the men in the cause that they exceeded the orders delivered by their chief.

Blueskin was strapped down to the hard wooden press and bound hand and foot by the cords.

These were chosen by the thieftaker's men that they might eat into his flesh—a piece of fiendlike cruelty worthy of their leader himself.

Then, to suppress his groans, he was gagged.

This was done with a gag so roughly fashioned and of such dimensions as almost to stifle the unhappy prisoner.

In vain he appealed to their hearts.

"Hearts" did we say? They had none, or, if this should be a literal impossibility, they must have been of the flintiest ever known in human breasts.

The expression of agony in the housebreaker's eyes must have touched any human being.

And so he was left for four-and-twenty hours.

A day and night of mortal anguish.

A day and night, making the very existence of the tortured wretch a hell upon earth.

The jailors, it is true, had to remove the gag twice during this period to give the sufferer food and drink.

Food he refused, but they forced it down his throat with the utmost barbarity.

The drink, too, for which he was parched nearly to choking, they delayed until the very last moment.

The poor wretch fainted under these horrors.

[THE DEATH OF THE MISER.]

Even then, as if these barbarities had not sufficiently repaid the unhappy John Blake for his aggravated assault upon the tyrant thieftaker, they had yet a store of punishment in reserve for him, of which we shall now proceed to treat.

Four-and-twenty hours passed.

Jonathan Wild made rapid progress, considering his dangerous condition.

Of course he was not yet prepared to quit his bed, but the strength of his giant will got the better of his physical infirmities.

The whole time he had never ceased speaking of the desperate prisoner undergoing such barbarities in the Newgate press-room.

And now he could not conceal his vicious desires, his eagerness to be once more face to face with his victim.

He rose from his bed.

Totteringly, he donned his garments, girded on his sword, and staggered from the room.

He could not be dissuaded from his object.

In vain did his attendants try every act of persuasion they could think of.

The only concession which he made, after no end of persuasion, was to allow two of the men to support his steps, one on either side.

And in this state the thieftaker reached the press-room of Newgate once more.

As he entered the chamber, and his eye lighted upon the prisoner, a gleam of vicious and intense satisfaction lit up his pallid countenance.

Blueskin, as we shall continue to call him till we have settled accounts with him in these pages, was just slowly recovering from his third fainting fit.

This one had been of so long a duration that the warders had been rather alarmed.

It was with no trifling satisfaction that at the moment of the thieftaker's entry they perceived signs of returning animation in the heaving of the prisoner's breast.

Jonathan Wild pushed his two supporters aside.

Then, with a supreme effort, he contrived to maintain himself in an upright position by resting on the huge hanger which was girded to his side.

The thieftaker would not give the prisoner the satisfaction of seeing the wreck he had made of him.

His throat had been most carefully bandaged with thick rolls of linen.

Over this he had tied a fashionable cravat edged with lace.

The very care taken in this part of his toilette must have told to the least observing eye that he had sustained no mean damage at the hands of the desperate housebreaker.

"Ah! ah!" he cried, smiling with pleasure, "you're bringing my friend Blueskin a little to his senses I find."

"And I am rather glad of it," said one of the warders.

"And I too," said Mr. Wild.

"I was almost afraid that he would not get round that last faint at all, Mr. Wild," resumed the former speaker.

"Ah?"

"He's been in queer street so long that we thought it was a croaker with him."

"Indeed?"

"He was gone as near as a toucher."

"It is a good thing for you," said Wild, "that he was not quite gone without me having the benefit of the show, for I'm hanged if it would not have gone hard with you."

The man looked frightened.

"I'm very sorry," said he, "but I didn't think that we was putting the pot on too strong."

"All right," said Wild. "Only if he'd gone before I'd seen him, I'd have had you strung up."

"Lor! what for?"

"Murder."

The warder shivered.

He well knew the serious nature of this threat.

Jonathan Wild revelled in a reputation for outrageous cruelties, a reputation which he had well earned.

He stood by, leaning upon his sword, and contemplating the woebegone appearance of his suffering victim, the unhappy Blueskin.

Presently the prisoner opened his eyes and glanced upwards.

In an instant his whole expression changed.

It was apparent that he was greatly chagrined to perceive that Jonathan Wild was yet able to be there.

The thieftaker saw it, and made a mental note of it.

It was to be added to the causes of enmity for which he was about to take a bitter vengeance.

"So, so, Master Blueskin, you're not gone yet, I find," he said.

"Not quite."

"Very nearly, though."

"Not more than you," retorted the prisoner faintly.

"That voice gives the lie to your words, Joe," said Wild.

"Joe Blueskin" was the prisoner's *nom de guerre* amongst the Romany pals.

"I shall yet live to see you out first, Mr. Wild."

"You lie."

"I shall."

"Not unless I go off before an hour's over," said the thieftaker.

"You may threaten me," said Blueskin, "but that's all, I know."

"Indeed?"

"Ay. You know it."

"And why, pray?"

"*It wouldn't be safe.*"

"Pshaw!" exclaimed the thieftaker. "You little know the man you speak to if you think that."

"I have heard something of your cruelties, Master Wild," said Blueskin, "but there is only one comfort I have, and that is that sooner or later you must get your deserts."

"Pshaw!"

"The touch in your throat, which you have managed to hide so neatly, is not a trifle, I know."

"Fool!"

"It may finish you yet."

"Silence!"

But the prisoner perceived, to his satisfaction, that he had hit upon a topic which caused his tormentor much chagrin.

"I wish I had you now in my fingers, with nobody near, I swear that I'd make you dance, hard as I've been knocked about by your devilish engines."

Wild lost all patience.

"Fool!" he said, hissing the words into the prisoner's ear. "You rush madly on to your doom."

"A fig for you!" retorted Blueskin.

And his woebegone face was momentarily lit up with some of his former air of defiance.

"Bring the press forward," said Wild.

The men paused.

They hesitated to obey such an order, for they well knew what it foreboded.

"Fools!" ejaculated the thieftaker. "Why do you pause? Do you think I don't know my business? The prisoner has refused to confess his share in the plot by which Jack Sheppard has managed to elude us once more."

The words were barely uttered ere they were repented of.

But it was too late.

A smile of satisfaction shone on the prisoner's face.

"You've let it out, Wild," he exclaimed.

"No, no!" said Wild.

"It's too late," said Blueskin, laughing. "The captain's off, and now you shall see how a brave man can die."

"You hear? He refuses to confess," said Wild, appealing to the men about.

"Yes, yes!" said the men.

"And you know, also," said the prisoner, "that I've nothing to confess, and that I've confessed nothing. I haven't been asked for a confession of anything, neither, or it's more than likely that I should have refused."

"You hear him?" cried Jonathan Wild. "He still refuses; so we must bring him to his senses. Put on the fifty screw."

This was a terrible engine, constructed of a weighty wooden frame, something of the form of a primeval printing press, and weighing nearly half a hundredweight.

This was borne by four men.

It was then placed upon the prostrate form of the prisoner.

His agony was shown at once, as the fearful engine of torture touched him.

His mouth opened wide, but even now he had the strength to suppress a cry of anguish as it rose to his parched lips.

"Now what do you say ?" said Wild.

Blueskin was silent.

"He is still obstinate. Suppose you pile on another twenty, and see what good that will do him."

The ruffian never once removed his eyes from the countenance of the unhappy prisoner as he gave these brutal orders.

But Blueskin guessed from his knowledge of the thieftaker's character that such would be the case, and, although suffering most intensely, he would not allow the faintest signs of it to appear in his face.

Another weight, similar in form to the former, but rather smaller, was brought, and placed upon the writhing body of the tortured wretch.

And now his agonies became fearful in the extreme to witness.

His hands were clenched so tightly that his nails dug deeply into the flesh.

His feet wriggled about, too, but, in spite of these signs, denoting how fearful were his sufferings, nothing of it appeared in his face.

"Do you confess ?" demanded Jonathan Wild once more.

The prisoner was silent.

"Obstinate still ?"

But Blueskin could not be persuaded to retort.

This was what Jonathan Wild desired him to do.

It is worthy of remark that as a rule the most vicious minded and unscrupulous desire some excuse, however feeble, for their villanies.

Even the thieftaker, callous as he was to this sort of thing, would have preferred being goaded on by the taunts and retorts of his victim.

However, as he could not succeed in making him break his continued silence, he proceeded with his cruelties.

His excuse to himself for these diabolical cruelties was the housebreaker's attempt upon his life.

His ostensible reason for applying the then recognised tortures for extorting confession (now happily done away with) was the prisoner's silence respecting the supposed plot which had been the cause of Jack Sheppard's escape.

"Is that enough, Mr. Wild ?" demanded one of the warders.

"No."

"Shall we put on more ?"

"Yes."

The men glanced from one to the other, but dared not presume to question his commands.

A third press was now brought and placed upon the other.

Then the whole were screwed down.

The torture now became the most awful ever known.

No secret inquisition ever boasted such horrors.

No refinement of cruelty could devise such a series of sufferings, protracted beyond human endurance.

At length the sufferings which the unhappy prisoner underwent baffled his determination.

In spite of his utmost endeavours to control his expression of pain, it burst from him.

A cry of deep anguish came from the sufferer.

His eyes seemed to protrude from their sockets as if about to burst out.

"This is something like satisfaction," said the thieftaker.

"Perhaps he'll confess now," suggested one of the men.

Wild was recalled to himself.

He thought that it was necessary to put the question once more as a matter of form.

"Do you acknowledge it now ?" he demanded of the prisoner.

But even this could not make Blueskin break his dogged silence.

"Screw on," said Wild.

And, although the men looked serious, they obeyed the order.

"Oh, Heavens !" groaned the sufferer.

"Ah ! at last !" said Wild.

"This is too fearful !"

"I thought you'd come round."

"Oh ! bloody dog !"

"Still obstinate ?"

"Inhuman dog !"

"*Screw on !*"

The fearful engine was again set in motion.

Now a fearful phase in this terrible scene was enacted.

A distinct crack was heard, as if the body of the unfortunate housebreaker was splitting like a lath.

"I die !" said Blueskin.

"Ha-ha !"

"Oh ! murder most horrible ! murder most fearful !"

"You should confess," said Wild, with a sneer.

"Oh ! thrice damned dog ! Your turn must come."

"You're an obstinate rascal," said the thieftaker.

"The captain's safe !" said Blueskin, with an expiring effort.

"He thinks more of that boy than of himself," said Wild.

It was true.

The housebreaker's whole thoughts — his very existence—appeared to be wrapped up in Jack Sheppard.

Blueskin never spoke more.

Presently, as the silence continued a long time, they examined him.

"How is he ?" said Wild.

"*He's dead !*" was the reply.

The answer was given in a whisper, so low that the thieftaker could not catch it.

However, he guessed from the tone the state of the case.

"Well," said he coolly, "this is satisfactory. Now I'll go back to bed."

And with this he sank upon the floor.

When the men went to raise him they found that he had fainted again.

The strength which had kept him up to witness the death agonies of his victim had gone.

Then, half lifeless, he was borne back to his chamber.

And with this fearful tragedy we draw the curtain over the press-room and its horrors.

CHAPTER CX.

JONAS AT WORK—PLOTS—DANGERS AND DECEITS —THE FOREST SNARE—MINA AT HAND—THE RUFFIAN—THE GIPSIES AT HAND—THE CHASE — AN AMBUSCADE — JONAS TRIUMPHS — THE MAIDEN'S PRAYER — A VILLAIN'S PURPOSE — BORNE AWAY — MISGIVINGS — ALONE—HELPLESS.

JONAS the gipsy at once took measures to intercept the arrival of Leonore with the gipsy tribe.

However, all his efforts were fruitless, as we shall see.

That is to say, all his efforts to intercept her arrival.

What further befell her after she had reached Epping with the tribe we shall show.

Leonore and Mina left the ruined house in Westminster the day following the departure of Lemuel.

Thus what information Jonas had gathered upon this head was of very little service to him.

He was two days late with his preparations, and it cost him much vexation and a goodly sum of money which he had saved up.

However, he determined to have full vengeance to compensate him even for this mishap.

Consequently he gathered together a body of unscrupulous ruffians—fellows of the lowest depths of degradation and ruffianism.

Every art which craft could devise was tried, but yet he failed to find an opportunity for removing Lady Leonore from the protection of the gipsies.

Open violence now alone remained as a final resource.

Accordingly he lay in wait for her about the gipsies' haunt at Epping.

Three days passed, however, and Leonore was yet safe.

At the expiration of this period an attempt was made which failed ignominiously.

It happened thus.

One of the fellows hired by Jonas was upon the look out when he happened to see Leonore stroll from the encampment and saunter into the forest.

Delighted at the chance, he sprang forward and seized her in his clutches without a word.

For a second Leonore was so surprised that utterance seemed to be denied her.

Then, when after a pause her speech returned to her, she uttered a loud and prolonged shriek.

"Curses upon her throat, the jezebel!" said the fellow.

And, throwing his arm around her, he lifted her up and bore her off.

The cry, however, had brought succour.

The instant after he was stopped short by finding himself face to face with Mina the gipsy queen.

The fellow uttered a cry scarcely less fearful than that of his intended victim.

"It's her second self!" he ejaculated breathlessly, "her double—her fetch."

The marvellous likeness which existed between Leonore and Mina now stood her in good service.

The fellow let her slip from his grasp to the ground.

Mina showed the greatness of her presence of mind in this emergency.

She held a swich in her hand—recently cut by one of the tribe from a hedge—and with a swing round she delivered the fellow a sharp cut across the face.

In an instant a livid blue line marked the place where the switch had struck.

At the same time she raised a small silver whistle to her lips, and blew a shrill note.

A scrambling amongst the bushes was heard, and the various members of the tribe came running along in every direction.

Never heeding the severe handling which he had received at Mina's hands, the ruffian started off.

"After him!" cried Mina.

"Who?" asked one.

"The ruffian who has offered violence to the sister of your queen—to your queen herself."

"When?"

"Which way?"

"Whither did he turn, Mina?"

"There through the brake."

"After him!" said the gipsies.

And off they dashed.

A most exciting pursuit at once commenced.

The fellow who had attempted to carry off Leonore fled wildly through the forest.

Dashed at impenetrable thickets, and tore his flesh and his clothes most cruelly.

The gipsies enjoyed the chase, and as he ran they amused themselves by pelting him with rubbish and stones which they gathered as they ran.

"Now he's down," shouted one.

It was true, but the fellow bounded to his feet again and was off and away with lightning rapidity.

It was an exciting spectacle.

Anything bordering upon the chase has always an excitement which is much liked by the English.

A man-hunt is of course the most exciting spectacle, as the chase becomes the more difficult.

This may be well understood by any one residing in this metropolis who has seen the crowds who rush after a hunted-down wretch upon the well-known cry of "Stop thief!"

The excitement was kept up by the gipsies for full half an hour, but, notwithstanding their own superior knowledge of the forest and its intricacies, they failed to overtake him, so desperate was the hunted man rendered by his danger.

Suddenly one of the foremost of the gipsies—it chanced to be Lemuel, the foster-brother of Jonas the outcast—called to his companions to stop.

"I hear Mina's whistle again," he said. "Let us return to her."

"Where?" asked one.

"In this direction."

"You must fancy."

"Not I."

"No, no, he does not," said another, "for I believe I heard it too."

"There it is again."

And now there was no mistaking it.

Shrill and loud, although apparently at some distance off.

"Follow me!" cried Lemuel.

"Nay, rather follow me," said Michael the Hare bounding forward.

A race to regain the side of their queen ensued, but Lemuel, although swift of foot, was soon distanced by Michael the Hare.

He showed the tribe then that he was not inaptly named.

As they proceeded the whistling was repeated, and they renewed their exertions to reach the spot.

They found Mina struggling with a cord by which she had been tied to a tree, and failed to release herself.

"What is it?" demanded a dozen of the gipsies in a breath.

Mina was so exhausted with her struggles that she could barely reply.

"There, there," she exclaimed breathlessly. "Follow again."

"What, another chase?"

"Leonore!"

"What of her, Mina?" asked Lemuel, stepping forward.

"Carried off?"

"Ah!"

"And by Jonas, the outcast of the Romany tribe!"

The boy uttered a cry of indignation, which was re-echoed by his companions.

"Are you sure, Mina?"

"Sure? Of course. Think you I could mistake Jonas, once having seen him? Never. 'Tis Jonas."

"But how has this happened, Mina?" demanded Lemuel.

"How? Ask me not; but if you would redeem your own good character, fly in pursuit."

"Mina."

"Fly, I say. Whilst we are wasting precious moments here in idle discussion Leonore is perhaps being dragged to misery and shame."

"Ah!" cried Lemuel.

"Perhaps death!"

"Mina, Mina, tell me how it occurred," said the gipsy youth.

"In a word, then," said Mina, "Leonore and I

were here alone. You had all fled from us after the dog who dared to offer her violence. This was doubtless preconcerted by Jonas, who must have been in communication with one of the tribe."

As the gipsy queen said these words she stared so fixedly at Lemuel that the boy coloured to the temples beneath her gaze.

"Lemuel," said she, "that guilty blush betrays you."

"Mina—"

"Not a word."

"Mina, I implore you."

"Silence. Admit your fault, repair the wrong you have done an innocent girl, or—"

"Mina, Mina."

"You will not?"

"Hear me," ejaculated the gipsy youth. "I feel that I have been to blame in some part."

"Ah!"

"He owns it."

"Nay, hear me first," said Lemuel. "I do admit that I have seen Jonas."

"Unhappy boy."

"But I know nothing of this, I swear by any oath which can bind the Romany," he said.

The tribe looked incredulous.

The admission of his partial guilt looked black against him.

"Then hasten to repair the wrong you have done the poor girl."

"Mina," said the gipsy boy, "I swear that I have done her no wrong. Could you but read my heart aright, you would well know that what I say is true."

"Then why have you dared, in open violation of my orders, to hold secret communication with Jonas, the outcast of the Romany tents?"

The boy hung his head before the violence of her wrath.

"He is my foster-brother you all know well," he murmured.

"What of that?"

"Pity me."

"Silence, boy! Were he a hundred times your brother, you should not be forgiven this imprudence, if indeed it be no more."

"Mina!"

"Silence!"

"At least believe in my truth."

"Never."

"Mina!"

"Spare your indignation, boy," said the gipsy queen. "What right has he who has once proved false to be angry at mistrust for the future?"

"But I have done nothing to compromise anybody."

"Foolish boy! Where is my sister?"

"I know not."

"Pshaw!"

"I would give this right hand to see her back here with us again."

Mina snapped him up sharply at these words.

"Stay," she exclaimed. "I take you upon your own conditions."

"What?"

"Either restore Leonore to me here, uninjured—and shortly too—or you know the consequences."

"What?"

"Your lot shall be a fearful one, I promise you."

"Nothing can be more fearful than the thought that I have been the cause—oh! how unwillingly!—of harm to your pale-faced sister."

"Then listen," said Mina, "for this is our decree."

The whole tribe gathered around the speaker to hearken.

Mina was beloved, and her master-mind respected by the whole of the wandering tribe.

It was a solemn occasion, and the most profound silence was preserved by one and all.

"Go forth now," said Mina sternly to the downcast boy, "and use such knowledge as you may possess of your outcast foster-brother to aid you in the search. Unless you restore Leonore to us uninjured and speedily, never more look upon us. You are an outcast from the tribe, a wanderer from the tents of the Romany—of your own people—who in my voice curse their traitorous brother!"

"Mina," said the youth, "I bow to your decree. I go."

"Remember."

"Fear not. I shall never show myself here or elsewhere unless I rescue Leonore from any harm which may have befallen her."

"Away."

"And that my absence may create no dissensions amongst my brethren—who I know are already dissatisfied by the absence of Jonas—I here freely avow that had not Mina pronounced my fate I should have choosen no milder punishment for my folly."

"Crime."

"Nay, folly, for folly alone it has been, believe me."

"Away, then."

"I go."

"Remember my compact."

"I shall not forget it."

"Farewell."

"Farewell until we meet again."

And, half phrenzied, the gipsy youth rushed away.

"Now," said Mina, "spread yourselves about the forest."

"Ay."

"Let each man arm himself and take a separate direction."

"Ay, ay."

"Away."

Mina's commands were promptly obeyed by all the men of the tribe.

The whole forest was scoured.

From north to south—east to west—yet no trace of Jonas nor of Leonore.

Most of them were so eager in the search that they did not make their way back to the camp for hours.

Some stayed even until the night was far advanced.

Scouts were posted in every direction, with the strictest injunctions to give the alarm upon the slightest sounds of passengers abroad.

Yet no result.

No signs of Leonore.

Hopeless and weary search!

*   *   *   *   *

It was thus that the abduction of Leonore—some of the immediate results of which we have just related—had occurred.

After the attack upon her by the ruffian, and the opportune arrival of Mina, the whole of the tribe had flown after the knave, leaving that part of the forest so nearly deserted as to offer a very fair chance of success to Jonas the outcast Romany.

Now the gipsy had never once removed his eyes from the spot, and he did not fail to take advantage of the opportunity which now offered itself.

As Mina and Leonore were discussing the attempted outrage, and the probable fate of the ruffian should he be overtaken by the gipsies, they were startled by a loud noise in the bushes.

Before they had time to utter so much as a cry three men rushed forth from the thicket and confronted them.

They had all three much the same appearance as the fellow from whom Leonore had so lately escaped.

The only difference was that they were all three masked.

One appeared to take the direction of the attack.

"Bind her to that tree," said he.

He held Leonore, struggling in his clutches, whilst Mina was in the hands of his two ruffianly companions.

"Help! help!" shrieked Leonore in the wildest terror.

"Silence, fool!"

And the ruffian, in spite of her struggles, lifted her easily in his herculean arms.

"Scoundrel!" said Mina, not at all heeding her own sad plight. "I know you through your mask."

"Ah?"

"Yes, the voice of Jonas, the outcast of his tribe, cannot be disguised from the ears of hate."

"Say you so?"

"Ay, and I tell you, more that as there is a just Heaven above us you shall pay, and dearly, for this outrage."

"Pshaw!"

"I shall denounce you."

"Beware, Mina!" said Jonas, now throwing off all disguise, and speaking in his own natural tones.

"Coward! Of what?"

"Of this."

"Pshaw! I despise you."

Jonas had produced a pistol, which he levelled at Mina.

"You may drive me to desperation by this," he said.

Leonore's shrieks at this rang out in the forest and must have been heard by the quick-eared gipsies, whose presence was then so much to be desired had they been less pre-occupied in the chase of the original cause of the mischief.

"Fire!" said the gipsy queen with withering scorn. "Fire! You dare not."

"Ah?"

"You dare not."

"Say you so?"

"I do."

"And why, forsooth?"

"Because you know that the Romany's vengeance for the crime would surely reach you."

"But what cares the true Romany for the consequences, so that he has the vengeance?"

"Much."

"Not a jot."

"Then why not fire?"

"Because—"

"Because you are a liar, as you are a coward at heart."

It was easy to perceive that Jonas was not a little moved by these taunts, but dared not to execute upon his former queen the vengeance which he nurtured in his heart.

His life he well knew would not be worth an hour's purchase if it were discovered.

Either of the tribe who should chance to come across him would think no more of cutting his throat than of snaring a rabbit.

It was a struggle between revenge and prudence, in which the latter gained the mastery.

"Away!" he cried to his men.

And, with Leonore still struggling in his clutches, he dashed from the spot.

As they left, Mina's struggles to set herself free were increased tenfold.

She had been so hastily secured that it was not a very long job to set her right hand at liberty.

This much accomplished, she did not pause to disengage the rest of the thongs which fastened her, but blew a shrill note upon the silver whistle, which had before stood her in such excellent service.

The rest of this portion of the adventure we have seen.

The remainder is to come.

In vain did Lady Leonore pray and beseech of her cruel captors to release her.

In vain did she beg them to tell her the motive for this outrage.

They were all silent.

Arrived at some distance from the scene of the outrage, they found a horse ready saddled, fastened to a tether.

The gipsy handed his trembling burthen to one of his villainous comrades whilst he mounted.

Then he placed her before him upon the saddle.

And now poor Leonore nearly fainted with fright.

Off they gallopped towards London.

Leonore was unable to resist any further the machinations of the cruel enemies who now surrounded her.

Utterly powerless—helpless once more in their hands.

Unhappy Leonore!

CHAPTER CXI.

LEONORE'S HOME — GLYDE HOUSE — MISGIVINGS —LADY GLYDE — MOTHER AND DAUGHTER — A FOND GREETING—WELCOME HOME—THE WAITING MAID—SUSPICIONS—STRANGE BEHAVIOUR —THE NIGHT VISITORS—THE DARK FIGURE— THE PHANTOM DRAMA — THE SLEEPING MAID —THE RUFFIANS — THE SECRET VAULT — THE WELL-HOLE—AGONY — THE SLEEPER WAKES— "MERCY!"— SILENT MURDER — THE VICTIM'S APPEAL—DEATH—AN ALARM.

SOME hours later than the events just recorded a man of a dark swarthy hue, wearing the unmistakeable mark of the vagrant Zingaro upon his face, arrived at the Glyde mansion, in one of the most fashionable of the West End squares.

This was Jonas.

He was accompanied by the Lady Leonore.

A strange mixture of sensations agitated her tender frame as she looked once more upon the home where she had first seen the light.

That home to which she had been a stranger for so many months.

Months of weary wandering and trouble.

Months of trial, of fatigue, and danger.

Months of deadly peril of life and limb.

Would her mother be glad to see her restored to her home?

But how restored?

If it had been her voluntary act to return to the Glyde mansion she might have hoped that the anger of Lady Glyde would be overcome by joy of her restoration home.

But no, it was not to be so; she had been dragged thither by brute force.

A ruffian of the lowest vilest class — an outcast gipsy and a vagrant—had dragged her back to her home.

Each stop in their return home caused her a new sensation.

As the hand of the gipsy lingered upon the bell she trembled from head to foot.

The footstep of the servant coming to answer the summons caused her to start violently.

"No, you don't," said Jonas, grabbing at her hand again.

He mistook the action, and fancied that she was about to fly.

But, now that she found herself once more by her home, once more about to be restored to her rightful position in the world, her dignity returned, and she waved the burly ruffian from her.

There was a singular dignity in her gesture which was not without its influence upon Jonas.

And all through the rest of the business he preserved a certain respectful demeanour towards her, when in the presence of a third person, which would have led few to imagine what Leonore had suffered at his hands.

The door was opened.

Leonore scarcely dared to look up.

"Lady Glyde?" said Jonas.

"Yes. Her ladyship is engaged," returned the domestic.

"She'll see us, I know."

"Her ladyship desired me particularly to say that—"

"Tut, tut! go and tell her ladyship that we wish to see her."

"Who?"

"Her."

Leonore thought that it was now high time to speak.

"Go," she said. "Take the message, as you are bid."

But the servant, who was a fresh addition to the Glyde household, could not recognise Leonore's authority any more than that of the gipsy to give him orders.

And it was with some difficulty that they succeeded in gaining an audience of the austere Lady Glyde.

At length, however, they were shown into an apartment, and there awaited her ladyship.

Leonore's reason for still keeping beside the gipsy was that she dreaded a scene before the domestics.

And she well knew that he would resist any attempt to quit his presence until she had been formally delivered into her mother's hands.

It is needless to say that the gipsy's object with all this was simply to avoid any quibble respecting the payment of the sum promised for Leonore's restoration.

Presently there was a footstep without.

Oh! how well did Leonore remember that tread!

How many times had she listened for it approaching her chamber door in sorrow and in apprehension!

The handle of the door was turned.

Leonore trembled violently now from head to foot.

The door opened.

In stalked Lady Glyde.

The daughter looked up in anxious expectation of her mother's greeting.

At first her ladyship was so thoroughly startled that she failed to recognise her.

In an instant it came to her.

"Leonore, my daughter!" she cried.

"My mother!"

The old lady threw open her arms, with a good theatrical effect, and the warm-hearted girl flew to her and embraced her with unaffected tenderness.

"My child, my child!" cried Lady Glyde, in a very deluge of maternal tears.

"Oh! mother, mother!"

"Restored to me at last!"

"You are pleased that I have returned?"

"My child! oh! how can you so cruelly and coolly put the dreadful question?"

"Forgive me, my mother."

We shall not dwell too long upon the tenderness which Lady Glyde lavished upon her prodigal daughter.

Presently, as if for the first time recalled to herself, she pointed to Jonas.

Jonas was sitting surveying his handiwork.

Not exactly satisfied with the result of it so far, it must be confessed.

He had hoped to have the gratification of seeing Leonore trembling before a stern harsh mother.

Bowed to the earth in deep lamentation before an iron-hearted father.

But no.

And so he had but the gratification of witnessing a great show of happiness.

Happiness which was indeed wormwood to the gipsy.

But to resume.

"Who is this?" asked Lady Glyde in a low tone of her daughter.

Leonore blushed.

"It is he who has restored your daughter to your arms."

"He?"

"Ay, mum—your ladyship—I'm the man, and so now hand over the mopuses."

Her ladyship's aristocratic ear was shocked by the vulgarity, but she dissembled.

Particulars were entered into, and Jonas sent to await her ladyship in the adjoining apartment.

"Go to your room, my child," said Lady Glyde. "Go, and dress yourself in a manner more becoming your station, whilst I go to settle with this worthy fellow."

"One word, my lady."

"Say 'Mother.'"

"Mother."

Lady Glyde drew her daughter to her, and embraced her, with a spontaneous burst of affection.

"Bless you, my child. But what is it you were about to say?"

"This fellow is a ruffian of the lowest vilest class."

"My love!"

"Mamma, I assure you."

"But how can I but treat him with every consideration?"

"Consideration, mamma?"

"Ay, has he not restored my darling to her mother's arms?"

"True, mamma."

"Then I must reward him."

"Ay. But that is all. You owe him no thanks. I have suffered much at his hands, believe me."

"Suffered?"

"Ay, much."

"My love—but no. I must dismiss this man, and return to you after. I will rejoin you in your dressing-room."

"Yes, mamma."

"Margaret, your maid to whom you were so much attached, is still in the house."

"Margaret? I'm so pleased."

"I could not get rid of a bird to which you were attached, my child, much less a human being who shared your love with me."

"Not shared it, mamma," said Leonore.

And the mother and daughter separated for a while.

The former to dismiss the gipsy, with his reward.

The latter to fly to her chamber, once more to welcome the familiar objects which she had not seen for so long.

Poor innocent guiltless Leonore!

She thought not now of the cruel treatment she had received at her mother's hands.

She thought not that it was by that mother's cruelties she was so long banished from her lawful home.

Banished to wander homeless, houseless, friendless.

She thought but of the greeting she had just received.

She thought but of the motherly affection which her ladyship had lavished so prodigally upon her.

Innocent guileless heart!

Leonore, you have yet another sad lesson to learn.

Another sad act in the weary drama of life to perform.

In the meantime Lady Glyde dismissed Jonas the gipsy with the reward in full.

As Jonas was leaving she eyed him sternly for a minute or so, as if to read his character.

"You are a desperate fellow, it seems to me," she said.

"My lady!"

"Tush! you know what I say. Now, would you undertake a desperate work?"

Jonas looked steadfastly at her before replying.

There was no doubt about her ladyship being serious.

"Yes," said Jonas coolly.

"You can?"

"For desperate pay."

"Good. Then be here again to-night with an assistant."

"I will."

"A trusty fellow, mind."

"Who?"

"The assistant."

"Ay, my second self."

"Good. Use discretion, and you can make a fortune."

"I'm yours, my lady."

"Away."

The time for his return was fixed, and Jonas, with a bow and a scrape, retired.

As her ladyship was turning to quit the room the rustle of a feminine garment caught her ear.

She darted to the door.

Dragged it open in time to hear a scampering upon the stairs, but to see nothing.

When Leonore arrived in her chamber her first care was to look about her to see if the articles of her wardrobe were as she had left them.

Then having obtained sufficient garments from the remnants of her once rich wardrobe to make herself presentable as the daughter of Glyde House, she rang for her waiting maid.

The door was thrown open and a girl rushed in.

She stopped short, stared at Leonore as if she had seen some spectre, and then gave a loud shriek.

"Margaret," said Leonore, "what is it? Are you not pleased to see me?"

"Oh! my dear, dear mistress," said the girl, "is it indeed you?"

"Of course, Margaret."

"Oh! bless you! bless you! How pleased I am! How beautiful you look! Dear! dear!"

And in an ecstacy of joy, and quite heedless of their respective positions, the girl rushed up to Leonore and embraced her.

Leonore returned the girl's greeting not a whit less warmly.

"Oh, dear, dear," cried the girl, laughing and weeping at once. "I have such lots to tell you."

"Have you been happy whilst I have been away?"

"No."

"Indeed?"

"Very unhappy."

"I'm sorry for that."

"And I shouldn't have stayed a day if I hadn't had a purpose in stopping."

"What purpose?"

The girl looked into the face of her young mistress with a glance brimfull of affection.

"To discover what they had done with you," she whispered.

"Ah!"

"Don't be angry, my dear lady," said the girl. "I know much more than I dare to say now. But you must keep your courage right, and it is hard indeed if together we cannot take your part between us."

As this sounded like a coalition against her mother, to whom she was but just returned, Leonore would fain have silenced the girl.

However, it was apparent that she spoke with some reason, and, moreover, that she meant her young mistress well.

"Put off all disagreeable matters for the present, Margaret," said Leonore. "We'll speak later of this."

"Willingly."

"For the present we must have only joys and happiness."

"I fear not."

"Hush!"

Lady Glyde's footsteps were heard upon the stairs.

The expression of the chambermaid's face changed upon the instant as if by magic.

"One word before my lady comes," she whispered hurriedly.

"What is it?"

"Beware of her."

"Margaret!"

"Hush! I listened just now at the door whilst she was with that gipsy man."

"Ah!"

"And heard that he is to come back again."

"Who is to come back again?" demanded Lady Glyde, entering.

But Margaret was not at all embarrassed at this.

"Joseph, my lady, whom your ladyship turned away for getting dr—ahem! tipsy."

"Oh!" said Lady Glyde drily.

"Yes, my lady. My young lady was inquiring after all the old servants."

"Very good. You may go."

Margaret made her obeisance and quitted the room.

"What did that silly chattering girl say?" asked Lady Glyde.

"Nonsense, mamma."

"About the servants only?"

"Nothing more."

Lady Glyde eyed her daughter sharply as she put the question with a casual air.

But Leonore had learnt from her mother's own cruelties to use a little deceit when necessary.

The glance accompanying her ladyship's words and the apparent difference between her tone and manner had put Leonore upon the *qui vive*.

At the same time it wrung her loving tender heart to find herself deceived again.

She had revelled for a moment—a brief happy moment—in a dream of happiness and love.

And now how utterly was her momentary vision destroyed!

Another interview took place between the mother and daughter.

Each appeared to lavish affection upon the other—to feel but love pure and deep for each other.

Upon Leonore's part we trust that it was not assumed.

Whether it was the same with Lady Glyde the process of events will show.

Yet Leonore was unhappy, very unhappy.

Her heart was again filled with restraint.

And it was but reasonable when she reflected.

And presently a terrible confirmation of her dismal forebodings was given her.

When she required the attendance of her waiting maid she was not forthcoming.

Leonore was informed that the girl had retired to bed.

According to established custom this was wrong.

If it had not been, she well knew that Margaret would have been too much delighted at her return to retire before again seeing her.

There was something in it.

Something more than our heroine could at present comprehend.

And she was determined to fathom the mystery.

However, she appeared to be satisfied without the services of her favourite attendant.

[THE MURDER ON THE THAMES.]

She accepted the story of her having retired so strangely to rest, and then, when all the house was wrapt in slumber, Leonore ventured from her bed-chamber.

With a small lantern in her hand she descended the stairs.

She knew where Margaret slept.

With stealthy strides Leonore made for the chamber.

As she neared it the sound of something stirring caught her ear, and she paused to listen.

"Great Heavens!" she murmured faintly. "Surely they never will—"

*   *   *   *   *   *

It was night.

The grim silent night.

Two men stood without a large mansion belonging to one of the highest families in the land.

Their object clearly enough was to gain admittance.

They were there upon a secret errand of the most desperate and deadly character.

After they had been there some little time one of them signalled some one within the house.

But this was only done after a deal of caution had been observed—unnecessary as it appeared to be.

Then the door was opened.

Who it was that answered this signal thus promptly no one could perceive from without.

The two men entered the house with slow and stealthy strides.

As they passed in the door closed behind them.

Noiselessly.

All transpired as if they were enacting a shadow drama.

So grimly silent.

Surely some deed of mystery and terror was about to be enacted.

We shall see.

When the two men passed through the hall, and gained the bottom of the stairs, they found themselves face to face with a dark figure enveloped in a long cloak.

So thoroughly was the outline of the figure preserved from view that it was not even to be seen if it was a man or a woman.

Without a word, with but a slow spectral movement of the right arm, it waved the two men to follow.

It would have been perceived by an observer, had there been any such, that the two midnight visitors were not a little impressed by this singular apparition.

Silently they followed.

The figure conducted them up the stairs.

Paused by a bedroom door, and motioned them to enter before him or herself, whichever it might be.

Now the first word was spoken.

" Is it sure she sleeps soundly ?" asked one of the men.

The breaking of the still silence of the night appeared to be very refreshing to the speaker's companion.

But the figure answered not.

An inclination of the head alone gave an affirmative response to the whispered question.

" Shall I strike as she sleeps ?" continued the man in a whisper.

The figure shook its head with a slow solemn motion.

The figure implied in a most impressive pantomime that the individual of whom they spoke was to be lifted from the bed and carried out asleep.

" What next ?"

An imperious gesture to commence operations at once told the fellow to await further instructions when he had executed this much.

He inclined his head in humility.

Turned the door handle gently.

Entered the room.

He found himself in a bedchamber, at the further extremity of which was situated a canopy bedstead, with coloured hangings drawn to.

He stole across the room with stealthy strides to the bed.

Drew back the hangings.

Then there lay revealed the plump and comely form of a sleeping girl.

After gazing upon her for a second he turned towards the door, and held back the bed drapery with one hand, whilst with the other he beckoned his companion.

His fore-finger warningly placed upon the lip directed the utmost caution.

With the same stealthy catlike stride, the second fellow followed his companion into the room.

The only light which they had was afforded them through the half open curtain upon the left.

Through this a clear but narrow streak of moonlight was admitted.

Avoiding this, he made for the bed.

Pushed back the bedclothes from the form of the sleeper.

Raised her in his arms.

The motion employed was so gentle that it did not in the least disturb her.

He was a powerful fellow, and the weight of the sleeping girl did not appear to hinder his movements in the least.

As they got to the door the figure who had conducted them there suddenly re-appeared.

Then resumed its former position of guide to the two men.

Thus led, the party proceeded down the stairs again.

They went through a kitchen upon the basement, crossed a paved yard, and entered a cellar.

Here the first thing which caught the eye was a wooden handrail, guarding a large opening.

It was a well.

Grasping his still slumbering burden firmly in his arms, the fellow, according to the directions silently indicated by the conductor, proceeded hastily towards the well.

Too hastily.

He chanced to jolt the sleeper so roughly that the deep slumber which even now continued was suddenly broken.

The girl opened her eyes.

Now they had to use wondrous promptitude.

One of the men suddenly threw a cloth over her head, drowning a startled inquiry as it rose to her lips.

Then he raised her to the level of the handrail.

Pushed a little way forward.

Now the girl began to understand that some wrong was intended her, and she struggled violently.

But what could the most frantic efforts avail her with this combination against her single frail strength ?

Alas ! nothing.

As he pushed her over she felt, although she could see nothing, that she was hanging over a precipice.

She dashed over the cloth with a sudden effort.

Grabbed sharply at the wooden handrail.

The fellow had now quitted his hold of her, and she hung suspended over the well-hole.

Her sole support, the feeble grasp she had of the sides of the well-hole.

It was fearful.

The depth beneath her was so terrible that not the faintest hopes of escape could the victim hope for who had once been thrust down its gloomy depths.

" Oh ! mercy, mercy !" she cried, struggling as she grasped the hand-rail.

Not a word was spoken.

Not the slightest answer was vouchsafed to her supplications.

The other executioner pushed her violently.

Still with the strength of despair the poor doomed creature clung to the side of the well-hole.

" Oh ! good heavens," cried the ill-fated girl, " if this is really some horrible dream, some cruel nightmare, I pray the Father of all mercy to waken me from it. It is too, too horrible !"

Still the ruffians thrust her back.

Still heedless of her appeal.

The agonised outpourings of a woman's heart could not touch their stony natures.

The murder was continued in fearful, dreadful silence.

As they could not get at their victim well enough to push her away from her hold, they bethought them of an idea still more horrible if possible.

One stamped upon her fingers with his heavy boots.

Crushed torn and bleeding.

The other with a stout thick bludgeon struck viciously at her head and face.

Then a savage attack was made upon her hands.

A single blow completed the business thus desperately advanced.

Murder was done.

Another of God's own creatures was sent into His presence to accuse her assassins.

But the vengeance of the Almighty little concerned them now.

Had there been any chance of earthly vengeance overtaking them it might have been otherwise.

But, by Heavens! this did not seem so very unlikely.

A wild unearthly shriek burst from some one close at hand.

And, singularly enough, at the very instant that the last echo of the murdered girl's cries died away in the fatal well-hole.

It was a fearful sound.

A shriek which threatened to alarm the whole house.

What could it mean?

Had the bloody deed any other witnesses than the three?

CHAPTER CXII.

RED RALPH IN TROUBLE AGAIN—OLD SCENES — HAUNTS OF FORMER DAYS—THE BOOZING KEN —RECOGNITION—A NOISE—A SCUFFLE—RALPH STILL A CONQUEROR—THE REWARD—FIVE HUNDRED ON HIS HEAD—THE CHASE — BILL JENKINS — THE CHURCH — THE STAINED GLASS WINDOW AND THE IVY WALL — A FRIEND IN NEED—THE CHURCH TOWER — RED RALPH AT BAY—A NEW FOE—TERRORS.

ONCE more we return to Red Ralph.

Once more do the pressing emergencies of the captain of the Yellow Band's position require our immediate attention.

For again is the bold Red Ralph a fugitive from justice.

Thus it is that the bloodhounds of the law, in their untiring energy and perseverance, have succeeded in tracking the fugitive robber hero to his lair.

One night, some little time after his visit to Newgate in company with Sir Harry Jerrold, in one of his fits of restlessness which had led to so many of his wildest adventures and misfortunes, the captain of the Yellow Band determined to pay a visit to one of the scenes of his earlier glories.

The Boozing Ken was chosen, as connected with more singular reminiscences than any other.

In it he had spent some of the most exciting moments of his mistaken career.

In it he had made many a triumph—many a fair conquest.

The latter, we may remark, were of the easiest, and required no seducer's arts to be brought into play.

In the Boozing Ken, too, he had, upon a memorable night, been forewarned of many events which had since transpired.

Upon these we have already touched as we proceeded.

The haunt we have alluded to the reader will well remember as being the rendezvous of the vilest characters that infested the metropolis and its environs at the period of our history.

It was here that we opened one of our earliest passages.

It was here that the captain of the Yellow Band had been warned by an old harridan that troubles innumerable beset his path and that a marriage of strange importance was about to occur.

This was before the robber's singular appearance at Glyde House, upon which occasion Lady Glyde and Jabez the hunchback had essayed to complete his destruction, after the outlaw's marriage with the helpless and lovely Leonore.

It is, therefore, little to be wondered at, when we reflect upon all this, that the Boozing Ken, in spite of its vile character, should still have some strange attraction and interest for the captain of the Yellow Band.

Accordingly, without any special object, did Red Ralph present himself at the haunt of former days, the Boozing Ken.

Many faces did the highwayman recognise amongst the assemblage he found there.

Many a desperado did he recognise beneath a mild and benignant exterior.

Many a ruffian of the lowest and most bloodthirsty nature did he discover lurking about there under an assumed name.

In the midst of all this, however, he little dreamed that he himself ran great danger of recognition likewise.

In spite of his beard, one of the company present spotted our hero the very moment he entered the place.

He was not sure of his man, however, and he therefore determined to test him before settling it positively in his own mind.

Accordingly he strolled up to one of the ruffians of the company, and addressed him thus.

"Well, mate, and what d'ye think is the latest news from the stone jug?"

"Can't say."

"Well, they've got Red Ralph in limbo at last."

He kept his eyes fixed upon the highwayman as he spoke.

Red Ralph started, but did not turn round.

He understood upon the instant that it was spoken at him, and he was greatly disgusted at his own want of presence of mind in allowing it to be perceived.

At present no further consequence resulted from it.

However, he could not hope to get off so lightly.

He knew the company into which he had ventured again.

A heavy price was set upon his head, so heavy as to tempt any of the poor wretches who were then present, he knew, to sell him to the law.

The saying, so popular in those days, of "honour among thieves" would not hold good, he knew, amongst such a depraved set as these.

Accordingly, whilst there was yet time, he determined to make good his retreat.

He rose to his feet, and sauntered towards the door.

At the same moment the fellow who had recognised the captain of the Yellow Band walked sharply up, and confronted him.

"Hullo! friend," he said.

Red Ralph eyed the fellow up and down with an air of supreme disdain.

"Hullo! friend, I say," repeated the fellow into Ralph's face.

"What would you?" demanded the captain of the Yellow Band.

"I? Nothing."

"Then stand aside."

"Gently, gently, master."

"Why do you presume to stand in my path?" said Ralph indignantly.

"Presume?"

"Ay, that's my word."

"Oh! that's your word?"

"By the way in which you echo me," said the captain of the Yellow Band, growing gradually warmer, "it would appear that you desire to quarrel with me."

"Oh! You think so?"

There was an intolerable sneer accompanying these words, which our hero could no longer endure.

He placed his hand upon the fellow's shoulder.

Clutched him with a firm grip, and swung him round out of his path.

As Red Ralph's strength, when exerted, was not to be despised, the fellow felt at once the danger of attempting to tackle such a rough customer alone.

As the bully rose to his feet a laugh of derision from those assembled in the Boozing Ken greeted his discomfiture.

"Ha! ha!" laughed one. "You got more than you bargained for that time, Morris."

"The biter bit."

"One for your cannister, Morris, that time."

This chaff stung the ruffian bully to the quick, and he rushed out after the captain of the Yellow Band.

Red Ralph heard him coming on behind, and he turned to face him.

The bold cool front which he presented had the effect of staggering the other for a while.

But only for a second.

"Now then, what is it you want with me?" demanded Red Ralph.

"Want? I only want to know what makes you so plaguey handy with your mawleys."

And he advanced threateningly.

"Look you," said Red Ralph. "If you would listen to a piece of friendly advice, you will stand off."

"Oh! should I?"

And as he spoke he drew nearer.

His intention was to engage the captain of the Yellow Band in conversation till he drew him off his guard and then make a vicious dash at him.

However, the wary highwayman perceived his intention, and would not suffer himself to be thus handled.

As the fellow drew too near to be pleasant he suddenly struck out.

Crack went his fist, full upon the imprudent man's face.

Down to grass he went, as if felled by a butcher's pole-axe.

This seemed to be so pleasant to him that he never stirred from that position.

Red Ralph, seeing the combat virtually at an end in this summary way, strode off.

One or two of the bosom companions of the fallen bully would have fain taken his cause in hand, but the strong right arm of the captain of the Yellow Band had secured him their greatest respect.

A second laugh at the expense of the fallen bully was, therefore, the sole result of his attack.

Red Ralph strode on unmolested—for the present.

Meanwhile the bully sprang up, and indignantly retorted upon the mocking crowd.

"Fools, fools!" he exclaimed. "You little deem whom you thus let slip through you fingers."

"Who? Who?" demanded a hundred voices in a breath.

"Is it warm?" asked one, smelling prey.

"A bulldog?"

"One of Wild's pups?"

"No."

"Who, then?"

"Why he's one as would fetch no less than five hundred couter this very hour, if we had him."

"Five hundred couter?"

"Ay, every farthing."

A groan went round the assembly.

"Why didn't you say so before, Morris?" asked one.

"I know."

"Why?"

"Because he's greedy. He wanted to have all of it himself."

"That's a lie," said Morris. "If I was greedy over it, why should I say anything about it now?"

"Oh! now! That's very different. Now," said the former speaker, "after you've got wolloped."

"Well, look here now, Tim Murphy, I ain't been wopped by you, have I now?"

"No."

"And I ain't likely to be."

"Unless you put your paws up again."

An angry reply brought the two men together, and a grand display of their abilities in the noble art of fisticuffs would have ensued had not the rest of the company interfered.

It must not be presumed for an instant that qualms of any description respecting the damage they might do each other caused them to restrain their movements.

Nothing but the thoughts that Red Ralph and five hundred pounds were slipping through their fingers could have stopped the much-loved exhibition.

Out rushed the whole tribe from the Boozing Ken in a regular scramble.

As they gained the road they saw somebody pass round the corner at a run.

Off they galloped in pursuit, with a loud cry.

They rushed wildly up to the turning in the road, and then perceived that they had been giving chase to a ragged-looking wretch—one of themselves, in fact.

Being quicker of perception than his associates, he had set off at once in pursuit of the captain of the Yellow Band.

Not with the intention or hope of securing his person be it understood, but simply in the idea that he could track him to some definite spot where he could take the necessary measures to secure him.

This he had done.

But the princely reward was not quite booked as yet.

"Hullo! hullo!" he cried, as he perceived the ragged mob advancing. "What's all this?"

"Hullo there!"

"Why who is it?"

"Only Bill Jenkins after all."

A groan of disgust went through the crowd at this.

"Why, what's up?" demanded Mr. Jenkins in surprise.

"Why, you know that fellow as pounded Morris up so?"

"Yes."

"Who d'ye think he is?"

"Don't know."

"Hold hard!" interrupted one of the slower runners, who only now came up. "He knows well enough. I see him bolt directly that Morris said as he was worth five hundred couter. Shiny Bill was off like a skyrocket."

"Well I don't know who it was any the more," grumbled Jenkins. "That I can swear."

"No matter, Bill, where is he now?"

"I've watched him into—now where do you think, my pals?"

"Can't say, can't say."

"Now out with it."

"Go on, Jenkins. You're wasting walleable time."

"Why, into a church."

"A church!" echoed a dozen voices in astonishment.

"Ay, and off I came to get a hand to go and make it right without loss o' time."

"Come on, then."

"What, all of ye?"

"Yes, yes, share and share alike."

Bill Jenkins growled disappointedly at this.

"Ah! Mr. Bill," said one of them. "You'd better not get too greedy over it. Morris was greedy, and Red Ralph gave him more kicks than ha'pence."

"Red Ralph?"

"Ay."

"Ralph?" reiterated the astonished Jenkins. "Was that fellow Red Ralph?"

"Yes."

"Sure?"

"So Morris says."

"Pheugh! Then I'm off, for one."

"What do you mean by that?"

"Why, I ain't a going to attempt to tackle Red Ralph."

"Not alone of course."

"No, nor with you either. I know what's what better than that."

"Well, of all the sneaking cowardly curs!"

"You may talk on as much as you please. I shan't make one of the party."

"Why not?"

"Because I know that if it is Red Ralph you are after, you might as well try to hunt down Vanderdecken the Flying Dutchman."

"Bah!"

"Bosh!"

"Humbug!"

"As you like, my pals," said Jenkins, "but I've had something to do with the captain of the Yellow Band before to-day."

"What of that? Red Ralph ain't no more dangerous than any one else I suppose."

"I don't know."

"Lor, Jenkins," said another, "Red Ralph the Yellow Boy may be a very good 'un in his way, but the very best man that ever prigged a fogle or cried 'Stand!' on the king's highway ain't no good again' a dozen."

"Try it on," said Jenkins. "You may do what you like."

"We will."

"Without me, my pals."

They saluted Bill Jenkins with a derisive laugh, and ran off after the rich prize.

At the bottom of the road they came upon the church of which Bill Jenkins had just spoken.

"This is it," said one.

"He's inside."

"Let's go in."

But the doors were locked, and no one was about to render them any assistance.

But here a word with Mr. Bill Jenkins is necessary.

No sooner had the mob of patrons of the Boozing Ken cleared off than Jenkins changed his route.

He vaulted over a gate and dashed across a newly-ploughed field towards the church.

By proceeding thus he made a short cut which brought him over the churchyard, and thus to the back windows of the church.

The wall was all overgrown with thick old ivy, which straggled across the stained glass windows up to the church turret, where the belfry had originally stood.

It was a fine old church, dating from the early Norman period, as might be more easily perceived by the many curiously carved old tombs of knights and crusaders which adorned it within and without.

About twenty feet from the ground was an open window.

Towards this Mr. Bill Jenkins at once directed his attention.

He could hear the murmurs of the mob on the further side of the church quite distinctly.

"I must be quick, or they will see my game here," he said to himself. "And yet it looks rather a nasty sort of job to climb up there. No matter, here goes!"

And with no more ado he clutched at the stoutest branch of ivy he could find, dragged himself up, and began the ascent.

Once he caught hold of a branch which was too tender to bear such usage and it gave way.

It very nearly precipitated him to the ground.

However, he contrived to regain his hold, with considerable presence of mind.

This little accident served to steady him.

Up he went.

The window was gained.

He scrambled through, and found himself in the organ loft.

He stepped lightly across to the gallery, and leant over the handrail to look about.

He could not see Red Ralph anywhere now.

"Singular!" he muttered. "And yet I dare swear that he has not had the time to leave."

He ran down the stairs into the centre aisle of the church and looked about him.

He heard a noise close behind him, and upon looking round perceived Red Ralph just rising from his knees from before a marble tomb.

The fellow drew back and would have retreated, in spite of the pressing emergency.

The most callous of us cannot fail to be impressed with such a scene as this.

"Why am I thus intruded upon?" demanded Red Ralph.

As he did not look round, the newcomer guessed that he was mistaken by the captain of the Yellow Band for the clerk or the sexton, whichever had admitted him into the church.

"I'm sorry to disturb you," began Bill Jenkins, hesitatingly.

Ralph turned sharply.

"Hullo! Who are you?"

"A friend."

"How came you here?"

"I'll tell you, Red Ralph."

"You know me?"

"Yes."

"Who are you?"

"One who wishes you well."

Red Ralph had instinctively clutched his sword-handle.

"Whoever you be," said the captain of the Yellow Band, "I pray you to withdraw and not molest me here. I would fain spare this holy place the desecration of an idle brawl or worldly dispute."

"I mean nothing of the kind," said Bill Jenkins. "I come in friendliness to serve you."

"How?"

"The whole ken of the boozers are after you. They know that you are Red Ralph, and have hunted you to the church."

"For what purpose?"

"Can you not guess?"

"Not I, 'i faith."

"There's a price upon your head."

"Ah?"

"A long one, too. Five hundred pounds ain't a trifle."

"And these miserable wretches would sell me for this filthy dross?" exclaimed Red Ralph.

"Ay, they would."

"And you?"

"Might have done the same if you hadn't done me a good turn once, Red Ralph."

"Who are you?"

"My name is Bill Jenkins. I dare say you have forgotten it. But I don't forget a service very soon."

"I'm grateful to you."

"You owe me no gratitude. Let me get you out of this scrape, and then even we shall only be equal."

At this juncture a murmur of voices was heard without.

This was followed by a spirited assault on the church door.

It sounded ominous.

"That door cannot stand much of that sort of thing I know," said Bill Jenkins.

Red Ralph looked about him for a means of escape.

"If you want to fly now," said Jenkins, "I've the means here."

"Where?"

"Follow me."

And they scrambled up the stairs to the organ loft.

Dashed up to the window.

Bill Jenkins was there first, but as he neared the window he waved Red Ralph back.

"Stand off!" he cried. "Stand off!"

"What is it?"

"They have discovered the window, and are climbing up the ivy!"

"Ah!"

"Wait."

"But how did you contrive to get in?" asked Red Ralph.

"This way."

"Then it is to be done?!"

"Easily."

The confirmation of what Bill Jenkins asserted was there.

A head and a pair of hands appeared upon the window sill.

"Now then, captain, down with him!" whispered Bill Jenkins.

Red Ralph took a pistol from his pocket and rapped the climber sharply upon the knuckles.

"Ah!" he cried.

And down he went, scrambling amongst the ivy as he fell.

"That's done for him!"

"Yes."

"But I fear mischief now."

"From what?"

"It has put them on the alarm."

"No matter."

"They will direct their attack upon the window alone."

"What of that? We can easily keep them off. It is a divided attack which we have more to dread from than that."

"So I see."

"Hush! They're at us again."

A second predestined victim was heard essaying his fortunes upon the ivy beneath the window.

This one was served rather worse than the former.

As soon as his hands touched the window sill Red Ralph clutched them firmly.

There he held the unfortunate wretch suspended by his wrists for several minutes.

"Help! help!" he shouted.

"What's got ye?" demanded one of the crowd from the Boozing Ken.

"The devil!"

"Eh?"

"Something's holding precious tight."

"You're quite safe, though, as far as that goes, for the present," said the former speaker. "The old gentleman wouldn't touch you on a church."

A roar greeted this sally.

"He'll wait his time," added the wit, thus encouraged.

"Murder! mur—"

Taking pity upon his agonies, the captain of the Yellow Band loosened his hold.

And down he fell.

There was a scramble to pick up the fallen man.

And thus the attack upon the window was finally repulsed.

The mob never ventured again to touch this side of the church.

However, retreat this way was an utter impossibility, for it was most effectually guarded.

Just as Red Ralph had made this discovery another not less important was made by Bill Jenkins.

The church doors were open, and the mob were pouring into the sacred edifice.

Oaths and cries alike attested in what little reverence they held the place.

They scattered and ran about in all directions.

Hither and thither, up the pulpit stairs, scrambling down by the communion table.

Bitterly did the old sexton who had admitted Red Ralph now regret what he had done.

The havoc which the unruly mob caused could not very easily be cleared away.

At length they heard the captain of the Yellow Band above.

A cry was raised, and off they ran in pursuit.

Red Ralph turned to fly.

He stopped short by the stairs.

"Come on, captain," said Bill Jenkins. "It's all up now."

"Never."

"Come on, then."

"No, no," said Red Ralph. "It shall never be said of a Yellow Boy that he basely fled before a pack of yelping hounds like these."

"Yelping hounds!" cried a voice from the crowd. "You won't fly from a pack of yelping hounds, eh?"

"Never!"

"We'll see."

And one of the persons below was seen to squeeze his way through the crowd and leave the church.

Red Ralph thought afterwards of this incident.

But in the excitement of the moment it had no effect on him.

"Give in, captain," said one of the foremost of the mob.

"Never."

"You're done up."

"Who'll take me?"

"That will I."

"Bravo, Morris!" cried the approving crowd.

"Have another tussle with him."

"Come on!" said Red Ralph, now worked up to the necessary pitch of excitement.

"We're after you."

And a few men made a step forward.

"At your peril!" said Red Ralph.

And he very effectually brought them to bay by presenting a pistol fully at them.

They paused irresolutely.

"Now stand back," said the captain of the Yellow Band, "and let me pass out free, or by my soul I swear I will slay the first man who opposes me."

There was a resolution in his tone which cowed them.

Determination to act up to what he promised in his gesture.

With his right hand clutching a pistol, the captain of the Yellow Band descended the stairs.

The mob moved back.

It looked like escape.

But no, not yet. His foot had barely touched the fourth stair when his ear caught a sound which caused him to pull up short.

The deep baying of hunting dogs was heard without.

The next moment they appeared at the entrance to the church.

Now there was no time to lose.

Red Ralph guessed at once what it meant, and it must be confessed that he felt alarmed.

He could take his own part to the very last against any man.

But to be hunted down to earth like a wolf was out

of all fighting annals which had ever been heard of by him.

He fled up the steps again.

"Up, up," he cried to Bill Jenkins, who had paused irresolutely.

"What is it?"

"The dogs!"

Jenkins turned pale.

"Dogs!" he faltered. "Surely they would never hunt a man with bloodhounds."

"Here they come to answer for themselves."

With this he dashed up a flight of rugged stone steps, followed by his companion.

He soon found himself upon the top of the church tower.

A flat-roofed tower, very much out of repair, and particularly shaky.

"They'll never venture up here," said Bill Jenkins.

"Well, no matter if they do," said the captain of the Yellow Band.

"We've done our best, and can do no more."

"It only remains to us to fight it out."

"I'll do that, captain."

"And I too, whilst there is a drop of blood left in my veins."

There was a pause in the attack from below.

They evidently did not like intruding upon two desperately hunted men who were now at bay.

"I shan't go," said one.

"Nor I. I ain't no food for powder yet awhile."

"Send up the dogs!"

A chorus of assenting voices was heard at this.

Sad music to the captain of the Yellow Band and Bill Jenkins.

With a deep baying, the bloodhounds, let loose at the foot of the stairs, made a terrific rush up.

Red Ralph was pale but determined.

He drew forth a short spring-back knife and opened it.

Drew his sword and laid it at hand in readiness.

Then hastily examined his pistols.

"Look out, captain," said Bill Jenkins. "Here they are."

"I'm ready!"

CHAPTER CXIII.

THE BLOODHOUNDS — A FEARFUL COMBAT — A STRUGGLE OF FURY — UNEQUAL ODDS — THE SHOT — VARYING CHANCES — THE IVY — THE LONELY HUT — THE MISER — A PRINCELY HOARD — THE MASKED ROBBERS — MURDER MOST FOUL — A DYING PRAYER — FIENDS IN HUMAN FORM.

WITH the deep baying peculiar to the bloodhound the dogs sprang up.

One made a rush at the captain of the Yellow Band.

But Red Ralph, quicker if not nimbler than the ferocious brute, perceived him in time to avoid him.

He sprang aside, and the bloodhound scrambled upon the parapet of the church tower.

Before he could regain his equilibrium Red Ralph sprang forward, and with a push sent him over the top.

So much for the first.

But yet a whole pack remained to be disposed of.

It was a fearful thought, and might have cowed the stoutest heart to contemplate it.

However, Red Ralph had fortunately no time to contemplate what had to come.

His whole attention was engrossed with the present.

A second bloodhound sprang up the stairs and leaped upon Bill Jenkins.

This fellow was less fortunate or less courageous than Red Ralph, and he got in sad grief.

The hound fixed upon him furiously, and tore his flesh in a most fearful way.

Up and down they battled fearfully for the mastery.

They rolled upon the ground over and over, but Bill Jenkins could not manage to shake him off.

It was a desperate battle.

The next brute that showed up leaped at Red Ralph, aiming at his throat.

So quickly did he spring that our robber hero could not jump aside soon enough.

He grasped his knife, shortened his arm, and dug fiercely at the hound.

So true did he strike—so well aimed was the blow—that the knife was buried up to the very hilt in the animal's carcase.

Its hold relaxed.

The jaw opened.

He fell to the ground dead.

A third coming up, Red Ralph cut at him with his sword, and with a well-timed blow succeeded in laying open its skull.

The poor brute fell groaning to the ground to expire shortly.

But whilst thus engaged two more of the bloodhounds made their way to the top.

With all the ferocious instinct of their race and breeding they flew upon Red Ralph.

Both sprang at his throat, and both succeeded in getting a hold.

Not at the throat itself, happily, or it would have gone hardly with the highwayman.

They got at his neckerchief and the collar of his coat, and tugged so unpleasantly at his throat that he experienced considerable difficulty in breathing.

He tugged and wrestled fiercely with the two hounds.

Fought with desperation.

Fought as only a man fights who battles for his life.

He could not contrive to use his knife now, or he would have had a great advantage.

Finding it impossible to shake off the two brutes, Red Ralph threw himself upon the ground.

Still they clung tenaciously to the bold captain of the Yellow Band.

Whilst thus engaged in tackling the bloodhounds one of his pursuers made his way up the steps.

He was the only one.

The others held the hunted highwayman in too much fear to attempt to draw any nearer to him than they were at present.

"Hold on, Snarley!" he said, clapping his hands. "Stick to them! Bravo, Pincher! Good dog!"

"Call off the beasts," said the captain of the Yellow Band.

"Ah!" laughed the man, "I thought you'd yield."

"Never!"

"Then you like it?"

"Call them off."

"I shan't. I want to see if there is any truth in the boast that you wouldn't yield to a pack of hounds."

"Call them off!"

"I shan't."

Red Ralph suddenly disengaged his hand and drew a pistol from his belt.

He levelled it point blank at the man as he stood.

"Now then," said Red Ralph, "call off your dogs, or I'll blow your brains out."

Without replying, the fellow would have retreated, but Red Ralph covered him with the pistol.

"Call them off, or I fire."

"Here, Pincher! Snarley, here," he cried, rather alarmed.

But it was no easy matter to make a bloodhound release a prey once fixed.

The dogs would not obey.

The fellow would not attempt a second time, but, dodging his head down, he made a sudden spring forwards.

At the same instant a flash and a report of Red Ralph's pistol accelerated his pace.

Over he went with a cry.

Down the steps he fell, bruising and tearing himself in a desperate fashion.

"Oh! oh!" he cried. "I am murdered—slain!"

Red Ralph threw his pistol from his hand and reached his knife again.

A sudden job at one of the animals settled his accounts without any more ado.

Over he went—dead.

A similar dig at the other brought him to the ground.

Red Ralph dashed up to Jenkins, and, seizing the hound which was so worrying him, he pressed his throat so fiercely that the animal was almost choked.

A knock upon the head with the butt end of a pistol settled his business at once.

They were released from the hounds.

"Now," said Red Ralph to Jenkins. "There is but one escape."

"There is none," replied Jenkins, binding his wounds.

"There is, if you have the courage to try it."

"Name it."

"The ivy."

"You surely would not trust yourself to so frail a support at this immense height?"

"You shall see. Follow or not as you please. I mean to do it."

"Go on, then."

"Good fortune to you."

"I'm with you."

* 　 * 　 * 　 * 　 *

We must change the scene.

In a poor country hovel not a hundred miles from the spot we have just quitted a man, stricken in years, thin and half-starved in aspect, with his garments sitting upon him in a loose way that would have been painful to a beholder, walked up and down in solitary woe.

Woe the most worrying that poor humanity is afflicted with.

The dread of poverty is his nightmare.

The canker that gnaws at his heartstrings.

For this old man is a miser. The love of gold is a fever with him—an unconquerable passion which eats him up body and soul.

A miser he is, and one of the very worst of his class.

He grudges himself the morsel of coarse bread—his daily meal—by which he contrives to keep body and soul together.

As we raise the curtain above his miserable hovel he is pacing the room uneasily, and rubbing his long famished-looking clawlike hands to produce warmth, for he is cold and sick at heart.

The gold fever and the famine fever have nearly completed their work.

The miser has not many hours to live.

Not many in the ordinary course of things, so reduced and emaciated has he become by the severity of his self-imposed penances.

He feels instinctively that the grim tyrant Death is approaching him, and he fears to die.

He fears and dreads to leave behind him that hoard of wealth—that princely fortune—which lies like a pearl in a hog trough, concealed from prying eyes, in that miserable hovel.

But little does the miser dream that what few hours' life he yet possesses is to be robbed from him within the hour.

"I'll look again, I'll look again," he muttered in his walk.

Then he stops and opens the door to look out into the road.

Apparently satisfied that he is free from interruption, he pushes the door to, but the latch does not catch.

This is a piece of carelessness quite out of keeping with his wonted precaution.

But the gold fever has him tighter than ever at this moment.

A wild paroxysm is upon him.

An unconquerable desire to be face to face once more with his treasure—the darling of his heart.

He walks totteringly up to the hearth, and, hastily placing a small knife beneath the edge of it, raises it up.

When high enough he eagerly dives his hand into the cavity and draws forth a bag of gold.

A weighty bag, and holding a fortune, for a poor man.

Just at this juncture a shadow darkens the window.

The shadow falls, momentarily over the hearth, and the old man tremblingly hides his treasure beneath his tattered coat.

But no, his fear works upon him he thinks.

He is deceived.

Alas! for guilty humanity, he is most cruelly.

Another minute, and he is satisfied that it was but his heated imagination working upon his fears and apprehensions.

The thirst for gold is strong upon his soul, and he eagerly raises the hearthstone once more.

Dives in and brings up bag after bag of treasure.

And now behold him there.

The picture of squalid misery and want—the very image of penury—in rags and tatters—at an age when one needs the cares and attentions of one's home and friends, sitting alone, gloating with feverish intensity upon a few paltry bags of dross.

Piles of bright beautiful metal, it is true, but their very brilliancy is hidden from the miser's greedy eyes by the coarse canvas bag which contains them.

"I think," he murmured, addressing the money-bags, "that I look upon you—darlings of my heart!—for the last time. Would that I could take you with me into the grave. But thank the god of gold—great Mammon be praised — I shall not have my last moments embittered with the thought that other hands shall clasp you after my death. Snugly you'll lie hidden from mortal sight then."

The door creaks behind him as he thus raves on.

But so occupied is he in his meditations that he heeds it not.

"Toil and struggle of years," he continued, "I must leave you."

"That's more than likely," said a voice in his ear.

"Ah!"

"Silence!"

"Help!"

Ere he could utter another cry a knife was buried up to the hilt in his back.

Whilst engaged in his sinful adoration of the gold he had so toiled and sinned for two masked men had been watching his movements through the window.

Then they had crept round to the front and found the door open.

It was propitious.

They stole in on tiptoe up to the miser, and one of them, as we have seen, closed the golden maniac's miserable career.

[RALPH DEFIES THE LAW.]

The old man fell across his gold with a hollow groan.

As he fell the blood founted out of his wound, and spurted over the murderer's face.

"Mercy!" faintly gasped the dying miser.

"Pshaw!" said the robber brutally. "What's the use of that now?"

"Oh!"

"You haven't half an hour's life left in you, old man."

He was right.

He had even stepped over the mark, for his victim had not half a minute's life left.

The miser sighed deeply, and, moving slightly, expired.

No. 38.

CHAPTER CXIV.

THE CHURCH TOWER — THE WHIPPER-IN — HIS
DOGS — LAMENTATIONS — RETALIATION — HOW
RED RALPH ESCAPED — A DESPERATE FEAT —
THE IVY WALL—THE SLIP—THE STATUE NICHE
— A LIVING MONUMENT — THE STONE — THE
PISTOL SHOT—THE FUGITIVES LOST.

THE church tower was for a few minutes deserted.

Then the owner of the ferocious bloodhounds appeared up the steps leading on to it.

He gave a very careful look around him at first and then stepped up.

The shot which Red Ralph had fired at him had made its mark.

A slight wound upon the forehead told its own tale.

The blood, which had flown copiously from it, had streamed down the fellow's face, and gave him a hideous appearance.

The non-appearance of Red Ralph and his companion was evidently a great mystery to him.

The first object which his eye encountered was the expiring hound which had first attacked the captain of the Yellow Band.

"Killed!" cried the fellow. "Killed! The best of the whole pack killed! Oh! Betsy, Betsy! What will the squire say to this?"

Already Red Ralph was avenged, but this was a brave addition to his triumph.

It had been a bold and desperate fight, but he had conquered—boldly vanquished!

And let him be what he may—nay, the vilest wretch amongst us — he must have our sympathy when contesting with the brute creation.

Ferocious and savage as the beasts of the forest, the hounds had been set upon the two desperate men.

With such prowess as has never been heard of, they had battled against the beasts.

Nay, more, they had gained the day, and slaughtered their panting assailants right and left.

But what seemed more and more extraordinary to the owner of the hounds, or rather the whipper-in (for they were, as the reader has divined from the lament just uttered, the property of some fox-hunting squire), was that he could only see two of the bodies.

The two combatants, too, had disappeared most mysteriously.

It was a problem.

Suddenly the whipper-in deemed that he had solved it.

With a cry he ran to the top of the steps again.

"Back, back!" he shouted.

"What's up?" demanded one of the mob.

"He's gone!"

"Who's gone? Surely not Red Ralph."

"He has, by jingo!"

"But how?"

"He's climbed down somehow."

"Down the wall?"

"I don't know. I suppose he's gone down by the ivy. Down you run, some of ye. Off! You'll stop him yet."

A scrambling was heard below after this exhortation.

The whipper-in ran up to the parapet where the green ivy just peeped above it.

He leaned forward, clutching the stone coping of the parapet, and peered down.

He fancied that he could perceive some agitation in the ivy a little lower down.

Yes, there was no mistaking it.

The ivy was shaking a bit, and the fugitives, or one of them, must be hiding there.

With his eyes still fixed steadily there, he stretched out his right hand, whilst he supported himself upon the left alone.

He clutched at one of the projecting pieces of stonework and dragged it backwards and forwards until it was loose.

Then he pushed it forward.

Down it fell over the parapet, avoiding the spot it was intended for by about half a dozen inches only.

"Curses on it!"

The words were barely uttered when he had an additional motive for choler.

A pistol was fired from the thick of the ivy, and

a bullet whistled most unpleasantly close to his cheek.

So startled was he that his left hand slipped from beneath him, and he was within an ace of being precipitated from the top of the tower.

"Help, help!" he cried.

Some one coming up the steps just at that moment gained the top of the tower, and ran to his assistance.

In the meantime the rest of the mob, hungry after Red Ralph's blood-money, had flown downstairs and rushed madly through the church.

Here they were brought to a stoppage as sudden as it was unexpected.

The doors were locked.

They were fastened so securely that to force them open was indeed no easy task.

However, their impatience could brook no delay, and they dashed at them furiously.

They were of a stout well-seasoned timber, and obstinately resisted a first and second assault.

However, a third, more vehement and desperate that the others, carried it by storm.

Out they dashed; like a pack of hungry wolves, shouting and raving in eager anticipation of taking the bold captain of the Yellow Band.

But Red Ralph was not to yield to this base rabble.

They flew, rather than ran, round the church, upsetting each other in their mad flight.

However, casualties did not excite much commiseration amongst these hardened wretches.

Several of the weaker of the mob were trodden down, and cruelly trampled under foot.

Oaths, shrieks, and yells were heard in plenty.

Surely never before was such a scene known around that sacred edifice.

The venerable pile was never before desecrated thus.

But a disappointment awaited the treacherous and vile horde of ruffians in this cruel chase.

They rushed, shouting and yelling, round to the ivy wall.

But no signs of Red Ralph could they discover.

Just as they burst from the church door a pistol-shot was heard, and this convinced them that he was yet within reach.

But no.

In spite of every endeavour—notwithstanding their most vigilant searches—no traces of the captain of the Yellow Band could be discovered.

High and low—far and wide—it was useless quite.

*   *   *   *   *   *

Let us see how the captain of the Yellow Band had so contrived to elude them.

As soon as the last and most ferocious of the hounds had been effectually dealt with he called to Bill Jenkins, who had so materially aided him in his desperate strait.

"I'm with you, captain," replied Jenkins, springing forward.

"This way."

"All right."

Red Ralph clutched the projecting stonework with a firm hand.

Then gradually he slipped over the side, and let his feet rest upon some of the thicker long stems.

It was a fearful height to look down.

If he had missed his footing, and been projected to the earth, a horrible and certain death awaited him.

But he did not pause an instant.

This was no time for indecision.

If the descent were to be effected it must be done quickly.

In another instant the mob would grow impatient, and rush upon the church tower.

The shot fired at the venturesome whipper-in of the ferocious hounds had staggered his pursuers for a while, he knew.

But only for a while.

A few minutes, and they would renew the pursuit with refreshed energy and vigour.

The result proved that his surmises were correct.

"You will not fear to follow?" said the captain of the Yellow Band to Bill Jenkins.

"No," replied the latter. "Or, rather, I shall be sure to follow you, whether I fear or not."

"Good."

"I'm with you."

"Steady, captain."

"Fear nothing."

But it looked so very risky that Bill Jenkins certainly did entertain the most lively apprehensions.

The bravest man cannot contemplate unmoved the risk of such a fearful death as this.

One—two steps downwards in the ivy were accomplished successfully.

As Red Ralph took his second hold the green plant, rotten with damp, came away from the wall, and he was left supported by one hand alone.

Jenkins gasped.

With dilated eyes, and his mouth wide open, he stood upon the top of the church tower, looking down upon the adventurous Yellow Boy.

Red Ralph looked up, cool and collected, and seeing Jenkins, as he had supposed that he would be, awe-struck at the misadventure, he nodded and smiled to re-assure him.

"All right."

"No danger, captain?" said Jenkins.

"None."

"I breathe again."

"Come carefully, though. It is very shaky."

"I see it is."

"Look after that."

"Yes."

"Begin further this way."

"Here?"

"Where you see that thick stalk."

"I have it."

And with no great eagernesss Bill Jenkins began to follow the desperate lead which the captain of the Yellow Band had set him.

He was even more fortunate than Red Ralph.

Having the benefit of the latter's experience and advice, he had happened to hit upon an excellent point for embarkation.

The ivy was thicker grown and much firmer there anywhere about.

He slipped along capitally, and regained his courage and presence of mind at once.

But four steps, however, had been accomplished when there was a commotion above.

It was then that the whipper-in of the hounds had ventured on to the roof.

The two fugitives exchanged glances of significance.

They did not dare to speak.

They looked into each others' faces for advice.

Red Ralph could but think of one thing.

The descent must be continued, and that more safely.

Their only chance now lay in flight, and that, too, of the fastest.

"On, on," said Ralph in a whisper.

"Good."

"Carefully—quickly."

"Ay."

And they stepped on.

But Red Ralph seemed to be in very bad fortune to-day.

A second time he slipped.

This time it was his feet, and he could find no footing at all.

He hung there, dangling by his two hands, for a painfully long time.

The more remarkable it was, too, that he could not touch the wall with his feet.

And now the ivy, which had supported him bravely enough at first, was not sufficiently strong to bear so weighty a strain upon it for long.

It gave way with him!

An exclamation of fear rose to his lips, but fortunately he subdued it ere uttered.

Jenkins was now on a level with him, but so occupied with his own personal danger that he could give scarcely a thought to the companion of his flight.

Red Ralph thought that at last his time was come.

The ivy bent nearly double, and—

He felt a hard substance beneath his feet.

A projection of stonework.

He glanced downwards again.

There, at his feet, at the very nick of time, was a stone ledge, projecting from a niche or opening in the wall, which was but very imperfectly hidden, now that he was close upon it, by the ivy.

He quitted his hold of the ivy by one hand, and clutched the stonework at the side.

Then dragged himself in bodily.

It was a dangerous feat, but the only thing which could work his salvation now.

Bill Jenkins had made a second step below the level of Red Ralph's resting-place, and had come upon a very ugly stage in his journey.

He was at a standstill.

In this predicament he looked up for advice or consolation from his companion.

Red Ralph was gone.

Disappeared.

For an instant Bill Jenkins imagined that the captain of the Yellow band had missed his footing and perished miserably.

But no.

This could not be.

He must have heard at least the noise of his fall, if nothing else.

He was growing hopelessly confused upon the point.

Suddenly a voice whispered cautiously from above.

Although the tone was low and wary, there was no mistaking the voice.

It was Ralph.

But where?

The ivy just above was pushed aside, and there Bill Jenkins saw, to his no trifling satisfaction, the captain of the Yellow Band snugly ensconced in the niche.

It had been originally intended for a statue, but Bill Jenkins thought that our bold hero filled it to much better advantage than the greatest of Michael Angelo's *chef d'œuvres* could have possibly done.

"Hist!"

"All right."

"Climb back," said Ralph.

"Room for another?"

"Come on—quick!"

Jenkins needed no second invitation.

He climbed up much faster than he had descended.

Three strides upwards and a few pulls brought him on a level with the captain of the Yellow Band again.

"Capital," said Ralph.

"Saved."

"I hope so."

"It couldn't have been better, just at the proper time."

He leaned out and glanced upwards, for they could yet hear the commotion over head.

"Be careful," said Ralph.

"All right, captain."

"Any one there ?"

"Yes."

"Who ?"

"That fellow who set the dogs upon us."

"I thought that I had settled him."

"No."

"Look out."

"All right."

"Ah ! he's looking this way. Ware hawk ! Here comes a stone !"

They drew back, and a huge stone, loosened from the top of the church tower, came rolling down, and passed harmlessly by.

"Missed !" said Jenkins.

"Vicious brute !" exclaimed the captain of the Yellow Band between his teeth. "Take that !"

And, stretching forth his arm, he fired a pistol straight upwards at the whipper-in.

CHAPTER CXV.

RED RALPH ON THE ROAD — THE LONELY MOOR — THE HUT — A FEARFUL SCENE — RALPH ON THE ALERT — EPHRAIM SKINNER — THE TWO BLACK MASKS — COMBAT — DEATH OF THE MISER'S ASSASSIN.

"HOLD !"

But it was too late.

The shot was fired ere the speaker could interfere, and the mischief, if any, was already done.

It was useless repining now.

"I fear, though," said Red Ralph, "that my imprudence may attract their attention hither."

"I hope not."

"We shall see."

"Hush !"

This exclamation was caused by their observing that all eyes were directed to that part of the wall.

Still they stood a fair chance of escape yet.

Their nook was so well sheltered by the ivy that the captain of the Yellow Band had not been able to discover it when only a few feet from the spot.

Accident alone, as we have seen, had revealed the existence of it to the adventurers, and this only at the very last moment.

No.

The howling mob below had grown silent in their eager search for the fugitives, so suddenly and mysteriously disappeared.

They waited for some considerable time, looking and hunting about in all directions.

Not a trace could they discover.

"They will never be tired of hunting us out," said Ralph.

"All in good time."

"Their perseverance deserves success," said the captain of the Yellow Band. "Don't you think so ?"

"I don't know that."

"In a better cause."

"Ah ! perhaps then."

"They are holding a consultation amongst themselves."

"I see."

"And, by Heaven ! they're clearing off."

"Yes."

"What can all that mean ?"

"I think they mean mischief."

"I see. Great goodness ! they are appointing one of them to watch here."

"Never one."

"Why not ?"

"No single man would venture to accept such a post."

"You will see."

"See, see, he refuses. They quarrel now, and they are all going away together, I believe."

"Right."

It was true.

The mob could not get any one of their number to accept the onerous post of sentinel.

Not even the promise of one-third the entire reward could induce any one to take so hazardous an office.

Yet they prudently kept in their hiding-place for a full hour after the mob had cleared off before attempting to descend.

Then with all haste they clambered down the ivy.

This accomplished in safety, they made gently across the churchyard, towards the quietest part of it, and climbed over a dwarf wall.

In the village, upon the further side of the church, they could plainly see a number of persons about in groups.

Still discussing, doubtless, the extraordinary scene which had occurred in the church.

They therefore avoided this part of the country, and, descending a gentle slope were soon lost to view.

They pushed on with energy for some distance.

"I shall leave you shortly now, captain," said his companion.

"Wherefore ?"

"To return to the Boozing Ken."

"But will not that be dangerous ?"

"No."

"Depend on it they will not hesitate to wreak their vengeance upon you for the disappointment they have suffered after all their labours."

"But they do not even know that it was I who aided you."

"Are you sure ?"

"Certain."

"As you will."

"I shall return there, captain ; but before going I should greatly like to see you exercise your craft upon some passing traveller."

"No," said Red Ralph. "That would be but strange gratitude for preservation from such a great danger as our recent one."

"But I have a great desire to see you on the king's highway."

"Wherefore ?"

"Because report says that you draw out a man's purse by looking at him."

"Pshaw !"

"That you can stop the boldest fellow on the road with a bow."

"Stuff !"

"So report says."

"Report's a common liar."

"Possibly. But there is generally some sort of foundation for what is given out."

"Well, well," said the captain of the Yellow Band, smiling good-naturedly, "since you insist upon forcing your compliments on me, you shall have a turn with me upon the king's highway."

"Good."

Mr. Bill Jenkins was uneasy now until they should come across a likely person upon whom the captain of the Yellow Band could practise his remarkable skill.

They walked on silently until they came upon an open flat country of sterile vegetation.

This was remarkable, as the spot they had just quitted was richly grown and beautifully wooded.

Some distance on they perceived a low cottage, or, rather, a hut.

It had a miserable aspect—cold, bleak, and deserted—on that barren moor.

"That's a dull dreary place to live in," observed Red Ralph.

" Ay, indeed."

" I could not contentedly pass my life there."

" Nor I, i'faith."

They walked nearer to it.

Presently Red Ralph perceived that it was the mark of observation for others than themselves.

Two masked men lurked about and peered through the window.

Then one opened the door stealthily, and, after peering in, entered.

" On my life," said Red Ralph to his companion, " there is some knavery working there."

" Ay."

" Let us draw nearer and see what it means," said Ralph.

" Come on, then."

And they ran as lightly as they could up to the hut.

But before they could get near enough to offer any opposition such a deed of blood had been wrought as is seldom heard of.

A helpless old man — a miser — half-starved and mammon-mad—had been slain.

Murdered in cold blood.

Slaughtered for the piles of gold which he had hoarded with such care for so many years.

As Red Ralph arrived at the window he peered in.

An exclamation of horror burst from him involuntarily.

There a bloody and distressing sight met his view.

Stretched upon the ground, bathed in blood, lay the old man who had met so fearful a fate.

" This is awful!" said Red Ralph aloud. " It is— it must be—divine retribution. I see another hand than these base assassins' in this bloody deed. Ephraim Skinner—false steward—false servant—'tis thus that your delinquencies are punished. But murder must not be done with this temerity. Might is right for me as well as these ruffians and murderers."

Darting forward, he stood before the door, and faced the two men as they left.

" Hullo!"

" What now ?"

" Villains !" said the captain of the Yellow Band. " Yield all your booty on the instant."

" Pshaw !"

" Put down your money bags and go ere I slay you."

" You ?"

" Even I."

" You are bereft of sense, my friend," said the masked robber, " to talk thus to two armed men."

" A fig for you and your arms," said the captain of the Yellow Band.

" Ah !"

" Draw and defend yourselves."

" Fool !" cried one of the masks. " You have pronounced your own doom in these words."

" I shall take my chance of that."

And with this he attacked both of the black masks with such vigour and agility that they had to beat a hasty retreat to recover their guard.

Red Ralph had sprung forward so suddenly that Bill Jenkins had scarcely divined his intention, and the events which transpired had followed so speedily that he had not had the time to join him.

Unfortunately he was without a weapon of defence of any kind whatever.

However he could not witness an unequal combat without desiring to take a part in it.

He crept up stealthily as he saw the captain of the Yellow Band in his turn hard pressed by the two assassins of the old miser.

He crawled along the ground to one of them, and, clutching him round the legs, suddenly upset him.

" Oh !"

" Too late," cried Jenkins.

Red Ralph, seeing this, made a sudden and furious onslaught upon the other, who was *hors de combat* in the space of a few seconds.

" See after them," said Red Ralph. " I'll go in and see if the old man yet breathes."

" It is useless," said the wounded mask.

" Ah !"

" He will never speak more."

" Villain !"

" Do with me as you will," said he. " The chance is yours. I have fairly lost the day."

The thrust he had received from the captain of the Yellow Band was more serious than it would have appeared.

With these words the assassin of the miser, Ephraim Skinner, sank back and expired.

CHAPTER CXVI.

THE STEWARD—EPHRAIM SKINNER—GOLD HEAPS —BILL JENKINS IN FEAR — AN OVERDOSE OF RICHES—THE INN—THE RUSTICS—A SURPRISE.

THE sight of the old steward quite staggered the captain of the Yellow Band.

Angered as he was against the base assassin who had so mercilessly robbed him of life, and, what was even yet dearer to him, his wealth, Red Ralph could not repress a feeling that these villains had been merely the instruments of retributive justice.

For gold had the old man toiled, lied, cheated, and robbed.

For gold had he fallen.

For gold had he been basely robbed, treacherously slain.

Piles upon piles of bright golden guineas did they find there bestrewing the ground.

" Don't fear to touch it, man," said the captain of the Yellow Band. " We have a right to take all."

" Of course."

" I authorise it."

" And I obey."

" Fill your pockets."

Mr. Bill Jenkins proceeded to obey this command with startling alacrity.

Truth to tell, it suited his humour to a turn.

However, he was hypocrite enough to pretend to have certain compunctions before Red Ralph, after the latter's strong indignation against the assassins, whom he had attacked with such signal effect.

Red Ralph's arguments were as convincing as singular.

" You need not pause, nor think to stain you hands with the old man's gold," he said. " I have such a right to it that did I speak further you would not hesitate an instant."

Nor did he.

It was truly an injustice which the captain of the Yellow Band did him in attacking his scruples thus.

Mr. Bill Jenkins was not very greatly troubled with matters of conscience.

He filled his pockets with such diligence that five minutes found him scarcely able to stagger along beneath the weight of his wealth.

But a misfortune happened to him which seriously deranged his interests in more senses than one.

His clothing was fearfully old and ragged, and the pockets were the only portion of the seedy suit which covered him that could be made to hold together a little.

Just as he loaded, and was struggling happily along under his delightful burden, there was a loud and ominous crack in the pockets of his nether garments.

Then the cold coins came clattering down his legs.

He clapped his hands upon his thighs, but could not stay the current.

The floor was literally smothered with the money.

With a very rueful expression, he stooped down to recover his scattered treasure.

The exertion proved too much for the other pockets, so greatly worn were they.

A tearing noise was heard, and was immediately followed by such a clattering upon the ground as quite startled both of them.

Such a clatter as neither of them had heard for many a long day.

With muttered curses Mr. Bill Jenkins scrambled all over the place, re-collecting his store of valuables.

At length they were gathered up again and placed carefully in a coarse canvas bag which Jenkins found in a corner of the hovel.

Then they started off.

"I tell you what, captain," said Jenkins, "we ain't safe with all this lot o' swag about us."

"Not safe?"

"No."

"Why not?"

"Supposing any one attempted to rob us? and these things will happen you know, captain."

"We should only have to defend ourselves, as we should have to do under any circumstances."

"True, but—"

"But—but the possession of a few guineas doesn't inspire you with such fear, does it?"

"I don't know, captain."

"If you have any doubts about it pray leave the money behind you."

"Eh?"

"There, there, bring it or leave it, it is all one to me, only look sharp."

"I'm with you."

A little further on his fears, which had only been silenced, not got under, broke out afresh.

"Don't you think, captain, that we had better bury the money somewhere?" he asked.

"No."

"But—"

"Throw it away."

"Never."

"Then do what you will with it. Stay, I've an idea. Would you like to become one of us?"

"One of you?"

"Ay, one of the Yellow Band."

"I should indeed."

"Then you've but to swear truth and loyalty to us, and you are a Yellow Boy."

"Good. When can I join the band?"

"As soon as you please."

"At once?"

"As you will."

"At once be it, then."

Red Ralph then gave the newly-enlisted Yellow Boy instructions as to where he should find the remnant of his bold followers.

As they walked on they issued out of the flat barren country into a well-wooded and pleasant part.

They passed along a very picturesque road, with a long row of overhanging chesnut trees, which made it a handsome grove, shutting out a great deal of daylight.

"A pretty spot," said Red Ralph.

"Yes, but—"

"But again."

"But rather dangerous."

"How dangerous?"

"For people carrying any property."

The captain of the Yellow Band burst into a loud laugh.

"Fore gad!" he exclaimed, "you are a marvel, Bill Jenkins."

"How, captain?"

"Do you imagine that we are to fall into an ambuscade here?"

The words were barely uttered ere a huge stone, hurled from an invisible quarter, whizzed past within an inch of Red Ralph's head.

Before speaking even the slightest word of surprise or fear the captain of the Yellow Band sprang aside and darted off.

Nor did he pause until he was fairly out of danger.

"Where could that have come from?" he exclaimed now.

"Ha, ha," said Jenkins.

"A hidden foe."

"Precisely. That's just what I've been trying to arrive at, captain—an ambuscade."

"Oh!"

"Well."

"An ambuscade, forsooth?" said the captain of the Yellow Band.

"Well, is it not?"

"An ambuscade?"

"Ay."

"Perhaps; but in a very mild form you will admit."

"Granted."

"And there is no great danger to be apprehended from such a cur as he who threw that."

"Perhaps."

"You are pusillanimous, Bill Jenkins," said Red Ralph.

"You slighted my warning before, remember," quoth Jenkins, "and this proves that I was not altogether wrong in what I advanced."

"Not altogether."

"No."

"But for such danger as that which I have experienced I wouldn't give a snap of my fingers."

"I wouldn't give anything for it," said Jenkins contemptuously.

"No," returned Red Ralph, "for in truth I believe that you would sooner be without the danger altogether."

"You've hit it there, captain."

"Come on, then."

"But how about this?"

"What?"

"This foe."

"Oh! that for him," cried the captain of the Yellow Band, snapping his fingers contemptuously. "That for him."

"At your service of course, captain," said the newly-enlisted Yellow Boy. "I would hunt him out."

"Why?"

"Who knows what may be his object in lurking there."

"Plunder, possibly."

"Or spying."

"And what have we to fear?"

"Much."

"I don't see it."

To this Bill Jenkins was about to make some hasty reply when a look from his new captain stayed the words ere they were spoken.

They walked on in silence.

The fears of Bill Jenkins were silenced only—not destroyed.

The captain of the Yellow Band thought nothing more of it.

It had been better for them if he had paid more attention to it.

Then he might have avoided many disasters.

Many mishaps were yet to befall our bold hero.

Whilst he walked on thus unconcerned a spy was lurking behind out of sight.

Yet never once was he or his companion lost sight of.

With the pertinacity of the bloodhound his steps were dogged.

After a couple of hours' hard march they paused to refresh themselves at an inn on the roadside.

Here they called for wine and something to eat.

The landlord obeyed them with alacrity, and they partook eagerly of the refreshment placed before them.

Whilst they were thus pleasantly engaged two farmers entered the room and saluted them.

The captain of the Yellow Band returned the salutation and continued his meal in silence.

The two farmers however grew chatty, and insisted upon not only taking part in the conversation, which they gradually drew Red Ralph and his companion into, but even in placing themselves at their table.

Ralph was good-humoured, and did not offer to resent this unwarrantable familiarity.

Presently two more men—apparently rustics—entered the room.

These, like the others, drew up to the table and joined in the conversation, which now began to take an unpleasant turn.

A dispute was forced upon Red Ralph in spite of himself.

Suddenly, and without any previous warning, one of the latest comers rose and walked to the fireplace, which was behind Red Ralph.

He then stole up to him, and, throwing his arms around him from behind, held him in a vicelike grasp.

The other drew a pistol and presented it full at our hero.

"Ah!"

"Hullo!" said Jenkins.

"Attempt not to stir," ejaculated the man holding the pistol, "for nothing can save you now."

"What mean you?"

"Red Ralph—"

"Ah!"

"You're my prisoner!"

CHAPTER CXVII.

A STRUGGLE FOR FREEDOM — THE WARRANT—
ARNOLD THE THIEFTAKER — AN OFFER OF
LIBERTY—A WAGER—"WHERE IS BILL JEN-
KINS?"—ESCAPED.

THIS was a startler.

But Red Ralph was not so thoroughly taken by surprise but that he was almost immediately alive to the emergency.

With a dash he endeavoured to shake off his assaillant.

It was a vigorous effort, but the man had him at such a disadvantage that to escape his toils was now a matter of impossibility.

He struggled and wrestled boldly, but all in vain.

And Bill Jenkins?

He had been so busily engaged in looking after his newly-gotten gold that he had fallen an easy prey to this strange ambuscade into which they had fallen.

The four rustics were speedily re-inforced until the place was swarmed with people.

To battle further against such fearful odds was sheer insanity.

No.

Escape, if indeed it was possible, must be effected by subterfuge and deceit.

But could anything avail him now?

We shall see.

When he had fought and struggled himself breath-less, leaving the evidences of his handiwork about him in all directions in the shape of broken furniture, glasses, black eyes, and many a damaged proboscis, he began to ask the reasons and their right for this unwarrantable attack.

"Right?" ejaculated one man, who had swallowed a couple of teeth in the struggle. "We've got you tight enough now; so as for the right, it doesn't matter a great deal."

"But you cannot—"

"Yes we can."

"Ha! ha! ha!"

"You cannot arrest me unless you have a warrant."

"We can."

"We have."

And another roar of laughter greeted this sally.

"As for that," said one of the men, stepping forward, "I can settle it with this."

His left hand contained a motley-coloured handkerchief, with which he was drying the blood and endeavouring to assuage the anguish of his bleeding nose.

His right hand held a warrant for the apprehension of a certain notorious robber named Red Ralph, the ringleader and so-called captain of a gang of notorious highwaymen known as the "Yellow Band."

Now the blood-stained handkerchief was as prominent as the warrant, and it was, for a moment, difficult to see with which he meant—to quote his own expression—"to settle it."

"What is that?" demanded the captain of the Yellow Band.

"A warrant."

"For what?"

"Your apprehension."

"Whose?"

"Yours—Red Ralph's."

"How know you that I am Red Ralph?" he demanded sternly.

"Plenty can identify you."

"Where?"

"Here."

"No one knows me here."

"Why I will tell you. Your companion shall settle it for you at once."

They turned and appealed to Bill Jenkins.

But from this worthy they could not glean much that was satisfactory.

Mr. Bill Jenkins was as tricky as a fox.

"Who is this?" asked one.

"That? Oh! that's my esteemed and honoured master, gentlemen," said Jenkins—"my master — Sir John Wingfield."

"What?"

"Pray spare him. Rob me, if you will, but spare him."

"What does the fellow mean?"

"Take all my money, but, oh! spare my master!"

"Is this really Sir John Wingfield?" demanded one of the men, already a little staggered by Bill Jenkins's bold assertion.

"No, no."

"He is."

"Will you swear it?"

"Ay. Propose the oath."

"Never believe him."

"He lies."

"No, I don't."

"He does," cried a voice from the back of the room.

"Who says so?"

"I."

And the speaker pushed his way through the crowd, and stepped up to the prostrate robber-chief.

"What?" said he. "Will you allow yourselves to be gulled by such a spooney as this?"

Jenkins was about to protest against the epithet when the other interrupted him.

"This fellow," he said, "you should all know well."

"Ah!"

"Who is he?"

Mr. Bill Jenkins grew just the least bit uncomfortable.

"Who? Why Bill Jenkins, the Rum 'un, to be sure."

"What, Bill Jenkins, the Plummy Dip?" cried one.

"The same."

Jenkins protested that he was Sir John Wingfield's servant, and none other.

But all in vain.

He swore by every saint in the calendar that he did not even know that such a person as Bill Jenkins was in existence.

But he might as well have spared his breath, as we shall see in an instant.

"It's no use, my friend Jenkins," said the rustic. "I know you too well. And as for the captain here, I can see that he has half recognised me, although he's puzzled to say where he has met me before. Is it not so, captain?"

Ralph was silent.

"I'll show you," said the rustic, "and settle your curiosity."

With this he took off a wig and false sandy whiskers, and stood there close-cropped and bald-faced.

A white smock was drawn off in a second, revealing beneath it the well-remembered uniform of the officers of the law.

The livery of Newgate.

The face, too, could not be mistaken.

It was Arnold the thieftaker.

Considerably altered from when we last saw him, but, nevertheless, sturdy again.

The tussle he had had with Red Ralph during the latter's convalescence, and the pistol wound he had received from the Yellow Boy's fair nurse, had left their marks.

But a stout frame and a strong constitution had powerfully resisted the evils thus wrought, and Arnold's pet revenge was now to devote his whole time—his entire wit and energy—to the capture of the bold leader of the Yellow Band.

"You know me, captain?"

Ralph nodded.

It was useless now to dissemble further.

"Tit for tat!"

He said this with a malicious grin.

"Not so," said Ralph.

"How?"

"You don't enjoy revenge enough to take all this trouble on my behalf for that."

"For what, then?"

"Money."

"Nay—"

"Oh! I know that too well. No man-hunter could have spirit enough to hunt down a poor wretch unless there were some bright golden guineas hanging to it."

"It's false."

"'Tis true, and you know it."

"'Tis not, I swear," said Arnold, earnestly. "For I would have had you had there not been a farthing to gain. I swore so when I got that infernal ball in my neck."

"You owe me no grudge for that."

"Not you?"

"No."

"Who then?"

"Ah! No matter. It was not my hand that fired the shot."

"Now, hark ye, Red Ralph," said Arnold, drawing near, and speaking in a low tone. "I'll show you that, in spite of your sneer, I am not quite so mercenary as you would suppose."

"Prove it."

"Tell me who fired that shot, and you are free."

Red Ralph looked earnestly into his countenance, and there he read only sincerity.

"No, Arnold," he said. "I believe you now, and fairly own that I wronged you, but—"

"You will tell me who it is?" said Arnold, eagerly.

"No."

"Why not?"

"Because the hand that fired that shot saved my life, did me great service, and was a friendly hand. Never shall it be said that Red Ralph betrayed a friend."

"Consider."

"I have."

"Your liberty."

"It is useless."

Arnold knew well the determination of Red Ralph's character, and forbore.

It was, as he saw, indeed useless to press him further upon the point.

Indeed he anticipated the result in proposing it, and did it more with the purpose of showing the Yellow Boy, after his sneer at the thieftaker's mercenary character, that even he could afford to pay for revenge.

"Before we start," said the captain of the Yellow Band to Arnold, "a word with you."

"A dozen, Red Ralph, if you wish," returned the other.

"What reward do you get?"

"For your capture?"

"Ay."

"Five hundred pounds."

"Good."

"But out of that I have about a hundred and fifty expenses."

And here he glanced around at the room-full of assistants about him.

"All your men?" asked Ralph.

"All."

"Regulars?"

"Redbreasts to a man."

Ralph was not a little surprised at this.

"What is it you have to say before we start?" asked Arnold.

"To be sure. Will you wager me fifty pounds that I am not out of limbo before forty-eight hours are over?"

"I will."

"Done."

The disguised thieftakers crowded eagerly round to hear this singular wager made.

They well knew that it was something more than an idle boast upon the part of the captain of the Yellow Band.

"You will lose that wager, Arnold," said Ralph, quietly.

"Perhaps."

"I know it."

"Enough, Red Ralph," said the thieftaker. "Let those laugh who win, you know."

"Do you deem me a braggart?"

"No."

"But you think that I overrate my powers?"

"Perhaps."

"Now, then, I'll tell you what. I will make you a wager also that before three days are past I will cry quits with you for this last turn you have done me."

Arnold hesitated.

[THE BOY SAVAGES.]

Every eye was turned upon him now, and he felt exceedingly ill at ease.

It was clear that he scarcely relished the proposal.

"What d'ye say?" quoth the captain of the Yellow Band.

"Now, Arnold," said one of the men, jeeringly, "your answer."

"Arnold doesn't care for it," suggested another.

"Looks queer."

"Funk fever."

"Death and furies!" ejaculated the thieftaker, thoroughly aroused by this. "What do I care for the boasting of a manacled prisoner who has more brag than brains?"

"O-ho!"

"Bravo, Arnold!"

"So, so," said the captain of the Yellow Band. "You are only reckless of the consequences because you deem it impossible that I should escape."

"No, no."

"It's clear enough."

"No matter."

"Do you accept my wager?"

Every one waited anxiously for the thieftaker's answer.

He could not get out of it with decency now.

"I do!" he cried. "Fifty pounds, Red Ralph, that you are not quits with me before three days are past!"

No. 39.

"Good."

His acceptance of the challenge was greeted by the whole room with a murmur of applause.

"Now then," cried Arnold, "let us move forward, or we shall never arrive. You, Quilter, take charge of Bill Jenkins."

"Yes, Mr. Arnold."

And the speaker turned to see where the prisoner was.

"Where is Bill Jenkins?"

No one could reply.

He had gone!

Vanished!

Disappeared as if by magic!

It was during the confusion which prevailed that Bill Jenkins, taking advantage of the all-attracting importance of his fellow-prisoner, had contrived to wriggle himself out of the parlour window.

Thence to the road, and he trusted to a clean pair of heels for the rest.

"Now," said Mr. Bill Jenkins, as he ran off, "I'll just go and put the captain's pals, Dick Turpin and King, up to this little job, and see what good they can do."

CHAPTER CXVIII.

THE RIVER—MOONLIGHT RACE—THE BOATS—THE WAGERS—A DESPERATE DIVE—SCUTTLING A BOAT—A GENERAL BATH—THE KNIFE—ARNOLD IN PURSUIT STILL—RED RALPH SQUARES RATHER EFFECTUALLY.

FOR a moment the reader must permit us to skip over twenty-four hours.

It was evening.

Starlight and moonlight illuminating the muddy Thames and making it sparkle with a thousand silver ripples.

Near to the haunts of the Alsatian bullies—glorious Whitefriars of notorious memory—a little rowing boat—one solitary frail barque—was launched upon the waters, and in stepped, as it was shoved off, two personages of whom this history has more than once treated.

Their movements appeared to be conducted with all possible secrecy and despatch.

They kept continually looking towards the shore.

With anxious eyes they looked from time to time down the coast, and listened intently to the faintest murmur they could catch.

"Now for it," said the last to get into the boat. "Off we are at last."

"Give me an oar."

"Nay, I'll take both. You steer—sharp into the middle of the river—that's it."

And plying the oars vigorously, they shot off.

In a few minutes they appeared out in fine relief in the moonlight.

The only object to disturb the beautiful monotony of the moonlit river.

"That was a desperate leap of yours," said the rower presently as he paused to breathe a while.

"True."

"And venturesome."

"But I had an object in view."

"Oh?"

"A particular aim to serve."

"I see."

"And by the will of Heaven I will yet serve it, if only to spite the cruel insidious foes by whom I am surrounded."

"You are an enigma, Ralph," said the other.

"Right, Dick," said Ralph, for it was our hero. "I can scarcely understand myself at times. Indeed

it very frequently is so; but upon the present occasion I had a double object to serve, else I swear that I never should have taken so much trouble to escape."

"It was worth the venture."

"Right."

They rowed on now in silence for some few minutes.

Both were taken up with the serene and quiet aspect of the glorious old Thames.

They were so much occupied with this that they did not notice that a boat had shoved off from shore.

The oars by which the second boat was propelled were muffled.

And moreover the occupants appeared to be very desirous of avoiding notice at all.

They kept to the side of the river, which was deeply shaded by the high-built warehouses and the private residences along its banks.

Ignorant of all this, Red Ralph and his companion went upon their silent way.

And yet to an observer it must have been clear enough that the second boat was following in pursuit of the first.

Their pace and movements were in every particular regulated by those of the other.

One man in the boat appeared to be giving directions.

Presently his gestures became more animated, and then, as they had drawn up to the other boat, within perhaps twenty lengths, and this unobserved, he gave a signal and they started off in real pursuit.

When this was seen by the occupants of the first boat their pace was visibly increased, and a gallant but unequal race ensued.

"Give me one oar, Dick," said Ralph.

"No, no, impossible, we cannot neglect the rudder."

"Why not?"

"We should be lost beyond redemption."

"Then we are certainly doomed."

"Ah!"

"Don't you see they gain upon us at each stroke they take," said Red Ralph.

"No matter. I'll tease them a bit."

"Stick to it."

"I will."

And he did with a vengeance.

The little misshapen dingey—so unfit for speed—cut through the water like a racer.

But the result was easily to be seen already.

What could one pair of arms do against three?

They could not hope for success under the circumstances.

The distance between the two boats was decreased with startling rapidity after a while.

When within about five boat's lengths the leader of the pursuing boat shouted to the fugitives to surrender.

"It's all up," he cried, "so give in, Ralph."

"Never."

"You'd better."

"Never. But anyhow give me the fifty pounds. I've fairly won it now."

"Granted."

"And the other fifty I'm going to earn."

"So you say; but, supposing that I won, how could I expect payment of the wager?"

"You can't win."

"How so?"

"You've lost one fifty. Now it's a double or quits wager."

"True."

"And if I win—"

"You will find your money ready. I've left it in such hands as will certainly make it reach you."

"Good."

" But how put an end to all parley. Surrender !"

" You have my answer to that."

" You will not ?"

" No."

" Then I shall fire upon you."

" As you like."

" You had best surrender."

" I think not."

" Capture is certain."

" Nay. Anyhow it can be but a chance, and do you know that it strikes me as being a very vague one ?"

" We shall see."

" Whilst, on the other hand, if we surrender, it is certain death."

" Not so sure."

" Oh ! but it is, after what has transpired."

" But—"

" It's no use. You cannot gammon me now."

" Then take that !"

A pistol shot was fired at the side of the boat, with very fair precision, but struck too high.

" Hullo !" said Dick Turpin.

" What now ?"

" It looks awkward."

" Why so ?"

" They mean to sink us."

" And can't you swim ?"

" Yes. But not as fast as they can row."

" We must chance it. Stay. They have given me an idea."

" What is it ?"

" You shall see."

Without further warning Red Ralph threw off his coat, waistcoat, cravat, and boots.

" Give me your clasp knife, Dick."

The other handed it to him.

" What are you going after, Ralph ?"

" You shall see. Row on. Keep them off a while yet."

" All right."

Red Ralph slid the knife into the waist of his breeches, and then as gently as possible rolled over the side of the boat into the water.

Down, down he went, with a deep dive, and disappeared.

" I fear me much of this venture," murmured Dick. " He's too much pluck in him, I fear, to make old bones."

* * * * * *

" What was that?" said Arnold.

A sudden shock was felt in the boat.

A strange effect, as if it had suddenly struck upon a rock.

The words were barely uttered when there was a second blow.

Still they could not comprehend it.

A little while longer, however, and the effect, if not the cause, became apparent.

" Hullo !" said one of the rowers. " I'm ankle-deep in water."

" By jingo ! so am I."

" And I."

" What can it be ?"

" She's been scuttled."

There was no mistake about this.

The boat was settling rapidly.

A few moments more, and all the boatload were scrambling in the water, struggling for their lives.

All could swim, more or less, and there was a general dash at the shore, which was happily at no great distance from the spot.

All struck out this way but one.

* * * * * *

Red Ralph scrambled up the side of the boat, panting and almost exhausted.

" I've done it !" he cried.

" What ?" asked Dick.

" Scuttled her !"

" By jingo ! you have," cried Dick Turpin. " And down she goes like fun. There's a scramble in the water."

" Who's that coming this way ?"

" Who? By Heaven ! 'tis Arnold. He won't leave me."

" He almost deserves to escape."

" True."

" But there's no placing any reliance in these thief-takers."

" No."

" Here he is."

Arnold struck boldly for the boat's side, thinking, doubtless, that he was unobserved.

However, before he could touch the boat Red Ralph hit him over the head with one of the oars, effectually squaring matters.

CHAPTER CXIX.

BILL JENKINS—HIS PLOTS — HOW HE SERVED A FRIEND IN NEED—AN OLD ACQUAINTANCE — SCHEMES — RED RALPH—WHITEFRIARS—JACK PILCH — TOM KING'S RUSE—THE MAGPIE AND STUMP—AN OLD DEVICE RESORTED TO—BOWS AND ARROWS — THE LETTER — TRUE FRIENDS AT A PINCH.

BUT before advancing any further in this direction a retrograde movement is necessary to explain how we find the captain of the Yellow Band in this position.

It will be remembered that we left him a captive once more in the hands of Arnold the thieftaker and an overwhelming body of his men.

Escape then seemed hopeless.

Yet his courage never once deserted him.

He kept up a bold defiant air, which had rather an alarming effect upon his captors.

They well knew that the captain of the Yellow Band—highwayman and robber though he was—was no ordinary prisoner.

They were well aware that he was by no means addicted to boasting or speaking idly of his prowess.

When he preserved such a demeanour under these circumstances it must be that he felt a wonderful certainty in attaining his object.

Precautions almost bordering upon the ridiculous were adopted against his escape.

He was surrounded by the men and a dozen eyes kept upon him all the way.

His slightest movement—his glance—nay, his very breathing was watched most jealously.

Escape could not then be attempted.

Not at present.

Arrived at the prison, the captain of the Yellow Band underwent a preliminary examination.

He was not a little surprised to find that a new charge was brought against him, and one of a most extraordinary and unlooked-for nature.

The clerk read off the formula of indictment prepared against our hero as follows :—

" Ralph, surname unknown and refused by the prisoner, and known as Red Ralph the Yellow Boy, being the ringleader of a band of highwaymen and footpads of criminal notoriety, you are placed here before us charged as follows :—That upon Thursday, the thirteenth day of October, seventeen hundred and ————, you did, by the aid and assistance of one William Jenkins, not now in custody of the law, maliciously slay and murder Ephraim Skinner, the steward and collector of the estates of the Right Honourable Lord Weirton."

Red Ralph could hear no more.

A cry of astonishment, wonder, and indignation burst from him.

"Murder?" he echoed.

"Ay, murder—murder most foul," said the clerk.

"By my hopes of mercy I swear that I am innocent!"

"Possibly."

"By all that's sacred—"

"Enough. A jury of your fellow-countrymen shall tell that."

"But this is a monstrous charge."

"'Tis one to be substantiated."

"Never on this earth!"

"It is."

"How?"

"By witnesses to the deed—eye-witnesses."

"Witnesses?" cried Ralph.

"Ay."

"Produce the perjured wretches, and let them confront me with this monstrous lie."

"They can do that," said a man with his arm in a sling.

He stepped forward as he spoke, and faced the prisoner.

In the space of a few seconds Red Ralph had recognised him, and the whole affair flashed across his mind.

This was the real assassin, whom the captain of the Yellow Band deemed he had slain.

It was he who had dogged his steps through the forest.

It was he who had hurled the stone at Red Ralph from a very secure hiding-place.

Then, failing in effecting a safe retaliation thus, he had calmly and patiently followed on at a respectful distance.

Chance had thrown him across Arnold the thief-taker, and information thus obtained had resulted in Red Ralph's overthrow, as we have shown.

"This man denounces me?" ejaculated Red Ralph.

"He does."

"Ay," said the assassin, "upon such sure proof as shall ensure you a speedy journey."

And here he gave his neck an expressive twitch upwards.

"Witness," said the clerk of the court sternly, "you must remember that this is a court of law, not a tavern. These observations are not permitted in court."

"Very good, sir."

The fellow hung his head and looked uncommonly sheepish.

"Prisoner, what have you to say?"

"To protest against this charge as monstrous—to denounce the base foul lie of that villain there."

"'Guilty' or 'Not Guilty' is all that we require of

"Not Guilty, upon my soul!" exclaimed Red alph fervently.

"Enter the prisoner's plea."

This having been done, some proofs were demanded by the court to warrant the prisoner's committal for trial.

"Stand forward," said the clerk to the witness.

"Proofs, your honour?" said the man. "My best proofs are my own eyes, besides which, if he was searched, the money of the old miser, which he robbed, would be found upon him."

"Has the prisoner been searched?"

Arnold stepped forward.

"Yes, your honour," said the thieftaker, "and this money found upon him."

"And another bag as well," said the prisoner immediately.

Arnold coloured to the temples, and immediately produced another bag from his pocket.

"Which I was about to put down," he said quickly.

The clerk of the court eyed him sharply, and then resumed the examination of the prisoner.

"Now, prisoner at the bar, what have you to say to this?"

"This," answered the captain of the Yellow Band boldly, "that from a distant turn in the road I saw this knave and another, both wearing black vizors, lurking about the hovel in which they basely slew the miserable old Ephraim Skinner. Before I could get up to the spot to offer any assistance they had entered and achieved their damnable purpose. The old miser was slain and robbed."

"Robbed?"

"Ay."

"By whom?"

"The murderer—the base assassin here."

"I protest—"

"Silence!" cried the clerk. "The witness has been heard."

"But, your honour—"

"Silence! If you cannot hold your peace you must be removed from the court. Respect for the court must be preserved."

"How is it, prisoner at the bar," demanded the clerk, "how is it, if the witness slew and robbed the deceased Ephraim Skinner, that you should possess the property about you?"

"That is easily explained."

"Explain it, then."

"The murdered man was scarcely dead when I got up to the spot. I went and accused the two assassins, drew upon them, and attacked them."

"Well."

"One I slew, as I believed, and left upon the ground for dead. The other fled for his life."

"And which of them do you pretend the witness to be?"

"The former."

"How do you account for the possession of the money, then?"

"I looked upon it as mine by right, after the death of the miser."

"A pretty right, truly," said the clerk of the court. "Prisoner at the bar, without further evidence I find here sufficient proof to commit you fully upon the charge of wilful murder of Ephraim Skinner."

Red Ralph bowed respectfully to the decision of the court, and was removed.

So far matters look rather black against our hero.

*   *   *   *   *   *

As soon as Mr. Bill Jenkins had wriggled himself out of the tavern window into the road, and escaped from the immediate danger, he began to turn his attention to the captive.

The captain of the Yellow Band had proved himself a staunch friend.

He had fought like a lion, and had proved himself frank and generous in the highest degree.

He had shared everything thus far with him, and, after himself, Mr. Bill Jenkins felt more affection for our robber hero than for any other human being.

"How can I aid him, though?" he mused. "First, I must see what they are going to do with him. Then I can think, and perhaps plot a little in his service."

This determined upon, he proceeded to put his project into execution at once.

Of himself he could not hope to do much.

The only way in which he could serve Red Ralph's cause was by hunting up assistance.

The first persons to apply to he well knew must be

Dick Turpin and Tom King, which two worthies were much attached to the captain of the Yellow Band.

It was no trifling undertaking to seek them out, for with such roving characters, who had no settled residence, he could not count upon finding them two days together in one place.

However, Bill Jenkins set himself to his task, and, by one of the luckiest of chances, he succeeded in coming across Dick Turpin at the third place he called at.

This was a well-known rendezvous for knights of the road of the first order of their class.

Lest this expression should sound oddly chosen to our readers, we beg to assure them that at the period of our story the roads were so badly guarded, and highway robbery so lightly looked upon, that, in spite of the punishment being a capital one for the offence, it was fearfully rife.

The highwayman was almost a member of society.

We do not think that our expression will be considered too strong when we reflect that Captain Macheath, "the ladies' highwayman," as he was called, was actually visited at Newgate, when condemned to suffer at Tyburn, by all the aristocrats of the day.

But we are digressing.

To resume.

Mr. Bill Jenkins, having found out Dick Turpin, lost no time in unfolding to the bold knight of the road the misadventure which had befallen the captain of the Yellow Band.

"He shall not be long in, then," said Dick Turpin when Bill Jenkins had concluded his narrative.

"I thought that you would aid him," said Bill Jenkins in glee.

"Of course I would."

"And, although I ain't exactly a genius, Dick," said Jenkins, "I can give you a hand in the job."

"Good."

"That is, if money is any object."

"Money?" quoth Dick.

"Yes."

"You've got some?"

"Some!"

"Of course I don't expect much," said the highwayman, noticing the emphasis upon his reply.

"No, no, I don't mean that. What I've got is yours to work with in this job, if it is wanted."

"Thank'ee."

"If it ain't, so much the better."

"Of course," returned the highwayman. "But never fear, Bill Jenkins, that a penny of it shall be used in any other cause than that of Red Ralph."

"Thank'ee, Dick. I know that you're a downright trump."

"But now to settle this little job. If you want to lend a hand you can run off to Tom King."

"All right. Where shall I find him?"

"At the 'Chairman and Crown.' You know the house?"

"Eastcheap?"

"Yes. Tell him to learn at once in what part of the prison Red Ralph is in limbo."

"Good."

"Then say that we shall meet him at the 'Checquers,' in Eastcheap, at dusk."

"Good."

"At midnight we shall go to work."

"All right."

"Stay—one word more. If there is any means of letting Red Ralph know that we are upon the lookout for him let it be done at once."

"All right."

"Off you go, then."

"And I'll meet you with Tom King at the 'Checquers' at dusk."

"Yes."

Bill Jenkins started off, and in a very short space of time found the redoubtable highwayman, Tom King, in the parlour of the 'Chairman and Crown' regaling himself.

King had a couple of fair but frail beauties upon his knees, and was very much flushed with wine.

At first Bill Jenkins scarcely deemed it prudent to confide so dangerous a mission as that upon which he was employed to Tom King in his present state.

However, the necessity for immediate action upon Red Ralph's behalf made him get over the difficulty very speedily.

With some considerable trouble he drew away the highwayman from his two mistresses.

"Well, my noble Jenk — Jenkins, what is it you want with Tom King?" he stammered.

"One word, my Trojan."

"Out with it, then."

"Not here."

"Why not?"

"It is too important to be spoken before so much company."

"But we are all fair and square here. Eh, lasses?"

"Oh! yes. To a man," returned one of the girls laughing.

This sally brought about much laughter and mirth, which threatened to spoil the object of Bill Jenkins's mission for a while.

"Tom, Tom," said Jenkins. "A word in your ear."

"Out with it."

"From Dick."

"What of him?"

"Come with me. It is serious."

Tom King steadied himself at this, and drew a long face.

"What do you mean? Dick's not in trouble again?"

"No."

"What then?"

"Red Ralph is, and Dick wants you to lend a hand at once."

"Ah!"

"But you are scarcely fit to aid us now, Tom, I fear."

"You shall see."

Then, to Bill Jenkins's astonishment, he ran off before he could offer a word of remonstrance.

He was away only a few minutes when he returned, looking quite refreshed.

He had essayed a cold water cure—a remedy which he frequently found effectual.

In other words, he had given the drawer a shilling, to pump upon his head until he came round.

"Now, Jenkins," said Tom King, "come with me, and I'll show you how I work the preliminary steps."

"You can?"

"I will."

They left the "Chairman and Crown," and proceeded at once to Smithfield, where Tom King introduced his companion to a low tavern, of a more doubtful reputation than the other.

As they passed the door Tom King glanced in before entering.

"Ah!" he whispered, pressing the other's arm hastily.

"What is it?"

"Stay here a while. The very man is there."

"Who?"

"Jack Filch."

"Of the jug?"

"The same."

"Pheugh! dangerous."

"Not at all. You come in shortly. Do not appear to have seen me previously. Don't recognise me unless I greet you first."

"I see."

And he pressed his forefinger to his nose in the most knowing manner.

Tom King nodded significantly, and entered the house.

Standing at the bar, drinking from a glass of punch, was a short square-built fellow with bandy legs.

He looked the picture of bulldog strength and ferocity.

His cast of countenance was, to say the least, repulsive.

A square villainous face, with a week's growth of beard upon it, a flat nose, little ferretty eyes, a low forehead, and a shock of thickly-matted mud-coloured hair, and we have the portrait of Mr. Jack Filch complete.

"Hullo, Jack!" cried Tom King, slapping him upon the shoulder as he entered.

"What! Tom?"

"The same."

"Why, where have you buried yourself all this time?"

"Been out of town."

"Where?"

"All over the country."

"Making a tower" (he meant tour) "of inspection of all the goals in the kingdom I suppose."

"No I ain't, you son of a gun," said Tom King. "I've been doing bad business."

"Have you?"

"Awful."

"Sorry to hear it."

And this was the sentiment of a prison jailor, publicly expressed in this fashion.

"Folks do say, Jack," said Tom King, "that you have got the fat job of the whole jug just now."

"What fat job?"

"One of the crack of cracks to look after, and that he has no end of visitors—and we all know what that means."

Here the highwayman slapped his pocket significantly.

Jack Filch shook his head.

"Devil a bit."

"Get along," said Tom King, nudging him in the side. "I know better."

"What do you mean?"

"Why, that Red Ralph, the Yellow Boy, is in limbo at last again, and that you have got him."

"Never."

"Who has, then?"

"Mat o' the Mint."

"How's that?"

"I don't know. All the bits of fat go to Mat now-a-days because Red Ralph managed to slip his darbies and bolt one fine night—the devil himself knows how, for I don't. They take every good job to the south side."

"The south side?"

"Yes. What's that?"

"Nothing; oh, nothing."

Tom King was so delighted at having drawn it out so easily that he could not restrain an expression of pleasure.

However, he speedily perceived that he had attracted Jack Filch's attention, and he changed his tone at once.

"However," said Jack Filch, "my turn must come again."

"Of course."

"Let him lose a prisoner, and then—"

"Gad! I wish he would!" said Tom King with fervour.

"And I too."

"You do?" said King eagerly.

"Ay, with all my heart."

"Well, to tell the truth, I should like to see this Yellow Boy slip his darbies again."

"And so should I."

"You would?"

Tom King pounced so eagerly upon the word that he excited Filch's attention again.

The latter looked up so astonished that Tom King cooled down upon the instant.

"What's all this eagerness for, Tom King?"

"Eagerness?"

"Ay."

"I'm not eager."

"I hope not. I hope you're not up to any games over the way."

"Not I."

"'Cause I'm one of the square—the very square, you know."

"Of course."

"And I wouldn't work nothing that was—"

"Not safe," suggested Tom King.

"Um—yes."

"Unless at a price."

"A price, eh?" And he leered into Tom King's eyes to read what was passing in his thoughts. "Eh? eh? Oh, no, not even at a price."

"Of course not."

"But you ain't a-tempting of a friend of course, Tom?"

"Not I."

Mr. Jack Filch looked rather disappointed at this.

Bill Jenkins, having entered during the foregoing conversation, here put in a word, for he thought that he perceived an opening to buy over Mr. Jack Filch.

"Hullo! Who's your pal, Jack?" ejaculated Tom King.

"He's no pal of mine," said Jack Filch, eyeing Bill Jenkins from his shoes to his crown.

"No pal?"

"No."

"Then it's like his cursed impudence to interfere in a conversation which doesn't concern him."

"So it is."

"But I say—"

"Get out!" cried Tom King with well-affected indignation.

Bill Jenkins slunk away at this, apparently abashed.

He took something to drink at the bar, and then strolled out to await Tom King near at hand.

Presently the highwayman appeared.

"Confound it, Jenkins!" he exclaimed. "You nearly ruined all."

"How so?"

"By your hastiness."

"But he was to be bought over, I am sure," said Bill Jenkins.

"Not he."

"Why, what did he say?"

"Pshaw! He merely threw that out as a feeler. I wouldn't trust Jack Filch any further than I could see him. He's as wily as a fox."

"Oh, if you know the man—"

"I do."

"That alters the case, and I'm sorry I spoke," said Jenkins.

"No harm done."

"Well," said Tom King, "that's done. And now for the next step. I'll show you what to be up to now."

"Good."

"You know the house opposite the west wall of Newgate?"

"The Magpie and Stump?"

"Yes."

"I do, well."

"Go there and wait for me. I shall join you within half an hour at the most."

Bill Jenkins did as Tom King directed, and true to the appointed time he was there.

He had a long green baize bag in his hand, which greatly puzzled Bill Jenkins.

"Can we engage the first floor for a while, landlord?" demanded the highwaymen.

"To be sure, your honour," returned the landlord.

"Good."

"Any commands?"

"A bottle of good sack, pens, and paper immediately."

"Yes, your honour."

They proceeded to instal themselves in possession, much to the mystery of Bill Jenkins, whose curiosity was excited to the utmost by these unexplained movements.

When they were fairly alone, and warranted against all fear of interruption, Tom King commenced operations.

First, he emptied the long green baize bag of its contents.

They were a bow and arrows!

"Hullo! What's that?" demanded the astonished Jenkins.

"A bow and arrows."

"I see. But what for?"

"Wait."

Tom King then proceeded to write upon a slip of paper, which he fastened to the arrow.

This done, he produced a ball of very thin twine, almost like thread, but of great strength.

This he twisted round and round the arrow with much patience in such a way as to have it evenly balanced, that it might not waver in its flight.

"What next?" asked Jenkins.

"Wait."

He coolly finished his preparations, and then began his explanation to Bill Jenkins.

"Now I'll tell you," he said. "I'm going to practise a feat of which I've often read in old romances."

"What?"

"You see that window?"

"The first?"

"No—the second."

"Yes."

"That is Red Ralph's cell."

"Ah!"

"I'm going to put this arrow into that window."

"Can you do that?"

"I think so."

"It is dangerous. If it should be seen they would double all their precautions."

"Ay; but I am an excellent marksman. I have practised a great deal at the bow."

Mr. Bill Jenkins thought the feat looked so difficult of accomplishment that he mentally settled Tom King must have been great at the "long bow."

However, he had an immense respect for the highwayman, or his muscles, and he did not venture to put his witticism into words.

"Now for it."

"One moment," said Jenkins.

"What now?"

"Won't you try the distance with another arrow. First judge of the distance."

"I cannot risk that. If it should fall in the yard and be seen, it might blow the whole concern."

"And if you miss?"

"We must try some other dodge."

"But—"

"Pshaw! man. Silence your fears. I don't shoot to miss."

"Undoubtedly."

"Look into the street. Is there any one about yet?"

"No."

"Throw open the window."

Jenkins did so.

"Now for it."

Tom King then took his stand by the open window and gently raised the bow.

There was an immense interest at stake and the caution which he observed in the execution of this portion of the business was worthy of the venture he tried for.

Breathlessly Bill Jenkins watched the result of the shot.

King slowly drew back the string.

It was gone.

The arrow—conveying intelligence to the captain of the Yellow Band which perhaps might turn his fate, make it life or death for him—had winged its flight through the air.

"Home!" cried Tom King, joyously.

"It has, it has!"

And Bill Jenkins was so immensely delighted at the success of the shot that he actually embraced the sturdy Tom King.

"Wait and watch," said the latter.

"What for?"

"The effect."

"If Red Ralph sees it?"

"Ay."

"But he cannot fail to."

They sat at the window motionless, gazing upon the cell which contained the captain of the Yellow Band.

But no notice was taken of the arrow.

A weary, weary time they waited.

"Perhaps he is guarded," said Jenkins.

"Not probable."

"Or too heavily ironed."

"More likely."

"Or—O Heavens!—"

"What now?"

"If it should not be his cell, after all your trouble!"

Tom King looked quite disconcerted for a minute at this suggestion.

"No, no," he said, "that's not likely either. Jack Filch was quite off his guard when he spoke, and —Ah, by Heavens! Do you see him?"

"Ay. Huzza!"

They could see a male form at the window, and that he made signs of understanding.

But they could not see his features from that great distance.

CHAPTER CXX.

NEWGATE—A STRANGE ENCOUNTER—THE GIPSY—RALPH'S WOES—THE CELL—NIGHTFALL—THE ARROW—THE ROPE LADDER—LIBERTY—ALARM—LAURA DELANE—A LATE VISITOR—DIFFICULTIES ANEW—MYSTERY.

RED RALPH was taking the regulation constitutional in the prison yard on the day of his capture, when an incident occurred to him which caused his captivity to sit upon him more irksomely than before.

It made his life a misery.

The bitterest anguish was his.

It was this.

Seated in a remote corner of the prison yard was a dark swarthy youth who appeared only to desire to court solitude and grief.

There was something about the boy which attracted our hero's attention.

His deeply bronzed skin pronounced his race at once.

As Red Ralph drew near to him he could not help thinking that, although he had not yet seen the boy's face, there was a something familiar to him in his outline.

We have already said that the captain of the Yellow Band spoke the Romany jargon well, and in this dialect he addressed him, in the hope of giving the boy some little comfort should he prove moderately worthy.

"What is the forest bird's grief?" asked Ralph.

The boy looked up, showing his fine dark eyes dimmed with tears.

Before he could reply Red Ralph had again spoken to him.

"Why, is it not Lemuel?" he exclaimed.

"The same," said the gipsy.

"And do you not remember me?"

"I do," said the boy, with a shudder, "and would that I had never seen you!"

"Why?"

"You have brought me sorrow."

"I? How?"

"Did you not bring into our tribe the beautiful pale-faced house-dweller?"

"My wife?"

"I know not if she be your wife. I mean Mina's pale sister."

"Yes—Leonore. What of her? She is all goodness—gentleness itself—and would not harm a dog."

"No, no, I know it."

"Then how can she have brought unhappiness into your tribe?"

Lemuel then related to his fellow-prisoner the abduction of Lady Leonore, his own share in it, and his vow to recover her.

He had, he said, traced Jonas the outcast to a fine house in a square near the water.

Here he had assailed him with reproaches, and, upon these being replied to by taunts, blows had been exchanged between the foster-brothers.

A disturbance had ensued, and he had been delivered over to the custody of an officer by some grand lady.

Red Ralph in an instant divined the full force of this misfortune.

The boy described the spot to him, and he found out at once that it was to Glyde House that Jonas the outcast had been traced.

Red Ralph was in a dreadful state of mind.

What might have befallen his beloved Leonore he did not dare to imagine.

However, it only served to strengthen his determination to escape, and that, too, without any loss of time.

When he returned to his cell he found that they had doubled their precautions.

Some of the heaviest irons which the prison contained were put upon him.

Still he did not despair.

Evening arrived, a few hours only having elapsed, although it appeared to Red Ralph that years had passed, and found him sitting moodily awaiting the final visit of the turnkey for the night, that he might commence his preparations.

For already had his fertile imagination been at work, devising a plot of escape of which he had the greatest hopes.

As he sat upon the corner of his wooden bedstead the rattle of something against the window caught his ear, and he glanced upwards.

An arrow flew into the cell, and fell upon the other side.

Scarcely deeming that it could contain such hopeful tidings as it really did, he hastened to secure it.

It was only achieved with the greatest difficulty, on account of the tremendous weight of his irons.

They seemed to bear him down to the ground.

He had no sooner secured it than he heard the dull regular tramp of the jailor without.

Quick as thought he snapped the arrow in two, and, doubling it up, thrust it under his vest.

The door was opened, and the jailor peeped in to see the prisoner.

Now Red Ralph was seated once more upon the edge of the wooden bedstead, looking the impersonification of peace and tranquillity.

The jailor nodded familiarly to the prisoner.

"Not gone yet, Red Ralph?"

"Not yet."

"I thought you would find it awkward this time."

"Perhaps."

"Oh! you will."

"I'm in no hurry."

"A good thing that."

"I can wait."

"Well, I can't," said the jailor, "and so I'm off."

And nodding his good night, the man disappeared.

Red Ralph, however, was so full of precaution, now that the moment for action had arrived, that he would not attempt to stir from the same peaceful attitude until he heard the retreating footsteps of the jailor die away in the stone-paved passages.

Then all his serene air disappeared of a sudden.

Up he sprang, in spite of the weight of his fetters, all life and activity for his enterprise.

"Now for my winged messenger," said the captain of the Yellow Band.

He drew forth the broken arrow, and pulled off the paper which was fastened to it.

It was writtten in one of the cyphers of which a select circle of *chevaliers d'industrie* only were the masters.

It ran thus :—

"*Dear Pal,—Your chum, the Monarch, watches your window from without, like a second Blondel with a Richard of the Lion Heart. Take the cord which is wound round the arrow, and preserve it whole. At midnight, after the third watch has gone its rounds, cast one end of it from your window to the right, over the wall. Something shall be affixed to it, which you will draw up, and then—Huzzah for liberty!*"

"Oh! this is gratifying," said Red Ralph in joy. "At least I find that I am not alone in the world, which is a solace to the heart."

He read and re-read this strange epistle, which was without a signature.

For some time he was not a little puzzled to understand from whence it came.

"'*Your chum the Monarch,*'" he read. "Ah! of course, *the King!* Glorious Tom King! Brave heart!"

He proceeded to unwind the twine from the arrow, and found it to be of sufficient length to reach a great distance.

He suddenly bethought him to look out of the window for his friend who watched for him.

He managed, with great difficulty, to move his bedstead to the window and look out.

Even now he could see no one, but he deemed (and justly) that he was watched from an unseen corner, and he bowed and made signs of recognition for his friend's satisfaction.

It was with great difficulty that he contrived to wait until midnight.

Two hours had not elapsed after the departure of the jailor ere he had contrived to cast off his fetters.

Then he clambered up to the window, impatiently to await the arrival of midnight.

[RALPH SHOWS HIS TEETH.]

At length the iron tongue of St. Sepulchre struck the midnight hour, and Red Ralph prepared for his escape.

He fastened a small stone to the end of the cord and cast it forth.

"Such a throw must import good omen throughout," murmured the captain of the Shadow Band.

He was successful the first time.

The stone fell without the high prison wall.

The trusty friends awaiting him soon affixed the promised implements to it.

He drew it up, feeling a tug at the end, which he interpreted aright as a signal, and found fastened thereto the end of a stout rope ladder of immense length, in one of the loops of which was inserted a fine sharp file.

"How thoughtful!" said the prisoner. "Well, well, it's hard if I can do nothing with this."

He completed the preparations, snapped through the bars, and ventured forth.

It was a fearful height—a desperate venture—but he was determined now to risk all or perish.

Arrived upon a level with the top of the prison wall, he paused a while for breath.

Then swung upon the rope ladder until he caught some of the projecting spikes.

Thus aided, he pulled himself on to the top of the

wall, and the rest of his escape became a comparatively easy matter.

He found Dick Turpin and Tom King awaiting him at the bottom of the wall.

Not a word was spoken.

They silently grasped each other by the hand, and led off the rescued prisoner to the end of the street.

Here they found a hackney coach awaiting them to bear him safely off.

The driver gave Red Ralph a signal of recognition as he jumped into the coach.

It was Bill Jenkins.

They had only gained the end of the street—the prison was yet in sight—when they heard a strange commotion in the courtyard of the prison.

"Discovered already?" said Ralph.

"Yes, the watch."

"Of course. But I thought that the last patrol had gone his rounds."

"It seems not."

Evidently the escape of Red Ralph had been discovered, though how it had been effected was as yet a mystery to the authorities.

"Drive on sharp," said Turpin.

"All right," replied Bill Jenkins. "I'm off, double quick."

And he drove on at a gallop.

Then a few seconds more, and the large gateway was thrown open, and out rushed a whole posse of jailors and officers.

"Drive for your life," said Tom King.

"All right."

It began to look like a chase.

He made with all speed for the "Checquers," in Whitefriars, where Red Ralph and Dick Turpin quitted their two companions.

Fearing pursuit now, they immediately made for the river, where they found a boat at the water-side.

They cast this loose and shoved off.

What followed we have already seen.

We take up Red Ralph's further movements from his moment.

Arrived some distance up the river, he landed upon the opposite side, and made for the house where he had quitted Laura Delane.

We cannot give an adequate description of the joy she manifested at seeing him return.

The deep love she bore him was apparent in every gesture.

"Oh! Ralph, Ralph!" she exclaimed, "I feared that you were lost to me—lost, I would say, for ever."

"Almost, Laura," replied the robber; "but, thank Heaven! I am restored to liberty again."

We shall not dwell upon their rapturous delight at being with each other again.

But it was doomed to a sudden rupture.

Whilst they were engaged in the house in chatting over his late escapade there came a mild modest kind of knock at the street door.

"O-ho!" said the captain of the Yellow Band, "a late visitor. Will you see who it is?"

She looked rather serious.

"Go, go," said Red Ralph. "It is only our friend Dick, I presume."

She ran off without another word.

The door was opened, and then Red Ralph heard a strange noise, which caused him to feel a little uneasy.

"Laura," he called.

But no answer came.

"What can have happened?" muttered Ralph. "Laura, Laura. Why don't you answer, my girl?"

Not getting a reply, he ran, sword in hand, to the door.

The door was wide open, but Laura Delane had disappeared.

Vanished.

There was no sign of her, or of the visitor who had arrived so late.

What could it mean?

Another chapter shall show.

CHAPTER CXXI.

RALPH'S SEARCH—THE PRIVATE INQUIRY OFFICE —USEFUL INFORMATION—THE THREE HORSEMEN — HO! TO THE RESCUE! — RED RALPH —THE SCUFFLE—A GENERAL SKIRMISH—WILD IN DIFFICULTIES.

RED RALPH was amazed.

Lost in wonder.

What could have become of Laura Delane in so short a space of time?

Some misadventure had befallen her—of that he was assured.

He could not rest in peace now.

Something seemed to conspire against his passing a day in undisturbed tranquillity.

He closed the door hastily and ran out.

At the corner of the street he encountered a man, to whom he addressed a dozen questions in an instant concerning Laura's strange disappearance.

The man was quite confused by his address, and could make no reply.

Red Ralph imagined that he perceived in the man's embarrassment some hidden knowledge.

A warm altercation ensued, and they were nearly arriving at blows upon the matter, for in those times the blow followed so quickly upon the word that squabbles were of alarmingly frequent occurrence.

However, Red Ralph recovered his temper in time to see that he was mistaken, and he made matters right with the fellow and left him.

His hot passion, however, had injured his cause in one way.

There was no possibility of pursuing the search now.

Still he could not rest.

He mounted his horse and rode off to his friend's house in Maddox Fields, where he passed the night.

In the morning he was stirring betimes, after a few hours' repose, and off on the same errand.

He called upon several trusty blades he knew, and made inquiries in every direction.

At length his searches were attended with some slight success.

This was in his last journey, to the house of one Matthias Black, a kind of private inquiry agent, who resided in the Mint.

It was the custom here to seek information of missing persons—a necessity, as will be readily understood, in a duelling age—for which a fixed sum was paid as a fee.

"What is it I can do for you, captain?" he asked as Red Ralph entered.

Ralph started.

"You know me?"

"By sight."

"Ah?"

"There is nothing so singular in that," returned Matthias Black. "You are known to many."

"Possibly."

"What is the nature of the business on which you seek me?"

"This. A girl, young, fair, middle height, and under some fear of the law, was last night arrested."

"Yes."

"You know it?"

"I do."

"Then my conjecture was right," thought our hero.

"What of her?"

"I wish to know what has become of her."

"She was locked up for the night."

"Where?"

"Newgate."

"On what charge?"

"A grave one—murder."

"Newgate?"

"Yes. But, as the offence was committed out of the district, she will be removed to the county jail to-day."

"Ah! when?"

"Before midday."

"Thank you."

He paid the fee and departed.

His first care now was to make his way with all possible speed to his trusty friend Dick Turpin.

He found the sturdy knight of the road ready for his service as ever, and apparently much pleased that Red Ralph had another job for him.

"What is the next little matter?" demanded the highwayman.

"You remember the girl I brought to the wood hut?"

"Ay."

"She told us her history."

"She did, poor girl."

"She is again in danger."

"And you would lend her a hand?"

"Yes. It is for that purpose I come to beg your assistance."

"It is yours."

"I guessed as much."

"Say how and where I can serve you, and I will be there."

"I knew it. By the 'Magpie and Stump,' towards midday."

"The 'Magpie and Stump?'" iterated Dick Turpin. "Is it possible that you have not had enough of that neighbourhood yet?"

"Not yet. You shall see that I have good reason this time."

"I doubt not."

"You'll be there?"

"Yes."

"I count on you."

"You may."

And they parted.

Towards midday two horsemen met by St. Sepulchre's Church.

They had not been long there when they were joined by a third.

They only conversed for a few seconds, and then separated.

The first to arrive stayed where he had met his friends, whilst the others took opposite directions.

The latter two drew up again at a short distance off, and then sat silently upon their horses, watching their companion by the church.

This horseman appeared in no way concerned about his two companions.

His only care appeared to be to watch the gloomy entrance to the dark frowning prison.

And there he sat with wonderful patience for fully twenty minutes.

At length his patience appeared to be rewarded.

The door opened, and forth issued some eight or ten officers, all mounted.

In the midst of them, also mounted, rode a girl, bound to her steed.

This was evidently a prisoner.

As soon as our horseman by the church caught sight of the girl he made a sign to his companions upon either side.

Then, burying his spurs deep into the horse's flanks, he dashed forward towards the group of officers.

With one wild bound he was in their midst.

His sword leaped from its scabbard, and he plied it so readily that the officers at first made way affrightedly before his hot charge.

Quick as lightning he was beside the girl.

One arm was flung around her shrinking form, the cords which bound her were severed in a moment, and she was lifted impetuously out of the saddle.

The next instant she was in front of the hardy horseman, dashing helter-skelter through the crowd.

It was a desperate feat.

A bold and daring one.

But would it succeed?

For the present it had, but would it ultimately? This has to be seen.

Before he could get perfectly clear of the gang of officers they had begun to recover from the surprise into which they had been thrown.

He was just upon the point of a glorious success when they closed in upon him with a shout.

It was now a critical moment.

"Yield thee, fool!" cried one of the officers, spurring on to him.

"'Fool' in your teeth!" retorted the gallant horseman.

And with upturned sword he met a desperate cut which was aimed at him.

A blow of his, quickly laid in, took better effect, and the officer, who thought that he had secured an easy prey, was sent reeling from the saddle.

"Ho! ho!" cried the officers.

"Down upon him!"

"Cut him down!" cried another.

"Maim his horse!"

One of the officers, who had probably more prudence than pluck—more stratagem than courage—pulled round his horse to attack the bold stranger in the rear.

But the eagle eye of the latter perceived the intention.

He pressed his toe ever so lightly into the horse's right flank, and caused it to rear up behind in the very nick of time.

"Ho! Nancy lass!" he cried. "Foes to the rear. Kick bravely, lass, and the day is yours, my beauty!"

And Nancy did kick with a vengeance.

The unfortunate steed bearing the officer who had displayed so much prudence suffered for his master's act by having his knees broken.

Down went the horse and rider, and the latter was trampled over by the intelligent Nancy.

"Confound it!" cried one of the officers. "After him, curse you!"

And with desperate impatience he cut through his own men and dashed at the bold horseman.

"What?" cried the latter. "Wild in the saddle again?"

"Ay, himself!"

"Thought you were dead."

"Not yet."

"Blueskin nearly did your work."

"Blueskin!" echoed Jonathan Wild, with an oath, which we suppress. "He can't say that I nearly did his! He's down below."

"Then you shall keep him company very quickly, Jonathan."

"This for your brag!"

And the thieftaker dashed viciously at the horseman.

But the latter, with wonderful coolness, turned aside the cut, and replied with a lightning thrust, which passed through Jonathan Wild's coat, and slightly grazed the skin.

"Curse you!" cried the latter. "You've done for me!"

"I hope so."

Wild indeed thought so, but it was merely one of those flesh wounds which are painful but harmless.

To take a speedy vengeance whilst there was yet time, he gathered up his whole strength into one final blow.

It was a mighty stroke, and was meant to terminate the combat in a summary fashion.

Indeed there is no doubt whatever that this would have decided the combat had it taken effect.

Thanks, however, to the intelligence of the adversary's steed, which seemed to anticipate the blow ere it fell, it was harmless.

"Ho! ho!" cried Red Ralph.

"Ho! ho!" answered echoing voices close at hand.

And the two horsemen whom he had been in conversation with by St. Sepulchre's Church rode up.

Sword in hand, they dashed into the fight.

"One for Tom!"

"One for Dick!"

"And one for Ralph!" cried the horseman who had rescued the prisoner.

And at each cry an officer was unhorsed.

"Ho! ho!" cried Jonathan Wild. "More men ho! To the rescue!"

"Ha-ha!" cried the first of the three horsemen. "You can't manage it alone, Jonathan Wild, after all your boast."

"Liar!"

"Prove it, and do your worst."

But the three officers who alone of the whole body remained in fighting condition seemed not inclined for the worst.

We must do Jonathan Wild the justice to say that he kept boldly to his share of the conflict.

As soon as he discovered that the wound which he had received was not so dangerous as he had at first imagined he applied himself to the contest with undiminished ardour.

Now he was the main point of the assailing party's attack.

All three of them appeared eager to get at him.

By this time the mobs collected were positively startling to behold.

The interest in the fray was immense.

"One more for Tom," cried one of the three bold horsemen.

And another of the three officers fell.

Matters were growing serious.

"Rescue! rescue!" cried Wild.

"Never."

"Help for the law!"

"Stand off, good people," cried the horseman with the rescued prisoner before him. "Death to the first who interferes!"

"Heed him not," cried Jonathan Wild. "Help, in the king's name! and a goodly reward is yours!"

"Stand off! Know, good people, that he who thus invokes your aid with false promises and lies is the arch-knave and traitor, Jonathan Wild."

A roar of execration followed this announcement.

"Death to the traitor!"

"Down with Wild!"

And a shower of stones, mud, and missiles of every description followed.

Wild was alarmed.

It not only looked like certain rescue for the prisoner, but great personal danger to himself as well.

The thieftaker knew that he was not at all popular amongst the people.

The transactions which afterwards brought him into disgrace with that tardy justice which he had so long been supposed to serve were already whispered about, and his name was detested.

"Help! help!" cried Jonathan Wild. "Help for the officers of the king!"

And he blew a signal upon a silver call which he had suspended by a cord from his neck.

"Look out!" cried one of the three horsemen.

"What now?"

"Fly!"

"And leave you? Never!"

"But consider the girl."

"Go, Ralph," said the other.

"Nay—"

"Tut tut, man! Off with ye! We're safe enough. As soon as you're free we'll follow."

"Good."

"Whither?"

"The Wheatsheaf."

"I'm after you."

"*Now, then, together!*"

And the three closed up their rank and dashed forward.

The two surviving officers fairly turned tail, leaving Jonathan Wild alone to contend.

"Now, Ralph, off with ye!"

"Farewell."

"Farewell."

"The Wheatsheaf."

"Look out!"

At this moment Wild had put in a vicious cut which nearly finished the gallant Tom King, who, as our readers have long since divined, was the "Tom" of the three bold horseman.

Dick Turpin turned aside the blow, and it fell on the horse's flank, cutting the poor beast in a frightful manner.

With a snort of agony it rolled over.

Tom King was nearly crushed by the fall.

A second later and there would have been no escape.

But with wonderful agility he rolled aside.

"Curse your chance!" roared Wild.

And he tried to run over him.

But Dick Turpin placed himself before his fallen friend, and combated boldly for him.

In the meantime Red Ralph had made clear off.

"The Wheatsheaf!" cried Jonathan Wild. "I shall be there to meet you, my lads. Look out."

"We shall."

"We do."

And at the very instant that the word was spoken the thieftaker's horse fell to the ground.

Tom King had rolled beneath the horse, and, shortening his arm, he buried his sword up to the hilt in the animal's belly.

"Now one for the rider!" cried Turpin.

He was about to strike.

"Quarter!" cried Wild.

"Give it him."

"Ay," said Dick Turpin. "I'll show that mercy which he would never give us. You deserve a dog's death, Wild, and you shall save your life for the gallows."

"I forgive you that speech," said Jonathan Wild, "and you shall have a chance with me when you are in trouble."

"I want no mercy," cried Turpin.

"Then you shall have it, in spite of yourself," said the thieftaker. "You shall see that even Jonathan Wild can show some gratitude at times."

"Ha, ha, ha!"

The idea of the thieftaker's gratitude struck them as being so excessively comical that they could not restrain their mirth.

Suddenly they heard a clank of musketry.

There was no mistaking the noise.

Dick Turpin looked up and perceived that a number of men had come out of the prison all armed with muskets.

"Now," cried the officer who appeared to command them. "Fire!"

There was a cry in the mob, a scuffle for a retreat, and all of them cleared off with amazing rapidity.

The muskets were brought up to their shoulders at the word.

"Look out Tom," cried Turpin.

"All right."

"Stoop!"

They both bobbed in their saddles, and a volley of musket balls rattled harmlessly over their heads.

"Off and away!"

"Ho! for the road."

"Stay, Tom," cried Dick Turpin. "Supposing that we should miss?"

"The Wheatsheaf."

"I'll be there," cried Jonathan Wild. "Look out and beware of me, for I mean you mischief now."

"You're welcome."

And, in spite of the united exertions of the officers, the two highwaymen beat their way through the crowd and got clear off.

But more of their fortunes in a future chapter.

For the present we have to deal with Leonore Glyde.

If the reader will follow us closely we will give a description of what further befel her after the tragical occurrence which had taken place upon the occasion of our last interview with her.

Events of a serious nature are about to transpire with our heroine.

To these we therefore think it but just to devote another chapter.

CHAPTER CXXII.

LADY LEONORE—NIGHT AND ITS SHADOWS—AWAY
—THE DISGUISE—WEARY AND WAYWORN—THE
OLD MAN—AN ENCOUNTER—CRUELTIES.

WE fear that we have too long neglected the fortunes of our hero's wife, the Lady Leonore.

We left her, as the reader will remember, upon the first night of her return home.

She had dreaded mischief, not understanding why her waiting maid Margaret had not been allowed to attend upon her as before, and descended in the dead silence of the night to the girl's chamber.

Here a fearful scene met her view, as we have already narrated many chapters since.

The horrors of the well-hole have been placed more vividly before our readers by the pencil of the artist than our pen could have done.

After witnessing the fearful horrors which were enacted at the pit of death by these murderous wretches a wild unearthly shriek burst from the girl's lips, and she fled.

The cry which had escaped her yet lingered upon her lips when she repented of it.

What could her horror avail the murdered Margaret now?

Nothing. No, the unhappy creature had fallen a victim to the blood cravings of this vile woman of the world—this civilised wolf who lived upon human blood—fed upon her own species.

It was too awful to have such a being for a mother.

She felt that she could no longer stay beneath that roof.

It was contamination to breathe the same atmosphere as that vile murderess who had hired assassins with base gold to take the life of a poor helpless and unoffending girl.

Leonore did not hesitate an instant.

Bounding down the stairs with alarming rapidity, she gained the street, and ran along as fast as she could.

She knew not and cared not whither she went so that she shut out the fearful vision which had just crossed her path.

Happily she had got a good start of the assassins before they had even discovered who it was who had given the alarming cry as the deed of blood had been accomplished.

She ran along until quite out of breath before she paused.

Then she found herself in an out-of-the-way place—quite an unknown locality to her.

It was a low neighbourhood evidently, from the small dingy houses and the close stuffy smell.

There is a peculiar unpleasant odour which tells of ten human beings or more reposing in a single chamber which ever characterises these localities.

It was quite dark here, and Leonore, suddenly growing nervous, would have retraced her steps had not the flickering light of a tallow candle stuck in a bottle caught her sight as she was returning.

She drew near and found that it was a poor wardrobe shop, and that the proprietor was yet stirring.

Leonore peered in and examined the wares there shown.

Male and female attire of every description was there.

This gave Leonore the idea of making a change in her apparel, for the superior appearance of her clothing at present would undoubtedly excite the cupidity of any one of easy conscience with whom she came in contact.

As she peeped in she could see an old woman seated behind a low ricketty counter half dozing over a parcel of clothes opened and spread out before her.

There looked to be no particular harm here, so Leonore thought that she would enter.

Accordingly she pushed open the door gently and went in.

"Hullo!" cried the old woman, tossing the parcel under the counter and starting up.

"I beg your pardon," said Leonore.

"What now?"

"I want you to sell me something."

"Sell? Oh! my dear, I can do that."

"That is, perhaps you could exchange some clothes with me."

"Yes, I can do that. What are they?"

"These I have on."

"For what?"

"A suit of male attire."

The old woman looked inexpressibly cunning at this, placing her forefinger to her nose, and winking in a most diabolical manner.

"Oh! that's your little game, my dear, eh? Well, well, we can do that much for ye."

"And quickly?"

"At once."

"Very good. Show me some clothes from which I may select."

"Yes, dear. I thought you was here on a very different errand at first, though."

"I do not understand you."

The old woman looked cunning again.

She winked, crossed her old parchment fingers, and gave her head a kind of flash jerk over the left shoulder, which perfectly mystified Leonore.

Seeing her look of astonishment, the old woman vouchsafed a word in explanation.

This, we would observe, left Leonore in a far greater state of bewilderment than ever.

"Don't ye see, my love?" she said.

"I don't know what you mean."

"I thought you was *on the cross!*"

This was as good an explanation as before, so Leonore gave it up.

The only conclusion which she could arrive at was that the old harridane was insane.

The bargain for the clothes was effected, and Leonore was robbed to the tune of about three hundred per cent.

She left the musty wardrobe shop, however, completely transformed from her former self.

A handsome delicate girl had entered.

A slim smart-looking youth, still handsome, left the shop.

Thus changed, Leonore started off upon her travels.

Her only plan was to seek out the captain of the Yellow Band.

But how and where to find him?

It was as difficult to commence such a search as this as any portion of her flight.

The only place at which she had the slightest hopes of hearing of her husband was the house in Whitefriars where he had made so many rendezvous.

To this, therefore, as an only resource, Leonore directed her steps.

That is to say, she determined to make her way to that part of the town as soon as she could inquire if it lay north, south, east, or west.

At present she was so utterly lost that she could not for a moment imagine where she was.

The first thing, then, was to inquire the direction of Whitefriars.

Now even this was no easy matter, for there was not a soul to be met with at that hour.

The only plan which Leonore could think of was to return with all haste to the wardrobe shop.

She began to retrace her steps at once, and looked about after the old woman, but all in vain.

She found all the turnings so alike.

Every street was but a repetition of the one she had just passed through.

Every house seemed in the dark night to be the same as its neighbour.

She was hopelessly lost.

She grew weary with long wandering, and the want of rest began to tell upon her sadly.

At length, thoroughly exhausted with her pilgrimage, she sat down upon a doorstep and wept.

"What a sad fate is mine!" she murmured through her tears.

And in this mournful frame of mind she continued, until, sitting there upon that cold damp doorstep, she sank into a kind of half sleep.

A dreamy kind of stupor came over her, scarcely sleep.

*　　　*　　　*　　　*　　　*　　　*

"My dear, my dear!"

And somebody was pulling gently at her coat-sleeve.

Leonore looked up in a sleepy kind of alarm.

"What now? What?"

"Lor! my dear, how you snap one up!"

Leonore found that the speaker was a miserly-looking old man, very old, apparently, and queer looking.

He wore a long coat, almost down to his heels, which was of the greasiest and most threadbare aspect.

In his left hand he carried an ivory-headed malacca cane.

This, by-the-bye, seemed to be the richest article he possessed.

It was so far superior to the rest of his attire as to be remarkable.

"What do you mean by going to sleep there, my dear?" said the old man.

"I was so tired."

"Well, then, go and be tired upon somebody else's doorstep."

"Oh! is this yours? I'm very sorry."

"Get up, then."

Leonore rose hastily, seeing that the old man was angered, but found that she had already grown cramped and stiff with the cold and damp.

She staggered and nearly fell down.

"Look here, my dear," said the old man. "You ain't well. What's the matter?"

"A little stiff, that's all."

The old man stood quite still, surveying Leonore in silence for several moments.

Before speaking he caught her by the wrist, so roughly as to startle her.

"Look here now, young un," he said. "What's your game?"

"Sir, I—"

"All right, I'm one of the downy ones myself, so out with it."

"I really am at a loss to comprehend your meaning, sir."

"Hoity-toity! you young blackguard. Where did you pick up all that teaser? It quite takes my breath away."

Leonore began to grow just the least bit alarmed now, and would have moved away.

But the old man would not hear of this.

He held her still firmly by the wrist, and she cou'd not possibly shake him off.

"Why do you seek to detain me?" she asked indignantly.

"Keep quiet, you young villain!" said he, "or I'll shake the life out of you."

And, as if in earnest of what was to come, he handled her so roughly that she cried out with pain.

"You hurt my shoulder," she said.

"I'll hurt your back if I lay my cane about it," cried the old man.

"What for?"

"I'll tell you that after."

"Unhand me, or I'll cry for help."

"You'll cry for help, will you? We'll soon see to that."

Then, suddenly raising his foot, he sent the door flying open, and, before Leonore could recover from her surprise she found herself in the passage.

"Help!" she cried.

But before a second sound could come she was flung back and dashed to the ground, the malacca cane which the old man carried cutting smartly across her shoulders as she fell.

Then she heard the bolts shot in the door and the lock turned, the key being removed at once.

This was growing awful.

She knew not what to do or say.

Tamely to submit to this kind of treatment was of course out of all question.

As quickly as possible Leonore rose to her feet, and crouched down in the shadow of the passage.

After the fastening of the door was completed the old man turned towards the spot where he had dashed the unfortunate Leonore.

"Now then," he cried.

But Leonore did not feel at all inclined to reply to this.

Silently she stood her ground, awaiting the arrival of the old ruffian who had so ill-used her.

"Why don't you answer?" cried the old rascal in a minute.

He paused another second or two for a reply, but none came.

Then he began to grow impatient, and he advanced a few steps, muttering aloud as he came, "Curse the young whelp! He's been and fainted, or some fine thing."

But another yard, old man.

One step more, and you will learn that the "young whelp" has not fainted, nor is he near it.

Up sprang Leonore, seizing the old man at random.

She chanced to get a hold upon his coat collar, whilst her left hand sought his neckcloth instinctively.

The grasp dragged him forward.

Then she thrust him violently back, before he could help himself, and down he fell with a crash.

This must have settled his opposition for some time at least.

At any rate, it partially settled accounts for such injuries as she had received at his hands.

Leonore was now thoroughly aroused, and she would not lose an instant in idle thought.

She rushed past the prostrate old ruffian, and made for the door.

Sad failure.

The locks, bolts, and bars which she had heard put up and fastened upon the door quit spoilt her chance of escape.

But for those she had been free.

But no.

Fate was against her this time.

"Ha-ha! my boy," cried the old ruffian, who was picking himself together. "You're puzzled, eh?"

Leonore's heart beat quicker and quicker.

Her hands flew over the door, and as soon as she lighted upon a chain or bolt it was withdrawn.

But yet the lock had to be turned.

Now it was stiff and rusty, and, notwithstanding her great exertions, and the speed employed in her work, she could not manage to effect it in time.

All had occurred so rapidly, too, that five minutes was not passed — not nearly — since she had been thrust into the house by the cunning old ruffian.

Up he rose and scrambled after Leonore.

She felt his long claw-like fingers upon her arm, and made frantic struggles to shake him off.

But all in vain.

Notwithstanding that he was an old man, whilst Leonore had youth and energy in her favour, she found that she could not hope to cope with him.

She struggled boldly, but it was useless.

With a strength of which few persons would have deemed him capable he seized her in his arms and bore her along the passage.

As they got to the end of it Leonore's courage was spent.

She could struggle no more.

Helpless as a new-born child she lay in his arms.

"Ah! my dear, it's all up with you," said the old man, grinning.

He was breathless himself with the struggle which had taken place, but yet he would not be conquered.

He hobbled off through the house, opened a glass door at the end, and crossed a stone-paved yard.

At the further end of this was a stout oaken door, thickly studded all over with iron nails.

It was fastened with an iron bar and a padlock of enormous strength.

Disengaging one arm, he sought a key in his waistcoat pocket and opened the padlock, loosened the bar, and pushed open the door.

As soon as the door was open he let Leonore slip from his arms.

Then he gave her a push forward, and she fell into the room.

She was no sooner here than the door was fastened in a trice, and the bar and padlock replaced.

"Mercy, mercy!" cried Leonore.

But he was gone.

She looked up in fear.

The place in which she now found herself was a low-vaulted cellar, damp and dismally lighted by a flickering oil lamp, suspended from the centre of the ceiling by a short brass chain.

"O Heavens!" murmured poor Leonore. "What horrible place is this? For what fresh horrors am I reserved now?"

She turned back to the door and beat it wildly with her hands.

But the only result from this was that she cut and bruised her delicate white flesh cruelly.

"Mercy, mercy!" she cried. "Pray let me go. I have no money. You shall have it all."

Yet no.

It was evident to her that, whatever might be the old man's motives in making her a prisoner, robbery was not one of them.

What then could it be?

Something worse.

Her heart sunk low within her, and she felt as near to fainting as ever yet she had felt.

"Oh, merciful powers!" she ejaculated. "Is there no escape from this awful place? No escape?"

She ran round the place, but no outlet could she see.

Suddenly her ear caught a faint sigh.

For an instant her heart stood still.

She held her breath, and paused to listen.

What could it be?

There was nothing further for several minutes.

Then a sigh rather louder than before.

In an agony of fear she made up to the oil lamp, unhooked it from the chain, and commenced a search round the vault.

Two steps, certainly not more, were taken, and she found herself before a human body.

Stretched upon the ground, and writhing in pain, lay a poor emaciated looking youth of eighteen or nineteen years of age.

He looked up into Leonore's face with a glance so full of agony that her own woes were forgotten at once.

"Oh! pray have pity! Have mercy upon my sad plight!" he exclaimed.

CHAPTER CXXIII.

THE VAULT — THE PRISONERS — MYSTERIES RE-
VEALED — THE BRUTAL PRACTICES OF OLD
DAN — HOW LEONORE SERVED THEM — THE
ARCHWAY — OLD DAN AGAIN — LEONORE IN
JEOPARDY—THE BOYS TO THE RESCUE—DAN
IN TROUBLE — THE BOYS' VENGEANCE — THE
HATCHET—A SCENE OF HORROR.

"WHAT is it, my poor boy?"

"I suffer, I suffer."

"What with?"

"Want o' grub," said another boy, whom Leonore could not yet see.

She held up her lantern, and found to her surprise that this miserable dark vault contained no fewer than seven or eight boys fastened to the walls with chains and cords.

One had an iron girdle round his waist, to which was attached a long chain.

Another had a pair of handcuffs on, which kept his wrists immovable.

A third wore a pair of iron anklets, from which a huge wooden log was suspended by a short chain.

And the remainder were secured with more or less ingenuity.

But in each instance the mode of securing these poor boys displayed cunning and cruelty.

They seemed to have been fearfully treated, to judge by their emaciated appearance.

Their cheeks were hollow and sunken, and their clothes in rags and tatters, in some instances barely covering their shivering limbs.

"What scene of horror is this?" exclaimed Leonore.

Most of the boys were afraid to speak.

They sat or crouched upon the ground eyeing Leonore askant, as if in fearful anticipation.

"What can I do for you, my poor boy?" she asked, leaning over the first boy who had spoken to her.

"Give me a little water."

"Alas! I have none."

"Get some."

"How can I?"

"Won't old Dan give you any neither?"

"Is he the cruel old man who keeps you all in here?"

"Yes."

"For what purpose?"

"For more purposes than one. He has taken out half my teeth."

"Your teeth?"

"Yes, to sell."

"Great Heavens! is it possible?"

"I'm not the only one."

"No," said the boy who had volunteered the information about the other's hunger. "He's served me the same, only I took out some of his molars too, with a right-hander straight from the shoulder. Only he couldn't sell them if they had been worth anything, 'cause he swaller'd 'em."

"But how came you tied down like this?" demanded Leonore.

"Old Dan did it."

"How?"

"One at a time, of course. If he had tried it on any other way we should have risen against him and put him down."

"It is really a mystery to me," said Leonore. "What can his purpose be?"

"Teeth is one of 'em."

"But after?"

"A knock on the head perhaps," said the boy.

"He dares not let you out after committing such an atrocity."

"No; yet I don't see why he shouldn't, for he picks us out artfully. Oh! he's as artful as the devil himself. He knows that we're most of us 'wanted.'"

"Wanted?"

"Yes, by the big-wigs."

"What for?"

"Stash your mag," said one of the boys, now speaking for the first time. "Don't you see as the cove's square?"

Leonore had in the course of her wanderings with the gipsy tribe picked up sufficient slang or Romany expressions to catch the meaning of the words which the boy uttered.

She comprehended it all now.

That hoary old villain, "Old Dan," as the boys called him, was in the habit of securing these poor misguided boys, who had early been trained to dishonesty, and actually bartered them like so much merchandise.

Atrocities of another nature were also reported to be in practice, of which Leonore had heard.

Boys had frequently been decoyed away, and, having disappeared, their bodies had been found in the hands of surgeons and students, who had purchased them of supposed resurrectionists, or bodysnatchers.

This then was no doubt one of the sources of profit to the old villain Dan.

He bartered the boys' teeth to the dentists, and then doubtless slew them by a slow poison before selling them to anatomists for dissection.

As Leonore thus reasoned a cold shiver went through her from head to foot.

What if she were thus horribly treated?

Supposing even that her life were spared, how could she hope to face her husband again, her beauty mutilated by the abstraction of her pearly white teeth?

"I say," whispered the boy who had given her all this startling information. "Will you keep mum?"

"What?"

"You won't peach—split, blab, blow the gaff on us if I put you up to a downy dodge?"

"No, certainly."

"You'll keep it all from old Dan?"

"I will."

"Then if you was to give us a hand we could all get out of this place as nice as ninepence."

"How?"

"Undo my blessed handcuffs."

"Tell me how."

"Bring the lantern. So. Now pick up that nail. Do you know how to use a picklock?"

"I'll try. Tell me how."

"That's it. Put the bent end in, turn it round and —so."

With a wild shout of joy he threw his arms in the air.

Such joy it is to experience freedom after bondage.

"Oh! give us a hand, Joe," said one.

"And me, Joe."

"And me."

"All right. One at a time. You must all of you thank this sweet cove."

"We do, we do."

"As for old Dan, he must have been groggy to let you in with us not chained up."

Whilst they were talking thus they had gone round to the suffering boys and one by one released them from their chains.

"Where's the hatchet?" said one.

"Here it is."

And he picked up a huge ugly-looking chopper from the middle of the vault.

"This is what he threatens us with if we cry," said the boy, holding it to Leonore.

"And this is what I'd give him if he was here now," said the boy whom Leonore had first released.

"Now for the door."

This had yet to be broken open before they were free.

One blow of the hatchet shivered the lock, and open flew the door.

Out they rushed in a body, Leonore slightly in the rear.

"Huzzah! huzzah!" they cried.

"Come on," said one of the boys, leading the way. "Through this archway. We needn't pass through the house, the old thief may have some mates there."

They darted with a shout of victory through the archway, Leonore following, and not a little overjoyed at what had occurred.

Not only had she herself escaped, but she had been the means of saving eight helpless boys.

Just as they had gained the archway, however, the back door of the house opened, and out rushed old Dan in pursuit.

He carried a large whip in his hand, and he flourished it threateningly as he ran.

Leonore was in the rear, as we have already said, and was the first to feel a smart cut across the shoulders with the whip, which set them tingling.

The next instant the old man had seized her by the back of her coat and dragged her off her feet.

The boys were on ahead.

"Help! help!" cried Leonore. "Do not leave me."

[CERTAIN DEATH.]

"No, no, no. Let's give the swell cove a hand."

Back they flew and fell upon the old man all in a body.

And now the old rascal got severely handled.

Leonore rose and would have begged mercy for him, but the boys had suffered so much at his hands that they would not hear of it.

They pommelled him heartily, until they were thoroughly exhausted.

Then one of them took up the hatchet and flourished it in his face.

"Now, old Dan, look out," he said.

"You wouldn't hurt me, Mikey, my dear?" whined the old villain.

"No, I wouldn't," said the boy. "Curse your old sneaking face! Give me back my molars."

"Oh, Mikey!"

"Where are they?"

"I haven't got 'em."

"Then take that, you old thief."

"Ah! ugh!"

The boy had given him a playful dig in the throat with the hatchet.

"Oh, spare him!" cried Leonore.

"Mercy, mercy, my boys."

"Never!"

"Cut him up!"

"Finish him!"

No. 41.

"Chop it off altogether!"

"Good. Then we'll collar the swag in his den that he's made out of us."

"Here's one for me," cried the boy holding the hatchet.

And down it came.

"Mur—"

The word was half out when his head was nearly severed from the body.

Horrors on horrors!

Leonore could no longer endure it.

With a cry of terror she fled from the painful scene.

CHAPTER CXXIV.

RALPH'S FLIGHT—THE "WHEATSHEAF"—PLOTS—THE THIEFTAKER—JONATHAN TRAPPED—RETALIATION—POSITIONS REVERSED.

As soon as the captain of the Yellow Band had got fairly off with the rescued prisoner the conflict around Newgate was virtually over.

It is true that it still kept lingering on, but nothing very marked occurred.

Jonathan Wild, it was remarked by a few—but only a few, for he took good care to leave when there was a grand confusion on—quitted the spot almost as soon as Red Ralph had gone.

Rushing into the prison yard, he called some of his picked men, and at once prepared for the pursuit.

"Do you think, Mr. Wild," asked one of his men, "that Red Ralph will really go to the 'Wheatsheaf?'"

"Of course. He said so."

"In boast, perhaps, to put you on the wrong scent. But you said you would be there, Mr. Wild."

"What of that?"

"That would surely put him off."

"Not a whit."

"But would he be foolhardy enough to go there with certain capture before him?"

"Once his word was passed—"

"As you will, Mr. Wild. You know the captain better than I do."

"Of course."

But still he was not without his doubts upon the matter.

The fact of it was, he was rather annoyed with himself for having been guilty of an imprudence, as he deemed it.

His great chance of success would have been to take the bold robber by surprise.

Now he had to go boldly to face him and capture him when he was prepared against surprise.

Properly he should not have appeared to notice the robber's words, and then he would have stood much more chance.

As it was, his only hope lay in the celerity of his movements.

If he were to gallop off now and ride there post haste he might perhaps overtake Red Ralph.

If not, it was probable that he would arrive there immediately after him.

Thus it would be a partial surprise, for he would not have expected so speedy a pursuit, and consequently not have prepared his resistance.

So thought Wild.

Now mark the captain of the Yellow Band himself.

He did not draw rein until he arrived in Maddox Fields.

Here he pulled up at the house of the friend who had been of such signal service to him upon several occasions, and left Laura Delane.

"Guard her as you would me," said the captain of the Yellow Band, "for there is danger abroad."

"I will."

"As for myself—"

"Do you not remain also?" asked his faithful friend.

"I must throw them off the scent in another quarter."

"At your own personal risk, I suppose, as usual. Alas! alas!"

"Dear Ralph," said Laura Delane, "do not run into such danger I implore you. Remain here."

"I cannot."

"But why?"

"If I stay here you will be hunted down at once. Be sure that I do all for the best."

"Oh, I'm well assured of that," said Laura—"the best for me."

"And consequently for myself as well," said Red Ralph.

Laura shook her head.

But it was useless to attempt further reasoning with the captain of the Yellow Band now.

His determination was taken, and it was not a trifle that could induce him to change it.

With a hasty farewell, and a promise of a speedy return, he took his departure for the "Wheatsheaf."

On his road he called upon a select circle of friends of easy conscience, with whom he made a little arrangement which was afterwards to act with startling effect upon his old enemy, Jonathan Wild the thieftaker.

As he reined in his horse before the "Wheatsheaf" out came old Jock the landlord.

He ran up to take the bridle of the traveller's horse, and assisted him to dismount.

"Good morrow, sir," said he, doffing his cap at Red Ralph.

"Good morrow, friend Jock."

The landlord looked up with surprise at this familiar gaiety.

"You know me, sir?" he asked.

"Ay!"

"I don't remember your honour just at present."

"Strange that, for we have often met before, and many a jolly carouse have we had together."

"'Tis perplexing."

"Here comes Mistress Margery," said the captain of the Yellow Band. "Let's see how she greets me."

The landlord's buxom daughter came up to the door where they were chatting and dropped Red Ralph a curtsey.

But this was far too courteous for the captain of the Yellow Band when such a comely lass was concerned.

He took her in his arms and kissed her heartily on both cheeks.

"Sir!" she remonstrated, repulsing him and colouring to the temples.

"My dear Mistress Margery, you are very distant and formal for such old friends as we."

"Old friends? I never saw you before."

"Oh, yes, you have. You have forgotten."

"No, I'm positive."

"So it seems to me, lass," said Jock. "But the noble gentleman says that he knows us well, and faith he seems to."

"Yes," said Red Ralph. "But I have grown a beard since we met, and the disguise it makes for me has deceived you, that is all."

"May I ask who you are?" said Jock.

"We shall wait until Captain Dick comes, eh, Mistress Margery? Ah, I see by your heightening colour that you know who that is. Now I'll warrant that you'll not forget him when he comes."

"Not I," said Jock.

"Nor I," said the blushing girl. "But who, sir, may you be? Surely you are not the captain?"

"If you mean Ralph, I am he."

"Never," said the girl.

"Never upon this mortal earth," exclaimed the landlord.

"Indeed it is, Jock, and nobody else, I can tell you."

"Why, Lor' love my eyes, so it is. Tip us your fives, captain. Why it's ages since we met. I declare that it's quite refreshing to the eyesight to see you again. Give me your fist."

And he wrung our hero's hand again and again in unaffected joy.

"Now, captain, the tipple?"

"The good old sort—brandy punch."

"And I will mix it for you," said the young hostess.

"Thanks, thanks, my dear mistress," said the captain of the Yellow Band, gallantly kissing the tips of his fingers at her. "It will go down all the sweeter for it."

"You are a sad man."

"Nay, I swear that I speak the truth. Ask Captain Dick."

Mistress Margery hung her head and blushed again.

Whilst thus speaking they had entered and seated themselves, whilst the landlord's daughter brewed the punch.

Just now there was a fresh arrival at the door, and off ran Mistress Margery, leaving the punch half finished.

"Captain Dick?" said Ralph, glancing up with a smile.

"I don't know," said Margery.

"Ah! no matter. Will you see?"

Yes she would, willingly.

The horseman alighted, and it proved to be no other than the bold knight of the road, Captain Dick—in other words, the daring highwayman Dick Turpin.

He caught the plump hostess in his arms and kissed her on both cheeks after the fashion of the age—keeping her (by the bye, a willing prisoner) in his arms considerably longer than custom ordained—and then inquired for Ralph.

"He's there."

"One word with him my lass, and I'll return immediately."

He ran into the parlour and grasped Red Ralph with fervour by the hand.

"Well met, Dick."

"Fortune favours the bold."

"But Tom?"

"Have you not seen him?"

"No."

"Then I fear some mischief has befallen him. I missed him in the skirmish."

"How did you contrive to get clear off? You were in the thick of it when I left."

"I cut my way through."

"Bravo!"

"But that wasn't so difficult a matter as it appeared whilst you were there, for the row began to grow general, the people joined in, and then it became an easy job."

"Did you see any of the cronies on your road here?"

"Yes. They will all arrive shortly."

At this portion of the conversation the tramp of horses was again heard.

This time there was a body of men, and Red Ralph at once concluded that it was his friends arrived.

A little surprise here awaited the highwaymen.

"Oh, father!" said Mistress Margery, rushing in, "whoever do you think is coming now?"

"Can't say."

"Mr. Wild."

"Jonathan Wild?" demanded the captain of the Yellow Band.

"The thieftaker?" said Dick.

"The same," replied the girl.

"Away, all of you," said Red Ralph. "We must have some fun with him now. Stand clear, Dick."

The latter would not dispute the Yellow Boy's wish, although, the truth to speak, his own inclination was to remain and see the fun.

They left the room, but Dick Turpin stood near at hand, to be in readiness in the event of his services being required.

A horseman, who was indeed Jonathan Wild, entered the house, followed closely by another of the officers.

"Good morrow, landlord," said the thieftaker. "Any company in the house at present?"

"Only in the parlour, Mr. Wild, and I don't see as you can have much business with them."

"You don't see? But you will see very soon."

Saying which, he knocked open the door, and entered the room.

Red Ralph was seated upon the edge of a table swinging his legs carelessly under it.

He glanced up and recognised Jonathan Wild immediately, in spite of a hastily assumed disguise which he wore.

He allowed the fellow who was with the thieftaker to walk round to the other side of him apparently unobserved.

Jonathan Wild already looked upon an easy victory as within his grasp.

Red Ralph's eye was upon him all the time, and he never lost the smallest movement.

When they had got pretty near to him he dived his hands into his capacious coat pockets.

At the bottoms of these were a pair of pistols of excellent finish, the primings of which had been very carefully examined by the captain of the Yellow Band before the entry of the thieftaker.

"Red Ralph," began the thieftaker, in a voice that was meant to be fear-inspiring, "you are my prisoner."

"Or might be."

"No, no chance on earth can now avail you."

"You think so?"

"It is sure."

"Not even this?"

And saying this, he produced his pistols, presenting one of them point blank at each of the thieftakers, who immediately sank into two chairs placed one on either side of Red Ralph.

"Your prisoner?" echoed the captain of the Yellow Band, with a derisive laugh. "Or else you are mine. It amounts to the same thing in the end."

CHAPTER CXXV.

HOW WILD REVERSED HIS REVERSE—THE SIGNAL—THE CHASE--THE DITCH--A HAVEN OF REFUGE—THE BARN—FLIGHT—THE PRECIPICE—A DEATH STRUGGLE—CERTAIN DEATH.

JONATHAN WILD was completely taken by surprise.

He was quite unprepared for such a master stroke of coolness as that displayed by the captain of the Yellow Band.

"So, so, my masters," cried Red Ralph, "you are outwitted, eh?"

The two thieftakers said nothing.

Wild gnashed his teeth in silent rage and disgust.

His man was far too alarmed to utter a word.

"Ho! Dick," cried Red Ralph.

"Here am I," said the doughty knight of the road, entering.

"Bring in the pals."

Half a dozen men, summoned by Dick Turpin,

rushed into the room and surrounded the two thief-takers.

"That's a settler, Mr. Jonathan Wild, I think," said Dick Turpin.

"No."

"It looks remarkably like it to my motion," said Dick.

"No. Outnumbered for the moment only," retorted the thieftaker, with a scowl of hatred.

And then, before a word could be uttered, ere the robbers could make the slightest movement, or even anticipate any further action upon the thieftaker's part, Jonathan Wild raised his call to his lips and blew a loud and shrill summons.

"Ah! drop that!"

But it was too late.

There was a rush at the door of the room, and a tramping of heavy footsteps.

"Look out!" cried Dick. "The Philistines are in force I find."

He was right. A whole mob of the thieftaker's men who were waiting in reserve came with a tremendous rush into the inn.

"Fly!" exclaimed Dick.

"I will," said Ralph.

And with a dash at Jonathan Wild which stretched him upon the ground, and a second attack no less sudden upon his man, Red Ralph sprang through the window.

It was such a leap as would have seemed impossible to the cool observer.

"I'm after you," said Dick.

And he was, in double-quick time, leaving the six fellows he had hired for this important service to shift for themselves.

But the interest of our narrative does not lie with these.

"Curses light upon his ever-ready wit," cried the thieftaker, scrambling to his feet. "Fire upon him!"

There was a scramble for the window, and in the space of a few seconds a dozen shots were fired.

But Red Ralph and Dick Turpin were too nimble for the thieftakers.

They were already out of the reach of shot.

"After them!" cried Wild. "Round the road!"

And a whole mob of the constables rushed wildly to the door.

Just as they gained the turn in the road—about a hundred yards from the house—they perceived the fugitives in full gallop.

They had found time to leap upon their horses and make for the open country.

"Mount and follow!" cried Wild. "To horse. After them!"

And now began a desperate chase for the highwaymen.

Jonathan Wild, with that perseverance which so characterised him in his hunt after those criminals for whom he cherished a private animosity, was the first in the saddle, and already far ahead of his men.

When he got within pistol shot he suddenly reined up, and, drawing one of his holster pistols, levelled and fired.

But he was too eager, and the shot missed.

Red Ralph turned in the saddle and waved his hat in triumph.

"Try again," cried Dick Turpin.

"Don't venture too near," said the captain of the Yellow Band.

This touched the thieftaker very nearly indeed.

Truth to speak, although of undisputed courage, he had so often met with severe reverses at the hands of Red Ralph that he scarcely relished the idea of getting at close quarters with him.

The rest of the pursuers came galloping past their leader.

"A hundred pounds to the man who brings Red Ralph down," said Wild.

A shout greeted this promise.

They buried their spurs in the reeking sides of their horses until they ran with blood.

The poor animals flew over the ground like lightning, snorting with pain and terror.

This brought them in a little time within shot of the flying robbers, and they did not fail to take advantage of such an opening.

A regular, or, rather, irregular volley followed, and down fell Dick Turpin's horse, dragging his rider with him.

"Curse the hand that fired that shot!" said Dick.

"Mount behind me," said Ralph.

"'Tis useless. Fly!"

"Never alone!"

"Leave me, I implore you. Save yourself."

"Never!"

Just then a second discharge was fired, and, by all that was unfortunate, down fell the gallant steed bearing the captain of the Yellow Band.

Red Ralph quickly disengaged himself from the fallen horse, and was ready for action.

"Leap the hedge, Dick!" he cried.

"I'm with you."

And, suiting the action to the word, he followed the captain of the Yellow Band, who bounded across a hedge in gallant style.

They flew nimbly across the field, and then threw themselves into a dry ditch.

"Over with you!" cried Wild.

But the very first man to essay the leap, which was by no means to be despised, found his horse lacked the pluck to take it.

A second was more fortunate, and was immediately followed by the thieftaker himself.

"Where are they?" he cried. "Which way did they go?"

"I don't know."

Nor any one. The query was unanswerable.

And now there seemed to be a moderate chance of their escaping.

A chance only, however.

"Dismount, some of you," said the thieftaker, "and beat the ditches and thicket there."

The men obeyed immediately, and the search was prosecuted on foot.

They searched all about with the utmost diligence, but without success.

And yet the secret of the two highwaymens' escape was the very simplest imaginable.

When we say "escape" we would imply momentary escape.

The ultimate success which would attend their ruse was yet extremely doubtful.

As soon as they were in the ditch, which was happily a very dry one, and deep enough to hide them standing upright, they ran along some considerable distance without straightening themselves, and thus escaped observation.

Arrived about three hundred yards from the spot where they had leapt over, they came to a dead stop, and had to look about them.

They were close to a large barn, apparently well stored, and they determined to secrete themselves here for a while.

They crept up, crawled in, and made their way up the ladder into the loft, where hay in large quantities was stored.

But unhappily they had not now quite escaped observation.

One of the men in the pursuit had seen them enter the barn, and, his courage heightened by the prospect of the tempting reward which Jonathan Wild had just offered, he started off in pursuit alone.

"By Heavens!" cried Dick Turpin, peering through a chink in the boards, "we are discovered. Yet no. 'Tis but one man."

"One man? No matter, he may betray us to the rest."

"What is to be done?"

"I will throw him off the scent."

"How?"

"Remain you here. I will leave in such a way that he shall perceive it, and as if by accident, too, and we can throw them all off."

"As you will."

"Stand close, Dick."

"I will."

"Farewell!"

Red Ralph at once quitted the barn, and sneaked off with much show of fearing observation.

On came the thieftaker, solitary, and eager for the chase.

He saw the captain of the Yellow Band, and was after him in a brace of shakes.

"Now, my friend," thought Red Ralph, "since you venture to follow, I'll put your courage to a stiff test."

He made direct for a high hill, overlooking an immensely steep declivity called the Giant's Leap.

A tradition was connected with this, from which it derived its name.

Of this, however, we cannot at present deal.

Just as Red Ralph got near the verge of the precipice he pulled up short, and turned to face his pursuer.

He could retreat no further, and therefore the man presumed that he was going to secure an easy prey.

Not so remarkably easy, however, as we shall show.

"Yield!" cried the man, running up.

"Come and take me, if you can."

"You can retreat no further."

"No, I cannot."

"Then give yourself up to me in a quiet and peaceable manner."

"Come and take me."

The man paused, for, truth to tell, he appeared scarcely to like the idea, now that matters were at a crisis.

As soon as the man got up with the captain of the Yellow Band the latter dropped his quiet peaceable manner, and turned savagely upon him.

With one dash at his waist Red Ralph had him in his arms, and bore him to the cliff.

"Now then," cried Red Ralph, "there is no sparing you. Over you go."

"Ah! mercy!"

"Not a whit."

And Red Ralph pushed desperately at him; but the man clung so tenaciously that he could not shake him off.

Red Ralph seized hold of the overhanging bough of a tree, and, thus aided, gave the other a more resolute push.

Suddenly there was a crack in the tree.

The branch gave way with a slight noise, and now Red Ralph hung half way between heaven and earth.

Is it death?

CHAPTER CXXVI.

LEONORE — EPPING FOREST — THE GLADE AND WHAT SHE SAW THERE—THE ASSASSIN INTERRUPTED—FLIGHT—LAURA DELANE—RIVALS—THE ROBBER'S WIFE—A SAD REVELATION.

LEONORE fled in horror from the fearful scene which she had just witnessed.

A terrible retribution had fallen upon the infamous old man who made such an unnatural traffic in human beings.

But there was one unpleasant circumstance in connection with this which caused Leonore to feel extremely ill at ease for a considerable time.

Her hand had indirectly wrought the tragedy.

It was she who had assisted the boys to escape.

After quitting the scene of blood she fled from the spot until once more she found herself in a respectable neighbourhood.

Then she began to look about her for some sort of conveyance, by which to reach a place of safety at once.

Unfortunately for Leonore, in those days travelling conveyances about the metropolis were but very few, and these were never out after midnight.

The only thing, therefore, was to make with all possible diligence for some spot where Red Ralph might be seen.

In Epping Forest she knew every nook in which he loved to lurk in his wild way of life.

To this part, therefore, she directed her steps after she had arrived at a fair starting point.

Fear lent her strength which she did not really possess, and she walked boldly through the night, until morning found her upon the border of the forest.

She made her way straight towards the glade, where she deemed that she was likely to find at least one of the Yellow Boys.

But, alas! she was most sadly disappointed here.

Not a soul was about.

It was possibly because the morning was not far advanced.

A little later, and doubtless all would be well.

Leonore had not long been here when she was startled by the appearance of a person whose face at once struck her as being familiar.

Fortunately she was so placed that she could see him without being visible herself.

It was a tall swarthy looking ruffian with a ragged shock of jet black hair and a slouching gait which bespoke the barn despoiling gipsy at a glance.

A second glance convinced Leonore that this same gipsy was none other than her old persecutor, Jonas, the outcast.

What extraordinary chance was this to throw the ruffian gipsy and his victim together after the latter had so recently escaped from the thraldom to which he bore her?

Leonore darted into the thicket as if by instinct.

We say "by instinct," for she had completely lost her presence of mind at the singular appearance of the gipsy Jonas.

It will be remembered that she had only a few hours previously quitted Glyde House, where she had left the ruffian Jonas with his companion in the execution of one of the vilest butcheries that were ever heard of.

Jonas came backwards into the glade, peering through the trees at some one advancing.

First he stood behind a large wide-spreading oak, a forest patriarch that had been there probably five hundred years or more.

Then, having assured himself apparently that the person as yet unseen was advancing in that direction, he hastily quitted this hiding-place for another more concealed.

By a singular chance he squeezed into the thicket only a few feet from the spot where Leonore was hiding in fear.

Now she did not dare to breathe, lest the gipsy should discover her presence.

In the space of a few minutes a third person appeared on the scene.

It was a young woman handsomely attired, in a

way, too, that was scarcely in accordance with the time and place.

As she advanced Jonas the outcast parted the foliage with his hands as gently as possible and stepped forth.

With stealthy cat-like strides he advanced.

An ugly-looking knife glistened in his hand, and Leonore, in an agony of fear, guessed the ruffian's purpose as he crept on.

Her eyes were fascinated, her lips closed with fear, and she could not utter a cry.

A few strides more, and he was up behind the girl.

The knife was upraised, greedy for the fatal stroke.

His arm moved already. Another instant and it must have been too late.

But at the instant—the fatal moment—a wild unearthly cry burst from Leonore—a cry so fearful that the whole forest re-echoed with it again and again—and the arm of Jonas the outcast fell powerless at his side.

The assassin was frustrated. The murderer was put off the execution of another crime to add to the fearful catalogue with which he stood accounted.

For an instant he paused, and then turned and fled precipitately—fled like the craven-hearted cur that he was—and Leonore sprang from her place of concealment towards the girl whom she had so fortunately preserved from such great peril.

"Ah!" cried the latter. "Have mercy I pray you."

"Fear nothing," said Leonore. "The danger is over now. See, he has fled in alarm."

"Then it was you who uttered that cry?" said the girl.

"Yes. I was here in quest of one—of one whom you cannot know—when I perceived this man draw near."

"Indeed. Then you saw him follow me?"

"Yes. In another instant he would have slain you. Even as I cried out his knife was close at your back."

Her hearer shuddered.

"How fearful!" she said. "But how can I sufficiently thank you for this great service?"

"Oh! you owe me no thanks," said Leonore, "for in truth I believe that it was more my own fears than aught else that caused me to cry out as I did."

"Nay. You would underrate the service you have done me."

"Not at all," said Leonore. "I have myself suffered persecution at the hands of that man and another, and the truth is that he who has fled alarmed me so that I could scarcely refrain from uttering a cry which so startled him."

"To that I owe my life."

"I am happy in having been instrumental in serving you."

"My thanks, my grateful thanks be yours," said the lady.

"May I ask what brings you here at this early hour?" asked Leonore.

"I came to meet one who—who (and she blushed deeply)—who is dearer to me than life itself."

"Who, may I ask?" said Leonore, a terrible suspicion crossing her mind for a moment.

"You will not know him."

"I may."

"Nay, I would rather not mention his name."

"As you please."

"You are not angry with me for refusing, after you have saved my life?" she said.

"No, not at all. Will you tell me to whom I am speaking?"

The lady was silent.

"I ask if you would tell me your name?" said Leonore, misconstruing her silence.

"I would rather not have given even that, but I am sure you would not harm me."

"I harm you?"

"No, no, of course not. But I am an outlaw, an outcast from my home and family, wrongfully accused of a murder of which I am innocent."

"Surely not Laura Delane?"

"The same."

"I have heard of the case," said Leonore. "This meeting is most singular."

They little deemed how singular it was.

"I should have been slain long since but for one who rendered me a service as you have done to-day. Escaping from justice, I fell into the hands of a villanous inn-keeper, who would have taken my life. Happily, one arrived in time to save me from their clutches, and 'tis he whom I now seek."

"Might I not ask his name?"

"I would rather not give it."

"Wherefore?"

"Because he is also proscribed. I could venture my own safety, but cannot imperil his."

"There is no danger with me," said Leonore. "But I think that I could give a shrewd guess of his name. 'Tis one of the Yellow Boys."

"Right."

"One of the followers of my husband."

"Your husband?" iterated the girl.

"Ay—Red Ralph!"

At this Laura Delane gave a wild shriek, and would have fallen to the ground had not Leonore caught her in her arms.

"What is it?" she asked. "Is it possible that it is he whom you love?"

"Alas! it is. Oh, say not that he is your husband."

"I spoke the truth. You cannot tell me that Ralph loves you in return?"

The girl hung her head and was silent.

"Oh, heavy day!" said Leonore. "I have passed through trials and terrors which would have slain many. I have been at death's door—I have been upon the scaffold—and yet I have not despaired. But now—oh, unhappy Leonore! love even is lost to you. Misery and woe can but be your portion!"

CHAPTER CXXVII.

DEATH — OUT OF DANGER — A SURPRISE — A GLOOMY WALK—AWKWARD POSITION OF THE CAPTAIN OF THE YELLOW BAND.

MEANTIME matters were indeed growing serious with Red Ralph.

The bold highwayman was left, the reader will remember, in a most critical position.

Hunted by the bloodhounds of the law to the verge of a precipice, a deadly struggle then occurred between our bold hero and one of the impetuous officers.

But soon had he cause to repent of his temerity.

Soon indeed had both of them cause to wish their ill fate had not led them to that spot to enter into so deadly a strife.

Hanging by the branch of a tree upon the very verge of the precipitous eminence, the captain of the Yellow Band was clutched with fearful tenacity by the desperate robber-hunter.

The heavy strain of the two bodies upon the tree caused it to creak most ominously.

Then some parts were heard to break asunder.

That one terrible sound cut short the breath of the two combatants, and seemed to ring out a death-knell in their ears.

But of the two it was clear enough upon whom it had the most effect.

The cheek of the officer blanched—turned of that

deadly pallor which is only seen upon the flesh of a corpse.

His jaw fell too, as if indeed he had really given up the ghost in that moment of mortal fear.

The sweat of deep bitter agony stood out upon his brow in round big beads, and the fear of death—violent and immediate death—was upon him in all its terrors.

The awful expression of his face so caught the attention of Red Ralph that, in spite of his own terrible position, he was moved.

Moved, but not with compassion.

To the bold highwayman personal fear, thus displayed too, was the most contemptible sensation which could agitate mortal frame.

"Coward at heart!" he exclaimed. "You earn the death you so fearfully anticipate."

Saying which, he pushed the officer from him with a sudden and violent exertion.

Down went the unhappy ill-fated man with a groan.

The action too had a good effect upon the desperate position of the captain of the Yellow Band, for as he pushed himself back from the falling body of his adversary he contrived to effect a better hold upon another branch of the same sturdy sprout overhanging the precipice.

His newly disengaged hand effected a firmer hold above, and thus he brought himself up the little incline on to *terra firma*.

Here he sat down, now that the struggle was over, for he was thoroughly exhausted and worn out.

"Pheugh! that was a narrow escape!" he muttered. "They hunt me closely, but yet I feel the warm blood of life too strongly within my veins to fear that death has any terrors for me yet. And yonder mangled corpse too. Ah! poor wretch! had he been bolder he might have been saved, or at least he would have had the satisfaction of perishing only with me. Ah! well. 'Tis a pity to see a fellow who fought with such undeniable pluck suddenly brought to such a contemptible end by the craven fear of death. And a man can die but once, as has been often said. Come when it will, I am ready for it. Heaven knows that I have courted it, although the instinct of self-preservation comes in full force upon me even at the eleventh hour, in spite of myself. And yet I get through all dangers with a marvellous run of fortune. Will it continue? Yes, I feel that destiny has already shaped my fortune pretty clearly, in spite of the reckless kind of existence which I follow. Time will show—time, the unraveller of the deepest mysteries."

Thus do we find the captain of the Yellow Band immediately after escaping from such a desperate encounter as the one we have just described turn to a contemplative mood—turn by a sharp transition from the most violent action.

After a few seconds passed in silent musing it struck him that he would go round and make his way into the valley below, to see if the officer still breathed.

It was just possible, although scarcely probable.

If he did, then he might be enabled to render some assistance.

With this view he began to reconnoitre the country around, and found that he was now far removed from any spot familiar to him. Not one of the landmarks could he remember.

He ran hastily down the hillside towards a long narrow gap at the bottom, apparently artificial, which led to the base of the precipice down which had fallen the ill-fated thieftaker.

Arrived here, he turned sharply off at right angles and ran down the slope to the bottom of the gap.

At the foot of it ran a gentle rippling stream of a beautifully picturesque appearance.

"Ah!" muttered Red Ralph, half aloud. "Then that settles all difficulties upon the point. The poor wretch has fallen into the water. Well, well, perhaps it is all for the best, for if he had not died upon the spot he could but have lingered on a few moments in his fearful tortures."

As he got thus far a light footstep broke off his soliloquy.

"What was that?" he muttered.

"*Stand!*" said a low voice close behind him.

"*Stand!*" hissed a second voice in his ear.

He turned round and found himself confronted by a tall burly-looking fellow in a long cloak.

Upon the other side was another of something the same build and general appearance.

Both wore long Spanish cloaks and broad-brimmed sombreros, which shaded two of the most villanous countenances which ever were fitted to mortal heads.

To add to the startling effect upon the captain of the Yellow Band, both held pistols to his head in the coolest and most determined manner.

"If you move one step forward or backward you are a dead man," said one of them.

"Thank you," said Red Ralph, recovering slightly from his surprise. "What is the meaning, may I ask, of this forcible detention?"

"Silence," said the former speaker sternly. "Do you think to escape the reward of your act with ribald jesting?"

"Why," returned the captain of the Yellow Band, "if you ask me for the candid truth, I must say that I wasn't thinking of it at all."

"You must go with us."

"With all my heart," said Red Ralph, not at all relishing the nature of the adventure, nor the tone of the two mysterious and threatening personages.

The two men were evidently puzzled by the light manner in which the captain of the Yellow Band treated their threatening speech and gestures.

It was done apparently more with the idea of producing a terrifying effect upon our hero than aught else.

"Vain man!" said one of them, "you don't know then that your guilt is known to us—that we have seen all?"

"Indeed?" said the captain of the Yellow Band. "And what then?"

"What then?" echoed the former speaker. "What then? Is it possible that you speak thus of a murder?"

"Stop that, my friend," said Red Ralph. "That's an ugly word to hear. I am no murderer."

"You have basely assassinated a man," said one of the men, peering at our hero beneath the shadow of the brim of his sombrero as if he would read his inmost soul.

"You lie!" said Ralph shortly.

"Ah!"

"Put up your knife," said the captain of the Yellow Band scornfully. "You cannot intimidate me with it. If I feared such a contemptible thing as you, depend upon it it would be rather your pistol I should dread than that little toothpick. Again I say, You lie!"

"Fool!" said the other man, who as yet had taken but little part in the conversation. "Know that we have seen it all clearly."

"Then you know as well as I that it was no murder."

"We know that it was murder of the foulest."

"Never. It was a fair and lawful combat, in which yon poor ill-fated wretch lost the day."

"What we could see of it did not assume the appearance of a combat, believe me."

"No matter. What became of him?" demanded the captain of the Yellow Band.

"The river has closed over your victim," was the reply.

"No victim of mine," said Red Ralph.

"You will have to prove that to your judges."

"Ah!" Then you mean to say that you are going to give me over to justice?"

"No."

"Then perhaps you will let me go free?"

"No."

"No, no," cried Red Ralph, fairly puzzled. "Then perhaps you will have the kindness to say in what way you intend to dispose of me."

"You shall learn that at our pleasure."

"The sooner then that it is your pleasure the greater will be mine," said Ralph.

"No jesting," said one of them sternly. "Follow me."

"Not I."

And with this he would have bounded away, but a glance convinced him that such a proceeding would have proved certain death.

Both held him so covered with their pistols that escape appeared to be an impossibility.

"Go on."

"Very well," said Red Ralph, glancing hopelessly upon each side, "I'll come. I'm not very particularly engaged just at present."

And the party moved forward, Red Ralph walking between the two cloaked men of mystery.

He glanced from side to side, and his very thoughts appeared to be interpreted by the man behind him.

"Checkmated?" he said to Red Ralph, with something bordering on a faint smile.

"No, not so—a continuer only; and one does escape from that by skilful play."

CHAPTER CXXVIII.

THE BOAT—THE OLD CASTLE—RALPH'S PRISON—
A STRANGE OFFER — THE TRIAL OF SKILL—A
TEST — THE BROKEN BAR AND THE SECRET
ORDER.

IN this singular way they led our hero along the bank of the river for some considerable distance.

Presently they came upon a small rowing boat moored alongside.

"Get in," said one of them to the captain of the Yellow Band.

Red Ralph scarcely liked the tone of command, but the two pistols were so steadily fixed upon him that he could not offer any further resistance.

"You see it is useless to resist," observed the former speaker. "You have no option but to obey."

"And why?"

"Because we have you in our power."

"Yes," said Red Ralph, pointing to the pistols, "and small credit to you for it with such backers."

"We have a stronger incentive than these playthings."

"What is it?"

"The power we have over you, we having witnessed your crime."

"I swear it was no crime. The man fell in fair and open combat."

"It is false!"

"Then you cannot have seen the struggle, as you pretend."

"We did—and we saw you hurl the man over."

"Never! It was his life or both. I preferred the former."

"No matter," said one of the captors of our hero. "Here you are now, and it is strange to me if you contrive to escape us."

Red Ralph said no more, and the two men exchanged not a word. The first to enter the boat silently took up the sculls and rowed vigorously, whilst the other remained motionless—or as motionless as the action of the boat would admit of—with his pistol fixed upon the bold Yellow Boy.

For full half an hour they continued thus, and during this time they could have proceeded no trifling distance, for they went with the current, and the rower plied the sculls with both skill and vigour.

At the expiration of this time they sighted an old-fashioned castellated building upon the bank of the river, surrounded by extensive grounds, rather wild in appearance, but of great beauty.

Near this the rower shot the boat ashore and jumped out.

"Follow," said the other to Ralph.

Our hero silently obeyed, and they resumed their march up to the building above mentioned.

Red Ralph perceived now that the old house was surrounded by an extensive moat, and was only approachable by a drawbridge, which was up.

One of the men produced a small whistle and blew a shrill note, which brought some one to the gate upon the further side of the moat immediately.

"Open, Geoffrey," said the other. "All friends here."

The bridge was let down, and Red Ralph was marched in in the same order as before.

Here he was conducted down a flight of stone steps of some depth along a subterranean passage, and through a stoutly barred doorway into a low vaulted cell.

This was but dimly lighted by a solitary grating, which struck an unpleasant kind of chill to the captive Yellow Boy as he crossed the threshold.

"So I am a prisoner," he said to his silent captors.

"For the present."

"For what purpose?"

"That you shall learn later," returned the man. "For the present make the best of your position."

"Ay, my bad best."

"No matter. It is the best that you can expect. Let that content you."

"I must."

The two men silently inclined their heads and left the dungeon.

"Content, forsooth?" soliloquised the captain of the Yellow Band as soon as he was again alone. "In truth I must, for I see no reasonable prospect of escape from here. No gallant Tom King—no rare Dick Turpin can aid me at this present straight. What can be the object of these two mysterious men with me? Faith, I cannot think of anything likely. Time must show me."

It is little to be wondered at that the bold highwayman felt somewhat perplexed—if perplexed alone —at this extraordinary adventure.

The strange aspect of the house in which he now found himself a prisoner was enough to arouse the curiosity of any mind.

The moat and the drawbridge, smacking so strongly of the mediæval, were alone a wonder in themelves, for at the period of our narrative baronial fortifications and armed retainers had long since disappeared and were almost as far removed from the people of that age as from those of ours.

A long and tedious captivity did it seem to Red Ralph.

An hour had barely past before he sighed for the refreshing atmosphere of freedom.

The novelty of the situation had worn away, and no longer had any charm for him.

About five or six hours passed on in silent gloomy meditation for the captive highwayman.

At the expiration of that time the ponderous door of the cell was unbarred, without any previous warning, and one of the two mysterious personages who had

[THE ASSASSIN.]

conducted the captain of the Yellow Band thither made his appearance, bearing a wooden platter, containg some eatables, and a jug of ale.

He put them upon the floor beside the prisoner.

"Eat and refresh yourself," said the man, "for you have that to do which requires a nerve of iron, a keen eye, and a steady hand."

"Pray explain yourself," said the captain of the Yellow Band.

"Eat, I say. You must be faint with long abstinence, and the work which we have in hand for you requires all your dexterity and courage combined."

"I don't comprehend you."

"No matter. Suffice it for you that you *must* eat. No want of food must hazard the skilful performance of that which we have for you to do."

"What is it?"

"All in good time."

The captain of the Yellow Band fairly lost patience at this tone of haughty supremacy.

"Look you, my friend," he said, "your manner ill suits me. I have a touch of your condition, which cannot brook the accent of command. Speak to me more fairly, or you will find that you have all your work cut out. I'll lead you such a dance—"

"Beware!"

"I will, in spite of your boguey threats. A fig for them."

No. 42.

"Eat and refresh yourself."

"Not a morsel, I swear."

The man scowled viciously upon his prisoner at this.

"Fool!" he exclaimed between his teeth. "Your temerity can but harden your position. Think not to escape us by your boastful temerity."

"Temerity?" echoed Red Ralph. "In truth I see no use for the employment of so big a word as that. It needs no great temerity to see that you talk twice as large as you act."

This roused the choler of Ralph's goaler mightily, although he endeavoured to hide it from the prisoner.

"Enough of this idle parlance," he said sternly. "Get up and follow me."

Red Ralph sprang to his feet with marvellous alacrity.

"That I will," he said, "for in truth I am already wearied of this place."

The man led the way out into a dark earthy passage, along which they passed in silence.

There was a damp earthy smell about it which told our hero that they must be passing beneath the moat.

After traversing this for some considerable distance they ascended a flight of steps, which, by the soft crumbling surface they presented, could not be the same flight he had descended on being conducted to the vault.

At the top of these they found themselves in something like daylight, which was quite a relief after the dead stillness and sombre hue of the place below.

"Now," said his conductor, "I am about to lead you into the presence of men of desperate character, and more desperate resources. Let me then counsel you to put a curb upon that insolent tongue, if you would not imperil your life."

The captain of the Yellow Band was stung to the quick.

This haughty tone goaded him to madness, but he felt that it would be dangerous to say anything now. So he bottled up his choler by a powerful effort, to be let out at the first convenient opportunity with redoubled fury.

He simply inclined his head to his conductor and followed him again.

At length their journey appeared to be at end.

The man paused before a dark wooden door, with heavy iron cross-bars upon it, and gave three loud taps, making a clear pause between each.

Then a small narrow grating at the top of the door, which Red Ralph had not before perceived, was opened, and a head appeared.

"Who is it?" demanded a voice.

"'Tis I, according to covenant," replied Ralph's conductor.

"Stanislaus?"

"Even he."

The grating was then closed, and the door opened.

"Enter."

Red Ralph obeyed, without a word, and found himself in the presence of a most singular assembly.

A spacious chamber was fitted up with dark tapestry hangings all round, and had somewhat of the general appearance of a hall of judgment.

All round the room were rows of seats, and in the centre, immediately facing the entrance, was a high seat or throne with a dais and a conical top.

Surmounting this, the tapestry hangings were brought up into the form of a canopy.

The front of this was decorated with some signs and insignia and puzzling hieroglyphic characters.

Each seat was occupied by a sombre and mysterious looking personage, the very counterpart of the two men who had conducted Red Ralph there.

On the throne sat an older man, who appeared to be the president of the meeting.

The effect upon our hero was startling in the extreme, as may be readily imagined.

The man conducting Red Ralph inclined reverentially before the president of the assembly, and walked across the chamber with slow and solemnly measured strides to a marble tablet, upon which was a small book.

This he picked up and held before him whilst he repeated some words to himself with a yet more serious air.

Then he kissed the book reverentially and replaced it, returning to his old position with the same measured strides as before.

"I wonder if they are all dumb, save my two friends who brought me here," thought the captain of the Yellow Band.

This was decided as the thought crossed him.

"Is this the man?" demanded the president of the person who had brought Ralph thither.

"Yes."

"And you are sure of him?"

"Ay, most worshipful master," returned the man.

"Ah!" mentally ejaculated the captain of the Yellow Band. "Master? I have it now. These are the companions of some secret order, and I am admitted to one of their conferences. For what purpose I shall soon learn I suppose."

"You have told him nothing?"

"Nothing."

"'Tis well. Draw nearer, man," said the president.

Ralph obeyed.

"Have you a sharp eye and a keen and ready hand?"

"I think so," said our hero. "It depends upon the purpose for which they are required."

"Silence!" hissed Ralph's jailor in his ear. "Your wanton tongue will undo you."

"You answer idly," returned the president, sternly. "Bring hither the test. Let us see if he has the skill to do our work."

Then, to the no small surprise of Red Ralph, two of them brought forward a pair of wooden blocks.

These they placed about three feet apart, and upon them they rested a stout bar of iron about three-quarters of an inch square.

"Can you strike fairly enough to sever that bar of iron?" demanded the president.

"Yes," returned Red Ralph, "with a suitable weapon—not with a court gallant's rapier."

"Give him a sword," said the president.

A stout weapon was placed in the prisoner's hands, and he was left alone to perform the feat.

It was one which our hero had before practised, and he felt confident of succeeding, notwithstanding that the strength of the sword was scarcely sufficient, compared to the stoutness of the bar of iron.

He raised it over his head, and then, with a dexterous whirl, brought it down, whizzing through the air.

There was scarcely a sound produced, and the iron bar lay upon the floor in two pieces.

CHAPTER CXXIX.

THE FEARFUL DOOM—RALPH'S TEMERITY—THE AXE AND THE BLOCK—A NEW HEADSMAN—THE MASKS—A DYING REQUEST—THE WHISPER—A SUDDEN REVERSE—DOUBTFUL ISSUE.

A MURMUR of approval ran through the hitherto silent assembly at this feat.

"Good," cried the grand master. "You spoke no idle boast."

"It is not my habit," said the captain of the Yellow Band.

"Your hand is both steady and true."

"Yes," said Red Ralph, picking up an end of the bar. "I will not deny that it is a clean cut."

"But could you strike as firmly if you had a human being there before you?"

"Yes."

"Are you sure?"

"Certain—provided that he had an arm of equal strength to protect him, and could boldly face me; and provided also that he has done me some grievous wrong."

This answer did not appear to be so much to the general satisfaction of the assemblage.

The president made some sign to the men who had brought the blocks and bar, and one of them was removed.

The remaining one was reversed, and the other end Ralph saw was grooved similar to an execution block, with a cavity large enough to admit a human neck.

The man then produced a block of softer wood, oval shaped, and narrow at the end, which was inserted in the cavity in the block.

Scarcely able to define his sensations, Red Ralph felt exceedingly ill at ease as he watched these proceedings.

The man who had handed him the sword quietly took it from his hand, and, all unseen by Red Ralph, whose attention was thoroughly engrossed by the block and its ugly-looking burthen, slid another object into his palm, resting one end on the floor, as the sword had done.

The cold iron handle caused Red Ralph to start.

He looked down at the object which had caused this, and found to his surprise that it was a long-handled axe of extra size.

"Strike!" said the president.

"What?"

"The block."

"For what purpose?"

"The test."

"And what if I refuse your test?"

"Refuse? You will not refuse, man. Beware how you would trifle with us."

It would be superfluous to say that the captain of the Yellow Band was no coward, and yet he felt an unpleasant chill steal over him as the command was issued.

Yes, there was no mistake about it. A command it was.

As he offered his objections he perceived a general movement upon the part of the members of this silent gathering, which led to his speedy acquiescence.

More than one cloak was thrown slightly aside, revealing the hilt of a dagger.

Resistance was certain death.

Red Ralph took up the axe and raised it to his shoulder. Then, grasping it in both hands, he brought it down upon the block, severing the wooden oval at the narrow end, as he felt was expected of him.

"It will do," said the president. "Take him hence."

"Stay," said Red Ralph. "One moment more. Let me be informed first what is the object of all this."

"Can you not divine?"

"A fearful thought crosses me."

"No matter how fearful. Be sure that it is but the truth. You have become the instrument of justice."

A faintness came over Red Ralph at these terrifying words.

"Speak to me more plainly," he said, "or I shall refuse to move a step in this business."

"A criminal, then, lies under sentence of death."

"And you mean—"

"That yours is doomed to be the hand to execute justice upon him."

Red Ralph started back with a cry at this fearful confirmation of what he half anticipated.

"Never, never, never!" he cried with energy. "I swear by Heaven I will not do it."

"Swear not by Heaven," said the president sternly. "You perjure yourself and send your soul to hell."

"I'll not do it."

"Then you will die."

"I can die."

"You shall, and briefly too," said the president.

He motioned to his companions seated around the chamber, and they rose with one accord and surrounded our hero.

Twenty bright daggers gleamed in as many resolute hands.

"At least let me die like a brave man should," said the captain of the Yellow Band. "Give me a weapon to defend myself."

"Silence," said the president sternly. "This is no idle quarrel which we have with you."

"Assassins!" said Red Ralph.

"Two minutes are given you to decide."

"Two seconds will suffice."

"Will you do it?"

"No."

"Will you do this deed, for the second time of asking?"

"No."

"Will you do this deed, for the third and last time?"

A score of daggers were upraised, and were about to be sheathed in the body of our desperate robber hero.

"Stay. Hold your hands," said Ralph.

"You relent?"

"One question first. Supposing I refuse, will your criminal escape?"

"Never."

"Who will do it?"

"I myself, if none other be at hand," said the president.

"And after I have perpetrated this murder?"

"You shall be free. All that will be required of you is an oath to secrecy of such a nature that you will not dare to break."

"I'll do it, then."

"Come."

First they conducted our hero into another chamber adjoining, where he was provided with some different clothing more befitting the ghastly office which he was to fulfil.

Then the axe was placed in his hand, and he was directed to follow his jailor.

At his request they furnished him with the sword with which he had severed the iron bar.

He stated, as his reason for asking it, that he feared to miss his aim at a first blow, and that he should feel more sure with a sword in reserve to give the *coup de grace*.

This settled, they conducted the captain of the Yellow Band into the cell of the prisoner who was to be executed in this awful secrecy.

All were masked now.

When they entered Red Ralph saw that the man doomed to death by the companions was young and handsome, and had an open and intelligent cast of countenance.

"So, butchers," he said as they entered, "you are here."

"You guess our errand?" demanded one of them.

"I do. Proceed, and mark you do it quickly. Here, my friend" (this was to Red Ralph), "let me feel your hand. Good. It is cool and steady. As you value the good opinion of a dying man, strike fairly. I don't think that any man would willingly cause another such agonies as are in store for me if you aim badly."

"I will not," said Ralph.

The prisoner pressed his hand in gratitude, and Red Ralph found that he had left a weighty purse in his palm.

"Now I'm ready."

"Are you still obstinate?" demanded one of the brotherhood.

"I am. Nay, do not seek to disguise your voice. Your mask cannot keep the hated face of Laman from my sight."

The man addressed started as if a serpent had stung him.

Evidently he was not pleased at being recognised.

"Proceed, then. I don't wish to waste time. Do your bloody work, and quickly."

"Fasten his hands behind."

The doomed man had already stooped over the block, with his neck stretched forth eager to receive the fatal stroke.

Ralph knelt beside him and whispered hurriedly in his ear, "Beg not to be pinioned."

A slight start told that he had caught the words so hurriedly uttered by the executioner.

"I have but one request to make," said the young man. "As it is a last one, you cannot refuse me."

"Name it."

"I would die a free man—not tethered like an animal for the slaughter."

"As you please." And they made Red Ralph a sign to let him go free.

"As you stoop," whispered Ralph, "take the axe from my hand."

The prisoner's eyes were of a sudden lighted with a wild joy as he looked his assent.

"You attack right and left. So now kneel."

The last words were uttered aloud, as a blind for the companions.

The prisoner bent his knee, but suddenly snatched the axe from Red Ralph's hand, and dashed at the companions on the right.

Red Ralph whipped out the heavy sword which had already done so much, and with a furious rush was upon the group to the left.

And now a fearful scene occurred.

The havoc which these two desperate men made was terrific.

CHAPTER CXXX.

THE CASTLE PASSAGES — A BATTLE — DEEDS OF DARING—THE PARLEY—MERCY TO THE DYING —TREACHERY—THE MEN IN ARMOUR—DESPAIR —A FIGHT FOR FREEDOM—HORRORS—RETREAT —THE CELL—THE BED AND THE SECRET PASSAGE—TEE FIRST GLIMPSE OF HEAVEN—HAPPY CONCLUSION—FRESH ALARMS.

IN the space of a few seconds the whole place resounded with the cries of the members of the brotherhood.

Before Red Ralph had long set himself to the work of vengeance no less than seven of the secret companions lay stretched upon the floor—five of that number never more to rise from thence—one so maimed as to be a certain cripple for life, if ever he should have the good fortune to recover, and the other insensible, with a ghastly-looking wound upon his brow.

This, however, although the more ill-looking, was in reality the least dangerous of them all.

The first shock of the assault over, full twenty bright daggers gleamed in the dull dungeon light.

But the prisoner, maddened with the blood shed up to the present, was in their midst in the space of a minute.

Grasping his bloody axe with both hands, he whirled it round his head.

The effect was terrible to behold.

He cut through all opposition with fearful desperation, chopping off heads, and mowing down the members of the secret brotherhood as if they were but ears of corn.

He had cut himself a circle, and stood bold and defiant in the midst of a huge and ghastly pile of mangled corses.

The captain of the Yellow Band was hotly engaged, as may be imagined, and yet he could not refrain from murmuring forth his admiration at the prowess of the bold young prisoner.

Presently there was a cessation in the hostilities.

The secret brotherhood, bold as they were, could scarcely be expected to carry on such a strife.

True they were overwhelming in numbers; but, to a man, they were unarmed save by a short dagger.

The wondrous activity and strength of their two enemies kept them so far distant that their weapons were of no service whatever.

They called off their members who were yet sound of limb towards the door to hold a consultation.

And now when the captain of the Yellow Band looked around him the scene which met his view was most horrible.

The dead and dying lay strewn about in every direction.

Groans, cries, and shrieks of anguish rent the air.

One fearful cry was heard above every other sound.

"Water, water, for the love of Heaven!"

"Heaven?" echoed the bold young prisoner. "You call upon us in Heaven's name now? You who would have slain me without hope of mercy?"

"Ay," added the captain of the Yellow Band. "And not simply that, but you would have been base enough to make me the instrument of your bloody vengeance."

"Water, water!"

"Not a drop."

"Monster!" said one of the wounded, crawling upon his hands and knees. "May such mercy as this be yours at your last hour."

"Curse on." And the prisoner simply rolled up his sleeves and bared his muscular arms for further slaughter.

"Merciless fiend!" continued the wounded man, with a gasp for breath, which was ebbing fast.

"Merciless?" repeated the prisoner. "And what mercy would you expect from a man whom you have doomed to the block?"

The wounded man merely groaned in dying anguish.

"What mercy can you hope for in the presence of the victim you would have slaughtered—before the man whom you would have abased by forcing him to become the instrument of your bloody-minded fury?"

"Nay," said the captain of the Yellow Band, who was touched by the fearful spectacle. "We must not be too hard upon these dying wretches. True, they have been merciless."

"Merciless?" echoed the prisoner. "In good faith they have."

"But they are dying now in bitter torment."

"It is their turn."

"Yes; but let us not rejoice in their agonies."

"Man, man," said the prisoner sternly, "I owe you much and would not prove ungrateful—"

"I know it."

"But you have not suffered as I have with them. You have not known what it is to have a parcel of hellish fiends taunt you to the quick, pluck you by the beard, doom you before your face to a fearful death, and discuss with torturing deliberation on the disposal of your carcas when they have slain you."

"True," said the captain of the Yellow Band,

"they have been remorseles—implacable. But let us show our superior minds by granting them such mercy as we can."

The prisoner merely shrugged his shoulders.

"As you will."

Red Ralph turned to some of the brotherhood who lingered about the door in anxious conversation.

"Bring your companions water," said he to one of them.

"We have it at hand," answered the man addressed.

"Bring it in then."

There was an eager movement at the door, which put Red Ralph on the *qui vive* at once.

"Beware of treachery I warn you," he said. "Who will enter?"

"I," said one.

"Throw down your arms then."

"I have none."

"That dagger beneath your girdle."

With a movement of assumed surprise the man drew the dagger from his belt, and tossed it on the ground.

"Now advance."

The man entered, holding a pitcher of water in his hand.

He made his way up to the more clamorous of the suffering men, and supplied their wants in turn.

One poor wretch was badly hurt at the shoulder, and it looked very awful with him.

"Hubert," he said, looking up piteously upon the prisoner, "I'm dying fast. Forgive me."

The young man turned away.

He had suffered so much at the hands of the secret brotherhood that mercy was quite banished from his heart for the present.

"Hubert," said the dying man in imploring accents, "mercy, I beseech you. Let me not leave this life at strife with my fellow-man."

Hubert was touched.

"What would you?" he asked.

"Your hand."

"There, then. And thus I perjure myself—risk my own soul—to comfort the parting moments of a man who has done his utmost to render my miserable existence of late a very hell upon earth. There is my hand."

Saying which, the late prisoner stooped over the dying man and grasped the hand which was stretched out to him.

The clutch was unnecessarily tight.

And now, instead of looking into Hubert's face, the latter could see that he and the brother who had entered with the jug of water were exchanging glances.

This probably saved Hubert's life.

The next instant the other had seized the pitcher in his hand, and made a desperate dash at the late prisoner.

Fortunately he had anticipated it just in time.

As the jug descended Hubert sprang aside, tearing himself from the treacherous grasp of the dying brother.

Down it came, full upon the face of the dying man, and settled his account upon the instant.

Thus was the death stroke wrought by his own perfidy.

"Treacherous to the last!" exclaimed Hubert sternly.

He slung his avenging axe upon his shoulder, and stood over the faithless brother.

"I can die, Hubert," said the man fearlessly, reading his doom in this stern glance.

"You shall."

"I know it, and am prepared."

"Plead for mercy."

"Never."

"Ask thy life."

"Never, I swear."

"Then you die. You are a brave bold man, and I would spare you if I could."

"Strike!"

"Farewell."

"*Strike!*"

"Are you prepared?"

"STRIKE!"

Down came the axe, chopping the desperate man clean through the skull, and inflicting instant death.

The captain of the Yellow Band shuddered fearfully at this fresh episode in the tragedy.

"Come, come," he said. "Let us away. This carnage is too awful."

"True," said Hubert. "I have been on many a hard-fought battle-field, but I never yet saw such a sight. For once I believe that God has fought in our cause."

"Yes; the avenging hand of Providence is here," said Ralph.

Saying which, he strode over the writhing forms to the door.

Here it was not an encouraging spectacle which met their view.

The whole passage was lined with members of the select brotherhood, thick as bees.

To cut their way through such a mass looked an utter impossibility.

The brothers were only armed with daggers, like those who had already fallen, but their numbers were overwhelming.

Red Ralph saw how matters stood, and being desirous of keeping from further bloodshed, if possible, he called a parley.

"One word," he said, "before we resume hostilities."

"Speak," said one of the secret brotherhood, stepping forward.

"We would avoid the further shedding of blood, if possible.

"'Tis easy."

"How?"

"Yield!"

"Yield?" echoed the captain of the Yellow Band and the rescued prisoner with one voice.

"Yield?" said the latter again. "After what we have done to prove ourselves the better men? Never, but with liberty."

"You will think better of it."

"Never."

"How can you hope to make your way through such hosts as we have to meet you?"

"No matter."

"Fools! You would rush upon certain death," said the speaker sternly.

"Not so certain," said Red Ralph, "to judge by what has already occurred."

"See here," said Hubert, pointing to the heap of dead and wounded about the cell.

"What of that?" demanded the brother spokesman.

"We shall strike as hard again."

"Ay—we shall."

"And we have numberless hosts to meet your two bold arms—two arms that shall never leave the castle in life."

"We shall see."

And the two desperate men prepared themselves to continue the bloody work.

"Hold!" said the brother spokesman. "Before you go on in your desperate work—before you devote yourself to certain destruction, hear me."

"Speak."

"Say on," said Hubert.

"Yield—and you—" (this was addressed to the captain of the Yellow Band) "shall be allowed to depart in peace."

"Do not trust them," said Herbert anxiously watching Red Ralph.

"Fear nothing," said the captain of the Yellow Band. "I am embarked with you in this desperate venture, and be sure I shall not quit you until we are both safely through it, or—"

And here he pointed his forefinger downwards in silent significance.

"Your hand upon it."

"There."

And the two desperate men, clutching each other's hands in a bold grip, sealed the compact of life or death.

"Foolhardy headstrong man!" continued the brother spokesman to our hero. "In that compact you settle your own doom."

"I care not."

"Death to all traitors."

A murmur of approval went through the throng of secret companions, reverberating through the whole place with a singular and fear inspiring effect.

It looked extremely doubtful, to gaze upon such a host of determined foes, if escape were possible.

Fearlessly, however, the two bold men made up their minds to follow out the work of desperation which they had set themselves.

Red Ralph threw off his jacket and stood bare to the waist—the picture of a Roman gladiator preparing for an arena of blood.

And a desperate work was there before him.

"Once more—do we pass out in peace?"

"Never, in life."

"Never!" cried the whole body of men, as with one voice.

"Then the evil light on you."

"We accept it."

"Then take it," ejaculated the bold Yellow Boy.

And with this he dashed forward and made a furious onslaught upon the nearest of the secret companions.

With a single stroke two of the devoted men fell.

"I'm with you!" cried Hubert.

"One for the Yellow Boys!" cried our hero again.

And again he plied his redoubtable weapon with startling effect.

Hubert, wielding his huge axe as if it had been a mere toy, joined his efforts to those of his liberator; and thus they fought side by side as none could fight for a less stake than liberty and life.

Their attack was so furious that the brothers retreated in spite of themselves.

Then they turned and threw themselves hopelessly upon the weapons of the two desperate men opposed to them—helplessly devoting themselves to death.

They could offer no resistance to the formidable weapons of the prisoner and Red Ralph.

"Open out," cried a voice at the back.

Red Ralph glanced up, and perceived that the speaker was none other than the president of the meeting at which he had been appointed the executioner.

"Ah! You do well to stop there," said the captain of the Yellow Band, "for we do not willingly stain our hands with others' blood."

"Silence!"

"Make us a clear passage, and let us pass out."

"Rash man! You shall repent this."

"Never."

"You shall."

"And if I do, I care not for death."

"Death may not be the worst treatment which we have to inflict upon you," was the reply.

"So you deal in torture as well?" said Red Ralph.

"As you shall find to your cost."

"I defy you."

Just then there was a great commotion in the crowd, and they opened their ranks to allow the passage of some fresh combatants.

What they now saw was anything but a refreshing sight for Red Ralph and the prisoner.

Six of the brotherhood stood before them armed from head to foot.

Their forms were protected by stout suits of chain armour, and steel casques or helmets protected their heads.

The two combatants looked into each other's faces for advice and consolation.

Matters looked ugly. How could they possible hope to hold their own against such odds as these?

"Now do you yield?" demanded the president.

"Not I."

"Nor I."

"Death to ye, then."

"Charge!" said one of the armed men in sonorous tones.

And they advanced towards the two combatants.

One of the men was a little in advance of the rest, and before Red Ralph could interfere Hubert had advanced to meet him.

"Here's for liberty!" he cried.

And he brought down his heavy axe with crushing effect.

The helmet and skull of the unhappy man were split fairly through, dividing the neck below them.

Not a sound—not a sigh escaped him as he fell to the ground.

A cry of wonder ran through the assembly, and the others drew up short in their advance.

But it was rather amazement at the prodigious feat than fear that caused them to halt.

Red Ralph was not a whit less astonished at the feat than were their foes, but he did not allow his astonishment to paralyse his movements.

On the contrary, he took advantage of the temporary panic thus occasioned to dash forward and attack his enemies with redoubled vigour.

He was well up in all kinds of fancy practice with the sword, such as pinning a card to the wall through the centre pip, and now was an occasion to bring this peculiar talent into play.

With his eyes fixed upon the point he was aiming at, he lunged out, carrying the sword fairly between the opening in the vizor of one of the men.

It was a fatal thrust.

The point of the sword entered the man's eye, and penetrated his brain.

"*Number two!*"

"Now what say you?" cried Hubert.

They were paralysed for a while at this terrible matter.

It seemed indeed as if some extraordinary chance was playing into the hands of the two desperate men.

A cry of horror greeted this second tragedy, and all remained terror-stricken at the sight.

"Now is our time," said Hubert. "Follow me. Quick!"

He clutched Red Ralph by the wrist, and dragged him back into the cell which they had just left.

Then he dashed to the door, and hastily fastened it.

"Quick, quick!" he said to the captain of the Yellow Band. "Barricade the door, and all is safe."

"What mean you?"

"Quick! Do as I say. I will explain as we proceed."

Whilst Hubert held the door Red Ralph caught up the block upon which he was to have taken the other' life, and drove it against the door.

"Now bring hither some of those carcases," said Hubert, pointing to the bodies of the slain brothers.

This was a job that our hero scarcely liked, and his repugnance manifested itself in his expression.

"Hold the door so."

Saying which, Hubert dragged up the yet warm bodies of the ill-fated brothers who had fallen by his hand.

He hastily piled them up on the block and around it, forming a very fair barricade.

"Now for liberty," said Hubert.

"How?" demanded Red Ralph. "I can't see how we are to gain liberty by shutting ourselves into this place."

"But you soon shall see."

"I'm all impatience."

"See here, then."

In the corner of the cell, at the back, was a rude bed of straw, which had been the prisoner's resting place for many and many a weary night.

"Here," said he to Red Ralph, "I made my only rest for more than fifteen months."

"Have you been a prisoner so long?"

"Yes."

"A weary captivity."

"True, and it might have been worse, had I not been engaged from the very first week in a labour which was a delight."

"Of what labour do you speak?"

"This."

He drew aside the straw, disclosing a cutting in the boards, forming a kind of trap.

He lifted this up, showing beneath it a dark hole big enough to admit the body of a man.

A flight of rudely constructed steps in the earth led down some six or seven feet, and from the bottom there was a narrow passage—so low that they had to pass along it in a stooping posture.

It sloped upwards along a steep incline.

"What is this?" demanded the captain of the Yellow Band.

"You shall see. This has caused me some labour and anxiety. Here is the finish of my work."

They had come now to a dead stop.

"What now?" asked Ralph.

"We have to continue it."

"Think you we can contrive to cut our way through?"

"Yes."

"And where to?"

"Liberty—beyond the castle moat."

"Ah! How know you?"

"I have calculated the distance to a mathematical nicety. We are not more than two feet from liberty."

"Sure?"

"As nearly as I can reckon from the poor resources I have had to aid me."

"To work then."

Hubert now set to work with the axe, plying it as a mattock, a much more effective instrument than any he had had the use of before in his labours.

The earth fell before his attack, and was scraped away by Red Ralph at once.

A few minutes proved that the prisoner had not calculated incorrectly.

The last piece of earth was scraped away, and they could see the starlit sky above their heads.

"Pardon me if I go first, good friend," said Hubert. "It is the first breath of the glorious free air that I have breathed for fifteen months."

"Speak not of it," said the captain of the Yellow Band. "I have tasted the bitterness of captivity too often not to understand your feelings now."

He clambered up through the hole, and was beside the entranced Hubert the next instant.

The latter could not speak a word.

His joy was so great that he could not shape it into words.

He stood there with his arms folded upon his breast, gazing upwards into the heavens in silent blissful gratitude for his deliverance.

Red Ralph looked about him.

He found that they had reached the surface of the earth at about eight or ten feet beyond the moat.

The castle looked weird and grim, and its turrets stood out boldly in the moonlight.

"Free, free," murmured the late prisoner in ecstacy.

"We had better be moving," said Red Ralph "for I see there is a commotion in the castle, which possibly relates to us."

A bell was rung with violence in the castle, and a rush was heard at the court-yard towards the drawbridge.

CHAPTER CXXXI.

THE HUNT AND THE POWDER BARREL.

SHIFT we the scene a while.

In a poor hovel at some distance from the spot where the stirring scenes which we have just narrated occurred two men were struggling under the weight of a small keg or barrel labelled "gunpowder."

The side bearing this startling inscription they turned down upon the hearthstone, evidently desirous of keeping it from view.

Their movements and speech were both hurried, and from their general demeanour the looker on would have supposed that they were anxious to get over the job before the arrival of some one whom they were expecting.

"Now then," said one of the men. "Quick as you please. That's it. Throw some straw on the top of it."

"There," said the other, obeying with such eagerness as to denote him to be the other's inferior.

"Some at the side too. That's it. There, that will do."

"I think that that's about the thing, Mr. Wild."

"Yes."

"No one would take that for gunpowder now, Mr. Wild."

The thieftaker, for it was he, turned upon the man, and aimed a savage blow at him.

Fortunately it just shaved his cheek.

Had it taken effect it would probably have damaged his beauty for some time.

"Keep a quiet tongue in that sheep's head," roared Wild.

"Lor, Mr. Wild," said the man, not a little pleased at having dodged the vicious blow. "I'm very sorry. How passionate you are!"

"You lie, you dog!"

"Oh! Mr. Wild."

"What do you want to bawl out all my affairs so that everybody can hear them for, eh? You jail-bird rascal, I'll slit your ears for you, depend on't."

"But—"

"Hold your hideous tongue!"

"There wasn't any one to hear," said the man in a breath.

"Oh! you won't keep quiet won't you?" said Wild. "We'll see."

And with no very amiable purpose he walked round the hut after the man, who retreated backwards, with his eye fixed upon his tyrant.

This roused the ire of the thieftaker, but he did not choose that it should appear.

He would not therefore quicken his movements, but, with a malicious purpose in view, he followed the man round and round the cabin until he got him off his guard.

The eye of Jonathan Wild was said to possess a peculiar kind of fascination for the victims to his tyranny. In this case it would almost appear to be verified, for the man could not remove his glance from the thieftaker.

Shortly the object of the malicious thieftaker was apparent in the disaster which befel the man.

Wild worked him towards the barrel of powder over which the man backed, and fell sprawling full length upon the hearth.

In an instant Jonathan Wild was upon him.

Thumps, kicks, and every variety of manual correction were resorted to, until Jonathan was thoroughly tired out, and the man was breathless and bruised all over.

"Mercy, mercy!" he roared.

"I'll teach you what's what, my fine fellow," said Wild.

"Have a little pity," groaned the fellow. "You'll spoil me for work to-day, Mr. Wild."

This had a most magical effect upon Jonathan Wild. He ceased his amusement upon the instant.

"Get up," he said.

"That's more easily said than done," replied the man, "after one has been pummelled as I have been."

"You villain, I've barely touched you," said Jonathan.

"That's a matter of opinion," said the man, rubbing his damaged portions.

"Silence!"

"But I'll be even with you one day," muttered the man doggedly.

"Ah!"

Anticipating a repetition of Jonathan Wild's pleasantry, the man dashed off round the hut, to the infinite amusement of the former.

"Fool!" he cried. "You're like some schoolgirl with your fears."

At this moment there was a noise without, and upon Jonathan Wild going to ascertain the cause of it he found two or three men running towards the hut.

"That you, Holland?" he cried.

"Hullo, ho!" answered one of the men.

"What now?"

"No good yet."

"Haven't you sighted him yet?"

"Yes."

"Then why haven't you done it?"

"He carries double."

"Who's his pal?"

"Don't know him—'tant a professional crack."

"Pshaw! I'll be bound that I should know him."

"Come and see."

"I'm with you. But we must go to work warily. He's a devil of a fellow if his blood's up."

"All right. Never fear for us, Mr. Wild," was the reply.

Wild turned to the man in the hut, bidding him remain until his return, and then started off with the newcomers.

As soon as the thieftaker was gone the man in the hut shook his fist after him, and then ran to the window and peeped out at his superior disappearing round the angle of the lane.

"He's off, and no mistake," said the man. "I was half afraid that it was only a trap to try me on. But no. Fortunately he does not suspect me. But I do him. I know as well as words could possibly tell me for what he has prepared that neat little contrivance."

The speaker alluded to the barrel of gunpowder which they had placed upon the hearth under the straw.

After another glance at the door, to assure himself that his tyrannical master was not in sight, he ran hastily back to the barrel in question.

Then, throwing off the straw rapidly, he rolled it out, and turned it over upon the end.

This done, with his knife he withdrew the bung, and, turning the barrel over again, shook out a great quantity of its destructive contents.

After this was done some little addition was made to the barrel which did not improve it in purity.

However, it made the weight of the barrel about the same as it was before, and this was something to compensate for the loss of the powder.

Then he carefully replaced the bung, turned up the barrel, and rolled it back to its place upon the hearth, where he covered it with straw.

"There," muttered the man. "That must have spoilt his game a little, and now I'll go and look after him—see if I can give a hand."

As soon as the man got out of the hut he ran out of the main road into a cross path.

Traversing with hurried strides a small but thickly-grown wood or shaw the man found himself in a small open patch of ground, which looked almost as if the wood had been cut down just there with some especial purpose.

"This leads to the lane again I know," muttered the man. "I must mind that I don't get on too fast."

He pushed his way across here and made for th thicket again, into which he plunged boldly enough.

The progress was slow and difficult here.

He had not got far before he heard the sounds of a scuffle.

"They're at it," he muttered, pulling up short.

Then there was a hollow groan, which appeared close at hand, and a voice heard in an angry tone of remonstrance.

"Villain! you shall repent of that blow. Dastard!"

"Come on. Leave him there."

"That's Jonathan Wild," murmured the listener at once.

"Bring him on to the hut."

"All right, Mr. Wild,"

"Come on, captain. It ain't no earthly use your kicking up all this rumpus, you know."

There were the sounds of a desperate scuffle taking place, which ended in the solitary individual's discomfiture.

When Wild next spoke his tone bore evidence of his having taken part in the broil.

"Fool!" he said, panting. "You shall be repaid all this."

"I fear you not, Jonathan Wild."

"You shall learn to."

"The man is not yet born that could teach me."

"I shall try."

"Pshaw! I spit upon ye, and defy you as before."

"Bear him along," cried the thieftaker, mad with passion.

"He's a magnificent fellow," thought the man from the hut, "and deserves to get out of such an ugly mess. It shall not be my fault if he doesn't. Yes, he shall yet find that I have even one sensation stronger than all else within me—gratitude!"

As the spot upon which the scuffle had taken place was now deserted, as far as he could hear, he pushed his way through the thickly-grown brushwood, to find himself once more in the open.

Here the first object which met his view was the inanimate body of a man stretched upon the green sward.

"Ah! They said he 'carried double,' I remember," muttered the man from the hut. "This is his pal. A good idea. If I was to give a hand here he might be able to go and put in a hand for the captain, and so I should be spared all danger in the matter."

He advanced to the wounded man's side, and found that he had been felled to the ground by a blow from some formidable bludgeon.

[THE MIDNIGHT EXECUTION.]

Upon his forehead he had a blue bump as big as a small egg.

His face was ghastly pale, and it was clear that the blow he had received had been no trifling matter.

"I must get some water," thought the man. "I shall never be able to revive him without."

But to get water was no small difficulty in this place.

It was a painfully long search.

However, his heart was in the work, and he flew about upon the errand with the greatest zest.

He found water in a rippling little brook, clear as crystal, and deliciously cool.

Using his hat as a vessel, he procured what he

could, and then made his way back with all haste to the swooning man.

The remedies were applied for a long time without avail.

Ultimately, however, his perseverance was rewarded with such success as the sequel will show.

CHAPTER CXXXII.

AN AMBUSCADE.

BUT now for a clear explanation of these doings. To give this it is necessary that we should return and take up the adventures of our hero and the lately rescued prisoner of the secret brotherhood, Hubert.

As soon as they heard the commotion within the castle they deemed it prudent to beat a retreat.

"Come," said the captain of the Yellow Band to his companion, who was unwilling to stir from the spot. "Come now, and we will return with such a force as shall shake this murderous castle to its base."

"But when?"

"Soon."

"Soon? That's vague. Oh! it's mighty hard to turn from such a scene with such a poor revenge for all the sufferings they have made me undergo whilst in their cursed hole."

"Poor revenge?" echoed the captain of the Yellow Band. "By my soul I think that we have not done badly, when we take the fearful odds and all disadvantages into consideration."

"No, no," exclaimed the late prisoner hastily, grasping the hand of his liberator. "You must not deem me ungrateful for all your services. You have saved my life, and it's yours when you shall claim it."

"There's not much danger of that," remarked the captain of the Yellow Band, smiling.

"Right. I speak idly."

"No, no. You have suffered much I know, and I can appreciate your feelings; but come away now. I promise so glorious a revenge that what we have already done shall appear as nothing to it."

"You do?"

"I swear it."

"Your hand upon it," said Hubert. "I have known you but a short time, but our mutual dangers have endeared you to me. Your word to me is as good as your bond."

"There's my hand," said Red Ralph, "and should nothing unforeseen occur to spoil the project, before three days are over our heads I can promise you such a feast of vengeance that shall satisfy your wildest cravings."

It was a singular proviso that Red Ralph had put in.

"Should nothing occur." It was almost as if he foresaw that some ill adventure was about to happen to him.

They had not taken a dozen paces more when there was a sudden scramble in the bushes.

"Look out!"

"Hullo!"

"Treachery! An ambuscade."

Before they could stir hand or foot to help themselves both were seized from behind in the grasp of a dozen unseen foes.

"The brothers are upon us!" cried Hubert.

And he struggled so desperately that, in spite of the numbers, it was more than possible that he would have got free.

But Jonathan Wild, seeing how matters stood, sprang forward and with a bludgeon delivered the unfortunate Hubert a terrible blow upon the forehead.

The gallant young man sank to the ground with a hollow groan, felled upon the instant like an ox from the butcher's poleaxe.

"Villain!" cried the captain of the Yellow Band. "You shall repent that blow! Dastard."

"Come on," said the thieftaker. "Leave the other there."

Red Ralph struggled boldly, but in vain.

His foes were a legion, and his utmost efforts failed to produce the slightest impression.

"To the hut," cried Jonathan.

Accordingly, the whole party pushed back again towards the hut, in triumph at their success.

Arrived here, Jonathan Wild ran on before and entered the hut.

"Snake!" he called.

But no answer came. The man he had left there was differently employed at present.

"You rascal!" shouted Wild. "If I thought that you would have sneaked off directly my back was turned, I wouldn't have let you off so easily. Confound it all! I didn't want those fellows to know what I was up to. It's so awkward in case of an inquiry. No matter. I must have my fun out of him. I've sworn to do it, and done it shall be at any price. I must trust to my luck to bring me through it afterwards if anything unpleasant happens."

He went to the door and beckoned to the men to advance with their prisoner.

"Bring him in," said the thieftaker. "Now you leave go of him. He can't get away from the others. There. Now help me."

Assisted by two of the men, Jonathan Wild rolled out the barrel again, endeavouring to keep the inscription from their sight.

However, this he failed to do.

He had intended it for Red Ralph only to see, that it might add an additional torture to those which he had already prepared for him.

"Hullo, Mr. Wild!" said one of the men. "You must have a mighty lot o' powder there."

The thieftaker scowled fiercely upon the speaker.

"Hold your tongue. See nothing," he said. "It is intended for other eyes, not yours."

"I smell," said the man, tapping his nose significantly.

"Now, then, strap him down to the barrel," said the thieftaker.

He tossed them some cords which he had already prepared, and in a few seconds the captain of the Yellow Band was fastened securely across the barrel of gunpowder.

"Now you can go," said Wild. "I'm going to stay a minute to see that he is all secure, and then I am with you."

"Shall we see after the pal of Captain Ralph?"

"Yes."

Off they ran at once upon this errand, and Jonathan Wild returned to his prisoner.

"Now, Red Ralph, I have you," he said. "Now there is no earthly chance for you."

"You think so?"

"Nay, I do not merely think. It is certain that we are both here alone, and that you are strapped immoveable to a barrel of pure gunpowder, which in another moment shall blow your body into a thousand fragments."

"Take your bugbears to frighten little children with, Jonathan Wild," said Red Ralph.

"You don't believe it?"

"No. I know that it is not true. I heard you say to the man but now that the inscription on the barrel was meant for other eyes than his."

"Ha! ha! ha! Then you took it as I intended it to be taken. I only hope that he so understood it as well."

"What mean you?"

"That what I said to the fellow was simply a blind to put him off the scent."

"For what purpose, pray, if your tale be true?"

"Your wit should tell you, Red Ralph, that government wouldn't work at such a little personal gratification as I am about to indulge in."

Red Ralph was silent.

What the thieftaker said was quite reasonable, and after all it might be true.

At any rate, he was assured that Jonathan Wild would not be restrained by any qualms of conscience.

"You believe it now, Red Ralph, I think."

"Not I. You foully lie."

"See then."

And he took his powder horn, and, opening the top

a little, he made a long train of powder from the corner of the cask, up by the bung hole, to the door of the hut.

Here he was obliged to make it into a thick pile and to damp it slightly, that the air might not blow it away.

After a second's absence from the door, completing the train, the thieftaker returned to the hut for a torch.

Then, having lighted this, he hastily made his way out.

"Farewell, Red Ralph," he cried.

"Monster!"

"Don't be unkind at parting. We shan't meet again."

"I hope not."

"Now, that's rude. You mean to imply that our destinations are different; but I don't think it. However, you'll probably know that first. Here goes, to satisfy your curiosity."

And with this blasphemous speech the thieftaker fired the train from outside the cottage.

"Ah!" thought Red Ralph, "my last minute."

* * * * * *

"Why, hullo!" cried the thieftaker, "Whatever's this?"

There was no explosion!

A faint sulphurous puff was the only result of his grand and elaborate scheme of vengeance.

He had run to some considerable distance, for he guessed that it would be a terrific explosion.

Now even he scarcely liked to return to ascertain the cause of the miscarriage of his project.

"Perhaps it's burning slow. When I damped it," he thought, "I may have put too much water."

But no train of gunpowder could take five minutes to explode.

Convinced of the folly of such an idea, he ran back to the hut to learn the truth.

The train had all burnt, but the barrel remained uninjured!

The barrel alone, too!

Red Ralph was gone!

CHAPTER CXXXIII.

THE HUT AND THE POWDER MINE—THE SPY—HOW HE DISAPPEARED—HIS RETURN—A CUNNING DEVICE—WILD ON THE WATCH—PUNISHMENT—FLIGHT AND CAPTURE—RED RALPH IN LONDON—THE MOB AND THE PILLORY—WILD'S VICTIM—RALPH IN A BROIL—A RING—FISTICUFFS A HUNDRED YEARS AGO—A FRIEND IN NEED — DANGER A-HEAD — "WE ARE WATCHED!"

"DEATH and fury!" cried Wild as soon as he recovered from the first shock.

But all the oaths in the world could not possibly mend the matter now.

Red Ralph was gone—mysteriously disappeared.

But yet his escape, like many other apparent mysteries, was in reality one of the simplest and most straightforward things imaginable.

Jonathan Wild had no sooner turned his back than the window of the hut was dashed open, and a man bounded through with a flying leap.

It was Hubert!

The bump upon his brow had greatly subsided, and in its place was an ugly wound, the result of Wild's brutal violence.

He had barely cleared the window when a second person sprang through and bounded into the hut.

This was the truant aid of the thieftaker, whose absence had caused his master so much chagrin and annoyance.

The cords which bound the captain of the Yellow Band were severed at one swift stroke of a knife, and he was free.

At this instant phiz went the train of gunpowder.

"Hush!"

"Flat on your faces! Down!" cried Red Ralph.

And he set the example himself by falling forward upon his face.

Hubert in an instant divined all, and threw himself upon the ground in a trice.

"All right," said the thieftaker's faithless man. "Jump up. There's no danger."

Ralph looked up.

"No danger?" he repeated quickly. "But I thought the cask was filled with gunpowder."

"Was filled, yes. But I took some out and doctored the rest."

"Then you have saved our lives," said Red Ralph.

"Then I am getting on," said the man. "And some day, no doubt, I shall be quits with you."

Red Ralph could not understand this speech exactly. There was something in the manner of this man which appeared familiar to him. His face, too, was well known to the captain of the Yellow Band, but where he had come across him was a perfect mystery to him.

"You don't remember, I see," said the man. "And yet we have met before, and that more than once."

"I know it, and yet I cannot think where, or who you are."

"My name for the present is Snake," returned the man.

"Your disguise then from your former self must be effective."

"So you said on the last occasion that we met."

"Then I recognise you at last. You are my old friend, the spy?"

"Right," returned Snake. "That was the name you knew me by for the want of a better. But come, we shall have our mutual enemy return to learn the meaning of all this."

"Of what?"

"Come. I will explain as we proceed."

They hastily quitted the hut, and made for the more thickly-wooded country, that they might be free from all hazard of pursuit.

Snake conducted them to a place of safety, explaining the events of that memorable day as they proceeded.

Then, putting them in the right track for the place they desired to reach, he quitted them, to return to the hut.

He hoped that he could yet escape suspicion from the thieftaker, should he reach the hut before him.

Fortune so far appeared to favour him, for when he reached the place there were no signs of the thieftaker or his men anywhere near.

"Good!" said the spy, half aloud. "Now I shall have the time for my little project, and I think that it will manage to throw as good a man as Jonathan Wild off the scent."

His project was this:—

He first proceeded to loosen his neckcloth and to rumple it in front to give it the appearance of having been rudely clutched by an unfriendly hand.

Then he tore open his vest at the top, disposing it with admirable effect to deceive the thieftaker when he arrived.

Mr. Snake next produced a penknife, with which he made a small incision in his arm, opening a vein, which bled profusely.

The blood he daubed upon his brow and face, and took care that it should fall over his hands and clothing generally.

Then he threw himself upon the ground, just inside the door of the hut, counterfeiting a swoon.

He had not assumed this positon two minutes when Jonathan Wild appeared upon the scene.

First, he peered round by the window, and glanced at the prostrate form of the spy.

Then, upon tiptoe, he crawled up to the door, and dragging it suddenly open, stood there, cudgel in hand, evidently with the idea of surprising the man.

However, he might have spared himself this trouble, for Snake had no intention whatever of moving—unfortunately for him, as will be seen.

In an instant, and before breathing a word, the thieftaker dashed at the spy, and delivered him a succession of such blows with the cudgel that the swooning man was awakened to consciousness immediately.

Not only to consciousness, but to the sense of pain, and right lustily did he roar for mercy.

"Take that, and that," cried Jonathan Wild, "you villain !"

"Mercy !"

"Devil a bit of mercy."

And he belaboured the unfortunate spy as long as he could stand over him.

"Now, you villain ! you thieving rascal ! you gallows bird ! do you think you're better ?"

"Oh-h-h ! Mr. Wild."

"None of your confounded hypocritical lies to me."

"But, Mr. Wild—"

"Silence ! Do you think you're better ?"

"No."

"Then you must have another dose."

"No, no, no !"

"I thought not, you traitorous dog ! You thief ! You sheep in wolf's clothing ! But you shall suffer for this."

"For what, Mr. Wild ?" demanded the spy, with well-assumed innocence.

"For what ?" iterated Wild. "For what ? Oh ! nothing. Oh, no ! You shan't get strung up for this little job ! Oh, no ! Not if I've got any influence at head quarters."

"Lor ! Mr. Wild," said the spy, with unmistakeable fright depicted in his countenance.

"Don't try on your hypocrisy with me again. If I hadn't seen you playing the fool with your face and your neckerchief I might have been gulled, but, as it is, you cannot throw me off the scent again."

"I'm sure, Mr. Wild—"

"Silence !"

"I'm quite innocent."

The thieftaker, enraged at his persisting in his innocence, threw his cudgel savagely after him, and, striking him upon the head, floored him as neatly as a ninepin.

Having recovered his breath, he dashed upon his victim, and pummelled him heartily again.

This time the spy did not see fit to stand all this tamely, and so he retaliated boldly.

The consequence was that a scrambling encounter upon the floor ensued, the two combatants rolling over each other until both were exhausted and breathless again.

"You rascal !" gasped Jonathan Wild, wiping away the blood, which poured in torrents from his mouth.

"Serves you right," retorted the spy as soon as he could speak.

"Ah !"

"Will you have some more ?" gasped the spy, growing bolder with despair.

The unfortunate man well knew what was reserved for him should he remain in Jonathan Wild's clutches now.

He felt that all was discovered, that he had been watched while preparing his elaborate deception, and that any further attempt was folly indeed.

His only hope now was to escape, and make his way to Red Ralph, for whom he had undergone all this.

The thought had occurred to him upon the instant to join the bold Yellow Band.

He staggered to his feet and made for the door.

Jonathan Wild, perceiving his intention, sprang up, and caught at his retreating garments, just missing him.

"Good bye !" shouted Snake.

"Stop !"

"Never ! Ta ta, Jonathan, my friend," returned Snake.

And off he ran.

The thieftaker was strong in spirit, but the flesh was weak. Struggle against exhausted nature as he would, he could not pursue the man with any hope of capturing him·

"Sdeath ! but the knave will escape me yet," cried the thieftaker.

"Ho ! ho ! hillo—ho, there."

No one answered. And then he had recourse to his whistle to signal his men, whom he knew could be at no great distance from the spot.

He was right in his conjecture so far, for instantly there was an answer to his signal, and several of the men came running up to the spot.

"Snake has betrayed us—let the prisoner escape. Fly after him. That way. Bring back Snake dead or alive !"

"Ay, ay, sir."

And away they flew, leaving their leader fretting and fuming impatiently.

For more than an hour did he have to endure this torment, and then he heard a shouting.

He ran to the door of the hut to welcome his men, and found to his delight that they had got the unfortunate spy, Snake, bound hand and foot.

A severe gash in the forehead from a sword cut gave his countenance a ghastly appearance, and told how desperately he had struggled for liberty.

"Ha, ha ! I have you now," cried Wild in ferocious joy.

The man turned his pale face to his brutal master, and glared into his stony visage imploringly.

But he might as well have tried to move a stone to pity.

Wild was remorseless.

"To London !" said he.

And the procession started off, bearing the unfortunate Snake to captivity and a doubtful fate.

What he suffered through his friendship to the captain of the Yellow Band it is impossible to describe.

Suffice it to say that he was the whole time beneath the charge of the ferocious thieftaker.

This will have due significance in the reader's mind when he remembers the end of the unhappy and misguided John Blake, or Blueskin, in Newgate.

Now Snake was brought to trial, and such false testimony did the thieftaker bear against him that he stoutly denied it all.

Then, taking this as an excuse for cruelty, Jonathan Wild made the unhappy prisoner acquainted with the press-room of Newgate and its attendant horrors.

The vice, the thumbscrews, and all the devilish contrivances of torture were brought into requisition.

His limbs cracked beneath the fearful pressure of the rack, and yet the animosity of the thieftaker was not appeased.

He was pressed by the most terrible of all engines—the one by which Blueskin was so cruelly slaughtered—until his ribs appeared upon the very eve of cracking.

He dared not go further than this, for a public

inquiry into these matters was beginning to be held, and it might chance to prove embarrassing.

All that the law permitted he would do.

And last, but by no means least, he reserved for him a public punishment which was by most persons deemed worse than anything, on account of the ignominy attached to it.

But bitterly was Jonathan Wild to regret this.

Bitterly, most bitterly did he repent of all that he had done to this poor wretch.

Success had made him grow bolder.

He ventured desperate chances with impunity. But this was not destined to continue.

But more of this anon.

* * * * * *

The project of the captain of the Yellow Band and the released captive, Hubert, advanced as well as they could wish.

What was the precise nature of this said project we shall take occasion to show a little later.

Suffice it to say for the moment that their present occupation brought them to London again, where we take up their movements for a while.

They were passing along one of the principal throughfares, when a large concourse of people, attracted by some unusual spectacle, called their attention.

The curiosity of our two adventurers being excited, they pushed their way into the crowd to ascertain the cause of the demonstration.

Red Ralph was elbowing his way up boldly, followed close behind by Hubert, when the man immediately in front of him turned round savagely and caught him by the collar.

"Hullo! friend," said the fellow, shaking our hero rather roughly. "Just look out next time where you put your feet."

Red Ralph did not deign to reply to this in words.

Twisting himself out of the brawny fellow's grasp, he turned sharply upon him, and delivered him a stinging blow between the eyes.

Back went the huge bully, staggering against his nearest neighbour.

"Hullo! gently there, gently," said the assailed person in his turn. "What are you about?"

"A ring, a ring!" cried the mob, all alive on the instant for a pugilistic encounter.

And accordingly a ring was formed for Red Ralph and the bully to display their fistic science in.

Boxing was in its zenith at the period of our narrative, and all the *élite* of society recognised it as a national institution.

The captain of the Yellow Band was, it is needless to say, a thorough proficient in the "noble art," and the marvellous manner in which he decorated the face of the bully quite excited the admiration of the whole crowd.

The fellow who had so imprudently assaulted Red Ralph was not devoid of skill, but his courage was of the meanest order.

He had only attacked our hero, counting upon his own superior size and strength.

But he had caught a tartar.

In the space of a few minutes he was so thoroughly drubbed by the captain of the Yellow Band that he took to his heels, bellowing for quarter.

Our hero coolly turned down his cuffs, and was retreating before the uproarous plaudits of the mob, when some one plucked him by the sleeve.

"*Beware!*" whispered a voice in his ear.

"Of what?" demanded the captain of the Yellow Band quickly.

"You are watched."

Ralph glanced up and perceived that the speaker was none other than Walters, the lieutenant of the Yellow Band.

"Walters?" he echoed.

"Ay, but mix with the mob. You are observed. We are observed now. Go."

Red Ralph beckoned Hubert, and they pushed their way into the mob still deeper.

"Do you see that poor fellow?" demanded Walters.

"No. Whom?"

"He in the pillory."

"Oh! then it is the pillory that the people are looking at?"

"Yes."

Red Ralph had pushed his way nearer, and saw the unfortunate wretch whom the mob were pelting and howling at like a mob of Maories.

"See, Hubert," he exclaimed. "Do you not recognise him?"

"Ah! by Heaven it is he. Poor unhappy fellow!"

They all recognised, in the tortured wretch, Snake, the spy and victim of Jonathan Wild the thieftaker.

CHAPTER CXXXIV.

THE ROBBER'S WIFE — LOVE AND SORROW — LAURA DELANE — LEONORE IN LONDON — ADVENTURE IN EASTCHEPE — THE GIPSY BOY — REVELATIONS — THE OLD HOUSE — PROTECTION — THE TRAP — THE SPY — DANGER.

IT is now time that we should resume the adventures of Leonore.

It will be remembered that we quitted her in the forest glade adjoining the old haunt of the Yellow Band.

Here she had been the witness of an attempt upon the life of Laura Delane by Jonas, the outcast of Mina's gipsy tribe, and here she had averted the impending catastrophe by a mere chance.

Here, too, had followed an explanation between the two girls which had caused them both much unhappiness.

The one had learnt that he to whom she had given her whole heart and soul belonged to another, whilst the robber's lady wife had found, to her bitter sorrow, that the captain of the Yellow Band was no longer faithful to his plighted troth.

After the explanation which ensued between the two girls they separated, each going in a different direction.

The sight of each other was odious to both.

Laura Delane fled the country for a while, and then, after a protracted absence, returned to England.

What further befel her after this we shall have occasion to note as we proceed a little later.

Leonore returned to London.

Here she had resources of many descriptions.

Many of her relations, not knowing, but more than half guessing, that all was not right at Glyde House, would have provided her with the means of subsisting in retirement and out of the way of Lady Glyde's machinations, but Leonore could not so far humble herself and disgrace her unnatural parent as to ask their aid.

All that she would accept at their hands was the means to provide her with a humble and secluded home.

Leonore found the very place she sought in an old-fashioned mansion in the east of London.

It was a fine old place, palatial in aspect, and containing many old nooks and contrivances, which invested it with great interest to Leonore.

Here she passed her time, if not pleasantly, at least in freedom from molestation upon the part of Lady Glyde or her emissaries.

She had been in this retirement for about a month

when as she was rambling through the streets she met with an adventure which led to another of such a character as will necessitate the relation of it.

She was passing through Eastchepe when she came upon a poor miserable-looking youth, who sat upon a doorstep in rags and wretchedness.

His deep-coloured swarthy cheeks were sunken so that there appeared to be very little more than skin covering the bones, which were fearfully prominent.

There was a pallor too apparent through the dark bronze hue of his sunburnt flesh which told of suffering and want, trials and privations.

Leonore's tender heart was touched.

Her hand and slender purse were ever open to assist the needy, and she stooped over the suffering youth and placed a piece of silver in his hand.

"Thank you, lady," said the boy, glancing into her face.

There eyes met, and there was a mutual sign of recognition.

"Lady Leonore!" ejaculated the boy.

"Lemuel!" exclaimed Leonore.

"Oh, lady, lady, you don't know how I have sought this meeting in weary wandering, and all in vain. How I have longed to gaze upon your beautiful face, to drink in the music of your voice, and look upon you thus."

And he fell upon his knees, grasping her hand and devouring it with kisses.

"My poor Lemuel," said Leonore. "How is it I see you thus, an outcast and a wanderer from your tribe?"

"You are the cause of it."

"I?" said Leonore. "I the cause of it, Lemuel?"

"Yes. Know you not that I am the foster-brother of Jonas?"

"I do."

"But do not too hastily condemn me unheard."

Leonore could see now that they were collecting a crowd, and so she left, bidding him again meet her at her home.

To the minute the gipsy boy kept the appointment, and then followed an explanation of all that had oc-curred since she had been abducted from the forest home of the wandering tribe.

"My poor Lemuel," said Leonore, "how much you have suffered upon my account!"

"Speak not of that, dear Lady Leonore," said the boy. "It is nothing."

"Nay, it is much, more than I can at present repay."

"Repay?"

"Ay. But at a future day—"

"Hold!" said the boy, drawing his half-clothed form up to its full height, while his deep hazel eyes flashed with scornful indignation. "What repayment do you speak of, Lady Leonore?"

"Such as it might be in my power to offer. I am not rich—"

Lemuel waved his hand impatiently at this.

"Lady," he said, "would you offer gold for payment of such sufferings as mine?"

Leonore was so astonished at his indignation that she could not reply to this.

"Pile up your dross, lady, until it reach the twinkling stars above us, and you cannot heal such wounds as mine. It is not gold I seek."

"What would you, then?"

"Gratitude."

"Gratitude?" repeated Leonore. "Gratitude for what?"

"When I shall have earnt it. Your money is kindly proffered I doubt not. I feel assured it is. But, oh, if you could but feel the humiliation of spirit which I experience when *you* offer me gold you would in pity refrain."

"You are a strange lad, Lemuel," said Leonore. "Truly I cannot comprehend you."

"You cannot understand that there should be aught that I could love better than gold."

"I don't say that."

"But you mean it. I know well the value you housedwellers put upon us birds of the forest."

Leonore smiled at the boy's vehement words.

"But, Lemuel," she said, "you know that the love of gold is not the weakness of the Zingaro alone."

"I know it. But I also know that you think the gipsy's soul is to be bought with your base dross."

"Not I."

"Then why have you offered your gold to me in payment of such love as mine?"

Leonore was completely staggered by the boy's words.

"What are you talking of, Lemuel?" she asked in wonder.

"Of you. Of you, oh! light of my eyes! Oh! Lady Leonore, you never can know how deeply I have loved you—how doubly severe I have felt the stigma cast upon me by the tribe and by Mina, to think that I should be suspected of complicity in the outrage of that bird of prey, Jonas. But I shall be avenged upon him—bitterly avenged."

As he said this his teeth were tightly clenched, and he shook his fist with determination which caused Leonore to tremble.

"Hush, Lemuel," said Leonore. "Would you speak of such things against your own foster-brother? Hush! I pray you."

"My brother?" iterated Lemuel vehemently. "My foster-brother? Were he my own twin brother, I swear he should not escape me now."

"Where is Jonas now?"

"I know not."

Leonore was glad to hear this, after the rash boy's desperate resolves.

"And the tribe?" she asked.

Lemuel shook his head sadly.

"I know not," he said, "for since I have been an outcast from the tents of my fathers I have not known anything of their movements."

"How long is it since you left them, then?"

"I cannot tell. So long seems to have passed that I have well-nigh lost all count of time."

"Poor Lemuel!"

"It is the first time that I have lived away from the tribe, and it has been a sore punishment to me."

"No doubt."

"But as sore will be the retribution that I shall seek upon Jonas the traitor."

"Hush!" said Leonore, shocked at the intensity of the hatred in his tone and words. "Speak not thus of your brother before me, Lemuel."

"Not if it pains you, Lady Leonore."

"It does indeed."

"Forgive me, then. But I have suffered so much, oh! so much! through his treachery."

"I do," said Leonore. "For, alas! I too know what that means."

"Yes. But have you no fear that he may dog your steps even here?"

"I had, but now I have grown bolder. I have learned at last to place dependence on myself alone. You shall see, Lemuel," why I no longer fear surprise when once within the walls of my citadel."

She led the way upstairs into her bedchamber.

Here she pointed out to the gipsy youth a square trap cut in the floor, which opened with a spring.

This she could set from the head of her bed by turning a handle, which was very skilfully concealed beneath the furniture at the back.

"You see, Lemuel," she said, "that upon the least

alarm at the door or window I can put a pit between myself and danger which quite ensures my safety."

"Yes."

"And this is not the only protection that I have. See here."

And she produced a pistol, which was snugly ensconced beneath the pillow.

Strange times, these, when one had to have recourse to such means to protect one's self.

A further conversation took place touching the present whereabouts of the gipsy tribe, and it was agreed that Lemuel should go and gather all the information which lay in his power upon the subject of their wanderings, and return the next day at the same hour.

But, in spite of all she could urge, Leonore could not persuade the boy to accept of money.

"I can bear anything rather than take money at your hands," said Lemuel. "You see, Lady Leonore" (and here he pointed to his wan and wasted cheeks), "I can even starve."

"Poor Lemuel!"

"Your pity is meat and drink to me," said the gipsy gratefully. "Farewell, lady."

"Till to-morrow."

"To-morrow."

And he was gone.

As he left the house he could see that a dark form issued out of a neighbouring doorway, and that his footsteps were dogged.

"Some one on the watch," he muttered. "I must see to this. It must portend evil. But to whom?"

CHAPTER CXXXV.

LEMUEL'S WATCH — THE VISION — THE OATH — VENGEANCE ON THE OUTCAST GIPSY.

THE next day, true to the appointed hour, Lemuel was there.

As he arrived before Leonore's dwelling he noticed a fellow in a huge beard, and wearing a large slouched hat, lurking near and casting furtive glances up at the house.

Seeing Lemuel draw near, he made off at once.

"There's something about that fellow," thought Lemuel, "that I know. That walk, I'm certain, is something that I've seen before."

At first he thought of following and finding out for himself, but impatience to keep the appointment that Leonore had made soon induced him to change his determination.

He entered the house, and was soon lost in ecstacy to be in the presence of the mistress of his boyish heart.

He had quite forgotten the loafing man in the beard.

"Lemuel," said Leonore, as soon as he arrived, "you are sure that no one now knows of my whereabouts?"

"No one."

"No one has watched you here?"

"Of course not."

"Because Jonas is just capable of placing spies to track you. But I don't fear for myself, since, as I have shown you, I am quite prepared for any violence that might be offered."

"But no one watched me hither. I am assured of it."

"That is well. I know of course that you would be careful if any thought of danger occurred to you, but I have endured so much that you cannot wonder at my fears."

"Poor lady!"

"You do not know all that Jonas has done to injure me."

The boy's eyes flashed fire.

"You do not mean, Lady Leonore," he said sternly, "that Jonas has ever dared to offer you wrong."

"No. Thank Heaven I have always been armed, to guard against extremities."

"In what way do you mean, then, Lady Leonore?"

"He has robbed me of a faithful friend and servant."

"How robbed?"

"He has slain her."

Lemuel was completely overpowered by the revelation of his brother's atrocity.

"Another cause, then, to help me on to the vengeance which I contemplate," said Lemuel.

"Nay, take my advice. Do not offer to molest Jonas. Rather shun him."

"Never."

"Consider that he is your own foster-brother."

"Were he twenty times my brother, he should not escape the just punishment that he has earned."

"Beware of him."

"I fear him not."

"But he is no ordinary foe. He is cunning, subtle, and crafty as the fiend. He may yet even talk you over to his own purposes."

"Think you so meanly of me?"

"No. But I know Jonas."

"He will harm you no further."

"Do nothing rashly I entreat. I implore of you."

"I will not."

"I rely upon your word."

"You may."

"Be careful, too, that you are not watched in leaving here. I mistrust Jonas so much, for I know his cunning and his duplicity as much as his ferocity."

"Lady Leonore," said the boy earnestly, "you have nothing to fear from Jonas."

"How know you?"

"I have a presentiment—a kind of inward monitor whose warning I cannot doubt."

"And this same monitor tells you that I have nothing to fear from Jonas?"

"Yes. And not that alone."

"Ah! What else?"

Lemuel looked up into her face earnestly before replying.

"It tells me also, lady, that I am not long for this world."

"Lemuel," exclaimed Leonore, "what a strange notion!"

"You will see it is true, though."

"What makes you think so?"

"Think? I do not think. I know. I have it here as surely as I know to whom I shall owe my death."

"To whom?"

"Jonas."

"Ah! Your own foster-brother. What horrible fancy is this that you are possessed with?"

"It is no fancy, but a presentiment of evil the earnest of which is assured to me."

"Then take the advice of a friend, Lemuel."

"A friend," said the boy gratefully. "Tell me what I may do that will please you, lady."

"Fly!"

"Whither?" demanded Lemuel, with a clouded brow.

"Away from danger."

"Whence?"

"To the tribe."

"They will only receive me back on one condition."

"What is it?"

"That you go with me."

"I? Impossible."

"Then, lady, you know the alternative," said Lemuel.

Leonore could not help being impressed by what the boy said. However, she did not like the idea of deciding the matter rashly.

"Hark you, Lemuel," she said. "I do not mean to decide at once. Let me see you again to-morrow, and perhaps I may."

"Oh! thank you, thank you. A thousand thanks, Lady Leonore, for that word. To-morrow, then. Oh! that it would come at once! If I could but pass over the lapse of time that must intervene in sleep!"

"Wherefore?"

"That I might not lose sight of your bright face."

Boy as he was, Leonore felt that she coloured beneath his ardent glances.

"There then, Lemuel," she said, looking up again quite angry with herself. "Get you home at once. See that you are here to-morrow betimes."

"Home?" iterated the gipsy bitterly. "Home did you say?"

"Yes. Have you no home?"

"None but the streets."

"And your bed?"

"The flags—a doorstep."

"Poor Lemuel!" said Leonore. "If you would but humble your proud spirit for once."

"To what purpose?"

"Take some money and get food and clothing, and a lodging."

"From you? Never."

Leonore saw that it would be useless attempting to alter his determination, and so she gave up the point in despair.

Lemuel left, with the understanding that he was to return at a later hour upon the morrow, so that if Leonore made up her mind to return to the gipsy band she could take her departure with Lemuel unobserved.

Now Lemuel did not wander far from the home of the idol of his boyish heart.

He hovered about the house which he had just quitted until the dead of the night, when he came and seated himself upon the doorstep of a building immediately facing the residence of Leonore.

Here he sat watching in silence beneath the window.

This weary vigil, however, could not long endure. He had been there but a little over an hour when he fell asleep, his head bowing on his chest.

A thick irregular breathing now told how deep was the slumber into which he had fallen.

Whilst he slept he had a fearful vision.

He lay back upon the doorstep with hands tightly clenched, and grinding his teeth as if he would pulverise them.

It would almost appear that he was half sensible of what was passing around him, without being able to interfere in the matter.

Some supernatural power appeared to chain his senses.

And still he slept.

*　　*　　*　　*　　*　　*

"Gently."

"I'm with you."

Two men, stalwart fellows, of the very build of the Whitechapel loafers of modern days, with huge brawny shoulders, bulldog faces, and a slouching flashy gait, denoting the London thief, crept up to the house opposite which the sleeping gipsy boy was reclining upon the doorstep.

"Do you mean to do it by the door, Joe?"

"No—window."

"What's the use of wearing masks then? It would only excite suspicion if any of the Charleys happened to pass by."

"What matters? We could fight our way off without being recognised."

"As you please."

"Hold the glim."

"Here you are," said the other, raising the lantern. Now tell me—shall I follow you in?"

"No. Keep guard at the corner of the street."

The entrance to the house was effected, and the window closed to as if nothing had happened.

The scout meanwhile was on guard at the further end of the street as agreed upon.

Suddenly the gipsy boy started from his slumber with a loud cry.

"Jonas!—dog!—devil!" he cried. "You shall bitterly repent this."

CHAPTER CXXXVI.

LEONORE — SLUMBER — THE AWAKING — SUSPICIONS — THE AGITATED BEDCURTAIN — MIDNIGHT MARAUDERS — AN OLD FOE — THE PISTOL AND THE TRAP—"I AM HIT!"

LEONORE had retired to rest with her head full of the meditated return upon the morrow to the camp of the gipsies, beneath whose tents she had passed so many happy hours.

The anticipations filled her with joy, for her heart yearned once more to be with Mina, whom she had learnt to love with true sisterly affection.

At length, after lying awake some considerable time, thinking it over, and brooding over all the dangers attending upon such a step, she fell asleep.

It was but a short and fitful slumber, for her ears yet rang with the words of ill omen which Lemuel the gipsy boy had spoken.

Presently she opened her eyes again so gently that she could not understand it.

She was wakeful at once.

No yawning, no fatigue now; but she felt herself fresh and vigorous as in the middle of the day.

This was the more strange, as she had not awakened with a start, and nothing appeared to have occurred to alarm her.

All was quiet within the chamber.

Leonore looked towards the door, and perceived that it was yet fast as when she had left it.

The window, too, was not tampered with, she was sure.

What could have put into her mind the idea to examine into these matters?

It was not habitual with her. Some instinct appeared to warn her of danger ahead.

Yes, there was this, and there was something more.

She was conscious by the self-same instinct of there being a strange presence in the room.

There was nothing to see or hear to confirm this notion.

And yet Leonore felt as sure of it as if she had seen the person whose presence caused her so much alarm.

With her eyes strained to the very utmost she sat in the bed looking forward into the darkness.

Presently she fancied that the curtain of the bed by the right-hand post moved.

This was unfortunate if it really were so, for then the intruder upon her privacy was between her and the trap in the floor, upon which she so much counted for safety.

She could endure this deathly stillness and suspense no longer.

"Who's there?" she demanded.

No answer.

[A HORRIBLE REVENGE.]

"Stand forth!" exclaimed Leonore excitedly. "I can see you there by the bedpost."

But it needed something stronger yet to draw him out of his position, if any one was really there, as Leonore supposed.

"Stand forth, or I fire!" cried Leonore.

"Ah! Say you so?" shouted Jonas the gipsy, springing out from the bedcurtains.

"Jonas!"

"Ay!" cried the gipsy, flourishing a murderous-looking knife. "And now you shall die I swear."

"Stand back, rash man!" cried Leonore. "You would rush madly upon your fate."

"Put down that pistol."

No. 44.

"Never!"

"Down with that pistol, I say."

"Never!"

Before Leonore could divine his intention Jonas sprang forward and clutched her by the wrist.

With a cry of terror Leonore sprang back upon the bed, disengaging herself from his rude grasp with a jerk.

At the same instant, almost by accident, she caught hold of the handle concealed in the bed furniture at the back.

Click! went the trap, and she could hear it as it slowly revolved and opened.

With a sudden and desperate clutch Leonore had

regained the pistol, which for a brief period had quitted her grasp.

"Ten thousand devils!" roared the gipsy. "Down with that pistol, or—"

"Back!"

"Dare oppose me further, and you will repent it bitterly," cried Jonas.

"Back, or I fire!"

"Fire! and I swear that I will yet seek vengeance even as the last breath leaves me."

"Rash man, I would not slay you in cold blood."

"Fool!"

And again he advanced to the bedside and clutched at the trembling Leonore.

But she was out of his reach.

He could perceive still by her manner that the girl was so thoroughly averse to bloodshed that she would not venture to fire yet.

Counting, therefore, dastard that he was, upon her forbearance, Jonas clutched yet further and with a desperate hold succeeded in dragging Leonore half out of the bed.

But even in this fearful position her presence of mind never entirely deserted her.

She struggled desperately with her assailant again.

But she felt that she could not much longer oppose him unless she took some desperate measures to rid herself of his assaults.

Gathering up all her remaining strength into one grand effort, she dragged herself from the gipsy's clutches.

Then, presenting the pistol, which she yet retained, without any hesitation she fired point blank at him.

"Curses!" roared Jonas. "I'm hit—I'm done for."

He staggered back a few paces.

Then, with a cry of execration upon the head of the girl he would have wronged, he fell backwards through the open trap.

Leonore heard the dull heavy thud of the falling body as it reached the floor at the bottom of the trap, and a shudder shook her entire frame.

CHAPTER CXXXVII.

WHAT FURTHER BEFEL RED RALPH BEFORE THE PILLORY—A DANGEROUS JOB.

RETURN we for a while for a brief glance at the movements of the captain of the Yellow Band.

We left him, as the reader will remember, in company with the rescued prisoner from the fortress of the secret brotherhood, gazing in astonishment upon the unhappy wretch in the pillory.

This was Snake, the victim to Jonathan Wild's brutality.

Just at the moment that they were pushing their way through, and whilst the captain of the Yellow Band and Hubert were laughing over the defeat of the fellow who had attacked Red Ralph and came to such signal grief at his hands, Walters the Yellow Boys' lieutenant accosted Red Ralph with a warning that he was watched, upon which they pushed their way further into the crowd, and thus avoided all chance of pursuit, as they thought.

What the result proved the reader will discover as we proceed.

Once out of the danger against which Walters had warned him, Red Ralph's whole thoughts were occupied with the idea of alleviating the sufferings of the unfortunate spy Snake, of which suffering he (Red Ralph) argued himself the indirect cause.

"Can nothing be done for him, Walters?" demanded Ralph.

"No."

"It is a sad pity," said Hubert," and upon my life I would give much to return the good service which he has so recently done both of us."

"And I too," said Ralph.

"Yes," added the lieutenant. "I'm nothing loth. He has proved himself a good friend to us. But how to help him? Could we bribe the mob to release him by force, think you?"

"No, no, no," said Ralph.

"It would be dangerous, I think," said the lieutenant.

"I, for one," said Red Ralph, "wouldn't countenance such a thing. It would be too risky."

Hubert regarded the captain of the Yellow Band in surprise.

"Too risky?" he said.

"Ay," said Red Ralph. "That is my word—too risky."

"But I thought that you liked risk," said Hubert.

"For myself I do. But with this case it is different. It would imperil others."

"If you mean us," said Hubert, indicating Walters and himself, "we can bear the hazard."

"Yes," said Walters.

"But there is the man himself. What of him?"

"He? Oh, he has nothing to lose."

"There you are mistaken. In the event of a failure to liberate him—a very probable termination, believe me—he would be so diligently watched that all chance would be lost for him."

The late prisoner of the secret brotherhood appeared to be struck with this simple reasoning.

"True," he said. "There is something in that after all."

"There is indeed," said Red Ralph, "for I have excellent reasons to know what close surveillance is kept on a prisoner who has once been caught attempting to break his bonds."

"Doubtless."

"We must wait patiently for our opportunity. It will be sure to offer."

"*Oh, yes, it will be sure to offer!*" said a voice behind them.

Red Ralph turned round, and found himself face to face with one of the officers, to whom he was aware that he was perfectly well known.

"Hullo, friend," said Ralph.

But before he could turn round or offer to retreat, if such a thought had occurred to him, he was clutched by the collar in a steady grip.

"At last," said the officer.

"What?" asked Ralph coolly.

"You are my prisoner."

The captain of the Yellow Band eyed him from head to foot with an amused expression.

"Your what?" he demanded, a supercilious sneer curling up the corner of his mouth.

"My prisoner."

"Pshaw!"

"Come, come, no nonsense. Move on with me, Red Ralph, or you'll get into trouble."

"You threaten me?"

"No, I warn."

"I tell you what," said the captain of the Yellow Band. "I warn, mark me; and unless you take your impertinent fingers from my collar, you'll find that I'm in no mood to brook your nonsense."

Without further reply, the officer attempted to drag Red Ralph away from the crowd.

But it was no easy task.

"If you don't take a civil warning you'll repent it," said Ralph.

"Oh! shall I?" said the man with a sneering laugh.

"Indeed you will. You will find yourself lying on your back there."

"Ah! how so?"

"THUS!"

And with this Red Ralph dived down suddenly, and, bending double, caught the officer in the pit of his stomach, and, raising him up with a jerk, pitched him a fair somersault over his head.

There he lay, as Red Ralph had promised, flat upon his back.

"Help! help! help!"

The bystanders, who had been watching the dispute with the greatest interest, here caught up the cry, and in the space of a few seconds the pillory and its unfortunate victim had lost all its charms.

Yelling and screaming, the mob tore round Red Ralph.

As soon as the officer was thus temporarily disposed of Red Ralph and his companions began to deem it expedient to look after their own safety by making a speedy retreat.

But the little fracas had gained them such notice from the crowd that they were most painfully lionised forthwith.

"Stop him! Stop him!" cried the officer, struggling to rise to his feet.

"What for?" demanded the nearest of the crowd.

"He's a robber."

"Hullo there! Good people, this man's a robber he says," quoth the man.

The words were barely uttered ere the lieutenant of the Yellow Band delivered him so smart a slap upon the face that he was most effectually silenced upon the instant.

But it was too late to be of any real service in their behalf.

The mob had already caught up the cry, and it was echoed from mouth to mouth with alarming rapidity.

Red Ralph and his companions, seeing now how matters stood, began boldly to push their way through the dense throngs around.

"Stop them!" cried the officer.

"Stop them! Stop them!" shouted a hundred voices at once.

"Let any man dare attempt it," said Red Ralph, drawing his sword. "At his peril!"

"I'm with you, captain," said the lieutenant of the Yellow Band.

"And I," said Hubert.

And the two latter drew forth their swords with a flourish that sent the mob reeling back with the loudest cries.

The three placed themselves back to back, forming thus a triangle of immense strength.

Three sturdier horsemen never yet met together.

And these three bold men thus challenged a whole mob—hundreds and hundreds thick.

But a mob without a ringleader is but a coward booby after all.

The whole of these people, desperate as they had been the minute before, were awed—cowed by the sight of three naked blades held in the grasp of three sturdy fellows.

"Stand back!" said Ralph, waving his weapon over his head.

"Stand clear!"

"Back with you!"

And the mob opened out for the three men to pass through.

Suddenly there was a cry in the crowd, which at once was felt by the captain of the Yellow Band to be of startling importance.

"Huzzah! huzzah! Here come the runners. Huzzah!"

Red Ralph looked up to see the cause of this alarming cry and perceived that, as the mob said, so it was.

A body of "runners," i. e., Bow Street runners, as they were afterwards called, appeared in sight mounted.

"The officers! the officers!"

"Now then," cried the captain of the Yellow Band to his two companions, "the Philistines are upon us, and we shall be cut to mincemeat by the weight of them, if we can't get clear of the mob."

"I should advise staying in the mob," said Hubert. It will afford protection from a mounted force."

"They will dismount, though."

"Cut your way through them."

"There's no time to wait."

And now they set to work in downright desperate earnest.

They waved their swords around their heads and dashed through the shrieking crowds, whilst the yells and cries of those who were touched with their weapons or crushed with the pressure of the mob rent the air.

One officer more eager than the rest made his way into the crowd in advance of the others, and unfortunately knocked down and rode over a woman and child, making the cause of justice fatally unpopular at once.

Curses and maledictions of the bitterest kind were called down upon the heads of the officers.

"Stone him!" said one.

The suggestion was met with the loudest shouts of approval upon every side.

The next minute a dozen missiles came flying through the air, and one of them, striking the officer at whom they were all directed, cut him severely over the right eyebrow.

It was a hideous wound in appearance, although of no great danger.

Down trickled the blood, giving a most ghastly appearance to the face of the unfortunate man.

It was a terrible thing this for the cause of the law. Blood appeared to arouse all the brutal instincts of the mob at once, and they thirsted for more.

And now the fearful example thus dangerously set was followed up with such effect that stones, bricks, and missiles of every description and size filled the air on all sides, and came falling amongst the officers in a way that naturally alarmed that gallant body of men not a little.

Two of their number were struck from their saddles.

"Wheel round!" cried the leader of the constabulary.

"Yah!" yelled the mob.

"Trot."

"Yah!" said the crowd again. "They are obliged to retreat. Off they go. A fig for the brave runners!"

There was no mistake about it, they did retreat.

And a most undignified retreat it was too.

And so we find that to the accident of a woman and child being knocked down Red Ralph and his two companions owed their safety.

CHAPTER CXXXVIII.

THE DARK ROOM—THE SCUFFLE AND THE OPENING CEILING—A FALLING BODY—JONAS—THE FIGHT OF THE GIPSIES—THE BRAND OF CAIN.

WHEN Lemuel, the gipsy boy, awoke from his slumber in the singular manner we have narrated in a previous chapter his first care was to examine the house of the Lady Leonore.

He had awakened from a horrible vision.

In his sleep it had appeared to him that the mistress

of his boyish heart, Leonore, was in the hands of the ruffian outcast, his foster-brother, struggling for life, and that he was then close at hand but powerless to aid her.

With a distinctness and vividness that made him doubt the unreality of the dream after he had awakened, he had seen Jonas the gipsy plunge a long knife into her snow-white bosom.

Then he had drawn it forth reeking with her pure blood, and repeated his hideous deed.

Then of a sudden his vision had changed, and Leonore was free, and—oh, joy!—unhurt.

At her feet lay the ruffian Jonas, unable to rise.

It was at this portion of his dream that Lemuel awoke.

He ran across to the door of Leonore's house to see that all was yet secure, so strong was the impression of the dream upon him.

All was safe there.

Then he looked about him to see if there were any other means of entry to the house.

There was the window, but this appeared to be secure. There was no sign of violence anywhere.

He tried the window as a last resource before returning to his hard couch.

It was unfastened!

Lemuel, not knowing why—certainly there was no reason—felt a chill all over him as he made this unpleasant discovery.

"Shall I venture in?" he thought. "No! I'll not. They might doubt the honesty of my purpose, and that would be death to me."

He paused a while to think it over, irresolute.

"And yet," he continued, "I had better. If harm happen here—and I have a strong presentiment of evil—I could never forgive myself. No! I'll risk even her displeasure. She may even think badly of me so that I but serve her."

And with this resolve the gipsy climbed up to the window, and entered the house as his foster-brother had gone before him but a few minutes previously.

But with what opposite intentions had they gone!

As Lemuel dropped from the window to the floor he fancied that some strange voice above caught his ear.

He listened intently for a while, and, not hearing it repeated, endeavoured to persuade himself that what he had heard was only his fancy.

He now began to look about him.

The place in which he now found himself was a dark square room, the only light which was admitted to it being from the small window through which Lemuel had effected his entrance. .

"There surely must be some door," thought Lemuel.

But none could he see. He groped his way all over the room, but no signs of a door could he discover.

This he knew must merely be something that he could not explain, for certain it is that there never yet was made a room without a door.

"Unless," went the gipsy's thoughts, "unless the people here go through the ceiling."

By a most singular chance, it was at this identical moment that he fancied there was a strange cracking noise in the ceiling above.

He looked up, startled.

Yes, surely enough, the ceiling did open, disclosing a trap some four feet wide.

And above he could distinctly hear voices in quarrel.

"Ah!" exclaimed Lemuel. "The trap in her room. And, by Heavens! 'tis the voice of Jonas!"

It is impossible to give an adequate description of the boy's sensation upon making this discovery.

To hear the confirmation of his most horrible fears taking place above him in the struggle for life between Leonore and Jonas the gipsy, and yet unable to stir hand or foot in her behalf, was too awful.

"Tremble, Jonas!" cried Lemuel. "I'm by your side."

But they heard him not in the chamber above.

Both Jonas and Leonore were so much engaged in the desperate combat that not even the booming of cannon could have taken their attention from each other.

Presently there was a shot fired.

Then, with a cry of execration and baffled rage, the outcast gipsy fell through the trap.

Lemuel chanced at this instant to be standing beneath shouting frantically, and so happened to do just the reverse of what he would have chosen.

Jonas falling glanced upon his foster-brother, and down they both fell.

However, the fall was broken, and Jonas the gipsy's back was probably saved by it.

"Jonas!"

"Lemuel!"

This was all that the foster-brothers could utter for a while.

"Jonas! devil! black-hearted fiend!" cried Lemuel. "You shall suffer, and bitterly, for all the wrong that I have suffered through you!"

"Curse you!" exclaimed Jonas. "I'm half dead already."

"Nor think to escape hence at all."

"Silence, boy!"

Lemuel had now regained his feet, and, although considerably shaken by the rough fall he had met with, he dashed forward upon his foster-brother.

The other grappled him as he came.

And now behold the two gipsy foster-brothers, nurtured at the same breast, locked in each other's arms, not as they ought to have been in amity and brotherly love, but in the deadliest hate, thirsting for each other's blood.

But it was very clearly seen how unequal was the contest between them.

Lemuel was as nothing in the other's brawny grip.

He struggled boldly, but all his efforts could avail him nothing.

Jonas remorselessly caught him in an iron grip by the throat, and held him down.

Then, with his disengaged hand he sought his knife, which had fallen to the floor.

"*Take that, boy!*" he hissed in the ear of the choking Lemuel.

And he plunged his weapon up to the hilt into his breast.

Lemuel's hold upon him immediately relaxed, and he fell back lifeless.

*　　*　　*　　*　　*　　*

A light appeared at the trap above.

It was held aloft and moved about.

"Who's there?" said the voice of Leonore.

There was no answer.

Leonore disappeared with the light, and presently there was a footstep without, and the door was opened, admitting Leonore.

We may here explain that Lemuel had failed to find this door because it was in a recess which had escaped his observation.

Leonore entered, holding the light in one hand and grasping a pistol in the other.

Judge, then, her horror and astonishment to find the unhappy Lemuel lying bathed in his own blood upon the ground, gasping for his last breath.

And Jonas?

He had flown.

Yes, notwithstanding his wound, the sturdy vagrant had contrived to escape, to wander the face of the globe, for ever to bear the brand of Cain.

CHAPTER CXXXIX.

THE DEATH OF THE GIPSY — THE JOURNEY TO
THE FOREST—THE DOCTOR—FATAL VERDICT—
AN AFFECTING SCENE — THE VOW OF VEN-
GEANCE — WOE TO THE MURDERER — AN EYE
FOR AN EYE—THE GIPSY TRIBE.

"POOR LEMUEL!" said Leonore, much shocked
at the dreadful spectacle which met her view.

"Ah! lady," said the gipsy boy, looking sadly
into her face.

And he held his hand clasped over the hurt, but
the blood gushed and founted through his fingers,
saturating his garments.

"This is very awful," said Leonore. "Who has
done this?"

"He!" gasped the boy.

"Jonas?"

Lemuel nodded, being now unable to speak.

"And he has fled! Which way?"

The boy glanced up at the window.

Leonore stooped over the bleeding gipsy and examined the wound in his breast. It was an
ugly gash, and an experienced eye would at once have
seen that the fatal instrument had pierced the lungs.

She took her handkerchief and, hastily tearing it in
two, bound it tightly over the wounded breast, at
once affording the sufferer a temporary relief.

"That is better," he murmured, looking up into
Leonore's face, with his eyes full of love and gratitude. "It seemed as if I breathed through the hole
he's made there."

"Poor boy!"

"Is it very ugly?" asked the gipsy, with a sickly
smile.

"It is painful, I suppose, but not dangerous," said
Leonore.

"You do not think so."

"I do."

"Then I know better. I've something that tells
me that I shall never recover this."

"Why do you think so?"

"I don't know. There's something within me
that tells me to look out for the end."

Leonore looked upon the face of the dying gipsy,
and, her woman's heart overflowing with grief, she
burst into tears.

"Don't weep, Lady Leonore," said Lemuel. "I
don't mind dying."

"But there is no danger."

Lemuel shook his head.

"I grieve alone for one thing," he said.

"What is it?"

"Jonas has escaped."

"For the present. Be sure justice will yet overtake
him."

"Justice?" echoed the gipsy boy, bitterly. "Talk
not to me of justice. I know too well what that means.
There is no law that will touch him."

"No law?"

"But Lynch law."

"Then, if the thought of vengeance can comfort
you now—though I would fain see other thoughts
occupy your heart at such a moment—"

"Ah!" said the gipsy boy, interrupting her,
"then you know that I am dying."

"Nay."

"It is useless, lady, attempting to keep the truth
from me. But I will not die until I have seen the
tribe again. I have yet some strength left."

He rose to his feet, and now, in spite of all that
Leonore could urge, he would insist upon quitting
the house.

Seeing that he was not to be put off this purpose,
Leonore would no longer oppose him, but now, un-

fortunately, when Lemuel was upon the point of
starting, the bandages around his wound got loose,
and the blood poured from his breast in a perfect
torrent.

Leonore was now in great trouble.

"I see," she said half aloud, "I must now do
what I should have done at first—send for a surgeon."

Lemuel caught the words.

Faint and suffering as he was, he was not to be deceived.

"It is useless sending for a surgeon for me, Lady
Leonore," he said. "I know well, better than you
can, that I am past surgery, yet I would, if possible,
once more see the band—breathe the pure air of the
open country. I stifle in this close city."

"I would do something for you, Lemuel, if it were
in my power," said Leonore. "Tell me what it is
that you desire."

"Nothing in life but to see the tribe again," replied
Lemuel.

"Nothing?"

"Nothing. Yet stay, there is one thing."

"Name it."

"Your love. Forgive me, lady. I am dying. I
have not many hours' life, perhaps not many minutes',
or I should not trouble you with my love."

"Hush. Do not speak to me thus."

"Pardon me, Lady Leonore," said Lemuel, taking
her hand, and raising it respectfully to his lips.

"I have nothing to pardon."

"Nay, but you have."

"To pardon, Lemuel?" said Leonore. "When I
see you thus, and all through my unworthy self?
Never! never!"

"Bless you, Lady Leonore!" said Lemuel, pressing
her hand to his lips. "It is such happiness to love
you, even though my time is so short."

In the meantime Leonore had rung for assistance,
and now her waiting maid, who had hastily dressed
herself, came upon the scene.

Her mistress hurriedly explained the state of the
case, and bade the girl assist the wounded gipsy into
the street, there to await her coming.

"Go on, Nelly," she said, "for I shall follow you
and Lemuel before you can reach the street."

"Lemuel, ma'am?"

"Yes, Lemuel Rook."

Rook was the family name of the gipsy.

Accordingly Nelly assisted him into the street, a
journey which was only effected with great difficulty.

Now Nelly had not been quite so attentive and
thoughtful to the wounded boy as her mistress, doubtless because she did not justly estimate the injury
which he had received.

The consequence was that when they reached the
street poor Lemuel was in a dreadfully faint condition.

"Can you not call a coach?" he asked in a low
tremulous voice.

The girl looked at him quite frightened.

She had only time to open her arms and catch
him, for he fainted away, a dead weight upon the
girl.

Nelly was so startled at this that she did not know
what to do.

First, though, she laid the inanimate body gently
down, and then began to think of calling her mistress.

Yet this was no use.

It was a surgeon who was wanted now, rather than
Leonore.

"What can I do?" exclaimed poor Nelly, wringing her hands in anguish. "Rook, dear Rook."

She looked up and down the street in every direction, but no assistance was at hand.

What was to be done?

"I must leave him here while I run for assistance."

Her resolution was no sooner taken than it was put into execution.

She ran swiftly down the street, turned to the left, and saw to her delight a doctor's red lamp some short distance along.

She ran to the door and knocked and rang with an eagerness that brought an immediate answer.

"Will you come, please, and see a young man who has fainted, sir?"

"Where?"

"In the next street. Come quickly, or he'll die."

Nelly's tearful earnestness brought out the doctor himself to inquire who it was.

She repeated to him what she had said to the page, and the doctor, thinking it a case of real urgency, merely waited to don his hat, and followed her.

Her impatience outstripped the doctor's methodical stride, and she was back to the spot where she had left the fainting Lemuel before he had turned the corner of the street.

We say where she had left him, for the gipsy had disappeared, leaving no trace behind.

She ran hastily here and there, but there were no signs of Lemuel, and when the doctor, panting with the exertion, arrived upon the spot, Nelly was quite startled with a string of the most violent vituperations which the amazed man of physic poured upon her offending head.

It was in vain that she explained. He would listen to no explanation.

The doctor was sure that some fraud had been contemplated in thus dragging him out of his snug bed at such an untimely hour of the night, and without any further parley he at once laid hands upon the girl for the purpose he averred of giving her over at once to the authorities at the nearest lock-up.

Nelly protested her innocence in piteous terms, and called upon her mistress to witness what she had said.

But our narration does not touch upon her difficulties any further, and therefore we shall leave her to get over these as best she may, whilst we see what has really become of Lemuel.

It was simple enough, although a puzzle to the distracted maid, Nelly.

Whilst the latter was gone for the doctor Leonore had performed a hasty toilet, and descended to the street.

Here, to her surprise, she found Lemuel fainting and alone.

Her first care was to call a sedan chair. She found one by chance not far off, and away they went.

Being cooler than her maid had proved, Leonore had the good sense to take the wounded boy at once to a surgeon, and have the wound dressed.

It was a duelling age the reader must remember, and the condition of the gipsy boy was not sufficiently strange to call forth any undue amount of attention upon the part of the doctor.

The man of science dressed the wound and shook his head gravely the while.

He would have ordered him to be put to bed and shrived without delay, but Lemuel would not hear of it.

"Give me something, doctor," he said, turning his full hazel eyes upon him imploringly, "to keep life within me until I reach the tribe."

"I cannot."

"Cannot?"

"Cannot guarantee your life for one hour," replied the doctor.

"Then I doubt your skill much, for there are a dozen old women in our tribe who could give me drugs beyond count to patch me up—perhaps to save my life."

The doctor shook his head with an incredulous smile.

"Impossible," he said.

"I tell you it is not impossible. They possess a knowledge of culling of simples and extracting balsams of life from plants which are entirely useless to the ordinary world."

"I should much like to know of such elixirs," said the doctor. "But here I can give you something which will revive your drooping strength a while. But I would not deceive you into entertaining false hopes of life."

The gipsy was greatly revived by the draught which the doctor presented him with, and they left.

Having succeeded in hiring a coach, Leonore, by the direction of Lemuel, ordered the driver to conduct them to the forest, to a certain house upon the border where he knew they could obtain information.

It was a long and tedious journey, for Leonore could not allow the coach to go fast, as the jolting punished the wounded boy severely.

It was morning when they arrived at the forest, and Leonore was overjoyed to find that not only had they arrived safely there, but that the tribe were also near at hand.

The coach was dismissed, as Lemuel insisted upon walking, and, half carried by Leonore, they sought the tents of the Zingari, where they yet lingered by-the-bye, in spite of the lark having heralded the new day some time since.

It were futile attempting to describe adequately the excitement created by the return of Lemuel and Leonore.

But when it was found that the former had but a few hours' life remaining, and had only lasted thus far by a miracle, a wild roar of execration burst from the lips of every member of the tribe.

Mina saw by the rapid transitions in the poor boys' expression how awfully near was the end, and with remarkable promptitude she called a council of the tribe to inquire into the matter whilst there was yet time for Lemuel to bear witness against his assassin.

"Speak, Leonore, my sister," said Mina. "Say who has wrought this mischief, that our tongues may curse him."

"And our hands avenge," said one of the gipsies.

This was greeted by the approving shout of every man, woman, and child of the tribe.

Leonore then described as briefly as possible the whole affair—her meeting with Lemuel in Eastchepe, the boy's visit to her residence, and her conjectures as to the cause of Jonas having learnt her whereabouts.

"Is this so?" demanded the gipsy queen of Lemuel.

"Yes. She says so. She can but speak what is true."

"I know it," said Mina, looking affectionately towards Leonore. "And I do but ask you to confirm what she says, that the tribe may hear it from the lips of their own murdered brother."

"They do, and will avenge me?"

This, being put by the dying boy as a question, brought forth a shout from the gipsies which made the neighbouring forest re-echo with the sound.

"Mina," said Lemuel, beckoning her to his side, and motioning away the rest of the tribe.

"Speak, Lemuel," said the gipsy queen, leaning over him.

"Promise me one thing before I go."

"Name it."

"Swear to have his life—Jonas. I'm not vindictive, and I would spare him for myself, but if he is not destroyed he will slay her."

"It shall be done," said the gipsy queen, pressing his hand.

"You swear?"

"Solemnly."

"I shall die in peace," said Lemuel, "since I know that she is safe. Guard her well."

"Do you so love her, then?"

"Better than anything—better than life. You can believe that," he added, pointing to his wounded breast.

"Enough, Lemuel," said Mina. "It shall be done. Strange," she added aside, "how everybody loves her, even this poor boy. Oh! all—all might, if *he* did not. But let me not think thus, or I shall doubt my own love for her—dear, dear Leonore."

As she turned round upon the boy again she perceived by another change in his expression that it was nearly all over, although apparently he was not aware of it himself.

He glanced up at Leonore tenderly, and she, happening to look him at that instant, caught his eye and was beside him instantly.

"How do you feel now, Lemuel?" she asked tenderly.

"Better."

"Do you want anything?"

"No. I want to sleep. May I hold your hand?"

"Yes."

And grasping her hand between his two, he glanced up into her fair face and smiled, as if bidding her a temporary farewell before reposing.

Then he sank at once into a gentle sleep, from which he never awakened.

In five minutes from that time Lemuel the gipsy boy was no more.

His spirit passed away so serenely that Leonore had not the faintest suspicion that all was over.

Indeed it was not until one of the old women of the tribe pointed it out to Mina by a sign that it was discovered.

*   *   *   *   *   *

"Over this cold clay of our departed brother Lemuel," said Mina to the tribe, who listened in silent reverence, "let us swear ourselves to vengeance."

"We do!"

"An eye for an eye, a tooth for a tooth, shall be ours."

"It shall."

"And Jonas shall die the death of a dog!"

"He dies the death of a dog!" responded the tribe in solemn unison.

It was an affecting scene.

Leonore felt her flesh crawl as she heard this wild people swear over a corpse such solemn dreadful vengeance.

But she could but acknowledge to herself that if vengeance were a human as well as a divine prerogative, now was the occasion to call it forth in all its bitter force.

Oh! Jonas! The day is at hand when the brand of Cain, which you have set upon your front, shall be bitterly washed away by your people.

Washed away, and in your own blood!

Beware of the knife of the Zingaro!

Fly to the furthermost corner of our globe, and you shall not escape your doom.

CHAPTER CXL.

JONAS AND MICHAEL THE HARE AT THE ALSATIAN INN.

JONAS the gipsy had not escaped unscathed after his brutal and bloodthirsty attack upon Lemuel, his foster-brother.

The shot which Leonore had fired had so severely injured him that, although he managed to make his way through the window and escape, yet he had not proceeded far before he fell upon the ground in a fainting fit, from which he did not recover for upwards of an hour.

Fortunately for him he had crawled out of the way some little distance, or Leonore would have come across him.

Here he had lain for about ten minutes after recovering his senses, when he heard footsteps approaching.

"If it should be that boy," he said, "or even the woman, for I think that Lemuel must now be surely safe from harming his *dear* foster-brother."

A sardonic grin was upon his countenance as he muttered these words.

However, he was evidently in no small pain at the thought of some one approaching, for, although he had been almost incapable of moving before, he now managed to rise to his feet and to hurry away into security.

His first care was to direct his still tottering steps to the inn in Whitefriars where he had hitherto found refuge.

It was a task to reach this, but he managed to accomplish it in time.

At length he arrived here, and then his courage—or rather his false strength inspired by fear—was at an end.

He sank prostrate as soon as he arrived upon the spot.

His wounds were attended to, and he was put to bed, where he remained through a long and weary illness.

He was particular to instruct the landlord of the inn to deny him to any one who should ask to see him.

The importance of this request the landlord interpreted in his own way. Suffice it to say that he promised to obey it; and to the best of ability he kept his word.

One of the tribe arrived there within three days after the terrible events which had ended so fatally to the gipsy boy Lemuel, as we have just narrated.

But the landlord, true to his promise, denied the presence of Jonas the outcast.

But the Zingaro who had come was not so likely to be put off.

The search for Jonas had now commenced in real and downright earnest.

Not a stone was left unturned.

The gipsies were not a people to be easily put from a purpose once fixed.

But Jonas was wary, and his host was ever upon his guard.

The reason of the latter being so was that he feared to lose not only a customer, but also the respectable character which his house had hitherto borne.

Six weeks elapsed, but yet no signs of any other foe of Jonas the gipsy outcast appeared in sight.

He grew stronger, and gradually, as his convalescence proceeded, he quitted his room and descended to the lower part of the house.

He was seated at the window of the parlour one day when, upon glancing out, he was greatly startled to see one of the gipsy tribe pass.

The man was lurking about evidently with some purpose, the nature of which Jonas too well divined.

He felt that he had earned a fearful punishment at the hands of his tribe, and he dreaded the meeting with any kinsman of his slaughtered foster-brother.

No sooner did he make the discovery that the gipsy was lurking about than he ascended to his own room and fastened himself in, bidding the landlord most positively to deny having seen him for some months past.

But even this could not secure him.

Vengeance was upon his track, and the revenge of the Zingaro he well knew was not of the same cold order as that of the house-dweller.

All that day he passed in fear and trembling of meeting with the tribe, but yet no one appeared.

Towards nightfall there was a knock at his bedroom door, and it was in the most nervous apprehension that he demanded who was there.

It was strange that he should ask the question, because he was always certain that at this precise moment no one but the doctor attending him could come.

"The doctor," replied a low voice without.

Jonas opened the door and admitted him at once, and in strode a tall thin man with a deal of beard and moustache of a singularly light hue for the swarthy tint of his complexion.

Jonas started back to see that this was not the doctor he expected.

"Dr. Grady has met with an accident," said the newcomer, "and he has sent me over to see you this evening."

Jonas fixed his eyes steadfastly upon the doctor and stretched forth his wrist for his pulse to be felt.

The man of science caught the wrist in an iron grip.

Then with his disengaged hand, instead of producing a watch to note the pulsation, according to the practice of the faculty, he whipped forth a long blade.

The cheeks of Jonas the outcast blanched with fear.

"Doctor," he faltered.

"No," thundered the doctor. "Your sickness has dimmed your perception."

"What mean you?"

"You don't remember me?"

"I—I—"

"Look now."

Jonas glanced up.

The doctor suddenly appeared bald-faced, and about his neck hung a rich profusion of jet black and glossy gipsy locks.

"Michael the Hare?"

"The same."

"What mean you, Michael?"

"Assassin!"

"Michael."

"Murderer! Thief of life and damned slaughterer of your brother, you are doomed. No power on earth can save you. You are ours!"

"Mercy!"

"Come!"

CHAPTER CXLI.

JONAS THE OUTCAST IN GRIEF.

JONAS attempted now to rally a little, growing suddenly ashamed of his weakness.

"What do you mean by this, Michael?" he demanded, with an attempt at his wonted bullying tone.

"Ask yourself."

"I do," replied Jonas, "and vainly I wait for an answer."

"Would you have me tell you, then?"

"Ay."

"Then know this. Lemuel fell by your hand."

"A lie, to begin with," interrupted the gipsy.

"'Tis yours, in your murderous throat," replied Michael.

At this Jonas half rose from his seat, clenching his fists with a revengeful gesture.

"Sit down, Jonas," said Michael the Hare sternly, "and don't venture to try on your tricks with me, or I may be tempted to rob our people of the vengeance which is their due, by slaying you here at my feet."

Jonas grew livid with mixed fear and disgust at the goading taunts of Michael the Hare.

"Beware, Michael," he said. "Beware, I warn you. I am no puny boy to be disposed of with big words. Have a care."

"What would you do?"

"What would I do? Crush you—grind you down beneath my heel."

"Bully was ever your name. Spare yourself your big looks. You know the value that I put upon them."

"Dog! I'll—I'll—"

"Pooh! pooh! Your anger may be potent against a stripling, a lad, a boy, but it can avail you nothing against a man. Grovel in the dust at my feet, crawl and fawn, and you shall not escape us."

"Begone."

"I go, but not alone."

"Indeed? With whom, then, Michael the Hare, would you go?"

"With you."

"And where?"

"To join the tribe."

"For what purpose?"

"That you will learn full soon, as you will find to your bitter cost."

"And if I refuse to go?"

"You dare not."

"Dare not? I do."

"Then I can find the means to make you."

"I should like to see you exercise your boasted power."

"You shall. And you shall say, too, that it is no boast. Once more, I ask you to return with me quietly."

"I will not."

"Then you see how we have means to compel you. I need not remind Jonas Rook that the gipsy's vengeance is none the less secure because delayed. From this moment your steps are dogged. The house is watched. Dare to step forth, armed to the teeth even, and you are ours. Jonas the Wolf is not safe night or day. Don't start back and fear me. I shall not strike *at present*. The vengeance must be executed in the presence of the tribe, who to a man have sworn your destruction."

"For what?"

"Murder."

Jonas shivered.

"But I deny this vile accusation. I know nothing of it at all, I will swear."

"Will you swear by the oaths of our tribe?"

Jonas started as if stung by an adder, and changed colour.

But he remained silent.

The oaths proposed evidently were of a terrible nature.

No gipsy was ever known false to such vows, and the perjured wretch Jonas hesitated, even with the possible release from the vengeance of his tribe to pay him for the taking of the oath.

"Cease all fooling, Jonas," said Michael, "and learn, to your discomfiture, that Lemuel lived to find us in our forest home to pour into our ears the tale of your villany."

This was apparently the heaviest shock of all to Jonas.

Now he deemed that all hope must be banished.

"You do not know all of that, Michael," he said in a fawning voice. "You know not what I have suffered through the boy."

[THE SPY IN THE PILLORY.]

"I do."

"He opposed me in the fulfilment of a vow that I had made. He struck me. You know what that means? You know that the Zingaro cannot bear a blow."

"I know that the Zingaro is false and treacherous."

"And I washed out the affront in the boy's blood."

"An eye for an eye, a tooth for a tooth. Lemuel has been basely, foully dealt with, and your blood only can appease the tribe. They will have it."

"Let them try to get it, then; and you, their bragging messenger, may return to them to say how much I value their empty words. They sent me forth to wander alone, and they shall find that I have in my turn cast them off. I do not value them that." And he snapped his fingers contemptuously.

"Beware, Jonas!"

"Silence, braggart, and begone."

Losing his temper at the taunts of Jonas, Michael the Hare sprang upon him, stretching him upon the floor, and would have strangled him as he lay.

Jonas at once, however, had seized the bell rope, and tugged it with such violence that before any damage could happen to him there was a rush without, and the landlord and the men came with a dash to his assistance.

Michael the Hare was dragged off panting with rage at not having wreaked his vengeance upon Jonas.

No. 45.

"No matter, Jonas," he said. "You will suffer for it yet, be sure."

"You shall," retorted Jonas. "You would not have dared to brave me thus had I been in fit and healthy condition. You know that well."

"You lie!"

"Away with him, landlord. Don't let me be disturbed by any one else, mark you—not any one."

As they were dragging Michael the Hare from the place he turned towards Jonas once more.

"No one can get in to see you perhaps," he said, "but, mark me, it will not be safe for you to venture out. A prisoner you shall be, here in your own room."

And with this he was borne away.

From this day forth Jonas lived in perpetual fear of the vengeance of the tribe.

He dared not step forth from the house lest any of them should be lurking near.

Six weeks passed over after the visit of Michael the Hare, and Jonas had regained his old strength and health.

The imprisonment to the house grew unendurable, and he began to get to the end of his ill-gotten gains which he had received from Lady Glyde.

The landlord began to grumble now that the payments for food and lodgement were not forthcoming.

Jonas made the resolution at last to go at all hazard, choosing the best time to avoid any one whom he felt it would have been awkward to meet.

Accordingly in the dead of the night he arose and donned his garments, and made into a parcel all the unconsidered trifles he could pick up about the house, not being particular as to their ownership.

Then he descended the stairs and quietly unbolted the door, sneaking into the street like the guilty thief that he was.

He looked about him now, notwithstanding the strangeness of the hour, in great fear of being observed.

But no.

By all that was fortunate the coast was clear.

He ran along until he turned the corner of the street, when a dark form sprang out of a doorway, and, confronting the startled gipsy, bade him stand.

Before he could offer the least opposition he was seized in a powerful grip from behind, and held whilst the man in front threw over his head a thick woollen cloak, which completely stifled all utterance.

In this state he was borne some little distance, when he could hear a carriage drive up, and he was thrust in.

*   *   *   *   *

The carriage stopped, and Jonas was lifted out.

It had been a long and tedious drive, as he had been in an almost fainting condition all the time, from the effects of the stifling bandage around his head.

The cloth was raised by one of the men, and Jonas, to his infinite astonishment and alarm, found himself in the midst of the gipsy tribe.

He quaked with terror and knew not what to say.

All around him he saw stern faces, and instinctively he began to make up his mind for the worst that could befal him.

CHAPTER CXLII.

THE ZINGARI'S VENGEANCE — THE FOREST — THE COUNCIL AND JUDGMENT — JONAS CONDEMNED — HIS VICTIM'S INTERCESSION — THE EXECUTION.

"WHAT shall be the doom of Jonas the outcast?" demanded Mina in a loud clear voice.

One solemn response came from the band simultaneously, as if but one big voice had given it.

"DEATH!"

Jonas trembled from head to foot.

"Is this your own unbiassed wills?" demanded the gipsy queen.

"It is."

"And what death shall he die?"

"The traitor's death—the gallows."

Jonas sank upon his knees in the most abject terror. His swarthy cheeks were blanched with fear, and he trembled from head to foot.

It is little to be wondered at. He found himself in the midst of a desperate and determined people, and wherever he turned he encountered but the sternest looks.

He had had his friends—comrades in the tribe—but not even these now greeted him with a friendly glance.

"Mercy, mercy, my brethren," he said.

"You appeal to your brethern?" said Mina sternly, "you who have murdered your brother?"

"Death to the assassin of Lemuel the Zingaro boy."

"Nay, at least, hear what I have to say in excuse before you go to extremities."

"Not a word."

"Nay—"

"Not a word."

"One moment," said Mina, and the murmurs were hushed upon the instant. "Let us hear what excuses the wretch has to offer. Let us know what excuse a man can give who has basely slain his own brother."

A murmur of approval went through the tribe, interrupted, however, by the few dissentient voices of the more violently angry.

"Speak, Jonas."

"Well then, this boy was ever in my path. He loved a house-dweller—loved one not of our people, mark you—and so he thwarted me at every trick and turn upon this account. At length he dared to raise his hand against me, and you know that no Zingaro can take a blow unless it be washed away in blood."

"Ay, ay, ay."

"I struck, then. I admit it. So far I am guilty," said Jonas humbly. "I acknowledge my fault—I can't call it anything worse, because it was done in the heat of passion, not with cold deliberation, as the house-dweller takes his vengeance, and I did not mean to slay the boy."

"You lie, Jonas," said Mina.

"I swear it, boys," said the outcast, turning from the gipsy queen to the tribe generally. "But you all know that Mina bears me no love. To her I owe all my misery—to her you owe the loss of the brave boy, Lemuel, whom I mourn no less than you."

And the ruffian shed a few crocodile tears.

A dead silence followed this speech, and Jonas began to interpret it to his own advantage.

We shall see if he correctly estimated his people's nature in this.

"What say you to this?" demanded the gipsy queen.

"Let it go on," said one.

"How?"

"To the end."

The coward heart of the fratricide sank within him at these terrible words.

They rung in his ears a fearful death knell.

As there was a mumuring in the tribe, the gipsy queen bade Leonore stand forth and bear witness against the doomed man.

"No, no, no!" said our heroine. "Oh! spare me this!" she said imploringly. "Pray let me go from this!"

"She here ?" ejaculated Jonas, now for the first time perceiving her. "Then all is lost!"

Now, pressed by the shouts of the gipsies to speak, Leonore stepped forward into the midst of them, and related in a clear calm voice the attempt upon her own life, and then the evidence she had to give respecting the murdered Lemuel.

This by far the most affected the tribe; but they were also much moved when Leonore, in a voice broken with emotion, gave the history of the fearful doings of which she had been a horrified witness upon the first night in Glyde House after her protracted absence.

When she described the slaughter of the fatal well-hole the tribe gave a howl of execration for the unnatural wretch who had slain the unhappy and faithful waiting maid, in addition to the many dastardly crimes for which he would have yet to account when the tribe had executed mortal vengeance upon him.

The gipsy queen advanced, and called to three of the tribe to proceed with the fatal business in hand.

"Isaac, Ishmael, Silas, do your work."

The three gipsies came forth, and then, before Jonas the outcast could think of offering any resistance, he was seized from behind again, and pinioned securely.

"Proceed."

A stout rope was produced, and one of the men, with awful deliberation, proceeded to make the end of it into a noose.

At this juncture the cries of the doomed gipsy became terrible to hear.

Leonore upon her knees besought them to have mercy, but her prayers were disregarded.

The gipsy had earned his doom, and they did not shrink in the execution of their vengeance as laid down, even though it had to be done upon their own brother.

Leonore was lifted from the ground in a state of semi-insensibility, and borne away to another part of the forest whilst the fatal business proceeded.

"Jonas," said the gipsy queen to the outcast as he stood beneath the tree with the cord about his neck, "before the last, have you any request to make ?"

"Yes."

"Name it."

"Shall it be done ?"

"Yes."

"If in reason," added the gipsy queen, fearful that his vindictive spirit might lead them to compromise themselves by too rash promises.

"Then I would have her throat cut."

"Whose ?"

"That woman's—Leonore's !" said Jonas, with his eyes full of the bitterest vengeance.

The ruling passion of his wicked wasted life was indeed strong in death.

The gipsies then went up in turn and shook hands with him, bidding him an eternal farewell, but he did not appear much inclined for this portion of the ceremony.

"Death to the traitor," said one of the patriarchs of the tribe.

Then at this signal the cord was pulled up, and Jonas the gipsy dangled in the air.

In the space of a few seconds he had ceased to breathe.

Right glad are we to draw the curtain over the dreadful scene.

Human vengeance upon humanity is ever a sad spectacle, and the present was scarcely less horrible in its features because the punishment doled out had been so richly merited by the gipsy vagabond who now swung a ghastly corpse upon the forest oak.

CHAPTER CXLIII.

THE PILLORY AGAIN—AN OLD FRIEND THERE—A TEMPTING OFFER — JONATHAN WILD — AN UNPLEASANT RECOGNITION — MOB LAW — THE PELTING AND ITS RESULTS — THE MILITARY CALLED OUT — A STREET RIOT A HUNDRED YEARS AGO.

THE day following the painful exposure of Snake the spy in the pillory another victim was exhibited in that disgraceful invention of justice, to humiliate and degrade criminal mankind to the lowest depths.

This was the third day that week that the excitement seekers of the locality had been gratified with this elevating spectacle.

It was, however, such an inspiring exhibition that it required something more than a three days' show of it to satiate the crowd.

The mob upon the third day was even greater than before, and the unhappy victim was jeered more vociferously than ever by the lively populace.

Missiles of every description were now hurled at the head of the offender, of whose fault even they were ignorant, illustrating with sad force how mankind only wants the faintest excuse for the exercise of cruelty, even upon its own species.

Eggs and vegetables in an advanced state of decomposition were amongst the more favourite projectiles of the wild crowd, and, as the reader will readily imagine, the unhappy criminal had not long been thus exposed before he was a pitiable object to look upon.

So disfigured did his face become with bruises and filth that before the half of his term of punishment had expired he was scarcely recognisable.

Like his predecessor in the pillory of the day before, the present culprit was not possessed of too much courage, and suffered in consequence thrice as keenly as a stouter hearted fellow would have done.

At first he did not murmur. He even appeared to bear the preliminary measures without so much as a sigh.

He had summoned up all his determination to bear the pain with stoical fortitude.

But, alas for the weakness of human resolution ! he had not endured the painful confinement for ten minutes before he began to weep and wail in a manner that was truly effeminate and lamentable.

He called upon his persecutors in piteous terms to release him from the cruel bondage.

This was of course about as probable, before the expiration of his hour, as that he would be rewarded for his offence, whatever it might be.

He begged, prayed, and entreated, but all alike turned a deaf ear to him.

Those who were within hearing, but out of reach of the missiles of the crowd, merely replied to his sorrowing by cruel jeers.

After his punishment had endured some time the pelting of the crowd was stopped of a sudden by the appearance of a posse of officers, who, armed with long staves, drove them back.

This created a deal of indignation, for pelting the unhappy wretches exposed in the pillory was recognised, whether legally or not we are not in a position to assert, as a legitimate feast of torture.

The reason of it was that one of the authorities—a man high in office, it was whispered—wished to confer with the criminal.

Then a man stepped forth, and made his way across the scaffold to the side of the prisoner.

"Well, my friend," he said in a cruelly pleasant voice, "and how do you feel by this time ?"

"Oh ! Mr. Wild," replied the culprit, "I shall die I'm sure."

" Perhaps."

The ready assent to the statement of which he expressed his conviction only appeared to alarm the prisoner, who perceived in the tone a hidden threat of fatal significance.

" Lor! Mr. Wild!" he exclaimed in anguish. " You don't mean surely that you contemplate anything worse than this ?"

" Possibly."

" Oh! I say, don't now."

" It's according how we take it, Bill Jenkins," said Jonathan Wild, with the coolest deliberation. " Now some people would not consider it worse to be turned off by Jack Ketch."

The prisoner's jaw dropped as low as the cruel engine he was confined in would permit.

" You don't mean—"

" Egad! I do, though," interrupted Jonathan Wild. " And not only do I mean it, but I mean also to see that no time is wasted in it."

The prisoner was beyond speech—he could only groan.

" You see, Bill Jenkins," resumed the thieftaker, " you have given us such a deal of trouble, and you are as slippery as an eel, so that I can think of no other means of securing you, unless, indeed—"

He paused.

" Unless what ?" exclaimed the culprit eagerly.

" Unless you feel inclined to purchase your freedom."

" Freedom ?"

" Ay. Not only pardon for all you have been guilty of—and many's the man that has been strung up for one tithe of what you have been guilty—many's the man, in fact, who has offended me a little, whose business I've managed at head-quarters when he has been perfectly innocent. Not only pardon, I say, but also liberty, man; hark you that. Liberty, upon one or two conditions."

" Oh! name them."

" Firstly, that you say where we could find your pal, the captain."

" Sheppard ?"

" No. You know that I can pop my hands upon him when I wish."

" Who, then, Mr. Wild ?"

" Don't be so confoundedly hypocritical!" exclaimed Jonathan Wild coarsely. " You'll do yourself no good by it, I can promise you. You know well who I mean."

" Not I, indeed, Mr. Wild."

" You lie, you dog. But you can do as you please. I shall derive more gratification at seeing you swing than in chasing down that devil, plague seize him !"

And he turned away, pretending to take his departure.

But he knew well that this was all that was needed to bring the man to his purpose.

He had not taken two steps before Bill Jenkins called upon him in piteous accents to return.

" Come back. Oh! come back, Mr. Wild !" he cried. " Don't, pray, leave me to my fate in that cruel manner. I'll do anything. I know who you mean."

" Curse you, I thought so."

" Don't be so violent, Mr. Wild."

" Don't fool away my time, then."

" No, sir. You mean captain Red Ralph ?"

" Of course."

" Yes, sir, what of him ?"

" Idiot! you insist upon misunderstanding what I say. However, yourself alone shall suffer for it, I promise you."

" Now don't, Mr. Wild."

" Silence! If you feel inclined to escape from that pretty position, and that nice little necklace, you had better tell me without delay all you know about Red Ralph."

" That's quickly done. I know nothing."

" Then nothing can save you."

And once more he turned upon his heel to depart.

And once again did the suffering criminal call him back in anguish.

" Stay one moment, Mr. Wild," he implored, " and I will endeavour to think if I know of anything."

" Now, I tell you what, Bill Jenkins," said the thieftaker. " I don't wish to make any bones of the matter, but I warn you that I'm just the least bit out of temper to-day. Now that's a thing that doesn't happen often to me, and so I would advise you not to trifle any more with me. I'm all the worse when I *am* just out. It's always the way with persons of an amiable disposition like myself. Now, if you fool any more with me, I shall grow unpleasant, I know I shall, and I shall leave you to your fate. It will soon be out of my power."

" Say what you want, Mr. Wild," cried Bill Jenkins.

" Firstly, to know where Ralph the Yellow Boy is to be found."

" I don't know, upon my—"

" Silence! and don't interrupt me. Secondly, you must aid us to capture him."

" The thing's impossible."

" Silence! Upon these conditions, and these alone, can you hope to escape from your just punishment."

" But how, Mr. Wild, can I help you to capture the captain ?"

" That's for your wit to discover. It *must* be done."

" I haven't an idea."

" Then I'll give you one. You can easily lure him to some convenient spot to do you a service. He's such a foolhardy fellow that he would even venture into the jug *incog.* to do you a service."

Bill Jenkins was silent.

" Well," said the thieftaker after a pause, " what say you ?"

" Let me out of this infernal pillory, and I will consider it over," returned the culprit. " I can't think here."

" I don't want you to think. Leave that to me. You have only to decide one way or another."

Bill Jenkins remained a long time undergoing a mental struggle. He could not readily bring himself to be false to one to whom he owed so much. And yet, upon the other hand, self was uppermost in his mind—a weakness he shared in common with men who were comparatively strong minded.

Whilst he was deliberating there arose a cry in the crowd.

One of the mob had recognised the thieftaker, who was universally unpopular, and a cry of execration arose.

This was followed by a shower of missiles—good hard substances—not such as had been thrown at Bill Jenkins.

One of these—a piece of jagged brick — struck Jonathan Wild upon the face, cutting him rather severely, to the immense gratification of the mob.

" My curses on ye all !" roared the wounded thieftaker. " A murrain light upon ye, one and all, ye dogs! Charge them !" (This was addressed to his men, who were below, pushing the mob back.) " Draw upon the scum! Chop 'em up! Cut 'em piecemeal! Curse me if they shan't rue it! And as for you, Bill Jenkins, you've taken too long to consider. I see in your hesitation a complicity with that thief, Red Ralph, and the Yellow Boys."

" Oh! Mr. Wild !"

" Fool! You would not consider my proposal, so

now let the law take its course. You shall find me no longer the soft-hearted fool I have been. You shall suffer for all this."

"I repent! I repent!"

"Too late."

"I'll tell all."

"You shall swing with him."

"I'll sell the captain."

"You will? Then—"

His speech was cut short by a second volley of projectiles, sent with more fatal aim than the former lot, and Jonathan Wild was forced to beat a retreat.

He left the scaffold, roaring with rage and pain from a series of small hurts received.

The blood was streaming copiously from his face from half a dozen wounds received in the short space of time.

He proceeded at once to call out a small detachment of military that was in attendance for fear of an *emeute* of this kind, and they charged upon the assembled crowds.

A riot ensued, in which several persons were severely injured.

Two old men, as we learn from the chronicles of the time, were killed outright—cut down brutally by the thieftaker's own hand.

This, however, could never be brought home to him, and thus, with fresh murder upon his soul, he pursued his guilty career with impunity.

But these are matters of history, with which it is not our purpose to deal here.

It had a result, of which we shall speak a little later.

For the moment matters more immediately connected with this narrative require our attention.

CHAPTER CXLIV.

LAURA DELANE'S JOURNEY—ITS PERILS—LEONORE'S PARTING GIFT—A TRUSTY GUARDIAN—WILD'S PLOTS—HIS ASSASSIN—THE INN AT DOVER—ALL'S WELL THAT ENDS WELL—FATAL CLIMAX—THE "GOOD INTENT."

LAURA DELANE, before she could flee the country as she had purposed, fell in with a very curious adventure, which, by the reader's permission, we shall give.

It does not exactly interfere with the thread of our narrative, and we give it more with the purpose of illustrating how far the brutality and personal animosity of Jonathan Wild could carry him, whilst we are upon the subject.

From his spies, of whom, by-the-bye, he had no few in his pay, he learned that Laura Delane was about to flee the country, and, although she contrived to elude his vigilance so far as to leave the metropolis in safety, he had set a trusty ruffian upon her track at the seaport town from which she was to ship.

Since the earlier legal prosecution of the unhappy girl certain facts had transpired which convinced the thieftaker that it would be hopeless to attempt now to procure a conviction for her.

To have her arrested and brought to trial, with the possibility of her escaping, would not at all have answered his purpose.

He therefore determined upon wreaking his private spite upon her by means which were not strictly legal.

He called one of his creatures to him—a wretch who had been condemned, and whose pardon Jonathan Wild had managed to procure for the purpose of making him his tool for life—and gave him instructions to proceed without delay to intercept her departure.

"You will ride hard for Dover," said the thieftaker. "Spare neither horse nor spur. Let 'em drop under you. No matter, I will pay all expenses. Ay, and a reward, too, that shall be dealt out with no niggard hand; but, mark me, you must reach before the "Good Intent" sails, or never let me look upon you again."

"It shall be done, Mr. Wild."

"Find her out. Here, on this paper, you will find her name and full description. The former I dare swear will not aid you much, as the girl has the cunning of the foul fiend to back her, but by the latter you must know her under any disguise. She has certain peculiarities of manner which mark her."

"Yes, sir."

"Now, for this girl I have the deadliest hatred. You know your part."

"Am I to go to extremes, Mr. Wild?" demanded the man, in a low significant whisper.

Wild regarded the man with a fixed irony glance which spoke most eloquent murder.

"*She must not leave the land!*"

This was all the instruction that passed between them.

"Go," said Wild, as the man departed. "Success and a rich reward attend you—or failure, and—well, never let me see your face more."

He never did.

But how or why we shall show, if the reader will follow us through the chapter.

* * * * *

Laura Delane travelled under the assumed name of Winter as far as Dover.

She reached the port in safety; but what was her chagrin upon arriving there to find that the weather was so rough that the "Good Intent" could not set sail until the following day!

She therefore made up her mind to rest contented until the morrow, feeling assured that no harm could possibly result from so trivial a matter as the delay of a single night.

In order to be prepared early for the departure of the vessel which was to convey her from her native shores, she hired a bed at an hotel close to the quay, an establishment, by the way, very different from those of our time.

Before parting company with Leonore, whom we should remark she had left in perfect amity, the highwayman's wife had given her some valuable advice and made her a few small presents.

Amongst the latter, curiously enough, was a pistol, one of a pair which she had kept by her for some time, observing that she would find no better guardian than that until she had left the land.

Laura was profuse in her thanks, and, more in gratitude than aught else, she followed the advice accompanying the present—viz., to keep it ever beneath her pillow, a custom which Leonore had adopted of late.

How singularly the use to which both put their several weapons corresponded is one principal reason for giving this incident, which, as we have before remarked, does not touch immediately upon the interest of our past or future narration.

Laura Delane retired to rest that night more happy and secure in her own mind than she had done for many a long and weary night.

The moon shone brightly through the window as she lay in bed, and she fell asleep, picturing the brightest things to herself.

A few short hours were to elapse, and these would rapidly pass in gentle slumber, and then—oh! joy!—she would be free.

The cruel restraint, the painful suspicions under

which she lay here would no longer have any fears for her,

She had not slept many minutes when she was suddenly and rudely awakened by a noise at the window.

With a start she raised herself up in bed.

Judge then of her horror and surprise when she perceived the dark outline of a man advancing to the foot of the bed.

He had seen that his entrance had aroused her, and he hastened to her side at once.

A long knife which he held in his grasp glistened brightly in the moonlight.

"Stand off!" cried Laura, "or I will fire!"

Her hand searched for the pistol—thrice welcome gift of the woman she had unintentionally wronged so deeply.

Instead of bringing the man to bay, as she supposed, it only hastened his movements.

With a cry he dashed forward at the girl, and struck a desperate and murderous blow at her, which, had it taken effect, would have settled Laura Delane's trials and struggles for this life.

But the courageous girl met the ruffian half way.

As he advanced she leant forward, and, pushing him back with the left hand, with the right she presented the pistol with certain aim and fired.

With a low hollow groan the assassin sank down.

The whole hotel was aroused.

Landlord, waiters, servants, guests, and all came rushing into the room, and found the midnight assassin breathing his last hard breath of life.

Jonathan Wild never did look on his face again.

A paper was found upon him containing a graphic description of Laura Delane, but it was not sufficient to trace the accomplices of the ruffian.

If it had been it would not have answered the purpose of Laura Delane to press an accusation.

The "Good Intent" *did* sail in the morning, and with it went Mrs. Winter, the girl who had so bravely defended herself from an attempt at assassination.

And Mrs. Winter (Laura Delane) was quite the lion, or rather *lioness*, of the voyage in consequence.

CHAPTER CXLV.

THE THREE TRAVELLERS — OLD RECOLLECTIONS — THE GLADE — THE TREE STUMP AND THE PASSAGE BENEATH THE FOREST — SUBTERRANEAN HOME OF THE YELLOW BAND — THE YELLOW BOYS GREET THEIR CHIEF.

RETURN we again to the forest where we have so often laid the scene of action during our history, and take up the adventures of Red Ralph.

It was at the well-remembered spot—the forest glade adjoining the hidden retreat of the Yellow Band—that our hero had made a halt, in company with Hubert, the sometime prisoner of the secret brotherhood in the moated castle, and Walters, the lieutenant of the Yellow Band.

As they pulled up their horses, Red Ralph, with that quietness which characterised all his movements, threw himself from the saddle, and made his way at once to the entrance to the thicket, which had to be passed to arrive at the entrance to the haunt.

"Follow me, Walters," he said to the lieutenant, "and bring Sir Hubert on after you."

"We follow, captain."

Red Ralph then pushed his way through the thick shrubs which grew straggling across the path in a most embarrassing manner.

"This way is apparently not in use much," said Hubert.

"Not of late," said Walters. "Our band is not what it once was," he added with a sigh. "When we were fifty strong you should have known us."

"Fifty! Is it possible? And what purpose were so strong an assembly for?"

"Oh! many."

"Moonlight birds?"

"Yes; but they have a bright side to their character, every man of them," said Red Ralph.

"I should say so," said Walters.

"And I too," said Sir Hubert, "to judge from their leaders."

They passed along in silence after this, until they arrived at the tree stump.

Here the reader may remember, in an earlier portion of our narrative, we have described how the gallant Tom King effected his entrance, which he discovered by accident, and had the startling encounter with the dwarf, who was afterwards so ruthlessly slain by Jonathan Wild's men.

Hubert was not a little surprised when he perceived the opening effected in the earth by the removal of the tree stump.

"This is a very wonder of singular devices," he remarked.

"It is ingenious, is it not?" said Red Ralph. "But we shall show you something yet more curious as we proceed."

"Indeed?"

"Yes. Step down fearlessly. It is dark, but the footing is none the less sure because you cannot see it at present."

Still Sir Hubert paused, not liking the look of it.

"Come. Fear not."

"Fear?" quoth Hubert indignantly. "That settles the matter. You shall see how much I fear anything whatever."

"The captain would not impugn your courage, Sir Hubert, I know," said the lieutenant of the Yellow Band.

"Not I, indeed. I know much better than you can, Walters, that this brave gentleman does not know the sensation of fear. Fear is for the vulgar and low-born; the patrician knows it not."

"Thus speaks the aristocrat," said the lieutenant of the Yellow Band, with a smile at the captain's vehemence. "It is a true axiom that what's bred in the bone is sure to come out in the flesh."

Hubert started, and was not a little surprised at the words of the lieutenant.

"What mean you?" he asked quickly. "Surely not—"

"Tut, tut," interrupted the captain of the Yellow Band. "I trust you will attach no importance to his words, Sir Hubert. We love each other well, and he, out of his great affection, would ever pursuade others with himself that I am noble."

"But, captain—"

"Silence, Walters."

The lieutenant was dumb.

"And he is right," said Hubert warmly. "You are noble, captain. You have that which constitutes true rank—nobility of soul."

Ralph shook his head.

"You are like Walters, over warm in my praise out of the respect you bear me."

"Nay, I swear."

"You speak somewhat rashly, never pausing to think that you speak of one who is proscribed by law —an outcast and a felon."

"No matter."

"Ay, but it does."

"Not a whit. Your hand, captain, your hand."

Red Ralph hesitated.

"You give it freely?" he asked, "in spite of my calling?"

"In spite of the whole world," said Sir Hubert. "If I heard the vilest things said of you now, captain Ralph, I should know what importance to attach to them. I have had the truest test that man can have of your worth—experience."

"There's my hand then," said the captain of the Yellow Band.

"I take it in love," said Sir Hubert. "Such affection and esteem do I bear you, so much do I owe you, that you have but to ask of me what you will, and if in my power it shall be granted."

"Then I have one favour to ask."

"Name it."

"If when our connection shall have ceased, and you have once more mingled with the world, you should hear my name mentioned, as you may, in loathing and execration—"

Sir Hubert interrupted him impatiently.

"I will not hear it," he exclaimed.

"Nay, but you may not be able to help it."

"The knave who utters a word against you shall recant before the whole world, or shall eat his words, I swear."

"Nay, I want not that."

"Say what you will."

"I was merely about to request you not to mention to any one that you had ever heard any absurd rumour of my being of noble birth."

Hubert looked with surprise at this singular request.

"I am not likely to hear such a thing I suppose?" he said, with an interrogation.

"No, no; but you might by chance. You understand?"

"Yes; but you may count upon my discretion."

"I do."

By the marked manner in which Sir Hubert now regarded him, the captain of the Yallow Band could see that the singular request had excited a deal of speculation in his mind.

Presently he held out his hand and addressed our hero in a tender tone of voice, accompanied by a kind of imploring gesture, as if inviting confidence.

"Tell me, captain—" he began.

"One moment," interrupted our hero. "Ere you put the question, which I anticipate before you shape it into words, let me beg you to refrain. There are subjects which are painful to all. I'm not a domestic man as you see, and so probably should not cite domestic proverbs, but forgive me if I remind you that there is a skeleton in every house. There is in mine."

Sir Hubert bowed.

"Forgive me, sir," he said.

"Nay," said Red Ralph, "there is nothing to forgive, or if there be it is rather upon my side than yours. Your curiosity, if I may so term it, is but natural."

This ended the matter for the present, and Red Ralph led the way on through the subterranean passage into the vaulted room where the memorable encounter above alluded to between the dwarf and Tom King had taken place.

They passed on into the next corridor, which issued into the chamber serving as the guard room, so to speak, of the Yellow Band.

As Red Ralph raised a piece of dingy drapery which hung over the entrance a singular scene presented itself.

All over the ground in picturesque groups were stretched the members of the famed Yellow Band, engaged in various amusements, the prevailing occupation being gambling of various descriptions.

Decimated, hunted, and destroyed as they had been by Jonathan Wild, and the myrmidoms of the law ever upon the track, they even now mustered some twenty strong.

At the approach of Red Ralph, Walters, and Sir Hubert a dozen men sprang to their feet with one accord.

"Who's there?"

"A visitor among us!"

"Spies in camp!"

A dozen exclamations such as these were muttered in a breath, and a dozen knives were whipped forth ready to drink the intruders' hearts' blood.

"Hold!" cried Red Ralph. "So soon forgotten?"

"'Tis the captain!"

A wild shout of joy greeted this announcement.

Then they rushed forward, crowding round their beloved leader, some actually clinging round his legs like a lot of overgrown children.

Such joy, such wild affection, was really touching to witness, and Hubert was not unmoved by it.

"One moment, boys," cried the leader of the Yellow Band. "You must let me introduce a friend. Sir Hubert, here, saved my life, and has made me eternally his debtor."

"Then a cheer for Sir Hubert!"

And a deafening shout rang through the vaulted chamber.

"What think you of this band of brave hearts, Sir Hubert?" demanded Red Ralph.

"Think?" exclaimed Sir Hubert. "I am lost in wonder."

"There's not a man amongst them but would lay down his life to serve me."

"I believe it. But how about their efficiency for the service?"

"You shall judge for yourself."

"Are they well armed?"

"Yes; but you shall see that also. I mean to proceed now upon no wild-goose chase. The world shall be rid of a pest."

"Your hand upon it."

They exchanged a hearty binding grasp upon it.

"Walters," said the captain of the Yellow Band to his lieutenant, "call out the men, and let them muster for parade up in the glade."

"Yes, captain."

CHAPTER CXLVI.

THE YELLOW BOYS—A REVIEW—EVOLUTIONS IN THE GLADE—AN ENTERPRISE DISCUSSED—THE ARRANGEMENTS AND THE TOKEN OF RECOGNITION—DEPARTURE ON THE MISSION—THE LIEUTENANT OF THE YELLOW BAND AND WHAT BEFEL HIM UPON THE ROAD—THE COURIER.

THE Yellow Boys were called up to the glade as desired, when it was found that they mustered one and twenty strong effective men, all ready to do or die in any cause in which their leader Red Ralph had an interest.

"To horse!" cried the captain of the Yellow Band.

With a shout the men ran off to prepare their steeds.

"Has every man in your band got a mount?" demanded Hubert, in surprise.

"Every one."

"Some perseverance and stratagem must have been employed to achieve this much," said Hubert.

"Both have been," responded the captain of the Yellow Band. "But we do not look at either when we have an object in view. We have to labour much harder in our wild and lawless way of life than any one in an ordinary occupation."

"Why, then, keep to it?"

"We love it."

"Is labour so sweet, then?"

"No; but we love the freedom that we have. We acknowledge no superior. No laws guide us here."

"It is a strange life."

"True; and a strange theory that binds us to it; but, outlaws though we be, we have such redeeming points to our characters that our crimes and frolics are forgiven here in consideration of the large set off of virtues."

"Virtues? I should think that virtue was a foreign word in the haunt of the Yellow Boys."

"Perchance the word may be; but you know us not yet. We are no ordinary footpads. We do not touch the poor and the needy. The rich and avaricious alone are our prey, and those I am bound to say bleed pretty freely for us."

"And is it possible that you contrive to keep up the band in such a state as this upon your—ahem!—in fact what you gather in the way of unconsidered trifles upon the road?"

"Not precisely. We have other resources."

"Would it be impertinent to ask what they are?"

"Well, frankly," returned the captain of the Yellow Band, "without desiring to make an unnecessary amount of mystery out of nothing, there are means that I have at my command, of which I do not even tell the boys themselves, and so I know that you will pardon my closeness."

"Nay; it is rather for me to ask pardon for my unwarrantable curiosity again," exclaimed Hubert.

By this time there was a rush of horses close at hand, and the whole band of the Yellow Boys rushed with a gallop into the glade.

They presented a fine and soldier-like appearance.

All wore long hangers at the side, and each saddle had its holster pistols of uniform size.

"Advance!" cried Ralph.

The movement was executed to the satisfaction of all.

"Form two deep. Single file! March! Halt!"

This was gone through with such military perfection and order that it excited the curiosity of Hubert beyond measure.

"Why, Captain Ralph!" he ejaculated, "where have your men learnt that? They have served."

"Most of them. They are either disbanded troopers or men who have deserted from various causes. Several have been unfortunate enough to incur the enmity of their superiors, and you know what that means."

"Alas, I do."

"An officer, you see, has the power of making the life of a man for whom he entertains a personal animosity one unceasing round of torment."

"True."

"The men have known of this resource, and have fled."

"To your satisfaction?"

"Yes."

"It must have been an addition to your Band worth having, for they are all good men."

"Yes; but it overdid itself."

"How do you mean?"

"They grew too numerous, and excited too much attention from the authorities," replied the captain of the Yellow Band.

"And you got troubled in consequence?"

"We did, indeed, seriously," said Red Ralph. "Imagine my grief when, upon returning to the haunt once, after a long absence, I found my men slaughtered, scattered, some dying, most dead."

"A surprise?"

"Yes, and a traitor in the camp. You will scarcely believe it possible, Sir Hubert, that we mustered nearly sixty strong once."

"Is it possible?"

"It is, indeed, a sad fact. Poor fellows! Well, well, it is of no use repining. One course alone remained for me."

"And that was—"

"To avenge them."

Hubert regarded the captain of the Yellow Band with a mixed glance of curiosity and wonder.

"Now, what think you?" resumed Red Ralph. "Are they fit and efficient for the service we want of them?"

"Undoubtedly."

"Then we start at once."

Red Ralph then called to his side the lieutenant of the Yellow Band, and gave him instructions to direct the men to disband and meet again upon an important service at a certain place.

They were to travel either singly or in couples; but not more than two were to ride together, lest they should excite attention.

To further ensure success in their mission and to avoid accidents, each man was to wear a small orange-coloured ribbon upon his left shoulder knot, not sufficient to attract the attention of any stranger, but that they might be easily recognised by each other.

Red Ralph, the lieutenant, and Sir Hubert were to carry a similar badge of recognition.

All the arrangements having been effected, the lieutenant gave the word to depart.

Every man had to provide himself with two days' rations, and was supplied with a sum of money sufficient to cover his expenses during the expedition.

This Sir Hubert would have provided, but Red Ralph would not hear of it.

"I give the services of my men, Sir Hubert," he said, with a slight shade of hauteur in his tone. "I do not sell them."

"Nay," replied Sir Hubert generously. "I would not, could not offer to purchase them. They are priceless."

Upon this they started off upon their several routes, with the understanding that they were to reunite at a given time and place.

Red Ralph and Sir Hubert rode in company, and the lieutenant took his departure last of all and alone.

This was a precaution against surprise of any kind, for it was well known to them that, in spite of the utmost vigilance they could exercise, they could not warrant themselves entirely free from the surveillance of the active and energetic authorities. The result proved this precaution to be a wise one.

The lieutenant before leaving paid a parting visit to the haunt, and examined all the exits and secret passages which as yet had not been discovered by the authorities.

All being right, he returned again to the glade, and, remounting his horse, rode away to the rendezvous.

It was a magnificent day, and the mild temperature was exceedingly well adapted to equestrian exercise.

The consequence was that he found the outset of his duty a most pleasurable part. For full five hours he rode on without drawing rein.

During the whole time nothing occurred of sufficient interest to record in these pages.

At length, growing a little weary of the ride, which had now begun to grow the least bit monotonous, and feeling some sensations of hunger and thirst, he drew up at a roadside house to bait his horse and attend to his own calls of nature.

Here he fell in with a little adventure which led to a series of trifling incidents of which we shall speak.

He was seated in the parlour draining a huge goblet of foaming ale when there appeared at the doorway a man booted and spurred like a courier.

[VENGEANCE.]

"Your servant, sir," said the man.

"Yours," answered Walters, his reply echoing in the pot, which he still held up to his mouth.

"You seem to be enjoying your liquor," said the stranger.

"Thank you, yes. Wanted it badly."

"Ridden far?"

"Some five or six and twenty miles," replied the lieutenant.

"A good pull at a single sitting," remarked the stranger.

"Yes. I have done much more, though, in my time," said Walters.

"And I, too. It is part of my trade," said the man. "But that north road is a bad one, and tires the horse greatly."

"Yes."

The man evidently did not anticipate such a curt reply as this to his observation.

"Have you come that road?" he asked after a pause.

"No."

"That east road is a miserable one. I don't wonder at your fatigue if you have done six and twenty miles of that."

Walters grew wary. "Confound it!" he thought, "the fellow wants to pump me; but its very little he'll get for his pains. He must be a courier."

For a while they sat in silence. The courier, having failed in getting up a continued conversation, was at a loss for a subject to start upon.

Presently, however, a peculiarity in the dress of the lieutenant of the Yellow Band caught his eye, and he remarked upon it in these terms :—

"You carry rather a gaudy top-knot on your shoulder."

"Yes," answered the lieutenant, "but a pleasant colouring."

"A love gift?"

"Yes."

"Are you sure that the fair donor is true to you?"

"Why do you ask?"

"Curiosity."

"Well, then," replied the lieutenant, "I presume that she is as true to me as I am to her. I am moderate in my dealings with women, and I ask no more of her."

"Very good so far," said the courier; "but in my ride to-day you are the fifth who has carried this gaudy device."

Walters felt that his cheeks were glowing like two live coals, not that he experienced any fear from the meddlesome stranger's words, but rather that the falsehood which he had intimated was discovered.

"Well, well," he said, rising to his feet, "I must be pushing onwards again. I have a long journey to go before nightfall."

"Indeed? How far?"

"Can't say precisely," replied the lieutenant shortly, and he immediately called the drawer and settled his reckoning.

Then, bidding the inquisitive stranger a good day, he turned and left the place.

"Good day, and a pleasant journey," said the courier. "If you had waited a little I would have accompanied you upon your journey. Wait but a little."

But Walters was gone.

CHAPTER CXLVII.

AN UNWELCOME COMPANION—"MONEY OR YOUR LIFE!"—THE WARRANT.

"THANK goodness that I'm fairly rid of that fellow," muttered the lieutenant as he resumed his journey. "He grew far too inquisitive and meddlesome to be pleasant."

The words had barely passed his lips when he heard some one pottering on behind him, and, upon turning in his saddle to ascertain the cause of it, he discovered the meddlesome courier, and the subject of his meditation, riding sharply after him.

Now the lieutenant's first impulse was to sharpen his pace into a trot, and thus avoid the stranger, but, upon maturer deliberation, it occurred to him that such a movement might possibly be construed into fear, and so he quietly continued without altering his pace.

In a few seconds the courier had overhauled him.

"Not left you yet," he cried, as he drew up with Walters.

"So I perceive," returned the lieutenant, with the slightest shade of displeasure crossing his countenance.

"No. I thought that I had better secure a cheerful companion whilst there was time than pause to refresh myself."

"Thank you."

"Oh! you have nothing to thank me for," said the courier. "I did it to please myself."

"Thank you again," replied the lieutenant. "But you are greatly mistaken if you think that it was to please me."

"No, egad?" said the courier, laughing boisterously.

"You are far out in your calculation if you did," added the lieutenant.

"No, no. I reasoned it thus with myself immediately after you had gone :—I can find houses of public entertainment anywhere on a frequented road like this, but cheerful genial company like yours (ahem!) is only to be met with upon rare occasions."

"Thank you again. But you will not find my company either cheerful or genial," said Walters.

"Pshaw! You do yourself an injustice. You're the jolliest fellow alive, if you only knew it."

"Well," answered Walters, "you don't know it, and so I feel that your company is forced upon me, as a premeditated insult to annoy me."

The courier could not longer pretend to misunderstand a speech which so clearly denoted anger.

"Hullo! friend," he exclaimed. "You are surely labouring under a great mistake."

"Not I," said Walters, "and I should advise you to quit my company."

"So-ho! sir, you threaten me?"

"No. I advise."

"Then since you choose to do it in that tone, I shall construe it as I please. I shall not leave you, lest you should have some absurd fancy that I fear you."

"You will not leave me?"

"No."

"Then I shall leave you."

"Indeed? How will you manage that?"

"Thus."

So saying, Walters drew one of his holster pistols and presented it full at the stranger—not a little to the other's surprise.

"Now," resumed the lieutenant, "you have refused my warning and advice, so you must pay for it. Your money or your life!"

"Villain, would you rob me?" exclaimed the stranger.

"Call it what you will. I certainly mean to have your property, alive or dead."

The stranger, without replying to this, felt for his holster pistol, keeping his eyes fixed all the while upon the lieutenant of the Yellow Band.

Walters perceived the movement, and before an eye could wink he gave the stranger a sharp rap upon the knuckles with the pistol barrel, and followed it up by a second with the butt end of the pistol upon the forehead, which sent him reeling from the saddle.

In the space of a few seconds Walters leapt from his horse, and was beside the fallen man, busily searching for his papers and valuables.

Valuables he could find but few. They consisted of an ill-lined purse, a large silver hunting watch, and a jewelled scarf brooch.

What few papers he could lay his hands upon he hastily thrust into his wallet and prepared to resume his journey.

It was well that he was so speedy in his movements for he had barely accomplished the rifling of the fallen courier when he heard the galloping of horses at no great distance from the spot.

No sooner had the lieutenant disappeared than two men rode up, and, seeing the courier stretched upon the green sward insensible, with a cry of recognition they dismounted, and hastened to restore him to consciousness.

As he came to his senses he muttered some few unintelligible words, and looked about him much perplexed and confused.

"Martin," said one of the men, "do you not know us?"

"What, Sloper ?"

"Ay. But tell us how this happened."

"Ah! I remember now. The traveller. 'Sdeath! The villain has robbed me. I knew it—this confirms it. By the dexterous manner in which he has cleared me out I can see that it was, as I supposed, one of the Yellow Boys."

"Surely not *the* one?" demanded one of the fresh arrivals. "Not Red Ralph?"

"Oh! no. I know him well."

"But has he really robbed you?"

"Ay. Before I could say a word he had given me a topper upon the sconce with a pistol butt."

"He has robbed you then. Gad! but it's a rare joke to take back to the bulldogs."

"Joke be hanged!" exclaimed the fellow surlily. "I see no joke in it. He has cleaned me out, and, worse than all, walked off with my papers."

"Confound it! Then the whole affair will be blown."

"You think so ?"

"Undoubtedly," replied the man. "Why the warrant is gone !"

* * * * * *

Walters rode at a dashing pace from the spot never pausing to examine his booty until he had put a good mile between himself and the fallen courier.

His disgust was great when upon opening the purse he found it to contain only three crowns and two or three small silver pieces.

"A vulgar dog!" muttered the lieutenant. "How dare he annoy me into stopping him upon the king's highway with only three dirty crown pieces in his pocket? The only consolation that I have in the matter is that I gave him that tap upon the head more as a reward for his impudence than in the way of business."

At first he even thought of carrying his disgust so far as to cast the money into the road, but then the wisdom of the axiom, "Half a loaf is better than no bread," occurred to him, and he pocketed the purse and his chagrin at the same time.

The only thing in connection with the matter now was that he felt that he should be forced to commit an injustice to his comrades.

It was the custom with the Yellow Boys to share all booty that was taken. But he could never own to having stopped a man on the highway for three paltry crowns.

"I wonder what the knave's papers can consist of," thought the lieutenant. "Washing bills, I'll be sworn. Tavern checks and tailor's accounts, as I'm a sinner, and not one receipted, or I'm no true man."

Whilst thus he rattled on he had opened one of the papers, which he found to be a printed form not filled in.

This he could make neither head nor tail of, and therefore he gave it up in disgust.

The next was also a printed form, but, unlike the other, it was filled in with writing.

"Why, hullo!" ejaculated the lieutenant. "Plague seize me if this isn't a warrant. I know the formula at the commencement too well to forget it. What can the fellow be? Surely not one of the bigwigs' bulldogs?" (*i.e.*, the cant expression of the day for the officers of the law). "'Sdeath! but it must be, though. Let me read."

He went on a little way until he was suddenly startled by coming across the name of Red Ralph.

"Confound it all!" cried the lieutenant again. "But this must be a warrant for the arrest of the captain. Then he was, after all, in pursuit of Red Ralph !"

It was indeed.

The ever vigilant officials had succeeded in tracking the captain of the Yellow Band back to the haunt recent as that had been.

Had it not been for the fortunate accident that had worried the lieutenant into silencing the presumed courier, he would be now upon their track.

Walters now understood why the fellow had remarked upon his shoulder knot and so pertinaciously forced his company upon him.

———

CHAPTER CXLVIII.

WHAT FURTHER BEFEL BILL JENKINS IN NEW-GATE — WILD'S ENMITY — THE ARTIFICIAL CALF — NOT A GOLDEN ONE — TEMPTING AND BRIBING — DIAMOND CUT DIAMOND — THE LETTER.

BEFORE resuming the movements of Red Ralph we will relate what befel Bill Jenkins after his release from the pillory.

He was taken off to Newgate, where Jonathan Wild at once waited upon him with further promises and threats concerning the revelation of Red Ralph's whereabouts.

But Jenkins was true to his word. He vowed never to betray the captain of the Yellow Band, and, as far as we have seen, he did not belie his promise.

"No matter," said the thieftaker. "We will soon see to this. If you do not think fit to reveal all you know—"

"Which ain't nothing," put in the unfortunate prisoner, with a lachrymose disregard of grammar.

"You shall taste a few of the delights of the press-room."

"Oh! Mr. Wild!"

"Think it over."

"But I ain't got anything to think over, I ain't, indeed, Mr. Wild."

"Very good. As you will you know. I am going—"

"Oh! don't go !"

"To order certain preparations for your superior comfort."

There was a tone of such cruel significance in the thieftaker's words that the unfortunate man shuddered.

He well knew that some horrible refinement of cruelty must be in contemplation for him if this were the case, for Jonathan Wild was only pleasant in this way when he meant something fatal towards his unhappy victims.

As soon as he was gone, therefore, Bill Jenkins set his wits to work to avert an impending catastrophe.

It was in vain that he attempted to bring his mind, such as it was, to bear upon the subject.

He could think of nothing but seeking the assistance of the captain of the Yellow Band.

He looked out of his dungeon window in longing. But the height from the ground was so alarming that he gave up all thoughts of attempting it at once.

No. The only thing was to send a trusty messenger to the captain of the Yellow Band.

But how to obtain a trusty messenger here?

This was no trifling difficulty.

As soon as the prisoner found himself alone he unbuckled his knee breeches at the right knee and slid down his stocking, revealing a nicely padded calf of paper money.

From this lot he carefully selected a bank note, and then replaced his stocking as it was before.

This done, he proceeded to fold the note carefully, and tear it through the middle, one half of which he rolled and folded in his neckcloth.

Then he patiently awaited the coming of the jailor, to whom he unfolded his heart warily.

"Morris," he began, "I have a job to put in your way."

"Have you?" growled the jailor. "And have you anything else to put in my way?"

"Yes."

"And have you got anything in the way of payment to put in my way as well?"

"Yes. A matter of ten pounds, if that's worth your while."

The jailor's eyes glistened greedily at this.

"Ten pounds, Jenkins?" he exclaimed. "What's to be done for the money? Out with it."

"Well, I want you to aid me."

The jailor turned from gay to grave at once.

"Stop there," he said, interrupting the prisoner. "You don't mean that you're going to try and tempt me to help you out o' limbo?"

"No. Now you don't suspect me of such a thing, sure-ly, Morris," said Bill Jenkins in a tone of wounded susceptibility. "I know too well that you are as faithful as the day to any one you serve."

"O' course. Nothing could put me from my duty," added the jailor.

"Of course not."

"Except at a price."

"Quite right, too, Morris," returned the artful Bill Jenkins, who was ready to pander to his weakness and vanities to any extent, as well as pay handsomely for the service he required, provided it could be achieved.

"Well, what is it you want?" demanded the jailor.

"Simply a note carried."

"Against rules."

"Who's to know it."

"Duty."

"Pshaw! Take my note as far as Whitefriars, to a given address, and the money's yours."

"Down with it."

"Oh! but you have to do the service first."

"Take the note first?"

"Ay, and let me write it too. For this you will have to get me some pens, ink, and paper."

"Stop a bit, Bill Jenkins. You don't mean to say as you can read and write?"

"Yes, of course."

"Now, before we go any further, Bill," said the jailor, "I warn you not to attempt to come the artful over me."

"Now, you don't suspect—"

"Don't I? I do."

"Well, then, you are a suspicious-minded man."

"Oh! no. Not by no means. Only when a man comes to ask a service of me, and he promises ten couter when he ain't o' course got ten pence in the blessed world, it's apt to make a fellow open his eyes rather wide."

"Yes; but I happen to have the ten pounds I promised."

"Gammon!"

"See that."

Upon which the prisoner flourished the half note before the jailor's eyes, much to his amazement.

"Hullo!" he cried. "Why, wasn't you searched when you came in, according to rule? I must do it at once."

Bill Jenkins began to regret his rashness.

"I have been searched," he said. "But what o' that? They'd never discover my secret."

"Well, we'll have a try."

"Stop," cried the prisoner as his jailor was moving off. "You don't think, Morris, that I'd be got over like that, do you? Now, I'll tell you what, attempt any of your games and I'll swallow the flimsey."

He crumpled it up in his hand and popped it into his mouth before the jailor could interpose.

Morris saw that he was now in real downright earnest, and so he forbore to trifle with him.

"All right, all right," cried the jailor. "Drop it, I say. I'll do it. What d'ye want?"

"Paper, pens, and ink. A note to reach Whitefriars before night."

"What house?"

"The Alsatian Bully."

"It shall be done—money down."

"No; half down."

"Half?" echoed the jailor. "How would ye manage that?"

"Simply enough. See here. This half the note is yours when the letter is written, and when you return from Whitefriars *with a written acknowledgement from the person of the receipt of it* you shall have the other half."

"Lor! Bill Jenkins!" quoth the jailor, in a tone of offended dignity. "How you do suspect!"

"Not I."

"It's what I call shabby."

"Fetch the paper."

The jailor grumblingly obeyed.

The note was written, and the jailor received half his bribe and departed in hot haste, eager for the "Alsatian Bully" in Whitefriars.

It was a notorious house and well known to the jailor; but the landlord informed him at once that Mr. Meadows, the traveller, was not then there. However, he knew where to get at him, and would see that the letter was transmitted to him without loss of time.

"Excuse me, sir," said Morris, "but what may this Mr. Meadows be?"

"What trade?"

"Ay, if any."

"Traveller for a trimming house."

"A bagsman?"

"Yes."

The jailor regarded the landlord fixedly for a few seconds, but could glean positively nothing from the steady stolid expression of his countenance.

"Well, Bill Jenkins," he said, as he returned to his prisoner-employer, "I've done it, and there's the landlord's answer written down. Give it me back when you've read it. I don't want no paper about."

"And here's the other half note. Now I shan't so much mind seeing Mr. Wild."

CHAPTER CXLIX.

JENKINS AND JONATHAN WILD AGAIN—THREATS —THE PRESS-ROOM—TORTURES—ARRIVAL OF AN UNEXPECTED VISITOR—WILD IN TROUBLE —AN EYE FOR AN EYE AGAIN.

THE morning following what we have just related Jonathan Wild the thieftaker paid a second visit to the cell of Bill Jenkins.

By his not proceeding to extremities at once it was clear that the thieftaker had yet hopes of gaining, either by fair means or foul, the information which he presumed Bill Jenkins possessed respecting the captain of the Yellow Band.

"This still augurs well for me," thought the prisoner; "for by a show of agreeing to what he wants I may escape the cursed tortures which he invents for me."

Presently Jonathan Wild entered the cell unannounced, which was, we should observe, his invariable rule.

It added to the dignity of his office he presumed, instead of lowering it.

At any rate, it helped to inspire his victims with that fear which he made it his purpose to create wherever he set his foot.

To see the wretched creatures shiver as he approached was joy supreme to the thieftaker.

Now Bill Jenkins was pretty sharp sighted, and he saw the thieftaker's weakness with a keen eye.

We have seen how he cringed and trembled and fawned before him to pander to the man's inordinate vanity and egotism.

It must not be supposed, however, that we would set up this degraded specimen of humanity us a model of courage and heroism, or even that he was to be admired for his wonderful diplomacy.

Jonathan Wild entered with a sternly severe look.

"Oh! good morning, Mr. Wild," exclaimed Bill Jenkins, rising with a servile bow. "Oh! good morning, sir. I'm so glad that you are come. I can't say how glad."

"Hold your tongue."

"Certainly—oh! certainly, Mr. Wild," said Jenkins.

"Have you thought over what I've said to you?"

"Yes."

"And what do you think?"

"Well, I'm still thinking, Mr. Wild, to tell the truth. I'm going on thinking. I like to think a good bit you know before doing anything rash."

Wild glanced up sharply at the prisoner.

There was actually a sound of jocularity or sarcasm in his voice, and he could scarcely believe it possible that the worm upon whom he could set his heel at any moment he chose would so far presume.

"Now hark you, Jenkins," said the thieftaker. "I have an idea that you are attempting to play the fool with me."

"Lor, sir!"

"Silence! Now, if for a moment I imagined such a thing possible I would think no more of having you turned off at Tyburn before the week was over than I would of cutting your ugly throat, if convenient."

Jenkins shivered.

"Do not be so violent, Mr. Wild, I entreat. Pity my nerves."

"Fool!"

"Yes, sir. You shall be sure, sir, before long, that I mean you fair, sir, I'm sure, Mr. Wild."

"Idiot! Do you think for one moment that I am condescending to make a compact with you? No such thing. I am giving you instructions, which you must follow out."

"Yes, sir."

"And woe to you if you don't obey me," said Wild.

"Trust me, Mr. Wild. I ain't such a fool as to throw up a good chance when I have one. They come too seldom for that."

"Good," said the thieftaker. "I'm glad to see that you have come to your senses."

"You see, Mr. Wild, that the atmosphere is so well adapted for cool and collected reasoning upon most subjects."

"I'm glad that you have found it so."

"Yes; and, as I said just now, I've been thinking how I can further the object of which you were kind enough to speak to me."

"At the pillory?"

"Yes, sir. By-the-bye, Mr. Wild, I was greatly grieved to find that you got hurt in that matter."

He drew a long face as he said this, but there was for the close observer a roguish twinkle in his eye which he could not manage to repress.

"No matter at that," replied the thieftaker. "I don't grieve greatly about it. The hand that threw the stone is no doubt now manacled—perhaps cold and stiff."

"Lor! you make me shudder to hear you talk so, Mr. Wild."

"I gave them a taste of my quality."

"And served them well right, Mr. Wild," said the prisoner.

"Yes. Well, I'm waiting for your decision."

"How, sir?"

"You're upon fooling bent, I find. As you will. I wash my hands of the matter from this time forth. The authorities may deal with you as they will."

Wild turned to leave the cell, and Bill Jenkins called him back in agony.

"Too late," said Wild, grinning maliciously. "I'm going to make some little arrangements below for your especial benefit. Good day, and more wit to you."

In spite of all that the unfortunate prisoner could do, the thieftaker left the place, and went, as he had promised, to prepare the little arrangement for his especial benefit.

An hour the prisoner passed in the greatest terror.

"If the captain doesn't look after me quickly," the unhappy Jenkins kept muttering, "I'm as good as gone."

But there were no signs of the captain—no result from the note which he believed to have been delivered by the jailor.

This was the form he put it in to his own mind, and then came the doubt, *was* it delivered?

After a little while there was a tramp in the passage without the cell, and then the door was opened once more.

Up sprang the prisoner, with an exclamation of joy at an anticipated arrival of assistance.

But great was his disappointment when, instead of the assistance he expected, who should enter but some of the warders.

"What is it now, my masters?" demanded the prisoner.

"You're to come with us."

"Whither?"

"*To the press-room.*"

* * * * * *

We shift the scene.

In the press-room of Newgate, stretched backwards upon the cruel engine which gave the title to the chamber, lay the unfortunate Bill Jenkins.

His countenance was already most fearfully distorted with pain and long suffering.

Thrice had the fearful instrument of torture been set in motion, and as many times had the hapless wretch shrieked in mortal woe.

And all the while by his side, and gloating upon his agonies, was Jonathan Wild the thieftaker.

No sympathy had he with the unhappy wretch, who shrieked and groaned fearfully beneath the crushing machine which was pressing his soul from his body.

"Oh! ugh! Hel—p!" groaned poor Jenkins.

"You should have been wise," said the thieftaker, grinning maliciously. "Had you been less pigheaded you might have saved yourself all this. As it is, you may rot for me. Curse ye! Put it on a bit more."

"Stay!" shrieked the unhappy wretch, writhing in torture. "Hold! I will tell all—everything!"

"Too late."

"You will slay me!"

"We will try," hissed the revengeful thieftaker in his ear.

"Mercy! mercy!"

"Go on," said Jonathan Wild. "Screw it up well. We'll teach him to play with the majesty of the law with impunity."

The press was again set in motion, and the prisoner was pressed until he could scarce breathe.

A faint and smothered sound escaped him again and again.

Yet still, with devilish ferocity, did Jonathan Wild gaze upon his victim, a sinister smile playing round his countenance.

At length, nature being thoroughly exhausted, he sank into a deep swoon, so closely resembling death that it was thought to be the grim tyrant itself.

The men employed at the press looked grave.

Whilst they were endeavouring to restore the swooning man to consciousness one of the warders ran in to say that a gentleman desired to see Jonathan Wild.

"I am particularly engaged," said the thieftaker.

"He *will* see you, sir."

"What? *Will?* And who is he who *will* see Jonathan Wild, I should like to know."

"Would you?" exclaimed a voice close behind him.

And, looking up, the thieftaker saw at his elbow no less a person than Sir Harry Jerrold.

The baronet was one of the most prominent men of the day, and had not only been a great public man, but was also high in favour with the first gentleman of the land—the king.

Now, as he made a dead set at the thieftaker, that worthy felt rather uncomfortable upon the matter.

"Well, Mr. Wild," said Sir Harry Jerrold severely, "is this the way that you treat a man of my rank when I express a wish to see you?"

"Sir Harry, I—"

"What? Out with it! Don't stand trembling there, man."

"I was not aware that it was your honour."

"And what business is it of yours who it was? You're a runner, Mr. Wild. You are rightly at the beck and call of every one who chooses, and if I find you remiss in your duties another time be assured that I shall take measures to report it in a quarter that you would find far from comfortable."

Jonathan Wild could only bow his head in meekness and humility, for he was a most despicable toady, and had a wholesome dread of the power possessed by Sir Harry Jerrold.

His men, too, to his no small chagrin, were overjoyed around him to see their tyrant forced to eat humble pie in this desperate manner.

"Hullo!" exclaimed the baronet. "Why what on earth have you here?"

"A prisoner, Sir Harry," responded the thieftaker.

"Torturing him?"

"Forcing confession."

"Of what?"

Jonathan Wild was silent.

He did not exactly care to own that it was something to the prejudice of the captain of the Yellow Band, as the worthy baronet had more than once expressed himself favourably towards our hero.

"Are you aware, Mr. Wild," demanded Sir Harry Jerrold, "that you are exceeding your duty in thus torturing a poor wretch?"

"No, Sir Harry. I thought—"

"Thought?" exclaimed the baronet. "And is it possible that you can proceed upon so light a matter as supposition to squeeze body and soul asunder?"

"No, Sir Harry, but—"

"But, but, but! Silence sir! How dare you? Don't tell me. Order that man's release."

Jonathan Wild hesitated to obey this order.

It was something galling in the extreme to have to set free a person secured with difficulty, and upon whom he was wreaking vengeance both on his own and Red Ralph's account.

"Do you hear me, Mr. Wild?" pursued the baronet.

"Certainly, Sir Harry."

And he grumblingly ordered the release of Bill Jenkins from the press.

Fainting, and scarcely possessed of life, they took out the unfortunate man, and set about applying restoratives, but it was long before they could bring him to his senses.

"Now, Mr. Wild," resumed the baronet, "I must know why you have thought proper to treat this unfortunate man thus."

"*Must* know, Sir Harry?"

"Ay. Why, the knave echoes my words! I *must* know. Now do you hear?"

"Well, then, because he aided and abetted the escape of Red Ralph, the notorious highwayman, and because he further refused to tell what he knew respecting him—to give information which would certainly have led to Red Ralph's capture."

"Oh, that's it, is it? Well, Mr. Wild," said the baronet, "I have long marked your virulent hateful temper. I shall take occasion to let it be known in the proper quarter."

"Oh," grumbled Wild, "you always had a fancy for thieves and highwaymen, Sir Harry."

"That's an impertinence," said the baronet, "and you will repent it, mark me. I have said it."

"Stay, Sir Harry. If an apology—"

"Too late."

In the morning the prisoner had sued thus to Wild, and he had rebuked him—scoffed and threatened him. It was now his own turn.

CHAPTER CL.

THE PRESS-ROOM OF NEWGATE—SIR HARRY JERROLD—WILD IN TWO CHARACTERS—THE TOADY REPROVED—A SAVAGE BLOW—THE BITER BIT—HOW JONATHAN WILD CAUGHT A TARTAR—A MISTAKE—JABERS THE THIEF-CATCHER—WILD IN PERIL—HOW HE SAVED HIS LIFE—RELEASE FROM THE BONDAGE OF A LIFE.

SIR HARRY JEROLD left Newgate, haughtily scorning the disgusting servility of the thieftaker.

Jonathan Wild fawned before Sir Harry, and cringed, and bowed, and scraped, and bowed again.

Like Sir Pertinax Macsycophant in the play, he "boo'd an' he boo'd," but in the present instance it was unhappily without much result.

The free-hearted baronet detested anything like hypocrisy such as Jonathan Wild's.

He was so sure of his own position that he wanted no crawling toadyism to put it before him.

"Hang it all, man," cried the baronet at length, thoroughly exasperated, "act like a man, if you are one. Drop the serpent before me. Fawn upon and lick the boots of some one of your own dirty kidney. I'm a man, and can't endure to see my own species degrade themselves below the level of humanity, to pander to my own weakness for vain power."

The thieftaker coloured to the roots of his hair (we had better have said his scratch wig, by the way), but he was silent.

Jonathan Wild was so prudent when he started upon a prudent course that it required something very strong indeed to shake him from his purpose.

He did not relish this treatment, nevertheless.

"Jabers," he said to one of his creatures who stood by him, "go and show Sir Harry to the gate."

"Let him keep a respectful distance—"

"Yes, Sir Harry."

"Because his presence reminds me of you," added the baronet, with killing sarcasm. "And I like to forget a thing of your nature as soon as it is no longer before my eyes."

Wild winced.

"Go on, fellow."

"Yes, sir," said the man with a smirk and a bow.

"Like you," exclaimed the worthy baronet. "Confound it! he beats you at it, Wild! Go on, Judas junior."

And he stalked out, leaving the thieftaker's men tittering audibly at their master's humiliation.

No sooner was Sir Harry Jerrold out of hearing than Jonathan's rage came out with a burst.

He could no longer control his choler. A small Vesuvius had been smouldering in his breast, and now it burst into a flame.

He turned with a cry upon his men—a yell it was, rather like the war cry of a North American Indian than anything we hear from an inhabitant of our cold island.

One of the men, who enjoyed the scene amazingly, but unfortunately had not the power of checking his mirth with prudence and controlling his expression at will like his comrades, wore yet a smile upon his countenance.

The thieftaker glared upon him with the ferocity of a wild beast.

Then glancing around for something wherewith to wreak his vengeance upon the unfortunate mirth-provoked man, he pounced upon a bar which had been used in the vice of the press.

Swinging the ponderous instrument once over his shoulder, he brought it down a tremendous thwack upon the unfortunate man's head, cracking his skull in an ugly-looking manner, and bringing him to the ground.

"Who's the next?" demanded Jonathan Wild sternly.

There was no reply to this unpleasant invitation.

The men glanced from one to the other and shivered.

"And so," said the thieftaker bitterly, "ye stand grinning like a pack of fools that ye are to hear me put upon by an upstart thief-protecting scurvy knave like that! And wherefore? Simply because he bears a handle to his accursed name. But do you think that I'll tamely submit to it? Never! The man who dares insult Jonathan Wild like that shall not do it with impunity. I swear it. That carpenter's apprentice dog dared to insult me—dared to put a hand upon me, and, by the mother that bore me, I swear he shall swing for it! Sir Harry Jerrold, you have roused the devil in me, and beware! beware! You shall bitterly rue the day that ever you said one word that Jonathan Wild could construe into an affront. I've sworn it, and when Jonathan Wild swears a thing it generally looks like earnest. With all my faults I generally am credited with keeping to a promise that I have once made."

He glared around upon his men, who were pale and mute at the downfall of their companion.

"Well, fools!" roared the thieftaker. "What d'ye mean?"

No one replied. No one meant anything.

"Why don't you pick up that dog there?" continued the thieftaker, pointing to the bleeding man upon the floor. "You want him to lay there and breathe his last gasp, curse ye! You want him to die off, that I may get into trouble about him, don't you?"

As he addressed himself to one man rather more particularly, the fellow felt it to be his duty to shiver, so he shivered.

"N—n—no, Mr. Wild."

"N—n—no, Mr. Wild," mimicked the thieftaker in a drawling voice. "Pick him up—lively, too, that

I may have the gratification of breaking his accursed sconce again when I'm in the humour, unless you would prefer me to deal in a like manner with you now. D'ye hear me?"

"Yes, sir."

"Away with him."

The men raised their fallen comrade in their arms, and bore him away when his hurt was properly tended.

Just as they were gone the man Jabers returned from seeing the baronet to the gate.

"Has that upstart fool gone yet?" demanded Wild.

"Who? Sir Harry, Mr. Wild?" asked Jabers.

"Who do you suppose I mean?" thundered Jonathan Wild.

"Well," replied Jabers, "I suppose you mean Sir Harry."

"You suppose?" mimicked Wild. "Well, well, things have come to a pretty pass when a man presumes to suppose here to my face—beards me to my very teeth."

"I, Mr Wild?"

"Yes, you, curse you! Whom do you suppose I mean?"

"Can't say I'm sure."

The words, surlily given, were barely uttered when the thieftaker sprang upon the man and caught him by the throat,

He was a tall and powerful fellow, this Jabers, but the thieftaker's attack was so sudden that he was toppled over.

Down he fell, sprawling upon the ground, with the thieftaker upon him.

But this man, albeit about as much of a toady as his fellows, possessed a little more courage.

His master might say what he pleased to him, but immediately it came to a physical demonstration of anger the man lost his temper as well as his master.

He could not brook a blow.

Jabers had been brought a prisoner to Newgate for having disabled his former employer for life.

He, the employer in question, had, in a fit of temper similar to Jonathan Wild's, raised his hand to his man, and Jabers turned upon him, maiming him for life.

His very existence had been imperilled for some considerable period, and Jabers would possibly have suffered the extreme penalty of the law but for the extenuating circumstances attending the conflict.

Jonathan Wild had taken the opportunity to make the fellow believe that his escape was the result of his power with the authorities, and so secured a bold and desperate fellow for his own service.

It was a desirable acquisition for such service as the thieftaker required of his men; but the very facts of his introduction should have made Jonathan Wild wary in assaulting such a desperate customer.

Jabers turned upon Jonathan Wild furiously.

Seizing him by the throat as he lay sprawling over him, he clutched him to his chest tightly.

Then with a sudden jerk he rolled him over upon the floor, nearly crushing him by his weight.

"Let go your hold!" said Wild.

The man's only reply to this was to squeeze the thieftaker even more tightly than before.

"Let go, you villain!" said Wild hoarsely. "Let go, I say."

"Never."

"I shall choak," said Wild.

His voice was by this time reduced to a whisper, and it almost looked as if he were speaking the truth for once in his life.

"I mean you to," hissed Jabers in his ear. "Curse you! You dare to lay your filthy paws on honest men. I have stood your bullying, your browbeating long enough."

"Rascal!" gasped the thieftaker. "You shall hang."

"Then I'll do something to make me earn the gallows."

"Help! help!"

"Call and struggle and kick as you will, you dog! you shall suffer for it. You say that no man insults Jonathan Wild with impunity. You have learnt that Jabers the thieftaker is not to be touched with impunity."

"I was enraged. I meant you no harm."

"I care not for what you meant. The wrong was there."

"But for your own sake consider," said the thief-taker.

"Too late."

"Mercy!" gasped Jonathan Wild, struggling like an infant in the vigorous clutches of his man. "You will be strung up for a certainty if you slay me."

"Pshaw!" said Jabers, shaking the thieftaker like a dog does a rat. "I slew old Thornbury, my master, because he deigned to lay a hand on me; and yet you see I live."

"Nay—"

"You would say that I owe my life to you," said Jabers. "Possibly. I admit it. At least you have often told me so. But then something else will turn up—somebody to get me off for murdering you. I mean it," he added, shaking Wild yet more fiercely than ever.

"Nay; no man escapes murder—no man," gasped the thieftaker.

"You lie."

"I swear it."

"You lie again. You can't reason me out of my revenge, Jonathan Wild. You would get me hanged for this if I let you off."

"No. I swear I couldn't."

"You saved me you say; so you could get me hanged."

"No, no," said Wild, before Jabers could begin a second bout. "I couldn't. No man could. I only said so. Thornbury did not die."

At this Jabers's hands fell from the prostrate thief-taker down by his side.

Up sprang Wild upon the instant, but Jabers, fancying it only a ruse to escape him, was beside him in an instant, clutching at him.

"Keep off, Jabers," cried Wild.

"You have spoken the truth?"

"I have."

"Thornbury lives?"

"I swear it. Disabled for life, it is true; but he lives in retirement. You shall see him."

"Then I am a free man again. I fear no Jonathan Wild, nor any man living. You may go free, Mr. Wild. Your information was worth the revenge."

CHAPTER CLI.

BEFORE THE MOATED CASTLE—FEUDAL TIMES RESTORED—A SCENE OF A PAST AGE—WALTERS THE HERALD—THE SUMMONS TO SURRENDER —THE HOLY BROTHERHOOD—SIR RUPERT OF CAIRGAL—TREACHERY—THE CAPTAIN OF THE YELLOW BAND ON THE ALERT.

WE shift the scene again. Before the moated castle of the secret brotherhood a large array of armed and mounted men were met to do battle with the secret society for their stronghold and their lives.

Thirty good and well-appointed men were there, besides their leaders.

These chiefs of the hostile force were mounted upon stout dun horses, which stood out from the uniform grey horses of the men.

Of the men we should observe that only twenty were mounted, the remainder being men-at-arms carrying muskets, pistols, cutlasses, pikes, bows and arrows for service when the ammunition should be exhausted, and other weapons of offence and defence.

Each man wore beneath his vest a stout breastplate of elephant's hide, warranted to resist anything short of a cannon ball.

At the same time it did not impede their movements as a metal plate would have done.

The three chiefs of the troop were dressed like the men, with the single exception of the head gear.

Whilst the men were protected by stout steel casques covered with a plain cloth, so as to avoid notice, the heads of the three leaders of the troop were unprotected save by the ordinary three-cornered hats of the prevailing fashion.

One wore a small white feather in the front of his hat; another had a similar feather speckled with dark drab; the third wore also a feather of a similar size, but jet black.

The attack upon the castle had not yet commenced, and by the eager and hasty movements of the knight of the white feather it was apparent that he was all impatience to commence the fray.

"Gently, Sir Hubert," said the knight of the black feather. "Let us proceed in the work, which is already rather out of practice, with all possible method in our movements."

"Method with such knaves as these to combat?" returned Sir Hubert. "'Twere an injustice to our cause."

"Would it not be wiser, captain," said the third leader, joining in the consultation for the first time, "to summon them to surrender the castle without delay?"

"Summon them?" echoed the knight of the white feather, or Sir Hubert, as we had better call him, since it is really none other than the sometime prisoner of the secret brotherhood. "That were, in fact, to put them upon their guard, for the result of the summons is assured beforehand."

"Nay," remonstrated the black feather, whom we shall in future call, as the reader has now some time known him, the captain of the Yellow Band. "The result is presumed, not assured."

"Pretty certainly assured, then, captain," said Sir Hubert.

"Granted pretty well assured, but not quite," said Red Ralph.

"And what has our friend here to say upon the subject?" said Sir Hubert, turning to the knight of the speckled feather.

"I? Oh! I agree with the captain," was his reply.

This was Walters, the lieutenant of the Yellow Band.

The questioner tossed his proud head impatiently at this response, but said nothing.

"What say you, Sir Hubert?" demanded the captain of the Yellow Band after a short pause.

"As you will."

"Nay, as you will."

"But if you are two to one in the matter, what signifies?"

"This, Sir Hubert," replied the captain of the Yellow Band quietly. "We would rather overrule you in a matter like this by a little reasoning than by a great deal of noise or by a majority. You may think that the lieutenant feels himself bound in duty to say as I say."

"Nay," responded Sir Hubert courteously. know the lieutenant too well to suppose him guilty of

[STORMING THE CASTLE.]

anything that could be possibly construed into meanness, and toadying anybody is a despicable meanness
of course.''

The lieutenant bowed in acknowledgement of this.

"My only object is," resumed the captain of the
Yellow Band, "to settle this matter as quietly as possible. Let it be amicably arranged, or there is no
possibility of an understanding.''

"Well, well," said Sir Hubert, "I am content. I
know that you speak for the best.''

"At least it is so according to my own conviction.''

"And you have a clearer reason than I can boast
of. Who shall be our herald for the nonce ?''

"That will I," said the lieutenant of the Yellow
Band.

Walters then, at a given signal—all the men being
removed from sight—advanced to the edge of the
moat facing the raised drawbridge, and, placing a
horn to his mouth, he blew upon it a loud shrill blast.

This being without a reply for some few minutes,
he proceeded to repeat his summons a second and a
third time.

At the third blast there was a commotion within
the castle, and upon the turret appeared one of the
secret brotherhood.

"Who is it that thus disturbs our holy fraternity
at the hour of devotion ?'' he demanded.

"I, Francis Walters, of Epping, in the name of the escaped victims to your tyranny—in the name of justice and vengeance—demand of you to give up your whole worldly wealth and possessions to us."

The absurdity and extravagance of the demand were such that the member of the secret fraternity could not comprehend his meaning at first.

He called upon the lieutenant-herald to repeat his summons, and then, in a burst of indignation, he bade the rude disturber of their peace depart.

"Begone!" he said in loud and austere tones. "I would have you know that we are armed against any dishonest men who would dare attempt to invade our sacred territory. Begone!"

"Again I call upon you to give up the castle," said the lieutenant, nothing daunted. "Give up in peace, and depart."

"Begone! or beware the vengeance of our fraternity," was all the reply now deigned.

"A third and last time do I call upon you to give up your possessions and quietly depart," said the lieutenant of the Yellow Band. "And if your mission here is as holy as you would make it appear, you will heed my warning, and save the lives of innocent men."

"What would you imply by that empty-sounding speech?" demanded the brother through a speaking trumpet.

"Simply, that if you do not give in to us in peace and accept the quarter and mercy which we perhaps wrongly offer, we will fight unto the very last; but we will raze your stronghold to the ground."

"Vain, idle talking! Man, beware how you would affront us. The holy fraternity of which I am a humble representative is a powerful and desperate one. The insolence is not taken to our own account, but is a slight to our holy mission here. As such we shall certainly avenge it in a way that will make you repent your idle and mad-brained boast."

"You refuse?"

"To listen to your empty boast, I do. Begone, and trouble us no more."

"The evil cannot be avoided I find," said the lieutenant. "Then let the evil light on you."

"So be it."

At this the impatience of Sir Hubert again burst through all restraint, and he advanced.

"Come back, lieutenant," he cried to Walters, "and let these guilty men take the consequences of their audacity."

"Who speaks thus?"

"'Tis I. Your blood be upon your heads!" cried Sir Hubert. "Bloody and remorseless wretches, you shall repent that ever you have known me."

"I know that voice's sound," said the brother from the castle turret, "but my memory fails to tell me where I have met it before."

"Tremble and learn, proud Laman!" said Sir Hubert. "It is I, Sir Hubert Fontenoy of Cairgal. I come for vengeance for the injuries I have received. I hurl defiance in your teeth."

"Ah! Hubert Fontenoy of Cairgal," cried the brother, "you have again ventured too near us to hope for escape."

"I seek it not."

"Vain man to venture near the lion's den when once away."

"The lion's den, vain boaster? The tiger's lair, traitor. Again we hurl defiance in your teeth, and call on you, as you would save whole your carrion carcases, to depart in peace."

While these empty-sounding menaces were being exchanged the captain of the Yellow Band in the background, still unobserved by the secret brotherhood upon the castle turrets, perceived some few men advancing stealthily in the rear of the others.

One crawled along the ground carrying an instrument which Red Ralph at once perceived to be an arquebus—an old-fashioned musket even then long since in disuse, and superseded by the matchlock, which in its turn gave place to muskets of many degrees improved form.

Suspecting treachery, he kept his eye upon this fellow until he got close to the top of the castle turret.

"Stoop!" he cried to Sir Hubert on a sudden.

Even as he spoke there was a flash and a report, and Sir Hubert Fontenoy of Cairgal was seen to reel in his saddle and fall.

CHAPTER CLII.

OPENING OF A FRAY—THE RIVAL HOSTS—THE OPENING VOLLEY—THE BATTLE GROWS FIERCER—PARLEY BETWEEN THE LEADERS—SURPRISE RESOLVED ON—BACK TO THE CASTLE—THE OLD SCENE—SIR HUBERT OF CAIRGAL—HIS DISAPPEARANCE—RED RALPH IN SEARCH—THE PRISON CELL AGAIN—HARD RECEPTION—ALIVE OR DEAD?

THE captain of the Yellow Band sprang forward with a bound, and in the space of a few seconds was beside the fallen Hubert.

"All right, captain," said the gentleman, springing up. "No damage."

"I thought you had been struck."

"Not I. I saw the treacherous dog firing the shot as you spoke," said Sir Hubert. "I ducked to avoid it, and lost my balance."

Whilst these few hurried words were being exchanged the lieutenant of the Yellow Band had advanced again to the edge of the moat, when, drawing forth one of his holster pistols, he took a quiet deliberate aim and fired.

Down fell the man, struck in the breast by the bullet.

"One to our side!"

"Well aimed, Walters," said Ralph.

"The treacherous dog!" exclaimed Sir Hubert, bitterly incensed at the fallen man's firing upon a flag of truce. "I'll wager a hatful of crowns that he did not duck to avoid the shot."

"Call forth the men."

The lieutenant sounded the call upon his horn, and out rushed the men from their several hiding-places, all eager to do or die.

It had been tantalising in the extreme for them to hear the firing without being able to join in.

"All loaded?"

"Ay, ay," ran along their lines from mouth to mouth.

"Present. Take steady aim for the turret, and—Fire!"

As the last words were uttered there was a flash all along the front row, followed by a rattle of some ten or twelve muskets.

A cry came from the battlements, and one man was seen to totter upon the edge of the wall, totter again, and fall over.

The waters of the moat closed over the ill-fated man, and effectually completed what the musket shot had commenced.

"So end all traitors!" cried Sir Hubert Fontenoy.

This appeared to be the veritable commencement of the fray between the Yellow Band and their recruits and the secret brotherhood.

Cries of rage were heard from the castle turrets, and then there was a rush of some twenty or more on to the battlements.

"Let the second division advance," cried the captain of the Yellow Band to the rear guard.

The men responded with a shout.

"To the front."

The party who had just fired fell forward upon their faces.

"Now then, my boys! my bold yellow lads!" cried their captain. "Bring them well up to the shoulder. Take steady aim. Fire!"

A second volley had a yet more startling effect.

As the men had aimed chiefly at the last to appear upon the castle walls, they were the chief sufferers.

They could be seen to drop three and four at a volley.

Then there was a short consultation amongst the secret brotherhood, and the result was anticipated by the captain of the Yellow Band, who perceived, by the fierce gesticulations employed to convey their meaning, that the worst passions that agitate humankind were aroused in these bloodthirsty men.

"Fall flat!" said Ralph.

"Ay, ay."

And down they fell upon their faces, with one cheer.

It was in time it is true, but only just. Another minute and it had been too late.

The volley from the battlements of the castle rattled harmlessly over their heads.

Not a man was scathed!

The enemy had evidently not understood this, for, as in the case of Sir Hubert Fontenoy, they imagined the sudden fall meant that the shots had taken fatal effect.

Something like a cheer was given upon the castle turrets, which was returned at once by the Yellow Boys, who sprang up from the ground in triumph.

"Pour it in again!" said Sir Hubert Fontenoy, in a state of high excitement now.

The men responded with loud cheers again and again.

A third volley was now poured in by the attacking party, and disastrous was the result.

The cries of the wounded resounded through the air, and, by the dull splashes in the moat, they could tell that the unfortunate men were falling to their fates in an alarming manner.

"They must have lost a goodly number already," said Sir Hubert Fontenoy to Red Ralph.

"Ay," responded the captain of the Yellow Band.

"See. There's another toppled over. 'Tis a glorious vengeance this, captain, eh?"

"A bloody one."

"'Tis as I would have it."

"Then 'tis glorious—too glorious almost," said Red Ralph significantly "It looks like butchering."

"What would you have?"

"I would fight with men who defend themselves."

"It seems to me that they do."

Red Ralph pointed silently around to their men, all flushed and excited with the fray.

Not one had fallen.

Sir Hubert Fontenoy at once comprehended his meaning.

"What would you have?" he asked. "You would not surely wish to see our men fall about us like the enemy?"

"Not I."

"Then how can we manage it? They or we must fall. By all means let it be they."

"So say I."

Walters joined the conversation at this moment.

"Captain," said he, "this is a sad carnage. Shall we go with a flag of truce and summon them again to surrender?"

"What says Sir Hubert?"

"Never with my consent!" exclaimed Sir Hubert. "Never will I consent to such a proceeding I swear.

What, after the base manner in which they met us but now? After this vile and base treachery? It would be simply to sacrifice the life of the man who bore the flag."

"So I think," said the lieutenant.

"As you will," said the captain of the Yellow Band.

"I think that after what has occurred we cannot venture to trust them."

"What must be done then?"

"What?" echoed Sir Hubert Fontenoy. "Let the battle proceed, and let those be conquerors who have the right upon their side."

"Or rather," said Red Ralph, "let us leave a party here whilst another lot tries the further side. By taking them by surprise, if it can be done, we may save much bloodshed, for it is certain that our men cannot hope long to escape unscathed thus. What says Sir Hubert?"

"As you please."

"Nay. 'Tis for you to say."

"I like the proposition."

"And will join us?"

"Yes."

"Good. Who shall stay here to conduct the attack?"

Then, as neither the captain of the Yellow Band nor Sir Hubert Fontenoy offered, the lieutenant felt himself bound to put up for the post.

"That will I," he said.

"Come, then, captain," said Sir Hubert. "Follow me."

"Alone?"

"Yes."

"We can return for aid in our enterprise I presume?"

"Yes—or, rather, I believe that it must be managed alone."

"Lead on."

"Good fortune to you, lieutenant, and ply them hard with powder."

"Yes, Sir Hubert."

"Stand well forward, and the day's our own."

"I will."

Sir Hubert and the captain of the Yellow Band went off at once, and made their way round by a circuitous route to the back of the castle.

The firing continued hotly in front all the while.

"Have you any plan of action?" demanded Red Ralph.

"Yes."

"What is it?"

"Can you not guess?"

"Not I i'faith! How should I?"

"Have you no idea how an entrance is to be effected into the castle?"

"One way perhaps—that is, if it be not discovered ere now."

"We shall see."

"I doubt it much."

As they were speaking they arrived before the excavation in the ground by which they had escaped in their remarkable flight from the castle.

The reader will remember that after the fearful havoc which they had made in the members of the secret brotherhood they had escaped through the cell in which Sir Hubert Fontenoy had been confined.

They made their way here, and to their no small satisfaction found the hole, which had merely been covered over with some turf and grass.

Red Ralph scraped away the grass and rubbish, and prepared to descend into the aperture.

"Nay—let me venture first," said Sir Hubert.

"Wherefore?"

"To see if anything be stirring below."

"Why not I, then ?"

"I am better acquainted with the place than you, and can see at once if all be well there. Keep close at hand, to be there if I should need your aid."

"Never fear."

Sir Hubert Fontenoy descended into the dark abyss, and all was still.

The captain of the Yellow Band listened intently above, but could hear nothing whatever to induce a belief that any mishap had occurred below.

The firing was continued in front of the castle all the while with more vigour than ever.

"What a glorious thing is war !" murmured Red Ralph, in ecstasy. "I wonder not it is love of glory that soldiers feel. Battle is assuredly man's noblest occupation. Oh ! I may even yet think of brave Sir Harry Jerrold's offer. In a foreign service I might win my way to renown and fortune. I'll think it over yet. Bravo, boys ! The Yellow Band still do honour to their fame."

This was because both the besiegers and the besieged had fired a volley together at each other, and with some great results, as he could hear by the cries.

But, Sir Hubert, where was he ? Where had he gone to all this while ?

It was only now that the thought of Sir Hubert crossed him, and as he reflected of the dangerous mission that he had gone on he began to grow very uneasy.

He peered down the cavity and called to him in a loud whisper.

"Sir Hubert ! Sir Hubert !"

But no answer came.

Red Ralph was now really concerned for the worthy gentleman, for he well knew the bold and venturesome character of the man, and he 'feared that some foolhardy stroke might put him in the clutches of the secret brotherhood.

If it did, then good bye to Sir Hubert Fontenoy of Cairgal.

He would indeed be as good as dead, for the foes to whom he was hurrying were as remorseless and cruel as they were unscrupulous.

"Sir Hubert !" again called the captain of the Yellow Band after a pause. "Answer me. Are you there ?"

Clearly he was not. If he had been, and in life, he would have replied.

He could bear this suspense no longer. It was a position of torture.

With stealthy and slow movements he began to descend into the excavation.

All was still.

He arrived at the spot where the straw of the late prisoner's bed covered the aperture at which Sir Hubert had worked so long and patiently for that liberty which he had finally secured.

It was yet covered over !

What could this mean ? Red Ralph asked himself.

If Sir Hubert Fontenroy had entered there, then he must have replaced the straw in its old position.

This augured well he thought, for if Sir Hubert had had the time to taken this precaution with such care and deliberation, then he must be in no very great danger now.

The only thing to fear was that, emboldened by success, Sir Hubert would carry his temerity too far.

One false step and all would be over.

Red Ralph pushed aside the straw and dragged himself up to the level of the opening to look round him.

His head was now projecting but a few inches above the ground when he heard a slight movement close at hand.

He turned round to see what it was when he saw something descending upon his head, so swiftly and suddenly that it is a marvel he perceived it.

Down it came with fearful velocity before he could entirely avoid it.

And down fell the captain of the Yellow Band back into the dark cavity below.

Alive or dead ?

———

CHAPTER CLIII.

HOW JONATHAN WILD PLOTTED — REVENGE ON ALL SIDES — THE COMPACT OF BLOOD — ITS PRICE — HUCKSTERS — THE ANONYMOUS LETTER — SIR HARRY JERROLD ON HOUNSLOW HEATH — THE STRANGE APPARITION — IT VANISHES.

BEFORE resuming the adventures of the Yellow Band and its leader before the moated castle of the secret brotherhood we must speak of an ugly little matter that befel Sir Harry Jerrold.

He left Jonathan Wild, as we have already described, in the press-room of Newgate.

What occurred between the irate and humiliated thieftaker and his creature Jabers we have already related.

After the severe handling that Jonathan Wild had received from his man's hands he determined upon a new line of conduct with him.

Jonathan was not the man to tamely submit to such treatment as he had received, and a complete vengeance was resolved upon, while yet he was receiving the punishment his bullying and outrageous treatment had earned him.

"Look you here, Jabers," he said meekly, as he adjusted his disordered dress, " I have a little proposition to make you."

"No use, Wild, now," said Jabers. "You've let the cat out of the bag, and I owe you nothing."

"Gratitude."

"Pshaw ! I've been your tool long enough. A fig for your gratitude !"

Jonathan Wild rolled his hypocritical eyes upwards with a sanctified air.

"It's the way of the world," he groaned, as if in bitter anguish of spirit. "It's the way of the world."

"What do you mean ?" said Jabers indignantly. " If I ever owed you anything it has been amply repaid, and more, in the brutal treatment I've received from you."

"Only hear him," said the thieftaker, addressing the ceiling.

"No. You've told me that I'm a free man, and so now we part."

"And what good can you do alone in the world, Jabers ?"

"That has yet to be seen."

"But I can put a job in your way."

"You can ?"

"And will."

"That depends upon the price," said Jabers doggedly.

"You shall have no cause to complain of that."

"What is it you want done ?"

"Hush. Don't speak so loud. Come here."

"No treacherous moves, Jonathan, or I'll settle your business," said Jabers.

"No, no. I mean you well, as you shall find. Do but as I wish you, and you are a made man for life."

"How's that ?"

"I mean a made man if fifty pounds will help you on."

"Fifty ?"

"Ay."

"Money down ?"

"After the performance of your share of the business."

"Bah!" said Jabers. "You don't take me for such a milksop. What security do you offer?"

"My word."

Jabers burst into a hoarse laugh.

"Your word, Jonathan Wild. Now hark you—if you really mean business—"

"Of course I do."

"Then don't talk such twaddle as your word. Say what you want done, down with the ready, and I'm your man."

"Nay, but—"

"Enough. You know well that I am a man to be relied upon. Trust my word if you will. If not, nothing can be done with me."

"Well, well, we will talk of that after. What I want is this—But first, may I rely upon you?"

"For what?"

"Keeping it mum if you don't chance to approve of my little proposition?"

"Certainly."

"You promise?"

"I do."

"Enough. You saw the villain who has just left here?"

"Who? Sir Harry?"

"Yes."

"What of him?"

"He has insulted me."

"I saw it."

"I am not a man, as you well know, tamely to take such a matter."

"I know that too, Jonathan Wild," said Jabers.

"I want you to avenge me."

"I? How? When? Where?"

"You are intentionally dull. Shall I speak plainer?"

"If you can. I hate these cursed quibblings."

"Well, then, plainly. I want him knocked upon the head."

Jabers started back affrightedly. The proposition which the thieftaker had been so long naming was of such an alarming nature that he could scarcely believe his senses.

He imagined that he perceived in it some fresh snare to catch him—probably as a means of vengeance for his late retaliation.

"I'm serious," said Wild.

"Impossible."

"You refuse?"

"Undoubtedly."

"You will have nothing whatever to do in the matter?"

"Nothing."

"And you will not touch the fifty pounds?" said Wild.

This brought Jabers to a standstill. Before such a sum he felt his scruples vanishing like smoke.

"Money down?" he demanded again as a feeler.

"Say half down."

"No."

"Half, and the rest upon completion of the job."

"And how would it be secured?"

"My word must suffice for that."

"It won't then," said Jabers resolutely. "Give it me in black and white, and I'll do it."

"What?" exclaimed the thieftaker. "Put such a contract in black and white? It would be simply to place a halter round my neck, and put the end of the rope into your hands."

"Then there's an end to it."

Jabers was turning to leave the press-room when the thieftaker called him back.

"One word more, Jabers. There, no squabbling. Say thirty down, and twenty when the job's done."

"No," returned Jabers. "I will make you one proposition, though, accept it or not as you please. That is the last word I shall have to say on the matter if you refuse."

"Name it."

"Thirty-five pounds down and twenty after it's done, or fifty down."

Jonathan Wild considered for a little time before replying to this proposal.

"Well, Jabers, I will," he said. "I have known you some time, and I will trust you. You may feel yourself complimented by that, for there's not another man I would trust in all the world — not my own brother."

"I should think not," said Jabers drily.

"When will you do it?"

"When you please."

"To-day?"

Jabers paused to consider for a minute or two.

"Perhaps I'd better," he said, "for if I don't do it whilst I'm hot upon it, I may not like to touch it afterwards."

"True," said the thieftaker. "It isn't pleasant for some men, Jabers, to sleep with such a matter on their conscience—not that I am often troubled that way myself."

Accordingly their preliminary matters were arranged, the first portion of the bribe was paid, and off started Jabers upon his mission of murder.

"He's gone," said the thieftaker to himself. "Now the next step is to send down to catch him at it. I have it! Yet no. I'll set Sir Harry Jerrold himself upon his guard if possible. But how? Ah! I have it this time. An anonymous letter will doubtless settle the matter. I'll choose a strange messenger, and despatch him without delay. A glorious idea, for then I work my vengeance upon both. If he kills Sir Harry or Sir Harry him, or they kill each other, I am avenged. Now, Mr. Jabers, you shall learn that it was better even to remain the tool of Jonathan Wild than work on such shakey business upon low pay."

Making at once for his own apartment, he wrote hurried note to the following effect:—

"One who values you highly, but who has unhappily earned your displeasure, has made the discovery that your existence is in peril from the hand of the assassin. Seek not to know more, for reasons of weight necessitate the confinement of the warning to these few words. Be yourself, then. Trust to a clear eye and a steady hand, and whatever you may think of this letter, do not slight its warning."

This done, he called a trusty messenger, a man upon whom he was certain that he could rely, and sent him off.

Sir Harry Jerrold by this time had not departed more than half an hour, and Jonathan Wild hoped that his messenger would catch him before he could get much further.

However, the man had particular instructions to proceed all the way to Hounslow in the event of not coming up with him before.

* * * * * *

Sir Harry Jerrold proceeded direct homewards after leaving Newgate.

Just as he was nearing the heath a masked horseman dressed in a long cloak, looking mysterious enough to frighten away the wits of any reasonable man, rode up at a gallop and placed himself in his path.

Sir Harry's horse was so startled by the strange and sudden apparition that it reared back on its haunches, well nigh unseating its rider.

"How now?" cried the baronet. "Friend or foe?"

The horseman touched his horse's flank with the spur, bounded to Sir Harry's side, and presented the letter.

Then he turned his horse round, and before a question could be asked he galloped away.

CHAPTER CLIV.

SIR HARRY JERROLD—THE HEATH AND THE ANONYMOUS LETTER—HOW SIR HARRY SLIGHTED ITS WARNINGS—HOW THEY WERE VERIFIED— THE ASSASSIN—A GOODLY BOUT—THE BLOODY CROSS.

SIR HARRY JERROLD was not a little astonished at these mysterious proceedings.

He looked up from the letter to find that the messenger had disappeared like lightning.

This being discovered he proceeded to break the seal and read the letter, the contents of which we have already given.

"Pooh, pooh," said the baronet. "If there is one thing more than another for which I have a most thorough contempt, it is an anonymous letter. This thing speaks for itself as a vile insinuation and a falsehood. If the purpose of the writer be fair, why not put his name to it? No, no; I will never believe that any man is so thoroughly disinterested as to seek to avoid recognition of services rendered. It's a forgery and a scandal, for some purpose of which I confess I have not as yet the faintest conception."

Sir Harry Jerrold rattled on against the practice of anonymous correspondence in this way, never thinking that his reasoning was scarcely the most correct.

To begin with, he could scarcely denominate such a document a forgery.

Again, since the correspondent was anonymous, he could not say that it was written with motives of self aggrandisement.

It was not as if the indentity of the writer were revealed in the paper in some ingenious hint, or in the character of a masked handwriting.

In spite of his words, it puzzled Sir Harry Jerrold.

He rode onwards at an easy pace, giving his horse his own time to perform the journey in, when on a sudden he was startled by hearing a footstep close in advance of him.

From the side of the road sprang a man masked and cloaked.

In his right hand he wielded a heavy sword, which looked a terribly formidable weapon.

Grasping the hilt with both hands, he held it across his shoulder, and at the very instant that Sir Harry Jerrold caught sight of him he was about to deal him a tremendous cut.

"Traitor!" cried Sir Harry.

At the same instant he pulled back his horse with a sudden jerk which brought it up upon its haunches.

Down came the sword, but Sir Harry was saved.

The sword, however, struck the horse's knees, bringing both him and his rider to the ground.

The force of the blow had prevented the assassin striking again very rapidly, or else Sir Harry had been a dead man.

As it was, Sir Harry was quickly disengaged from the fallen animal, and held his own promptly-drawn weapon to oppose a slanting-down cut.

The worthy old gentleman had yet enough youth in him to enjoy a brush of this description, and the great risk he had just run added an additional charm to the encounter.

He was upon his feet immediately, and boldly facing the assassin with an uplifted sword.

"Villain!" he cried. "You shall pay for this bitterly."

The man's only reply was to make a vigorous and determined onslaught upon the baronet.

It needed all Sir Harry's presence of mind and address to ward off the shower of blows which the would-be assassin rained upon him.

Cut and thrust were fairly exchanged on both sides.

"Villain!" cried the baronet, upon the occasion of a pause in the encounter for breathing time. "I know your purpose, and I know who has despatched you upon this errand."

"I care not if you do," returned the mask doggedly.

"But hope not for success. Your treachery shall meet with the reward it deserves. You shall take back a broken pate to your master."

"Say you so?" cried the man. "Then have at you!"

The baronet with considerable coolness turned a well-aimed blow aside, and returned it.

No damage was done, however, upon either side.

"Now look to it," cried Sir Harry. "For I swear by the bones of my fathers that you shall not escape without some mark of my displeasure."

"Stand to your sword," said the assassin jeeringly. "You waste your breath in idle brag."

"Knave!"

"Go on."

"Varlet! Dog!"

"Rail on, Sir Harry. You're not out of the wood yet, remember."

"Nor you."

"Nor would I be if I could until your business is despatched."

"That will never be."

"Here's one for it."

And down came a terrific cut that no blade could have parried.

Sir Harry Jerrold saw this at a glance, and he sprang aside to avoid it with great nimbleness.

Then, quickly recovering himself, he dashed forward ere the assassin could regain his guard, and put in a cut which, had the aim been more precise, would have settled the combat in a summary manner.

As it was, it chopped off a piece of the villain's brow and glanced on to his shoulder.

However, it served to bring him to the ground.

Sir Harry with a second blow knocked from his hand his sword, which the fallen ruffian still grappled with remarkable tenacity.

"Quarter, quarter, Sir Harry!" exclaimed the man.

"Quarter?" iterated the baronet. "Audacity!"

"Quarter, my noble foe."

"Never."

"Then you are no noble foe, and I would disdain to receive quarter at your hands."

"Have you the audacity to ask quarter of the man whom you would have slain but a few minutes since in cold blood?"

"But Sir Harry Jerrold claims to be of a higher order of man than I. I follow instincts blindly, such as they are placed in me—blood and gold."

"The avowal is frank, at any rate," said the baronet.

"I start with bad thoughts and a murderous bringing up—have no education to tone down my evil passions."

"That's a gross lie," interrupted the baronet. "For without some cultivation of your mind you would never show the nicety of judgment displayed in your remarks. Therefore, if you would attempt to excite my pity by showing up your ignorance, you but deceive yourself. You have just done the reverse, for I perceive a certain elevation of thought in your words which makes your vile attempt upon my life utterly inexplicable, as well as inexcusable.''

The man only groaned with the pain of his hurt.

"Think as you will, Sir Harry," said the man. "Do as you will, Sir Harry, so that you but spare me."

The baronet looked upon the grovelling miserable wretch with a smile of contempt.

"Enough, rascal!" he said. "Your miserable existence is spared you, rather that my honest sword shrinks from such base-born blood as yours than for your solicitations. Your life is spared."

"Thanks, thanks, Sir Harry," said the man in fervent gratitude. "And now, vile base assassin as you deem me, you shall not find me deficient in gratitude."

"Curse your gratitude! I want it not, you rascal!"

"I could tell that which would prove of use to you."

"Keep it to yourself."

"I could tell you who put me on."

"Ah! you may do that."

"I thought, Sir Harry, that you would like to learn—"

"Yes. But stay. I would not delude any man with false hopes. You cannot escape me scatheless. I will set my brand upon your front—"

"Ah!"

"That honest men may shun you."

"Forbear, in mercy."

"Not a whit."

And, in spite of the man's struggles, the baronet drew upon his forehead with the point of his sword a bloody cross, similar in shape to that of a recognised criminal.

The fellow shrieked with the pain of the hurt, which, coupled with the cuts and thrusts already received, caused him to sink into a dead swoon.

"He's dead," said Sir Harry, without much regret in his tone. "So be it. But I must not practise my good steel upon his carrion."

And the baronet rode away.

CHAPTER CLV.

A GLANCE AT MINA THE GIPSY QUEEN — LEONORE IN THE GIPSIES' FOREST HOME—EVENING WAN- DERINGS—THE RUINS OF THE WOOD HUT — BY- GONE RECOLLECTIONS—DOUBTS AND FEARS— SISTERLY AFFECTION—EXPLANATION OF EARLY MYSTERIES.

WHILE we have been so engrossed with the adven- tures of the captain of the Yellow Band, his lieutenant, Sir Hubert Fontenoy of Cairgal, and the thirty trusty swords aiding them in their dangers before the moated castle, we fear that we have sadly forgotten the for- tunes of Leonore, the virgin wife of our robber hero.

These are scarcely less important to our narration than those of Red Ralph himself, and must be given forthwith.

At present, too, Lady Leonore is with the gipsy tribe —with the gipsy queen Mina, whose adventures no less belong to our romance than those of Red Ralph and his wife.

Up to the present she has perhaps played a com- paratively unimportant part in these pages; but in future chapters she is destined to stand out a heroine indeed.

The extraordinary resemblance existing between Mina and Leonore is not, as the reader doubtless has guessed, entirely accidental.

However, the moment for explanation of this and other matters of the deepest interest to our story has not yet arrived. A startling mystery has yet to be dealt with in connection with this remarkable portion of our duties. But of this anon.

The death of Lemuel, the gallant Zingaro boy, and the subsequent summary justice executed upon his traitorous foster-brother are yet fresh in the reader's mind we doubt not.

These tragic events threw a gloom upon the whole tribe for many a long day. No longer were they in appearance the rollicking youthful Bohemians we have seen them. No longer did they rise from their dew- damp pillows with the same lightheartedness which ever marked the Zingaro. No longer did they join in the camp round the watchfire at sunset with bois- terous merriment and with their wild and fantastic song and dance as of yore.

They had passed through an era of blood, and it hung yet heavy upon their souls.

We would not endeavour to create an impression that the morality of these forest children was so shocked.

Acknowledging no legal code, no house-dwellers' laws, they had peculiar notions of their own, which would startle the steadier propriety of the inhabitants of towns or cities.

The blood of two of their brethren had been shed by violence—that of one by the hand of his foster-bro- ther, and that of the other the (fratricide) in judgment by themselves.

For many and many a day the influence of this sad episode remained visible in the tribe.

The spot in the forest where their just vengeance had been executed was studiously avoided by the tribe, from the youngest child who could run alone to the oldest beldame.

It was evening, and growing rapidly into night, and Mina the gipsy queen and Leonore arm-in-arm wandered silently through the forest.

Both were in thought—deep thought. And both unconsciously were thinking upon the same matter.

As they wandered onwards they came upon a heap of blackened and charred ruins—a pile of burnt tim- ber with not a square foot of good wood in it.

Mina looked up from the brown study into which she had fallen with a smile of recognition.

"See, Leonore," said the gipsy queen. "Do you not recognise this?"

"What?" demanded Lady Leonore glancing up- wards.

"This pile of ruins."

"No. I see that something has stood once here."

"And you do not remember?"

"No."

"Ah! Leonore," said the gipsy queen, half reproach- fully. "You do not look back to an event in connec- tion with this spot with the same joyful satisfaction that I do."

"What event do you speak of, dear Mina?" asked Leonore.

"Let me bring it back in its former state ere I tell you. Picture to yourself here, where all now is but a pile of ruins and cinders, a small wood-hut."

"Yes."

"Ah! you begin to remember what I allude to now. A lost wanderer knocks for admission at the door, and is refused—"

"At first."

"But, persevering earnestly, the only occupant of the hut appears—"

"Yes, yes."

"And then both the owner of the wood hut and the weary night wanderer who has walked through the woods into a new day—both of these, I say, are almost dumb-stricken by a marvellous phenomenon. Do you follow me now, dear Leonore?"

"I do, I do."

"You know that I allude to yourself and your gipsy sister?"

"Yes, yes, dear Mina," said Leonore, embracing her fondly. "And that was our first meeting. How wrong of me to forget the spot!"

"Nay. One could scarcely expect you to remember it. That hut was built for me by the tribe, and although of rude construction and accommodation, yet it was endeared to me by fond recollections."

"But one question, Mina."

"A hundred if you will."

"One will suffice for the present. You will not think me rude, dear Mina?—curious or prying in troubling you with my questions?"

"Nay; that is cruelly put. Ask me any proof whatever of my love for you, and you shall not find me wanting in readiness, dear Leonore."

"Well, then, there is always a portion of your life which to me is an impenetrable mystery."

"The greatest mysteries are but simple matters when an explanation is given."

"I know it."

"What is it, then?"

"Firstly—"

"Oh-ho," interrupted the gipsy queen, with a light laugh. "I thought that one question would suffice."

"Well remarked," said Leonore, smiling. "You do well to mention it, dear Mina, for I promise you that, tempted by your candour and frankness, I was about to launch out into a rush of questions and impertinences which would have overwhelmed you."

"Nay. I know that to be impossible," said Mina.

"To overwhelm you?"

"No. That you could ask impertinences, as you call them."

"You have not seen my curiosity fully developed as yet."

"I have seen something better. I have seen your forbearance since we have been together, and I don't think that so many of our sex could have so long refrained from questioning me, the more especially as the circumstances under which our acquaintance began were so peculiar. A rather strange circumstance, a fatal mystery, surrounds my doings immediately before my acquaintance with you. Deeds of violence had been wrought by this hand."

Leonore shrank involuntarily from her at this.

"Pray, Leonore, do not draw from me. They were but just deeds, as you shall hear."

"How can such deeds be justified?"

"Ah! Leonore," said the gipsy queen, sadly, "I see that we are even alike in disposition, both so eager to jump at conclusions before we have scarcely an idea of the subject."

"Perhaps you are right," said Leonore. "We should hear before judging—at any rate, before condemning."

"Ay, we should, indeed. Think what misery you might have been spared. Think how you have judged Red Ralph upon the bare word of an unknown—a woman who is avowedly an outcast, a fugitive from justice, with a price upon her head."

Leonore started.

"You think me unjust, cruel to my love, Mina?"

"I would not grieve you, Leonore," answered the gipsy queen. "But I must be cruel to be kind. You have been hasty in your judgment of your husband."

"I would I could think so."

"It would be well if you could."

"Alas! I know it."

"I would not endeavour to persuade you that Red Ralph is all truth and perfection, because few men are."

"Then he has fallen, you think?" said Leonore, with sad eagerness to learn her misery.

"Perhaps yes, perchance not. Allowances, however, should be made if he really has."

"Allowances?" iterated Leonore indignantly. "You have never loved, Mina. You do not love him."

Mina clasped her hand to her heart, and her face grew so suddenly of a deathly pallor that Leonore was quite startled.

"How much you wrong me there," said Mina, "you do not, cannot even, know."

"Forgive me, Mina. I have struck some tender chord."

"Nay, it is past now. I was about to remark, dear Leonore, that man's sins should be judged in proportion to the temptations outspread before him."

"I cannot admit that reasoning. Have I not had bitter temptations even before me?"

"Truly."

"Am I not a weak woman cast suddenly upon the world? Reared in the lap of luxury and affluence, of a sudden by cruel chance I have been cast forth, and yet I—I have escaped the ordeal."

"And why?"

"Why? It answers itself."

"Yes. You are right, Leonore. It answers itself thus: Woman is the safeguard of society, and no half measures can be admitted with her. She must be all pure or all bad. This keeps many a would-be sinful woman in the right track, and—"

"And inborn virtue goes for nothing, then?"

"Nay, I do not say that. I would merely point out that man's vices cannot be measured as woman's. Society admits the one and not the other."

"Well, well, dear Mina," said Leonore, "we cannot look upon the question in the same light, and, therefore, can never agree. But we have wandered from our old subject with all this."

"Yes. Your question."

"I may ask it, then?"

"I await it."

"Why did you have that wood hut built?"

"Oh! Your question was nothing more harmless than that?"

"Why what did you expect?"

"I thought perhaps—but no matter. That hut was built by the tribe for two reasons: it was necessary that I should be separated from the tribe."

"Indeed?"

"Yes. One of those reasons you are in some way connected with."

"How so?"

"I was being pursued by Jonathan Wild the thief-taker for a crime of which I was morally as innocent as yourself."

"But could you escape pursuit, then?"

"It was so deemed. But the result proved that we were mistaken."

"And your other reason?"

"I had a long and severe illness, and the old women of the tribe said that I had better be removed to a house to be nursed."

"I thought that you always tended your sick in the tents."

"Yes, those born in the tents."

"And you, then?"

"I am a house-dweller. I see that you are astonished. I shall give you some day an explanation of that too. Well, I would not quit my people, and so they constructed that rude wood hut to shield me from the keen forest air during the crisis of the fever which laid me low."

"And it was, then, after this that I met you?"

"It was."

"But can you account for the strange appearance of Jonathan Wild just after I got to the hut? He

[MURDER.]

could never have tracked me through the forest on that fearful night."

"No."

"It has always puzzled me."

"I can explain it; but to do so will necessitate going a little back into the past. Give me your ear, and I will explain something of the mystery which to you must enshroud me—"

Leonore interrupted her,

"One moment, dear Mina," she said. "Is there anything in your history which might tend to lessen my affection for you?"

"Nothing, Leonore."

"Proceed then."

"Yours is but a slight love, after all, Leonore."

"Mina—"

"Nay, I speak but reasonably when you fear that a word of mine may shake it."

"You misunderstand me."

"Nay. Nothing in life could shake my love for you."

"Not if you learnt that I had been guilty of a great crime?"

"No. That would endear you to me the more, because I should know that yours was a suffering soul —a repentant heart, that had need of consolation."

Leonore seized her in her arms, and embraced her with passionate affection.

"Dear, dear Mina," she said, "you are all affection, and worthy of a better love than mine."

Mina kissed her forehead in reply.

"A better love, dear Leonore, does not exist," said the gipsy queen, "for, after all, I find that yours is a pure and chaste love. I can understand why a soul so pure as yours should shrink from contamination with a baser spirit."

"You forgive my words, then?"

"Don't ask it."

"Then I promise that nothing that you utter shall shock me. I am sorry that I spoke of estranging your affection. It is impossible. Nothing that you can say can affect me."

"Believe me I have nothing of so very shocking a nature to say. What I have to say shall be said, though, without further delay, for the evening grows cool, and I would conclude whilst we are yet before the ruins of my little wood hut."

Clearing her throat, as if in promise of a lengthy narration, Mina the gipsy queen commenced her recital.

But as it is an important subject, inasmuch as it will throw a light upon the obscurity of a former episode in these pages, we think that Mina's history deserves a new chapter.

———

CHAPTER CLVI.

MINA'S HISTORY — HER EARLY LIFE — THE LIBERTINE SQUIRE AND THE FALSE ZINGARO — AN ABDUCTION — THE PRISON CHAMBER — THREATS AND PERSUASIONS — THE GIPSY QUEEN DEFENDS HER HONOUR — ESCAPE — THE CELLAR FLAP — WHAT SHE HEARD AND SAW.

"I SHALL not, dear Leonore," began the gipsy queen, "go very far back in my history. The facts of my connection with the tribe must for the present remain a secret and a mystery to you. Suffice it to say that shortly after my joining the tribe I attracted the attention of a house-dweller, one Rupert Fairfax, a county squire of some property, and reported to be descended from a great republican general of the Commonwealth. It was a few years since, and I was pretty attractive."

"Was?" said Leonore reproachfully: "And you are what?"

"That I leave others to judge."

"Then I will pass judgment. You are handsome and beautiful, and good as you are beautiful."

"Fie! What vanity to praise my looks when we are the very counterpart and presentment of each other!"

"True," returned Leonore, blushing and laughing at once. "I never looked at it in that light."

"Well," resumed Mina, "I had got to Squire Fairfax I think?"

"Yes."

"This squire was a handsome young man, but one of rather loose principles. He had succeeded when very young to a large estate and fortune, and was soon surrounded by a parcel of toadies and fortune hunters, who praised up his follies and vices, smoothed over his worse defects, and pandered to the very utmost to his evil desires, until he became as unscrupulous and wicked as the worst passions, when they are not only allowed to run riot, but pampered and fed well, will make a man. He saw me with the tribe whilst we were camping upon his estate. I must confess that I put myself in his way, for Squire Fairfax was in everybody's mouth. He was beloved by his tenantry because he had once dragged his arbitrary steward through the horsepond for seizing on an old decayed farmer, and because he was not over particular in collecting his rents. He was immensely rich, independently of his landed property, a mere percentage of which satisfied his wants. I put myself in his way, with no intention of catching his notice, as heaven is my witness, but merely to see what kind of man was this prince of landlords—this paragon of squires. Well, the squire saw me, and was smitten. He paid a visit to our camp at once, and laid violent siege to my affections. I will not say that I was not flattered by his attentions. I should not be a woman if I were not. At length Squire Fairfax, mistaking a free open manner for something worse, ventured to make proposals to me such as no honest girl can bear without the blush of shame and indignation mantling her cheeks. I could not reply to him, so thoroughly was I astounded by what he had said; so I fled from the spot. He pursued me, overtook me, and again poured into my ears a tale of passion that made them tingle with shame. I turned upon him a look of supreme contempt and disgust, and ordered him away. He only laughed, and called me a coy gipsy—a forest bird of paradise—and even attempted to lay hands upon me. At this I called some of the men of our tribe to my aid, and he desisted.

"'No matter, Mina,' said Fairfax, turning upon me a look of baffled rage. 'You have foiled me once. Your cursed prudery not only ruins your own prospects and advancement, but checks me in my pleasures; so look to it.'

"I was so indignant, so thoroughly incensed against the man, that I could not reply. He left me, and I returned into my own tent to weep."

Leonore at this expressed her astonishment.

"To weep, Mina? Rather to rejoice at your deliverance."

"Nay, Leonore," replied the gipsy queen sadly. "I had almost begun to love that man."

"Is it possible?"

"Alas! yes."

"And can a heart so deceive one? One would almost think that love is so divine that instinct would guide the heart to the bosom which truly reciprocates its passion."

"Yes. But you know that I was there with the tribe, surrounded by rude and uncultivated men. The squire, Rupert Fairfax, appears, and makes such a demonstration that— Yet no. Had I been wise I should have understood that a proud and rich gentleman would never woo a gipsy vagrant girl, as he deemed me, with honourable purposes."

"You have nothing to blame yourself for, it seems to me, Mina."

"No. The youthful heart of a maid is easily moulded into love. I loved and was deceived."

"Well, did you see no more of this lover?" demanded Leonore.

"Yes," replied the gipsy queen, with a shudder. "There is yet a fearful sequel to my history."

She paused and brushed her hand across her eyes, as if to force back a flood of tears.

"Do not continue your story if it pains you," said Leonore.

"Nay," returned Mina. "I have set myself a task, and I will go through with it to the end."

"Some days after what I have just related I was wandering through the woods surrounding our encampment musing regretfully, and—I blush to own my girlish weakness—in tears at the falsehood of my lost love, when I came suddenly upon two men holding an earnest conference in a low hushed voice. I drew up short before they discovered me, and judge of my amazement when I found one of them to be

Rupert Fairfax. The other was one of my own tribe—a guilty man who has since expiated this and other crimes in a fearful manner."

"Jonas ?"

"The same."

"For what purpose was he there ?"

"I listened. I don't shame to confess this much, for instinct told me that I was the subject of their conversation. I found that my conjectures were correct—nay more, that, in spite of the scorn and indignation with which I received the squire's guilty proposals, the unmanly fellow still was determined upon accomplishing my ruin. I leave you to judge with what horror, shame, and indignation I heard one of our people coolly discussing my forcible compliance with the libertine's views."

"Poor Mina !"

"I shall yet have much greater need of your sympathy."

"And this was Jonas ?"

"It was."

"The traitor !"

"No matter for Jonas now," said Mina. "He will no longer trouble any of us here. Fearful as it is to take divine prerogatives into our own hands, from the character of the man it is certain that nothing else could have secured us from his malice."

"No. Yet still—"

"You do not hold with what we—what *I* have done in this ?"

"I think," returned Leonore evasively, "that the law—"

"Law ?" interrupted the gipsy queen impatiently. "Do you not see that the Zingaro acknowledges no law, no rules, no code so binding upon him as the judgment of his tribe—of his queen."

"Perhaps you are right," said Leonore, with a shudder. "But to me it seems a fearful thing to kill a man in cold blood."

"But this was no man. He was but a dog, a toad, a reptile, whom it was the duty of every honest man to crush."

"Truly, he was a traitor."

"At heart. But enough of Jonas. How far he was concerned with this Squire Fairfax you have yet to learn. I could not wait for more. My heart was young. I was not then trained in duplicity. I had not then acquired the lessons which I have since so well imbibed."

These last words were given with much bitterness.

"Poor Mina !" said Leonore, pressing her hand sympathisingly.

"You will pity me I know."

"I do."

"Well, dear Leonore," resumed the gipsy queen with a flushed cheek. "I was returning in hot haste to the encampment, when I found myself confronted in the wood, in a retired lonely path, by two strange men. Before they had spoken a word, or made the slightest demonstration, I guessed their purpose in their faces. One seized me in his arms and I was powerless. I would have cried out for assistance, but fear seemed to paralyse me. My tongue clove to the roof of my mouth. Before I could recover myself sufficiently to utter a word a cloth was thrown over my head from behind, and I was borne off."

She paused for breath.

"I scarcely know what happened to me then, but I suppose I fainted, for when I recovered I found myself in a strange house. I was alone, but still in fear. A terrible presentiment naturally occurred to me. I instantly guessed that I was in the power of Squire Fairfax—alone, and at his mercy. I examined the chamber in which I found myself, for the purpose of discovering if there were any means of escape. I found that there was no hope—no chance. Not the faintest loophole had been left open by the cool and calculating villain, so well had he laid his plans. I had not long recovered when the lock of my door turned, and the man I expected made his appearance. It was Fairfax.

"'Well, my scornful proud gipsy,' he said on entering, 'and how fares it by this time?'

"'Ill, Mr Fairfax,' I replied, 'and I implore of you to open your doors and allow me to depart in peace—to return to my tribe.'

"He laughed at my words.

"'Why I find my coy gipsy is silly as well as pretty,' said the squire. 'What, let you go now after all the trouble I have been at to snare you? No, no, no.'

"'Villain !' said I.

"'Nay, Mina, my love. Come, give me one kiss.'

"'Never !' I shrieked. 'Sooner would I slay you there at my feet. Begone !'

"'Slay me ?' he repeated, somewhat startled by my vehemence.

"'Ay, I mean it.'

"'You talk idly, my dear,' said the squire, with an attempt to smile, which sadly failed.

"'Not so,' I said, 'for I have the means about me now.'

"'Nonsense.'

"As he put this half in the form of an interrogation I reiterated my assertion.

"'Look upon me, Rupert Fairfax,' said I, 'and tell me if I look like a liar. Do I resemble your own black-hearted self?'

"He laughed uncomfortably, but did not offer to approach me.

"'I shall find the means to ascertain if you *have* spoken the truth,' he said, with a deep significance which caused me to shudder apprehensively.

"He left the room, closing the door after him. I sprang forward, but too late. The door was locked securely against me. But now I could not rest. The lock securing my door was but a rude and feeble contrivance. I will not dwell upon these details. Suffice it to say that towards night I contrived to force my way out of the room and through the house. Here I met with some serious obstacles to further progress. The door at the front of the house was fastened securely, and the key removed.

"Had it not been for this mishap I should have retreated in safety, so quietly had I managed to escape from the chamber in which I had been a prisoner. I did not pause to lament my hard fortune, but, urged on by the immediate necessity of action, I made my way into the basement.

"As I was nearing the basement steps I found that a cellar flap at the end of the hall had been left open. Just as I reached this open flap the sounds of an angry altercation reached me from below. I looked down, and there I witnessed a sight that turned my blood cold in my veins.

"Spellbound and silently I looked on. It was a fearful sight, and ended fatally, when a word from me might have saved bloodshed. It was no fault of mine, however, for fear held me dumb, although I afterwards suffered as if I had indeed been guilty."

"Hard fortune !" said Leonore.

"Truly. But not for me alone. You shared in the wrong."

"I ?"

"Yes. You are surprised, but you shall hear how."

CHAPTER CLVII.

MINA'S HISTORY CONTINUED — WHAT FURTHER
BEFEL HER IN THE LIBERTINE SQUIRE'S
POWER — JONATHAN WILD'S HAND IN THE
BUSINESS — BOLD DEFIANCE — HOW MINA GOT
FROM THE CHAMBER — THE OPEN CELLAR
FLAP — A SCRAMBLE — WHAT SHE SAW THERE
— THE DEATH OF THE GIPSY — CAPTURE —
IMPRISONMENT — FALSE WITNESS AND CON-
DEMNATION — RESCUE — THE RUFFIAN VIL-
LAGERS — WITCHCRAFT — A NARROW ESCAPE —
THE SLUR IS REMOVED FROM THE NAME OF
MINA THE DAUGHTER OF NIGHT.

"FROM what I afterwards learned, dear Leonore,"
continued the gipsy queen, "it appears that I had no
sooner disappeared than the whole band professed
themselves both wonder and horror stricken. Singularly enough, not one of them had an idea that I had
become the victim of the machinations of Squire
Fairfax. It was the more strange, as they one and
all were aware of the vile proposals that Squire
Rupert had dared to make to me. The forest was
scoured, and, of the whole tribe, as I afterwards
learned, none was more apparently earnest in the
search than Jonas—the traitor Jonas.

"In the tribe at the period I speak of was one
Ephraim, a young man, who possessed a wit and
shrewdness of no mean order. It was the cunning
of the Zingaro more fully developed. Ephraim con-
ceived the idea that my disappearance was due to the
squire, and he set himself at once to watch the place.
We learned the facts afterwards from one of the tribe,
to whom he confided his project under a pledge of
secrecy.

"Ephraim dogged the squire's steps night and
day, and, at length finding something to confirm his
half-formed suspicions, he broke into the house
through the basement, and chanced to come across
the squire and one of his creatures, a bold burly
ruffian—one of the two who had been instrumental
in carrying me off.

"A scramble ensued. It was this that I witnessed
down the open cellar flap from the hall.

"With breathless anxiety I saw the squire advance
and seize the luckless Ephraim by the back of the
head, and, dragging him back, endeavour to throw
him to the ground.

"Ephraim was supple and active, as well as strong.
He jerked himself from the grasp of his murderous
assailants, and, seizing Rupert Fairfax around the
middle, he raised him from his feet and cast him
stunned for a while to the further extremity of the
cellar.

"Before he could regain his presence of mind,
however, the ruffian I before alluded to rushed upon
him, toppled him over upon the ground, and there he
held him at his mercy with his left hand, whilst his
right hand sought a knife which he had concealed in
his breast.

"The action was too plain to be mistaken, but,
although I saw the life of poor Ephraim in danger,
as I told you before, I had not the power to utter a
cry or sound—to say that word which might have
saved the life of a fellow-creature.

"Spellbound and dumbstricken I gazed upon the
now unequal combat. I saw the glittering of an upraised knife, I saw the fatal weapon descend, and—
ugh! all was over.

"Poor Ephraim gave one piercing unearthly shriek
before he expired—a cry that will ring in my ears
until my dying hour. That cry was caught up by
me before it had died away upon his lips, for the
spell which chained my senses — benumbed every

faculty and speech—was broken, and my cry might
have sounded like the echo of the dying Ephraim's.

"'Hullo!' cried one of the men from below,
a wretch whom I afterwards knew but too well.
It was Jonathan Wild the thieftaker. The villain had
been engaged by Squire Fairfax as a fit instrument
for his dastardly rascality.

"'Some one there?' demanded the squire, coming
forward.

"'Yes, squire.'

"'Who?'

"'The gal.'

"'Plague seize her!' he cried. 'That's devilish
awkward. What shall we be up to?'

"'Up to?' echoed Jonathan Wild. 'Why after
her.'

"Then followed a scramble, and I knew that the
murderers were about to come in pursuit of me. I
fled I knew not whither—I thought not whither. I
only sought to fly, but in my agitation I rushed into
the danger I might then, in the confusion which prevailed, have easily escaped. I found myself confronted by the squire upon the top of the basement
stairs.

"'Foolish girl!' he cried. 'You have got yourself
into something like real danger now by your obstinacy.'

"I resisted him with such desperation that,
breathless as he was from his late struggle and fall, he
could scarcely match me.

"In the struggle which ensued I dragged him
towards the open flap, and then, by accident rather
than design, I pushed him down it.

"After this I even contrived to get from the house,
but was overtaken by that ruthless merciless destroyer
of the innocent—that false witness and swearer away
of men's lives—Jonathan Wild the thieftaker.

"In spite of my prayers and entreaties I was taken
off, but now not to the squire's house.

"Judge then, dear Leonore, to what horror and
consternation was changed my rejoicing at this when
I found myself consigned to a prison."

Again did Mina the gipsy queen pause in her narration, overcome by the fearful recollections which it
conjured up.

"A prison?" iterated Lady Leonore, aghast.

"Ay, a prisoner."

"But you? How, in heaven's name? For what
purpose?"

"Ah! Leonore," returned Mina, "now comes a
portion of my history yet more appalling in its details than anything which has gone before. I was
actually arrested, imprisoned, and brought to trial
upon the charge of murder."

Leonore shrank back, horrified at the fatal word.

"Do not draw from me," said Mina in a tone of
sad reproach. "I am as innocent of the crime as
yourself."

"I believe you."

"And whose murder do you think I was charged
with?"

"I cannot guess."

"Ephraim's."

"Ephraim's? What he whom you had seen slain
by the hand of Jonathan Wild?"

"The same."

"Is such atrocity, then, really possible?"

"Alas! it is, as we see," said Mina. "But I will
not pain you by dwelling upon these horrors. All the
tortures, miseries, terrors I experienced during that
imprisonment culminated in a conviction. Start not,
dear Leonore. The only evidence of the fearful crime
of which I stood charged was the false witness of
Jonathan Wild. Strange as it must appear to you,
dear Leonore, it is nevertheless a fearful fact. I was
to have been executed.

" Upon the eve of the day appointed for the execution I escaped. There was nothing very remarkable about this, for ever since the conviction I had preserved such an apathetic demeanour that the authorities, I presume, grew negligent, deeming the ordinary caution unnecessary. But, horror-stricken as I was, I never once lost my presence of mind, and the occasion no sooner presented itself than I took advantage of it.

" I must tell you, Leonore, that in my escape I was aided by the tribe, who were always upon the look-out for me. I returned at once to the tribe—an imprudent thing to do, as you will doubtless say, under the circumstances.

" So it proved, as you shall hear.

" While I had been away it appears that Rupert Fairfax had been stretched upon a bed of sickness—his life had almost been despaired of. Now Jonathan Wild, with the cunning of a very devil, had spread about the village a report that he had been ensnared and bewitched by certain potent charms, which I, as queen of the gipsies, was supposed to possess the power of working.

" The reason he adduced for this gave a certain colouring of truth to the tale fabricated with such diabolical ingenuity, and it well nigh proved fatal to me.

" He avowed that, captivated by the manly presence of the squire, I had actually sought his love, and that he had resisted my fascinations and urged me to return to the tribe.

" To this end he further stated that he had procured the assistance of Ephraim, in the hopes that, being of my own people, his persuasion might induce me to forego my guilty hopes."

" Merciful powers !" ejaculated Lady Leonore.

" I wonder not at your amazement, dear Leonore," continued Mina. " But you do not yet know all. A yet more deadly phase in my horrible romance remains untold."

" Is it possible ?"

" You shall hear. The good people of the village were credulous, and Jonathan Wild's artfully-worded story gained their faith. Mystery and witchcraft were highly-spiced excitements, and all they had to stir them from the dull monotony of their existence, and were consequently acceptable to them."

" Is such ridiculous nonsense, then, still put faith in ?"

" To my cost I found that it is. I had no sooner appeared in the village than a cry was raised, for I was well known and at once recognised. I was denounced by the whole assembled village as a murderess and a witch."

" Your life in this particular episode greatly resembles my own ill-fortune," said Leonore.

" The cause is natural. Our resemblance you see."

" Ah !" ejaculated Leonore, with a burst of intelligence. " I see it all now. The witchcraft. It was for you that I so nearly suffered death."

" You ?"

" Yes, within an ace."

" How ?"

" At the stake."

" Strange that in all our confidences, dear Leonore," said the gipsy queen, " you never once alluded to that terrible adventure."

" Not strange either," said Leonore, " for I dreaded to recal those terrible times to mind."

" Well," resumed Mina, " to conclude my narration. for the night draws on apace, and we must return to the encampment. I was seized by the villagers and dragged off in triumph with loud acclaim." They purposed putting me through the recognised tests of witchcraft, commencing with the trial of water. You are well acquainted doubtless with all that, so

I will not go into details. Then I was to be burnt at the stake. For a long time it looked very ugly indeed with me, for when assailed I had only two of the tribe with me, and they were of course powerless to aid me in contending with the whole assembled village. However, one of the two had the presence of mind to return promptly to the camp and bring assistance. But you may judge of my sufferings when I tell you that I had reached the stake before assistance arrived. Nay, the faggots were already piled up around the post to which I was bound, and all was in readiness. But a dozen sturdy Zingari, armed with sticks and knives, soon scattered the whole lot of village loons. I was rescued and borne off by my own people to the tents.

" The excitements which I had undergone during that week proved too much for me now it was all over. Before night I was in a raging fever—prostrate and helpless as a babe. And now, dear Leonore, I come to the wood hut. At this time I had not been sufficiently long with the tribe to become inured to all the rough treatment our way of life necessitated. The old women of the tribe saw and understood this, and would not guarantee my recovery unless I was removed to the protection of four walls.

" The events to which I owed the illness which had prostrated me precluded all possibility of openly seeking advice, and we dared not go into the town or village, where attention might be excited. Moreover, it was not now convenient to remove me far. For this purpose the tribe set diligently to work, and in a single day and night constructed my rude wood hut —of which we see before us all that now remains, sole evidence of horrors now happily over. I feel a strange sensation of sadness steal over me as I look upon them.

" Come, dear Leonore, let us return to the encampment."

This, then, is the explanation of the seeming mystery with which our narration commenced.

But an explanation of several matters important to the interest of our story is yet due to the reader.

The extraordinary resemblance existing between the gipsy queen and our high-born heroine surely admits of some explanation.

We shall see. In the meantime other matters of higher interest and excitement call our attention.

We must return to the moated castle, and see what has occurred whilst we have been duly telling the reader the bygone history of MINA THE DAUGHTER OF NIGHT.

CHAPTER CLVIII.

THE BATTLE AT THE CASTLE STILL — A GOODLY FIGHT—THE DRAWBRIDGE—ATTACK AND REPULSE — THE AVALANCHE FROM THE CASTLE TURRET — DANGER — THE MOAT — SUCCESS — HOW THE DRAWBRIDGE WAS LOWERED — A BRAVE CONTEST — "RED RALPH AND THE BOLD YELLOW BOYS !"

THE fight around the moated castle yet raged with fury.

Oaths, groans, and shrieks of the wounded and dying were mingled with the rattle of muskets, which grew less frequent as the fight went on, denoting that the ammunition was beginning to run low.

Thrice did the lieutenant of the Yellow Band lead on his men to take the place by storm.

Thrice did he conduct them to the assault, which was made with great determination.

But thrice were they repulsed, and once with great danger.

They had by this time several of their number *hors de combat.*

Not a man had been very seriously injured, however. Several had cracked crowns, and one or two a fracture of some limb or other, but not a man was killed yet.

The drawbridge was held up by a chain, which resisted every effort to dislodge it.

It was too stout to give beneath the feeble blows that the besiegers stormed upon it.

They might have succeeded had they possessed any favourable instruments for the assault, but unfortunately no one had any weapon of greater strength than a sword.

Yet it was boldly persevered in by the lieutenant.

He made a vigorous attack upon the chain, but the only effect was their broken swords, whilst the chain remained intact.

This was not the only difficulty either.

From the castle turret the besieged had discovered that attempts were being made in this direction, and a whole body of this numerous order was posted immediately above, furnished with all kinds of aids to harass and worry the lieutenant.

Missiles of every size and form were hurled down by the dozen upon his devoted head.

Still he kept to it boldly, only once exchanging his hat for the stouter head-gear of one of the fallen men.

The missiles hurled at him either fell wide of the mark or glanced off his head or shoulders without effecting much damage.

Presently, as Walters was driven from his position for the third time by the hot shower of projectiles hurled at him, one of the men ran up to his side.

"Beg pardon, lieutenant," he said, touching his hat.

"What now?" asked Walters.

"Would a hatchet do better for your job than a sword."

"A hatchet?"

"Ay, sir."

"Of course. But where is there one to be got?"

"Here, sir."

Saying which, he produced a small but stout axe with a wooden handle, which Walters snatched from him with an angry exclamation and an oath.

"Why on earth, man, have you kept this hidden?" he asked. "No matter. Take your musket."

"Yes, sir."

"Call six men hither."

Six of the besieging party were before the lieutenant in a few seconds.

"Now, my men," said the lieutenant, "I want you to keep me undisturbed at the drawbridge."

"Ay, ay, sir."

"You understand?"

"All right, lieutenant."

"Aim well, and I can promise you that if you can keep me free from their attention for ten minutes—nay, less—I will open the drawbridge, and the rest is easy."

"We'll do it."

"And you will no less contribute to the success of the day than myself — than the captain and Sir Hubert."

The men answered this piece of judicious flattery upon the part of the lieutenant with a shout.

Armed now with the hatchet, Walters returned to the chain of the drawbridge, getting as close under the shelter of the wall as possible, to avoid the attention of the members of the secret brotherhood assembled immediately above.

One of the brotherhood, however, soon spied out the means of harassing the lieutenant at his post.

From the angle of the turret he could catch a glimpse of the Yellow Boy, but to make himself effectually annoying he had to place himself in a far more prominent position than was agreeable, considering the hot attack kept up from below.

He raised his cross bow to his shoulder, but before he could discharge it a shot from below struck him in the chest, and with a groan he sank back lifeless.

Upon a man-of-war during an engagement sailors have been known to say that no two shots touch the same spot, and the safest place is to ram one's head into the hole left by the last ball that has passed through the bulwarks of the vessel.

Probably upon this same principle the brother had no sooner fallen a victim to his enemy than his place was supplied by a second.

However, it was clear that the saying did not hold good in his case, for he had no sooner taken up his position than he was driven from it by three shots fired in rapid succession.

And the lieutenant of the Yellow Band belaboured at the chain of the drawbridge unmolested.

Upon the point of his attack he had already done some little execution with the three swords which lay broken upon the edge of the moat in evidence of his handiwork.

The chain was now half cut through.

The drawbridge shivered and vibrated with the sturdy blows delivered with wonderful precision by the lieutenant's steady nerveless hand.

Upon the ramparts above it was remarked by the secret brotherhood, and the importance of the work on hand was duly appreciated by them.

One of them, who appeared to be in authority, called a learned council upon the matter.

"My brethren," he said, "if that sacrilegious dog now swimming on horseback in the moat be not disturbed, we shall have cause to repent it."

"We shall," replied the brotherhood with one accord.

"Then something must be done at once."

"Ay, and no time wasted in idle parley."

"See how the bridge shakes."

"Had the fastening been less secure it would long since have fallen."

"Truly, the sacrilegious infidel plies his weapon well."

"And that shows the double importance of frustrating his plans. If he strikes thus upon the chain, his aim will not be the less sure when he has only the devoted members of our holy brotherhood to oppose him."

"What to do, then?"

"This. Do you take the left angle of the turret there."

"Yes."

"Away. Spare not shot nor aim, for it is the most important portion of this bloody fray. To your work, and let not this infidel dog escape."

"Count upon me."

"And you," continued the chief of the holy brotherhood, "take the right angle there."

"Facing Isaac?"

"Yes. And let your aim be true as is the purpose for which we oppose these infidels."

"It shall."

The second of the secret brotherhood being thus disposed of, it left the more time to mark the best positions for the remainder of the men summoned for this important service.

Singularly enough, although the work was so pressing and so important, only the two first disposed of appeared to be serving in the object.

Presently an arrow, shot from the right angle of the castle turret came so near the lieutenant that he felt some lively apprehensions for his safety.

" Now, my men," he cried to the six men covering his work, " pick that fellow off."

But it was far more easily ordered than accomplished, for the man had snugly ensconced himself behind a pile of hastily-erected stonework, where for a while he contrived to shoot away unmolested.

Had he possessed a moderately decent aim Walters would have been a dead man half a dozen times.

But the vigilance of the Yellow Boys was more than they could oppose with any success.

One of them, more alive to the nature of the defence adopted than his fellows, darted round, and mounted hastily into a tree.

Here, from one of the topmost branches, he got a fair view of the brother who was worrying the lieutenant, and a couple of shots sufficed to dislodge him.

" Another stroke for the Yellow Band ! " cried Walters.

And, finding himself freed from the attack of the right, he belaboured at the chain again with redoubled vigour.

" Bravo, lieutenant ! " shouted a dozen of the admiring band.

Incited by the cheers of his men the lieutenant of the Yellow Band struck boldly at the second chain— the first being summarily disposed of—and with one blow did such execution upon it that a few strokes of this description threatened to demolish it.

Judge, then, the chagrin and consternation of the lieutenant when, in the moment of success—upon the very edge of accomplishing his dangerous mission— he found himself exposed to a hot fire of musketry and arrows from the left.

He was forced again to retreat.

Close under a projection lining the top of the moat he stood again.

This not only served as a shelter from the attack from above, but, the moat being shallow here, his brave steed found a good resting-place.

" Stand to it, my men ! " he cried to the six Yellow Boys.

" All right, lieutenant."

" Give me another blow at the chain, and the drawbridge is down."

" Hurrah ! "

" This done, you know how easy is the rest. I promise good sport."

The attack from the left turret was silenced by the Yellow Boys forthwith, half a dozen of whom rushed out of the general attack to aid in this important service.

Walters turned his horse's head again round to the drawbridge.

But now an unexpected difficulty presented itself.

The noble animal was so exhausted by its efforts that it refused to take the deep water again.

All that the lieutenant could do now was of no avail.

In vain did he apply spur and stroke to the poor animal's back with the flat of his sword.

It would not move.

" Plague seize thee for an obstinate cowardly brute ! " said Walters. " But I will not be baulked by such a mischance in the moment of success. Since thou'lt not aid me, I must do it alone."

And with this the lieutenant scrambled upon the horse's back and stood up.

Then, leaning forward, he made a sudden and desperate spring, and caught at the edge of the upraised drawbridge, upon which he hung until he had made good his hold.

Then he scrambled up, and, perching himself astride the chains, he drew the axe from his belt, where he had temporarily placed it, and struck boldly again at the chain.

One stroke, and the drawbridge appeared only to be held by a thin wire of the chainwork.

" Here goes the last stroke ! " cried Walters.

And down came the hatchet with fearful force and precision.

And down, with the selfsame stroke, came the chain and drawbridge.

Walters had calculated his danger, and prepared for it. Yet withal, as it fell, he was very nearly shaken into the moat.

Fortunately, however, he grasped one of the broken chains, and, pulling himself upwards, secured his footing upon the drawbridge.

Suddenly there arose a fearful cry from his men— one awful shout, as if some unavoidable calamity were about to demolish their host.

" Stand clear ! "

" Jump, lieutenant ! "

" Into the water with you ! "

" Down ! down ! "

Walters comprehended some great danger instantly. He sprang to the edge of the drawbridge, and clutched it with both hands, whirling his body round under it for protection. The danger he divined by instinct could only come from above.

Simultaneously with this movement upon the part of the lieutenant of the Yellow Band there came from above an immense pile of stonework, hurled down to demolish the devoted Yellow Boy.

It was this that the Yellow Boys had seen, one and all.

So great was the mass intended to hurl the lieutenant to destruction that it took the united exertions of no less than eight of the secret brotherhood to push it over the turret of the castle.

It glanced upon the side of the drawbridge, shaving some of the planks upon the edge, and carrying the splintered wood into the moat with it.

And the lieutenant ?

He had disappeared !

Awe-stricken, the Yellow Boys looked on, not one of them offering to retaliate upon the eight men who had hurled the fatal projectile.

For fatal they deemed it.

Then some six or seven of the Yellow Boys rushed to the edge of the moat, and two of the number plunged in.

The remainder of the band meanwhile protected their advance.

" The lieutenant is gone ! "

" Dead ? "

" Ay."

Several minutes had now elapsed, and it was deemed impossible that he could yet survive the long immersion.

*   *   *   *   *   *

A few seconds after they had pronounced his fate a struggle was observed in the water beneath the drawbridge.

Then the lieutenant's horse, which yet stood beneath the stonework projection where its master had left it—trembling as if the poor beast were stricken with ague, at the fearful din of battle around it— with a loud neighing dashed into the water it had previously with such obstinacy refused to take.

One stroke of its forelegs brought it beneath the drawbridge.

The horse bent forward its gracefully curved neck, seized something between its teeth, and then turned for the shore.

With a cry of joy, one of the Yellow Boys still swimming in the moat struck out for the bank and scrambled up.

Then, regardless of his own state of exhaustion, he stretched forth his hand and grasped the horse's bridle.

With his other hand he clutched at the object which the faithful animal held between his teeth with such tenacity, and tugged at it with desperation.

The struggling steed redoubled its efforts, and scrambled ashore panting.

And there by the coat collar it held the slim insensible form of Walters, the bold lieutenant of the Yellow Band.

* * * * * *

A few minutes, and the indefatigable lieutenant was armed and ready for service again.

"Give me a spare coat if there is one," said Walters as he threw off his own dripping garment.

But, impatient of the delay in satisfying this demand, he refused it when it came.

"Now for the assault!" he cried.

The excitement at this amongst the Yellow Boys was immense.

"You will take the command of six men upon this side, Morris," said Walters; "and—Jeffries—"

"Here, sir."

"You will have the command of six men upon this side."

"Yes, sir."

"You understand that your duty is to protect our advance."

"Yes, lieutenant."

"You will cover at once any of the enemy who may show above there as we make the assault."

"Yes, sir."

"I will lead the assault myself."

"Nay, lieutenant," said one of the men. "You had better withdraw."

"What?" ejaculated Walters.

"Yes, lieutenant, indeed you had, until you are a little better again."

"Plague seize any man who talks of withdrawing."

"Only a few minutes," they urged.

"Not a second."

And so he persisted, in spite of all that they could urge.

The men were then formed into a body and arranged with such precision and judgment that a military observer would have supposed the leader accustomed to this kind of attack.

"Now," cried the lieutenant. "Ready—follow me—charge!"

And a dozen horsemen armed to the teeth rattled over the drawbridge at a gallop.

"Red Ralph and the bold Yellow Boys!" shouted Walters.

"Red Ralph and the bold Yellow Boys!" cried the men.

The doors now opposing them were of stout oak thickly studded with iron nails.

At the first shock they resisted boldly.

The men withdrew, and a second attack was made more impetuously than the first, carrying down the portals with a terrific crash.

"Red Ralph and the bold Yellow Boys!" cried Walters, excitedly.

And again did the men catch up his war cry as they rushed in after him.

In the court yard of the castle a numerous array of the secret brotherhood was drawn up to greet them.

A shower of arrows—apparently the favourite war implement of the brotherhood—were discharged without much effect.

The Yellow Boys had been ordered to lower their leathern hats to protect their brows, and the arrows glanced off from them and their stout doublets harmlessly.

"Give them a volley!" shouted the lieutenant.

The men replied with a cheer.

The volley was fired, visibly thinning the ranks of the enemy.

"Charge them!"

"Hurrah!"

"Red Ralph and the bold Yellow Boys!"

Pistols were grasped by their long barrels and used as clubs. Swords flashed from their scabbards—a dozen trusty blades in sinewy muscular grasps.

On came the bold little phalanx with another rush, bearing down their foes by scores.

And yet every inch of ground was contested boldly by the secret brotherhood.

Bold and desperate men were they, preferring death to an infringement of their rights or an intrusion into their fortress.

"Strike for the bold brotherhood and the right of justice and innocence!" cried the chief.

But his brethren needed no words of encouragement to incite them to the performance of their duty.

They let themselves be thrown down, but never did they stir a step.

The lieutenant, being the foremost in the action, was the first to suffer any disaster.

One of the fallen brotherhood as he was being trampled underfoot stabbed the horse which Walters rode, burying a long knife up to the hilt in the poor beast's belly.

Down came the lieutenant, but his falling horse crushed its destroyer to death, thus avenging both its master and itself at a blow.

Walters soon disengaged himself from the fallen steed, and was up brandishing his sword round his head in an instant.

The brothers, seeing the leader of the enemy falling, gained courage and attempted to close round him.

But Walters was too wary for this. With his back to his own men he carved himself out a circle of blood.

His quick eye and ready hand opposed any one attempting to pushing beyond the limit, and death was sure to follow.

"To it, my lads," he cried.

"Hurrah!"

"Red Ralph and the bold Yellow Boys!"

The men caught up the cry once more and charged more vigorously.

Their weight alone crushed the comparatively unarmed brotherhood.

And inch by inch the ground was contended; but still the Yellow Boys steadily advanced.

Suddenly a voice from the interior of the castle issued some command to the opposing brothers which the Yellow Boys could not comprehend.

The effect, however, was by no means encouraging to the attacking party.

The secret brotherhood suddenly retreated with a rush, opening out on either side, and allowing the Yellow Boys to follow up their impetuous course some half a dozen yards unmolested.

But only this distance.

Judge, then, their consternation at finding themselves on a sudden opposed to a fresh body of the secret brotherhood some twenty strong.

CHAPTER CLIX.

RESUMES RED RALPH'S ADVENTURES—HOW SIR HUBERT FONTENOY FARED — RALPH IN JEOPARDY—A GOODLY FIGHT—TWO MORE—A DESPERATE STRAIT—AT DEATH'S DOOR—SURPRISE AND RELEASE — THE CASTLE FALLS — SIR HUBERT AND RED RALPH ARE REVENGED UPON THE SECRET BROTHERHOOD.

WHILST we have been engaged in matters of such excitement we have greatly neglected our hero.

The reader will remember that we left the captain

[A STRUGGLE ON HORSEBACK.]

of the Yellow Band in rather an unpleasant predicament. After awaiting Sir Hubert Fontenoy of Cairgal for nearly twenty minutes at the entrance of the subterranean passage which communicated with his sometime prison Red Ralph had grown impatient at the delay, as well as alarmed at his protracted absence.

Unable any longer to remain in such anxious doubt as to the fate of Sir Hubert, he also penetrated the gloomy depths of the passage, and made his way up to the opening, which, at the period of their memorable escape from the castle, was concealed by the straw couch of the hapless Sir Hubert Fontenoy, when in the power of the unscrupulous order.

Here, upon making his way upwards, the captain of the Yellow Band had received a blow which sent him reeling backwards.

Down he fell the whole depth of the excavation.

There he lay for several minutes, half stunned by the blow he had received and the effects of the fall.

When he had sufficiently recovered himself he began to grow alarmed at this mishap. It was now decided, he thought, that something serious had occurred. Sir Hubert was in danger—possibly captured, or worse!

This, then, was the explanation of his long silence.

"Oh! Would that I had insisted upon his remaining," thought the captain of the Yellow Band, " or at least have insisted upon accompanying him."

No matter. It was useless repining.

Moreover, it was quite out of Red Ralph's practice. With him to think was to act, and he now set himself to work to obviate the difficulties and dangers created by Sir Hubert's resolve.

There was but one thing to do—return he must at all hazards by the secret cutting into the cell.

Noiselessly, and with all due caution, the captain of the Yellow Band advanced once more, climbing up the steep rise with great difficulty under the circumstances.

He gained the top.

"Now, then," he murmured mentally. "Now for another trial."

It was neck or nothing.

With one bound he was up in the cell—his right hand grasping his naked sword, which he flourished around his head, awaiting an assault.

He found himself opposed to about eight or ten men, all armed with long swords!

As his eagle eye scanned the numbers he could not but note that they were, to a man, big sturdy fellows—men whose breadth of limb and muscular development appeared to denote that they had been rather born for the sword than the gown.

"Death to the rude despoiler of our home!" cried one of them.

And they advanced with threatening gestures towards Red Ralph.

As they moved out Ralph could see what had become of Sir Hubert Fontenoy of Cairgal. The gallant gentleman lay stretched upon the ground in a state of insensibility.

At a first glance Red Ralph believed him to be dead.

However, he was soon convinced to the contrary by a heavy sigh which broke from the swooning knight.

Red Ralph threw himself into position to receive his foes.

Undaunted, he faced the whole host.

And these were, to a man, armed like himself, save the pair of pistols he carried at his belt, and which he had taken the precaution to load before venturing on his dangerous enterprise.

The men advanced upon him with threatening gestures.

Red Ralph waited patiently until they were within a few paces, and then, presenting both pistols with a deliberate aim, he fired.

Before the smoke of the pistols had cleared off he had fallen upon them and taken them by surprise.

Thus assaulted, the men could scarcely defend themselves, and when Red Ralph could witness the work of destruction that he had caused he saw that no less than six of the secret brotherhood had fallen.

Two now remained to be disposed of, but these were tough customers.

One made such a vigorous onslaught upon our hero that he could not but think how little chance he would have stood had the foes taken the initiative, instead of awaiting his attack.

From this foe single-handed Red Ralph had to beat a retreat before he could make a fair stand.

The second man, seeing this, very promptly followed up the attack from another side, and the captain of the Yellow Band had his sword beaten from his grasp.

Another moment, and he was helpless and at their mercy.

At this disaster Red Ralph's sole sensation was of disgust at having been beaten thus in the moment of victory.

Six men out of eight there to oppose him had he

worsted in a trice, and now he found himself in turn at the mercy of two—nay, almost of one, it might be said, for the one man had but arrived in time to follow up the other's work.

"Villain!" said one of the brotherhood, standing over Red Ralph.

"Despatch him quickly," suggested the other.

And he made a step forward, as if with the purpose of following up the proffered advice with his own hand.

"Hold!" said the former, interposing. "Do nothing rashly."

"Nay, but it were but justice."

"Undoubtedly."

"Your justice," said Red Ralph. "Might is right with you."

"Justice is right."

"And you would have justice upon your side in slaying me in cold blood?" said the captain of the Yellow Band.

"Yes."

"Then, whatever your faith may be, it is a convenient one."

"You blaspheme."

"Despatch him!" urged the other.

"Strike away!" said Red Ralph, not moving a muscle, not quivering an eyelid.

"You are a bold man," said he who had so well wielded his sword.

In spite of his sacred calling, he appeared to look with great admiration upon our hero as a man who could look upon death with such stoical calmness and serenity.

"Why do you hold your hand?" demanded Red Ralph.

"Are you so eager for death?"

"I care not when it comes."

"Weary of life?"

"Perchance."

"Then there is less due to you than I imagined," said the brother. "I took your indifference for boldness of heart, not for contempt of life."

"What care I?"

"Care? Hush, guilty man. You blaspheme. How do you value the gift of life—such a gift—when you can part with it so readily?"

"My friend," quoth Red Ralph, "my word on't, you are better with the sword than the cant of the cloth."

"Vain man!"

"Pshaw!" said Red Ralph. "But I am fain to confess, upon a little deliberation, I find your argument not devoid of some reason."

"To what purpose is all this idle parley?" said the other brother impatiently. "End it at once."

"How?"

"With the sword."

And again he advanced threateningly.

This time the other of the fraternity, who was more humanely inclined, did not offer to oppose him in the execution of their vengeance upon the hapless Ralph.

It looked ugly for our hero. In another minute he would have been annihilated.

But the same marvellous fortune which has followed him throughout his life, during the period, at least, that we have had any dealings with him, did not desert him now.

At this instant a great outcry was raised in the passages without.

A great rush was made, and some ten or twelve of the brotherhood entered the cell, driven by a few of the Yellow Boys.

"Saved! saved!" cried Red Ralph.

"The captain!"

No sooner did they recognise their leader than a tremendous cheering ensued.

The prison cell re-echoed with their cries.

The two captors of our hero had now all their work to do to attend to themselves, and Red Ralph once more escaped unhurt.

At this instant Walters rushed into the cell.

" Where is the captain ?" he cried.

" Here."

" Safe ?"

" And sound."

" Thanks for that assurance, captain," said Walters fervently. " Truth to tell, captain, I had almost begun to despair of finding you."

" A few seconds more and I doubt if you would have done so."

" What mean you ?"

" I should have been a corpse."

" In trouble, then ?"

" Nearly in grievous trouble."

" These knaves have dared—"

" You see how much they have dared," said the captain of the Yellow Band, pointing to the prostrate form of Sir Hubert.

" Dead ?"

" No."

It is well for them he is not. It would have gone hard with them if he had been," said Walters.

" Ay, it should."

Sir Hubert Fontenoy was only stunned for the time, and he partially recovered as they spoke. His first question was for the success of their enterprise.

" The greatest," said Red Ralph. " None better could we have hoped."

" Good."

And then he asked for Walters and several of the members of the Yellow Band in whom he had at first professed himself greatly interested.

It were impossible to describe the knight's joy at finding them all safe and sound.

By this time the whole of the force had penetrated the castle.

As they passed each place had been ransacked in turn.

The men were heavily loaded with spoil of all descriptions.

One of the men who attracted Sir Hubert's notice was earnestly engaged in kneeling over one of the brotherhood, endeavouring to force him to confess where their principal treasures were hidden.

But, like all his brethren, the fellow was obstinate.

With a courage that excited the admiration of all—even the Yellow Boy, who threatened him with all kinds of fearful tortures—the man refused to speak.

" Don't waste good time there," said Sir Hubert Fontenoy.

" It is not waste, Sir Hubert," returned the Yellow Boy.

" Nay, but it is."

" I seek for a purpose."

" Which I well divine," was the knight's rejoinder.

" For I have heard your threats."

" You do ?"

" Ay. But follow me, some of you, whilst the remainder keep watch here. I know every nook and cranny, and you shall have a rich feast I promise you."

He led the way to one of the underground vaults, where prizes of uncommon value were discovered snugly ensconced.

The men proceeded to load themselves with remarkable expedition.

It was impossible to estimate correctly the value of their booty. Suffice it to say that they ransacked the whole place and transferred every object of the smallest value to their own pouches.

And then the victorious enemy began to think of retreating.

It was well that they did so, for before many minutes had elapsed one of the scouts came in to announce the arrival of a strong body of men mounted and armed to protect the secret brotherhood.

But before they could draw near to the spot Red Ralph and his men were ready to depart.

They left the castle, and in every direction was scattered the evidence of their prowess.

It was a glorious day for the captain of the Yellow Band.

It was gratifying in the utmost degree for Sir Hubert Fontenoy.

And the lieutenant ?

Well, in retreating from the castle an event happened to him which we shall chronicle as we proceed.

But of this in a fresh chapter.

CHAPTER CLX.

RETURNING IN TRIUMPH — AN ALARM — THE OFFICERS—WALTERS SEES AN OLD FRIEND—THE COURIER AGAIN—A CUNNING DEVICE—HOW THE COURIER WAS LED TO DANGER—THE GATE — A TUSSLE — WALTERS VICTORIOUS A SECOND TIME.

LADEN with spoil, the Yellow Boys filed off out of the castle, headed by Red Ralph, Sir Hubert Fontenoy of Cairgal, and the lieutenant of the Yellow Band.

The alarm which had been previously given of the approach of a body of mounted men proved to be not without foundation.

A large body of men were certainly seen advancing, and these men ascertained to be, upon a mere cursory glance, officers of the law.

But the fight was lost and won.

The fray was over, and the officers proved themselves the true antecedents of the police of our own day by coming too late.

" It is as we were told," said the captain of the Yellow Band.

" Constables ?"

" Ay."

" What's to be done ?" asked the lieutenant.

" Done," said Sir Hubert Fontenoy, with his wonted peppery tone. " Why, sir, if they mean us any harm let us walk into them—smite the rascals hip and thigh."

" I'm not for that."

" Nor I," said Walters.

" It would ruin us."

" Pshaw ! How ruin us ?"

" We must not be known."

" But it is impossible to avoid discovery."

" Not a whit."

" How are we to act ?"

" Call a halt. Nay, retreat if necessary, and scatter ourselves."

" So that a few whom they may choose to pick may be cut down without hope of mercy."

" No fear of that."

" But there is great fear."

" Do but as I request, and there is none," said Red Ralph.

" Nay, let me propose something," said the lieutenant of the Yellow Band. " Let all go their ways but me."

" And you ?"

" I shall remain here."

" To be captured."

" Fear not for me."

" What would you do ?"

" No matter," said Walters. " I'll engage success. Away with you, or we are lost."

In spite of Sir Hubert's objections, he was bustled off by the captain of the Yellow Band, who knew his lieutenant well, and placed the most implicit reliance in everything he did.

Their triumphant band were called to a halt, and received their instructions without a murmur.

They would have liked a skirmish with the officers, notwithstanding the amount of severe fighting that they had just got over, but they had a heavy booty with them, and understood the necessity of keeping it secure.

They were well used, too, to sudden manœuvres, and the order issued by the captain was readily and smartly obeyed.

In the space of a few seconds all had disappeared but Walters. He remained, awaiting quietly the approach of the troop of officers.

Then, when they were within a hundred yards of him, he turned his horse round and rode off at a trot.

This had the effect of bringing out the foremost man of the troop in pursuit of him at a gallop.

Walters presently looked round to ascertain if anything were to be dreaded from the single officer who ventured upon his pursuit unaided, and found that the man was far behind.

"Hullo! friend," said the officer as he rode on. "So we meet again."

Nothing can equal the surprise of the lieutenant of the Yellow Band upon discovering that this was none other than his old enemy the courier.

"So-ho!" cried the lieutenant, "I must have some fun with my friend here before we part."

He slackened his pace a little until the courier got near enough to recognise him, and then he again set spurs to his horse and galloped away.

The effect upon the pseudo courier was startling. He could scarcely believe the evidence of his senses.

"Come on," cried Walters, laughing. "Come on, my friend, if you have the courage for a ride."

"Rascal!" shouted the courier.

The lieutenant laughed, and waved the other to come on.

"I'm after you!" shouted the pseudo courier.

And out he rode at a desperate pace, right away from his comrades and their protection.

Walters cunningly contrived to keep sufficiently near to tease him into pursuit without allowing him to get up to him.

But there was one little matter that he had never contemplated until now.

As soon as the courier got within a short distance of him a loud report and the whistle of a bullet unpleasantly close to his ear reminded him that he was within pistol shot.

The lieutenant set spurs to his horse, and flew onwards with a jeering laugh, goading his pursuer to madness.

"Rascal!" he screamed. "I'll have you yet, or I'll die with you."

And on they rode, a race of desperation—a race of life and death.

Walters turned out of the main road and made for a high gate laying at a turn upon the right.

He drew in a while, and then, giving his horse the rein, dashed full at the gate, clearing it in gallant style.

On came the courier.

Nothing daunted, he rode at the gate, but his horse refused the leap.

"Ha, ha!" cried Walters jeeringly. "I was really afraid for you, friend. Come, come, try again."

With a cry of rage the courier wheeled round his cowardly brute and tried it again, but again it refused the leap.

There was no help for it. He must descend and open the gate.

Walters saw that it was no lack of courage upon the horseman's part, but he could not forego the malicious pleasure of taunting him with cowardice.

"I'll wait for you, friend," he said. "Come on. Take your time."

"You dare not."

"Pooh, pooh."

Walters drew in his horse, and quietly awaited him.

Just as he had gained the side of the lieutenant off the latter started, but now he was too late.

Before he could get off the courier had grasped him by the collar.

"Now!" he cried between his set teeth. "Now we shall see who's master."

"We shall."

And the lieutenant turned in his saddle and grappled with the courier.

At the same instant he buried his spurs deep in his horse's flanks, causing him to rear and smart with pain.

Then off he started at a rattling pace.

But the courier would not let go his hold, nevertheless.

Side by side they galloped thus for full ten minutes, until the patience of the lieutenant of the Yellow Band was well nigh exhausted.

"I must put an end to this," he said. "Let go your hold."

"Never."

"Fool, remember the lesson of this morning," said Walters.

"And you shall have a lesson now to remember."

"You'll not desist?"

"Never."

"Then down with you."

With an almost superhuman effort he dragged him out of his saddle, end threw him heavily to the ground.

Down he fell, and lay where he fell motionless as a statue.

"Number two to me!" cried the lieutenant in a voice of triumph.

And away he rode to rejoin the captain of the Yellow Band.

Thus were they freed from the pursuit of the officers by the ingenuity of Walters.

And the bold Yellow Band rode home in safety, to bear to their haunt in Epping Forest one of the richest booties that it had been their fortune to secure ever since they had commenced their wild and lawless career.

CHAPTER CLXI.

JONATHAN WILD MUSES OVER HIS LATEST SCHEME —HOPES AND FEARS—WAITING FOR THE VERDICT — AN UNLOOKED-FOR CONTINGENCY — FEARS PREDOMINATE—A CLIMAX—THE VISITOR.

BEFORE proceeding with the movements of Red Ralph and his colleagues we must recur to an event to which the reader has hitherto attached, we presume, but too little importance.

We allude to the attempt at assassinating the worthy baronet, Sir Harry Jerrold.

The gallant manner in which the worthy gentleman disposed of the knave who made the attempt has doubtless remained fresh in the recollection of the reader.

After Sir Harry Jerrold had quitted the foiled ruffian, and had disappeared, the miserable wretch crawled from the spot where he had lain until Sir Harry was out of sight.

After looking anxiously in the direction that the baronet had taken he rose to his feet.

Truth to tell, he was more shaken than hurt.

"So, Mr. Wild," he muttered to himself, "it is thus your fine project ends. Well, well, it might have been worse. And now what ought I to do? Should I, in justice to myself, follow up this iron-handed old man, and complete by stealth what I have so signally failed to accomplish by boldness? Or should I let him rest? He certainly spurned me, and that should prompt me to revenge. But, on the other hand, he spared my life, and that should secure my forgiveness. I must think it over."

The would-be assassin limped on a few paces musing upon his revenge.

Suddenly he came to a halt.

Just before him, at his very feet, lay a scrap of paper crumpled up.

In spite of its crumpled appearance it bore something the signs of a letter.

He turned it over with his foot, and then picked it up, and, spreading it out, read it over carefully twice.

It was the anonymous letter that Sir Harry Jerrold had received, warning him against the assassination.

At the first glance a change came over the face of the foiled assassin—a change so marked and so full of significance that it would appear that he had recognised the handwriting and drew some inference from the document which caused him to feel annoyed.

"So, so," he muttered between his set teeth, "this is the way that you keep faith, Jonathan Wild, is it? You would play double-faced with me to the last. As you please. You have had your vengeance in this, doubtless, you conceive. You shall see that mine is to come. You shall learn, too, which vengeance is the most sure—yours or mine. Jonathan Wild, you shall bitterly repent the day that ever you played fast and loose with me. From this day forth I dodge you like your shadow until I have hunted you to the death— until the gallows has made you its own—until I see you swinging a ghastly hideous corpse upon the fatal tree. Sleeping or waking, I am by your side—your shadow, until you shall dread the name, the very thought of Jabez!"

And with this the foiled assassin limped slowly away.

* * * * * *

Jonathan Wild in the meantime was chuckling with joy at the depth he had displayed in the expedition upon which he had engaged Jabez.

The day following that appointed for the execution of the deed of villany upon which his creature Jabez was despatched the thieftaker was all over the gaol smiling benignantly upon everybody.

Hence everybody who knew him intimately was sure that some piece of villany was either about to be concocted or had just been executed.

A third day passed, and no Jabez appeared.

This looked conclusive, and Jonathan Wild was in an immense state of excitement.

"Ha! ha!" he laughed. "Brave doings and a noble plot—a very noble notion I must say, although it was my own, and that may sound like conceit upon my own part. No matter, we are all more or less conceited. The only modest man is he who knows how to veil his conceit the best from his fellows. So let us not attempt to disguise our weaknesses from ourselves, whatever we may do with our stronger faults."

By this we see that joy at the presumed success of his projects excited the thieftaker into a bit of philosophy.

When we think of the nature of this and the nature of the philosopher, it will appear the more remarkable to us.

"One of 'em is certainly gone," thought Jonathan Wild, "and that one is certainly Jabez I should say; but I must learn more positively. How can I get some information from Sir Harry? Let me think— let me think. Ah! I have it. I'll send a messenger to his house at once with a letter of apology—just a softener for any little rudenesses of which I may have been guilty when he was here. I know that he put me into a bit of a tantrum, and although I kept it pretty well under, flesh and blood can't stand too much of that sort of thing. I dare swear that I exploded a bit. I'll write at once and despatch my note —insist upon my fellow seeing Sir Harry and getting a verbal answer. A glorious notion! I shall kill two birds with one stone again. *Kill two birds!* Gad! that sounds ominous! Can I hope for such luck? No, no. It can't be possible. I can't even hope that they have so much as maimed each other. We shall see, we shall see."

The joy at the remote prospect of such an amiable contingency was too much for Jonathan Wild, and he fell into a brown study.

During this he painted the brightest things imaginable in his wonderfully vivid imagination.

He fancied that he saw both Sir Harry Jerrold and Jabers struggling upon the ground with each other, with the life blood streaming from many wounds in various parts of their bodies.

So vivid did this agreeable mental tableau present itself before him that for a while, in his blissful reverie, he imagined it to be real.

"And yet," he muttered, "it is scarcely just that I should be out of all these delights. It is scarcely just, after the insults and the injuries that these two have heaped upon me, that I should allow them *quietly and peaceably* to drop each other off, without so much as a look or a word to assure them that I was enjoying their little vagaries. Gad! I almost begin to wish that they were not dead yet. It would almost have been as well to look forward to the treat of seeing them pop off—groaning musically as they went. Oh, I wish now that I had that to look forward to."

Even Jonathan Wild found pleasure in looking ahead.

But where was his philosophy now?

Alas! the great thieftaker, in common with the weaker of humanity, had drained the cup of pleasure, in this instance, to the dregs—had given full vent to his passion, and, like a hot-blooded youth rather than the cool old villain that he was, he had at once grown satisfied with the bare ideas that his vivid imagination had conjured up.

But a reaction was at hand.

Supposing that Sir Harry Jerrold should not be dead —supposing that the worthy baronet, forewarned by the anonymous letter of which he (Jonathan Wild) was thinking so much but a few minutes before, had surprised Jabers in his murderous attempt and beaten him into confession of the whole affair.

Ugh! from this point of view the question looked decidedly ugly.

The influence of Sir Harry Jerrold with the highest authorities of the land was such that the thieftaker feared the worst should he suspect him for an instant.

"Confusion!" muttered the thieftaker, now working himself up to the greatest agony point. "If it has miscarried I am a lost man. Oh, fool, fool! why did I not foresee such a contingency? But it never crossed me until now. Pheugh! I feel a cold perspiration all down my back at the thoughts of it."

If the thought created such an impression, what would the reality of it do?

That has yet to be seen.

However, his fears, which he had by this time worked to a very feverish pitch, had not yet arrived at a climax.

They culminated in a regular hot bath of agony when a jailor came in to announce a visitor.

"A gentleman, Mr. Wild."

"Who?"

"Wants to see you."

"Who, fool?"

"Yes, Mr. Wild, immediately."

"Who is it, idiot?" thundered the thieftaker. "If you're deaf, why didn't you say so?"

"I am a bit hard o' hearing," replied the man in a whisper.

"Who is it?"

"Gent, sir."

"What name?"

"Sir Harry Jerrold."

Wild sank half lifeless into a chair.

It had an effect upon him that the most stirring adventure would have failed to produce.

Thus we see that conscience can operate more potently upon us at times than any actual danger that can face us.

"Confusion," muttered Wild, wiping his forehead. "No matter. I must see him."

"Yes, sir."

"Show him up."

"Yes, sir."

"Get out. Oh, he's deaf. SHOW HIM UP! Get out, fool!"

CHAPTER CLXII.

SIR HARRY JERROLD—WILD'S MISSION—TROUBLES—FAILURES AND DISASTERS—HIS JOURNEY TO THE KILN—THE LONELY COTTAGE—BILL JENKINS—A STARTLING RECOGNITION.

"WELL, Mr. Wild," said Sir Harry Jerrold, entering the room, "and so we meet again."

The thieftaker dared not raise his eyes to the baronet.

"I say we meet again, Mr. Wild."

"Yes, Sir Harry. Oh! yes, precisely," stammered the thieftaker.

Sir Harry Jerrold stared in astonishment at the hesitation with which he mumbled forth these words.

"Do you know my object in coming here, Mr. Wild?" pursued the baronet coldly.

"N—n—no, Sir Harry."

"Then I'll tell you."

Wild was perspiring at every pore as if in a vapour bath.

"I'm all attention, Sir Harry."

"I have lost sight of that unhappy wretch you wanted to murder here."

"M—murder?"

"Ay. Oh! legally of course."

"Oh! Sir Harry."

"Silence! and listen to what I have to say, without comment."

"Yes, Sir Harry."

"Now I've a notion that you know something about him."

"I swear—"

"Silence!"

"I have never set eyes on him."

"Oh!" said the baronet sarcastically. "And so I suppose you insist on having all the say to yourself. As you like. Only, if you insist, I know what to do."

He turned to the door, unconsciously adopting a line of that teasing aggravation that the thieftaker was so given to towards his unfortunate victims.

Wild rushed up, and placed himself in his way.

"Don't be hasty, Sir Harry, pray," he implored. "You have only to say what you want of me, and you know that I ask nothing better than to serve your honour."

"So it seems."

"Let me know what it is you want, Sir Harry, and you shall be attended to."

"Bill Jenkins must be found."

"Yes, Sir Harry."

"And you must do it."

"Yes, sir."

"As you are perfectly capable of doing."

"Yes."

"'Sdeath!" cried the baronet in triumph. "The knave admits it. You know where he is. Don't attempt to deny it, you rascal."

"No, no. I didn't mean that, Sir Harry."

"No matter. He must be found."

"Very good."

"See you obey, and that it is seen to quickly."

"Yes, Sir Harry."

"I have a bone to pick with you yet, Mr. Wild. Upon the ready performance of this job depends your present safety. You mark that — present safety."

"Yes, Sir Harry."

"I promise nothing more."

"No, Sir Harry."

"Before to-morrow let me hear from you."

"Yes."

"And the better your tidings the better reception you will have at Hounslow."

"Yes, Sir Harry."

"Remember."

And with this final admonition the baronet departed.

Jonathan Wild was half beside himself with joy at having got off so lightly.

However, he knew that it was no idle threat that Sir Harry Jerrold had made. The baronet had the power, and he doubted not would exert it.

Wild was well aware how unpopular he was with Sir Harry Jerrold, and he understood his object in pressing the search after the missing Bill Jenkins.

The fact was that after his incarceration in Newgate the unhappy wretch had been so thoroughly terrified that, when once he regained his freedom, he fled far away, and lay hidden in various places in dreadful anticipation of the thieftaker's further enmity or the hold that the law might take of him.

Immediately the baronet had gone Jonathan Wild despatched half a dozen messengers in different directions upon the search.

Every house of call for the light-fingered generation was searched in the course of an hour or so, and the slender information that they had gathered was brought back to him.

No one knew anything. Only one man suggested that he might have taken a fancy to return to the "Kiln."

This was a fanciful title that Mr. Bill Jenkins's confrères gave to his dwelling, on account of its being somewhere in the vicinity of a lime kiln.

Jonathan Wild well knew every haunt of every vagabond of the day, but the possibility of his man returning there had not as yet crossed him.

However, he was determined to ascertain this, and so he started off without loss of time upon his errand.

Mounted upon a sturdy horse, he reached the place in about a couple of hours.

It was a small cottage, standing alone in a large waste of land, and at no great distance from the lime kiln.

When Wild came within two hundred yards of the cottage he dismounted and fastened his horse by the bridle to a tree stump.

Then he made his way to the house, carefully concealing his pistols.

His object in this was to induce a belief that he was unarmed, that Bill Jenkins's wife might let him into the house in hopes of plundering him.

The thieftaker was not very charitable in his ideas, as the reader will doubtless guess from the very summary manner in which he reckoned up the character of Mrs. Bill Jenkins.

He could see no one about, so he made his way up to the cottage and knocked with the handle of his whip upon the door.

There was no answer.

"The house must be deserted," thought Jonathan Wild.

He knocked again louder than before, and shouted out repeatedly in loud tones—

"House, house. Anybody within here? Ho, ho!"

He fancied that he could hear a window above opening.

He glanced up and saw a head protruding from the open window with two staring eyes looking at him.

His very man.

"Bill Jenkins himself!"

"Jonathan Wild!"

Such were their mutual exclamations of astonishment. For the thieftaker was scarcely less amazed at his good fortune than Bill Jenkins was astounded and alarmed.

"Bill Jenkins," said Wild, "come down."

"Not if I know it," replied Bill Jenkins sharply.

He withdrew his head, and no persuasions nor threats upon the part of the thieftaker could induce him to appear again.

Wild was at his wit's end.

He could not imagine what to do.

Presently, after he had tried every inducement in his power without success a third character appeared upon the scene.

It was a woman bearing a babe in her arms.

"So-ho," said the thieftaker readily. "This is Bill Jenkins's wife I suppose. I'll try her."

His ready wit had already hit upon an expedient to overcome this difficulty.

But it was not so easy of performance as he at first imagined.

He had to resort to extremities, which, however, as we have had plenty of opportunities of witnessing, was not always distasteful to the thieftaker.

But more of this in another chapter.

CHAPTER CLXIII.

THE BEGINNING OF A VERY EXTRAORDINARY ADVENTURE.

ONE morning all London was astonished. All the dead walls bore a poster which was the cause of considerable wonder and alarm among the worthy citizens who perused the announcement therein made.

His Majesty King George had graciously offered a reward of one thousand pounds for the capture of a famous highwayman.

Who was the depredator whose body was deemed so valuable?

The reader need scarcely be told that he was the hero of this strange story—none other, in fact, than the redoubtable Yellow Boy, the great Red Ralph.

All classes of society were soon occupied and interested in this intelligence.

They talked the matter over in the drawing-rooms of St. James's, they discussed it at the coffee-houses and the taverns, on the Stock Exchange, in the streets, in the shops, in the little back parlours, behind the shops, and, among other places, in the stable yards of the old coaching inns, and notably in the yard of the one in Holborn.

"So Mr. Red Ralph is to be nabbed at last," said the coachman of the "Flying Lightning." It flew almost six miles an hour at high pressure.

"So he's to be nabbed, sir, and nabbed he will be."

With which remark Joe Leathers, as honest a man as ever handled the ribbons, dipped his red nose into the froth of a tankard of Yorkshire stingo, a liquor which the landlord, a West Riding man himself, always kept on the establishment.

"There's not no manner of doubt about that," said the guard, John Jenkinson, "not a ghost of a doubt," and then, to make the matter still more certain may be, he added, "not half a ghost."

"A jolly good job too, I say," said Joe, when he had lifted his nose out of the tankard, feeling a good pint the better.

"The same here," observed John Jenkinson. "Them's just my sentiments, sir, to a hair's breadth."

When John Jenkinson had drunk his share of the stingo, and the passengers were safely tucked away inside the coach and stowed away outside, so swaddled up in overcoats and wrappers that all human resemblance was well nigh obliterated, he and Joe took their places.

Then the horses' heads were let go, and the horn was blown, and the "Flying Lightning" flew away (at the usual rate) right ahead towards Yorkshire.

Before, however, it had reached its destination—a good way short of it, indeed, if you must have the truth—no further away from town [than Hampstead Heath—something unpleasant occurred.

It was night and foggy.

From the fog came forth a loud voice calling on the coachman to stop.

Through the fog came a gigantic figure—fog magnified—which proved to be a highwayman, and no other than Red Ralph himself.

He was alone and single handed, and you might have supposed he would not have proved a very formidable enemy.

Nothing, you might have thought, could have been easier than for Joe or John, assisted by some of the passengers, to seize the robber and bind him hand and foot.

Had they done so there was one thousand pounds waiting for them, with His Majesty's best thanks.

Somehow, though, one was afraid and, as the saying is, the other dared not.

The consequence was that Red Ralph was not captured that evening.

On the contrary, he rode off with twenty golden guineas in his pocket, the property of the travellers.

Also a silver watch, also a pair of bracelets, also a couple of snuff boxes, and a diamond brooch.

Altogether not such a very bad twenty minutes' work for a foggy evening.

The "Flying Lightning," on the other hand, instead of flying on to Yorkshire, turned tail rather sheepishly, and crawled back to Holborn to tell the sad story of its disaster.

Of course the Bow Street runners and Mr. Wild's men were immediately applied to.

They laid their heads together and pondered, and went on pondering throughout that night and the following day.

It was then unanimously resolved that something must be done. What the something was to be was not, however, yet decided on.

Next night the mail coach on Hounslow Heath was stopped by a single highwayman, which highwayman was again no other than our friend Red Ralph, who on this occasion carried off about a hundred and thirty pounds' worth of property.

Next morning all London was wondering again more than ever.

Again the walls were covered with posters, but this time His Majesty King George graciously expressed his willingness to increase the reward to two thousand pounds.

Everybody now made up his mind that Red Ralph's career was pretty well ended.

"Perhaps it will be worth some one's while to catch him now," some said.

"No doubt of it," said others.

"And he will be caught."

"Of course he will, if they try to catch him."

"So we shall see him hanged at last."

"Let us hope so."

"At any rate, let's have a glass together on the strength of it."

That night the Chelmsford coach was stopped, and a rich stockbroker who had the misfortune to be travelling by it lost two hundred pounds in gold and notes.

"What's your name, fellow?" asked the stockbroker, as he handed the money through the coach window.

"Red Ralph, at your service," replied the highwayman.

"What, the famous Ralph?"

"I believe I have the honour to occupy a good deal of public attention," said our hero, with a smile and a bow.

"If you take my advice, young man, you'll occupy it no longer," said the stockbroker.

"How so?"

"You'll clear out, I mean, before they catch you."

"But I haven't made enough to retire on yet."

"You ought to have made a good deal."

"I am rather extravagant, to tell the truth, and am soft hearted where the ladies are concerned, but I mean to work hard and be steady, and put something by in future."

"What do you call working hard, pray?"

"Doing what I'm doing, to be sure."

"The devil you do!" exclaimed the stockbroker. "However, let me give you a word of advice."

"Another word?"

"Yes. Being a highwayman, in a bright scarlet coat, and on a thoroughbred horse, is a very fine thing I've no doubt, but hanging is undignified, look at it any way you will."

"Are you a fatalist, sir?"

"No."

"I am, then, and I believe in fate. I shall not die under Jack Ketch's fingers I have a notion."

"Have you? Well, I should not like to run your risk, that's all."

At this Red Ralph burst out laughing, and, putting spurs to his horse, galloped away.

Little did Red Ralph think that that very night he was doomed to meet with one who would be instrumental in bringing him face to face with death.

Great and glorious had been his career, but the sky above was dark and threatening.

The end was nearer than he thought.

A fearful end it was—a hideous doom.

But we must not anticipate.

We must approach the goal step by step.

*   *   *   *   *

That night in the bar parlour of a little tavern in Lambeth a man sat drinking.

He was a large raw-boned fellow, shabbily dressed.

He was a countryman, and at first sight you might have been inclined to put him down as a drover.

He was in reality a very rich farmer, the owner of upwards of a thousand acres in the best part of Kent.

Although when first we make his acquaintance we find him sipping his grog at the Boar's Head, yet you must not run away with the idea that Job Hardstaff was anything of a toper.

He was, on the contrary, a very careful abstemious man, and had a good banking account.

He was very proud of his bodily strength, and had one of the best constitutions in England.

He could thrash any man his own size and weight he said, and he certainly had polished off one or two a size larger, who had been rash enough to quarrel with him.

He had one great boast, though.

He had never been robbed.

He prided himself not only upon his strength, but his sagacity and cuteness.

"I can make money, sir," he said, "and by George I can take care of it."

Up to now so he had.

Upon this particular night, sitting here in the parlour of the Boar's Head, he got into conversation with the company in the room respecting highwaymen.

"Who's this man the bills are stuck up about?" asked Job. "Red somebody."

"Red Ralph, sir," said a little man, the parish clerk, peeking up. "Haven't you heard of him?"

"I can't say I have not, sir," replied Job. "I've never seen him, though. Luckily for him, he's never come across my path."

"He's rather a tough customer they say."

"Is he?"

"Very—so they say."

"However tough he is, he'll find a tough 'un in me I can tell him."

"No doubt of that, sir," said the little man hastily, for he had no desire to try Job Hardstaff's toughness.

And here the conversation ceased for a few minutes until the former took it up again.

"I hear a good deal of talk about these highwaymen fellows," he said, "and how they rob one person and another. I'll tell you whom it is they do rob if you like."

"We shall feel much obliged to you, sir, if you will," said the little man.

"It's cowards."

"Oh!"

"That's whom it is, if you want to know. They haven't the pluck to tackle a strong man, and if they did so by accident, and he was to show fight, and—"

"Yes, sir."

"What would they show do you suppose?"

"The white feather?"

"The seats of their unmentionables, if they wore any."

Delivering himself thus, Job Hardstaff laughed a loud triumphant laugh and drank up the remainder of his liquor at a gulp.

Opposite to him, in a dark corner, where his face was hidden by the shade of an angle in the wall sat a stranger.

Strangers were not popular in this tavern parlour, but this stranger was a very modest and retiring young man, with whom nobody could easily take offence.

He seemed to be a clerk or a small tradesman.

He had light curly hair and mild blue eyes.

He had a very soft mild voice, too, when he spoke.

When Job Hardstaff had finished his laugh the modest young man coughed timidly behind his head and made an observation.

"This robber person called Red Ralph isn't generally supposed to be a coward, sir, I believe," said he.

"Oh, isn't he?" cried Job. "Ha! ha! I dare say not. I've never had the honour of meeting with him myself."

"You may perhaps."

"I hope I shall."

"Then you will be able to give us a better account of him perhaps."

"Perhaps so."

"Perhaps so," repeated the young man, with a quiet smile.

Job Hardstaff stared at him, but the young man averted his eyes.

[A DEED OF HORROR.]

The eyes of the assembled company turned upon the young man in wondering curiosity.

He was a stranger very clearly, or he would never have ventured to talk thus to the great Job.

Job had used that parlour once or twice a week for many years past, and he was well known and his opinions respected.

Anyhow he had a good hard fist, and that made his arguments unanswerable.

He was not accustomed to be chaffed, and felt somewhat uneasy.

He must set himself right without loss of time, that was certain. Therefore said he—

"There's one thing that I'm pretty certain of, without waiting until I've seen this Red Ralph, and that is, that I shouldn't be afraid to meet any living highwayman, and, furthermore, I should advise highwaymen to think twice before they cross my path."

Mr. Hardstaff rose with this and prepared himself for the road.

While they were saddling his nag he added a few more words, evidently for the benefit of the misguided young man who had ventured to address him.

"If a highwayman thinks it worth his while to risk a broken pate or a bullet though his skull, and he got the best of me, he would find it worth his while, perhaps, to empty my pockets, for at this present speaking I have a hundred pounds in Bank of England notes in one of them.''

"I think you run a great risk by carrying so much," said the young man.

"Oh, not a bit of it. I come to town to sell my corn or sheep, and I take back the produce of the sale. I have done so any time these ten years always safely.''

"You may try once too often."

"Ha! ha! I'm not afraid. See here."

As he spoke he produced a pistol from his pocket.

"I carry this by the side of my money."

"Allow me, sir," said the young man, as Job held it out towards him.

"You keep it loaded I see.''

"To be sure."

"A very murderous weapon.",

"Very little doubt of that."

"A pleasant journey to you."

"Thank you. Good-night, gentlemen all.''

Job's horse was by this time ready.

He climbed into the saddle and trotted away."

The young men followed very shortly afterwards, mounted on a horse waiting for him at the street corner, and galloped in the direction that Job had taken.

Poor Job, he little thought what was coming.

CHAPTER CLXIV.

THE CONTINUATION OF JOB HARDSTAFF'S ADVENTURE.

THE storm was brewing. It had been threatening throughout the day. Since morning huge dusky masses of clouds had overshadowed the town. Now and then a violent gust of wind, bearing a pattering shower of rain, rushed through the streets, lashing the sloping roofs.

But then the torpid calm resumed its sway.

The clouds, partially rent and scattered, rebuilt their vapourous masses.

Then again would descend, with all its lowering influences to weaken and depress the energies of every living and breathing thing, that close stifling sensation which proclaims the brewing of a storm.

The day passed away and evening darkened into pitchy night.

From time to time a hollow moaning gust would sigh through the air full of threatening import.

Just as Job Hardstaff was about to leave the inn the storm so long brewing gave indications that at length it was about to descend in all its fury.

"I should wait for a short time if I was you, sir," said the ostler.

"Why so?"

"We are going to have some rough weather, if I'm not mistaken."

"I am not afraid of a wet jacket," said Job.

"Of course you know best, sir."

"I ought to do."

"You'll get a soaking, my friend," said the ostler to himself as Job rode away.

Then, turning to re-enter the stable yard, he ran full butt against somebody who was hurrying out of the inn.

It was the young man with the light curly hair.

"Who are you shoving?"

"Get out of the way, you fool."

"Fool yourself. I'll teach you to give me bad names."

And the ostler threw himself into a boxing attitude.

But next moment he was lying flat on his back. A terrific left-hander had knocked him off his legs.

The young man had struck him a tremendous blow between the eyes.

For some moments, as he lay there gasping, he was by no means sure whether or not his head had been left upon his shoulders.

When at last he was able to scramble to his feet he found the young man had disappeared.

"He has run away. I knew he was a coward."

As Job Hardstaff rode along he looked wistfully up at the sky.

Somehow, in spite of his courage, something, a dim forboding of impending danger, took possession of him.

The silence was profound.

The darkness was intense.

A few large drops of rain came splashing down.

Then there was a pause.

Then suddenly a stream of blue lightning tore across the darkness.

Upon the flash came instantly the thunder peel—not the usual hoarse roar, but a sharp ringing, rattling din like the discharge of artillery.

Then another flash, vivid as the first.

Two great portions of the sky appeared masses of lurid flame.

Between them leapt a forked and jagged stream.

The thousand buildings stood out with spectral distinctness.

Then again the thunder seemed to strike into the very brains of the listeners.

Job Hardstaff, trotting on briskly, had got quite half a mile away from the inn before the first flash of lightning.

Before the flash came he had heard in the distance a noise he took to be thunder.

It was not thunder, but a horse's hoofs.

Somebody was galloping behind him. A runaway horse, perhaps, he thought.

As the noise approached he thought he would draw his own horse on one side to avoid a collision.

The idea came a little too late.

In the midst of the first vivid flash of lightning the galloping horse came full upon him, and his own nag, staggering beneath the violence of the assault, came heavily to the ground.

Its rider too rolled in the dust.

Very soon, though, he was on his feet again, swearing savagely.

The cause of the accident had not fallen from his horse, but the animal itself had come to a sudden standstill.

The second flash of lightning revealed its rider sitting motionless.

Job Hardstaff in amazement recognised the face of the young man he had met in the inn parlour.

"I am very sorry for what I have done," said he, "but it was so dark."

"All the more reason why you should not have been galloping like a madman."

"But, my dear sir, do you know why I was galloping?"

"How can I tell?"

"It's very easy to guess, though."

"I don't feel inclined to waste the time."

"Then I'll tell you."

"Thank you."

"There's no occasion."

Job grunted savagely. He was getting into a passion.

"I rode after you because I wanted to catch you up."

Job knit his brows mistrustfully.

"Why?" he asked.

"I heard you were going my way."

"Oh!"

"So I thought I should like to ride with you."

"Why?"

"For protection."

Job was silent for a moment and pondered.

Voluntarily he felt in the pocket where his money was.

It was safe.

By its side also reposed the pistol.

From what you said, sir, about highwaymen, I thought it would be much safer to travel in your company if you would allow me do so.

Job made no reply. He was helping up his horse.

"Allow me to assist you," said the young man.

Job still made no answer, but the young man dismounted.

Very expertly he contrived to get the nag upon its feet again. Then he passed his hand down its forelegs.

"Knees are all right," he said.

Job, growling to himself, mounted into his saddle.

Then they rode on for some time silently.

The rain was now coming down heavily, and it seemed as though it were by no means likely to leave off for some time yet.

"It would have been a wiser course for you to have stopped at the inn until to-morrow morning," said Job, with a grim smile.

"I could not do that, unfortunately."

"As it is, you will probably get washed to the skin."

"I don't mind that."

"That's all right, then. I don't care for it myself."

Now this was not strictly the truth, be it known. Job would have been inclined to seek shelter, and had he been alone would have sought it.

But thought he, "I'll give my young friend here a drenching. He won't leave me for fear of Red Ralph. I'll keep him out until there's not a dry rag on him."

This amiable idea made Job chuckle, and they rode on silently.

They had now got past the last house of what could be called London, and were in a country road with hedges on either side.

They soon passed the last inn which was to be found for a mile or so, and now the notion of shelter must perforce be abandoned for some time to come.

After all, the storm was short-lived.

By the time they got half way to the next inn the rain had ceased.

They had reached an open place very lonely and desolate.

The young man looked around inquiringly.

"Thinking of the robbers?" suggested Job.

"Yes, I was."

"Don't frighten yourself. No harm shall happen to you," said Job, with a laugh.

"I'm not afraid for myself."

"For whom, then?"

"You."

Job stared in astonishment. Then his brows darkened.

"For me? What do you mean, sir?" he asked, after a moment's pause.

"Only this," replied the other, laying one hand upon Job's shoulder, "I am the Red Ralph for whom you have several times expressed contempt, and I should feel obliged by your handing over the contents of your breast pocket."

"Part of the contents will be enough for you perhaps."

And as he spoke Job produced his pistol and presented it full in the highwayman's face.

Ralph laughed insultingly.

"What, you mock me, do you?" cried the other. "Your blood be on your own head, then."

Job pulled the trigger, with an oath.

The pistol flashed in the pan, but without any other result.

Ralph laughed sardonically.

"It's my turn now, my friend."

And he presented his own pistol at Job's head.

"Hand over your money," said he, "or I shall blow your brains out."

"You may blow them out. I shan't give you the money."

"My dear sir, why do you unnecessarily risk your life? Do you think that my pistol also is going to miss fire?"

"I won't give up my gold without a struggle."

"There'll be none. I shall shoot you dead."

"Will you, villain? We shall see."

With that Job Hardstaff sprang upon him so suddenly and unexpectedly that the other had not time to pull the trigger.

The violence of the shock flung Ralph back upon his saddle.

In a moment, dropping his pistol to the ground, he also grasped his antagonist by the throat.

Together they fell heavily to the earth.

Locked in a tight embrace, they rolled over and over.

Furiously they struggled.

Each tried to choke his foe.

Each strove madly for the mastery.

As they rolled over each other upon the ground Job Hardstaff's superior weight was greatly in his favour.

When he lay upon the other's breast he seemed to crush his breath out of his body by his huge bulk.

But Ralph was slippery as an eel.

He writhed and wriggled himself from under his grasp.

At last, when Job had got him down fairly, and had got his knee upon the highwayman's throat, Ralph freed himself by a gigantic effort.

With a sudden exertion of a strength which was almost superhuman he hurled Job over his head.

The former ploughed the wet mud with his nose, and then rolled over on his back and lay panting.

In half a second Ralph had regained his feet, and had taken a spring at his foe, was uppermost, and held him by the throat.

As thus he held him, too, the lightning flashed out again.

It showed him his pistol lying within reach, and he seized it.

But it also showed him the farmer's face, muddy, bleeding, ghastly.

He no longer panted. He no longer struggled. The fall had caused a dreadful wound on his forehead, from which the blood was flowing fast, and he lay silent and senseless.

Ralph's anger had been so aroused by the other's resistance that had he still continued weakly struggling there is very little doubt that the robber would have slain him.

But seeing him thus perfectly helpless and in his power, Ralph's generous nature prompted him to be merciful.

The money was there, and could be taken easily. Why should he further pain its owner?

"Poor devil! he has perhaps got his death wound as it is."

So thinking, Ralph plunged into the fallen man's breast pocket and brought forth the money.

Putting it safely away, he rose to his feet.

"I must not leave the poor beggar lying like this in the middle of the road, or he will get run over to a dead certainty."

He took hold of Job by the shoulders, and dragged him towards the road side.

Close to the spot there was the entrance to a field guarded by a five-barred gate.

He raised Job up in a sitting posture against the gate, out of harm's way.

Then he turned to go.

But a thought struck him.

He took a piece of paper out of his pocket, and scribbled these words upon it :—

"*I spare your life this time, having no occasion to take it.*

"*A word of advice—Don't cross my path again.*
                                "RED RALPH."

Ralph put the scrap of paper on which he had written this polite note in the pocket from which he had taken the money.

Then he mounted his steed and rode forward laughing to himself.

"A thick-headed pig. I hope he's not killed. If he is, though, it's certainly his own fault. If he hadn't tempted Providence he wouldn't have got hurt."

Ah! Ralph, Ralph, if you had only known, you too would not have tempted Providence by crossing this man's path.

Our hero rode onwards for some time, meditating on the recent adventure and upon other matters, when it suddenly occurred to him that it was coming on to rain again harder than ever, and that already his coat was wet through.

"I'd give the world to be at home in bed," he said to himself. "But the worst of it is my bed is a long way off."

He looked about him. Not a hundred yards off was an inn, through the window shutters of which a light was glimmering.

"I should like to take up my quarters there," he said, "for they keep a good tap, but—"

There certainly was a drawback.

"It's ten to one that when they pick up my friend the farmer they'll bring him to this inn. In that case, perhaps, it won't be the safest place I can choose for shelter."

He was dreadfully weary, however, and once having got the notion into his head of seeking a bed somewhere, in his usual reckless style he determined to carry out his intention, let the risk be what it might.

He scanned the horizon eagerly, hoping somewhere else at a short distance to see a light which might indicate the whereabouts of another inn.

Sure enough there was afar off a faint glimmering.

He put spurs to his horse and pressed forward.

Down in a little hollow about forty yards further on there was a low building.

Over the door something swung backwards and forwards, creaking in the wind.

When Ralph reached the portal he found that this object was, as he had supposed, a signboard.

"Yet," he said to himself, "it's rather strange that I never noticed it before, because I thought I knew all the inns and taverns hereabouts."

He heard the sound of several voices within, talking in a low tone.

"There's company here," he thought. "I hope the beaks are not among them. Anyhow, here goes."

Raising his whip, he knocked with its handle upon the panel.

Instantly there was silence within.

Then a low whispering.

"Hullo!" thought Ralph. "What does that mean?"

The whispering continued for a moment.

Then all was still as the grave.

Then a stealthy footfall approached the door from within.

"This doesn't look pretty to begin with," thought Ralph. "But who cares? I'm in the mood for an adventure."

CHAPTER CLXV.

THE DEN OF THIEVES—A NIGHT OF HORRORS.

IF our hero were desirous of an adventure, with plenty of danger in it, he seemed certainly to have come to the proper place to find that for which he sought.

The door was opened by a black-muzzled ruffian, who shaded his own face from the light of a candle he carried so that it fell upon Ralph's handsome features.

"What is it?" the man asked.

"A night's lodging."

"How many of you are there?"

"What you see, my friend."

"I can't see very clearly."

"Two, then, if you count my horse."

"We can accommodate both. Step inside."

As Ralph hardly supposed that he intended that both he and his steed should step in together, he alighted.

Another man appearing took charge of the horse.

Ralph followed the first man into the house.

The appearance of the person who had answered the highwayman's summons was certainly anything but inviting.

If he had been only half as prudent as he was brave Ralph would surely have beaten a retreat while there was time.

It was rather late now.

The horse had been led away.

The door was closed.

He was facing the danger.

He was hemmed in, and retreat was cut off.

Round the fire-place sat a group of ruffians six in number—as ill-looking scoundrels as ever our hero remembered to have met with.

They had been watching him curiously.

"What the deuce are they I wonder," he said to himself.

They were not men who earned their living by any honest trade, that was pretty sure.

They were not cracksmen or knights of the road.

Ralph stared at them very hard, and they returned the compliment.

They were heavy thick-set fellows, and wore great boots and blue or striped shirts surmounted by shaggy overcoats.

A light dawned upon Ralph as he glanced at the table.

On it there were several curiously-shaped flasks and bottles.

"They're smugglers or pirates," thought he. "And to think that I never found their hiding-place out before."

He might have got on as well, as things turned out, had he not found it now.

But he felt no fear, and, flinging himself down in a chair, called to the man whom he took to be the landlord for some drink.

When Ralph had given his order he sat lashing his boot with his whip and affecting an indifference which he did not exactly feel.

The landlord was a long while bringing the liquor, and for a moment he peeped up at him from under his eyelashes.

What he saw was calculated to startle him.

But he did not exhibit any sign of having seen anything.

On the contrary, he dropped his eyes again instantly.

What it was that had occurred you shall hear.

When he raised his eyes just at that identical moment the landlord, at the other end of the room, was pouring something from a tiny bottle into a glass of hot spirits.

One of the smuggler-looking men was standing by his side and whispering to him earnestly.

The smuggler held a candle, the light from which fell upon the landlord's hand.

But all this was occurring behind Ralph's back.

How then did he see it?

At the opposite side of the room, facing our hero, was a looking glass. As he raised his eyes he saw in it the picture described.

He dared not allow them to think that he had seen anything to excite his suspicions.

Therefore he looked down again directly, and went on lashing his boots, whistling as he did so.

To himself, though, he could not help thinking, " I should have been much better on horseback with my wet clothes on than in this nest of assassins."

His meditations were cut short by the landlord approaching him.

" Here's the grog, sir."

" Thank you."

Ralph took it in his hand and sipped a teaspoonfull, and then placed the glass on the table beside him.

Just as he did so one of the piratical gentlemen before the fire rose and stretched himself.

" It's most time we were going I think," said he.

" It's quite time," said another, consulting his watch. " We ought to sail in less than an hour."

" I'm off too," said a third. " Who goes my way ?"

" I do, for one."

" I'll be with you, mate."

" Come on, then. Let's be moving."

The whole party rose and began to button up their coats and adjust their comforters.

" Good night, landlord," said one.

" Good night, landlord," chorused the rest as they moved towards the door.

The landlord hurried forward and drew the bolts for them to go out.

" Good night to you all," he said, " and a pleasant voyage to you, and luck."

" The same to you, old man."

They went away with this, laughing among themselves.

Ralph watched them out.

There was surely nothing very suspicious in their behaviour, although their appearance at first sight might tell rather against them with an over fastidious person.

" After all, I'm probably not going to have my throat cut," was Ralph's reflection.

There were only two men left now.

One was the landlord, the other the man who had stood by him when he was mixing the grog.

They were talking together in the same corner, and Ralph could unobserved watch their actions in the glass.

Presently both turned their backs.

Ralph seized the moment.

In it he tipped over three-quarters of the glass of grog into a spitoon standing close by the table.

The two men came forward, and Ralph fancied that they both glanced towards the glass.

" It warms one up a little," said Ralph. " The wet seems to have penetrated to my very bones."

" Better get to bed, sir, as soon as possible. Shall we dry your clothes against the morning ?"

" Can you let me have a fire instead in my own room ?"

" Oh, to be sure we can. My man will be in directly, and he shall light one for you."

The landlord's friend here broke in, saying, " I must be toddling, Mark, or they will be tired of sitting up for me."

" It's early yet."

" It's as late as I can stop I think."

" Well, you know best."

The man went to the door and the landlord let him out, letting in at the same time the man who had taken away Ralph's horse.

" Have you put up the horse, Jem ?" asked the landlord.

" Yes. It'll be nice and comfortable till the morning."

" Go and light a fire there in the front room for the gentleman, and be as quick as you can, for I'll be bound he'll be pleased to get to bed."

" Yes, I shall," said Ralph.

" Have some more grog, sir ? I see your glass is empty."

Such was the case, for Ralph had tipped it over again, watching his opportunity for so doing.

Another thing he had also managed to do unseen.

He had wiped the bottom of the glass with his finger, to scoop out the sediment, if there was any there.

There was a little—a very little, though.

Ralph presently touched it with the tip of his tongue.

It tasted bitter.

" I was right, then. They meant foul play, by heaven."

What was to be done ? Should he go upstairs to bed, wait until all was quiet, and then effect his escape ?

The question was, Would he be able to do so when he was upstairs ?

Why not now ?

But after the last man had taken his departure the landlord had securely bolted and barred the door.

If they meant to rob and murder him they would never allow him to depart under their very eyes.

To express a wish to depart would be a certain way of arousing their suspicions, and of urging them on to some decisive course of action.

No, the best plan decidedly would be to wait for a while.

" I'll go upstairs and immediately escape by the window."

This was the determination he arrived at.

The man came downstairs directly, saying the fire was lighted and the bedroom ready.

Ralph then followed the landlord, who carried the candle, upstairs.

He stopped at the door of a room on the first floor, opened the door, and showed him into the apartment, and, leaving the candle upon the mantelpiece, bade him good night. Then he retired, shutting the door after him.

It was a poverty-stricken place, with bare boards, save a tiny piece of carpeting by the bedside.

When the door was shut Ralph listened to the landlord's departing footsteps.

Then, stepping lightly across the floor, he approached the window.

He raised the blind.

Then he let it fall again, with an oath.

The window was secured by strong iron bars.

" No getting out that way," muttered Ralph. " What's to be done ?"

As he spoke a sound in the house below smote upon his ear.

He listened attentively.

It was the sound of the bolts in the outer door being drawn back.

Still he listened.

Presently he heard a footfall on the floor.

Then the sound of voices whispering.

" One of them has come back, at any rate. Perhaps all the lot. I'm in a nice trap this time."

Again he approached the window and tried the bars.

They would not yield, in spite of his efforts.

He then walked across to the door.

There was no key, and the bolt was but a very feeble one.

There was, however, no other means of securing it.

The only furniture the apartment contained was the bed and one ricketty old chair.

"They'll be up presently I suppose, and I shall have to fight for it."

He had brought up with him the second glass of grog.

There could not be much danger in drinking this, because he had watched it made, and he was pretty sure it had not been drugged.

He was right.

The first glass had the sleeping potion in it, and the landlord probably had thought that it was no good wasting any more, as what Ralph had had was sufficient to send half a dozen strong men fast asleep for a week at a stretch.

Ralph therefore thought that no great harm could come to him if he took the liquor.

"I'm horribly wet and cold," he said. "And, besides, it will keep my pecker up."

He did not want any false courage, for he was brave enough without that. But still it would do him no harm.

He therefore drank up the liquor, and felt much the better for it.

What was to be done next?

The candle supplied to him was only an inch long.

If it had not been for the fire he might have expected very soon to be in the dark.

To guard against this he stirred the fire up. But in so doing he committed a rash act. The fire newly lighted would not bear stirring.

When he stirred it again he made it worse. As he got desperate he kept on lunging at it. The result was that in ten minutes the fire was out.

There was nothing left now but the candle.

The case was very desperate.

"I hope they'll come while there is yet a little light," said Ralph to himself, as he crept to the door and listened.

He listened intently with a throbbing heart.

As he did so he drew forth from his pocket the pistol which he always carried, and noiselessly examined its loading.

It was all right. His knife also was ready to his hand.

Again he listened. This time he distinctly heard footsteps upon the stairs—stealthy footsteps—approaching the door. By this time they calculated that the opiate would have done its work—that their victim would be senseless and at their mercy.

He prepared himself for the struggle, clutched his knife, and stood ready to make a spring.

A notion, though, suddenly occurred to him, upon which, without a moment's hesitation, he acted. He took off his coat, wrapped it round the bolster, and heaped it up in bed in such a way that, in the dim light, it seemed very much as though he occupied its place. Then he himself crouched down upon the other side of the door behind the ricketty chair, with which, with the aid of a pocket handkerchief he fashioned a meagre sort of ambush.

Then, placing the pistol within reach, he grasped his knife and crouched, tiger-like, ready for a spring.

All was silent in the house. Not a sound was to be heard—not a creak—not a word—not a whisper.

The candlelight gleamed upon Ralph's passionate face, and on the bright blade of his dagger.

He waited and listened. The suspense was terrible.

At last—creak! creak!—they were coming.

As well as Ralph could guess by their footsteps they were two in number, and they approached on tiptoe.

Reaching the door, they paused to listen.

Then, from a fumbling noise, he concluded that one of them was peeping in through the keyhole.

He held his breath and listened.

He could hear them breathing softly.

Then he heard them whispering.

"Is he asleep?"

"I don't hear any noise. I fancy he is."

"Is there a light?"

"Yes."

"Can't you see the bed, then?"

"Yes, and I think he is lying in it."

"All right. Let me come first."

Ralph could not help smiling.

"If he only knew what I had got waiting for him," he thought, "he wouldn't be so eager."

The handle of the door was turned.

Then the door was pressed upwards a little and gently shaken.

"I can't loosen the bolt."

"Curse it! I meant to alter it. Let me try, though."

Again the door was shaken.

"Lift it from the bottom."

The robber's fingers crept stealthily in underneath the door. Ralph the same moment leant forward and raised his knife.

There was a crushing, grinding, sickening sound.

Then a shriek of agony.

CHAPTER CLXVI.

THE HORRORS CONTINUED—A FEARFUL FIGHT —A SURPRISE—CAPTURE—RALPH A PRISONER ONCE MORE.

EVERY moment Ralph expected that the robbers would rush in upon him in savage fury.

But he was mistaken.

He waited with the reeking blade of the knife upraised.

But he waited in vain.

A death-like silence once more prevailed in the passage.

After the robber's first uncontrollable howl of agonised pain no cry was made.

After a time Ralph heard the sound of retreating footsteps.

Then, afar off, something like smothered groans, as though the wretched creature were endeavouring to stifle the sounds which the torture of his mutilation wrung from his labouring breast.

Ralph could not expect, though, that the fight was to end thus. They would soon be back again, and then there would be a deadly struggle.

While he waited the candle, which for some time past had been flickering faintly, went suddenly out.

"All the better," said Ralph. "We can fight fairer in the dark when the odds are so large."

He took his pocket handkerchief and bound his dagger knife securely in his hand, so that it could not possibly be knocked out of his grasp.

Then he placed his pistol ready cocked in his bosom, so that it would be ready at a moment's warning.

Then again he crouched and waited.

So intense was the silence, as he waited, that every sound, the very faintest—a rain drop on the window pane or the shivering of the dead cinders on the hearth —seemed to beat like a hammer upon his brain.

Ah! there was again a sound upon the stairs.

A sound of laboured breathing.

A footstep.

A hand laid upon the handle of the door.

Then there was a scratching noise. The person outside was endeavouring to force back the bolt with the blade of a knife.

At length he succeeded.

The door opened very slowly and the assassin stole into the room.

He only came in about a foot and a half, and then stood still to listen.

He listened as intently as Ralph had done for his approach.

He was listening for Ralph's breathing, but the highwayman held his breath.

Hearing nothing then, the assassin came to the conclusion that after all the drug must have operated and the victim must be in a state of stupor.

He crept towards the bed.

Ralph rose and crept after him.

But the man must have heard him coming, for he turned suddenly.

Ralph's knife fell, but it went through the man's shoulder, instead of through his back into his heart, as it would surely have done had he not twisted round.

The fellow staggered back a pace or two, clutched at the window blind, and in falling tore it down.

In a moment Ralph was upon him and plunged the dagger again into his breast.

The man struggled frantically, the blood spirting from his mouth.

But, like hail, a shower of furious blows descended.

Then, at last rising from the gashed and gory corpse, he turned towards the door.

At that instant a light was seen approaching.

The door was flung wide open, and the landlord rushed in, his face ghastly white and blood-stained.

One of his hands, the hand Ralph had mutilated, was tied up; in the other he brandished an axe.

With a wild howl, he rushed upon the leader of the Yellow Boys.

But as he came Ralph suddenly produced his pistol and fired.

He was in too great a hurry to take a good aim, but the shot took effect in the man's jaw, shattering it fearfully.

With a piercing shriek, the ruffian fell back into the passage, and lay there weltering in his gore.

Not a second was to be lost. Ralph sprang forward over his prostrate form, trampling it down recklessly as he went.

But the coast was not yet clear.

Holding the light in the passage was a third man, armed with a pistol.

As Ralph saw him he stumbled, and the stumble saved his life, for at that moment the man fired, and the shot passed over his head.

In another instant the gallant captain had closed with him.

Locked in each other's arms, they fell to the ground.

The light was extinguished, and they struggled furiously in the pitchy darkness.

But Ralph was pressed down beneath the other's weight.

His antagonist had got his knee upon his breast, his fingers grasping his windpipe.

Then Ralph heard a clicking noise which could not be mistaken.

His foe was cocking a pistol.

In another moment it would be too late to make an effort. But Ralph was not yet mastered.

The hand which still held the dagger was lying between their bodies.

He exerted all his strength, twisted round for an instant, plunged it into the body of his antagonist, and literally tore him open with one furious slash.

Then, shaking off the writhing wretch, he leaped to his feet, and fled, all blood-besmeared, downstairs.

Not yet, however—not even yet—were his perils over.

Alas! far greater evils awaited him.

As he reached the tap-room there arose a loud thundering at the door, and a cry of " Open, open!"

The sound of many voices was without.

Were they the voices of the smugglers returned?

While he was considering what he ought to do, however, the door, with a terrific smash, flew wide open, and a mob of men rushed into the room.

At the first glance, aided by torches which they bore, Ralph saw that they were not the persons he had supposed.

Before he could answer his own question as to who they were he found himself the centre of an eager group.

A loud cry then arose—

" 'Tis he! 'Tis Red Ralph! Secure him!"

With a wild effort at self-preservation he raised his dagger, and, striking out right and left, plunged madly forward.

But, having escaped from the room, he found himself in the midst of a mob of armed soldiers without.

Overcome by numbers, he was beaten down.

Then, securely handcuffed, they placed him on a horse, and, guarding him on every side with loaded carbines, led him away captive.

CHAPTER CLXVII.

JENKINS AT HOME—THE LIME KILN—WILD IN GRIEF—DESPERATE REMEDY—THE ROBBER'S CHILD — HORRORS — HOW JENKINS AVENGED HIS MURDERED CHILD—THE YELLOW BOYS TO THE RESCUE.

WE must ask the reader to return with us to the " Kiln," where, he will remember, we left Jonathan Wild vainly striving to induce Bill Jenkins to come down and open the door.

After spending some considerable time in this fruitless task a third person appeared upon the scene, who turned out to be none other than Mrs. Bill Jenkins, bearing a child in her arms.

The thieftaker remained in the shade of the doorway until the woman had nearly reached the cottage.

There were no other means of concealing himself at hand, as the place was utterly devoid of vegetation of any kind. Indeed, so sterile was the surrounding land that one might almost have thought it was subject to eruptions, like Vesuvius and Ætna.

However, night—that cloak of evil deeds—sufficed for the nonce, and the woman was close upon him before he discovered himself.

" Mrs. Jenkins, I think."

As he said this he stepped forth from the shade and confronted her.

She was so startled that she fell back as if the thieftaker had been an apparition.

" Lor—"

" Mrs. Jenkins?" repeated the thieftaker, sharply.

" Yes, sir."

" I thought so. Where is your husband?"

Mr. Jenkins was about to begin some rambling statement when the thieftaker stopped her short.

" Enough. Don't trouble yourself with any unnecessary lies. He is there, I have seen him, and I must speak with him immediately."

" Yes, sir,"

" So open the door and let me in, or it won't be good for his health I can promise you."

Mrs. Jenkins, quite alarmed at the thieftaker's bullying way, was about to open the door precipitately when the window above was thrown open and Bill Jenkins appeared again.

"Stand clear, Bridget," he called. "Don't mind what he says. If you open the door I'm a lost man."

"Lor 'a mercy, Bill."

"'Tis Jonathan Wild."

The woman gave a shriek and ran a few paces off.

The fact is that Jonathan Wild had secured himself such a world-wide fame for brutality that Mrs. Jenkins, in common with the rest of the world, shrunk from him in fear and horror.

But yet she had one difficulty to contend with.

Her own fears were increased by a mother's anxiety. At her breast was a babe, who should have been put to rest some time since.

"Bill," she said, "what am I to do with the child?"

"Keep it there."

"*I'll* see to that, since you're so obstinate," shouted the thieftaker.

And he made a grab at the child, but a mother's eye defeated his purpose, and the woman flew away like the wind.

"Jenkins!" he called in despair at the window, "Jenkins!"

"It's no use, Wild."

"But I mean you well, I tell you."

"Bah!"

"I'll give you ten pounds if you come with me."

This appeared to make Mr. Bill Jenkins open his eyes.

"Ten pounds?"

"Ay; money down."

"Oh, of course. Because I suppose that there is fifty pounds offered for my apprehension."

"No; I swear not."

"Don't care, I won't come."

"Don't be a fool, Jenkins," said the thieftaker. "I tell you that unless you come you will not only do yourself a serious wrong, but you will ruin me."

This was an unfortunate admission.

No sooner had Jonathan Wild said these words than Bill Jenkins threw up his arms and shouted with wild joy.

"Hurrah! Hurrah! That's a settler, Jonathan. You don't see much of me."

"I say, Jenkins."

"Never."

"Come, come."

"Ha! ha! Me come? And with the prospect of ruining you if I stay away? Ask any reasonable man what he would prefer to do. No, no, Wild. I have suffered too much through you to let slip the opportunity of taking a little revenge. It's so easy, too. Oh! I can enjoy this."

"Rascal!"

"Ha! ha!"

"Scoundrel!"

"Ha! ha!"

"You shall repent this."

"I never can."

"You shall see. I have yet means in my power of making you dance."

"Pooh!"

"You shall see."

Mrs. Jenkins and Master Jenkins, or Miss Jenkins, whichever it might be, were at some little distance off, the former awaiting in trembling the thieftaker's movements.

But, alas! she did not have long to wait.

The determination of Jonathan Wild was taken upon the instant, with what cruel purpose we shall show.

He made a dash in the direction of the poor woman and her babe.

With a startled cry, she flew away as soon as she saw the movement of Jonathan Wild.

But, alas! poor woman, encumbered as she was with the weight of the child, she could not make much progress.

And the thieftaker came on with great strides.

By this time they were within a dozen yards of the smoking lime kiln, and scarcely that distance separating her from Jonathan Wild.

With a shout of rage the thieftaker was upon her.

"Ah!" she shrieked. "Mercy! mercy!"

The thieftaker's only reply was to tear the child from her.

"You shall see what mercy I show," said the thieftaker.

"What would you do?"

"This."

He darted up the slope leading to the mouth of the blazing lime kiln—holding the baby with one hand aloft.

The woman, with a mother's instinct, divined his purpose.

She flew like the lightning flash to his side, and caught his upraised arm with her two hands.

But what could her feeble strength avail her against the bold desperate grasp of the thieftaker?

Nothing, positively nothing.

He shook her off with a growl.

"Let me go, woman," he said, "or you will repent it I promise you."

And even as he spoke he seized her by the hair, which was long and black, and glossy as the raven's wing.

He held the babe aloft in a nervous grasp, and then—

* * * * * *

From the cottage Bill Jenkins could see the lime kiln well, and all that transpired there.

He could actually perceive his wife struggling with the thieftaker, and yet he was too great a coward at heart to venture a step to her assistance.

But presently he saw something which stirred his sluggish cowardice.

"By Heavens!" he cried. "The accursed thieftaker has got the child. Ah! great Heavens! oh! how horrible. He has dashed the baby into the blazing lime kiln!"

Flesh and blood could not endure it.

A father's love triumphed over the brutal and disgusting cowardice of the man, and he must fly to the aid of his child if even his life were sacrificed.

He hastily snatched up a pair of pistols from the table where he had lain them ready loaded in case of an emergency immediately upon discovering Jonathan Wild's presence there.

Then he rushed from the house like a madman.

Darting along the path, he gained the lime kiln.

At this moment—the helpless child having been hurled to its fate so awfully and so suddenly—the brutal thieftaker was endeavouring to drag the mother to the edge of the lime kiln by the hair of the head.

"Damnable villain!" cried Bill Jenkins, rushing upon him.

With one blow upon Jonathan Wild's right arm the woman was released from his murderous clutch.

"Ah!" cried Will.

"Villain!" said Jenkins, his face now blood red with passion and indignation.

"You are my man," said Wild. "Why didn't you come before?"

"You will find that I have come too soon. Dastardly scoundrel and villain, who wars against women and children, nothing else could rouse me, as you see, but now I swear by all my hopes of life and hereafter that you shall follow that child."

In spite of himself, the thieftaker grew pale at the thought.

The despised cowardly Bill Jenkins had grown alarming by the justice of his wrongs.

[LIFE OR DEATH?]

Not an instant did he hesitate, but grappled boldly with the thieftaker.

"Let go your hold!" said Wild.

"Never!"

"Fool! You shall repent this."

"Never shall I repent that I sought vengeance upon the destroyer of my child," said poor Jenkins.

"Down with you, then!"

And Wild attempted to drag him to the verge of the lime kiln.

Bill Jenkins appeared to desire nothing better.

He allowed the thieftaker to drag him to its very edge, and there, grappling him with desperate tenacity, he hung over—hung between life and death.

"Follow your precious chick!" said Wild, now utterly lost to all sensations but that of revenge.

"Not I!" cried Jenkins.

"Who, then?"

"You!" roared Jenkins, half frenzied.

And with an effort almost superhuman the positions were reversed.

And now Jonathan Wild was hurled headlong into the blazing lime kiln.

As he fell Jonathan uttered a loud and piercing shriek.

It echoed shrilly and awfully through the still night air, like the yell of one in mortal agony.

But, fearful as was the cry, it would not have

No. 51.

moved the murderer to pity—it would not have saved the blackhearted thieftaker's life had it not reached other ears than his.

As Wild's luck would have it, though, it was heard by others.

Scarcely was it uttered than, as though by magic, a band of horsemen galloped on to the scene.

They crowded round the mouth of the pit.

In frantic tones one called to the rest for a rope, which, being passed forward, was lowered to the miserable wretch.

But he could not hold it in his burnt hands.

Half raised from the pit, he fell back again.

Once more they lowered the rope.

This time, however, they lassoed him, and so dragged him to the surface.

He fell to the ground, groaning dismally. But they raised him in their arms and bore him away to a house where measures could be adopted for restoring him.

While a number of the horsemen were thus engaged the rest had fallen upon Jenkins.

They did not know the rights of the case, and this was not a moment to listen to explanations.

In spite of his wild prayers and entreaties the unhappy man was cut down.

Then a score of swords traversed his body.

It was not until it was almost hacked to pieces that his corpse was deserted by the band.

But, the bloody work being finished, there suddenly arose a cry.

"Yellow Boys, this way. Quick, quick!"

The Yellow Boys, for such were the horsemen, rushed to the sound of their leader's voice.

"See," cried Ralph, "who it is we have saved. It is our arch enemy Jonathan Wild."

"Back to the pit with him!" yelled the indignant band.

"Nay, that were too horrible a death for even such a miscreant as he is."

"No, no. It serves him right."

"Hold, boys, I forbid you to touch him. Fire is God's punishment hereafter. On earth he deserves a dog's death on the gallows. Let us pray to live to see the sentence of the law carried out."

Frightfully burnt and mutilated as he was, the villain heard them, and, half raising himself, shrieked out—

"Your time will come before mine, Red Ralph, and the rest of you. I shall see you all hanged. Ha! ha! I shall see you all hanged."

The Yellow Boys with one accord rushed upon him with drawn swords.

But Ralph dashed forward, and flung himself between them and their intended victim.

"Let him be. His time will come, and perhaps it is not so far distant as he supposes."

They left him thus, and rode away.

They left him groaning and cursing—blaspheming on the brink of eternity.

Horribly disfigured—more than half dead—still his devil's heart prompted him to revenge.

"Red Ralph," he cried, "I will never rest now till I hunt you down. Where's Jenkins? Is he dead? Ha! ha! that's well. And Jabez—curse him!—he shall rue it also. I'll be equal with them all. I'll—I'll— Oh! my God! what agony I suffer! My flesh is falling from my bones. I—I— Curse them all! Oh! oh! I wish they were in the furnace. I'd not help them out. Oh! oh!"

And, raving thus, he lapsed into insensibility.

CHAPTER CLXVIII.

THE SOLDIERS AND THEIR CAPTIVE—THE LANDLADY'S PRETTY DAUGHTER—A BOLT—A MEETING.

RETURN we again to Red Ralph, who when we last saw him was again a captive, handcuffed, and surrounded by soldiers bearing loaded carbines. One would have thought the danger of his position at this juncture sufficient to have cowed even the bravest, but yet Red Ralph's pluck and presence of mind did not desert him in the dreadful fix in which he found himself placed.

The soldiers were foot guards, and about thirty in number. The horse upon which they mounted Red Ralph was his own, and had been the cause of his capture.

The men were all laughing and joking among themselves, in high glee at the notion of the reward which would probably be divided amongst them.

"When the captain's had his share of the swag," said one, "there'll be enough left for a jolly good drink or two among the rest of us."

"And easy enough earned by some of us who did not come in for a scratch of Ralph's knife."

"He's killed poor Jackson, though."

"Ah! and spoilt Mason's beauty."

"Well, we shall have the satisfaction of seeing him swing for it."

"That's a sort of comfort."

"I say, Mr. highwayman," said one of the men, addressing our hero, "I should advise you, the next time you try to hide yourself—"

"He won't get another chance in this world, Jack, so you needn't tell him."

"Well, what I've got to say won't do him any harm. He'd better hear it."

"Yes, perhaps I'd better hear it," said Red Ralph, with an insulting laugh. "There's no knowing what may happen."

"To be sure not. Well, then, when you hide next time—if you ever get a chance, that is—"

"Granted."

"Which you're not likely to do."

"Certainly not—according to your opinion."

"Well, then, when you hide, don't leave your finger-post up outside the door."

"What do you mean?"

"Why your horse, to be sure. We should never have guessed you were there if we hadn't seen it in the stable."

"Oh! that's how it was, was it?"

"How came you to choose a place so near the scene of your last exploit? That wasn't wise."

"I'm afraid you're right," said Ralph. "However, what is to be is to be you know."

"And so you're to be hanged."

"Bless me, no. I never said that. I was to be caught, that's all."

"That't jolly well half way to it you'll find."

"Shall I? I don't think it."

"Everybody has a right to an opinion. Anyhow, we shall see—"

"What we shall see."

"No doubt of it."

They pursued their way, laughing and joking as they went. They were merry fellows these soldiers.

The large sum of prize-money, too, which was to be divided among them put them into good spirits.

Their captain was the jolliest dog among them, and it was jollyness which was the cause of their subsequent long faces, as you will see.

Before very long they came to a tavern, the one at which Ralph had at first thought of putting up for the night.

He was known there, and some of the inmates of the house were not unkindly disposed towards him.

These inmates were the handsome black-eyed landlady, and the landlady's prettier daughter.

With both these ladies our gay highwayman had had his little love passages.

When they saw him come up, therefore, with his handcuffs on, and the soldiers' cruel guns pointed at his breast, their gentle bosoms swelled with pity.

The leader of the soldiers, being, as has been said, a jolly dog, and a gay fellow too, when he came in front of the tavern had two ideas occur to him.

One of these ideas was that he would like a few minutes' chat with the ladies, and to flourish a little as the captor of the famous Red Ralph.

The other idea was that a glass of rum and milk would be acceptable this very chilly morning.

Therefore he called a halt.

The soldiers were glad enough to stop, as you may suppose.

Two of the guards, with loaded guns, remained by the side of the prisoner.

The rest betook themselves to strong ale.

But when they had been drinking for a few moments Ralph's head began to droop forward, and he looked as though he was going to fall off the horse.

"What's the matter?" asked one of the soldiers by his side.

"Nothing," said Ralph.

But his head still drooped.

"It must be something. Are you ill?"

"I'm only a little faint. It will go off directly."

But the landlady's daughter was watchful of this little scene.

She approached the captain of the soldiers, who was flirting with her mother.

"Look at your prisoner," she said.

"What's amiss, my dear?"

"He's very ill."

"It's fear most likely."

The young lady's eyes flashed fire.

"You know the signs from personal experience perhaps."

But then, changing her tone, she said in a wheedling way—

"Mayn't I give him a glass of brandy, captain?"

"Well, I don't see why you shouldn't, my dear, if it pleases you. Only allow me to say that I do not think he is worthy of your sympathy."

"We ought to feel for any poor creature in distress, ought we not?"

The captain only smiled, so Miss Mary got the brandy, and went with it in her own fair hand towards the prisoner.

As she approached he did not raise his eyes.

"Poor prisoner," she said, "take this. It will do you good."

He stooped down towards her and murmured softly—

"Send away one of the guards."

"The poor man is dreadfully ill," she said aloud. "Oh! Mr. soldier, do go and call the captain here for half a moment."

Then in a low tone she said to Ralph—

"For Heaven's sake try nothing rash. You will be shot down."

"I'll risk it," he answered. "Pretend to be wounded, and fall back into the other man's arms. Leave the rest to me."

As he spoke he raised his hand, as though to strike her.

She gave a shriek and fell back against the soldier, about six feet distant.

Involuntarily he rushed forward to save her.

In an instant then Ralph had cast off his handcuffs, and, saying but one magic word to his faithful steed, was galloping across country at lightning speed.

With a loud cry the soldiers sprang to their feet.

In an instant they had seized their guns and had fired wildly after the fugitive.

But he lay forward upon his horse's back.

The shots whistled harmlessly about his ears.

He rapidly undid the bridle, which was knotted up, and turned the horse's head towards the fields.

Over the hedges they flew, as though no such obstacles barred their way.

The ditches were crossed as easily as though they had been but dry land.

He had no occasion to use his spurs: the faithful animal which bore him seemed to know that its master's life was at stake—that upon its efforts alone did his hopes depend.

It is better sometimes to place one's faith in the fidelity of a dumb animal than in a human being.

Much better was it in such a strait as that in which Red Ralph now found himself.

The amount of money set upon his head was so large that it was almost too strong a trial for the constancy of even his faithful followers.

But a thousand or two pounds did not represent the value of a feed of oats in his good horse's eyes.

On—on they went.

The soldiers were soon knocked up and out of breath.

So long, however, as they were in sight it was not safe to halt for an instant.

Onward, still onward.

But at length, turning round in his saddle, Red Ralph saw that he was alone, and that at least a mile of open country lay behind him, and on it no sign of his pursuers.

Once more he was free.

It was scarcely credible; nevertheless, it was the case.

He had escaped for the present.

"By Jove, though," said he, with a laugh, "it's time for me to retire on my laurels. This dear old native land of mine is getting a precious deal too hot to be pleasant."

What he said was quite true. But there was a little difficulty: "I've nothing to retire upon." There was the rub.

He was such a reckless extravagant ne'er-do-well that the money no sooner came into his hands than it slipped through his fingers.

What had become of Job Hardstaff's coin, for instance?

Gone, every penny of it.

It was now in the possession of the captain of the soldiers.

"There's no help for it," said Ralph. "I must start afresh, work hard, and make a bolt of it directly I've scraped together enough to clear out with comfortably."

He was now riding along a field which was separated from a narrow lane by a high hedge, and he was busily searching for the weakest place to force his way through.

"What I want first of all is a disguise," said he, "and the first man I meet, by the Lord Harry, I'll change clothes with him."

Just then he found the open place desired.

He forced his way through, and on reaching the opposite side found himself confronting—

Who do you think?

CHAPTER CLXIX.

FACE TO FACE—AN UNPLEASANT MEETING—A ROBBERY—THE TOILET IN THE WOOD—THE RUSTIC WITH THE PIPE—A CONVERSATION—HOMEWARD BOUND.

THE man of all men in the world whom Red Ralph

least wished to encounter was the man who met him face to face in the lane.

That man was Jonathan Wild !

Astonished as he was at the unexpected sight of the thieftaker's villainous countenance, yet Wild was even more surprised than he.

Leaping suddenly through the hedge, and confronting him, it appeared to Wild that Ralph had been lying in ambush waiting for his arrival.

Jonathan's first act was to seize his pistol.

The next to level it at the highwayman's head.

This sort of thing, though, would not do for our hero.

He was unarmed.

There was only one way open for him, except of course surrendering himself a prisoner—an act which with but one drop of blood in his body he would have hesitated about having recourse to.

The only way, then, was to wrestle with his foe.

The notion passed through his brain with the rapidity of lightning.

The project was no sooner formed than it was put into execution.

He made a sudden tiger-like spring.

He flung himself full upon Wild and dashed him from his horse to the earth.

There he lay helpless on his back stunned by the violence of the fall.

Ralph, on the contrary, was unhurt.

The pistol had been discharged into the air as he fell.

"Ha ! ha !" said Ralph. "Nobody would believe now that the terrible thieftaker could be so easily overcome. What shall I do next ?"

He might have made his escape now easily enough, but he did not think of that.

He might do something else.

Had he not often vowed to take Wild's life ?

Now was the time.

Now he could strike the fatal blow.

"But no," Ralph thought with a bitter smile. "He shan't get off so easy, after all. Why should I let him go by the back door ? No ; I'll see him hanged instead. That will be the best revenge."

Having come to this conclusion, Ralph was about to take his departure when something came to his recollection.

"To be sure," said he. "I'd very nearly forgotten it."

He peered cautiously around.

No one was within sight.

He stooped and placed his ear to the ground.

No one was coming along the road in either direction.

"Now for it," said he aloud. "I'll trouble you for your outfit, Master W."

As Jonathan was not in a position to offer any resistance, Ralph set to work.

He unbuttoned the thieftaker's clothes and pulled them off.

He took coat, waistcoat, breeches, hat, neckerchief, etc.

He left Wild his shirt, for decency's sake, and his boots, because they would not fit him.

He made a bundle of these effects, took Wild's pistols and sword, mounted his own horse again, and rode off.

In less than a mile further he came to a small wood.

Leaping his horse over the hedge which divided it from the high road, Ralph forced his way into the thicket, and, having found a quiet spot, began to make his toilet.

"There's nothing in any of my pockets. The soldiers looked to that."

Saying this, he stripped off his clothes and flung them in a heap among the long grass and low brushwood, kicking them out of sight.

Then he dressed himself in Jonathan's apparel.

Then he tied a red handkerchief round his head to hide his golden curls.

Then slouched his hat over his eyes and remounted his horse.

Riding out from the wood again, he leaped back into the road and trotted onwards.

He had not gone a great distance, however, before he saw sitting on a gate a rustic smoking a pipe.

"Hullo !" cried the rustic.

"Hullo !" responded Ralph, pulling up short.

"Are you going to pass an old friend in that way ?"

"An old friend ?"

"To be sure."

Ralph fancied he knew the voice.

He rode up to the gate, and stared in the man's face.

The rustic took off his wide-awake and laughed loudly.

"Why," cried Ralph, "it's Walters."

"Walters it is."

"What are you doing here ?"

"I was looking for you, captain."

"Looking for me ? " said the other, frowning slightly. "What do you mean ?"

"Captain," said the other, "I know what's passing in your mind. Look me in the face fairly, as you used to do, and tell me whether you believe me to be true."

"Walters, give me your hand."

"There."

"There."

As they spoke the two old comrades joined hands in a cordial grasp.

"The whole of the Yellow Boys are scouring the country in search of you, captain. We have been frightened out of our lives on your account since those infernal bills have been plastered on the walls."

"I got an anonymous letter thrust into my hand the other night, Walters."

"I know you did."

"You do ? And you know—"

"Its contents."

"Give me the villain's name, then, who sent it."

"I cannot quite do that, because I am not certain, but I can make a pretty close guess."

"Who was it ?"

"Your old friend, Jonathan Wild."

"The scoundrel ! I met him half an hour ago, and I might have paid him out."

"We shall never be safe until he lies below the earth."

"Or swings above it."

"That's a far distant event, though, I fear."

"We all of us have been scouring the suburbs because we feared that you might believe the warning to have some foundation in it."

"What was Wild's motive do you suppose ?"

"That is very easily explained. He meditates an attack upon our haunt, and wants to have the leader of the band out of the way."

"You know this for a fact."

"Yes."

"And his presence in these parts, can you account for that ?"

"No, not yet. But I hope to do so."

"Have you a clue ?"

"I fancy I have, captain, to a strange dark mystery, the particulars of which I will at once reveal to you."

CHAPTER CLXX.

JONATHAN WILD THE SECOND — AN ARTFUL DODGE — "MEET ME AT THE FOOT OF THE GIBBET"—THE DRAUGHT—THE TREACHEROUS GUESTS.

WHATEVER the mystery was, we must reluctantly reserve it for the present, the proper time for the revelation not having arrived.

Suffice it to say that some papers which Ralph found in Jonathan Wild's pockets very materially assisted the investigation.

Ralph lost no time when the conversation was concluded in turning his horse's head homewards.

Two hours later he was asleep in the cave.

Several hours' repose succeeded.

When the captain opened his eyes he found Walters standing by his couch.

In his hand he held a printed paper.

"This is the last thing out," he said.

Ralph took it into his hand, and read as follows :—

£2500.

HIGHWAY ROBBERY.

The above reward is offered for the capture of
RED RALPH.

The placard then set forth the particulars of the recent robbery of Job Hardstaff, and gave Job Hardstaff's address, with a promise on his part to add £500 to the £2000 previously advertised.

"Poor Job!" laughed Ralph.

"He wants all his patience if he waits for you, captain," said Walters.

"I'll tell you what, Walters, we must have this five hundred."

"How?"

"I have got a notion. Give me a pen and ink."

Walters obeyed.

The captain wrote in a bold hand :—

Sir,—As you are anxious to capture me, and as I intend to give myself up to justice, I shall be very happy to give myself up to you for the sum of money you mentioned—namely, £500.

"*Therefore please to meet me, if you dare, alone at midnight on Hounslow Heath beneath the gibbet.*

"*Take care you come alone.*

"*Take care you bring with you the money.*

"*Beware that you do not play me false.*
"RALPH THE RED."

"What time is it now, Walters?"

"Five o'clock in the afternoon."

"Let one of the men gallop off directly to my friend Job Hardstaff's house."

"Certainly, captain," and Walters took the letter.

When he came back Ralph was dressed in Jonathan Wild's clothes. He had also darkened his face and put on a black wig.

"Why, captain, what are you going to do now?"

"I am going to Hardstaff's of course."

"What to help to catch yourself?"

"Exactly. You shall come too, if you like."

Sure enough, while Job Hardstaff was pondering over Ralph's mysterious letter, who should knock at the door but Jonathan Wild (for the time being) ?

"Mr. Job Hardstaff, I believe," said the sham Jonathan.

"My name, sir," responded the farmer.

"Mine is Jonathan Wild. I believe you caused these bills to be circulated."

"To be sure I did."

"And you offer five hundred pounds for the capture of this man?"

"I shall think the money well laid out if it buys him a halter."

"I agree with you, sir, but still I hope that we may catch him without wasting your money."

"I shan't object to that."

"You may have heard of the capture of his friend Tom King."

"I have not. However, what has that to do with the business ?"

"Everything. Tom King is charged upon strong evidence with the robbery in reality committed by Red Ralph, who I'm certain will not allow King to suffer on his account."

"Ah ! I begin to see."

"If King does not manage to escape from Newgate, which I do not think likely, this Ralph certainly will deliver himself up in his stead."

"I should not have believed in the existence of such generosity."

"Ah! he is a noble fellow, though I say it, who perhaps shouldn't."

"Praise from you is praise indeed."

"Right you are."

"But what plan do you propose, then, by which we may trap our friend and save my money ?"

"I will explain. The two thousand already advertised will be reward enough for me if I can manage to pocket it all, but I shall want the temporary loan of your five hundred to assist me."

Mr. Hardstaff looked a little glum.

"When I say a loan of course I mean that the money shall never leave your hands."

Mr. Hardstaff brightened up.

"I am quite at a loss to understand your meaning," said he.

"You must make an appointment with Ralph, and tell him that you will have the five hundred pounds in your possession."

"For what reason ?"

"There's the difficulty ; but we shall get over that with a little trouble I dare say."

"What would you say, Mr. Wild, if I suggested a motive ?"

"I should be very much obliged to you."

"Ralph has suggested one himself. Look at this letter."

And as he spoke Job produced the document in question.

Ralph could not refrain from a slight smile.

"It's been a long while coming," he thought to himself. "I began to be afraid that the letter had not reached him."

"What do you think of that ?" said Hardstaff.

"Of course you won't go, my dear sir."

"Well, I don't know. Do you think it's a trick ?"

"I know it's Ralph's handwriting, for I have often seen it."

"Well, then, why should I not meet him ?"

"Because he would probably take your money and give you a thrashing."

"Will he, by Jove ? I should like to see the man alive who could do it in a fair fight."

"But he has done it, hasn't he ?"

"It's a lie," roared Job.

"I am sure I beg your pardon, and if you are not afraid of going, we'll go together."

"I'll go alone."

"No, you must not do that. I wouldn't answer for the consequences."

"Hang the consequences, sir. I can take care of myself."

"Very well, then. I'll tell you what we had better do. You must take the money with you, and we will all three go as far as the heath—you, and I, and my man. Then you shall go on first. Take this Red Ralph chap by the nape of the neck and bring him to us.

We'll tie him head and heels and carry him off to Newgate. There you see the whole plan is cut and dried, and Red Ralph almost as good as hanged."

"I agree," said Hardstaff. "And if we are successful I promise you five hundred for your share of the trouble."

"That's very kind of you, and I won't refuse the offer. By the way, I saw a very pretty gig out in the yard. Suppose we go in that, and I'll send on our horses to the Old Bailey."

"That will be the best way I think."

Things being thus arranged, the horses were given in charge of a third Yellow Boy, who turned up at the moment in the dress of a farm labourer.

Half an hour afterwards, having previously partaken of the best that Hardstaff's larder could produce, the two robbers and their guileless victim set forth in the gig with the five hundred pounds.

As they rode along, said Ralph (that is to say, Jonathan Wild), "It's very chilly to-night. I've something very choice here which we took the other day from a smuggler. Will you taste it?"

So saying, he passed a flask to his companion.

"It's very nice," said Job, "but it's very strong."

"Try a drop more. It won't hurt you."

*   *   *   *   *   *

"It's very extraordinary," said Job, "but I feel quite giddy. Will you take the reins?"

"With pleasure."

*   *   *   *   *   *

Next morning Job Hardstaff was picked up in a state of insensibility in a lane near Hounslow Heath, and a gig was sold the previous evening at a tavern near Smithfield.

Not a halfpenny of the five hundred pounds returned to the pocket of their much injured owner.

CHAPTER CLXXI.

A NIGHT IN A TOMB.

"I AM thinking of breaking up the Yellow Band," said Ralph, "and sharing our booty, and then myself going abroad."

"Oh, no," cried Walters. "You must not think of deserting us."

"We can't hope to go on with impunity for ever," said the captain. "We have been very lucky, and I feel that we are reaching the close."

His companion was silent and thoughtful.

"Before we wind up, though," said Ralph, "we must distinguish ourselves. I have one or two schemes, and one expedition which I mean to undertake by myself."

Walters endeavoured to persuade Ralph to allow him to be of the party, but the captain was obstinate.

A few hours afterwards Ralph, disguised as a countryman, was sitting in the taproom of a village inn a few miles from London, on the Northern road.

There was a great excitement in the neighbourhood. Lady Glengowen was to buried in state at midnight in the vault of the Glengowens, beneath the parish church.

There was great talk among the villagers concerning this strange event.

It was not every day in the week that a lady of title was buried in those parts, and as for a midnight funeral, such a thing had never been heard of.

One was quite certain it wasn't legal.

But another said, "Bless you, lords and ladies can do what they like."

Another added, "That's true enough." Several there were who were better informed than their fellows and could explain why the funeral was to take place at midnight, instead of during the day.

These had read all about it in the county newspaper, which had copied it from the London papers.

It was in the latter that our hero had also seen the particulars of the extraordinary occurrence.

The facts were these:—Lady Glengowen was a spinster. In her youth she had been disappointed in love, her betrothed husband dying upon the very day fixed for the wedding, he having been shot in a duel.

The shock she had received was supposed in some measure to have turned her brain. At least, she ever afterwards was counted very eccentric.

Among her other peculiarities, until the day of her death she always wore the jewels in which she was to have been married, which had been presents from her lover.

Although a peeress, these costly decorations were, nevertheless, at times somewhat unsuitable.

In her will she had strictly directed that she should be carried to the churchyard in an open coffin and buried in all her jewels.

Extremely unpopular was this arrangement with the young ladies of the family, but still it was generally understood that it would be carried out.

The family lawyer, however, made a suggestion, the result of which will very shortly appear, though to say what it was just at this moment would rather spoil our story.

Ralph listened to the conversation around him and, chuckled.

"I saw her lying in state," said the landlord, "and, man alive! the rings on one hand would pretty well have set me up in a London tavern."

"What a shame to give such a feast as that to the worms!"

"Hang me if it ain't enough to bring the London bodysnatchers down on us."

"Bodysnatchers?" said the landlord, with contempt. "Do you mean to say, Giles, that you believe those cock and bull tales the cockney fools get up to frighten one another with?"

"Well, I don't think it's very likely, certainly, but one does read of such things."

"Read, indeed? If they didn't put a lot of lies in books, what would they fill them with?"

"I should have to be much poorer than I am, and that's the truth, before I should go to rob a corpse."

The great affection which Lady Glengowen had enjoyed among all who knew her summoned hundreds to her lying in state.

Her funeral took place by torch-light, with great pomp.

A long procession of mourners belonging to all classes followed the bier, and the coffin was lowered into the vault after an affecting funeral oration.

About two hours after the funeral, and when the church was again deserted, a dark grey figure glided noiselessly among the graves in the church-yard.

No one was there to see it working at the door of the church, and soon the skeleton keys had done their work, and it glided noiselessly down the aisle towards the vault where lay the newly-buried dead.

It was Ralph who had undertaken this perilous adventure.

He had brought with him his skeleton keys, chisel, picklocks, crowbar, and pincers, but these tools did not avail him much, as things turned out.

He climbed over some palings surrounding the mausoleum, but it was not an easy task to get into the vault itself.

A carefully locked iron gate, eight feet high, formed of spikes, placed in a semicircle almost to the top of the arch, was the first difficulty.

With much trouble, and no small amount of pain, he contrived to climb over the spikes and squeeze himself through.

The space, though, was very narrow, and he very nearly ripped himself up by slipping his foot.

However, having mastered the gate, he prepared for further difficulties.

A double trap-door closed the vault.

It was made of stout oaken planks.

" The deuce is in the locks," said he. " My keys are no good here."

He must prise open the door, but this was very difficult, for it fitted very closely.

At length he contrived to insert his chisel.

Then he worked it about till he could get in the crowbar.

Then he exerted all his strength.

It was a terrific weight.

He panted and perspired.

But at last he succeeded in turning back one of the trap-doors, which weighed only a hundredweight.

It, however, had taken more than one hour to get thus far.

" I must not waste time this way," said Ralph, " or I shall have daylight surprise me."

He turned the door back creaking on its hinges, but a new difficulty then met his eyes.

There were no steps, as he had expected, leading into the vault.

The depth he could not fathom with the aid of his dark lantern.

Evidently it was very great.

It was far too deep to think of venturing on a jump.

What was to be done ?

Having reached his object so nearly, Ralph was not the man to think of abandoning it very readily.

He had nothing that would serve him.

There was no other way than to climb back over the top of the gate, and look for a pole.

With a great deal of pain he squeezed his way back into the church.

He searched everywhere, but in vain.

At last he went out into the churchyard.

There he found a young tree, which he cut down, and, lopping off the branches, took it back with him to the vault.

But all at once he slipped.

He tried to save himself; but in vain. He was overbalanced: the weight of the pole dragged him down.

He fell headlong into the black yawning chasm.

* * * * * *

He fell twelve feet, and, striking his head in the descent, lay for some time in a state of insensibility.

When he opened his eyes again he found himself jammed between two coffins.

The lantern fastened to his belt had been extinguished by the fall, but he had matches in his pocket.

He soon struck a light and began his examination.

He looked round carefully for the new coffin, but it required a lengthened search to find it, as the outsides all looked one about as old as the other.

At length he found it.

After removing the oilskin coverlid Ralph came across some unexpected obstacles.

In spite of all his exertions, he could not remove the coffin lid, in consequence of two padlocks which were unpickable.

He had left his other instruments on the trap-door and did not think it worth while to go in search of them.

With an exertion of his great strength he contrived to break off a hasp and tore the padlock from the lower end of the coffin, while the other resisted all his efforts.

Still he was enabled to seize the coffin lid with both hands, and raise it so as to see the corpse lying inside.

Very horrible it looked, with its phosphorescent face contrasting with the sable velvet.

It was awful to contemplate, and—

There were no jewels !

No. It was a fact.

He put his hand and felt beneath the body.   There was not one that he could find.

He exerted all his strength to the utmost, straining every nerve, and with an almost surperhuman effort wrenched off the lid.

Then he took the body out.

But still he gained nothing.

What was to be done now ?

Clearly nothing but to get out of the vault again as soon as possible.

But now came the difficulty.

The pole that had dragged him down, and on which he had calculated for his escape, was too smooth and too short.

All Ralph's exertions to climb it were in vain.

He was caught in a trap.

The sides of the vault were smooth as glass.

There was not a foothold to be found.

Ralph sat down on a coffin to consider.

" I've done it this time," said he.

There was little doubt of that, if he meant that he had got into an ugly predicament.

What could he do ?

There was nothing for him to do but to wait until somebody came who could help him.

" And who will, I should like to know, " said he. " They'll take me for a ghost."

At that moment the church clock struck four.

" Another hour to daylight, and my light is failing."

Yes ; the lantern sure enough was going out for want of oil.

In five minutes more he was in the dark.

Then he sat in an awful silence and pitchy darkness waiting for daylight.

Alone with the dead !

CHAPTER CLXXII.

IN THE GRAVE—A FOOTSTEP—THE OLD MAN—A THIEF, AND NOTHING TO STEAL—THE STRUGGLE—THE FALL—THE THREATS—VOICES WITHOUT — THE MOB — A RUN FOR IT — CAUGHT AGAIN — THE MYSTERIOUS WOMAN IN THE DARK.

A FEARFUL night was this which Red Ralph passed in the tomb.

Long hours of protracted horror, enough to have shaken the reason of one less brave than the lion-hearted robber chief.

It was not, however, any supernatural fears which possessed him.

Nor indeed was it the fear of the punishment which he might expect at the hands of the law when next morning he was discovered.

It was the idea of his shame and degradation which distressed him—that he, the great highwayman—the hero of a hundred deeds of daring—should at last be caught and put into prison for such an affair as this.

And to be caught in such a way, too—that was the most humiliating part.

To be caught like a rat in a trap.

To be punished by the stocks, perhaps—the pillory —the whipping post.

Great Heavens! could he outlive such humiliation ?

When they came would it not be best to declare himself to be the celebrated criminal he was?

But in that case there could be only one result—Death!

As Ralph thus reflected he worked himself into a perfect fury.

Backwards and forwards he strode the length of his hideous prison house.

Deep were the curses he heaped upon his own folly.

"If I only get out of this one scrape," he said.

What projects for the future he formed! But what chance was there of the future?

He applied himself once more to the tree trunk.

Once more he struggled desperately.

But in vain. He was a captive. There was no hope for him. He must make up his mind to wait until somebody came to release him.

He flung himself upon the floor, and tried to curb his impetuosity.

"What time was it?" he wondered. He could not recollect what hour he had heard the church clock strike last.

Perhaps it had struck while he was stamping to and fro, and he had not heard it.

It could not possibly be that it was only an hour since he had heard the last chimes.

He tried to be patient and wait.

He held his breath and listened intently.

The singing noise in his head, bred of the intensity of the death-like silence, almost drove him mad.

The pitchy blackness seemed to grow thick and suffocating.

He felt an almost irrepressible inclination to shriek aloud.

All at once, though, he fancied he heard a faint sound.

Yes. He could not be mistaken. There was a noise in the church.

Ralph held his breath and listened.

Then the sound of a door being closed very cautiously fell upon his ears.

Then came a stealthy footfall in the aisle.

Ralph waited in a fever of anxiety.

The steps drew nearer.

Nearer still.

Then he heard the gate of the vault shaking.

Then the grating of a key in the rusty lock.

Grasping the trunk of the tree in his hand, Ralph set his teeth and waited.

The gate creaked on its hinges, and slowly opened. The rays of a lantern straggled in at the mouth of the pit.

In the faint glimmering light behind it Ralph could discern the harsh outlines of an old man's face—a face surrounded by white straggling locks and a grizzly beard.

The owner of this head held on high his lantern, and peered into the darkness with a scared and haggard face.

At sight of Red Ralph's face white and motionless in the abode of the dead the old man uttered an exclamation of terror, and the lantern almost fell from his trembling hands.

"Who's that?" he shrieked. "Who are you? Speak!"

"I'm not a ghost," replied Ralph hastily. "Don't be afraid."

"Eh? Oh! not a ghost. Thank God for that."

And he summoned up courage to have a good look at Ralph's face.

"I don't know you," he said. "Who are you?"

"Well, who are you?" asked Ralph in return.

"I'm Jarvis the sexton."

"Oh! are you?"

"Yes, I am; and what are you doing down in this grave?"

"I'm not here by choice, you may be sure of that."

"How did you come here?"

"I fell in."

"And what are you doing?"

"Waiting to be helped out."

"And who do you expect is going to help you?"

"You are, of course."

"You think so?"

"To be sure."

The old man was no longer terrified—at least, to judge by his tone.

Quite the contrary, and Ralph felt a trifle uneasy.

The more so when he heard a certain ominous click, which there is no mistaking when you know the sound.

The old man was cocking a pistol.

When next he spoke he presented it at Ralph's head, and said—

"Hand up the jewels."

"What?" gasped our hero.

"Hand up the jewels."

"I haven't got any."

"You have."

"I haven't."

"Who has, then?"

"How the deuce do I know?"

"You came here to steal them."

"Well?"

"And you've stolen them I suppose."

"You suppose wrong, then, for once, old gentleman."

"Give them up, I say, or I'll blow your brains out."

Ralph was puzzled what to do next.

"Don't be violent, old gentleman," said he; "when there's no occasion. Just let's talk the matter over quietly."

"I've no time to waste."

"It won't be wasting time if it saves your neck from the halter, I should think."

"What have you got to say?"

"Just to ask you what you intend to do."

"To have those jewels."

"But if I refuse to give them up to you?"

"I shall shoot you dead, and rifle your corpse."

"But the noise of your pistol will probably arouse the neighbours."

"What then? They can't come in until I have done my work."

"But, my worthy friend, when they find my dead body lying here, and the jewels gone, won't they naturally suppose that you've collared the swag?"

The old man seemed to hesitate.

"No," said he presently. "I can easily explain it by saying an accomplice of yours ran away with them before I could interfere."

"Ah! I don't think that will wash, though, my fine fellow. They'll examine the footprints in the aisle; and then you'll have to keep the jewels dark for many a long month. Besides, allow me to add that I am one of a band, that I have been sent here, and, if you kill me, one of my pals will creep into your cottage while you are asleep and cut your throat as sure as you're a man."

"If I help you out, will you—"

"Of course I will. I'll share fairly all I've got."

"You swear it?"

"I swear it."

The old man put down his lantern, and, fastening the end of a stout rope to the iron gate, lowered the other end into the vault.

Ralph seized it, and in another moment was by the old man's side.

[THE BESIEGED HUT.]

"Thank Heaven for that!" said he, drawing a long breath.

But the old man did not relish any long delays. He seized Ralph by the arm.

"Come, shell up," said he.

Ralph looked down on him, and smiled mockingly.

"What were you pleased to remark?"

"Hand over my share."

"Poor old person," said Ralph, with a laugh. "You never made a more woeful error than you've done this time."

"You won't, then?"

"No, and for one simple reason."

"Which is—"

"That I can't."

"You can't?"

"No. I haven't got any jewels. There were none."

"Were none? You lie! You've stolen them."

"Just satisfy yourself by feeling in my pockets, if you don't believe me."

The old man eagerly adopted the suggestion.

"I can't feel anything. What have you done with them? Tell me, I say. You shan't go. Tell me, or I'll scream for help."

And he clung frantically to the highwayman.

"Now look here," said Ralph, producing as he spoke a loaded pistol from his breast. "Don't make an idiot of yourself. There were no jewels in the coffin. We've both been sold, and there's an end of the matter."

But the old man, instead of being pacified, was wild with rage at hearing this.

Suddenly he seized Ralph, and strove to hurl him into the pit.

But he would have had no chance with his strong antagonist had not Ralph slipped his foot.

Dragging the old man with him, he fell once more into the grave.

He was not stunned this time, although he was much bruised and shaken.

As for the sexton, he was well-nigh knocked silly.

He lay on his back, gasping like a stranded codfish, his toes quivering like the toes of a dying frog.

The lantern standing at the edge of the pit threw a faint light down into the old man's face.

"You're not dead, are you?" asked Ralph.

"Not quite. Every bone in me is broke, though."

"Well, try and get up."

"I can't move."

"Try. Here, I'll help you."

He lurched the old man up as he spoke.

"Oh dear! oh dear! I'm nearly dead."

"Not quite, though. You'll be better presently, when we're in the open air."

"How are we to get out? I pulled the rope up again."

Here he was, then, once more in the trap.

"Look here, old fellow," said Ralph. "You knocked me down, so you must help me up. Let me stand on your shoulders and scramble out."

"No, let me stand on yours."

"Not if I know it. I won't trust you further than I can see you."

"I won't help you, then."

Ralph placed the cold nose of a pistol against the sexton's forehead, saying as he did so—

"If you don't make a back against that wall without any further parley I shall murder you. Now understand, I'm not joking. My name is Red Ralph. There's over two thousand pounds set on my head, whether I'm taken dead or alive, and if I'm taken, I shall be hanged. Your paltry life will make no difference one way or the other, so I shall shoot you."

"No, no! Mercy! mercy!"

And the sexton fell on his knees.

"Enough of this. Do as I bid you."

With many groans the sexton made a back against the wall. Ralph then mounted up, and climbed out of the grave.

"Help me out, too," said the sexton.

"Not if I know it."

"But they'll think that I came here to rob the vault."

"That's your look-out."

"I shall be hanged."

"Serve you right."

As, however, our hero was always as generous as he was brave, he had no intention of deserting the old man, and he prepared to lower the rope.

But at that moment there arose a great clamour at the church door—the sound of heavy blows and of angry voices.

Probably the sexton had been suspected and watched, and they were come to seize him.

At that moment there was a loud cry of, "Jarvis! Jarvis!"

"I'm lost!" groaned the old man.

"It's your own fault if you are. Take hold of the rope."

But the sexton was paralysed with fear, and unable to help himself, and there was no more time to lose.

Ralph was compelled to look to himself.

At that moment the church door gave way, and a mob of villagers rushed in. Ralph looked hurriedly around. Where could he fly to?

Suddenly he remembered that on his way to the vault he had passed a flight of stone steps, evidently leading to other vaults below the church.

Catching up the lantern, he hurried in that direction.

He was scarcely a moment in doing so, and before the villagers had caught sight of him he was engulfed in the subterranean passage.

But no sooner had he disappeared than the crowd came hooting and howling all over the lower part of the church.

Ralph rushed on. At a little distance he saw a light. It was the moon shining through a small window.

Grasping the bars with both hands, he wrenched and tugged at them furiously.

The ironwork was old, and eaten into by the rust, and soon came tumbling down beneath the Yellow Boy's gigantic strength.

In another instant he had sprung up, and forced his way out into the open air.

Arrived there, he found himself in the yard of a house. Very high walls surrounded him. In front, however, was the back door of the house, standing ajar, and in that direction he bent his steps.

He entered cautiously, proceeded on tiptoe down the passage, and was about to place his foot on the lowest stair of a flight in front of him, when suddenly two arms were flung round his waist, evidently those of a woman, clasping him in a vice-like grasp.

CHAPTER CLXXIII.

THE STRONG FAIR ONE — "LET ME GO!"—A RIDE
UPSTAIRS — A NOVEL EXPEDIENT—AN ESCAPE
—THE BAGSMAN — A STRUGGLE — A CHASE.

WHO on earth was this strong-armed fair one who had taken Ralph captive?

He could hear the shouts of the men in the church. In all probability it would soon be discovered that he had effected his escape by the window. They would follow in the same way, and he would be taken —that is, if he waited until they came to catch him.

But how to get away?

The beautiful white arms were clasped round him as tightly as though they had taken root and grown to his sides.

Ralph struggled desperately to free himself.

But he struggled in vain.

The worst of it was that in his struggling he was restrained from properly exerting his strength for fear of hurting his assailant.

If it had been a man he would not have hesitated to use his heels and his elbows.

If he could get away, though, without hurting her he would do so. But if she would not leave go of him, what was he to do?

The voices grew nearer, and he was growing desperate.

"By Heaven," Ralph cried, "if you value your life, you'll unloose me."

"What, would you kill me, you miscreant?"

"There's no doubt about it. Leave go, will you?"

And he made believe to cock a pistol.

"Oh! you murdering ruffian! I'll hold you till they come, and then I'll give you up to the constables, and when you're tried and sentenced I'll come to see you hanged."

"Well, I'm hanged if you will. Come now, once for all, leave go. This is the last time of asking."

"I won't. Help! Thieves! Murder! Help!"

By this time Ralph had put up with as much as he could.

"If you won't let me go," he cried, "you shall go with me."

And without another word, he drew himself up to his full height, swept her right off her legs and rushed upstairs with her as though she had weighed no more than an empty sack.

Finding herself thus unceremoniously dealt with, the lady's shrieks grew louder and shriller.

She struggled and kicked; but she could not make the "fiery untamed steed" come to a standstill.

Yet she clung to him with persevering tenacity.

Ralph had run to the front door, which was on the basement floor.

He found it locked and bolted, but he undid it, in spite of the fair one's struggles.

Then, having opened it, he found himself in the village street. It was empty and deserted, for all those who were out of bed had flocked to the church.

There were a good many persons, though, who had not got up, and among them the inhabitants of the house he had just rushed through.

As he turned on the door step the first streaks of daylight showed him the face of his captor over his shoulder.

She was the servant maid who had got up early. She was a very pretty, buxom lass, and one with whom Ralph felt that under more advantageous circumstances he could have fallen in love.

But now his only object was to get rid of the obstreperous beauty. But how?

Really no more time could be wasted. The people in the house, alarmed by her shrieks, were coming downstairs. Heads were to be seen at the windows of the adjoining houses.

What was he to do?

All at once a grand idea occurred to him. He could not shake or push her off, and he did not want to strike her. There was only one way, and that was to pull her head towards him and kiss her till she let go.

Jerking round suddenly, he got his arm round her neck and fastened his lips to hers.

The effect was magical. She let me drop as though he had been a hot coal, and struggled frantically to escape.

He would not let her go, though, before he had taken at least a score of kisses.

The moment he released her she turned and fled, shrieking in the greatest terror.

He, on his side, took to his heels and went down the village street as fast as his legs would carry him.

"I'm a free man at last," said he.

But he was very much mistaken.

Leaving the street as soon as he possibly could, he rushed up a lane by the side of the principal inn, and ran with all the speed of which he was capable.

Was he free at last?

No. Some one was coming from the opposite direction. It was a horseman, who at sight of him pulled out a pistol and levelled it at his head.

"If you advance another step," cried the stranger, "I'll shoot you down."

"Why so?" roared Ralph, with what breath he had left. "I don't mean to hurt you."

"How do I know that?" cried the horseman. "I shall shoot you if you come a step nearer."

The fact was the stranger was a bagsman, and was frightened out of his life at the sight of Ralph.

He had made up his mind that the highwayman meant to rob him, and nothing could have persuaded him to the contrary.

This was not exactly the moment for an argument.

Ralph fancied he could hear footsteps and voices approaching from the village street.

He made a dash forwards. But as he did so he slipped. It was lucky for him that he did, for as he came the bagsman aimed at him and fired.

The bullet whistled over him half an inch from his skull.

But the bagsman at once pulled out another pistol and levelled it at him.

Then Ralph's anger burst forth.

"Curse you!" he cried. "Your blood be on your own head, you infernal idiot!"

As he spoke he himself drew forth a pistol, levelled it, and fired.

It struck the bagsman in the shoulder, and he reeled and fell heavily to the ground.

At the same moment a crowd of villagers appeared.

Ralph immediately seized the horse's bridle and sprang into the saddle.

But before he could start he was surrounded by the villagers.

Pulling tight the bridle, he dashed his heels in the horse's flanks, and charged amongst them.

They fled at his approach. But he trampled them down and galloped on.

Luckily they had no firearms, and at best could but send a shower of stones after him, which fell harmless, and very soon he was in the open country.

He rode on as fast as he could, until he was out of harm's way, and then slackened his pace.

"This has been an awful night," said he. "I wonder what is in store for me."

Something a good deal worse than what he had gone through. That was very certain.

CHAPTER CLXXIV.
CONCLUSION.

THE night was clear and starlit. The moon was up.

As Red Ralph rode along he came upon a forked road with a finger post pointing in each direction.

He rode up to inspect this nearer, when it suddenly occurred to him that the spot was a familiar one.

"Strange!" he murmured half aloud. "I know this spot well. Let me see. Ah! I remember now. This is the anniversary of an event which befel me at this very spot. It was here that I met for the second time one whom I dread to think of. One whom—"

He paused.

The singularity of the coincidence was enhanced by the fact of it being at the same hour, in addition to the self-same spot.

"How very remarkable!" continued Red Ralph, a strange sensation creeping over him.

The words were barely uttered when there was a hasty shuffle in the foliage, and forth sprang a horseman, parting the thickly-grown bushes and shrubs.

Red Ralph started back, quite alarmed by this sudden apparition. But, becoming ashamed of such a display of weakness, he rallied and confronted the stranger.

"How now, sir," he cried. "What do you mean by this?"

The stranger, upon hearing Red Ralph's voice, uttered a startled cry and galloped away.

"You do not think to get quit of me thus," cried the captain of the Yellow Band. "I'm after you."

He buried his spurs in his horse's flanks, and dashed after the stranger, and in a few minutes had overtaken him.

"Stand and deliver!" cried Ralph.

"Never with life," returned the stranger, drawing his sword.

Red Ralph, anticipating what was to follow, wheeled his horse sharply round just in time to avoid a slashing cut aimed at his head by the stranger.

"Since you mean fighting," cried Ralph, "I am for you."

His sword was out in the twinkling of an eye, and with immense spirit he returned the other's attack.

One blow sent the stranger's sword whirling from his grasp, and at the same time knocked off his hat, revealing his long pale face and grizzled beard in the bright moonlight.

Ralph stood stock still as if suddenly transfixed.

"Merciful Heavens!" he gasped.

"Unhappy boy!" cried the stranger. "I told you to beware the last meeting. You meet me for the third time by hazard, or by predestination, according to the terms of our legend. Strike, boy, and fulfil the doom of our house!"

Ralph let fall his sword to the ground and sprang from his horse, prostrating himself before the traveller.

"Nay, sir," said the highwayman humbly. "I am not so base. Here in all humility I kneel before you and beg forgiveness for your outcast and repentant son."

The stranger appeared all amazement one minute; but the next he sprang from his horse with an eagerness rivalling that of the robber himself, and threw his arms around the prostrate Ralph.

"Come to my arms—my heart, my son. I will believe in you, and you alone."

"My father! Oh! my father!" said Red Ralph, embracing the other tenderly.

Whilst they thus hung in each other's embrace—father and son, separated by such cruel fortunes for so long—there was a sudden noise, and some six or eight horsemen appeared, headed by one who seemed by his dress to be a farmer.

"Seize that fellow there!" he said. "That's the fellow—Red Ralph—the slim one."

"How now?" cried Red Ralph, starting back in surprise.

"See, too," cried the farmer, who was no other than Job Hardstaff, "here is a proof of the gallow's jack's calling. He has already murdered this man."

Red Ralph turned to see what they meant, and found that his father, so lately recovered, had fallen lifeless to the ground.

"Poor devil!" said Hardstaff, with a shrug of the shoulders. "He's dead."

"Dead?" cried Red Ralph. "Then thus is the doom of our house fulfilled! Oh! cruel fortune! to tease us with the vain hope that it was averted. Do with me as you will now. I care not."

* * * * *

Ralph was borne away to prison, and, in further evidence of his identity, his captors took with them the insensible form of his father. We use advisedly the expression, "insensible form," for when arrived at their destination it was found that the strong emotion caused by the recovery of his son had merely thrown him into a strong swoon.

When recovered from this he was well nigh frantic at his son's new danger.

"Fear not for me, father," said the highwayman. "I have faced worse dangers ere now, and come safely through them. All I want is your love."

"Nay," said his father. "Can you not see in this the working out of our doom? To avoid the fearful curse of our race, the last of our long line is doomed to ignominy and a shameful death."

"Never believe it, father," said the highwayman. "I have one resource that can always be used at the last extremity."

"What? Is it suicide? My son, I pray you—"

"Nay, fear nothing," said Ralph. "Take this ring. Bear it to the king. He will know it. Recal to his mind a promise he made me one night, with these particulars."

He then sketched out briefly his interview with the king, and the promise his Majesty had made. Before his father left, too, he related the history of his marriage with Lady Leonore, and the atrocities of her mother.

The father of the highwayman departed upon his mission, and was informed at the palace that the king was taking the air in the gardens (St. James's—since thrown open to the public as St. James's Park), and that he was attended by a large suite of courtiers.

Ralph's father flew at once to the spot, and found the king near the artificial river, engaged in a rather heavy flirtation with a lady of middle age.

However, he made straightway for the royal presence, and presented the signet, with his petition.

No sooner was the name of Red Ralph uttered than the lady with the king became interested.

"Well," said the king, "we remember well. And as it is fitting that a royal promise should be kept, your knavish son shall be spared, or—"

"Your Majesty," said the lady beside the king, "a word, I pray you, ere you decide. This man you would spare is the vilest of the vile—an assassin."

"How, my lady?"

"He has taken from me the affection of my child."

"What now?" cried Ralph's father. "Who is this woman?"

"S'death! ye unmannered varlet," said the king. "This is my Lady Glyde."

"And I charge this woman with all the atrocities of which she would accuse my son. She is a murderess. I have full proofs of it."

"Your Majesty," said Lady Glyde, changing colour, "surely does not give any credence to the lies of this robber's father—"

"Lies in your teeth, madam," said the other, thoroughly aroused. "I speak as a true and loyal gentleman—as Francis, Earl of Weirton!"

This came down upon the guilty woman like a thunder clap.

The earl had much influence at court, although he had been an absentee from the royal presence for some years.

He demanded the arrest of Lady Glyde, and brought forward overwhelming proofs of her guilt; but before they could remove her from the gardens she took a swift poison and fell a corpse by the gates.

The king pardoned Red Ralph, the captain of the Yellow Band (now Lord Weirton), conditionally.

He was for a certain period to remain abroad until the affair had blown over, for the king was a thorough aristocrat at heart, and would not have the world speak lightly of the patrician heir of Weirton.

Red Ralph at once acquiesced, and now, restored to his beloved Leonore (who succeeds at length to the wealth her guilty parents had so long kept from her), he took his departure for the continent, where he soon obtained a commission in a foreign regiment.

His faithful Yellow Boys followed him, and did some famous execution in the ensuing wars as "The English Band," earning themselves an undying reputation.

Is, then, our story told? Not quite. Of the strange adventures of Leonore and Laura Delane, and of the mysterious gipsy, Mina, we have more to say, but in another place. In the history of "Wild Will; or, The Pirates of the Thames," will be also found the future life of Red Ralph, and the account of the awful doom which in the end awaited him.

THE END.

THE LOND⬛⬛⬛ COMPANY.